Jackie Collins

Lovers and Gamblers

PAN BOOKS

First published in hardback 1977 by W. H. Allen & Co. Ltd

First published in paperback 1978 by Pan Books

This edition published 2009 by Pan Books
an imprint of Pan Macmillan, a division of Macmillan Publishers Limited
Pan Macmillan, 20 New Wharf Road, London N1 9RR
Basingstoke and Oxford
Associated companies throughout the world
www.panmacmillan.com

ISBN 978-0-330-47825-0

3 5 7 9 8 6 4

A CIP catalogue record for this book is available from
the British Library.

Typeset by SetSystems Ltd, Saffron Walden, Essex
Printed in the UK by CPI Mackays, Chatham ME5 8TD

Visit **www.panmacmillan.com** to read more about all our books
and to buy them. You will also find features, author interviews and
news of any author events, and you can sign up for e-newsletters
so that you're always first to hear about our new releases.

For all the Lovers and Gamblers I have known

Especially Oscar

BOOK ONE

1

Al King slammed and locked the bathroom door. He ran the shower until it was pleasantly warm, then let the water cascade on his body for at least five minutes. He soaped himself vigorously, turning the shower onto ice cold and marvelling at the sudden shrinkage of his cock. Amazing. Never failed.

He climbed out of the shower and studied his nakedness in the full-length mirror. A week at a health farm had done him the world of good. The slight paunch he had suspected was gone, his stomach was flat as a pancake. Forty push-ups a day helped there. He turned sideways. Pretty good. The body was in fine shape. Lean, tanned, hairy, masculine. Al allowed himself a pleased smile, and leaned forward to study his face. Everything seemed in order except for an incipient blackhead lurking on his chin. He squeezed it carefully.

Yes, he still looked pretty goddamn good.

In fact he looked better than ever. The recent operation to remove the bags under his eyes had been an unqualified success, and the new teeth-capping job was excellent.

Physically he was in perfect shape for his forthcoming tour across America, an event he was looking forward to with mixed feelings. It was two years since he had been on the road, and although he wouldn't admit it to anyone he was worried that he could keep up the pace. Jesus Christ – so many cities – and every one of them would expect a peak performance. His voice was in pretty good shape, but the tour promised a gruelling schedule – and the press, the critics, would be the first to pounce if he wasn't up to his previous standard.

He opened the bathroom door carefully. The redhead and the blonde were both waiting, lolling on the bed in an

3

advanced state of nakedness. He headed towards them. Time to play. Time to get it on.

An hour later his enthusiasm was turning to boredom.

'Al!' exclaimed the blonde for the tenth time, 'you are the greatest!' She smiled a vacant pretty smile and concentrated once more on pleasuring him. Earlier in the day, when they had first met, she had promised him in a heavy southern drawl, 'I am gonna *pleasure* you honey, like you ain't *never* been pleasured before!'

He was still waiting.

'Al!' mumbled the redhead, mouth full, 'you are *too* much! Just too too much!'

Al wasn't really listening. He lay naked and relaxed in the shuttered hotel room, his arms casually behind his head. With his eyes half-closed he endured the attentions of the two women. He had no plans for getting involved or of even participating. Why should he? Let them do all the work. After all he was a star, wasn't he? They were lucky to be in his bed, his room, his life.

Al King was a rock-soul superstar. A singer who drove women mad the world over with his low throaty growl and his sexual gyrations. At thirty-seven he had reached the peak of his success. He had everything.

Money. Plenty of that. Off-shore investments, and lots of ready cash for the useful little things in life like a two hundred thousand pound house in London. A new red Ferrari, plus matching Rolls and Bentley.

Love. Well, he had a wife of sixteen years standing, a fair-haired sensible woman called Edna, who stayed out of the way because that was how Al wanted it. For more exciting sex there was always a selection of ready and able ladies. Any shape, size or specification.

'Al,' suggested the blonde, shifting so that her well-developed mammaries hung invitingly over his mouth, 'Al, baby, why don't we fuck?'

The redhead paused at what she was doing and expressed great interest in the blonde's suggestion.

Al grunted. Stick it into these two. They must be kidding.

'Just keep at it,' he pushed the redhead back into position.

Women had never been a problem. Always plenty to go around, even before he was famous. With the fame came the classy bits. Falling over themselves for a piece of Al King cock. And what ravers!

He could feel no sign of an orgasm. The trouble was that he just couldn't be bothered to make it with the casual pick-ups that crowded his bedroom. He started off thinking – yeah – great. And he ended up thinking – why bother? Lately it had to be a very special girl – and how many of those were there around?

It was four o'clock in New York. It was the middle of July, and hot. Of course the room was air-conditioned, but still it was a strange sort of coolness.

Al said, 'Get dressed, girls, I've had enough.'

They both chorused their disappointment. He hadn't even touched them.

'I could make you come,' the blonde said, 'if we got rid of *her*.' Scornfully she indicated the redhead.

Al got off the bed and headed for the bathroom. Whatever gave her the impression he would *want* to come with her? 'Dressed and out in five minutes,' he snapped.

'Hey . . .' objected the redhead.

Al took another shower, you couldn't be too careful. This time when he emerged from the bathroom the girls had gone. Good. Sometimes they stayed to argue. He pulled up the window shades, flooding the bedroom with sunlight.

He contemplated phoning his brother Paul, but he was with Linda, and she wouldn't be too pleased. Linda wasn't bad, too strong for Paul though, it wouldn't last. Anyway, she wouldn't stand a chance against Paul's wife, Melanie. Now she was a real little toughie. She liked the money, the big house, and all the perks of being Al King's sister-in-law. She would never stand for another woman in Paul's life.

Al yawned. Now *his* wife was another proposition. Sweet, faithful Edna. He had met her when she was sixteen, knocked her up, done the right thing and married her. Well, her father had been very persuasive, he had given Al two thousand pounds to set him up in a record shop. However, being shut up in a shop did not appeal to Al. What he really wanted to do was sing. He was well known locally. Whenever there was a wedding or an event people would say – 'Get Al to give us a few songs.' He made the odd five pounds here and there, but he would have done it for nothing.

Paul was the brains of the King family. He had just finished a course of business accountancy and was working for a chartered accountant. Al had persuaded him to leave his job and open up the shop with him. 'After all, it's just the two of us now,' he had said. Their parents had recently died within months of each other.

Soon the shop became the local musicians' hang-out, and a group called 'Rabble' invited Al to sing with them. Paul took over their management, and within two years it was 'Al King and Rabble'. Within four years it was just Al King, and the ride to superstardom had really begun.

Edna had never complained. They had started married life in one room. Al was out all day working, and then, when he joined 'Rabble', he was out all night too. Edna looked after the baby, helped out in the shop, cooked, cleaned, struggled to make ends meet. She had been a softly pretty girl when Al had met her. Now, at thirty-three, she was plump and matronly, and she stayed very much in the background of her husband's starry life.

Al's family was important to him. His sixteen-year-old son, Evan, received everything he wanted, although to Al's chagrin he never seemed to appreciate anything. He was a skinny, sulky boy with acned skin and greasy hair. *'You're* Al King's son?' People would question in disbelief when they first met him. He was a poor scholar and hated school. Al had promised that at the end of the present term he could leave and perhaps accompany him on his tour. Evan had shown unheard-of enthusiasm. Al had decided it would do the boy good to get away from his mother. Edna fussed round him too much, the boy was stifled.

As a boy Al had never been stifled. He had engaged in sexual relations at the ripe old age of thirteen with one of the local hookers. Evan, at the ripe old age of sixteen, never seemed to notice girls, let alone screw them.

Al had plans to change all of that. Get the boy away from his mother, show him what it was all about. Yes, it was about time he gave some of his attention to Evan. Get rid of those spots. Put some weight on the boy. Get him royally laid. Yes.

The hell with it, Paul should be at his disposal – not

Linda's. He picked up the phone. 'Hey Paul baby, you want to shift your ass up here and discuss more important things than getting your rocks off?'

'What's up, Al? Can't it wait?'

'No. I need company.'

'Give me a few minutes.'

Al switched on the television.

Wrapped in a black towelling bathrobe he poured himself a bourbon and coke – fattening but favourite – and settled down on the bed.

He clicked the remote control dial. Quiz game. Western. Cookery. Chat show. He stopped there.

'Well,' said the interviewer, 'who shall we pick out to talk to next amongst this bevy of beauties?'

The camera switched to a group of about fifteen girls in swimsuits clustered together at the front of the audience. 'Miss Philadelphia,' continued the interviewer, 'would you like to step up here, dear.'

Miss Philadelphia was a skinny, nervous girl, with long legs and freckles. She smiled jumpily.

'Gee, honey,' said the interviewer, leering at his audience, 'I'm not going to *eat* you. What do you think your chances are of winning the "Miss Coast to Coast" title tonight?'

'I'd like to,' she replied breathily.

'What would you do if you did?'

'I want to travel. Then I guess I'd just like to settle down and be a good wife and mother.'

'Wonderful. Isn't that wonderful, everyone?' The audience obediently clapped.

'Bullshit!' exclaimed Al, and he was just about to change the channel when Miss Los Angeles stepped forward. She was wearing a black shiny bikini, and she had a body that stopped even Al in his tracks. Big bosom, long legs, finely muscled stomach, small waist. He dragged his eyes up to her face and it was not a disappointment. She was great looking, with a wide luscious mouth, and long streaked blondish hair which fell past her shoulders in soft waves.

'Not bad!' exclaimed Al out loud, and he felt himself slightly aroused, which was a good sign.

He would have her. He would get his brother to arrange it.

For Al King nothing was impossible. He could have any woman he wanted, and he usually did.

☆

'Why do you always have to run whenever he calls?' demanded Linda.

'Because,' explained Paul King patiently, 'that's why Al and I have such a good relationship, and that is why we are still together.'

'Christ!' exclaimed Linda crossly, 'you make the two of you sound like an old married couple.'

'That's right,' agreed Paul, 'a manager and his star have a very sensitive relationship. It *is* sort of like a marriage, and Al and I have a good one.'

'God! You and your bloody marriages! It's not only your wife I have to contend with, Al is a lot more demanding than any woman.' Linda Cosmo climbed out of bed. She was a thin woman in her early thirties, with Elizabeth Taylor eyes, and straight black hair. She was strikingly attractive.

'Come back here,' demanded Paul.

'Why? For a quick one? You know I don't appreciate quick ones. Anyway, I thought you said he would be busy this afternoon – *all* afternoon. It's only just past four.'

'I expect he got bored, you know Al.'

'Yes. I know Al. He's a pain in the ass. I really don't know why you stay with him – you have plenty of money, you don't *need* Al King any more.'

'Cool it, Linda,' Paul followed her out of bed, 'you should understand.'

'Oh sure, I *do* understand. I understand about Al, and about your wife, and about your kids. What time does that leave for *me*? How often are we alone together?' She locked her hands behind Paul's neck, 'You know I love you,' she continued softly, 'but love needs attention too.'

He kissed her, running his hands down her naked body. She was right, he did neglect her. But what could he do? He had so many other commitments.

'How would you like to come on the tour?' He had blurted it out before really thinking about it.

She looked at him suspiciously. 'I'd love it – you know that. But how?'

'Officially, that's how. I'm appointing you tour photographer.'

'You're kidding!'

'I'm serious. Only stop giving me a hard time about Al.'

'You really mean it?' She wrapped her arms around him, kissing him long and hard. 'We can be together, and it's a terrific challenge. I always did get turned on by a challenge.'

She kissed him again? and he pushed her away, laughing. 'If I'd known I was going to get this good a reaction I'd have given you a job sooner! I feel like a Hollywood producer!'

She grinned. 'I'll join you on the casting couch later!' Then seriously she added: 'I won't let you down, I promise you that.'

'On the casting couch?'

'On the tour, you fool!'

'I know you won't let me down, you never do.'

He guided her back to the bed. 'Why don't we put the casting couch into action now?'

She laughed softly. 'Why not indeed? There's nothing I like better than screwing the man with the most beautiful cock in the world . . .'

As usual it was the best for him. Linda Cosmo was the only woman that he genuinely liked making love to.

He had met her a year previously. New York. Opening night in cabaret for Al. Noise. People. Booze. Food. She had been sent by a magazine to photograph the event. Paul had seen her, fancied her, moved in before Al. He usually gave Al first crack, but that time it had been different.

They had been together on and off ever since. The on was when he was in America. The off was when he was in England.

He was pleased with the idea of bringing Linda on the tour. She was an excellent photographer, and they would be able to be seen together.

Later, as they dressed, Linda asked, 'Can I tell people?'

'Tell them what?'

'About the job?'

'Not yet. Let me cue Al in first. And I've got to break it to B.S. – you know what he's like, he may struggle a bit.' B.S., better known as Bernie Suntan – was Al's American publicity man – the best, but somewhat nervous and temperamental. He might object. Then again he might be delighted with the idea. Whatever he thought it was tough shit. Only Al could influence Paul's decisions.

The reasons that Paul and Al were in New York was because of the Al King Supertour. A spectacular odyssey across America. There were a few minor details to sort out – things that Paul could have really taken care of on the phone – but he had wanted to make the trip if only to be with Linda. Al had decided to come along at the last moment. Fresh out of the health farm he was ready for some action.

The tour was immensely important. In the last year Al's record sales had been slipping. Nothing desperate, just a slow, hardly noticeable slide. But Paul had noticed, and coupled with the fact that Al's last two singles had failed to make the top of the charts, he realized that it was time to bring Al back in front of the people. Too much time in television and recording studios created a vacuum between a star and his public. On stage Al was pure dynamite.

The trip was meticulously planned. Al would travel in his own lavishly equipped plane – that way all travel hassles would be taken care of.

So far Al had made no mention of bringing his wife, and Paul was sure that the matter would not come up. Paul was relieved because it gave him a beautiful excuse with his own wife. If Edna wasn't allowed on the trip, then Melanie certainly wasn't. Not that Paul would compare the two women. Edna was a doormat and Al treated her as such. Melanie was a sharp lady, which was why Paul had to play it very carefully with Linda. If Melanie got a whiff that he was serious about anybody – well . . . He didn't like to think about it.

He had been married to Melanie for ten years – since she was eighteen, and they had two young children. Melanie was an ex-dancer. She was very pretty, but oh what a bitch! And a nag. And somewhere in the back of his mind Paul knew for sure that she had slept with Al. He had no proof, knew nothing for certain, but he just had a feeling . . .

Linda was dressed and ready to leave. 'Later?' she asked.

'As soon as I'm free.'

'Come to the apartment, I'll cook dinner.'

'We may have to go out with Al, I don't know what he's got in mind but I can't leave him alone.'

Linda laughed sarcastically. 'The great Al King alone – never!'

'Watch it, you'll be working for him soon.'

'I don't understand it,' Linda mused, 'you're better looking, taller, and a whole year younger. Why aren't *you* the superstar?'

'Because I can't sing, and whatever you may think about Al he's got a bitch of a voice. Besides, I like being the manager, it means I score the best birds.'

'Oh, really?'

'Oh, really, yes. I got you, didn't I?'

'Yeah, you got me hooked like some stupid fish. There I was, looking for a stable relationship, and I get some dumb married man who spends his life wetnursing superschmuck!'

'You've got a big mouth, but I love you.'

That's *why* you love me.' She glanced quickly at her watch, 'Hey – you're going to be late – better move it.'

'I'll call you later.'

'Fine, I'm photographing the "Miss Coast to Coast" competition tonight. It shouldn't take long. I'll call you.'

'Can't you cancel it?'

'No way, I need the bread.'

She left, and Paul finished dressing in a hurry. Out to the elevator, up two floors, and then he was knocking on the door to Al's suite. A waiter let him in.

'Where the fuck have you been?' Al asked rudely. 'I ordered you a steak sandwich, you took so fucking long I ate it.'

'I'm not hungry. What happened to your companions?'

'Jesus! Dogs! Horrible. I had them out of here in double time.'

'I warned you.'

'How would *you* have known? In the lobby they looked like two real little darlings. I'll tell you what though, I saw one I *really* fancy.'

How many times had Paul heard *that*. Growing up together had been a checkered path of fame, fortune, and women. Al had always fancied anything that moved and was female.

'Who is she?' enquired Paul, 'and where did you find her?'

'*You're* going to find her,' corrected Al, 'I don't know her name. I spotted her on television – there's some beauty competition tonight – she's in it.'

'Miss Coast to Coast?'

'Yeah, that's right. How did you know?'

'I'm a detective on the side. Only how do we find the girl if you don't even know her name?'

'Miss Los Angeles.'

'Dinner tonight. It's as good as done.'

2

Dallas licked already shiny lips. She stared at herself in the full-length mirror and adjusted the Miss Los Angeles sash. She wished that she could take it off, it ruined the whole effect of the leopard skin bikini.

Later in the evening, when she won, she would have to put on the stupid crown and cover herself with the fake ermine cloak. What a drag!

Dallas knew she would win. She had taken steps to make certain she would.

'You wearing a hair-piece?' Miss Long Island asked bitchily, craning to see herself in the mirror.

'Yeah,' agreed Dallas, 'around the crotch!'

Miss Long Island retreated angrily.

Dallas peered at herself once more in the mirror. She did look her absolute best. She deserved to win. There really was no contest. Still, it was just as well that she had taken out insurance.

'The judges are being introduced!' someone shouted with excitement and the girls in the dressing-room crowded round the closed circuit television set in the corner.

A smile hovered round Dallas' mouth. Five judges, and she had taken care of three of them. On those odds she could afford to feel secure.

'First, the ladies', the announcer on television said, 'and I would like to hear a big round of applause for that wonderful screen star, Miss April Crawford.' April Crawford appeared, swathed in mink.

'Now, someone we are always reading about – leader of fashion and fun, Lucy Mabel Mann.'

'Isn't she *pretty*!' one of the girls exlaimed.

Yes, agreed Dallas silently. And I should know, for it was only this morning that I visited her in her Central Park West duplex, and gave her the greatest head job she has ever had!

'Now let's hear it for Ramo Kaliffe, the man with the million dollar eyes.'

Hello Ramo, thought Dallas. I took care of you last night, and you were more than grateful.

'Petro Lorenz, writer and television personality. And lastly, Ed Kurlnik, of Kurlnik Motors fame.'

Ed gave that short embarrassed smile that Dallas had grown to know so well over the last few months. She had been taking care of Ed for exactly sixteen weeks. Twice a week, Mondays and Fridays. It was no secret that he was a married man.

The girls were being summoned together and hustled out the door. The parade was about to begin.

Dallas shook out her mane of hair and strode confidently onto the stage.

☆

Dallas Lunde, born twenty years previously at a small zoo her parents had off the main highway outside Miami. An uneventful childhood, no brothers or sisters, but plenty of animals to play with. Her parents didn't believe in school, so they never bothered to send her.

Sometimes, when he had the time, her father would tutor her in various subjects. He was particularly fond of geography and real life adventure.

The three of them lived a very tight life; her parents had no friends. They were some kind of religious maniacs – following a cult all their own – which made them reject any contact with the outside world. The animals they looked after were their whole life.

Dallas grew up alone. The zoo was off the beaten track, and the only other people she ever saw were the two-dollar-a-day visitors. Once a month her father went into town for supplies, and it wasn't until Dallas was sixteen that he took her with him. She would always remember that day. The shops, the people, the cars and the noise. Along with the supplies her father collected a young man called Phil, who was to come and help out at the zoo. Unbeknown to Dallas he had also been picked out as a husband for her. She was given no choice. On her seventeenth birthday she and Phil were married.

At the time it didn't occur to her to object. Her parents' words were law; she had never argued. She knew nothing of the world outside. She had never even seen television or movies. The only books she had ever read were about animals and wildlife.

Phil was tall and nice-looking. He spoke softly. It was a shock when that evening he threw off her nightgown and violently deflowered her. The only sexual education she had received had been from observing the animals, but even they behaved with more gentleness than the man who was her husband.

Night after night Phil demanded his rights. He never kissed or caressed her, merely lifted her nightdress and thrust himself in. Dallas accepted this. She worked hard during the day, and at night she cooked and cleaned and suffered her husband's attentions, because this was the way she thought things were. When her mother became ill, her father decided they needed more help at the zoo, so he employed a young black couple named Burt and Ida Keyes. Dallas liked them immediately, they were always laughing and giggling, and they seemed so fond of each other. She couldn't help watching them. She noticed the way they kept on touching each other, and the secret smiley little looks they exchanged.

After several weeks she plucked up the courage to discuss this with Ida. 'You and Burt are always feeling each other, kissing, things like that. Do you like it when he does ... well ... you know?'

'Like it!' Ida make a sucking sound of enjoyment. 'I just couldn't live without it!'

Dallas studied Burt with new eyes. What made him so different from Phil? It couldn't only be his black skin. It wasn't long before she had the chance to find out. They were alone together one day cleaning out one of the cages, when Burt reached out and lazily pushed the hair off her forehead. Then he cupped her face in his hands, and kissed her long and hard. The feel of his tongue exploring her mouth created a vacuum of excitement in Dallas that she had never known before.

He undid the buttons on her blouse, and exposed her breasts. All the time he was whispering endearments.

Dallas could not have moved even if she had wanted to. She was powerless, thrilled, on the brink of a fantastic new discovery.

Burt bent his head to her breasts, and she leaned back hoping the moment would last forever. Then she saw the blood as it fell on her breasts from the cut above Burt's eye. She heard the cursing as Phil lifted the stick to strike once more. She felt the shame sweep over her in a great wave.

She jumped up, covering herself. Oh God, how could she ever face her friend Ida again?

She ran back to the house and collected a few belongings, then she took twenty dollars from the dresser and fled.

She had no idea where she was going, she just ran.

On the highway she thumbed a ride, and it was only when she was settled in the front seat of the Ford car that she stopped to think.

'Where to, sweetie?' inquired the florid driver of the car, and he reached over and patted her on the knee.

☆

'Miss Los Angeles. A beautiful young lady of twenty whose vital statistics come out at a staggering 39–22–36. Dallas by name, a model, whose life ambition is to marry a fellow American – because – and I quote the lady herself – American men are so big and strong and handsome. Wowee folks, that's *some* compliment.'

Dallas paraded across the stage. The spotlight felt hot on her almost naked body. Stomach in. Bosom out. Head high. Fixed smile. Walk tall.

She glanced briefly at the judges. Ed was regarding her like a proud father, and well he might. What was that sweet old-fashioned phrase? Sugar daddy. Yeah – that's what he was, her sugar daddy.

She had met him in Los Angeles, and he had transported her to New York and set her up in a very nice apartment. When she had heard he was to be a judge on 'Miss Coast to Coast' she had asked him to pull a few strings. He had done so, flown her to Los Angeles where she won the local contest, and now here she was. With connections it was as easy as that.

Ed Kurlnik could pull a lot of strings if he so cared. He

was an important man, head of the Kurlnik Motor dynasty – a vast corporation almost as large as the Ford empire.

Dallas turned and flashed a smile at the television camera. Ed was most impressed at the fact that she was only twenty. He was sixty-one, and looked it. Money could buy most things, but it couldn't turn back the clock. Having a young girlfriend made him feel virile and alive.

'Honey-blonde hair, green eyes, five foot seven inches of beautiful woman. Let's hear it for Miss Los Angeles – the lovely Dallas.'

She turned and smiled one last time, then she was off the stage, and running back to the dressing-room.

She unhooked the top of her bikini, stepped out of the tiny pants. Then, totally naked, she inched her way into a long green tube of a jersey dress. Nine hundred dollars worth, Ed had bought it for her. It fitted like a second skin, skimming her hips, clinging round her breasts, plunging back and front. She fluffed out her hair, licked her lips. She was ready.

She watched the other contestants on the closed circuit television. Some were pretty, some cute, but none could hold a candle.

'You sure think you're hot shit!' Miss Long Island hissed.

'Served your way. Right up the ass!' replied Dallas calmly. They were all jealous of her and well they might be. She was going to win. Of that there was no doubt.

☆

The man in the car had taken her to a motel. She was grateful to him, she had nowhere else to go.

He was about her father's age. He wore a brightly patterned sports shirt, and baggy beige trousers.

'Say, girly, what ya gonna do lo make an old man happy?' he asked.

Dallas sat quietly on the corner of the double bed. What was she going to do?

'Make yourself comfortable,' the man suggested, 'and I'll go and get us some beers.'

Dallas sat unmoving. She didn't know what to do. If she hadn't met this kind man she would still be out on the highway thumbing a lift. She had made the move, she couldn't go back. Phil would kill her. Her parents would never talk to her again, and as for Ida . . .

The man returned, carrying a plastic bag from which he produced a six pack of beer, and a box of Ritz crackers. 'We'll have ourselves our own little party.' He switched on the television, and drew the curtains. Then he snapped open a can of beer, and handed it to her. He was sweating a lot, small rivulets running down his face.

Dallas sipped from the can. She had never tasted beer before. Her eyes were glued to the television set. So much going on. So many new experiences.

'You gonna get undressed?' the man inquired, licking his lips and sticking a fat fist into the Ritz crackers.

'Why?' asked Dallas carefully, not at all sure what it was he wanted from her.

'Ha!' exclaimed the man, 'I'll take care of you, girly, don't worry on that score.' He unzipped his trousers and struggled out of them. He had sunburned thighs, and underpants that matched his shirt. 'Come on, girly,' he insisted, 'let's go.'

So this was the price of a bed. Dallas sighed. She knew what he wanted now. Well, it couldn't be any worse than it was with Phil.

She felt nervous and unsure. But if it meant a bed for the night . . .

She had no money, no choice. The only alternative was returning home, and she couldn't do that. This man would look after her, he was a fatherly type, he had behaved kindly.

She stood up and removed her jeans, and the man moved forward and took off her pants. Then, sweating more than ever, he removed his own pants, and pushed her back on the bed. He was struggling with a rubber thing, fitting it over his penis.

Dallas closed her eyes, bit down on her lip and counted silently. With Phil she never got as far as fifty, with this man it only took to fifteen, and then he was grunting and heaving, and it was over. He hadn't been as rough as Phil. It was almost painless.

'You're a little beauty!' exclaimed the man, you been at it long?'

'Oh,' said Dallas vaguely, 'I guess so.' She went to the bathroom and put her pants and jeans back on. She stared blankly at herself in the mirror. Her eyes were tear-filled, but she couldn't cry, nobody was forcing her to do anything. Quietly she went back into the bedroom and settled on the bed in front of the television.

Half naked, the man was asleep, his snores hardly disturbing her.

In the morning she awoke with a start. She had fallen asleep in front of the television still in her clothes. She looked around for the man, but he was gone. On the beside table there was a note and a twenty-dollar bill. The note read – 'Vacate room by twelve, all paid for. Thank you.'

Where was he? Why had he deserted her? Maybe she hadn't pleased him. Why had he left twenty dollars? Did he know she had no money?

Puzzled, Dallas ate the rest of the Ritz crackers while watching television. Then, at twelve o'clock, she was back on the highway.

☆

There were six finalists. Nervously they huddled together backstage waiting for the results.

Dallas stood slightly apart, aware of the fact that a television camera was trained on them to catch every nuance of disappointment. She tried not to look too confident. She smiled slightly and parted her lips appealingly. Let all the guys in the audience drool. She knew she looked great. She knew she was a winner.

They were announcing the three winners now.

Miss Kansas City was third. She squealed with delight and kissed the girl nearest to her before rushing onto the stage.

Miss Miami Beach was second. 'Oh my God!' she muttered, the colour draining from her face. And she had to be pushed onto the stage.

Here it comes, thought Dallas, here comes my little bit of fame – here comes my passport to better things. If any of those sonsofbitches have double-crossed me . . .

'And now the winner – "Miss Coast to Coast" – The beautiful – Dallas! Miss Los Angeles!'

She pulled in her stomach, threw back her shoulders and walked confidently onto the stage.

Flashbulbs were popping, the audience was applauding and cheering. Maybe she would have won it without taking out insurance . . . She seemed like a popular choice.

The MC was grabbing her excitedly – 'Miss Coast to Coast! Miss Coast to Coast!' he kept on screaming.

She smiled towards the television cameras. The previous year's winner was placing the sash around her. Ramo Kaliffe was placing the crown on her head. 'Later,' he whispered.

'Maybe,' she whispered back. Maybe not – she thought. Wouldn't do to let Ed find out there were others . . .

Out of the corner of her eye she spotted Ed, he was smiling proudly. He had been smiling the first time she had met him, but that had been for different reasons . . .

☆

Dallas thumbed a lift into Miami with a truck driver. He chewed gum and barely spoke to her. When he stopped the truck to let her out she had hesitated.

'Whassamatter?' he asked.

'I thought you might want to keep me with you . . .' she ventured.

'Aw, shit!' he spat on the sidewalk. 'I got daughters older than you. Go peddle it at the Fontainebleau.'

The truck drove off and she was left standing there. Go peddle it at the Fontainebleau – what did that mean?

'Excuse me?' she asked a woman at a bus stop. 'Is there a Fontainebleau Street?' The woman shook her head. 'Fontainebleau Hotel,' she suggested, 'but that's over on Collins Avenue.'

'How do I get there?'

The woman looked her over. 'Goin' for a job?'

'Er – yes.'

'Come with me on the bus, I'll tell you when we get there. Hadn't you better smarten up?'

'I will later,' agreed Dallas. She was wearing her standard clothes of old jeans, a T-shirt, and sandals. Perhaps she should brush her hair and wash her face. She was beginning to feel extremely hungry.

The Fontainebleau Hotel seemed a large and formidable place. Dallas hung around outside for a while and watched the people emerging and collecting their cars. Two girls walked by in beach clothes, and Dallas fell into step behind them as they entered the hotel. The huge air-conditioned lobby seemed even more formidable, so Dallas followed the two girls into an elevator. They took it down to a lower level, and emerged into an arcade of shops. She smelled the restaurant, and wondered how much a sandwich would cost. While she stood outside wondering, a group of men appeared. They were middle-aged and jolly. They were shouting at each other in friendly tones, and clapping each other on the back.

'Excuse me?' Dallas asked the nearest one, 'how much is a sandwich?'

This question produced much hilarity, and they crowded round her, staring and laughing.

'What you doin' here?' one of them finally asked.' You don't look like you belong here.'

'I'm . . . er . . . looking for a job.'

'What sort of a job?'

Dallas shrugged. 'Anything where someone will take care of me.'

'If you'll have a bath, I'll take care of you,' one of them suggested leeringly.

'All right,' said Dallas seriously.

'I think I just got lucky!' he joked to the others.

Dallas stared at him. 'What's your name?' she asked. This time she wanted to know, then maybe he couldn't run off in the middle of the night.

'Frank' he said, 'you can call me Frankie.'

The others were walking off into the restaurant. 'I'll see you guys later,' volunteered Frankie.

'Make sure she takes a bath,' one of them said as a parting shot, 'don't want to carry anything back to Irma!' They all departed laughing.

Now they were alone Frankie lost some of his strut. 'You look awfully young,' he said, 'you sure you old enough?'

'Twenty dollars' stated Dallas, 'and a sandwich.'

She was learning fast.

3

'I'm sorry,' said Linda firmly, 'but she wouldn't come.'

'Wouldn't come?' echoed Al and Paul in unison.

'That's right. You got it in one.'

'You didn't tell her it was me,' exclaimed Al in disgust.

'Of course I told her it was you. I said – Al King – the famous singer – would like you to be his guest for dinner tonight.'

'And?'

'And she smiled, flashed those lethal teeth, and said, 'that's nice but I'm busy.'

'Busy!'

'She probably *was* busy. After all, the girl just won "Miss Coast to Coast". There were horny little guys all over the place, I was tripping over them.'

Al shook his head in amazement. 'I guess she didn't believe you. I suppose she thought you were putting her on.'

'Maybe,' said Linda irritably, 'I don't carry an official document stating I am a certified pimp for Al King.'

'Perhaps you should,' said Al, 'that way you . . .'

'Come on, you two,' interrupted Paul quickly, 'the girl's probably married or engaged or something.'

'Since when has that made any difference?' asked Al, moodily.

'I have, however, managed to acquire a consolation prize,' stated Linda. 'Miss Miami Beach is waiting in the lobby for us, so *someone* believed me.'

'Fuck Miss Miami Beach!' said Al dourly.

'I thought that was the whole idea,' replied Linda. 'She's downstairs, gorgeously pretty, and creaming her white lace panties at the thought of meeting you!'

'Great!' exclaimed Paul. 'She came second, didn't she? Shall I get them to send her up, Al?'

'I thought we were going out to dinner,' said Linda coldly. She was fed up with the whole thing. She hated Paul when he was with Al, she wished that just once he would tell his brother to shut up.

'Tomorrow,' said Al, 'I'll have lunch with her tomorrow.'

'With who? Miss Miami Beach?'

'The original one – the piece that won – Dallas – that's her name.'

'*I* can't arrange it,' said Linda quickly..

'I wouldn't ask you to. Paul can take care of it, can't you, boyo? Come on, let's go, I fancy some Italian food. How does that grab everyone?'

Linda bit back a swift retort. It didn't grab her at all, in fact it was the last thing she fancied. But she had learned not to argue with Al. What Al wanted – Paul wanted – and she was not ready to put her relationship with Paul to the test. If it came down to the crunch, who would Paul side with? One day she would be ready to find out. But not now, not yet.

☆

Miss Miami Beach waited in the lobby. She was a creamy-looking blonde with puffed-out hair and baby blue eyes. She leapt up at the sight of Al. 'Oh my goodness!' she exclaimed, 'this is like a wonderful dream!'

Al smiled and took her by the hand. 'Why didn't *you* come first? You're the prettiest.'

'Oh, thank you. I won two thousand dollars. I'm going to go to Hollywood for a screen test too. It's the most heavenly evening of my life. And now meeting you . . .'

'Are you wearing knicks?'

'Pardon me?'

'Knickers. Drawers. Panties.'

'I don't understand . . .'

Linda shot Al a cold look. 'He's joking,' she said, 'his sense of humour is sometimes obscure.'

Al laughed. 'Oh Linda. If only you and I had met first, what a couple we would have made.'

'Yeah,' agreed Linda sarcastically, 'a real fun couple.'

'What was the girl that won like?' Al turned his attention back to Miss Miami Beach.

She wrinkled up her nose. 'Horrible. Nobody liked her. She wasn't friendly at all.'

'But a great looker.'

'If you like that type. I never thought she would win. We were all hoping she wouldn't.'

'Naughty little girls. Were you mean to her?'

'*She* was mean to us. She was a – well she was a bitch.'

'We're going to eat spaghetti, with clams and meatballs. Then we're going to come back to the hotel and I'm going to let you breathe garlic sauce all over my cock. You do know what a cock is, don't you?'

'Oh. Er – yes.'

'Good girl. You and I are going to get along fine.'

☆

Two hours later their table for four had swelled to ten.

'Al shouldn't drink,' Linda complained, 'who *are* all these people?'

'You know Al,' replied Paul, 'he likes to have people around.'

'I wish you'd stop saying – you know Al. Yes, I know him, and most of the time I find him a big fat pain.'

'I wish the two of you would get along. It would make *my* life a lot easier.'

'I can't help it, he just behaves so badly, bossing people around, intimidating that little blonde – he's done nothing but make obscene suggestions to her all night.'

'She loves it.'

'She doesn't love it. She's just too overawed to object. He makes fun of people – cruel fun.'

'You take things too seriously.'

'Maybe I do. Maybe it's because I hardly ever see you, and when I do I want us to be alone together. I want to cook for you, and make love to you. I don't want to watch you being a yes man to your brother.'

'Your bitching is starting to get on my nerves.'

'So *sorry*.' She felt tears sting the back of her eyelids and she fought for control. If only she didn't love Paul so goddamn much. If only she wasn't so jealous of him. When he left her he had another life neatly waiting for him. A wife. Two kids. A home. And what did she have? A lousy apartment and a half-assed career. It wasn't fair. She had so much to give to the right man. Was that man Paul? She was beginning to wonder.

☆

'Take off your clothes,' said Al. He was sitting fully clothed on the bed in his hotel suite.

'Now?' asked Miss Miami Beach hesitantly.

'No – tomorrow,' Al replied sarcastically, 'Come on – strip off. Let's see the form that made you number two.'

'Can we turn the lights off?'

'I don't want the lights off.'

'I've got a scar.'

'What sort of scar?'

'Appendix. It sort of embarrasses me.'

'Bullshit. Clothes off or out.'

Slowly she unzipped her dress and stepped out of it. She was wearing a flesh-coloured bra and lace briefs.

'Will you sign one of your albums for me?' she asked.

'I'll do better than that, get that felt pen from the dresser and come over here.'

She did as she was told.

'Take your bra off,' he instructed.

She did so.

Roughly he grabbed her left breast, and holding it steady he scrawled Al. He repeated the process with King on the right one.

She was breathing heavily, and her breasts signed with his name were featuring erect nipples.

'Get dressed,' Al sighed, 'go home. I'm tired.'

'But . . .' she began.

Why did they always have to argue? Wasn't it enough they had spent time with him, been seen with him?

'Out!' said Al sharply.

Miss Miami Beach snatched up her clothes, and turning her back she began to dress.

Al waited impatiently. Why were the majority of females quick as a flash at getting *out* of their clothes, and yet it took them forever to put them on again?

At last she was finished, and she turned towards Al. 'Was it something I did?' she asked meekly.

Al shrugged. Conversation she wanted now!

'Well,' she sighed, 'I guess I'll always remember tonight. Maybe I'll see you in Hollywood.' She waited for him to reply, but he had shut his eyes and was feigning sleep. 'Goodbye then,' she said softly, and tiptoed out.

He waited until he heard the door shut, then he got up, switched on the television, fixed himself a scotch and coke. It was four in the morning and he wasn't tired. He felt like a little action – a game of poker or craps. But this wasn't Vegas, and he didn't know where it would all be happening. On impulse he decided to phone Edna. There was no delay, so he got right through.

'Al?' questioned Edna sleepily, 'is anything wrong?'

Edna had a hangup about spending money. She still

assumed that to go to the expense of telephoning from America meant instant disaster.

'Nothing's wrong,' assured Al, 'just thought I'd see how you were,'

'I'm fine. You only left yesterday. Are you *sure* nothing's the matter?'

Oh God. Why couldn't she just accept the fact that he had called for the pleasure of hearing her voice. 'Is Evan around?'

'He's asleep. Al, these calls are so expensive, I wish you wouldn't waste your money.'

It was always your money. Never our money. If Edna had her way they would still be living in one room. She had never learned to accept his success gracefully. She always predicted gloom. If the truth were known she was a miserable woman. He had to twist her arm to get her to go out and buy herself a new dress.

'Wake him up, Edna. I want to say hello.'

'He's got school tomorrow.'

'OK. So *don't* wake him up.'

'I'll tell him you phoned.'

'All right, tell him in the morning.'

'Goodbye, Al.'

'Goodbye, Edna.'

She couldn't wait to hang up. Waste not. Want not. Her favourite motto.

Edna probably would have been the perfect wife for a guy with no money. But as the wife of a superstar she was a total loss.

Al phoned room service. Bacon and eggs. Christ – but he must keep a sharp eye on the weight. Al knew what was happening every minute of the time. On stage he had to look great, and to look great he had to be thin. It was a lot easier to keep your weight down when you were twenty-seven. At thirty-seven, bulges appeared where they shouldn't, and they were hell to get rid of. However – one portion of bacon and eggs, some champagne to swill it down with. He would cut out breakfast. He would save himself for lunch.

Dallas – funny name for a girl. She was certainly a great looker. If he was lucky she just might be able to hold his interest for an afternoon.

Probably another dumb bitch though. They were all dumb.

Starstruck pushovers. They would fuck for money. Fame. Power. Whatever happened to good old lust?

☆

Bernie Suntan stretched in front of the Beverly Hills Hotel pool. 'Jesus H!' he exclaimed. 'If they were givin' out tickets for happiness this would be it!'

'Mr Suntan,' a female voice boomed through the loud-speaker. 'Telephone for Mr Suntan.'

Bernie heaved himself up. Two hundred and sixty pounds of fifty-two-year-old flesh, every inch – except a few crucial ones – heavily suntanned. He wore white boxer shorts trimmed with a Mickey Mouse motif, purple sunglasses, a white peak cap which bore the legend 'Everybody Likes It', and a lot of solid gold jewellery. Underneath the cap the dome of his head was totally bald, but halfway down his scalp a profusion of blond curls sprouted and luxuriated well past the back of his neck.

'I'm the oldest hippie in the business!' Bernie would often announce. And nobody ever argued with him.

En route to the telephone Bernie stopped to greet people. 'Hey, Rod baby, where's the kilt?' 'David Tebet – my favour-ite man – when did you get back? Good to see you.' 'Princess! How do you look! How does she *look*?'

He finally reached the phone and snapped into a rapid business dialogue. Apart from being the oldest hippie in the business Bernie Suntan had the reputation of being one of the top press agents. If you wanted action, call for Bernie. It would cost you, but it would be worth it. Right now he was setting up the public relations side of the Al King tour. And setting it up right. Every city had to roll past like clockwork. No riots. No trouble with the local police. No drugs. No bad publicity.

He didn't worry about Al too much, the only thing you had to watch out with him was the women and gambling. But the others on the tour could cause trouble, and by doing so give the whole caboodle a bad name.

For a start Bernie was doubtful about the three black girls who were to be Al's backing singers. The Promises. Three beautiful girls – if you liked spades – and frankly that wasn't Bernie's particular scene. So they sung up a storm, but what about their private lives? One of them married to a drummer who just drew three for dealing. One of them making out with a certain minor mafioso. And the third young enough to be definite jailbait. Three ding-a-lings. Bernie wasn't happy about having *them* along.

Then he had also heard talk that Al was planning to bring his son. Well what was *that* all about? A sex symbol superstar dragging along his teenage son. Bad image. Very bad image. If he did come he would have to be pushed very much into the background. Like completely out of sight.

Bernie had big plans for Al in Hollywood. As far as he was concerned it would be the publicity pinnacle of the whole trip. The stars would be brought out in force to meet the great Al King. There would be parties, receptions, interviews. There was so much to get together before the start of the tour. Everything had to be planned down to the last detail. Nothing could go wrong. Bernie was staking a lot on this tour – he had been offered an incredible deal that would take him out of the publicity business forever and into the heady world of production. If all went off without a hitch Bernie had no doubt the job would be his.

'Hey,' he yelled into the phone, 'I want the best. Everywhere we go – the best.'

4

Edna King sat in the kitchen with eyes downcast, trying to shut out the slightly hysterical voice of her sister-in-law.

'It's bloody disgusting!' shrieked Melanie. 'Honestly, Edna, I just don't know why you stand for it. *I* wouldn't, I'll tell you straight.'

'It's all lies,' muttered Edna, going over to the fridge, opening it, and staring vacantly inside.

'*You* know that, *I* know that. But don't think that everyone who reads it is going to think that. They'll eat it up. The public loves a bit of juicy gossip. What *are* you looking for?'

'Nothing.' Edna shut the fridge and came and sat back at the table.

'Anyway,' continued Melanie, 'what about Evan? It can't be much fun for *him* reading all this junk about his father.'

'I'll hide it from Evan.'

'The boys at school will show him.'

'Oh, Melanie!' Edna's eyes filled with despairing tears, 'What can I do?'

Melanie smiled triumphantly. 'You *know* what you can do, I've told you enough times. If you *really* want to put a stop to all the gossip and lies, you can go on the tour with Al.'

'But . . .'

'No buts. I know what you're going to say. Al likes to travel alone. He worries when you're along. He likes you in the background. Well, shit, Edna. If you want to put a stop to the gossip you *must* be seen by his side.'

'Maybe you're right . . .'

'Of *course* I'm right. And I'll come too, you won't be alone. Will you tell Al? Or do you want me to?'

'No.' Edna jumped up nervously. 'I'll mention it.'

'Don't mention it – *tell* him.' Melanie stood up. 'I've got to be off, hairdressing appointment. Now don't forget, when he gets home tomorrow *tell* him.'

Edna nodded unsurely.

Outside the house Melanie climbed into her new white Simca sports car. Edna wouldn't tell him. Edna was scared shitless of him. If only *she* was married to Al. Oh boy, but things would be different then. Unfortunately she had picked the wrong brother. Paul just basked in the aura of a star – what *she* needed was the real thing.

Al liked her, he had always liked her. In fact . . . Melanie smiled. If *she* was married to him he wouldn't have to spend his life whoring around. Edna was a drag. Fat and dreary, not even pretty. What on earth had Al ever seen in her?

Melanie wanted to go on the tour. She would give any-thing to go on the tour. But – and it was a big but – as long as Edna wasn't going there was *no way* she could be aboard. She had nagged and cajoled Paul, but he had pointed out that as long as Al wasn't taking Edna it would be impossible for him to take her. And of course Al had no desire to take Edna. It would restrict his activities.

So Melanie was stuck, and the only hope was to prod Edna into a little action – and that was a difficult task. Edna thought the sun shone out of Al's ass, and even if she actually caught him screwing some hooker she would have a mouthful of excuses ready on his behalf.

Melanie pulled up her car on the double yellow line outside 'Mr Capones' and got out. She was blonde and pretty, with slightly pointed features, fashionably thin in all the right places, with a reasonable-sized bosom, and long dancer's legs. It was her legs that had first attracted Paul's attention. It was her legs that first attracted *everyone's* attention. She remembered, with a little smile, Manny Shorto, *the* Manny Shorto – famous but elderly American comedian. He had started on her legs and worked his way up . . . But then the bastard had run out on her . . . And she had met Paul. She had been one of the dancers on an Al King television spectacular. Paul had invited her out, and a year later they had married. Materially she had everything she wanted. It wasn't enough.

She swayed into 'Mr Capones', throwing her jacket at the receptionist. Mr Capone himself stepped forward to do her hair.

'Hi there,' she smiled lazily, catching his attention with her eyes, and holding it.

Mr Capone responded with a lingering look of his own. He was all tight trousers and teeth. He ran his hands through her hair. 'What do you want today?' he inquired.

Melanie smiled. 'Paul's coming back tomorrow, so you'd better make it something fuckable!'

☆

Edna didn't smoke or drink. Her weakness in times of crisis was eating. As soon as Melanie had departed she returned to the fridge and stared yet again at the contents. There was nothing she fancied. Nothing with chocolate or cream or pastry.

The maid came into the kitchen, and Edna shut the fridge guiltily. She could never get used to the servants. She hated having them around. A maid to do the work. A cook to prepare the meals. A chauffeur to take care of the shopping. What was there left for her to do?

'Can I get you something, madam?' asked the maid.

'Nothing, thank you.' Edna picked up the newspaper with

the vitriolic gossip item that Melanie had brought over and left the kitchen. She wandered into the garden: it was a nice day, sunny and warm. She hoped that the good weather would last over the weekend. Al enjoyed sitting by the pool, it did him good to be able to relax.

Maybe Melanie was right. Maybe she should go on the tour. She didn't relish the thought much, doing anything with Al publicly was a frightening experience. But it *would* put a stop to all these terrible rumours . . .

Al had mentioned he might take Evan along. She didn't like *that* idea at all, the boy was difficult enough as it was. Bad tempered, lazy, untidy, rude. However, without Evan at home it would be so quiet, and she could handle him, she understood him. He was a growing boy and needed the presence of his mother close by.

Edna sighed. Perhaps she should have gone to the hairdressers with Melanie. She wanted to look pretty for Al, she had been trying to diet but it wasn't easy. Anyway he was always saying that he liked her just the way she was. 'I like something to grab hold of,' he would comment.

On the other hand Melanie was always nagging at her to do something with herself. 'You *must* lose weight,' she would insist, 'why don't you come to the health club with me?' Edna remembered her day at the health club with cringing embarrassment. Perfectly made-up girls in white mini dresses who looked like they had come straight from the hairdressers verbally pulled her to pieces. 'You're *very* overweight.' 'Your skin is in a neglected state.' 'Your hair is lifeless.' 'You need massage, sauna, scalp treatment, colouring, tinting, skin therapy, a professional make-up.'

Edna had got through the day somehow, and she had to admit that when she emerged she did look almost glamorous. But the price had been ridiculous, and Al had hardly noticed any difference. That had been three months previously and she hadn't bothered to go back.

'Do you want to swim, Mrs King?'

Edna jumped. It was Nelson, the odd job man, who also attended to the maintenance of the swimming pool.

'No thank you, Nelson.'

'You sure? Won't take me but a minute to get my equipment out.' He leered knowingly at her.

'No.' Edna shook her head. She didn't like Nelson, there was something not quite nice about him. He had only been with them six weeks, and when she had complained to Al about him he had said, 'Give him a chance. It's not that easy to get people to work for you today.'

Nelson was watching her, and she tried to avoid his penetrating stare. It was no good, she couldn't feel at ease in front of him. Abruptly she turned and went back into the house. Was it her imagination or could she hear Nelson laughing? She would really have to talk to Al about him again.

☆

Evan King sat chewing on his fingernails in the back of the chauffeured Rolls. He huddled into the upholstery hoping as usual that not too many people would notice him. He was a very thin boy, with acned skin and greasy brown hair.

He resented the fact that every day he had to be ferried to and from school in a Rolls Royce. 'Why can't I take my bike?' he constantly demanded of Edna.

'It's not my decision,' she would reply. 'You know that your father insists on security.'

'Balls!' Evan would mumble in reply. He hated his bloody father. Bloody Al King. What a burden it was to go through school with someone like that for your father. The other kids gave him hell about it. Evan looked forward to the end of term with unconcealed joy. It was his *last* term, the end of school forever. He couldn't wait.

The Rolls dropped him off in front of the house, and Evan kicked at the gravel drive moodily. He anticipated his mother's questions. Hello, dear. Did you have a good day? What was for lunch? Who did you talk to? Is anyone coming over?

She bloody *knew* no one was coming over. They never did, except maybe once to check out Al King's house, and then to sneer. *Three* colour televisions. A *billiards* room. A *swimming* pool.

'Evan! Evan!' Nelson was calling to him from the side of the house.

'Yes?'

'Come here for a minute, got something to show you.'

Evan followed Nelson to the shed he used. 'Seen these?' said Nelson, proudly thrusting a pile of magazines upon him.

Evan squatted down on the ground and leafed through the magazines. They featured titles like 'Sun Child', 'Birds of Nature' and 'Pussy'. They consisted entirely of females in various stages of undress.

'Where did you get them?' asked Evan, slowly.

'I found them. Nice, aren't they? Some lovely little birds in there, real tasty little pieces. Nice. Aren't they nice then? I'll sell you the lot for a quid.'

'OK,' agreed Evan quickly. He stuffed the magazines in his school satchel and fished in his blazer pocket for some money.

'I could get you the real thing for a tenner,' offered Nelson, slyly. 'Ever had the real thing?'

'Course,' said Evan weakly.

'Yes,' agreed Nelson, 'I expect your old dad passes a few your way.' He laughed knowingly. 'I bet he's got crumpet knee deep.'

'See you,' said Evan, and headed for the house. Now if he could only avoid his mother he could settle down and *really* get a good look at the magazines.

'Evan, dear.' Edna sprang at him from outside the kitchen. 'How was school today?'

'OK.'

'You father telephoned from New York last night. He sends you his love.'

'What did he want?'

'Just to see how we were.'

'Did he mention the tour? I *can* go on it, can't I?'

'I suppose so. Whatever your father says. I was thinking that perhaps I might come too.'

'*You*,' stated Evan scornfully, 'why would *you* want to come?'

'I just thought it would be nice for both of us to go . . .'

'That's a lousy idea. It stinks. I don't want to go if you're going.'

'Oh, Evan.' Edna bit her lip, 'why ever not?'

'Because you spy on me. You're always asking me questions. Anyway, I'd like to be with dad alone.'

Edna nodded miserably. Where had they gone wrong with Evan? They had given him everything, denied him nothing. Yet he was full of hostilities and resentments. 'Is anyone coming over?' she asked.

'No.'

'Do you want some tea?'

'Yes.'

Edna scurried off to the kitchen to prepare him a tray. He was going through a difficult time. It was his age. She understood. He was just a child. Although when *she* had been sixteen she had been pregnant, and shortly after, married.

Edna sighed. She wished Al was home, she hated it when he was away.

5

Things were beginning to grow hazy. She had won. She was a star. And prepared as Dallas had been, the fuss and activity around her was startling. Photographers. Television cameras. People. Men. And a sudden tinge of respect reserved for a person who was about to become a personality. Dallas liked it, in fact she loved it. But she wanted to get rid of the cheesy cloak and crown. Most of all she wanted a drink.

At last the photographers were finished, and she was escorted back to the dressing-room to collect her belongings. The organizers of the contest seemed intent on taking her over. She was their 'Miss Coast to Coast', and as such they expected to make quite a bit of money promoting her for the year she would carry the title. She had won ten thousand dollars prize money, a screen test, and the chance of making a lot more money by accepting the various contracts to promote products that would be waved in her direction. For the time being she was being given a suite at the Plaza for a week, a car and chauffeur for the same period, and a list of immediate engagements that she would be expected to fulfil.

She was also being given a permanent escort, Mrs Fields, a middle-aged lady hired to keep a firm eye on the winner, and an even firmer eye on the winner's reputation. 'Miss

Coast to Coast' was supposed to represent the young, good, clean image of American girlhood. Dallas couldn't help giggling at *that* thought.

☆

Dallas Lunde survived the hazards of staying in Miami with hardly any money, no permanent residence, and no job, for almost three months.

She quickly picked up the pattern of the way things were. No man was permanent. They came and they went, and the trick was to find one who wasn't just a one-nighter.

The conventions were the best hunting grounds, and sometimes Dallas found herself with a man who might even stay as long as six or seven days.

She soon developed a routine. She got up late in whichever hotel room she had spent the night. Then she would order a substantial breakfast, watch television for a few hours, and if the man she was with had checked out, she would saunter down to the beach or swimming pool and look for a likely replacement. There was no shortage of replacements. She began to use make-up, bought herself some new clothes. In a way it was a whole exciting new life.

She had started to copy the way people talked on television. She loved the old Lana Turner movies, and moulded herself on the good-time girl with a heart of gold.

It did not occur to her that the type of life she was leading might be wrong. Sexually she derived no enjoyment from her encounters with the mainly older men she slept with. They seemed more than delighted with her, and she tried to please. They didn't bother her, they didn't hurt her, and most of the time she was free to watch television which was teaching her so much about life.

Then one day she met Bobbie.

It had been a fairly normal week. A married man in his fifties had kept her in his room for three days. He was in from Chicago on a toilet tissue convention. On his last night he became restless. 'Know any other broads?' he questioned.

Dallas shrugged. 'Nope.'

'I fancy a sandwich, a nice thick juicy little sandwich. Rye one side, white the other. Can you handle that?'

Dallas smiled vaguely. She had no idea what he was talking about.

The man phoned the desk clerk and made some mumbled

requests. Half an hour later Bobbie arrived. She was a tall black girl, wearing denim hot pants, boots, a lace-up sweater, and a curly wig. She had an incredible rounded jutting-out ass, and a flashing dazzling smile.

She greeted the man with a friendly kiss, and a 'Hey baby sugar. We gonna have ourselves a party!' *Then she requested a hundred dollars which she tucked safely into her boots. 'This your* wife?' *she asked, indicating Dallas. She had a habit of emphasizing the last word of every sentence.*

'Just another hooker,' the man said, and a thick excitement was creeping into his voice.

Dallas sat watching bemusedly.

'Well!' exclaimed Bobbie, arms akimbo, 'watcha want, man? What's your pleasure?'

'Undress me. Both of you.'

'Sure, sweetie honey. Bobbie will do a job on you that you ain't never gonna forget.' She turned and smiled at Dallas. 'You gonna help out, sister?'

Dallas stood up. She was wearing a red bikini.

Bobbie grinned at her, 'We all gonna have ourselves a little fun. *Good clean dirty* fun!'

She wriggled out of her hot pants, revealing a thick bush of wiry pubic hair. 'Take your drawers off,' she instructed Dallas, 'let's get this dude really in the mood. I don't want no limp dicks come hangin' out at me when I peel down his pants.'

Dallas slipped off the bottom half of her bikini, and for the first time since Burt Keyes she felt a strange sexual stirring.

'Let's get this show shakin'. Lie down, mister, I'm a gonna give it to you good!' Bobbie slithered his clothes off him as he lay immobile. Dallas stood watching as Bobbie casually hoisted herself on top of him.

'Come on, baby,' Bobbie encouraged, 'show him your titties, sit on his face, do somethin'!'

The situation was strange to Dallas. She didn't know what to do. And all the time there was this strange building excitement. She unhooked her bikini top.

'Hey momma!' shrieked Bobbie, bouncing happily up and down, 'you have got yourself a real pair!' *She climbed off the man, leaving him gasping. 'Wanna see a show, daddy? Wanna see a little* female *action?'*

The man nodded, his face red, his eyes bulging.

'So!' stated Bobbie, and she smiled at Dallas. 'Watcha say, sister? You wanna be the fella? Or will you leave it all to big bad Bobbie?'

'I don't know . . .' stammered Dallas. This was one situation that television hadn't *covered*.

'Lie down,' said Bobbie with a wicked grin, 'I always did like virgins!'

☆

'You're a very lucky girl,' Mrs Fields said crisply, as they sat in the limousine whisking them to the luxury of the Plaza.

'Yeah,' replied Dallas in mocking tones, 'a lucky little girl.'

Mrs Fields looked at her sharply; she hoped this one wasn't going to be difficult. The previous year's winner had been a sweet child, but the year before that the girl had been a bitch and caused everyone a lot of trouble.

'There will be a photo call at nine thirty in the morning. Usual thing, sitting up in bed wearing a nightie and the crown. Then we're to go to the office for you to sign some contracts. Lunch will be with a representative of a wool firm, if they decide to sign you it could be most lucrative. In the afternoon you open a supermarket, and in the evening you will go to the premier of *Guns at Dawn*. Do you have a boy-friend?'

'No.'

'Good. Much better that way. Boyfriends can get very jealous. This title will make a lot of difference to your life, you will be amazed at all the important people you'll meet. "Miss Coast to Coast" 1966 married a Senator. She was a lovely girl.'

'Was he?'

'Pardon?'

'Joke.'

'Oh. Well anyway, there are a few things you would do well to remember. You will be in the public eye for a year, and if you conduct your private life discreetly it will be much better for all concerned. A lot of men will be after you, but as far as this title is concerned morals are most important. My advice to you – and I have been looking after "Miss Coast to Coast" for thirteen years – is to not let it all go to your head.

Remember your home and your family. Remember your grass roots.'

Dallas choked back a laugh.

'I shall be staying at the Plaza with you for a week,' Mrs Fields continued, 'during that time your year's reign will be planned, and we will find you a suitable place to live, and of course, after that, I will accompany you on any out-of-town trips, and I will always be available for help and advice.'

'Sounds like a heavy schedule.'

' "Miss Coast to Coast" 1972 made a hundred thousand dollars. She was dedicated. She worked hard and she never complained.'

Dallas was silent. A hundred thousand dollars was a lot of bread. Not bad. She had entered the contest for a joke, an ego trip. Now perhaps she should look at things more seriously. She would have to ask Ed's advice, he might not be too thrilled now she had won. She would ask him later at the party.

☆

Dallas went to live with Bobbie. It was nice to have a proper home again after so many hotel rooms.

'Twenty dollars a lay!' Bobbie had scoffed, 'and all-nighters too! Kid – you bin givin' it away! From now on you're with me, and we don't do nothin' under a hundred apiece. Stick with me, baby queen, and we will all get rich!'

Bobbie lived in an untidy one-room apartment with mice roaming the kitchen, shabby furniture, and a closet full of kinky outfits. She had connections with most of the hotel clerks and her phone never stopped ringing. Most important, she had television, colour, twenty-eight-inch screen.

She taught Dallas everything she could. At first Dallas was a reluctant learner, but as her body responded to Bobbie she began to enjoy their relationship. Bobbie was the first person to come along that seemed to care about her.

Making love with men had never triggered any response, but with Bobbie it was different, and sex took on new meanings.

Bobbie organized their business engagements. She told Dallas what to do, what to wear. She taught her how to turn men on in exciting, new and inventive ways.

'You can fuck 'em shitless,' she advised Dallas, 'but it's only a job – keep it businesslike, never let them get to you. I'm the only one can get to you – right, sugar sweet? Right.'

Dallas agreed. But she didn't really agree. Deep down she knew that Burt Keyes could have got to her.

Six months went by. Then one night there was a call from a motel on the highway.

'Shoes. Chocolate sauce on your tits. Raincoat.' Bobbie instructed. 'I know this old dude, all he wants to do is lick the sauce off and come in your shoes,' she giggled, 'he's old!'

Bobbie drove them to the motel in her battered Ford. She was laughing and chattering all the way.

Dallas felt strange with the chocolate stickiness on her breasts, and her nakedness sticking to the plastic raincoat.

The man was indeed old. Bobbie had forgotten to mention the fact that he would be wearing pyjamas with his shrunken penis hanging limply out.

'He must be about ninety!' Dallas whispered, 'I don't think I can stand it.'

Bobbie threw her a stern look. 'I never back out on a promise. I'll make it up to you later. Let's go.'

They took off their raincoats, and the old man's eyes shone with a long lost desire. He lay down, and Bobbie leaned over him, dangling her chocolate-coated nipple over his mouth. Dallas did the same. The old man licked feebly.

After a few minutes Bobbie took off her shoe and held it over the old man's slightly aroused penis. 'Let's do it for mamma!' she crooned.

He started to come in great heaves and jerks.

Dallas turned away. Was that the moment she decided that this wasn't the life for her?

Suddenly there was a strange, groaning, rattling noise, then silence.

'Oh Holy God!' exclaimed Bobbie suddenly, 'the old bastard died on us. He died!'

Dallas turned slowly round. Surely Bobbie was making one of her usual jokes? But when she saw the old man lying there, she knew that he was dead.

Bobbie slapped him on the face. 'Wake up!' she commanded, 'wake up.'

'If he's dead,' stated Dallas blankly, 'what are we going to do?'
Bobbie gathered her raincoat up. 'Get the hell out of here, that's
what we'll do.'
'But what about the police? They'll know we were here, the desk
clerk called you, he'll tell them.'
'We didn't kill him.'
'I don't want to see the police.'
'I'm with you, sister. We'll get the hell out. Nobody will find
him till the morning, we can be in LA by then.'
'Have we got enough money?'
'Sure and he hasn't paid us.' Bobbie looked for his bankroll,
found it, started to peel off two hundred dollar bills, thought better
of it and pocketed the lot. Let's go, sugar, baby. Let's get our asses
out of here.'

☆

Dallas was the star of the party, and she positively glowed in
the limelight. Everyone wanted to talk to her, men and
women alike.

Ed Kurlnik hovered nearby. He had to be cool, couldn't
be obvious. Ramo Kaliffe flashed Arab white teeth in her
direction. Lucy Mabel Mann smiled sweetly and invited her
to lunch.

'Miami Beach has gone off to meet Al King,' Miss Boston
volunteered, 'isn't *she* the lucky one.'

Dallas smiled, and vaguely recalled some photographer
offering her the chance of a night with Al King. Who needed
that scene? Stars were boring. Boring people. Boring fucks.
All they did was talk about themselves and break a leg to
reach the mirror first.

'I think I'll stay at the apartment tonight,' Ed managed to
inform her.

'I thought you always had to go home on Saturdays?'

'Tonight will be an exception.'

She had only won a matter of hours earlier, and already
Ed was prepared to make exceptions. 'I have to stay at the
Plaza for a week.'

Ed raised his eyebrows, 'You don't *have* to.'

'But I think I will.'

Ed frowned. 'Why?'

'Why not? I've always wanted to stay at the Plaza.'

'Why didn't you say so before, we could have done so any time.'

'Any time, Ed?' He was scared to even walk down the street with her. If wifey ever knew she would clamp down on his seventy million dollars like a vice.

'If you like,' Dallas offered slyly, 'you could come and see me at the hotel later.' The thought of Ed Kurlnik sneaking into the Plaza to visit her brought tears of laughter.

'I can't do that,' replied Ed, outraged. 'You *know* I can't do that.'

They were interrupted by a photographer snapping random shots, and Ed nipped smartly out of the picture.

Dallas yawned, it had been a tiring day and she was exhausted. But so what? She was a somebody. She was 'Miss Coast to Coast', and she couldn't flake out on her night of triumph.

This was her night and she was determined to enjoy it.

6

Al woke late with a feeling of apprehension. He didn't feel that good, in fact he felt dreadful.

He lay in bed, opened his eyes, and did not feel like getting up at all.

He knew why he felt bad, it was fear, plain honest to goodness fucking nerves.

The forthcoming tour was bugging the hell out of him.

Why was he so nervous? He had tried to figure it out. It wasn't like he had never been on the road before, he had done many successful tours. But the last one had been two years previously, and two years was a long time between gigs. OK, so there had been the cabaret dates, the television spectaculars, the records. But basically what Al *liked*, what he *wanted*, was that contact with a huge live audience. Going out there and doing your thing was what it was all about. The ultimate high.

He had made so much money in the last few years. If he wanted to pack it in and never work again he would be more than set. So the records weren't selling so well, they tried to keep it from him, but he was well aware of every happening in his career. So what did the tour *really* mean to him?

It meant finding out how the people felt. Were the same fans who had been out there two years ago still going to be around? Were they still going to react with the same degree of enthusiasm? Was he still the tops? Or was he, at thirty-seven, a little too old for the adulation and hysteria? Would he now be regarded as just another establishment star?

He still looked great. He still sounded the same. Was that good or bad? Would they expect him to have changed?

And would his voice still be up to it? Would it survive the strain of God knows how many performances in vast stadiums?

Al coughed nervously. He wished the goddamn tour would start already. Every morning he woke up to the same fears and it was getting him down. He couldn't even discuss his thoughts with Paul, he didn't want to give voice to his doubts. Maybe when he got home he would tell Edna, but knowing her she would probably suggest that he cancel the whole tour and stay at home. Her secret dream was that they would lose all their money and move back into one room.

Edna was still the same sweet simple girl that he had married. She hadn't changed with his success. She hadn't grown.

In a way Al was grateful, but in another way he resented her. Why didn't she read more? Entertain? Wear beautiful clothes? *Improve* herself?

He had changed, and he was glad of it. When he had started in the business he had been very rough, a right layabout. Now he could go anywhere, meet anyone, and feel perfectly at ease.

Edna was more like a mother than a wife. Always there. Always uncomplaining. Hot meals. Clean shirts. She was the one who took his cock out to massage his balls because his stage trousers were too tight. That was about the only time she took it out too. He sighed. Every day the bridge seemed to get wider.

Of course he should never have got married. But then he would not have had Evan, and it was wonderful to have a son, even if the boy did need taking in hand.

How many happy marriages did he know of? How many

that lasted longer than five years? In the world he moved in now – not many. At least he could trust Edna. She would never think of looking at another man. And she loved him for himself, the whole Al King bit meant nothing to her.

He sighed again. Then he remembered Paul was supposed to be arranging lunch for him with – what was her name – the beauty contest winner – Dallas. Yeah. Al grinned. Not a bad bit of crumpet.

He consulted his digital watch to discover it was eleven-thirty. He hauled himself out of bed, and launched into thirty push-ups. Christ, but they got more difficult every day.

Lunch with a girl called Dallas. What would she be like?

Like the rest. Pretty but dumb. Either posing in front of a mirror all the time, or allowing him to scrawl his autograph across her ripe and ready breasts. Women – they were all the same.

Disgust built in Al's gut. Disgust at himself for using women, and contempt for the women for *allowing* themselves to be used just because he was a star.

Fuck it. To hell with a girl called Dallas. He picked up the phone and dialled Paul's room.

☆

Paul had not spent the perfect morning.

He had left Linda's place at 6 a.m. while she still slept. She had woken at seven and phoned to inform him that she was not pleased.

He was not pleased either. He had fought off a stoned mugger and been unable to find a cab for ten blocks.

Mental note. Get Linda an apartment on the better side of town.

Now he was going through one big hassle trying to arrange a lunch date for Al with 'Miss Coast to Coast'. He had finally convinced the organizers what a great coup it would be, but apparently Dallas felt otherwise.

Paul wondered who or what would placate Al. Turn-downs were rare, in fact Paul could not recall the last one.

The phone rang. It was Al.

'Ah,' said Paul cheerily, 'how we feeling today?'

'In good shape. What's new?'

'Mention of the tour in all the columns. Bitch item in

Reporter. Nothing heavy.' Paul was damned if *he* was going to mention the lunch. Maybe Al had forgotten.

'About that lunch I wanted you to arrange . . .'

'Oh, yes. Well, it's like this, she . . .'

'Cancel it.'

'Cancel it?'

'You heard me. 'Who needs it?'

'You're right. I'll wipe it out immediately.' Paul hung up relieved. He was off the hook. Now Al would never know he had been turned down.

Paul was very protective towards his brother. He liked things to go smoothly for Al, he always had. Even at the beginning Paul had only told Al the good things that happened. He never mentioned the recording companies and theatre managers who had not wanted to know . . . He spoke only with glowing enthusiasm of Al's future career, and he pushed and pushed until he made a crack big enough to send Al into orbit.

He had willed Al's success, and he had also worked his ass off to make it happen.

There was a knock on the door. 'Morning,' Linda said brightly, 'I was a bitch on the phone and I'm sorry.' She put her arms round his neck and stretched on tiptoe to kiss him.

The phone rang, and Paul went to answer it.

Linda lit a cigarette and wandered over to the window. She felt the usual tight feeling that she always got when Paul was leaving. He came into her life. He went out of her life. He was like the goddamn sea. It was most unsettling. She was just his New York girlfriend, someone to hump while he was away from his wife. She had made up her mind though that *something* would have to be settled on the tour, or that would be it.

'Trying to get hold of Bernie is impossible,' Paul complained, hanging up the phone.

Linda laughed, 'What about "Miss Coast to Coast"? Did you line her up for lunch?'

'Funny thing, she turned us down flat. Can you believe that? First time that happened in . . .' He was interrupted by the phone jangling. It was Bernie Suntan. He launched into a business conversation.

Linda was just lighting another cigarette when Al came in.

43

He swooped down on her with a kiss and a hug. Standard Al King greeting, but it made her uncomfortable. He had a habit of thrusting a knee intimately between her legs. She had learned to automatically back away, but this time she was not quick enough.

'You smoke too much,' Al admonished.

'It's *my* cancer.' Linda replied defensively.

'Funny. Hope you're not laughing all the way to the grave.'

'So "Miss Coast to Coast" was *still* not available,' Linda snapped, 'hate to say I told you so!'

'What do you mean? *I* was the one who cancelled out on the lunch.'

'Oh come on, Paul told me she turned you down flat.'

Al's smile faded. 'Paul – what is this shit?'

Paul waved vaguely. He was busy on the phone and had not heard their conversation.

'He's talking to Bernie,' Linda explained.

'Fuck Bernie. When I want to talk to baby brother, I talk.' Al walked over and cut off the connection with a vicious slam of his hand.

'What the hell are you doing?' complained Paul, 'I've been trying to get hold of Bernie all morning.'

'Did you fix up that beauty queen bitch for lunch or did you not?'

'You said you didn't want to have lunch with her.'

'I know that. But was she coming?'

'I don't really know – I was . . .'

'Cut the shit . . . She said no. Right? As your girlfriend so nicely put it, she turned me down flat. Right?'

Paul glared at Linda, 'What does it matter? You didn't want to have lunch anyway.'

'I've changed my mind. Get her.' Al slammed his way out of the room.

'What can I say?' mumbled Linda.

'I think you've said enough. You *know* what he's like, why couldn't you just keep quiet?'

'I guess I'll go home.'

'I guess you should.'

Once again Al had come between them. Well screw him, she wasn't going to creep out. 'If you like,' she ventured, 'I'll see if I can fix something. I have some pictures I could drop by the hotel – maybe I could talk to Dallas.'

'Anything would help.' He softened. 'Look, I know it's not really your fault, I should have told you not to say anything.' He kissed her. 'I'll be waiting for your call, do what you can.'

7

Her photograph adorned the front page of the newspapers, and she studied it intently. It was a thrill, a great big crazy thrill. On the same page there was an article about the President, and there was a picture of him also, a small picture, *much* smaller than the one of her. Suddenly she was *somebody*, no longer a faceless hooker, but a person whose photograph was larger than the President's!

She was staying at the Plaza Hotel and she didn't have to fuck anybody. She was a free agent. She had a cheque for ten thousand dollars, and she hadn't lain on her back to earn it.

She felt incredibly elated. She leapt out of bed, threw open the window, and admired the view.

☆

'Check out the view, sugar baby!' Bobbie insisted when they flew into Los Angeles, 'Mind blowing!'

They went to stay with a friend of Bobbie's who was white, miserable, and addicted to heroin.

'I can't stand it here!' Dallas insisted after a few days. 'Aren't we going to get a place of our own?'

'Yeah,' agreed Bobbie, 'we gotta get back in action.'

So she found them an apartment off the Strip, and renewed her connections.

Things in Hollywood were different. No longer out-of-town schmucks set on getting laid. Instead, sophisticated, jaded people, who required much more than a simple fuck. Dallas started to complain immediately.

'Shit man!' exclaimed Bobbie, 'just shut your eyes an' think of nothin'. Their money is just the same.'

'No,' insisted Dallas, 'I won't do it.'

'OK,' agreed Bobbie, 'we'll only book you out to the straights.'

So Dallas found herself alone most of the time. She cleaned the apartment and did the cooking; it kept her busy while Bobbie was out working. She also learned to drive – an essential for California living.

But it wasn't long before she started to feel a revulsion at Bobbie's advances. At first it had been something new, but now, with Bobbie coming home from a twenty-handed orgy, it began to pall when she wanted to make love.

'You got yourself another girlfriend?' Bobbie asked accusingly.

'No, I'm just tired.'

The more she resisted Bobbie, the more the black girl started to do for her. She bought her presents and flowers and chocolates. She became like an attentive suitor.

One day Dallas packed her things and left. She was fed up with the whole situation. She moved into a bungalow at the Beverly Hills Hotel with an impotent writer who liked her to walk around naked. That was all he required of her, and he was quite friendly and nice. He didn't pay her, but she had free board and lodging at one of the best hotels in town, and the use of his Cadillac. It was a convenient arrangement, and occasionally Dallas would pull a trick on the side and make some extra money. There was one man who came to the hotel pool every day and offered her a thousand dollars to star in a porno film. Dallas declined. 'Why?' he had questioned affronted, 'ain't ya ever heard of Linda Lovelace?'

She had heard of her, but it wasn't the kind of stardom she wanted. In her mind she knew there was a better life for her somewhere. Television had shown her the American dream, and she saw no reason why there shouldn't be a piece of it for her.

Bobbie found her five weeks later. She was waiting when Dallas returned from a shopping trip. 'Get your ass packed and out of here!' she snapped.

Dallas stopped in amazement. How had Bobbie found her?

The writer, somewhat nervous, but smiling bravely, said: 'I think that you had better do what your – uh – friend says.'

'You goddamn right she better do it!' snapped Bobbie, tossing her wig impatiently, and tapping green-taloned nails on the table.

'Are you asking me to go?' Dallas inquired of the writer.

'Well – er – yes. I didn't realize that you were – that you had a – uh – well permanent sort of – er – friend.'

He was deeply embarrassed and would not look her in the eyes.

I don't have to go,' Dallas stated flatly.

'Oh yes you do, sugar sweets,' interrupted Bobbie quickly, 'I got things to say to you that you ain't gonna want no-one to hear.'

Dallas packed. One suitcase of possessions was the sum total of her belongings.

'Goodbye,' she said to the man she had lived with for five weeks.

'Bye,' he mumbled, redfaced. God knows what Bobbie had told him.

'See ya!' yelled Bobbie cheerily, 'any time you wanna free one give me a call.' Under her breath she muttered, 'No balls, you sure picked a loser, kid,'

Outside, in the car Bobbie said: 'I bail ya outa the shit in Miami, give you a home, clothes, work my black ass off fuckin' pigs so that you can take it easy, and what happens? What the frig happens? Soon as I turn my back you all hightail it outa my life for what you think will be forever. Well, sugar baby, life just ain't that simple. I knew I'd find you, and I did.' She smiled triumphantly. 'Shoulda bin a friggin' detective.'

'What do you want? I didn't take anything.'

'I didn't take anything!' mimicked Bobble sarcastically. 'Kid, you are green all the way up. You an me are together, a team. We know too much about each other to split up. You dig what I mean, baby doll? Cast your mind back to a certain motel and a certain old dude, a very old dude. You get it?'

'I get it.'

'Good girl. I knew you would understand once I explained it to you real simple like. Now we can get to work – you an' me. I think it's about time ya got used to the Hollywood way of life. Shit, baby – I am through protectin' you – from now on it's togetherness – all the way. You dig?'

☆

The photo call was fun. Sitting upright in bed, low-cut nightie, crown on the head, and fifteen guys struggling to get the best picture. Smile. Flash. Laugh. Flash. Sexy look. Flash.

Mrs Fields allowed them an hour, and then it was up and dressed and over to the offices of the organizers to sign some contracts.

Dallas wouldn't sign. 'I have a friend who I'd like to check them out with first,' she explained sweetly.

'Sure,' they agreed, but they were all pissed off.

'By the way,' Mrs Fields said, 'Al King, the singer, would like to take you to lunch. We could arrange it as a nice little publicity thing.'

'I thought I was supposed to be having lunch with some wool firm?'

'We could postpone that.'

'Don't. The more things I do as "Miss Coast to Coast" the more I'll like it.' Offhandedly she added, 'Let's face it, Al King's probably only looking to get laid and really, I'm not that sort of a girl.'

'Quite,' agreed Mrs Fields, and she sighed, because suddenly she realized that it was not going to be an easy week.

'Now,' said Dallas brightly, 'have I got time to spend some money before lunch? I've always wanted to go into Saks and spend *my* money.'

☆

Life with Bobbie was no longer the same. The black girl's easygoing friendliness was gone. Instead she was tough, flip, and businesslike. She spelled it out to Dallas in no uncertain terms. They had killed a guy, together, and because of that simple fact they were stuck with each other.

'You had better get used to it, kid,' Bobbie warned, ''cos if you run off again I'll find you, and next time I ain't gonna let you off so easy.'

So began a year of complete and utter degradation for Dallas. She had not believed that people with such devious and perverted tastes existed. Bobbie made sure that she came across every one of them.

'They're clients,' Bobbie would explain, straightfaced, 'it's just another job.'

It was a year of gradual hardening for Dallas. The only way she could face the things she did for money was to shut everything out. They could have her face, her body, but they could never get into her mind. She became as good and as practised at her job as Bobbie. And like the black girl who had been a hooker since was was thirteen, she became hard, cynical, tough and unfeeling. Unlike Bobbie, she wanted no other comforts, she didn't turn to women for a relationship, she cut that side of her life out completely. Sex was her profession, and that was all.

Bobbie and she lived together increasingly uneasily.

*They did not resume any personal relationship, and Bobbie –
who had always been into smoking pot, started on other little habits.
By the end of the year she was into heroin, and Dallas knew she
had to get away.*

*She waited for the right opportunity, and as soon as she set eyes
on Ed Kurlnik she knew that this was a chance she mustn't blow.*

☆

Mrs Fields accompanied Dallas around Saks.

'I want this – this – and this,' Dallas snatched dresses off
the racks. 'Oh and the black evening gown from the window,
and does it come in any other colours? Great, I'll take it in
every colour.'

'Your money won't last long at this rate,' Mrs Fields said
warningly.

'I know,' laughed Dallas. But oh the thrill of spending her
own money. She had a charge at Saks that Ed had opened for
her, but buying this way was much more satisfying. She
managed to spend three thousand dollars in half an hour,
and she was giddy with excitement. She breezed through
lunch with the wool firm representatives full of charm
and laughter. They wanted her to sign to an advertising and
promotion contract immediately. Mrs Fields was impressed.
'They usually take weeks to make up their minds.'

'I want double the amount they have paid before.'

'They'll never pay more.'

'Wanna bet, baby!' Dallas laughed, 'they'll pay, and be
pleased to.'

'I'll tell the office,' said Mrs Fields, tight-lipped.

'By the way,' inquired Dallas, 'what's the fee I'm getting
for opening the supermarket this afternoon?'

'I don't really know.'

'Find out, 'cos if it's not enough I'm not doing it.'

Mrs Field nodded. She had been right, this one *was* going
to be difficult.

☆

*Ed Kurlnik and Dallas Lunde were side by side in their respective
cars at the traffic lights. Dallas recognized him immediately, she
had seen him on television only three days previously.*

Ed Kurlnik. Head of the Kurlnik Motor dynasty. One of the

richest men in America. Married. Two children. Sixty-one years old.

And here he was, driving a Kurlnik Leopard, completely alone. Dallas couldn't believe her luck.

The traffic lights changed, and his Leopard sprang away with surprising speed. Without hesitation Dallas slid into the lane behind him. She knew exactly what she would do.

He stopped at the next red light, and Dallas, in her battered old Buick, careered into the back of him. It wasn't a bad smash, but it was enough to dent her fender and break one of his rear lights. She slumped forward over her wheel and waited.

It was that easy.

He was concerned. He took her to his hotel for coffee.

'I must have fainted,' she explained.

He was kindly, fatherly. He asked her out for dinner. She told him she was a student. He took her out again. She told him she was a virgin. Another date. She became an orphan.

When he suggested the apartment in New York she hesitated at first. When he insisted she finally agreed. But what to do about Bobbie? She would never let her go, and if she did manage to get away, Bobbie would come looking for her, and then Ed would find out the truth and that would be that.

Dallas puzzled over what to do. This was her chance and she didn't want to blow it.

The answer when it came to her was incredibly simple – she would kill Bobbie.

☆

'Not enough,' Dallas stated. 'If you want me to open super-markets I get a thousand dollars.'

'They won't pay that.'

'Then I won't open them. It's that simple. Now I'm taking the afternoon off and I'll see you back at the hotel later. Don't worry, I'll be there in plenty of time for the première.'

She left Mrs Fields sitting rigid-faced in the offices of Beauty Incorporated Co. – the outfit that organized the 'Miss Coast to Coast' contest.

If they thought they had hold of another dumb girl to hustle and promote for a year, they were on the wrong track. She had her own idea of the way things should be, and that way was *her* way.

She took a cab over to the apartment in the hope that Ed would be there, but he wasn't. Probably pissed off about the previous evening. She phoned him on his private number at his New York office. He *was* pissed off.

'Listen, sweetie,' she cooed, 'it's just all been so exciting. I'm sorry about last night, were you lonely? Why don't you come over now and I'll surprise you.'

He wasn't hard to persuade.

She took a quick shower, and then surveyed her closet of Ed's favourite outfits. What would surprise him today? Something subservient, something apologetic.

She finally hit it. Martha the Maid.

Humming softly to herself she slid into the short black dress with the white starched collar and cuffs, the sheer black stockings, the neat black shoes, and as a final touch a small adornment of white lace ribbon in her hair.

One thing about Ed, he loved surprises.

8

The stewardess smiled winningly. 'Everything all right?' she asked for the twentieth time.

Al ignored her.

'Perfect,' replied Paul, returning her smile.

'More champagne?'

'I think we're well topped up.'

'If you need anything just give me a buzz.'

'Wouldn't hesitate.'

She smiled and lingered. 'Mr King,' she said directly to Al, 'I *loved* your last record, I just had to tell you.'

Al looked her over. She was sleek and blonde with a well-developed bosom straining at the confines of her regulation blouse. 'Do you fuck?' he asked crudely.

She didn't even blush. 'It depends,' leaning forward slightly she added, 'Are you offering?'

Paul wished that he was somewhere else. Al was impossible when he was in one of his 'I hate women' moods, and that was the mood he had been in all day.

'When?' inquired Al.

'Tonight, tomorrow.'

'Screw tonight, tomorrow. I want it now.'

She laughed. 'I'm on duty.'

'All I want is a little service.'

Paul got up. He was not enjoying being in the crossfire of their conversation. He wandered over to the magazine rack.

A few minutes passed and then Al got up and vanished into one of the toilets, followed shortly by the stewardess.

Paul went back to his seat. Casual sex had never appealed to him, it gave him bad vibes. It always reminded him of the way animals went at it. Sniff Sniff – I fancy you. He preferred to get into a woman's head first, her body second.

He thought about Linda. She was all the woman he had ever wanted. Intelligent, attractive, independent. If he wasn't married to Melanie . . . But he was and somewhere along the way, she had changed. She had become one of life's grabbers. Gimme . . . Gimme . . . Gimme. Bigger house, bigger pool, bigger car. She demanded the best of everything, and nagged the hell out of him if she didn't get it. If it wasn't for the children . . . married man's lament, and he knew it. But they were both so young and vulnerable, and they needed him.

Al returned to his seat, strapped himself in, and resumed gazing out of the window.

'Only another two hours,' remarked Paul.

Al nodded. He had become completely uncommunicative ever since Paul had been unable to arrange lunch with Dallas. It was his way of showing disapproval.

He was a *star* for Chrissakes. If he wanted something, he should have it *immediately*.

☆

Melanie King went to the airport in Al's white Rolls Royce to meet them. She enjoyed being the centre of attention, and some of the airport photographers took her photo.

Al and Paul came walking through from customs, and the photographers sprang into action.

Melanie darted forward and kissed Al, she followed this up with a quick peck for Paul, then hanging firmly onto Al's arm she walked with them both to the car.

'Edna's cooking dinner,' she volunteered, 'steak and kidney pud, she slung the cook out and she's having a ball.'

'She hasn't fired the cook, has she?' asked Al, alarmed.

'Oh no, just got rid of her for the night. The maid too. I don't know how she manages.'

'She enjoys it,' sighed Al. 'My wife the worker!'

Melanie squeezed his arm. 'Tell me about the trip, I want to hear all about it. I hope you two didn't get up to anything naughty,' she giggled, 'bet *you* did, Al. It's all right, I won't tell Edna.'

☆

Edna opened the oven and prodded the sizzling potatoes with a fork. They were just the way Al liked them, cut into thin slices and covered with onions and herbs. The steak and kidney pudding simmered on the cooker, and all she had left to do was to whip the cream that would accompany the baked jam roll dessert.

All Al's favourite things, and yet she couldn't remember the last time they had eaten such delicious food. Al usually instructed the cook on what they would have for dinner, and it varied between steak, plain chicken, or fish, always with a salad. Al insisted that he had to watch his diet. 'Cholestrol,' he would mention ominously if Edna suggested so much as a cottage pie. In the old days they had lived on cottage pie, sausages, mashed potatoes, and chips. In the old days Al had loved his food, and for once Edna wanted to be sure that he got something he enjoyed.

She hummed softly as she busied herself in the kitchen. It seemed such a long time since Al had been home, although in point of fact it was only a couple of weeks. New York, and before that the health farm.

Everything in the kitchen seemed in order, so Edna went upstairs and changed out of her pinafore dress into a long plum-coloured shirtwaister. She powdered her face, added lipstick, too much rouge, and blue eyeshadow which immediately streaked. She had never been much good with make-up, but Al liked her to try. She dabbed on some perfume, and brushed her short mousey brown hair. As she was surveying herself in the mirror Evan slouched in.

'What are *you* all dressed up for?' he asked sneeringly

'I want to look nice for your father.'

'Well, you look awful. All that stuff on your face doesn't suit you. It looks stupid, I don't know why you bother, he *knows* what you look like.'

Edna frowned. Perhaps he was right, perhaps she did look ridiculous. But it was too late to do anything about it; she could hear a car pulling up on the gravel outside, and excitedly she ran downstairs.

☆

Al got out of the car and Paul pulled Melanie back and snapped, 'Do we *have* to stay for dinner?'

'Yes,' snapped back Melanie, 'Edna's prepared it specially.'

'I wanted to see the children.'

'Nobody's stopping you. Pop over, kiss them goodnight, and come right back. I'll go in and make some martinis, I shouldn't think Edna could cope with that.'

'All right,' agreed Paul. 'I'll be back in a minute.'

Al and Paul had adjoining houses. They had acquired the land at a reasonable price some seven years previously, and they had divided it neatly down the middle and built respective mansions. Al's was ranch style, Paul's white and modern. They both had swimming pools, garages large enough for four cars, billiard rooms, and saunas. Paul often thought it was stupid and nouveau riche to have both built swimming pools, but Melanie had *insisted*. 'I don't want to feel like a poor relation,' she had complained when he had suggested they didn't need one.

His children were sitting up in bed washed and scrubbed, and nanny was reading them a story.

'Hey, kids!' exclaimed Paul, 'did you miss daddy?'

They leapt excitedly out of bed and threw themselves at him, until he was a tangle of arms and legs and kisses. It was a good feeling. Love. Pure and unblemished. The only true kind.

Nanny got them off him and settled them back in bed.

'Mustn't get too excited,' she admonished, 'otherwise we won't sleep, will we?'

Paul knew when he wasn't wanted. Nanny hated having her routine screwed up. And Melanie bent over backwards to please nanny. 'Do you realize,' she, had once informed

Paul, her pretty face grimacing with horror, 'if nanny ever left us I'd have to look after the children myself!'

On impulse Paul went downstairs to his study, locked himself in, and direct dialled Linda's number in New York. She was there.

'I miss you,' he said.

'I love you,' she replied.

He wondered very seriously what Melanie would say if he asked for a divorce.

☆

'Hello there, fatso!' Al walloped Edna on the behind. 'All tarted up. Are we going out?'

Edna blushed. He *had* noticed.

Melanie hung onto Al's arm. 'How about a delicious cold martini? Shall I fix us some?' She led Al into the living room and called over her shoulder, 'Ice, Edna.'

'Where's Evan?' Al demanded. 'Funny kid, you'd think he'd be here to greet me.' He went to the foot of the stairs and screamed out, 'Evan!!'

The boy appeared at the top of the stairs, white-faced and pasty.

'Don't I get any sort of greeting?' demanded Al. 'Come down here,'

Evan walked slowly down the stairs and Al grabbed hold of him in a bearhug.

'How's it going, boyo?' he asked cheerfully, 'still the randiest little bugger at school!' He winked at Melanie. 'Just like his dad. I thought about nothing but girls when I was his age.'

'Have things changed?' giggled Melanie.

Al burst out laughing. Evan scowled.

Edna came bustling in with the ice. 'Where's Paul? Dinner's nearly ready.'

'He'll be right back, he just popped over to see the kids.' Melanie busied herself behind the bar.

'Was New York nice?' Edna asked.

'Not bad,' replied Al, 'business, business, business. I just want to relax now. Christ, but it's a noisy city.'

'I love it there,' interrupted Melanie. 'The shops, and the theatres. Wouldn't you love to go, Edna?'

'Not really . . .' she caught Melanie's look and added lamely, 'Well yes, I suppose I would.'

Al wasn't even listening, he was staring out into his garden. 'Who's been fucking around with my apple tree?' he demanded.

'Don't use that language,' said Edna, 'not in front of you know who.' She glanced stealthily at Evan. 'You know I don't like it.'

'Who,' said Al coldly, 'has touched my apple tree?'

'I did,' scowled Evan, 'I cut off a few rotten branches.' He turned to Edna. *She* told me to.'

Edna blushed. 'I didn't think you'd mind. The bad apples were falling in the pool. I didn't think you'd mind . . .'

'Jesus H!' exclaimed Al. 'What the fuck do you think I employ a gardener for? It's too bad, Edna, just too bloody bad . . .'

Her eyes filled with tears. 'I'll see to dinner,' she mumbled.

'Martini!' said Melanie brightly, and she handed Al a glass.

Paul returned, and Al took him to one side. 'I've had a great idea.'

'Yeah?' questioned Paul with relief. At least Al was talking to him again.

'We finish off the TV special next week?'

'That's right. There's just the locations left to shoot.'

'Great. You know the number "Lady"?'

'The song you sing to Katy May?'

'Right. Where are we shooting it?'

'South of France.'

'Terrific. Now Katy just sits there, right?'

'We start off with a shot of you and her in an open car driving along the coastline, then the beach, swimming, fooling around. Should be fantastic'

'Have you ever seen Katy in a bikini?'

'Why?'

'She's short. Oh I know she's cute and cuddly, and a lovely little singer, but . . .'

'And very popular.'

'I give you that.'

Paul sighed. He smelled trouble. 'What are you leading up to?'

'I don't think it's going to look right my singing "Lady" to Katy.'

'She's the only female guest on your show.'

'She doesn't have to be.'

'Who do you want? Raquel Welch?'

'I want "Miss Coast to Coast". Perfect little spot for her. She'll do it if we pay her the right amount. Call New York and arrange it. And Paul – this time don't fuck it up.'

'Dinner's ready,' called Edna. She had recovered her composure, and proudly set out all Al's favourite foods in the middle of the dining-room table.

'When you get a hard-on . . .' muttered Paul.

'Humour me. After all, I *am* the star of the family. Evan! Come on, boyo, dinner's ready.'

Melon to start. Al liked melon. He wolfed it down, then got up from the table and said, 'None of this other crap for me, I've got to watch the old weight.'

'I've cooked all your favourite things,' wailed Edna. 'Al, you *must* eat.'

'Sorry,' said Al cheerfully, 'can't let the paying public down. Anyway, I'm not hungry. Evan, fancy a game of tennis?'

Evan scowled. That was the last thing he felt like doing.

Edna's eyes brimmed over with tears, and, streaked with blue eyeshadow, they fell silently down her cheeks.

One thing stardom had done for big brother, mused Paul, it had turned him into a right bastard.

9

When Ed Kurlnik left, Dallas fixed herself a large vodka on the rocks. She put on a bathrobe, curled up in a chair, and nursing her drink, she mulled over the previous scene.

Ed Kurlnik. Powerful. Rich. Married

Ed Kurlnik. Little sixty-one-year-old boy who liked to play games. Naughty games.

She reached beneath the chair she was sitting on and fished out a recent magazine. Ed Kurlnik was on the cover with his wife, Dee Dee, a strong, respectable-looking woman with steely grey hair and icy blue eyes. A woman in her middle fifties – fifty-six the magazine said – who was still attractive in a lady of the manor way.

Dallas opened up the magazine and turned to a picture of two girls. The Kurlnik twins. The Kurlnik heirs. Rich bitches, with cool blonde hair and wide-spaced grey eyes. Twenty years old. The same age as she was. One of them wore riding clothes, the other a neat skirt, sweater, and pearls.

Dallas laughed aloud. Pearls indeed! She would fuck their father wearing pearls, she would make him buy them for her. Or maybe he could borrow them from his daughter, now *that* would be a laugh . . .

She read the article through for the hundredth time. It was like reading about a stranger. And yet she knew him so well, or thought she did. 'Ed and Dee Dee Kurlnik are one of the happiest married couples on the island.' She read about their holiday home on Fire Island. 'There is nothing better Ed Kurlnik likes to do than pitch a barbecue and feed his family.' Dallas could think of many things he liked to do better than that. 'Ed Kurlnik has always been the perfect father. Work or play, he always puts his family first.' Did they still make love? Ed and the well-preserved Dee Dee. Dallas bit hard on her lip. She didn't want him making love to anyone else, she wanted to be the only one.

'The twins never bother or worry their father. Dana is studying nursing, and Cara is interested in social work.' Crap! No one family could be *that* perfect. Dee Dee was probably an old lush, and the twins raving nymphos.

Dallas stuffed the magazine back under the chair.

How would life have been if Ed Kurlnik had been *her* father? Would she have worn riding clothes and studied nursing? Would someone have *cared* what she made of her life?

She had left home at seventeen and *nobody* had cared. Nobody had come looking for her. She had become a hooker, a whore. Nobody had forced her to, she had just drifted into it. And nobody gave a shit. She wondered if her parents or her husband or even Burt and Ida Keyes had given her a second thought. Probably not. Life at the zoo had probably just kept going.

What would they all think of her now? A beauty queen, a

title holder, girlfriend of one of the richest men in America. They still probably wouldn't give a shit. They were like that.

Dallas sighed. She had got over the hurt a long time ago. So they hadn't come looking for her. Big deal. They wouldn't even recognize her now, she had changed. Before she had been a pretty little nothing, now she was a beauty, a show-stopper, a breathtaker, a winner.

She downed the rest of the vodka, dressed, and took a cab back to the Plaza.

Mrs Fields was waiting impatiently. 'Where have you *been*?' she demanded.

'Did my shopping arrive? I want to wear the black dress tonight.'

'I hung everything up.'

'How kind of you. Just like having a personal maid!'

☆

Once the decision to kill Bobbie was made, Dallas fantasized hundreds of ways to do it. She hadn't been watching television steadily for four years without having learnt a thing or two. There were several workable methods.

Poison. Fire. Gunshot. Drowning.

Dallas finally picked on drowning as the neatest method. Bobbie had never been a very good swimmer, she attacked the water like a dog – thrashing around in all directions. 'I like the water, but it scares me,' she had confided to Dallas, 'I think my old man tried to do me in under a fire hydrant one hot and funky summer!' Pity he hadn't succeeded.

Bobbie had become very dependent on her heroin, and because of her habit she was not insisting on such a vigorous professional schedule. That was a relief as far as Dallas was concerned. It gave her time to see Ed, and also time to plan what she was going to do. Her constant fear was that Ed might find out her line of work. He wouldn't want her if he knew, he would want nothing to do with a common hooker. She vetted every job Bobbie arranged. Who would be there? How many? What was involved?

'Don't start getting high hat again,' complained Bobbie, 'I need the bread.'

Half the time she was incapable of performing at all, and Dallas was tempted to leave, just vanish off to New York with Ed. Bobbie would never find her in the state she was in most of the time. But if she did it would blow everything ... No, it was a risk Dallas couldn't afford to take.

She felt no remorse about what she was planning to do. The things that Bobbie had forced her into ... The humiliations, the degradations, the sexual nightmares of beatings and animals and sado-masochist happenings ...

She watched one night while Bobbie fixed herself up, then she produced good Mexican grass, turned on, and invited Bobbie to join her. She cooked a sensational dinner and made love to the black girl for the first time in a year.

'Wow!' Bobbie exclaimed, 'What's happenin', man? What'd I do?'

Dallas smiled. 'Like old times, huh?'

'Like – yeah sugar. Do that again.'

Dallas obliged, then later she suggested they go down to the communal pool and swim.

'Skinny dip?' inquired Bobbie, 'I love to feel that warm water go ridin' up my hot little pussy!'

'Sure,' agreed Dallas, 'only quietly. We don't want to wake everyone up.'

They twisted towels around their nakedness, and crept down to the pool.

Dallas slid in the water first. It was cool and dark. 'Come on,' she called to Bobbie.

'Hey, I'm cold,' Bobbie complained.

'It's lovely in the water, come on.'

Bobbie sat gingerly on the edge of the pool in the shallow end and dangled her legs in.

'Let's go, baby,' whispered Dallas.

'Aw – I think it's too cold.'

Suddenly Dallas gripped her by the ankles and pulled her sharply into the water. She kept a firm hold of Bobbie's ankles, raising them above the water so that the top half of the black girl's body was completely submerged.

There was no sound, just the sudden splash when she had first pulled Bobbie in. For seconds Bobbie, was still, and then all at once she started to struggle, and it was like holding a fish. Dallas moved slowly back into deeper water, but Bobbie's struggling was becoming so intense that she managed to free one leg, and was kicking out with it. Dallas hung firmly on to the other one.

How long did it take to drown? How painful was it? Jesus Christ – what was she doing? *This wasn't some TV film, this was life, this was happening, this was* now.

Abruptly she let go of the struggling girl, and spluttering and choking, Bobbie surfaced. She thrashed her way to the side of the pool and crawled out. She lay by the side retching.

Dallas climbed silently out. She wrapped the towel around herself.

'*You fuckin' bitch!*' *Bobbie groaned,* '*you tried to kill me. You want me out of your life that bad you fuckin' got it. Get out of my apartment – and don't you* never *come back!*' *She started to retch again, and Dallas left her lying there. She went up to the apartment and packed her things.*

Maybe she hadn't meant to kill Bobbie at all. Maybe she had just wanted to frighten her . . .

Yes, that was it. She had only wanted to frighten her and it had had the desired effect. Dallas nodded to herself. She wouldn't have hurt her, really she wouldn't.

☆

Ramo Kaliffe was Dallas' arranged date for the première, and Ed would not be pleased about *that*. She froze him out of thinking there would be any action. Screw him. He had served his purpose. 'Did I not please you last time?' he asked in a hurt voice at the end of the evening.

'Please *me*?' she said incredulously. As far as she could remember she had spent three quarters of an hour going down on him, and he had kindly dipped his head to her for a fast two minutes. Not that she minded, sex was no turn-on whichever way it was served. Sex was a means to an end. Sex was Ed Kurlnik and pleasing *him*.

Back at the hotel someone had dropped off an envelope of photos, and she devoured them with her eyes.

They were ten by eight glossies of her taken at the 'Miss Coast to Coast' contest. Enclosed was a brief note, 'Dropped these by as souvenir – would like to get together and do some more. Please call Linda Cosmo.' And there was a telephone number.

It was still early, before midnight. Dallas picked up the phone and asked for the number.

Linda answered sleepily.

'Hi, this is Dallas – "Miss Coast to Coast". I got your note. I'd love to do some photos.'

Linda stifled a yawn, she had been fast asleep. 'Marvellous. When are you free?'

'Tomorrow morning?'

'Wonderful. About ten o'clock.'

'Couldn't be better. What shall I wear?'

'Can I look at what you have when I get there?'

'Sure.'

'See you tomorrow then.' Linda hung up and switched on the light. Too late for Al King, but it would be a good scoop to do some photos of the girl. She might be able to place them in *People* or *Newsweek*.

Dallas hung up the phone and flopped out on the bed. She felt drained, it had been a busy day. The first day of her new life. Beauty Incorporated were probably going to be furious that she had arranged her own photo session, but that was just too bad. For once in her life *she* was going to be the decision-maker, and doing a photo session with a female photographer appealed to her. Guys were always on the make, trying to hustle, making suggestive comments. It would be nice to have some good photos taken, sexy but decent. Not like the murky photos from her past. Photos where she had tried to keep her face out of the picture. And it had been easy really, it wasn't her face they were after. Gyno shots, Bobbie had called them – 'Snatch money! The easiest way to make it!' she had joked. But Dallas had hated posing for that kind of picture. What kind of sick people paid for that kind of photograph? Guys who couldn't get it up ... Or maybe guys who didn't want to ... Dallas finally fell asleep, surrounded by the glossy pictures of her as 'Miss Coast to Coast'.

10

The sun at Nice Airport was blazing down. Photographers were jostling for shots of Al as he disembarked from the Air France plane. Tourists were gaping. Officials were pushing forward to greet him.

He wore a white sports shirt, white trousers, and a thin

black alligator belt that clasped together his initials in gold. His black hair was just long enough and carefully tousled. His black eyes hid behind grey-tinted shades.

He had spent the previous week at his home in London lying by the swimming pool and acquiring a perfectly respectable golden tan. London had been having a heat wave, and Al had taken full advantage.

Paul, by his side, was more conservatively dressed. But the women, when they had stopped eyeing Al, turned their attention to him and wondered who he was. He was a couple of inches taller than Al, leaner, with finer bones and smokey eyes. The brothers were by no means plain.

Al was in a very good mood indeed. Dallas had been booked for the show, and everyone seemed pleased about it. The producer had been delighted, and the only person who was somewhat put out was Katy May.

The English press played the whole thing up to the hilt, with photos of Katy in a swimsuit looking dejected, and recent shots of Dallas.

Bernie Suntan had telephoned from California. 'Ace publicity – great starter.'

With Melanie's coaching Edna had finally said to Al that she would like to come to the South of France with him. 'Forget it,' he had replied, 'I'll be working all day, you'll be stuck in a hotel, and I'll be worrying about you.' That had been that. No Edna. No Melanie.

A convertible Cadillac met them at the airport and sped them off to the Hotel Voile D'Or, at St Jean Cap Ferrat.

'This is the life!' exclaimed Al. 'Give me the sun and I could become a real beach bum.' He admired the passing girls. 'Place is jammed with little darlings!'

He had not mentioned Dallas to Paul since the night he had told him to get her for the show. It was almost as if he had forgotten all about her, and when Paul had told him it was arranged he had just nodded. Paul understood. The girl had said yes and that was that. Al knew that he could have her, so the thrill was gone.

They arrived at the hotel, and Paul went off to meet with the director and camera crew. Al changed into white swim shorts and a short towelling jacket, and sauntered down to the pool. He enjoyed the buzz that went up when he appeared, but it was a sophisticated group and no one came running over for his autograph.

He acquired a beach bed and lay out. A girl in an orange bikini was openly staring at his crotch. The myth of Al King and his tight stage trousers was alive and well and bulging in his swim shorts.

The sun was delicious, burning into his dark skin and causing thin rivulets of sweat to moisten on his hairy chest.

He tried to empty his mind and think of nothing. But the tour kept on drifting uneasily into his thoughts, and his stomach turned mildly in anticipation of the ordeal. He had spoken to Edna of his fears. He had lain next to her warm comfortable body in the night, and confessed his terror. She had held him close and crooned, 'Don't go, stay with us, stay with Evan and me.'

That wasn't what he wanted to hear. He wanted encouragement. He wanted building up. And if Edna couldn't give him that, who could? Who else knew the real Al King? They all saw the strutting, cocksure, virile star. They didn't want to see just another man with insecurities. They wanted glamour. He gave them what they wanted. Why else did he force himself to diet, have plastic surgery to remove that extra chin, re-cap his teeth so that the famous Al King smile remained whiter than white.

☆

Later Al hosted a dinner at an open-air restaurant called 'The African Queen' for some of the crew, and an assortment of local talent rounded up on the Croisette in Cannes.

It was a boisterous evening, the wine flowing freely and food likewise. Around midnight Al got bored, and he brushed aside the girls swarming round him, and suggested to Paul that they split and carry on to Monte Carlo where they could indulge in a little gambling.

Paul was only too pleased to oblige. He discreetly settled the bill, and they escaped.

Al wanted to drive. He handled the Cadillac restlessly, and drove it too fast along the winding coastal road.

'Let's *get* there at least,' muttered Paul.

'You nervous?' laughed Al, putting his foot down harder, and nearly colliding with an oncoming Citroën.

'Cut it out,' mumbled Paul.

'Trouble with you is you don't want to live dangerously. You live a safe life – you're even faithful to your girlfriend! Didn't you fancy *any* of them tonight?'

'Didn't *you*?'

Al sighed. 'I don't fancy any of them any more. They're all a bunch of scrubbers. Get the clap as soon as look at them.'

'So don't look,'

'Do me a favour. You know the score. I've got them comin' out of my ears! Who has to look? They're grabbing at me before I even fart in their direction!'

They drove straight to the Casino in Monte Carlo.

Al could feel the adrenalin flowing. He headed over to the nearest roulette table and surrounded twenty-six and twenty-nine with fifty franc chips. Seventeen came up. He repeated the procedure, doubling his bet. Six came up. He piled some chips on black, and once again chevalled twenty-six and twenty-nine. Zero came up. He changed tables and piled chips on number five. He was lucky first time, and the croupier pushed stacks of chips in his direction.

'It's my night, boyo!' he gleefully told Paul.

Two hours later they left. Al was three thousand pounds down.

'It's a mug's game,' announced Paul.

'Horseshit. I'll come back tomorrow night and beat the shit out of 'em.'

11

Dallas sat on the Pan American jet, sipping champagne and marvelling at the events of the previous week.

So much had happened. So many exciting things.

Now here she was sitting on an aeroplane heading for Europe. She could hardly believe it.

A passing stewardess smiled in a friendly fashion and asked, 'Everything all right, Dallas?'

She nodded to indicate that everything was fine. In the space of a week people recognized her, they treated her with that special kind of deference reserved for the famous.

Getting the Al King show had been a terrific break – all she had to do in the show was look pretty – but it was a beginning, and everyone had to start somewhere.

The photos that Linda had taken of her were selling well, and Linda was nice, easy to work with, friendly, and someone to rap with. Of course Dallas wasn't into the confiding bag, she had too much to hide, but just discussing what was happening to her now was a relief.

Ed had taken her sudden rise to mini fame in a different fashion. He was used to having her completely available, and now that she was in the limelight it made things more complicated. Strangely enough, he was pleased when he heard about the trip to Europe. 'I'll meet you there,' he promised, 'I'm about due on a business trip to London, and I'll fly down to the South of France after.'

She had not been exactly thrilled, but then again why not? It was progress, and why was she with Ed Kurlnik if not to make headway in the affair? If he ever left his wife for her . . . Well, that would be worth more than all the transient fame could ever be.

The 'Fasten Your Seatbelts' sign was flashing on. They were due to land in London where Dallas had a one-day stopover to organize her clothes for the television special. She had managed to dump Mrs Fields. 'This whole chaperone scene is not for me,' she had flatly informed Beauty Incorporated. They had not been pleased, but Dallas carried the scent of success, and they stood to make a substantial amount in commissions, so for once they relaxed their rules. Mrs Fields had muttered ominously, 'This girl means trouble.' But money spoke louder than words.

At London's Heathrow airport Dallas was met by a bevy of photographers.

She was wearing a white suit, and she obligingly shrugged off the jacket, and posed provocatively in a tubular, strapless sweater, which clung like glue round her sensual unfettered breasts.

The picture was on the front of all the evening newspapers. In England she was an instant celebrity.

By the next morning she was on another plane to the South of France. Briefly she thought about Al King, wondered what he would be like. Linda – who knew him – had merely commented, 'Steer clear, he's a prick.' The way she had said it gave Dallas the impression that she didn't like him at all, but further questioning had produced nothing, so Dallas had dropped the subject.

She didn't much care anyway. They were all the same. Men. Sonsofbitches. Perverts. Sex-mad little boys.

And stars. The worst kind.

She should know, in her former business capacity operating in the heart of Beverly Hills she had met enough of them.

Case one. A hero of the West. Always the good guy, never the villain. What would his loyal faithful public do if they knew that in private he indulged in horseback activities that Would *never* find their way onto the screen.

Case two. Baby-faced former child star. He liked nannies and governesses, and a good solid beating daily.

Case three. A football player. Adored by women the world over. Could *only* get it up when clad in women's clothes with a dildoe up his ass.

Dallas knew of many more examples. Where were all the *normal* people? *She* had certainly never come across any. But then of course she hadn't exactly led what could be termed as a normal life.

At Nice airport, things followed the same pattern. Photographers. A press agent to meet her. She posed, this time in a clingy red dress. God, but there was something mesmerizing about a camera lens. She could communicate with a small piece of engineering, much more so than with people. Mouth slightly parted, moisten lips, head back so that hair flowed, body muscles tensed. She had it down to a fine art.

'I'm Nicky,' said the television assistant who accompanied the press agent. He was a young man, with pimples and red hair.

Dallas smiled, and Nicky was immediately captivated.

'I'll take you to your hotel. They want to do a rehearsal after lunch. Was it a good flight?'

Dallas nodded. She was busy looking around her and taking in the strange sights and sounds. It was a thrill to be in Europe, something that she had never expected to happen to her. She had known that Ed Kurlnik would be the passport to a better life, and now – just a few short months after meeting him – things were moving at a pace almost too fast for her to keep up with. Occasionally she was bothered by the thought that her past might catch up with her. Some sly-faced man from the shadows might see her photo and step forward to announce, 'That girl is a hooker, nothing but a common little whore.' She was prepared if that ever happened. She would just smile sweetly and deny it. After all, who could *prove* her former life style?

Bobbie. The name stuck nervously in her throat. She had neither seen nor heard from her since the night at the pool. But Bobbie must have seen her picture in the paper, she must know what had happened to her. And it was not like Bobbie to miss a going opportunity. Dallas was quite prepared for the fact that she would eventually appear, and she was alert for when it did happen. She wasn't about to be blackmailed and have her whole new life hang on a thread. If Bobbie reappeared she was ready far her. And this time she wouldn't screw it up.

☆

'Al King,' he announced coolly. *So you're the bitch that stood me up for lunch.*

'Dallas,' she replied, equally cool. *Conceited bastard. I have met your type before. Linda was right.*

'Did you have a good flight?' *If you play your cards right I'll take you back to my hotel and give you a glimpse of Al King cock.*

'Fine, thank you.' *He wants to get laid. They all want to get laid.*

'Good.' *Christ, but she's a knockout. Green eyes. Soft lips. Soft hair. A body that should be labelled instant hard-on.*

'The Atlantic crossing was a bit bumpy.' *If I was into men, I guess this is what they would look like. Dark and hard. Bastards.*

They had met at the scene of the location. The opening shot of the particular sequence they were to do together was of the two of them in an open sports car driving along. The camera crew were busy setting up.

Nicky had escorted her to the location, and Al had sauntered over and introduced himself.

'Dallas, dear,' announced the director, an effeminate gentleman in tomato red trousers with a bandana round his head, 'can we have you in the car, dear.'

'I'll have her in the car!' joked Al.

Dallas shot him a frosty look. I only do it for money. Ed Kurlnik's money.

'You too, Al,' continued the director. 'I want to start with a long shot of the car, nice scenery, hair blowing, everyone wishes they were there. Then we come in for close-ups. Dallas gazing adoringly at you – you singing. Sound – put the machine on, let's get some atmosphere here.'

The sound mechanic switched on a portable machine, and Al singing 'Lady' came blaring into the afternoon sunshine. It was a funky soul song, with Al's incredibly sexy gravelly voice playing sensually with the lyrics.

Al leapt into the car and started miming –

> Lady you are pretty
> Lady you are witty
> Wanna be my Lady
> Wanna drive me crazy
> You got eyes like hot molasses
> Hey baby
> Hey maybe
> Hey Lady
> Lady Lady Lady
> You are foxy Lady

Dallas climbed into the car and openly yawned.

'Great!' exclaimed Al, 'a yawn I get.'

'Now, darling,' fussed the director, 'I want you to *gaze* at Al. Don't take your eyes off him. I want love, romance, a touch of sex.'

'I wouldn't mind a touch of that,' interrupted Al.

'I'm sure you'll never go short,' sniffed the director. 'Dallas, sweetie, you understand what I want? Every woman watching should be aching to change places with you.'

They rehearsed the shot several times until the director was satisfied, then they broke for lunch which was served from a mobile canteen. Nicky helped Dallas get a plate of cold meats and salads and hovered reassuringly by her side. They sat on the nearby bench. Al retired to a private caravan.

'How do you like our star?' asked Nicky.

'Silver, plastic, and tarnished.'

Nicky laughed. 'Don't let anyone hear you say that. Oh, here comes his brother.'

Paul had been delayed at the hotel on long-distance calls, and as soon as he arrived Al said, 'She's here. Go find her and tell her to join me for a glass of wine and a quick fuck.'

'Are you serious?'

'About the wine. The other I'll ask her myself.'

'Terrific. I hope it will have all been worth it.'

'Got a feeling it just might be.'

Paul spotted her immediately. You could hardly miss her with that tangle of sun-streaked hair and incredible figure.

He approached briskly. 'Hello, I'm Paul King. Al would like you to join him for a drink.'

Dallas smiled. 'I bring love and kisses from Linda. She said to tell you New York misses you.'

'That's nice.' He shot a wary look at Nicky. It wasn't exactly *discreet* of Linda to send that kind of a message, suppose Melanie had been with him? 'How about the drink with Al?'

'Gee, thanks. But I think I'll just stay out here. The sun is *so* lovely, I'm really enjoying it.'

'Oh. You see Al thought it might be nice if the two of you got to know each other a little better.'

Dallas winked. 'I know.'

Paul felt suddenly awkward. The village pimp. 'Sure you won't change your mind?'

'Not unless it's part of my contract.'

'No, it's not,' Paul said stiffly, and he walked away.

Nicky shook his head in admiration, 'Wow! Mr King is not going to like this.'

'Mister King is not going to get this.'

'This is the second of his television shows I've been on and he gets *everything* he wants.'

'So he's just going to have to be deprived. I'm sure there are plenty of ladies around who wouldn't mind him jumping on their bones, but I am *not* one of them.'

Nicky grinned shyly. 'Would you come out with me tonight?'

'How *old* are you?'

'Twenty-two. We could go dancing. There's a good disco in Juan les Pins.'

'Sounds like fun, Nicky. And I know that you wouldn't even *think* of jumping on my bones.'

'Certainly not.' He smiled proudly. 'So it's a date then?'

'A date.' Even Ed couldn't get mad about her going out with a kid like Nicky, and she didn't want to sit in her hotel, she wanted to get out and see something of the Riviera.

☆

'So what's the matter with the bitch?'

'I don't know, Jesus, Al, I don't even much care. You'll nail her – you always do.'

'I know *that*,' agreed Al coldly. He lit a cigarette, thought of his voice, stubbed it out, and swore softly. 'I felt like having her now.'

'So you'll have her tonight – big deal.'

'Yeah. I'll have her tonight. Arrange dinner – set something up.'

'Christ!' exclaimed Paul, 'I think the message is she wants you to ask her yourself.'

'You're right. That's the problem – she wants *me* to ask her. OK, boyo. Book me a table somewhere horny, order flowers, champagne. Jesus H, she had better be worth it.'

Paul frowned. Orders. Sometimes Al treated him just like another lackey. Linda was right. Maybe he should stop wetnursing Al and put a manager on the job. Then he could relax, enjoy his money, and organize everything from the air-conditioned comfort of his suite of offices in Park Lane. Maybe after the tour. He knew what Al was going through now, it wasn't the time to start making changes. Al didn't mean to issue orders, he didn't even realize he was doing it. Having everything done for him had just become a fact of life. It was all part and parcel of being a star.

'You could take her to dinner at the Colombe d'Or in St Paul de Vence. Romantic. Private.'

'Ask her, Paul.'

'I thought *you* were going to ask her.'

'You give it another try.'

'Oh shit – Al.'

'Arrange it. I'll romance her first and fuck her later!'

☆

71

12

Edna King awoke to the sound of the phone ringing. It was eight o'clock, she was usually awake by that time, but lately she had been taking sleeping pills and they seemed to make it more difficult to get up in the mornings.

It was Melanie on the phone. 'Have you seen the papers?' she demanded shrilly.

'No,' replied Edna, already resigned to the bad news they would no doubt contain.

'I *warned* you, I *told* you we should have gone with them.'

'What is it?'

'I'll be right over.'

Edna climbed reluctantly out of bed. She knew what it would be, some item about Al and another woman. There were always items about Al and other women. Ignore them, he had continually told her. Never believe anything you read in the papers. Melanie appeared to take every word as gospel, and she never allowed an item to slip by Edna unnoticed.

The kitchen was already occupied by the maid and Nelson, who were enjoying a bacon and egg breakfast.

The maid, a strapping Italian, asked in her careful English, 'Something, madam?'

'Coffee,' said Edna nervously, 'for two. In the lounge.' What she really wanted to say was, 'Get out of my kitchen, my house, my life.' What she really wanted to do was make herself a hot sweet cup of tea, and some thick fattening toast liberally spread with strawberry jam.

She had ordered coffee because it was what Melanie preferred. 'Tea is for peasants,' Melanie would sniff.

The newspapers were in a neat pile on the hall table, but Edna purposely left them untouched. Why spoil Melanie's fun?

She walked in the lounge and gazed out of the French windows into the garden. It was the start of another beautiful day, and the pool gleamed invitingly. Swimming was good exercise, maybe she should swim more. If only Nelson wasn't always lurking round the pool. When she put on her bathing suit he seemed to stare at her in a peculiar way, a penetrating way. She would have to ask Al to get rid of him. It really wasn't fair of Al to tell her not to be silly, it wasn't him he stared at.

Melanie came striding purposefully across the garden. She was wearing a purple track suit, and without make-up her prettiness faded, and was replaced with a petulant, pinched look.

Edna unlocked the French doors and let her in.

'Take a look at this!' Melanie thrust a paper at her.

On the front page there was a photograph of Al sitting in an open car smiling at a girl who gazed back at him with a faintly mocking smile. She was a very beautiful girl, with long legs propped on the dashboard, and a seductively unbuttoned shirt. The caption read 'Al King Meets His Queen', and underneath, in smaller print, it said, 'Al King enjoys a get-together with American beauty queen, Dallas. They will appear together on Al's forthcoming television spectacular.

'It's nothing,' Edna explained, placing the newspaper carefully down, 'just publicity.'

'Just publicity,' jeered Melanie, '*just publicity*. Are you blind? Look at the way he's looking at her.'

'It's publicity, Melanie. Al has to do these sort of things. *I* don't mind, so I don't see why *you* should.'

'Oh, charming! I'm trying to help you, Edna. If you're too naive to see what's going on, *I'm* not. Al is making a fool of you, and if I've told you once I've told you a thousand times, you should be by his side – otherwise one of these days you're going to *lose* him.'

The Italian maid came in with the coffee. 'Where, madam?' She smiled knowingly. Had she heard? Edna gestured to the table. Damn Melanie and her loud voice.

'I can't stay for coffee,' Melanie snapped, 'I have a masseur coming over. *Think* about what I've said. *Think* about the position you may find yourself in. It's not too late – yet.' She flounced out the same way she had come in, leaving Edna in a state of flux.

Lose Al. Impossible. Absolutely impossible. But was she being naive? *Was* Al making a fool of her? Edna shook her head in disbelief. She trusted him. She always had and she always would. Melanie was just trying to cause trouble for no reason.

Edna gulped down the hot coffee. If only her sister-in-law would leave her alone. If only everyone would leave her alone. If only she could go back to the days when it had just been her and Al ... Just the two of them. No money, but what wonderful times they had enjoyed together.

Perhaps before he went off on the American tour they could go away somewhere. Maybe Brighton, where they had spent their honeymoon. What a week *that* had been. In the last few years Edna had noticed Al's gradual slackening of interest in sex. At first she had been relieved, in the early days he had wanted it constantly, she shuddered at the memory of his demands. Morning, noon, and night. Day after day. Even when she had been *pregnant*. Now he seemed content to just lie beside her. It had been months since he last made love to her. Of course she didn't mind, she knew that his work took a lot out of him. But a week in Brighton would do him good, even just a few days. She resolved to discuss this with him.

Satisfied with her decision she finished her coffee, and then drank Melanie's. It wouldn't do to *waste* it. Anyway, it went well with the packet of Bourbon Cream biscuits that the maid had thoughtfully provided.

☆

Upstairs in his bed Evan stealthily inspected his collection of magazines. He found studying them a diverting pastime. He had his favourite girls and would quickly turn to the relevant pages and study the female of his choice. There was Bertha. Blonde. Eighteen. Hobby – breeding horses. She liked big dominant men who knew what they were doing. She wore pearls, and see-through nylon knickers, and appeared in a variety of poses with her legs apart.

Then there was Maralyn. A big girl, Maralyn, with enormous jutting breasts which she seemed to take a great deal of pleasure in playing with.

He really could fancy a night with Bertha or Maralyn. Oh yes. Actually he could fancy a night with anyone. Sixteen and still a virgin. It was ridiculous. None of the other boys at his school were in that position. They had all had 'experiences'. Evan had heard them discussing various aspects of what appeared to be highly exciting sex lives.

He brooded about his lack of female companionship, and anxiously perused his magazines, of which Nelson seemed to have a never-ending supply. He often thought of Nelson offering him the 'real thing'. How much would it cost? Would he know what to do? Where would it take place?

He had at last decided to ask Nelson to arrange it.

Meanwhile there remained Bertha and Maralyn. He just had time for one of them before school.

He chose Bertha with her nylon knickers, and clutching her firmly under his arm he made his way to the bathroom.

13

He wanted her, and he was pushing. Gradually it dawned on Dallas that the only reason she was on the Al King television spectacular was because Al King himself had ordained it. It all fell into place. The offer of a drink on the night she had won the contest. The lunch she had never attended in New York. The request for her to join him in his caravan. And now a dinner invitation – which she had turned down.

'I wish you would change your mind,' Paul had said tightly at her refusal.

'I'm busy,' Dallas had replied. 'Anyway, I don't go out with married men.' Lies. Lies. Lies. What about Ed Kurlnik jetting in the very next day. Nobody was more married than Ed.

'Al is just extending his friendship,' Paul explained.

More like his cock, Dallas thought, and I am not for sale any more.

During the afternoon they taped the beginning of Al's song in the car. Dallas just had to sit there gazing at him. He was good-looking. *Too* good-looking. Arrogant, with an assurance that came from getting everything he wanted. Well, he wasn't going to get her. She wondered if his brother had told him yet.

Photographers buzzed around snapping numerous shots. She smiled at him, licked her lips, and threw her head back.

'You love it, don't you?' said Al.

'It's fun,' she replied carefully

'I like your tits.'

'Good for you.'

'Why don't you want to have dinner?'

'I'm not in the mood for getting chased around a table.'

'What table? What are you talking about?'

'Oh come on. *You* know what I mean.'

'Don't flatter yourself, kid. Girls like you are fallin' off the trees to get me.'

'So go find a tree.'

The afternoon passed quickly, and shortly before they finished for the day, Nicky came over and in an embarrassed voice told her that he wouldn't be able to take her out after all. Poor kid, somebody had warned him off. Probably the brother. Well, screw all of them. So she wouldn't see the sights. She would go to bed.

'Dinner, darling?' the director inquired.

'I'm too tired,' she excused herself.

'See you in the morning then.'

☆

'I don't believe it!' Al exclaimed, 'she's a dyke, must be.'

'Yes,' agreed Paul, although privately he thought nothing could be further from the truth.

'She's sharp too. Answers back. Maybe I could convert her.'

'Why not just forget her. She's a headache.'

'I'll fuck her, I'll forget her. It's that easy.'

'And if you don't fuck her?'

'Ah, boyo, that's the problem. You know me when I don't get what I want.'

Paul frowned. Indeed he did know.

'Violette Victor is in town. She's having dinner with us.' Violette Victor was a young French movie actress in current vogue.

Al's interest perked slightly. 'Have you met her?'

'I met her agent this afternoon. She's looking forward to meeting you.'

☆

Later, on the Carlton terrace, they met with Violette and her agent. She was tall and skinny, with straggly brown hair and luminous almond-shaped grey eyes. Wide-mouthed, she smiled a warm greeting, and clutched Al firmly by the hand.

Paul breathed a sigh of relief. If *she* didn't take Al's mind off Dallas nobody would. She was a star, and her reputation as a nymphomaniac was well known.

The four of them had dinner up in the hills, and then Al and Violette vanished up to her suite at the Carlton, and neither was seen again until morning.

Al arrived an hour late at the location.

'You look like you haven't slept for a week,' stated Dallas.

'Are you a lesbian?'

'What a sweet old-fashioned question. If I was, it would be none of your goddamn business.'

'So you are.'

'No, I am not.' Why had she answered him? He had no right to know either way. She thought of her relationship with Bobbie and shuddered. Those were scenes better forgotten. No, she was definitely *not* a lesbian.

'Let's have dinner tonight.'

'I don't want dinner with you.'

'Why not?'

'You're too – I don't know – you're just too . . .'

'What?'

'*I don't know.*'

'If you don't know let's have dinner and find out.'

'You're too obvious.'

'Obvious?' He burst out laughing, 'Obvious! You can talk, with your tits hanging out from here to kingdom come!'

'You want to get laid.'

'I just got laid. Tonight I'd like dinner with you. We could talk, like get to know each other.'

'Why?'

'Why not?'

'Anyway I can't. My boyfriend—' she stammered over boyfriend, realizing she had picked the wrong word, 'is coming to town?'

'Who's your boyfriend?'

'Just a friend.'

'We could all have dinner.'

'No thanks.'

The director had lined up the shot and was calling for

action. Al started to sing, and Dallas did the full adoring gaze. Idly she wondered who he had been with the night before, and then suddenly, for no reason, she felt a sexual excitement grip her, a feeling she had only ever experienced with Burt Keyes, and the beginning of her affair with Bobbie. She wanted to close her eyes and hang on, it was such a *good* feeling, and in spite of the life she had led, such an unusual feeling. She didn't understand it. What had caused it?

The sound machine boomed Al's voice over loud and clear. Oh Christ! Not feelings for this creep in tight trousers.

She could feel her nipples hardening, and she saw Al notice. Then the bulge in his trousers started to grow. He stared at her, casually slipping the clothes from her with his eyes. Bastard. He knew what was happening.

'Cut!' the director called, 'that was sensational, no retakes. Coming in for close-ups. Everything OK, Al?'

'Couldn't be better,' and he winked at her, 'could it?'

She turned away and let the make-up woman attend to her face. What had happened? And why? She couldn't think straight. Thank Christ Ed would be with her soon. If only she could manufacture that special feeling for Ed. If only . . .

☆

'How was last night?' Paul asked.

'Not bad.'

'Not bad. I hear she's a killer.'

'Boney.'

'One of the biggest movie stars in France and all you can say is boney.'

'Do you love Linda, Paul?'

'That's a hell of a question.' They had never really discussed it before. 'Why?'

'Does it kick you in the gut when you see her? Like – pow. Know what I mean?'

'I know what you mean. Yes, I love her.'

'And Melanie?'

Paul shook his head. 'It's difficult. Melanie's my wife, mother of my kids. What's with the questions?'

'Just thinking.'

Violette Victor arrived for lunch and the photographers

had a field day. She was not averse to publicity, and posed moodily in a faded denim jump suit.

Dallas was suddenly ignored, and she felt sharp pangs of jealousy at the switch of attention.

Al and Violette Victor. She imagined them in bed together.

Nicky came over to complain about being told he couldn't take her out the previous evening. She brushed him aside, and watched as Al and Violette disappeared inside his caravan. A lunchtime fuck. Charming.

Stupid, conceited, *star*.

In the afternoon they shot the second half of Al's song. They had to leave the car and run from the beach into the sea. Dallas had to throw off her dress, underneath which she was wearing a white bikini.

'You look absolutely marvellous, darling,' exclaimed the director, 'You remind me of Ursula Andress in that Bond film.'

'Who?' questioned Dallas.

The director raised an irate eyebrow. 'Are you kidding dear?'

Violette Victor had departed and Al seemed in good humour.

'You're happy,' remarked Dallas.

'I had a good lunch, know what I mean?'

She knew what he meant, and then before she could help herself she said, 'Get your cock sucked, did you?' She could have kicked herself as soon as she had said it.

Al started to laugh. 'Oh, boy! Little Miss America. What naughty words you come out with. Yes, as a matter of fact I did.'

Why had she said it? What did she care? It made it look like she *did* care. It made her sound like a really tough broad. Which of course she was, but that was supposed to be *her* secret. Oh shit, why had she said it?

'Good for you.' And for some inexplicable reason her eyes filled with tears.

'Changed your mind about dinner?'

'I told you, I'm busy.'

'Pity. I can see that you and I would get along really well.'

'Don't count on it.'

Al grinned. 'I'm counting on it. Anyway if you can't make dinner come to the Casino in Monte Carlo later, bring me some luck.'

'Doesn't Violette Victor bring you luck?'

'Violette Victor doesn't fill a bikini like you.'

'But she sucks good cock, right?'

'Right.'

Oh God, not again. What was she trying to do. She was carrying on like she was jealous or something ridiculous like that. Miss Toughie. Shut up, Dallas, you're behaving like a cunt.

'I think you and I could have one helluva good time together,' Al said seriously. 'Why don't you dump the boyfriend, whoever he is.'

Was he kidding? Dump Ed Kurlnik. Never.

'Not possible. Anyway I don't want to.' Her eyes dropped to his impossibly filled swim shorts, 'besides, he has more to offer me than you do.'

Now what a lie *that* was.

☆

Ed arrived in a black chauffered Kurlnik Supreme, looking dapper in a dark blue suit.

He had ordered adjoining suites in the Hotel de Paris, and he kissed Dallas chastely on the cheek and booked an immediate phone call to Mrs Dee Dee Kurlnik on Fire Island.

So the immaculate Dee Dee was holding the fort at their holiday mansion. With or without the lovely twins? Dallas wondered viciously if she was screwing any of the local talent. Maybe she would dip her immaculate toes in the ocean and get eaten by a shark.

'How's it going?' Ed asked, as he waited for his phone call.

'Terrific,' replied Dallas, kneeling to unzip his trousers.

He turned away. 'Not while I'm on the phone.'

'Why not? I've missed you.'

Flattered, he turned back to her. 'Make it quick while I'm waiting for the call to come through.'

What other way was there but quick with Ed?

☆

Al didn't fancy her. Movie star or not, she was just not his scene. Skinny body. Hairy armpits. Grating accent.

He had performed the night before, but that was it.

Lunchtime she had serviced him. Now she expected the compliment returned.

'We'll have dinner first,' he suggested, 'Paul's meeting us at The African Queen. You like pizza?'

Disappointed, she slipped into a dress. 'Later, then,' she said, as if to reassure herself.

'Wouldn't miss it.'

He drove the Cadillac at his usual erratic pace. He wondered if Dallas would turn up at the Casino. God, she was beautiful. And that body. Quite unbelieveable. And he liked her style, she wasn't prepared to take the shit he dished out to everyone else. It was a pleasure to find a woman who answered back. He had known she would be different. He had sensed it. And he had to have her. Had to.

Dinner was a succession of autograph hunters. The tourist season was in full swing, and they went after Violette and Al endlessly.

Al couldn't wait to get to the Casino. The adrenalin was flowing. He needed some excitement.

He hit the roulette table, covering all his favourite numbers. 'Tonight's my lucky night,' he told Paul.

Zero came up.

☆

Dallas and Ed dined at a small discreet restaurant overlooking the harbour. Conversation was sparse. It was so strange to be out in public together. Dallas drank most of the wine, and Ed told a long and boring story of a business transaction.

If they were married is this what their life would be like together? A succession of boring dinners. She had longed for the day when he would actually take her out, and the anticlimax was awful. Of course in New York it would probably be different. There everyone knew him, and it would be exciting to be seen together.

Mrs Ed Kurlnik. What respect *that* title would conjure up.

'Shall we go to the casino?' she asked casually after dinner.

'I don't gamble,' Ed replied.

I bet you don't, mustn't risk the precious millions. 'But *I'd* love to go. Can we?'

'Well . . .'

'*Please.* She slipped her hand onto his thigh under the table, 'we'll do what *you* want later.'

'Just for a short visit then.'

He paid the cheque, undertipped as was his habit, and they climbed into the comfort of the Kurlnik Supreme, and were whisked over to the Casino by the chauffeur.

Dallas had chosen her outfit with care. A plain white dress. Long. One shoulder exposed. A thin silver choker, silver bangles on both arms, and gypsy hoop earings.

Ed, not known as a giver of compliments, had volunteered that she looked very nice. She knew she looked beautiful. She knew the dress emphasized every curve of her body.

She didn't know why she was in such a state of excitement about seeing Al King. But she was. She wanted him to see her with Ed Kurlnik. She wanted him to realize that she wasn't just another dumb, pretty girl, available to any star who beckoned. Maybe then he would leave her alone.

☆

'Sonofabitch!' muttered Al in disgust.

'We go now?' inquired Violette.

'Just another roll. Only one.'

'You'll lose again.'

'I like faith. Can't you try positive thinking?'

'I try. But your luck is *merde.*'

'Your enthusiasm kills me.'

Carefully he covered the table. Cheval twenty-six and twenty-nine. A wad of chips on red. Cover seven, eleven, seventeen, twenty, thirty-five. Musn't forget twenty-five and thirty-two.

The croupier spun the wheel. Al sucked in his breath. The ball rolled lazily round. Come on you bastard. He was down by ten thousand pounds. Enough by anyone's standards, three years' wages when he had been working on the roads.

Come on baby – roll into one of my numbers. The ball jumped into thirty-five, wavered, jumped out and landed firmly on twenty-six.

'Baby!!' screamed Al, and he looked up in time to see Dallas. For a moment he forgot about winning, and thought, Jesus Christ, I have to have her. Then he noticed the small elderly man with her, and his eyes swivelled back to the pile of chips being propelled towards him. With gambler's instinct he let the cheval on twenty-six ride, doubling it. It came up again. He had known it would. While Dallas was there he was a winner.

☆

'Don't you gamble at all?' Dallas asked, her eyes scanning the room finding Al, and returning satisfied to Ed.

'It's a fools' game, for children.'

'But you love games,' she squeezed his hand, '*I* should know.'

He allowed himself a smile.

She nuzzled close to him. 'One drink and you can take me home to play, OK?'

'Yes.'

Paul had been trying his luck at blackjack. Gambling wasn't really his scene, but he didn't mind playing for fun, and anything was better than standing behind Al watching him go beserk. He saw Dallas come in, and recognized Ed Kurlnik at once. So here was the reason that she didn't want to know about Al. Sonofabitch. No wonder she played it cool. Ed Kurlnik. Who would have believed it.

He scooped up his minimal winnings and went right over to them.

Dallas was charm itself, carrying out introductions, and asking innocently, 'Is Al here?'

'He's playing roulette.'

'Why don't you all join us for a drink?'

'Great. I'll see if I can tear Al away.'

Ed was not pleased. As Paul departed he instructed, 'Tell them we just bumped into each other.'

Dallas widened tiger eyes. 'Of course, baby. I'm a friend of your wife's in New York. Or shall I be a friend of your daughters'?'

Ed pursed his lips. What kind of fool was he to be seen in public with this girl. He should have kept her shut away. He should *never* have arranged for her to win that beauty contest. She was changing from the lovely innocent girl he had first met in Los Angeles. She was becoming pushy.

Eventually Al came strolling over hand in hand with Violette. 'Why don't we go to Regines?' he suggested, 'it's just next door.'

Ed was quite pleased at meeting Violette Victor. He had seen a private screening of her new film where she had performed a most explicit sex act with another girl. He wondered if Dallas would consider . . . Maybe later . . .

The five of them went to Regines, an exclusive discotheque overlooking the sea, where they were given the best table in the room, and where the disc jockey immediately played Al's most famous record, 'Random Love'.

'An oldie but a goodie,' Paul laughed. God, that record had been the beginning of it all.

Violette, realizing who Ed Kurlnik was, and being no slouch, engaged him in a lengthy conversation about a film she wanted to do, but for which nobody would put up the money as it was a very offbeat project.

Dallas let her have him. She wasn't jealous, she knew whose bed he would be in later.

She sipped her Pernod on the rocks, and exchanged stares across the table with Al.

Women kept coming up to him, whispering little messages, giggling, slipping him notes.

'Doesn't it drive him mad?' Dallas asked Paul.

He shrugged. 'He's used to it, it's part of the game. Did anyone show you the papers today?'

'No . . . Why?'

'You and Al are all over them.'

'I'd love to see them.'

'I'll see you get copies.'

'Thanks.' Was he being nice to her now that he had discovered Ed Kurlnik was her man? No longer was she being treated as just another little ding-a-ling to lure to Al's caravan for a quick one.

Al removed a faded blonde from his left shoulder and stood up. 'Dance?' he questioned Dallas.

She glanced at Ed deep in conversation, and stood up also. 'I guess there's nothing better to do around here.'

The record was Ben E. King's 'Supernatural Thing' and Al started to gyrate his hips in the way he had made famous all over the world.

'You move like a stud waiting for some action,' laughed Dallas.

'That's just the way it is. Want some?'

'No thanks.'

'OK, big eyes. Just don't come begging later.'

'I promise I won't.'

'Promises are made to be broken.'

They danced silently, enjoying the feeling of togetherness the beat gave them.

Bobbie had taught Dallas how to dance. 'You gotta let it all hang loose,' she had instructed, 'pretend you're balling a really *fantastic* guy – just let go – ya dig?'

Dallas had understood exactly what she meant, but had never put it into practice until now.

'Supernatural Thing' faded away, and Aretha came on at her best, singing 'You'll Never Get to Heaven'. Al pulled her close, very close, and they rocked silently together on the crowded dance floor. Like a roller coaster the feeling hit Dallas again. Great waves of sexual excitement.

She could feel him grow hard against her thigh, and she pressed towards him shutting her eyes.

'Let's get out of here,' he murmured.

'Let's not,' she whispered back, but her voice was shaky and she had to struggle for control.

'You mean to tell me you're really tight with the old guy?'

'That's right.'

'Bullshit.'

'Let's sit down.'

'Let's wait till I'm in suitable shape to sit down.'

She drew away from him. 'Can I get you a glass of cold water?'

'Only if you personally throw it over my cock!'

She couldn't help smiling. A man who gave her incredible sexual waves *and* made her smile. Impossible. If things had been different maybe she would have done something about it. But no. She was too smart. She had been around. Stars. They were all the same. Wham bam. Thank you M'am. Then on to the next little pushover.

Back at the table Ed was getting restless, 'I'll drop you at your hotel,' he told Dallas, fooling no one. 'Where are you staying?'

'The Hotel de Paris,'she replied demurely.

'See you tomorrow,' said Al, 'bright and early.'

'Goodnight,' said Ed, and to Violette, 'don't forget to write me the details.'

As they were leaving Dallas clung tightly onto Ed's arm. 'What was *that* all about?' she asked.

'She needs backers for her new film.'

'Ooh – backers, huh? And what would she give *you* in return?'

'Don't be stupid.'

'Stupid I'm not. You fancy her, don't you? Come on, tell me the truth, I don't mind. Come on, daddy . . .' Half laughing she threw her arms around him. And that was the precise moment when the camera flashed, and Ed Kurlnik and Dallas had their first photograph taken together.

14

The scandal affected all three of them. The newspapers pounced on the situation with glee, and the photographs of Al and Dallas taken at the location were used in conjunction with the one of her and Ed leaving the nightclub so that it looked like she was conducting two different love affairs at the same time.

Denials came thick and fast.

After threatening to sue the photographer, Ed Kurlnik stated that Dallas was merely a casual acquaintance who had happened to be leaving the nightclub at the same time as him.

Wasn't it strange, replied the newspapers, that Mr Kurlnik happened to have been a judge on the 'Miss Coast to Coast' competition. And by further coincidence, was he aware of the fact that he and Dallas happened to have adjoining suites at the Hotel de Paris? They had been wanting to get something on Ed Kurlnik for years, and this was the perfect opportunity.

Al made a formal statement to the effect that he and Dallas were merely professional colleagues, and he couldn't understand the fuss, as everyone knew he had been happily married for sixteen years.

Dallas safely said 'No comment' as she had been advised to do in a sharp phone call from Beauty Incorporated.

Ed had flown immediately back to the safety of Dee Dee and Fire Island. 'We'll discuss it next week,' he had tersely told Dallas, 'just don't admit anything.'

She had finished the taping of the television special. There had only been half a day's work left, and an attentive Nicky had taken her to the airport. Al had been friendly but cool, he made no more mention of personal matters. End of the affair that never was.

Back in New York she received a lecture from Beauty Incorporated on the morals of being 'Miss Coast to Coast', and they hinted that if there were any further scandals they would have to think seriously of asking for her resignation.

Her phone never stopped ringing. Chat shows. Interviews. Playboys around town. She waited for the call from Bobbie, but it never came. That was *one* good thing.

She enjoyed all the attention she was receiving, so much so that she took no notice of the fact that there was no word from Ed. He would be scared to appear in her life again too soon. He would want a little time for things to simmer down. In the meantime she could enjoy her notoriety. Although she didn't feel she could go as far as accepting any dates. If she went out with anyone it was bound to be publicized, and Ed wouldn't like that. Or would he? It might be good to be seen out. She could always tell Ed it was to protect him.

She didn't quite know what to do until Ed solved the problem. He waited a week, and then a male secretary appeared at the apartment and packed up all his personal belongings. Dallas watched the secretary numbly. When he was finished he handed her a typed envelope and inside was the lease for the apartment in her name, and a cheque for ten thousand dollars. Bastard! Who did Ed Kurlnik think he was?

She could not believe that he would treat her in this way. She tried to contact him, but he had changed his private office number. For a while she was in a state of shock. Ed had been her passport to a whole new life. With him behind her she had felt completely protected. And now what did she have? Some ratty title, and a bit of half-assed fame. The thought had always hovered at the back of her mind that one day the immaculate Dee Dee would be divorced, and that she – Dallas – would become Mrs Ed Kurlnik.

Ten thousand dollars. What a paltry pay-off *that* was from a man of his wealth. Why, goddamn it, he was treating her like some little hooker. The irony of that was not lost on her.

She went out on the town with anyone who asked, drank too much, and was photographed everywhere. Let Ed Kurlnik see how much he mattered to *her*. Let him eat his heart out – senile old fool.

Beauty Incorporated called her in for yet another lecture on morals. She had certain standards to keep up. The unseemly publicity would have to stop.

She made a half-hearted effort. Stayed home two nights in a row, stopped drinking. Then the contract with the wool firm fell through just when she was on the point of signing. Not quite the right public image, she was told. Screw that.

Beauty Incorporated wanted her to go on a field trip to entertain troops abroad with Manny Shorto, a randy old comedian. 'How much?' she asked.

'The publicity is enough,' was their answer.

Screw *that*. 'I want to make some money,' she told them, '*real* money.'

'You're very uncooperative,' they replied. 'Frankly, the best thing would be if you resigned.'

No way.

Days later Beauty Incorporated fired her, and Miss Miami Beach stepped simperingly into her shoes. The newspapers went to town on that one.

Dallas didn't care. She had a movie test to do, and a lucrative contract for a suntan commercial which she had arranged herself. She had also met Kip Rey, nineteen-year-old heir to the family shoe fortune. He was tall and blond, and the ex-fiancé of Ed's lovely daughter Dana. Somehow it seemed like poetic justice.

They had met at a party. She had gone to use the John, and Kip was already in occupation, throwing up.

'Hey – you all right?' she asked.

'If I was all right I wouldn't be spewing up the godawful food they served at dinner. You drive?'

'Yes.'

'Take me home.'

She had been at the party with a faceless man that she couldn't care less about. She didn't mind dumping him.

'Sure,' she agreed.

He had a Maserati parked in the street, and she had some trouble with the gear shift, but he instructed her, and she soon got it together.

They ended up driving down to Coney Island and paddling in the sea. They snared a few joints, and he made her laugh. He didn't want anything from her, so she started to see him every night.

He was a young man with a lot of problems. He hated his rich family, didn't want to work in the family business, and used drugs like they were going out of style.

'Bad news,' Linda Cosmo informed her on one of their lunches.

'But I can relax with him,' protested Dallas, 'he doesn't hassle me.'

She and Linda met regularly. They got along exceptionally well, and Linda took incredible photos of her. They had already had five magazine covers.

'How did you and Al make out?' Linda had enquired upon her return from Europe.

'We didn't,' had been Dallas's somewhat terse reply.

'Good,' Linda had announced firmly – and that had been that.

Dallas did find herself thinking about him sometimes. His black eyes and hard body. Al King. SuperCock. Yes. She had made the right decision. Who needed to be just another one of the girls?

Kip took her to Puerto Rico for the weekend, and they stayed at a friend's house, and spent the entire three days bombed out of their minds on a variety of goodies that Kip supplied. They slept together for the first time.

Dallas felt nothing. His tall blond body did nothing for her. No waves. No jolts. Just plain professional fucking. No charge, kind sir, I am out of the business now. I don't even have to fake orgasms. I can be my good old-fashioned self.

'Don't you enjoy it?' he would mumble, too stoned to really care.

She would stare at him and not reply. What was there to enjoy when your body was anesthetized?

They played James Taylor and Dylan records, ate chocolate, went riding and swimming.

The night before they returned to New York he broke down and cried. 'I'm no good,' he confided, 'I'm a weak sonofabitch. I don't even know how you can stand to be with me.'

Dallas shrugged. 'I like you, it's that simple.' But if she was truthful she would admit that the only reason she liked him was because he made no demands on her.

'I'm rich,' he told her, 'goddamn rich. When I'm twenty-one I get over three million dollars, then the bastards can't touch me. Let's get married, Dallas.'

She agreed. It seemed like a wonderful idea. Only she knew his family would never allow it, and it was two years before he was twenty-one.

They announced their engagement. Once more she made headlines.

Kip was whisked back to the family compound in New York to explain matters.

Dallas had to fly to Los Angeles to shoot the suntan commercial, and do the screen test.

Kip assured her everything would be all right. They would meet again in a week's time in New York and discuss their plans.

Going back to Los Angeles made her nervous. So many bad memories. However, everyone connected with the commercial couldn't have been nicer. She worked hard all day, and collapsed exhausted into bed at night. Kip didn't call, but then she didn't expect him to.

She had a bungalow at the Beverly Hills Hotel and remembered the writer she had lived with there. Where was he now? Would he remember her? Out of curiosity she called the desk to inquire of his whereabouts, but they knew nothing of him.

When the commercial was finished she made her screen test. All the time she was there she half expected Bobbie to appear, but she never did. Maybe she had died – trashed out on one of her drug trips – what a relief *that* would be.

On the day that she was due to fly back to New York, Kip Rey was found dead of a drug overdose.

15

Brighton was sunny, hot and crowded with day trippers. It was a mistake.

Al and Edna arrived at lunchtime, checked into the hotel, and by four o'clock they were on their way home.

'I don't know why I listen to you,' Al ranted. 'Paul said it was a ridiculous idea. Brighton for crissakes!'

'I thought it would be nice,' ventured Edna timidly.

'Nice!' roared Al, 'With me getting pawed by every little old lady in sight. I've bought you a beautiful home where we have absolute privacy. What's with the Brighton bit?'

'We spent our honeymoon there.'

'That's because I couldn't afford anywhere else. Grow up, Edna, don't go chasing the past.'

'Slow down, Al, you drive too fast.'

'Don't nag. You're becoming a prize nagger lately.'

Her eyes filled with tears. How could she nag him when she hardly ever saw him?

'I've been thinking,' she ventured.

He grunted.

'I've been thinking it would be a good idea for me to come with you on the tour. Not *all* the time, just when Evan is with you.'

'What the hell for?' he snapped. 'You don't even want *me* to go, you've made *that* clear. And anyway – you hate the whole bit – photos, questions. No, Edna, you stay at home, I'll feel happier that way.'

'But I *want* to come. We're never together any more.'

'No, Edna.' His tone of voice indicated that he no longer wished to discuss the subject, so Edna lapsed into a miserable silence.

He had returned from the South of France, furious She had hardly dared mention the fact that the English press were going to town on his so-called romance with Dallas. 'There's no truth in it, is there?' she had finally asked.

'Are you kidding? Don't tell me they've got you believing it now?'

'Of course not.' And she felt guilty for ever having listened to Melanie.

When Edna had suggested Brighton, to her surprise, Al had said yes. They had left the very next day, and now, only a few hours later they were on their way home.

'With this traffic we'll be lucky to make it by seven,' he grumbled, 'I should have brought the chauffeur. I don't know why I let you talk me out of it.' He zoomed out of lane to overtake, and shuddering, Edna hunched down in her seat.

☆

'All set,' leered Nelson, pocketing the five pounds Evan had just handed him. 'She'll be here at six, back door. Let her in and take her up to your room.' He snickered. 'You'll find her a willing little partner. Don't be shy now.'

'I'm never shy,' said Evan aggressively. Although secretly he was shaking with fear at the very thought of it all.

'What's her name?'

'Her name? Oh – er, her name. Let me see now – Trudie, yes that's it – Trudie. Ever such a pretty bit. Better than the magazines – Oh yes, better than the magazines.' And he nudged Evan sharply in the ribs. 'Don't forget now, six o'clock.'

'Six o'clock,' repeated Evan numbly.

Nelson left, and Evan consulted his watch. Four o'clock. Two hours to wait. He didn't know how he would get through them. Thank goodness his parents were away for the weekend. To have the house to himself was a golden opportunity not to be missed.

He raided the bar and took a bottle of vodka and some glasses to his room. He drank a little of it, and felt his courage grow.

By six o'clock he was waiting anxiously by the back door. By six-thirty he was walking down the road looking for Trudie. By seven o'clock he was back in his bedroom with the realization that he had been conned. There was no Trudie, Nelson had been lying. And who could he complain to about his five pounds? Nelson knew that there was no one he dared tell. Sod rotten Nelson. He drank some more of the vodka, and never even heard his parents arrive home.

☆

Al was in one of his moods. He screamed abuse at Edna. Stupid cow. 'I'm going out,' he announced, 'on the piss with the boys, so don't wait up.'

'But you haven't had a thing to eat, I'll make some . . .'

He slammed the door in her face. Jesus, but he was uptight. He needed thawing out. He jumped into the Ferrari and roared next door.

Melanie answered the door. Brittle, horny, little Melanie. 'What happened to Brighton?'

'Piss on Brighton. Where's Paul?'

'He's at the office. Why don't you come in anyway?'

'I'm going to the pub, tell him to meet me there.'

'I could make you a drink.'

'Thanks but no thanks.'

She laid a hand lightly on his arm. 'Why not?'

He shook himself free. 'I'm not that much of a bastard.'

'And I am. Is that what you're saying?'

'One time was bad enough.'

'Oh, thanks a lot, you certainly know how to make a person feel good.'

'Melanie, sweetheart, I'm in no mood to mince words. You wanted a fuck one night – I gave it to you. I've felt pretty lousy about it ever since. Nothing personal but I don't ever want to repeat the exercise.'

She smiled tightly. 'I was offering you a drink, Al, that's all, a drink.'

'Terrific. But if you don't mind I'll get it at the pub.'

He jumped back into the Ferrari and roared off. He would always regret having given Melanie one. It had been a mistake, and one he hoped she would never be stupid enough to tell Paul.

☆

At his office Paul checked the final arrangements for the tour. It was all looking good, tickets were selling briskly, Bernie Suntan was doing a marvellous publicity campaign. They would open up in Canada to iron out any kinks, then straight into the big one at Madison Square Garden, New York.

He placed a call to Linda. He seemed to be missing her more than ever. She was out, and he wondered where. Did she go out with other men when he wasn't there? He had never asked her, but suddenly he was feeling very possessive, and if she did, it would have to stop. Lately he was fantasizing how it would be if he was married to her and not to Melanie. Would it be great? Or would it be great for a couple of years and then turn into the state of war that existed between most married couples he knew?

It was only a dream anyway. He could never leave his kids.

☆

Edna unpacked the suitcase that only earlier in the day she had so carefully packed for Brighton.

Al was so touchy lately. She knew he was worried about the tour, but why did he have to take it out on her?

She put her new nightdress on the bed. It was long and blue with discreet frills round the dipped neckline. She would wear it tonight. Al needed her. And when he got home he was prepared to forget the rantings and ravings. She would put him to bed and comfort him. She would do the things he had often urged her to do in the early days of their marriage, things that she had always considered slightly dirty and perverted. That would surprise him. That would please him.

That would at last make him *notice* her.

☆

In the private bar of his local pub Al found plenty of hangers-on to sit with. They laughed at his jokes, allowed him to buy them drinks, and basked in his limelight.

He relaxed in their company. He forgot about Brighton and Edna and the whole aggravating day. He boozed it up on scotch and coke and became suitably drunk. He realized in the middle of it all how unhappy he was. He had everything. And yet he had nothing. Was that it? Was the fact that there was nothing left to reach for the reason for his unhappiness?

God, but he needed the tour. He needed to get away. He needed Dallas.

Needed Dallas? He almost laughed aloud. How had *she* crept into his train of thought? Some two-bit broad with a rich boyfriend and a body. Who needed her?

But she was a challenge. She would give as good as she got. And how! Christ, he got horny just thinking about her, and that *was* unusual.

Now all that newspaper shit had petered out maybe he would see her again in New York. Not too long to wait. He would get Paul to arrange it . . . Yeah – good idea.

Paul arrived in time to drive him home. He was in no fit state to do so himself.

Edna met him at the front door and helped him up to bed. She laid him down and undressed him. He shut his eyes while the world weaved up and down.

Her hands stopped as they drew off his undershorts, and although he wasn't hard her head bent to kiss him.

He imagined himself in a shuttered hotel room with yet another fan and he pushed her away. 'Leave me alone,' he muttered. 'Why don't you all just leave me the fuck alone.'

☆

Evan woke up with a splitting headache and a dreadful sour taste in his mouth. He lay in bed wondering what to say to Nelson. He wanted his money back, maybe he would threaten to tell his mother. Nelson would laugh and jeer and call his bluff. Nelson wouldn't give him back his money. Evan knew that for sure.

Sun was streaming through the windows hurting his eyes. What are you supposed to do for a hangover?

He decided to take a shower in his father's bathroom, and was surprised upon reaching his parents' bedroom to find Al sprawled across the bed asleep. He had thought they were in Brighton. Wow – they must have come back early – perhaps it was just as well Trudie hadn't turned up. Evan blushed at the thought of his mother catching him with a girl. Crikey! She would have been furious.

Al suddenly stretched his arms and opened his eyes. 'Evan!' he exclaimed smiling, 'what's new, boyo?'

Evan clutched his pyjama trousers together, they gaped embarassingly. 'You're back,' he stated stupidly.

'No, we're still in Brighton,' Al laughed, and climbed out of bed. He was stark naked, and Evan's eyes rushed feverishly round the room searching for somewhere to focus other than his father's huge penis.

'Gotta take a piss,' Al said, 'don't go away, I've been wanting us to rap, but I never seem to *see* you. Where do you go all the time? Got yourself a girlfriend?'

'No,' muttered Evan, wishing he could tell his father about Nelson, but too ashamed to.

'Come on, a randy little sod like you.' The sound of Al peeing in the bathroom filled the room.

Evan edged towards the door. Perhaps his father wouldn't notice him go.

Al strolled cheerfully back in the bedroom. He was still naked, but to Evan's relief the size of his penis had subsided. Vaguely he wondered if his father was deformed. Or, crikey – maybe he – Evan – had an exceptionally small one. He would brood on *that* subject later.

Al was scratching his stomach. He studied his son. God, the kid was scrawny. He needed building up, he had no muscles. And that hair, shoulder-length grease.

'If you want to come on the tour you'll have to cut off some of that hair.'

'Why?'

'Because it doesn't suit you, that's why. It looks like shit, don't you ever wash it?'

'Sometimes.'

'I wash mine every two days, and I have it cut and styled every six weeks. I think I'll take you with me next time. You've got to be more aware of your personal appearance.'

'Why?' sneered Evan, 'I'm not a *pop* star.'

'No, and you never will be if you look like that.'

'Don't want to be.'

'OK. OK. Nobody is forcing you. What are you doing today? Want to come to rehearsal?'

'No thanks.'

'Want some money? Are you going out?'

'Can I have five pounds?'

'Sure, take it, only don't tell your mother, you know she doesn't like me giving you money.'

Evan grabbed five pounds from the dresser. Edna insisted he manage on three pounds a week pocket money, at least Al understood *that* side of things.

'I'll see you at dinner then,' said Al.

Evan nodded. 'I can come on the tour, can't I?' he blurted out, 'you promised I could. And *she's* not coming, is she?'

'Who's *she*?'

'Ma.'

'No she's not, and don't call your mother she. Maybe I'll take you.'

'You promised.'

'I didn't promise, I said maybe I'll take you. Don't hassle me. Get your hair cut and we'll see.'

☆

Al threw himself into weeks of vigorous rehearsal schedule. He worked all day, and at night was exhausted and uncommunicative. Then he would come home, work out in his gym, eat a spartan meal, and collapse in bed.

Again he read about Dallas in the newspapers. It seemed you couldn't help reading about her, everything she did seemed to make news – from getting fired as 'Miss Coast to Coast' to getting engaged to some rich kid. It all seemed to happen so fast.

Al felt sorry for her – he had really liked her, and maybe without all the hysterical publicity they could have got something together. But he had a certain public image to maintain – and he wasn't stupid enough to blow it for an affair that would last how long? A week? Two weeks? Forget it.

Meanwhile the newspapers kept on dragging up the same old pictures of him with her from the television special, and hinting at a great romance still lingering on. He wanted to laugh. He hadn't even seen or spoken to her since the South of France. And he certainly had never given her one.

On the Saturday before Al went off to a health farm, Edna invited Melanie and Paul to dinner. Al decided he wanted one fast blow-out before starvation, so they went to Tiberio, a fashionable Italian restaurant in Mayfair.

Edna was uncomfortable. She was supposed to open up the conversation about joining the tour, then Melanie would back her up. Words stuck in her throat, and they were at the coffee stage before Melanie finally flashed: 'Only another week and you two will be off, how lucky can you get.'

Paul snorted. 'Lucky indeed. It's a circus.'

'Don't you think,' ventured Edna, 'It would be nice if Melanie and I joined you, maybe in California.'

'It's not *your* cup of tea, Edna. You would hate every minute of it. Crowds. Riots. *You* know what these things are like.' Paul paused, and waited for Al to join in, but Al was playing eyes across a crowded room with a young movie actress, and was not about to be interrupted. Paul plunged on. 'Of course I know Al would love to have you there, as I know I would love to see Melanie. But these trips are murder, and we wouldn't subject you to it.'

'I think,' said Melanie sharply, 'it would be fun. Don't you think so, Edna?'

'Yes, I'd like to be with Al, I'm sure I could put up with a little discomfort.'

'So!' stated Melanie brightly, 'let's arrange it. We can meet you in Los Angeles. Edna and I can do some shopping, and get some sun. It will be like a holiday for us.'

Paul frowned. The thought of Melanie and Linda face to face was too much to bear. 'Al,' he said sharply, 'what do you think?'

Al was dragged reluctantly into the conversation.

'Forget it,' he said, 'I've promised Evan the trip and you know what he's like, Edna, he'll think you're spying on him.'

'But, Al . . .'

'Stop nagging. I'll take you for a holiday when we get back.'

'If you've got the energy,' murmured Melanie, sourly.

'I'll have the energy,' Al replied sharply.

Melanie flushed. 'It looks to me like they don't *want* us along. Will we cramp your style?'

'Oh for Christ sake shut up,' interrupted Paul.

'Why? I've heard what goes on when you go on one of these tours. little groupie girls to cater to your every whim.'

'I said *shut up*, Melanie.'

'Don't get excited. Edna and I will stay at home like good

wives, only don't be surprised if we turn up somewhere along the way to *surprise* you. A flying visit, now you couldn't object to that, could you?'

Paul signalled for the bill. The conversation was progressing in decidedly the wrong direction.

Edna brooded on Melanie's remarks, and when they were in bed she said to Al, 'Have you ever been unfaithful?'

He yawned. 'What kind of a crappy question is that? It's one o'clock in the morning, go to sleep.'

'I know you must be exposed to temptation. I know it can't be easy for you. What about that Dallas?'

'Edna, be a good girl. Stop listening to your cunty sister-in-law and go to sleep.'

'You know it's not easy for me to talk about things like this. You haven't made love to me for months. Is there someone else?'

'Jesus, Edna. Are you complaining? There are other things on my mind besides sex.'

'I've never refused you.'

He knew that. She lay on her back, parted her legs, and expected him to do all the work. Well, he just couldn't fancy that scene any more. 'I know, I'm just off sex, that's all.'

'I could,' she hesitated, 'well, you know, I could put you in my mouth like you always wanted me to.' She could feel the blush sting her face.

Al sighed. Oh no, Edna. It's too late, Edna. Oh Jesus! 'I'm tired. We'll talk tomorrow.' He turned his back. As far as he was concerned his marriage was over. The only problem was telling her.

Thank Christ for the tour. A chance to get away, think things out. He drifted into sleep, lurched into a nightmare. He was on stage. He was fat, and he was old, and when he opened his mouth to sing nothing came out. In his sleep he moved into the comfort and security of Edna.

BOOK TWO

THE TOUR

16

Bernie Suntan was sweating. What the fuck? Whoever sweated in London? Who knew it was a razzle dazzle heatwave for crissakes?

His blue and white striped cotton trousers stuck uncomfortably to his thighs. His red T-shirt emblazoned with AL IS KING was damp with perspiration. His feet flopped damply in his stars and stripes sneakers.

Paul King, beside him, was the picture of cool. Pale beige Yves Saint Laurent lightweight suit. Striped shirt. Dark shades.

They were at London Airport waiting for the star. Everyone else was aboard.

The plane, sleek and black, loaded with champagne, caviar, and liberal supplies of scotch and coke, waited patiently on the tarmac. AL IS KING decorated each side in bold gold lettering. From within, speakers roared out with the sound of Al's latest album.

An elite group of press waited on the tarmac, sipping iced Daiquiri cocktails, and nibbling small smoked salmon delicacies handed round by a bikini-clad hostess.

'What the fuck—' expanded Bernie, 'nothing but the best for the press.' And he winked at a lady interviewer of great power, and said, 'I never knew you had such insane legs!'

She blushed, taken aback for the first time in years.

Al's arrival was heralded by the white Rolls gliding over the tarmac and stopping nose to nose with the plane. The photographers jumped forward. On cue Al climbed out.

He was as thin and fit as possible. White trousers clung. A gold belt. White shirt open to the waist. Several gold medallions.

He grinned, strolled over, kissed the girls, posed for photos, answered questions.

'I must say you do look marvellous, Al,' enthused the lady reporter.

'Thank you, darling.' Bitch. Cunt. It was she that had written in her column only a few months previously that if Al King had anything else lifted the whole lot would collapse. He kissed her on the cheek for a photo, and nearly recoiled at the aroma of BO.

'Is this the start of a tax exile?' inquired one over-zealous reporter.

'No way,' replied Al, 'I'd miss my wife's cooking too much!'

'What about the former "Miss Coast to Coast". Will you be seeing her?' asked Bitch. 'I understand you two were quite cosy on that television special you did together.'

Al smiled calmly. 'My wife might see her. As I've said before they're old mates, perhaps if Edna joins me we will all get together.'

'What fun!' Bitch sneered unbelievingly. She needed a good seeing-to, that was her problem. 'And *will* Edna be joining you?'

'I hope so.' No way.

'How about having the girls out for a picture with Al?' suggested Bernie.

Everyone agreed it was a good idea, and 'The Promises' were called from the plane.

They were three stunning black girls. Rosa, at twenty-three, the eldest. Tall and reed-slim, with straight long hair and Chinese eyes. Sutch, twenty, curvy body and afro red hair. Nellie, small and slight, seventeen years old, delicately pretty. They wore identical outfits of white hot pants, thigh-length white boots, and AL IS KING red T-shirts. They grouped round Al, and the cameras clicked.

Paul glanced at his watch. Time to go. He gave Bernie the word. Linda was meeting the plane in Canada, he didn't want to keep her waiting.

It took another half hour before everyone was safely aboard and the plane was finally taxi-ing down the runway.

Al went right back to his private bedroom, an elaborate room – featuring a circular bed, leopard print padded walls, and thick pile carpet. A small bathroom led off to one side reached through a concealed door. He stripped off his clothes, put on a towelling dressing gown and picked up the glass of iced champagne waiting for him. Forget the scotch and coke for a while, too fattening. He smoked a cigar. This was it. This was the beginning, and he could feel a mounting excitement that nothing else compared with. Not even sex. And when had *that* last been exciting.

Maybe he should see a doctor. Hey doc, I've got this slight problem – too many beautiful girls, can't seem to be *bothered* any more. Can't seem to make the effort.

Paul came through. 'Everything all right?'

'Fine. Terrific'

'Voice OK?'

'Never better.'

'Great, kid. You'll kill 'em!'

'Don't I always?'

☆

Girls screamed when Al disembarked at Toronto. There was a healthy crowd. Banners proclaiming 'WE LOVE AL.' Policemen to protect him, hustle him to his limousine, ride him to his hotel.

His elation was building. Adrenalin flowing.

At the hotel there were flowers, fruit, booze, telegrams. A young girl smuggled her way in with room service and begged to suck his cock. When he declined she offered to suck Bernie's because he was 'close' to Al. Security removed her.

'Things ain't changed,' shrugged Al, 'Christ but it's good to be back!'

'What the fuck,' agreed Bernie, 'this is one scene that splits your head open more ways than one. We'll have a time, Al baby. Anything you want, just yell.'

Should he yell for Dallas, or should he put her out of his mind where she belonged? If he could forget about her that would be the best thing. Just another body, and he would be falling over them on this trip. He would not yell. He did not want her *that* badly. He would survey the available action and put Dallas away once and for all.

'You get some sleep,' suggested Bernie, 'Luke gonna put

in time outside the door. He's a tight guy, be beside you all the way – but *nobody* gets past him. I tell you he's the bionic man. Anyway I'm goin' over to check out the Gardens. Pick you up for the television interview in a coupla hours.'

Bernie waddled off. Al opened the door and checked out Luke, who was to be his bodyguard on the trip. The bionic man was right. Luke was six foot four, black, and mean-looking. His muscles rippled before he even moved.

'Hey there, man,' greeted Al, 'want a beer or something?'

Luke shook his head.

Al went back in his room. Time to shower. Order a steak. More champagne. Gargle, So where was Paul?

Should he call Edna? He had promised he would. But he didn't feel like listening to her moans. He had promised Evan he could join the tour in Nashville, and Edna had wanted to come too. No way. No thank you. After sixteen years Edna was nagging her way right out of his life.

☆

'I've missed you,' confessed Paul.

Linda hugged him, 'I've missed *you*, twice as much.'

'Only twice as much?'

'Well . . .' she laughed softly, 'maybe more. How was London?'

'The same. Work, work, and more work.'

'But you love it.'

'I wouldn't do it if I didn't love it.'

'Shall we stand here making small talk, or shall I slide you out of your lovely suit and have my way with you before big brother calls?'

'I wish you'd have your way with me. I don't think I can wait much longer.'

She grinned. 'You really have been missing me.'

'I really have.'

They started to undress each other, fumbling and pulling at belts and zippers.

'Oh my goodness, Paul, you've been saving up!'

'Just for you. I hope you appreciate what you're getting.'

They were silent for a while, delighting in each other, moving slowly, quietly. Then the phone rang. Paul groaned.

'Don't answer it,' begged Linda, 'at least not for a minute.'

The phone continued to jangle. 'I've lost my concentration,' Paul grumbled, reaching for the phone.

'That's not all you've lost.'

'Yeah, who is it?' he asked abruptly.

'Paul, boyo, where are you?'

'I'll be right there, Al. I was just coming.'

'Oh yes!' whispered Linda.

'Who are you with? Is Linda there?'

'Yes, she's here.'

'Bring her with you. Come on up, boyo. I'm fidgety, feel like a little company. Check out the lobby and see if there's anything worth giving one to.'

'What do you want, the groupie clap?'

'Shit. You're right. Who has numbers for Toronto? Find out and get me a piece, I need something before the show.'

'I'll try.' Paul shifted his body away from Linda.

'Do that.'

Linda sat up and reached for a cigarette. 'What did he want?' she asked tightly.

'To get laid.'

'Does he never stop?'

'I thought he had, but the urge is once again upon him. Pardon me while I make a few calls.'

'I didn't know you pimped for him too.'

'On tour I do everything for him. You had better get used to it.'

'Oh – that's great. Are we finished then? Shall I get dressed?'

Absently Paul replied, 'Yes.' He picked up the phone and called the desk.

Angrily Linda marched into the bathroom. One minute they had been making love – and now it seemed the furthest thing from Paul's mind. Well, he would have to beg for another chance. If this was a taste of Paul on tour he could shove it.

She dressed, brushed her hair, and touched up her make-up.

Paul came into the bathroom and nuzzled her from behind. 'All fixed,' he said cheerfully.

'Oh good.'

'What's the matter?'

'Nothing.' Her voice dripped sarcasm. 'Should there be?'

'Come on, Linda. You promised you would understand. We'll have plenty of time together later.'

She forced a smile. 'I understand.'

'Good girl. Come on, let's go, he's waiting.'

17

Where had all the money gone?

Dallas shook herself awake from a massive hangover and surveyed the pile of bills that had just dropped through the mailbox.

She was spending faster than she was making. Ed Kurlnik's paltry pay-off she had blown on jewellery and furs. The money from the commercial she had frittered away. Clothes, clothes, clothes.

She squeezed orange juice, and sipped it slowly. What time had she arrived home? She could hardly remember, but she did remember with a smile fighting off Aarron Mack in his chauffeured limo. *The* Aarron Mack, Swedish czar of Mack Cosmetics. Friend of Ed Kurlnik. Old fart.

He could not believe that they were not going to end the evening in her bed. She had been giving him a strong come on all night. From the moment they had met at a party she had set him firmly in her sights. A friend of Ed Kurlnik's was far too good an opportunity to miss, even if he was somewhat older than Ed. He was in his early seventies, but well preserved, with a strong bullet head, and a fine set of white sparkly false teeth. Short though, barely five seven, and she towered over him in her Walter Steiger shoes. It didn't seem to put him off, he seemed to love it.

'Why not?' he had demanded when she wouldn't allow him to come up to her apartment.

'We've only just met,' she demurred.

'Are you an old-fashioned girl?' he had asked, grabbing for her breasts.

'No, but I like a little time to get to know a person.'

'You want money?'

'Please don't insult me.'

His hands were all over her. 'What *do* you want?'

She moved his hands. 'Time.'

'Dinner tomorrow?'

'I'm busy tomorrow.'

'The day after?'

'If you like.'

He squeezed her breast triumphantly, and she elbowed him sharply away. If she played her cards right Aarron Mack was a very viable proposition. His wife had recently died, and he was equally as rich as Ed Kurlnik.

Old rich men with hard-ons. It seemed to be her destiny. Kip Rey might have been her salvation; he had been fun to be with, but always so stoned, and sexually there had been the usual void. Absolutely no turn-on. She had cried at his death, but more at her loss than at his.

Since he had died she had slept with no one. There had been no reason to do so. She had thrown herself into the New York social scene. Getting fired had made her a celebrity, and she was invited to all the openings and parties. She enjoyed having her photo taken, and all the attention she received. She also enjoyed turning down countless sexual propositions. *That* was the real kick.

Men didn't understand her. She was young and beautiful, why wasn't she out fucking her brains out?

The doorbell rang. It was three dozen yellow roses and a box from Cartiers. She opened the box; it contained a diamond flower-shaped brooch. She tossed it to one side; might come in useful to sell one day.

Aarron Mack took her to dinner at The Four Seasons. She ordered caviar and Steak Diane, then left it all. She drank wine, and brandy, and Pernod on the rocks. Nowadays it took a lot of booze to get her where she wanted to be.

Later they went to Le Club, and they danced, his bullet head nuzzling discreetly against her bosom. She drank three Irish coffees, but obliteration seemed nowhere near. He suggested she visit his triplex penthouse for a nightcap. She agreed. Going up in the elevator he unzipped his fly and crammed her hand in. For an old man he was surprisingly erect. She snatched her hand away.

In the apartment they went out on the roof garden, and a butler appeared with champagne.

The city was spread out before them, a sea of lights.

'Get on your knees,' Aarron instructed.

One diamond brooch and she was supposed to get on her knees. Dallas laughed aloud.

'Please,' he added, and he was shaking himself free as if preparing to pee.

'No,' said Dallas slowly, 'you get on *your* knees.' And she opened the slit in her skirt provocatively.

'Later,' husked Aarron.

'Now,' insisted Dallas.

'I can give you wonderful presents,' Aarron promised, 'be a good girl and do as I ask.'

Dallas flicked her skirt briskly together. Her mind jumped back to a certain motel, an old man lying dead on the bed, Bobbie deftly pocketing his bankroll.

She turned to leave. 'I'm going home, Aarron. Find someone else to buy wonderful presents for.'

'You can't go,' he objected.

'Oh yes I can, I can do what the hell I like.'

She walked through the sumptuous apartment to the elevator. It could all have been hers if she had cared to get on her knees. But why should she? It didn't make her happy, nothing made her happy. For the thousandth time she wondered why her parents had never come looking for her. Life at the zoo with Phil sticking it in every night must have been better than this.

It occurred to her that if she went home and took an overdose of sleeping pills nobody would care. Not one single person. Maybe it wasn't such a bad idea after all.

She took a cab home. It was three o'clock in the morning. Idly she wondered if she had enough sleeping pills to do the job properly. How many did you need? The booze was finally hitting her, and by the time she arrived home she was weaving on her feet.

She nodded at the desk porter. He was asleep.

The apartment was on the fifth floor. The apartment that Ed Kurlnik had rented for her. The apartment where she had entertained him in so many different guises. He would be hard put to find a woman as versatile and imaginative as she was. Perhaps she should leave him a note. That would really put him away with Dee Dee. She couldn't understand why tears were rolling slowly down her cheeks, and yet she was smiling, giggling even.

She fumbled for her keys. Funny, the door seemed to be open, and there was a smell that she couldn't quite place.

She put her bag down on the hall table and groped for the light switch. Before she could reach it an arm enclosed her from behind. 'Don't scream,' a voice warned, 'I've got a knife and I'll split you from end to end. You hear me – bitch? You hear me?'

18

Toronto was a sell-out. Fifteen thousand Al King fans waiting expectantly for the master.

Al was at tension pitch. Paul stayed solidly by his side. Whatever Al wanted, Al got.

It was hot. Before going on Al was sweating in the black satin jump suit that clung to him like a second skin. He swigged down a bottle of Perrier water, and watched from the side of the stage as 'The Promises' finished their set.

They rocked in unison – 'Easy baby – stay with me baby – give it to me baby – Easy baby.'

He could see the sweat rolling off their gleaming bodies and sticking to the suede skins swathed round their supple forms.

'Easy baby – make it baby – shake it baby – make me come . . . to you . . . OOOh baby . . . OOOh babee . . .'

The crowd roared its approval. 'The Promises' were just starting to hit it. Their latest record was zooming ahead in the charts.

Al had worked with them once before in Las Vegas, and they offset him perfectly.

They came running offstage, breathless, happy. 'The vibes are wailin' tonight, man,' said Rosa. 'Jeese – it is but *beeeautiful!*'

Al's musicians were starting up. The conga, the drums, the guitar, the tambourines.

He strode on stage.

> Who's gonna give it to you tonight
> Who's got love that's outasight
> I'm your lover

I'm your man
Hey momma – shake your can

The crowd screamed. Al was one of the few white singers
who sang soul the way it should be sung – the black way.

And yet that wasn't all. His amazing voice could turn
from pure funk to sing the clearest ballad around and then
double back to a horny throbbing rasp.

Out front Linda took photographs, and marvelled at the
magic Al created on stage. It was almost as if he lifted
the audience up and took them with him on his own private
trip. She watched a girl shaken by her own tears. Another
who simply could not look at him. Row upon row they were
under his spell, wriggling, squirming, trying to keep the
excitement under control but not succeeding. Then suddenly
screaming, storming the stage, clawing at the security guards.

And Al, under the spotlight, singing, moving, thrusting,
tempting them in his black satin, stretched tight over what
appeared to be a giant cock.

You wanna make it tonight
You wanna shake it tonight
We're gonna do it together
The way that we should
We're gonna love together,
Like I knew we would

A thin, pale girl fainted, and was passed casually over
people's heads and taken outside. By now everyone was
standing, caught in his spell, rocking, swaying.

Al was caught up in his own spell. This was it. This was
the ultimate. This was *the* orgasm. He could use his voice to
far more effect than ever he did his cock. And his voice was
ready, his whole body was ready.

He was making love to fifteen thousand people simultaneously and it was the absolute high. He never had got
involved in the whole drug scene, and the reason was
patently clear. Could a sniff of coke, a shot of H, a handful
of mescalin, even begin to compare with this? No way.
No fuckin' way.

He was singing with his everything. His heart. His soul.
His guts. And they knew it, and they loved him for it. And
he was a part of them and vice versa.

When it was over he was drained, in a state of shock. Paul and Luke bundled him under towels and raced him to a waiting car, and he was spirited away before the audience realized he was gone.

If the people had got hold of him they would have torn him to loving pieces.

He came out of it slowly. Back to reality, back to ground level. A shower. A massage. Gargle with the warm harshness of brandy.

'Incredible,' Paul told him, 'goddamn incredible.'

And he knew it was true. He never kidded himself on the quality of a performance. Relief flooded through him, and the tensions and insecurities of the previous few months were gradually exorcised. He had done it. He was better than ever. They had loved him. And *this* was only the first stop.

'Let's party,' he told Paul. 'Let's have us a time.'

☆

Linda made her own way back to the hotel. She had no choice; by the time she got backstage Paul had vanished. Not that she expected him to be waiting for her, but he could have *told* her. She called his room, but there was no reply. She contemplated phoning him at Al's but decided against it.

She went downstairs to the lobby and bumped into Bernie. She had yet to prove her worth as a photographer and Bernie regarded her with a certain amount of suspicion. However, who wouldn't feel expansive after Al's performance. 'What the fuck,' said Bernie, 'you comin' to the party?'

'Wouldn't miss it. Where?'

'The Dragon suite. Go on down.'

She made her way to the lower level of the hotel and located the party.

Al and Paul were not there. It was full of newspaper reporters and Toronto personalities. 'The Promises' were flitting about being charming.

She took a glass of wine, and looked around for someone she knew. There were enough people connected with the tour, but no one she had really talked to. She sighed, wow – this was really going to be fun.

'Hello.'

She turned to confront the speaker.

He was a middle-aged man in a plaid suit with baggy eyes and a crew cut. 'Lonely?' he questioned.

'Not particularly,' she replied.

'I didn't think you *were*, I just thought you *might* be.'

'Thanks anyway, but I'm not.'

'The name's Hank Mason, newscasts are my game – Mason's the name.'

Linda looked desperately around for Paul.

'How's about us splitting from here, and I could take you to a nice cosy little place I know?'

'Thank you, but I'll pass.'

'Don't be like that. You looked lonely.' He belched discreetly. 'You're a pretty girl, don't get uppity with me for trying.'

'Look Mr er . . .'

'Mason.'

'Mason. I am not lonely. I appreciate your offer, now please leave me alone.'

He leered. 'I like 'em difficult.'

'Oh for Christ's sake – go away.'

'I bet you like 'em rough. A smack round the bottom – you like that, don't you?'

'Fuck off.'

'Or maybe you like girlies. Is that your kick?'

'Am I being too polite for your pin-sized brain? Go fuck yourself, buster.'

Before he could reply she saw Paul, and hurried over.

'Hi, sweetheart.' He kissed her absently. 'What are you doing down here?'

'Waiting for you.

'You're in the wrong place.'

'How am I supposed to know that.'

'If you had waited in your room I would have told you. Wasn't Al sensational?'

She nodded. Maybe coming on the tour hadn't been such a good idea. Or maybe it had been a terrific idea. She was seeing a whole new Paul.

'Run upstairs and fetch your cameras, the party's in Al's suite.'

'Where are you going?'

'I've got to sort out some people here, I'll see you up there.'

So he hadn't even come looking for her. She frowned, but Paul was already drifting off. They were all shits, Dallas was right. They had become quite friendly in New York. Dallas was a toughie, but honest with it, and Linda had found that to be a surprisingly refreshing quality in a woman.

OK, Paul. I can be tough too. You want to play the casual bit, I can play too.

☆

Al basked in it. He sat back and accepted the compliments. Christ, but he felt he deserved them. He had starved his ass off to be in prime physical shape, and rehearsed non-stop for what seemed like months.

And it had all been worth it. God, the feeling he had now could not be beat. He was exhausted but elated. He felt like an athlete who has beaten every possible record.

The room was crowded with people anxious to join in his triumph. His musicians, a few select groupies, and a mixture of freaks who had talked their way in.

Three girls hovered nervously near him, ready for a wink, a nod, anything. They would slit each other's throats to get near him first should he give a signal.

He didn't bother. He felt perfectly satisfied. Anyway he had sent Paul off to look for some real local talent. Groupies gave him no charge. Beneath their bland young faces lay sharp little brains armed with tape measures and plaster casts.

He knew that he should call Edna. She would be waiting by the phone anxious to hear what had happened. But goddamn it, she had wanted him to fail, she had wanted him to stay home. She wouldn't be ecstatic about his success.

'The Promises' came flitting in. He had screwed Rosa that time they had been in Vegas. Once or twice between shows, it had been nice. But she had been involved with some gangster – and Al had decided the risk was not worth the prize. He wondered if he should renew old acquaintances. But getting involved with someone on the tour could turn out to be a drag. Whoever said never mix pleasure with business was a genius.

Rosa was coming over anyway. She kissed him. 'Babee, you were *the* best – you hear me – the best!'

He hugged her.

'We gonna have good times this trip, huh?'

'Yeah,' agreed Al. 'Oh yeah.'

19

Dallas stood perfectly still. The arm that enclosed her from behind was steel-strong across her back. Fear shoved the alcohol out of her system, and she could feel the heavy, panic-stricken beating of her heart.

'Don't scream,' the voice warned again, 'and don't turn around.'

She recognized the smell. It was the strong aroma of pot hanging heavily in the air. Whoever it was in her apartment must have been there for some time. In the gloom she made out two suitcases stacked near the door, and her television set standing alongside them. She breathed a little easier. A robbery.

'Take the things and go,' she whispered. 'I won't do anything, I won't call the police.'

'Shut up.' The arm tightened round her neck, and the front door was kicked shut.

She could not see her assailant, but from the sound of his voice he was youngish. She could feel his body up against her. He was tall and skinny.

They stood silently in the darkness, then suddenly, inexplicably, he started to rub himself against her.

Oh God! She felt the vomit rise in her throat. He was going to rape her.

She was wearing a long silk jersey dress with nothing underneath, and his free hand roughly plunged into the top of it and released her breasts.

He giggled, a high-pitched maniacal laugh. 'Better than the grandma I had last week,' he boasted, 'she had tits on her like hangin' onions!'

She started to shake, shivers racking her body.

'I like 'em young,' the voice continued, rubbing the palm of his hand roughly across her breasts, 'young an' juicy with big tits. You like big cocks? I got a big one, m'am. You are gonna see a whopper.' He released his arm from around her neck, and both hands grabbed her breasts. 'Shall I give it to you up the ass?' he asked conversationally, 'I did that to a girl the other day, she screamed and hollered. You wouldn't do that, would you? I had to cut her a little to make her stop, real little cut across her throat.' He laughed again. 'Man, she sure was *screamin'*. I . . .'

Dallas spun suddenly round, arms crossed over her exposed breasts, eyes blazing with fury.

She was right. He couldn't have been more than eighteen. He had no knife, and he stepped back in surprise.

'Well?' blazed Dallas, 'where's your big cock then? I thought it would be ready for me. I like 'em big. Big and juicy. You got a juicy one, sonny? Want to show it to me?'

He looked alarmed.

'*Come on*,' insisted Dallas, 'don't tell me you're all talk?' she took her hands away from her breasts. 'Nice, huh? Big, huh? Just the way you like 'em.'

'What are you?' he muttered nervously, 'some kind of nut, some freak . . .' He was backing towards the door.

'Don't go,' said Dallas, 'thought we were going to have a little *rape* here. Come on, sonny, show me what you got. I *like* it up the ass, do you? Come one, sweetie. Or can you only get it up when you have some scared shitless woman on the floor? Well? Is that it?' Her voice became taunting, 'Only get it up *then*, sonny, is that right?'

'Jesus!' He opened the door. 'You're mad, you know that? You're some kind of freaky person. Jesus . . .'

He ran off towards the elevator, and she slammed the door, slid the chain on, and then started to shake. She sat on the floor, huddled her arms around her knees, and rocked back and forth. To hell with fear. To hell with standing there and just letting it happen. Fuck him, whoever he was. Because he was *stronger* than her, because he was a *man* she was supposed to stand there and let him do and say what he wanted. And after, when he left, when she was lying there, when the police came. What then? Did you *know* him? Were you a *virgin*? Oh well, how many men have you had then? Open your legs for the police gyno, and don't mind the policeman standing at the back of the room, he's used to it.

Fuck that.

But what if he had a knife? What if he hadn't been such a kid? Every day you read about murders. She shut her eyes. The shock started to hit her. She forced herself into the living room and swigged from a brandy bottle. The room was a wreck. He had shit on the carpet, thrown garbage round the room. In her bedroom and bathroom he had scribbled obscenities in lipstick all over the walls. Sick kid. He had probably copied it from some movie.

She knew she should call the police, but she also knew the publicity it would entail. Who needed that? After all he hadn't gotten away with anything. She had frightened him off empty-handed.

Meanwhile she couldn't stay there. No way. Never again.

Methodically she cleared up. By eight in the morning she had packed everything she wanted to keep. She called her only friend in New York, Linda Cosmo, and the telephone message service gave her an out-of-town number where she could be contacted.

She phoned, and a sleepy Linda instructed her to move into her apartment. 'I'll be back in a few days,' she explained, 'then we'll sort something but.'

Dallas called for a cab, picked up Linda's key from the janitor, and moved in.

She stocked up with food, double-locked all the doors, and stayed there until Linda got back.

20

The show at the Civic Centre Arena, Ottawa, was the same razzle dazzle smash hit as Toronto. Even better, perhaps, as Al gained full confidence.

Rave reviews filled the newspapers, and the tour's slogan – 'AL IS KING' was widely used. The concerts were a sell-out across America. A side rip-off industry sprang up amongst people lucky enough to have purchased blocks of seats. Soon tickets were going at five or six times the original price. A limit was set on people only being allowed two tickets per person, but the hustlers soon got round that.

Linda took an incredible photo of Al on stage. Like a

God he stood before the masses. She had captured him in a moment of stillness above a sea of female hysteria. The picture was used world-wide to illustrate his triumph.

Bernie accepted her as an integral part of the tour from that moment on. Paul, however, didn't. He seemed offhand and disinterested. He was annoyed because she had apparently insulted a Toronto newscaster called Hank Mason, who had been the only person to knock Al in print.

'So what?' Linda had questioned, 'he was rude to me first.'

'Never insult the press,' Paul had warned, 'they can make or break us.'

Linda had considered the whole incident ridiculous. Al was an undeniable smash hit, how could one little newscaster affect that? Anyway *Al* hadn't insulted him, *she* had.

'He knows you're with the tour, that's why he knocked Al,' Paul had said, 'try and be nice to everyone.'

'Oh, sorry. Maybe I *should* have gone home with him and let him smack my bottom. Should I have?'

Paul had not bothered to reply.

Linda could not understand what had happened to them. They had waited and longed to be together, and now that they were it was an anti-climax. Paul seemed to spend his entire time finding girls for Al. One after the other they were paraded up to the Master's suite for his inspection, but so far not one appeared to have passed muster.

Find 'em – fuck 'em – forget 'em – had once been Al's motto. Now it seemed to be find 'em – forget 'em. He couldn't even be bothered to try. They were boring, all of them. He wondered if age had finally caught up with him. But it wasn't that, he knew it. No problem getting it up, but it had to be for something better than a parade of dumbells looking to screw a star.

He tried it with Rosa, and it was good, but not good enough to try again.

He didn't need it anyway. The moments on stage were enough. The power orgasm. The joy of thousands of women having you at once. The mass fuck.

He looked forward to New York. That was the *real* start of the tour as far as he was concerned. His insecurities had swept away. His voice was better than ever. The fans were still there, still loved him, still wanted him. He felt like a weight had been lifted from his shoulders. Christ – to have failed, or only achieved moderate success. What would he have done then? Retired? He could never retire, singing was his life. But it couldn't go on forever, and if he did go it had to be at a peak.

He had finally phoned Edna.

'What's the weather like?' had been her first question.

What the fuck did the *weather* matter? He wanted her praise. He spoke to Evan.

'When can I come?' The boy had asked truculently.

What a family! Didn't they read the newspapers? Didn't they know that Al was King again?

He allowed a stoned blonde to give him a mediocre blow job before going to bed. She was delighted at the honour. He thought about Dallas, once, briefly, and wondered where she was and who she was with. Now there was a girl who would never do anything in a mediocre fashion.

He slept, and in his sleep he was surrounded by applause and warm bodies, and he slept well.

☆

Linda said, 'I had a call from Dallas.'

Paul was reading *Variety*. 'Who?'

'Dallas. She had some kind of bad experience. I lent her my apartment.'

'Why did you do that?'

'Because she needed a place to go.'

'I didn't realize you were *that* friendly.'

Linda gazed out of the aeroplane window. 'What's the matter, Paul? What's happening with us?'

It was the first chance they seemed to have been alone together. Four days in Canada, and every night a party.

'Nothing's the matter. I *told* you what I'm like on tour.'

'Do you wish I wasn't along?'

He folded his *Variety* and stared at her. 'Do you?'

'I asked *you* first.'

'I don't know. I thought it was a good idea, it *seemed* like a good idea. But Al has to come first, and I know that bugs you.'

'OK, so he comes first. Understood. But I'm not even

running a poor second. Since that first day you haven't even touched me . . .'

'There hasn't been time. You know Al likes me to stay with him after a show. He can't sleep, he needs to talk, play cards, just relax. And when I do get to your room you're asleep and I'm bushed.'

'Wow! We sound like a couple of real swingers!'

'New York will be different. He'll probably find a girl he likes, then I can be with you.'

'What about Dallas? He likes her, doesn't he?'

'It's not mutual. She gave him a hard time. He doesn't need that whole bit.'

Doesn't he? mused Linda. We shall see. If she got Dallas and Al together. If they hit it off. Well – maybe her problems would be solved.

Dearest Al, I am offering you a swop. You may have Dallas, and I, thank you very much, will take back Paul.

Linda smiled. It wasn't a nice thing to do to a friend, but all is fair in love and war, and this was war.

☆

New York was blisteringly hot. Crowds and photographers were at the airport to meet the plane. Al was whisked off to do a television interview and Paul, of course, went with him.

Linda took a cab into the city. She was hot, tired, and more than a little disappointed at the way things were going. She wanted a bath, and a think, and maybe a man – a transient stud purely for medicinal purposes.

Sometimes the only way to really relax was to lose yourself in a totally physical pastime. Linda had found that an occasional sexual scene was the only way she could turn off, and clear out her head. It did not mean that she loved Paul any the less, or that he wasn't a good lover, it was just that sometimes sex without emotional complications was a great therapy treatment.

She contemplated phoning Rik. She had seen him a few times over the last few months. He was a dumb actor with a beautiful body. They had met at their mutual supermarket.

She stopped the cab and made the call.

'You haven't called me for weeks,' Rik complained.

'I've been out of the city.'

'You could have let me know.'

'Sorry. I thought I might pop over.'

There was silence, then Rik said truculently: 'You really are a bitch, you *use* me.'

'Don't you want me to come over then?'

'Yes, of course I do.'

'I'll be there soon.'

She hung up and sighed. Rik was right, she did use him. But why should *he* complain, he had been using women for years.

She gave the driver his address and sat back. She felt no guilt. Why should she? Paul was still sleeping with his wife, and maybe an occasional groupie too – God knows, there were enough of them floating around.

She lit a cigarette and hoped that Rik was not going to start giving her a heavy about not calling before. She had never allowed him her phone number or address and it bugged him. If he started getting uptight he would just have to go.

He was easily replaceable.

☆

Al smiled his way through the television interview. Stock questions. Stock answers. The interviewer was a well-known woman by the name of Marjorie Carter, who had her own news programme. She kept on giving him penetrating moody stares. She had formerly been a Washington journalist, and some said she had once had the ear of the President. Which one Al wasn't quite sure, probably Kennedy, as she was about forty, but strikingly attractive in that groomed, designer-label clothes way.

'That was fun,' she said, after the show. 'At least you can *talk*.'

'What do you mean by that?' Al asked.

'I keep on getting supposed superstars on the show who sit transfixed by their own image on the monitor. So out of it they can barely string their ums and ers together.'

'Sounds like a laugh.'

'I have tickets for your performance tomorrow. Is it worth seeing?'

Al smiled. Now they were off camera she wanted to put him in his place. 'Depends what you're looking for.'

'Excitement.' She had hot, frustrated eyes.

'I think I can help you there.'

'I'll come then.'

'Do that, and drop by the party later.' Maybe if she was lucky he would give her one.

Bernie came rushing over. 'Sensational! Al, you came over great – but right on. Jeeze . . .' He mopped at the sweat streaming down his face with a coloured handkerchief. 'Word's out you're here – we gotta make a quick side exit – like, cement yourself to Luke and move like you gotta crap.'

Bernie hustled Al up, and Luke – forever hovering – gripped onto his arm, and with Paul the other side they headed swiftly for the exit it was least expected they would emerge from.

Neither Bernie nor Paul revealed to Al that while he had been on the show they had received a death threat. A telephone call from some displaced head – 'I'm gonna kill that mothafukin' bastard son of a bitch . . .'

Nothing unusual about threats, but you always had to take them seriously. You never knew when some nutter would decide to do something about it. Once Al had been on tour, and a disgruntled husband had managed to smash his way into the dressing-room with an axe. It was only Paul's quick thinking that had saved Al. He had tripped the maniac up and sat on him until help had arrived.

They made the car in safety, sped to the hotel, entered through the underground garage.

'Set me up a poker game,' Al demanded of Paul, 'and a girl, lots of tit and ass and blonde hair.'

Paul frowned. *Another* girl. Al seemed insatiable on this trip. He raised eyebrows at Bernie and Bernie winked in reply. 'I've got just the lady . . .' What the fuck – Al would never know she was a hooker.

21

Alone, holed up in Linda's apartment, Dallas did a lot of thinking. She was twenty years old. She was beautiful, and

God knows she was at least as talented as half the girls who were making it in television and movies.

What was she *doing* with her life? She was bumming around New York going out with guys she didn't like, didn't want to lay, and only wanted to give a hard time to. Was this the revenge she was supposed to be getting for Ed Kurlnik splitting? Some revenge.

She was spending all her money at an alarming pace. And when that was gone – what then? Back to hustling? No thank you.

She was drinking too much. And if that freak hadn't broken into her apartment, God knows what she would have done. Perhaps she should thank him. OK, so she had no one – not one person who cared about her. But she had her health, her looks, her talent, and goddamn it she was going to make something of her life. Success was not such a distant dream. She was known, she had done a TV show and a commercial. She was always in the gossip columns. She wasn't some little unknown Miami hooker any more.

She formed a plan of action, and getting out of New York would be the first step. She would sell her jewellery and furs, and rent her apartment; that would give her capital. Then she would go to Los Angeles. She had received letters from a couple of agents who were anxious to meet her. She could go to an acting class there, she could study and learn. And if she was lucky enough to make it, she could have a baby. The thought delighted her. A human being. Flesh and blood that would belong to her. A little girl or a little boy, what difference, there would be someone she belonged to, someone who would eventually care.

☆

Linda arrived back in the early evening.

'What happened?' she asked, disappearing into the shower. 'Make some coffee and we'll talk.'

Dallas made coffee, and without being dramatic told Linda exactly what had taken place.

'Jesus!' exclaimed Linda, 'it's unbelievable!' But she knew it happened fifty times a day. 'Why didn't you call the police? Don't answer, I know it's a dumb question. Anyway I'm glad you came here. I just can't believe you *talked* him out of it. Weren't you petrified?'

Dallas shrugged. 'I guess I just baulked at becoming another victim. I was so angry I forgot to be frightened.'

'The trouble is if they ever caught him all he'd probably get would be a telling off and a three-month suspended sentence. Girl at my school got raped, she was fifteen and so was the boy. They ignored the fact that he held a knife to her throat – naughty, naughty, they said, and he was back in school the next week. The girl became a raving dyke and nobody cared.'

'I feel together now. It was rough at the time but I'm over it. Thanks for the loan of your apartment, it's so cosy here. I just crawled into bed and glued myself to the television. I can split now you're back.'

'You can stay if you like. I'm only here for a couple of days and I'll be sleeping over at the hotel.'

'Thanks, but I've got this urge to get out of New York. If you don't mind I might stay while I sort things out. Who do you know that will give me a good price on my jewellery?'

'Hey, if you need money I can come up with some, you don't . . .'

'No. I want to sell it. Thanks anyway. Really, Linda, you have been great, I don't know how to thank you. I mean I could have moved in and ripped you off – anything . . .'

'I knew you wouldn't do that. You needed help – I was able to. If *I* need help any time I'll be at your front door like fire!'

Dallas laughed. She had a friend, and it was a good feeling. Maybe Linda might have cared if she had taken the pills – maybe just a little.

'How was Canada?' she asked.

Linda made a face. 'Al was a sensation as I'm sure you've read everywhere. Paul was busy holding his hand. I took some good pictures.'

'I haven't seen any papers.' Dallas paused. 'How is Al?'

'He's screwed his way through Canada. America here he comes! I was going to ask you the ultimate favour and see if you would come out with us tonight, but I changed my mind

– after what you've been through I certainly couldn't inflict Al on you.'

'I wouldn't mind . . .'

'You wouldn't? Hey, that would be great. Paul seemed to think that you and Al were deadly enemies. According to Paul you're the only female around who ever gave him a sharp no. As far as Paul is concerned Al has access to every woman in the world! I think Paul would be surprised if the Queen said no!'

'Listen, I'll come out, that doesn't mean I'll say yes.'

'Sure. Look, I'll give Paul a buzz and set it up.' Linda smiled to herself. This was going to work out just fine. Maybe Paul was right, maybe Al *was* irresistible to most women.

She shut herself in the bedroom and called the hotel.

'How did the television show go?' she asked.

'Didn't you watch it?' Paul sounded pissed off. Nothing unusual, lately Paul always seemed pissed off.

'I forgot.'

'That's great. Al will be delighted to hear that when he asks your opinion.'

Linda almost laughed aloud. 'Since when has Al wanted *my* opinion?'

'Are you coming over?'

'I thought we were going out.'

'Al's tired.'

'Maybe he'll revive when he hears who I've got him for a date.'

'Who?'

'Dallas. All set. Can we eat somewhere decent?'

Paul glanced over at his brother. He was immersed in a poker game with three men. The blonde hooker was draped over the back of his chair looking bored.

'It's a little late in the day for that lady to start changing her mind.' Paul lowered his voice, 'Al's well taken care of for tonight.'

'You mean he doesn't want a date with Dallas?'

'No way.'

'Did you ask him?'

'He's sitting right here.'

'Let me speak to him.'

'Linda, don't push it. Are you coming over or not?'

'Not.' She hung up the phone. Now why had she done *that*? A sudden show of independence, not such a bad thing. Let's play see if Paul will call me back.

Dallas was washing her hair. 'What shall I wear?' she asked.

'Forget it. Al's taken a pill and gone to sleep.'

'You're kidding. It's early . . .'

'He's got a big show at Madison Square Garden tomorrow. Tell you what, would you like to come and see it?'

Dallas shrugged. She felt suddenly let down. 'I don't know, can I see how I feel tomorrow?'

'Sure. But it's worth seeing. The master is at his peak, and it's some show.'

'I'm sure it is. But right now I feel like taking each day as it comes.'

'Of course. I'd feel the same way after what you've been through. What do you say? Shall we venture out to dinner on our own?'

'Why not?'

They went to a small Italian restaurant, ignored the stares of the men, gorged on salad niçoise and fettucini, and talked.

'Shouldn't you be with Paul tonight?' Dallas asked.

'He's holding big brother's hand.'

'Even while he sleeps?'

'Al demands full attention at all times.'

Dallas shook her head in amazement. 'I don't know how you can stand it.'

'I don't know myself. Listen, strictly between us Paul has become a pain in the ass. I think maybe my being on the tour is a bad idea, and this is only the beginning. Can you imagine how I'm going to feel about him in a few weeks?'

'It's probably a good thing. Get your head together on your real feelings for him.'

'Right now my real feelings are – ugh! *Never* get involved with a married one, kid.'

Dallas laughed. 'You're telling *me*. What the hell do you think Ed Kurlnik was? Married. Single. They are all shits.'

Linda sighed. 'Sometimes they can be nice shits.'

'Oh come on. You know better than that.'

'You're very bitter, Dallas. Don't let one guy who tried to

rape you put you off the whole race. You're too young and too beautiful . . .'

Dallas laughed. 'Some day remind me to tell you about my past. That one guy was just one of many who formed my opinion on the entire male sex.'

When they got back to the apartment the phone was ringing. Linda picked it up quickly.

'Where the hell were you?' Paul sounded pissed off.

'Out getting laid.'

'Charming, really charming.'

'Dallas and I went to Pinos and had some food.'

'Oh. Do you want to come over?'

'Just me?'

'No, bring ten or twelve of your neighbours if that's what gets you going.'

'Funny. I meant . . .'

'I know what you meant. Listen, sweetheart, I know she's your friend and all that, but for Al she is bad news. I can sense it, got a feeling. Know what I mean?'

'No, I don't know what you mean. But if you're offering me your fine English body I'll be right over.'

'I'm offering.'

'I'm there.' Linda put the phone down, turned to explain to Dallas, but she had gone into the bathroom. Linda knocked, but there was no reply. 'I'm going,' she called out, 'see you tomorrow.'

Dallas stared at her reflection in the mirror. Bye-bye Linda. He calls. You run. No wonder he treats you like shit. She waited until she heard the apartment door slam, then she emerged from the bathroom. It was twelve thirty. She felt very alone. She bolted the apartment door, double locked it, checked that all the windows had safety catches fastened. There didn't seem much else to do.

Reluctantly she went to bed. But sleep was a long time coming, and when it did creep up on her it was full of bad dreams.

☆

22

The bomb scare came five minutes before Al was due to go on.

Bernie happened to take the call, and his heart lurched into a series of sharp palpitations as he heard the quiet, nondescript voice explain to him that three bombs would go off at three-minute intervals during the course of Al's performance.

'Fuck you,' Bernie managed to scream down the phone before the line clicked dead in his hand.

'Another fan?' asked Al dryly.

Bernie nodded, his mind racing. How the fuck had they gotten through to Al in his dressing room anyway? And why call him? Why not the newspapers? The police? Anyone but him. Why should he have to be the one responsible for the fact that there may or may not be three bombs waiting to blow up hundreds of Al's fans? Jesus, wasn't it enough that he had the press to deal with? Wasn't that punishment enough?

Anyway, there was heavy security. It must be another hoax. Bernie frowned. Just pretend it never happened. Just sweat it out.

'See you, man.' Al was buoyant.

The gladiator off for the kill.

'What the fuck,' replied Bernie, 'give 'em your balls, baby.'

Al grinned. He was on top. Right on top. New York lay responsive and waiting like a particularly accommodating whore. He could do what he wanted. They had paid their money and they were ready to enjoy him, devour him, give him the greatest come of his life.

He strode on stage and was drowned in a mass sound-wave of screaming. He felt himself grow hard. The power hard-on. Boy, if he was fucking instead of singing he could go all night. He gave a boxer's salute, waved, grabbed the microphone and launched right into 'Blue Funk Rock'. The audience roared its approval.

☆

Watching him, Dallas felt that she didn't know him at all. She didn't know him that well anyway. A few brief conversations, one dance, a strong attraction, that was just part of his whole charisma.

Watching him made her realize just how right she had been not to get involved.

This man rocking and weaving around the stage was public domain. He belonged to 'them', the people. He was, quite rightly, a superstar. She could see why. She could look at him objectively.

It all became clear. She had wanted him sexually because she was supposed to want him sexually. He was selling sex. So he had a great voice, but so did a lot of other singers. His appeal was the combination. The sexuality that radiated a message to every woman watching him.

Dallas smiled, it was a relief. She didn't need him, she didn't need anyone.

She glanced quickly at the fag hairdresser whom she had brought with her. He was entranced, his eyes bright, his body moving to the sound of Al.

She looked around her. Al seemed to have everyone mesmerized. She could recognize a few celebrities. Linda had given her exceptionally good tickets. Wasn't that Marjorie Carter? And God – Ed Kurlnik. What was *he* doing here? The cheap bastard. She wasn't sure, but it looked like he was with one of his daughters. Was it Dana? If it was they had both been engaged to Kip Rey, so they had much in common. Kip had told her stories Ed would *never* believe about his darling daughter.

She wasn't concentrating on Al. He had slipped away from her, a living, moving, phallic symbol, vocalizing obscene lyrics.

She forced herself to watch him, and gradually she too was caught up in the magic he weaved, the sheer magnetism of the man. But this time she knew, and by knowing the game she was safe, she could relax.

☆

Al came hurtling off the stage, soaked to the skin.

Paul hugged him before he returned to his army of lovers.

Linda captured the shot. If Paul loved anyone it was Al.

She wondered what an analyst would have to say of the situation. Latent fag? Brother envy?

Why was there Al? Wasn't the wife and kids enough?

Although she couldn't deny that Paul had been wonderful the previous evening. Kind, considerate, a caring lover. And they had talked long into the night and reconciled their differences.

They had both agreed that if her being on the tour screwed up their personal relationship then she would leave.

'I love you,' Paul had told her, 'and when the kids are older . . .'

He should package it and Al could sing it!

☆

The party was so jammed that Dallas nearly turned around and left. Her hairdresser wouldn't let her. He pursed his lips and surveyed her coldly. 'Truman might be here, darling, you can't deny me *that*.'

The rumours abounded that simply everyone in town *was* there, and it seemed to be true. The photographers all but ignored Dallas and went in search of bigger game.

'I think I'll get drunk,' she told her hairdresser, as if he cared. He had spotted someone who looked remarkably like Jackie O. and was entranced.

Dallas lifted a glass of wine from a passing tray. She could see Ed Kurlnik across the room, and it seemed like too good an opportunity to miss. She made her way over to him, ready for some sort of confrontation, not sure what to expect.

'Hi, Ed,' she said softly.

He was startled, panic flashed across his face, but he recovered quickly remembering that Dee Dee was safely in Europe. 'Hello, Dallas, dear.'

The girl standing next to him was staring. It was his daughter Dana, a cool, classy-looking blonde. 'Daddy?' she questioned, moving protectively close to him.

'It's all right.' He gave her a short angry little shove. 'Why don't you go and get a drink, I'll join you in a minute.'

Dana glared at Dallas, a high flush suffusing her glacial features. 'If you're sure . . .'

'I'm sure,' Ed snapped, nervously cracking his knuckles, a gesture that made Dallas wince.

They waited in silence while Dana moved off, then Ed said, 'For Christ's sake if you see a camera pointing in our direction move away. You don't know what I've had to go through.'

'What *have* you had to go through?'

He scowled. 'Bloody murder. And I've missed you, goddamn it I've missed you. I don't think we should talk here. I'll come to the apartment later.'

'I'm not at the apartment any more.'

'Why not? I bought it for you, didn't I? You got my cheque, didn't you?'

'Yes, I got the kiss-off money.'

Ed frowned. 'It wasn't kiss-off money. Just a little something to tide you over until we could meet again.'

'You didn't *say* that. In fact you didn't say anything. Not even a phone call, Ed.'

'I had to be very, very careful. I shouldn't even be talking to you in public now.'

Dallas shrugged. 'I just thought I'd say hello.' She turned, as if to go.

Ed restrained her with his hand on her shoulder. 'Where can I see you later? We must talk.'

'Why, Ed? I thought everything was over.'

'Nothing's over,' he hissed, 'I can't do without you. God, people are staring. Where? Just tell me where and I'll be there.'

Dallas thought quickly. Why not string the old bastard along? What was there to lose?

She smiled suddenly, dazzlingly. 'Dress up time later? Is that what you want? Slave and master? Teacher and pupil?'

His voice was thick and heavy. 'Oh yes, oh yes.'

'The Essex House. Apartment eighty-nine, eighth floor. Come straight up.'

'What time?'

'In a couple of hours.'

'I'll be there.'

'I'll expect you.'

She watched him walk away. A small scared shitless billionaire with a hard-on. He rejoined his daughter. What a shock he would get when he showed up at The Essex House in the middle of the night and started hammering on the door of a strange apartment. She stifled a giggle. If only she could have been there to witness it.

☆

Crowds of fans had gathered outside the club where the party for Al was being held.

Luke, Paul and Bernie formed a human guard and shoved Al through. He was immediately besieged by the photographers. They wanted photographs of him with this celebrity – that celebrity. Smile, Al. Turn on the charm, Al. Turn on the bullshit.

He found himself being introduced to Ed Kurlnik, and he muttered, 'We've already met.' And Ed Kurlnik's daughter was holding too long onto his hand, and squeezing ever so slightly, and saying in dulcet Grace Kelly tones: 'You must come out to the house sometime. How about this weekend?'

After a while Marjorie Carter approached him. 'I've come to rescue you from the boring masses.'

'Who said I needed rescuing?'

'I did. How many times can you listen to people telling you how sensational you are?'

'All the time.'

Marjorie laughed. 'Modest, you're not. My car is parked out back for a painless getaway. My simple little apartment awaits your pleasure. Champagne, caviar, all your favourite things. Shall we go?'

Al surveyed her warily. He didn't like his women quite so dominant.

But she was a challenge, on the cover of two national magazines that very week, and supposedly the highest paid woman in television.

'Let's go,' he decided. It would make a change.

'Follow me,' said Marjorie, 'I've become an expert at escaping out back entrances.'

Al started after her. Luke fell into step behind him.

'Leave it tonight,' Al instructed, 'I'll see you back at the hotel.'

Luke shook his head. 'Got orders not to leave your side.'

'Fuck your orders. Who do you think you're working for anyway?'

Paul moved over. 'What's the problem?'

'Tell him to get lost.'

Paul sighed. 'This is New York, Al. It's just not feasible for you to be on your own. We've had a lot of threats . . .'

Marjorie joined in. 'My chauffeur is a karate expert, Al will be perfectly safe with me.'

Paul stared in surprise. 'Well . . .' he started to say. But they were gone.

On the way out Al thought he saw Dallas. Of course it wasn't her. He was always imagining he saw her. A girl in the street with the same kind of walk. A face in a car with the same wild abundance of hair. He shook his head. Why was it that she was the only girl he couldn't get out of his head?

He followed Marjorie Carter into the back of a black Lincoln Continental, parked, as she had promised, in the quiet of a back alley.

Marjorie Carter lived in some style in a penthouse apartment with spectacular views over New York.

'Are you married?' Al asked.

'Divorced,' Marjorie replied shortly, 'and not about to get trapped again. I enjoy my independence. Open the champagne, I'm going to change.'

Al felt like he was partaking in a scene from an early Hollywood movie. The ballsy career woman off to slip into a negligee. Shades of Joan Crawford. He remembered her movies from when he was a kid. Paul and he had always slipped into the local movies through an open window in the ladies toilet. In fact Marjorie Carter even reminded him of Joan Crawford.

Raven hair, strong features, a direct way of speaking. He didn't fancy her, couldn't fancy her. There had been a teacher at the grammar school he had attended who had also reminded him of Joan Crawford. She had caught him jerking off at the tender age of eleven, and reported him to the headmaster. Eight strokes of the cane. A very nasty memory.

Marjorie returned. It wasn't quite a negligee, it was a long fall of silk jersey, and she had quite obviously removed her underclothes.

Al coughed. Where was all his witty repartee, his sexy come-ons. Somehow, 'Want to fuck?' or 'Show us your tits' did not seem the right phraseology to throw at a Marjorie Carter.

She accepted a glass of champagne from him, dipped a minute cracker into the silver jar holding the caviar. Her breasts joggled through the thin material, dangerously close to drooping.

'Well,' she said, sitting on a leopard-covered sofa and clicking on a remote control television, 'shall we watch ourselves?'

'Huh?' asked Al nervously.

'A videotape of our interview.'

'Oh, yes.'

Their images flashed on to the television screen.

'You look beautiful, Al,' she purred.

Shouldn't *he* be saying that to *her*? But how could he?

On the television screen she was attractive in a stern, no-nonsense way. He could understand her success, she handled the interview in a masterly fashion. But of course she had done it so many times before.

'I think it would be nice,' she said, when the programme was half-way through, 'if we made love here. Or do you prefer the bedroom?'

There was no getting out of it. He hardly dared argue. And oh the magic of a little authority. His body was responding nicely.

'Here will do.'

'Good.' She stood up and slipped off the robe. 'My body is nice, don't you think?'

She had full, over-ripe breasts, that dominated a short body, stretch marks on her thighs, and a high mass of jet black pubic hair that seemed to trickle down her inner thighs.

'Very tasty.'

'You should have seen me when I was nineteen. Then I was really something.'

'How old are you now?'

'Does it matter?'

'No, just curious.'

'Five years older than you.'

'I'm thirty-six,' he said quickly.

'You're thirty-seven. I know every little detail about every guest I have on my show. Secret of my success.'

He put his arms around her waist and buried his head in her stomach, 'What else do you know about me?'

'That you're supposed to be very good, and I like a man who knows what he's doing.'

He reached up, squeezed her over-ripe breasts.

'Why don't you undress?' she asked.

Thank God he was hard. He stood up, slipped off his clothes.

'The great Al King, the legend lives!' Her tone was faintly mocking as she fondled him.

He started to push her head down.

'Don't!' she objected sharply, 'I like to fuck.'

She made him angry enough to straddle her immediately. Hammer it into her, the bitch, who did she think she was?

Her legs clasped him firmly behind the neck, her arms too. He noticed that she didn't shave under her arms, and for some strange reason that excited him further.

'Tight, aren't I?' she asked. 'I had the operation. Nice, isn't it. Some women have their faces lifted, I get right down to where it really matters.'

For the first time in months he found himself ready to come. Oh Jesus it was good. Ride along with it, wait for the moment.

She suddenly twisted free.

'Hey . . .' he objected, 'I was ready . . .'

'I wasn't. Are you out of practice or what?'

Him, out of practice. She had to be kidding.

He moved on top of her again.

'Don't forget,' she said sharply, 'ladies first.'

'I didn't know there were any around,' and he slammed it into her, and came with an explosion that nearly blew his ears off.

Marjorie was furious. 'I should have known it was all reputation.'

Al dressed quickly. He was sorry he had ever gone with her. There was more feeling in the abortive scenes he had with the groupies and hookers.

Marjorie turned the volume up on the television and lay back on the sofa. 'See yourself out,' she said, and from underneath the sofa she produced a black plastic vibrator.

Al didn't wait to hear the buzz.

23

Dallas saw Al at the party. She thought he saw her, but it was only a brief glance across a crowded room, and why should that make him stop?

After the fiasco in Monte Carlo he had probably never given her another thought, and indeed why should he? She was just another beautiful girl. His life was probably full of them.

She was hurt. She had thought there had been something between them. Well screw him – Mister Big Star.

Linda was edging towards her – 'You made it! What did you think?'

'Quite a show.'

'Horny little thing on stage, isn't he?'

'If you like that type.'

Linda laughed. 'I know, I know, *you* don't.'

Dallas just smiled.

The next morning she awoke early and took a cab over to her former apartment. No more hanging around New York. With the apartment rented at least she would have some sort of income.

Downstairs the janitor handed her a telegram. 'Came a coupla days ago,' he explained.

Dallas tore it open. It was from an agent she had met on her trip to the coast. Brief and to the point it read – 'Interesting proposition. Call collect. Cody Hills.' And there was a phone number.

She tucked it firmly in her purse, it would be something worth looking into, especially as she was on her way out there.

'Mr Mack's chauffeur bin trying to find you,' the janitor confided. 'Bin here every day. What shall I tell him?'

'Just tell him I've gone to Los Angeles.'

'Sure,' agreed the janitor. Maybe the chauffeur would be handing out another ten bucks for the information.

Dallas' next stop, was the shop where he had left her jewellery to be appraised the previous day. The price they offered her seemed fair, so the deal was done.

Now she had income and capital. She felt excited about getting away. No ties. A new start. Why wait?

Three hours later she was on a plane. Linda had not been at the apartment, and the only place she could think of contacting her was at Paul's hotel, but she did not want to phone there, so she had left a note of thanks, and a present – an expensive Gucci hold-all Linda had admired. It was the first present she had ever bought for anyone and it was a good feeling.

The flight to Los Angeles was bumpy, but she managed to sleep in spite of the persistent attentions of a fat businessman in the adjoining seat.

'Call me,' he wheezed, as the plane came into land, 'if you ever get lonely.'

That was really funny. She was always lonely, but he would be the last person she would call.

Los Angeles was balmy and sunny. She took a cab to the Beverly Hills Hotel. The plan was to stay there only until she found a suitable apartment.

She called Cody Hills immediately. He suggested they meet for a drink, and she agreed.

The Polo Lounge was crowded as usual. Dallas looked around for Cody Hills, not even sure if she would remember him – their previous meeting at the studio had been very brief. She needn't have worried. He found her, authoritatively took her by the arm, settled her at a table.

'You look even better than I remember,' he remarked briskly. He was a pleasant-looking man in his late twenties, medium height and build, brown hair combed carefully forward to conceal the fact that he was going prematurely bald.

'Remember me?' he asked.

'Of course,' lied Dallas.

'Of course not. Redford I'm not. But I haven't been able to forget you, and when this thing came up I knew you were the right girl.'

'What thing?'

'First things first. What are you drinking?'

'Orange juice.'

'Fantastic. You take dope?'

'No. Hey – what is this?'

'It's just that the girl I'm looking for has to be a clean-living lady. Gotta think of the sponsors.'

'What sponsors?'

Cody glanced conspiratorially around. 'I am going to make you and me rich. Very, very rich. Does that grab you in all the right places?'

'I guess so, as long as I don't have to . . .'

He held up a hand. 'You don't have to do anything. Just trust me. Just keep looking the way you look, and trust me.'

'Can you please tell me what this is all about?'

'Certainly.' He waved at a passing friend. 'This is the situation. Saw your test – it stunk. Nothing new – all the beauty queen tests stink. They knock 'em off – just a formality. If you're lucky you end up in a Dean Martin movie stickin' out your whatsits and looking dumb. However – you are an incredible-looking young lady. I saw the television show with Al King. You looked spectacular. Racquel, Farrah, Sophie, you have a little bit of each of them – but something plus, something wild.'

'If the test stunk . . .'

'Don't go getting sensitive. Paradox Studios are launching a big new television series – "Man Made Woman" – sort of a late night "Bionic Woman" with sex. They have a girl signed – I happen to know they are not going to be able to use her.'

'Why?'

'Because she's a sex change. Looks sensational, but you cannot make a coast-to-coast star out of a girl who used to be a sailor! So, who better than "Miss Coast-to-Coast" herself?'

'But I've never even acted.'

'So they'll teach you. Honey, believe me, when they see you – you are in. I know it. I feel it. I was even prepared to pay your .fare out here. And we will be able to negotiate a peach of a contract – a million dollar contract. They'll see you. Want you. That's when we move. They'll be in a bind, they have to start shooting next week.'

'Don't they know about the sex change girl?'

'They will. Tomorrow. Authenticated evidence.'

'So what do you want me to do?'

'Just stay out of sight until I call you. No lounging round the pool, going to restaurants, shopping. Just fall in love with room service until I call you.'

'I was going to look for an apartment.'

'Honey, believe you me, after next week it will be houses you'll be looking at – big ones with pools and tennis courts.'

Dallas smiled, 'I guess I have nothing to lose . . .'

'And everything to gain. You *are* a bona fide female, I take it?'

The smile snapped off her face. 'Mr Hills. Is part of the deal me proving that to you?'

'Dallas. I would love to answer yes to that question, but I'll take your word on it. Besides, silicone doesn't move the way you move, and I'm late for dinner at my mother's house. I'm a second-generation Portnoy.'

'A what?'

'A nice Jewish boy.'

Later in her hotel room, Dallas thought about Cody Hills. He was the first man who had ever offered her anything without expecting dividends in return. Of course it might all be pie in the sky, but he seemed so enthusiastic, so sure.

She wondered if she should confess to him the fact that she was an ex-hooker. But what good would that do? She decided against it. What was the use of lining up strokes against yourself before you had even begun?

☆

Two days later Cody called her.

'Pack a bikini, things are in motion. I'll be up to fetch you in half an hour.'

He drove a dashing red Mustang. 'Climb in,' he instructed, 'I'm afraid I'm going to have to inflict my mother on you, but it's the only place I can think of where you can get a tan in private.'

'Why a tan?'

'To make you look even more delectable, delicious, and just a little bit savage.'

'I'll be savage if this all ends up as a pile of shit.'

'Shhs . . . Nice girls with sponsors don't talk like that.'

'Fu . . .'

'Dallas. Please. Not on the way to my mother's house!'

She couldn't help smiling. 'Where does your mother live?'

'The Valley. Nothing extravagant, but for God's sake don't touch anything unless you can put it back *exactly* where it came from! I'm afraid I'll have to leave you there for the day, and the minute my back is out of there she'll be after you like the CIA.'

'Now look . . .'

'Nothing about you. Just about me. How long have you known me? Where did we meet? When are we getting married? The usual Jewish mother questions.'

'Sounds like fun. What shall I say?'

'No comment. Act like a star, you may as well get some practice in.'

Cody's mother was a round, neat little woman. She settled Dallas in a sun lounger, settled herself close by, and revealed the family history.

'Cody is a good boy, a good son. But show business! The movie business! A *meshugenah* profession!'

Dallas found out that he had been an agent for five years. Before that he had worked around the studio doing anything he could. The industry was his life. Eventually he wanted to be a producer.

'He don't usually bring his girlfriends home,' Mrs Hills confessed. 'But you – well, it's good to see he has taste.'

'I'm not a girlfriend, I'm a client,' Dallas explained patiently for the third time.

'Of course you are,' agreed Mrs Hills with no conviction, 'but my Cody will make some girl a wonderful husband, a Jewish girl of course. A Jewish actress if that's what makes him happy. Elizabeth Taylor he won't get – but a nice girl like Streisand – what a voice? I hear she's got a hairdresser for a boyfriend. At least she gets her hair done for free . . .'

Another two days passed before Cody imparted the news that they had an appointment. 'Lew Margolis himself. Head man at Paradox. One look at you . . . I know we got it made.'

They decided what Dallas would wear. A white safari suit in the softest cotton, and a white Stetson hat with her hair tucked under it.

They planned every move together. She would enter Lew Margolis' office with Cody and sit quietly whilst they talked. The first question that Lew directed at her she would slowly remove her tinted shades, and stare directly at him. The second question the hat would come off. After that, the jacket, under which she would be wearing a clinging T-shirt.

'It will work – by the fourth question we'll be in. Don't forget, right now they are *desperate* – and there just aren't any girls around with such perfect physical qualifications for the part.'

Cody's confidence was catching, and Dallas found herself almost sure of the fact that the part would be hers. What a wonderful start to a new life.

The night before the interview Cody took her to the 'Aware Inn' for an early dinner. They talked about general things, almost scared to trade the strong excitement they both felt. When he dropped her off at the hotel he kissed her chastely on the cheek.

'Tomorrow,' he said firmly, 'think positive.'

'I will,' she replied, grateful that he wasn't trying to rush her into the nearest bed, although she sensed that he wanted to.

'Pick you up at eleven.'

'I'll be ready.'

'Goodnight, star.'

'Goodnight, producer.'

'How did you know . . .'

'Your mother.'

'I guess you know all about my circumcision too.'

'Intimately.'

'See you tomorrow.'

'Tomorrow.' She leaned forward and kissed him softly on the lips before walking into the hotel.

The morning was bright with very little smog. Dallas breakfasted on figs and orange juice. Did her exercises in front of the open window. Made up and dressed with painstaking care.

Cody picked her up exactly on time. She noticed he had washed and plastered his hair down more carefully than ever. He wore a suit, Californian lightweight, but still a suit.

They drove in silence to the studios. A large sign proclaimed 'Paradox Television, The Greatest'.

Lew Margolis sat behind an Italian marble desk littered with various silver and gold awards. Framed photos of his family took pride of place on a marble side table. The floor was marble, the walls were marble.

Dallas didn't really notice any of this. She didn't notice because she was too busy remembering.

Lew Margolis had been the mystery client whose house Dallas had gone to with Bobbie on her last and final orgy.

Lew Margolis would know instantly and irrevocably that she was a paid whore.

24

Rave reviews on the Madison Square concert brought only a thin smile to Paul's lips. He was so furious at what he considered Al's irresponsible behaviour that it eclipsed all else.

Linda had never seen him so angry, and in a curious way the fact that he was ranting and raving about Al brought them closer together.

'Death threats here, mobbings there. Kidnapping and everything else, and he runs off with a woman *I* wouldn't even look twice at, and takes a *stroll* back to the hotel.'

'He's a big boy.' Linda pointed out.

'Let him be a big boy on his own time. This is business, and if anything happened to him. Jesus, Linda, you should see the crank mail he receives. There's a lot of husbands running wild who would be only too happy to take a slice off his balls.'

'I'm sure he can look after himself.'

'On the New York streets, at night, Muhammed Ali can't look after himself!'

'I should have offered to fix him up with Dallas. That would have kept him off the streets.'

'Do it. Tonight.'

'I don't know if she'll still want to.'

'Try.'

Al, for his part, awoke strangely refreshed. He blocked out the bad vibes of the previous evening and remembered only the fact that he had been able to screw and come. A rare achievement these days.

He lay in bed, ordered champagne, and read and re-read his rave reviews.

Dana Kurlnik phoned him at three o'clock. 'This week-end,' she said in imperious tones. 'What time shall the helicopter collect you?'

'I didn't say I'd come.'

'You didn't say you wouldn't. I'd like you to meet my twin. We're identical, you know. Don't you think that's fascinating?'

'Absolutely. Do you fuck together?'

'Absolutely. What time did you say you wanted the helicopter?'

'Twelve in the morning. Tomorrow. There'll be three of us.'

'Can't wait.'

'We'll only be staying the night.'

'Don't bet on it.'

American girls, they didn't half come across strong. Al yawned, got up, inspected himself in the mirror. He didn't like the bags that appeared to be forming yet again beneath his eyes. Something would have to be done about *them*.

He buzzed Paul, Linda answered.

'He's gone out,' she informed him, 'back in about an hour.'

'Why don't you come up. Want to talk to you.'

'Are you out of bed?'

'You're perfectly safe. I don't jump on my brother's girl. Not unless she asks me to.'

'Ha Ha. Can I bring my cameras?'

'If it's candid shots you're after I look like shit.'

'So what else is new?'

☆

Al's suite was on the floor above, so Linda walked up, said hello to Luke stationed outside, and went in.

Al greeted her in a towelling bathrobe. 'Seen the reviews?' was his first question.

'Of course. Sensational, naturally.'

'Where's Paul?'

'He's not in a very good mood. He's gone to double check security for tonight's concert.'

'Is he pissed off at me?'

'It wasn't a terribly smart move was it? And why walk home? Anything could have happened.'

Al shrugged. 'I don't know, love. Felt like it. Listen – you, me, and Paul have been invited to the Kurlnik place for the weekend. I said we'd go, might be a giggle.'

'I wouldn't mind. When?'

'Tomorrow, we'll just stay the one night. Then on to Philadelphia for the show on Monday.'

'Sounds good to me, as long as Paul says yes.'

'He'll say yes. He always does what I want – you should know that by now.'

Linda sighed. 'Thanks a lot, you certainly know how to make a person feel good.'

'You want me to be honest, don't you?'

Linda lit a cigarette. Al always made her smoke more than usual. 'Not particularly, but if it makes you happy. By the way, nothing definite, but how would you feel about seeing Dallas after tonight's show?'

'Is she here?' Al asked, 'Jesus – that wasn't her at the party last night, was it?'

'The very same.'

'Why didn't anyone *tell* me? I'd like to see her, sure I would. Can you fix it?'

'I think so. She's staying with me. I've been trying to call her but she must have gone out.'

'Why don't you go on home, wait for her. Bring her to the concert. We'll go somewhere nice for dinner.'

'You're very anxious.'

'I like her. Is there anything strange about that?'

'Oh sweet! Our superstar has feelings too.'

'Jesus, Linda, you are some smart ass.'

Linda smiled. She felt she had scored a minor victory. 'I'll go home, then.'

'Do that. And call me. Better still have Dallas call me.'

'I'll try. She might be busy.'

'Fuck you, Linda. You enjoy every minute of me not getting what I want. You could have told me she was staying with you before this.'

So Paul hadn't told him. Bad Paul. 'I didn't know you cared.'

Al shrugged. 'I don't care. Like she's all right, we'll have some laughs. I don't *care*.'

'OK. OK. I'll call you later.'

If only he had been sure it was her at the party. He could have dumped Marjorie Carter easily enough. He had thought about Dallas so many times since the South of France. He had run and re-run the videotape of their television show on numerous occasions. He had read about her fiancé dying. He had seen the occasional photo of her in the gossip columns. She looked gorgeous. She always looked gorgeous.

He wasn't sure if she would still be talking to him. After the incident in the South of France he had frozen her out. Business relationship only. Screw the newspapers and all that publicity. It had petered out now. Even Edna had believed him when he swore there was nothing in it. And there *was* nothing in it. He had never touched the girl. Perhaps that's what was bugging him.

Anyway, that would all change soon. After the concert. Maybe before the concert if Linda got hold of her in time. He watched a bad quiz show on television, impatiently waiting to hear from Linda.

Finally she rang, terse and to the point. 'Our little bird has flown, jetted off to good old LA.'

'Oh shit!' said Al, and he was surprised at how disappointed he suddenly felt.

☆

Fire Island was enveloped in a sea mist, but it didn't alter the sultry humidity. The Kurlnik estate jutted out towards the sea. It had its own private beach, indoor and outdoor swimming pools, tennis courts, and a mini golf course.

Dana Kurlnik was there to greet them. She was tall and bronzed, coolly groomed in tennis whites.

'My mother's away,' she informed them, 'and daddy is quite busy in the city. So it's just myself and Cara. Come, I'll show you the house.'

It was quite impressive. Picassos nestled next to Hockneys on the walls. Priceless antique furniture mixed unashamedly with ultra-modern.

'You must be hungry. We'll lunch on the terrace. Fifteen minutes all right with everyone?'

'Fine with me,' agreed Al, 'it doesn't take me fifteen minutes to take a piss.'

Paul and Linda exchanged looks. Dana appeared not to have heard.

'What a house!' exclaimed Linda.

'Yes,' said Paul wistfully, 'makes my place in England look like a shack.'

They were given a room with an old oak four-poster bed, and a sea view.

'This is lovely,' enthused Linda, 'veree romantic – you think so?'

'I think,' said Paul slowly, 'that we are the beards, and that Al knew all along old man Kurlnik wouldn't be here.'

'I did want to meet him. Dallas never mentions him. I think she was more upset than everyone supposes.'

Paul grinned. 'I think Al wants to get his own back through the daughters.'

Linda started to undress. 'Judging from the one we've seen I think she would welcome any getting his own back Al cares to give her.'

'Linda, why are you almost naked?'

'All the better to make love to you. After all, we have got fifteen minutes before lunch, why waste them?'

☆

Cara Kurlnik appeared for lunch. Blonde, like her sister, and equally cool.

Linda couldn't help reflecting how old they both seemed to be. Not in looks, they were certainly good-looking enough. It was just their demeanour, sort of a weary, glacial, seen it all, done it all, attitude. And of course they probably had. Being the daughters of one of the richest men in America probably did not lead to a quiet and sheltered life. Their conversation was peppered with famous names and places.

Lunch was delicious. A mixture of seafoods and salads laid out invitingly on silver dishes.

Al gorged himself, swigging back the champagne the girls had thoughtfully provided. For dessert there were bowls of strawberries with thick cream ladled on top.

'Here goes my diet,' remarked Al.

'Do you have to diet?' questioned Cara. 'How boring.'

'Only when I'm working,' said Al quickly, 'I like to keep in shape, like a boxer.'

'Oh, you mean training. I would have thought it was only your voice you had to worry about.' Dana stared at him as she spoke. A cold, grey-eyed, stare.

'Al uses a great deal of physical energy,' Paul joined in. 'He's like a wet rag when he comes off that stage.'

'Does training include no sex?' inquired Cara.

'Are you kidding?' laughed Al.

Linda had been fiddling with her cameras. 'Anyone mind if I take some photographs?' she asked.

'Go right ahead,' replied Dana, 'would you like us to pose for you?'

'That won't be necessary – I don't work like that. Just carry on doing whatever you're doing.'

'I thought we might go ski-ing,' said Cara, 'the boat's all ready. You do ski don't you, Al?'

'Yeah, I ski.' He had learnt in the South of France, his first holiday after success had started to creep up on him. He had known it would come in useful one day. Edna had never learned. She had sat on the beach and complained that it was a dangerous, stupid sport. She had been quite surprised when after three abortive attempts he was up up and away. Perhaps if Edna had been the kind of woman who had learned to water ski their marriage might not be on the rocks today. And it was on the rocks. He knew there was no going home after this trip.

With all his success he had nothing, no one. Plenty of everything. But what did that mean when you were alone in bed at night. And whoever it was that shared his bed he still ended up alone.

He envied Paul. He had Linda. A strong, ballsy woman who obviously loved him very much. And what did Al get? He got the slags, didn't he? The star fucks and groupies. The ballbreakers like Marjorie Carter, and the nymphos like the Kurlnik twins. He could smell a nympho a mile off, however much money she had. And he would accommodate them, if he was able. And he would probably enjoy it, on a momentary basis. And they would say – 'Wow – what a stud Al King is'. And that was his life. Superstud. Superfuck. There must be something better somewhere.

'Are you going to change?' asked Dana.

'What for?' responded Al, 'it's private here, isn't it?'

'Yes, of course,' said Dana.

'In that case it's everyone in the raw.'

'I'd love to photograph the event, but I think Paul and I will sit this one out. Is it all right if we use the swimming pool?' Linda took Paul's hand and pulled him up, 'OK with you?'

'Yes, sure,' Paul replied, almost reluctantly. There had once been a time, in the early days, when identical twins would have meant a good time for both of them. Al had always been the puller, but Paul had never been averse to joining in. Until he grew up. Al never grew up.

'Well, girls,' announced Al expansively, 'lead me to your boat, and if you're good girls you can put on a ski each.'

'Don't you mono ski?' asked Cara, in patronizing tones.

'The hell with the fancy stuff. I like to keep it simple.'

'Naturally,' drawled Dana.

She would be the first to get it, Al decided. Stuck-up rich little snob.

Cara drove the Riva, while Dana and Al skied. Both girls were wearing bikinis under their tennis whites. Al had ended up in his Y-fronts feeling slightly foolish. Dana, of course, only needed one ski, whilst Al, next to her, felt clumsy and inadequate on two.

Cara zoomed the speedboat expertly across the sea, until at last she cut the engine, and Al and Dana subsided into the water. Dana slipped easily out of her ski, and had swum to the boat long before Al came struggling aboard trailing his skis behind him.

As he climbed into the Riva he noticed both girls had discarded the tops of their bikinis. It didn't make much difference as they were both built like boys. Four indifferent, identical tits. He grinned, thought – what the hell – and slid out of his ridiculous wet Y-fronts.

Dana was busy rolling a joint. 'Hey – hey—' she exclaimed, 'the legend lives!'

Cara turned to stare, running a small pink tongue nervously across her lips.

The boat rocked gently in the waves. The sun had cut through the mist, and Cara started to lay out striped mattresses on the back of the boat.

'What have we got to drink?' Al asked.

'Champagne, of course,' replied Dana, 'isn't that your favourite? In the ice box at the front.'

He got out the champagne, popped the cork, found some glasses, and took it all to the back of the boat.

They lay out on the mattresses, with him in the middle. Cara produced a tape recorder, and the sound of Al singing joined them. Dana passed the joint around. He declined.

'I thought all musicians smoked,' said Dana in surprise.

'He's not a musician,' replied Cara dismissively, 'anyway most of the over thirty-fives prefer to drink.'

'Don't talk about me as if I'm not here,' interrupted Al. 'Grass doesn't do anything for me, why the hell should it?'

'Nobody's forcing you. How about some coke? Believe me, ski-ing when you're out of it on coke is a beautiful experience.' So saying Dana reached into a bag and produced a glass phial of white powder. She was wearing a small gold spoon on a chain around her neck, and she took off the chain, removed the spoon, filled it with white powder and snorted the stuff delicately and expertly into each nostril. 'Here,' she offered it to Al, 'it's the best.'

Al fingered some cocaine from the spoon, snorted just a little. Why not? He had been working hard, he deserved some relaxation.

Cara leaned across him to reach for the joint. He felt her nipples brush his chest. He looked down and watched himself harden. They all watched.

'Random Love' played loudly on the tape recorder.

Nobody seemed in any kind of hurry. Al snorted a little more coke, took a drag on the joint. He was starting to feel really good.

Cara took her glass and slowly tipped the champagne from it over his chest. He felt his nipples come erect, and Cara bent to lick the liquid off him. Dana joined in from the other side. He closed his eyes to the burning sun, sealing off the identical faces that were now administering to him from both sides.

'Jesus!' he muttered.

'Good, isn't it?'

Their heads were travelling down in perfect unison, licking, biting, kissing. Then they were attending to his balls with feathery, identical tongues. It was an incredible sensation, so incredible that he could hardly bear it. He needed to screw, to jam it in. But which one first? Lazily he rolled towards Dana, but she shoved him away.

They continued to work on him, slowly, methodically. It was sensational – but – 'I'm going to come,' he warned. He turned to reach Cara, but they held him down, and as he came, spurting all over himself, one of them snapped an amyl nitrate under his nose.

His orgasm seemed to go on for ever as he jerked and thrust up into nothingness. It was amazing, but it was frustrating. All the times he couldn't be bothered to screw, and now, when he wanted to, it was denied him. Still he couldn't complain. Although it was a strange sensation to come into nothingness.

Slowly he opened his eyes. Cara and Dana watched him expectantly. 'Good?' they chorused.

'Bloody good,' he agreed.

'Why don't you wash off in the sea?' Cara suggested.

'Yes.' He was covered in his own sperm. 'There's no sharks around here, are there?'

'Only the human ones – inland,' replied Dana coolly.

He slipped over the side. The water was invigoratingly cold. He swam away from the boat. It felt good swimming in the raw, it always had, even when he was a kid and stripped off to swim in the canals. He did a strong crawl, dived under the water, couldn't see much. Pity they didn't have diving gear aboard – although they probably did – they seemed to carry everything else.

He surfaced. The boat appeared to have drifted some distance away.

'Hey!' he yelled. But he couldn't see the twins. What if there *were* sharks? He felt a small stab of panic. Rapidly he started to swim towards the boat. He felt tired, a bit muddled. It was all the champagne, the joint, the coke, the ammi. Jesus, he could *collapse* out here. What the fuck were they doing?

He felt the sudden stab of cramp in his right side. It slowed him up. The boat was getting further away, the cramp was getting worse. Was it his imagination or was the sea getting rougher?

'Hey!' he screamed out. But nobody appeared to hear him.

25

Dallas stood in the doorway of Lew Margolis' office staring at the man who had the power to create a marvellous new career for her.

She pictured him not behind his marble desk, but at the door of his magnificent house in Bel Air, wearing nothing but a smile, and an orange-coloured bathrobe.

☆

A year ago. Lew Margolis. She had known him only as 'Dukey'. Bobbie called all their clients 'Dukey'. 'Makes 'em feel wanted – kinda special,' Bobbie explained, 'cancels out the hooker dude relationship.'

Who was she *kidding?*

Dallas was nervous and edgy that evening. Things had already started with Ed Kurlnik, and if he ever found out what she really did . . . To protect herself on professional engagements, she tried to look as different as possible.

Tonight she had tucked her long hair out of sight under a red afro wig. And she wore much more make-up than usual, and raunchy, hooker-type clothes.

'Come in, ladies,' Lew Margolis ushered them into a huge, white living room.

'She-e-et man, this is nice,' approved Bobbie, already stoned out of her head. 'Any other comers or is this just a cosy sweet stuff threesome?'

'Just the three of us,' replied Lew pleasantly. He was a man of about sixty with abundant dark hair and a prominent nose. He wore steel-rimmed glasses and walked with a limp.

Dallas took in her surroundings quickly. Nice house. The guy obviously had bread. He wasn't completely unattractive, so what did he need with them? She noticed two photo frames placed face down on a corner table. How many times had she seen that done. Mustn't let the family watch.

'So, Dukey, Babe,' trilled Bobbie, 'give me the action, and we're on.'

'You two cunts get your clothes off,' the pleasant tone had vanished from his voice.

Bobbie smiled. 'Money first, honey second. Three hundred for an hour. Fine with you Dukey, babe?'

He reached in his bathrobe pocket, extracted a stack of notes, counted off three hundred, and handed it to Bobbie.

She checked it through, stuffed it into her purse. 'Seems cool to little 'ole me. Clothes off, girl.'

Whilst Bobbie stripped provocatively and elaborately, Dallas peeled her clothes off quickly. Each time it became more difficult. She remained impassive and unsmiling, leaving the jokes and fun up to Bobbie.

When they were both naked his attention focused on Dallas.

'Well? questioned Bobbie, hands on hips, legs astride, 'what we gonna play? You wanna little show? Or maybe a massage? What's it to be, man?'

'Upstairs' he said thickly.

He led them up to a beautiful bedroom, dominated by a king-size bed. On the wall there was a portrait of the film actress Doris Andrews, noted for her portrayal of 'good girl' parts.

Lew flung open a closet of women's clothes. 'Dress yourselves,' he commanded, 'everything. Tights. Panties. Bras. An outfit. It doesn't matter if they fit or not.'

It was a peculiar request. But Dallas was used to peculiar requests. She sorted through the shelves, drew on some black tights, found a pair of black lace knickers. Whoever the clothes belonged to had expensive taste. She chose a black silk bra, and it fitted her perfectly. Over the top she slipped on an Yves Saint Laurent suit.

The clothes were much too big for Bobbie, and by the time she was dressed she looked ridiculous.

Lew Margolis watched silently until they were both finished. Then he handed them two identical wigs, and told them to put them on. The wigs matched the hairstyle of the woman in the portrait exactly.

'We're going to play pretend,' Lew said.

'Like – wow!' shrieked Bobbie, 'who you want me to pretend to be? Charlie Chaplin?' She imitated Chaplin's walk, then collapsed laughing on the floor.

Lew Margolis didn't smile. 'Downstairs. In my study. I will be a dentist.' He stared at Dallas. 'You will be the patient. Mrs M. And you—' he indicated Bobbie, 'just announce her.'

'Sounds like fun . . .'

They followed him downstairs. Bobbie making faces behind his back. He went into his study, closed the door.

'This dude is fuckin' nuts' whispered Bobbie, 'a real head case. He wants us to look like his fuckin' wife! Why, I bet it's her clothes we got on. I bet . . .'

'Announce her,' shouted Lew, from behind the closed door.

Bobbie knocked, waited for his, 'Come in.'

'Mrs M. for her dental appointment, sir.'

'Show her in'

Dallas walked into the study. On the desk the photographs were face down.

'Sit down, Mrs M.' said Lew pleasantly, indicating a chair. 'Nurse help Mrs M. to get comfortable. Take her jacket.'

Bobbie helped Dallas off with her jacket. Lew had removed his orange bathrobe and was wearing a white dental coat and nothing else.' Wait outside, nurse, I'll call if I need you.'

Bobbie went out, shut the door.

'Lean back, Mrs M. I'll just have a look at your teeth, see that everything's all right. Now, open your mouth wide.'

Dallas did as she was told. Then suddenly he leapt on a stool next to the chair, and jammed his penis into her mouth. It was unexpected. She gagged, nearly choking.

'Take it easy, Mrs M.' he said soothingly, 'It's what you come here for, isn't it? Everyone knows. Everyone. Even your husband. It's the talk of Beverly Hills how you're fucking around on your husband. You whore!'

They stayed three hours, collecting a total of nine hundred dollars. And they played doctor, hairdresser, dressmaker, head waiter, gynaecologist, gardener. And every game ended with his little speech about Mrs M. wanting it, getting it, and everyone knew, even her husband.

Driving them home Bobbie said, 'Now there is a dude with some problem. Do you think the wife is out fuckin' everything in sight?'

'I don't know and I don't care. I just hope I never have to see him again.'

☆

Lew Margolis stood up from behind his marble desk. 'Come in, sit down. Cody has told me lots of good things about you.'

Slowly Dallas walked into the office. He hadn't recognized her – yet. But then of course she had the protection of her hat and shades. When she took those off . . .

More than anything she felt bad about Cody finding out. He would feel so let down. She should have told him. But how did you casually reveal an item of information like that? Oh, by the way, Cody, forgot to mention it, it's probably not important anyway, but I used to be a hooker. Worked doubles with a stoned black kid, we must've laid half of Hollywood.

'Didn't I tell you?' Cody was saying excitedly, 'didn't I warn you she was sensational? And *who* could be more right for the part?'

'Yes,' agreed Lew, 'she is a lovely girl. How old are you, dear?'

'Twenty.' She took off her shades and stared at him, just as she had stared at the dentist, and the hairdresser, and the gynaecologist.

'Perfect age,' he looked her up and down, 'perfect everything.'

'Thank you.' With one gesture she removed the Stetson, and shook her mane of hair free.

'Has she done anything?' Lew asked Cody, 'Is there any film on her we could see?'

'An Al King television special and a commercial,' replied Cody quickly, 'I can arrange for you to see them within the hour.'

'Yes,' said Lew, 'but I imagine she photographs like she looks.'

'On camera she's even better.'

'I don't know about the name . . .'

'It's unusual.'

'Yes, it's unusual. Ever acted, Dallas?'

She removed her jacket. Surely he would remember now? 'I've acted quite often. I've been told I'm very good.'

'We'll see about that. You certainly look the part. Why don't you run over to costume and make-up. We're all set to shoot a test on you. All right with you, Cody?'

'Fine, Mr Margolis.'

'You go with her. If the test hits the spot we're in business.'

Cody stood and extended his hand. 'I think we're going to be in business, Mr Margolis.'

The rest of the day seemed to pass in a dream. Dallas didn't think she would have got through it if it wasn't for Cody. He didn't leave her side, encouraging, admiring, boosting her confidence. And all the while she waited for Lew Margolis to suddenly remember.

He didn't. Anyway, if he did, it appeared to make no difference.

She tested, doing three different scenes which she had to learn there and then. Cody led her through every word. 'Unless you're the worst actress in the world the part is yours,' he confided, 'and when they see the test and realize how great you are, that's when I get called back to the big man's office. And that, sweetheart, is when schmucky little agent, yours truly, Cody Hills, shafts them right between the two big ones. We go for broke. A million dollar deal or nothing. That's when you have to hang in there and trust me. They'll kick, but in the end they'll pay. And they can afford to.'

'Whatever you say, Cody. By the way, is Lew Margolis married?'

'Where have *you* been? He's married to Doris Andrews. So you have no worries about bed being part of the deal. Why? He hand out any horny vibes?'

'No, not at all. I just wondered.'

'Wonder no more. Doris Andrews keeps a twenty-four-hour eye on Lew, and him on her. No, you've got no problems with him – he's straight.'

Poor misinformed Cody. Lew never could tell him, because by revealing her he would reveal himself. Dallas sighed. Why couldn't things be nice and simple?

Two days later, as Cody had predicted, they called him in to negotiate. He told them what he wanted. They told him to forget it.

Three days later Dallas signed a million dollar deal to star in 'Man Made Woman'.

It was an option deal, but if they picked up on all options, and there was no reason to suppose that the series wouldn't be a giant smash, then, as Cody comfortingly told her, she would not only be a huge star, but rich as well, with every opportunity to do the one movie a year her contract allowed.

It was an exciting time. Much more exciting than winning some stupid beauty contest.

Cody could not conceal his absolute delight, and went around the entire time grinning from ear to ear.

'I'm giving up the agency business,' he informed her. 'Going into production.'

'Production?' she questioned, 'production what?'

'*Our* production company. You concentrate on becoming a star. I'll concentrate on finding you the right property for your first movie.'

'Hey, mister, hang on there. I may be a big flop.'

'"Man Made Woman" will top the ratings. First season, you'll see.'

'Your confidence is very reassuring.'

He took her hand, held it tightly. 'Stick with me, it's catching. Even my mother thinks you're going to be a star.'

'I'm going to try, God knows I'm going to try. I've dreamed about a chance like this.'

'So has my mother!'

She couldn't help laughing. Cody, it seemed, could always make her laugh. She had started to lean on him, turning to him for advice on everything. He was looking at houses for her, something small to start off with, and then who knows? She had put herself entirely in his hands business wise. But she trusted him absolutely. After all, he had started the whole thing.

Cody Hills was the first man she had ever respected. Perhaps because from the very beginning he had always treated her nicely. No heavy come-on. No sexual hassle.

Maybe sex with Cody might mean something. There had been no one since Kip Rey, and that had not been a happy scene. She didn't crave sex, she didn't even think about it. But she did want to let Cody know she was grateful for everything he had done. And to her way of thinking sex was the only way to say thank you. So that evening, when they were enjoying a celebratory dinner, she suggested he came back to the hotel and spend the night.

'Who me?' protested Cody. 'Me and you? The princess and the frog?'

'Frog? Are you stupid. You're a very attractive man.'

'I am?'

'You am.'

'I'll probably kick myself black and blue in the night, but right now I don't think we should complicate our warm and businesslike relationship with things that go grope in the night.'

'Are you saying no?'

'I am saying that you ask me again when things are not as bright as they are now. When you're tired, and fed up with being at the studio six a.m. five days a week, and pissed with your vacation time because it's not long enough, and sick of posing for publicity stills, and . . .'

'Are you . . .?'

'I am not a fag,' he interrupted, 'and if we slept together my mother would find out and expect us to get married or something sloppy like that. Let's put it this way – something special is worth waiting for. So please can you wait . . .'

'*Funny!*' She laughed until tears swelled her eyes. And she understood he wanted more than sex, and he wanted her to know that.

'Now that we're nearly rich,' he said, deftly changing the subject, 'how do you think I'd look with a hair transplant?'

'Horrible!' laughed Dallas, 'I like you just the way you are.'

☆

A week after the contract was signed Lew Margolis summoned her into his office. He smiled warmly, asked her to sit down, offered her a drink. Then, from the floor behind his desk he picked up a bundle of women's clothes and flung them at her.

'Put these on, million dollar cunt,' he said, still smiling.

She should have known when she walked into his office. The photo frames on the marble table were all turned face down.

26

What would happen if he died out in the middle of the Atlantic ocean? Drowned, whilst two stoned little rich girls rocked and rolled on their private speedboat unconcerned about his fate.

What would Paul say when they arrived back without him? What would Edna say? And the newspapers of course would have a marvellous time.

Grimly he swam on, the pain in his side getting stronger and stronger. But fortunately the wind seemed to have dropped a bit, and he did appear to be making some progress towards the boat. He could hear his own voice echoing raunchily from the tape recorder. 'Random Love' again. His first big hit. How long ago that all seemed. Must be ten years. His first television appearance on a pop show to promote the record. A live audience of randy groupies. They had stormed the stage and tried to rip his clothes off.

Girls. Girls. Girls. From that moment on there had been a constant supply. What was it about fame that attracted women? He didn't flatter himself that it just happened to him. He had seen a wizened old comedian who could command the instant attention and availability of the most beautiful of girls. He had seen a very famous politician, fat and grotesque, who regularly bedded every female in his path.

It wasn't flattering to be aware of the fact that you could have any one you chose *only* because you were famous. If he was Al King, road digger, he would hardly be out here, drowning, with the fabulously rich Kurlnik twins. And he would not have been invited back to Marjorie Carter's body. Oh no. *That* type of woman wouldn't second glance him, however good-looking he was. And he was thirty-seven years old. According to all the books he had read on the subject he was past his sexual prime.

The hell he was.

He had reached the boat, and he hung onto the side, too exhausted to haul himself aboard. The cramp gradually subsided, and wearily he pushed himself up the ladder and into the boat.

The Kurlnik twins were on the mattresses at the back, their bodies entwined. Oblivious to all else they were making love to each other.

Al stared in disgust. He could have drowned, and all they cared about was each other.

Angrily he slid into the driver's seat, and gunned the Riva into action. It shot off, nearly dislodging the girls on the back.

Cara crawled to the front of the boat, her eyes blazing. 'You stupid bastard!' she yelled, 'you could have drowned us!'

They left Fire Island later that afternoon.

'I don't understand,' Linda complained, 'I thought we were staying the night. What's the problem?'

Paul shrugged. 'I've given up asking Al for reasons. Something must have happened while they were out ski-ing. He's burning, just leave him alone.'

'Don't I always?'

'You know what I mean. Stay out of his way. No photos.'

'*Yes, sir*.'

They returned to New York and Al closeted himself in his hotel suite. 'No calls, no birds, no games. I just want some peace.'

'I'll hang around,' Paul volunteered.

'No way, baby brother. I want to be alone.'

'What happened out there?' asked Paul, as curious as Linda.

'Nothing important,' stated Al blankly, 'that's the whole goddamn trouble – nothing important.'

'They seemed like nice girls . . .'

'Piss off, Paul. I don't need conversation.'

'I'll be around if you need me.'

'I don't. I'm going to sleep. Wake me an hour before we have to leave tomorrow.'

'If you're sure . . . Luke will be outside if you want anything.'

'I know that.'

Reluctantly Paul left. This was a mood of Al's he had never encountered before. Al wanting to spend a night by himself – unheard of. Especially at the peak of his success.

When Al was alone he phoned Edna. He hadn't spoken to her since Canada. Suddenly he missed his home, his son, even his wife.

'Hello,' she was anxious as always, 'is everything all right, Al?'

'Of course it's all right. Hasn't there been anything in the papers there?'

'Oh yes, the newspapers are full of you. Pictures, write-ups. I'm sticking them in the scrapbook.'

'That's nice. Evan around?'

'He's upstairs. I'm worried about him. He never wants to do anything or go anywhere. He spends all his time alone. And I found some magazines in his room . . .'

'Yeah? It's just a problem age. Tell you what, now that things seem to be moving so smoothly I thought I'd have him with me sooner. We go to Philadelphia, Monday – he can join us there.'

There was silence from Edna's end of the phone, then in a small voice she protested, 'But, Al, I'll be alone in the house. You know I get nervous when I'm alone.'

'That's crap, Edna. You've got a maid, a cook, Nelson. And goddamn Melanie right next door.'

'I know, but . . .'

'But nothing. He was joining us in Nashville anyway, so he'll come a week sooner – big deal. You said he's stuck in his room all day, this will give him a chance to see a bit of life.'

'Melanie says we should come too . . .'

'Melanie is a pain in the butt. Do I have to keep on reminding you how you hate these tours?'

'I know. You're right. Al, the shower is broken in our bathroom and . . .'

'What are you telling me for? Since when did *I* last mend showers? Tell Nelson, he'll fix it, what do you think I pay him for.'

'I still don't like Nelson.'

Al sighed. 'Jesus, Edna, I'm not asking you to jump into bed with him . . .'

'Al!'

'Have him mend the shower, and anything else that needs doing.'

'All right.'

'Call Evan, I'll tell him the news.'

There was a five minute wait until a surly Evan came on the line.

'You're joining us Monday,' Al enthused, 'so get yourself together.'

'I haven't got any decent clothes.' Evan complained.

'Don't worry, you can get it bigger and better here.'

'Yes.'

'Is that all you've got to say – yes? This will be the trip of your life, boyo, *I'll* see to *that*.'

Al hung up the phone.

☆

As each day passed the thought of divorce grew stronger and stronger. For a moment he had thought he missed Edna, but speaking to her on the phone, listening to her whiney voice, well, he knew it was finally over.

It would be difficult to tell her. He could imagine the scenes and tears, but it had to be done.

He climbed into bed, took a couple of sleeping pills, and fell asleep watching Johnny Carson on television.

☆

The show at the Spectrum, Philadelphia, was another smash.

As the tour progressed, so momentum picked up, and Al and 'The Promises' just got better and better.

'Beautiful show tonight, babee,' cooed Rosa, her dark skin agleam with sweat. She had said goodbye to her mafioso boyfriend in New York, and was once more available.

'Not bad,' agreed Al.

Bernie was throwing a small party in his suite at the hotel, just a private gathering for people connected with the tour.

'I hear you're bringing your boy out,' said Rosa, licking full red lips, 'your wife comin' too?'

Al shook his head, looked around for Paul.

'I left my man in New York. Won't see him until LA. Sure gets lonely at night.'

'*You*, lonely? Can't believe that.'

She pouted. 'Hey, Al. What's the matter? We had good times before, why not now?'

'I can't get involved, Rosa.'

'Hey man – *involvement* is the last thing in this little girl's head. Just a few good times, a few laughs. How about it, sport?'

'Not this trip.'

'I thought we were pretty good together.'

'So let's hang onto our memories.'

Rosa smiled. 'Sure. No hassle.' Her eyes drifted over to Luke stationed motionless by the door, 'You ever give that hunk time off?'

'You want him, he's yours.'

'He's a big mother! Real big and mean. Think I'll just hustle on over and hear the story of his life. By the way – you hear Magno Records all set to sign us to a *fantastic* contract? New billing – "Rosa and the Promises". Next year it will be *me* can use a bodyguard!'

'I heard. It's great news. Congratulations.'

'Thanks to you having us with you on the tour. We were almost there, but this pushed the button.'

She undulated over to Luke, thin, black and beautiful. Al could remember the desire the first time he had seen her. He had been there, the desire was no longer present.

He finally caught Paul's eye and beckoned him over. 'I'm going to bed . . .'

'It's early,' protested Paul. 'I thought you might want a gin game.'

'No. I want to be at the airport in the morning, meet Evan myself.'

'You feel OK?'

'I feel great. Why?'

'No girls tonight. The blonde in the corner is hot at the sound of your name . . .'

'So why don't you fuck her? Why does it always have to be me?'

'Huh?' stuttered Paul, confused, 'I thought . . .'

'Goodnight, Paul.'

☆

Bernie Suntan wiped the sweat from his brow with a large cotton handkerchief. He was too fat, that was the trouble, too goddamn fat. What the fuck was he doing running around airports in this unbelievable heat. He should be sitting in an air-conditioned office arranging deals – that was *his* forte in life. And with any luck, when this tour was over, that's just what he would be doing.

A ground hostess approached him, she was fresh and smiling. 'Your flight is just clearing customs, Mr Suntan. Our man will bring young Mr King right through.'

'Thanks, babe. You've been a big help.'

'Anything to help out Al King,' her eyes sparkled, 'I don't suppose there is any chance of getting tickets for tonight's concert?'

Bernie reached in his pocket. 'You just gotta mention it, babe, just gotta mention it.' He handed her two complimentary tickets, scribbling a number on the back. 'Give me a call later, there may be a party after. And bring a girlfriend – a pretty one.'

'I *will*! Is it possible that we might get to meet Mr King?'

Bernie regarded her through narrowed eyes. She *was* pretty. 'If you're lucky, babe, you may get to do more than meet him!'

She giggled and blushed.

'No shit,' continued Bernie, warming to his theme, 'Al's a wow with pretty little things like you.' He patted her reassuringly on the bottom 'wear something sexy. What's your name anyway?'

'Betty-Ann-Joe.'

'Well, Betty-Ann-Joe, tonight just might be your lucky night.'

She was positively glowing. 'Really? You think so?'

'Shit, babe, I *know* so.' He gave her a little hug, 'don't forget to call.'

'Oh, I won't.'

Outside the airport building, in a long Cadillac with black-tinted windows, Al waited impatiently.

Luke sat impassively in the front next to the chauffeur.

'Hey – here comes my boy.' Al jumped out of the car. 'Evan! You look great! How was the trip?'

'I feel sick,' complained Evan.

'Get in the car, you'll be all right. Hey, Bernie – they take good care of him?'

'The best. Al, say hello to Betty-Ann-Joe, she saw Evan got through customs with no hassle.'

Al hardly glanced at her.

'Mr King,' enthused Betty-Ann-Joe, 'I have all your records, every single one. It's been a real pleasure to help you out.'

'Sure,' agreed Al absently, climbing back in the car. 'Come on, Bernie, let's get this act together.'

☆

Of course it was a mistake. Nothing Al said or did brought a smile to Evan's pinched and spotty face. He remained unimpressed. The truth of the matter was that being in his father's presence made him more insecure than ever.

He knew that people expected Al King's son to be something special, and when they were confronted with him it was all they could do to keep the surprise off their faces.

But anything was better than being stuck at home with his mother. And Nelson – slimy, horrible slob. He had expressed great surprise at the fact that the girl he had arranged for Evan had never turned up. 'Little scruff, knew I shouldn't trust her.' But he had said nothing about returning Evan his five pounds, and when Evan had mentioned it days later he had assumed a hurt expression and said, 'I haven't got your money, I gave it to the girl.' The subject had not come up again. And Evan had been reduced to the cold comfort of his magazines. That was until his rotten mother found a stack of them and burned them in a ritual heap at the bottom of the garden.

'What's been happening?' asked Al, 'everything in good shape at the house?'

'There's a drought,' mumbled Evan, 'they've banned using hosepipes. Your grass has all burned up – looks like straw. Your apple tree's full of worms.'

'Any more good news?' asked Al ruefully. Evan knew how he loved his garden.

'Nothing much. Auntie Melanie scratched up her car. I think the swimming pool's cracking.'

'Terrific. Apart from that everything's fine though?'

'I think so.'

'He thinks so!' Al shook his head. 'We'd better get you some clothes. Tonight you'll watch the show, then after we'll have a party for you. How does that grab you?'

'All right.'

☆

Later Al had a private conference with Paul. 'The kid needs to get laid,' he informed his brother. 'Those spots are signalling a desperate message. We've got to find him a girl for tonight. A young hooker who knows her job. He mustn't guess. Can you arrange it?'

'Al, for you we all pimp. But for Evan too? I think you're asking too much.'

'So have Bernie arrange it, I didn't mean you personally.'

'Why don't you ask him yourself? It's not like it's part of his job . . . he's already taken the kid shopping . . .'

'Fuck his job,' snapped Al suddenly, 'do I have to beg to get a favour done around here? Isn't it enough I sweat my guts out on stage every night so that everyone around me can get fat? Even you, Paul. Where would you be without me?'

'I never thought I'd hear you say that,' replied Paul with tight-lipped control, 'who the fuck do you think got you where you are today?'

'You helped, but I'd have made it anyway.'

'And so would I. I've got artists in London waiting for me to stop tagging along tucking you in nights and concentrate on their careers. And they'll be stars – the bloody lot of 'em, when I give them some time.'

'So why don't you go then? Fuck off. I can manage without you.'

Paul was white-faced. 'I think I will.'

Al stalked off into the bathroom and slammed the door. He felt incredibly tense and uptight. He needed a woman to vent his fury on.

Bernie had taken Evan out shopping, they wouldn't be back for a while. He picked up the phone and asked for 'The Promises'' suite.

A soft voice answered.

'Rosa?' Al questioned.

'Rosa's out, this is Nellie.'

It flashed across Al's mind that she was only seventeen.

But it was only a flash. 'Why don't you come up for a drink,' he suggested.

The hell with it. He needed a woman, anyone would do.

☆

Paul nursed a large scotch. 'I have had it. Up to here. I'm not some frigging little gofer he can spit on when the mood takes him.'

'Calm down,' soothed Linda, 'I'm sure Al didn't mean it.'

'Ha!' snorted Paul, *'you're* sure Al didn't mean it. There's a twist. *You're* the one that's always telling me what a cunt I am to cater to him the way I do. And you're right. That's what I am. A grade A cunt.'

'Make it a prick and I'll be the first to agree with you!'

'Don't make jokes, Linda, please. If it wasn't for you, I'd be on the next plane out of here.' He handed her his glass for a refill. 'You think I need all this? I've got a young kid – writes all his own songs – sounds like Tom Jones ten years ago – could knock spots off Al. All he needs is a push. And I'm the one that can do it for him.'

'So what are you waiting for?'

'You know why I hung back. I thought Al needed me on this tour.'

'He probably did at the beginning. It could have been a disaster – then he *would* have needed you. As it is, he's a sensation. He needs no one.'

'You're right. You're always right.'

She nuzzled his neck. 'That's why you love me and that's why one of these days you'll marry me . . .'

Together they said: 'When the children are older!'

Paul couldn't help laughing.

'You see,' said Linda, pleased, 'I can even make you laugh when you're at your blackest. Now let's make love and forget about the whole thing. If you are going to make any moves at all I want you to have a clear head, so stop guzzling scotch and guzzle me instead.'

'How do you guzzle a person?'

'You've never heard of guzzle? What are you – a boy from a sheltered family? Come here and I'll show you!'

☆

'What you done to Nellie, man?' Rosa's green eyes flashed dangerously.

'Screwed her. Is it a crime?' Al was still in a filthy mood as he sat in his dressing-room dabbing his face with pancake.

'You bastard!' spat Rosa. 'Motherfuckin' bastard! She's only a kid. Whyn't you pick on someone your size?'

'Is she complaining?' sighed Al patiently.

'No, she ain't complaining. She's all starry-eyed, thinks marriage is just around the corner.'

'So disillusion her.'

'Do your own dirty work,' stormed Rosa, 'I think you're a mean bastard pickin' on a kid like her. Ain't you got enough groupies and God knows what hangin' around you?'

'Leave it out, Rosa. I'm in no mood for lectures – especially from you.'

'*We* could have had some laughs, but that wasn't enough was it, you had to go shaggin' after little kids.'

'Get lost, Rosa.'

'You bet your ass, whitey.' She stamped out of the room.

Bernie, on the phone in the corner, pretended not to hear. But his stomach was already warning him that things were not going to progress as smoothly as he had hoped.

'Fix anything?' snapped Al.

'They got a girl of twenty. Redhead. Big knockers. Name's Susie. She'll be at the party.'

'Is she all cued in?'

'She will be. I'll see her myself when I pay her.'

'Good.'

The phone rang, and Bernie automatically reached for it. 'Yes?'

The voice, slow and distinct, was instantly recognizable. 'Tonight,' it whispered, 'the three bombs due to go off in New York, they'll be set tonight instead. Three-minute intervals.' The phone clicked dead before Bernie could say a word.

'Who was it?' asked Al.

'Wrong number,' sweated Bernie. His stomach had not been wrong. The thing that worried him was that this had sounded like a local call. Same thing in New York. OK, so nothing had happened in New York, but maybe this was the build-up. And where did the quiet, nothing voice obtain the private dressing-room numbers?

He would have to discuss it with Paul. Maybe it would be wise to contact the police.

Luke appeared at the door.

' "The Promises" just went on,' he informed Al.

☆

Sitting near the front Evan felt nervous being amongst so many strangers. The girl next to him chewed gum and wore the AL IS KING T-shirt. She joggled around on her seat like a caged puppy. On his other side were two middle-aged women in flowered dresses. They chatted together in low, controlled voices. They reminded him of his mother.

He was glad when the lights dimmed and a red flash from the darkness of the stage produced 'The Promises'.

He fell in love instantly. She was the most beautiful girl he had ever seen. She stood to one side of the tall black girl in the middle. She was coffee-coloured, with long jet black hair, and a beautiful little face. She was dressed the same as the other two, but on her, somehow it looked different. The other two were stridently sexy. She was almost demure.

They swayed together –

Come on sweet stuff
Sure can't get enough
Ohhh – you're sugar sweet
Ohhh – babee
Ohhh – babee
Love you like a bomb
Gotta love you long
Ohhh you're my desire
Ohhh – babee
Ohhh – babee

Evan opened up his souvenir programme, found their picture. Her name was Nellie. She was seventeen. Only a year older than he was. And he would meet her, of course he would. They would be travelling across the country on the same plane.

☆

169

'This is my son.' Proudly Al introduced Evan to everyone at the party. They all gave him the scarcely hidden look of amazement. At least Evan thought they did.

'Have some champagne, son.' Al thrust a glass at him. 'Go on, drink it up, get used to the good things in life early.'

'I've never . . .'

'Drink it down like a man, won't do you any harm.'

Evan gulped at the fizzy liquid. It had a revolting taste, much too bitter.

'You liked the show?' asked Al.

'It was all right,' mumbled Evan. He had liked 'The Promises', but when Al had come on, his toes had curled with embarrassment. Was that man on the stage posturing and gesturing really his father?

The girl sitting beside him had gone into a frenzy of madness. Even the two middle-aged women on his other side had appeared to go beserk.

The whole place was full of screaming women. They must be mad.

'It's a good job that I know all right from you means sensational!' laughed Al. 'You're Mr Cool. I don't think I've ever seen you crack a smile!'

Evan smiled weakly, and gulped at the champagne just to have something to do. He didn't see Nellie until she was right behind Al putting her hands over his eyes from behind.

'Peekaboo!' she trilled.

Al removed her hands. 'Oh, it's you,' he said, 'this is my son, Evan.'

'Hi there, Evan.' She had a very high sing-song voice. She was even prettier off stage, wearing red trousers and a peasant blouse. 'Lovely show, Al, really something,' she tucked her arm into Al's, her eyes shone with adoration.

Al deftly removed her arm. 'Nellie's one of "The Promises". She'll look after you a minute, I've just got to see about something.' He strode off, leaving them together.

Evan was speechless. Frightened to open his mouth in case his voice let him down and cracked horribly – a circumstance that had been occurring of late.

'I didn't know Al had a big boy like *you*,' sighed Nellie in her funny little voice, 'how old are you?'

'Sixteen,' replied Evan, his voice staying at a nice deep level. 'I'll be seventeen soon.' Soon was about six months off. 'You don't look like him.' Nellie narrowed her eyes. 'Not at all.'

Evan was glad to note that he was taller than her. He drew himself up to his full height and thrust his glass at her. 'Have some champagne,' he suggested. Unfortunately his voice broke right in the middle of champagne.

Nellie giggled, but she took the glass anyway, sipped a little, sighed dreamily, and said, 'Your old man sure is something, *really* something.'

Al returned at that point with Bernie, and a hard-faced redhead.

'This is my son,' announced Al, 'Evan, say hello to Susie.'

Evan nodded quickly, and returned his attention to Nellie, who was taking sips of the champagne like a little bird.

Susie said in a loud voice, 'Hey now – what a looker! You told me he was nice – but what a *looker!*'

Evan stared at her in amazement. She was talking about *him*.

She placed her hands firmly on her waist and rocked back and forth, 'Hhmmm . . . If you're an import – then I'm in the import business!'

Nellie giggled. 'I think you all just got lucky,' she whispered at Evan.

He blushed. Susie reminded him of one of the girls from his magazines. She was wearing a green dress, low-cut and split up the side. She had jammy red lips, and flinty brown eyes. Her red hair straggled down her back. She winked at Al in an obvious fashion. 'Mind if Evan shows me around?'

'Around where?' croaked Evan anxiously.

'Go ahead,' said Al, 'show Susie the rest of the suite.'

'But there's only the bedrooms,' objected Evan.

'I *love* bedrooms,' enthused Susie, 'I love to see how other people decorate. That's what I am, y'know. A decorator.' She grabbed Evan by the arm. 'Come on, handsome. Show me the sights.'

Tensely Evan pulled away. Firmly Susie hung onto him again. 'Pretty, please,' she pouted, 'be a good boy, you won't regret it.'

Panic-stricken Evan turned to Al. 'Show her around,' said Al smoothly, 'We'll see you later.' And he turned away.

Susie dragged a reluctant Evan towards the bedroom.

'See no one goes in,' Al instructed Bernie.

'What was *that*?' asked Nellie, 'she looks like a hooker.'

'She is a hooker,' agreed Al. 'Little present for Evan.'

'Some present!' Nellie rolled her eyes. 'Poor kid was frightened to death.'

'He'll love it.'

'Oh yeah?' questioned Nellie, 'with a gorilla like that?'

'You should have seen *my* first fuck. Next to her that one's a princess!'

Nellie giggled. 'You are *bad*!' Then her voice softened, and her fingers touched his cheek. 'It was wonderful today, somethin' I bin dreamin' about since Vegas. You know I was fifteen then, just a little kid.'

'Listen, Nellie, don't go getting big ideas. This afternoon was nice but . . .'

'Mr King! Remember me? Betty-Ann-Joe. We met at the airport this morning and Mr Suntan got me tickets for your show and you were sensational but of course I knew you would be and I just had to come over and tell you how I felt because . . .' She droned on with a breathy enthusiasm whilst Al inspected her. Pretty, young, clean-looking. He had had it with celebrities and rich bitches. What he needed was a girl who wouldn't answer back. A girl who would be over-whelmed just by being in his company. He certainly didn't need Nellie, with fawn-like love shining out of her eyes. Best to discourage her right from the start. He regretted the fact that he had ever invited her to share his bed. Rosa was right – he *was* a shit.

He put his arm around Betty-Ann-Joe. 'So you liked the show. Come with me, young lady, and I'll show you something you'll like even better!'

Paul watched the scene from across the room, Linda by his side.

'I don't know how he does it,' she commented dryly. 'How come he's not a walking advertisement for the clap? I mean do you realize how many there have been in the last couple of weeks?'

'He's always been like that,' replied Paul. 'Now that he

can have anything he wants I guess he feels he'll be losing out if he doesn't.'

'He can't *enjoy* it. Do you think he enjoys it?'

'Who knows? I don't discuss his sex life with him.'

'Oh come on – of course you do.'

'Of course I don't.'

'He's probably a lousy lay, always having to prove himself the way he does.'

'That he's not.'

'How do *you* know?'

'I just know.'

'Oh. Have you indulged at the same time then?'

'When we were young – yes.'

Linda laughed. 'Confessions of a raver. And I always thought you were so straight.'

'I was about eighteen at the time.'

She kissed him on the cheek. 'I wish I'd known you when you were eighteen.'

He looked around anxiously. 'I told you to be careful when Evan's around.'

'He's not around. He's locked in the bedroom with that dreadful hooker. I think it's an awful way to treat a young boy, it could put him off sex for life.'

Paul shrugged, 'My brother – he knows it all. Meanwhile little Nellie's in a state over there – apparently he found time to give her one this afternoon . . .'

'Oh, no.'

'Oh, yes. See if you can cheer her up before Rosa zeros in. I can see the shit hitting the fan any day now. Go on, I've got to have a talk with Bernie.'

☆

'Take your clothes off,' commanded Susie for the fifth time.

Evan sat miserably on the corner of the bed. 'I don't want to.'

Susie sniffed. 'Jesus, kid! I'm trying to do a job of work around here, but you are not makin' it easy.'

'I haven't asked you to do anything,' snivelled Evan, wishing he was back in England, wishing he was anywhere except trapped in a hotel bedroom with this large red-haired monster.

'Listen, kid,' said Susie firmly, 'I got orders to fuck you. F-U-C-K. You understand what that means? I got paid already. I gotta reputation to consider, so at least unzip your fly, at least do that, goddammit!'

'I don't want you,' muttered Evan, scarlet with humiliation. 'I don't know who paid you and I don't care.'

'Your daddy paid me. Your daddy wants you taken care of.' Suddenly she took off the belt of her dress, and the whole thing seemed to disintegrate, falling to the floor, and leaving her stark naked, except for a laddered pair of tights. 'OK, sonny. Here's the goods. *Now* can you flip it out?'

'Go away,' mumbled Evan, 'go away and leave me alone, I think I'm going to throw up.'

'Sheeit!' Susie scooped up her dress and threw it back on. 'Why couldn't I have had the daddy? Listen, kid, I ain't givin' nobody back no money. You want me to go, say somethin' happened. All right?'

'Yes.'

'Oh, and say it was great, outasight, mind-blowing! OK? I've got me a reputation to consider.'

'Yes.'

'Right on, kid. We're a team.' She inspected herself in the mirror, smiled secretly and added, 'You don't know what you're missing . . . Tell your daddy to give me a try – no charge.' She winked and left.

Evan remained huddled on the bed. He was so confused. He had wanted a girl. But not like this. Not paid for and arranged by his father. And what about Nellie? Did she know? If she knew he wanted to die, simply and quietly die.

Damn his father. Damn his bloody famous father. He wished something terrible would happen to him, something really terrible . . .

27

'I think,' said Dallas slowly, 'that you have made a mistake.'

Lew Margolis chuckled. 'A mistake! Don't talk crap. I recognized you the moment you walked into my office. No one could possibly forget *that* body.'

'Am I supposed to be flattered by that remark?'

Lew leaned back in his chair, enjoying every minute of the confrontation. 'You can be what you like, suit yourself – *Mrs Margolis*.'

Dallas shook her head in amazement. 'You're sick, you know that? You're really sick.'

'Why?' he snapped, suddenly angry.

'Because if I *was* the girl you thought I was . . .'

'Which you are . . .'

Dallas ignored the interruption. 'If I *was* that girl, what makes you think that in a million years I'd go back to doing what I was doing?'

'Everyone has a price,' said Lew flatly, 'and all women are whores anyway. Take my wife,' he picked up a photo frame and stared at a glossy smiling photo of Doris Andrews. She had a scrubbed fresh look familiar to moviegoers the world over. 'She'd screw a snake if it had the bad sense to venture onto our estate. I know all about her, so I take my revenge. Can you blame me?'

'Divorce would seem like a better idea.'

'Why should I divorce her? I love her. Take your clothes off, Dallas, put on those things, I only have fifteen minutes. I want to be a real estate agent, this is my office and you've come to discuss selling your house and buying a bigger property.'

'Forget it.'

'Don't be a silly girl.'

'What are you threatening me with if I don't, Mr Margolis?'

He raised his eyebrows in a gesture of surprise. 'I am the man who is going to make you into a star.'

'I know. I signed the contract already.'

'Contracts can be broken.'

'People can sue.'

'In this town power rules. Surely you know that by now?'

She shrugged, trying to conceal her sudden nervousness, trying to maintain an outward calm. 'People can also tell true life stories.'

Lew laughed loudly. 'Who would believe *you*? A girl who got fired because she wasn't a good enough actress for the part. Besides, you're forgetting, I'm married to Doris Andrews – her reputation is public domain and pure, pure white. Anyone trying to throw mud would end up covered in it.'

'Why did you hire me? Why did you agree to pay me all that money? Why would you even *think* of making me a star?'

'Because your agent was correct – you *are* the right girl for the part, and as you know, we need someone immediately. But no one is irreplaceable, there are other girls, maybe not as good as you – but available – and accommodating.'

She brushed her hair back with her hands, and fought to keep the tears of frustration from appearing. 'Let me get things straight,' she said slowly. 'I want to be absolutely sure I understand you. The contract is only good if I do what you want, is that it?'

He nodded.

'And if I don't, I'm out. Right?'

'Right, I'm afraid. Does Cody Hills know of your former occupation?'

'Keep him out of it,' snapped Dallas quickly.

'He'll have to know,' stated Lew blandly, 'if I drop your contract he'll have to know.'

'Why?'

'He seems like a smart young man. I'm sure the moral implications will put him off sueing.'

'You've worked it all out, haven't you? Either way I get screwed.'

She wanted to scream and shout and hurl abuse at him. She wanted to claw his filthy little eyes out, kick him where it hurt, smash his mouth in. Instead she managed to smile coolly while she gathered up the clothes he had thrown at her and placed them in a neat pile on his desk. Then she leaned over the desk, selected a cigarette from his silver Dunhill box, lit it, leaned back, and said, 'OK, Mr Margolis. You win, and why shouldn't you – you're holding all the cards. But not now, not while you only have fifteen minutes.'

'But . . .'

'No buts. It's my turn to take control. You want me to be in control, don't you? We can have more fun that way, lots and lots of fun . . .' How easily the hooker dialogue returned. The stern bantering that most men loved. 'Now you be a good boy and do things my way. I promise you a trip, sugar, that will blow your little mind.'

'When?' he asked eagerly.

'Tomorrow. Not here, but at my house.'

'I can't be seen going to your house.'

'Who will see you? The virgin queen doesn't have you followed, does she?'

'No . . . but . . .'

'We can play swimming instructors, wouldn't that be wild? Do you swim?'

'I used to . . .'

'And you will again.' She smiled, blew him a kiss with her fingers. 'I'll be Mrs Margolis – you can be Mark Spitz if you like. She would like him, wouldn't she? Young, strong . . . Can you play the part?'

He nodded, a pleased expression covering his features. 'You know what I want don't you? You're a smart girl. I knew you'd see things my way. There's no reason we can't both enjoy it.'

The smile was stuck on her face like a mask. 'No reason at all.'

She left the studio in a controlled state of fury. She drove her rented car to her rented house in the Hills.

She walked around, stripping her clothes off as she went, then naked, she dived into the kidney-shaped pool, only letting her tears come when the water hit her.

She swam up and down the pool, powerful strokes cutting through the bland blue water. And she cried herself out. Exhausted herself, until at last she clambered out of the pool, flopped down on the grass, and lay spreadeagled to the sun, thinking.

Blackmail. Pure and simple blackmail.

You pull my schlong, and I'll pull the strings for you to be a big and beautiful star.

But what if she was a star already? What could Lew do then? 'Man Made Woman' would make her a star. It wouldn't take that long. How many visits from Lew Margolis would she have to endure? The thought of even one made her flesh creep. Once a hooker always a hooker was bullshit. She would sooner wait tables than go back to that life.

There had to be an answer.

At first, staring at Lew as he sat smugly behind his fine marble desk spelling out the way it was, she had wanted to kill him. That's why she had suggested the swimming bit. But of course it hadn't worked with Bobbie, so why should it with him? But oh the satisfaction of dragging him under, feeling him squirm, seeing his fear when she let him up.

It was just a dream. She was incapable of murder – indeed the thought disgusted her – just as Lew Margolis disgusted her.

She was often haunted in dreams by the corpse of the old man so long ago in that Miami hotel. She would wake sweating, her legs shaking, her heart pounding.

If only she could turn to Cody for help. But he would be so disappointed in her, and even more disappointed as he saw their million-dollar deal go flying out the window. She wondered if he would be shocked. Were people shocked by things any more? He would be hurt, that was worse. She would have let him down, and no way did she want to do that.

She rolled onto her front. What to do? Lew Margolis was blackmailing her, there must be a way she could turn the tables on him.

It came to her in a series of thought waves, piece by piece. Photographs. Everyone believed photographs.

Lew and she. One time. Repugnant thought. But if she could get photographs.

How?

She had never held a camera in her life. But if she could hire someone . . . Silly thought, it would only lead to more blackmail . . .

But it was the answer. The living room and bedroom overlooked the pool. Huge glass windows, an unimpaired view. How did she find a photographer? How did she trust anyone? Linda.

The name sprung into her mind. Linda would help her if she told her the truth. If she agreed, it was the perfect solution. Perfect.

Dallas relaxed at last, giving herself to the sun, and deciding the best way to ask Linda. She certainly couldn't tell her over the phone, maybe there would just be time to find out where she was, get on a plane, and if Linda cooperated they could fly back together and get everything organized for Lew Margolis' visit the next evening.

She was about to get up when she heard footsteps approaching, then Cody's voice, 'Hey, lady, your slip is showing, but don't panic, my eyes are covered and I can only see what I let myself.'

She rolled over, stood up, and wrapped a towel around herself sarong style. 'You can look now.'

'God, you're a tease!' He uncovered his eyes and grinned. 'You promised to call me the second you got back. What did he want?'

She shook her head, playing for time, wondering what the hell to tell him. 'I don't really know,' she said at last, 'sort of a pep talk about morals, I guess.'

Cody nodded. 'I thought it would be something like that. He's running scared after his he/she shock. Are you all right? Your eyes are red. Have you been . . .?'

'Cody, I got a call from my aunt. Remember I told you I had this aunt back East that I lived with until I was sixteen?'

'You told me she was bad news . . .'

'I know I told you that, but she still brought me up. If it hadn't been for her, after my parents were killed, well . . .' She shrugged helplessly. 'She needs me. A personal problem. I'm going to see her.'

'You can't go. Are you mad? You start shooting in three days. You're supposed to be resting, getting a tan, studying your lines.'

'I can study my lines on the plane. Look – I've got it all arranged, flight booked, everything. I'll be back day after tomorrow, I promise you. Back in time to get twelve hours' sleep before the big day.'

Cody frowned. 'The studio will never allow it.'

'The studio doesn't have to know.'

'It's a stupid move.'

'It's one I have to make.' She clasped his hand, squeezed it. 'I wouldn't let you down, surely you know that much about me?'

He nodded in resignation. 'Yeah, I suppose so.' Then more vigorously, 'So get packed and dressed and I'll drive you to the airport for my sins.'

'Your sins you can keep. I'll take my own car to the airport, leave it there, it will be simpler that way.'

'I could meet you tomorrow.'

'Cody, I want a producer not a chauffeur.'

'I could come with you . . .'

She feigned annoyance. 'I don't think you trust me.'

'Of course I trust you.'

'Then please, be a sweetheart and haul your ass out of here so I can get ready. I'll call you the moment I arrive. I promise.'

He was reluctant to leave, but she finally got rid of him.

Poor Cody. What a pack of lies she had fed him. But it couldn't be helped, it was all in a good cause;

Some good cause, saving her own ass.

She located Linda in Miami. It *would* have to be Miami.

She was on a plane there within the hour.

28

The push-ups were tiring Al out. 'Forty-seven, forty-eight, forty-nine, fifty.' He collapsed on the floor gasping for breath. 'Your turn, Evan, boyo.'

Evan watched his father through narrowed eyes. No way was he going to compete with him. 'I don't feel like it, dad.'

'Give it a try,' commanded Al, 'you want to stay scrawny *all* your life?'

Reluctantly Evan squatted down on the floor, but fortunately the phone rang before he was forced to humiliate himself.

Al picked it up. 'Yes?' he questioned. Pause. Then – 'Oh, Edna, it's you again.' Pause. Then – 'I told you yesterday he was fine, there's no need for you to keep phoning.'

When he hung up he was in a filthy mood. Edna hadn't bothered to call him once, but now that her precious little Evan was around she was on the phone every day. He had been right to get the boy away from her. Evan was a mummy's boy, frightened if anyone so much as farted. And his spots were as bad as ever. He still looked skinny and a misfit in spite of all the new gear.

Al would have liked to have discussed the boy with Paul,

but since their argument there had been a certain coolness between them. A coolness that Al now regretted.

Being a star meant never having to say you were sorry. But he *was* sorry, although he didn't know how to say so.

The tour was taking on a certain sameness. Philadelphia a smash. New Jersey the same. Kansas City ditto. And now Miami – gateway to the retired sun-seekers of the world.

Installed in a suite at the Fontainebleau, Al could not even venture out. To do so meant instant mobbing from droves of beehive-hairstyled ladies in town on a hairdressing convention.

He had discovered that Evan was not the ideal travelling companion. The boy was a permanent fixture, not allowing Al the freedom he needed. Somehow he had thought that underneath all the whiney crap Evan would be just like him. Misguidedly he had thought that if he stuck a cigar in his mouth, plied him with champagne, and turned him on to pussy, the boy would miraculously change.

No such luck. Evan remained his usual surly self. Refusing champagne, choking on cigars, and backing away in a panic if a member of the female sex hovered anywhere near.

Al walked over and stared out of the window at the crowded swimming pool many storeys below.

'Bullshceet!' he said slowly, 'Bullsheet you fuckers!' He was bored. Horribly, restlessly bored.

'What are we going to do this afternoon?' ventured Evan.

Al throttled back a vicious reply. He had become a fucking entertainments director!

What he would like to do, what he needed to do, was spend the afternoon in bed with a dumb blonde. A really dumb blonde who wouldn't bother him with any talking.

'I don't know,' he said, 'maybe Bernie can take you somewhere. I'm tired, thought I might go back to kip.'

'Oh,' the boy's voice was disappointed. 'But you promised we could go scuba diving.'

'How can we do that?' asked Al, exasperated, 'when you can't even swim?'

'I can watch from the boat.'

'Tell you what,' Al had a sudden idea, 'you can have a swimming lesson, I'll call down and arrange it.' That would give him at least an hour free.

'I'll never learn,' complained Evan, 'I've had lessons for years.'

'Can't give up on it,' insisted Al, 'it's only a matter of time, then pow – it's like fuc . . . dancing – you never forget.'

'I can't dance.'

What can you do? Al felt like asking. I've lavished everything that money can buy on you, and you still can't do a fucking thing. Thank you, Edna. Before my very eyes you have raised a pain in the ass.

Ignoring Evan he picked up the phone and called the desk. A swimming lesson was arranged instantly. As soon as he got rid of the boy he hoped that a blonde could be arranged equally instantly.

Actually all he had to do was saunter out of his room and take his pick, but who needed that trip?

He called Paul, but someone at the desk informed him that Mr Paul King had gone out on a yacht for the day with Miss Cosmo.

What the fuck did they think this was – a vacation? He hoped in a moment of malice that Melanie called and got the same message.

Evan had changed into swimming shorts.

'Take you socks off, for Christ's sake!' snapped Al. 'You look like a walking advertisement for the English abroad.'

Grimly Evan peeled off his socks. What a rotten trip this was turning out to be. His father either completely ignored him, or went out of his way to embarrass him. Al King's son. What a cross *that* was to bear.

He allowed his mind to linger fleetingly on Nellie. She was so pretty, and sweet and nice. He could admire her from afar, it was better that way. If only it had been *she* that his father had arranged for him. That would have been wonderful, instead of that monstrous big Susie girl. And the embarrassment of facing Nellie after that evening. But she had been sweet about it. Hadn't mentioned it. In fact there had been no chance for him to talk to her since then. She seemed to go out of her way to avoid Al. Maybe she didn't like him, and Evan could understand *that*. However, Evan enjoyed the fact that sometimes he felt her eyes in his direction, but he was too shy to stare back.

He wished he could be more like his father towards women.

He wished he looked like his father.

He wished he was famous and rich and everyone jumped when he spoke.

He wished his father was dead.

☆

Finally rid of Evan, Al decided to take off for the afternoon. He was sick and tired of playing nursemaid. Fuck it. He was a star. A superstar. *He* should be the one out for the day on a yacht, not Paul.

He rifled through the piles of invitations littered around the suite. Parties. Receptions. Mostly from people he didn't know and didn't even want to know.

What to do? He had to get out. To stay meant the imminent return of Evan, and even if he was locked safely in the bedroom with a blonde it wouldn't be the same.

He picked up an invitation to attend a luncheon party for the English Ambassador, got dressed quickly, had Luke summon his limousine, and they were away.

☆

'This is nice,' Linda murmured. She lay in a sun chair, sipping a Banana Daiquiri, and observing the frenetic activities of the other guests on the yacht as they scurried from group to group frightened of missing something or someone.

'Not bad,' agreed Paul. But he was frowning, and he couldn't help wondering if Al was all right. Since the argument they had maintained a cool business relationship, or at least Paul had. Al, in his way, would have been quite happy to pretend the whole incident had never happened. But Paul was deeply hurt, and childish though it was, he wanted an apology, and he was determined to hold out until he got one.

Linda was delighted that she suddenly had Paul all to herself. He attended to business, saw that the shows went smoothly, and then he was all hers. No hanging around to see what Al wanted to do. No hand holding, ass kissing, pimping. It was a refreshing change.

When Paul seemed to weaken she reminded him that Al

had Evan with him anyway, and Bernie and Luke were in constant attendance to see to his every need.

That was fine, reasoned Paul, but he could see Al becoming more and more restless as the tour progressed, and he thought to himself – fuck you – stubborn bastard – apologize for Chrissake and I'll be there to smooth things over – look after Evan – find you prime pussy – whatever you want.

'I *like* the rich life,' Linda remarked. 'Why don't *we* buy a yacht and just take off where no one can find us. You've got enough money, haven't you?'

Paul grimaced mockingly. 'So! It's my money you're after.'

'Never! It's your body, it's always been your body ... Come here, you sex machine. Come here, you big ...'

'Stop it! Hands off, someone will see.'

'Don't be so English.'

'Don't be so American, and get your hands off my ...'

'All right. All right!' Linda stretched languorously and laughed. 'Am I getting brown?'

'Not bad. You like lazing around in the sun, don't you?'

'Yes. I could see myself living this kind of life. You know, I don't see why we can't—' she began, then stopped abruptly, her mood changing mid-sentence. She knew why they couldn't buy a yacht and take off. She knew why they couldn't be together. She reached into her purse, produced a cigarette, lit it, drew deeply, stared at Paul. 'I hate the fact that you're married,' she stated flatly, 'I really hate it.'

'Why are you bringing that up. I never tried to hide it,' he defended.

'Nope,' Linda laughed in a brittle fashion, 'I guess you never did.' She thought of the unknown enemy, the wife, and for the thousandth time wondered what she was like – even more important, what Paul was like when he was with her. Did they make love? Well of course they must do. Was it good? Linda bit deeply into her lip. She wasn't going to ask. She wasn't going to behave like the other woman. She was just going to cool it, like she always had. And in the end – where the hell did it get her? Nowhere fast, that's where it got her. If she was smart she would cast her eyes around for someone new, someone free.

She sighed, shivered slightly, drained her drink and said:

'Let's circulate, Paul, let's see who else is on this floating piece of ostentation.'

Maybe she should start to play games. Maybe *that* was the way to get through to him. But oh Christ who needed all that game-playing crap, not at her age, that was stuff for teenagers.

'Do we have to?' Paul groaned.

'Yes,' insisted Linda. 'I thought I saw Ramo Kaliffe a minute ago, and I'd love to meet him.'

'Lead the way,' said Paul resignedly. And he wondered what Al was doing.

29

Arriving at Miami Airport hit Dallas like a giant shock wave. It brought back every bad memory. Was it really only two years ago that she and Bobbie had fled the city like a couple of thieves?

She remembered the night in detail . . . The old man dying on them. Bobbie pocketing his bankroll. The mad dash to their crummy apartment where they packed up in record time. And then the airport where Dallas had felt that at any moment a hand would descend on her shoulder and she would be arrested . . .

She jumped as a voice growled, 'Wanna cab?'

'Yes, please.' She climbed in and directed the driver to the Fontainebleau.

More memories. She had practically started her career at the Fontainebleau. She shuddered when she realized how many men ago *that* had been.

'Al King concert at the Sportatorium tonight,' the driver remarked, 'it's a madhouse over there, big hassle with forged tickets. You here on vacation?'

'No.'

'You look familiar, like I know you. You on TV?'

'No.'

'Had a girl in the cab last week. An actress – English. She . . .'

Dallas tuned out as the cab driver droned on. She found

herself wondering if her parents were still at the zoo. If her husband was with them. If any of them had ever given her a second thought.

If she had more time she could drive out there. Not of course to go in, but just to see if the zoo was still there . . .

Bastards. She had been seventeen years old and they had just let her walk out in to the world on her own. A girl so innocent that she had thought the first guy that screwed her was doing *her* a favour.

The cab pulled up at the Fontainebleau.

'You sure do look familiar . . .' the driver mused.

She ignored the remark, paid him, and walked up the steps into the hotel.

Linda was not there. Paul was not there. But the desk clerk pointed out Bernie Suntan waddling across the lobby on his way out.

Dallas hurried over to him. 'Mr Suntan,' she said quickly, 'I . . .'

He continued walking. 'Sorry. No free tickets, kid. Kaput. All gone. Follow us to Chicago and I'll see what I can do.'

'I don't want tickets,' she said. 'My name is Dallas, I'm a friend of Linda Cosmo, and I have to get hold of her immediately. It's most urgent. Can you help me?'

Bernie stopped, stared, let out a whistle. 'Jeeze, you are one beautiful lady! Saw the TV thing you did with Al, excuse me for not recognizing you at once but this tour is ageing my facilities! For you I gotta ticket.'

'I don't want a ticket,' Dallas explained patiently, 'I just want to see Linda.'

'Of course you do,' agreed Bernie, rubbing sweaty palms together, 'and we shall share a car to the Sportatorium and we shall find her for you.'

'Thank you.'

☆

The cab driver had been right about it being a madhouse at the Sportatorium. Huge crowds roamed around outside surging angrily in different directions. Mass blocks of tickets had been forged, and many genuine ticket holders had been unable to gain entry.

'If we could catch the rip-off merchants life would be a lot easier,' Bernie complained, as their car edged its way through the crowds. 'Gonna take you to Al's dressing-room while I find Linda, she's a good kid – takes a bitch of a picture. You should see the show.'

'I did. I saw it in New York.'

'You did? Wish I'd known, could have done a nice little thing with you and Al. Pictures . . . old friends. Could have been a nice plug for you.'

'I don't think that's such a good idea. I think Al's nervous of his wife.'

Bernie burst into raucous laughter. 'Al? Nervous of his wife? Craperooney, baby – pure craperooney. Al's screwed everything that moves on this tour. No offence . . . I mean what the fuck . . . *everyone* knows about Al.'

Dallas agreed. 'Sure. So if you were a girl would *you* want to be photographed with him?'

Bernie laughed some more. 'If I was a girl I'd piss my way out of his sight in record time. He treats 'em all like shit.'

'Him and who else?' stated Dallas dryly.

'You're something,' guffawed Bernie, 'I like you. When I'm a producer gonna keep you in mind.'

'How kind of you.'

'What the fuck . . . If you can't help friends in this life who can you help?'

'Quite right,' agreed Dallas briskly, 'do you think we can find Linda now?'

☆

'The Promises' were on stage belting out 'Love Power', shimmering in black sequin boiler suits.

Al was in his dressing-room, drinking hard. He had already demolished a bottle and a half of scotch, and did not feel like doing the show. Fuck the show. Fuck the people. What was he, a puppet?

Evan, in one corner of the dressing room, puffed uneasily on a cigarette.

Luke had rushed off to summon Paul.

Bernie, unaware of any dramas, waddled in with Dallas behind him.

Al didn't see her. He scowled at Bernie in the mirror and said, 'Where you been, Bernie? Out water ski-ing? Or maybe

Disneyland took your fancy? Don't know why you took the trouble to come here at all. Why do any of you bother? I do the work, the rest of you should stay away, just pick up the money. You shitass. Here's a nice little item for you. Al King will not appear tonight. Al King is all fucked out and just wants to sleep. You like it? Does it grab you by the balls?'

'Al!' protested Bernie. 'Baby! what's the matter? I just got off the phone to Chicago setting everything up. I would have been here sooner if . . .'

Dallas backed quietly out of the room as Bernie spoke. She did not need this whole bit. Al King was obviously every bit as impossible as she had thought he would be.

Paul was striding towards her. 'What's going on?' he snapped in an irritable fashion. 'What are *you* doing here?'

'Question one – I don't know. Question two – looking for Linda. Is she here?'

'She's photographing "The Promises".'

'Thanks, I'll find her.'

'Did you see Al?'

'Some other time, I think.'

Paul nodded, and went into the dressing-room.

Dallas located Linda at the side of the stage. She watched as Linda went about her business, not disturbing her until she stopped to change film. Then she stepped forward and Linda nearly dropped her camera in surprise.

'I have to talk to you. Can we go somewhere?' Dallas asked.

'Sure, I'm about finished. Why are you here?'

'It's a long story, and I need your help. That's why I'm here.'

'We'll take one of the cars back to the hotel,' Linda decided. 'I don't think tonight's the night I'm going to miss the shot of the century. Hey, Larry,' she called to one of the roadies, 'tell Paul I had to go – catch him later.'

Dallas had thought long and carefully about how much she should tell Linda, and in the end she had decided that only the truth would help. Of course, certain things she would leave out – such as the old man dying, and her attempt to drown Bobbie. But apart from that she had planned to be quite open about everything. Linda was too smart to fall for any phoney story. To acquire her help she had to be honest, and that meant the whole messy story. If Linda was the friend she hoped she was, she would help out.

They sat in Linda's hotel room, ordered drinks from room service, and Dallas began her story. She talked for two hours, with only occasional nods from Linda to encourage her. And when she was finished she was surprised to find that she was crying.

Linda handed her a Kleenex, and Dallas said, embarrassed, 'I haven't cried since I was a kid.'

'It's a sad story,' commented Linda, 'God, Dallas, I never knew any of this. I mean I never thought you were the virgin type, I knew you'd been around – haven't we all. But this . . . Jesus!'

'It's funny, y'know talking about it and all, it seems so remote. Like half the things happened to someone else. I can't really believe I did all those things, screwed all those men. I can't believe it was me. And now this sonofabitch wants me to go through it all again. He'll make me a star but I'll be his paid whore.'

'I'll help you,' said Linda quickly. 'I'll take the pictures. But you haven't thought it out clearly. If you're in the pictures with him he can turn the whole thing around. *You* can't be in the photos, we'll have to hire a professional.'

'He won't go for that.'

Linda lit a cigarette. 'He will if you're in it too. We'll get hold of a black girl – someone that will remind him of Bobbie. You'll be there – involved, but I'll make sure the only photos I get are with him and the other girl.'

'It's a marvellous idea. But I am not exactly in a position to come up with a black hooker between now and tomorrow night.'

Linda frowned. 'LA must be crawling with them. Bernie might be able to help out there – he knows everyone.'

'But you promised not to tell anyone.'

'Of course not. Is asking him for a girl telling him anything? I'll make up some story, I'll have to for Paul anyway – he is not going to be thrilled to discover I'm off to LA for the day.'

'Listen,' said Dallas seriously, 'anytime, anything. One of these days I hope I can pay you back.'

Linda laughed. 'Wait until the job is done before you

thank me. It won't be *that* easy – but with a little luck we'll make it. Now come on, let's take ourselves over to Paul's suite – they should be back soon, and I'll give him the news of my impending absence. Probably do him good – maybe he'll miss me. Only maybe mind you – but it's a chance!'

☆

Paul persuaded Al to do the show. He finished the bottle of scotch, reeled on stage, and the audience screamed. He did a lousy show but the only person who knew about it was him. The screaming never let up for a minute, so who could possibly hear that his voice was slurred and not up to par. He even inserted the word fuck in place of love on several occasions, and no one was any the wiser.

'Morons!' he mumbled as he was bundled into his car and sped back to his hotel. He wanted to party, but passed out instead, and Paul left him on his bed with Luke watching over him and strict instructions to contact him when he awoke.

It was time to forget about their fight, Paul decided. He had not realized that Al was heading into one of his states, he had thought he was flying high. Thank God he hadn't left the tour in a fit of ego. Al really needed him, and he would be there.

When Linda told him that she had to go to Los Angeles for a couple of days with Dallas he didn't mind a bit. It was a relief in fact, giving him absolute free time with Al – a fact that Linda would have bitched about.

Linda noticed his attitude, and she smiled coldly saying, 'It might even be longer than a couple of days.'

'Take as long as you need,' Paul replied absently.

Sonofabitch. What did he care? If only she could summon the strength she wouldn't come back at all.

☆

They arrived in Los Angeles early the next morning and drove straight to the house. Linda prowled around inspecting the facilities she would have for her photography.

Bernie had come up with the phone number of a black call girl. As Linda had thought, he had a special little book with a listing for every preference. His eyes had bugged out as to *why* Linda wanted the number of a black hooker in LA. But she had just smiled and said, 'Everyone to their own, Bernie sweetheart,' and left it at that.

The girl – exotically entitled Diamond, answered the phone on the second ring in a lazy Southern drawl. Linda said they had a proposition, and could they talk. Diamond agreed, noted the address, and said she would be with them in an hour.

She turned up two hours later, a dazzlingly pretty girl in her early twenties with an abundance of long black hair and a Diana Ross smile. Her only problem appeared to be short legs and a dropped ass. Apart from that she was a knockout.

Linda fed her some story about a married man whose wife needed pictures of him in action.

Just as Diamond was objecting, Linda mentioned a fee of five hundred dollars, and the deal was clinched.

Diamond left in a cloud of Hermès perfume promising to return later.

'We're all set,' Linda announced, 'do you think you had better call old Lew and make sure he'll be here?'

'He'll be here,' said Dallas bitterly. 'I just hope I can go through with it.'

'Come on!' chided Linda, 'just think of the outcome … Think of the time when *you* can screw him.'

'Yes,' agreed Dallas, 'I can just imagine his face when I show him the photos. It would never occur to him that I'd have the brains to work this out. He thinks I fucked my brains out when I was a working girl.'

'Listen, kid, I hate to say it, but they all credit women with minimal thinking capacity. Hey – you know what I think? I think a few drinks around here would not go amiss. And how about a little grass – you got any?'

'In a red box under the fridge. Linda, isn't it ridiculous – I'm nervous.'

Linda smiled. 'Aren't we all? But forget about it, relax. Tonight we're going to win for a change, I just know it.'

☆

30

Al awoke with one of the worst hangovers he could remember. His head pounded in a series of drumbeats, his eyes hurt, even his teeth ached.

He tried to remember ... Jesus, the show. What had happened with the show? Had he appeared? He honestly couldn't remember.

He lay very still, trying to ignore the fact that he had to piss, trying to concentrate.

He remembered going to some lousy afternoon party. Some gathering full of snobbish English exiles. Miami-based chinless wonders. Tinkly-voiced, horse-faced girls who regarded him as some kind of freak. It had somehow brought back every bad memory of the days before the fame.

He had left the party abruptly and gone to a whore-house. The man least likely to have to pay for it had selected a jolly little Cuban girl, and spent three hours getting boozed in her pathetic little room.

He hadn't screwed her, merely humiliated her. And after, he felt like a real shit, and had continued on his drinking jag all the way to the concert.

He remembered vaguely Evan joining him somewhere along the way. And Bernie, and Paul arguing with him. But had he gone on? He truly couldn't remember.

The desire to piss was too strong to resist, and by the time he came out of the bathroom Paul was sitting on his bed. They regarded each other warily. Neither quite sure what terms they were on.

'Fuck the push-ups this morning,' mumbled Al, 'What I really need is a couple of gallons of orange juice and a new head.'

Paul picked up the phone and requested a jug of fresh orange juice from room service. 'Food?' he questioned.

Al made a face.

'So,' said Paul, hanging up, 'what's the problem?'

'No problem. Just felt like cutting loose.'

Luke had filled Paul in on Al's activities of the previous day. 'What made you go to that party?'

'What did you want me to do? Sit here and play footsie

with Evan? You'd all pissed off – I couldn't even find Bernie.'
He hesitated. 'How did the show go?'

'You staggered around a lot. Insulted the crowd. Fortunately there was so much screaming you could have stripped off and sung Bollocks and no one would have noticed. At least we got you on.'

'Where's Evan?'

'I sent him down to the coffee shop.'

Al held his head. 'The kid is driving me nuts, gotta get him off my back. Gotta send him home. *You'll* have to tell him, *I* can't.'

'Thanks a lot. The boy idolizes you. If you send him home it's going to be an A one rejection – he'll become even worse. I think you should give him another chance.'

'Another chance at what? He won't drink, smoke, or screw. Watches me like a hawk – I can't take it, makes me nervous.'

Paul opened the door for room service, and poured Al a hefty glass of orange juice. 'Just leave him alone. Stop worrying about him. First of all it's wrong to have him in your suite – we'll get him his own room in future. Don't have him follow you everywhere – let him make his own friends.'

'I wish he would.'

'Leave him alone and he will. I'll have Linda take a friendly interest in him when she gets back.'

'Where's she gone?'

'To Los Angeles with Dallas – she has some problem – Linda's helping out.'

Al's interest perked. 'What problem?'

Paul shrugged. 'Don't know. Dallas flew in, grabbed a hold of Linda, and they flew off this morning. I think that . . .'

'Dallas was here?'

'Last night.'

'Why didn't you tell me?'

'I just did.'

'That's great, isn't it. He tells me when she's gone.'

'*You* were gone last night. You were lucky to do the show. You were . . .'

'Do me a favour, Paul. Piss off. Your voice is pounding into my head and I can't take any more.'

'Sure. Plane leaves in two hours. Press reception and

television interview arranged to take place at O'Hara Airport upon arrival. Kup show to be recorded this afternoon. Party in your honour tonight at the Macho Mansion.'

Al groaned. 'If I'm not dead by that time . . .'

Paul smiled thinly. There had been two calls that there was a bomb secreted on Al's plane, and at this very moment the plane was being thoroughly searched. 'You'll make it.'

Al grinned. 'Sure I will. Sauna. Massage. Stomach pump. By the way – you got a phone number for Linda?'

'I didn't know you cared.'

'I do. She's lovely but taken. Do you mind if I phone Dallas?'

Paul wrote a number on a piece of paper. 'Be my guest.'

After Paul left, Al felt relief. Things were back to normal between them. It made him feel a lot better. God almighty, if Paul couldn't understand his moods by now . . .

He poured himself some more orange juice, gulped down several Bufferin. Forced himself to take a cold shower, then decided he couldn't miss doing his push-ups and got through half of them before collapsing.

Only then did he pick up the telephone and ask for the number Paul had given him. He didn't know what he was going to say if Dallas answered, but he wanted to talk to her, just say hello again. Of course she would have to fly into Miami the night he was pissed out of his mind. It seemed to be fate that they kept on missing each other.

The operator told him to hold on. He waited impatiently and was surprised at how disappointed he was when he was informed that the number did not answer.

Shit! What *was* it about Dallas?

He folded the piece of paper with the number on it and put it carefully into his pocket. Later, he would call again later.

☆

Edna King peered at herself in the bathroom mirror. Melanie had persuaded her to have her hair cut. She had dragged her to a place called Mr Capones, and a tall, thin, leering Italian had chopped off her shoulder-length mouse, and she had emerged with short blonde curls.

Reluctantly she did have to admit it looked better.

Although what Al would say she didn't know. He would probably be furious. He was always telling her he liked her just the way she was – well, that was what he used to tell her. He hadn't told her much of anything in the more recent times they had spent together.

She stood up and admired her new svelte figure. Thanks to Melanie watching her like a hawk she had lost ten pounds. And her make-up was much better since Melanie had taken her to that place where they had taught her to apply things in a more subtle fashion. But what would Al say when he found out how much she had spent on a whole new wardrobe of clothes? He would be furious. 'Don't be silly,' Melanie had argued, 'he spends more on clothes in a month than you have in your entire married life.' That *was* true, but still, *he* was the star of the family.

Edna smiled at herself tentatively in the mirror. Melanie has persuaded her to go to the dentist and have her crooked front tooth capped. It still surprised her to smile and see the difference.

She sighed. She just hoped that Al wouldn't be too angry.

Melanie had laughed at her fears. 'You look wonderful. Younger, prettier, smarter. Al will be knocked out, just you wait and see.'

And it wouldn't be that long to wait. Melanie had booked the tickets already which would fly them both to America on a surprise visit.

Edna rubbed nervously at her subtle brown eye-shadow, blending it in even more. At least Melanie was right about one thing, she did look much better, whether Al approved or not.

☆

Macho was the giant success men's magazine of the seventies. What *Playboy* had been to the sixties, and *Penthouse* to the early seventies, *Macho* was now. Its enormous sales left all its rivals trailing in its wake. The appeal of the magazine was that it had something for everyone. Month after month it featured beautiful, nearly naked, very famous ladies. Nude men with vibrant hard-ons. Unknown Nymphets indulging in near porn. Incredibly elegant fashion lay-outs. A very comprehensive Arts section. Political writers of great esteem.

In fact it was the cream of all the top magazines combined into one.

Van Valda, owner, founder, and editor supreme, had set himself up in a Chicago mansion bigger even than Hefner's former palace. He lived there in splendid isolation surrounded by an ever-changing procession of Nymphets.

To be a Nymphet you had to be between fifteen and seventeen, very pretty, and quite dumb. Any job which phased you out at eighteen did not appeal to intelligent girls.

At the Macho Mansion a huge party was being prepared for Al King, and his reputation had preceded him. Nymphets fluttered back and forth squealing with joy. It wasn't often that a true life superstud honoured them with his presence. Usually they had to make do with Van – who couldn't get it up. Or visiting important men who could only just get it up.

'I wonder if he's as sexy as he sounds,' breathed one pink and white fifteen-year-old.

'Better!' assured a more sophisticated sixteen-year-old. 'I know a girl who knows a girl whose sister has had him! She says . . .'

Hot little rumours flitted back and forth all day. And six baby Nymphets crowded onto Van's giant bed to watch Al's arrival on Van's giant-sized television screen.

Van smiled paternally. He was a thin, undistinguished-looking man of forty, whose one desire in life had been to make a lot of money, and surround himself with beautiful and sexy females. The money part had gone without a hitch, but somewhere along the way his hard-on had vanished, and for two years he had been painfully impotent. Painfully, because the desire was still there, but the implement was not.

He fondled a gorgeous little thing's right breast, always hopeful. She smiled and encouraged him. He put his hand down the pants of another girl, and she wriggled around.

He stopped both activities. He would sooner watch one of his famous porno home movies. Maybe Al would be interested in seeing one later. He could run the Ramo Kaliffe, always good for a laugh.

'What time will he be here, daddy?' burbled a sweet little redhead. 'Will he fuck us? Will he fuck all of us? Wouldn't that be fun, girls, wouldn't that be really boss?'

They all squealed their agreement.

Van climbed off the bed. Better get his equipment together, this was one movie he didn't want to miss.

☆

Mob scenes at the airport heralded Al's arrival. He stepped from his plane, impeccable and sexual in an all-black outfit. He made a boxer's salute at his fans, smiled for the cameras. Behind him Paul marvelled at his tenacity. A few hours before he had been a complete wreck, now he was like a new man.

He handled his press conference beautifully. He combined just the right amount of aggressiveness with a humorous charm, and the ladies and gentlemen of the press loved it, especially the ladies.

Bernie hovered protectively, ready to combat any difficult questions. But they didn't come, and everything went off smoothly.

Paul noticed Evan scowling in a corner, and he went over to him. 'How's it going? Enjoying yourself?'

Evan shrugged and mumbled, 'S' all right.'

Paul felt guilty that he had paid hardly any attention to his nephew. But he didn't want him finding out about his relationship with Linda. Evan would tell Edna. Edna would tell Melanie. Melanie would go raving mad.

'Spoken to your mum?' Paul inquired.

'Yes,' muttered Evan.

'Everything OK at home?'

'Yes.'

A great conversationalist Evan was not.

'I suppose you miss home.'

'No, I don't miss it. Don't miss anything.'

'Yes ... Well ...' Paul was lost for words. No wonder Evan was driving Al mad. Maybe the best idea was to pack him off home.

Evan watched his uncle walk away. He must think he was stupid or something. Ignoring him all the time, and now suddenly finding the time to speak to him only because that woman had gone away. Through the glass windows he could see 'The Promises' being ushered into a limousine. A trail of photographers had followed them; he was glad they hadn't *all* stayed with his stupid father. Tonight he would talk to

Nellie. He would say something, anything, he had made up his mind. He would wear his new jeans suit, wash his hair, use some of his father's make-up to cover his spots. He would do it. Definitely. She had looked at him on the plane today, really stared. He had been surprised that Al hadn't noticed, he had been sitting right next to him. But of course his father never noticed anything about him. Why should he? The only important thing in *his* life was himself.

The press conference was over and everyone was walking out to the cars. Evan trailed behind. If he stayed far enough behind he would be put in the car *after* Al. He had learned *that* little trick in Miami. Who wanted to travel with the star? People peering in the car and making remarks. Ugh!

Paul was beckoning to him but he pretended not to see. It was easy when you knew how. Head down, shuffle a lot, play deaf.

When he looked up, the car with Al in had gone.

At the hotel there was a long handwritten letter waiting for Al from Van Valda. It welcomed him to the city, wished him every success on his tour, gave him an enthusiastic rundown of the party in his honour, and insisted most profusely that Al check out of his hotel immediately and move into the Macho Mansion. In a childish scrawl Van had written:

> There is plenty of room for you and whoever you care to bring. We are at your service – I have a cook on duty twenty-four hours – a choice of over a thousand movies to run at any time – and any other kind of entertainment you desire. We do hope to welcome you as more than just a party guest.
> Sincere regards,
>   Van

'Sounds good,' commented Al. 'Why aren't we staying there?'

If you remember,' replied Paul, 'Bernie checked it out with you in New York and you said no way. You agreed to the party but that was it.'

'Yeah – I think it's coming back to me. Wants me to do a naughty picture for his rag.'

'Right on. They were willing to pay whatever you wanted.'

Al laughed, 'Sure! Me, a hard-on, a suntan and a caption saying King Cock!'

Paul joined him in his laughter. 'They have been after you or Warren Beatty since the magazine started.'

'So let them get Warren.'

'You're kidding. If they are lucky they'll end up with Woody Allen. I hear rumours that his price is a million and a false nose!'

They both fell about laughing.

Later Al was driven over to the television studios and recorded the Irv Kupcinet show. He had done the show before on a previous American trip, and Irv was the perfect host. It all went very well.

By the time it was over Al was tired and half contemplated cancelling going to the party. But as it was in his honour he could hardly do that. So he went back to the hotel, changed, killed half a bottle of champagne, and set off with Paul, Bernie, Evan, and 'The Promises' for the Macho Mansion.

Another evening of fun.

He could have done without it.

31

Nervous as she was, Dallas managed to greet Lew Margolis with a dazzling smile. She looked incredible in a black halter top and long silky trousers.

Linda and Diamond were safely out of sight. Stevie Wonder played softly on the stereo. The champagne was open and waiting.

Lew seemed delighted by the entire set-up.

'Nice little place,' he murmured, 'private. Cosy, nice. No – I don't want any champagne – get me a Perrier water.'

'Don't you drink?' asked Dallas.

'Bad for me.'

'Oh come on, one glass won't hurt you.' She thrust a glass at him, and was relieved to see him sip at it.

He consulted his watch. 'I can only stay an hour,' he warned.

'I've got a surprise for you.'

He narrowed his eyes. 'I don't like surprises.'

She smiled, 'You'll like this one.'

'I don't like *any* surprises. Get your clothes off.'

'My clothes off? I thought you wanted to play games, I thought we were going to play swimming instructors.'

Lew scratched his head. 'I don't know. I don't think I need to.'

'Don't need to what?'

'Play games.' He laughed, pleased with himself. 'This could be game enough, just having you and knowing what I know.'

Dallas forced the smile to stay on her face. What a pig!

'Let's go out to the pool,' she suggested, 'it's such a beautiful night. I have such beautiful plans.'

'I've been looking for a cunt like you,' Lew sneered harshly. 'Good-looking, ambitious, ready to do anything. You will do anything for me, won't you? Christ! I can get it up just talking to you. You know what that means?'

She took him gently by the arm and guided him out to the pool.

Reclining on the diving board totally naked, apart from silver sequins decorating her nipples, was Diamond.

Dallas thought how gorgeous the girl looked. When she was lying down you didn't even notice the short legs or dropped ass. And she had big rounded breasts which were emphasized by the decorative sequins.

Diamond propped herself up on one elbow. 'Mr M,' she trilled, 'how good to see you again. How really exciting. Why don't you just come on over here and play with my hot little pussy while your lady wife goes and prepares herself for her swimming lesson.'

Lew turned to Dallas. 'Surprise!' she said, giving him a little push in Diamond's direction. 'Go and have fun, I'll be with you in a minute.'

Lew didn't argue. The sight of Diamond was too appealing, and anyway he probably thought that Diamond was Bobbie, and that they were reliving old times. Even if he realized that they were different girls he would just think that Dallas had tried to recreate a scene that he had obviously enjoyed.

With a sigh of relief Dallas watched him limp off towards Diamond. Then she hurried into the house and alerted Linda.

She drew the drapes halfway across the huge glass windows, turned the lights off.

Linda knelt down with her cameras. 'If he looks straight through the window he'll see me,' she warned.

'I know, I know. Don't worry, we'll keep him much too busy to notice.' As Dallas spoke she slid out of her trousers and top. Underneath she wore the briefest of bikinis. She gulped quickly from the champagne glass. Oh God! This was the moment she had been dreading. Taking a deep breath and holding her head high, she went back outside.

☆

Dinner at his mother's house was the usual bringdown. She was a nice old lady but she nagged the shit out of him.

When was he going to get married? Buy a new car? A house? Have children? Go to the dentist? *Stop* going to the analyst?

Cody pulled his car up at a stop light, glanced at a girl in the neighbouring Pontiac. He thought she smiled at him, but she had driven off before he could definitely decide. He felt depressed, although for the life of him he couldn't understand why. He was on the threshold of having everything go the way he had planned it would. He was on the brink of recognition and success. People who had formerly ignored him on the street would now start accepting his phone calls.

Hollywood. What a town. You could live and work there all your life as he had done, and unless you made waves nobody knew that you even existed.

He was about to make waves. Big ones.

He was the man that had discovered Dallas.

He was the man who had negotiated her a million dollar contract. And soon the whole town would know about it, and schmucky little nothing agent Cody Hills would suddenly be a big man. An in-demand man. The personal manager and agent they would all want.

In short, he would be hot.

Of course he had planned the way things would be. And when Dallas had first arrived in Hollywood to do the screen test he had known that somehow she was going to be his big chance. He saw in the wild-haired, sensuous girl more than just a great body. He sensed the smell of stardom. Sure the test stunk. Why not? The cameraman should have been retired, the director was someone in authority's brother, and the actor they tested her with was a fag. Testing beauty queens was a routine job that talented people wouldn't touch.

Cody always made it his business to be around when they were shooting those tests. You never knew when someone would come along. Someone special. Someone like Dallas.

He had watched her, and waited patiently for an opportunity to use her. 'Man Made Woman' turned out to be just such an opportunity. The girl they had originally signed had been big, blonde and beautiful. Too big, too blonde, and with a deep husky voice that didn't quite match.

Cody had done some private investigation, and come up with facts that surprised even him. He knew that when the truth was revealed no way could the studio use her.

But he took his time. First he wired Dallas, and when she called him and was already in Los Angeles he was delighted. He quit his job at the agency – they had never appreciated him but they soon would. And he concentrated all his efforts on getting Dallas the job. He never wavered. He named the terms he wanted for her, and would not budge. Sharp instinct told him the terms would be met. They were.

Everything had gone according to plan. Well almost everything.

He pulled into a gas station and stared morosely out of the window. What he hadn't planned on. What had come as a complete shock – was the fact that he had fallen – corny as it was – yes, fallen straight in the deep end love with his client. How un-smart could you get? Cody Hills caught in a trap he had so deftly always managed to avoid.

Living in Hollywood, being an agent – successful or not, being a male, meant there was *never* a shortage of female company.

He had had girls. Oh, had he had girls!

Irene, short and dark, who used to knit him socks and try out the Kama Sutra with him.

Evelyn, who shared a mutual difficult relationship with her mother.

Connie, who shared his analyst.

None of them beauties, true. But they were warm and female and loving.

'You are not Paul Newman,' his mother had announced to him recently, a slight note of surprise in her voice as if secretly she had half expected he was. 'You'll soon be thirty. What about marriage?' She made it sound like an offer! Marriage did not feature in his future plans. Irene, Evelyn, Connie, they would all make wonderful wives for someone. But not him, no way him.

So where did that leave Dallas? Right up front, that's where. But God! A woman like her. It would be an insult to even approach her in the way he wanted to. And of course she was the gateway to the main chance, and he couldn't even think of jeopardizing their business relationship.

But it was not going to be easy. Oh God, no.

She had gone away for one day and he was a seething mass of nerves. Where was she? Who was she with?

She had phoned him from New York she said, but when he checked with the operator he had found the call had come from Miami. Why was she lying to him? Well, why not, she probably had a boyfriend that she didn't want him to know about.

Miserably Cody paid for the gas, consulted his watch. It was only nine o'clock, too early to go home, too late to call Irene, Evelyn, or Connie.

What he would do, he decided, was drive up to Dallas' house, check it out, see everything was all right.

Good idea. He switched on the car radio and set off down Sunset.

☆

Linda glanced at her watch. It was exactly nine o'clock. She was dying for a cigarette, but there was no time for such luxuries. Quickly she changed the film in her camera. It was difficult in the dark but she managed it without too much trouble.

Training her telephoto lens to the window once more she was able to immediately catch another revealing shot of Diamond and Lew Margolis. He was enjoying himself now, clad only in his sports shirt and socks.

Dallas stood back from the couple, still wearing her bikini. Ingeniously she had thought of a ruse which had been successful in making her a non-participant. Allowing

Diamond and Lew time alone together at the beginning had sharpened his interest in the black girl. When Dallas had emerged in her bikini she had become very businesslike.

'My swimming lesson,' she told Lew firmly, 'and keep your hands to yourself.'

That had surprised him, and when his hands had started to try and remove her bikini she had immediately rebuked him.

'I'm *Mrs* M.,' she told him witheringly, '*The* Mrs M. And I don't like strange men trying to touch me. Only my husband can touch me. Understand?'

Diamond had been right there to comfort him. 'Poor baby, poor little swimming instructor. Don't want to mess with those *married* bitches, they only mean trouble. Come teach me how to crawl, babe!'

Lew loved the game. He loved doing things to Diamond whilst Dallas watched. It was almost as good as if the *real* Mrs Margolis was there. Miss Prissy Lips. Miss No Fuck Your Husband but screw everything else in sight.

He smiled as he reached his finale in Diamond's mouth. Linda captured it all.

☆

As Cody approached the house he was surprised to see several cars parked outside. He was even more surprised when he realized that one of them was Dallas'. For a moment he couldn't quite collect his thoughts. She had gone away, taken her car to the airport, phoned him to inform him that she would not be back until the following morning. Well, she was back all right.

He didn't turn into the drive. He parked his car on the roadway and walked by foot towards the house.

He didn't mean to spy on her. He had no intention of sneaking around. But why hadn't she let him know she was coming back sooner than expected? And who the hell did the other two cars belong to?

His better judgement told him to get in his car and go on home. Dallas was a free agent, she could do what she wanted. She didn't have to check with him every time she sneezed.

But he couldn't do that. He was burning with curiosity about who she was entertaining.

He contemplated marching straight up to the front door, ringing the bell, and, when she answered, saying: 'Surprise, surprise – just happened to be passing and saw the lights.' But then he realized that there were no lights on, and anyhow he couldn't possibly be just passing when she lived at the top of a hill.

He could hear music coming from around the back, the swimming pool area. Slowly he edged through the bushes, hating himself, but determined to see who she was entertaining.

The tableau that greeted his eyes was not what he had expected. Dallas standing, arms akimbo, clad in the briefest bikini, watching a couple on the diving board making the most intimate form of love.

Slowly Cody backed away. His head was churning with mixed emotions. Was that how the love of his life got her kicks? Watching other people? Or maybe things were just beginning. Maybe later she would become a participant . . .

He felt more depressed than ever. Christ! This was the girl he was risking his future on. A deviate. A voyeur.

Jesus! What if the studio ever found out?

☆

Coldly Dallas watched Lew Margolis struggle back into his clothes. He was hurrying, obviously late for some event.

Diamond had discreetly vanished.

'Not bad,' Lew remarked expansively, 'but you missed out. Next time I'll spend more time, service both of you, wouldn't want you going to bed with a twitchy cunt!' He laughed happily at his own humour. 'Next week. I'll let you know what night.'

'Yes,' murmured Dallas. She just wanted him out of her house as quickly as possible.

'I think . . .' he began. But the ringing of the telephone cut him off.

Dallas stared at the phone. She couldn't answer it. It might be Cody, and she had told him that she wouldn't be back until the following morning.

Lew waited expectantly.

The phone rang insistently.

'Aren't you going to answer it?' growled Lew.

Dallas shook her head.

'Why not?' he wanted to know. 'Boyfriend checking up on you?'

She shrugged.

'Answer it,' Lew commanded. 'Answer it and talk dirty to your boyfriend. I got a few minutes.'

She snatched the phone off its cradle, 'Yes?'

From far away in Chicago, Al King said, 'Hey, beautiful, this is Al. How come you and I are always just missing each other?'

'I can't talk now,' Dallas snapped, and she slammed the phone down.

Lew belched: 'You've got to learn to do what I say.'

'Next time,' she replied tightly.

Lew withdrew a stack of notes from his jacket, looked at them reflectively and then stuffed them back in his pocket. 'I almost forgot. Don't have to pay for the services any more.' He laughed again, squeezed her right breast harder than was necessary, and finally left.

She listened to his car draw away. Bastard! What a bastard! He thought he had her good and tied up. Well, she would show him.

Linda was in the kitchen.

'What do you think? Dallas asked breathlessly.

'I think he's a dirty old man,' commented Linda. 'I'm shocked! I didn't know such things went on outside of magazines and movies.'

'Did you get what we wanted?'

'He got what *he* wanted. And that girl – wow – that's what I call a professional. She handled him like a fish!'

'Linda . . .'

'Yes, I think we got exactly what we wanted. Of course can't really tell until I develop them, but I think we are in business.' Diamond appeared, fully dressed and groomed. She smiled. 'Everything cool?'

'You were wonderful, and thank you,' said Dallas.

'Old guys are so pliable,' remarked Diamond, still smiling, 'you wouldn't think they've been screwing all their lives, they're just like little children. I got two regular clients – I think one must be eighty – why he's like a naughty *schoolboy*.'

'Do you enjoy your work?' ventured Linda.

Diamond shrugged. 'What's not to enjoy. I don't work myself too hard. I got my own apartment, car, plenty of clothes. And a stud whose looks would blow your brains!'

'Doesn't he mind?' asked Linda, unable to understand how such a great-looking girl could sell her body for money.

'Mind?' laughed Diamond. 'Honey, he is in the same business. And if ever either of you two ladies are in the market for a great big beautiful screw – well, I can recommend my guy. He is the *best*!'

'Oh,' said Linda, suddenly embarrassed, 'well I don't think that . . .'

'Don't knock it,' interrupted Diamond, 'the long cold night may come when you had a fight with your husband, fella, whatever. Well y'all might feel a little horny. Now you don't want to go cruisin' for some stud who'll just as soon as give you a social disease. What you'll need is a few hours of my man. He is pure funk. You can't go wrong.'

'Don't you get jealous?' enquired Linda, intrigued about the whole situation.

'What's jealous?' laughed Diamond, 'I still get my piece of the action.'

Dallas finished counting out the five hundred dollars and handed it to Diamond. She wished that she had looked on the hooking profession in the same easy-going fashion that Diamond appeared to. But every memory she had of it was bad. Being used, like a commodity. Ugh! She shuddered.

Diamond left, and Linda got down to work. She converted the kitchen into a dark-room and got right into developing the rolls of film.

It wasn't until the images of Lew Margolis and the black girl started to take shape that Dallas suddenly remembered about Al King phoning. Linda was busy pinning the pictures up to dry when Dallas told her about it. 'What do you think he wanted?'

Linda stood back to survey her work. 'Your body, I expect, he's always had a yen for you. Wow – I think I could get a job with *Macho* any day – just look at these shots!'

'Just what I needed. Linda, you're a genius!'

'Tell it to Paul, if he doesn't get our act together soon I might just be tempted by the thought of Diamond's big beautiful boyfriend!'

'I'll tell him, I'll tell him.'

Linda inspected another picture fresh from the solution. 'Dallas, babe, I think you and I are in the blackmail business!'

32

Van Valda had assembled a cast of stars. Anyone who was a harassed personality and who happened to be in Chicago was invited to the party to honour Al King.

There was a brilliant but drunken writer who weaved about insulting everyone. There was an elfin-faced movie star recently featured naked between the pages of *Macho*. There was a socialite lady of chiselled beauty who trailed an outrageous fag gossip columnist. There was Marjorie Carter, in town to do a taped interview with Van Valda, and she froze Al with a look. There was a male movie star with bedroom eyes and a pocketful of cocaine that he was being more than generous with.

And amongst this group of luminaries frisked at least twenty special hand-picked Nymphets.

They all wore the same uniform, which consisted of crotch-hugging hip shorts and minuscule fluffy sweaters, short enough to show off plenty of tummy, and if the arms were stretched up, the underside of bouncy baby bosoms.

Some of the ground rules for being a Nymphet contained the riveting information that no panties or bras were to be worn at any time, and that a Nymphet's bust measurement must be no less than 34 (C cup) or more than 36 (B cup).

Van Valda had laid down the rules himself.

Nymphet of the month was a freckle-faced redhead named Laurie-Poo, who because of her position was allowed first crack at Al. She sprang to his side the moment he arrived, announcing coyly, 'I am your Nymphet for the night, my name is Laurie-Poo, and anything you want you just have to ask me. Any thing,' she added, in case he was too thick to get her point. 'Now what can I get you to drink, Mr King, sir?'

'Rustle up some champagne, sweetheart.' He looked around and made a face at Paul.

Then Van Valda came strolling over clad in a silken Kung-

Fu jacket and velvet trousers. Van extended a firm masculine handshake, nodded at Paul, and confided, 'I can have any woman in this room, so can you, Al, so can you. I don't expect there are many men who can say that.' He puffed proudly on a phallic-looking pipe.

'Henry Kissinger,' suggested Al drily.

Van chose to ignore that remark. 'Glad you could make it,' he said, 'the Macho Mansion is at your disposal. Anything you want is yours,' he paused, then added meaningfully, 'anything.'

'I'm getting the message,' replied Al pleasantly, 'but right now all I want is a drink.'

Van looked outraged. 'You don't have a drink yet?' He hooked his fingers into the shorts of a passing Nymphet, 'Mr King doesn't have a drink yet,' he said sternly.

'Oh dear!' she cooed.

'We only just got here,' remarked Paul.

At that moment Laurie-Poo returned balancing a tray professionally on one hand. It was loaded with full glasses of champagne, and little dishes filled with Polynesian titbits. She placed the tray on a table, a glass of champagne into Al's hand, and a fried shrimp into his mouth.

Van nodded his approval. Al nearly choked.

Across the room, marooned by the door, Evan stared around in amazement. He had never seen anything like it. Is this how people really lived? The Macho Mansion was an incredible place, and Evan felt awed that he had been allowed in. Perhaps there *were* some good points to being Al King's son after all.

He stood at the door to a huge luxurious living room. A Macho fantasy room filled with chocolate leather couches, chrome and marble tables, marvellous quadrophonic sound equipment issuing forth the voice of Al King, giant television screens on every wall with headphones for any guest who did not wish to miss their favourite programme.

In the middle of all this luxury was a sunken bar, set firmly in the centre of a miniature lake. Nymphets tripped lightly back and forth across a small bamboo bridge, holding aloft loaded trays.

Evan could recognize at least two movie stars. His mouth dropped open at the daring outfit of the female one. Why, her breasts were completely visible through some type of gauzy top. He stared, completely mesmerized.

'Hey – close your mouth – somethin's gonna fly right in!' It was Nellie by his side. She giggled. 'Some set-up huh?'

'Yes,' croaked Evan, overwhelmed at her sudden attention.

'So how ya doin'? Havin' all sorts of fun?'

He looked around quickly to make sure she was talking to him. She was.

'It's not bad,' he managed.

'Yeah,' she agreed, 'know what you mean. I guess you must feel the strain too. I mean being with Al all the time – I guess he's not that easy to be with – kinda tied up in knots, tense, never sure of what he wants.'

Evan was not quite sure how they had arrived at discussing Al, but anything was all right as long as she stayed next to him.

She looked particularly pretty in a yellow boiler suit which emphasized her delicious dark skin.

'Have you been here before?' he ventured.

'Where? Chicago?'

He nodded.

'Oh sure, bin through every crummy joint in the town. Never rated an invite *here* before. It's kinda unreal, like one of those men's magazine lay-outs.' She tossed her long black hair back. 'Believe me, *I* understand the pressures Al has to go through. You can tell him that from me, tell him Nellie says she understands. Right?'

Evan sensed that she was about to move off. He gripped her by the arm and blurted out quickly, 'You're the prettiest girl here.'

She giggled, surprised. 'Why thank you – I never knew you cared!' Then seriously she added, 'Don't forget to give Al my message.' And she was gone, plunging into the centre of the room, immediately surrounded by an admiring group of men.

☆

Al found the whole scene oppressive. He did not care for Van Valda, a boring man who puffed smugly on his pipe and groped every female who came within range. He did not care for the other guests, mostly hangers-on who grouped around the celebrities and told them how wonderful their last book/film/record/concert was. Their conversations were interchangeable.

The whole party was bullshit.

He couldn't even fancy the plastic baby Nymphets. Especially not the one who had attached herself to him like glue.

Looking around he suddenly thought of Dallas, and of how she would stand out in this crowd. A real woman. The best-looking woman he had ever seen.

And why hadn't he had her by now? Where was the King magic? A little persuasion and she could be his.

He reached in his pocket, found the bit of paper with her number on, and instructed Laurie-Poo to take him to a private phone.

She led him into an office of which one entire wall was an aquarium. She waited expectantly.

'Get lost,' he told her, 'I don't need my hand held for a phone call.'

'I'll wait outside,' she stated primly.

He gave the operator the number he required in Los Angeles, and leaned back in the plush leather swivel chair. He smiled as he listened to the phone ringing, planning what he would say Nothing heavy. Just some light conversation, and then casually he would suggest she catch the show, he could send the plane for her.

She picked up the phone, her voice brusque.

'Hey, beautiful,' began Al easily, 'this is Al. How come you and I are always just missing each other?'

'I can't talk now,' she snapped, and bang, his connection went dead.

For a moment he was stunned, hurt. Then anger took over. She had hung up on him. The bitch had put the phone down! He couldn't believe it! It had never happened to him before. Who the hell did she think she was? So she was beautiful, big fuckin' deal. Hundreds of girls were beautiful. Bitch! Bitch! She was under his skin. She was getting to him. Women were not supposed to get to you. Women were supposed to be ready, available and accommodating.

Angrily he got up, marched out of the room, brushed past Laurie-Poo. He found the movie star with the cocaine and indulged himself generously. Then he noticed Evan, still huddled ignored by the door. He turned, located Laurie-Poo right behind him, and whispered in her ear.

She listened, disappointment suffusing her chubby features. Then she set off in Evan's direction.

Van Valda was at his elbow. 'Everything all right, Al? Feel like a private party?'

Al followed Van and a select group out of the living room and into a private elevator. Apart from himself there were the two movie stars, male and female, and the drunken writer. The female movie star trailed her fingers lightly over his fly. Her elfin face glowed. She attended to Van in the same way.

The elevator took them directly into Van's bedroom. The room appeared to be all bed and mirrors and video screens. The carpet was thick fur.

The female movie star flung off her clothes, such as they were, and collapsed, spread-eagled, on the fur carpet.

Male movie star immediately started to service her with his tongue.

Discreetly Van set his hidden cameras in motion. This would certainly be a good one for the library. He then sprung a switch, and photographs of six different girls leaped onto the screens.

'Choose whichever you want,' he suggested blandly.

'Give me the little Chicano,' moaned the female movie star, 'is she as talented as she looks?'

'More so,' replied Van smugly.

Al studied the photos. Two busty blondes, a black girl, the Chicano, an ugly redhead with giant knockers, and a delicate Chinese.

'I'll take the redhead,' Al said. 'Are they real?'

'Of course they are,' replied Van, offended.

The writer rubbed himself reflectively. 'Bring them all in,' he mumbled, 'I can't choose.'

Van smiled. This was going better than he had expected. He pressed a series of buttons, and within seconds the girls came filing in.

The redhead went straight to Al. She was very tall, perhaps six foot in the black ankle-strap shoes she wore with black stockings and an old-fashioned suspender belt. Van had found from experience that men over thirty-five were distinctly turned on by stockings and suspenders. And as most of his famous guests were in that age group he always made sure that at least two of the available girls wore them. Tonight it was the redhead and the Chicano.

The redhead was quite thin. A fact which accentuated the enormous boobs which sprung forth from her body like two particularly lethal weapons. Apart from the shoes, stockings, and suspenders, she wore an open-nipple bra of black fur.

At the sight of her Al started to laugh. She was like a walking dirty picture.

Van, although he did not indulge himself, had allowed a small pouty Nymphet in, carrying a tray of drugs. Cocaine, grass, even methadrine for the really dedicated.

Al smiled. How the Kurlnik twins would love it here! He helped himself to a joint. Dragged deeply. Sat on the edge of the giant bed.

The girls who had filed in stood in a silent line waiting to be summoned.

The writer staggered over, pawed at one of the blondes, 'C'mon baby, get 'em off.'

She was wearing a purple jump suit zippered down the front. 'Help me out of it, daddy!' she purred.

The writer lurched against her. He was so drunk he could scarcely stand up.

Al glanced over at Van. He did not seem about to participate. 'Which one is yours?' inquired Al in a friendly fashion.

'Don't worry about me,' replied Van blandly, 'Rita!' He gestured to the redhead. 'Take your bra off. I think Mr King would like to see what you're hiding.'

Rita obeyed, slipping and sliding out of the bra like a seasoned stripper. She did indeed have the most enormous boobs Al had ever seen.

Van smiled in a paternal fashion. 'I heard they were your weakness,' he confided, 'and Rita's are all her own, she's not just another Los Angeles silicone job, y'know.'

Female movie star sat up to take a look, select a joint, then she vanished down on the floor.

By this time everyone except Van and Al had taken time out to remove their clothes. The Chicano and Chinese had joined the movie stars on the floor. Rita, stripped and ready, and the black girl, in a see-through Andy Warhol T-shirt, stood around waiting.

Van sat one side of the big bed. Al the other.

'Please do go ahead,' Van offered, watching the writhings around him with all the excitement of a dead fish. 'Rita, help Mr King with his clothes.'

Rita and her outsize protuberances bore down on Al. He held her off with a hand. 'Van? Which one is yours?'

Van puffed quickly on his pipe. 'Don't worry about me, go right on and enjoy yourself.'

'While you watch?'

Van looked offended. 'If it bothers you . . .'

'You bet it bothers me.' Al stood up, his mouth tightening into a disgusted line. He indicated Van's other guests. 'What are we all supposed to be – the cabaret?'

'Now Al – please. I arranged all this for you. I thought you would enjoy . . .'

'No shit?' interrupted Al coldly, 'and I'd like to bet my ass that you're photographing the whole event.' He moved threateningly close to Van, 'Am I right, buddy boy?'

Van squirmed uncomfortably. 'Any pictures or film taken of my guests is never used other than for my personal library.'

'Horseshit,' said Al tensely, 'get 'em stoned, get 'em fucking. Your personal library must be worth a fucking fortune.'

'If you like,' suggested Van, quickly, 'I could show you some films

'Jesus!' Al laughed in disbelief, 'you don't let up, do you.'

The redhead, still standing, shifted uneasily and raised her eyebrows at the black girl. The black girl, stoned and bored, ignored her.

'You're a slimy sonofabitch,' Al said, heading for the elevator. 'I didn't like you on sight, and now I like you even less.'

'But, Al. The party, I did it for you . . .'

'You don't even *know* me. I'm not the asshole you seemed to think I would be. Porno photos yet!' He indicated the movie stars writhing about on the fur carpet oblivious to the fight going on above them, 'and when do you break the news to those poor schmucks? Hey – listen – have I got some

photos of *you*! And hey presto – they're in your pocket from
that day on. Right?'

'You've got the whole thing wrong,' argued Van wood-
enly.

'Bullsheeeeet! Who are you kidding – you prick.'

He stepped in the elevator and as the doors closed he saw
the female movie star surfacing yet again, and enquiring in a
sweet girlish voice, 'Anyone for head?'

Later, back at the hotel, Al and Paul had a good laugh
about it.

'You just wouldn't have believed it,' Al explained,
'Uptight, sitting on his bed getting ready for the action like
an old queen.'

'Maybe he is. Maybe that's his scene.'

'Who, him? Surrounded by eight million girls. Come on.'

Paul rustled up a poker game and they played late into
the night.

It wasn't until he was alone in his bed that Al allowed
Dallas to intrude into his thoughts.

He had to have her. And one way or the other he was
going to see that he did.

33

Dallas awoke in a fog. She was awake, but she could not
manage to open her eyes. She lay very still whilst the fog
cleared, and she could collect her thoughts.

Briefly she remembered the previous evening. It had all
gone so smoothly. And thank God it was over.

She opened her eyes. There were still things to do. It was
time to get up. She glanced at the bedside clock. Ten o'clock.
Naked, she jumped out of bed, shook her hair loose, flung on
a thin silk robe.

Linda was in the kitchen making coffee.

'Where are the photos?' Dallas asked anxiously.

'Don't worry. The negatives are in an envelope ready for
you to take to the bank. And two separate sets of prints are
in here.' Linda indicated a kitchen drawer. 'Phew! I've got to
tell you I'm glad it's over.'

'*You're* glad it's over.'

'It was an education though. To think that funny little gimpy guy runs a studio, is married to Doris Andrews, *and* plays games with hookers on the side. Wow – how many hats of different colours can a person wear?'

Dallas shrugged. 'If I told you some of the things I know . . .'

Linda gulped her coffee. 'Don't! Enough is enough. I don't think I can take any more right now. I've spent the entire evening dreaming about Diamond's boyfriend. I didn't even know there were such things as *male* hookers. I'm a sophisticated New York girl of thirty-two, and I *didn't even know about male hookers*. I think I want one!'

Dallas couldn't help smiling. 'What on earth for?'

'For what do you think? I mean the thought of going to bed with a guy who is there purely for your pleasure. Terrific! Don't get me wrong – Paul is marvellous in bed, but sometimes I think to myself wouldn't it be sensational to be absolutely selfish. Just lie back and give the orders, and don't worry about whether it's good for him or not. Bliss! It comes to me in a sudden flash why female hookers have always been so popular! Imagine telling a husband or lover to give you head for four hours – he'd laugh you out of bed. But a male hooker – the pursuit of personal pleasure would be limitless!'

'You could always buy one of those vibrating tongues they advertise in *Movie World*.'

'Dallas! Where's your sense of togetherness. I don't want a vibrating tongue. I want the whole man! Hey – how much do you think they charge?'

'You're not serious, are you?'

'Why not? When I was in analysis my shrink always used to tell me not to hold back. "Experience the fruits of life," he would say.'

'Why did you stop?'

'He wanted me to experience his penis. Right in the middle of a fifty dollar session! He was about eighty and totally bald. I'm sure you can understand why I declined.'

Dallas toyed with her coffee. 'I . . . I really don't understand.'

'Huh?'

'I mean I don't understand people's – er – hang-up with

sex. And believe me, Linda, I've had so many men. Bald, eighty, young, rich. You name it, I've had it. And you know, it all means nothing. I couldn't care less if I never went to bed with another man. Sex turns me off – not on.'

Linda nodded. 'I can understand your attitude. Christ, you've told me enough about your life for me to realize the problems you must have.' She looked thoughtful, 'Analysis would be really good for you, help you sort things into perspective. And then you need a really terrific guy to get you together in bed. You need a *loving* relationship.'

'I was thinking of Cody . . .'

'The agent guy you told me about?'

'Yes. He's been so kind. He's really nice, and I know that he wants to go to bed with me.'

'Do you love him?'

Dallas laughed bitterly. 'What's love, Linda? That's one scene that will never come my way.'

'Don't be so sure . . .'

'Of that I'm sure. I like Cody. I guess I respect him . . .'

'And you would grit your teeth and sleep with him. Right?'

'Right.'

'Forget it. You need a little passion in your life if it's ever going to work for you.' Linda drained her coffee, refilled her cup. 'I'm going to make a really bizarre suggestion, you'll think I'm nuts, but think about it before you say no. You've spent most of your life operating as a hooker, servicing guys, seeing that they get their rocks off in just the way *they* want it. Any perversion goes, right?'

Dallas nodded.

'Well,' Linda continued, 'who more than you could use the ministrations of a male hooker? For me it would be a luxury. For you it could be a necessity.'

'Oh no, I don't think . . .'

'Wait. Give it some thought. What's to lose? Right now you hate sex. Well, you're an intelligent girl, *you know* that is not a normal attitude. Not the gateway to a balanced and happy life. Cure yourself. Find out what *you* like. Find out with a guy who is there *just* to give *you* pleasure.'

They were both silent for a moment, digesting what Linda had said.

'Do you know,' Linda continued, 'that in sex therapy they pay partners to give you pleasure. It works. Thousands of men and women have been cured. Frigid women. Impotent men. Premature ejaculation. All kinds of things. I'm not saying that's *your* problem – but whatever your hang-up I'm sure it can be cured with the right treatment. I have to confess to you that I find sex one of the joys of life – and you're my friend – I don't want you to miss out. You are so young and beautiful. Sort yourself out now. Put the past behind you. Jesus, I'm talking too much. Give me a cigarette and shut me up.'

Silently Dallas handed her a cigarette, and shook one from the pack for herself, although she didn't normally smoke.

'It's not such a bad idea, Linda,' she finally said, 'I guess it does make sense. There have been times – far and few between – when I've realized sex can be a kick . . .'

'Terrific. At least you know what I'm talking about. Touching, feeling, giving way to pure sensual delight. Nothing like it, kid.'

'Maybe a sex therapy clinic . . .'

'Maybe not. You want the world to know your secrets? Soon you'll be famous, television makes you a star overnight. A male hooker – maybe Diamond's guy. Much more discreet. He doesn't have to know your secrets, he's just there to give you a good time. A clinic will investigate you like the CIA!'

Suddenly Dallas began to laugh. 'Honestly, Linda! Can you imagine *me* paying for it! What a switch!'

'Stranger things have happened . . . Hey, I think you should get dressed and get those negatives over to the bank. I think I'll feel better when they're locked up.'

Dallas stubbed out her hardly-used cigarette, 'Yes, boss.' She got up, glanced out of the window at the California sunshine.

'Linda? You don't *have* to leave today, do you?'

Linda drained her coffee, thought briefly of Paul. Realized that he hadn't even bothered to call her yet.

'No, I guess I don't.'

'That's great. I'll call Cody, let him know I'm back, then he can take us out to lunch – I do want you to meet him.'

'Can't wait.'

'You'll like him, I know you will.'

Watching Dallas, Linda was surprised at the gradual change in her. When they had first met, Dallas had been a very withdrawn, cold person. Of course she understood the reasons why now, but it was wonderful to observe the emergence of a much freer, warmer personality.

'I've got a fitting at the studio at two thirty,' Dallas was saying, 'maybe after, we could drive down to the beach. If I didn't start work tomorrow I would really show you around. Perhaps when the tour finishes you could come back, spend a couple of weeks – a month – as long as you like. That's if sleeping on the couch isn't too awful.'

'It's very comfortable. I might take you up on that. Somehow I don't think I see Paul whisking me back to London with him. Did I remember to tell you *never* to get involved with a married man?'

'Hang on there – I'm all booked out to a male hooker!'

Dialling Cody's number Dallas felt bad about the line she would have to feed him. Lies. God how she wished that she didn't have to lie to Cody. But it was for his own protection – for their mutual protection.

He answered on the fourth ring. 'Cody Hills.'

'Dallas,' she replied, copying his businesslike tone.

'Oh, you're back,' his voice was flat.

'Such enthusiasm! This is your star, don't I get more than an "Oh, you're back"?'

He hesitated then, 'Sorry, been on business calls all morning. Was everything all right?'

'Perfection. I sorted it all out. Hey – do I merit a lunch at least? My girlfriend, Linda, is with me and I want you to meet her.'

'I'm supposed to be viewing office premises . . .'

'Terrific. We'll come with you. Where shall we meet?'

Aggravated he gave her the address. He hung up the phone, went in the bathroom, took a handful of stomach pills. An incipient ulcer had been lurking for years.

He was mad at himself for not being able to conceal his annoyance with her. But annoyance wasn't even the right word. Jealousy would be more like it. And Christ, you really had to be a schmuck to be jealous of a client.

If he wasn't careful he would give himself away. 'What was that orgy at your house last night?' 'That was no orgy, that was my idea of fun.' Shit! Her personal life was none of his business. If he was smart he would keep it that way.

He had a sudden idea, and glancing at his watch he quickly picked up the phone.

☆

After securing the negatives in a safe deposit box, there was time to do a little shopping. They wandered down Rodeo Drive peering in shop windows. Linda bought an Indian ivory choker and matching bangle.

'Looks amazing with your hair,' Dallas assured her. 'If only we had time we could drive down to Palm Springs and go to the Indian reservation, they have a shop right at the top of a mountain where they sell all silver and turquoise stuff they make themselves. Cody told me about it. I'd love to go.'

'So would I. I really don't know why I cheated myself out of a trip here before. I'm an American who has never seen America!'

'You're seeing it now with the tour.'

'Hotel suites. Limousines. Concert halls. Sports stadiums. Boring parties where everyone hangs around Al. Oh, and did I tell you his son has joined us now?'

Dallas looked surprised. 'His son?'

'Poor kid, I feel sorry for him. A spotty teenager who is obviously petrified of his father – and Al in his stylish way keeps on throwing grotesque whores in his direction.'

'What about his wife?'

'What about her? I don't think she's allowed out. Who knows if she even exists. Al is the supreme chauvinist. An egotistical son of a bitch.'

'You really like him, don't you?'

'I see right through him.'

'A man like that must have tremendous problems.'

'The only thing tremendous about Al is his dick! And boy – is he spreading the news – as well as the legs of every female who crosses his path.'

'He hasn't changed then?'

Linda laughed. 'Al, changed? You must be kidding!'

Dallas launched into another subject of conversation, but her thoughts lingered with Al. His timing on the phone call had been bad. What else could she have said to him with

Lew Margolis standing right there. Anyway what was there to say? Hello. How are you. Goodbye.

She remembered his arms around her the night they had danced together in Regines in Monte Carlo.

She remembered the sudden warm excitement when he looked at her. When his black eyes travelled down her body.

She remembered the way they had joked together. The conversations loaded with sexual innuendo.

As she thought about him her body responded, and suddenly, walking down Rodeo Drive, she was seized with a strong sexual longing. A feeling so powerful she could hardly believe it. It was a feeling she had experienced so little in life. One time with Burt at the zoo. A couple of times with Bobbie. And now.

Maybe Linda was right. Maybe a man who would think only of her pleasure was what she needed. Or Cody, if only she could will this feeling in Cody's direction.

They had reached the car. Thankfully Dallas slid behind the wheel. She banished Al from her thoughts and tried to concentrate on what Linda was saying. Al King was bad news. Even *she* knew that.

Cody saw the car Dallas was driving approach, he managed a wave, indicated the parking lot attached to the building, and then turned to Irene who stood demurely beside him. Irene had been his brilliant idea – well, actually Evelyn, not Irene – but Evelyn had been in the midst of mother problems and unable to make lunch. Irene was second best, and she looked it. He had not seen her for several weeks and she appeared to have gained ten pounds. And why had he never noticed how hairy she was? Throughout their two-year intimate relationship he had never before noticed the fact that she had the suspicions of a moustache. She did have great legs though – short but great.

'It's nice to see you again, Cody,' Irene said, 'I couldn't imagine why I hadn't heard from you.'

'I told you what with leaving the agency and everything I've just been so busy. But I'm really glad you could manage lunch today.'

She squeezed his arm. 'I have missed you. When am I going to see you—' she paused meaningfully, 'properly?'

He wondered briefly if a moustache and an extra ten

pounds would affect their previously quite erotic sex life. He decided it probably would.

'I don't know. Work, work, work – you know how it is.'

'Oh I know, I know. You don't have to tell me. Why this week my boss . . .'

'Here they come,' interrupted Cody, and as usual he was knocked out by Dallas. She really was the most unbelievably beautiful girl. She strode towards him like a graceful leopard, her long hair blowing around her face. Her body emphasized by the thin silk shirt tucked into white jeans. He hardly noticed the girl with her, every female seemed to be non-existent next to Dallas.

'Hi there,' she said, presenting him with a hug and a kiss, 'told you I'd only be away a minute. This is Linda, she's going to be spending a few days with me.'

He smiled at Linda, blackly wondering if she had been involved in the previous night's orgy.

Irene stepped forward. 'My name is Irene Newman,' she announced formally, pumping Dallas by the hand, 'no relation to Paul!' giggle, giggle. 'I'm so pleased to meet you, Cody has told me all about the wonderful contract he's gotten you.' She paused, squeezed Cody's arm in an intimate fashion. 'If there is anything I can do for you, please say. Cody tells me you're new in town, I know he's rented a house for you, but y'know – any girl things I can help out on – beauty parlour, gym – oh and I have a marvie place where I get a discount on sports clothes. If you like I can . . .'

Cody listened in amazement. Irene the talker. Was there no end to the surprises she had in store for him?

They viewed the office space, Irene chattering throughout.

'What do you think?' Cody asked Dallas.

'Wonderful!' replied Irene. 'You could move in tomorrow, all you need is a desk, and a nice chair. I know a place on Fairfax . . .'

Dallas shrugged helplessly.

On the way down in the elevator she pulled Cody to one side. 'I think we'll pass on the lunch. I didn't realize you had a date, why didn't you say?'

'It doesn't matter, she's just an – er – old friend. Come on – you must have lunch.'

Dallas glanced at her watch. 'No, really I have to be at the studio by two, I won't have time. Linda and I will grab a hamburger somewhere.'

He nodded miserably. What a bad idea Irene had been. I'll call you later, then.'

'Dine,' she dazzled him with a smile, 'maybe we can have an early dinner.'

'I don't know, I might be tied up.' He could kick himself for being so petty and stupid, but he couldn't help it.

She looked disappointed.

'But I'll try,' he added lamely.

'Do that,' she replied with an understanding smile.

34

Bernie had noticed the two girls in every city they had visited. He had seen them only as part of huge crowds of girls who hung around the hotel entrances and concert venues. They had not really registered properly until Chicago, when he had suddenly realized that they were following Al across the country. They were both quite young, but neither of them was very pretty.

He ambled over to them, and found out their names. I mean – what the fuck – these two were true fans. A little publicity wouldn't go amiss. He could throw a few free tickets their way, some souvenir programmes, a T-shirt or two.

Plum was nineteen and fat, a little larger than Bernie himself.

Glory, on the other hand, was extremely skinny. Sixteen, with freaked-out hair and a funny pointed face.

They were ecstatic that they had finally been noticed. Plum informed Bernie that they had pooled their savings, given up their jobs, just to be close to Al. Sometimes they hitched across country, sometimes took a train. From Miami to Chicago they had invested in plane fares to get them there in time.

'Well, girlies, today you just got lucky,' Bernie announced, 'be back here around six and I'm gonna take you in and let you meet the big man himself. How does that grab you?'

'I'll faint,' quavered Glory. 'Man, I'll just faint right away!'

'Can you give us tickets for tonight?' asked Plum shrewdly.

'Sure,' agreed Bernie. 'You mean you came all this way and you don't have tickets?'

'Yean we *got* tickets. But like we need the bread – so we'll make a little green stuff on ours – *use* yours.'

Bernie shrugged. 'Whatever turns you on.'

Glory giggled. 'Al turns me on. Like he turns my legs to jelly, man. Like when I'm not even stoned, he *turns me inside out*. Ain't no one can do that to me less I'm out of it.' She gripped Bernie's arm tightly. 'You know him, you're tight with him – tell him if he wants a trip will blow his head off . . .' she paused, scratching desperately at her frizzy hair, her eyes glazed over, she almost fell.

'She's just hungry,' said Plum stoically. 'We haven't eaten since the plane yesterday, and the crap they expect you to eat. I wouldn't give that crap to a cat.'

Bernie fished in his pocket, counted out five dollars, handed it to Plum. 'Get some food, and a wash or something. Fix yourselves up, I'll have photographers here.'

'On five bucks we're gonna eat, wash, and fix ourselves up? Who you kiddin'?'

'So don't eat. You want to meet Al be back here at six.'

Plum scowled. 'Cheap.'

Glory, revived, muttered, 'I could blow the brains off a monkey!' and lapsed back into a daze.

Bernie peeled off another five dollars. 'Buy her a steak, make her human.' He started to walk away.

'Don't forget our tickets,' Plum snouted after him.

☆

Al had slept most of the day away. Then at five he had woken, decided he needed a woman, and Paul had tracked down Rita of the pneumatic boobs for him.

'Don't tell Van I'm here,' she had pleaded, 'he wouldn't allow it. I'm supposed to work exclusively for him.'

'Are you a pro?' Al asked.

'Of course not. I'm a model. Van pays me – very generously, so sometimes I do him little favours.'

'Open your legs,' Al said crudely, 'I want to see if you've got a camera hidden up there!'

She did not appreciate the joke. But she did service him expertly, and left him with a strong feeling of disgust.

He did not take kindly to Bernie's suggestion of a photo session with two fans who were trailing him across the country. But Bernie insisted. It was a story bound to make all the newspapers, and a nice human interest story for either *Time* or *People*.

Glory and Plum turned up promptly at six in full battle-dress. Bernie would have bet that Plum had used the money to get Glory a shot of whatever she was hooked on. From a quiet little zombie she had turned into Miss Personality.

Plum looked even fatter in blue jeans and a satin jacket. Glory even thinner in red stockings on stick legs, and a voluminous sweater.

They pawed at Al like a couple of agitated puppies whilst the cameras clicked away. He smiled, joked, put his arms around them, presented them with signed photos.

The cameras kept flashing.

Glory whispered in his ear, 'I'd like to swallow your cock all down in one piece, right into my stomach.'

Al pushed her pleasantly away, extracted himself from Plum. 'Enough, boys,' he said to the photographers.

'Dynamite!' wheezed Bernic. 'World-wide coverage tomorrow.'

'Get 'em out of here,' hissed Al, 'I've got a show to think about.'

☆

When he strode on stage nothing else mattered. The disgust, the problems with Evan, the boredom, Edna, Dallas. Everything was obliterated as his music came crashing protectively round him.

He opened up with 'Blue Funk Rock', followed it with 'Keep It' – both his own compositions. Then he launched into a medley of songs made famous by some of his favourte artists. Al Green's 'Let's Stay Together', Bobby Womack's 'I Can Understand It', Wilson Pickett's 'Midnight Mover', Stevie Wonder's 'You Are the Sunshine of My Life'. And to finish, Isaac Hayes' 'Never Can Say Goodbye'.

The audience loved it. They would love it if he stood on his head and whistled 'Dixie'!

He was halfway through 'Random Love' when it happened. An explosion so muffled that only the people in the immediate vicinity were affected. But as some of those people were blown to bits, the panic and chaos spread within seconds.

One moment Al was on stage singing his guts out to an ecstatic screaming audience of thousands. The next he was being dragged off stage by Luke and Paul, whilst pandemonium raged below.

The bomb, a small one, had been placed beneath a seat. It killed two people, mutilated seven, injured fifteen. By the time police and security guards were able to gain control of the panicking crowds five people had been trampled to death in the rush to leave the stadium. Fifty-eight people had been injured, and hundreds were in shock.

It was an Al King concert many would never forget.

Why? was the question everyone asked. How could anyone be so twisted and deranged as to want to kill innocent people?

If a man with a gun had got up and shot Al it would have been understandable. After all any public figure from a politician to a rock star knew he lived under constant threat of assassination. That was one of the hazards of making it in the envy-ridden sixties and seventies.

But to maim and injure like this . . .

Two seventeen-years-old girls killed. A boy with his leg blown off. A woman without a foot . . . The list of horrors was endless.

Bernie thought of the voice on the phone and shuddered.

Fortunately he had reported the threats to the police. But there had been no telephoned threats in Chicago. No sick and twisted voice telling him what was going to happen . . .

The police questioned him at length. They took charge of the hate mail Al received. They questioned everyone connected with the tour. They even questioned Al.

By the time they were finished it was 4 a.m. and Bernie felt drained and exhausted. He collapsed into his bed at the hotel, not even bothering to remove his clothes. Fuck it. He needed sleep. The next morning he would have the world press to deal with. He had already spoken to the overseas news agencies. This kind of publicity . . . Who needed it? It would either make or break the tour. People were funny, if they got scared . . . Jesus – what the fuck. He swigged from a bedside bottle of scotch and then let his bulk sag onto the bed. His eyes closed, only for a minute it seemed because immediately the phone was ringing. He snatched it up – 'Bernie Suntan,' he said quickly.

'I told you,' the voice whispered, 'I warned you. I gave you a chance to stop him from performing his vile obscenities. God will punish sinners. This is just the first of many.'

The line went dead.

Wearily Bernie struggled awake and called the police. Why did this maniac, whoever he was, have to pick on *him* to confide in?

☆

Lying in bed Al could not sleep at all. If it was not for him none of this would have happened. If he had not been appearing at the concert the crowds would not have been there – the bomb would not have been placed – the people would not have been killed and maimed. Once before, early in his career, something dreadful had happened. As he was escaping from a theatre one night a girl had somehow or other got enmeshed under the wheels of his car. She had not been killed, but crippled for life. He had not been driving, it was not his responsibility. But he had never forgotten that girl, and over the years he had sent her a continual stream of money and gifts.

Guilt money.

In a way he did feel guilty that he had so much. But Christ knows he worked hard enough for it. Each show he did seven pounds of sweat rolled off him. Hard physical work. It was harder than digging ditches.

He thought of phoning Edna to let her know that he was OK. A news flash had probably reached England by now. But would she care? It was Evan *she* cared about.

Evan was asleep in his own room somewhere in the hotel. Thank God he had not wanted to attend the concert that night. It had been a good idea of Paul's to suggest that he didn't keep him in the suite. They had been too much on top of each other, that's why the boy had been getting on his nerves. Now things seemed much better. He gave Evan money and told him to go out and enjoy himself. Evan had not objected.

Evan, in fact, was quite enjoying it. He had amassed one hundred and sixty dollars from the money his father threw his way. And he was free to buy girlie magazines, and candy, and sit in his room and enjoy them.

He put on the colour television and hardly budged from his room. Nobody bugged him. Occasionally Al would call him on the house phone and ask him if he wanted to come up to the suite. He always had an excuse.

He had been watching a repeat of 'Kojak' when the news came through about the bomb at Al's show. For one icy, hopeful, moment he thought that maybe his father had been killed. But no such luck. He listened with fascination to the reports of the bomb. Then anxious to see for himself, he left the hotel and took a cab over to the stadium.

He couldn't get anywhere near because of ambulances and fire trucks. He tried to push through suddenly thinking of Nellie, but he got shoved back along with the rest of the ghouls who had come to watch.

Surprisingly there appeared to be an air of cheerfulness amongst the crowds. Smiling, happy faces, hoping to get a glimpse of someone else's misery.

A television crew roamed around, sticking microphones in front of people's faces to get their comments.

'Why did you come here?' A girl reporter asked a woman carrying a baby.

'Better than television,' the woman laughed, 'like it's real drama – y'know. Wouldn't wanna miss it.'

'Were you at the concert?'

'Naw – jest came over when I saw the news.'

Evan realized there was nothing to see. He had missed all the good bits. He looked around for a cab, but there was none about. He had no idea how to get back to the hotel, but he started to walk anyway, hunching his shoulders into his denim jacket, cursing the fact that he had not chosen to attend the one concert where something decent had happened.

He did not notice the group of boys following him, boys about his own age.

He did not notice them closing in on him, surrounding him, jeering.

He stopped, unable to proceed anyway. Fright made him go cold.

'Hey, asshole!' screamed the tallest boy, 'you got any money, honey?' They all laughed, circling him.

'W-w-what?' stammered Evan.

'Green sticky stuff, asshole. Give it – *now!*'

Terrified, Evan groped into his pockets, found some change, handed it over.

'Wowee – fifty fuckin' cents! We found ourselves a real rich little motha!'

Evan thought quickly of the one hundred and sixty dollars in twenties stuck in the back pocket of his jeans. They wouldn't get that.

'I haven't got any more money,' he said quickly, his voice breaking.

'What's with that accent, asshole?' questioned the leader, 'You foreign or sumpin'? Jeeze! Now listen, prick . . .'

'Pigfuckers!' yelled one of the boys, and they melted away into the night as if they had never existed in the first place.

Relieved, Evan ran over to the patrol car cruising by. He informed them who he was, where he was staying, and what had happened.

They told him off for walking around alone at night, shoved him in the car, and took him back to the hotel.

In exchange he had to promise to produce Al for them to meet with their wives next morning. He had no idea how on earth he'd fix *that*.

Safe in bed, his hundred and sixty dollars in a neat pile on the bedside table, he relived the scene. All of a sudden he was the hero of the piece. He had told *them*. Oh boy – he couldn't wait to tell Nellie all about it. Maybe now she would like him. Maybe now he could ask her out.

He fell asleep and dreamed that *he* was Al King. A far brighter star than the original.

When Al found out about Evan's adventure the next day he was pissed off to say the least. He posed with the police-men and their wives because he could hardly do anything else. But it was the last thing he needed. There was so much else going on. A trip to the hospital to visit the victims. Interviews to keep the world press happy. Television appearances.

Marjorie Carter came to the hotel with her camera crew. She was a professional to her fingertips. The interview was real human interest stuff. How did he *feel*? What would he *do*? Did this tragedy change his plans for the future?

Neither of them mentioned the night they had spent together. They were both excruciatingly polite.

The concert that evening was cancelled in deference to the victims, but Al promised that he would return to do another show sometime in the future.

He had no intention of ever setting foot in Chicago again.

He balled Evan out. Why had he come running over to the stadium? Why was he so fucking stupid that he walked the city's streets alone at night? Didn't he know people could get *killed* that way?

Evan was contrite. He had only come because he was worried about Al. He had only hurried over to see if he was all right.

Al felt a sudden rush of warmth and love towards the boy. He wasn't such a bad kid after all.

Van Valda sent a long and tearful letter of regret that such a thing could have happened in Chicago. He seemed to have forgotten all about Al's insults on the night of the party. 'Please come back and stay with us at Macho Mansion,' he begged.

Al threw the letter away.

Edna phoned, absolutely hysterical. Al calmed her down. Assured her that he and Evan were okay. Assured her there was no further danger, and wished he could be sure of that fact himself.

By six o'clock the entire Al King entourage was aboard his private plane, and without a backward glance they took off into the cloudy skies. None of them was sorry to leave.

35

Dallas had been working on 'Man Made Woman' for a week, and it couldn't be going better.

The crew were friendly. The director, Chuck, was interesting and sharp. His wife, a striking black girl called Kiki, was designing the clothes, and some of the outfits were incredible.

Cody arrived every day to have lunch with her. He seemed to have gotten over his recent strange mood. Dallas had put it down to the fact that maybe he had been having problems with his girlfriend. She had been surprised when he had turned up that day with Irene. Funny, but she had never really thought about him having another life away from her. He had spent so much time with her. He had always been available. The fact that he suddenly produced a girlfriend had been something of a jolt. She had complained to Linda.

'Hey,' Linda had pointed out, 'the guy's normal. What did you think? That he jerked off in a closet?'

'Just didn't think about it.'

'Well, you should have. He's a sweet guy, he's probably got lots of girlfriends.'

'But I . . . Oh shit, forget it.'

She didn't want to talk about Cody's love life. She didn't want to admit that she was secretly annoyed that he wasn't waiting patiently in the wings for her. After all she had offered herself to him. And what was it he had said – in the nicest possible way of course – he had said that they shouldn't complicate their business relationship. Terrific. The one guy she would sleep with didn't want to.

More and more her mind flicked over the possibility of calling Diamond and asking for the services of her boyfriend. What was there to lose? Maybe she would enjoy it. Maybe she should at least give it a chance . . .

Linda had left. Dashed off at the first news of the bomb in Chicago. As Paul's girlfriend she was anxious to be by his side. As a photographer she was desolate that she had missed the event.

Dallas couldn't help wondering how Al must feel. She had even tried to call him in Chicago to offer a few words of sympathy, but he had already checked out of the hotel.

Every time she thought about Al, she got that feeling. It swept over her leaving her in a state of agitation. It didn't please her. She, who had always been so much in control

She knew that she needed a man. Her skin was breaking

out, and she was becoming irritable for no reason. Several guys at the studio would be happy to oblige, but they were all your usual macho merchants, horny studs looking to screw anything that crossed their paths.

Lew Margolis had not intruded on her personal life since the one night with Diamond. She had seen him once when he turned up to view the week's taping. He had barely nodded in her direction.

She was prepared for him. The negatives locked securely in her safety deposit box at the bank. The photos hidden beneath her bed.

She dreaded a confrontation, but it had to come, and the longer it took, the better.

Meanwhile she was working hard, doing her best, and enjoying every minute of it.

☆

Cody kept a firm eye on things. The series was going to be as sensational as his every expectation. Dallas was positively glowing, and on camera she looked like a dream.

He had decided to swallow his feelings, and devote himself entirely to looking after her again. She seemed to have no more secrets. She was open and warm with him. Perhaps that one night had been an exception. Everyone went a little wild on one occasion. He could remember the time when an early girlfriend had insisted that he tied her to a bed and beat her. He had done it, felt guilty but done it anyway, and the girl had been delighted in spite of her screams. Every time he had stopped she had screamed, 'More! More! More! Harder! Harder! Harder!'

Now if anyone had witnessed *that* little scene . . . He shuddered to think about it.

After the lunch Irene had phoned him constantly. *He* knew it was over. Why didn't she?

She sent him a pair of hand-knitted red socks, and when they had no effect she sent him a blue pair with his initials on.

He sent her back a potted plant with a please forgive me note.

She visited his apartment and scrawled 'Bastard' all over

his front door in lipstick. He knew it was her because who else wore 'Crimson Pirate' lipstick.

The new office was nice. He bought an odd antique desk, a leather swivel chair, and hired a buck-toothed sixty-year-old secretary. They both sat back staring at each other, waiting for the phone to ring. It didn't.

Becoming a hot agent and personal manager was not instant. It was obviously going to take a little hustling on his part. He had to let people know he was available, ready for new clients. They probably all thought he was too big time now.

In the meantime he read scripts, and novels. He was looking for Dallas' first film. It would have to be a big one. 'Man Made Woman' was just a beginning.

☆

Saturday, Dallas was on location all day. Everyone was working overtime to get the first show out on schedule.

They were shooting at the beach, and it was a glorious day. Hot, sunny, no smog.

Kiki had designed her the most incredible swimsuit. White strips of leather winding round her body.

'I'm going to get the most peculiar suntan!' she joked to Cody when he appeared in the afternoon.

'You look great,' he enthused, 'it's a shame you're so ugly!'

She stuck out her tongue and wiggled it at him.

'Talented as well as ugly!'

'Why don't you shut up, Mr Hills. I *was* thinking of inviting you to dinner and watching you barbecue some delicious steaks I am planning to buy – or maybe *you* could buy them. What do you think? An evening at my house?'

'The thing I love about your invitations is that they always involve *me* paying out money.'

'Oh, I'll *pay* for the steaks. I just don't know when I'll have time to *get* them.'

He kissed her lightly on the cheek. 'I can't, beautiful client. My mother has got a sister in town from Cleveland who can't get through the evening without her very successful Hollywood agent nephew coming by to tell her inside stories of John Wayne and Doris Day.'

'*John Wayne and Doris Day!*'

'I told you she's from Cleveland. They've never heard of any other movie stars there. Unless you count Lassie and Rin Tin Tin.'

'Rin Tin who?'

'Don't make me feel old, I'm only twenty-eight.'

'And sexy with it.'

The assistant called Dallas over for the next shot.

Cody watched her. He couldn't take his eyes off her. None of the men could.

Two takes and she was back beside him.

'So no dinner tonight then? Stood up for an old lady from Cleveland.'

He sighed. 'I told you earlier this week that I would be tied up tonight. I'd ask you to come but they'd marry us off before the end of the dinner! Tell you what – I'll drop by after.'

'Nope. I wouldn't mind an early night. I *am* kind of exhausted.'

'We could barbecue tomorrow. Maybe ask Kiki and Chuck.'

'Terrific.' She smiled brightly. But she didn't feel bright. She felt disappointed and lonely. However, she didn't want Cody to know she felt that way. If he knew, he would cancel out on his mother and cause family problems. She knew what a difficult relationship he had there. Talk about love/hate. So she smiled and said she didn't mind and joked and laughed with him.

Maybe an early night *would* do her good. She had been working like a dog. Up at all hours, falling into bed at night completely flaked out.

But it wasn't going to work out. She was too keyed up and restless. She needed someone . . . something.

She knew that tonight was the night she would try out Diamond's boyfriend.

36

The crowds were larger than ever. It had been the same way in Nashville and Memphis. And now at the Coliseum in Houston, Texas, they were out in force.

If Al King had been a superstar before, he had now become almost a cult figure.

'Al is King! Al is King! Al is King!' chanted the mobs who did not have tickets and were stuck outside.

The bomb in Chicago had triggered off the most amazing reaction. Both Paul and Bernie had been worried that it would affect attendances, and that there would be a lot of returned tickets. But quite the reverse had happened. A ticket for an Al King concert was like gold dust. On the side the rip-off merchants were selling them at astronomical prices.

Gratifying as he found it, it also made Al nervous. So many people expecting so much. He sensed an attitude of expectation from the hordes that he couldn't quite fulfil. He knew what it was. They wanted blood. They wanted excitement. They wanted another bomb.

Every crank in America wrote threatening letters. Three lunatics confessed to having planted the bomb. Security was rigid everywhere he appeared. Concert halls, theatres, stadiums were searched before anyone was allowed in. Then began the painstaking task of frisking the audiences as they filed slowly towards their seats. To attend an Al King concert you had to arrive at least two hours early.

'The Promises'' manager wanted them to quit the tour. Paul was furious, and wouldn't allow it. They had an iron-clad contract, and no way could they slip out of it.

Paul knew *why* they wanted to quit. All the stuff the manager was handing him about the girls being frightened was so much crap. The truth was they had an amazing new record contract, and had been offered their own television series.

Rosa's mafioso boyfriend arrived from New York, and caused nothing but trouble. He hated Al, in spite of the fact that Rosa insisted nothing had ever gone on. He lurked around wearing three-piece black suits with an obvious shoulder holster, and patent leather shoes. He watched Rosa like a hawk, and even she started to get a little jumpy.

Nellie was getting sick. She had lost a lot of weight, and looked like a skeleton. She kept bursting into tears for no reason. Everyone knew about her enormous crush on Al. Everyone, that is, except Evan.

Evan was enjoying himself. He had managed to save

another forty dollars, making a grand total of two hundred. He was delighted, and counted it lovingly every night.

He was left to his own devices. No one bothered him. As long as he showed his face occasionally things were cool. His hair grew very long. His skin even more spotty as he consumed nothing but candy. He had found magazines on sale that surpassed anything he had ever seen before. People actually *doing it*. Girls showing everything. Animals. He was sickened and excited. God, if Nelson ever saw *this* collection *he* would have to pay. Evan snickered at the thought, and packed his magazines neatly at the bottom of his suitcase.

Linda had returned to the tour to find Paul preoccupied with business. Twice during the week he had had to fly back to New York for meetings, and not once had he offered to take her with him.

She took her pictures, and brooded, and decided maybe when they reached Los Angeles she would stay there. Christ! A year was long enough to screw up your life for any man. Yes – in Los Angeles she would give Paul an ultimatum. If he went running back to his wife and kids – which she knew he would – then at least she could get over him in the sun surrounded by lots of horny would-be actors. Good therapy.

Al was invited to a lot of parties in Houston. The city seemed to be full of oil millionaires with randy wives all waiting to throw their palatial mansions open for Al's inspection – not to mention their legs.

He did the party bit. He even screwed a couple of the wives and one daughter. Nothing memorable.

When they flew out of Houston he was glad. He could never understand why all those rich people fell over backwards to entertain him. And the husbands didn't even seem to mind him having it off with their wives. On the contrary – they seemed positively *proud*.

The next stop was Oklahoma.

Al lolled on the big double bed in his private bedroom on his private plane. He wasn't tired, but he didn't feel like socializing with the others. He was bored with the endless games of backgammon and gin rummy. He was bored with listening to his musicians discuss their last lay. He was bored with Rosa's flinty-eyed boyfriend staring at him, and

Nellie giving him tearful looks, and Sutch *always* playing Stevie Wonder tapes on the cassette player that never left her side.

He was bored with Luke.

And he was extra-bored with Evan, who looked like shit, and complained every time you talked to him.

Bernie bored him with his endless talk of this publicity break and that. Didn't Bernie realize that his job was a piece of cake? Didn't he realize that Al King would fill the newspapers with or without the help of Bernie Suntan?

And Jesus, what was with bringing those freaks aboard for the ride – those two clap-ridden groupies. Whose plan was this, for Christ's sake?

Angrily Al buzzed for Paul.

'What's up?' asked Paul, coming in cheerfully. 'Thought you wanted to sleep.'

Al scowled. 'I'm sick and tired of my plane being used as a travelling knocking shop.'

'Huh?'

'I want Rosa's boyfriend off. He wants to follow her across the country let him do it on his own money.'

'Hey – Al . . .'

'Hey Al nothing. The creep gets up my ass. And tell Bernie I don't ever want to see him bring those two freaks aboard again.'

'They ran out of money. Bernie thought . . .'

'Tell Bernie to shove his thoughts right where it will do them most good.'

'OK, Al.' A sudden air pocket nearly jolted Paul off his feet.

'What the fuck is the pilot doing?' demanded Al.

Paul did not dare tell him that the pilot was showing Evan how to fly the plane. Al was not the only one who was bored, the tour was getting to all of them. Personally, in spite of the gigantic success it was, Paul could not wait for it to finish. He had so much to do. The offers Al was receiving were incredible. Above all expectations. There was a new record contract to negotiate. Two films. A tour of Australia that promised enough money for instant retirement. He would have to sit down with Al and find out what he wanted to do.

Just a formality really, because Paul made all the career decisions. He had already decided that Al should do one of the films. There had been many offers in the past – indeed, early on in his career Al had appeared in a bad British comedy as a horny milkman – but nothing that had been just right. Now both these films he was being offered seemed tailor-made. Of course the main thing was that neither part would tax Al's acting abilities. And quite frankly who knew if he had any to tax?

Lost in thought, Paul didn't notice Glory squeeze quietly into the room behind him. It wasn't until Al roared, 'What the fuck is *she* doing in here?' that Paul saw her edging along the side towards the bed. He grabbed her quickly by the arm. God, but her arm was so thin he thought it might snap off!

'I had to put my eyes on your room, man,' she mumbled, 'like where does the master sleep, y'dig man? Like give my eyes your body and I'll die happy.' She rolled wild eyes in her pointed face, licked dry lips. 'You are . . .'

Before she could finish, a red-faced Plum came bursting in, followed by an even redder-faced Bernie.

For one horrible moment Al thought the two freaks had come to rape him. The fat one and the thin one throwing themselves on his body, ravishing him. He shuddered.

Everyone was speaking at once. Plum was screaming complaints at Glory. Glory was mumbling inanely. Bernie was blustering 'What the fucks' all over the place, and Paul was coldly shoving them all out.

When they were gone, with the door shut firmly behind them, Al said, 'I think that proves my point, Paul. No more strangers on this plane. Do you realize if that little freak had had a gun she could have blown my head off? So much for all my fucking protection *then*.'

'You're right,' agreed Paul, more shaken than Al could see. The skinny girl had been totally out of it, stoned shitless. 'I'll talk to Bernie.'

'Don't *talk* to him. Blast his fuckin' bollocks off!'

'Right.' Paul left the room hurriedly.

Linda tried to stop him as he rushed past. 'What's happening?'

He could see Bernie and the fat girl arguing and gesticulating near the front of the plane. 'In a minute,' he told Linda, and strode down to Bernie. 'I want them off,' he said sharply, 'as soon as we land.'

'Yes,' agreed Bernie, embarrassed.

Plum turned to Paul, fat red cheeks blazing. She indicated Bernie. '*He* said we could see where Al slept. He *said* so. He promised. We both gave him blow jobs an' he *promised*.' She glared balefully at Bernie, who was gazing out of the window. 'He's a fat slob,' she continued, 'I wouldn't have sucked his fat cock if it hadn't of meant gettin' near Al. Nor would she.' She indicated Glory, spread out on a seat, staring disinterestedly into space.

Paul's anger dissolved. He wanted to laugh. Naughty old Bernie getting it off with these two outlandish little girls.

Bernie was scarlet-faced at having been caught.

'Well,' said Paul, 'what can I say? I guess you thought you had a deal.'

'Yes,' replied Plum, still annoyed.

'Al doesn't like to be disturbed. Bernie shouldn't have made promises he couldn't keep. And you shouldn't do things you don't want unless you have a contract. At least you've had a free ride.' He smiled, after all they were Al's fans and he didn't want them leaving the plane pissed off and ready to sell their stories to the nearest newspaper. 'Have you got tickets for the show in Oklahoma?'

'Can we have six? asked Plum quickly.

'Six?'

'We've got friends there.'

Paul kept smiling. 'Fine. Six tickets. You want a couple of T-shirts and some pictures?'

Plum nodded. 'You're nice – you know that. Nice.' She leaned down and prodded Glory who had fallen asleep with her mouth open. 'Say thank you to this one, he's nice.'

Glory opened red-rimmed eyes. 'You want me to suck his . . .'

'No!' said Paul quickly.

Plum grinned, revealing a missing front tooth, 'We wouldn't mind. We both wouldn't mind. I mean you're nice. Besides, you're his brother, and that's family.'

Paul backed away. 'I'll get you the tickets, hang about.'
'We wouldn't move,' leered Plum.

☆

Evan didn't know what was going on. He didn't much care
either. After an interesting half hour with the pilot he had
manoeuvred himself into a seat next to Nellie, and they had
been making idle, wonderful conversation.

'I don't understand these girls who follow stars,' said
Nellie crossly, 'it's so dumb. Don't you think it's dumb?'

'Yes,' agreed Evan. He would agree with whatever she
said. He would agree if she told him to throw himself off the
plane.

'*I* could never do a thing like that, *I* could never throw
myself at anyone.' She placed a small, delicate hand softly on
his knee. 'Did you give Al my message?'

Message. What message? He couldn't remember any
message. 'Yes.'

'What did he say?'

'He er um, he was er. He said – um, he was pleased.'

'Pleased!' Her pretty face lit up. 'Pleased. Oh I knew he
would be. I knew it!'

'Yes.' Evan paused, then plunged on with – 'I've saved
two hundred dollars. I mean I've got two hundred dollars.
I wanted to – um – buy you a present.'

'How lovely,' she giggled, 'I think I'll go and see Al.'

'What?'

'I think I should. I mean if he's pleased . . . Well I think I
should just – you know – tell him personally.'

'Tell him what?' Evan was confused.

'My message, silly.' She leaned over and kissed him lightly
on the cheek, 'You've been such a help to me.' And then she
was clicking off her seat belt, and heading for Al's private
room.

Evan watched in amazement. What had he said? Why had
she gone?

Rosa stopped her as she passed. 'Where *you* goin', girl?'

'I just got a message,' Nellie replied, eyes shining.

Rosa shook her head in disgust, 'Do yourself a favour and
forget him. He's just a user.'

Nellie smoothed down her long black hair. 'I don't need advice.'

Rosa shrugged. 'Don't come cryin' to me again. He's only gonna give you another glimpse of the magic horn – then it's onto the next. I *know* it, girl. Don't forget – I *bin* there.'

'Oh Rosa, don't be jealous!' said Nellie, kindly, 'it's not *my* fault he likes *me*.'

Rosa sent her eyes heavenwards. 'Jesus, save the children, or what's left of them.'

Nellie reached Al's door. Knocked. He didn't answer so she opened it tentatively, saw he was asleep, and crept in.

She silently approached the bed, stared down at him. She remembered how good it had been that one time in Miami. So very good. Spoiled by the fact that he hadn't wanted to speak to her since. But now that she knew her message had pleased him. Well, that made things different. He wasn't mad at her after all.

On impulse she peeled off the dress she was wearing, wriggled out of her panties, then quietly she snuggled into the big bed with him.

He was in the foetal position. She curled her slight body into his back, following the curves of his body.

He turned lazily, still asleep, but hard. She opened her legs and he entered her. She breathed his name softly, moving to accommodate him.

He came very quickly, eyes still closed. Then he mumbled, 'Go to sleep, Edna,' and turned his back on her.

Edna! Nellie lay there unfulfilled and trembling.

How could a man make love to a woman and still remain asleep? Unless of course he thought that woman was his wife.

Oh God! She was so humiliated.

She crept out of bed, frightened lest he wake. She dressed. It was her own fault, she should have wakened him.

How *could* she have done it?

She slipped out of the room, bumping straight into Paul.

'Oh!' she jumped nervously.

Paul gave her a suspicious look.

'I just wanted to talk to Al about something,' she stammered, 'but he's asleep.'

'Do me a favour, Nellie,' said Paul pleasantly, 'don't go into Al's private room unless he invites you. He does not like being disturbed. Any problems, come to me. OK?'

'Sure, sure Paul. I just er – I just, y'know, wanted to ask him something. Nothing important.'

He watched her walk away. Poor kid. Everyone knew how she felt about Al.

'She was in there for ten minutes,' remarked Linda, whose seat was nearest to Al's door. 'Perhaps she's murdered him.'

Paul glared at her, but walked into Al's room anyway. His brother slept peacefully.

What he would have to do, Paul decided, was station Luke outside the door. Al's private bedroom was becoming more like Grand Central Station every day.

☆

Edna King felt uncomfortable in the masculine striped suit.

'Latest fashion,' Melanie had assured her, 'suits you very well.'

Melanie herself was wearing an Yves Saint Laurent dress in a flattering blue colour. The sort of colour that looked good on Edna.

They sat together side by side on the huge jumbo jet. Edna had never liked flying, and her palms were wet with nerves as she waited for the take-off. Melanie was calm and collected, smiling at a man across the centre aisle, arranging her *Vogue* and *Harper's* and daily newspapers in a neat little pile.

Edna wondered wildly what would happen if they crashed. Al would be furious with her. And what would happen to Evan? Why oh why had she ever let Melanie talk her into this trip? It was sheer madness. 'The boys will love it,' Melanie had assured her. 'Once we're there, they'll love it!'

Of course the deciding factor had been Al's birthday. He was to be thirty-eight years old in two days' time, and Edna had spent every birthday with him since the day they were married.

'You'll be his present,' Melanie had enthused, 'just think how thrilled he'll be!'

Melanie had gone ahead and arranged everything. Even the bomb in Chicago had not put her off her plans. They were to fly directly to New York, stay there two days, and then fly to New Orleans, arriving on the evening of Al's birthday.

Melanie had called Paul before they left, and told him that she and Edna were off to a health farm for a few days and would be incommunicado. Paul had said what a good idea, and asked to talk to the children.

Melanie knew that Paul would be furious when they arrived. But so what? She was his wife, Al's sister-in-law, she was entitled to *some* of the glamour. Things had been quiet with Paul and Al away. Thank goodness Mr Capone was around to while away several boring evenings. He might only be a hairdresser, but he did give an incredible blow dry!

Melanie smiled, patted Edna reassuringly on the knee. 'I never thought I'd get you this far,' she said brightly.

'Nor did I,' replied Edna, and she shuddered as the huge jet roared into life.

37

Dallas hurried home from the location and immediately phoned Diamond before she changed her mind.

'Julio will be delighted to visit you around eight o'clock,' Diamond said, the perfect secretary.

Julio! Dallas realized that she didn't even know what he looked like. He could be five foot tall and seventy-three. And she was going to pay him for a service that at one time men had paid *her* for.

She drew a long, warm, bubble bath, tried to relax in it, couldn't. She brushed her hair, creamed off her make-up, wrapped herself in a towelling bathrobe. After all it wasn't like this was a date. It was a business appointment. A thera-peutic trip.

She smoked a little grass, not too much, just enough.

This whole scene was Linda's idea. Why wasn't she here to hold her hand?

At exactly ten to eight the doorbell rang, and Dallas nearly jumped out of her skin. She peeked at herself in the mirror. Wrapping her robe tightly around her she opened the door.

Cody stood there, smiling, and holding a brown paper

carton. 'I ate dinner at a record pace. Listened to ten boring stories about Cleveland, and decided you *were* business, so I did have a legitimate excuse to get the hell out. My mother wasn't pleased, but the only thing that would please her would be me marrying Golda Meir's daughter – and I don't even know if she's got a daughter!' He handed Dallas the carton, 'it ain't barbecue – but it's Jumbo Jims from Dolores', and chocolate malts, and banana cream pie. I thought we could live a little.'

Silently Dallas took the carton.

Cody walked inside. 'You look like you were just going to bed. I bet you didn't even bother to eat.'

Dallas shook her head. Food had been the last thing on her mind.

'So we'll eat, then I'll let you get some sleep.'

'I thought you already ate,' Dallas ventured.

'You call my mother's cooking eating? You must be kidding!'

Dallas didn't know what to do. She didn't want to hurt his feelings, but at the same time she wanted him out of there fast. She cringed at the thought of him bumping into Julio. And oh God – if he found out what Julio was doing there . . .

Why had she ever arranged it? Goddamn Linda and her stupid ideas!

Cody sat himself down on the couch. 'It's been a great week,' he said enthusiastically, 'you're even better than *I* thought. I didn't know you were going to turn out to be an actress on top of everything else. Is there no end to the surprises you have for me?'

'Cody. The hamburgers were a lovely idea, but you *did* tell me you were busy tonight.'

He stood up. 'You want me to go.'

'No, don't be silly. It's just that I did sort of arrange a date, and he'll be here any minute.'

Cody hit his forehead with the palm of his hand. 'Stupid me! I should have called. No problem, I'll just take my hamburgers and go.'

'It's not that I wouldn't have sooner spent the evening with you . . .'

He laughed, but she could tell that she had hurt his feelings.

'I understand, sweetheart. Don't worry about it.' His eyes flicked quickly over her bathrobe and unmade-up face. 'I could leave you the food. I'm not really hungry. It will just get wasted.'

'*I know*,' said Dallas, suddenly, 'you sit down. I'll get rid of my date. How's that? He was second choice to you anyway.'

'Wouldn't dream of it.'

'Well I would. Just sit down and shut up. I don't want him to see you.'

'Look, Dallas, I really think . . .'

At that moment the doorbell rang. Dallas made a gesture for Cody to be quiet. She shut him in the living room and went to the front door.

Julio was six foot two, black, and the best-looking man Dallas had ever set eyes on. He was about twenty-nine, beautifully dressed in a white silk shirt and French-cut black slacks. He smiled, displaying perfect white teeth. Parked behind him in the driveway was a gleaming white Ferrari. Business must be good.

'Hi,' he said easily, 'I'm Julio.'

'Oh,' replied Dallas blankly. She was not sure what she had expected, but it certainly wasn't Mr Perfect. What's a nice boy like you doing in a business like this? She was tempted to ask. But instead she said, 'Julio. There's been a slight problem. I'm afraid it's not possible for me to keep our er appointment tonight. I'm sorry you've been troubled, but of course I'll pay for your time. How much do I owe you?'

His smile remained. He took her hand, kissed it, 'I have not been troubled. Perhaps you would care to make another appointment.'

She shook her head, kept her voice low, 'I can't right now.'

'But you'll call when you can?'

'Yes.'

'In that case – no charge.'

'But I've wasted your time.'

'My time is never wasted.'

'If you're sure . . .'

'Of course.'

She shrugged. 'OK then, another time.'

'Another time.' Still smiling, he turned, got into the Ferrari, and roared off, saluting her with a friendly wave.

She leaned against the door. Oh if Linda had been here to witness *this* scene. She wanted to laugh, it all suddenly seemed so funny. If Cody hadn't turned up she would have invited Mr Perfect in to make love to her. And she was sure he would have been excellent. But no way could she have gone through with it, no way at all.

She thought of Cody sitting in her living room waiting for her. Dear, sweet, Cody, with his thinning hair and sense of humour. Why was she looking elsewhere? He wanted her, she was sure of that. So why not?

☆

He didn't mean to sneak a look, but he couldn't help himself. He was sorry when he saw a really great-looking black guy climbing into a white Ferrari.

A black guy. Let's digest *that* little bit of information. Oh sure, he was as liberal as the rest. He had supported civil rights, equal education, job opportunities. He had watched 'Roots' along with everyone else.

But shit. Sexually. Well, everyone knew that sexually they were hung like the Taj Mahal! Once a girl went to bed with a black man she didn't want to know about a white man. Direct quote from his mother. Like *she* would know.

Why the hell had he pushed his luck and come running over like a schoolboy. Of *course* she wouldn't be sitting around on her own just because he wasn't free. Why hadn't he learned his lesson the other night? Call first, schmuck.

Dallas came back in the room, 'All taken care of.'

Cody stood up. 'I think I'd better go.'

'Hey—' she pushed him playfully, 'I just cancelled my date for you.'

'But I still think . . .'

She wound her arms around his neck, moving her body close to his. 'That means I want *you* to stay.'

They were the same height. If she wore high heels she would be taller than him. He wished he had had a chance to clean his teeth after eating his mother's cooking. All these thoughts rushed through his mind as they kissed. He felt rooted to the spot. With Irene or Evelyn he would know what to do next, but with Dallas . . . She could feel his instant hard-on through her bathrobe. Christ, she would be able to feel it if she was wearing armour plating! He could not remember being this excited since high school when Janet Dell had jerked him off in the back of her father's car!

Dallas was undressing him. 'Hey,' he objected weakly.

'Hey—' she agreed, manipulating him out of his trousers. 'Oh yes,' she added, when she noticed his bulging jockey shorts.

He was embarrassed. He didn't want to touch her. He knew if he touched her it would be all over.

She was fiddling with the belt on her bathrobe.

'Let's go in the bedroom,' he suggested weakly.

'Let's,' she agreed.

It was dark in the bedroom, and when she switched the light on he turned it off.

She took off her bathrobe and lay down on the bed.

He had never seen a body like it. Legs like it. Breasts like it. Skin like it.

'Come here,' she said, holding out her arms.

As if he needed an invitation. But it was a mistake. He knew it was a mistake.

Ten seconds later his fears were realized. Instant come. He didn't even get it inside.

She laughed it off. 'Such enthusiasm!'

But he felt destroyed, like a young boy. And he couldn't get it up again, in spite of her kindly administrations.

'I'm sorry . . .'

'Don't worry about it.'

'It's never done that before.'

'It's a naughty boy.'

Shit! She had it in one.

He closed his eyes and wished for death or something along those lines. With Evelyn he could go all night. With Irene he was Mr Playboy personified.

'Why don't you sleep here?' Dallas suggested.

'I think I'll go home. Expecting a call.'

'If that's what you want.'

She didn't even argue, and who could blame her? If she

got rid of him early enough she could call up Superspade and really get it on. But he knew he was being unfair, it was she that had suggested he stay.

Miserably he dressed.

She didn't seem too put out. Any other girl would have been screaming for equal orgasm by this time.

She stayed in bed, modestly covering herself with a sheet, and when he was dressed she said, 'What about the hamburgers?' And he brought the carton into the bedroom, and she munched a cold hamburger with great relish whilst he watched.

'See you tomorrow, then,' she told him cheerfully when he was ready to leave. She didn't seem upset by his performance – or rather lack of it.

He kissed her chastely on the cheek and made his escape.

Dallas watched him go, sorry that he had not wanted to stay the night. She had been right about Cody. He was a genuinely nice guy, and she was touched by his obvious lack of experience in sex. He wasn't a groper, a jumper, a lecher, pulling at her body in a lustful frenzy the way most men did. He was a little bit shy, a little bit reticent. She sat up and hugged her knees. He was the kind of man she could live with.

OK, so he didn't make any bells ring. But she hadn't expected he would. Sex had never been a turn-on, just a way to make some money. Linda was wrong about it all being so wonderful.

Yes, Cody was the guy for her, of that she was sure.

But in the back of her mind was a feeling of disappointment. No sexual waves. No incredible flooding of the body and emotions. No hot and cold thrills. For a second her thoughts lingered fleetingly on Al King, then sternly she shut him out. Cody Hills was the man for her. Cody Hills was the man she wanted to marry.

38

Evan didn't know how it happened – well, not exactly. One moment he had been enjoying a more than friendly conversation with Nellie, and ten minutes later, when she had come back from a visit to Al, she seemed distant and upset. She didn't even sit down next to him, she went and huddled alone in a seat at the front.

He didn't have the courage to follow her. What if she snubbed him?

Probably his bloody father had hurt her feelings. He was good at doing that. As long as *he* was all right he didn't care what he said. It amazed Evan why people were still so anxious to jump at his every command. He treated them all like dirt.

When the plane landed, Evan hung back as usual. There was always such a fuss at every airport. Photographers, crowds, two-faced smiling officials. Evan hated it all.

He was concentrating on staying out of the way, when the fat girl spoke.

'Hi,' she said, bringing her face and bad breath very close to him 'whachasay we all ride inta town together.' She wasn't asking him, she was telling him.

'I don't think . . .' he began.

'You got a ride, dontcha? Glory an' I don't take up no room. Like we got no bread left. Like not even bus fare.'

'Yeah,' agreed Glory blankly, hitching up a laddered red stocking.

'OK,' muttered Evan. He knew who they were. They followed Al everywhere.

He got in the last of the fleet of black Cadillacs sent to meet Al and his entourage. The girls squeezed in with him. A couple of the musicians were already in the car.

'Get lucky, Evan?' one of them laughed, nudging his colleague.

'Aw shut y'face,' snapped Plum, 'after what we done f'you guys on this tour y'd think *one* of you would see we got a ride.'

'Anyone riding you needs insurance!' laughed the musician.

'Don't come to me next time you want it,' spat Plum. 'Y' all stink anyway.' She turned to Evan. 'Friggin' animals. Don't 'preciate nothin'.'

'Nothin',' echoed Glory, scratching at her frizzy mop of hair.

The car drove straight to the hotel. The two girls followed Evan into the lobby, and waited while he collected his key.

He pretended not to see them as he headed for the elevator. But they fell into step, one on each side of him.

'Y'don't mind if we use y'room for a few minutes,' stated Plum. 'Gotta wash, pee. You're real nice. Know that?'

No. He didn't know that. But it was nice to hear. In fact he had never been told that before. He warmed slightly towards the big fat girl.

They crowded into his room. 'Jeeze, I'm hungry!' exclaimed Plum. 'D'you think we could have room service? Jeeze – what I could do with a coupla cokes and a 'burger.'

Why not? He didn't have to pay for it. 'Order what you like,' he said magnanimously. After all if they thought he was nice he didn't want to spoil their opinion of him.

After scanning the room service menu, and choosing a mammoth meal, the two girls vanished into the bathroom. They stayed locked away until a knock at the door announced the arrival of the food. Then they emerged, wearing different outfits, although how they managed it Evan didn't know, for they possessed one scruffy-looking carry-all between the two of them.

Glory seemed to have perked up considerably. 'Nice room!' she exclaimed as if seeing it for the first time.

'Big! Too big for one guy all on his own. Food! You sure are one wonderful person. Cute too.' She winked at him. 'Wish we had some booze. Got any booze?'

Evan shook his head.

'Booze makes me do veree dirty things!' Glory added, rolling her slightly protruding eyes, 'how 'bout you?'

'Don't drink,' muttered Evan.

'Never?'

'Champagne.'

Glory fell about laughing, 'Shit man! Champagne. 'Scuse me for bein' in the same room!'

'Leave him alone,' interrupted Plum quickly.

'I ain't hassling him. Honest I'm not. He's the man. Like look at this food – got me droolin'.' Glory picked up some french fries with her fingers and stuffed them in her mouth. 'Yum! Good stuff.' She narrowed her eyes at Evan. 'Ain't you all eatin'?'

'I might have to eat later with my father.'

'Oooh! With my father!' Glory mimicked his accent, whilst Plum mouthed 'shut up' at her. 'French fries no good for your spots anyway,' yawned Glory.

Evan reddened.

'Don't go gettin' uptight 'bout your spots. *I* got spots too. All over my bum. Wanna see?' She started to unzip her jeans.

'Not *now*,' objected Plum, 'I'm eating.'

'Tell you what,' laughed Glory, 'you can squeeze my spots if I can squeeze yours! A deal?' She stuck out a skinny hand with nails bitten down to the quick. Evan took it. They shook solemnly. 'You're a real nice person,' Glory smiled, 'I think we're all gonna get along just fine.'

☆

'How do you like our city?' the girl interviewer asked.

'The best!' replied Al firmly. He knew what they would all ask, and he gave them all the same answers. 'Saw a great show when I was a kid – *Oklahoma*. Howard Keel singing his whatsits off.'

'Howard Keel?' she questioned, smiling politely.

'Yeah – Howard Keel – you remember . . .' He trailed off. How could she remember? She was only about twenty something. The young, smart ones. They always sent the college ladies to interview him. Why didn't he ever get an old bag? Someone who knew what the fuck he was talking about.

I will be thirty-eight in two days' time, he thought. Two years after that I will be forty. And I don't want to be poncing around the world dodging randy females when I'm forty. I don't want to be married to Edna either.

'I beg your pardon?' said the interviewer.

'I beg your pardon what?'

'I – I thought you said something.'

'Just your ears playing tricks on you.' He took a swig of champagne and surveyed the girl. She was pretty in a *Cosmopolitan* way. He leaned forward, fixing her with his deep black eyes.

She moved uncomfortably on her chair. 'I wanted to ask you,' she began.

'Let's forget about the boring questions,' he said, 'let's just get it all off and fuck.'

'Oh!' She blushed.

'Come on,' insisted Al, 'this is your chance for an exclusive. Isn't that what all little girl reporters want?'

She opened her mouth to reply. Didn't know what to say.

'Clothes off,' suggested Al. He leaned back and waited. Wouldn't it be nice if she said no. But no such luck. She was soon unzipping, unbuttoning, and unhooking.

He yawned. What could you expect from a girl who had never even heard of Howard Keel?

☆

Bernie Suntan conferred with the security heads at the Fairgrounds Arena. Everything seemed tight.

Goddamn weather. The goddamn heat never seemed to let up. He had to carry a supply of T-shirts because he sweated his way through six of them a day.

Goddamn tour. He wished they were in LA already. His town. A civilized place where you could walk by the pool at the Beverly Hills Hotel and see *other human beings*.

He was sick of being nice to morons and bums and nothings. Little people with small minds and little jobs on hick newspapers. Douche bags all of them.

He swigged from a can of beer. He was still smarting with embarrassment at the scene on the plane. Those two pigs that should never have been allowed out without a leash. Jeezus! That they should tell Paul about what they had done to him. Jeezus! Ugly would be an overestimation of their condition!

Had he not been stoned and extremely horny he would not have put his tool in their direction in a million years. But Jeeze – he had been working his balls off, and where was the thanks? Major coverage in every city. Magazine pieces that you would sell your mother for. Every television show. What the fuck – he was doing a GREAT JOB!

Of course if he had had the time he could have found himself a sweet piece. But who had time? And those two gorillas had been available and grinding their teeth for a thrust of what he had to offer.

Fat he may be. But he could cream chicks with the best of them.

He finished his beer, crumpled the can. What the fuck.

They were out of his life now. He had told them in no uncertain terms to quit hanging around him.

Roll on LA.

☆

After half an hour Al was bored. He sent Miss Girl Reporter packing and lay morosely on his bed studying the ceiling. Hotel rooms. He hated them.

Paul called to say they would be leaving for the Arena in an hour.

Al hauled himself into the shower, soaped his body, rinsed away the previous half hour.

He shaved. Studied his face. Plucked out a few eyebrow hairs that were daring to cross the bridge of his nose. He brushed his teeth, played with some dental floss.

He didn't look like a person who was nearly thirty-eight. Squinting at himself in the mirror he decided he looked no more than twenty-nine – well, thirty at the most.

Satisfied with his appearance he decided to phone Evan. He felt a bit guilty about the fact that he hardly saw him any more. But it was a relief – having Evan in his pocket had started to drive him crazy.

Evan answered the phone in his room with a surly, mumbled 'Yes?'

'Coming to the show tonight?' Al asked cheerfully.

'Yes,' answered Evan.

'Good. Why don't you come to the suite and we'll drive over together.'

There was a short, muffled silence, then Evan said, 'Think I'll see you there. Can I have some extra tickets? I've got some friends I want to bring.'

He had friends! At last! 'Sure, sure. How many do you want? I'll have Bernie arrange it.'

' 'Bout six.'

Six friends! When he worked, he worked quickly! 'They'll be at the box office. You and your friends want to come to the party after?'

'I dunno. We might.'

'Try to make it. You need any money?'

'Yes.'

'Come over and I'll give you a fifty.'

'Can't. I've got someone here.'

'A girl?' Al was delighted.

'Yes,' muttered Evan. 'So can you leave the money at the desk for me?'

'It will be my pleasure, son.' Al hung up the phone well pleased. So Evan had finally got himself connected. What a relief! Not that he had been worried. He knew the kid was normal – after all he was Al King's son, wasn't he?

☆

'I got you the tickets,' Evan said.

'Clever!' sighed Glory.

'Why did you want six?'

'To sell of course. Gotta make bread every way y'can. Know what I mean?'

Evan nodded. Why hadn't *he* thought of that.

Plum was smearing lipstick on. 'We'd better get moving. We've got – let me see – yeah we got twelve tickets to sell now. Reckon we'll make at least two hundred.'

Glory whistled. 'Like – rich, man.'

Plum nodded. 'It'll keep us goin'.'

'My father is leaving me fifty dollars at the desk,' Evan announced proudly.

'So we're all rich!' laughed Glory, latching her thin arm through Evan's equally thin arm. 'We can buy us some real good poppers and come back here and like – y'know – have a real *mean* time. Wanna do that, Evvaan?'

'Yes,' he said quickly, 'let's do that.'

Plum threw her arm around him. 'You're one of us now, man,' she said kindly.

He positively glowed. He was one of them.

☆

Bernie spotted them first, Al's kid and the two barracudas.

He complained to Paul, who didn't believe him. 'Evan, with those two? You must be mistaken.'

'You want me to tell them to leave the kid alone?' Bernie blustered. 'Mistaken I ain't. The three of 'em bouncing around out front as tight as thieves.'

'Let me ask Al,' Paul decided. It was up to Al to decide the company Evan should keep.

Al said 'Jesus!', shook his head and laughed. 'I guess it can't do any harm. Leave him alone if that's what he wants.'

Paul passed the word to Bernie, who snorted with disgust. If it was his kid . . . Aw – what the fuck . . . Fortunately it wasn't.

☆

They counted out the money.

Two hundred and sixteen bucks!' exclaimed Plum in delight.

Glory slid her arm tightly around Evan's waist, 'Wanna add your fifty?' she asked slyly, 'wanna be our partner?'

'Yeah,' agreed Plum, 'if you go with us y'gotta pool your bread too. S'only fair.'

'OK,' squeaked Evan. He reached into his jeans' pocket for the money, pleased he hadn't told them about his two hundred dollars.

Plum took the fifty, added it to their money, and then placed the wad of notes firmly in her bra. First she extracted a twenty which she handed to Glory. 'She'll score for us,' Plum explained to Evan, 'now you're our partner you can join in *all* the fun.'

He shivered in anticipation. They weren't Nellie, but they liked him, accepted him, and if he couldn't have Nellie . . . Well . . .

Glory vanished off into the crowds who had not managed to get into the concert.

'She won't be long,' Plum informed him confidently, 'she's gotta nose f' the best score. Few quacks be just right.' She nudged him knowingly. 'You're not into the heavy stuff are you?'

He wanted to ask what heavy stuff? He wanted to ask what quacks were? He wanted to know score what?

He stood silently. Maintain an aura of being one of them. Mustn't ask questions. Mustn't act like a fool.

Once, at school, one of the seniors had been caught smoking grass. He knew what grass was. His father had offered him some once, stuffed a vile-smelling cigarette in his mouth and said: 'Drag on that and if you ever want it again come to me; I don't want to catch you doing it behind my back.'

Glory returned, skipping and laughing. Both girls seemed to have forgotten about the concert, indeed they had sold all the tickets, including their own.

'Let's go back to the hotel,' Plum suggested, 'an' have a good time.'

Glory giggled shrilly. 'Can you give us a good time, Evan? Can you? Can you give *both* of us a good time?'

He smiled bravely. Why not? If his father could do it why couldn't he?

'Yeah,' he croaked, 'let's go.'

39

Dallas waited for their relationship to develop. She waited for Cody to tell her something corny like he loved her. She waited for him to make love to her again.

He did none of those things.

He phoned her on the Sunday to tell her his mother was sick and he couldn't come over.

He turned up at the studio on Monday for lunch as usual. And it was as usual. No mention of what had taken place between them. No words of love. No physical contact. He was exactly the same as he always was. Sweet, charming, funny. He had a script he wanted her to read. He had two important magazine interviews he had arranged for her. He had a franchise on 'Man Made Woman' T-shirts he wanted to discuss with her. He had a top photographer coming in from New York specially to photograph her.

What with working and doing all the things Cody had arranged she did not have much time free.

At first she was hurt by his attitude. But the hurt soon turned to a cold anger, and she felt used and debased.

How dare he treat her like this. Cody Hills. Short, balding, not even rich – yet. And she had gone to bed with him, given herself to him – and he didn't want to know.

When the call from Lew Margolis finally came she was in just the right mood for it.

'I'll come to your house,' he informed her, no doubt hoping she would arrange a second session with the luscious Diamond.

'No. I'll come to your office,' she insisted, 'I have a surprise for you.'

The date was made, and she went home, selected some of the best photos, and slid them into the cellophane pages of a leather-bound album. It was a touch she was sure Linda would have appreciated.

☆

Cody was destroyed. Dallas was everything he had ever dreamed about in a relationship. But Christ! What did she want with him? She could have anyone.

He loved her. He loved everything about her. But he knew it was a love that would destroy their relationship. And God Almighty – ultimately theirs was a business tryst. And that's the way he had to keep it.

Regarding things clearly and logically he could see where it was all at. She was looking for something – someone, and he just happened to be there. Yes – it could be great, until she found what she was *really* searching for. And then what? Wasn't he better off being her agent, manager and friend? That way he would always be around.

Mr Cody Hills regrets that although he would give his left leg to keep on trucking, his head rules his heart (fortunately), and he is too smart to screw up a golden opportunity.

He hated himself. He knew she was hurt. But one of these days she would thank him. This is where analysis got you. Made you so smart you cut off your own balls!

On the Sunday, after being with Dallas the previous day, he had steeled himself into action. He had phoned Connie.

'My God! I figured you died! she exclaimed, 'where have you been?'

'Working,' he explained, 'can I come over?'

'I was just washing my . . .'

'I'll be there in time to dry it!'

'Haven't changed, have you?'

He hoped not. He rushed over to her apartment on Fountain, and within fifteen minutes had talked her into bed – wet hair and all.

She did not have a body like Dallas. No one had a body like Dallas.

He did not come all over her in one schoolboyish spurt. He indulged in twenty minutes polite foreplay and seventeen minutes of polite fucking. He then spent a further half hour being affectionate and considerate. Fell asleep for an acceptable hour, and then went home.

Things weren't what they used to be.

☆

Lew Margolis looked through the book of photographs once, then a second time. He didn't speak.

Dallas, sitting across from him, lit a cigarette and tried to appear as calm as possible.

Lew studied the photos yet again.

'Like them?' Dallas inquired. She couldn't stand the silence. Let's get this show on the road and over and done with.

'Is this the surprise you had for me?' he asked at last.

'I thought I'd show them to you first. Thought it might make rather a nice anniversary present for your wife. I understand you've been married nine years next week.'

'Once a cunt always a cunt,' he said wearily. 'How much?'

'How much for what?'

'The pictures.'

'No charge, Mister.' She glared at him. 'Just no more private meetings between us. Get your rocks off on somebody else's time.'

His lips tightened. 'We had an arrangement, you agreed.'

'I agreed shit. You blackmailed me, and now I'm throwing the ball back into *your* court.'

'I can make or break you.'

'Likewise.'

They stared at each other, then finally he said, 'You don't want to fuck me means you're a silly girl. You got the pictures means you're smart. But it's all a game – remember that – just a game. And I am an *ace* player – *an ace*. What are you? Some down-and-out hooker I gave a break to.'

'Thank you, Mr Margolis,' her voice was thick with sarcasm, 'may I please go now?'

He flicked through the photos again. 'Yeah. Go. You've

won this round – but if Doris ever sees these pictures you'll find yourself washed up on the beach one morning along with the rest of the garbage. Remember that, it's not an idle threat.'

'I'll remember. But *you* remember there's a letter with my lawyer should anything happen to me. And the negatives will become very public property.'

'You've been seeing too many movies. Get your ass back to work. If I can't hump you I may as well make money out of you.'

She stood up. Christ! Was it worth it? She felt more dirty than if she'd slept with him a hundred times.

'Get lost, cunt,' he added. And it was the last she saw of him until Cody received an invitation for the two of them to attend a dinner party at the Margolis residence two days later.

'I don't want to go,'she told Cody.

'Are you kidding?' he argued. 'An invitation to one of their dinners is like the seal of approval in this town. He must really like you.'

She had no alternative but to accept the invitation. To refuse would certainly make Cody suspicious. Besides she was curious to see what Lew had in mind.

☆

The dinner party was on a Saturday. Dallas spent the day doing pictures with the photographer from New York who was an outrageous, amusing fag. He was full of gossip about the so-called Beautiful People, and told the most scandalous stories. He also took magnificent photos, and she continued her love affair with the camera. It was the only love affair she had.

When Cody picked her up she was tired, irritable, and not at all looking forward to dinner at the Margolises.

'You look wonderful,' Cody told her.

'Wonderful enough to make love to?' she questioned. It was the first time either of them had mentioned it.

Cody was prepared. He knew that eventually she would have to say something. He pulled the car over to the side and turned to her. 'You want to hear a really corny speech?'

'Try me. I'd like to hear *something*. It's our anniversary,

you know. Exactly one week ago we made fast abortive love
– or rather we *nearly* did. And I'd like to know why you've
been trying to forget it ever happened.'

'I . . .'

'How do you think I *feel*?' she continued, her emotions
rushing to the surface, 'I don't enter into relationships easily,
you know. You have no idea what it took for me to sleep
with you.'

He was temporarily speechless. He hadn't expected *this*.
What about the night he had sneaked up to her house and
seen her taking part in an orgy? What about her big black
boyfriend?

'Well?' she demanded. 'What's the problem, Cody? Don't
I turn you on?'

Another laugh. She turned him on so goddamn fast it was
over before it had even happened.

He took her hand. 'You know I adore you . . .'

'But?' she interrupted.

'But I think if you and I indulge in any sort of a thing
you're going to regret it.'

'Oh, come on!'

'I mean it, Dallas. Don't you understand this is just the
beginning for you. Once a week you're going to be on
millions of TV sets all over the country. Your face – you –
will be public property. You'll have all the pressures of being
a star, plus all the advantages, *I* don't want to get in the way
of all your advantages.'

'What are you talking about?'

'You know what I'm talking about. You'll be able to have
any guy you want, and I don't want to be shoved in the
background like some schmuck. It may surprise you but I've
got an enormous ego.'

'Terrific,' said Dallas coldly, 'really terrific!'

'What?'

'Your opinion of me.'

'It's not my opinion of you. I love you – and because I
love you I don't want to put you in a position of feeling
guilty.'

'Ha! We haven't even made it properly and already I've
discarded you for ten other men!'

He sighed. 'Basically I'm being selfish. I don't want to get kicked in the teeth.'

'But I wouldn't . . .'

'But the chances are you would.'

'Chances? What chances? I think you're full of shit.'

'So does my mother – that's why she wants me to get married to a nice kosher lady who'll stuff me full of Ex-Lax hidden in the chicken soup!'

Dallas couldn't help laughing. She felt better after their talk, and in a way she understood how he felt, but that was only because he didn't know her very well. 'Take me to the party, Cody. Maybe I can get drunk and rape you when you're not so busy protecting your *enormous* ego. I think we have a future together – let me see if I can convince you.'

The first person she saw at the party was Ed Kurlnik.

The second person she spotted was Aarron Mack. The two of them were engaged in an animated conversation – well, about as animated as two elderly billionaires could be.

Two of the richest men in America, and they had both wanted her. Not bad for a girl who had had to make it on her own.

Lew Margolis was bearing down on her, a fatherly smile suffusing his false teeth. 'Glad you two kids could make it,' he said warmly.

Tonight she was kid. What had happened to cunt?

'Mr Margolis,' eagerly Cody shook hands, 'so nice of you to think of us.'

'My pleasure. Got to look after my little star!' He winked at her. 'Right, Dallas?'

'Right, Mr Margolis.'

'Call me Lew, no need to be formal. Come, I want you to meet my wife.'

Dallas had seen Doris Andrews in so many movies that meeting her was like coming face to face with an old friend. The same wispy brown hair, cornflower-blue eyes, kindly smile, a little girl voice. 'So pleased to meet you, Dallas dear. Lew has told me all about the wonderful series you're doing for him. It sounds such fun.'

Dallas could hardly imagine the ordinary-looking Doris

Andrews seducing every man she came in contact with. Lew's games were probably a figment of his very vivid imagination.

'Let me introduce you around,' said Doris, adjusting the Peter Pan starched white collar of her dress. She certainly lived up to her screen image.

Both Ed and Aarron had spotted her at the same time, and their conversation was abruptly terminated, whilst they both tried to wander over in an unobtrusive way.

Aarron reached her first, as Ed was waylaid by a woman who Dallas realized with a shock was Dee Dee Kurlnik.

'Dallas!' exclaimed Aarron, clutching both her hands, 'you leave New York just like that. No word, no address. I am hurt.'

She stared down at his bullet head. God, all the money in the world couldn't make you tall.

Doris smiled. 'Aarron, I didn't realize you knew our little star,'

There were a lot of things Doris didn't realize.

'Yes, we are old friends.'

'Of course you are,' Doris grinned, 'you know every beautiful girl in America! He's such a naughty boy, Dallas, you'll have to watch him!'

Naughty boy! The man was seventy-three years old!

Dallas smiled weakly and looked around for Cody. He was in deep conversation with Ed and Dee Dee. Oh Christ! This was a nightmare. Lew Margolis must have planned the whole thing.

A waiter hovered with a silver tray. She snatched a glass of champagne and gulped it down.

'Now that I have found you again,' Aarron said smugly, 'escape will not be so easy.' He leered at her breasts. 'I have thought about you many times.'

She remembered their last dismal date. Such fun that she had contemplated suicide. She remembered him exposing his withered penis to her, expecting her to immediately get on her knees.

'I think I had better circulate,' she said.

'Why?' he wanted to know.

'Because I think I should.'

He shook his head in admiration. 'I like your spirit. I liked it in New York. You don't care about my money, do you?'

'Not particularly.'

'I like that. Most women will do anything for money.'

'Really?' Her sarcasm was lost on him.

'You'd be surprised,' he brooded darkly, 'but you are so different. I knew that at once.'

'Good for you.'

'I am in California for only three days. I want you to keep those days free. We shall be together.'

'I'm working.'

'Tomorrow is Sunday. We'll take my plane to Palm Springs.'

'I don't want to go to Palm Springs.'

'We'll go where you want. I like your fiery spirit. You remind me of my dear departed wife. She was Swedish, you know. We were married for forty-six years. She was an independent woman – like you.' He coughed, bending over and choking vigorously.

Dallas took the opportunity to escape. She walked out beside the Olympic pool and hoped that Aarron wouldn't follow her.

So this was a chic Hollywood dinner party. Not quite what she had imagined. Apart from Cody and herself everyone was so old.

She sipped her champagne and marvelled at the mosaic initials embedded on the bottom of the pool. Inside she could see Cody still talking to Ed and Dee Dee. Aarron was looking around wondering what had happened to her.

She recalled the last time she had visited this house. As a hooker. Who would have thought that she would come back in such a different position; Oh come on, Cody – what the hell are you talking to those two old farts about?

Beautifully laid out tables were in position on the huge patio. Six tables, ten places per table. Sixty people. Some small dinner party.

She circled round the tables glancing at the delicate engraved place cards set in their exquisite silver holders. The names read like a Who's Who of Hollywood. She found her own name positioned between two men she had never heard of. Now if she could only find Cody's place – a quick switch and no one would be any the wiser. Dallas was still innocent of Hollywood party procedure. Doris Andrews had spent hours sweating over who should sit next to whom.

'You want some help?' A waiter who had been hovering on the sidelines approached her.

'No, it doesn't matter, thank you.' She headed back for the house.

Doris Andrews was just emerging. 'Ah, Dallas, dear. What are you doing out here? Aarron's looking for you. I think you made quite a hit there. I didn't even know you two knew each other. He's such a sweet, sweet man, and so lonely.'

'And so rich,' Dallas added drily.

'But of course. Isn't everyone?' Doris touched her lightly on the arm, then hesitating slightly she asked, 'You do like men, don't you?'

'What do you mean?'

Doris's fingers drummed a light pattern on her arm. 'Sexually.'

'Sexually?' Dallas questioned, suddenly at a loss for words.

Doris laughed throatily. 'Men are such brutes. Big and hairy. Rough. Unthinking. A woman's touch is so much softer . . . kinder . . . Do you know what I mean now?'

'I think I'm getting the message.'

Christ! Doris Andrews dykesville! Public image – Miss Clean – Husband's image – Miss Randy. Lew – you are playing the wrong game!

'Well, dear. Perhaps you and I will take lunch together one day. I can give you the benefit of my experience. Twenty years in this shitty business – you have to know how to handle yourself. I can see you're going to be someone special . . .' She trailed off. 'Must get dinner organized. You run along and enjoy yourself.'

'Yes,' agreed Dallas, still in a state of shock. Doris Andrews. The only screen virgin left in Hollywood!

She wandered back into the house to be pounced on immediately by Aarron demanding to know where she had been.

'I went for a walk,' she replied, annoyed at being questioned. Then she saw Cody free from the Kurlniks at last, and beckoned him over.

He came on the trot, eager and delighted by the entire party. Before she could introduce him he was pumping Aarron by the hand and saying, 'Mr Mack. It's a real pleasure to meet you. My name is Cody Hills. I am Dallas' agent and manager.'

'Good,' wheezed Aarron, 'then you can instruct her to come to Palm Springs with me.'

Cody laughed with just the right amount of deference. 'Mr Mack, unfortunately I can't instruct Dallas to do anything. A very headstrong young lady is Dallas.'

They both regarded her with patronizing smiles.

She was furious. Headstrong indeed!

'Mr Mack, I know why you are in Los Angeles,' Cody continued. 'It's the big search, isn't it? You are looking for the new Mack girl. Well, has it ever occurred to you that Dallas is just the girl you're looking for?'

'Is she not signed for a television series?'

'Yes, she is. And that could be just the tie-in to make the new Mack girl *really* exciting. 'Man Made Woman' as *your* Mack girl – wearing *your* cosmetics – *your* perfumes. Think of the excitement *that* would generate. Of course ... she doesn't come cheap.'

Aarron was impressed with the idea. His small eyes gleamed.

'What do you think, Mr Mack. Is this a great idea or is it a great idea?'

Dallas walked away. Neither man noticed her go. Cody would have made a great Coca Cola salesman. She had never seen anyone so turned on by his own ideas. Maybe he was right. Maybe he wasn't the man for her. She was seeing a side of him that she wasn't sure she could stomach. Mr Kiss-your-ass. She had kissed too many asses in her life to go through that scene again.

'Dallas!' Ed Kurlnik had stationed himself behind a potted palm and was hissing her name.

She marched over to him. 'How dare you stand me up in New York!' she said loudly.

'Sshh!' he mumbled.

'Don't sshh me. I waited at Essex House all night. You never came.'

'I did,' he whispered.

'Your wife's coming over. Are you going to introduce us?'

'What?' he jumped. 'Dallas, I . . .'

She strolled away feeling good.

Two of the richest men in the world grovelling for her favours.

Wow – if this was a taste of being a star – she liked it.

40

'**Look out** the window,' said Paul.

Al, emerging from the bathroom, went to the window, and saw, eighteen storeys below, crowds of girls blocking the street outside. They held a giant banner aloft – 'Happy Birthday, Al – You are King.'

'I think you should make an appearance,' Paul said, 'they've been there all day.'

'How's the security?' snapped Al. He was starting to get slightly paranoiac about his personal safety.

'There are cops all round the hotel. The management suggested you give 'em a wave from a first-storey balcony. Then we can smuggle you out to City Park through a back entrance.'

'OK. Fine with me. That flight knocked me out this morning. I guess I've slept the day away.'

'It's your birthday – do what you want.'

'I thought I always did anyway.'

'Yeah – every day's a birthday for you Al.'

'Right on, baby brother – right on!'

'You get yourself together then, I'll let them know you'll be out on the balcony in an hour. Does that give you enough time?'

'Yeah.'

Paul left. Al switched on the television. It would take him five minutes to dress. Idly he switched channels until he found a Western. Christ! Paul Newman looked young. An unlined, un-lived-in face. Must be a really old movie. Of course Newman still looked terrific – but you knew he was just another old guy that looked terrific. What was it that aged a person?

Al rushed to the mirror and studied his own image. A thirty-eight-year-old superstar. Thirty-eight. Wasn't that nearing middle age? Al King middle-aged – never. The thought filled him with dread. His life was speeding along and leaving him behind. Dreary days – only the nights – lit up with champagne, and cigars, and women, offered any diversions. And was it worth the hangovers?

Of course the hours on stage were still magic. A level of communication he could reach nowhere else in his life. But suddenly it wasn't enough. He wanted more. More what? He didn't really know, if he did he would buy it.

He lit a cigar, too soon after waking for a smoke, but what the hell. Maybe cancer would save him from ever being senile. He smiled grimly. As it happened he didn't feel too good, nothing specific, just a sort of draggy feeling that he couldn't put a name to.

He slouched in front of the television, not really watching it at all. He was worried about Evan, worried at the company he was keeping.

At first it had been a joke – Evan and the two freaks. Al had thought it would have been a five-minute relationship. But Evan let them attach themselves to him with a vengeance. He even asked if he could bring them with him on the plane from Houston. Reluctantly Al had said yes. Against his better judgement, but Christ Almighty it was the first time the kid had made friends, and he didn't want to come the heavy father bit. He had tried to discuss the girls with his son, but Evan refused to carry on conversations – he just mumbled inaudible yes's and no's.

What they had, Al finally realized, was a communication problem. And sod it – it wasn't *his* fault – he had given the boy everything that money could buy. Evan just didn't appreciate things.

The whole problem was Edna's fault. Christ! She would have a blue fit if she saw him now.

Al sighed. He would let it go. Let Evan get them out of his system. After all, he too had banged a few slags in his time.

☆

Linda bumped into Paul in the lobby.

'I got some great shots!' she enthused.

'I think he's depressed.'

'Who?'

'Who! Only you would ask who.'

'So-rrry.'

'Did you manage to wrap everything yet?'

Linda mock saluted. 'Naturally, I have not forgotten it is Big White Master's Birthday.'

Paul glanced at his watch. 'Listen, I've got to move. Be sure to get everything organized.'

'You betcha ass, black eyes. See you later.'

He kissed her cheek. 'Later.'

Linda watched him walk across the lobby. Sentimental bum. He was making as much fuss about Al's birthday as if it were for a child. Rather sweet really. But then that's what had hooked her on Paul in the first place – his inherent niceness.

She observed Evan enter the lobby, his two bizarre companions flanking him as usual. She wished that Paul had not put the block on her photographing them – because wow – what a picture *that* trio would make.

'Hello,' she said, as they passed on by.

Evan's glazed eyes flicked briefly in her direction. She wondered if Al knew that these two freaky girls had got his son flying on some drug or other. Probably not.

She wondered if she should be the one to tell him. Probably not. She sighed. Some birthday present.

☆

As the lights dimmed, the audience roared its approval. Their patience was stretched to the limit, even 'The Promises' had had trouble holding them. They wanted Al. They didn't want to wait.

As the total darkness swept over the audience the sound of drums started slowly, to be joined by tambourines, then the guitar and congas.

The opening bars of 'Random Love'.

Suddenly Al standing centre stage bathed in brilliant spotlights.

The audience was on its feet as one, screaming their appreciation.

The waves flooded over him. He assaulted them rhythmically – swaying, moving, bending, leaning – until they were almost a part of him. Total fucking.

The spotlights tracked his every move, following him like relentless slaves. He swigged from the champagne bottle waiting on top of one of the amplifiers, and the mob screamed 'Happy Birthday Al' and surged dangerously near to crushing the mass of security guards in front of the stage.

He decided against doing his usual set, and switched into a rasping parody of Jagger's 'Satisfaction' – then Stewart's 'Maggie May' and his own 'All Night Stand'. The crowd went mad.

'S'good to be in New Orleans,' he told them. They screamed. He did some very funky, very beautiful Bobby Bland hits. Then he rasped into a medley from his new album which was to be released any day. And then 'Bad Black Alice', his current single, which was racing up the charts.

He was halfway through that when the crowds broke through security and came clambering up on stage like small mad locusts. He felt panic and terror as he saw the mob descending. He was paralysed with fear. He just couldn't move.

A girl grabbed him round the neck before he even realized what was happening. She was thrown bodily off him by Luke who appeared miraculously quickly. Another girl gripped him round the legs, her hands clawing and strange little grunts emitting from her throat as she too was pulled off him.

It was like a bad dream. One moment music and harmony – the next the dark eruption of violence as Luke and Marvin half dragged him from the stage kicking and shoving the locusts out of their way. His feet hardly touched the ground. That's how fast they got him out to the car.

'Holy shit!' He exclaimed as the car raced off, 'What the fuck happened?'

I told 'em they didn't have enough guys out front,' Luke said stoically. 'I told Bernie they'd break through.'

'What did he say?' asked Al, sudden anger coursing through him.

'You know Bernie, but I told him.'

Sure. Al could just imagine. Fat Bernie had probably

shrugged and said 'What the fuck.' After all it was no skin off his nose if Al got torn to pieces by his fans. Think of the publicity . . .

☆

Evan, Plum and Glory were near the front when it happened.

'Jest fall with the crowd, man,' Plum yelled with excitement, 'and hold on!'

Panic swept over Evan as pressure from the crowds behind propelled him forward. Hold on to what?

Glory was laughing and scrambling towards the stage. Plum grinned solidly. Neither girl seemed in the least put out by the sudden chaos.

Evan saw people swarming over the fallen security guards using them as footrests to get a hoist up towards the stage. It didn't seem to matter that Al was no longer on the stage.

'Hang on in there, man,' trilled Glory, 'just keep on a movin'.'

He could hardly do anything else. And then from behind he could hear pain-filled screams as more security guards moved in wielding heavy truncheons in all directions.

He wanted to get out of there. But there was nowhere to go, nowhere to turn. Then suddenly he felt himself falling, knees buckling. And he knew if the mob behind him didn't stop he would be trampled to death.

☆

Edna didn't like New York. And – momentous decision – after all those years she finally admitted to herself that she didn't like Melanie. She had always known in the back of her mind that her sister-in-law was a pain – but suddenly she found that she could come right out and think it – maybe even say it – only to Al of course, she wouldn't want to be disloyal to the family. The thing was that Paul was so nice. She had always been fond of him. Like her, he only had Al's best interests at heart. Together they had supported Al on his climb to fame, and together they were still the only two people really close to him.

To see Melanie at work was a shock. Edna had always suspected that she played around, but to see her blatantly flirt with every man who crossed her path was disgusting.

Melanie had arrived in New York armed with a book of telephone numbers. People she had met, friends and business acquaintances of Al's and Paul's. She didn't care who she called. 'I'm not sitting in a hotel room for two days,' she had told Edna when she objected, 'I'm going out to have fun!'

Edna sat in the hotel room by herself whilst Melanie did just that. The first night she didn't arrive home until 4 a.m. The second she didn't bother to appear at all and breezed in with room service delivering breakfast. 'Do you honestly think that Al and Paul aren't out having themselves a good time?' she demanded of Edna.

'I'm sure they're working very hard,' Edna insisted.

'Oh sure! And the rest. Don't you know these tours have girls following them across the country? Girls who will do anything. A man would have to be the Pope to resist *that* kind of temptation. Paul and I have an understanding.'

Edna tightened her lips and didn't pursue the conversation. Melanie was just not a nice person. It was quite obvious she had used and manipulated her to get her to agree to the trip. Now that they were almost there she didn't care any more. Edna was no longer useful.

The flight to New Orleans from Kennedy Airport was delayed by three hours. Melanie was furious, and bounced around the airport trying to cause a fuss. She finally caught the attention of an airline official who settled them in a private lounge, and plied Melanie with vodka.

Edna leafed through magazines and willed the plane to be ready to take off soon. She didn't want to miss Al's birthday. After all, that was the whole point of the trip.

☆

'Thank Christ you weren't there.' Paul took Linda's face in his hands and kissed her.

She wriggled free. 'I miss all the good things. When I think of the pictures I could have gotten . . .'

'You could have been crushed to death. I've never seen anything like it, it was frightening. Christ knows how many injuries we're going to have with this one.'

'Is Al all right?'

'A little frantic. We're still trying to locate Evan. No one seems to know whether he was there or not. Since he's been hanging around with those weirdos he does his own thing.'

'I saw him earlier with them in the lobby, but that was long before the concert.'

'Bernie's at the theatre, I'm going to take a ride over to the hospital. Now what I want you to do is to put a time stop on all the party arrangements – just a postponement – I hope we can go ahead later. Meanwhile do me a favour and go and sit with Al – and if Evan turns up, contact Bernie.' He kissed her. 'I'll be back soon, sweetheart.'

Linda did as she was told. What a wonderful secretary I would have made some lucky executive, she thought, as she darted around the hotel issuing instructions.

Wife – no. Secretary – yes.

Everything done she made her way up to Al's suite. He slouched morosely on the couch watching a late newscast of the event on television.

'Some birthday!' he said bitterly.

'It's not over yet,' she replied briskly. 'Any word on Evan?'

'Nothing. I should never have let him go wandering off all over the place with those two freaks.'

'You didn't know this was going to happen.'

Al made a face. 'This, that. I should know where the fuck he is. I was just so goddamn relieved he had found some friends that I let him do what he wanted.'

'Can I fix you a drink?' Linda asked, going over to the bar and sorting through the bottles.

'Bourbon and coke. Heavy on the bourbon.'

'Coming right up.' As she was mixing his drink the phone rang. 'Shall I get it?' she inquired.

'Yeah. I don't want to talk to anyone unless it's about Evan.'

She picked up the phone.

'Got him!' announced Paul triumphantly, 'a little worse for wear, but still in the land of the living.'

'Wonderful!' exclaimed Linda. She handed the phone to Al. 'Paul's found Evan, he's all right.'

'Thank Christ for that,' Al replied, relief sweeping on him.

☆

The girl was totally naked apart from gold paint all over her voluptuous body. She emerged from the giant cake holding aloft another smaller cake with thirty-eight candles burning brightly. 'Watch out you don't singe your tits!' somebody shouted, and there was much raucous laughter.

Al accepted the smaller cake from her, weaving unsteadily on his feet. 'Gotta thank everyone,' he slurred, 'for makin' this a great evening. 'Specially Paul.' He patted the naked girl on her bottom. 'You another present darlin'?'

'Yeah – go on give 'er one!' A musician shouted. 'An' if you don't want her send her over here!'

Al sat at the head of a long table. On one side of him was Evan, surly and bruised, with his arm in a sling. On the other side sat Paul, and all along the table were the other members of the tour.

The birthday dinner party had turned out to be a big success, with everyone getting good and drunk to relieve the tension of what had happened earlier.

Al had loved his presents. A solid gold digital watch from Paul. Cufflinks shaped like a nude woman from Bernie. A leather-bound book of the best photos of the tour from Linda, and numerous sweaters, shirts and novelty gifts from everyone else.

Evan had not given him anything; and Nellie had embarrassed him with a thick chunky gold identity bracelet inscribed 'Love from Nellie always'.

'Cut the cake,' Linda enthused, 'it looks delicious.'

'Sure,' agreed Al, 'you want to get off the table, darlin'?'

The naked Golden Lady allowed herself to be helped down to an accompaniment of lewd remarks.

'Get her a chair,' demanded Al, 'sit down next to me, darlin' – have some champagne.' He offered her a glass, but moved it out of reach when she went to take it. He did this three times, and she went along with the joke. Then – wham – he threw the glass of champagne all over her, and the rivulets of liquid mixed in psychedelic patterns with her gold body make-up.

She laughed along with the rest of them, and sat down.

'Want some cake?' Al asked, warming to his audience.

'Oh no . . .' she began, but too late. Al had picked up the

cake and aimed it directly at her chest. Chocolate sponge, soft cream, and icing squelched its way across her bosoms.

'Anyone for dessert?' Al laughed.

Further down the table Nellie got up and hurried from the room.

Evan watched her go and wished that he could follow her. His arm hurt, his body ached, and he wished he knew where Glory and Plum had vanished to.

'Hey, Evan, boyo,' Al was nudging him, handing him a spoon. 'Have some cake, help yourself. Go on, son, have yourself a time!'

41

'If a day in Palm Springs will turn you into the Mack girl, why won't you go?' Cody persisted.

'I don't understand you,' raged Dallas, 'are you dumb or something? The guy wants to get laid – LAID. Is that what you want me to do to become the Mack girl? Because if it is just tell me and then we'll both know where we stand.'

'You can handle him.'

'Ha! I can handle him. Sweet. Lovely. But I *don't want* to handle him. Are you with me? I *don't want to*.'

'Not physically, stupid.'

'Don't you call *me* stupid. I have had a tough life – and if I was stupid I wouldn't be here today.'

'What sort of a tough life have you had? A girl with your looks.'

Dallas laughed bitterly. 'Oh boy! You're not even interested in my background. What do you care? Here I am – all ready for you to promote. What does my *past* matter. *You* don't give a shit.' She paused, stared at him wearily, 'Why don't you just go on home, Cody?'

They stood outside her house arguing. She was tired and angry. She had hated the party. Hated the bullshit. And hated Cody for even suggesting she go along with it.

'Aarron Mack is calling me first thing,' Cody said, 'I promised him I'd talk to you.'

'Why don't *you* go to Palm Springs with him?' Dallas

suggested sweetly. 'He liked you, he's old, almost senile –
I'm sure he won't notice whether it's you or me pulling on
his rocks.'

'You really can be disgusting.'

'Almost as disgusting as you and your suggestions.'

'I am not suggesting anything,' argued Cody desperately,
'I'm just saying that if you went to Palm Springs with him
the Mack girl contract would be ours. You could fly back the
same day. He just wants to be seen with you – that's all. I'll
come too if you like.'

'God, you're naive! How can anybody live in this city,
work in the film business, and *still* be naive!'

'Trust me, Dallas. I got you "Man Made Woman", didn't
I? I got you an unbelievable deal didn't I? Well, I'll get
you a million dollar contract to be the Mack girl. You want
it? Come to Palm Springs and I will not leave your side –
I promise.'

'You promise?' She was starting to weaken.

'Naive agent's honour!'

'Oh God! You really are a hustler!'

'I know. Will you come?'

She sighed, smiled. 'I guess a million dollars *is* tempting.
But you must not . . .'

'Leave your side,' he finished for her, 'I'll call you first
thing and give you the schedule.'

☆

Palm Springs was gloriously hot. Aarron kept a small house
there. Six bedrooms with bathrooms en suite, a gigantic living
area, Olympic-size pool, and modest golf course.

'Nice little place,' Dallas observed drily.

'I don't use it much,' Aarron explained, 'two or three times
a year. If you would ever care to avail yourself of the facilities
please feel free to be my guest. Do you play golf, Cody?'

'Sorry, no.'

'Don't be sorry. I don't play myself. I just have it for my
guests.'

'I'd like to sunbathe,' Dallas decided.

'Of course,' Aarron agreed, 'and then I have arranged a
small luncheon party for you.'

'For me?'

'As it was such short notice I was not able to contact many people. But twenty-five should suffice.'

'Oh yes,' nodded Dallas, winking at Cody. 'Small but nice!'

She changed into a white crochet bikini, and lay out on a yellow striped chaise longue.

Aarron sat on a chair, clad in a bathrobe, and sheltered by an umbrella. He never took his small beady eyes off her.

Cody reluctantly climbed into his swimming shorts. He wasn't athletic, never had the patience for exercise and keep fit. He was decidedly flabby around the middle – and embarrassingly white for a person who had lived all his life in California. He was ashamed for Dallas to see him, but with the clever use of a towel he managed to negotiate a spot somewhere between her and Aarron without revealing too much of himself.

After regarding Dallas intently for some length of time Aarron finally said, 'You've changed.'

She shielded her eyes from the sun and glanced up at him. 'I have?'

'Very much so. In New York you were different.'

'I was?'

'I felt there that you were a girl who would go out with a man simply for his money.'

She yawned. 'It didn't get you anywhere though, did it?'

'I apologize if I insulted you in any way. I see now that you are not that sort of a girl at all.'

'Thanks,' she replied sarcastically.

Cody tried to get up unobtrusively, tripped, and fell in the pool. He wasn't fond of the fact that Aarron Mack was conducting a conversation over his head as if he didn't exist. If it wasn't for me, Aarron, old sport, she wouldn't even be here today.

He decided to swim the length of the pool ten times. Get rid of some of his flab and give them a chance to talk.

'Would you *like* to be the Mack girl?' Aarron asked.

'Would you expect any personal favours in return?' Dallas replied coolly.

Aarron shrugged. 'I am an old man. I am not demanding.'

That's not an answer.'

'I could offer you more than you've ever dreamed of . . .'
'And wonderful presents.'
'What?'
She laughed softly, 'Just remembering, Aarron.'
'Will you think about it?'
'Nope.'
'Why not?'
'Because my body is not for sale – whatever the price.'
'I could marry you . . .'
She sat up. 'Could you really?' Her voice dripped sarcasm.
'Isn't that what you want?' He was puzzled and hurt.

What she wanted was to laugh in his face. Screw Cody for forcing her into a position like this. A proposal of marriage! Shit! From *the* Aarron Mack. Double shit! A few months ago this would have been it. The Golden Opportunity. Just lie back, open your legs – your mouth – whatever – and revel in the money. But things were different now. She was a person. An individual. And no one – but no one – could buy her.

'I'm sorry, Aarron,' she said in a kindly fashion, 'I'm very flattered, but I just don't want to get married.'

'You don't want to get married,' he repeated blankly. 'Then what do you want?'

She opened her arms to the sun, lay back. 'To enjoy life. To do the things *I* want to do.'

'Do you *want* to be the Mack girl?'

'We just had that conversation.'

He hesitated. 'No strings.'

'No strings?'

'You have my word. But we shall be friends, and maybe in time . . . who knows . . .'

She sat up again, her eyes shining. 'Of course I would adore to be the Mack girl. And I thought you were just another dirty old man!'

He smiled tightly, his perfect false teeth gleaming brightly in the sun. 'I'll talk to your manager after lunch. There are a lot of things to be worked out.'

'Thank you, Aarron.' She stood up and kissed him lightly on the cheek, 'You're really a very nice man.'

☆

Cody was elated. Persuading Dallas to spend the day in Palm Springs had been a master stroke on his part. He had personally seen to it that she never had to spend one minute alone in old man Mack's company – and it had been easy really. All those interesting and influential people turning up for lunch, staying all afternoon, and then, when they left, Cody had reminded Aarron that Dallas had to get back to LA, and Aarron had put his plane at their disposal.

It was only when they were leaving the house and saying their goodbyes that Aarron took him to one side and told him that he wanted him to fly to New York to discuss a contract. 'You'll fly in with me on Tuesday,' Aarron said, 'that suit you?'

Yes, it suited him.

Negotiations took place. Cody made his points – business-wise he was sharp as a razor. Dallas ended up with a contract that would pay her more money than either Lauren Hutton and her famous Revlon deal, or Margeaux Hemingway and Fabergé.

Once again Dallas was news. Every newspaper carried her photograph. Every magazine wanted to do a cover story on her.

Cody's phone did not stop ringing. The deal he had made for his client was world-wide news, and whereas the 'Man Made Woman' contract might have been a fluke, the Mack girl contract really clinched the fact that he was hot stuff. Suddenly clients were lining up to avail themselves of his services.

He didn't plan to handle just anyone. He wanted a small stable of three or four clients who were the tops. Maybe his thinking was old-fashioned, but what he wanted to provide was a very personal service. He wanted to mould and guide and direct, and not push his artists into the hands of lackeys and hangers-on. If you were lucky enough to get taken on by Cody Hills – by God, you wouldn't get lost in the shuffle.

In exchange he demanded a straight twenty-five per cent of all earnings. Considering some stars were paying their agent ten per cent, and another twenty per cent to their manager, this wasn't a bad deal.

Within days he had signed a top rock star, an English

comedy actor, and a young stud who had just finished his first movie.

Cody's stable was complete.

☆

The smile was set on Dallas' face, so much so that her facial muscles ached.

'Last one!' promised the photographer, 'you *look beautiful.*'

The camera clicked, her smile collapsed. 'Terrific!' she exclaimed, glancing at her watch. 'I think I have a fast five minutes left for lunch.'

Kiki, the clothes designer, smiled. 'These photos will be worth missing lunch for.'

'Tell that to your husband when I faint in the middle of this afternoon's shooting. I'm starving! Is Cody around?'

'He called, said to tell you he'll be over later. Come on, let's get you out of the dress and I arranged for a salad tray to be left in your dressing-room.'

'Thanks, Kiki. Do you and Chuck work as a team? I never seem to be out of sight of either of you.'

'Yeah,' replied Kiki laconically, 'I get you to be photographed in my clothes on condition I have you back on the set in time. It seems to work.'

'For everyone except me! I don't want a salad. I want a fat juicy steak with french fries, and a couple of thick chocolate malts. I don't even get time to go to the bathroom any more!' But Dallas smiled as she complained. She felt marvellous. On top of everything, before the first 'Man Made Woman' had even been shown she was a star. Before the first Mack girl photos were on every billboard, in every magazine, she was a star.

Everyone was clamouring for her services. Cody was inundated with scripts and books. The representatives of commercial products were knocking at his door, anxious to use Dallas. All the television game and chat shows desired her presence. Every magazine thought a cover story on her was a great idea. All the Hollywood eligibles wanted to date her. Party invitations abounded.

Cody said, 'We shall proceed slowly. It would be easy to grab at everything, but it would also be a mistake.'

She agreed with him. He had made it happen for her, and she was prepared to accept his decisions.

Since the party she had neither seen or heard from Lew Margolis, and she took this as a good sign. Perhaps now he would leave her alone.

Aarron Mack had of course returned to New York, and he made a daily solicitous phone call to her. She didn't mind that, in fact she was rather flattered that his original lechery had turned into an almost fatherly concern.

She was not interested in dating the Hollywood rota of known studs – a rather boring group of pseudo-sophisticated macho-hams who liked to notch up every new famous female on an imaginary fuckbelt.

Parties she had never enjoyed. Perhaps the word party was too synonymous with orgy in her mind.

She enjoyed working, and posing for pictures and becoming a somebody. She enjoyed bumming around with Cody, Kiki and Chuck in the evenings. No chic restaurants, or discotheques. Just little places where you could get a great meal, and not get involved in all that table-hopping shit.

Watching television, barbecuing, and staying home were favourite. Or dropping by Tower Records on the way home and picking up some great new albums and playing them on the incredible stereo equipment she had invested in.

The question of sex did not arise. Cody seemed determined never to mention the subject again, and she didn't want to push him into anything. If he wanted to wait – well, let him wait. She would just have to prove to him that she wasn't about to rush into bed with every superstar who asked – and they were all asking. With a little patience on her part Cody would eventually come around, of that she was sure. He was a man, wasn't he? And he was just the sort of man she wanted as a husband. He would make a great father, she could see him with dozens of kids . . .

'What are you grinning about?' Kiki inquired, 'can we share the joke?'

'It's not shareable – not yet. But I promise that you and Chuck will be the first to know.'

'Come and eat your salad, starvation is making you too mysterious.'

Later that evening Dallas came face to face with Al King,

and for one short moment she forgot about Cody, and her plans, and the waves of excitement came flooding back.

She stood very still, breathed deeply, and surveyed the huge display of Al King albums in Tower Records. He seemed to be staring at her from every angle. Not only was there a full-colour photo of him on the cover of the album, but the sleeve opened up to present a double-space pin-up. A three-quarter shot of Al baring his chest, his teeth. Brooding with his eyes. His black hair curled in an almost gypsy fashion. An ivory horn hung phallicly on a thick gold charm around his neck. The album was called *Al IS KING*. Dallas decided not to buy it.

She wandered around bumping into piles of Al King albums stacked up on the end of every aisle. There was no avoiding him. A huge poster leered down from the wall.

She chose a new Temptations album, a Marvin Gaye Greatest Hits, and a Linda Ronstadt for Cody. On the way to the checkout she picked up a copy of *AL IS KING*. What the heck – may as well buy it, he did have a great voice.

She drove quickly home, guilty and excited. Why guilty? Nothing had ever happened.

She ran in the house, kicked off her shoes, and extracted the record from the sleeve.

It wasn't until she had put it on the turntable that she realized she was not alone.

Sitting in the corner, huddled in a chair, was Bobbie.

42

The plane finally took off. Melanie, slightly sloshed, fell into an open-mouthed sleep immediately.

Edna sat tensely by her side, unable even to close her eyes. She stared out of the window and wondered for the hundredth time what Al's reaction would be at seeing her. He wouldn't be pleased. You were not married to a man for sixteen years without knowing how he would react in certain situations. He hated her coming on tours because he knew *she* hated it. But this time *was* different. This time Evan was there, and he at least would be pleased to see her. And she wouldn't stay long – whatever Melanie said. If Al wanted to send her home she would go. The last thing in the world she wanted to do was upset Al. Maybe Evan would come home with her. Maybe he had had enough. She comforted herself with that thought, and at last fell into a fitful sleep.

☆

'You got beautiful pair tits,' slurred Al, rolling across the bed with the naked Golden Lady.

She laughed. She could afford to laugh. She was one of the highest-paid call girls in New Orleans – and sleeping with Al King was no hardship.

'You want I should shower?' she asked, in a high nasal twang. Remnants of birthday cake mixed with the gold paint still on her body.

'I want two of you,' he demanded, 'got a friend?'

She pursed golden lips, 'Won't *I* do, honey? Just lil' ole me all on my ownsome?'

'Want two,' mumbled Al, 's'my birthday, y'know. Want two.' He reached for her silicone boobs and kneaded them roughly.

She jerked away. 'I guess I could call Lynn . . .'

'Yeah – call Lynn.'

'Yeah, I'll call Lynn. Only whose gonna pay . . .' She stopped speaking abruptly. Paul King had given her strict instructions about not admitting to Al that she had been paid.

Al was gulping scotch from a bedside bottle. He hadn't heard her.

She climbed off the bed. 'I'll go in the other room an' call Lynn,' she announced. 'Whyn't you take a shower, honey? Be nice an' sober for the two of us.'

'Who's drunk?' roared Al. 'Who – my dear girl – is drunk?'

She stifled a rude laugh and muttered, 'Bombed outa his skull,' to herself, and she wasn't surprised, for she had witnessed some of his drinking downstairs, and oh boy could he pack it away. Any other man would be laid out cold by now. She was a little zingy herself. Not too much – a professional girl always made sure it was never too much – but just enough to have a real good time.

She left him on the bed and went into the other room.

First she called Paul to ask him if it was all right to bring in another girl. Paul said to get six girls if that was what Al wanted, and the money would be left at the desk.

She then called Lynn, who was asleep after a heavy evening at an advertising reunion, and said no way was she doing any more work that night.

'It's Al King,' whispered Golden Lady.

'Shit! Whyn't you say?' complained Lynn, 'I'll be right there.'

☆

'Who was that?' demanded Linda, as Paul hung up the phone.

'The girl from the cake. Al's calling for more troops.'

Linda stretched. 'I don't know how he does it. Did you *see* what booze he got through?'

Paul reached for her. 'It runs in the family, cast-iron stomachs.'

'Yeah, and the rest!'

☆

Evan lay on top of his bed wondering what he should do. His arm hurt, his body ached, and he still bristled with the humiliation of his father's birthday party.

The whole evening was a daze, from the moment he had been knocked flying at the concert. People had trampled over him, and then more bodies had fallen on top of him, and that was the last he remembered until waking up to the sound of an ambulance horn blaring – and he had been in the ambulance along with others – and they had all been taken to a hospital – and fleets of nurses and doctors had descended on them prodding and pushing and stitching and bandaging.

'You got a sprained arm,' a doctor informed him. 'The rest is just bruises and shock. Guess we'll keep you in overnight just in case. Give your details to the nurse and we'll contact your parents.'

They had shoved some sort of injection into him, and an elderly nurse had appeared with a sheaf of forms and asked him his name. 'Evan King,' he mumbled, 'I'm Al King's son.'

'I think this one's delirious,' she told the doctor.

Fortunately, shortly after, Paul arrived. He signed some papers and said, 'Thank Christ you're OK. Your father's going mad. Get dressed, we're getting out of here.'

Evan felt distinctly groggy. The injection had been a sedative, and he wouldn't have minded at all spending the night at the hospital and sleeping it off. But Paul had other plans. The party must go on. Nothing must spoil Al King's birthday.

Evan sat through the party half asleep. He picked at his food, gagged at the champagne, and blushed with embarrassment when the naked girl came climbing out of the cake. Not that he hadn't seen a naked girl before. He had. Both Glory and Plum had initiated him into the disgusting joys of manhood. But that was different, they were his friends, he was one of them.

Now, lying on his bed, inspecting his watch and discovering it was two thirty in the morning, he wondered for the hundredth time where they were. The last time he had seen them was at the concert. They had run forward with the crowd, smiling and laughing, not trying to hang back like he had, getting knocked down and trampled on. They hadn't even tried to help him, although he was being unrealistic even thinking that they could. But where were they? Ever since they had become friends the three of them had been inseparable. They all slept in his room, taking it in turns to use the bed. Why – all their possessions were in the one shabby carry-all standing in the corner. That at least gave him some security. They couldn't take off anywhere without their things.

He wished he had one of the pills that Glory called quacks. They really made you feel good, sort of full of confidence and ready to talk to anyone. Glory took them by the handful, but he stuck with Plum and used them sparingly.

'She needs them more than us,' Plum explained sagely, 'like she's trying t' get over the heavy stuff – she was in a real bad scene for a while. She's fine now – had a gig in hospital – that's some straightener.' Evan had nodded wisely as if he understood what on earth she was talking about.

Now they were both missing, and he felt lost without them. Maybe they had got hurt after all. Maybe they had been taken to another hospital ... Just as he was beginning to panic there was a muffled knock at the door. He hurried to open it, and there they were, Glory hanging limply onto Plum.

'Where have you been?' Evan demanded, for once his voice not breaking.

'Sshh, man,' whispered Plum, 'she's not feelin' so good. Let's get her on the bed.'

Glory was indeed extremely pale, her eyes glazed and popping out of the sockets alarmingly. Evan helped Plum to drag her onto the bed, and she immediately curled into a tight ball and began to snore.

Plum yawned. 'I guess that's her for the night,' and she started to remove the patchwork smock top she was wearing.

'*Where have you both been?*' hissed Evan, '*I* was in the hospital. My arm – look at my arm.'

Plum regarded him wearily. 'S'your own fault. We told you t'move with the crowd. You gotta flow, man, or y'get the shit kicked outa you.'

He sat on the end of the bed, defeated, and watched as Plum unzipped her jeans, and lumbered out of them. She wore no pants, and now she was clad only in a dirty bra which might once have been pink. Her body, although fat, was surprisingly smooth. Acres of smooth white flesh. Evan felt himself stirring. She noticed. He ripped off his clothes clumsily with his one good arm. He wasn't at all embarrassed. She had seen him naked before, they both had. They had admired his skinny body. They had stroked it, and fondled him. They had taken his private parts into their mouths and they had told him he was all right. They had opened their legs for him and allowed him to do whatever he wanted. He had looked and marvelled, and finally he had put it in. Now he wanted to do it again, and although he preferred Glory, Plum would do.

'I'm wiped out, man,' Plum complained, 'just split from a wild party. Anyway we can't use the bed – she's out.'

'The floor,' Evan mumbled, 'we can use the floor.'

'Shit!' complained Plum. But she lay down anyway and parted her massive thighs.

Evan leapt upon her like a randy dog. Plum farted

delicately. It didn't put him off. Perhaps at last he was his father's son.

☆

Arthur Sorenson sat at the reception desk and consulted his new stainless steel watch with the fluorescent dial. It was an eighteenth birthday present, an event he had celebrated two weeks previously. The dial read two forty-five exactly. He had been on duty for one and three-quarter hours and soon it would be time for coffee.

He glanced around the deserted lobby, proud of the fact that he was in charge all on his own. Mr Ridley usually shared the evening shift with him, but tonight Mr Ridley had called in to say his daughter was sick – caught up in the riot at the Al King concert. Mr Ridley had said it would be all right for him to do the evening shift on his own, as long as he didn't leave the desk, not for *any* reason. Mr Ridley had worked for the hotel for twenty-two years. Arthur Sorenson had worked there for two weeks. He felt pleased that Mr Ridley had chosen to trust him after such a short time.

He whistled tunelessly, and watched as a cab pulled up outside, and let off a lone male passenger. By his foot was an emergency button which connected straight through to the police station. These days you couldn't be too careful. His foot hovered near it as the man approached the desk.

'Good evening, sir,' he said politely, wondering if maybe he should amend that to, 'good morning', in view of the time.

'Two twenty – key,' the man growled. He was fat and sweating and outlandishly dressed.

'Yes, sir.' Arthur's eyes glanced quickly at his book, ascertained the party's name, reached for the key, and said, 'Thank you, Mr Suntan, sir.'

The fat man grabbed the key and vanished into the elevator.

Arthur glanced at his book again. Bernie Suntan. What a name! Of course he was part of the Al King party, that would account for it. They were a rowdy group. One of the maids had told him about the party earlier. What a wow that must have been! And only five minutes earlier a woman had arrived at the hotel. A strange woman wearing dark glasses and a belted mink coat. Strange, as it was the middle of summer, and hardly the weather to be wearing a mink coat. She had asked for Al King's room, and while he telephoned to check if it was okay to send her up she had examined a run in her tights, examined it all the way up to the top of her thigh. It was quite obvious that her entire outfit consisted of only tights and a mink coat.

If he let himself Arthur could get quite excited at the thought. He tried not to let himself. He watched her into the elevator and wondered at the stamina of Al King. A riot. A wild party. And now this.

Arthur wondered if perhaps he should think of following a singing career rather than that of a hotel clerk. Everyone said that he had a nice voice. But then of course show business was an erratic profession – and being a desk clerk could lead to all sorts of things. Mind you – it didn't seem to have got Mr Ridley far.

Arthur sighed, glanced at his watch again, and wondered if taking a coffee break would count as leaving the desk. After all it would only take him a few minutes to fix a cup of coffee, and anyway who would know?

☆

Melanie complained from the moment the plane landed. They couldn't get a cab. There were no porters to carry their luggage.

'I just don't know!' Melanie exclaimed in disgust, 'you stay with the cases, Edna, I'll soon get something organized.'

Edna stood forlornly by the luggage trying to ignore the attentions of a drunken businessman who had arrived on the same plane and was also having trouble getting transport.

She wanted to cry. She was tired, fed up, and she had missed Al's birthday by hours. By the time they got to the hotel it would be nearly three in the morning. Al would be asleep, and probably not at all pleased at having his rest interrupted.

Damn Melanie and her stupid plans. The whole point of this trip had been to arrive on Al's birthday.

A lone tear of anger and frustration rolled down her cheek. The drunk was at her side in a flash, 'Mustn't cry,' he mumbled. 'We'll all have a party. Want a party, little lady?' His lewd wink was the last straw, she turned her back and the flood of tears started in earnest.

'What's the matter with you?' Melanie asked scornfully upon her return. She brought with her a good-looking airline official, who piled their luggage onto a trolley, and in no time at all was driving them into the city himself.

By the time they reached the hotel he and Melanie were exchanging addresses and long meaningful looks.

A slow worker Melanie was not.

☆

'Ha Ha! Gotcha!' Lynn shrieked. She had discarded the mink coat and the tights, and was joining in a game of spray the shaving foam with Al and Golden Lady.

Spurts of white foam were all over the place. Golden Lady was giggling hysterically as Al massaged some foam into her pneumatic breasts.

'Not so *hard*,' she hiccoughed.

'Frightened they'll drop off,' jeered Al.

'If they do she can always buy another pair!' laughed Lynn, who was rather proud of her own small but natural boobs.

'Bitch!' shrieked Golden Lady. 'Jealous bitch!'

They launched into a mock struggle, an act that had obviously been staged before for many a satisfied customer.

Al watched, his interest waning, his head pounding. Why didn't he just give them some money and send them both home. He knew they were hookers. So what? At least with a hooker you knew, where you were, at least they didn't come running at you with an autograph book between their legs.

His interest revived as slowly their struggle turned into something else. Golden Lady was sliding her hands up the inside of Lynn's thighs, her thumbs were spreading the forest of black hair, and she was kneeling in front of the dark girl. She bent her head. So that's why they called it head. Sweet old American expression. In England it was going down. In America the only going down you did was in elevators!

'Yeah!' Al encouraged. He felt himself hardening, the first

time that night. Golden Lady with all her efforts had not managed to get it up.

She glanced slyly over at him, relieved that at last something was working. For a moment there she was worried that she might have lost her touch.

Lynn was arching her body back, moaning and sighing. The girls worked well together, complimenting each other by their very different colouring.

Lynn's screams, whether simulated or the real thing, indicated the end of that particular episode, and Golden Lady rose triumphant. She headed towards Al, her body a mixture of gold paint, remnants of cream cake, and shaving foam. She had a hard but pretty face which would age into craftiness. She bent to his toes, licking them, prostrating herself on the floor, her tongue travelling quickly up his legs, her mouth dying to enclose him.

Lynn, making a fast recovery, came over and started to knead his nipples. It was the Kurlnik twins all over again, but these two hadn't quite got their act together. Whereas the twins had merged into one woman with four hands and two tongues, these two were stimulating him in a distracting way. He wanted to come quickly and get rid of them both. But as soon as he tried he knew it was going to be an effort. All the booze he had put away was slowing him down, and no amount of tongues or mouths was going to make him come in a hurry. He would just have to sweat it out. And try to enjoy it.

☆

'Wouldn't you know it!' exclaimed Melanie sharply, 'nobody at the desk. What kind of a place is this?'

Her attentive escort smiled. 'One of the best hotels in town.'

'You could have fooled me,' complained Melanie, and she stamped her foot childishly.

'It *is* three o'clock in the morning,' Edna pointed out.

'Don't I know it,' whined Melanie, 'I'm exhausted,' she raised her shrill voice, 'is anyone around?'

Her escort shrugged helplessly, 'I hate to leave you lovely ladies like this, but I have to get back to the airport. I'm supposed to be on duty, I should never have left.'

Melanie fixed him with her cornflower-blue calculating eyes 'You've been marvellous,' she said, sotto voce, 'just one more, little favour . . .'

'Name it.'

'Hop over the other side of the desk and tell me the room numbers for Al and Paul King. I'm certainly not going to wait here all night.'

'Is that all?' He smiled, and vaulted in true macho-man fashion over the desk.

Melanie nodded her approval.

'Let me see now . . .' He rummaged around, found the current reservation book and read out, 'Al King – penthouse suite, twenty-ninth floor. Paul King, suite 120, twelfth floor.' He checked a panel beneath the desk and came up with two keys. 'They're doing a wonderful job of looking after their guests in this hotel – anyone could just saunter in here and take their pick of who to rob. All set ladies?'

Melanie leaned forward and kissed him lightly on the cheek, 'You're a doll.'

☆

Returning to the desk a few minutes later Arthur Sorenson was most disconcerted to find a pile of luggage sitting in the middle of the lobby. No people, just luggage.

Goddammit, he had only gone for a cup of coffee. Why had whoever it was chosen that particular time to arrive? And where the heck were they?

His eyes slid automatically to the two elevators. When he had left on his coffee break they had both registered lobby, now one of the indicators showed that the elevator had travelled all the way up to the twenty-ninth floor.

Goddammit, if Mr Ridley found out he had left the desk . . . This was his first job, and he liked it. He enjoyed working the early morning hours, it left him plenty of free time during the day.

He eyed the luggage suspiciously. Those suitcases belonged to someone, and that someone had just dumped them in his lobby and calm as you like gone on up to the twenty-ninth floor. He realized with a sudden sinking feeling that Al King was ensconced in the Penthouse suite on the twenty-ninth floor, and nobody but nobody was supposed to go up there without clearance. Al King was some sort of security risk.

Arthur frowned. What to do?

If Mr Ridley was around he would know what to do. But Mr Ridley wasn't around, and Arthur Sorenson didn't know what the heck to do. So he did what he considered was the safest bet, and that was exactly nothing.

When he was fired early the next morning he wondered why.

☆

Al shoved the golden head, 'Suck it!' he commanded.

The lady obliged, until he pulled her away by the hair and gave the dark-haired girl her turn.

He stood naked in the middle of the living room, both women kneeling on the floor in front of him. All the lights were on, the television spewed forth a decrepit Western. The room was a wreck, furniture overturned, shaving foam everywhere, clothes littered about.

He pushed down on the dark-haired girl's head, forcing her to take him deeper into her mouth.

'Come on, baby,' he crooned, 'take it all, swallow it down.'

The dark-haired girl did her best.

None of them heard the key in the door. None of them noticed the door tentatively open. They were all fully absorbed.

'Suck, suck . . . Shit!' Al started to reach orgasm, the dark-haired girl hanging on in there, Golden Lady twisting herself round his legs, determined to get in on the act.

Edna stood in the doorway transfixed with shock. At first she had thought it must be the wrong room, but as she tried to back quickly out she realized it must be the right room because that was Al standing there, *her* Al, with those two filthy women doing things to him, disgusting things, degrading things. And the funny thing was he was *letting* them. He was just standing there allowing them to molest him. Allowing them to suck on his private parts like vultures.

Edna felt the vomit rise in her throat, she couldn't control it.

Golden Lady saw her first. 'Who the frig are you?' she demanded, unwinding herself from around Al's legs and standing up.

Al saw her next, but didn't recognize her for a moment. The clothes, the hair, everything was so different. Realization dawned like a nagging stomach ache.

☆

Melanie let herself quietly into Paul's suite. She switched on the lights in the living room and looked around. It was really quite nice, although she was sure that Al's was probably better.

She checked herself in the mirror. Yes, she looked good, a little tired, but certainly a restful night's sleep would take care of *that*.

She was pleased with the way things had been going. One smile and they came running after her in droves. If she hadn't had Edna trailing along behind her she *really* could have had a good time. As it was she had had fun.

She smiled secretly to herself. Paul didn't realize how lucky he was having a wife like her.

She peered round the bedroom door and saw a huddled shape in bed. Carrying her toilet case she went quietly into the bathroom. A nice refreshing shower and she would surprise her husband in bed.

43

It was a tremendous shock, but at the same time it was no surprise at all. For all along Dallas had known that eventually Bobbie would turn up. The only question in her mind had been when.

Bobbie didn't say a word. She just huddled in the chair staring at Dallas, her afro wig curled to ridiculous heights, her eyes red-rimmed and watery.

Calmly Dallas switched off the stereo. 'How did you get in?' she asked.

'Hey, sugar sweets, aintcha never heard of pickin' a lock? Sweetstuff, I was *born* on the street – ain't never come across a lock to defeat me yet.'

'You chose the wrong profession – you should have been a burglar,' said Dallas drily. She refused to be intimidated by this person. 'What do you want?' she added coldly.

'Some greetin'!' complained Bobbie, 'some shit ass greeting from such an *old* friend.'

Dallas glared at her steadily, 'Cut the crap, friend. Tell me what you want and get out.'

Bobbie seemed to have developed a nervous facial tic. It looked like some kind of obscene wink. She stood up, and Dallas noticed how painfully thin she had become. She wore white shorts and scuffed boots and her thighs had an unattractive hollow appearance. Her face was thick with make-up. She seemed to have aged years.

With a shudder Dallas remembered her relationship with this girl. Personal and business. It all seemed like another world away.

'How about a drink?' Bobbie asked, attempting a camaraderie that had ceased to exist long ago, 'you all are doin' pretty fine – guess you can afford a shot of somethin' for good ole Bobbie.'

'Do you need money? Have you come here to blackmail me?'

'*Blackmail!* Shit, girl. I taught you everything you know. If it wasn't for me you'd still be peddlin' it for twenty bucks a night. I got you out of that scene. Blackmail – shit! You were some green little kid with a foxy pair of tits and a hot box. Blackmail! Ain't that a bitch!'

Dallas picked up her purse, 'I can give you two hundred dollars, it's all I have in cash. But get this straight – don't come back for more. I'm not giving you this money because I have to. I'm giving it to you because I'm sorry for you.'

Bobbie laughed uneasily, 'Sorry for me! You paranoid or something? Ain't *nobody* gotta be sorry for me. I'm together, like really in tune. You wanna give me two hundred bucks – sure I'll take it. I don't need it, but shit I deserve it.' She snatched the money and stuffed it in the waistband of her shorts. She seemed uncertain as to whether to continue the conversation or not, but Dallas made up her mind for her by walking to the door and flinging it open.

'Goodbye, Bobbie, don't come back.'

'Some welcome!' Her facial tick seemed to get worse, but

her mind seemed to be on the money tucked into her waistband. She headed for the door, and as she passed, Dallas
noticed that her whole body was shaking. On a sudden
impulse Dallas grabbed the black girl's arm and pushed up
the sleeve of her sweat shirt. The whole arm was a mass of
angry red tracks. 'You really did it, didn't you,' Dallas said
in a rush of sympathy.

Bobbie pulled her arm sharply away, 'Go fuck yourself,'
she growled, 'you fuckin' big time motha! Don't you go
givin' me your shit ass "what a *bad* girl Bobbie is" crap.'

'You need help . . .'

'Fuck help. I ain't *never* had any.' She laughed in a cavalier
fashion, 'dontcha know? I was born with a pair of cement
balls – they'll keep me going.' She walked in a jaunty way
out of the door. 'You'll need a friend one day. Don't come a
runnin' to my door, sweet stuff.'

Then she was gone, walking off down the hill in her
scuffed boots and ridiculous wig.

With a heavy feeling Dallas knew that she would be back.
The two hundred dollars was only a beginning. A girl with a
habit like that to support was going to run out of money real
fast.

☆

'I think you should handle me,' the girl said. She was
incredibly pretty, with an abundance of blonde curls, and a
devastating smile. Her tongue flicked out and licked full
glossy lips. 'I don't know why you're fighting it, you know
we'd be good for each other, I'd be a very cooperative client.'
She emphasized cooperative, leaving Cody in no doubt about
what the cooperative would encompass.

He cleared his throat, glad that his desk stood protectively
between them. 'Well, Carol . . .' he began, continuing with a
quick line of bullshit that he was getting quite proficient at.
He called it his 'don't call me I'll call you' line.

It was amazing the people who had wanted to become
clients. If he was just after a quick buck he would have signed
all of them.

Carol Cameron was not an unknown little starlet. She had
starred in two very successful sex horror movies – not hard
core either. The trouble was she couldn't act, and she had

screwed half – if not all – of Hollywood to get where she was today.

Cody did not fancy her, and even if he did it would not make any difference to his decision. Sex would not get in the way of business. He had proved that with Dallas.

Carol knew a turndown when she saw one. She stood up, smoothed down the revealing jersey dress she was wearing. Her nipples strained to escape the confines of the material. 'Think about it, Cody. Why don't you drop by my house later and have a drink?'

'I'm having dinner with my mother,' he replied quickly. Sometimes his mother came in very useful.

'So later,' Carol purred, 'you're not going to sleep with your mother, are you?'

He laughed at what he supposed was a joke. Very bad taste, like the lady who had made it.

'I don't think I can . . .' Why was he making excuses? Why didn't he just tell her no. 'No,' he said.

'No?' she questioned.

'No, I er can't.'

She pouted, 'Shame! Perhaps another night. I'll call you.'

Mental note. Tell secretary he was always out to any calls from Miss Carol Cameron.

'Wonderful! I'll look forward to it.'

She blew him a kiss and undulated out of his office. It was horribly old-fashioned to undulate. Dallas strode – long purposeful, sexy strides, like a beautiful leopard.

Thinking of Dallas reminded him it was late, and she would be home from the studio by now. Kiki and Chuck were coming over, and they were going to barbecue. He had promised to pick up the steaks, and agreeing to see Carol Cameron had made him late. He swore softly, gathered up some papers he wanted to go over later, and left the office.

☆

Dallas was drinking too much. She had dived into the vodka before dinner, heavily indulged in the wine during dinner, and now was into her third Cointreau on the rocks.

'I thought this was going to be a quiet evening at home,' Cody said, following her into the kitchen whilst she stacked the plates in the dishwasher.

'So it is,' she replied brightly, 'everyone's having a good time, the steaks were great.'

Gently he extracted the glass from her hand. 'You're working tomorrow.'

She snatched it back, 'I'm working every day,' there was a hard edge to her voice, 'I'm a working girl, always have been.'

'What's the matter?' Cody asked patiently.

'Matter?' Her eyes filled with sudden tears. 'Why should anything be the matter?'

Kiki breezed into the kitchen, 'I'm taking my man home,' she announced, 'sorry about eating and running, but if I don't get him home now he's going to be a permanent fixture in front of your TV!'

'Take him home and give him one for me,' Dallas shot a baleful look at Cody. That's about all I'll get tonight!'

'Oh boy!' exclaimed Kiki. 'We'll get out before the dishes fly!' She winked at Cody.'See you all tomorrow.'

She thought it was all a big joke. A lovers' quarrel. Everyone thought that Dallas and Cody were lovers.

'I hate you,' Dallas said spitefully when Cody returned from seeing their guests off, 'I really hate you, and what's more I think you're a fag. You hear me – a FAG.'

Her anger at finding Bobbie in her house was finally erupting. And Cody was the nearest target.

'You're drunk,' he said quietly, 'why don't you go to bed.'

'Fag!' she jeered, 'closet queen!'

His mouth tightened. 'I'm going home. We'll talk tomorrow.'

'Yeah, go on home – or better still why don't you run on over to mommy's?' She tore off her shirt and faced him menacingly, her naked breasts perfect in their splendour. 'I'm offering you for free something that other men have had to pay for. But it's too much for you, isn't it? You'd sooner sink it into some nice tight ass . . . You'd sooner . . .'

He approached her swiftly, gripped her by the shoulders. 'What do you mean – other men have had to pay for it?'

She was suddenly sullen, 'Nothing.'

He shook her, 'What do you mean?' He was now as angry as she was.

She tried to shrug him off, but he had her in a tight grip. 'I said nothing . . .' she muttered.

His anger collapsed. 'I don't know you, do I? I worship you and I know nothing about you.' He let go of her and turned to go.

She ran after him, pulled him round to face her, 'I was a hooker,' she screamed, 'a cheap twenty dollar hooker! Does that satisfy you? Does that make you feel better? No wonder you don't want to fuck me . . .' The tears came on top of the anger and she fell on to the couch sobbing.

He was shocked, genuinely shocked. But then he knew that he had never investigated her past because he was frightened of what he would find out.

He went to her, held her in his arms, comforted her while she poured out her life.

She left out Lew Margolis and the pictures. She left out Bobbie and their relationship. She left out her marriage at sixteen.

She told him what it suited her to tell him. She told him what she thought he could accept and still keep loving her.

In the early hours of the morning they chartered a jet, flew to Las Vegas, and got married.

Cody knew when he was needed.

44

When Melanie slid confidently into bed alongside her husband, she was aghast to find herself embracing feminine curves. Linda had been similarly aghast, and Paul had been hopeful that perhaps a freak earthquake might hit New Orleans.

Meanwhile Edna was in a state of shock, seeing her beloved husband indulging in the sort of activities that she had thought only existed in perverted people's minds. As she threw up she could think only of the fact that she was ruining somebody's carpet, but somehow, for once in her life, it didn't seem to matter, and she stood there vomiting, oblivious to the hostile state of the Golden Lady who Al had kicked half-way across the room.

'Jeeesus Chriiist!' exclaimed Lynn, as Al wrenched her head off him, 'what *is* this?'

'It's my wife,' explained Al, sobriety hitting him like a hammer. 'Get the hell *out* of here!'

It wasn't the first time that Lynn had been caught in a similar situation. Wordlessly, she grabbed her mink coat, flinging it over her nakedness. 'Come on!' she said to Golden Lady, who was grovelling around on the floor looking for her clothes.

Al said, 'Edna?' As if not quite sure it was really her.

She looked at him with pain-filled eyes. 'I'm sorry . . .' she began.

'*She's* sorry!' huffed Lynn, pushing past with Golden Lady who was in a most bedraggled state. 'If I was you, dear, I'd get a new lynx coat at least!'

Al waited until they were gone, then he walked over to Edna, took her arm, and led her to a chair. He slumped on the sofa next to her and muttered, 'Why didn't you tell me you were coming?'

'Put some clothes on, you'll catch cold,' she said in the normal voice of a mother scolding a child. Her eyes refused to meet his, they darted nervously round the room. She got up, 'Where's the bathroom? I want to clear up that mess.'

'Leave it,' he commanded.

'I can't leave it,' her voice was all choked up, 'I can't leave it, Al. And I'm sorry I came, and I'm sorry I upset you. I knew it wasn't a good idea. I told Melanie . . .' Her voice began to quaver. 'How could you? How *could* you?' She broke into tears. 'I only wanted to be with you on your birthday . . . That's all. Oh, Al, why did you do it?'

Why did I do it? Because I've been doing it for years one way or another. Because when I get off that stage I'm about ready to explode. Because you've never been around when I've really needed you. Because you think sex should take place in a bedroom, in the dark, once a week, using one position only. And whenever I've suggested anything else you've backed away in horror.

'You can divorce me,' he stated blankly, and was amazed at the relief that came flooding over him as soon as he said it.

'I don't want to do that,' she interrupted quickly, 'we're

very happy. I love you. I think that in time I can forgive you. After all if it was only this once . . .' She trailed off, waiting for him to assure her that it was only this once.

He said nothing.

'Where is Evan?' she ventured.

It hadn't taken her long to ask about her precious son.

'He's all right,' Al replied brusquely, 'you can see him in the morning.'

'Yes, she agreed, 'we'll all feel better in the morning. This will seem like a bad dream in the morning.' She sighed deeply, and summoned a tenacious whisper of a smile. 'I'm going to try and forget it ever happened, Al. I'm going to forgive you.'

☆

'You sonofabitch!' Melanie shrilled. 'I could understand you having it off with some little tart – but *sleeping* with the bitch, spending the *night* with her. Who is she?'

Paul shrugged, 'It doesn't matter who she is.'

'It doesn't matter who she is!' mimicked Melanie. 'You can bet your boots it doesn't matter who she is – because *you're* not seeing her again! That is if you ever want to see your *children* again.' She paused triumphantly, knowing she had gotten to him with *that* threat.

They had been bickering ever since Linda had left. God, Linda handled it well, Paul thought. After the initial scene of French farce she had leapt from the bed, coolly shut herself in the bathroom, dressed, and left without a word to either of them – in spite of the temptation of Melanie's spiteful verbal attack. Paul had wanted to applaud her dignity.

'I should have thought,' sniffed Melanie, determined to get as much mileage as possible out of the event, 'you could have done better than that. I should have thought that while you were picking it might have been a nineteen-year-old nympho. Or are you losing your touch? Are all the best ones going in Al's direction? Was this hag one of Al's rejects?'

Paul wanted to slap her right across her pretty pointed face. But he knew it was important to stay calm, appear cool. If Melanie so much as suspected that Linda was anything serious .

'She was some girl I picked up in the bar,' he admitted, 'some nothing girl.' Christ! If Linda could hear him she would never talk to him again.

'Absolutely charming! And I suppose if you had got syphilis or something from her *I* would have been the one you would come running home to with it.'

'Don't be silly.'

'Oh – don't be silly,' Melanie narrowed her eyes and glared at him, 'what are you? A fool? You *could* have got infected, she looked like a tramp. I want you to go to a doctor tomorrow.'

'All right, I'll go to a doctor if it will make you happy,' Paul muttered.

'Thank you. I think it's the least you can do.' She yawned, ready to forget the incident for the time being. Actually it had been rather exciting catching dull old Paul like that. He *had* become exceedingly dull in the last few years, only interested in business and making money. Well, she couldn't complain about that – but it certainly was a change from the man she had married. A man whose sole interest in life had been getting her into bed.

She felt a tingle of excitement, and she thought of the good-looking airline official who had driven her to the hotel, and the tingle became an itch. She thought of the naked woman climbing out of bed with Paul. She had not been an old bag. She had been a very attractive female, a fact that Melanie would never admit.

She moved closer to her husband. 'Did she have nice boobs?' she asked, her voice becoming babyish.

He knew what to answer. He was not a fool. 'Not as nice as yours.'

'As mine?' She feigned surprise, 'but mine are only little. Do you like them little?'

He was relieved that forgiveness had been so quick, and he reached for his wife and massaged her small breasts the way she liked him to. She moaned immediately, and lifted the slip she was wearing. He pulled off her panties, all the time thinking about Linda. He bent his head to her breasts, and she moaned even louder, One thing he enjoyed about Linda was her delicious silence. He did not have an erection, but fortunately Melanie did not bother to notice. She had other ideas. She was pushing his head down and opening her legs.

'I can't let you make love to me properly,' she gasped, as he attacked her with his tongue, 'not until you've had a doctor look at your thing. I don't want to catch anything, do I?'

☆

In her room Linda was busy packing. She was numb with fury, number with disgust – and both emotions were directed at Paul. Her lover, her big brave man. He had practically shit himself with fear.

She relived the evening in her mind. The party, everyone had had a good time, everyone had still been recovering from the events of earlier, so a lot of drinking had gone on, and when she and Paul had returned to bed they were both slightly out of it. They hadn't even made love. They had kissed goodnight, cuddled up, and gone to sleep. Just like an old married couple.

The next thing that Linda could remember was hands on her, hands that snatched themselves off her in double quick time, and a high-pitched voice screaming, 'Who the hell are *you*?'

Paul had woken, switched on the light, and recoiled in horror at the woman who appeared to have joined them in bed. He said one startled word – 'Melanie!' That had been enough for Linda. Wordlessly she had left the bed, found her clothes, and gone into the bathroom to dress.

She didn't know what else to do. Paul was struck speechless, and the skinny blonde – his wife – was screeching insults at him.

He was still speechless when she came out of the bathroom. The blonde stared at her, started to say something. But Linda didn't wait to hear, she got out of there – fast. And when she was out of there, and in her own room, she suddenly saw the whole scene in a much clearer light.

Bloody hell – she wasn't a hooker, for Christ's sake. She was Paul's long-standing girlfriend, he professed to love her. And yet he had not uttered *one* single word. He had not tried to protect her in any way, shape or form. He had been scared shitless.

Yes, she could understand that it was unexpected. But it *had* happened. It *was* a confrontation, and he *could* have dealt with it like a man.

Grimly she finished packing. She had no intention of hanging around to listen to his excuses. First plane out in the morning to New York – and fuck Paul King.

☆

Evan awoke to the sound of the phone ringing. He had not slept properly anyway. How could you sleep properly three in a bed? Glory was in the middle, lying on top of the covers with all her clothes on, still fast asleep. Plum was squashed on one side, her vast nude body covered only partly by the sheet. She lay on her back and emitted harsh snores. Evan had about three inches of space on the other side. He felt worse than ever, his arm throbbed violently, and his body ached all over.

He licked dry lips and picked up the phone. On the other end was his father who didn't waste any words.

'Get those two slags out of your room if they're with you. Clean yourself up and get yourself up to my suite.' There was a short pause, a heavy sigh, then, 'your mother is here.'

Holy crap! His mother!

Evan glanced guiltily at the two sleeping girls. *His mother!* If she should ever find out . . .

He didn't know what to do first. Dress. Wake them. Hide.

He ran in the bathroom, peered at his spotty face, ran back to the bedroom, shook Plum, who merely groaned and turned over.

Frantically he grabbed Glory by the shoulders, and she sat bolt upright, startling him. 'Wassashitsamatter?' she mumbled.

'My mother,' he explained, his panic-stricken voice uncontrollable, 'she's *here*. She's with my father, *she's here*.'

'So what?' Glory questioned, her thin mouth set in a mean line.

Evan was speechless. He had expected Glory to react in the same way that he had. He had expected her to leap up, dress, wake Plum, and get the hell *out* of his hotel room.

Glory was lying down. Glory was preparing to go back to sleep.

'You've got to go,' Evan said quickly, 'you and Plum. If my mother comes down here, sees you . . .'

'So what?' repeated Glory, even more meanly than the first time. She was not pleased at being woken.

'She'll go mad,' stammered Evan.

'Take away your train set, will she?' mocked Glory, 'smacka naughty little boy's ass?'

Evan reddened, his spots standing out lividly.

'Shit!' exclaimed Glory in disgust, 'You're just like all the rest. Had your good time – now we can just piss on off.' She gave Plum a vicious kick, 'Wake up, fatso, we're gettin' the push again.' She climbed off the bed and gave Evan a bitter stare before going in the bathroom, 'And t'think I thought you were one of us. What a laugh!' She slammed the bathroom door, leaving him with Plum who had sat up and was looking at him suspiciously.

'Why have you upset Glory?' she asked.

'I didn't,'he protested.

'You must have.'

'I woke her up because my mother is here and . . .'

'You want us to go,' finished Plum.

'I don't *want* you to go. But my mother . . . Well . . .' He shrugged helplessly.

'You're frightened of her?'

'Not frightened . . .'

'I know, I know. You've got some shitty mother hang-up. Think she knows best and all that guff. *I* had hassles with my mom – old bitch. One day I walked, no more hassles. It was that simple.'

There was a crash from the bathroom.

'You *have* upset Glory,' accused Plum. 'Why'd you have to do that? It will take me all day to get her together.'

'I didn't mean to . . .' said Evan miserably. 'I wouldn't upset either of you. You've both been . . .' His eyes filled with tears which he tried unsuccessfully to blink away.

'Aw, c'mon,' comforted Plum, 'don't *you* go gettin' upset. Anyway, I think I got an idea. Whyn't you go an' see your Ma – try an' grab some bread from Al, and I'll talk to Glory, try and get her to go along with my idea.'

'What idea?' Evan asked hopefully.

'You'll know. I'll tell you when y'come back. But it's a trip

– a real head trip f' us all. Now don't forget – get some money – steal it if you can – he'll never notice.'

More cheerful now that Plum had taken control, Evan nodded. He was still one of them. Nothing had changed.

☆

Al did not sleep well at all. It had been some birthday. First the riot, then the drama with Evan. The party, and following orgiastic goings on with Golden Lady, and her friend, and then the sudden appearance of Edna.

It had all been too much.

He had terminated further discussions on his sexual goings on by telling Edna of the riot. She had been suitably sympathetic – in fact in no time at all she was acting as if nothing had happened, but when he mentioned that Evan had been slightly hurt she had gone mad, and he had to forcibly restrain her from dashing down to his room. Somehow, Al thought, she would not take too kindly to the sight of her son and the two queens of freaksville! If indeed they were still with Evan. Certainly a double discovery in one night would not be to anyone's advantage. Al had persuaded her into bed – purely for sleeping purposes. And he had spent a restless night lying by her side wondering how he could tell her that their marriage was over.

He got up early, while Edna still slept, and crept into the living room to phone Evan.

He then phoned Paul, wondering how *he* had fared.

'Paul,' stated Al tersely, when his brother answered the phone. Two questions. Where was Luke – who according to you never leaves the outside of my door. And how did Edna get my key?'

'What can I say . . .' began Paul, his voice destroyed.

'Nothing,' flashed Al. 'Call me back with some answers.'

'I *have* the answers. Do you think I've slept? Luke got the shit kicked out of him spiriting you off stage yesterday – he went off duty outside your room after he saw you safely inside from the party, *I* told him it was all right. Did *I* know?'

Al snorted, 'Some fucking security!'

'The key is another matter. I think we can sue the hotel. The manager has already dumped the night clerk. Have you seen the papers?'

'The papers? Is the fact that my wife caught me with a couple of hookers in the papers?'

'No. But it's not too good. Some joker got a picture of you at the party feeling up that blonde from the cake – the bastards ran it on the front page next to a kid all bashed up from the riot.'

'Oh, that's fucking marvellous isn't it?'

'I've been on to Bernie. He's working on killing it already. It's the kind of spread can go world-wide.'

'Just what I need.'

'On the good side "Bad Black Alice" made number one today.'

Al felt the depression lift for a moment. He was number one again. Top single selling record in America.

They had all thought he was past it. They had all labelled him a has-been. But he had shown them – Christ! Had he shown them! The tour was a smash. Now the single was at number one. What the hell had he been worried about anyway?

'I think,' Paul was saying, 'before we leave today you should visit some of the kids in the hospital with Edna. We'll have photographers there, get it out on the news agencies. Fortunately there were no serious injuries – the worst is a broken arm. The rest seem to be bruises and shock and the aftermath of hysteria.'

'Arrange it.'

'I think it's a good idea.'

'Don't give me speeches. I said arrange it.'

'I thought you'd say yes. Bernie's already got it in hand.' Paul paused. 'Was everything all right with Edna?'

'Sure,' answered Al sarcastically, 'there I was with my cock in some slag's mouth. Edna was delighted. I said – "Hello, darlin', come in and join the orgy." She was thrilled.'

'As bad as that, huh?'

'Worse. She's forgiven me. And what about you?'

'I'll tell you later.'

☆

It didn't take Paul long to discover that Linda had packed up and checked out. He could hardly claim to be surprised. In fact he was relieved. It would have been an impossible situation if she had stayed, and Melanie had discovered who she was . . . Christ! What a situation. If he hadn't been caught in a compromising position he would have given Melanie the bollocking of her life. How dare she take it upon herself to come and surprise them. It certainly can't have been Edna's idea – Melanie must have been jollying her up for weeks.

Paul wasn't worried about Linda's sudden departure. She knew the way things were. She understood. She was just being discreet. God, but she was a wonderful woman, as soon as he had time he would call her. She was probably a little mad, well, disappointed really. But he would find a way to make it up to her. As soon as he could pack Melanie off, Linda would be back by his side.

It was *his* turn to work on Edna now to get her the hell out of America and back home safely to England.

With Al's support – which he had no doubt would be forthcoming – it shouldn't be too difficult.

☆

Edna was shocked when she saw Evan. In a way it was worse than seeing Al with those two terrible women.

Evan was thinner than ever, battered and bruised, tired-looking, and *filthy*. His hair hung in lank, greasy strands. His acne formed a pattern of angry relief against his dull pallor. His clothes – certainly not an outfit *she* had bought him – looked like he had slept in them for a week.

She stepped forward to hug him. He pushed her away, mumbling about his arm.

For the first time since leaving England she was glad that she had come. God, in his infinite wisdom, had sent her to fetch her son. Rescue him might be a better word.

Al obviously noted nothing amiss. 'How's it going, Evan?' he asked in an amiable fashion. 'Arm OK?'

Anger formed in Edna's breast. An anger she had never known existed before.

'When did he last eat?' she snapped at Al.

He shrugged, 'I don't follow him around with a tray.'

'I can see that. He looks half starved. Evan! When did you last eat?'

Evan scratched at a spot, 'I dunno . . . I'm not hungry.'

Edna shook her head bitterly, 'What does he look like?'

She turned to Al, her voice unnaturally sharp. 'I thought you were going to look after him. I thought I could trust you. Why, he's not even in the same room as you,' her voice rose, 'and thank goodness for that. Has he seen a doctor?'

'He was at the hospital yesterday.'

'Did *you* speak to the doctor?'

'No, I . . .'

'I want a doctor for him *now*. I want him properly examined. I want his arm X-rayed. I want him to get the sort of treatment you expect for yourself.'

Al was amazed. Edna had never spoken to him like that in her life. She was positively bristling with anger. She even looked different.

He wanted a divorce. All Edna cared about was Evan, she had now made that painfully obvious.

'I'll get him a doctor,' he said dully. 'I'll get him what the fuck you want.'

Evan wiped his nose with the back of his hand and regarded his parents blankly. All he wanted to do was to get out of there and back to his friends.

'Don't swear in front of him,' hissed Edna. 'I don't want him to learn your gutter language.'

'Can I go?' mumbled Evan. 'I feel like lying down.'

'You can lie down here,' replied Edna. 'You can also have a bath and put on some clean clothes. Give me your key and I'll fetch your things.'

'Oh no,' squeaked Evan, flushing, 'I'll get them.'

As Edna started to object, Al interrupted, 'Let him go. We have to ride over to the hospital for the photographs now, then the airport. Go get packed, Evan. You'll come to the airport with Paul.'

'But . . .' began Edna.

Al silenced her again. 'He's all yours in Tucson. You can bathe him and feed him and get him all the doctors you want. Right now turn a little of your attention in *my* direction.'

Edna, appeased with promises, was meek again. 'Yes, Al,' she said, 'but after Tucson I think it would be best if I took Evan home.'

'I think you're right,' agreed Al, relief flooding through him.

And neither of them noticed the look of panic that swept across Evan's face.

☆

Bleary-eyed Bernie jostled amongst the photographers and reporters at the hospital. He winked and joked and laughed while they all marked time waiting for the star.

He personally felt like shit. What the fuck . . . Why was it always him that got all the flak? Was the riot *his* fault? Was security *his* bag? How about brother Paul stepping forward for a little of the blame. It was Paul who put the ceiling on what they were going to pay for security – and if he hadn't been so busy with foxy Linda he would have realized that as the tour gained momentum so the crowds got wilder. Jesus Christ – if he – Bernie – was in charge, things would be different. He could go nuts just thinking of the way it would be.

He had a monster hangover. After Al's party he had taken himself off to a very famous New Orleans cat house. A place that hadn't changed a thing – except the girls – in fifty years! The madam was seventy-three years old. A character of gigantic proportions in a curly red wig and New Frontier dress.

Bernie had chosen himself a genuine French girl who had known all the tricks of the trade and used them in an expert fashion. It had been a pleasing experience, far different from the grubby little groupies he had used on the trip.

What the fuck . . . In Los Angeles girls queued up to be seen in his company. Beautiful girls.

Bernie Suntan. In Los Angeles he was a celebrity himself.

Al arrived at the hospital. There was a buzz amongst the photographers. Bernie noted how good he looked. Nothing seemed to phase Al.

'Put your arm around Edna,' Bernie reminded.

Al obliged, smiling, turning on the famous King charm.

Bernie handed him a stack of record albums, and watched as he walked around the ward talking to the kids in their beds and signing records for them.

The cameras flashed, recording every moment. With any luck these pictures would be syndicated, wiping out the nasty taste of the riot and Al with the naked Golden Lady.

The public would love it. He was leading a life they all envied. The wife. The hospital visit. That was the good image. On the other hand everyone suspected he was a great lover and had a wild side.

Perfect combination. The good and the bad.

Al had it down to a fine art.

☆

Linda was back in New York by lunchtime.

She took a cab straight to her apartment, where she shut herself in the tiny kitchen, and smashed every dish she possessed.

It was a very satisfactory relief of tensions. One that a psychiatrist had taught her in her early days of analysis.

Afterwards she swept up the mess, dumped it in the hallway garbage shute, and made herself a strong cup of black coffee.

The tiny apartment did not please her. It had a musty smell, the furniture looked tacky. Originally she had furnished it from junk shops, and at the time it had been fun, not to mention cheap. Now, eight years later, it was an unsatisfactory dump. She had known that for a while, but somehow she had imagined Paul *would* leave his wife, and then would be the time for changes.

'Dumb schmuck!' she muttered to herself. Taken in by the oldest line in the world. He loved her – but . . . And the but was bigger than both of them.

Enough was enough. And she had definitely had enough.

She called her agency to let them know she was back. Her Al King pictures were selling all over the world, and she was gratified to learn how much money she was making.

She was tired, but after a shower she picked up the phone and called her actor friend, Rik. He was distinctly unfriendly because she had not contacted him as promised.

'I *tried*,' she lied, 'but your number is always busy. Can I come over?'

'You always do this,' he complained.

'I've been working,' she explained. 'You're the first person I've called since I got back, which is approximately one hour ago.'

'Am I supposed to be flattered?' he ask petulantly.

'Aren't you?' she cajoled.

'Hmmmn,' he was ready to forgive her, 'Did you miss me?'

'Of *course* I missed you. I thought about you lots.'

'I think I might have a job,' his voice perked up. 'Only off Broadway, but . . .'

'That's great!' she interrupted, I'm on my way over – OK?'

'I suppose so,' he relented.

She hung up. God Almighty – what you had to go through to get a good fuck these days!

☆

The hospital visit was a success. Al was in good spirits again. On the way to the airport he formed some plans in his head. Edna sat silently by his side forming plans of her own. She was shocked at the condition of Evan, and she wanted to get him home as soon as possible. Never mind about what Melanie wanted to do – *she* was going home.

Al was thinking that it wasn't such a bad thing Edna turning up the way she had. In fact it was a good thing. She had caught him in action, and that could be his lever for a divorce. Edna, I'm just not good enough for you. You've seen the truth at last. I can't go on doing this to you. I refuse to hurt you any more. The perfect solution. How could she argue with him? He was doing it for her.

And he could handle the whole thing long distance. Too ashamed to face her and all that shit. Of course he would see she had everything she wanted. The house in England, plenty of money. In fact in a way he *was* doing it for her. She had been a loyal wife. He did treat her badly. She deserved some nice un-famous schmuck – which with all the money she would have would be no problem. He would have to make sure no con men came sniffing around. He would work something out with his lawyer to take care of everything.

It was a very satisfactory decision. He would put it into motion as soon as she left.

Another bonus was the fact that she would also be taking Evan off his hands. The responsibility of having the boy along was too much. In the meantime he would go out of his way to give them both a good time in Tucson. A last family fling.

More photographers waited at the airport, and Al waved and laughed, one arm around Edna, as he boarded his plane. Fuck it. He was a superstar. He was number one. How could he have ever doubted himself?

Paul was waiting on board with Melanie. He looked uptight about something. Probably she had been giving him a hard time.

Al grinned, thumped him on the shoulder. 'Hey – baby brother. We should be celebrating – what's the long face for? Let's get the champagne in action, let's . . .'

'We can't find Evan,' Paul said tightly. 'He's gone. Vanished.'

'Huh?' Al could not believe what he was hearing.

'He's done a split with those two freaks. Here's the note that was left for you.' Paul handed Al a grubby bit of paper.

It was written in Plum's untidy scrawl – TAKIN' EVAN ON TRIP. DON'T WORRY. SEE YOU IN L.A.

Al read it through twice, unwilling to digest the information.

Edna would go ape shit.

There went his plans.

'Jesus!' he said at last, 'Jesus H. Christ! The kid's a worse fuckin' moron than I thought he was!'

Paul nodded. 'I hope that's all it is. I just hope. But don't blow out the possibility that they may have kidnapped him.'

45

Cody impressed upon Dallas the importance of keeping their marriage a secret.

It would be bad for her career.

Lew Margolis wouldn't like it.

Her future fans would feel cheated.

Aarron Mack wouldn't like it.

The main reason, he kept quiet about. His mother. Bad enough that Dallas wasn't Jewish – but an actress too! He would have to break it to his mother gently.

It was no hardship keeping the event a secret. They had flown to Las Vegas late at night, instructing the pilot to be ready to fly back to LA within the hour. They had taken a cab along the neon-lit gaudy strip, and finally chosen a 'Little Chapel of the West' advertised in flashing lights as a twenty-four-hour wedding parlour.

The preacher had slipped a creased suit over his pyjamas. His wife, with rollers in her hair and a cigarette dangling from jammy lips, had served lukewarm white wine in glasses advertising a nearby gambling salon.

Two witnesses were pulled in off the street for a few dollars each. The wedding ring was a cheap cigar band. The whole ceremony took no more than ten minutes.

'We'll do it properly later,' Cody promised her in the cab on the way back to the airport.

'Yes,' agreed Dallas, wondering why she didn't feel suddenly secure and happy.

They were back in LA in time to get a few hours' sleep before Dallas was due at the studio.

'Shall I stay?' Cody asked.

'Of course,' replied Dallas. What the hell did he think they had got married for if not to be together?

She showered, brushed her teeth, and went to him naked.

He stroked her body, muttered words of love, made love to her in a perfectly adequate way – a vast improvement on the time before.

She hated every minute of it. She hated the feel of his hands, his tongue, his male organ. There was no joy, no waves. He could have been a customer – another trick. He did the same things, went through the same motions.

'Did you come?' he asked anxiously when they were finished.

A man who needed to ask would never know.

'Mmmn,' Dallas mumbled, turning her back to him so that he wouldn't see the tears.

She had made a mistake. It wasn't his fault. He was blameless – only wanting to do what made her happy. But he had been right, they should have waited.

'Goodnight, Mrs Hills,' Cody murmured. 'Did I remember to tell you that I love you?'

☆

A week later Bobbie was back.

This time she appeared at the studio, thin and jumpy in

studded suede hot pants and a see-through shirt. She was hanging around outside Dallas' dressing-room, and pounced on her during the lunch break.

'Hey, sugar sweets,' she greeted cheerfully, as if they were the best of friends. 'What's happenin'?'

Dallas hustled her quickly into the dressing-room. 'How did you get here?' she questioned, her voice weary. She had expected Bobbie back, but not this soon.

'I got influence,' Bobbie's facial tick went into sudden uncontrollable action, and she started to rub her red-rimmed eyes. 'I need some more bread,' she mumbled, 'just a fuckin' loan 'til I get myself back in action.'

'No more money,' Dallas replied. 'I told you that before.'

'Dontcha get tight-assed with me,' suddenly Bobbie was screaming, 'you owe me plenty – *plenty*.'

'I owe you nothing.'

Bobbie rolled her eyes, 'Sweetshit! You got no memory on you, girl. I dragged you out of that pisshole you was givin' it away in. *I* discovered *you*. We go back a long way together. We got memories – mutual memories . . .'

Anger was starting to bubble up inside Dallas. Anger and frustration. The unfairness of it all.

'Go away, Bobbie,' she said tightly. 'Go away and don't come back if you know what's good for you.'

'Just another coupla hundred,' cajoled Bobbie, her mood becoming pleading. 'Just two hundred and I'll leave you alone. I know you don't want me around. I know I'm an embarrassment – but shit, girl, try and see it my way.'

'I do see it your way. I see you've got your eyes on what you think is a bank.'

'You're doin' pretty good . . .' whined Bobbie. 'What's a coupla hundred to you? I got a need . . . I gotta pay the man . . .'

Dallas stared at the black girl. She was pathetic. But pathetic or not she had to get her off her back. Lew Margolis was enough to have hanging over her, she didn't need this too. She dug into her purse, came up with sixty dollars. 'It's all I've got,' she said flatly.

Bobbie snatched the money from her. 'It'll do,' she sneered, 'for now. I'll be back next week. Get a bundle together for me and I'll leave you alone. It's only fair y'know.

You gotta see things my way, sweet stuff – I am responsible for you gettin' this all together – without me you'd be nowhere.' She shoved the money up the leg of her hot pants and sighed, 'We girls gotta stick together. You and me had some good times.' She ran her hand lightly over Dallas' arm. 'Remember, honey? Remember?'

Dallas pulled her arm away. 'You try remembering the swimming pool, Bobbie. No more money – get it? *No more money.*'

Bobbie giggled, 'Yeah – I remember that little scene. But you had nothin' to lose then. Now you're riding high. By the way, sugar sweets, how's Mr M? Still the same sweet old-fashioned guy? He remember you? He remember that hot juicy box? He remember the *good times*? Maybe I should pay him a visit, give him a little reminder. What do you say?' Her eyes glazed over whilst she was talking, and she patted the money reassuringly. 'Think about it, kid. I'll pay you a visit in a coupla days and we'll talk some more, gotta go now – gotta get my head together.' She teetered off on ridiculous high-heeled wedgies.

Dallas slumped into a chair. Oh God! What was she to do? Lew Margolis hadn't stumped her, why should a stupid stoned hooker be a problem.

She pressed her fingers into her temples, massaging, thinking. Her mind remained a blank. Nothing. No solution. Somehow she would have to figure something out. In the meantime she would just have to keep on paying.

☆

Cody patted his stomach, 'Delicious!' he exclaimed, 'the best spaghetti I've had all day!'

Dallas smiled, 'It will get better.'

Cody held out his hand, 'Come and sit down, I'll do the dishes.'

'You mean you'll load the machine.'

'I mean I'll scrub the pans.'

'You're so good to me.'

'Gotta treat a star like a star. I want you to read that script tonight.'

'I can't tonight, Cody, I'm really wiped out.'

He was immediately sympathetic. 'Tough day?'

'It's just tiring.'

'Only four more weeks and they'll have the first six in the can. We'll have a honeymoon – go anywhere you like.'

'I can't wait. It's some schedule.'

'They have to work this way. A segment every six days – that's the way to make money. When you figure it out over a year it's not bad at all. You make twenty-four shows a year – that's only five months' work and the rest of the time is yours.'

'Thanks a lot. With the Mack thing – personal appearances – and hopefully a movie – I'll have no time left at all.'

'What do you want time for?'

'I want to have a baby.'

Cody sat bolt upright, 'You want to *what*?'

'A baby. I want a baby.'

He laughed. 'Married a week and she wants a baby! We've got all the time in the world – next year we'll cut 'Man Made Woman' down to twelve shows a year. Think you can wait?' She glared at him. He thought she was joking. Well, to hell with him – she didn't need his permission – she only needed his cooperation – and she wasn't short of that. Now that they were married he expected to make love all the time, and each experience made her more withdrawn physically. It was as if he was making up for lost time. Not that he didn't try to please her. He tried too goddamn hard, forcing his tongue in every possible crevice in his vain attempts at giving her pleasure. 'Don't do that,' had become her battlecry, and although she tried to make her tone pleasant she wanted to scream 'Leave me alone – don't touch me.' And of course he knew he was doing something wrong, and because of that tried all the harder.

'I think I'll go to bed,' she said.

'I think I'll join you.'

'You don't have to, it's early.'

'I want to.' Christ, did he want to! And yet what was going wrong between them?

His original instincts had been right. He should have stuck to his guns, given her time. Now they were married – married for crissakes! And she didn't even want him. He knew it. He sensed it. And his gut reaction was never wrong. He should have taken his own advice and left her alone. He had known it wouldn't work. But to turn out this bad so soon? Without even another man edging him into obscurity. He just couldn't figure it.

She had wanted *him*. There had been no gun at her head. And now with the baby talk . . .

She lay in bed totally wiped out. Bobbie. Fucking Bobbie. What was she to do?

For a moment she contemplated telling Cody – handing the whole bag over to him. But the things Bobbie would probably tell him . . . She couldn't face *that*. No – the best thing was to just keep paying – and paying and paying.

Her eyes filled with tears, and she turned her back as Cody climbed into bed beside her. His hand tentatively caressed her shoulder and she lay rigidly still. The hell with him – he could whistle for it tonight.

☆

Doris Andrews – Mrs Lew Margolis – turned up at the studio the next day. She behaved like a queen visiting her subjects, and they all bowed and scraped in her direction. She smiled graciously, accepting compliments as she picked her way carefully across the set of 'Man Made Woman', finally stationing herself beside the camera operator.

'Hello, dear,' she waved at Dallas, who was just about to do a third take on a difficult scene. 'I've come to take you off for lunch.'

Dallas smiled weakly. Just what she needed. Lew Margolis' dykey movie-star wife.

She did the scene, Chuck called cut, and there was nothing else to do but be enveloped in clouds of *Joy* as Doris kissed her firmly on both cheeks.

'I've been meaning to visit you for days,' Doris said in her girlish voice. 'I wanted to congratulate you on becoming the Mack girl. Wonderful news. So good for your career. But didn't I tell you at my party that I knew you were destined to be someone special?' She chuckled intimately. 'Some of us have it – some of us don't. You've got it, darling girl. I could tell as soon as I set eyes on you. And I should know – Lord, should I know. Twenty years in this business . . . God – that sets you up . . .' She trailed off, her cornflower-blue eyes misting over momentarily. 'I've arranged lunch in Lew's private dining room. Just the two of us – Lew's not here today, he's at home, a slight chest cold, but I always insist he stays home if there's the tiniest thing wrong with him. He loves me to baby him.' Her lips tremored slightly. 'All men like to be treated as children. Remember that, my dear, and you'll never have any problem keeping a man. Not that you would of course – with that fine figure, those lovely breasts ... Tell me, do you exercise to keep them so firm?'

Dallas said quickly, 'I never eat lunch, Mrs Margolis.'

'Doris, my dear, call me Doris. All my friends do.' She linked her arm through Dallas'. 'And I'm sure we're going to be friends. I feel a very warm closeness towards you, as if we had known each other for many years. Today you *shall* eat lunch. A little salad, a few slivers of smoked salmon. Some fresh pineapple. I ordered it specially for you.'

There was no getting out of it. Dallas made a face behind her back as she followed Doris out to a powder-blue Corniche which whisked them over to Lew's office. First the husband, now the wife. Why the hell didn't they both leave her alone?

Lunch was laid out and waiting. A bottle of white wine to go with it. 'I don't drink when I'm working,' Dallas objected.

'Of course,' agreed Doris, but she poured her a glass anyway. 'Now, Dallas dear, tell me all about yourself. Were you born out here?'

Picking at the food Dallas fabricated a suitable background for herself. Doris nodded over every word, her blue eyes misting over at references to parents killed in a car crash and – the truth at last – a fiancé dying of a drug overdose.

'I've never taken any kind of drugs,' Doris admitted in a breathy whisper. 'I suppose when I was growing up drugs just weren't an issue, and of course Lew would never want me to experiment now.' She gave a self-conscious laugh. 'Lew's a very straight-laced man you know.'

'Really?' questioned Dallas, cramming smoked salmon into her mouth and spooning some pineapple onto her plate. The sooner this lunch was over the better.

'Oh yes,' continued Doris, giggling like a naughty child, 'he has ruled over my career with an iron hand. Love scenes confined to an occasional kiss. No naughty words. All my films have appealed to a wide family audience.' She hesitated, then – 'He even censors our private life together.'

Dallas really didn't want to hear about it. She studied her pineapple and wished that Doris would shut up.

'He's a very jealous man. Has me followed, watched. I'm never allowed to be alone with another man – never. But I don't mind.' She leaned forward intently. 'You see, Dallas dear, my interest has never been in other men ... Do you understand me?'

'I've always enjoyed your movies,' Dallas replied brightly, 'I think I must have seen them all on television. Why even ...'

Doris patted her gently on the arm. 'Am I embarrassing you, dear? I wouldn't want to do that. But somehow I sense in you a kindred spirit. You see I feel that you too have been used by men. Before I married Lew ... Well, I came to Hollywood when I was seventeen – a young innocent farm girl – and between seventeen and Lew Margolis I sucked more hot cocks to get work than I care to remember. Enough to last me a lifetime.' She patted at her lips delicately with a lace handkerchief. 'Perhaps I sound crude to you, but sometimes it is such a relief to find someone with whom you can be totally honest. I feel so close to you, Dallas. You see my husband has never been able to get an erection, and I don't mind, I don't mind at all. We have a marriage of the minds. Sex is not important to me. But when I see a girl like you. A beautiful sensual girl with breasts I want to touch ...'

'Mrs Margolis – Doris,' Dallas interrupted quickly, 'please don't go on. I'm not into that scene, really I'm not.'

Doris smiled softly. 'Don't be frightened to admit it.'

'I'm not frightened.'

Doris's blue eyes bore into her. 'I can sense these things, dear, you can't deceive me. Perhaps you're not ready for a relationship just yet, but you will be – you will be. Just a little time in this town. The men are vultures, they'll eat you up and spit you out. I just want you to know that we can be friends and perhaps lovers. I hope lovers.'

Dallas nodded. She wanted to say – don't call me, I'll call you – but somehow she didn't want to make fun of this woman – this world-wide star of family entertainment whose husband could only get it up for hookers.

'I understand, Doris,' she said softly, suddenly enormously sorry for her.

Doris smiled, 'Good.' She glanced at her neat gold watch.

'My goodness – I must get you back to the set. I'm glad we've had this little lunch.'

'Yes,' agreed Dallas.

They drove back to the set in Doris' powder-blue car, and lounging around outside, carelessly chatting to an electrician, was Bobbie. She was becoming a permanent fixture.

'Hey, babe!' She teetered over to Dallas, balancing precariously on outrageously high-heeled boots worn with the perennial hot pants. ' 'Bin lookin' for you all over.'

'You're not wasting any time,' muttered Dallas bitterly, at the same moment waving and smiling at Doris as she drove off.

'Yeah, man. Well, like how long sixty bucks gonna last me? You're rollin' in it, sugar sweets – let's not get tight-fisted when y'all got soooo much to lose. Lay a thousand on me and I'll flit outta your life like a fast shit!'

'I don't have any money on me. I gave you every last cent yesterday.'

'So get it.'

'I can't get over to the bank. I'll give you a cheque.'

'No cheque, sugar sweets. Cash. Today.'

Dallas thought quickly. If a thousand dollars would keep Bobbie off her back for a while it would be worth it. She could always send someone over to her bank to cash a cheque. At least it would give her some thinking space. She needed time to figure out what to do about Bobbie.

'I'll get it for you.'

Bobbie blinked nervously. 'Good girl.'

'Where shall I send it?'

'Bring it yourself. No messengers.' She scribbled down an address. 'I'll be waitin'. Oh – an' chicken – none of your smartass ideas 'bout hittin' on me. I gotta friend with a letter. Anything happens to me you got yourself up shit creek.'

Dallas nodded grimly. They must have been watching the same television programmes.

Bobbie wobbled happily off.

Kiki, on her way to the set, linked arms with Dallas. 'Who was *that*?' she asked.

Dallas shrugged. 'Some freak chasing autographs.'

'I wonder how these people get on the set,' Kiki complained. 'Tell me about your lunch – Chuck says you were last seen being spirited off by Doris Andrews. What's she like?'

☆

Cody spent two hours on the phone locating the best house he could in Acapulco for their honeymoon. He wanted to surprise Dallas. Wanted her to have something nice to look forward to.

When it was all arranged he got nervous in case she wouldn't want to go to Acapulco. He had sent off a heavy deposit, but the hell with it . . . If she didn't want to go there he would sacrifice his deposit. True love indeed.

He had been thinking about what she had said. A baby. At first an unthinkable idea. But on second thoughts, if that was what would make her happy. After all she was a girl with no family. She had had a rotten life. If she wanted a baby . . .

It could be worked out. If only she would be prepared to wait a few months; Long enough to get twenty-four of the shows in the can, and all the Mack girl photos for the initial six months. It wasn't such an impossible idea after all. And his mother – maybe it would soften the blow. A baby to look forward to.

He would have to think about it seriously. If that was what would make Dallas happy – well, it *was* a possibility. It *could* be planned. He remembered with horror the one and only time he had knocked a girl up. She had been a secretary at one of the studios. It had been *she* who had insisted on an abortion. In fact she had planned the weekend together in Tijuana, and treated the whole thing as one long jaunt. Shocked at her callous attitude, he had dutifully spent the weekend with her, paid all the bills, and never seen her again. At least it proved he was potent.

☆

Dallas left the studio at six. She consulted the scrap of paper Bobbie had scribbled her address on. It was on Santa Monica Boulevard – the massage parlour and porno shop end.

Christ! Dallas wasn't pleased, but she had the money stacked neatly in her shoulder bag. And she had a little speech planned to lay on Bobbie. No more blackmail. If she wanted it Dallas had decided she would pay for her to take a cure. If she didn't want it – too bad. This thousand dollars was the last payment.

The traffic on Santa Monica was heavy. It was going home time – and everyone seemed to have decided to go home via Santa Monica.

Dallas scanned the numbers looking out for Bobbie's address. She hadn't bothered to call Cody to tell him she might be late, as she hadn't realized Bobbie lived so far away.

At last she found it. A seedy walk-up apartment house sandwiched between a used army clothes shop and an 'ORAL SEX – The Only Way' neon-lit parlour. She hadn't expected Bobbie to be living in the lap of luxury – but this – what a dump.

She parked the car a half block away and walked back. A drunk sat by the shabby open door. A sign read 'Rooms by the hour'. Dallas shuddered. Suddenly she didn't want to go in. Didn't want to climb the narrow staircase and search for Apartment 4B which was probably only a room anyway.

The drunk reached for her leg and she stepped smartly past him and up the stairs. Rock music blared from behind a door marked 1A, a baby crying from 1B. Both rooms on the second floor seemed silent. She continued up to the third floor, and jumped when the door of 3A opened and a hollow-eyed youth emerged, stared at her, and clattered off down the stairs.

She paused to catch her breath, anger creeping over her that she had allowed herself to get in this position. If only she could wipe out her past, just erase the whole lousy memory. Lew Margolis, Bobbie ... Why did these people have to keep on reminding her ... And who else was waiting out there to reveal her?

Wearily she reached the fourth floor. A door stood uninvitingly open, she checked the number, it was 4B.

'Anyone around?' she called, unwilling to enter the small darkened room.

'Fuck off!' screeched a woman's voice from behind the closed door of 4A. This was followed by a man's laughter.

Bobbie lay on the floor naked and shivering. She had been

badly beaten up. Her face looked unnatural; swollen and cracked lips, trickles of blood coming from her nose, and one eye so puffed up that you could hardly see it.

She rolled towards Dallas with a groan and an attempted smile. 'Hey, sugar sweets,' she mumbled, 'y'all bring the money? I need it man, like I *really* need it. They're comin' back, and next time they're *really* gonna work me over!'

46

Al issued instructions that complete secrecy must prevail concerning Evan's disappearance.

But too many people knew, and items of gossip leaked out and were exaggerated.

Edna was completely hysterical and had to have a doctor in constant attendance to keep her sedated and quiet.

Upon arrival in Tucson a private detective was hired. 'He'll pick him up in no time,' Paul assured Al.

'If you had been watching out for him this would never have fucking happened,' spat Al, his anger hissing out in the direction of anyone who came his way. 'Why wasn't someone watching him? Goddammit, I'm supposed to be the singer on this tour. Am I supposed to do everything else too?'

Paul shrugged. What could he say? He returned to his suite, and Melanie, and recounted the conversation with his brother.

'He's right,' agreed Melanie, peering in the mirror and applying powder blusher with a brush. 'Poor Al, you *should* have been keeping an eye on Evan.'

Jesus! Paul was speechless. Linda would have comforted him, told him that of course it wasn't his fault – which it wasn't.

'You always side with Al,' he complained. 'Maybe you should have married *him*.'

'Maybe I should,' agreed Melanie crisply. 'I would have been much better for him than that whining hag he's stuck with.' She finished applying the blusher. 'There! How do I look?'

'Like the bitch that you are.' He stormed out of the room. What did he need it for? A stupid, vain, nagging little bitch!

Linda was right. He should face up to it and leave her. He would still be able to see his children. He would have visiting rights. But, God, they were still so young . . . Maybe if he could just stick it out for another couple of years.

☆

They were in a park on the outskirts of town.

'Move up,' Glory giggled. 'Shift that skinny ass an' give me some space, man!'

Evan shifted around awkwardly in the sleeping bag. Glory shifted with him. They were both so thin that their bones crunched together.

Plum, huddled in her own sleeping bag next to them, mumbled, 'Shut y' face. Gotta get some sleep.'

They had bought the sleeping bags as an investment against staying in hotels. As it was summer they provided adequate warmth and comfort, and during the day folded neatly into back packs which were quite easy to carry.

Upon leaving the hotel in New Orleans they had taken a bus out of town, then left it after an hour and hitch-hiked back the way they had come. 'Throw any snoopers off our tracks,' Plum explained. 'Daddy is sure to try an' grab you back.'

Evan had no desire to be grabbed back. For the first time in his life he felt like a free person with his own identity. It didn't occur to him that his mother would be worried sick. He knew he could look after himself, and it was about time she realized it.

'You gotta hard-on?' Glory was asking. 'Little me feelin' horny. You feelin' horny Evvvan?' She was wriggling her hands down between them, feeling through his Y-fronts, pulling his very erect member out.

'How can we do it in here?' Evan asked, excitement flooding through him so strongly that he almost came at her touch.

'Keep still,' she commanded, manoeuvring him between her legs. She giggled. 'Easy does it. Push. C'mon, man, push for shit's sake.'

He felt himself slide inside the familiar contours of her body. She was different from Plum, more slippery and slidey.

'Put your mouth to mine, man,' she whispered. She had a

pill in her mouth which she transferred skilfully to his.
'Swallow it,' she encouraged, 'swallow it down an' keep on
fuckin'!'

☆

The little sod had ruined everything. Screwed every one of
Al's plans, and now he was stuck with a hysterical Edna who
seemed to think that he was entirely to blame for Evan
running off.

'He split because of you,' Al said at last. 'You've always
mollycoddled the crap out of him. He probably couldn't face
it any more.'

Edna shook her head in pain. 'I trusted you with our son.
I trusted you . . .' She started to cry.

Al left the room. This was all he needed. Stuck with Edna.
How could he be expected to work under these conditions?
He needed space . . . He needed to drink without her complaining every time he took a swig. He needed to get laid. It
was essential to have a dumb and busty blonde ready and
available.

He stormed down to Paul's suite, but there was sister-in-
law Melanie in a low-cut yellow dress thrusting tits (too
small) and sympathy (too close to home) at him. He didn't
need *that*.

In the elevator on the way back to his suite he bumped
into Nellie. Sweet dark-haired Nellie, who touched his arm
and said, 'I understand, Al. I understand.'

There was the afternoon to get through, so he said, 'You
want to buy me a drink?'

Her face lit up. 'Oh, yes.'

'What are we waiting for? Let's go to your room.'

He vaguely remembered another afternoon he had spent
with her. But it was only a hazy memory.

He went to her room, lay on the bed while she fussed
around drawing the shades, pouring him a drink, loosening
his clothes.

'I knew you'd come back,' she whispered. 'I was sure
you'd come back to me.'

He wasn't really listening. His mind was going in a dozen
different directions.

'Do you want to make love?' she was asking.

Make love. Is that what they called it?

She had taken off her dress to reveal black silken skin and small breasts with hard extended nipples. He liked more voluptuous women, but she would do.

'You knew it was me on the plane. You did, didn't you?' she asked.

He didn't know what the hell she was talking about. 'Yeah,' he agreed, ''course.' Her long black hair fell in a sweeping curtain as he pushed her head down on him. He wanted no more than a blow job. He didn't want to become involved with her face or body. He just wanted release.

After fifteen minutes he shoved her away. He couldn't come.

Goddammit, Evan, you have even ruined my sex life.

'What's the matter?' Nellie asked softly, 'Am I doing something wrong?'

He rolled onto his stomach ignoring her. He would have been better off with Sutch, big-titted Sutch whom he had never had. Or even fiery Rosa. Or better still, all three.

'What room is Sutch in?' he questioned.

'Why?' asked Nellie, blinking nervously.

'Don't bug me,' snapped Al.

'She . . . she's in the room opposite.'

He climbed off the bed, zipped up his trousers.

'Later,' he said, and walked out.

Nellie ran to the door, watched him through the spyhole. He walked to the room across the hall, knocked. Sutch opened the door clad in a pink silk kimono. Al said something, Sutch grinned, and he walked in and closed the door.

Nellie stuffed her fist in her mouth to stop herself crying out.

All this time she had thought . . . imagined . . . but she meant nothing to him, absolutely nothing.

She walked into the bathroom and slid a razor blade out of the wall dispenser.

She sat on the side of the bath and stared at the sharp glint of fresh steel. Slowly she brought it to her wrist, and slowly she cut deeply into the taut flesh until the blood ran in a heavy river down her naked body.

☆

'I wondered when you'd get around to me,' laughed Sutch. 'Honey – I ain't bin countin' the days, but I *sure* knew the day would come!'

She poured him a hefty scotch and wrapped her kimono firmly round her, emphasizing her large unfettered breasts.

She had what he was looking for, and he reached for them.

She slapped his hand away. 'Say please!' she chided, tossing her afro mane of orange hair.

'Please,' he said, ripping her kimono down the front, allowing her ripe and juicy body to be exposed.

She shook her boobs at him provocatively, as he had seen her shake them many times on stage – although on stage they had always been covered by flimsy strips of material.

'Nice,' he said.

'Nice,' she agreed, 'nice 'n yummy. Want a taste thrill, baby? Suck on a tit, I'll roll us a joint.'

Why hadn't he discovered Sutch before? She was more than enough to while away a boring afternoon with her plump sexy body and laid back humour.

He followed her to the bed. Stevie Wonder was belting away on a portable tape machine. Sutch propped herself against the bed back and proceeded to roll a joint from the equipment she had on the bedside table. Al threw off his clothes and joined her.

'My, my,' she exclaimed. 'Bless my little cotton socks! It's *all* true – every goddamn spunky inch of it!'

'Turn over,' he commanded, 'get on all fours. We'll have the joint later.'

'Yeeeessireeee!'

☆

Melanie wandered around the suite picking up things and inspecting them. Invitations, magazines, gifts from fans.

Edna sat in a chair wrapped in a dressing gown, her face white and drawn.

'I don't know,' Melanie was saying, 'I'm sure he's all right. You know what boys are like. If he's with those two girls . . . Well, they'll look after him. He's probably having a wonderful time.' She spotted a mirror, and leaned forward to study herself intently. 'I look so tired!' she wailed, 'Fine trip *this* has turned out to be. All I've seen is the inside of an aeroplane and lousy hotel rooms.' She adjusted a curl, coaxing it into place with some spit, then turned once more to Edna. 'Why don't we go out tonight?' she suggested. 'After the show. It would do you good. You could put on some make-up, and one of your new dresses. I can get Paul to book a table at the best place in town.'

'No,' said Edna flatly.

'Why not?' persisted Melanie. 'Aren't you bored? We've been stuck in this hotel for two days. I'm going out of my head, and fat chance *I've* got of getting taken anywhere without you and Al.'

'Too bad.'

Melanie wasn't sure she had heard Edna correctly. 'Huh?'

'I said too bad,' snapped Edna. 'I don't care if you are bored. *I don't care, Melanie.* You're a selfish bitch. Yes – I said it – a bitch.'

'Edna!'

'Don't Edna me. I wish I'd never let you talk me into this trip. If I hadn't come here none of this would have happened. I blame you, I really do, so don't come whining to me because you're bored.'

'Thank you very much. I love you too.'

'Just go away and leave me alone.'

'A pleasure!' Melanie flounced from the room, turning at the door to give a parting shot. 'Fine thanks I get for making you look halfway decent instead of the frump you usually are.'

Edna ignored her. She didn't care what she looked like. She just wanted Evan back.

☆

The press were on to something. More of them than usual were at the Community Centre, milling around getting in everyone's way. With 'Bad Black Alice' being number one with a bullet, interest in Al was at its peak. The Rock papers had all sent representatives in the hope of getting an exclusive interview

Bernie had organized an informal party after the show just

to keep the press happy. He hoped to persuade Al to give a mass interview – with maybe a promise of some exclusives for the more important papers the next day.

A thin girl from *Rolling Stone* kept on cornering him. 'Word's out Al's son been abducted. True or false?' she asked.

'False,' sweated Bernie. 'Where did you hear that?'

'Word's around.'

Yeah. Fucking word would be around. All they needed was the rumour to make the papers put the idea into those two freaks' heads that they could get *money* for returning little Evan safe and sound.

The crowds were packing in. Al arrived in the company of Sutch. The photographers leapt forward.

What the fuck was he doing with *that* one? Bernie groaned. Out of the three Promises she was the wild one. Her husband was in jail on a drug bust, and she never set foot on stage unless she was out of her head on coke. The other two were angels in comparison to Sutch. Rosa, the lead singer, stuck with her mafioso boyfriend and kept to herself. Nellie was just a sweet little girl whom everyone loved.

Al strode into his dressing-room, swigged from the bottle of Jack Daniels set out and waiting for him.

'Any news?' he asked Bernie.

'Paul's on the phone now.'

'Security good?'

'The best.'

'It better be. One more fuckup and I walk.'

Bernie scratched absently under an armpit. 'If you could make a press conference tonight – after the show. I set up a party. Booze. Food. I think you should do it.'

'If I feel like it,' allowed Al.

If he felt like it. Who the fuck did he think he was all of a sudden? You never played superstar with the press if you wanted to stay up there. You kissed ass and sucked cock – metaphorically speaking of course – although certain stars were not averse to doing the real thing if it kept their name in lights.

Rosa appeared at the door of the dressing-room. She ignored Al as she always did except when on stage.

'Where's Nellie?' she directed at Bernie.

'I don't know. Where is she?'

'*I'm* asking *you*. Didn't a car go to fetch her?' Rosa had taken to staying at different hotels on the tour, and making her own travel arrangements. Her 'boyfriend' preferred it that way.

'Yeah, of course. Didn't she arrive with Sutch . . .?' Bernie trailed off, remembering that Sutch had arrived with Al.

Rosa twitched her head angrily. 'Find her, Bernie, we go on in twenty minutes. She's probably sittin' in the hotel waitin' for Sutch.'

'I'll call the hotel. No panic'

'Sure, man, no panic. Only we don't go on unless there's three of us.' She swept off.

Al had started to apply his make-up. Dark pancake base. Slight kohl emphasis on the eyes. He swigged continually from the liquor bottle.

Suddenly Bernie got that feeling. It slipped in under his gut, a nagging ache that warned him of trouble. Sweet shit . . . What the fuck . . . They'd soon be in LA. Couldn't be soon enough for him.

☆

Two days on the road and already Evan was feeling tired. Of course he was enjoying it, having a wonderful time. But didn't either Plum or Glory ever think of taking a bath? And greasy hot dogs washed down with Coca Cola did not seem to be a very *balanced* diet. And when they were hitching, the two girls seemed prepared to climb into anything that stopped. What if a maniac stopped? A maniac all set to rape and murder all three of them. He had read dreadful things about what happened to hitch-hikers.

His arm still hurt. His bruises still hurt. And the novelty of being squashed in a sleeping bag alongside Glory was wearing off. She snored, and she never washed, and she was always stoned.

Also he noticed in panic in the mirror in a men's room that his spots were getting *worse*. Soon his face would be one large red patch.

'Why don't we stay in a hotel tonight?' he suggested.

Come on? laughed Plum. 'Are you *serious*, man?'

'Why not?' he persisted. 'We can afford it.'

'We can?' questioned Plum. 'I'm holdin' the bankroll, man, and we are almost busted.'

'But what about my two hundred dollars and the other money we had?'

'S'nearly gone.' Plum was unconcerned by this fact.

'How can it have?'

Plum fixed him with a mean look. 'You want a written account? We *spent* it, man – like *used* it, y'know. Sleeping bags, food, an' how do you think Glory's bin payin' f'all the goodies she's scored?'

He didn't argue further. But he thought with a certain longing of a warm bed, a juicy steak, and a hot bath.

They were riding in the back of a truck and Glory, asleep in a huddle, suddenly awoke. 'Where are we?' she asked, yawning and rubbing her eyes.

'Who knows?' snapped Plum. 'I'm gettin' a big heavy question session 'bout where all the bread's gone.'

'Yeah?' Glory was not really interested. She was reaching in her jeans' pocket and digging out some pills. She stuffed several in her own mouth and then offered the remaining few to her friends. Plum shook her head. Evan took two, swallowed them. Without water they stuck in his throat, but he knew they would eventually dissolve and then he would feel better – much better.

☆

'You mothafucker!' screamed Rosa at Al. 'You stinkin' mothafucking sonofabitch!'

Bernie had called the hotel to locate Nellie. The car was still out front waiting for her. There was no answer from her room. An assistant manager at the hotel had been dispatched to her room with a pass key. He had found her on the bathroom floor in a pool of her own blood. She was still alive, but barely. At the same time that Bernie was being informed on the phone an ambulance was rushing to the hotel.

Within five minutes Nellie was receiving emergency treatment on her way to the hospital.

Bernie had broken the news to Rosa who had gone mad with fury. She had stormed into Al's dressing-room and started screaming at him.

Assorted news media gathered in a fascinated group outside the door.

'Pig!' screamed Rosa. 'If it wasn't for you . . . You white piece of *shit*! You hear me, prick – *you hear me*!'

'The whole of Tucson hears you!' intervened Bernie. 'Please, Rosa, it's not Al's fault.'

She shook free. 'Don't give me *that* shit. Ever since the day that mothafucker crept into her bed she ain't been the same girl. She *loves* him – this piece of white crap – she *loves* him. The kid lived for a look – a smile. I could *kill* him.' She sprang suddenly, like a pouncing tiger, all red sequin dress and clawing fingers.

Bernie dragged her off Al, who just sat there staring at himself in the mirror.

'Enough,' said Bernie, holding her against his massive bulk.

She went limp in his arms. 'Get me a car to the hospital,' she muttered, 'and get me out of the sight of that mothafucking prick.'

Bernie half carried her from the room and back to her dressing-room.

Sutch had her head cradled on the dressing table and was sobbing. Make-up ran in colourful rivers down her face.

'I'll arrange a car,' said Bernie. He didn't feel too good himself. Nellie had been everyone's favourite. 'What about the show?'

'Fuck the show!' spat Rosa. 'Let superprick do it on his own. I ain't *never* sharing a stage with him again as long as I live!'

☆

A little more scotch. Gargle. Spit out. Got to do the show alone. So what? Why not? He was the star for Crissakes. He was the one they had all piled in to see. Al King. Number one with a bullet. Number fucking one.

'Are you all right?' asked Paul.

'Sure,' laughed Al. Why shouldn't he laugh?

It wasn't *his* fault some silly little girl had slit her wrists. It *wasn't* his fault – no matter what anyone said. So he had given her one. So what? If all the girls he had ever given one to slit their wrists . . . He laughed. Jesus! What a sight. There wouldn't be room for them in all the hospitals!

He went to swig from the scotch bottle again but it was empty. Empty! Would you believe that? A star with an empty bottle.

'Hey Paul – bring another bottle.'

'You've had enough, you're going on in five minutes.'

'Don't tell me I've had enough.'

'You've drunk *the whole bottle* yourself, goddammit.'

And another half bottle with Sutch. And two fine joints. And a touch of coke to keep him in peak condition. And some pretty good fucking. Just like old times. Why hadn't he discovered Sutch earlier?

'More, Paul,' he demanded, and he stood up and the room swayed. But that was OK. The room had rhythm – just like him. He laughed aloud. Paul's worried face swam before him.

'Point me to the stage,' he demanded. 'Wait a minute – gotta piss.' He unzipped his fly and let out a stream of urine in the general direction of the wall.

'Al!' Paul turned to Bernie. 'He'll never make it. We'll have to cancel the show.'

'Cancel and we got ourselves a riot,' pointed out Bernie.

'The show muss go on . . .' slurred Al.

'Let's get him on and let's get it over with,' said Paul quickly.

Bernie shrugged. What the fuck . . . It wasn't *his* funeral.

☆

Evan awoke stiff and uncomfortable. He wriggled out of the sleeping bag and surveyed his surroundings.

The girls had got them all invited to a party in an empty house. When the party had finished they had stayed on utilizing the bare floorboards as a home for the night. Some party. A lot of drugged people swopping partners. Evan had huddled miserably in a corner. He did *not* want to join in. He did *not* feel like one of them.

Glory had jeered at him – 'Poor little baby mommy's boy,' she had taunted. 'Frightened to show his pee pee!'

Perhaps it had not been such a good idea to have decided to travel to Los Angeles with them. His parents never taunted him – never. They were a pain – but from what he had heard all parents were the same.

He prowled around the empty, depressing house, and his thoughts turned to bacon and eggs, sizzling sausages, and hot coffee. His stomach grumbled with hunger. He had eleven dollars. If he didn't wake the girls that would be enough to buy himself a decent breakfast. He glanced at his watch. It was only 8 a.m. and the girls never stirred until ten at the earliest – wherever they were sleeping.

He pulled on his jeans and crept from the house. He didn't even know what town he was in, but he set resolutely off, and within two blocks spotted a drug store.

He took a stool at the counter, and was just about to study the menu when the headline of the newspaper on the rack caught his eye. 'AL KING SENSATION' it screamed in heavy black newsprint.

☆

The show was a near-miss disaster. Somehow Al managed to stagger his way through it. A performance punctuated with raging expletives, half-forgotten lyrics, and general sloppiness.

The screaming fans prevented themselves from seeing the real truth. But the press were there with their pencils sharpened.

The worst point was when Al fell. Sprawled happily in front of thousands of people, gave them the V sign, and staggered back on to his feet. There was almost a moment when Paul thought Al might repeat his bizarre performance in the dressing-room, and pee all over the audience with the famous King Cock. But he restrained himself, albeit reluctantly.

Once off stage he was wrapped in towels and rushed to the hotel where Paul had a doctor waiting to see him. The doctor examined him and pronounced him on the verge of a complete breakdown.

'Bullshit!' screamed Al. 'Bring on the girls!'

The doctor injected him with a sedative and warned Paul that he should have complete rest for at least a month. 'Impossible,' Paul muttered under his breath. He knew Al was as strong as a horse. But there had been a lot of additional strain. The bomb. The riot. Edna's arrival. Evan's disappearance. Nellie's suicide attempt. He wished that Linda was around to discuss things with. She had a habit of always coming up with the right decision.

Maybe he *should* cancel a few of the concerts. Give Al a rest. After all, going on like he had tonight was going to do him no good at all. And they did have to replace 'The Promises' – even if Nellie recovered – and it was touch and go at the moment – she wouldn't be able to work again for months. Besides, Rosa had threatened never to appear with Al again.

Maybe if he cancelled all the gigs before Los Angeles – that would give Al a break – enough to get himself together. He could always do the cancelled gigs later – something could be worked out. Yeah – that might be the answer. With the single at number one it wouldn't do Al any harm – and Jesus – the state he was in it could only do him good.

'I'll order you some food,' he said, 'then you should get some sleep. Edna wasn't feeling well – she's sleeping in another room.'

'Fuck Edna!' slurred Al truculently. 'Frigid bag! Get me 'nother bottle of Jack the Lad.'

'Listen, Al . . .'

'Listen, brother,' mimicked Al, weaving round the room, 'I did the show, didn't I? I did the fucking show. That's all anyone cares about, isn't it? Now piss off an' leave me alone.'

Reluctantly Paul left. He knew better than to argue with Al when he was in that mood. Luke was stationed outside the door. 'Don't let him out,' Paul warned. 'I'll be in my room if you need me.'

In the middle of the night they needed him. A terrible crashing noise was coming from behind the locked door of the suite. By the time the manager was called, the pass key found, and they managed to get in, the crashing had stopped. Al had completely wrecked the entire suite. Slinging what he could out of the window, breaking and smashing whatever else was in his way.

He lay in the middle of the wreckage fast asleep, snoring and smiling.

In the morning he remembered nothing about it.

'I've often wanted to do what you did myself!' sighed the manager, as they tried to work out the cost of the damages.

'Double whatever the bill is,' Al said magnanimously. 'Wreck a room on me!'

The next morning the papers screamed news of Al's bizarre concert performance, and Nellie's attempted suicide, and without actually saying so they managed to give the impression that Al was responsible.

Paul kept the newspapers away from both Al and Edna, and after a conference with Bernie he issued a joint statement from Mr and Mrs King expressing their deepest sympathy about Nellie who was a dear and close friend of both of them.

☆

Evan never spent his eleven dollars on breakfast. In fact he never had breakfast at all. He read with a sweeping horror about Nellie. *His* Nellie. And his heart lurched at the filthy allegations about her and his father.

He had to get to Tucson. He had to get to the hospital.

He spent his eleven dollars on phoning Tucson and tracking down Uncle Paul. He didn't care if they were angry with him. He didn't care about anything except getting to the hospital and seeing Nellie.

Paul seemed relieved to hear from him, and gave him instructions on what to do.

Whilst Evan hung on the phone Paul looked up a car hire firm in the area – which fortunately was only about a hundred miles away – and arranged for a car to pick Evan up. 'Don't get lost on the way,' he warned.

Get lost! No way! Nothing would stop him getting back to Nellie.

He had forgotten about Glory and Plum safely tucked up in their sleeping bags. Even if he remembered, it wouldn't have worried him. They could look after themselves. Nellie couldn't.

☆

Paul broke the good news to Edna. She was perfectly composed. 'Book us on the next flight to London,' she said calmly.

'Are you sure?' ventured Paul.

Al was still under sedation in the bedroom.

'Yes, I'm sure,' said Edna quietly. 'Very sure.'

This was a different Edna to the one Paul had known for so many years. The other Edna wouldn't have dared make such a decision without consulting Al.

'Melanie will go with you,' said Paul.

'I'd prefer she didn't.'

'Why?'

'Because I don't like her. I'm sorry, I know she's your wife, but I have to be truthful.'

Paul stared at her with a sudden admiration. He didn't like Melanie either – but he would never have the nerve to say so. What had happened to Edna? Had she suddenly sprouted balls?

'That's fine, Edna. I'll just book seats for you and Evan.'

'Thank you. I'm going to pack.'

He watched her leave the room and felt good for her. She was walking tall for the first time since he had known her.

☆

The car ride to Tucson took three hours. Evan sat stiff-backed and anxious all the way. He told the driver to go straight to the hospital where Nellie was.

'I'm supposed to take you to the hotel,' the driver complained. 'Deliver you personally, not let you out of my sight.'

'I *have* to go to the hospital first,' Evan insisted.

Reluctantly the driver agreed. The kid looked desperate.

They stopped him at reception at the hospital. He knew he must look a scruffy sight.

'I'm Al King's son,' he told the receptionist, 'I have to see Nellie – she's expecting me.'

The receptionist eyed him suspiciously. She didn't believe him. She had been bugged by press and fans all morning. 'She's dead,' she said coldly, 'died this morning at eight o'clock.'

47

The first reaction Dallas had was to turn and run – get the hell *out* of there.

But how could she go? How could she leave Bobbie in the state she was in?

One part of her warned, 'Don't get involved.' On the other hand you wouldn't leave a dog like this. After all, at one time Bobbie had befriended her – abortive as that friendship had turned out to be.

Decision made, Dallas slammed the door behind her shutting out the muffled sounds of love-making coming from the other apartment.

She didn't know what to do. Should she try to move Bobbie? What if something was broken?

An Indian bedspread was draped across the window secured only by string. Dallas removed it and covered the shivering black girl's body. She couldn't help noticing the gnarled tracks of heroin addiction covering both of Bobbie's arms. The veins were bruised and discoloured, covering old scars where she had injected herself over and over again. Unable to find more space on her arms she had started on her legs. Dallas shuddered.

Bobbie was rolling her eyes around and around. Dallas placed a dirty pillow under her head. 'What happened?' she asked. 'Who did this to you?'

'Hey,' mumbled Bobbie, focusing at last. 'The man, baby. Who else? I tole him I was gettin' the bread – I tole him.' Her head rolled to the side. 'Get me a shot of scotch – s' over there – kitchen.'

Dallas took quick stock of her surroundings. A small, dark room. Couch that doubled as a bed. Table littered with make-up, magazines, clothes. A jagged piece of glass propped up in the middle to do duty as a mirror.

The kitchen consisted of a cracked Formica unit in the corner.

Amongst crowds of empty bottles littering the top, Dallas located one a quarter full of scotch.

She handed it to Bobbie, who sucked greedily from it.

'Is there a phone here?' Dallas asked.

'You don' wanna phone, sugar,' mumbled Bobbie. Her voice was very weak.

'But you need a doctor.'

'Yeah. But I don' need the shit goes with it. I'll be fine. You just hand me the bread and get out before they come back.'

'Before *who* comes back?'

'Whadda you care? I'm leanin' on you for bread – that's all. So be wise – like I taught you.' She tried to sit up, but couldn't make it. 'I need some stuff . . . I got a beeeg need . . . Be a nice girl – reach outside the window – there's a ledge – pass it to me. Those cocksuckers don' know it all . . .' She wiped blood from her mouth and looked at it with surprise. 'One shot and those bastards can take a flyer up their own assholes . . . I'm gonna own the world . . . the world, man. Like I'll have myself a house. Best fuckin' house in LA. Best fuckin' girls . . .' Her eyes were rolling again. 'You wanna come an work for me, sugar . . . Wanna be my star . . . Wanna be my lover . . .' Her mumbling was becoming incoherent. 'Nevah was given a fuckin' thing in my life . . . Worked ass . . . Hey – get me the stuff – get me the magic . . .' Her eyes closed. She had passed out. The bottle fell from her hands gurgling the remains of its contents out on to the threadbare rug.

Dallas picked it up. This was it. This was the bottom line. Bobbie had sunk pretty low – but whose fault was it? She had started off with none of the breaks. Hooking at thirteen. And now hooked in another direction. Heroin. The land of peace and glory for those that had nowhere else to go.

Dallas cradled her head and tried to remove some of the blood. 'It'll be OK, Bobbie,' she crooned, 'I'll look after you. I'm going to get you into a hospital, get you cured.'

Bobbie's eyelids fluttered. But she didn't open her eyes. She seemed to be breathing in a very laboured way.

'I've got to get help,' Dallas muttered. She ran from the apartment and hammered on the next door.

'Get lost!' shrieked a woman's voice.

'I need help!' pleaded Dallas.

'Honey, don't we all!' replied the voice.

'Please! The girl next door is very sick.'

'That little junkie! She can drown in her own piss for all I care.'

Nice place. Was it worth trying the other apartments, or should she go down to the street and try to find a phone? She decided to try the street, and started off down the stairs. On the second floor her way was blocked by two men coming up.

'You know where's the nearest phone?' she asked.

They made no move to let her pass. One was a heavy-set black, the other a tall skinny white man with yellow hair and jumpy eyes.

'Whatcha' all needin' to telephone for?' asked the black.

'I need some help ... with a sick friend.' As she spoke she knew with a feeling of dread that these two men were the 'they' that Bobbie had been mumbling about.

'Move on up,' stated the black firmly. 'Y'all must be the friend Bobbie said was bringin' her a present. Gotta admit we di'nt believe her.'

'I'm going to call a doctor,' Dallas said, trying to keep her voice controlled.

'Y'all goin' to pay us her little debt first.'

'How much does she owe you?'

'How much you got, foxy? And how come I ain't nevah seen you around?' His hand moved like lightning, brushing over her breasts, removing her shoulder bag. He opened it, found the stack of bills, whistled admiringly. 'Must be over a thou here ... Business pretty good, baby?'

'Does she owe you all that?' Dallas asked coldly.

'Don' worry that foxy little head 'bout it,' he smirked. 'She gotta habit to support she gotta learn how to support it. Who you work for? Might just pay you a visit – a *free* visit. Wouldn't wanna see you all messed up like your friend.'

'You did that to her? Why?'

He laughed. 'Why? She wants to know why.' He cackled some more,' ' 'Cos I'm *mean*, bitch, real fuckin' *mean*.' He reached forward and squeezed her breasts.

'Let's get outa here,' said the other man, 'we got what we came for.'

'*You* may have got what you came for. I wouldn't say no to fucking this sweet piece – fucking her good.'

'Another time. We got work to do.'

'Another time. I'll get your address from Bobbie,' his hand slid down her body, pushed between her legs, 'remember it'll be for free.'

She shoved him away, thankful that she was wearing jeans.

Cackling he started off down the stairs. 'Keep it hot for me, foxy. Y'all are in f' a thrill.'

She bit her lip to stay silent. She knew what men like that

were capable of doing. She had seen what they had done to Bobbie. And Bobbie was her prime concern.

There was a telephone in a bar half a block away. She called emergency and told them to send an ambulance.

If you were smart – she told herself – you would get the hell out of here and go on home. But how could she leave until she saw that Bobbie was properly looked after? Besides, she wanted to let them know that she would be willing to pay for Bobbie's treatment, and then a cure. A private nursing home where she would be well looked after.

She ran back to the seedy apartment house, hurried up the four flights of stairs, pushed open the door.

Bobbie had dragged herself over to the window, managed to get her heroin, managed to inject herself with the help of an old belt pulled tight to locate a welcoming vein, and a plastic syringe.

She was slumped on the floor by the window. The belt hung loosely round her arm. The syringe was on the floor beside her.

She managed to smile at Dallas. 'Hey – glad you're here.' She was groggy and rubbing her eyes. 'Feel kinda funny – kinda bad. Pills. Booze. Little shot of H. Guess I mighta overdid it, sugar. Like we had some laughs once . . .' Her voice turned into a rasping choking gurgle, and her eyes rolled back for the final time.

She was dead.

From the next apartment a woman could be heard screaming in the throes of orgasm. A man laughed, a harsh unkind sound. Rock music drifted up from the second floor. In the distance came the blare of the ambulance.

Dallas hurried from the room. There was nothing she could do now.

☆

Cody paced angrily around the house, glancing at his watch for the twentieth time. She was late. Very, very late. And he had checked that she had left the studio on time. He had checked with Kiki and Chuck, and she hadn't gone home with them.

So where was she?

She was with another man, that's where she was. Maybe

the black stud with the white Ferrari. Or maybe the little group he had spied her orgying with that night. Or maybe the guy she had flown off to see when she had lied to him she was visiting an aunt.

He felt sick with jealousy. An emotion he had never felt in his life.

It was all so wrong – he should never have gotten involved. *Never.* She was playing him for a sucker ... She was his *wife*. His *wife*. And she was out screwing another man.

It was to have been such a great evening. A celebration. He had completed a terrific deal that afternoon for his English comedy actor to star in a top movie. It proved to him that his magic touch wasn't confined to Dallas.

He had booked a table at the Bistro to celebrate. And he had planned to tell Dallas about the house he had rented in Acapulco, and also that he was delighted with the fact that she wanted to have a baby, and having thought about it decided that they could definitely slot it into their schedule.

So where was she?

She was impulsive. Maybe she had just moved out. They hadn't argued, but he was only too painfully aware that she wasn't happy.

Maybe she had had an accident. But she was a good driver.

He was getting dumped sooner than he had thought.

He heard her car in the drive, and sat down trying to compose himself. Stay cool. Stay calm. See what she had to say.

She entered the house, flopped down in a chair and stared into space. She seemed almost unaware of his existence.

'You're home,' he stated, rather unnecessarily in the circumstances.

She looked dishevelled. Her long hair mussed, her face tired and drawn. Some fuck, he thought, some good fuck. He didn't want to think it, but the thought was there and refused to go.

'Where have you been?' he asked, although if he knew her at all he knew he should leave her alone.

She glanced at him with indifference. 'Out,' she replied.

'Where?' he asked pointedly.

'Driving.'

'Driving where?'

'Why don't you leave me alone?'

'Why don't you tell me where you were?'

'Why don't you fuck off?'

He stood up. 'I guess it's no use my asking who he is.'

She didn't reply, just looked at him coldly.

He shrugged, trying to conceal the hurt he felt. 'You wouldn't listen to me. I told you this would happen. I knew it . . .'

She sighed. 'You're wrong.'

'I'll do whatever you want. But let's get out of it now – with dignity – without the screaming and accusations. Without the shit I want to throw at you.'

'Whatever you want, Cody.'

'I don't want to call you names . . .'

'So don't.'

Her apparent indifference infuriated him. He walked slowly, stiffly, to the door. 'I'll stay at a hotel tonight.'

She didn't stop him. She sat in the chair and stared into space, and he left before the tears slid silently down her face.

☆

Once in his car Cody immediately regretted leaving. Hasty – much too hasty. So anxious to get out before she said things he didn't want to hear. Anxious to preserve his dignity – sanity.

So she had been with another man – so big deal. It was him she had come back to. But he didn't want to be in that position. The jealous husband, the schmuck waiting at home for the crumbs of her company.

He would get out now. Immediately. A quickie divorce. And then, things could go back to the way they were. Friendship. Business. So he wouldn't have her body, but he wouldn't get torn to shreds every time someone else did. Or would he?

He drove furiously along the strip. Maybe he should have listened to what she had to say. Who was he kidding? She had had nothing to say. She acted as if he didn't exist, didn't matter. He had tried to forget about her past – what little she had told him of it. So she had been a whore – but that was a

long time ago. And she had stopped being a whore. Whore –
what a beautiful old-fashioned word – probably one of his
mother's favourites. But could he ever forget?

Why the hell had she ever told him? He slammed his foot
down hard on the accelerator.

He had nowhere to go. He had given up his apartment.
Going to his mother's was out. A hotel was too depressing a
thought.

Feeling sorry for himself he headed in the direction of
Connie's apartment. A little sympathy was the order of the
day.

☆

Dallas remembered the good times.

The beginning of her relationship with Bobbie. The fun.
The laughs. Of course hooking wasn't everyone's idea of
having a terrific time – but in Miami with Bobbie it hadn't
been *bad*. Just another way to make some bread. And they
had had each other. The first *real* relationship Dallas had ever
experienced. The first person who gave a shit.

Bobbie had taught her to cook, dance, fuck, laugh. Bobbie
had taught her how to look after herself, protect herself, get
herself through the day.

And then had come the old man in the motel, the trip to
LA, and the sudden disintegration of everything that was
fun.

And the drugs. Bobbie had been fairly straight until LA.
Tinsel city had scored again. Shit! It could have been *her* that
had gotten hooked on drugs. There but for the grace of Ed
Kurlnik . . .

Dallas shuddered, hugged her knees to her chest.

She thought of Bobbie's skinny pathetic body lying on the
floor of the shabby room. The two animals who had beaten
her up. They should be in jail . . . But there was no one to put
the finger on them – only her – and she knew enough not to
get involved. Forget *that* scene.

It was funny – she should be glad that Bobbie was dead.
She should be out celebrating – after all, it was the perfect
solution. And yet she could only feel sorrow. A sense of loss.
Ridiculous really – but that's the way it was.

Vaguely she remembered Cody walking out. Poor Cody –

he thought she had been with another man. If only he knew
... If only she could have confided in him ...

But it was better this way. Much better.

She was a loner, she didn't need anyone. Better that Cody
should realize this. Besides, his opinion of her was the lowest.
He had immediately assumed she had been with another
man ... Screw him ... Tomorrow she would give him the
good news that they weren't really married anyway. She
had pretended to forget, but she had known all along that
she still had a husband in Miami.

☆

'What in heck do you think you *want*?' questioned Connie,
keeping Cody firmly in place by way of a chain lock on the
door.

'Let me in and I'll tell you,' he replied, feeling like an
unwelcome door-to-door salesman.

Connie stood her ground. 'Our mutual shrink tells me that
you treat me like dirt. He says that you are a user and that I
should throw you out of my life. Period.'

'Did you tell him my name?' asked Cody, alarmed at
losing face with his analyst,

'Certainly not. You – better than anyone – should know
we deal only with initials. And by the way, why haven't you
been to see him for three weeks?'

'How do you know that?'

'I just know ... You should go see him, you've got
problems. Any man who treats women as sexual objects
needs help.'

'*Me?*'

'Yes, you. How do you think you've treated me?'

A woman emerged from the apartment opposite and
stared.

'Let me in, Connie,' whispered Cody urgently.

'No. I'm sorry – but I'm a person. A human being. I am
not here for your sexual convenience.' She started to close the
door.

'*But I don't want sex!*'

Connie gave him a superior smile. 'Of course you don't,'
she said understandingly, and slammed the door shut.

The woman opposite cackled, and darted back into her

apartment before Cody could think of a suitable remark to throw in her direction.

He had been seeing Connie on and off for two years. Why the sudden cold shoulder? Didn't she know he was going to be rich and powerful? Didn't she care?

He knew who would care. Her name sprung to mind immediately. Carol Cameron would not close any doors in his face. She would throw everything open – everything.

He drove to the nearest bar – looked her up in the phone book – somehow he had known she would be listed – and drove right over to her address.

She answered the door of her small house after a long pause. Clad in shorts and a T-shirt over very obviously nothing, she looked younger than she had in his office. She was not wearing make-up, that was why. And her hair was more tousled and natural-looking, not teased into lacquered curls.

'Cody!' she exclaimed. 'Why didn't you call? I look a mess.'

'You look lovely.'

'Gee, thanks.'

'I'm accepting your offer of a drink.'

'That's marvellous. Just come in, settle yourself down – I've just got to take care of a few things.' She led him into a pink living room strewn with fluffy toy animals. 'What can I fix you?'

'Vodka.' He glanced around.. Pictures of Carol lined the walls. A nude portrait had place of honour.

'I won't be a minute,' she said, 'just make yourself comfortable.'

'I'm not interrupting anything?'

She giggled. 'Nothing I can't finish at another time.'

She left the room and he could hear a whispered conversation, then a few minutes later a door slammed. Goodbye boyfriend. Don't kid yourself it's on account of your irresistible sex appeal, Cody, my boy. The fact is most girls are career girls – and career comes first.

He flipped through some magazines. They were full of pictures of Carol in various forms of undress.

She was taking a long time. He glanced at his watch.

Why had he come here anyway?

A little company, a little warmth. Who was he kidding? He wanted to get laid. He wanted to feed his bruised ego.

'Hello,' said a childish voice. Carol stood in the doorway, posing. Her face was a mask of make-up. Her hair (or was it a wig?) carefully curled.

She wore very high-heeled furry pink mules, pink frilly panties with a strategic open heart on the front revealing bleached pubic hair. And a frilled pink bra with an open heart dead centre both sides allowing amazing nipples to point threateningly at him.

'You are going to handle me, aren't you?' she lisped. 'Baby *wants* to be handled by you.'

Yes. He was going to handle her. But not in the way *she* expected.

Oh God, if his mother could see him now!

He stood up. Decadent Hollywood here I come!!

48

The rest did Al more good than Paul could have hoped for. They went to ground in an Arizona ranch house that did not even have television. There was just Al, himself, Luke, and a Mexican couple who looked after the house.

Al spent his days soaking up the sun by the swimming pool, and occasionally going riding. There was tennis and squash, billiards and table tennis. The house was completely cut off with only one telephone for emergencies. Paul had borrowed it from a millionaire who occasionally liked to get back to the simple life. It wasn't that simple, but it *was* completely isolated.

Edna had flown back to England along with a reluctant Evan.

Melanie had been a problem, but Paul had solved that by allowing her a two-week vacation in New York by herself before flying home. 'It will be too boring for you to stay here,' he had explained. She hadn't argued.

Bernie had flown on to Los Angeles to set everything up. Al would now do two concerts there – then a special charity event in Las Vegas – and then they would take the plane on to South America where Al was getting a million dollars for just two concerts. It had been an offer that Paul could not refuse. And it would more than compensate for the lost revenue of the cancelled shows.

So Al was drying out. No booze. No drugs. No women. Sun. Exercise. Healthy food. Rest.

He had lost weight, gained a suntan, and looked and felt good.

Meanwhile 'Bad Black Alice' remained at number one with a bullet. And the album – *AL IS KING* – was fighting it out for the number one spot with Rod Stewart.

A new group had been hired to replace 'The Promises'. Three black girls who called themselves 'Hot Fudge'. Paul had flown to Los Angeles to see them, and signed them on the spot. They were sisters, and their mother travelled with them, so Paul foresaw no big problem there. They were also sensational on stage – dynamic, fresh and sexy.

Everyone had been upset by Nellie's death. Al more than anyone. He had told Paul about that fateful afternoon. 'I never knew she *cared*,' he explained, 'if I had known I'd never have gone near her. I thought she just wanted some laughs.'

'Sure,' Paul agreed. But privately he thought how anyone with half an eye could see that Nellie was besotted. The fact was that Al never noticed anyone's feelings except his own.

Paul had called Linda the very moment that Melanie was on a plane. But she never seemed to answer her phone. All he could get was the answering service, and after five calls where he left his name and number it occurred to him that she had no intention of calling him back. At first he was angry—What right did she have to do this to him? But gradually he realized that she had every right. There were no ties between them. She was a free agent.

He suffered in silence. Brooding about what she was doing, who she was seeing, who she was sleeping with . . .

Al didn't even bother to ask where she was. But then Al didn't even begin to understand what a real relationship was all about.

After three weeks they were ready to move on. Paul had never seen his brother look so good – which was just as well because Bernie had lined up a gruelling schedule of television appearances, press interviews, and parties.

It was back to the grind. The glare of the spotlight.

Was Al ready?

He was as ready as he'd ever be.

☆

'Got a cigarette?' asked Linda.

She was in Rik's depressing small apartment, in Rik's lumpy bed, having just eaten Rik's over-active and engorged penis.

'No smoking, honey, you promised.' He lay on his back, arms propped behind his head, a pleased smile on his face.

'I want a cigarette!' she snapped.

'All right, all right.' He leaned over her and reached under the bed producing a packet of filter tips. It was *his* idea that she give up smoking, certainly not hers.

He lit the cigarette for her, placed it in her mouth. 'Bad for you,' he admonished.

She drew deeply, inhaling the delicious poison into her lungs. She glanced at Rik. He was back in his supine position, still smiling.

He was beautiful – but God he was boring! She had been seeing him for three weeks on a regular basis, and he was driving her nuts!

She had thought that a good steady screwing would take her mind off Paul. But she had been wrong.

She got out of bed and started to dress.

'Where are you going?' asked Rik, the smile vanishing from his face.

'I feel like a walk.'

'I'll get dressed.'

'Alone.'

'You promised you'd stay the whole night.'

'I can't.'

'But you promised.'

'Listen Rik, I don't think that we had better see each other again.'

'Whaaat?'

'For a while anyway.'

He leaped off the bed and held her firmly by the shoulders. 'Why?' he pleaded. 'What have I done?'

She shook free. 'It's nothing you've done, it's just that,'

she shrugged, 'I don't know, I'm beginning to feel hemmed in, like trapped.'

His lips tightened. 'That's ridiculous.'

'It may seem ridiculous to you, but it's the way I feel.'

He turned his back on her. 'Why didn't you tell me earlier?'

'Earlier when?'

'Before we made love.'

'What difference does *that* make?'

'It makes a lot of difference.'

She tried to make light of it. 'Hey listen, kid, I never turn a great lay down!'

His hurt face made her realize she hadn't said the right thing.

'I'll call you, Rik,' she said, 'in a day or two.'

He stared at her. How come she was using all his lines?

'You never call when you say you will,' he muttered.

She smiled brightly. 'This time will be different, you'll see.' And before he could object she was out of his apartment, on the street, hailing a cab, and making some decisions.

☆

Back in England, back at her house, a cowed and silent Evan by her side, Edna did something she had been wanting to do for years. She fired the cook, the maid, and with the most pleasure of all – Nelson.

He was not easy to get rid of. He leered at her and said, 'I'll be seeing Mr King about it when he gets back.'

'No,' replied Edna, 'you're seeing me now, and I'm telling you that I'd like you to leave – today.'

Nelson narrowed mean eyes. 'So that's the way it is, then. Pushed out without so much as a by your leave.'

'I'll pay you two weeks' money,' said Edna firmly.

'That's not enough,' Nelson grumbled, 'rich people pushing us poor around. You think with money you can do what you want.'

'Is four weeks' wages enough?' questioned Edna.

'Make it six, missus. That's only fair.'

'All right.' She would have agreed to anything to get him off the premises.

She counted out the money and Nelson snatched it greedily. 'You'll be alone, then, all alone 'til the master gets back.'

'Thank you, Nelson,' she said brusquely, dismissing him.

Insolently he picked at his nose. 'I'll have to pack up me things,' he said, 'you don't mind that, do you?'

She turned away, filled with relief that she had been able to fire him. 'That will be all right,' she replied curtly, 'but please make it fast.'

He sniggered. 'Yes, *m'am,*' and ambled off down the garden muttering to himself.

She had done it! Soon she would be alone in the house. *Her* house. She could cook meals without feeling like an intruder. She could clean her own furniture, dust her own shelves. She could swim in the pool without that horrible man leering at her. She could tend to the garden, grow her own vegetables. And if Al didn't like it when he came back . . . Well, he would just have to lump it. She was going to do what made *her* happy for a change.

Upstairs Evan lay on his bed, his eyes open and unseeing. If he hadn't run off . . . If he had been there when she needed him . . . *He* was to blame for Nellie's death. It was *his* fault.

Tears trickled down his face, weaving their way through his acned skin.

He didn't know what to do. He just didn't know . . .

☆

Jetting into Los Angeles was a trip unto itself. The California faction of the Al King fan club were out in force. The police held the crowds back while he was transferred to the obligatory long black limousine.

'Welcome Welcome Welcome!' screamed the fans, holding their banners of undying love aloft.

A female journalist of much clout was waiting in his limo for a taped radio interview. The programme was syndicated all over America.

Bernie Suntan was on hand looking fat and sleek and happy. This was *his* town. Here, he was in control. He handed Al a typed list of top Hollywood hostesses who all wished to give parties in his honour. In the Hollywood social circles giving parties for visiting celebrities was *the* thing to do –

whether you knew them or not. They were all vying to do the honours for Al.

☆

Al ticked off Doris Andrews – because he had always loved her movies; and Karmen Rush – because she was *the* female superstar of the moment, and while not exactly beautiful, she had a charisma matched only by her sensationally powerful voice. He didn't fancy either of them, but more important he was a fan of them both.

Bernie was well pleased with Al's choice – national coverage on both events would be guaranteed. Karmen Rush and her entourage had already requested tickets for both of Al's concerts.

The stars were turning out in legion to see Al, and Bernie was delighted to see how well he looked. In Tucson he had been puffy-faced, tired, and drawn-looking. The transformation was remarkable.

☆

Linda arrived in Los Angeles on the same day, although she wasn't aware of that fact until later when she saw all the press and television coverage. She had not planned it this way. In fact she had not planned anything. She had just decided that she had to get out of New York for a while – so she had packed a few clothes, her cameras, and here she was. Free. She wanted to stay that way. Just because Paul was in the same town didn't mean she had to see him.

She called Dallas at the studio, who insisted that she come and stay with her.

'My plan is to get a little apartment,' Linda told her. 'But while I'm looking, your place would be just wonderful.'

'Come by the studio and pick up the key,' Dallas said, 'I'll leave it at the main gate.'

☆

As soon as he was settled in his bungalow at the Beverly Hills Hotel Al handed Paul a slip of paper. 'Call her,' he said.

Paul looked at the number blankly, 'Call who?'

'Dallas.'

'Dallas?'

'You going deaf?'

'I thought . . .'

'You thought what?'

'Goddammit, Al, you know what. She always gives you a hard time. You need all that crap?'

'I'll decide what I need.'

'Anyway, she's a heavy number now. You can't pick up a magazine or paper without finding her picture or a story.'

'So?'

'Well . . .' Paul hesitated, then plunged ahead. 'She didn't want to know about you before. What makes you think . . .?'

'Just call her. Your opinions I can do without. I pay you to do – not think.'

'You *pay* me?'

'Don't split hairs,' snapped Al in an irritable fashion. 'Call her, tell her I'd like her to be my guest at the concert tomorrow.'

'Sure, boss,' drawled Paul sarcastically. They had had three weeks of peace and rest. Al had actually started to behave like a human being. Now he was back to his old self. Christ almighty! To say that he *paid* him – it was an insult. Maybe Al thought that he could stroll onto the street and just hire anyone who could do the job that he did. Why, without him, Al would have drowned in his own juices long ago.

When this tour was finished they were going to have to get some things straight. Either his brother treated him with some respect or it was *over*.

Paul left the bungalow, screwed the piece of paper up with the phone number on and threw it into the bushes. It was pointless to call anyway. She would only turn Al down. She always did.

Besides, Bernie had two thick black books that were going to keep Al more than busy.

49

Dallas had slept badly with the help of two Seconal – which *hadn't* helped.

She got up an hour before she was due at the studio and

packed up all of Cody's things. Two suitcases. Most of his personal stuff he kept at his mother's. Thank God he hadn't *told* his mother.

She was so relieved it was over almost before it had begun. If Cody was agreeable they could just continue the way they were before. It had been *her* mistake. She didn't love him – whatever love was. And she certainly couldn't put up with the sex – no way.

She swam, fixed orange juice and toast, and tried to blank the whole Bobbie business out of her mind.

She couldn't. She kept on seeing the dingy little room, Bobbie lying on the floor . . .

If only she could arrange a decent funeral, at least send flowers. But to get involved was hopeless, and she knew it.

The phone rang just as she was leaving. It was Cody.

'I'm sorry, I'm sorry, I'm sorry,' he said, 'I was suspicious, jealous, I didn't wait for you to explain, I . . .'

She cut in. 'You were right, Cody, you called the shots, I lived up to your non-expectations. I guess it's the way I am.'

'But I didn't . . .'

'Look – we have to talk. Can you come by the studio for lunch?'

He agreed to meet her. She sighed, it wasn't going to be exactly easy telling him that they were never married, that it was all a put-on. Maybe he would be relieved . . . She was.

☆

Carol Cameron slept nude, wearing only a black sleep mask and massive ear plugs. If a rapist broke in she would probably never even know he was there!

Cody slid from her king-size bed early in the morning, and fixed himself coffee in her chintzy kitchen. He was exhausted. He had never known making love could be so *energetic*. If they ever gave out an Oscar for energy and initiative in the sexual stakes Carol Cameron would be sure to win!

He wondered what she thought of him. Good? Bad? Indifferent? Excellent?

He remembered the first girl he had ever slept with. A secretary (he had a history of secretaries!) several years older than himself – he had been twenty – a late starter due to his mother monitoring his every move. Anyway, after the big bad deed he had waited patiently for her verdict, but she hadn't said anything, until finally he was forced to ask. 'How was I?' 'Adequate,' she had replied with a yawn.

Adequate! The word had stayed with him all his life.

Did Carol Cameron think of him as 'adequate'? He thought not, remembering the compliments she had showered upon him. 'Enormous!' (untrue) 'Never seen anything like it!' (unlikely) 'You're the best!' (could be true, but with her track record probably not).

Hmmm . . .

In the clear light of morning he was sorry that he had come here. He was a married man, and whatever Dallas had done did not give him the right to rush out and do it too.

Now Carol Cameron would put the word around that he was an easy lay – especially when he told her he wasn't going to handle her. Maybe she would put the word around that he was enormous and he could spend the rest of his life disproving it . . .

What was he thinking of? He had a wife. Dallas had never commented on his sexual prowess at all. She was always very silent and undemonstrative. She seemed to have enjoyed it more the very first time when he had been unable to get it up for more than a few seconds.

Of course with her previous record, sex was probably not the ultimate turn-on. But he had hoped to change all that. Maybe other guys were changing it every day. Maybe she could only get it on with big black studs . . . Group scenes . . .

He mustn't think like that.

He picked up the phone and called her.

☆

'Cut!' shouted Chuck. 'Okay – print it. Let's break for lunch.'

'You want to have lunch with us?' Kiki asked Dallas.

'No thanks. Cody should be here – oh, there he is.' She strode over to him. 'Hi.'

He kissed her chastely on the cheek. 'Hi.'

They walked in silence to her dressing-room. He sat on a chair while she unzipped herself out of the silver track suit she had been wearing for the scene.

He marvelled at her body as he always did. The long legs,

finely-muscled stomach, magnificent breasts. She shrugged her way into a loose kimono and lit a cigarette.

'I've got a confession,' she said, 'I think as my almost husband you should know.'

He was confused. 'What are you talking about?'

'Us. We were the marriage that never was.'

'Huh?'

'We were never married. I wasn't quite straight with you – you see I already have a husband.'

'Is this some kind of joke? If it is I don't think it's very funny.'

'It's no joke, Cody. I was married at seventeen to a guy in Miami. We never got divorced. So you see . . .'

He stood up knowing that his skin was turning a dull red with anger. 'I see.'

She stood up too. 'It's best this way. No hassles. You were right, I should have listened to you.'

He stared at her. God, she was beautiful. But God she was a bitch. Didn't she realize she had just cut off his balls?

'It can all be like it was before,' she was saying, 'business and friends.'

Now she was handing them back to him neatly packaged, the way she wanted it.

'I packed up all your things – maybe you could collect them this afternoon before I get back. I don't think we should string things out.'

'No, of course not,' he said tightly. He wanted to hit her, strike out. But he had never hit a woman in his life, and besides – she was still Dallas – and he still loved her.

She kissed him lightly on the cheek. 'I'm sorry I lied to you. I don't know why I did – but I guess you understand.'

Oh sure. He was a schmuck, wasn't he? Schmucks always understood.

'Do you want any lunch?' she was asking him casually.

Don't tell me she was going to eat at a time like this? He could throw up all over her.

'No,' he said quickly, 'there's things at the office needing my attention.'

'Well . . .' she stretched. 'Shall I call you tomorrow?'

'Yes, of course.' He just wanted to get *out* of there.

She moved very close to him. 'You're *sure* you understand?'

He forced a laugh. 'What's to understand?'

He drove around in a daze for two hours afterwards, finally stopping at a drive-in for a coffee. He still couldn't face eating.

The coffee rumbled uncomfortably around in his stomach. He felt sick. He had to find a hotel – it was either that or back to the comforting Miss Cameron. He couldn't face the office.

He drove up to the house to collect his suitcases which Dallas had so thoughtfully packed for him. Boy – when she wanted somebody out there was no hanging about. But he couldn't hate her. He had known this would happen – not quite so soon perhaps – but eventually.

Why would a girl like Dallas want to be married to a guy like him? He couldn't think of one good reason, and he realized it was time to go back to his analyst for a fast course of self-esteem.

☆

Linda picked up the key and drove her rented Mercury up to Dallas' house. The sun was shining. The Californian disc jockey blathered on about nothing on the radio. The attendant in the supermarket she had stopped at had given her a ripe juicy cantaloupe as a gift along with the big bag of groceries she had bought.

Los Angeles was a nice city. Warm and friendly. Fun. She wanted to have fun, she had been working much too hard. She was planning to relax, take it easy, photograph a few movie stars.

A man was putting suitcases in a car outside the house, and she recognized him as Cody Hills. God, she hoped he wasn't moving out on *her* account.

She honked the horn. 'Hello there,' she shouted.

He turned to look at her. Blank, No recognition.

'Linda Cosmo, Dallas' friend,' she said, jumping out of the car.

'Oh, hi.' He looked glum.

'I'm coming to stay for a few days – just 'til I find an apartment.'

'Good.' He was about as interested as a frog.

'Gorgeous weather,' Linda remarked. She had always had a compulsion to make inane conversation.

He was busy slamming the boot down on his car. He was quite attractive really, a little more hair, lose a few pounds . . . She tried to remember what Dallas had said about him – something about him being nice . . . too nice . . . Was there such a thing as a man who was too nice?

As she was thinking, she was carrying the groceries from the car, trying to manage her large Gucci hold-all, and all of her camera equipment. It didn't work. She tripped and dropped everything. Oranges and apples were rolling about wherewhere. A yoghurt lost its top and spilled out. A carton of eggs smashed.

'Shit!' she exclaimed.

Cody got out of his car. He had been just about to drive off.

'You want me to help you,' he stated.

'I want you to help me,' she agreed.

He looked at her properly for the first time. She had the most direct, deep, interesting eyes. She looked like the sort of woman you could *talk* to.

She smiled. He smiled back.

'You chase the oranges,' she said, 'and I'll get the eggs before they turn into an omelette!'

Suddenly he was very, very hungry.

☆

Doris Andrews' well modulated nasal twang said, 'I want you to come to a party I am having on Saturday night. A very *special* party.'

Dallas held the phone away from her ear and made a face. She had just walked into the house and been caught by the phone ringing. She was grimacing at Linda who was waiting to greet her.

'Hey – listen – I really *hate* parties,' Dallas said.

Doris chuckled. 'I know just how you feel, dear. But there are certain parties you have to be seen at, and I'm sure you'll agree that mine is one of them.'

'I don't know . . .'

'You're not turning me down are you?' chided Doris softly.

'It's just that . . .'

'I won't take no for an answer, dear. Nor will Lew. There

will be many important people here, people you should meet.'

'OK,' Dallas agreed reluctantly, 'but I have a houseguest. Is it all right if I bring her?'

'Is she pretty?'

'Not *your* kind of pretty!'

'Dallas! What we discussed was between us.'

'I know, I know, I was only kidding. Can I bring her?'

'Of course. What's her name?'

'Linda Cosmo.'

'Fine. Placement, you know. If she's pretty I'll seat her next to Aarron, with you on the other side. Oh, by the way, the party is for Al King. Lew is trying to get him for a picture. See you Saturday, my dear, between seven and seven thirty. No later.'

Dallas put the phone down.

Linda rushed over, hugged her. 'Good to *see* you. Am I a surprise?'

'Tonight is full of surprises,' said Dallas. That was Doris Andrews . . .'

'The movie star?'

'Who else? I only get calls from stars now, you know. *Anyway* – party on Saturday night for – guess who?'

'Al King.'

'How did you know?'

Linda shrugged. 'Girlish intuition or some such crap.'

'Are you and Paul . . .'

'Split. Yes. Weeks ago. His wife caught us in bed together. How do you like *that* little scenario?'

'Sounds cosy.'

'*Not* a trip to be recommended.'

Dallas smiled. 'Tell me a trip that is? Are we going to the party?'

Linda shrugged. 'Whatever . . . I don't care . . .'

'We'll go, then,' Dallas decided. She couldn't resist the opportunity of seeing Al King again. Not that he meant anything in her life . . . But what was there to lose?

☆

50

Two days of interviews, photographs, television, and work. Rehearsing with 'Hot Fudge'. Ordering some amazing new outfits from Nudies – the renowned Beverly Hills tailor shop. Catching up on all the latest albums – sent over to him with a magnificent stereo music-centre by his record company. Meetings with a producer he wanted to use on his new album.

'I spoke to Dallas and her answer is still no,' Paul lied, 'but has Bernie got some numbers for you! I . . .'

'Forget it,' snapped Al. 'I'm not in the mood.'

Paul had never known a time when Al was 'not in the mood'. Especially after three sexless weeks in Arizona. Especially with a big concert coming up. Why wasn't he demanding a big-breasted dumb blonde? Some rock stars sniffed coke, got high, shot speed, to get it on just before a show. Al's vice had always been a woman. A faceless, big-breasted blonde. Now – in Los Angeles – city of the quintessential ding-a-ling – he didn't want to know. Paul couldn't understand it.

Al had spoken to Edna once a week since her return to England. Short, flat conversations, dealing with the trivia of domesticity. Had the garage sent a man to wax his cars? Did she forward all the tax forms on to the accountant? How was Evan?

Evan was in bad shape. He was in a state of extreme nervous tension, although Edna thought he was his normal surly self, and as part of her new policy left him alone.

His arm was better. His bruises had faded. But he had a new, more pressing problem. Something terrible had happened to him. Something so horrible that he was at his wits end about what to do.

He had a venereal disease.

Oh, he knew what it was all right. He could remember in vivid detail the films they had shown at school during a sex education class. The frightening pictures of a diseased penis – withered, dripping, covered in sores. And of course he remembered the teacher's warning words about impotency and pain and sometimes even death!

God! He had it. He knew he had it. He would probably *die* from it!

He couldn't possibly tell anyone. The shame and embarrassment would be too much to bear. Perhaps dying would be the best thing.

He sat in his room and brooded over his symptoms which seemed to get worse. If he did die his mother would surely find out. If only his father was home . . . He would understand. He might even be sympathetic. He would certainly help him.

Three and a half weeks of pain culminated in the fact that he couldn't even pee any more without going through the most excruciating agony. That decided him. He forged his mother's signature on a cheque, cashed it – there was no problem as they knew him at the bank. He then told Edna a friend had invited him to stay in Scotland for a few days, hiked out to London Airport, and got on the first available flight to Los Angeles. It was the first time in his life he had gone to his father for help.

☆

The concert at the famous Hollywood Bowl was a sell-out.

'Every fuckin' celebrity in town 'bin fighting for tickets,' exclaimed Bernie happily, 'don't know how I'm squeezing 'em all in. You think I'm gonna turn away Streisand and Beatty? Best fuckin' turn-out this city's seen for a long time. Is Al in good shape?'

'He's sober, straight – don't know, what's the matter with him,' Paul replied. 'I've never seen him put on such a low profile.'

'Don't knock it,' urged Bernie. 'We don't need another Tucson scene. I got a truckload of photographers grabbing my balls for a piece of the action tomorrow. You think Al would mind if *Newsweek* came in the helicopter?'

'Ask him.'

'Come on, Paul, *you* ask him. *I* can't talk to him – nobody can talk to him any more except you.'

Paul hadn't realized it before, but what Bernie said was true. Al had retreated into a non-communicative state with everyone. Maybe it had been a whole better scene when he was drinking – maybe not.

'I'll ask him,' said Paul. 'If there's room I'm sure he'll say yes.'

'There'll be room,' wheezed Bernie. 'Now about tonight, I've arranged for the car to pick you up six forty-five. I think as guest of honour Al should arrive early. Doris Andrews won't have any photographers in the house – except *Women's Wear Daily* – but she's laying on facilities for the press outside – and if her guests don't mind having their picture taken that's straight with her. She's not a bad broad – the old man's a pain in the ass . . .'

'I know,' interrupted Paul, 'I had a meeting with him yesterday.'

'Anything exciting?'

'He's got a property he wants Al to do.'

'Shall I leak it?'

'Hold back, Bernie. I don't know – Al's not in the mood for making decisions. He's going to read the script – I'll let you know the strength in a day or two.'

'Right on. Karmen Rush's boyfriend bin buggin the shit outta me 'bout *their* party for Al tomorrow. Should be some wild gig.'

Paul nodded. 'As long as they know it's got to be after the concert.'

'Sure they know. They're all gonna *be* at the show.' Bernie smirked with pleasure. Had he done a job on Al. His city – *his* fuckin' town – and he had made Al a hero. Tonight the Doris Andrews/Lew Margolis bash would have the crême de la crême of Hollywood society. The older group. A mixture of the A and B groups – the elite Beverly Hills moneyed talent. The respectable movie stars and their suitable partners. The moguls and their wives, with a beautiful girl or two thrown in for added flavour.

The, Karmen Rush party after the show tomorrow would be pure freaksville. The young side of Hollywood. The new Hollywood. Millionaire rock stars and their old ladies. Groupies. Druggies. Models. Designers. Promoters. Hustlers. Porno magazine chiefs. And Girls Girls Girls.

Bernie was looking forward to it. Karmen Rush had made her home in a fantasy mansion on the beach at Malibu. She had started off owning one smallish house, and over the course of five years and much fame had gradually purchased six neighbouring houses and joined them all together making one wide strange incredible mansion. Karmen's house was almost as famous as she was.

Bernie had only ever attended one party there – but it would remain in his mind forever. He had gotten stoned out of his head – the drugs were flowing – and had woken up in a rubber dingy in the *ocean* with a spaced-out starlet!! Fortunately they had not been too far from shore, but he could still summon a shudder at the memory. The ocean for crissakes! What the fuck – that's what living was all about.

☆

'Why are you wearing that?' asked Linda.

Dallas turned in front of the mirror. 'Don't you like it?'

'For a snack at a drive-in it's perfect. But for the party tonight?'

Dallas frowned. 'Why should I get all dressed up? A room full of dirty old men leering all over me – ugh!' She was clad in a huge black mohair sweater over trousers. She had pulled her hair back in a ponytail and scrubbed her face of make-up. 'Do you think I look awful?' she questioned. 'Maybe if I look awful they'll all leave me alone.'

'Kid – *you* could never look awful. If that's your kick for the night do it. I should care. But – and please take this in the way it's meant – isn't being the Mack girl more than your photos all over the magazines? Isn't it creating some sort of image? I mean Aarron Mack might take one look at you tonight – clap himself on the head – and say "holy shit! I made a mistake!" And then you'll be out how many zillions of dollars?'

Dallas couldn't help laughing. 'Very funny. Do you mind hanging around getting drunk or something while I change. It means we'll be late – probably ruin Doris' "placement" – but I guess you're right.'

She inspected her clothes. If she was going to change she may as well do it in style. There was a little white jersey number – a Halston – understated and clinging. She slipped into it – it was no longer understated.

She untied the rubber band holding her hair back, and bending forward brushed it vigorously. Then she sat at the dressing table and smudged kohl round her eyes, gold on her cheeks and eyelids, shiny lip gloss on her mouth. She added emerald earrings – the one gift of Ed Kurlnik's that she had kept – and she was ready.

'Why did I tell you to change?' sighed Linda. 'I looked pretty good before. Now I feel like the poor relation!'

'Nonsense. You look great. I wish *I* had your kind of looks.'

Linda laughed. 'You're such a flatterer.' As it happened she did feel pretty good about the way she looked. Two days in the sun had taken away her New York pallor, and she had gained a few pounds in places where it flattered her. Most women had to diet, but Linda was a natural-born skinny. It didn't bother her – clothes always hung better on thin women – but sometimes she yearned for the kind of curvy body that most men lusted after.

Screw it – men had never been a problem to get. It was marrying them that was the trick. She thought of Paul, tried to blank him out, couldn't, wondered if he would be there tonight. Hoped he would, wished he wouldn't. 'Are we ready?' asked Dallas. 'We're ready. Whose car?'

'You can drive if you don't mind – they'll have parking service.' They set off. Both beautiful in their individual ways. Dallas, tawny and sunstreaked – all teeth, hair, and body. Linda, slim and chic, darkly arresting.

They were good friends – *close* friends. In the last few days they had both done a lot of talking. Dallas had confided to Linda about Cody – unaware of the fact that Cody had already told Linda – but she didn't give him away. In fact she didn't tell Dallas she had seen him. He had asked her not to, and she had respected his wishes. She could understand and sympathize with both of them.

Who was right?

They had both made a mistake. Cody was a really nice guy. He deserved more than Dallas was prepared to offer him.

And Dallas   well, she was very special. She needed a strong macho man who would control and look after her – and at the same time be father, brother, lover to her. All the men she had missed out on.

Linda wondered if such a man existed. If he did she wouldn't mind grabbing him for herself!

☆

'Al King!' Doris Andrews clutched him by the hand, and memories of a dozen movies flitted through his head. He had grown up with Doris Andrews, along with Tony Curtis, Rock Hudson, Janet Leigh . . . He felt like he knew them all. It was just like meeting an old friend.

'Hello, Doris,' he said, kissing her warmly on both cheeks. He had never wanted to fuck Doris Andrews – Janet Leigh yes – but Doris had always been the big sister type. 'I've wanted to meet you for years,' he continued, treading carefully because he knew how pissed off *he* got when a well-meaning fan said, 'I love you, I've always loved you – ever since I was a little girl.' And it was usually some middle-aged hag who looked ten years old than him. Of course Doris probably wasn't *that* much older than him – seven or eight years top whack – which would make her forty-six or seven. She looked in very good nick.

'It's *my* pleasure, Mr King. I'm so glad you're letting us have this little party for you tonight. I only hope I've managed to include everyone you would enjoy meeting.'

Janet Leigh? What a kick to meet *her*. He looked around, recognizing several world-famous faces. And they had come out to honour *him*. Dressed up in their best glad rags to see *him*.

He nudged Paul. 'Not bad, huh?'

'Where? asked Paul, immediately assuming that Al had seen a girl he fancied. Al's abstinence was beginning to worry him.

The turn-out, schmuck! Just look around.'

Doris was summoning a waiter. 'What will you have to drink, Mr King?'

'Call me Al, and I'll call you Doris.'

She gave him the famous twinkling perennial virgin smile. 'Lovely! Now – who would you like to meet?'

☆

The boy who took the car said, 'You're late, ladies.' He was about nineteen, with a Ryan O'Neal face and a Burt Reynolds body.

Dallas ignored him. Linda smiled. He smiled back.

'Hey . . . How about . . .'

Dallas dragged Linda inside before he could finish.

'Not bad!' Linda exclaimed.

'They're hanging off the trees in this town,' Dallas drawled laconically. 'Every good-looking stud in America gravitates to LA all ready to become a movie star. Didn't you ever listen to the words of "San José"?'

'I knew there was a reason I came here!' Linda said. 'Prime Californian cock!'

'Linda! You're really disgusting.'

'What's disgusting about it? Why shouldn't I be honest? I'm not out to murder anyone – I just want to get nicely laid – by young randy studs. Ain't nothing wrong with *that*.'

Dallas laughed. 'You're incorrigible! It's lucky you never saw Julio.'

'Who's Julio?'

'Diamond's boyfriend. Remember? The male hooker.'

'You *saw* him?'

'Nothing happened. I made an appointment and backed out.'

'*You* would. What was he like?'

'I don't think I'd better tell you.'

Linda licked her lips. 'That good?'

'That good. Even *I* thought so. Hey – come on – we'd better go in – we can't stand in the hall all night – Doris is going to be furious as it is.'

☆

The entire pool area was tented, pink and white candy-striped awnings with fairy lights hanging in little clusters.

Tables surrounded the pool covered in plain pink cloths. Silver and fine glassware glinted at each place setting. There were ten tables seating twelve people per table.

Al was at a table with Doris Andrews on one side of him and Mrs Harmon Lewis on the other. Mrs Harmon Lewis was extremely rich, extremely ugly, and extremely powerful. She was head of one of the largest talent agencies on the coast. She had been married to Harmon Lewis – the famous four-foot-ten-inch cowboy star of the forties. Since his early demise at the age of thirty – falling off a box while making

cinematograph love to a five-foot-eleven-inch Swedish star –
Mrs Lewis had been enamoured by very short men. She
herself was a healthy five foot four inches – but she seemed
to get her kicks from wearing the highest possible heels and
the shortest possible men. She had managed to propel to
fame a five-foot-one-inch matinée idol, and a five-foot-
nothing comedian. 'There'll never be another Harmon!' was
her constant lament. But it did not stop her from looking.

Al, of course, was much too tall to ignite even the smallest
flicker of her interest. But he was the star guest, and everyone
knew Mrs Harmon Lewis insisted on being seated next to the
star guest.

Al, trapped between the two women, decided the time had
come to break his boycott on liquor. Fuck it. He felt great,
looked great, what harm would it do to go back on the booze?
Nellie's death had hit much harder than anyone cared to see.
The whole Tucson scene had frightened the shit out of him.
Losing control was not his bag. So he had stopped drinking
just to prove that he could – and he could – any time he wanted.

He reached for the wine.

Doris – the perfect hostess – immediately gestured for a
waiter.

'Changing your mind?' she inquired.

He laughed. Earlier he had told her he didn't drink. 'Why
not? That's what minds are for, isn't it?'

☆

Dallas stood at the top of the steps leading to the patio, and
gazed down at the beautifully laid-out tables, and the people
eating and chatting.

Linda, a step behind her, muttered, 'Talk about making a
late entrance . . .'

'The only kind,' Dallas murmured.

And she was right, because one by one every pair of eyes
stopped to look at them, until a hush hung over the gathering
– only a momentary hush – but it was enough to make an
impact.

Doris came trotting up the stairs. 'You naughty girl!' she
hissed. 'You're *so* late. I had nearly given up on you!'

'I'm sorry. Car broke down. Doris, I'd like you to meet my
friend, Linda.'

'Hmmm,' absently Doris shook her by the hand. She was more concerned about her placement. 'I've had to move you around. I couldn't leave Aarron with two empty seats beside him. I've put your friend at Lew's table.'

'That's all right,' Dallas said.

Doris replied somewhat huffily, 'I should hope so. Come, let's sit down.'

☆

Seeing Dallas was like getting an electric charge. Al had forgotten quite how beautiful she actually was. The sensual face framed by the streaked mass of hair. The body in the clinging white dress, with quite obviously nothing underneath. Every man in the place was staring at her.

Al went to stand up as she passed, but stopped himself in time. Let her come to him.

But she didn't. She glided past and sat down at the next table. She did not appear to even notice him.

As luck would have it they were seated almost back to back.

He swivelled round and tapped her on the shoulder. 'Don't you say hello any more?'

She turned and stared at him with her incredible green eyes. 'Hello.'

Doris came back to the table, squeezing between them. Dallas turned her attention back to Aarron Mack, who was toasting her with champagne.

Her thoughts were not on Aarron. They were on Al. It was like chemistry. She was drawn to him like a magnet. As soon as she saw him strange things happened. Things that she could hardly control. Her head felt light, her skin flushed, her stomach knotted into a sort of sick feeling. What the hell *was* it about him?

Aarron said, 'You look beautiful, beautiful. I toast your beauty.'

She lifted her glass and clinked it together with his before swallowing the champagne down.

Behind her she was only too aware of the fact that Al was only inches away.

☆

Lew Margolis was talking business. He did not acknowledge his wife's introduction of Linda as she sat her down at his table.

Linda didn't mind. But she wondered if *he* would mind if he knew it was *she* who had taken the pictures Dallas had shown him. How different he seemed from the man beside Dallas' pool that night. How tempting it would be to say, 'Excuse me, Mr Margolis, but I have seen you in action. Uncensored action!'

The fact that he was talking business with Paul – who hadn't even seen her – did not help matters. She looked around the table. Strangers. Famous strangers. No one was taking the least bit of notice of her.

On one side she recognized a television star of a cop series. On the other a fag screenwriter. They were both engaged in conversations on *their* other sides. Charming! How to be really, really popular! Was there something her best friends had failed to tell her?

She tapped the TV star firmly on the shoulder. She couldn't let Paul see her just sitting there. 'Hi, I'm Linda Cosmo. I was wondering if I might do a photo lay-out on you? I'm out here from New York sort of scouting interesting stories. You may have seen my Al King cover on *People* a few weeks back.'

The TV star had been about to give her a brush. After all, at a party like this who was she? But the words 'photo lay-out' and '*People* cover' changed all that.

'Yeah—' he said enthusiastically, 'I was wondering why they hadn't gotten around to me yet. Yeah – I'd like that. When do you want to do it?'

Linda smiled. Mention publicity to an actor and you were away and running. Pity his reputation as a closet queen went before him.

☆

Dallas could not force one morsel of food down her throat.

Aarron said, 'Are you not feeling good?'

'I'm feeling fine, I'm just not very hungry.'

Aarron summoned the waiter. 'More champagne at this table.'

Dallas drained her glass. Goddamn it – the presence of

Al King right behind her was turning her into a nervous drunk!

Aarron patted her on the leg. 'It's good to see you relax.' His hand lingered just that moment too long.

She could not summon the strength to remove it.

'When you come to New York for the launching I have something very serious I wish to discuss with you,' Aarron said, 'you must promise me you will give it your full consideration.'

She nodded. Why the hell had she come to this party anyway?

Turkish coffee was served, with wafer-thin imported peppermints for the ladies, and the best illegal Havana cigars for the men.

A small group of musicians started playing romantic Italian sounds. Room was cleared to make a dance floor.

Mrs Harmon Lewis eyed the short bass player and said, 'Doris gives the best parties in town!'

Al was busy receiving a stream of celebrities who were playing musical chairs – dodging back and forth between tables. He had made a discovery. The worst star fucks of all were the stars themselves! They were positively fighting for a few minutes at his table. *Him!* Al King. Ex-road digger. Ex-Janet Leigh-inspired wanker!

He should be flattered. But he found it funny. And all he really wanted to do was to grab hold of Dallas and get out of there.

☆

'When did you get here?' asked Paul, in a tone of voice which clearly said, 'What the hell are *you* doing here?'

'Few days ago,' smiled Linda. 'Why?'

They were talking across the table which didn't make things easy.

'I tried to call you,' Paul said. 'You never called back.'

'Shall we dance?' the TV star suggested to her.

'Love to,' replied Linda. She shrugged slightly in Paul's direction as if to dismiss his question.

He glared at her.

☆

'Excuse me,' said Dallas, getting up from the table. She was dying to go to the bathroom. She made her way inside the house. The guest powder room was occupied.

She made her way upstairs. Mr and Mrs Margolis' boudoir. Memories! Memories!

She walked into their bathroom. More memories!

The champagne was beginning to make itself felt. She was very lightheaded. She went to the john, brushed her hair, applied more lipgloss.

She didn't hear the door open behind her, she didn't realize anyone was in the room until the smell of *Joy* enveloped her, and Doris had her enclosed in a strong embrace – one hand cupping her left breast.

'I love you, Dallas,' she whispered, her little girl voice strained, 'I love you.'

Dallas only felt revulsion. She tried to push her away, but Doris was strong and held on.

'I'm not *into* women,' protested Dallas.

'Oh yes you are!' insisted Doris, 'I'm never wrong – never. Open your legs for me and you'll never want another man.'

'Leave me *alone*!' snapped Dallas. 'Just *leave me alone*.' She shoved Doris off and rushed from the room.

Why didn't anyone ever believe her?

☆

'If you can spare the time perhaps *we* can dance,' said Paul coldly.

Linda was just sitting down after dancing with the TV star for the third time.

'If you like,' she said.

He got up and came round to her side of the table. 'Having fun?' he hissed.

She smiled coldly. 'About as much fun as you and your wife have had for the past four weeks.'

'My wife left shortly after you did.'

'How shortly?'

'A matter of days. Haven't you read about what's been going on?'

'I was sorry to hear about Nellie.'

'We all were.'

'Including Al?'

'It wasn't his fault.'

'Sure.'

'There's no need to use that sarcastic tone.'

'Oh sorry. I wasn't aware that I had to check with you about what tone I could use.'

'Don't let's argue. I've missed you. Come on, let's dance.'

☆

Al watched Dallas walking back to her table. Mrs Harmon Lewis was regaling an intimate item of scandal. He wasn't listening. He couldn't give a toss. He gripped Dallas' wrist as she passed.

'You and I are going to dance,' he stated.

'But . . .'

He stood up, 'No buts.' He guided her to the dance floor and, at last, held her. He was immediately hard.

'You remind me of an Arab I once knew . . .' she murmured demurely.

'*An Arab?*'

'Yes. Didn't you know they consider it a great compliment to get a hard-on as soon as they dance with a woman.'

'Who told you that crap?'

'This Arab I knew – Charles something or other. It's like burping after a meal if you enjoy the food.'

'Horse crap!'

'That you have to fart for!'

'Nice. Very nice.' He pulled her even closer. 'Why haven't you returned my calls?'

She looked surprised. 'What calls?'

'Don't give me that . . .'

'Don't give *me* that. You haven't called.'

'No, but Paul has.'

'He hasn't.'

'He hasn't?'

'He hasn't.'

'Sonofabitch! I'll kill him. I've been thinking about this since the South of France. Remember?'

How could she ever forget? 'Nope.'

'Regines. Dancing together.' God she felt marvellous.

'Oh yes – wasn't that shortly before I got the icy treatment?' She tried to edge away from his persistently hard body.

'Who's talking about icy treatment? What about the time I called you from Chicago?' He pulled her firmly towards him.

'You're holding me too tight. I can't breathe.'

He released her slightly. 'Why don't we split from this boring party?'

'And do what?'

'What do you think?'

'Oh, no!'

'Oh no why not?'

'Because I do not want to.' Liar! Liar! For the first time in her life she did.

He shrugged. 'We can do what you want. Drive to the beach, grab a hot dog, take in a strip show, buy some new sounds at an all-night record shop.'

'OK.'

'OK what?'

'OK to everything. It sounds like fun.'

He laughed. 'You'd really sooner do all that than . . .'

'Yes!'

'What are we waiting for then?'

'You can't leave.'

'Why not?'

'You know why not. You're the guest of honour.'

'So what? I don't know any of these people, and what's more I don't think I want to.'

Out of the corner of her eye Dallas saw Doris emerge from the house. She seemed completely recovered from the incident in her bathroom. She was smiling and nodding. Lew was sitting at a table with his cronies. Dallas was thankful not to have had to have talked to him.

'I can't leave Linda,' Dallas said.

'Linda's all right.' Al indicated that she was dancing with Paul.

'Why don't we ask them to come with us?'

'Whatever you want.'

'You're being very nice tonight. Whatever *I* want. I thought it was always a question of what *you* want.'

'If it was a question of what *I* wanted we'd be in a bed somewhere screwing our . . .'

'No way.'

He smiled, enjoying her company, enjoying the thought of what he knew would happen later. He threw up his hands in mock despair. 'I'm not arguing!'

She laughed, happy for the first time in weeks. 'You'd better not!'

☆

Giggling and laughing they collapsed in the back of Al's limousine.

'What did she *say*?' Dallas asked again.

'She said, "Mr King – you are the rudest man I have ever met." Her eyes filled with tears – and I said, "Darlin' I've got a headache, what can I do?" And *she* said, "You can stay, you prick!" I nearly fell over. Doris Andrews using language like that. Disgusting!'

Dallas giggled. 'I could tell you worse things about Miss Andrews than that.'

'You could? Go on – tell.'

'I can't.' She indicated Luke, who was driving the car. 'It's secret.' She felt extremely lightheaded, almost carefree for once in her life.

'Where to first?' asked Al.

'You promised the beach.'

'You heard the lady, Luke. The beach it is.'

'What about Paul and Linda?'

'I said we'd meet them in an hour at "Pips". He wanted to square things away with old man Margolis. You know Paul – business first.'

'I didn't get a chance to talk to Linda. I was so busy sneaking out before Aarron grabbed me – was everything back to normal with her and Paul?'

'Didn't ask.'

'You're so concerned.'

'I'm concerned with being alone with you. Anyway – Paul lied to me. He told me he'd called you. Who the fuck does he think he's playing games with?'

'Maybe he thought he was doing you a favour.'

I'll pick my own favours.' He took her hand and held it. When was the last time he had held a girl's *hand*? When was the last time he had bothered to *talk* to a girl? He was enjoying every goddamn minute of it.

The car sped silently down the winding curves of Sunset.

'What about some music?' Al asked. 'Who would you like to hear?'

'Bobby Womack,' Dallas replied.

'Bobby Womack! How about Al King?'

'Bobby Womack please. Or Rod Stewart. Or David Ruffin. Or . . .'

He silenced her with a kiss. Burying his hands in her mane of hair. Holding her head so that she couldn't move.

He could not remember the last time he had kissed a girl. He was Al King. He did not need the preliminaries. It was either fuck or out.

Kissing Dallas was more exciting than any of the dumb bimbos he had screwed.

He was exploring her mouth with his tongue. Wow – he had forgotten what fun kissing could be. He was so horny he could have come there and then.

At the beginning she had returned the kiss, but now she was pushing him away.

'I want you,' he muttered. 'I want you . . .'

She leaned back in the seat, gazed out of the window. 'No,' she said.

He reached for her magnificent breasts. He could see her nipples were hard through the thin material of her dress.

She slapped his hand away. 'Forget it!' she snapped.

'What's the matter?' he asked in a puzzled voice.

'Do I have to have a reason for not wanting you? Or is it part of the ride to have sex with the great Al King if he takes you in his car?'

'I thought you felt the same way I did.'

'You thought wrong.'

They sat in silence for a few minutes, then Al said, 'Luke, we got any Womack tapes?'

Silently Luke slotted the *Home Is Where The Heart Is* tape into the machine, and the sexy voice of Bobby Womack serenaded them with 'How Long'.

'OK?' demanded Al.

'Terrific,' replied Dallas.

He took her hand again, and they listened quietly to the music which was assaulting them from all four speakers.

Nearing the coastal road Al spotted a drive-in. 'Hot dog time?'

Dallas replied, 'It's on our list, isn't it? Plenty of relish.'

'Luke – two hot dogs – one ketchup – one relish.'

Luke swerved the big car into a parking bay, and got out. 'What do you want to do at the beach?' Al asked.

'Can we take a walk along the seashore?'

'We can do whatever you want.'

Luke returned with the hot dogs and they munched them hungrily.

'Been reading about you,' Al said. 'It's all happening, huh? Long way from that old guy you were with in the South of France.'

'That old guy is one of the richest men in America.'

'Is that why you were with him?'

'How's your wife?'

'What's my wife got to do with this conversation?'

'The same as my old guy – exactly nothing.'

Al laughed. What a change to find a woman who answered him back. She hadn't even said yes the first time. Of course she would the second time – but that was only to be expected.

Dallas breathed deeply. She was with him. It was nice. It was fun. But it was all a crock of shit. He was just another superstar on the make. All he wanted was her body. All he wanted was to add her to his list. He was a married man – at the most it would be a few nights of good times. Who needed that? She certainly didn't. So what was she doing with him? She couldn't explain it.

They walked along the beach hand in hand. Dallas had taken off her shoes, and Al had rolled up his trousers. They talked about inconsequential things. A television show they both liked. A book Dallas thought he might be interested in reading.

'Hey – why don't we swim?' Al suggested.

'You're kidding – I'd feel like that girl in *Jaws*!'

'Come on, it would be great. Look at those waves.'

'*You* swim.'

'Is that a challenge?'

'Go ahead.'

'Hold this,' he handed her his jacket, stripped off his shirt, took off his trousers. The hell with it – he stepped out of his Y-fronts. Let her see the treat he had in store for her.

She didn't bother to look, just said, 'Be careful, I'm not very good at mouth to mouth resuscitation!'

He ran into the dark sea, ducked under a huge wave, and was swimming strongly out to the calmer waters. He trod water and looked to shore. She was standing there holding his clothes. 'Come in,' he shouted. 'It's like a warm bath.'

She waved. She couldn't hear him.

Dallas sat down on the sand. Why – when he kissed her – had she not shoved him away immediately? Why had she dissolved into soft mushy pieces? Why had she wanted him with a passion she had never felt in her life before? It had taken every bit of will power she possessed to push him away. How come he was invading her feelings?

In the distance she watched him swimming back to the beach, and come staggering out of the sea. He ran towards her. 'It's freezing when you get out,' he laughed: 'Real brass monkey time! Hey – can you run up to the car and see if Luke's got a towel or blanket or something I can dry myself with.'

She did as he asked, and the impassive Luke gave her a large rug which she carried back to Al. He wrapped himself in it. 'You missed a treat.'

'Yeah. Why are you shivering then?'

'Smartass.'

'Get dressed, we'll be late for Paul and Linda.'

He tried to put his arms around her.

'You're all wet!' she complained.

'So help me get dry.'

Laughingly she pushed him away. 'I'll see you in the car. Hurry up!' She didn't trust herself with him.

Waiting at 'Pips' the Beverly Hills discotheque they found a disconsolate Paul. 'Your friend,' he complained to Dallas, 'what does she want from me? I said I was sorry. Does she want it written in my blood? Why is you hair wet, Al?'

'Went swimming.'

Paul shook his head in amazement.

'Where's Linda?' inquired Dallas.

Paul said, 'You may well ask. I tried to talk to her but she doesn't want to know. Maybe *you* could talk to her for me.'

'Yes – *you* talk to her for him,' interrupted Al, 'just like *he* called you for me.'

Paul glared. 'I was only doing what I thought was . . .'

'Shut up,' said Al amiably. 'Order champagne, Dallas and I are going to dance.'

They pressed together on the crowded dance floor, and once again Dallas could feel his insistent hardness.

'Having a good time?' he asked.

'Not bad.'

'That's what I like – enthusiasm!' He hugged her tightly, unaware of the fact they were getting a lot of attention and stares. 'You're going to come to my concert tomorrow. Then after, Karmen Rush is giving a big party for me. Yes?'

'I don't know . . .'

'Stop giving me a hard time. I've got the message you're not an easy lay. I'm asking you to a concert and a party, not a twenty-handed orgy. Right?'

'Right.'

'I still want you . . .' he whispered in her ear. 'Don't tell me you aren't feeling the same way . . .'

She was saved from answering by Cody Hills. Cody in a suit and tie, dancing with the definitive dumb blonde.

'Cody!' she exclaimed, surprised to see him. 'What are *you* doing here?'

☆

It was obvious to Cody that to get through the whole traumatic experience with Dallas he was going to need outside help.

Carol Cameron was ready, willing, and available. She was also very pretty. And if you had an ego that needed repairing – well, she was the best sexual mechanic around – and where better a place to starting restoring a shattered ego than in bed?

Of course after a few days her conversation did begin to pall. It was always about herself. Her new photos. Her acting classes. Her clothes. Her hair. Her face. Her *career*.

Because he felt it was only fair to do a trade – she wasn't

giving him her body for *nothing* – he took her on his books and got her the small but interesting part of a hooker in a double-part 'Kojak'. She was delighted, and dragged him to 'Pips' to celebrate. Whereupon who was the first person he bumped into? Dallas of course. Dallas nuzzled on the dance floor with Al (goddamn English sex maniac) King. And why did she stare at him in a state of surprise and say, 'What are *you* doing here?' As if he was some kind of freak who should only be seen during business hours.

He managed to give her a cool smile and mumble something about he came here often.

Meanwhile Carol was freaking out over Al King, and digging Cody in the ribs muttering, 'Introduce me! Introduce me!'

Cody did as she asked, and Al dismissed her with hardly a glance, and who could blame him when he was dancing with Dallas.

When they were out of earshot Cody said, 'Let's go home.'

'Let's stay,' enthused Carol, jiggling about in her tighter than tight gold pants and lurex sweater.

'We're going,' Cody insisted. At least with this one he was going to be the boss.

'If you're going to *force* me . . .' she pouted.

'Yes,' he said. She didn't argue further.

☆

Dallas and Al left 'Pips' at two in the morning, Paul tagging along with them.

News had leaked out that they were there, and several photographers sprung into action. Paul tried to shield his brother.

'Forget it,' said Al. 'I'm not bothered.'

He might not be bothered now, mused Paul, but he would not be too thrilled in the morning when his picture was flashed all over the newspapers. Especially when the news services flashed it all the way to England, and Edna got a load of it.

They all got in the car. 'Where to now?' asked Al.

'Drop me at the hotel,' said Paul.

'You'd better take me home first,' suggested Dallas.

'We haven't finished our list,' objected Al. He sneezed.

'You've caught a cold,' Paul accused. 'You should get

some sleep before tomorrow. All we need is for you to lose
your voice.'

'I can sleep all day.'

'You're taping the Johny Carson show in the afternoon.'

'Anyway, I'm beat,' interrupted Dallas. 'Whacked out. So
if you want me to come tomorrow . . .'

'If I take you home now is that a promise?'

'I suppose so.'

'OK, we'll drop Paul . . .'

'We won't drop Paul. You're both at the Beverly Hills,
aren't you? So drop me first.' She gave Luke the address.

'I thought . . .' began Al.

'I know what you thought, and you thought wrong.'

He grinned. It was good to be in on the chase once more –
gave the whole game a little excitement. The big E had been
missing from his life for far too long.

They dropped Dallas at her house. 'See you tomorrow,' Al
said.

'Probably,' she replied.

'Don't give me that – its a definitely.'

'Well . . .'

'Tomorrow,' he said firmly.

'If you say so . . .' She walked in the house and they drove
off.

Al felt marvellous. Paul was glum.

'Put on one of my tapes,' Al instructed Luke. 'No – don't.
Put on the Womack tape we were playing before.' He sang
along with it. 'Isn't she great?' he asked Paul. 'She's the kind
of girl I could really like – you know, she's different, kind of
ballsy. She's there. Know what I mean? She's not just standing around waiting to get humped. Makes a nice change.'

For how long? Paul wanted to ask. None of them lasted
more than five minutes. He only liked this one because she
was giving him a hard time.

At the hotel the red light was flashing on Al's phone
indicating there were messages. A memo pushed under his
door read, 'Contact the front desk – urgent.'

Perhaps Dallas was calling him to tell him she had
changed her mind.

He picked up the phone. 'Al King here,' he snapped.
'What's the message?'

'One moment please, Mr King, I'll put you through to the front desk.'

There was a pause, then a man's voice came on the line. 'Mr King. Sorry to bother you – but we have a young man here claiming to be your son. An Evan King. He has a passport from England verifying the fact. Shall we send him over? I didn't want to do anything until I'd checked with you.'

'Send him over,' said Al dully.

What the fuck was Evan doing here?

51

Linda saw no reason why she should hang around and watch Paul discuss business with revolting Lew Margolis.

Paul had apologized to her. 'I'm sorry my wife caught us in bed together but what was *I* supposed to do?' If he didn't know, she wasn't going to be the one to tell him. Now he was saying Al wanted them to join him at 'Pips'.

Did he honestly expect one little apology to make everything all right? If he did he was more of a fool than she had thought. And to add insult he was already saying, 'Al wants us to . . .' Well, screw what Al wanted. *She* didn't have to trip ass over elbow to do what Al wanted. Let them all run – Dallas too, if that was her scene. But she was free, white, and twenty-one . . . Well maybe not exactly twenty-one – but free and white for sure.

She slipped quietly away from the party, and she hadn't given the parking boy a second thought until he gunned her rented Chevrolet up the drive for her, hopped out and said, 'I'm getting off now. Could you drop me on the Strip?'

She looked him up and down. Surveyed him as she would a prime leg of lamb in the supermarket. He was young, but certainly experienced. That cocky grin – she tried not to laugh at her choice of adjectives – bulging jeans, muscle-bound T-shirt.

'Sure,' she said casually, 'jump in.'

He slouched in the passenger seat, chewing gum. 'Where's your friend?' he asked.

As if you don't know – she thought. You saw her leave and planned your exit with me because I'm the only woman on my own and you probably do this all the time, you randy little stud. 'She had to leave.'

'Yeah?' He blew a bubble with the gum.

Bubble gum yet! She really was baby snatching!

'You connected with the movie business?' he asked.

'I'm a photographer.'

'Neat!' he sat up very straight. 'I'm an actor, you know.'

'Oh really?'

'Yeah – I'm just parking cars for a friend – like helpin' him out. I've been in a "Marcus Welby" and "Bionic Woman".'

'That's exciting. How old are you?' If he was over eighteen she would allow him to have her. She would even pay for the motel room. Younger, and he was on his own.

'Nineteen, nearly twenty,' he said.

She smiled.

Two hours later they lay on their backs, smoking pot that he had thoughtfully produced, in a Westwood motel.

'Again?' he asked.

'Why not?'

He rolled her onto her stomach, forcing her on all fours, entering her from behind. He performed like well-oiled machinery. In. Out. In. Out. All pistons working. He was bringing her to her fourth climax. She groaned. He mumbled what she took to be a few obscenities. 'I'm gonna come,' he announced.

It was his first time. 'Go ahead,' she murmured, 'you deserve it!'

He exploded inside her – wiping out all thoughts of Paul. He didn't collapse. He was still rock hard. She came a little after him. She had to force him off her. 'Enough!' she gasped, 'I can't take any more!'

Why was it would-be actors were such amazing lays? And how come when their star rose their cocks diminished?

She giggled softly. It was a problem she would probably never find the answer to.

Dallas was asleep when Linda finally got back to the house at 4 a.m.

She took her clothes off and swam in the invitingly warm pool. She had dropped her parking boy off on the Strip as she had promised him hours before.

'I'll call you,' she had said.

'I'm not on the phone, I'll call you,' he had countered.

'Impossible,' she had said. 'You must have a number where I can reach you.'

Reluctantly he had produced a number where she could leave a message for him. 'Why can't I have *your* number?' he had complained.

She hadn't answered. She had blown him a kiss and driven off.

The danger was in trying to make a relationship out of one night of lust. Men had learned that lesson long ago. Women were only just beginning to learn.

In the morning the doorbell rang waking them both up at the same time.

'Linda – you there – can you get it?' yawned Dallas from the bedroom.

'Got it,' retorted Linda, inspecting an amazing array of flowers through the spyhole in the door.

She signed for them, baskets and baskets of red roses. The card was addressed to Dallas. Paul wouldn't know about displaying such unbridled generosity.

'Here.' She wandered in the bedroom handing Dallas the card. 'There's a flower shop outside.'

Dallas opened up the card. 'Al' was typed neatly in the centre. Nothing else, just 'Al'. She handed Linda the card to look at.

'He really likes to commit himself, doesn't he?' mused Linda. 'But you're one up on everyone else, I've never heard of him sending any of his girls flowers.'

'I'm not one of his girls,' snapped Dallas irritably.

'Don't tell me the great A.K. struck out?'

'I'm telling you.'

Linda clapped her hands together. 'Hurrah! The Master has finally failed.'

Dallas stretched and yawned. 'But I must admit I was tempted. If it hadn't of been for what I *knew* about him . . .'

'The original fuck and run merchant,' interrupted Linda.

'I know. But, Linda, you know me. I am *never* tempted. I don't even like sex.'

'So what makes you think things would be different with Al?'

'It's just a sort of feeling – more a sensation. He held my hand, it was so goddamn exciting I wanted to faint!'

'Oh Christ!' exclaimed Linda. 'You sound like you're in love.'

'In love! Are you kidding? I've *never* been in love. I wouldn't even know what it felt like.'

'Exactly. Did you get stomach cramps? Couldn't eat? Sweaty armpits? A feeling of euphoria?'

'Well, now that you mention it . . .'

'Shit!' Linda clapped herself on the forehead. 'Why did you have to pick on a creep like Al? Couldn't you propel those feelings in a nice guy like Cody's direction?'

'We bumped into Cody last night. He seems to have taken the whole thing very well. He was with a blonde who resembled that dragon he turned up at lunch with in no way whatsoever.'

'What do you want him to do – sit at home and cry?'

Dallas climbed out of bed. 'I'm going to look at my flowers. By the way, what happened to you?'

'San José.'

'Huh?'

'The song – remember? Would-be actor pumping gas and parking cars. He was pumping all right!'

'You didn't?'

'I did, and it was a truly beautiful experience – apart from which he's a great lay!'

Dallas screwed up her face in disgust. 'I don't know how you could do it.'

'*You* did it for long enough.'

'That was for money.'

'Well this is for like. I *like* screwing.'

'But what about Paul?'

'He's different. I love him – correction, I loved him – I'm not sure how I feel any more. But while I'm finding out I'm certainly not going to give up my sex life. Coffee?'

'If you're making.'

Dallas arranged her flowers around the house. They looked beautiful. She showered, washed her hair and dressed. She couldn't stop thinking about Al. Aarron phoned.

'Why did you leave so early?' he wanted to know.

'I didn't feel good,' she lied.

'Why don't you come to Palm Springs with me today? I'll fly you back in time for the studio tomorrow morning.'

'No, Aarron. It's my only day off and I want to do a lot of things around the house.'

'I'm going to New York tomorrow. Perhaps next week-end.'

'Perhaps.'

'I'll telephone you on Wednesday.'

She hung up. He had behaved like the perfect gentleman with her apart from hands that lingered too long on her knee. She knew if she wanted to she could get him to marry her. She could be Mrs Aarron Mack. He was old. How many years did he have left? But the days of wanting to be married to a rich man were far behind her. She wasn't sure what she wanted now – but it wasn't that.

Al phoned at four o'clock. He sounded different – edgy and cold. 'I'll send a car for you,' he said, 'there's no room in the helicopter.'

'Hey – listen,' she replied, 'maybe I shouldn't go.'

'I *want* you to be there.'

'Well I'm not traipsing out there all alone in a car.'

'Christ! Don't *you* be difficult, I've got problems enough.'

'I don't want to add to your problems,' she snapped icily, and hung up on him.

He phoned back immediately. 'What's with you?' he demanded.

'What's with *me*? What's with *you*?'

'Aw – shit. My son arrived out of the blue, just flew in and dumped himself on me.'

'Why don't you send him back?'

'It's not as simple as that – he's got problems.'

'What problems?'

'If you're really interested he's got a dose of the clap.'

'Oh!' She was silent. There wasn't really much to say to that.

'Did you get the flowers?'

'They're fantastic. Thank you.'

He sighed. 'Look, how about if you bring Linda to the show?'

'I don't think so . . .'

'Why not?'

'She's busy.'

'Have you got any other friends could come with you? We could take them with us to the Rush party after.'

She thought of Kiki and Chuck. They would probably love to go. 'I'll make a phone call. Can you call me back?'

'Please understand if *I* can't call you back – I'm right in the middle of an interview. Bernie or Paul will call you. Tell them how many tickets you want. The plan is we'll meet back at my hotel after the show, we'll go to the party from there. Does that suit you?'

'If you say so.'

He hesitated. 'I wish I was with you now. Did you sleep?'

'Yes. Did you?'

'No. I lay awake thinking of what you and I *should* have been doing.'

She laughed softly: that was exactly what *she* had been doing.

'Listen, I'll see you later,' he said. 'Don't let me down.'

'I'll be there.'

'I'll be singing just for you.'

Sentimental bullshit! She hung up the phone and wondered how the hell she had got into this state. She had been determined not to be affected by him, and for some stupid reason she was walking on air at the sound of his voice.

Linda was crosslegged in front of the television watching a rerun of 'Starsky and Hutch'. 'He's a horny little devil!' she remarked.

'Who is?' asked Dallas.

'Little Dave Starsky. Who else?'

'I thought perhaps you were talking about your boyfriend from last night.'

'You're kidding – I've forgotten about him already.'

'I don't suppose you fancy coming to Al's concert at the Hollywood Bowl tonight, and after, a party for Al at Karmen Rush's?'

Linda lit a cigarette from the butt of one she was just finishing. 'I honestly don't think I could sit through one more Al King concert. Besides it would mean seeing Paul, and I really don't want to.'

Dallas nodded. 'I knew you'd say that, although I can't

understand why you don't want to see him. He was in a terrible state last night – really miserable.'

'Good. Let *him* be the unhappy one for a change. I've had it with his weak excuses – *other* people get divorced when they have young kids. What's so different about Paul?'

'Maybe he's frightened about the money she would take him for.'

'He's too smart to get taken financially – she would get exactly what he wanted her to get. Did you know he's tight to the point of being mean? He's never even bought me so much as a flower!'

Dallas glanced at her watch. 'I've got to call Kiki – maybe she and Chuck will want to make it tonight.'

'While we're on the subject of phone calls . . .'

'Yes?'

'If you don't mind . . .'

'What?'

Linda grinned. 'Would it bother you if during your absence I made an appointment with your male hooker?'

'My male hooker?'

'Well – Diamond's. I'm really in the mood for an expert.'

Dallas started to laugh. 'I don't believe *you*!'

'Do you mind?'

'Why should I mind? Be my guest. He's black, you know.'

'I couldn't care less if he's orange!'

Dallas sighed. 'You really want to pay for it?'

'Why not? It's all part of life's rich field of experience. Besides – I never screwed around when I was with Paul – well, not much anyway. Now I want to make up for lost time before I hook myself up with another married schmuck.'

'I'll find you the number.'

☆

Bernie had lined up two sycophantic, siliconed, typical Hollywood blondes for Al's use.

'Forget it,' snapped Paul, who was not in the best of moods. 'He's not asking so I'm not pushing.'

'I'll keep them around anyway.'

'Do what you want with them.'

Bernie had already done *that*. He had auditioned them personally and was ready to pass them on.

Al glided through interviews, taping the Johnny Carson show, and the helicopter ride to the Hollywood Bowl in perfect humour. The only sour note was created by Evan, who had sprung himself on Al in the early hours of the morning. In the longest conversation he had ever had with his father he had confessed to a 'problem' that he had been unable to confide to his mother. With patient questioning Al discovered what the 'problem' was – and in no time at all had summoned a doctor who had examined an embarrassed Evan, given him a shot, and said it was nothing more serious than a mild dose of the clap.

Al did not know what to do. He should be mad at the boy – but what the hell – it took balls to climb on a plane to America just like that. And it was good to know that Evan – for the first time in his life – had come to him with a problem instead of running to his mother.

Of course Edna would freak out. And once again he was stuck with Evan. But he didn't have the heart to send the kid on the next plane home. At least not until he got him cured.

Meanwhile – how to tell Edna. And not just about Evan. But about the fact that he had made up his mind that he wasn't going back to her. He wanted a divorce. He had made his decision, and he wasn't about to change his mind.

☆

The crowds congregating at the Hollywood Bowl stretched for miles. A steady stream of cars searched for parking spaces. The stars rode by in their chauffeur-driven limousines with the special window stickers allowing them the closest drop-off points.

'There goes Karmen Rush!' the fans screamed, banging on the tinted glass windows of her black Rolls Royce. She acknowledged them with a queenly wave, only her sphynx-like eyes betraying the fact that she was stoned out of her head.

'Ramo Kaliffe, Ramo Kaliffe!' The fans chanted as the Arabian matinée idol zoomed past, flanked on either side by two girls who looked exactly like the two blondes Bernie had on standby for Al.

Bernie, in the press enclosure, was sweating more than usual. Jeeze! What a turnout. The photographers were having a field day as the stars rolled up. Rock stars. Movie stars. Sports stars. Television stars. It seemed they had all decided to make the pilgrimage to watch Al perform.

Waiting to stride out into the spotlight Al felt remarkably calm. A can of beer was the only alcohol beverage he was imbibing.

'Is she here yet?' he asked Paul for the fourth time.

'Yes,' said Paul, although he really didn't know and didn't particularly care. He wasn't sure if he liked the fact that Al was obviously struck on Dallas.

'I told you she'd come,' smiled Al.

'Hot Fudge' were swaying and weaving their way onto the stage. They wore black satin cat suits with no sides, and the longest tightest boots imaginable.

Their sound was stronger, more funky than 'The Promises'. They were more raunchy altogether.

Al had decided he preferred them. He listened to the applause. He noted their mother – a fat black lady jiggling about and mouthing each word at the side of the stage. She caught him studying her and winked broadly. He winked back.

'Hot Fudge' were on their closing number. The applause was enthusiastic. They ran off the stage into the excited arms of their mother.

Al tensed himself for his entrance. The MC was cracking a couple of jokes. The audience were shifting around impatiently. Come on, man, we've sat through 'Hot Fudge' – we've made the right noises – so what are we waiting for?

'And now—' the MC was shouting, 'the man you all want to see – the man you've been waiting for – the man himself – *Al King*!!!'

BOOK THREE

52

The sun was shining in Rio de Janeiro. It was a perfect, cloudless day.

'Fetch your mama her robe,' Jorge Maraco requested of his daughter.

'Sure, poppa,' replied Cristina, leaping up from her position by the family swimming pool and running into the house.

Jorge turned to his blonde wife, 'You see,' he said, 'I don't know why you worry about her. She is polite, considerate, obliging.'

'To you,' replied his wife pointedly. 'She'll do anything for you.'

Jorge puffed on his cigar. 'She is a good girl. A credit to her family.'

'You only see the side she *wants* you to see. I tell you, Jorge, I am worried about her. Some of the company she keeps . . . It's not right. After all she is only seventeen, still a child.'

'She has a woman's body.'

'What difference does *that* make? You should be *more* concerned because of that fact.'

Jorge reached lazily for his wife, and patted her affectionately on her bare thigh. Evita Maraco was wearing a one-piece white swimsuit which showed her voluptuous body off to full advantage. She drew away from her husband. 'You are not taking me seriously,' she accused.

'I am,' he protested, 'I always listen to everything you say.'

'Yes, and I am always right. Hasn't eighteen years of marriage taught you that?'

'It has taught me never to argue with a beautiful woman.'

'In that case you must talk to Cristina – today. Her thoughts and actions should be taking her in a more serious direction. Why, when I was her age, you and I were engaged to be married.'

'I paid your mother for the privilege.' Jorge chuckled at the memory. 'You were my poor little carioca washing clothes to take home the money for mama.'

'Lucky for you I washed *your* clothes,' snapped Evita. 'An old man like you not married – you were a disgrace to your family!'

'I was only forty,' protested Jorge.

'Forty! A spoilt rich child. *I* saved you.'

'Yes,' agreed Jorge, 'you saved me from a life of wine, women, and . . .'

'Boredom!' snapped Evita.

He reached for her thigh again.

'Stop it!' she chided. 'Are you never satisfied?'

He sighed, 'Never. Eighteen years wanting the same woman. I would not have believed it possible.'

Evita could not help smiling. She *had* tamed him. When they had married his reputation as a womanizer had been legendary. Jorge Maraco – the slippery millionaire industrialist – still single at forty. A world-wide dallier with some of the world's most beautiful women. What a catch he was. And who had caught him? A penniless working girl from the slums.

She had been seventeen, the same age as her own daughter was now. But what a different kind of life she had led. A life filled with poverty, despair, and work. It was only her beauty that had saved her. Her long white-blonde hair which was so unusual, her cinnamon elongated eyes, chiselled features, and full ripe body.

Jorge had come across her in the kitchens of his house one day, and fallen irrevocably in lust. Love, of course, had followed – helped by the fact that Evita refused to go to bed with him until they were married. Her virginity was the only possession she had to bargain with, and she used it wisely.

Cristina had been born a year after they were married, and until recently she had given them no problems. She was a bright scholar, and had always mixed with the right friends. But now – Evita felt uneasy. Cristina remained her usual polite and charming self to her father – but when he was not at home she became mean, moody and extremely rude. It was only a recent occurrence, a matter of months really. Before that Evita had been hoping that Cristina would become engaged to a boy she had grown up with. Up until a few months previously they had been steady companions – but then suddenly the change. And Cristina had become secretive and mysterious about where she was going and who she was seeing.

It could not go on. Evita had made up her mind that Jorge should talk to his daughter, find out exactly what *was* going on.

☆

Cristina Maraco stared at her reflection in her mother's dressing-room mirror. She was not thrilled with what she saw. How unfair that she should be the image of her father – dark and squat – why couldn't she have inherited her mother's classy blondeness?

Jet black hair hung in a tangle of thick frizzy curls around her olive-skinned face. She had a boyish body, wide shoulders, small breasts, sturdy legs, wide ass.

She *hated* the way she looked! Boys didn't. Boys said she was sexy. Boys were always trying to grab her tits or ass. Or kiss her sulky pursed lips.

Boys were a pain.

Nino wasn't. Nino was different.

Nino didn't grab. Nino said, 'I want to sleep with you, Cristina.'

Nino was only nineteen. But he wasn't a boy – he was a man.

Not like Louis – the boy her mother liked. The boy her mother wanted her to *marry*. Louis was draggy. Full of himself and his family's money. Just because his father was unbelievably rich.

Money was bad. Money was corrupting. Nino had taught her that.

She grabbed her mother's robe from the closet and held it up against herself. Ugh! Silk, in some yucky print. It had probably cost a few hundred dollars. Enough to clothe some poor family for a year.

Her mother spent a fortune on clothes. And her jewels! She had diamonds and emeralds as big as marbles!

Cristina wandered over to her mother's dressing table and idly sorted through the many bottles and jars. Evita was beautiful. What did she need all this junk for? If she was ugly it would be understandable. But she was exquisite, and young, and *it wasn't fair* . . .

Cristina grabbed up the robe from the floor where she had thrown it, and ran downstairs.

'You were a long time,' remarked Jorge, withdrawing his hand from Evita's thigh, but not quick enough for Cristina not to notice. They were always at it – her dear parents.

'Couldn't find it.'

Evita stood up and slipped the robe over her swimsuit. 'I'm going to rest,' she announced. She stared meaningfully at her husband. He gave an imperceptible nod.

Cristina dived into the pool. She was a very fast swimmer, churning her way up and down the pool at a record pace. She did fifteen lengths, then climbed out, shaking her head like a wet puppy.

'You swim well,' Jorge remarked.

Cristina flopped down beside him. 'Poppa, I've swum well since I was three years old. Why are you telling me now?'

'I remember when you learned to swim,' he said. 'Your instructor threw you in and out of the water like a sack of potatoes. I thought your mother would have a fit.'

Cristina smiled politely, and wondered how long it would be before her father followed Evita into the house. It was their Sunday ritual. Out by the pool after lunch. Into the house before five o'clock. It was the only day Cristina saw Jorge. The rest of the time he was at the office or visiting his factories, and when he returned home he usually preferred a private dinner with Evita.

Nino had said it was wise to present herself to her father in a good light. She had told him what a bitch Evita could be, always questioning and prodding for information about what she was doing.

'I don't see Louis at the house any more,' Jorge remarked. 'Is he sick?'

Cristina shrugged. 'It depends what you call sick, poppa.'

'What do you mean?'

She made a face, 'Oh – *you* know.'

'I know *what*?'

'Boys. They're always . . . Well – *you* know what I mean.'

Jorge sat up. 'Do you mean to tell me that Louis . . .'

'Yes.'

'He didn't . . .'

'No.'

'Thank God for that!' Jorge chuckled. 'You're a sensible girl. I never doubted that. Perhaps you could explain to your mother . . . She would understand. You see, we give you so much freedom, Cristina, and I think it worries her. Other girls have chaperones, strict parents. I have never believed that is the way. But I know you would never let us down . . .'

'*Never*, poppa.'

Jorge smiled. He had talked with his daughter. She was a good girl. *He* had never doubted the fact.

'Well, Cristina, I think I shall go inside now. Are you going out?'

'Yes, poppa.'

He kissed her absently, anxious to get inside to Evita. She would have showered by now. The sheets would be scented. The shades drawn down. They would make love passionately. They always did on Sundays.

'See you, poppa.' Cristina kissed him lightly on the cheek, and jumped back into the pool.

'Yes, yes.' He hurried into the house.

Cristina watched him go. He was fifty-eight but he looked much younger really. He had the same sturdy body as she did, all his own teeth, and his eyes were strong and clear, not bloodshot and runny like some of the old men who were his friends.

She snorted. His friends! What a bunch they were. At parties and barbecues they could hardly keep their rheumy old eyes off her! They thought she was the sweet little virgin daughter. Good little Cristina. Sweet little Cristina.

Oh how sweet to see the surprise on their faces if they were to learn the truth.

She, Cristina, was not a virgin.

She was a woman of the world. A woman of experience.

She had been sleeping with Nino for six whole weeks!

She turned on her back in the pool and let her thoughts take over.

Nino. Even his name created a warm dark excitement.

The first time she had seen him she had known that here was someone different. She had been with a large party enjoying the carnival ball at the Municipal Theatre. She had been wearing a spangled outfit – her mother's choice, but nice all the same. And her hair had been threaded through with silver streamers, and her make-up had been a fantasy of silver patches and dots.

He, of course, typical Nino, had taken no trouble with his appearance at all. With his looks he didn't need to. He was nicely thin, with hidden muscles, and a stomach so hard it was like wood. His hair was black – even darker than hers, and he wore it just as it grew – a tangled mass of jet curls. She had since copied the style, nagging and cajoling her hairdresser to get it exactly right.

His eyes were the most amazing thing about him. Black, fringed with the longest lashes. But it was the way he used them. His gaze was so penetrating, so intimate. His eyes seemed to bore right through you.

Louis, on the other hand, was the sort of boy parents liked on sight – and of course they liked him even more when they realized who his father was.

Before Nino she had quite liked Louis. But after Nino, she had realized he was just another nothing little rich boy with no point of view towards life.

'He has no fire,' Nino had explained simply. 'I do not want you to see him any more.' So she hadn't.

Her first meeting with Nino had been a disappointment. He had ignored her. He was with a rich American girl who was vacationing in Rio, and she had known some people in Cristina's party, so they had all joined up. Cristina had been immediately struck, but he had dismissed her with a cursory glance.

'Who is he?' she had asked Louis, 'and why is he so rude?'

Louis had grinned. 'He wouldn't be so rude if he knew who you were. He only goes out with girls who have money. He's a trouble-maker.'

'How do you know?'

'School. He had a scholarship there. Nobody liked him. He is not one of us. His family are nothing.'

She had tried to ask Louis more, but he changed the subject, and took her off to dance, and she had watched Nino with the American girl, whispering to her, and nuzzling into her neck,

Cristina had not been sorry when she heard three days later that the American girl and her parents had been robbed of thousands of dollars worth of jewellery and travellers cheques.

She had not seen Nino again for two months, until one day she was out shopping with her friend, Marie Therese, when she saw him striding down the street. 'Hello,' she had said, and he had stared at her with those black intense eyes, and said, 'Who are you?'

She had started to stammer. 'Cristina Maraco, don't you remember, we met at the carnival ball – I was with Louis Baptista. You were with an American girl. You must remember?'

His eyes had strayed to Marie Therese who was extraordinarily pretty. 'I remember,' he said, staring straight at Marie Therese. 'You girls coming to the beach this afternoon?'

'Yes,' Cristina replied quickly, 'where will you be?'

He shrugged. 'Ipanema.'

'Whereabouts?'

'You'll find me,' one last penetrating stare in Marie Therese's direction, 'if you want to.' He strode off.

'Who was *that*?' Marie Therese asked, her cheeks flushed pink. 'My parents would *never* let me go to Ipanema beach on my own. Who is he, Cristina?'

'Not a very nice type,' Cristina said dismissively; and as soon as she could get rid of Marie Therese she had rushed home and changed into her briefest tanga, and rushed off to Ipanema, where it took her two hours to find him.

'Where is your friend?' he had asked.

'She had work to do,' Cristina explained. 'She is studying French with her fiancé.'

Later, when they knew each other better, they had laughed about Cristina making up a fiancé for Marie Therese. 'But it was always you I wanted,' Nino would say mildly. 'Always you.'

He was with friends at the beach. A different class of people than Cristina was used to. One girl paid particularly close attention to Nino. She kept on grabbing his leg and trying to pull him down on the sand beside her. He resisted her advances, and indulged in polite conversation with Cristina. What did she do? Where did she live? When she told him who her father was he said, '*The* Jorge Maraco?' After that he took her swimming, and spoke sharply to the girl who touched his leg, and they walked along the beach and he held her hand.

Later, when she said she had to go, he had asked when he could see her again. They had made a date for the following Friday, and she had rushed home on winged feet, spent a boring evening with Louis, and lived only for Friday.

From that day on her life had changed. Nino had taught her so much. He had explained about poverty, about how the rich had everything, leaving nothing for the poor. He had taken her on his motor scooter for a tour around the Favellas – a shanty town of rotten shacks on a hill overlooking the affluence of the more fortunate. She had seen filthy babies playing in the mud, old people so thin that their bones stuck through their ragged clothes. Mothers with ten children struggling to see they got one decent meal a week.

She had been horrified.

'One day,' Nino assured her, 'we will change all this. My life is dedicated to seeing equality amongst our people.'

He took her to visit his grandmother, a wizened old woman who was his only living relative. She, too, lived in a shack. She had no teeth, hardly any hair, a skin disease. She looked a hundred years old.

'You would not believe she is only fifty,' Nino said. 'That is what a life of poverty has done for her. My mother died giving birth to me in that same shack. Now perhaps you will begin to understand my bitterness.'

That night Cristina cried herself to sleep.

Two days later Nino asked her if she would be willing to help.

'What can I do?' she had asked, 'I have some old clothes ...'

'We don't want your charity,' Nino had spat with a venomous anger.

'Well . . . what?'

'Your parents have friends. People with a lot of money. Do you think they would feel it if they were relieved of some of their possessions?'

Cristina was startled. 'What do you mean?'

'You know their houses. You could find out their movements . . .'

'No! I couldn't. I know what you are asking me to do and it wouldn't be right.'

'All right.' He had taken her in his arms and kissed her. 'I respect your feelings. I won't ask you again.'

He lived in a small one-roomed apartment. They had spent many hours there together. She allowed him certain privileges – privileges she would never have allowed Louis. They would kiss, and caress, and sometimes she would allow him to remove her sweater and bra. She never permitted him to go further than that.

'I want to sleep with you, Cristina,' he had told her that evening. 'We are not children playing silly little games. I need a real woman.'

'It's impossible,' she had replied, 'I couldn't . . . It would be shameful. My father would never forgive me.'

'Your father need not know. And as for being shameful – God – I thought I had changed your mind – opened up your head – but if you can still harbour petty bourgeois ideas like that . . .' He trailed off in disgust.

'I have to wait,' Cristina said hesitantly.

'Until when?' snapped Nino.

She was blushing. 'Until I marry.'

To her surprise Nino burst out laughing. He leapt off the bed and said, 'Time to go home.'

She was relieved. She thought he had dropped the subject. But the next day when he did not turn up at the time they had arranged to meet she was worried. She waited three days for some word from him. He did not contact her. In desperation she went to his apartment. He opened up the door wearing only jeans which he was busy doing up. He looked surprised to see her, and blocked the door.

'Where have you *been*?' she asked accusingly.

He shrugged. 'Around.' From behind him there came a woman's laugh, and then the woman herself. She was half wrapped in a sheet. She hugged Nino from behind, and said in a teasing voice, 'Come back to bed, sugar plum, Pussy's lonely . . .'

Cristina's face blazed red. Nino shrugged. 'I am a man . . .'

Cristina had left. And after two days of crying and thinking things over she had made up her own mind.

She dropped Nino a note asking him to meet her.

He had turned up at the appointed time looking better than ever. He was casual and friendly, as if nothing had happened. They talked. She told him of her decision, and hand in hand they strolled back to his apartment.

She didn't smoke, but he made her puff on a special cigarette which he said would relax her. She was so nervous. But he was calm and in charge.

He undressed her slowly, mouthing compliments about her body. Then he made her lie on the bed and watch while he stripped off. She could hardly breathe with excitement. She had seen him nearly naked on the beach so many times, naked except for the tiny bikini shorts he wore. Now he was throwing off his shirt, unzipping his jeans, and walking towards her.

She gasped. She had seen men with no clothes on before. Her father in the shower once, pictures in a magazine.

But never like this, never so turgid and swollen. It was like a weapon.

He lay beside her and started to kiss her. She was used to that part, even the part when he brought his head down to her breasts. But she wasn't used to the feel of his penis so hard and insistent on her leg.

'Hold it,' he instructed her.

She did so, ridden with guilt at the thought that what she was doing was wrong.

'Stroke it, here – I'll show you how.'

She rubbed it in the way he told her to, and he started to groan – low animal noises that both disgusted and excited her. Then he pushed her quickly away, and pulled open her thighs, and thrust his head down between them. She froze, unable to move, not wanting to move. His tongue began to open her up, probing, investigating. Until at last she too started to make her own animal noises.

'Are you ready to try?'

'Yes,' she whispered. 'Yes, yes, yes . . .'

He moved his head up, and reached for a package beside the bed. 'I'm going to wear protection,' he told her matter of factly, 'but I don't usually like to. It spoils it for me. Next week I'll send you to a doctor I know and he'll fix you up.'

It crossed her mind that he was very experienced, but then he was a man – why shouldn't he be?

He rolled the thin tube of rubber over his penis. 'Bring your knees up, try to relax,' he told her. 'It may hurt a little, but only the first time, only this once.'

She looked into his eyes. His deep, brooding, intense eyes. 'I'm frightened . . .' she began. But he wasn't listening, he was on top of her and forcing his way between her legs. Thrusting, pushing . . . It hurt in a pleasureable way.

'Relax,' he kept on saying, 'just relax.'

She began to make more animal noises, and a feeling of tenseness built up inside her. A tenseness that wanted to burst right out.

'I love you, Nino, I love you,' she cried out.

He was silent. Sweat beading his forehead. He balanced his weight on his arms, and churned in and out of her.

She was gasping now, reaching for the climax. Reaching . . . Reaching . . .

Then she was caught up in something so pleasurable that she could not control herself. Her legs twisted themselves around his back, her nails raked into his skin. 'Nino, Nino, Nino . . .' she yelled, 'Niiiinnno . . .'

It was over for her. The strength flooded from her body. She felt positively euphoric.

Nino was pumping into her harder and harder. His eyes were closed. His mouth set in a thin line. Then he too reached his orgasm. 'Rich bitch!' he screamed. 'Rich capitalist bitch!' He collapsed on top of her, groaned, rolled off, turned his back.

She lay very still. She felt so *good*.

She turned and studied the outline of her lover's ass. So tight and firm. So much nicer than hers. Gently she put her hand on it. He rolled to face her.

'That was wonderful,' she sighed, 'why didn't you tell me it would be like that?'

'It usually isn't,' he replied. 'Are you sure this is your first time?'

She giggled. 'Of course, silly. When can we do it again?'

That had all taken place six weeks previously. Six glorious weeks of what it was like to be a woman.

Cristina lay spreadeagled in the warm water of the swimming pool. Nino had never said he loved her, but she was sure he did. He would tell her in his own good time. She had *proved* that she loved him beyond doubt. She had told him about her parents' friends, the Von Cougats. She had drawn him a map of their house, and pinpointed the safe and alarm system control. She had also told him of a ball they would be attending, and Nino and his friends had acted without hesitation. The Von Cougats had been relieved of over a hundred thousand dollars' worth of jewellery.

Cristina had understood. Nino was right, the Von Cougats wouldn't even miss it.

'We need as much money as we can get,' Nino told her. 'With money we can buy power – we can buy the instruments of terror – we can *force* the rich to listen to us.'

'Yes,' agreed Cristina, although she really didn't understand what he was talking about.

Nino was a member of some mysterious organization. He attended secret meetings, and talked about his 'leaders' with an air of reverence.

When Cristina asked about it he silenced her with the words, 'Not yet. When you are ready I'll take you to a meeting.'

When would that be? He wouldn't tell her.

'Soon,' he would tell her, 'we will have enough money to start our campaign. Then you will see some changes in this city – then you will see the capitalist pigs brought to their knees.'

Cristina had nodded. All that mattered to her was Nino. As long as she had him she didn't care what happened.

Enough thinking. She leapt out of the pool and ran into the house. The door to her parents' bedroom was firmly closed.

If they only knew what she had been up to ... She shuddered at the thought. They would lock her in the house and never let her out again!

☆

Evita stretched and sighed. There was no getting away from it, her husband was a selfish lover. She could hear him singing happily in the shower. Jorge Maraco.

How surprised everyone had been when he had chosen her as his bride. It had taken years before his friends had accepted her. Now her early days of poverty seemed like a bad dream. It was almost as if her life had begun the day she had set eyes on Jorge.

She had not been a disappointment to him. She had come to his bed a virgin, and he had been the only man she had ever slept with. Although it was not for want of other men trying – she had often received secret notes and phone calls from Jorge's so-called friends. She had turned them all down. She had been absolutely faithful. Except ... She blushed at the memory. One lapse in eighteen years of marriage. Her blush deepened. One lapse ...

Three years earlier Jorge had taken her to Acapulco. There was a film festival in progress, and the town had been filled with movie stars, directors, and producers. Jorge appeared to be on nodding terms with everyone. He loved the gaiety and excitement. Evita was somewhat intimidated by it all. She encouraged Jorge to go out and about, attending receptions and screenings, whilst she stayed mostly at the hotel, lying under a large umbrella beside the swimming pool.

It was during this time she had struck up a friendship with the American film star Doris Andrews. Doris' husband was in the entertainment business and he too seemed to be out all day. Doris and Evita became close friends, sharing gossip, ordering long cool Planters Punch together, exploring the tourist shops.

Evita had never suspected that Doris was anything but completely normal. Until one day, returning from a shopping trip, they had both collapsed exhausted from the heat in Doris' suite. They had lain side by side on the large bed, giggling, laughing. Doris had slipped off the pink mu-mu she was wearing. It had seemed perfectly natural, after all it *was* hot, so Evita had slipped out of her beach dress also.

They lolled on the bed clad only in panties.

'What lovely breasts you have,' Doris had said, and she had leaned over and touched them and murmured, 'so full, so firm.'

Evita had smiled. Her breasts were lovely. She was proud of them.

'I wish mine were better,' Doris had complained, cupping her own small boobs. 'What do you think of them?'

Evita hadn't really thought about them at all. But she looked, and noted the erect nipples, and noted that her nipples were also extended. And it had seemed perfectly natural when Doris had started to stroke and caress her.

One lapse . . .

And she had not repeated it. She had insisted to Jorge that they flew home that very evening. He had been surprised, but hadn't argued. He never argued with her.

Jorge emerged from the bathroom, a towel tied round his middle. 'I spoke to Cristina,' he said. 'I told you we have nothing to worry about. She is a good girl. It is Louis we have to worry about. He tried to take liberties with her. She refused him. That is why she sees different friends now.'

'But who are her new friends? She never brings them home, we know nothing about them . . .'

'If it will make you happy I'll tell her we must meet them.'

'Yes. I think we must.'

'Of course.' He dropped the towel and approached his wife. His penis was erect and ready.

Just once Evita wished he would use his tongue instead. Doris Andrews had used her tongue . . .

'Evita!' Jorge sighed, positioning himself above her. 'My darling Evita!'

53

Melanie King was still in New York. If Paul knew he would be furious. She had taken elaborate precautions to make sure that he didn't find out. His only concern was the children, she didn't kid herself on *that* count.

She phoned nanny and made up a mass of lies as to why nanny should say she was back in London if Mr King phoned.

Nanny sniffed her disapproval. 'About my time off . . .' she began.

'You can have two weeks to visit your mother when I get back,' Melanie promised rashly.

'Very well, Mrs King.'

Melanie had hung up relieved. That took care of *that* end of things. She had herself to take care of. She was twenty-eight years old, and she wasn't getting any younger. Paul was dull and boring. She had thought when they married that being Al King's sister-in-law would bring a lot of excitement into her life. It had brought nothing of the sort. It had brought a boring life stuck in a house next to boring Edna – and *it just wasn't good enough.*

She had come to New York determined to have a good time before returning home. She hadn't counted on running into Manny Shorto again. Now that she had . . .

She had first met Manny eleven years ago. She had been seventeen, pretty, innocent, and stupid.

Manny Shorto, the famous American comedian.

Eleven years ago he had seduced her, used her, tricked her, trapped her.

She had been one of the dancers on the television spectacular he had come to England to star in. He had promised her the earth, delivered her three mediocre screws, and flown back to America leaving her confused and pregnant.

She had been forced to sleep with two film extras and a camera operator to get enough money together for an abortion. Then, a few months later she had met Paul King. Without hesitation – when he asked – she had married him. She had never loved him. She had always expected something better to be just around the corner.

Now Manny Shorto was back in her life. And he didn't even remember her! The bastard.

But he wanted her – oh how he wanted her. His wife had died of cancer, and he lived alone in a large hotel suite surrounded by hangers-on. He was more than a star – he was an American legend.

They had met again at a party. He asked her out – she said no – he sent her some presents – she said yes – he tried to screw her – she said no – he sent her some more presents – she still said no.

She was his type. There was no denying that. 'What do you want?' he asked. 'Name it – you got it.'

She wanted to be Mrs Manny Shorto. *She* wanted to be the star's wife.

Now if she played her cards right . . . If she could only stay in New York long enough . . . This time *she* was going to screw *him*. This time *she* would win.

☆

The Hollywood Bowl concert was a smash. Even Bernie had to admit that he had never heard Al in better voice. He grabbed the audience in his fist, and held them there in a dazzling performance. They screamed their approval – stars and fans alike. At the end of his 'tribute to other singers' he dedicated Bobby Womack's version of 'We've Only Just Begun' to a 'wild-haired, green-eyed lady out front'.

Dallas, sitting with Kiki and Chuck, smiled slightly. No one knew it was for her. It was their secret.

He over-ran by half an hour, and everyone stamped and clapped and cheered for him to stay longer – but it was time to go – and he gave them his boxer's salute and vanished.

'Wow!' exclaimed Kiki, 'he is *too* much – but the best. I never realized what impact he has. Jeeze – I'm weak at the knees. That is one horny man!'

Chuck laughed. 'I'd look horny if my pants were cut to within an inch of my life!'

Kiki giggled. 'You're horny anyway, baby.' She hugged him, 'In fact – you are the horniest! I can vouch for that!'

They got caught in a huge traffic snarl-up, and it seemed like hours before they reached the Beverly Hills Hotel. There was a hassle to get directed to Al's bungalow, and Chuck nearly got involved in a fight.

There was a mob of people at the bungalow. Dallas found Paul and asked what was happening. 'Go through to the bedroom,' he said. 'He's waiting for you.'

She edged through the crowd, and Luke ushered her into the bedroom.

Al was lying on the bed in a towelling dressing gown. He sat up when he saw her and said, '*Where have you been*?'

'The traffic . . .'

He reached around her waist and pulled her onto the bed with him. 'Let's fuck,' he said urgently, 'I was thinking about you all the time . . .'

She shoved him away. 'What is it with *you*?'

He leapt on top of her, pinning her arms down. 'What is it with *me*? I haven't had a woman for weeks. I can have my pick, but I've been waiting for you . . . Do you know what it means for me to wait?' He lowered his mouth onto hers. She flicked out her tongue to meet him. He relaxed his hold on her arms and pushed his own tongue into her mouth.

She bit his tongue sharply, at the same time springing free and rolling off the bed. 'I don't want to screw you. Get it? I'm not another one-night lay. Another silly little star fucker.'

He started to laugh. 'Is my tongue bleeding?'

'I don't believe you,' she huffed, picking herself up from the floor. 'I walk in the room – you *attack* me. There's a million and one people right outside. Honestly . . .'

'I love you,' he laughed. 'I really love you.'

'Good,' she replied. 'Now get dressed and we'll go to the party.'

He saluted, still smiling. 'Yes m'am.'

She couldn't help smiling too. 'And don't get smart, or we won't go.'

☆

Karmen Rush wanted him.

She was a lady who always got what she wanted, or all hell was let loose.

She was a not too attractive female who had styled herself into a devastating cult beauty. Her aquiline features she emphasized with deliberate shading. Her too-close-together myopic eyes she hid behind black contact lenses, and emphasized the outer eye and lid in a dramatic Egyptian fashion. Over her thin mouth she drew a shape of a more inviting nature, which she filled in with a dark brown lipstick. She dieted fanatically to keep her thinner than thin figure. And her hair she had dyed a jet black, and wore it very long with the help of various hair pieces.

Her magic voice was all her own.

She was one of the very few bankable female stars in the world.

At the age of thirty-two, she had devoured three husbands, and was currently sharing her sumptuous house with a young dress designer by the name of Keeley Nova. His friends sometimes called him Keelin' Over, on account of the fact that he was always stoned out of his head, and had a habit of falling down flat at the most inopportune moments. Karmen never seemed to notice. She sailed through everything like a queen, her face an impenetrable mask. As long as she was never disturbed during the three hours it took for her to get herself together every day – then she seemed unruffled by anything.

When Al arrived at her house she took him by the hand and husked, 'Beautiful . . . Beautiful . . .' in his ear.

He had always wanted to meet her. She did not leave go of his hand, and she had a grip of steel.

The house was alive with freaks – music issued forth from every corner – an old Shirley Temple movie played soundlessly on a giant screen.

Karmen fixed him with her deadly eyes. 'Come with me,' she whispered, 'I want to tape record our first conversation.'

Dallas gave him a little shove from behind. 'Go on,' she urged, 'I'll be fine.'

'But . . .' Al began.

'Go on!' insisted Dallas. 'I don't mind – really.'

'I'll be back in a minute then.'

Karmen dragged him away.

'I can't get over this house,' Kiki was saying, 'Dallas, have you looked around – it's insane!'

The house was indeed weird. Not furnished in the conventional sense – but littered with exotic cushions and rugs, and only iit by long black candles that were stuck in holders ranging from exquisite silver to wine bottles.

On the walls priceless Picassos jostled next to old movie posters. The back of the house was sheets of glass which led out to the beach and the ocean. Various huge dogs wandered about apparently harmlessly. Word had it that at a gesture from Karmen they would attack and kill.

'Kinda cosy!' joked Kiki. 'What do you think, Chuck baby, shall we take it?'

'Christ! Be careful what you drink!' Chuck replied. 'There's not one normal person here. They'll slip you acid before you can say hello!'

Dallas wandered onto the beach. She didn't mind the fact that Karmen had spirited Al off. In fact in a way she was pleased. If he was so anxious to get laid let Karmen do him the honours. At least it would give her an excuse to stop seeing him. And she wanted to stop seeing him – she wanted it to be over before it had begun. That was the only way she would be safe.

☆

Paul arrived at the party a little later. He had stayed behind to get rid of the people at the bungalow. He couldn't spot either Al or Dallas, and assumed that they had finally got it together and were hidden away somewhere consummating the relationship. Good. That would mean the end of Dallas. It didn't seem right for Al to be so hung up. Paul preferred him the way he knew him – this whole Dallas trip was unusual.

He looked around. It was pure freaksville. What was he doing here? Why wasn't he out trying to get Linda back?

A stoned redhead swayed over to him. 'What star sign are you, lover?' she asked. 'If you're a Scorpio we're in luck. My horoscope promised me a Scorpio today and you look like a beautiful human being.'

'No, no,' he backed away. He couldn't turn on to women the way Al did. He couldn't produce an instant hard-on with a complete stranger. It just wasn't his scene. He needed more. He needed a certain mental communication before anything physical could happen.

He wanted to leave. This wasn't his kind of party. Quietly he headed for the door.

☆

Karmen said, 'Your vibes are reaching me, Al. I knew you and I were tuned into the same thought waves.'

They were in her bedroom. A room painted black with no ceiling. The ceiling was the sky littered with stars.

'Like it?' she asked. 'I designed the whole house myself.'

'Nice.'

'Nice! It cost me a goddamn fortune! Listen, Al. We can lock ourselves away from the party. We can party on our own – just the two of us. You want to snort a little coke? I've got the best stuff – or is grass your treat? Whatever. Name it.'

'Hey,' he objected, 'thanks for the offer, but I came here with someone.'

'So? Who is she? Some nothing chick you can hump any day of the week. I'm offering you *me* – Karmen Rush.' With a gesture she undid a clip, and the black halter-neck dress she was wearing slid to the floor.

Her body was so thin that her ribs were visible, and her hip bones jutted out, emphasizing the fact that she had shaved off every inch of pubic hair. Her nipples were black flowers – painstakingly designed. A black heart was tattooed on her waist.

She stared at him. 'Don't tell me you're not king. Don't tell me all I saw up there on that stage was a pair of old socks.' She turned her back on him and walked contemptuously over to the black fur bed. She flopped onto it, opening her legs.

He could see everything. There was no black bush impairing his vision. He had not had a woman for over four weeks. Besides which, this was Karmen Rush – *the* superstar lady – asking him – begging him . . .

He wanted to get back to Dallas. He wanted to . . .

He unzipped his trousers. One quick fuck wasn't going to make any difference.

☆

Twice Linda nearly dialled the number. Twice she copped out at the last minute. What was it about California? She felt *so* horny. Was it something they put in the water? Or was it just her way of getting Paul out of her system?

The parking boy had been fun, a laugh, a one-night stand. But a hooker – wasn't that taking things a bit too far?

Men had been using hookers forever. Yeah – but probably men who couldn't get it on for free elsewhere. Either that or they wanted to do things they didn't want to do with their wives.

But what the hell. She wanted something different. She wanted a man who was dedicated to pleasing her. Dedicated. Not some dude who expected as good as he gave.

Determined, she picked up the phone again. But just as she was dialling, the doorbell rang.

She slammed the phone down and went to the door. It

was Cody Hills. He looked distraught. 'Where is Dallas?' he demanded.

'She went to the Al King concert at the Bowl. You want to come in? You look like you could do with a drink.'

Morosely he followed her inside. She fixed him a vodka on the rocks and he gulped it down.

'So what's up?' she asked, 'you look in a state.'

'Yes,' he agreed, 'I have to get hold of Dallas. I've got bad news – really bad news.'

☆

Dallas sat on the beach for a while, and the while grew into a long time. So she went back inside, and found Kiki and Chuck. There was no sign of Al. No sign of Karmen. 'I'll be back in a minute' indeed. What bullshit!

'I'm going to leave,' she said, trying to keep the hurt out of her voice.

'But what about Al?' Kiki asked.

'He's a free agent. There's nothing between us, you know.'

'Sure,' agreed Kiki, 'just an electric charge you could cut with a knife.'

'Yeah – so electric he's run off to screw rent-a-witch.'

'Who?'

'Do I have to draw you a picture? Our lovely hostess. Listen Kiki – I don't give a shit, I'm splitting.'

'Wait until we finish eating and we'll come with you,' Chuck joined in. 'After all – it's up early again tomorrow – back to the grind.'

Dallas nodded. She was tired. She only had to hear the words 'up early' and it was instant yawn time. She would go home, get into bed, and forget about Al King.

If she had been smart she would have forgotten about him in the first place.

☆

Edna rose at seven. There was so much to do, and with Evan away visiting friends she planned to spring-clean his room.

The house was looking wonderful, sparkling clean, the way it had never looked before. She had been horrified at the filth she had found. You pay people to look after your home, and what did you get? You got dust swept under couches, cobwebs in the hall light fixtures, thick grease in the oven, a permanent rim around the bath, unpolished silver, unmoved furniture.

Edna had soon taken care of all that. She had personally scrubbed the house from top to bottom. Now all she had to do was maintain it.

She made herself a cup of tea. Oh, the luxury of an empty kitchen! Then she strolled round the front of the house and picked up the newspapers from the mail box. On the front page of one of them, there was a large picture of Al and Dallas. They were laughing, looking at each other. Al's expression was of rapt interest.

Calmly Edna read the blurb.

'Al King Meets his Queen Again'. That was on top. Underneath the story read: *Los Angeles, Saturday, Superstar Al King (38) and Ex 'Miss Coast to Coast' Dallas (20) seemed to find plenty to laugh about at a party in his honour given by Doris Andrews (43). Earlier in the year Al's name was romantically linked with Dallas. The claim then was 'just good friends'. Isn't it wonderful how friendships last?'* Edna folded the paper carefully and returned to the house.

She couldn't make up her mind what to do first. Wax the kitchen floor, or start on Evan's room. She decided on the kitchen floor. Humming softly to herself she switched on the radio.

How nice to no longer have Melanie coming around to try and rub her nose in it. Because, quite frankly, she couldn't care less.

☆

'I'm sorry,' said Karmen blankly, 'I must have given you too much.'

Al, struggling his way to consciousness through a throbbing headache muttered, 'Too much what?'

'Ether,' replied Karmen matter of factly. 'I put a pad over your face when you were coming – it usually produces the most hallucinatory effects. I guess you must have breathed too deeply or something. You've been asleep for hours, the doctor was quite worried.'

Al did not believe what he was hearing. Ether! She could have *killed* him. The woman was totally insane.

He wanted to throw up. He felt terrible. 'You stupid bitch!' he slurred. 'You're mad, fucking mad.'

She pinched the bridge of her nose with dangerously taloned black-painted nails. 'I tried to wake you. I did everything to wake you.'

Al focused on her boyfriend standing behind her. He looked very spaced-out and very nervous.

Al tried to stand. 'I want to get out of here,' he said, 'I don't need fucking maniacs in my life. Where is the doctor anyway?'

'When he saw you were coming to he left. He doesn't like to get involved.'

'Jesus!' Al spat in disgust. 'Get me my driver – Luke. I want out.'

'Sure, man,' Keeley said, 'I'll arrange everything. Don't you worry about a thing.' He unlocked the bedroom door and exited.

Al staggered to his feet. He noticed he was fully dressed. The last thing he could remember was giving this ugly bitch a good hammering. Then – pow – nothing until now. Ether! Christ Almighty!

'Who dressed me?' he demanded.

'Keeley.' replied Karmen. 'You could have just slipped quietly away. I didn't think you would want to go with your pants off.'

Al glared at her. What could you say to a psycho screwball? She was nuts.

She stared impassively at him, unruffled by the whole event.

Keeley came bouncing back in the room followed by a concerned Luke.

'Where the fuck were *you*?' Al demanded, not waiting for a reply. 'Get me to the car.'

Karmen fluttered her hands vaguely in the air. 'It could've been a beautiful experience,' she murmured. 'You could've *thanked* me.'

'Sod off, you dumb bitch.' He followed Luke through a side door and out to the car. He still felt weak. 'How long was I in there?'

'Nearly three hours,' replied Luke. He didn't dare to ask what had happened

'Where's Paul?'

'He came and left.'

'Dallas?'

'She left hours ago.'

'Figures,' said Al glumly. Nobody had been concerned. Nobody had been worried. They had all thought he was having the hump of a lifetime – why disturb him?

Fuck it. He deserved it. He had been so hung up with Dallas . . . Then the first superstar that had exposed her skinny body had pulled him. Terrific. What will-power. What strength of character. What a pile of shit.

He was disgusted with himself.

'Stop off at the first liquor store we pass and buy a couple of bottles of Jack Daniels,' he instructed Luke.

What the hell . . . Dallas wouldn't want to know about him now. She wouldn't believe him whatever story he told her. He had blown her out in front of her friends, humiliated her. He didn't even have the courage to call her. For one lousy star fuck he had crapped on the first relationship he might have had in years.

The concert had been such a triumph. He had been riding on a natural high. Was his ego so insecure that he'd felt obligated to screw Karmen Rush? Or was it just that he was plain horny after being without a woman for so long, and when she had taken off her clothes . . . When she had opened those white thin superstar legs . . .

Luke stopped the car at a liquor mart, and ran inside.

Al slumped back in the car. A few shots of Jack Daniels would soon get him together again.

☆

Kiki and Chuck were very kind. Too kind. They chatted about all sorts of unimportant subjects as they drove back to Beverly Hills.

Dallas wanted to scream, 'I don't care! I don't mind! Al can have who he wants, it doesn't bother me!' But she knew they were only trying to pretend they hadn't noticed the fact that Mr King had done the fastest walk-out on her on record.

'That Rush woman is really creepy-looking,' Kiki gushed. 'Did you *see* the make-up? *Three* inches of white base.'

'To cover her famous spots,' Chuck joined in.

'Yeah,' Kiki continued, 'do you know she never even appears at the studio without her make-up – I swear to God – 6 a.m. she marches in *fully made-up* – then she throws out the make-up guy – locks herself in his room – takes off all her "going to the studio" make-up – and does a whole new job on herself! Martha Scott told me – she did her hair on her last picture. Now the hair is another story . . .'

Dallas tuned out whilst Kiki droned on. She couldn't care less about Karmen Rush. It could have been anyone. She had known about Al's reputation up front – that's why she had held back. And thank God she had. At least this way she could walk away from it feeling no pain. If she had slept with him . . . If she had liked it . . .

Well she hadn't. It had taken extreme self-control, but she hadn't.

What a laugh that a man like Al King could turn her on where all others had failed. A superstud. A type of sexist pig that she should really loathe. Maybe he would have struck out too. Maybe if she *had* gone to bed with him it would have been as distasteful as it was with everyone else.

Oh well . . . No use wondering about *that*. Forget him. Concentrate on work. Concentrate on becoming a star. Concentrate on *herself*.

'Isn't that Cody's car?' Kiki was saying.

Dallas glanced out of the window. It was indeed Cody's Mustang parked neatly beside Linda's rented Mercury. What was he doing there? Fortunately she couldn't spot a white Ferrari, so Linda must have changed her mind about Julio. 'Coming in for a drink?'

'Sure . . .' began Chuck.

'No,' interrupted Kiki hurriedly. 'I'm beat, I really am. We'll see you tomorrow.'

Dallas knew what *she* wanted. She wanted to see her back together with Cody.

They said their goodbyes and Dallas walked into the house.

Cody jumped up when he saw her. His face was white.

'What happened between you and Lew Margolis?' he snapped. 'Because whatever it was Lew wants you *out* – off the series. What was it, Dallas? For Christ's sake what was it?'

54

'I can't,' insisted Cristina.

'Why not?' replied Nino, lazily.

They lay on the beach, hands entwined.

'I keep on explaining to you why not.'

'Because it's *your* house. Because it's *your* mother's jewels. If you really think about it – then you would say – yes, Nino – I'll tell you when it is a good time, Nino – I'll tell you where the safe is . . . how to open it.'

Cristina pulled her hand away and sighed. 'You ask me too much. First the Von Cougats, then the Bogatos – now you want to rob *my* house – my parents' house.'

Teasingly Nino threw sand over her stomach. 'So. It is fine to rob *other* people's houses. But when it comes to you . . .'

Cristina blushed. 'It's not just that. You stole from the Von Cougats – the money your organization gets for the jewellery goes to help the poor. No one was hurt. They are insured. As you said, no one will even miss it.'

'Yes,' his hand massaged the sand lightly into her stomach.

'So I told you about the Bogatos. *I* made it possible for you to rob them.'

'You were very helpful.'

'Yes, Nino,' her eyes filled with tears, 'but you didn't tell me that you and your friends would have to kill the dog . . .'

'It attacked us . . .'

'And wreck the house. Cover the walls with slogans, rip up priceless paintings.' She started to cry. 'I wasn't going to mention it – I felt too sick to mention it. But now – what you are asking me . . . it's impossible.'

His hand moved slowly down her stomach, his fingers hooked into the thin knot of cord holding the bottom half of her tanga together. 'I think we should go home,' he whispered.

She stopped crying and shivered slightly. He had her under some kind of unbreakable spell. 'It's early,' she protested weakly. 'I thought we were going to surf.'

He laughed. 'Who wants to surf when we have better

things to do?' He stood up and offered his hands to pull her off the sand.

They walked slowly back to his apartment. Her body was tingling with the anticipation of what he would do to her.

'Ah, Cristina, Cristina,' he sighed when they were in his room, 'what a baby you are, what a little innocent.' He was undressing her as he spoke.

'Do you *love* me?' she blurted out, unable to hold back any longer.

'I love you as I love the stars, the sky, the beach, the ocean.'

It was no real answer, but she was satisfied. It was more than he had said before.

'I love *you* she crooned, 'oh how I love you, Nino.'

He did not reply. He silenced her with his mouth.

Later, when Cristina had left, he lay on his bed and stared at the ceiling. The paint was cracking and peeling, sometimes little flakes would fall down onto him whilst he slept. He never slept well. He was always restless. His dreams were always full of nightmares. He craved for some action. He craved for his organization to start its reign of terror. The preparatory work was boring – at least the work he was stuck with was. 'You're the good-looking one, Nino,' his leaders had told him. 'You're the one who will be able to captivate the ladies – the *rich* ladies.'

Fund-raising was his job – whilst the others were out buying arms, making stockpiles of bombs – and compiling lists of victims for Operation Kidnap – *he* was satisfying women in bed. It was not a job he enjoyed. He had a girlfriend – Talia – a tough, intelligent twenty-three-year-old, who worked in the smuggling side of the operation. For the last few months he had hardly seen her at all. It was a most unsatisfactory situation. When he made love to Cristina he shut his eyes and tried to pretend it was Talia. It never worked. Talia was a woman of fire, whilst Cristina was just a silly little rich girl.

Cristina Maraco. Just how useful could she be? Her father was a very rich man ... Blackmail or kidnap had been discussed, unless she could be used in some other way. Her mother's jewellery would be a help. Perhaps she would be able to supply more information on families such as the Von Cougats and the Bogatos. 'String her along some more,' were Nino's instructions. At least she was better than the Americans. He shuddered at the thought of the American women he had serviced. Big women with big demands. 'Do this, Nino, baby.' 'Do that, Nino, sweetheart.' 'Just there, don't stop.' 'One more time, Nino.' Ugh! How he hated them. Capitalist pigs from the worst capitalistic country of all.

His eyes were closing. Sleep was coming. The nightmares were coming. No use fighting it. He succumbed.

☆

'Where have you been all day, Cristina?'

Wide-eyed and innocent. 'Just to the beach, mama. I *told* you I was going to the beach.'

'You look so . . . flushed.'

'I have a headache, mama, I think I will go and lie down.'

Evita nodded. She didn't know what it was, but she just had a feeling that Cristina was up to something. When Jorge returned home late in the evening she tried to explain her feelings to him.

'Up to *what*?' He laughed.

'I don't know. I can't explain.' She paused thoughtfully. 'I think she has a boyfriend.'

Jorge grimaced. 'According to her she has a lot of new friends. And after what Louis tried on I don't blame her.'

'I think,' Evita said hesitantly, 'that she is sleeping with someone.'

'Impossible!' Jorge shouted, his complexion turning a dull red. 'How can you say such a thing?'

Evita shrugged. 'It's just a feeling I have.'

'You're wrong. She's a good girl, that much I know about my own daughter.'

'We've allowed her too much freedom. How do we know what sort of people her new friends are? At least with Louis we knew his family. Do you know that she never even has time to see Maria Therese – her best friend.'

Jorge frowned. 'On Sunday I will tell her to bring some of her new friends to lunch. We will meet them and make our own judgement.'

Evita nodded. 'Yes, I think that would be a good idea. *You* ask her, she will only find some excuse for me.'

Jorge kissed his beautiful wife lightly on the lips. 'Problems, problems, as if I don't have enough all day! But you are wrong, my darling, I know you are wrong. Cristina is a good girl. I would bet my life on that!'

☆

Evita took one look at Nino and saw immediately the Favellos in his eyes. She knew without doubt that here was a boy who came from exactly the same background as she did.

He was good-looking, marvellous-looking in fact, with his wild curly hair, and intense jet eyes. Evita could certainly see what attracted her daughter physically. But he was obviously a boy who lived on his wits. His clothes were the standard dress of the young – a uniform almost. The tight faded jeans, a collarless shirt, old tennis shoes. But round his neck hung an expensive gold chain with some sort of religious medallion, and Evita couldn't help thinking it was a present from a rich female. His kind always had rich women – she had seen so many boys like him who would sell their bodies to the tourists for whatever they could get out of it.

All these thoughts were churning quickly through her head as Cristina introduced him. Jorge had requested that Cristina bring her new friends home – but she had turned up with only one – this boy – and Evita could understand why. Her daughter was in love. It was quite obvious as she gazed at Nino with naked admiration shining from her eyes.

Jorge shook Nino firmly by the hand. 'Do you two youngsters want to swim before lunch?' he asked.

Cristina looked quickly at Nino, questioning him with her eyes.

Nino nodded, glancing around at his luxurious surroundings with a mixture of contempt and envy.

'Go ahead,' offered Jorge. 'Cristina, show your friend to the changing room.'

'Not necessary,' said Nino, unzipping his jeans and fixing Evita with a sudden moody stare.

'Don't do that here,' Cristina said quickly. 'Poppa doesn't like a mess of clothes round the pool – Come on, I'll show you where to change.'

Nino zipped his jeans up again. 'Sure,' he said, still staring at Evita.

She returned his stare with a polite smile. She hated him on sight. He represented a certain type of male she loathed. Arrogant. Mean. Conceited. A sexual aggressor. Young as he was, his character was quite clear to her.

Cristina grabbed Nino by the hand and led him off down the gardens towards the changing rooms.

Jorge turned to his wife, a complacent smile suffusing his face. 'You see,' he said triumphantly, 'he seems like a nice enough boy.'

'Don't be a fool,' snapped Evita in reply. 'You haven't said two words to him. Who is he? Where does he come from? What does he do?'

Jorge frowned. 'Give me time. I can't start questioning him the moment he walks in our house.'

'He's from the Favellos.'

'How do you know?'

'It's in his eyes, it's in his smell.'

'Evita. Don't condemn him before we even know him. He's Cristina's friend, she likes him.'

'She more than likes him.'

'What do you mean?'

'Your daughter is a woman – she likes this boy as a woman would like him. Did you see the way she looks at him?'

'No I didn't,' replied Jorge irritably. 'I wish you wouldn't always jump to conclusions and make hasty decisions about people.'

'I have an instinct for knowing things. This boy is no good.'

Jorge turned away from his wife. Sometimes she could be very annoying with her 'instincts'. A year previously he had been forced to terminate a lucrative business deal because Evita didn't like the man he was dealing with.

'You will be fair,' Jorge insisted, 'you will not judge this boy on two minutes – you will judge him after we have spent the day in his company. I am sure if he is a friend of Cristina's he will turn out to be nice, polite and respectful.'

☆

'Hold this,' urged Nino.

'I can't, not here!'

'Hold it. Stroke it.'

'Nino. My parents are just down the garden. They'll wonder what we are doing in here.'

'Put it in your mouth.'

'Nino!'

'Do it. I command you. Get down on your knees and put it in your mouth.'

'No!'

'If you love me you will.'

Her eyes were filling with tears. They stood in the changing room close together. She in her tanga. He with his jeans around his ankles, his brief swim suit around his knees, and his penis swollen and distended.

'If you loved me you wouldn't ask,' said Cristina miserably.

'I *have* to ask. I can't go out like this. It's *your* fault I'm like this.'

Reluctantly she sunk to her knees. 'But if they come looking for us . . .'

He grabbed her head and guided himself into her mouth. 'Ah!' he sighed, 'that's good, that's very good.' Slowly he rocked back and forth. It was the first time she had allowed him into her mouth, although she wasn't averse to the feel of *his* tongue.

He was excited because of the woman. The beautiful woman with the glacial features and white-blonde hair. *She* was the kind of woman he had always dreamed of having. A madonna in a white bathing suit, with the body of a lush peasant girl. The combination was irresistible.

The joke was that she was Cristina's mother. A woman Cristina had called a bitch and a hag, and God knows what he had expected – some sort of old, jewel-ridden bag! The joke was on him. Cristina's mother was cool, ladylike, and so young.

'Aaach!' He climaxed quickly, pushing himself deep into Cristina's mouth. She gagged and tried to push away. He wouldn't allow her to until he was finished. Then he withdrew, satisfied – doubly satisfied because of where the event had taken place.

Evita watched the young couple emerge from the changing rooms, and turn towards the pool. She had known he would wear the smallest of swimsuits. She had known his body would be deeply suntanned, finely muscled and hard. After all he probably lived by his body, therefore it had to be in perfect condition.

What did he want with Cristina? Did he want to marry her? Was he foolish enough to believe that they would allow it?

Cristina was no great beauty. Oh, she was pretty enough, attractive, but she was not the sort of girl that would have a boy like that running around after her unless there was something in it for him – something more than just sleeping with her, because as she watched them cavorting in the pool, she was sure that he was indeed sleeping with Cristina. When you started life living in a shack amidst a sea of other shacks you developed an antenna for sexual knowledge. Evita knew at a glance.

She sipped slowly the glass of chilled white wine Jorge had poured for her. How lucky she had been to meet him. What a miraculous escape it had been for her. If not for Jorge . . .

'So this is how my little rich girl lives,' breathed Nino, surfacing behind Cristina and grabbing her round the waist, 'your own swimming pool, all the luxuries. I never even knew what a *bath* looked like until I was fourteen years old.'

'That's not *my* fault,' objected Cristina, wriggling free and striking off down the pool.

He swam after her, keeping his voice low so that her parents couldn't hear him.

'Do *you* think it's fair? Do you?'

'You know I don't, but there's nothing *I* can do about it.'

'But there is.'

'Please don't let's discuss it here.'

He placed his leg between hers under the water.

'Don't!'

'Why not?'

'You *know* why not. *Please* behave yourself, Nino.'

'And if I do, will you promise to do something for me?'

'I thought I just did!'

'Not that. Something important. Something that will help the organization.'

'If I can . . . You know I'll help if I can . . .'

Jorge was clapping his hands together beside the pool to attract their attention.

'Have you two had enough yet? Lunch is ready and I am hungry.' He glanced quickly at his watch. He had a schedule to adhere to. He didn't want to miss his afternoon siesta with his wife. It was all very well Evita wanting to meet Cristina's friends, but if it was going to interfere with his schedule . . .

Cristina swam to the edge of the pool, and hauled herself out. 'I'll have to change, poppa, I'll be as quick as I can.' She threw Nino a towel, 'You can use the changing room, I'm just going into the house.'

Nino caught the towel, smiled politely at Jorge, and glanced covertly at Evita. She wasn't kidding *him* with that glacial expression, she had noticed his body, she had noticed how great it was. Young, hard, virile. He strolled with deliberate slowness to the changing room.

Cristina ran into the house and up to her room. She had not wanted to tell Nino, but the thing he had made her do to him before they swam had made her feel sick. She rushed into her bathroom and rinsed her mouth out with strong mouthwash, then she cleaned her teeth. It had been mean of him to force her to do *that*. Especially in the changing room, within earshot of her parents. He had known she would not dare to object too strongly. He was so wonderful, and yet at times he could be so mean. He teased her a lot. He said her legs were too short – her breasts too flat – her ass too low. Then, just when she would be near to tears, he would kiss her, and laugh, and insist that he wouldn't want her any other way.

There were times when she wished that she had never set eyes on him. There were also times when she did not know how she had ever managed to exist without him.

If he asked her to marry him she would. Whatever her parents said.

She was amazed that he had agreed to come and meet them. 'If it will help you out,' he had shrugged. 'We don't want them locking you away 'cos they think you are mixing with undesirables. We'll show them what a fine upstanding guy I am.'

☆

'What do you do, Nino?' asked Evita.

She and Jorge sat at the luncheon table with him, waiting for Cristina.

'I study,' replied Nino, trying to engage her in a moody stare, but not succeeding.

'Oh yes, and what do you study?' Her tone was ever so faintly mocking.

'Politics.'

'Very good,' boomed Jorge, 'excellent. Hoping to be President one day, eh?'

'Not exactly.'

'Where do you study?' inquired Evita.

'What is that girl doing?' complained Jorge, glancing impatiently at his watch.

'Shall I go and find her for you, sir?' volunteered Nino.

'No, no, I'll send Maria.' He summoned the maid, a fat, surly girl. 'Go and tell Miss Maraco we are waiting, and to come at once.'

She bobbed a nervous curtsey. 'Si, señor. I tell her.' She rushed off.

Jorge indicated the plate piled high with delicious chunks of melon in the middle of the table, 'Let's start. Help yourself, Nino. Make yourself at home.'

'Thank you,' replied Nino politely, and he shot another look in Evita's direction, but she seemed to have decided to ignore him. Bitch! She thought she was too good for him. He helped himself to some melon.

'Where is your home?' inquired Evita.

Questions, all she could ask was questions.

'My family were killed in an automobile accident when I was very young,' he replied smoothly. 'I live with an aunt who has always taken care of me.'

What lies! 'Oh. Where is that?'

He was saved from answering by the appearance of Cristina. She had changed into jeans and a shirt similar to his. Somehow it really annoyed him that she tried so hard to look exactly like him.

'All that time to end up looking like a ragbag,' complained Jorge. 'You have such pretty dresses. On a Sunday it would be nice if you could wear them.'

'Oh, poppa! Sometimes you are so old-fashioned.'

'Old-fashioned,' sniffed Jorge, 'old-fashioned because I would like to see my daughter wear something that makes her look like a girl. What do you think, Nino?'

Cristina looked to him for support. He said, 'I must agree with you, Mr Maraco. I like a girl to look like a girl.'

You weasel, Evita thought. You nasty little weasel.

Cristina blushed a dull red. 'I don't care,' she said defiantly. 'Anyway, Nino, it was *you* that said it was wrong to waste money on clothes.'

'Really?' said Evita, 'did you say that, Nino?'

Now it was his turn to be embarrassed.

'I didn't mean not to buy any clothes at all.'

'What *did* you mean?' Evita had him on a spot.

'Well – you know,' he looked around helplessly at Jorge in his hand-made silk shirt and immaculate French trousers, Evita in her three hundred dollar towelling beach robe. 'I just meant that to own an excess of clothes when there are people starving on the outskirts of the city is wrong.'

'Starving?' questioned Evita, 'I hardly think they are starving.'

'You wouldn't know,' flashed Nino.

'And *you* would?'

She had caught him. He had been determined not to get involved in any arguments or discussions with them. He knew these kind of people. One threat – even a minor one like him – and they would order him out of their daughter's life. It wouldn't do to have their luxury rocked by a would-be revolutionary hanging around.

He shrugged. 'No, I don't know.'

Evita laughed coolly. 'And I thought you were going to be a young man with a cause.'

He shovelled some melon in his mouth. 'No cause.' Bitch! Bitch! Bitch!

The rest of the lunch passed without incident, and at exactly three o'clock Jorge rose from the table and said, 'I know you young ones will excuse us,' and helping Evita from the table, added, 'It's been nice meeting you, Nino.'

As soon as they were out of sight Cristina giggled. 'No cause,' she mimicked.

Nino turned on her angrily. 'What did you *want* me to say? That I think the way they live is disgusting? That their outlook is selfish and bourgeois? That they should do something useful with their money instead of sticking it on their backs and fingers and wrists?'

'Poppa supports many charities.'

'Charity!' spat Nino. 'The people shouldn't have to accept charity. By right, if all the money was divided, *everyone* would have enough. There would be no need for *charity*! Come on, let's get out of here, the stink of useless money is making me sick.'

☆

Jorge stripped, preparing for his shower. 'Quite a nice young man,' he commented.

'A trouble-maker,' replied Evita. 'I know his kind, I grew up with his kind.'

Jorge held her by the shoulders, helping her off with her robe. 'You can be a hard woman.'

'We must stop Cristina from seeing him.'

'And how do you propose we should do that?' He began to peel down the straps of her white swimsuit.

She shrugged, the gesture freeing her breasts. 'I don't know, it's something we must talk about. Maybe a trip – a long trip.'

Jorge fingered his wife's breasts. 'Whatever you want,' he said. 'You know you always get what you want.'

☆

'I want you to start seeing Louis Baptista again,' Nino said.

He and Cristina lay naked on his bed having recently finished making love.

She sat up. 'What?'

'Now don't get excited. I have my reasons.'

He pulled a pile of newspapers from under the bed and laid them out. He picked up one and read an item that had been circled in red.

'Rock/soul superstar Al King has accepted millionaire

impresario Carlos Baptista's offer to do two concerts in Brazil. His fee will be an astounding one million dollars.'

'Why are you reading me this?' Cristina asked.

'One million dollars is a great deal of money.'

'Of course it is.'

'Can you imagine what the organization could do with a million dollars?'

'I don't under . . .'

'Stop saying you don't understand and listen to me. I am trying to explain to you. If the great Al King was kidnapped – what a simple matter for them to pay one million dollars to get him back. The money is already available – instead of paying him, they pay us. Get it?'

'Don't be silly, Nino. It would be impossible – people like Al King are guarded all the time – and anyway – kidnap is a bad crime. If you were caught . . .'

Nino jumped off the bed irritably. 'We just talk about it and already I am caught! What faith you must have in me.'

'I do have faith in you. I know you can do anything you want to. But how could you possibly kidnap Al King?'

'With *your* help.'

She was startled. '*My* help?'

'You and your friend Louis – Carlos Baptista's son. You told me he was mad about you.'

'I stopped seeing him when you and I started to see each other.'

'That doesn't mean he will not be thrilled when you telephone him and resume your relationship.'

'But I don't want to.'

He sat down on the bed again, reached under her shirt and started to caress her. 'But for me you will. If you love me you will.'

'Why?'

Was she being deliberately dense? 'We have three weeks. Right now Al King is resting in Arizona, then he goes to Los Angeles and then he comes here. Three weeks will give you more than enough time to grab young Louis with your charm and newfound talents. From him you will be able to get all the information we need about Al King. We will be able to plan the best form of action.'

'But . . .' He silenced her by pressing his mouth down on hers.

She would cooperate. Of that he was sure.

55

Las Vegas. A razzle dazzle city in the middle of nowhere, filled with lovers and gamblers, con men and hookers, entertainers and mafiosi, winners and losers.

Las Vegas. If Los Angeles was the City of Angels, Las Vegas was the City of Devils. Blackjack. Craps. Roulette. Poker. And many other harmless little games to part a man and his money. Or a woman. Although their Las Vegas role was slightly more servile. Women worked according to their looks and their age. The beautiful, tall, spectacular show girls, baring it all. Their more energetic, but equally pretty sisters were the dancers. The attractive girls with dipped necklines dealing you in blackjack. The not quite so attractive girls donning black tights and cute shortie costumes to serve you free cocktails. The over-thirty ladies, with the same shorty costumes, baring ass and tit, patrolling the lobbies and restaurants, trying to sell you tickets for Keno, or some such fun games. And then the motherly waitresses in sensible white uniforms serving you Corned Beef Hash and Frank Sinatra sandwiches in the various delicatessens that no decent hotel would be without.

Al flew into the city in a suitably drunken haze. A haze that he had existed in since the fateful Rush party.

At first Paul had been delighted to see big brother back to normal. But three days and ten blondes later he wasn't so sure.

Al was back to normal with a vengeance.

A series of events had taken place.

Item one. Al had phoned Edna to explain to her about Evan. Not the whole truth, just the fact that he was with him, and safe, and that he would keep him there a while longer.

Edna, to Al's surprise, had received the news calmly. Then, just as he had been about to end the conversation, she had requested a divorce. Edna had asked *him* for a divorce! No hysterics, no crying. Just a matter-of-fact statement that they would both be better off without one another. Of course the thought had been in his mind for some time. But for Edna to suggest it! Jesus Christ! It was an outrage! How dare she!

He had mumbled something about they would talk about it later, and hung up. The next day Edna had announced it to the newspapers. The newspapers yet! Edna who baulked at having her photo taken with him! She had given an intimate interview to a hard-nosed bitch who made him out to be a combination between Casanova and Dracula!

Item two concerned Dallas. The fact was she lived up to his expectations, refused to speak to him, sent back his flowers, and in a face-to-face confrontation outside her house told him to go fuck himself. He had given up after that. Battles he didn't need.

Item three was the film Paul wanted him to do. The script was right, the money and percentages were right, the contracts were being drawn up. Paul had negotiated the deal with Lew Margolis. Somehow Al had doubts. He was a singer. What gave everyone the impression he could turn into an actor overnight? As far as he was concerned he hadn't made up his mind yet, whatever Paul thought.

Meanwhile, in Las Vegas, he concentrated his energies on going straight to the tables. A path was created through the tourists whilst whispers of 'Al King, Al King, Al King' reverberated through the place. An admiring crowd gathered around the roulette table he picked, and oohed and aahed as he proceeded to lose thirty thousand dollars.

He shrugged, grinned, moved over, to the crap tables. The crowd followed him.

A florid-faced dress manufacturer was just about to roll the dice. His face broke into a huge smile when he spotted Al, and he handed him the dice. 'Here you go, Al, you take 'em – maybe it'll change my luck.'

He took the dice, squeezed them hard – 'Five thou on the line,' he told the houseman. The houseman turned to the pit boss for confirmation. The pit boss gave an imperceptible nod.

Al rolled. The crowd were silent. He threw a five and a two. The crowd cheered its approval.

'Let it ride,' he told the houseman. The man added five thousand dollars' worth of chips to the stack already there.

He blew on the dice, rolled again. This time a four and a three. Lucky total of seven again.

'I knew it!' The florid-faced man exclaimed, scooping up the chips he had won betting on Al's throws, 'I knew you were a lucky devil.'

Several females were edging as near to Al as they could. A particularly large-bosomed redhead was making the most headway.

'Let it ride,' instructed Al. He hurtled the dice down the table. Five and a two again. He was up twenty thousand dollars. Not bad. But of course he was down thirty thousand on roulette. If he let the twenty ride and he won he would be up ten thousand. What the hell, it was only money.

'Again,' he said.

The crowd held its breath, then, just as he was about to roll, the big-bosomed redhead grabbed his hand holding the dice, and gave it a wet and sloppy kiss. 'For luck, baby,' she breathed, nudging him with her bosom.

It was too late for him to stop. But he knew he would crap out. Knew the redhead had blown his luck.

He was right. Two miserable ones showed up on the dice. The crowd groaned.

'I could offer you a consolation prize,' the redhead suggested.

He ignored her, signing the chit the pit boss handed him. So he was down fifty thousand dollars. So what?

'Could I have your autograph?' a very fat lady was asking, 'for my little niece. Charlene. C H A . . .' She spelled the name as he scribbled an almost illegible Al King on the book matches she had given him.

He walked away. The redhead followed him. 'Buy me a drink?' she suggested. She had nothing much to offer except the boobs and the hair.

'Are you a hustler?' he asked.

'Of course not!' She appeared deeply offended.

'Shame. I thought you and I could work something out.'

She bit her lip, then coyly said, 'What did you have in mind?'

'A good fuck.'

☆

Paul was on the phone. Lately he seemed to spend half his life on the phone. It was a bad line and he could hardly hear. 'I'll call you back, Melanie,' he said. He had been trying to reach her for days, but she always seemed to be out. Finally he had left a message for her to telephone him. He wanted to talk to her before they flew off to South America. Who knew what the phone connections were like there?

'You can't phone me back, I'm not at home,' Melanie's voice seesawed down the phone.

'I can hardly hear you,' complained Paul.

She said something that he couldn't hear at all, then,' ... can't see there is any point.'

'What?'

'I can get it in Mexico,' she screamed.

'Get what?'

'A divorce.'

He thought she was talking about Edna. 'Why does she want to go there?'

There was a series of electronic noises, then the operator interrupting, saying: 'You've been cut off. I'll try to reconnect you on a clearer line.'

He banged the phone down. It rang again immediately. It was the manager just wanting to inform him that Al King had signed chits totalling fifty thousand dollars. Terrific. Now he would have to haul Al away from the tables before he did any more damage. He had only been down there half an hour.

There was a knock at the door, Bernie stood there sweating.

'Have you seen Al?' Paul questioned.

'Yeah. He just boarded the elevator with a real water buffalo. Jeeze – you've got to have a grudge against your tool to go near a barracuda like that.' Bernie wheezed his way over to the table with the booze on, and poured himself a shot. 'With his money he should buy himself a new wife!'

'At least he's away from the tables.'

The phone rang and Paul snatched it up.

Melanie's voice came through clearly. 'I'm glad you agree,' she said, 'I've even decided to let you have the children.'

'What?'

'You want them, don't you? They'll be better off with you.

Manny and I will be leading an erratic life – not the sort of life children will fit into.'

'What the hell are you talking about?'

'Aren't you listening to me?' Melanie shrilled. 'Do I have to go through it all again?'

'You want to go to Mexico with Edna. Is that it? Well, I can tell you now . . .'

'You fool!' snapped Melanie, '*I'm* divorcing *you* in Mexico. I'm marrying Manny Shorto and we want to do it as soon as possible.'

Paul did not believe what he was hearing.

'You can keep the children,' Melanie shrilled on, 'as I said before they'll be better off with you. Of course the Mexican divorce will be a temporary step until we can arrange a proper English divorce. Manny wants everything to be done properly, he . . .'

She talked, whilst Paul sat down and listened unbelievingly. She had never gone home. She had stayed in New York. She had run into Manny, an old flame. Jesus – old was the operative word – he must be at least seventy. They had rekindled the flame. This time it had been too big for both of them . . .

Paul replaced the receiver, cutting off her voice. First Edna, now Melanie. What was going on? He slumped into the couch.

'Everything cool?' inquired Bernie, scratching under a sweaty armpit.

'You're going to love it,' replied Paul, still in a state of shock. 'Melanie's divorcing me. She's getting married to Manny Shorto.'

Bernie laughed, 'Come on, man . . .' He trailed off when he realized Paul was serious. He didn't know what to say. Paul was slumped out like a man in an accident – yet he had been balling that Linda Cosmo most of the trip – so the wife couldn't mean *that* much. But who knew with married couples . . . What the fuck . . . For the first time in his life Bernie was at a loss for words.

☆

Al sat fully dressed in the living room of his luxury suite whilst the redhead danced for him. She had discarded every stitch of clothing except for her shoes. The huge knockers were a silicone job, with sad inverted nipples. Her frizzy red pubic hair grew down the inside of her thighs. She was not the most tempting sight he had ever seen as she weaved and swayed somewhat clumsily in front of him.

He could make them do anything. What were they, dumb zombies? A half hour ago this woman had been a total stranger, now she was prepared to do anything for him. If he asked her to lie down and open her legs so he could take a few photos she would do it. She would do it for Marlon Brando, Robert Redford, Al Pacino . . . Any famous man. The list was endless. She would probably even do it for Richard Nixon – and definitely for Jimmy Carter.

Al was just deciding how he could get rid of her when Paul came bursting in.

The redhead stopped dancing abruptly, and looked for something to cover herself with.

Paul ignored her. 'We made a winning double,' he announced, 'Melanie's divorcing me – wants to marry Manny Shorto. Are you ready for that?'

Al started to laugh.

Paul said, 'What the hell are you laughing at?'

Al was doubled up with laughter – 'She got herself a star. For Christ sake – surely you can see the funny side of it?' He beckoned the redhead over who had decorously covered herself with a cushion, favouring her lower half.

'What would you do, darlin', if Manny Shorto wanted to marry you?'

'Huh?'

He reached for a siliconed tit and bounced it playfully. 'Would you say yes? Come on – truth now – would you say yes?'

'I'm married,' she replied, not quite comprehending the question.

'Married!' he exclaimed. 'What the fuck are you doing here then?'

'Separated,' she added quickly.

'The bitch never even went back to England,' Paul said morosely. 'She shacked up in New York with that old prick – leaving the kids all alone.'

Al gave the redhead a little shove in Paul's direction.

'Want to give her one?' he offered, 'wham bam it out of your system?'

'No thank you,' said Paul, at the same time as the redhead objected with – 'Hey – what is this?'

'Oh sorry,' Al apologized, 'you only fuck stars, is that it?'

'I think I'll get dressed . . .'

'Do that,' Al agreed, 'pack the silicone away – oh and next time your husband's home borrow his razor and shave your thighs – right now you remind me of King Kong's mate.'

'My husband could beat the shit out of you,' she hissed, 'who do you think you are?'

'Just a superstar,' he sang.

'I can't get over it. After all I've given her.' Paul sat down, shaking his head.

The redhead picked up her clothes and put them on as fast as possible. Two bright spots of anger burned into her cheeks.

'Faggot!' she spat at Al as she was leaving.

'For you – any day,' he minced in reply. 'Never could get it up for a gorilla!'

She slammed the door with a resounding bang.

'Did I interrupt something?' asked Paul, startled by the noise of the door.

'Absolutely nothing. Why don't you fix us a couple of belts and tell me the whole story.'

☆

Dallas lay in bed, shivering slightly, unable to sleep.

Who the hell did Lew Margolis think he was playing games with? Some out-of-town hick? Some dumb little girl?

She would soon show *him*.

She relived the latter part of the evening in her mind. The part where Cody was waiting for her to get home, his face drained of colour and worried.

What had she done to upset Lew Margolis, he wanted to know. What *had* she done? Because Lew Margolis had summoned him to his house on Sunday and informed him 'Man Made Woman' was being cancelled. 'Dallas just doesn't come across, just doesn't make it,' Lew had said – his face as impassive as a snake's. 'I'm opting out now, no good throwing more money into it.'

'Now?' Cody had stammered.

'As of today,' Lew agreed, 'tell your client not to bother turning up tomorrow. She won't be needed.'

Cody knew that something was desperately wrong. He had seen the daily rushes himself. Dallas came across like a million dollars. She looked magnificent, and her acting abilities were more than adequate for the part.

'What about her contract?' Cody had asked.

'It will be honoured up to the first option date,' Lew replied. 'That's only fair.'

Cody had been speechless. The whole thing was ridiculous. Lew Margolis must be some kind of nut. Then it came to him. This had to be a personality clash. Something had happened between Dallas and Lew. Something big enough to cause this lunacy. For it was lunacy – Lew's studio stood to lose if they opted out on 'Man Made Woman' before it even reached the television screens. Everyone stood to lose.

'So what happened?' Cody insistently questioned Dallas. She shrugged. 'Nothing.'

'It can't have been nothing,' he snapped. 'You were at his party last night. It must have been something that happened there . . . something you did or said. Did he ever try to come on with you?'

Dallas didn't dare to glance in Linda's direction. She wanted to tell Cody not to worry. Everything would be fine in the morning. Everything would be fine when she reminded Lew Margolis of a certain set of photographs. 'No, he never did. The only approach I've ever had from that family has been strictly female.'

'Female?' echoed Cody, puzzled.

'Doris.'

Cody made a disbelieving face.

'She's a dyke,' Dallas insisted. 'She tried to grab me – I turned her down.'

'Come on, Dallas,' he said patiently, 'this is *the* town for gossip, and not a word of Doris Andrews being a lesbian has *ever* got around. If she was, the world would know.'

'Well, she is,' insisted Dallas stubbornly.

'Hmmm . . .' Cody was still sceptical. 'We'll have to work out a press release – we'll have to tread very carefully. I just don't know . '

'Let's all sleep on it. Tomorrow might change everything. Besides, I am bushed, I can't even think straight . . . Hold any statements until we speak tomorrow.'

He nodded. God, she was taking it well. Any other actress would be hysterical by now. He wondered if she fully realized what she was losing. Not just the money, but the shot at instant fame, the shot at becoming a household name in a matter of weeks. Without that cherry the other offers might dry up. After all, who was she? And the big question would be why had she been dropped? Acting was like gambling in a way. One minute you were hot – the next cold. It could happen to anyone. But when you were cold – oh boy – nobody wanted to know.

Thank God she had the Mack contract. Although he would have felt a lot more secure if her face was on every billboard. Aarron Mack was no fool. He would want to know why Lew Margolis was firing her. And what was Lew Margolis going to say? Cody didn't even want to think about it.

'Another drink?' Linda offered.'

He declined. He had to find a hotel to spend the night in. The thought of another evening with Carol Cameron was too much to take.

☆

Dallas was up at six. She drank endless cups of coffee, and at nine o'clock she called Lew Margolis at the studio and got his secretary who said that he wasn't in yet. Of course she could phone him at home, but Doris would be there, and that just wouldn't be wise.

She waited until ten, and called the studio again. 'Mr Margolis is in a meeting,' the secretary said.

'Tell Mr Margolis to call me back as soon as he can. It's urgent.'

Linda was just waking. 'What's the plan of action?' she asked.

'I'll make that bastard sorry,' Dallas replied, her eyes steely. 'Who the fuck does he think he's messing with?'

Linda said, 'You need any help, I'm here.'

Dallas nodded. 'Thanks. But this creep I can manage all on my own. He seems to have forgotten about the photos.'

'I know that now is probably not quite the time to ask –
but I'm busting to know. What happened with you and the
great white master last night?'

'He's a prick,' replied Dallas dismissively. 'I guess you
were right.'

Linda didn't probe. She could see that Dallas' mind was
elsewhere.

Lew Margolis did not call back.

At eleven o'clock Dallas drove to the studio. She drove
past the studio gates with a wave, and parked near Lew's
office. His secretary looked flustered to see her.

'It's all right,' Dallas said, 'I'm sure he's expecting me.'

Unsure, the secretary buzzed her boss.

'Send her in,' he commanded.

Dallas strode scornfully into his office and perched on the
side of his marble desk.

'Hi, Lew. What seems to be the problem?'

His small eyes flicked over her body. He chomped steadily
on a thick cigar. 'No problem.'

'I think there is.'

'Yes?'

'Yes. I think you've made a couple of hasty moves. I think
you're forgetting a few things.'

His nostrils twitched, a nervous habit he had acquired
twenty years previously. 'Cunt,' he said evenly, 'stupid cunt.
I took a lot from you, but when it comes to messing with my
wife . . . You filthy whore.'

'What are you talking about?'

'You know goddamn right well what I'm talking about,'
he sneered. 'Pervert! Degenerate! I took a lot of flak from you
– but when you try to put your stinking hands on my
wife . . .'

Gradually it dawned on Dallas that Doris had been
making up stories. She got off the desk. Stood facing him,
shaking with fury.

'You're screwing your facts up. *I* never tried to touch your
wife – she came after me.'

'Lying cunt,' stated Lew, not believing a thing she said.
'You go near my wife again and I'll have you fixed perma-
nently. I'll have your legs broken – you face smashed up.
Please believe me, these things can be arranged.'

Dallas attempted to keep her voice even. 'I don't know what Doris has told you, but . . .'

Lew ground the remains of his cigar into an ashtray. 'Don't even mention her name,' he warned.

'I'll mention what I like,' she flashed back. 'I'll mention certain photos I have of you that Doris might be interested in seeing. Keep this shit up, and they'll be in her hands today.'

Lew laughed. It wasn't a pleasant laugh. 'What photos?' he jeered.

'You know what photos.'

He laughed again. 'Do you think I'm a fool? Do you think I have got where I am today by letting cunts like you get the better of me? Those photos don't exist any more – they ceased to exist weeks ago. The set hidden in your house – gone. The set you gave me – destroyed.'

'You're forgetting the negatives.'

'I'm forgetting nothing. Go to your bank – check out your safety deposit box.' He chuckled. 'Sometimes it helps to have power in this town.'

'You're bluffing.'

'Don't count on it. I was going to keep you on in the series – you were good – you could have been a big star. But when you tried to lay your filthy whore's hands on my wife you went too far . . . So get out.' His eyes gleamed with malice. 'You never honestly believed you'd got the better of *me*, did you?'

She left the studio in a hurry, drove straight to her bank. He had to be bluffing – how the hell could anyone open another person's private safety deposit box. Banks were places of trust, it was impossible.

She requested her box, went in a private cubicle to open it, stared in dismay. It was empty.

She wanted to scream. It was so unfair.

'Who has been to my box?' she asked the clerk.

He looked at her in surprise. 'No one m'am.'

What did he know? Nothing. She could complain, make a fuss, it would all be to no avail.

Tears of frustration filled her eyes. Men. They had been screwing her all her life – if not physically then meta-phorically.

She wanted revenge. Lew Margolis was not going to get the better of her. No way.

A plan was already forming in her mind. A plan that would need a certain amount of working out.

She strode out of the bank to her car. Thoughtfully she drove home.

Al King was sitting in his chauffeured limo outside her house. He leapt out when he saw her and started mouthing apologies. She brushed past him. 'Go fuck yourself, Al,' she muttered, and slammed the door in his face.

☆

Doris Andrews said, 'This is a very sweet house, dear.'

'Thank you,' replied Dallas demurely. 'Can I fix you something to drink?'

Doris laughed softly in her breathy fashion. 'Much too early for me. But maybe an orange juice if it's freshly squeezed.'

'Sure,' said Dallas brightly, 'it will only take me a sec. Why don't you sit out by the pool?'

Doris said, 'What a sweet pool,' and took herself outside, and settled on a lounger.

Dallas rushed into the kitchen, grabbed some oranges, cut them in half, and squeezed the juice out.

She reached for a half-smoked joint she had left in an ashtray, and dragged deeply. It was her third one that day. She knew the only way she would be able to go through with her plan was if she was well stoned.

It had been easy to persuade Doris to come to her house. One phone call. A hint of promise.

The difficult part had been getting Linda to go along with the plan. 'Not again!' she had complained. 'I think you're playing it too close. Lew Margolis is obviously a man with connections – it could be *dangerous*.'

Dallas had been her most persuasive, and a reluctant Linda was ready to do her part.

The orange juice was squeezed. Dallas poured it into a glass crushing a speed pill in with it. Wouldn't do any harm in case Doris suddenly developed inhibitions. She carried the juice outside. 'I should be very cross with you,' she said, 'you've been telling your husband things about us that aren't strictly true.'

Doris widened blue eyes – a famous screen gesture that had saved her from countless villians. 'I only hinted. Just the teensiest little hint. You see I was jealous,' she giggled self-consciously, 'when I saw you leaving my party with that – that – monster!'

Dallas said, 'Your teeniest little hint got me fired – you know that? Booted out of the series. Is that what you wanted?'

Doris looked immediately contrite. 'Oh no! My dear, I'm so sorry. I had no idea . . .'

Not much – thought Dallas – you conniving jealous bitch. You saw me leave with Al after turning *you* down, and your ego couldn't take that. So you screwed me – but good.

'I didn't think you did,' she said, 'but all the same . . .' she shrugged, 'I'm out, and I just don't know what to do.'

Doris quickly said, 'I'll talk to Lew, I'll tell him I made a mistake.'

'You know it won't do any good. You told me yourself how jealous of you he is.'

Doris nodded sadly. 'That's true. Oh dear, what have I done?'

You've used *your* power – just like your husband used his. And you both think you've fixed me. But I am no shrinking out-of-town hick. You'll both see how smart I am.

Dallas patted her gently on the hand. 'Don't worry about it, drink your orange juice. Do you mind if I swim?'

'I feel so badly . . .' Doris started to say. But the words stuck in her throat as Dallas stepped out of the shorts and halter top she was wearing, revealing her totally beautiful naked body.

Doris stared.

Dallas ran her hands casually over her own body, lingering for a second on her erect nipples. 'You going to swim?' she asked Doris. 'It's quite secluded here, au natural is the order of the day.' She reached out and started to unbutton Doris's silk shirt. 'Here, let me help you.'

Doris didn't move. Dallas finished unbuttoning the shirt, took it off her. Then she unhooked the white bra Doris was wearing. It was padded, giving Doris curves she didn't possess.

Slowly Doris lifted her hands and cupped Dallas' full breasts. She said, her voice no more than a breathy whisper, 'I knew you would be beautiful,' and she pulled the younger woman close to her so that she could take her breast in her mouth.

Dallas closed her eyes tightly. Just pretend you're not even here. Just hope that Linda is already in action capturing photos that Lew Margolis will *really* find interesting.

☆

Cody went along with Dallas' request that he release no statement to the press. 'It would be better coming from us than from the studio,' he suggested.

She was adamant. It was almost as if she expected some miracle to happen and that she would be reinstated as 'Man Made Woman'. Unbeknown to her, the studio had not cancelled the series at all. They had merely replaced Dallas with another girl. Chuck had told Cody. 'It's ridiculous!' he had exploded on the phone. 'How can you change the star of a television series halfway through? Anyway Dallas was marvellous in it – they've replaced her with a girl who has nothing – the public will never buy it. Everyone here thinks Lew Margolis has blown his stack.'

Cody agreed. He remembered the outcry when the 'Bionic Woman' had guested on a couple of 'Six Million Dollar Men' segments and been killed off. The public just wouldn't accept it, and to its cost the studio who owned the series had had to bring her back to life.

Cody knew that when the series was shown the public would want Dallas. As far as he was concerned Lew Margolis had gone stark raving mad. The man was a fool, and eventually he would have to pay for it – Cody would personally see to that.

Meanwhile he had Aarron Mack to worry about. He was anxious to meet with Dallas and have a private discussion.

'I have heard certain disturbing rumours,' he had told Cody on the phone, 'and I wish to see the young lady and discuss them. I will send my plane for her to meet me in Palm Springs tomorrow.'

'I'll come with her,' Cody said.

'I'd sooner meet with her alone.'

Cody had a bad feeling. His gut reaction was not in good shape. Either that or it was his developing ulcer.

☆

Linda lit a cigarette. Her hand was shaking.

God! Miss Sophistication. One lesbian scene and she was a mass of nerves.

How could Dallas do it? It was difficult to understand. This whole blackmail thing was going too far. Once – to help a friend out. Twice – Linda was disgusted with herself. It was sickening. And to have had to have watched Dallas and Doris Andrews together. Ugh! She was certainly no prude. But two women together . . . It was not that they had done much of anything – a man and a woman doing the same things would have been fairly tame stuff – but two women doing it. Linda couldn't reconcile herself to *that*. Lesbian tendencies she had never had, and this had put her off forever.

She went into the bathroom and lifted the photos out of the solution. They were good. Clear. Revolting.

Dallas had shut herself in the bedroom and Linda was glad. In a way she was almost embarrassed to face her. It made things somehow different between them.

As soon as she had finished the pictures she wanted to get away. Dallas had asked too much in return for sleeping on her couch. The very next day she would find herself an apartment.

☆

Dallas lay on her bed staring blankly into space.

What had happened to her Californian dream? A nice home, a steady career, a baby. What did she want now?

She had her house, that was okay. But the desire to have a baby was gone. Who needed to bring children into a world like this? Career was important too. The desire to be someone. And she enjoyed working. When she was before the cameras she could really forget everything and become the character she was playing. So why couldn't they all leave her alone? Why did she always have to be on her guard, scheming, planning, plotting a way to come out on top?

Bobbie had known how to escape the pressures of just existing. Heroin. It had killed her. Maybe she was better off.

Dallas turned over and lay on her stomach. She had showered when Doris left, scrubbed her body thoroughly. Sex became more and more of a hassle. She hated it. She went through the motions with a complete lack of feeling. The scene with Doris had been particularly difficult.

Why did they want her? The face. The body. Is that all they saw?

She shut her eyes, squeezing them tightly so that the tears that had suddenly formed couldn't escape.

Cody had phoned earlier to tell her that Aarron Mack requested her presence in Palm Springs the next day. What did he want?

She reached on her bedside table for the bottle of Seconal pills – took one – two – three.

Soon she was asleep.

The insistent ringing of the telephone woke her the next morning. She could hear the ringing, hoped that Linda would pick it up. Goddamn it. The phone kept ringing. She reached for it, mumbled hello.

It was Cody, cheerful and bright, reminding her that he would pick her up in an hour to take her to the airport.

'*Why* do I have to go?' she complained.

'Because we don't want to blow *this* deal – he needs jollying up.'

'Terrific. Play with his balls and lick his ass.'

'I'll ignore that. You know how to handle him.'

'Sure.' Sourly she hung up.

She got out of bed, stretched, yawned. She felt terrible – heavy and hungover. She reached for a joint, lit up. Soon she felt better.

There was an envelope and a note from Linda in the kitchen. The envelope contained a set of photos complete with negatives. The note read, 'Here you go – guess they are what you wanted. Got great deal on apartment – so am moving. Will call you. Thanks for everything – Linda.' Dallas crumpled the note in her hand. She didn't blame her.

Critically she examined the photos. They were better than she had hoped. Doris revealed as Lew had never seen her before, and obviously not a reluctant participant. Good.

She carefully chose two, sealed them in an envelope, and addressed it to Lew marked 'Personal and Private.' Then she sealed the negatives in another envelope, which she planned to deposit at a bank near the airport under a false name. Let Lew find them there. The remainder of the photographs she hid around the house. As long as the negatives were safe it didn't matter if Lew found these.

She dressed. Smoked another joint. Packed a small bag in case she stayed overnight in Palm Springs.

Cody picked her up on time, chatted inanely all the way to the airport. He thought he was cheering her up. Before boarding Aarron's plane she squeezed his hand, 'Don't worry, kid, everything's cool.'

'I know, I know,' he agreed, 'let me know what time you'll be back and I'll meet you.'

She giggled. She suddenly felt great.

Cody realized she was stoned, but it was too late to stop her from going.

'Don't call me, I'll call you,' she chuckled. 'Be a good fella.'

He didn't like to see her in that kind of state. He wished he was still around to look after her. 'Watch it,' he said sternly. 'Don't do anything you don't want to. Remember we have a contract, he has to honour it.'

'Course I'll remember.' She winked lewdly. 'I won't even fuck him unless he asks me!'

She slept on the short flight to Palm Springs. Slept in the car on the way to Aarron's estate.

He sat beside the swimming pool, a gnarled, nut-brown figure in snappy red-striped bathing shorts.

He kissed her hand, offered a choice of champagne or mineral water. 'Are you hungry?' he asked solicitously 'Shall we eat lunch now or later?'

She opted for later, changed into a bikini, and flopped out beside him, immediately falling asleep.

He watched her sleep. How could he believe what he had heard about her? She breathed deeply, her magnificent breasts almost escaping from the brief bikini top. He wanted to reach over and touch her. He didn't care what he had heard. He was determined to possess her.

She slept for almost three hours, then she woke, stretched,

rolled into the swimming pool, splashed around, emerged, and said, 'I'm sorry Aarron. Did I sleep for long?'

He nodded, 'You must have been tired, it's past four. I'll tell them to serve lunch.'

'Great! I'm famished.' She excused herself, went into the house, got a joint from her purse and smoked it in the John.

Lobster, caviar, and smoked salmon with an array of salads waited. She ate heartily, and then polished off half a delicious chocolate cake.

'That was good!' she exclaimed.

'You were hungry,' Aarron stated.

'Yeah. I guess I've been working too hard. It's really nice to have a few days off.'

'A few days off?' He paused, obviously puzzled, 'but I thought—'

'Oh, don't tell me you've heard the rumour about me being off the series too.'

'Yes.'

'Don't believe it. I'm having a week off.'

'But Lew Margolis telephoned me himself.'

Dallas laughed. 'Poor old Lew. I think he's getting senile. It's all a mistake. I told him I needed a rest, he seems to think I want more money. Everything's a bit confused, but I can promise you I'll be back on the set next Monday. By the way, what was it you wanted to discuss with me?'

She had Aarron completely puzzled. He had prepared a speech, but it didn't seem to fit now. Finally he said, 'I am really most perplexed.'

'Why?' she asked, pouring herself some more champagne.

Aarron shook his head sadly. 'I have known Lew Margolis for many years. We are not close friends but we are old acquaintances. I should warn you that he is saying some very strong things about you.'

Dallas widened her eyes in surprise. 'About me?'

'Of course I do not believe what he is saying,' Aarron hastened to add, 'but all the same, they are disturbing things, and I think we should discuss them. You see, being the Mack girl will identify you very closely with all the Mack products, and should there be even the slightest grain of truth in what Lew is saying...' He paused to have a short coughing fit. 'I can be quite frank with you, Dallas. Mack cosmetics is my company, but I am getting on in years, I have had to make certain tax provisions for my family. I have a son and a daughter, they are both married. I have five grandchildren.'

'So?' questioned Dallas impatiently. She didn't want his life history, she wanted him to get to the point.

'I make the final decisions, but there is a family board of directors at Mack cosmetics. They are happy that you are to be the Mack girl, but any scandal . . .'

Dallas laughed. 'I thought we had a contract?' she questioned mockingly.

'Oh yes,' agreed Aarron, 'with options of course.'

'Of course.'

'If anything Lew Margolis is saying about you is true . . . Then you would be paid up to the first option . . .'

'And not used.' She finished for him.

'Exactly.'

She sipped her champagne, her green eyes glinting dangerously. 'So tell me, Aarron, what exactly is Lew saying about me?'

He looked uncomfortable. 'I don't believe it. I know it can't possibly be true.'

'But you felt you had to ask me anyway, just in case.' Suddenly she hated him, sitting in his Palm Springs mansion so rich and secure.

'Yes.' He was relieved she was so understanding.

'Spit it out, Aarron, I can't wait to hear.'

'He said that you were a prostitute. That you and a coloured girl used to work together. Also that you were a lesbian and the two of you used to give shows.'

Dallas threw back her head and roared with laughter. 'He said *that* – about *me*. It's unbelievable! And anyway, even if there was the slightest bit of truth in it, how the hell would *he* know? The whole thing is utterly ridiculous – I mean it's absolutely laughable!'

'I knew it couldn't possibly be true,' said Aarron quickly. 'I just wanted to hear you deny it.'

'Deny it? It's hardly worth denying, it's so ludicrous. Who could possibly believe it? I told you the man is getting senile.'

'If you wish I can have my lawyer draft a letter on your behalf to restrain him from repeating such a vicious story. It would be best to stop him now.'

'Yes. I think we should.'

Aarron leaned across the table and patted her fondly on the shoulder. 'I knew there was no truth in it. I remember in New York when we first met how you wouldn't even let me touch you.'

She lowered her eyes. 'I'm like that, Aarron. A man must be prepared to wait with me.'

He sighed happily. 'Yes, yes. I understand. In spite of your looks, at heart you are really just an old-fashioned girl.'

She hid a smile that threatened to break into uncontrollable laughter.

'Yes, Aarron, you are so right. At heart I'm really just an old-fashioned girl.'

At Aarron's request she decided to spend the night. Why go rushing back to LA. For what? Anyway she wanted to wait until Lew received the photos. Let him stew a little before she contacted him. Let him call Cody and beg to have her back on the series. Let him suffer when he saw the intimate pictures of his wife.

Aarron wanted to take her out to dinner, but she pleaded a headache, and retired to the guest suite, where she sat in bed watching TV and smoking another joint.

There was an interview with Al King arriving in Las Vegas. He was there for a big charity concert the next day. She stared at his image on the screen, dragging on the joint, and beginning to get the feeling that seemed reserved only for him. He was a bastard. He had stood her up for a skinny bag. Screw him.

Why not? He was available. Why not get him out of her system once and for all?

Yeah – why not? She had nothing better to do.

She grinned. She could just imagine his surprise when she turned up in Las Vegas.

☆

56

Cristina telephoned Louis Baptista. He was delighted to hear from her, even though she had given him a most abrupt and hurtful brush several months previously.

'Can we see each other again, Louis?' she asked sweetly.

He was hesitant, he had started to date other girls, started to forget the hurt. 'What did you have in mind?' he questioned falteringly.

'I don't know. I've been thinking about you a lot. Maybe we could go riding in Tijuca forest like we used to.'

'Yes, all right.'

'If you *want* to, that is.'

'You know I want to.' His voice was gruff.

'Tomorrow?'

'I'll collect you from your house at noon.'

'That would be fine.' She banged the phone down, and stuck her tongue out at Nino, who stood by her side. 'Satisfied?'

'Excellent. I bet he was thrilled.'

'Of course.'

'Is he still mad for your childish body?'

'I expect so.'

'I told you it would be easy.'

'I *knew* it would be easy. I just didn't want to do it.' She threw her arms around Nino. 'Do I *have* to see him?'

'Only for a few weeks. It won't be so bad. Then when it's all over, if you still want to, we can go to your parents and tell them we want to get married. And if they don't approve, we'll do it anyway.'

She hugged him. 'I wish we could do it now.'

He removed her arms. 'You know that's impossible. Listen, I have a meeting this afternoon. You had better run on home.'

'Can't I come with you?'

'No.'

'Why not? If I'm going to be a part of it why can't I come?'

'Because they wouldn't like it.'

She pouted. 'Who are *they*? And why wouldn't *they* like it?'

'How many times do I have to explain things to you? Before you can become a member of the organization you have to have *proved* yourself. After all you are not one of us.'

'I should think setting up these two burglaries would have proved whose side I was on.'

'*I* know whose side you are on, and after the kidnapping – if all goes well – you'll be accepted. But not now – not yet. Don't push.'

'All right. But when I'm your wife they'll *have* to accept me. *Then* I'll be one of you.'

He laughed bitterly. 'Yes. Poor.'

'I'll go home now. Shall I come over after seeing Louis tomorrow?'

Nino hurriedly said, 'No. Certainly not. Concentrate on Louis. I don't want to see you for a week.'

'A week! Nino, that's impossible. I couldn't live that long without seeing you.'

'In three weeks, if this is successful, you won't have to live two minutes without me. Isn't that worth giving up something for?'

She sighed. 'I suppose so . . .'

He cupped her face and kissed her gently. 'A little something to be getting on with. Well – child, I'll see you in a week.'

'If I live, and don't call me child.'

'I'll call you woman when you have proved that you are.'

'I thought I had done *that*.'

'Maybe – we'll see how you get on with Louis.'

She stuck out her tongue again. 'Pig!'

'Child!' He guided her to the door.

'I'll phone you every day,' she said.

'No. Not even that. I want *all* your energies to go in *his* direction.'

'But, Nino . . .'

He placed a finger on her lips and moved her gently out the door. 'Goodbye, my love, do a good job.'

When she was finally gone he let out a groan of relief. A whole week! It was too wonderful to contemplate. He would be free to see Talia, spend some time with her, sleep with her. A solid diet of Cristina was so boring. Now if it had been her mother . . .

Louis was essential to the plan. As Carlos Baptista's son he would obviously have access to places Al King would be – and access was the most important part. Unbeknown to Cristina the kidnap had been planned. Why should he tell her? Who was she but a stupid little rich girl whose mind could be manipulated by his body. And his body was going to become famous and powerful as a result of the Al King kidnap.

He smiled. When this plan proceeded to its triumphant conclusion he would no longer have to tout his body. He would automatically become one of the leaders. He knew it would be so. Besides, his fortune had been told, and it was in the cards.

Nino was confident that the cards never lied.

☆

The week dragged by as far as Cristina was concerned. Louis, thrilled to be reinstated in her life, was happy to spend every day with her.

They went riding in Tijuca forest twice. They took the cable car to Sugar Loaf Mountain, which was a really tourist thing to do, but which Louis said would be fun. They went to the Botanical Gardens, the Museum of Modern Art, the Jockey Club, the Yacht Club.

Cristina found herself mixing once more with all her old friends. How childish they all seemed to her. How unaware of what was happening in the world. All they seemed concerned with was parties, new cars, and having fun.

The girls would group together and giggle about the boys. '*He* tried to put his hand up my shirt.' 'Santiago is a *great* kisser.' Such silly things. Cristina could hardly believe that only months before *she* had been a part of this juvenile group. Oh, the things she could tell them now! How she could shock them!

One afternoon she was cornered by Marella Bogato who insisted on telling her the gory details of the robbery her family had experienced. 'It was so dreadful, Cristina, you just can't imagine. They cut off the poor dog's head – *cut it off.* Then they wrote terrible things all over the walls *in his blood.*'

Cristina shuddered. She was sure Marella must be exaggerating. Nino and his partners in crime couldn't possibly be that cruel. Thank God she had never allowed them to rob *her* house.

'These people must be sick,' Marella continued. 'They must be animals. Mama has had a complete breakdown, and we are selling the house. It's not what they took, Cristina, it's just the horrible feeling that their senseless violence has left.'

For a moment Cristina felt sorry for what she had done. Then she thought of Nino – of his impassioned appeals for equality – his sincereness about his cause. He was right. To redistribute some of the wealth was a good thing.

She ached to be with him. Louis was sweet, he had always been sweet. But he was a baby. A rich, spoiled baby.

On the day before she was due to see Nino, Louis took her to an open-air concert outside the Opera House. After, he said he wanted to surprise her, and he drove his red sports car up into the mountains to a small country house his parents kept there. He had obviously been there earlier in the day because the table was laid for two, with candles waiting to be lit, and a cold supper in the fridge.

'Surprise!' he said. 'I wanted tonight to be special.'

'But I thought we were going dancing.'

'We can go later if you want. I just thought it would be nice if we were alone together. We always seem to be surrounded by people.'

Suddenly he was all over her. 'I like you, Cristina. You know how much I like you. I thought for a while that we were finished – you became so cold. Now we're together again I want to ask your father's permission for us to be married next year.' He reached into his jacket pocket and produced a small box. 'Here, I've brought you a ring. I love you, Cristina, I always have. We were meant to be married.' He plunged his mouth down on hers, kissing her frantically.

Nino had not instructed her how to deal with *this* situation. She had another two weeks to go. If she shoved Louis away and told him her answer was no, that might spoil everything. Instinct told her she had to play him along. So although she didn't feel like it, she kissed him back, and let his hands linger for a moment on her breasts before pushing him away.

'Don't, Louis.' she reprimanded him sharply.

'I'm sorry. I don't mean to take liberties with you. It's just that I want you so much, I always have.'

Idly she glanced at the ring he had presented her with. It was a heart-shaped sapphire surrounded with diamonds. It must have cost a fortune. It *was* beautiful. She took it from the box and slipped it on her finger. It fitted perfectly. She could wear it for two weeks . . . Give it back to him when she told him that they couldn't marry.

'Do you like it?' Louis asked anxiously. 'If you don't we could change it.'

'It's very pretty.'

'*You're* very pretty.' And he was grabbing her again, exploring her mouth with his tongue, allowing his hands to slip from her shoulders to her breasts.

In spite of herself she felt excited. He wanted her so much that she couldn't help feeling a surge of power. She was a woman and he didn't even know it. How surprised he would be if he knew how experienced she was.

She had noticed the bulge in his trousers, and that gave her a feeling of power too.

Louis was a good catch. Marie Therese had been mad about him for years, and Marie Therese was much prettier than she was, but it was *she* he wanted.

'Have you ever been with a woman?' she gasped, pushing him off once more, and watching him to gauge his reaction.

'No,' he said, flushing.

'But you must have,' she insisted. 'All boys of your age must have had *some* sort of experience.'

He turned away from her. 'I don't think I should tell you.'

'Of course you must tell me. If we are to be engaged, I must know everything. There can be no secrets.'

'When I was seventeen my father took me to a whore house.'

'How exciting!'

'Cristina! It wasn't exciting. It was disgusting. Old women with floppy bellies. I did what I had to do and never went back. My father thought that made me a man.'

'And did it?'

'It made me sick. I swore I would wait until I found the girl I loved.'

'And here I am,' Cristina teased.

Louis was very serious. 'Yes. Here you are. And I am glad that I have waited, because we will be able to start out together. It's the way it should be.'

She wanted to laugh in his face. How young and naive and romantic his words were. Poor Louis. He was such a baby.

☆

Evita could not understand it. One moment her daughter was starry-eyed about the boy called Nino – the next – Louis was back in her life.

Jorge was triumphant. 'I told you not to worry about her,' he crowed. 'She probably quarrelled with Louis because he tried to take liberties with her. Now he realizes he cannot get away with that kind of behaviour. Our daughter is a good girl.'

'Perhaps,' mused Evita. But she wasn't satisfied. Something wasn't quite right, and she decided to go ahead with plans to take Cristina off for a long trip somewhere.

Her plans were shattered when Cristina flashed an engagement ring under her nose.

'Louis wishes to meet with poppa,' her daughter said. 'Some old-fashioned idea about getting his permission.'

'It's wonderful. I'm so thrilled for you, my darling,' Evita said. But still she had a feeling of disquiet. Cristina did not appear to be particularly excited at the prospect of being engaged to one of the richest young men in Brazil.

'We'll throw an engagement party,' Evita said. 'We'll make it a marvellous occasion. Would you like that?'

'Oh, mama, I don't want a fuss. Can we wait a few weeks?'

'Certainly, dear.' But Evita couldn't imagine why she would want to wait. 'Whatever happened to that young man you brought home? What was his name? Nino?'

'How should I know?' replied Cristina crossly. 'He was just a friend.'

Evita was quick to catch the evasive quality of her daughter's voice. Somehow, in spite of the engagement, she felt that they had not heard the last of Nino.

☆

He lay on his crumpled bed and grinned and said, 'You didn't waste any time then?'

Cristina grinned back as she stood beside the bed. '*Some* people find me irresistible.'

He patted a space beside him. 'Come join me and collect your reward.'

'I can't. I have to get home, Louis is picking me up. We're spending the day at his house.'

'How nice. No time for me any more. I can see you did manage to live the week through without me.'

'Nino! I'm doing it for us. *You* were the one who said I have to concentrate on Louis absolutely.'

Nino raised his eyebrows. Yes he had said it, but he hadn't expected her to take him quite so literally. He had imagined she would come running to him, unable to wait to leap into his bed. He hadn't wanted to sleep with her, but he had steeled himself to the fact that he must. Now she obviously didn't want to. Was he losing his touch?

He rolled off the bed and held her loosely round the waist. 'Time for a kiss at least?'

She giggled. 'Please! I'm engaged to another man. We can have none of this.'

Suddenly he was angry. 'Are you sure you are not taking this game too seriously?'

She was contrite, showering his face with kisses. 'I'm sorry – sorry – sorry. I'm only doing what you *wanted* me to do.' Secretly she was thrilled, because Nino seemed almost jealous.

'Yes, of course,' he said. 'So what information do you have for me?'

'Plenty. I've found out everything I can. Louis thinks that I am Al King's greatest fan! I can't even stand him – my mother buys all his records.'

'Well?' questioned Nino, impatiently.

'Let me see now.' She paused provocatively, enjoying her small moment of power. 'He's arriving in Rio the day before the concert . . .'

'What time?'

'I don't know.'

'Find out. It's important.'

'He's travelling in his own plane.'

'Who with?'

'I don't know yet, but apparently Louis' father will be getting a list. Mr Baptista will be meeting him at the airport with television, photographers – a whole big deal. Then in the evening there's to be a big party for him, to which I am naturally invited.'

'Good. Be sure to meet him. Be sure he will remember you.'

'How do I do that?'

'We'll think of something, but it's important that he knows you.'

'Why?'

'I'm supposed to be asking the questions. I have a lot to work out.'

'Anyway – I don't know what he'll do the next day – but in the evening there is the concert, and apparently he'll be leaving for the airport immediately after. Something about he's nervous of crowds and wants to get out before the people leave the stadium. I think Louis said a helicopter will be waiting to take him to the airport.'

'You've done very well.'

'I try to please. When do you think you will take him?'

'I don't know.'

'If you manage it before the concert I guess they'll pay you the money quickly. How many hours will you hold him? You won't hurt him, will you?'

Nino shook his head. How stupid she was. 'Everything will be fine. Nobody will get hurt.'

'I've got to rush. Can I see you again this week?'

'Phone me as soon as you find anything else out.'

She kissed him. 'I love you so much, Nino. I'll be glad when this is all over and we can be together.' She left quickly.

Nino sat thoughtfully on the side of his bed. She was playing games. She didn't realize this was for real. She didn't even realize the major part she was going to have to play in it.

Oh well – she would learn. If she wanted him she was going to have to pay for the privilege. And she would. He would make sure of that.

☆

57

Dallas hailed a cab at Las Vegas airport. 'Take me to your leader!' she giggled at the driver.

'Hey, lady – you wanna go somewhere – tell me – I'll be happy to oblige. You wanna play games find another cab, I gotta livin' to make.'

She mock saluted. 'Yes, officer.'

'So – where to?'

It suddenly occurred to her that she had no idea where Al was appearing. 'Big charity telethon show,' she mumbled – Christ but she was stoned. 'Al King.'

He gunned the cab into action. Fortunately he seemed to know what she was talking about. She was delightfully out of it – spaced halfway to the moon.

She giggled quietly to herself. Wouldn't do to annoy the driver. 'Mustn't annoy the driver . . .' she found herself mumbling out loud.

He clacked his lips in disgust and ignored her. Dumb hooker. Any woman arriving unescorted in Vegas was automatically a dumb hooker. And this one was worse than most – with her messy clothes and tangled hair. Pretty enough – but who the hell did she hope to pick up in the state she was in?

'I've been here before,' Dallas announced. 'Came here with a friend called Bobbie coupla years back. She died, y'know.'

'I didn't know that,' the driver replied, his sarcasm lost on her.

She shook her head. 'It doesn't matter.' She tried to recollect her day. It seemed she had just woken up and here she was. No. Somewhere along the way it had been a long day, and now it was night. She giggled quietly, and reached for the remains of a joint stuffed in her jeans pocket. She lit up.

'Put that out,' snapped the driver, 'you think I wanna get busted?'

'Think I wanna get busted!' mimicked Dallas.

'Watch it, sister.'

She started to sing, 'I ain't your sister whacha say to that mister?' Then she laughed so hard she couldn't continue singing. Wasn't life fun? Why had she never realized it before? 'I was in Palm Springs this morning. Woke up there – beautiful day, so I swam, lay around in the sun.'

'Why didn't you stay there?' asked the cab driver sourly.

'You know something – I nearly did. But hey – how would *you* like to fuck an old guy of seventy?'

He swerved the cab over to the side of the road with a great mashing of brakes. 'Out!' he commanded. 'I don't havta listen to your foul language in my cab. I gotta daughter your age.'

'Oh Christ!' muttered Dallas.

'*Out!*' he screamed.

'Shit! Don't go gettin' your balls in a sweat, sugar! Hey – I sound just like Bobbie. You know Bobbie?'

He was red in the face.

Dallas climbed out of the cab, and he threw her bag out after her.

'Scum!' he muttered.

'Bum!' she replied, still laughing, unperturbed at being dumped at the side of the road.

Yes. She could remember Palm Springs. She had left there sometime in the afternoon, been flown to Los Angeles in Aarron's private jet. At LA airport she had booked herself out on the next flight to Vegas. Didn't want to see anyone. Didn't want anyone to know where she was.

Let them all sweat. She would return when *she* was ready.

On the plane she had met a lovely lady with freaked-out hair and granny glasses, who had sold her a fine supply of Qualudes and some good grass. Fortunate, because she was starting to run out.

Why had it taken her so long to find out what a good time you could have when you were stoned? She had smoked joints on and off for years without much effect. But suddenly – jeeze – use enough – mix in a few amphetamines, a little speed, and you could be flying in no time at all. It was a *wonderful* feeling. Pure. Clear. Mind-expanding. For the first time she could understand Kip Rey's hang-up. And to think she had been the one to criticize him, put him down, when all he had been doing was escaping to wonderland. Of course, he had died. Accident. Unfortunate.

A truck was pulling over to the side of the road, the driver whistling at her. 'Need wheels, baby?'

She smiled. Nice, kind guy. 'Sure.'

'Climb aboard.'

She threw her bag into his cab, jumped in.

'You got a great pair,' he said. 'They for real?'

''Bout as real as your balls.'

He laughed, jamming the big truck into motion. 'Where to, big eyes?'

'Caesars Palace,' she said mentioning the first place that came to mind.

'I'll give you door-to-door service, 'cos I like you. What you gonna give *me* in exchange?'

'Whatever turns you on, sugar sweets.' Pure Bobbie dialogue. It amused her to use it.

He opened his legs slightly, patted his crotch. 'I could use a hand job.'

Wasn't this where she had come in?

She waited until the truck stopped at a traffic light, jumped out.

'What the f . . .' began the driver.

'You're too late,' shouted Dallas, 'I gave it up. Give *yourself* a hand job, sport. You might enjoy it!'

She looked around. Where the hell was she? Shit. What a lousy idea *this* trip had been.

☆

Three numbers, but they were screaming for more. Al looked to the side of the stage and shrugged. The sooner he was off the sooner he could get back to the tables. Fifty thousand down was a bummer – a loser's trip. He was a winner – and he was going to win it back – every goddamn dollar.

The redhead had been the catalyst, if she hadn't huffed and puffed all over his dice he would have won. She was a definite loser – thank Christ he hadn't touched *her*. She probably would have given him a dose.

One more chorus of 'Bad Black Alice'. These charity telethons were a pain in the ass. But he had agreed to do it. Every goddamn star in California had agreed to do it. The money was being raised for invalid children and as far as Al was concerned that was one charity you did anything for. Top priority.

Karmen Rush was waiting at the side of the stage to follow him on. He ignored her.

Christ it was hot – he was sweating like Bernie. Jeeze!

Luke was waiting with towels. Paul was waiting with a choked expression – he was more pissed off about Melanie giving him the boot than Al was about Edna. Poor sod. He should be dancing in the streets with joy – after all *he* had the children – his prime concern.

Al knew what he was going to do. He had made up his mind. After South America he was going to return to Los Angeles. He was going to buy himself the best goddam house around – and he was going to do the movie – give it a try. Then he was going to take six months off to write some new songs – stuff he really wanted to do.

Beyond that he didn't know. By that time his divorce should be through. He would be free.

Free to what? Fuck America?

He was sober again. Cold stone sober. The telethon hadn't given him much of a high. After playing such large venues a small audience was a bit of a come-down – millions had been watching him on television – but that wasn't the kick. The real thrill was having them out there before you. Feeling them. Smelling them. Peaking with them. The ultimate orgasm. He was looking forward to Rio. Two hundred thousand in one fell swoop. What an experience *that* should be.

The patrol car cruised to a stop beside Dallas, and one of the policemen leaned out. 'What are you doing out here?' he asked.

'Some creep gave me a lift and tried to rape me. I jumped out and here I am!'

'Hop in,' the cop said, 'where you headed?'

Thankfully she climbed in the back of the car.

'I want to get to the big charity telethon that's going on here tonight.'

'You got a ticket?'

'No, but I got a friend.' Stay straight, she warned herself, don't let them see you are out of your head.

'You hitch all the way here?'

Did she look *that* bad? Come to think of it she hadn't looked in a mirror all day. She had just thrown a T-shirt and jeans over her bikini when she left Palm Springs – all right in a hot little asshole of a town during the day – but not quite right for now. 'Yeah,' she said. Who needed conversations?

'You looking for a job here?'

'Not really.'

'It's a tough city if you don't have a job. My cousin can always use pretty waitresses – Joe Vondello's on the strip – tell him Mac sent you.'

'Thank you, Mac.'

He laughed self-consciously. 'Any time.'

They dropped her outside the hotel where the telethon was taking place.

'I'll stop by Joe's in a coupla days – see how you're doing,' the cop said.

'Thanks,' she waved. Wow! Close! They could have taken her in for being out of control of her own body! She giggled at that, and wandered in a side entrance of the hotel and found a ladies' room.

Her appearance in the mirror sent her into gales of laughter. She did look a wreck. No make-up, uncombed hair, staring wild eyes. She fished some dark shades out of her bag and covered her tell-tale eyes. Then she popped a couple of pills, and realized that she hadn't eaten all day, and the nagging pain she had suddenly acquired was hunger.

She drifted out amongst the slot machines and roulette wheels. 'Where can I find Al King?' she asked a security guard.

He looked at her blankly. 'Who?'

'Forget it. Where's the telethon?'

'In the Princess Room – it's all full – booked weeks ago.'

'Yeah?' She weaved slightly, moved away from him, and on impulse sat down at a roulette table. She fished in her bag, found a fifty and slid it over to the house man. He handed her a stack of dollar chips in exchange. She piled half of it on twenty-nine. The other half on thirty-five. Twenty-nine came up. She had won just under nine hundred dollars. 'Let it ride,' she said.

The houseman gave her an imperceptible wink from

beneath his green-tinted head shade, and spun the wheel. Twenty-nine showed again.

A buzz went around the table. The houseman paid her thirty thousand six hundred and twenty-five dollars in placques. She tipped him the odd six hundred and twenty-five. The pit boss stepped forward to see what was going on.

'My lucky night,' laughed Dallas. Wow! Even money was easy to make when you were stoned!

'Dallas?' a voice questioned, 'Dallas babe. What the fucker-ooney *you* doin' in town?'

She turned to see Bernie Suntan. Big, fat, sweaty Bernie.

'I came to see Al,' she smiled, 'is he around?'

'For you he'll be around. You feel all right? You look a little shaky.'

'Terrific, just terrific.' She pushed her stool away from the table, went to stand up, felt sick. Then the room was spinning . . . spinning . . . spinning . . . And she blacked out.

As she fell the last words she heard were – 'Thirty thousand bucks . . . who wouldn't faint at winning that.'

☆

'You want to make the party?' Paul asked. 'Everyone's going to be there.'

Al stepped out of the shower. He felt refreshed.

'I'm going to give the tables my undivided attention,' he said. 'You want to join me?'

'Your undivided attention lost you fifty thousand dollars earlier. That's a lot of money.'

'You're telling the man who is just about to make one million dollars for two days' work that fifty thousand dollars is a lot of money?'

Paul frowned. 'Stop jerking off, Al. You owe a fortune in taxes in England, and I suppose Edna is going to squeeze you 'til your balls drop off.'

'Edna might have changed, but not that much. I will take a bet with you she asks for nothing.'

Paul laughed disbelievingly.

'As for my English tax situation – it's all in hand, isn't it? And now that I'm a tax exile . . .'

'You are?'

'I told you I'm not going back.'

'Then you should have left before April.'

'Now he tells me.'

'I've been telling you for years. You never wanted to leave before.'

'I had Edna to think of.'

'Since when did you ever think of Edna?'

Al began to dress. 'You know your problem?'

'Please tell me.'

'You need to get laid. You're becoming like an uptight old lady.'

'We can't all solve everything with a stiff prick.'

'We can't all get stiff pricks either. You got a problem there too, Paul?'

'I'm going to the party. Go lose all your money, you stupid fuck.' Paul stalked out.

Al felt sorry when his brother had gone. He knew he was going through a bad time what with Melanie giving him the push and Linda pulling a number about not wanting to resume their relationship. But Jesus! What was *he* having – a picnic?

The trouble with Paul was he thought he was perfect. Nobody was perfect. What Paul needed was to go out, get good and bombed, and jam it into some randy blonde. He thought he was too good to do that. That's what really pissed Al off – why was it okay for him and not good enough for Paul? Al could remember the days when they had gone at it together. Share and share alike. But his brother had changed through the years. He had gotten uptight.

The hell with it – what was he worrying about Paul for – he could look after himself. Let him go to the party and mix with the stars – personally he couldn't give a shit. What he had in mind was a good hot poker game. Should be easy enough to find *that* in Las Vegas.

He finished dressing and was just about to leave the suite when the phone rang. He indicated to Luke, who was reading a magazine in the living room, to pick it up. 'I'm not here,' he mouthed.

Luke picked up the phone, listened for a moment, turned to Al. 'I think you'll want to be here for this. It's Bernie Suntan – says he has that lady downstairs – the one you like.'

It was the longest sentence Al had ever heard Luke utter. 'What lady?'

'Dallas.'

'He says . . .'

Al grabbed the phone. 'Bernie? What's happening?'

'Like – your friend Dallas is here. She seems kinda out of it. I just hadda pick her up off the floor by the roulette table.'

Al couldn't imagine Dallas being any other way except in complete control. 'Is she ill?' he asked urgently.

'Well . . .' Bernie scratched his head and stared at Dallas – who was lolled out giggling on a chair in the manager's office. Who was he to tell Al she was stoned out of her head? 'I think she'd like to see you.'

'Bring her up – what are you calling me for, schmuck? You *know* I want to see her.'

'Sure,' agreed Bernie, banging down the phone. You could never do anything right for Al. If he had taken Dallas up to Al's suite without asking he would have gotten a right bollocking. 'Come on, sweetheart.' He took Dallas by the arm. 'The big man is waiting.'

She giggled. 'Mustn't keep him waiting, huh Bernie? Mustn't keep the great white master waiting.'

Bernie was disappointed. He had thought this one was different. The few times he had seen her she had appeared to have conducted herself with a certain amount of class. But now she was just like all the rest. He could imagine what would happen when Al got a load of her in this state. One bang and out. Anyway, they were off to South America in the morning . . . What the fuck . . . Al would have been much better off taking advantage of some of the numbers in his little black book. Did he have some hot numbers! After all – Los Angeles was *his* town, and he could have imported anything Al wanted to Vegas – anything!

He thanked the manager, and guided Dallas out of the office. If she was what Al wanted then she was what Al was going to get.

They made an incongruous couple. The fat man in the lewd 'I choked Linda Lovelace' T-shirt teamed with white bermudas and tennis shoes, and the giggling girl with a mass of tangled hair and dark glasses.

'You got your cheque somewhere safe?' Bernie asked. The manager had exchanged her chips for a more secure way of carrying her money.

She patted her jeans pocket. 'Yeah.'

They boarded the elevator, attracting curious stares. Dallas started to sing in an out-of-tune voice. She smiled at two middle west matrons and their gaping husbands. 'I'm a gonna get laid,' she announced, 'I'm a gonna make it with Mister Superstar himself. Isn't that exciting?'

The two women turned away, clicking their mouths in disgust. The men glanced at each other, grinning with embarrassment.

Bernie nudged her to shut up.

She nudged him back. 'For a man who choked Linda Lovelace you sure are shy.' She winked at the two men. 'Right, fellas?'

The elevator stopped and emptied out.

'What's the matter with you?' Bernie muttered, pressing the button for them to ascend even higher. 'You turned into some kind of exhibitionist?'

'My, my. What long words you know,' she drawled. 'Al teach them to you?'

He pressed his mouth into a tight line. Fresh broads he didn't need. The sooner Al was shot of this one the better.

☆

After stalking from his brother's room, Paul got to thinking that perhaps what Al had said was true. Perhaps he *did* need a woman. How long was it? Long enough. He had been choked and mortified to have suffered from a wet dream two evenings ago. A horrible experience, and something that had not happened to him since he was sixteen years old. Physically he needed a woman. For once in his life he would just have to do it without the mental stimuli.

He wondered for the fiftieth time what Linda was doing. She wasn't the type of woman to just sit around. She enjoyed sex – she wouldn't go this long without finding another partner. He hadn't had much success at winning her back. He knew it was because he was just offering her the same old deal. Now things were different. Now Melanie had forced his hand. *She* had left him. And he had what he wanted, he had his two children. How would Linda feel about becoming an instant mother? He wasn't too sure she would know how to handle it. He wasn't even sure any more if she would *want* to handle it. All that talk about how much she loved him . . . Of course if he phoned her, told her that *he* had left Melanie . . .

In the meantime he was going to follow big brother's advice and get laid.

☆

'Where is she?' Cody's voice on the phone was desperate.

'I don't know,' Linda replied. 'I moved out yesterday morning. How did you track me down?'

'I called your agency in New York. Are you sure you don't know where Dallas is?'

'Of course I don't know. If I did I would tell you. Anyway, I thought she was going to Palm Springs.'

'She did. Stayed there last night, and was flown back to LA on Aarron's plane this afternoon. She never arrived back at her house.'

Linda glanced at her watch. It was eleven in the evening. 'Maybe she's visiting some friends.'

'I know all her friends. I've checked them all out.'

'Maybe there are a few you don't know.'

He was defeated. There were probably legions he didn't know. 'Yes,' he agreed miserably. 'I do have to talk to her, it's really urgent. You have no idea where I could find her?'

'No idea. What's the panic anyway? Is she back on the series?'

He was surprised. 'How did you know?'

'Just a feeling . . .' Lew Margolis certainly hadn't wasted any time. One glimpse of his wife's picture . . .

'They want her at the studio first thing tomorrow – got to re-shoot this week's segment – they're already out three days.'

'She'll turn up, I wouldn't worry about Dallas, she can look after herself.'

He was irritable. 'I know *that*. The whole situation is so strange, it's almost like she knew Margolis would change his mind. You know she didn't want me to release a press statement, and she was right.'

Linda yawned. 'Sixth sense, I guess. Listen, Cody, I was just going to sleep, so if there's nothing else . . .'

'I'm sorry,' he was immediately contrite, 'I hope I didn't wake you. I just thought you would know where she was. Can I give you my number in case she contacts you?'

'She won't contact me. She has no idea where I am.'

'Did you two have a fight?'

'No. I just felt the time had come to move on. You know, being with Dallas the whole time can sometimes become stifling.'

She was telling *him*. Ruefully he said, 'Yes I do know that. What do you have now – an apartment?'

'One room on Larrabee. Very pretty, communal pool – you must come by sometime.'

'I'd like that.' He hesitated, then, 'If you're not busy for dinner tomorrow . . . Do you like the Aware Inn?'

'Lovely.'

He was pleased. 'I'll pick you up around eight then, and in the meantime if you hear anything . . .'

'I won't hesitate to call you.' She put the phone down and wondered why she had accepted a dinner date with him. He was nice – that's why. He was attractive and kind and thoughtful, and why the hell couldn't Paul be like him?

Cody hung up and wondered yet again what kind of game Lew Margolis was playing. He couldn't figure it out. What was the point of it all? And where was Dallas? Didn't she realize he would be worried about her? Didn't she care? He was finally facing the fact that she didn't. There was only one person in Dallas' life, and that was herself.

☆

'You're looking terrific,' Dallas giggled, 'horny and virile. Doesn't he look *great*, Bernie? A real sexy hunk of man! Hey Al – did you ever think of posing for one of those women's magazines – like *Playgirl* or *Viva*? I mean you *should* – you've got the body. Hasn't he got the body, Bernie? Great pectorals, I bet!'

Bernie backed out the door. 'I'll see you at the party, Al. Gotta rush now. Gotta change.'

'Oh – no more Linda Lovelace,' lamented Dallas. 'Shame! I bet she would have enjoyed being choked by you!' She kissed an amazed Al lightly on the cheek and wandered into the suite flopping down on the couch.

'She's out of it,' Bernie hissed. 'You want Luke should get rid of her?'

'Is she drunk?' Al asked.

'Stoned, baby – son-of-a-bitch stoned.'

'I'll handle it,' Al said shortly. 'Luke – you can take off, I won't be going out.'

Luke edged past Bernie. 'I'll get something to eat, then I'll be outside if you need me.'

Bernie said, 'Aw, Al, you should show your face at the party.'

'Forget it. Those things are a pain in the ass.'

'But . . .'

'Goodnight, Bernie.' He slammed the door in his face. Then he turned and walked slowly into the living room. Dallas was still on the couch. She had lit a joint and was dragging happily. She smiled at him, offered him a drag.

He shook his head.

'Well,' she said, 'wanna fuck now or later?'

He stared at her. This was the one woman he had desired and been unable to have. This was the one woman that was going to be different. She was different all right. She was full of surprises. *She* was speaking to him like *he* usually spoke to them.

So – here was the opportunity. Why wasn't he stripping off his clothes, going at it, and sending her out of his life? What was he waiting for?

He had wanted her desperately – he still did. But not like this, not while she was obviously spaced out and unaware of what was going on.

'What are you doing in Vegas?' he asked quietly.

'Came to see you, sugar sweets. Came to consummate our meeting of the minds.' She giggled uncontrollably. 'Came to get *fucked*. By the *King*. Al is King, isn't that what I'm always hearing? So prove it, man, show me. I'm ready, willing and able.' She broke into song, 'Ready, willing and able! Hey, sugar, come and kiss me, huh? Come and see if you're gonna be the one lights this baby's fire!'

'What happened? What got you into this state?'

'*State!* like *what* state?'

'Come on, you know what I mean.'

She rolled off the couch, bumped onto the floor, giggled, dropped the joint, attempted to stand, swayed against him. 'Shall I take my clothes off?' she slurred. 'Want to see what I'm offering you? I thought you *wanted* me. That's why I'm here babe, service with a smile – and no charge. You like that – no charge.'

He held her firmly by the shoulders. 'Where are you staying? I'm taking you home.'

She grinned. 'I am not staying anywhere. I am with you. Hey – you got any coke? May as well make this a big trip. Whatcha say?'

He guided her into the bedroom and eased her on to the bed. 'Why don't you rest a minute, you look tired. I'll get you some goodies . . .'

She threw her arms wide. 'Wow – whole room is spinning – like it's a whole roundabout trip.' She closed her eyes. 'Gotta make sure . . .' she mumbled, 'goddamn dyke . . . nice to be here . . .' She lapsed into sleep. He had known she would. Whatever she had been taking apart from the shit had finally knocked her out. Anyone could see she was exhausted. She looked terrible, unkempt and dirty.

He sat on the side of the bed and watched her. In the morning she probably wouldn't be talking to him again. If he had done what she wanted he *knew* she wouldn't have been talking to him.

Al King. Gentleman. When had *that* transformation taken place?

He gently removed her shoes, and pulled a cover over her. She was still muttering in her sleep, but nothing intelligible. He went in the other room and emptied out the contents of her bag. Amongst the jumble of clothes and make-up he found two bottles of pills and a tin with about eight rolled joints in. He confiscated them all. Then he called her house in Los Angeles hoping to reach Linda. There was no reply.

What to do? He wasn't about to just fly off and leave her in the morning. Then it occurred to him that she could come too. His plane had to stop off in Los Angeles to pick up Evan, and he would surely reach Linda by then, so maybe she could come to the airport and collect Dallas.

Three days in South America and he would be back. And when he returned that was the time to work something out with Dallas. She wasn't just another dumb piece of ass – she was the woman he wanted – and she was just going to have to realize that. Maybe tonight would prove it to her. He could have done anything he wanted – but he hadn't. When it happened, he wanted them *both* to know about it.

No way was it going to be a one-way fuck.

No way.

58

Cristina was kept so busy that she hardly had time to think. Louis took care of that. After asking her father's permission to marry her, and receiving it, he plunged them both headlong into a series of engagements.

In spite of her protests everyone wanted to give parties for them, and she could hardly refuse.

Louis showered her with gifts. He was sweet, and fun. In spite of herself she was having a good time. She had never felt so important before, suddenly she was the centre of attention. Her girlfriends were consumed with envy. 'Cristina, you are so lucky,' Marie Therese sighed. 'Louis is so nice, everyone adores him. I've had my eye on him for ages – especially when the two of you broke up. He always wanted you though – can't imagine why!'

'Cat!'

'I'm just jealous, that's all. I'm sure I won't find anyone to marry me for years – probably not until I'm ancient – twenty or something. And you'll have such a wonderful life together. Oh, you are so lucky!'

For a moment she agreed with Marie Therese. She *was* lucky. Then she remembered the truth of the situation. Her marriage plans were merely a smokescreen. Nino was to be the man in her life. She shivered at the thought of his hard, dark body, so different from blond Louis'. Different in every way. Louis was rich. Nino was poor. Louis came from an excellent family. Nino's family consisted of an aged crone who lived in the slums. Louis adored her. Nino – well, she wasn't sure *how* Nino felt. He *said* he loved her, but only

when she asked him outright. Louis would give her everything – a beautiful home, clothes, jewels. Nino scorned
material possessions, they would probably have to live in his
small one-roomed apartment.

It crossed her mind that she might be making a terrible
mistake, and there was no one she could discuss it with. No
one she could turn to for advice.

At the end of the week she didn't telephone Nino at the
appointed time. She had meant to, but somehow it slipped
her mind.

He phoned her the next morning and insisted that she
came over to his apartment at once.

'I'm going sailing . . .' she objected.

He was furious, 'You are coming here,' he insisted.

Sulkily she had cancelled her meeting with Louis, making
up some excuse about having to go to the dentist.

Nino greeted her with a kiss which surprised her. She
had expected him to still be angry, as he had been on the
phone.

'I've missed you, carioca,' he whispered, 'my body has
been screaming for your touch.' His hands started to caress
her. 'Have you missed me? Have you wanted me as I have
been wanting you?'

For the first time in their relationship she felt that what he
was doing was wrong. She attempted to move away from
him, but he was all over her, his hands under her sweater,
up her skirt.

'You still love me?' he whispered. 'You still want me to
touch you?' His hands were busy, and her objections soon
turned to moans of acquiescence. She clung to him, emotions
rushing to the surface. 'I do love you, Nino, I do, I do.'

He laughed softly. 'You sound like you've been having
second thoughts.'

'Don't be silly, as if I could.'

He started to undress her, but suddenly he stopped. 'I
don't know,' he muttered.

'What is it?' she asked anxiously. He had tuned her body
to a fine pitch, and she was more than ready for him.

'Maybe it would be better if I didn't touch you.'

'Why?'

'I don't know – you just seem – different.'

'But I'm not, I'm not. Please, Nino, please. Make love to me and everything will be like it was.'

He spread her legs, lowered himself on top of her.

She arched her back, twisted her legs behind his neck.

As he plunged inside her she suddenly thought of Louis and was ashamed. What would he think of his fiancée if he could see her now?

When they had finished making love, Nino produced a pad and pencil and started to question her about Al King. Details. Details. She told him what she could.

'We only have a week,' Nino reminded her.

Only a week? She shuddered at the thought.

'You must telephone me every day,' Nino said, 'report on every little thing.'

'But what *is* the plan?'

'I can't tell you yet. Be patient, you will know soon enough.'

She was suddenly frightened. 'Nino, I won't be involved, will I?'

'Of course not.'

'But you said before, you mentioned something about Al King must be sure to know me. Why?'

'Purely for access. No one will know you have anything to do with it.'

Nervously she bit on her nails. 'And us? Don't you think it would be better if we waited a few weeks before running off together. It might be suspicious if I drop Louis immediately.'

He shrugged. 'Whatever you say.'

'It's not that I don't want to be with you as soon as possible . . .'

'I understand.'

How he controlled his fury he didn't know. He waited for her to dress and leave and then he let rip. 'Rich, capitalist, bourgeois bitch!' he screamed, punching the mattress in anger. 'I'm good enough to service, madame, but not good enough for her to run off with!' He could read her stupid little mind. She *liked* being engaged to Louis Baptista. She was enjoying it. Well, she would be sorry – very, very sorry indeed. They would *both* be sorry by the time *he* had finished with them.

Cristina rushed home feeling relieved that she had settled things with Nino. She would help him as much as she could with information – she had promised that much. But after – well, she just wasn't sure any more. She wanted time to think things out. Maybe she wasn't as much in love with Nino as she had thought. Maybe it was just a sex thing. She had heard stories about people becoming trapped sexually. She shuddered at the thought. It couldn't happen to her – could it?

Perhaps she should try a few things out with Louis. Experiment sexually. *He* wouldn't be averse to trying. If she enjoyed it just as much with him . . . Well . . . After all, Louis had so much more to offer . . .

☆

Evita read the letter through a second time. It was written in neat girlish script on lilac notepaper. Anyone else reading it would find it to be an innocuous exchange of greetings between two friends. Evita found it a frightening reminder of her one lapse.

'How are you?' Doris Andrews wrote, 'I have often thought of you and Jorge in the past year.' Words leapt out at Evita – 'short vacation . . . Must get away . . . Would love to see you . . . arriving next week . . . will phone you . . .'

Jorge, sitting across the breakfast table from Evita, said, 'Who is the letter from?'

'Doris Andrews,' Evita managed to reply calmly. 'You remember, don't you? The American film star we met in Mexico last year . . .'

Jorge reached for the letter. 'Yes, yes, of course.' He scanned it quickly. 'How nice. You liked her, didn't you? Why don't we invite her to stay with us?'

'Oh no,' Evita replied quickly, 'not now, not with all the bother with Cristina . . .'

'Your daughter is engaged to a wonderful boy and you call it bother.' He shook his head in bewilderment. 'A couple of weeks ago you were complaining because you didn't know who she was seeing . . . What *would* satisfy you?'

'I will be satisfied when she and Louis are safely married.'

Jorge's eyebrows rose. '*Safely* married?'

'I just don't feel right about her engagement. Why won't she allow us to have a party for her?'

'We'll have a party for Doris Andrews if it's a party you want. I think it would be a nice gesture, don't you?'

'I don't know . . .' Evita fluttered her hands vaguely.

'Well, I do,' Jorge said decisively. 'You love giving parties. All that plotting and planning that you are so good at. Yes. We shall definitely have a big party. Go ahead and organize it, my dear.'

Later, when Jorge had left for his office, Evita read the letter through once more. She had never expected to hear from Doris again, never expected to have a rude reminder of her one indiscretion. A letter was bad enough. But the fact that Doris was coming to Rio . . . If only she could go away somewhere, hide. But that was impossible, already Jorge was planning a party. He had known that she and Doris had become close friends; if she wanted to leave as soon as Doris arrived it would look strange. Jorge was no fool. Eventually he would work things out.

Evita sighed deeply. If Jorge ever found out . . . She would sooner die. She would be so ashamed.

And yet . . . If she was honest she would have to admit that she had enjoyed every minute of her sexual interlude with Doris. Jorge thought he was a wonderful lover, but his hands were hard and strong, whereas Doris' had been soft and demanding in a completely different sort of way. And her tongue, so intuitive, finding every secret place of excitement within seconds. Evita thrilled at the memory. What if it happened again? She wasn't sure if she would be able to stop Doris. She wasn't even sure if she would want to . . .

Quietly she went to her desk and sat down in preparation to compose a reply.

'My dear Doris, how nice to hear from you after all this time. Yes, I too remember what a delightful time we spent together in Acapulco. Jorge and myself are so pleased you will be visiting our city. Perhaps you would allow us to give a party in your honour . . .'

☆

Louis was breathing heavily.

'Kiss me again,' Cristina whispered. 'Kiss me properly.'

They were clutched in each other's embrace in the front seat of Louis' sports car.

Louis groaned. 'Do you know what you are doing to me, Cristina? Every night I have a terrible stomach ache ... I go home and I cannot sleep. We will have to be married as soon as possible, I just can't go on like this. I can't control myself for much longer. We must arrange a date, we must talk to our parents.'

'I said kiss me again.' She was glowing with power. Louis was under her spell, he would do anything for her. She captured his mouth once more, pushing her tongue out to meet his. His hands slid to her breasts. For once she didn't push them away. After a few minutes he snatched them away of his own accord. 'I can't go on like this,' he muttered in a strangled voice.

'We don't have to,' Cristina whispered. 'We're engaged. Anything we do together would not be wrong.'

He wasn't sure that he had heard her correctly. 'Are you saying ...'

'I'm saying let's go to your house in the hills. Is it empty?'

'Yes. But, Cristina, are you sure?'

She felt that she was such a woman of the world. 'Yes, Louis,' she replied softly, 'I am sure.'

Wordlessly he started the car. Cristina smiled to herself. He was so anxious.

The small sports car sped up into the mountains. Cristina felt quite calm at what she was about to do. It was an experiment. If Louis could satisfy her in the same way that Nino could ... Well then, why *shouldn't* she marry Louis? After all, Nino with his theories and ideas would be so demanding. Besides she *liked* having money, a fact she would never dare confess to Nino.

Louis had to break a window to gain access to his parents' weekend house as he did not have a key with him. 'I never thought you would ever allow me to do this,' he said, as he let her in the front door. 'Are you sure? Are you really sure?'

'Of course I am, silly. I don't want you going home every night with stomach ache, you could do yourself harm.' She looked around. 'Where shall we go?'

He took her by the hand. 'Upstairs.'

Halfway up the stairs they heard voices. Louis froze.

'Who is it?' Cristina whispered, alarmed.

'I don't know,' Louis whispered back. 'You go out to the car, I'll investigate. Hurry.'

She rushed back to the car which was parked around the back. Suddenly she was nervous.

Louis joined her within minutes. His mouth was set in a grim line. He jumped in the car, took off the handbrake and allowed the car to coast silently away from the house.

'What is it?' Cristina hissed.

'My dear father,' Louis replied, obviously upset, 'in the bedroom with a woman.'

'Oh! You mean we caught him?'

'You could say that. Only he didn't see me. I looked through the keyhole. Tonight he's supposed to be in São Paulo.'

'What a lucky escape! Can you imagine if we had burst in on him?'

'You would think he wouldn't take a woman to a bed he shares with my mother,' Louis complained.

Cristina tut-tutted in agreement. But secretly she was intrigued at the thought of portly Mr Baptista in bed with a woman. She wondered if her own father did such things . . . The thought excited her. 'Stop the car, Louis,' she whispered urgently, 'I want to do it with you. I want to do it with you now!'

☆

When they met, five days later, Nino sensed the change in Cristina immediately. He was furious. After all, she did not know that he had not been completely serious about his intentions. As far as *she* was concerned he loved her and was preparing to marry her.

A lot she cared. He had misjudged her. She wasn't the pliable, stupid, little girl he had thought. She was stupid all right – but devious stupid.

'I'm so tired,' she complained to Nino. 'Parties, parties, parties.'

He managed to smile sympathetically. Only a few more days . . . keep her sweet for a few more days. 'You look well on it, carioca,' he assured her.

'Do I?' she asked, knowing full well that she was

positively glowing. The experiment with Louis had turned out to be an unqualified success.

'Do you have a copy of the list of everyone travelling with Al King for me?'

She fished in the straw bag she carried, and produced it. 'I took it from Mr Baptista's desk. Honestly, I felt like a private detective in one of those American television serials!'

'Clever girl.' He took the list and studied it.

'I can't stay,' she said quickly. 'Today Louis is taking me to Paqueta Island. He wants to know where I am every minute. You know, I've been thinking – I don't know if we should see each other for a while. It might not be wise.'

Carefully Nino placed the piece of paper on a table. He held Cristina playfully around the waist. 'Do you mean we will not have time to make love today?'

She attempted to squirm free. He held her extremely tight. 'Well, carioca? Not today, huh?'

'No, not today, Nino.'

He held her even tighter. 'You still love me though?'

'You're *hurting* me . . .'

'Not as much as I could.' Suddenly he let go of her and she lost her balance and fell back on the bed.

He stood over her, slowly unzipping his jeans.

She lay back, frightened at the menace in his eyes.

'You know what I want you to do,' he said.

'I told you . . .' she began.

'I thought you loved me,' he mocked. 'If you love me you'll do anything for me.'

'Next time.'

'And when will that be?'

'Soon. I promise you.'

'And this is the girl who was not sure if she could live three weeks without me. What happened, carioca? Does Louis have a bigger one than me? Or is it just the fact that his is coated in money and mine is merely coated with the slime of the Favellos?'

She reddened. 'Don't be silly, Nino.'

'Don't be silly,' he mocked. 'Do you think I am a fool? Do you think I don't know what is going on?'

She lowered her eyes. 'I'm sorry.'

'You're sorry!' he exploded, 'just like that – you're sorry. And what about me? What about my plans?'

'I'll still help you,' she said quickly. 'I promised I would and I haven't let you down. I got you the list, didn't I? And if I find out anything else I'll let you know . . .'

'Thanks,' sarcasm dripped bitterly from his lips, 'how kind of you.'

She attempted to sit up. He pushed her back with one hand.

'I'll tell you the plan,' he said coldly. 'Listen carefully.'

She was frightened, his eyes were alive with a hatred and contempt that she had never seen before.

'Al King arrives on Thursday – in two days time. Naturally you will be at the party Louis' father is throwing for him. Be sure to meet him, talk with him and the people close to him. Be sure they know you are to marry Carlos Baptista's son. Friday is the day of the concert – you attend – but early on you and Louis slip away and go straight to the airport. You make sure that you reach there before Al King does. I will meet you there. That is all you have to know for now.'

'What are you talking about?' Cristina gasped. 'I can't do that. What are you thinking of?'

'I'm thinking of the Von Cougats and the Bogatos. I'm wondering what they would say if they found out it was sweet little Cristina Maraco who had provided the plans to their houses – in her own sweet handwriting – plans that enabled them to be robbed. I'm also thinking of your father. Would it interest him to know about his daughter and me? Would he like to know what you and I do together? Would your mother be pleased to hear from the doctor who fitted you for a diaphram? The doctor I arranged for you to see?'

Cristina's face drained of colour. 'You wouldn't . . .' she whispered in horror.

'Try me,' Nino replied arrogantly. 'Or maybe I could compare notes with Louis on your performance.'

'You pig!'

Nino shrugged. 'Of course if you help me out with Al King then I will have no need to tell anyone anything – ever.'

'But how could I explain going to the airport, leaving in the middle of the concert, to Louis?'

'I'm sure you could think of something.'

'But why do you need us?'

'For access. To board his plane. Don't worry – you will be in the clear. I promise you no one will know we are connected. Once I'm on the plane you can go – we need never see each other again.'

She covered her eyes with her arm. What a mess she had got herself in.

'Do we have an agreement?' Nino persisted.

She took her arm away and stared at his handsome arrogant, hateful face. 'All right,' she muttered. What choice did she have?

'Good. I will contact you by phone to give you further details – times and places, and I want a report from you twice a day in case any plans get changed.' His mouth twisted into a thin smile. 'Well, my little carioca, shall we make love before you go? Or are you still in a hurry?'

59

Dallas woke up slowly, stretched, spread her arms out, opened her eyes, and wondered where the hell she was.

She felt hot, and kind of sweaty, and realized that she still had her jeans and T-shirt on.

She tried to remember, but everything seemed to be a vague blur, the clearest memory being Palm Springs.

She sat up, looked around the ornate hotel bedroom, located the bathroom, and locked herself in there. She stripped off her clothes and stepped under an icy shower. The cold water refreshed her. She grabbed some soap and washed herself thoroughly, including her hair. Then she wrapped herself in a towelling bathrobe which was hanging behind the door, and turbaned her hair in a towel. There was a tube of toothpaste lying on the side, and she squeezed some onto her fingers and rubbed it over her teeth, rinsing her mouth out with water.

Things were becoming clearer. She could remember getting on a plane to Las Vegas and meeting a frizzy-haired girl who had fixed her up with a lot of good things. Wow – that was it. She had gotten good and stoned, and come to think of it a joint and some pills wouldn't be such a bad idea now. She felt depressed and down. Al King ... Al King ... Hadn't she been following up some wild idea of visiting him? Christ! She *must* have been stoned!

She walked out of the bathroom looking for her bag. Then she noticed that there were men's clothes around the room, and a suitcase that wasn't hers.

She tied the bathrobe tightly around herself and walked into the living room.

Al King was sitting at a room service table drinking orange juice and reading a newspaper. He looked up when she came in. 'Good morning. How did you sleep?'

She stared at him, waiting for recollection of the previous evening to come flooding back. Nothing. She bit her lip. Now her goddamn head was beginning to throb.

Al smiled pleasantly at her. 'Want some breakfast?'

She shook her head. Breakfast wasn't what she wanted. 'You seen my bag?' she muttered, disgusted with herself for what obviously must have happened.

'It's over there.'

She picked up the bag and headed back to the bedroom, emptying the contents out onto the bed. A bikini. A T-shirt, denim shirt, some shorts. Bottles of make-up, a hairbrush, small hair dryer, several packs of chewing gum, a hand mirror, box of Kleenex, tube of suntan cream, and a make-up bag. That was it. The entire contents.

She turned the bag upside down and shook it. A few hairpins fell out. Where the hell were her pills? Her joints? Shit. She *couldn't* have demolished them *all*.

She went in the bathroom and picked her jeans up off the floor, rifling through the pockets. She pulled out a cheque and squinted at it in amazement. Thirty thousand dollars. Made out to her. She went back in the living room waving it in the air. 'Where did I get this?' she demanded.

'Don't you remember?' Al asked innocently.

'If I remembered I wouldn't be asking, would I?' she snapped.

'What *do* you remember?'

She glared at him. 'Nothing.'

'I'm not surprised. You were flying without wings. Maybe you can tell me what happened to set you off.'

She slumped into the chair opposite him and picked at a bread roll. 'I feel like Doris Day,' she said miserably. 'Every old movie I ever see of hers she wakes up with some guy and doesn't know whether they made it or not. You know – like she was drunk or something. So come on Rock Hudson – fill me in.'

'You won the money at roulette. We didn't make it – oh, you wanted to – but I figured it might be more fun to wait until you knew who you were screwing. Old-fashioned of me, I know, but I'm like that.'

She laughed suddenly, clutched her head and said, 'Ouch! That hurts. You mean I *won* thirty thousand bucks? Wowee!!'

'I thought you were going to say "you mean you didn't screw me? Thank you Al, I always knew you were a first class gentleman"!'

She laughed again. 'Doesn't really matter one way or another, does it? I'm not a virgin like Doris Day – or didn't you realize?'

'I realized.'

'Never mind. For one me, there's always hundreds of others. What am I doing here anyway?'

'*You tell me.*'

She shrugged. 'Don't know. Guess I had this stupid idea of you and me finally getting together. I'll be honest with you, Al. I find sex no great turn-on – I thought maybe with you . . .' She trailed off.

'I could have had you doing cartwheels last night. In LA you didn't want to know about me. Why the sudden change of mind?'

'Can I have some orange juice and coffee? And maybe some eggs. I feel like I haven't eaten for six years. Hey – I had some joints in my bag – you seen them?'

He shook his head. 'I'll order you breakfast. How do you want your eggs?'

'Scrambled. Oh and some toast and jelly – and some crispy bacon.'

He phoned room service, glanced at his watch. Time was running tight.

'I should call Cody,' she mused, 'he's probably going out of his head.'

'I thought you were working.'

'I have taken a week off, courtesy of Mr Margolis. Do you know him? Such a charming man. He and his lovely wife.'

'I think I might do a movie for him.'

'Lots of luck!'

'You still haven't told me how you managed to appear in Las Vegas stoned out of your head.'

She made a face. 'It wasn't easy.'

'I'm glad you're here though. I wanted to explain about Karmen . . .'

She held up a hand. 'Nothing to explain, *I* don't care.'

'But that's it. I *want* you to care . . .'

'Oh, Al, please. Don't get corny with me. I understand. I'm a very understanding lady. You can screw who you want.'

'Then why wouldn't you talk to me in LA?'

'I could *really* appreciate some grass. With your influence couldn't we summon some up?'

'You're changing the subject.'

'What subject?'

'Look, I have to be on my plane in an hour. We're stopping in LA to pick up my son . . . Then I have a couple of gigs in South America, and I'll be back in a few days. Why don't we plan on getting together when I get back?'

'Just like that, you're flying to South America today?'

'I can drop you in LA.'

'Terrific. What makes you think I want to go back there?'

'Don't you?'

She reached over and drained his orange juice. 'Where's the food? I'm getting desperate.'

An idea was forming in his head. 'I said don't you?'

'As a matter of fact I don't.'

'So why not come to Rio with me? No strings – I won't touch you – or I'll touch you. Whichever you want.'

'Why do you want me to come?' she asked suspiciously.

'Because I like you. I think we understand each other. I think we could have some laughs.'

'I have to be back in LA next week.'

'We will be.'

She smiled, dazzling him. 'Why not?'

☆

Paul nudged the girl who was asleep beside him. He had been nudging her on and off since 6 a.m. in the hope that she would wake up and leave. It wasn't that he didn't like her. She was an attractive girl of twenty-nine, intelligent, articulate, good in bed. She was one of the producers on the telethon, not some little nothing groupie. They had made love once, quite satisfactorily as far as he was concerned. But he had been unable to rise to the occasion a second time, and far from being put out, she had produced a life-sized penis substitute from her purse, and requested most politely that he use it on her. He had done as she asked, albeit reluctantly, and he had been somewhat put out by the amount of orgasms she had proceeded to achieve. With his cock – one. With a plastic substitute – multiple. It didn't seem right somehow.

She obviously had no intention of ever waking up, so he got out of bed and stamped his way around the room a lot before going in to shower and shave.

He was halfway through shaving when she strolled into the bathroom, squatted on the John and peed noisily.

'How are you this morning?' she asked amiably.

'Rushed.'

'Shame. I thought we might . . .'

'No time.'

'That's cool. I have a lot to do myself. If you want to reach me in LA you can call me at the network.'

'I will.' He knew he wouldn't.

'You're better-looking than your brother,' she remarked, getting off the toilet and running the shower. 'Not that I'm into looks – but you are.'

He wasn't flattered. He didn't enjoy being compared to his brother in any way.

He finished shaving, hurried in the bedroom and dressed. He wanted to call Linda. He wanted to tell her that he loved her. He wanted her to tell *him*.

Instead he booked a call to London. He was worried about his children being all alone in the house with just the nanny. He wanted to assure them that he would be home soon.

The girl producer strolled nakedly into the room and started to dress. He watched her, willing her to hurry. She retrieved panty hose from the floor, sat on the bed and slid them on. Then a skirt from a chair, high-heeled shoes, and lastly a shirt which showed off her perky nipples.

She collected her purse, picked up the penis substitute which sat lewdly on the bedside table.

He wondered why she carried it. In case nothing better came along?

'I'll see you around, Paul,' she said casually, 'give me a buzz when you get back.'

'Yes,' he said. No – he thought.

He waited until she closed the door, then he placed a call to Linda.

He paced the room, expecting both calls to come through at once. They didn't. The operator informed him that there was no answer at the number he had given her for Linda. And he had to wait half an hour before he got a line to England.

Nanny was most huffy. 'This isn't good enough, Mr King,' she informed him, 'I haven't had my day off for weeks.'

'I'll pay you double,' he promised her. 'Just wait another week and I'll be back.'

'I think it's disgusting,' she sniffed, 'absolutely disgusting!'

'Yes,' agreed Paul. 'We'll discuss it when I get back, nanny.'

'We certainly will!'

He checked his watch. Better call Al to make sure he was awake. It was a long trip, he could always sleep on the plane if he had been up all night. He wondered how much money he had managed to lose at the tables. The sooner he got Al away from Vegas, the better.

☆

Evan waited impatiently at the airport in Los Angeles for his father's plane to pick him up. He felt a lot better, the few days in a private clinic had not been too bad. Everyone had been very nice to him, one young Puerto Rican nurse in particular – of course she had known he was Al King's son, which was probably why.

He had watched a lot of television, and the time had passed quite quickly. They had treated him with a course of injections, and apparently all he needed now was some follow-up shots and everything would be fine. No sex until after your check-up, the doctor had warned him sternly. Chance would be a fine thing. Now that Glory and Plum were out of his life who would look at him? He missed them, in spite of the fact that they had given him the dreaded disease. After all, they hadn't known. He kept on wondering what they had done when they realized that he had just walked out on them. Did they miss him? He had no way of contacting them. His only friends. He had thought that maybe he would run into them in Los Angeles. After all that's where they had been heading. But no such luck. His father had dumped him straight into the clinic – to get him out of the way no doubt. There was no reason for him to stay in a clinic, he could have received the treatment as an out patient. But no – the famous Al King didn't want his horrible spotty son around – so he had hidden him away.

At least he was going to Brazil. That was *something*. And to be fair to his father at least he hadn't been sent home.

He flicked through the bunch of magazines he had purchased. *Playboy, Penthouse, Macho*. Idly he wondered if the doctor's no sex instructions had included masturbation. After all – you couldn't give a magazine centrefold a dose of the clap, could you?

☆

On the plane Dallas said, 'I must call Cody. Really – otherwise he'll be contacting missing persons.'

'I'll have Bernie get in touch with him when we land at LA. Does that suit you?' Al replied.

'Yeah, that's fine. Have him say I'll be reporting back for work on Monday. Oh, and Al – I know I keep on asking you – but can't we have Bernie score a few joints for us? I'm in the mood to get stoned.'

'Where is he going to score at the airport?'

'He can make a call, can't he?'

'By the time they get out to the airport we'll be long gone.'

She made a face. 'Big fuckin' star and I can't even get high.'

He laughed. 'You need to be high to travel with me?'

'I must have been high to agree to come. What am I doing

here? I don't even have any clothes. Maybe I should get off in LA.'

He took her hand. 'I want you to stay. You can pick up some clothes in Rio, anything you need.'

'I need *some* grass. *Someone* on this plane must have a joint.'

'You're really that desperate?'

She shrugged, smiling. 'Not desperate. But if I don't get one I'm going.'

He wondered how angry she would be if she knew that it had been he who had confiscated her supply.

'Stay where you are,' he warned. 'Don't move – I'll see what I can do.'

'Oh yeah?'

'Oh yeah.' He set off down the plane to where Bernie was playing gin rummy with some of the musicians. He sat down ostensibly to watch, but once out of Dallas' sight he pulled her tin box out of his jacket pocket and extracted a joint.

'Gonna join us for a game?' Bernie wanted to know.

'Not today,' Al replied. 'Got other things on my mind.'

'I'm down three hundred bucks,' Bernie complained. 'If this goes on, by the time we make Rio I'll be busted out.'

'So learn to play,' chided Al. He glanced over at Paul, sitting alone on an aisle seat studying some papers. 'How'd the party go?'

Paul nodded. 'It was nice.'

'You take my advice?'

'What advice was that?' Paul replied tightly.

'To get laid, schmuck!'

'We can't all . . .'

'I know, I know,' Al interrupted. 'We can't all go through life with a stiff prick. But it beats the hell out of wanking!' He laughed at his own humour, and made his way back to where Dallas was sitting. He could have suggested that they sat in the bedroom – but he didn't want to rush things. She was with him of her own accord, let things happen nice and naturally. One joint wasn't going to turn her into the stoned zombie she had been the previous day.

He gave her the cigarette. She lit up, inhaling deeply, leaning her head back, finally allowing the smoke to drift lazily out of her nostrils.'Better!'she sighed.

'You like that?'

'Why not? Don't you?'

'I can take it or leave it. Give me a healthy slug of scotch any day. Something that hits you in the gut with a punch you can feel all the way down to your balls!'

'I don't have balls.'

'Oh no? You could have fooled me.'

Playfully she punched him.

'I *like* a ballsy woman,' he objected. 'I can't get anything going with most of the doormats that come my way. I could shit all over some of 'em and they wouldn't object.'

'From what I hear you usually do,' she remarked dryly.

'So what do you hear?'

'That you are Mister Super Prick – in both senses of the word.'

He groaned. 'What a reputation! Is that why you wouldn't go out with me?'

She dragged on her cigarette. 'Maybe.' She studied him through slitted eyes. 'Maybe not.'

'You and I together . . .' he began.

She quietened him with a finger to his lips. 'Let's take it minute by minute. No promises. No crap. No commitments. I don't want you to change for me.'

'But you make me feel different.'

'So be different – until the next Karmen Rush comes along . . .'

'I didn't . . .'

'Goddammit, Al. *I don't care.* Be Mister Super Prick, I really don't care. We'll have a few laughs – I won't give you any heavies. We'll have a good time, no strings on either side.'

It wasn't good enough. His stomach churned at the thought of her with another man. He hadn't even had her yet, and he knew that she was all he would ever want. In the past, with other women – he had never given a monkeys about what they did when they weren't with him. They could have laid the entire team of the Harlem Globetrotters for all he cared. Even Edna. Of course Edna never would have . . . But if she had been that way inclined . . . Well, so what? Now here he sat next to a woman he hardly knew and he felt he could kill for her. He wondered how *she* felt. Surely she must feel something. Surely she must notice the electric current which surged between them? An invisible magnetic force that drew him closer and closer. He had never felt like this in his life.

'Mr King. Please can you fasten your seat belt.' The stewardess interrupted his thoughts. 'And extinguish all cigarettes. We are coming into land at Los Angeles.'

'Sure, Cathy,' he smiled at the girl, then he took the joint from Dallas and stubbed it out.

'Careful,' she admonished. 'Or is there more where that came from?'

'How many do you use a day?'

'Whatever I feel like. Why – does it bother you?'

'Only when you fall down.'

'I promise not to fall down. Only in the direction of your bed – does that suit you?'

No, it didn't suit him. He didn't want her to speak like that.

With a sudden surge of dread he realized that Evan would be boarding the plane shortly. Evan, who had to be told about the divorce Edna wanted – unless he had already read it in the newspapers. Christ! Why did *he* have to be the one to tell him? Couldn't Paul do it?

He glanced at Dallas. She had shut her eyes. Mussed and untidy she was still the most beautiful girl he had ever seen.

☆

Linda was all set to photograph the television star she had met at the Margolis' party. She was looking forward to it – it marked the start of her career in California. She had definitely decided to live there for a while, maybe permanently. Who needed the hassle of New York when you could make a living in Lotus Land? Deep down she knew it was just a temporary move, a time to get herself together. She *needed* the excitement and energy of New York – she *needed* the hassle. But this would do – for the time being.

Just as she was leaving the apartment the phone rang. She knew it was Cody.

'I haven't heard from her,' she said into the receiver.

'You haven't heard from whom?' It was Paul's voice.

'Who is this?' she asked falsely.

'It's Paul. Don't play games – you *know* it's me. Look, I'm at the airport, I've only got a minute. I tried to call you last night – it would be nice if you told people when you changed your number.'

'I didn't know *people* would be calling me.'

'Well, I am.'

'I noticed.' She placed the hold-all with her camera equipment on the floor. 'How did you get my number?'

'Dallas told me you had moved, so I called your agency. She's travelling with us.'

Linda nearly dropped the phone. '*Dallas* is travelling with you? Cody is doing his nut looking for her – he's really going mad. Does he *know*?'

'Yes, I think Bernie's contacting him now. Listen – I don't want to talk about Dallas, I want to talk about us.'

'Go ahead.' Yeah – go ahead, you bastard – tell me all about how your wife doesn't understand you and now that she's safely out of the way I can come back.

'I've decided to leave Melanie.'

There was silence.

'Did you hear me?' Paul continued. 'I'm going to divorce her. I mean it, Linda. We can be together. We can get married. Anything you want.'

'Ohmigod!' she gasped, she could hardly believe what she was hearing. 'Are you kidding me?'

'I'm not kidding you. I mean it, and I've told her – and does this prove to you that I love you?'

'I'm in shock, Paul. Honest to God I'm in shock.'

He laughed. 'Look – I can't really talk now – the plane is waiting. I'll try to call you tonight. I'll be back in four days, then I want to fly straight to England. I thought you could come with me.'

'I don't know what to say . . .'

'Say yes. It's what you wanted, isn't it?'

'Of *course* it is. Oh darling, it's wonderful. Did you tell her about us?'

He hesitated for a fraction of a second, then, 'Yes. I certainly did.'

'You told her it was me at the hotel in Tucson?'

'Does it matter?'

'Sure it matters. What do you think we've been fighting about?'

'I told her.'

'You told her you loved me?'

'Yes. Yes. Yes. I have to go now. I'll try to call you later. Start packing.'

'Paul?'

'Yes?'

'I love you.'

'You too.'

She put the phone down, and shakily reached for a cigarette. Mrs Paul King. Linda King. Should she change her name on photo credits, or should she just add to it and become Linda Cosmo King – sort of like Farrah Fawcett Majors. She giggled. It was all so unexpected. Jesus! She would be a married lady! He had done it, he had finally done it. He had left his wife for her.

Where would they marry? What should she wear? Could she have one last fling with Julio – male hooker supreme – before giving up all other men forever? Would she really have to give up all other men? *That* was a sobering thought for a start. Not any? Ever? Not even birthdays and Christmas?

Mrs Paul King. She would see England, meet his family, his children.

Children. How did she feel about them? Frankly she had never had anything to do with children. Weren't they all supposed to be nasty little monsters, especially other people's. And Paul's children were half Melanie's. Would they have straggly yellow hair and shrill voices?

Maybe they shouldn't marry at once. Now that they could, maybe they should wait. Perhaps living together would be fun, just for a while, just so she could get used to the idea.

She noticed the time. Running late for the television star. Just time to try and call Cody, make sure he knew where Dallas was. The line was busy. She didn't have time to try again. Picking up her camera hold-all she rushed out the door. Soon to be married or not she still had a living to make.

☆

Al greeted Evan warmly. 'Everything all right? They treated you good? You look fine.' The sight of Evan's acne – worse than ever – made him wince. 'How about something to eat?'

'No thanks.'

'Well find a seat, get settled.'

'Where are you sitting?'

'I'm at the back – got an – er – friend with me. Why don't you sit with Paul. I know he wants to talk to you. Cathy – put Evan next to Paul.'

The stewardess took Evan's arm and steered him to a seat.

Al returned to Dallas. She was still asleep, her head balanced at an awkward angle. He got her a cushion and inched it under her head. She grunted. He smiled to himself. This must be love – since when did he ever bother about a girl's neck?

☆

Linda took a series of marvellous photos. The television star seemed to be prepared to do anything for a camera, and by the end of the session she had him reclining across the bonnet of his imported Rolls Royce wearing an orange caftan and holding a can of beer. Let his fans work *that* one out!

'You must have lunch,' he insisted when they were finished, and led her out by the pool where a neatly dressed Mexican had laid out twin lobster salads on a poolside table.

His butchness was dropping rapidly and his closet queen tendencies were coming out full force. 'That woman I work with is a bitch!' he confided. 'Everyone thinks she is such a dear. But I know, believe me I know. I had to kiss the bitch the other day.' His voice rose in disgust. 'Kiss her! And do you know what she did? The bitch ate onions for lunch. Can you imagine?'

Linda smiled in sympathy.

'You don't know what it's like working on a series,' he further confided, 'stuck with the same people day in and day out. Only the guest stars change – and who do we get?' His voice filled with contempt. 'Out-of-work movie actors who look down their nose at me. I'm a star, baby, a *star*. But do they appreciate that fact? Oh no. You can bet your sweet ass they don't. What a drag to be stuck in a television series, they say – when most of them would give their left tit to be in my position.' He picked disconsolately at his lobster. 'That bitch, my co-star, thinks *she's* the star of the series. *She really thinks so*. If I left, the whole thing would fall to pieces. Who do you think gets the ratings?'

'I'm sure it's you,' said Linda kindly.

'You bet your sweet ass it's me. Do you think anyone would switch on their set to see that bitch?'

The Mexican appeared silently and respectfully and informed the television star that he was wanted on the phone. 'I won't be long,' he said. 'Help yourself to anything you want.' He vanished into the house.

Linda smiled. The sun was shining, everything was working out, she felt marvellous.

She picked up a newspaper to glance at. The gossip column was a who's who of what was going on in Hollywood that week. Al King was mentioned – an obtuse item that tied him together with Karmen Rush. She read on, suddenly transfixed, and could hardly believe what she was reading. *'Paul King, younger brother and manager of the great Al, was as surprised as everyone else to find his young and extremely pretty wife Melanie announcing her engagement to the one and only Manny Shorto. Slight snag is the fact that she will have to divorce Paul first. Better hurry, Melanie – Manny celebrates his seventieth birthday next week.'*

Linda slapped the paper back on to the table. 'Bastard!' she said out loud. 'Rotten lying stinking bastard!' And to think she had fallen for his lies. 'I've left her, Linda. I love you, Linda. I've told her all about us, Linda.' The hell he had. Wifey had given him the boot, and he was settling for second best.

Well, screw him. He could stick his marriage proposal right up his lying ass. Second best she was not!

☆

Dallas was only half asleep, but she kept her eyes closed anyway. She didn't feel like making conversation. The joint had taken the edge off her nerves and she felt nicely relaxed.

She was trying to figure out why she had agreed to come. Was Al King really what she needed in her life right now? He was a selfish, bossy, womanizing chauvinist. Why was he the only person who created a spark of excitement? Why did she want to be with him?

She had to find out. If it was a sexual thing she had to know. Three days in South America should be long enough to get him out of her system once and for all. She had made up her mind what she was going to do. She was tired of the struggle. Tired of fighting the Lew Margolis' and Doris Andrews' of the world. When she got back to Los Angeles she was going to marry Aarron Mack. Marrying him would protect her from all the hassles – and if there was one thing she felt she needed it was some protection in life. As Mrs Aarron Mack she would automatically be treated with the respect that all his money deserved. So she didn't love him. So what? The time had come to put herself first – and she intended to.

60

The excitement at the airport in Rio was tense. The usual assortment of crowds, fans, police, photographers and television crews waited impatiently for the Al King jet to land.

Cristina found herself boxed into a private enclosure with Louis, his father, Carlos and several of his assistants. It had been Louis' idea. 'Would you like to come to the airport to see Al King arrive?' he had asked. 'Yes,' she had nodded. He thought she was the singer's greatest fan. And why shouldn't he? She had done nothing but ask questions about the man.

Oh God! How she wished she had never heard his name. How she wished she had never agreed to help Nino.

But it was too late to back out now. Nino had trapped her with his insidious form of blackmail. Her most fervent wish of all was that she had never set eyes on him. How ashamed she was of that relationship – if it wasn't for her shame she might have confessed everything to Louis. But what would he think of her? How could he possibly still want to marry her after her confession?

No, the only solution was to go along with what Nino wanted her to do. If she helped him this last time she would be free of him.

☆

Al pushed Dallas gently. 'Seat belt on,' he commanded.

She opened her eyes. She really had fallen asleep. 'Are we there?'

'Coming in to land.' He had changed into skin-tight black trousers, a black silk shirt, and a positive gold mine of chains.

'Ready to face your public?' she asked.

'But of course. You like the gear?'

'You look terrific, Mister Superstar,' her tone was faintly mocking.

'You don't look too bad yourself.'

'I look horrible. I want a bath, some decent clothes, and a make-up job.'

'I like you just the way you are.'

'I bet you've been using the same old lines for years – they're *so* corny. How do I get off this plane without being seen?'

'What's with the not being seen bit? You're with me.'

'No thank you. *You* look prettier than me right now. I want privacy.'

'Funny.'

'I mean it.' She put on her tinted shades. 'I'll see you at the hotel later.'

He nodded. 'If that's what you want. You can go with Paul and Evan – I think you should meet him anyway.'

'Why?'

'Why what?'

'Why do you want me to meet Evan?'

Al frowned. 'He is my son, you know.'

'So?'

'So . . .' Al faltered. Why *did* he want her to meet him? He had never introduced any of his girlfriends to Evan before. Why start now? 'I don't know . . . We're all travelling together . . . Jesus! Do I have to have a *reason*?'

She laughed. 'Be a good superstar and bring me some grass to the hotel.'

He was annoyed. 'Don't keep calling me that.'

She laughed some more. 'Aren't we the touchy one!'

The plane was swooping in to land. Al could see the crowds from the window.

'You stay on board until Paul fetches you,' he instructed.

Maybe having Dallas on this trip hadn't been such a brilliant idea after all. She could be some smart ass.

'Yes, sir!' She saluted. 'Anything you say, sir! Oh – and don't forget the joints, Al, I'm depending on you.'

☆

Evan sat sullenly in his seat. The plane had landed, the star had disembarked. Now all that was left were the remnants. Everyone had gone except the woman at the back of the plane. His father's woman.

Evan hadn't really been able to get a good look at her. But now she had moved into an aisle seat, and he could see masses of hair, dark sunglasses, and jeans and a shirt.

He hated her, whoever she was. It was women like her who had broken up his parents' marriage. Paul had told him about the impending divorce. 'It's for the best,' he had said. For whose best? Evan wondered. Certainly not *his*.

Where would he live? Which one of them would want him?

He wished that he'd never come back. He wished that he was still travelling across America with Glory and Plum, having good times, having fun. If it hadn't been for Nellie . . . Poor beautiful Nellie. And her death was his father's fault too.

Evan scowled. Why was he unlucky enough to be born with a father like Al King?

Paul reappeared. 'All clear,' he shouted. 'Let's go.'

Evan gathered together his magazines and set off towards the exit.

Dallas followed him. Paul took her arm. 'Tremendous reception Al got,' he said.

Dallas smiled. 'Paul, you're a man of connections. You think you could get me some grass?'

Paul frowned. First Al. Now Dallas. Why were people always asking him to do things for them?

☆

Nino was in the lobby of Al's hotel when he arrived, heralded by a rush of photographers. He leaned unobtrusively behind a pillar and watched the star.

Al King was older than he had expected, and taller than he appeared in photos. But he was good-looking all right.

Nino picked at his teeth with the side of some book matches, and watched Al all the way into the elevator. He took note of everyone around him. The tall black man who hovered watchfully in the background was obviously Al's bodyguard. The others appeared to be the usual hangers-on that stars collected around them. Nino watched the indicator light on the elevator ascend to the tenth floor. It paused there, and within minutes returned to the lobby! The fat man who had accompanied Al up got out and waddled towards a cluster of photographers standing in the lobby.

Slowly Nino strolled towards the busy reception desk. He smiled at a girl working there. 'Time for your coffee break, Didi?' he asked casually.

Her face lit up, 'Nino! You are early.'

'Only ten minutes. Can't you get away now?'

She looked quickly at her watch. 'I don't see why not.' She called to one of the boys behind the desk, 'Drago, I'm taking my break now.'

He nodded.

'One minute,' she instructed Nino. 'I'll get my purse.' She vanished into a room marked 'Employees Only'.

Nino strolled over to the magazine stand. Didi had been so easy. They were all so easy. A little sweet talk. A few false declarations of love and passion, and they were yours.

He had manoeuvred a meeting with Didi nine days previously, as soon as Cristina had told him what hotel Al King would be staying at. Within two days he had slept with the girl. Within five she had agreed to give him the information he required. He had fed her some story about a thesis he was working on. The life and times of the very rich.

Didi came hurrying over. She clutched his arm, and kissed him warmly. 'I've missed you,' she declared.

'We only saw each other last night,' he replied.

'I know. But I have still missed you.'

They walked from the hotel, arms linked, Didi chattering on about the injustices of working in a hotel. If Nino had more time he might have considered recruiting her for the organization. She was perfect material, and she would be able to furnish invaluable information about the guests who booked into the hotel. However, she would need working on, and Nino didn't have time for that now. He had much more important things on his mind.

'Did you get me what I asked for?' he questioned.

'Yes,' she replied smugly, 'I have a duplicate list of the Al King party and what rooms they are in. I copied it out first thing this morning when the reservations were confirmed.'

'Good girl.'

Didi smiled. 'I have an hour's break. Will that give us time to go to your room?'

Nino hid a grimace of disgust.

'Of course,' he replied, 'isn't that the reason I came to see you?'

☆

'Shall I open the shutters, señorita?' the bellboy asked. Only he wasn't such a boy. He was tall and muscled, dark-haired, with knowing eyes.

Linda would adore him, Dallas thought, Linda would probably ravish his fine young body. 'Hey,' she said, 'you look like a guy knows his way around. Can you get me some grass?'

'I beg your pardon, señorita?' the boy replied carefully.

'Grass. Shit. Hash.'

The boy continued to look wary.

'Something to *smoke*—' Dallas pantomimed dragging on a joint, then she rolled her eyes and indicated joy. 'You get me?'

'Ah!' the boy said at last. 'It is expensive . . .'

'But you can get it! I knew you would be able to help me. And some pills,' she pantomimed popping pills into her mouth, 'something good. Qualudes if you can – anything, it doesn't matter. Something to get high – you with me?'

He nodded. 'It is expensive . . .' he began.

'Sure it is,' agreed Dallas, fishing in her purse, and producing two fifty dollar bills, 'and I need it *fast*,' she came up with another fifty, 'like in an hour.'

He grabbed the money hungrily.

'*I'll* open the shutters. *You* get going.'

He hurried from her room.

She giggled. That would fix Al – because she knew *he* wasn't about to come up with anything. And now that she had discovered how much fun life could be – with a little help – well, she wasn't about to give it up.

If only she had realized before. All that misery she had gone through. The shame of hustling guys – no wonder Bobbie had felt no pain. Being high was a whole new way of life. A way of living where nothing much mattered – everything was cool.

Marrying Aarron Mack would be a wonderful experience. No longer was he a dirty old man trying to grab a thigh. He was a beautiful human being. He would give her money, and protection, and respect, and money, and a position in the rat race, and money. She laughed out loud. Maybe she wouldn't even bother going back to work on Monday. Who needed all that fame shit? Who needed getting up at 5 a.m. and spending hours being beautiful?

She thought briefly of Cody. Bernie had told her he had called him for her. 'He's kinda uptight,' Bernie had understated. 'He says they were waiting for you all week to show up at the studio. I told him you'd make it first thing Monday. Maybe you should call him yourself.'

She didn't want to call him. He would only tell her off for disappearing. Who needed that trip?

So she would finish the series. Yes – for Cody she would finish it. Then they could all go to hell. She was *through* catering to other people. What had other people done for her except screw her rotten?

She threw open the shutters and was suitably impressed by the view. A magnificent stretch of white beach, bright blue ocean, and in the distance fantastic mountains. The beach was crowded with bikini-clad people. Cars lined the periphery. Transistor radios wafted out the sound of samba.

Dallas was glad that she had come here. It looked like the kind of place you could have a good time in. A place where you could forget your problems and just be happy.

She caught sight of herself in a mirror, and it reminded her that she was supposed to purchase something to wear for the party that evening. Al had thrust a thousand dollars in her purse and told her to get whatever she liked.

She had accepted the money. Why not? Once a whore always a whore. Wasn't that how the saying went?

✩

In the jewellery store Al tried to decide between a small diamond heart to hang around her neck, or a lavish aquamarine and diamond ring. The heart won. If he started giving out rings someone might get the wrong impression.

'Send the bill to my hotel,' he instructed, and for good measure picked out a chunky gold identity bracelet for himself. Then, feeling generous, he purchased a slim digital gold watch for Paul, and a rough gold lion pendant for Bernie. He thought of Evan, but couldn't decide what he would like, maybe money would be best. But then he noticed a rough gold penknife, and that seemed suitable, so he got him that.

'Anything else, Señor King?' the wide-eyed manageress asked. She was a redhead, voluptuously squeezed into a green dress. Under normal circumstances Al would have considered giving her one. The thought didn't even occur to him.

'That's it,' he said, then he remembered Luke waiting outside the shop. He walked to the door, put his head out, asked Luke his birth sign, then came back in and chose a thick gold chain with the appropriate medallion hanging from it. That took care of everyone. Paul would organize minor presents for all the others on the tour.

Al walked out to his limousine. He felt really good. The concert the next day was a real challenge, and he was looking forward to it. Two hundred thousand people in one go, and according to Carlos Baptista it was a sell-out.

Dallas would be there to watch him. If things worked out she would be watching him for weeks – maybe even months.

He hoped she would hold his interest. He hoped this affair was going to be different. Tonight he would have her. No – they would have each other. He felt himself harden at the thought. Christ! He had wanted her long enough, it was about time.

✩

Evita entered Cristina's room. She was wearing a dramatic black dress which bared one shoulder, and was held in place by a massive diamond clip. Her white-blonde hair was piled high in a severe chignon. 'Darling, are you ready?'

Cristina scowled at her own reflection. 'I look fat!'

'You do not.'

'Beside you I do.'

Evita sighed, 'It's because I am wearing black.'

'I wish I could wear black. I hate this dress.' She twirled in front of the mirror, and the red dress she was wearing twirled with her. 'I look like a little girl!'

Evita laughed. 'How could you?'

Cristina made a face at herself in the mirror. 'I wish I could wear jeans,' she muttered, 'I knew this dress was a mistake.'

'You look perfectly delightful,' Evita assured her daughter, 'Louis will be quite bewitched.'

'He already is,' replied Cristina sourly. She was becoming more and more tense. All she could think of was stupid Nino, and the stupid things he wanted her to do. How on earth was she supposed to get Al King to notice her? She had been introduced to him at the airport and his stupid glazed smile had not even focused in her direction.

How on earth was she to get Louis to take her to the airport in the middle of the concert? The whole thing was ridiculous. Nino was asking too much.

With a shudder she remembered what Nino had threatened to do if she did not cooperate. Oh God! The shame! Louis would never speak to her again.

'I think you should take a wrap,' Evita was saying. 'You're shivering. Do you fell unwell?'

'I'm fine,' replied Cristina, wishing her mother would go away and leave her alone, 'perfectly fine.'

☆

Al wore a dinner jacket of black brocade with matching vest, and pale blue evening shirt, and the tighter than tight trousers which were his trademark. He didn't feel tired, in spite of a day that had included the plane trip from Los Angeles to Rio. Television interviews. Photo calls. Press reception. And now a large party in his honour.

Paul said, 'Do you want me to fetch Dallas?'

Al shook his head. 'You take care of Evan and go in the car with Bernie. Here – a little something.' He handed his brother the package with the watch in.

Paul opened it. He was amazed. It was the fifth watch Al had presented him with in the last two years. Didn't he realize? 'Great – thank you,' he said, taking off his Cartier and replacing it with the new watch.

'Solid gold,' Al pointed out unnecessarily.

'I can see,' replied Paul.

'Cost a bomb,' added Al.

Yes. No doubt. Paul knew he would have to settle the bill in the morning. Al never dealt with the money side of things. He just spent. Sometimes indiscriminately. Frankly Paul thought he should never have shelled out a thousand dollars to Dallas. She had just won thirty thousand, let her spend her own money.

'I'll see you there then,' said Paul.

'We'll be right behind you,' assured Al.

He waited until Paul had left, and then he checked himself out in the mirror one more time. He looked good. Couldn't argue with facts.

He wondered if he should have a drink – maybe a fast blast of Jack Daniels. Six bottles stood unopened on a table, compliments of Carlos Baptista. He decided against it. Tonight he wanted to have all his wits about him. He wanted to remain razor sharp. Maybe later he and Dallas would share a bottle of champagne. But only if she wanted to.

He picked up the box with the diamond heart in, and dropped it into his jacket pocket, then he set off to fetch her.

☆

The bell boy had not let her down. Six joints and two bottles of pills, and no change. But she hadn't minded that. The hell with it, it was only money.

She smoked three of the joints, and swallowed a few pills. She didn't know what they were, but the bell boy assured her they would have the desired effect. They certainly did. This time she was *really* flying.

When Al called to say he would be picking her up in twenty minutes she had not even started to dress. In fact the six hundred dollar gown she had purchased was still in its box. She had been lying out on the balcony admiring the view. The twinkling lights fascinated her. The parade of cars driving along the promenade that separated the hotel from the beach. The samba music which never seemed to stop.

She threw off her jeans and shirt and stood under a warm shower. It was so pleasant that she stayed there for ten minutes. Wet and naked she danced around the room drying off. Who needed towels?

She opened the box and extracted the dress, a gorgeous funnel of white silk jersey. She slipped into it, unaware that it was back to front and that her breasts were totally exposed.

She applied some make-up in a smudgy fashion, and shook her hair which was in a wild tangled mass.

Al's knock at the door coincided with her lighting another joint, and she stubbed it out hurriedly. He wouldn't be pleased. She must appear absolutely normal. Mustn't disappoint him.

She flung the door open. 'Hi, Al.' And she started to giggle. 'Good to see ya!'

The smile vanished from his face. 'Where did you get it?' he asked coldly. He had told all of them. Bernie. Paul. Luke. They all knew if she asked to say no.

She weaved back into the room. 'I'm ready,' she slurred, 'ready t'go t' the party.'

His eyes travelled down her body, fixing on her breasts, and suddenly he wanted her so badly that nothing else mattered.

He walked towards her, took her in his arms, kissed her.

Her mouth was slack.

He moved his hands over her incredible breasts.

She slumped in his arms.

'I want you,' he said, his voice fierce, 'can you understand that? I want you.'

She fell back on the couch, still giggling. Her legs parted. The folds of white jersey parted. She was wearing nothing underneath.

'G' ahead,' she giggled, 'be my guest, man.'

He turned away, smashing his fist into the palm of his hand. 'Why?' he screamed, 'Why? Why? Why?'

'You all gonna wake the neighbours, sugar sweets,' she

slurred. 'Come on over here and I'll give you a blow job – calm you down. A *professional* blow job. Did I ever tell you I was a *professional*? Fucked my way from here to Kingdom Come! Hey Kingdom Come. That's funny – get it? Get it? Al Kingdom come . . .' She dissolved into peals of laughter.

He threw off his jacket, dragged her from the couch, ripped the back to front dress off her. Lifted her like a sack of coal over his shoulders and carried her into the bathroom where he dumped her unceremoniously in the bath.

'Hey,' she grumbled, 'you're rough.'

He turned the shower attachment on, and icy water cascaded over her.

She tried to struggle up, gasping. He shoved her back.

He soaked a towel and wiped it over her face. She spat a string of obscenities at him. He ignored her.

He went in the other room, tipped out the contents of her purse and found the remaining joints and the pills. He marched back in the bathroom. She was climbing out of the bath. He held the bottle of pills up to her face, 'What are they?' he demanded.

'How the fuck do I know,' she snapped.

'Throw up,' he said sternly, 'stick your finger down your throat and throw up. You don't know what this junk is.'

'The hell I will.'

'The hell you won't.' He grabbed her by the hair and forced her head back. 'You going to do it or shall I?'

'Get lost,' she hissed.

'OK,' he said, 'OK.' He prised her mouth open, jamming two fingers in.

She bit down sharply, drawing blood. He didn't withdraw his fingers, and she felt the vomit rising, could do nothing to stop it.

She threw up half over him, half over the floor.

He let her go. She slid to the floor. He threw a towel over her and marched back into the other room wrapping Kleenex round his bleeding fingers.

He called room service, ordering a pot of black coffee. Then he stripped off his ruined vest and shirt.

She was sobbing on the bathroom floor, still stoned, but manageably so. He scooped her up, dumped her back in the bath, this time he let the water run warm, and she didn't struggle.

'Goddamn it,' he said. 'You know how to be difficult.'

She hunched her knees up, covering herself. He took this as a sign that she knew what she was doing. 'Don't go away,' he said, 'I'll be back.'

He set off down the corridor to his suite, startling the maids who lapsed into torrents of excitement.

Luke, waiting outside, did not bat an eyelid at the state Al was in. If Al had something to tell him he would do so, if not, well, he was the boss man, that was his prerogative.

Al collected two bathrobes – he always travelled with at least six – and went back to Dallas' suite.

She was in the same position, her head slumped on her knees.

'Out,' he said, gently but firmly.

She stood up docilely, and he tried to ignore the body, but Christ! Even under these conditions he was getting a hard-on.

He helped her into a bathrobe, and she accepted his help silently.

'We're going to talk,' he said.

She nodded.

He took her into the living room, sat her on the couch.

'Wait,' he commanded.

Again she nodded, slumping back and closing her eyes.

He went in the bathroom, took off his trousers and put on the bathrobe. Then he cleared up as best he could.

Al King, superstar, clearing vomit off a bathroom floor?

Who would believe it?

Even he didn't believe it.

The Kleenex wrapped round his fingers was soaked with blood, and the two fingers hurt like hell. He held them under the cold tap and wrapped them in fresh tissue.

He could hear the phone ringing, but he didn't rush to answer it. He knew who it would be – either Paul or Bernie wanting to know where the hell he was.

Dallas appeared to have fallen asleep. This was getting to be a habit. Only tonight was supposed to be special. He snatched the phone up in a fit of temper. 'Yes?'

Paul's voice. 'Where are you, for Crissake?'

'I am at the hotel,' replied Al, evenly, 'I should have thought that was obvious due to the fact that you just telephoned me here.'

'Cut it out, Al. Half of Rio has turned out to meet you. Carlos Baptista is getting jumpy.'

'Am I getting paid to do a show tomorrow? Or am I getting paid to attend Carlos Baptista's party?' Al's voice was icy.

Paul knew the danger signals. Best to placate him. 'Will you be long?' he asked pleasantly.

'As long as I fucking please!' snapped Al, banging the phone down.

Screw Paul for bothering him. But at the same time he knew he was being unfair to his brother.

He walked to the door, whistled for Luke. 'Call Paul at the party,' he instructed, 'tell him I can't make it – he can give them any excuse he likes. And inform the front desk *no* calls – either my suite or Dallas'.'

☆

Nervously Cristina skirted the room. She had danced twice with Louis, once with her father, and where was the famous guest of honour that she was supposed to get to know? Everyone was asking the same question. Where was Al King?

His brother was there. His son was there. His publicity man was there. But where was the star himself?

Cristina spotted her future father-in-law deep in conversation with Paul King. She took a deep breath and walked over.

'Hello,' she said gaily, 'have you seen Louis?'

'What?' snapped Carlos, not at all in a good mood.

'Er – Louis,' stammered Cristina, 'I seem to have lost him.' She turned to Paul King. 'Hello again, we met at the airport earlier today. Cristina Maraco, Louis Baptista's fiancée.'

'Run along, dear,' interrupted Carlos brusquely, 'we're in the middle of a business conversation.'

'Oh – sorry.' She felt herself blushing, and was furious with Nino for having put her in such an undignified position. Paul King completely ignored her. The two men resumed their conversation as if she had never interrupted. So much for getting to know the people surrounding Al King. Then she noticed the son, at least someone had *said* it was the son, although she could hardly believe that the spotty, insignificant boy standing in the corner was actually the great Al King's son. She could not remember seeing him at the airport.

Resolutely she walked over to him.

'Hello, I'm Cristina Maraco, Louis Baptista's fiancée. I don't think we have met,' politely she extended her hand to him.

He seemed to back away, hiding his hands behind him.

Cristina dropped her hand. Stupid boy, no manners, and what a horrible skin. 'Louis is Carlos Baptista's son,' she continued by way of further explanation of her position, 'I'm looking forward to meeting your father. Where is he?'

'Don't know,' mumbled Evan, highly embarrassed by this strange girl picking *him* out for conversation.

'Oh,' said Cristina, momentarily at a loss for words, then, 'what's your name?'

'Evan,' he replied.

She smiled, 'Nice. Want to dance, Evan? You do samba, don't you?'

☆

'Where is the star?' Evita asked Carlos.

'My dear Evita, if I knew – he would be here. His brother tells me he is tired and is sleeping. I arrange this party for him. Two hundred of the most interesting people in Rio to honour his arrival in our city,' Carlos made a gesture of despair, 'and he is tired. He is sleeping. What can I do?'

Evita smiled sympathetically. 'You can get me another glass of your delicious champagne.'

Momentarily distracted, Carlos said, 'You are looking as beautiful as ever, Evita. My God you are a wonderful-looking woman. Couldn't we . . .'

'Here comes Jorge,' Evita interrupted lightly. She was used to Carlos' vaguely erotic suggestions. She laughed them off as she laughed off all the propositions she received. Jorge would never believe how unloyal most of his friends could be when it came to his wife.

Jorge approached, smiling 'Where is . . .' he began.

'Please!' interrupted Carlos, 'do not ask. My one prayer

now is that he turns up for the concert tomorrow. Two
hundred people I can explain to. Two hundred thousand
might present me with a problem!'

☆

Al allowed Dallas to sleep for a couple of hours. He paced
the room and wondered what the hell he was doing there.
He couldn't find an answer. He had started off wanting a
girl, a body – and now here he was – *concerned*, for Chrissake.

He drank the coffee which arrived, then stood on the
balcony gazing out at the breathtaking array of twinkling
lights.

The smell of the sea drifted up, and he thought about the
evening he and Dallas had walked along the beach at Malibu,
and he had swum and she had sat waiting for him. God –
she had seemed like a different girl then. Together, sure of
herself, in control. He wondered what had happened to get
her going on this destructive drug trip. And it was a destructive trip, any fool could see that. Okay – a couple of joints
never did anyone any harm if that was your scene – but once
you started indiscriminately popping pills at the same time –
then you were headed in the wrong direction. She seemed to
be striving for total oblivion. Where was *that* going to get
her?

Christ – *he* knew about total oblivion. He was an expert.
But he had always had people around to look after him.
Dallas seemed to have no one who really cared.

When he woke her she was subdued like a small child
who has done something naughty and been found out. She
huddled in his large bathrobe, legs tucked underneath, and
regarded him with watchful green eyes.

'Hungry?' he questioned.

'Starving,' she replied.

He called room service and ordered her some scrambled
eggs and himself a steak sandwich.

'We missed the party,' she said solemnly.

'We sure did.'

'Is it too late? Couldn't you still go?'

'I don't want to go,' he replied.

'But it was in your honour . . .'

'I know.'

She shrugged helplessly. 'I don't know why you stayed with me.'

'I can't quite figure it out myself. But I intend to find out. You and I are going to talk – I mean really *talk*. No bullshit. I want to know what's happening with you. I started out wanting to get into your body – now it's your head I'm interested in.'

'Settle for the body, Al. I think I owe it to you.'

'With no charge?'

She flushed. 'What?'

'When you're stoned all you can talk about is giving it away for free.'

She turned her head away from him. 'Take no notice of what I say when I'm stoned.'

He leaned forward, put his hand under her chin, and forcibly turned her face to look at him. 'I want to know about you, Dallas. I want to know it all. Everything.'

She laughed bitterly. 'Why not? Why don't I tell you the whole pretty story.'

'Yes, why don't you.'

She shifted uncomfortably. Her head was beginning to ache. Christ – why was he bugging her? What did he want from her? 'You really want to know?'

'I wouldn't be here if I didn't.'

Fuck it. She would tell him. Get rid of him once and for all. 'You asked for it,' she said roughly, then adopting a singsong voice she began.

'I was born twenty fun-filled years ago in the house back of a crummy private zoo my dear parents owned in a backwater off the main highway leaving Miami. I was a real event in their lives – something else to study – like the chimps or bears. Only I wasn't kept in a cage – not a visible one, that is. I had no schooling, no playmates except the animals, no toys, no books.' Her eyes filled with angry tears. 'I had fuck all if you want the truth. I wasn't even allowed to talk to the paying visitors in case they would corrupt me with stories of the outside world where *real* people lived. When I was sweet sixteen my father took me into town to pick up the monthly supplies – the first time I was allowed out. Can you believe that? Some guy rode back in the truck with us – kept on giving me fishy looks. It wasn't until later I found out he'd been picked as a husband for me . . .'

Talking about it was like a catharsis. She had never told anyone the truth before. Even with Cody she had tailored the story to suit herself. Now it all came pouring out – everything. Bobbie. The old man in the motel. Her months of degradation in Los Angeles. Meeting Ed Kurlnik. Trying to kill Bobbie. Fixing the judges on 'Miss Coast to Coast'. She didn't try to hide a thing. If Al wanted the truth that was exactly what he was going to get.

The food arrived and they both ignored it. He poured her some coffee, and she gulped that as her voice wavered and shook and neared tears as she told her story.

When she reached the part about Lew Margolis and his blackmail attempt, Al stood up and walked to the balcony. She told him about Diamond and Linda helping out with the photographs. Then about Bobbie coming back, Doris Andrews, her short marriage to Cody, Bobbie's death. She didn't leave out a detail. Finally she told him about Lew's latest attempt at blackmail, and the steps she had taken to resolve it.

'That's it,' she said at last, her voice blank. 'You wanted it – you got it. Can you blame me for wanting to get stoned? Can you blame me for not wanting to know myself? Jesus Christ, my parents knew a long time ago I was worth nothing. They never came looking for me – never gave a shit. I've been in every newspaper – on the cover of nearly every magazine in the country. They still don't want to know. They have never attempted to reach me. I'm telling you – they knew right from the beginning. They must have been delighted when I took off. They didn't lose a daughter – they lost a maid. I guess they hired a replacement the very next day.'

Al hadn't uttered a word. He stood by the balcony, his face impassive.

'Why don't you go?' asked Dallas brusquely. 'Piss on off while you've still got the chance. You know all about me now. A hooker. A dyke. A murderer. A blackmailer.' She laughed grimly. 'Some record!'

He turned slowly. 'Do you *want* me to go?'

'Sure. Go. I'm a big girl. I can take care of myself. I've got a cheque for thirty thousand dollars somewhere – I'll make it back to LA and I'll see you around. You know, Al, you and I would never have made it – we're just too different.'

'Different!' he snorted. 'Different! You've got to be kidding! So you were a hooker – you slept with guys for money. Well I slept with women for free – hundreds, thousands probably. I didn't like them any more than you liked the guys you went with. *But we both had our reasons for doing it.*' He paused to light a cigarette. 'You're not a murderer. You didn't kill Bobbie. And the old guy in Miami had a heart attack. It was an accident. How do you think I feel about the bomb killing two girls at my concert in Chicago? I feel like shit about it – but it was not my fault – I don't think of myself as a murderer. *It was an accident.*' He walked over to her, held her roughly by the shoulders. 'Blackmail. I blackmail people every day of my life. You do this for me and I'll do that for you. Only I call it by another name – business. And you want to call yourself a dyke – go ahead. Only a couple of homosexual experiences do not make you into a dyke. We all experiment with sex – when I was a kid I tried it with everything except sheep! What I'm trying to say, Dallas, is don't pin labels onto yourself. Don't put yourself down. So you had a rough past – so *forget* it.'

'How can I forget it when I'm still forced to do things I hate myself for?'

'Who's forcing you?'

'I have to protect myself . . .' she began hesitantly.

'Tear up the photos of you and Doris – destroy the negatives.'

'But . . .'

'It will be all right. I can promise you that. You'll still be "Man Made Whatever" if that's what you really want. Forget about yesterday – start living for today. Hey – are you as hungry as I am?'

Softly she said, 'Yes.'

He phoned room service, but as it was now four in the morning they had closed down.

'Well—' suggested Al, 'how do you feel about a cold steak sandwich?'

61

The Maracana soccer stadium had been transformed into a vast theatre in the round. In the centre of the pitch a platform had been erected, littered with microphones, amplifiers, and musical equipment.

Two hundred thousand people chanted and sang patiently. Police guards were stationed all around the inner circle of the stadium a foot apart. Some of them had dogs with them.

Carlos Baptista was justifiably proud of his security arrangements. No star in his care had ever been involved in any kind of riot – he made sure there was always more than adequate protection. That was one of the reasons he was always able to get the biggest stars. That, and the fact that he was always ready to pay top dollar. He was paying Al King one million dollars for two concerts – but he still expected to make money on the deal – what with the entrance fee and the various concessions he had arranged. Television rights alone had fetched in a princely sum. What a stroke of genius it had been on his part to have thought of hiring the fabulous Maracana Stadium as a venue for Al King. Perfect.

The star himself had been charm personified at a meeting that very morning. He had apologized profusely for not turning up at his party, and when Carlos had been introduced to his girlfriend he could understand why. She was the most beautiful, sensual woman he had ever seen. A streaked mass of hair, strong sexual face, burning green eyes, and a body that defied description. Carlos had professed himself honoured to meet her, and he had meant every word of it.

Now she sat next to him at the concert, but alas, on his other side sat his wife – a magnificent seventeen-stone lady.

Carlos sighed, and patted Dallas delicately on the leg. 'More champagne, my dear?'

She shook her head. Who needed champagne? She was high enough. And without any outside aids. Just Al. He had been so wonderful to her. So understanding and kind.

They had talked until the dawn. Exchanged thoughts and feelings – rapped about themselves until she felt she knew him better than anyone she had ever known. And he certainly knew her. Yet he hadn't been disgusted. He had listened, and sympathized, consoled, and advised. He had understood.

She had always thought that if she ever told anyone the truth about herself they would back off. Al had stayed. He had given her a feeling of inner strength – a feeling she knew she could begin to build on.

And he had not touched her.

He had proved beyond doubt that he did not want her for her body. And yet they both knew it would happen, and when it did it would be clean and good and everything that she had ever imagined.

A sudden roar went up from the crowd as Al appeared. He stood in the middle of the platform holding both arms aloft in greeting, allowing the audience's adoration to pour over him.

Suddenly Dallas knew if there was such a thing as love – this was it.

She loved the man giving himself to the crowds. She loved him with her whole being.

☆

'I changed my mind, I just don't want to go – that's all.'

Louis frowned. 'I just do not understand you, Cristina. For three weeks I hear nothing else but Al King this, Al King that. When is he coming? Where is he staying? Who is he with? Now comes the big moment – the concert at Maracana Stadium – we are on our way there – and you make me stop the car, and tell me you do not wish to go.'

Cristina attempted a gay laugh, although she did not feel at all gay.

'Louis – you know what I'm like. I get moods, sudden desires. I can't be conventional.'

He nodded resignedly.

'What I really feel like doing now is driving to the airport. Does that sound crazy?'

'The airport.' Louis was disgusted. 'Why the airport?'

Cristina shrugged. 'I don't know. I just *feel* like it. Maybe we could see Al King's plane – I heard your father say he has a *bedroom* in it. A bedroom! Can you imagine!'

'All our friends are at the concert, they will wonder what has happened to us.'

'Let them wonder. Who cares? We'll tell them we were making mad passionate love somewhere,' she moved her hand onto his knee – tiptoeing her fingers up towards his crotch. '*That* would make them all envious as anything. They're jealous of us anyway. Marie Therese is beside herself because *I've* got you.'

He let out a strangled groan. 'Don't do that, Cristina, you know what it does to me.'

Teasingly she replied, 'What does it do, Louis? Tell me, please tell me.' She felt him growing beneath her fingers.

'Oh God!'

'I know what, I'll make a bargain with you. If we can go to the airport I'll do what you begged me to do the other night. Remember? The mouth thing. Would you like me to do that to you?'

'Yes,' he agreed urgently.

'OK, drive somewhere quiet. Then after, do you promise we can go to the airport?

'I promise.'

He started the car, and Cristina took a deep breath. *One* hurdle accomplished.

☆

He was out there for one and a half hours. Alone most of the time apart from his musicians, and joined on two occasions by 'Hot Fudge'.

The crowds were going mad, screaming for more. Carlos Baptista was beaming from ear to ear. Better than he had expected. A sensation in fact. Al King generated the most excitement he had ever seen.

Bernie was hustling around getting everyone together for the helicopter trip to the airport. Dallas, Evan, Paul, Luke. They would take the plane directly to São Paulo, and it would return for the others, plus all the equipment, in the morning. It was only a short hop.

Bernie assembled everyone while Al was still singing – got them all aboard the orange helicopter – so now all they needed was Al to be rushed straight on with Luke, and they would be away before the crowd stopped cheering.

All it took was a little organization.

☆

Nino took a bus to the airport. He was early, but he had meant to get there early. Now that the wheels were in motion he felt pretty good. He felt important. He knew he *was* important.

He headed straight for the information desk where he had arranged to meet Juana – a plump girl who worked at the airport as a ground hostess.

She was duly waiting. He greeted her with a kiss, pinched her fat bottom. She gazed at him with adoring eyes. 'Last night was . . .'

'Shhh.' He quietened her with a kiss. 'Tonight will be better, my little carioca, much, much better. Did you find out what I wanted?'

'Naturally. I can show you exactly where the plane is, and where Mr King and his party will be boarding. Nino, tonight . . .'

'Later, we'll talk about it later. Did you get me the uniform?'

'Yes. Are you sure no one will know I helped you?'

'Of course not. And so what if they do. I'm only going to interview Al King, not shoot him.'

Juana giggled.

'Think of the money I will get for an exclusive interview,' Nino reminded, 'and think of who will benefit from it.'

Juana giggled again. 'Me?' she suggested coyly.

'Yes, you. Now quickly, where is the uniform? Where can I change?'

☆

In the helicopter Al held Dallas by the hand.

'You really did it!' she said.

'My inspiration was in the audience,' he replied, squeezing her hand hard.

Sitting behind them Evan couldn't help eavesdropping. Horrible woman. How he hated her, taking up all his father's attention. Why, Al was virtually ignoring him now *she* was around. He hadn't even asked him how he liked the show, and he always did that.

Evan picked viciously at a spot and glared out of the window. He didn't even know what was supposed to be happening after South America. Were they going back to England? No one had bothered to tell him. He didn't matter. *He* was only Al's son – not his stupid girlfriend.

☆

'I've got a confession,' Cristina said nervously, 'I promised someone I would do them a favour.'

'What favour?' asked Louis easily.

They stood in front of the newspaper and magazine stand at the airport.

'Remember Nino? Cristina asked.

'That rat bag,' replied Louis dismissively, 'why do you mention *him*?'

She bit deeply into the side of her lip. 'He's not so bad.'

'*You* hardly know him.'

Desperately she thought of what lie would make everything all right. 'I know his sister,' she stammered.

'How do you know his sister?' he asked curiously. 'I didn't even know he had one.'

'She works at the hairdresser I go to,' Cristina lied, 'my mother likes her – feels sorry for her. Sometimes she comes to the house.'

'Look, why don't we buy some magazines and go on home,' said Louis, suddenly bored by the whole thing. 'They have American *Vogue*, and look – a new edition of *Motor Sport*. He took out his wallet. 'Anything else you want?'

'I'm doing this favour for my mother,' Cristina said quickly, '*she* asked me to help Nino's sister.'

'What *are* you talking about?'

'Nino's going to meet us here. I promised we would help him see Al King's plane.'

Louis stared at her. 'Are you mad? How would that help his sister?'

'It's a long story, very complicated. *Please* help me, Louis. Honestly it's *very important*. I *promised* my mother we would help, I *promised*.' She was near to genuine tears.

'This is crazy,' he said, completely bewildered.

'If you love me you'll help me.'

'But, Cristina . . .'

'Oh look, here comes Nino now. *Please*, Louis, *please*. I'll explain it all to you later, but *please* don't ask questions now.'

☆

There were no press at the airport. Al's departure had been kept a secret. They were able to transfer from the helicopter to the plane with no fuss at all.

Holding Dallas' hand he strode through the jet to his private bedroom at the back, barely pausing to nod at his two stewardesses.

Bernie greeted them with his usual dirty jokes, and they laughed and asked about the show.

Paul sat down, opened up a table and laid out some contracts that he wanted to go over.

Evan strapped himself into an isolated window seat, and continued putting work in on the spot he was attacking.

Two key journalists had been invited along for the trip. They sat up near the front hopeful that Al would eventually emerge.

'Is that everyone, Mr Suntan?' stewardess Cathy inquired.

'That's it,' replied Bernie. 'We're empty this trip.'

'We'll close up then.'

As she spoke Cristina Maraco came running along the ramp leading onto the plane. She was flushed and breathless.

'Oh!' she gasped, 'we made it!'

The two journalists looked at her in surprise. Bernie waddled over. 'What do *you* want, girlie?' he asked, thinking she was a fan. 'And how the heck did you get on here?'

'The man at the desk let me through. He said it was all right. I'm Cristina Maraco – remember – we met at the airport when you arrived – and at the party last night. I'm Louis Baptista's fiancée. Louis, Carlos Baptista's son. Didn't Señor Baptista telephone you?'

'Should he have?'

'Oh yes – he said he would. You see he wants you to take us to São Paulo with you – he wants Louis to be there early to organize some things to do with the concert tomorrow.'

She spotted Evan and waved. 'Hi – good to see you again. Oh and there's Señor King's brother,' she called out desperately. 'Hello – remember me?'

Paul hardly glanced up.

Bernie scratched his head. 'So where is Louis?' He remembered him, a nicely-spoken boy, and he vaguely remembered her. Hadn't she spent quite a time dancing with Evan the previous evening?

'He's just coming, it is all right then?'

'I don't see why not. Let me just check it.'

He walked over to Paul, who plainly did not want to be bothered.

'Carlos Baptista wants his son and fiancée to come with us. Is that OK?'

'If Carlos says so.'

'So I'll tell them it's fine?'

'Yes. I suppose so.' Paul returned to studying the contracts.

Bernie waddled back to Cristina.

'Yes?' she asked anxiously.

'Yeah. Only hurry your boyfriend Up, we're waiting to go.'

Cristina rushed off the plane to where Louis and Nino stood waiting in the tunnel which joined the embarkation point to the plane.

'It's OK,' she said.

Nino and Louis moved forward, Nino walking slightly behind Louis in his mechanic's uniform. In one hand he carried a shabby airline bag. The other hand was buried deep in his overall pocket clutching onto a gun which was pointing straight at Louis' back.

62

Van Howard glanced at his co-pilot and raised a questioning eyebrow.

'Five minutes,' Harry Booker assured him, removing his radio head set. 'The runway's clearing now.'

'Good,' Van was tired, and was looking forward to finishing off the short hop to São Paulo and getting some sleep. He had not slept at all the previous evening. Truth to tell he had had a lousy evening. The problem was Cathy, his wife.

At first the idea of captaining Al King's private jet across America, with the opportunity of taking Cathy along in a professional capacity – had just seemed heaven-sent. He had recently quit his job of seventeen years with a commercial airline, and he had been looking around wondering what to do, when a friend had mentioned the Al King job.

Van had attended two interviews, and been hired over eight other equally experienced applicants. Cathy being chief stewardess had been part of the deal.

What an opportunity it had seemed. The money was great, and it would get them out of the ten-year rut their marriage seemed to have become stuck in.

Everything had started off all right, but gradually Van noticed Cathy changing. He had married her when she was seventeen, and as far as he knew had been her only boy-friend. Their marriage had seemed quite stable – the only black spot being the fact that they seemed unable to produce children. Privately Van knew it was her fault. At forty-seven years of age he had had more than his share of girlfriends with unwanted pregnancies. However, they had both sub-jected themselves to various undignified tests, and although there seemed to be nothing clinically wrong, still it had not happened.

Van had hoped that this trip might do the trick. Different environments. Different places to make love. But as they progressed across America Cathy became more and more withdrawn.

She had finally told him the previous evening. Told him after drinking a bottle of wine to give herself dutch courage.

She had fallen in love with one of the musicians on the tour. A twenty-four-year-old long-haired freak who made his living strumming a guitar.

'Are you mad?' Van had asked her.

'I'm leaving you,' she had replied. 'As soon as the tour is finished I'm leaving you.'

'All set, chief,' Harry Booker interrupted his thoughts, 'we just got clearance. Seems we've taken on three extra passen-gers. Shall I inform control?'

'Doesn't matter.' Van shook his head. It was impossible to

keep a proper passenger list on these flights. People popped on and off from city to city. Journalists, photographers, groupies. Van never knew who was aboard. He glanced round at the navigator and flight engineer, men he had been allowed to pick personally.

'Are we ready?' he asked. A question he always asked before turning on the power.

Their nods were affirmative.

☆

In his custom-built flying bedroom Al tossed Dallas a bathrobe.

'Make yourself comfortable,' he suggested, 'I'm going to.'

She looked around her. 'This is unbelievable!' she exclaimed.

'You like it?' he asked proudly.

'It looks like something out of *Macho* magazine! Even a hick like me can see it's in the worst taste possible! It's nothing but a travelling knocking shop!'

'I'll have you know I've caught up on a lot of sleep in this room.'

'I'll bet!' She shook her head in amazement at the circular bed covered in black silk sheets, the fake leopard padded walls, the thick pile carpet.

'Bathroom's over there,' he indicated a hidden door in the padded walls, 'what shall I order for you? A drink? Food? You name it – we've got it.'

'This whole thing must cost you a fortune!'

'Tax deductible.'

'I'll have a Bloody Mary. You *are* going to allow me to have alcohol, aren't you?'

He grinned. 'Bout as much as you allow me. I'm sweating like a pig – I'll have a shower as soon as we take off.' He threw off his clothes and put a bathrobe over his undershorts. Then he picked up an intercom phone and snapped, 'Cathy – two Bloody Marys right now. How long before take-off?'

☆

Cathy Howard hung up the intercom phone and made a face. She wished Al King could be like everyone else and *wait* for his drink. Didn't he realize she had other things to do just before take-off? Besides that, she felt terrible. Telling Van the truth last night had been a tremendous strain. Why couldn't he have taken it like a man instead of dissolving into pitiful tears? She had been shocked. Van had never shown one ounce of emotion throughout their ten-year marriage. Perhaps if he had, things might have been different . . .

She busied herself in the small galley with tomato juice, vodka, and ice cubes. Al liked his drinks just so – he always insisted that she fixed them personally.

Wendy, the other stewardess, rushed in. 'Did you get a load of the mechanic with the Baptista party? she asked. 'Mmm . . . tasty. I wouldn't sling *him* out of bed!'

'*You* wouldn't sling *anyone* out of bed,' Cathy replied crisply.

Wendy had started the trip as Harry Booker's girlfriend. That had lasted all the way to Chicago, when they had both decided to go their own ways. Since that time Wendy had undertaken her own personal survey of the sexual habits of the American male.

'Who are the drinks for?' Wendy asked.

'Mr King of course.'

'You want me to take them?'

'I can manage, thank you.'

Wendy pouted, 'Why do *you* always have to do everything for him?'

'Because I'*m* chief stew. Anyway, he likes me.'

'Given half a chance he could like me,' Wendy muttered. 'Are you feeling OK? You look terrible.'

'Well enough to take him his drinks, thank you.'

☆

The FASTEN YOUR SEAT BELTS NO SMOKING signs had flashed on.

Bernie was sitting up front rapping with the two journalists.

Paul was engrossed in the contracts, making notes on a separate piece of paper.

Evan had settled into a secluded seat at the back, near the door to Al's private bedroom, and he was studying his latest batch of girlie magazines, trying to decide between Elvira, who loved horses, and had the biggest knockers he'd ever seen, or Yana, whose widely spread legs displayed a healthy abandon for wide open spaces.

Cristina sat opposite Louis and Nino, a table separating them. She had paled beneath her suntan, and her eyes were wide and alarmed. Under her breath she whispered. 'Help me God – Please help me. I promise to be good. I promise to do everything my parents want. I promise to be the perfect daughter. But please please God help me out of this mess.'

And what a mess it was. Nino had turned up to meet them all right. He had smiled, his eyes blazing intently. And he had said, quite politely, 'How are you, Louis? How does it feel to have a gun pointing at your belly?'

And she had laughed, thinking it was a joke, thinking he was kidding. But he had moved insidiously towards her, pressing himself against her so that she could feel the pressure of the metal, and he had said, 'Tell your boyfriend to do as he is told, Cristina. Tell him or I'll blow his guts out.'

With a sudden fear she had known that this was no joke. 'Do as he says, Louis. He means it.'

Louis had stared at her with an expression of disbelief. 'What is this . . .' he began.

'Shut up and start walking,' Nino had interrupted. 'Walk ahead of me, I'll tell you where to go. *Both* of you ahead of me.'

She hadn't dared to argue. She hadn't dared to say another word. She had just followed Nino's instructions, and now here they were bound for São Paulo where she didn't know what would happen.

Louis hadn't looked at her once. He just stared straight ahead with a stony expression. He probably thought she was a part of it. He probably thought she had tricked him. And the horrible truth was that she had – but she hadn't meant to, hadn't wanted to. And had certainly not been aware of the fact that Nino would have a gun.

The jet was taxi-ing down the runway, preparing for take-off. A stewardess touched Cristina on the arm, and she jumped.

'Sorry,' said the stewardess, 'did I startle you? Just wanted to check that you have your seat belt fastened.'

She smiled provocatively at Nino. 'All done up?' she asked, flashing admirable teeth.

He nodded, returning her smile, stripping her with his eyes.

'I'll be back to see what you'd like to drink as soon as we're airborne,' she said, instinctively smoothing down her skirt.

☆

'You've got everything organized,' Dallas remarked.

'Sure,' agreed Al, 'I like my privacy.'

He had settled them both into a small couch with concealed seatbelts. He indicated a niche for her to place her glass in.

'How many ladies have you had on this plane?'

He grinned. 'No ladies.'

The jet began to pick up speed, thundering down the runway, then lifting up into the sky with a lyrical ease.

Al leaned over and kissed her, softly, insistently. She parted her mouth to accept his kiss, teased him with her tongue. 'I think,' he said gruffly, 'I'm going to like this flight.'

'I think,' she replied, 'we both are.'

☆

Nino licked dry lips. His throat was parched, and he was dying for a glass of water. No time for that though. No time for anything except putting his plan into operation.

He glanced swiftly at Louis sitting silently beside him. He had been easy enough to handle. Rich boy frightened of getting a bullet in the stomach.

Cristina was staring at him with an accusing expression. He knew she was beside herself to speak to him – but she couldn't – didn't want to let her precious Louis know that she had been in on it.

Nino allowed himself a small, tight smile, and his hand caressed the gun in his pocket lovingly. What power it gave him. What wonderful incredible power.

The jet had stopped climbing and was levelling out. The SEAT BELT and NO SMOKING signs flashed off.

Out of the corner of his eye Nino saw the two hostesses spring into action bustling around taking drink orders. Rock music filtered through the speaker systems.

'I'll tell you what we are going to do,' Nino said in a low voice, 'lean forward and listen, Cristina.'

She did as she was told. Louis glared at him, wanting to speak but not quite sure if he dared.

'This plane has three bombs aboard. Only *I* know where they are. Shortly I will tell the rest of the passengers. If everyone cooperates with me no one will get hurt – if they don't' – he shrugged – 'too bad for all of us.'

Cristina gasped. 'Nino! Are you mad?'

Louis joined in. 'He's not mad, he's bluffing. I know for a fact that Al King's plane is searched by security guards before he boards it.'

'An hour, sometimes two hours before he boards. Plenty of time left for a mechanic with an authorized pass to come aboard and do what he has to do.'

Louis said, his voice strained, 'What are you doing this for?'

'Ask your girlfriend, she knows all about it. Now I want you two to sit here quietly while I go and have a word with the captain. I should advise you not to tell anyone – I shall do so soon enough. Should anyone attack me, try to knock me out – that would be very unfortunate. The bombs are due to go off at fifteen-minute intervals half an hour from now. Only *I* can stop them. And please don't forget the fact that I have a gun – a weapon that I am quite prepared to use.' He undid his seat belt and stood up. 'The safest thing for you two is to just sit tight. I wouldn't *want* to hurt either of you, but I can assure you I would.' He set off down the centre aisle of the plane towards the flight deck.

Cristina looked helplessly at Louis. 'I'm sorry . . .' she began, 'I didn't know . . . didn't realize . . .'

'Didn't know *what*?' hissed Louis, 'how much *did* you know? *You* arranged to meet him. *You* got us on the plane. This all must have been planned . . . you *knew* all along.'

'I didn't know what he planned. I didn't know he had a gun, bombs. Do you think I would have helped him if I'd known that?'

'So you *were* helping him?'

'I only . . .'

'Shh – he's talking to the stewardess. As soon as he's out of sight I must tell someone.'

☆

Wendy was fixing drinks for the journalists when Nino came up. She winked. 'Can't wait, huh? In that case what's your pleasure?'

'I'd like to talk to the pilot.'

'Sorry – forbidden ground. Now what do you want to drink?'

'I have a gun in my pocket,' Nino said pleasantly, 'it's pointing right at you.' He gestured with the outline of it. 'Shall we go?'

'Oh no!' said Wendy. 'Oh, Jesus, no!'

'Come on. Move. Walk in front of me and keep smiling.'

☆

They were always trying to screw you.

Always trying to make points.

Always slipping in goddamn stupid clauses that a twelve-year-old would spot!

Angrily Paul made copious notes. Who the fuck did Lew Margolis think he was dealing with? A bunch of amateurs, for Crissake? A bunch of schoolkids?

Paul always checked the contracts before passing them on to the lawyers. He could spot things that the lawyers wouldn't even notice. What did they care? As long as their astronomical bills were paid.

And who did all the work? Who saved Al thousands of pounds by going through the small print? He did of course. Baby brother. The schmuck who never got any appreciation. The schmuck who was treated like a combination of Bernie and Luke. Chief gofer.

Linda was right. Linda had always been right. And where the hell had *she* been last night? It was difficult enough getting through to Los Angeles – but he had managed it three times – and three times her phone had rung and nobody had picked up. It was just too bad. He had told her he would probably be phoning. The least she could have done was stay in.

He had promised her marriage – wasn't that what she had been angling for? Wasn't that what she wanted?

It just wasn't good enough. She was playing games with him and he didn't *need* that crap.

Louis Baptista slid into the seat beside him. Christ! Conversation he didn't need either.

'Don't panic – don't panic—' Louis's voice was high-pitched and nervous – 'we're being hijacked – he's got a gun – bombs. He's with the pilot now.'

'Whhaat?'

'Nino. He's mad – quite mad. What shall we do? What shall we do?'

☆

Van Howard knew at once what was happening. As soon as Wendy pushed her way onto the flight deck – every drop of colour gone from her face – the dark boy behind her – he knew.

Every pilot had imagined himself in the situation a thousand times. They even used to give lessons on what to do at the airline he had worked for. Stay calm. Don't panic. If it's not possible to disarm the hijacker/hijackers then go along with what they say. Reassure the passengers. Under no account put their lives at risk. Try and maintain radio contract with control. All of this flashed through Van's mind before the terrified Wendy uttered a word.

'He's – he's got a gun in my back,' she gasped.

☆

Al finished showering and called out, 'You want to join me?'

'No thanks, I find showering in the middle of the sky absolutely crazy!' Dallas sat cross-legged in the centre of the bed and sipped her Bloody Mary.

'Don't knock it if you haven't tried it,' Al walked back into the bedroom knotting the cord of his bathrobe. He joined her on the bed and started to laugh.

'What's the matter?' Dallas asked.

'First time I ever shared a bed with a girl I haven't given one to.'

'Your English expressions are so cute!'

'Fuck you.'

'Another cute expression!'

'Now look . . .'

She smiled at him, stopping him in his tracks.

'I think . . .' he said.

'I think so too.'

He stared at her earnestly, 'Are you sure?'

'I'm as sure as I'll ever be.'

He reached for her, and she moved towards him willingly.

'I've waited a long time for this,' he whispered, shrugging off his bathrobe.

'Me too,' she whispered back, running her fingers lightly over his chest.

'Christ!' he muttered, 'you want to see what I've got for you?'

'I can see, I can see.'

'Just a minute,' he reached over to the panel surrounding the bed and pressed a few buttons.

'What are you doing?'

'Locking the door and turning off the intercom. Now nothing can disturb us.'

☆

By the time Louis had garbled out a story that Paul understood, it was too late. Van Howard's voice was booming out through the speaker system. 'This is your captain speaking,' he said calmly, as if he was just about to give them a weather and altitude report. 'We seem to have a slight problem here.'

Cathy, busying herself with a tuna fish sandwich and a chocolate milkshake for Bernie, stopped to listen. What slight problem? It was a beautiful clear night, no turbulence, a short hop. What problem?

'It seems we have a gentleman on board who would prefer us to land elsewhere. He has asked me most persuasively, and for the safety of all of us I feel that I must comply with his wishes.'

'What the fuck?' said Bernie, who had been only half listening. 'Did I fuckin' hear right?'

One of the journalists nodded nervously. 'I think maybe we are being hijacked.'

'Hijacked!' Bernie boomed, 'the fuck we are.'

'There is absolutely no need for any kind of panic,' Van's

voice continued, 'we have a full tank of fuel, and I would like you all to move to the back section of the plane and sit together. Please do that now. Cathy – please organize this procedure.'

She couldn't believe it was happening to her again. Two years previously she had been working a flight hijacked by three Arab guerillas. The passengers had panicked, and two of them had got shot. The plane had crash-landed in the desert, and there had followed two days of captive hell before they were rescued. The whole incident was a nightmare – the reason she had stopped working for a major airline.

'Cathy,' Van was repeating, as if he knew she would be rooted to the spot, 'please move all the passengers to the back of the plane, see they are strapped in, and sit with them yourself. If you all cooperate everything will be fine. Under *no circumstances* attempt to take matters into your own hands. I repeat – *under no circumstances.*'

Automatically Cathy sprang into action. Remember the rules. Don't panic. Appear calm and in control. Be reassuring but firm. 'Come along, everyone,' she said, 'let's make our way to the rear of the plane.'

Bernie and the two journalists were nearest the front. 'Bring your drinks with you if you want,' Cathy said. She could do with a drink herself. She took the female journalist by the arm. 'Come along now.'

Bernie said,' Jeesus Chee-rist! What the fuck's happening?'

Cathy managed a wan smile. 'Think of the publicity, Mr Suntan.'

'Who's hijacking us, for Crissake? Al will go fuckin' nuts!'

'I think it must be the young man who came aboard in the mechanic's uniform. He seems to be the only one missing – he must be on the flight deck.'

'Well, let's rush him, for Crissakes.'

'No,' said Cathy firmly, 'if the captain says we should take no action then we must obey him.'

'The fuck we must!' Bernie turned as if to head for the front of the plane.

Quickly Cathy blocked his path. 'Mr Suntan. We are in an emergency situation. We must obey the captain. To disregard him would be foolish.'

'Aw – shit,' grumbled Bernie. But he allowed himself to be herded with the others towards the back of the plane.

Cristina sat rigidly in her seat.

Cathy shook her by the shoulder. 'Come along, miss,' she said softly. She could see the girl was in shock, 'there is nothing to worry about.'

'He forced me,' Cristina mumbled, 'he blackmailed me.'

'Yes,' agreed Cathy, 'come along now.'

Cristina allowed herself to be helped from her seat. 'Louis isn't talking to me,' she said sadly, 'Louis hates me.'

Paul was already standing in the aisle as Cathy encouraged her small group of passengers towards the back of the plane.

'What can I do?' he asked urgently. He knew about the previous experience Cathy had gone through, and considered her an expert on the subject.

She didn't feel like an expert, but she did know that they all had to do what Van said. 'Just stay calm,' she replied, 'and help everybody else to do the same.'

Evan, already seated at the back of the plane, was startled to suddenly be descended on by a whole group of people. He shut an obscene centrefold quickly, and took off the earphones attached to his portable radio – the reason why he had not heard what was going on. Quickly his uncle brought him up to date.

'Crikey!' he exclaimed, quite excited by the whole prospect. And he bundled his magazines together and dumped them under his seat.

☆

'I'm going to tell you something,' Al said softly. 'All my life I've been fucking. This is what I call making love.'

'I know,' she whispered in reply.

They sprawled across the bed together, naked, exploring each other's bodies with their eyes, their hands, their fingers.

They had done no more than to stroke, to touch, to marvel. It was enough for the time being. In a way they were both nervous, neither of them wanted to rush things.

'You do have the most marvellous, beautiful, untouched body I have ever seen,' Al told her.

'Untouched?'

'Yeah. That's the way I feel about you. Do you know what I mean?'

She nodded. She knew exactly what he meant. It was the first time in her life she had felt like this. So peaceful, and warm, so soft and expectant. Climbing a mountain, slowly, lazily. Stopping to rest every so often. No rush to get to the peak.

☆

'What about Al?' Bernie asked Paul, 'the shit'll fly when he finds out.'

'I don't think he's going to find out,' Paul replied, 'not until we land anyway. He's incommunicado. Doors locked. All speakers must be turned off. And you know his bedroom section is completely soundproofed from out here. There is no way we can reach him.'

'Thank God for small mercies,' Bernie snorted. 'But somebody's balls will get minced when we end up in some asshole communist dump. Cuba probably. How far away are we?'

Paul shrugged. 'What makes you think Cuba?'

'Isn't that where all hijacked planes go?'

'Cristina,' Paul leaned in to talk to the girl. They had sat her next to Evan. 'Do you know where this Nino character plans to take us?'

She was ashen-faced. 'I don't know,' she mumbled.

'But you were helping him, you *must* know,' Louis spat.

'I don't. I don't.' Tears started to trickle silently down her cheeks.

'Leave her alone,' said Cathy. 'Can't you see she's in shock.'

'Look – if she can help us . . .' Paul began.

He was interrupted by the crackle of the speaker.

'I am talking on behalf of my people,' Nino's voice announced, 'the oppressed, the sick, the poor. There are three bombs aboard this plane . . .'

'Aw-Jesus!' exclaimed Bernie, 'we're dealin' with a fuckin' commie psycho.'

'Three bombs that I can trigger off at any time. The captain has agreed to cooperate with me. I advise you for your well being to do the same. My organization – the P.A.C.P. – People

Against Capitalistic Pigs – requires only money. We will land in a safe and secure place, and when the money is paid you will be released. If you behave you will not be hurt.'

The speaker shut off.

'Money,' muttered Bernie, *'we're* the capitalistic pigs and *they* want the money. Assholes.'

☆

'I have to contact flight control,' Van insisted, 'I have to get air clearance.'

'No. You will follow the course I have given you.'

'But we could be in another plane's flight path.'

'It has all been checked beforehand,' Nino intoned, 'just do as I tell you.'

'Is it an airport you want me to land at?'

'I'll ask the questions. You follow my instructions.'

'I have to know. I can't just land this plane anywhere. We need certain conditions – a proper runway.'

'You are a first-class pilot. I am sure you will manage.'

'We're flying blind without radio contact. You have taken us off the radar path – we're flying blind.'

'Follow the instructions I have given you.'

Van glanced in exasperation at Harry, and then turned around to his navigator and flight engineer. They both seemed quite calm. At least he had an experienced crew. But flying without radio contact, on a new flight path, in a strange country, at night, was dodgy to say the least.

'Can you let the girl go back in the cabin with the others?' Van asked. Wendy was huddled in a corner quite obviously terrified.

'She stays with me,' Nino said sharply, 'if anyone doesn't cooperate she will be the first to get a bullet.'

☆

Cathy peered anxiously out of the window. They had been flying for quite some time, long past the time they should have landed at São Paulo. Since the two speaker announcements there had been silence. She wondered how Van was coping. He was a good pilot, a professional to his fingertips. He would stay calm, she knew that. She had risked going to the galley and made everyone coffee, and she had brought a couple of bottles of brandy and some packets of biscuits back with her. It was getting cold, and she had pulled down blankets and pillows and told everyone to try and get some sleep.

Van would have been proud of her. She was very together and in control when she could so easily have lapsed into hysteria at the memory of the other time.

She thought about her long-haired musician, and wondered what he would do when he heard.

São Paulo must have realized the plane had left its flight path long ago. Perhaps other planes had already been sent out to search for them. After all it was Al King's plane, with the great superstar himself aboard. And Carlos Baptista's son was with them, although from what she could make out nobody knew he was aboard. Anyway – a major search would be launched immediately.

It had begun to rain – little driblets of water were trickling down the windows. She hoped she was mistaken, but she thought she heard thunder. She hated flying through storms. A stewardess friend of hers had been killed in a plane struck by lightning.

'Perhaps I should go up to the flight deck and ask if I can make them all coffee,' she suggested.

'I don't think you should,' warned Paul. 'If he has a gun he may be getting jumpy. You busting in could set him off.'

'You're right. But I bet they sure could use a cup of coffee.'

☆

The weather conditions were worsening. What had started out as light rain had turned into a thunderstorm.

As far as Van could ascertain they were flying over the interior of Brazil – probably somewhere over the Amazon, heading in the general direction of Peru. Fortunately they had plenty of fuel, but it wouldn't last for ever.

'How soon can we expect to land?' Van asked. He was getting tired, the sleepless night had not helped.

'I told you – don't ask questions,' Nino replied.

Harry said, 'Weather conditions ahead are really bad. I suggest you tell us where and when we put this thing down.'

'Shut up,' snapped Nino. He had a blinding headache. If they read and studied the instructions he had given them they would *know* where to land. It puzzled him that they kept on asking questions – *he* didn't know. The organization had told him it was a disused airport somewhere – it was all in the instructions. When they landed other members of the organization would be waiting to take over. Nino would be flown out of there, back to Rio, where he had a new name and a new apartment waiting.

'Just follow the instructions,' he said grimly.

'Let's have the rest of them then,' snapped the navigator.

'You've got them.'

'Up to here I have, there must be another page.' He held up the paper to Nino.

'I gave you both pages.'

'Only one.'

'Both!' screamed Nino, suddenly panicky. The instructions – written out in navigational terms by a former airline pilot were on two sheets of white paper. He was sure he had handed them both over.

Van and Harry exchanged glances. They sensed a crisis.

'Look for it – you fool, perhaps you dropped it,' Nino raged.

'*You* look for it,' shouted the navigator, '*I* never bloody had it.'

'Is this some trick?' screamed Nino, and he pulled out his gun.

At that precise moment the plane hit an air pocket and plummeted several feet. It was enough to throw Nino off balance, enough to precipitate his trigger finger, and the gun went off, the bullet lodging firmly in Van Howard's right shoulder.

63

Cody was angered by Bernie Suntan's phone call. Dallas regrets she will not be able to make the studio until Monday. How on earth had Dallas known that the studio required her? For all she knew she was still out on her ear. And why had she not picked up a phone and spoken to him herself? Too cowardly no doubt. Frightened of the major blast she would get from him. And he *was* angry. His anger overshadowed the relief he felt at the fact that she was all right. She *knew* how concerned he must have been. How could she just vanish without so much as a word? He had spent a sleepless night imagining her raped or murdered or something equally horrific. Instead she had been unconcernedly shacked up with Al King. And now she was hopping off for a quick weekend in South America. Lew Margolis would love that. And *he* was the one stuck with telling him.

In fact Lew took the news surprisingly calmly. 'Oh,' was all he said. A resigned and weary 'Oh.'

'She'll be on the set bright and early Monday morning,' Cody assured him.

'Yes,' replied Lew vaguely.

Cody had expected fireworks. All he got was a damp squib. He was puzzled. Anyway – at least she was back on the series, that was the main thing. He just hoped that she wasn't going to turn up stoned on Monday morning, she had been in bad shape when she had set off for Palm Springs. He sighed. Well, of course he had known the first time he set eyes on her that it wasn't going to be an easy ride. But he had expected the traumas and temperaments when she had made it – not on the way there.

Thank God he was emotionally untangled. Getting involved in that way was suicide time. It was good it had been so brief.

Carol had worked as far as restoring his ego was concerned. But she had become too much of a good thing – and he had moved out and taken a short lease on a furnished house on Miller Drive. Nothing spectacular, but it would do to be going on with.

His business was going well. Apart from his English comedy actor signing for a major movie, he had just completed a very lucrative deal for his young stud actor to make a film in England. If things were sorted out with Dallas, and everything seemed to be going smoothly, then he saw no reason why he couldn't make a quick trip to Europe. He had never been there, it would be an experience.

His secretary came into the office. She was apologetic. 'Miss Cameron is *insisting* upon speaking to you. This is the fourth time she has called today.'

'Tell her I'm in a meeting.'

'I told her that three hours ago.'

'Tell her it's a long meeting.'

'Yes, Mr Hills. Oh, and your mother called again, said she was waiting for you to call her back.'

He made a wry face. 'I'll do that now.' Big agent or not you couldn't keep mother waiting. If he did she would nag the pants off him, and *that* he didn't need.

☆

Linda peered at herself in the mirror. Here she was, thirty-two years old, living in California, and going out on a date, for Crissakes. She hadn't been on a date since she couldn't remember when. Her relationships had fallen into either the Paul or Rik categories. A commitment or a screw. Who went on dates any more?

She looked good. Black hair, clean and shining. Make-up not over emphasized. Figure, slim and enticing in a beige pants suit and matching shirt.

She decided she looked exactly what she was. A no-nonsense career girl who was prepared to meet anyone on equal terms. For a brief moment she wanted to kick her cool together image. Why couldn't she look wild and sensual like Dallas? Why couldn't she have a ripe luscious body that drove men to distraction?

She laughed softly at her thoughts. Might be all right for a night, but to be saddled with that kind of image? Forget it. Anyway, in her own quiet way she hadn't done too badly.

The afternoon she had spent indulging herself on a soothing shopping trip around Beverly Hills – purchasing the suit, and shirt, some boots, a slew of make-up, six new hardback books, and a new lens for one of her cameras. Pure extravagance. But she had enjoyed every minute of it. Anything to get her mind off that asshole Paul and the number he was giving her. Christ – but he must think she was an idiot. And that was the most insulting thing of all – to think that she would believe his crappy lies – with Melanie King and Manny Shorto plastered over every fucking paper in town.

She had stormed back to her apartment after her therapeutic shopping trip, still fuming. She had contemplated phoning

Julio and making a quick appointment. But why waste him on a quickie? If he was as good as he was supposed to be – why rush?

So now she was hanging around waiting for her date to pick her up. She should have arranged to meet him at the restaurant – much better idea. Now she would have to offer him a drink, and make idle stilted chit-chat. *He* would probably want to talk about nothing but Dallas, and *she* would be bored stiff. She just wanted to forget about Dallas and that whole scene for a while. Images of Doris Andrews – wholesome idol of the American screen – kept on floating around her head. Doris naked. Doris kissing, biting, sucking . . .

She wondered if it was too late to phone Cody and cancel. Who needed a date? She needed a session with her parking boy or some such faceless male.

The doorbell buzzed, and ended *that* escape route.

Cody stood there washed and clean and nice looking. He had brushed his sandy hair forward, and wore a well-cut jeans suit. And he carried – Oh no! A box of ribbon-wrapped candy!

'You make me feel like I'm back in high school,' Linda grinned, accepting the box from him and dumping it on the small bar which divided the kitchen and living areas.

'This is nice,' said Cody, looking around.

'It's cheap, and I don't know how long I plan to make it home.'

'Why didn't you stay on with Dallas then?'

One minute and she was already a part of the conversation. 'I like my privacy. Can I fix you a drink?'

'Vodka would be fine – on the rocks.'

He prowled round the room. Perfect set-up for a bachelor girl who planned to move on. Nothing cutesy. Nothing personal. 'You got a place in New York?'

'A sleazy apartment which I love.' Why was she lying to him? She hated it. Paul hated it. It was a dump. It was in a lousy neighbourhood – but it had been home for quite a few years.

'Anyone living there while you're away?'

'Why? You want to borrow it?'

'No – I just er wondered.'

'Like you want to know if I live with a man – right?'

He looked embarrassed. 'No . . . I . . .'

'I have had an on/off relationship with Paul King – Al's brother, manager, general wet nurse and pimp – for one and a half *very* long years. At the moment – for reasons I wouldn't dream of boring you with – it's very definitely off. Apart from him, my other attachments are only momentary. How about you?'

'I told you about myself and Dallas . . .'

She handed him a vodka, swirling the ice cubes with her fingers. 'Yes. You told me.' Please don't tell me again, Cody. If you do I'll scream! She was not in the mood to listen to stories about other women.

'Since then I've spent a little time with Carol Cameron.'

'Carol *who*?'

'Cameron. She's an actress.'

'In this town they all seem to be actresses,' Linda remarked drily. 'In New York they are models. In Hollywood – actresses. I think those two phrases encompass a huge spectrum of professions!'

Cody laughed. 'You're a bright lady.'

'Am I supposed to curtsey and say thank you, kind sir?'

'I meant it as a compliment.'

'Why? What's complimentary about calling someone bright? How would you like it if I gave you a look of amazement and said – hey – you're really quite intelligent.'

He gulped his vodka. 'Point taken.'

'I'm not in a very good mood,' she confided, 'in fact I'm pissed off at the world. Maybe we should just forget about tonight.'

'I'm not in a very good mood either. What do you say to going out and getting good and plastered?'

'Man to man?'

'Whichever way you want it.'

'I'm on.'

☆

They had a good time. They started off with a bottle of wine over dinner, then Irish coffees, then lethal tequilas at a jazz bar Cody knew, and finally Brandy Alexanders at a high-class strip joint.

'I'm having a *marvellous* time,' Linda revelled, 'hey – Cody. Don't they have any *guys* in this place?'

'What do you want – a sex show?'

She patted him on the shoulder, her voice attempting to register an even keel. 'No, buddy. No sex show. I mean jus' guys. I mean we got tits every way you look – tits over there – an' there – an' there.' She pointed out two topless cocktail waitresses, and a stripper, then unexpectedly she stood on her chair, rocking dangerously. 'How about a few dicks?' she yelled. 'How about it, fellas? Show us what you got!'

'Get down,' laughed Cody, 'you'll get us thrown out of here.'

'Equality!' Linda yelled. 'I want to see some great big joints!'

A few females sitting round about joined noisely in. 'Yeah!' 'Get 'em off fellas!' 'Let's see the great white wonder!'

The cocktail waitresses looked at each other and sniggered. The waiters, all three of them, backed warily towards the bar.

With a drunken leap Linda left the chair. 'Ladies united. Let's debag 'em.'

'Jesus . . . Linda . . . stop . . .'

Cody was choking with laughter.

Linda advanced on a waiter reaching for his fly. He socked her straight on the jaw. Because she was so drunk she fell with a delicate easy grace.

She woke up five minutes later in Cody's car.

'We got thrown out,' he solemnly informed her, 'but I screwed 'em. I refused to pay the cheque!'

'I'll sue that sonofabitch for assault,' she wailed. 'My jaw feels like a side of beef!'

'I'll take you home and put an ice pack on it.'

'*Your* home – not mine.'

'I thought this was a man to man evening?'

'I'm a bright girl – I can change my mind, can't I?'

☆

Evita watched the Al King concert at the Maracana Stadium. She even enjoyed it in a detached sort of way. And after, at a small dinner for twenty-five people that Carlos Baptista had arranged, she danced and chatted, and admired the exotic cabaret of eight voluptuous samba dancers.

But all the while her thoughts were elsewhere. Her thoughts were concentrated on the following morning when Doris Andrews was due to arrive.

How should she treat her? Should she be cool, warm, enthusiastic, distant?

Should she *say* anything? Or just try to pretend their sexual dalliance had never occurred?

Jorge was enthusiastic about the party he had insisted she should plan. It was to be on Sunday and everything was arranged. She had even purchased a new dress for the occasion, and requested Jorge to collect her emerald and diamond jewellery from the safety deposit box at the bank.

In one way she was dreading Doris' arrival. But in another way it had excited her to fever pitch.

She was dancing with Carlos. The portly, rotund man reeked of cigar fumes.

'A magnificent evening – heh – heh? What did you think of my American star – heh – heh?'

'I thought he was English.'

'He is, he is. But you know what I mean. He is an *international* great. They loved him, didn't they? Did you hear them scream?'

'My ears are still ringing.'

He gave her an intimate squeeze and wistfully sighed. 'If only Jorge and I weren't such friends . . .'

'Yes?' she teased, 'and what would you do, Carlos?'

'I would . . . *Merda!*' He was being summoned to the phone.

Evita drifted quietly back to the table where Jorge was involved in an animated discussion of politics.

She watched him, her handsome distinguished husband, and wondered why he wasn't enough. Wondered why the need had been there for Doris Andrews to find and take advantage of.

'Where do *you* think the children could have got to?' Carlos' wife, Chara, was asking – interrupting Evita's thoughts.

'I really don't know,' Evita replied politely. She didn't really like the fat, gossipy Chara.

'So impolite,' Chara complained. 'Carlos is furious. Louis will be in trouble when *he* gets home. Wasting expensive tickets – two empty seats for everyone to see. I can assure you *Louis* will be in trouble.' She waited for Evita to assure her that Cristina would also be in trouble, but Evita just smiled, nodded, and looked around for someone to rescue her.

'The young people today have no manners,' Chara continued, 'no discipline. Why – when I was a girl I wasn't allowed out of the house without a proper chaperone,' she waved fat bejewelled fingers in the air. Today all they have is freedom – freedom – and no respect.'

Idly Evita wondered why both Chara and Carlos used words in double sequence.

'Of course I blame the parents.' Chara continued, getting in a dig at Evita. '*We* have always been very strict with Louis – very strict.' She stuffed a candied grape into her mouth. 'He is a good boy—' she sighed regretfully, 'but easily influenced by others ... Tell me, why does Cristina wear such funny clothes?'

Evita smiled sweetly. 'It's her style. Personally I think at seventeen it doesn't matter what you wear. As long as you are young and pretty ... Chara, do please excuse me, but I've been meaning to ask you – does obesity run in your family?'

☆

Linda woke up with a bearable hangover. It was a long time since she had been so drunk – in fact hadn't the last time been over some sort of job crisis?

She reached over and touched Cody who was still sleeping. She had broken one of her golden rules – stayed overnight. But who had been able to summon the strength to drive home? Anyway – come to think of it – who had wanted to?

Cody Hills as a lover had been a delightful unexpected surprise. They had started the evening as mates and ended up as lovers – and she didn't have one single regret. In fact the whole situation reminded her of the first time with Paul. But of course Cody had none of the complications. He wasn't married. He didn't have children. He lived in America. He didn't work for his brother – indeed he didn't even *have* a brother. What a plus *that* was.

She laughed softly to herself, and climbed out of bed.

Cody started to wake, stretched out his arms to her.

She blew him a kiss. 'Coffee for two,' she said, 'black, extremely strong and I'll bring it to bed so stay right where you are.' She turned at the door. 'Oh, and do you take sugar?'

'Three spoons. What's your name?'

She treated him to a rude gesture. 'Get lost!' and exited.

Cody bounded from the bed. He felt marvellous. He went into the bathroom, scrubbed his teeth, took a piss, and climbed expectantly back into bed.

Linda was the best thing that had ever happened to him. She was *very* attractive, witty, intelligent, warm, funny. She was *everything* he had ever wanted in a woman. And in bed she did not make him feel inadequate – she made him feel like a giant! She wasn't Dallas – lying limply there suffering his advances. She wasn't Carol Cameron waxing false enthusiasms over his every move and exclaiming like a hooker at a convention. 'Ohhh Marvie!!!' 'You can't go near me that that huge thing!!!' 'You're soooo fan-tas-tic – *really* you are!'

He couldn't wipe the wide smile off his face. To find a woman like Linda so soon after the débâcle with Dallas. It was wonderful. *She* was wonderful. Of course he still loved Dallas – but it was a protective love – a brotherly love – an *agent's* love.

Linda walked back into the room carrying a tray with two steaming cups of coffee, and the papers which she had picked up from outside the front door. How many girls would think of doing *that*?

'Can you cook?' he asked.

'No – but I open a mean can!'

'In that case what do you say about moving in?'

'I say let's give it some time. OK?'

'If I can have an option on your evenings.'

'I'll talk it over with my agent.'

☆

Carlos Baptista didn't want to break up the party. He puffed on a giant Havana cigar and wondered what to do.

His wife was talking to Evita. The rest of his guests

seemed to be enjoying themselves. What to do? Tell them? Tell them what? That he had just had a report that Al King's plane had failed to turn up in São Paulo. That all radio contact had been terminated shortly after the plane left Rio.

What had happened? No one seemed to know. The weather between São Paulo and Rio was good. It was a bright, clear night. The whole thing was a mystery.

Carlos was an optimist. He had every confidence that the plane would turn up, after all it couldn't just vanish.

He decided anyway to keep the news to himself. No point in breaking up a good party.

He caught the eye of his latest mistress, a lovely exotic girl married to one of his minions. He winked at her. With a slight incline of her head she indicated the dance floor. He noted Chara still busily chatting away, and he nodded at his girlfriend.

Life was too short to worry – Al King had obviously for some obscure reason instructed his pilot to go elsewhere – these stars were very temperamental. As soon as he turned up at another airport Carlos would be notified. Frankly he didn't care *merda* what Al King did. As long as he turned up on time for the concert in São Paulo the rest of the time was his own.

Carlos beamed, and swept down on his girlfriend. 'Senora Jobin, my turn to dance with you I think.'

☆

Linda spent the day in a daze. She was knocked for six. It was all so unexpected. One second she had been contemplating murdering Paul – the next he was out of her mind, a past memory, and she knew for a fact that she *didn't love him any more*. Just like that she was freed, and the relief was incredible!

Not that it was instant love with Cody. No – he was nice, she liked him a lot, but it was a relationship that would have to be gradually built up. She was quite prepared to give it a try and see what happened. If it worked out – great.

She got through the day, drove over to Cody's house, and they barbecued steaks and talked and talked and talked. It was good. It was meaningful.

When they fell into bed at 4 a.m. it was even better than the night before.

'Where'd you *learn* all this stuff?' Linda murmured appreciatively.

'Tonight. Now,' Cody replied.

'He knows all the right things to say too!'

'He's a bright boy!'

The word bright had become their own private joke.

When they finally slept Linda kept on waking up.

'Wassamatter?' Cody asked sleepily.

'I don't know. I feel kind of strange. I have the weirdest feeling. I keep on thinking of Dallas and Al ... As soon as I drift into sleep I see them both clearly. It's like they are in some kind of trouble ...'

'Do me a favour – go to sleep. You know what an analyst would say, don't you? He'd say you were really thinking of Paul.'

'Thank you very much.'

'Goodnight, Linda.'

'Goodnight, analyst.'

64

The sudden plummeting of the large jet frightened everyone. But no one was hurt as they were all strapped firmly into their seats. The only damage was some spilled drinks, and verbal hysteria from the lady journalist, 'Ohmigod! Ohmigod! We're going to crash! We're going to crash! Ohmigoooood!!' The last word developed into a panic-stricken wail.

'It's nothing to get excited about,' Cathy said as calmly as she could, 'we just hit an unexpected air pocket, nothing unusual.'

The plane was jumping around all over the place, and Cathy wondered what the hell was happening up front. For the first time she felt frightened.

'Stay calm, everyone,' she said in her most reassuring tone, 'we seem to be going through a rather turbulent patch.'

'Where the fuck are we?' demanded Bernie.

'I don't know,' Cathy replied, furious with Van for leaving

her stranded back here with a bunch of soon-to-be-hysterical passengers. He must know they would be getting anxious, the least he could do was make some sort of announcement – anything. But maybe he wasn't allowed to.

The lady journalist was still wailing and screaming, whilst everyone else sat silent and white-faced as the plane lurched around the sky.

'Chree-ist,' exclaimed Bernie in disgust, 'this whole friggin' plane's gonna bust apart if this keeps up. His comment induced further hysteria from the lady journalist. 'Will you shut up, you douche bag!' Bernie shouted. 'Keep your fuckin' screams to yourself.'

She was shocked into silence.

'This plane is built to withhold any kind of turbulence,' Cathy assured them. 'No chance of it breaking up, Mr Suntan.'

'Bullshit,' he muttered.

☆

Dallas and Al were being thrown around the bed giggling and laughing.

'Do you believe it?' Al asked. 'Do you believe we've waited all this time and just when we are about to finally do it we run into a storm!'

'It's a sign from above,' Dallas said jokingly.

'I'll give *him* a sign. Come on – haul yourself over to the couch and strap yourself in.'

Staggering and bumping around they managed to get into bathrobes and strap themselves into the couch.

'It's not dangerous, is it?' Dallas asked.

Al laughed. 'I've been through turbulence that makes this look sick.' He held her hand. 'Nothing to worry about – got the best pilot money can buy – anyway we'll probably be landing soon, and you know the first thing we're going to do?

'No, what?'

'I'll give you one guess.'

☆

As the bullet entered his right shoulder Van Howard lost consciousness. He slumped over the controls, and for seconds everyone on the flight deck was immobilized. Then, as the big plane lurched and bucked, Harry Booker sprang into action. He hauled Van out of the cockpit as best he could, and took over flying the plane himself.

By this time Nino was on his feet and screaming a string of expletives. Wendy was sobbing hysterically, and the navigator had ripped off his jacket and placed it under Van's head. It was now extremely crowded on the flight deck, and the storm and general turbulence were rolling the plane in all directions.

'I'm going back,' Harry Booker yelled, 'I'm turning round.'

'No, you are not!' Nino shouted in excited frustration.

'There's no other way, you've lost the rest of the flight plan. If we don't know where we're going eventually we'll run out of fuel.'

'I have not lost anything!' Nino screamed. 'He is hiding it – it's him.' And he turned his gun on the navigator.

☆

'I think one of us should go to the front of the plane and see what's happening,' Paul said, more worried than he cared to admit.

'I'll go,' volunteered Louis.

'No, I'll go,' said Cathy. 'I'm less likely to alarm them.'

'We need you here,' Paul replied. 'I can go.'

'Please . . .' Cristina spoke for the first time. 'Please let me go. After all it is partly my fault we are all here.'

'Partly!' snorted Louis.

'Nino knows me. He will tell me what is happening. Please let me go.'

'Let her go,' growled Bernie. 'If she knows the guy maybe she can talk some sense to the prick.'

Paul had to agree that Bernie was right.

'Be careful then,' he warned, 'don't upset him. Just try and find out how long it will be before we land, and where.'

'I'll do my best,' Cristina replied, unstrapping her seat belt and setting off down the rolling plane.

☆

'We have no alternative,' Harry Booker said stubbornly. 'I'll try and make radio contact.'

'No!' screamed Nino, his gun wavering back and forth between the navigator and Harry.

'What do you suggest then?' said Harry, his temper beginning to snap. 'We're flying out here in the middle of nowhere, we don't know where we're supposed to be going. We're flying blind, the weather conditions stink, and apart from all those pluses – that man is probably dying.' He indicated Van lying on the floor, Wendy crouched over him attempting to stem the flow of blood from his wound. 'What's the penalty for murder in your country?' Harry sneered. 'Come on, let me turn back. We might just be lucky enough to make it. When we land you can keep me, the plane, whatever you want – as hostage.'

'I don't want you,' Nino said with contempt. 'I want a million dollars for Al King.'

'They'll give it to you,' Harry said persuasively, 'they'll give it to you for saving him.'

'Do you think I'm a fool?' spat Nino. 'Do you think you are dealing with a boy?'

As they argued Harry was putting the plane into a very slow unobtrusive turn. He didn't know where he was, but surely it would be better to head back from where they had come.

'I think you should listen to me,' Harry said. 'I think right now you're in a big mess, and I want to help you get out of it.'

Nino brought his free hand up to his head, and pressed his throbbing temple. He was confused. He didn't know what to do. He had the plane. He had Al King. Single-handed he had achieved that with only the help of a gun and three crude home-made bombs that were not even primed.

Now they wanted him to go back. They said they didn't have the second page of the instructions. But they must be bluffing. They *had* to be bluffing.

He had given them *two* pages of instructions – or had he?

Yes. He was sure of it – or was he?

The constant buffeting of the plane didn't help him think clearly. The rain smashing into the windscreen. The roar of the thunder. The angry flashes of lightning.

☆

'What is going on?' Al said suddenly, after a particularly sharp burst of turbulence. 'I hired a guy like Van Howard so I wouldn't have to go through this shit. If there's a storm he knows enough to avoid it. This is like a goddamn roller coaster – the fucker must be drunk.'

Dallas placed her hand on his knee. 'Don't get excited.'

He forgot the vibrating plane for a second. 'With you beside me . . .'

She leaned in to kiss him. Their lips met and were jolted apart.

'Fuck this!' said Al. He undid his seat belt and lurched over to the bed. He pressed a switch marked 'flight deck' and picked up the intercom. 'Howard!' he yelled. 'Howard!' He jiggled the switch – 'Great. Can't even answer the phone. Howard! What the fuck's happening?'

☆

Paul glanced around at everyone. They were mostly silent, huddled in their own private thoughts. Bernie was the only one who seemed to have developed verbal diarrhoea, muttering vague obscenities and curses of prophetic doom.

'Shut up, Bernie,' Paul snapped, 'keep your thoughts to yourself.' He wished that Al would emerge from his private retreat. Christ! He couldn't be sleeping or even screwing through this. And surely he must realize they had been in the air hours too long.

But of course he never bothered checking schedules. He had no idea how long the trip to São Paulo was. And he had Dallas to distract him. The beautiful Dallas, who like all the others had fallen into the appropriate position – bed.

Paul scowled. He knew what would happen. When they landed at whatever Godforsaken place they were heading for, Al would emerge. 'Where are we?' he would demand. And wherever they were, he, Paul, would get full blame.

He knew it. Everything was always his fault – so why should this occasion be different from any others?

☆

On the flight deck everything happened at once. As Al's voice boomed from the internal intercom demanding to know what was happening, Cristina pushed through behind Nino, startling him even further. Instinctively he pressed the trigger of his gun, and a bullet ricocheted round the cabin, grazing the side of Harry Booker's head. Blood started to drip from a superficial wound.

'Nino!' Cristina screamed, flinging her arms about him in an attempt to wrestle the gun from him, 'stop it! Give up . . . Give up – you can't win. You must give up.'

Nino tried to throw her off, tried to club her with the butt of the gun.

The navigator, seeing this as a good opportunity to disarm the madman, left his position and joined in.

Blood was dripping across Harry's eyes. He felt like he had been zonked on the side of the head with a hammer. He raised his arm to clear the blood with his sleeve. He never saw the lightning explode in a huge flash of white hot burning light straight in front of the plane.

He never saw it hit the right wing of the plane, which immediately burst into flames.

He only knew that the plane was out of control, plummeting crazily.

☆

'Brace yourselves,' Cathy yelled as the plane rocked violently, 'bend your heads forward – clasp your ankles.'

'We're going to crash – we're going to crash,' shrieked the lady journalist hysterically.

Jesus God! For the first time Paul felt fear. A cold fear that gripped him around the stomach. A fear that said – 'This is it – this is the final curtain.' He thought of his children, their faces flashing before him. He thought of Linda – how disappointed she would be. Then ironically he thought of Al screwing happily away in his private soundproofed bedroom. How fitting that he should go on the job.

'Holy shit!' exclaimed Bernie, 'the fuckin' plane's on fire!'

Vainly Cathy pleaded, 'Please stay calm. Everything will be all right. We have a very experienced pilot.'

Silent Luke suddenly burst into loud prayer, his resonant voice somehow comforting.

'Cristina! Cristina!' Louis screamed, struggling with his seat belt, 'I must get to Cristina!'

'Please stay seated,' begged Cathy. But she couldn't

prevent him from staggering off down the lurching sinking plane.

Cathy tried to peer out of the window, but there was only darkness and rain, and bright yellowy orange flames shooting over the wing. If Van could get them out of this . . . Oh God – if Van could save them she wouldn't leave him. She would stay with him. She would be a faithful wife. She would give up her long-haired musician. Oh God – please let Van save them.

Evan was throwing up. Vomiting in uncontrollable bursts all over himself. He had wet his pants also. But he didn't care. Didn't care at all. He wanted his mother. She would take care of him. She would know what to do. Tears rolled down his cheeks. He wanted mummy.

☆

Al was thrown violently across the padded bedroom.

He could feel the plane dropping, being buffeted around by the wind. He knew that something was terribly, dreadfully wrong.

He hauled himself across the floor and managed to belt himself in next to Dallas.

Her eyes were huge with fear. 'What's happening?'

'I wish I knew.' He wanted to go through to the passenger compartment, but the plane was plunging so crazily he didn't dare move. He was lucky to have made it back to his seat.

Somebody's head would roll for this. When they made firm ground, somebody was going to pay for putting them through a trip like this.

It did not occur to him for one moment that they might not make firm ground. The possibility of a crash was unthinkable.

He took Dallas' hand, and she clung on to him tightly.

'Don't worry,' he said, soothingly, 'we'll soon be landing.'

☆

The plane hurtled blindly down.

Harry Booker wrestled helplessly with the controls but there was nothing he could do. He was trying to stabilize the plane, get it under some sort of control.

He knew he would have to put it down, blindly, wherever

they were. But if only he could get hold of the bastard . . . He pulled back on the wheel with all the strength he could muster, and forced the thrust levers into full power. 'Come on, you mother . . . Come on . . .' Painfully, slowly, the nose of the plane started to climb. But it was much too slow, and the fire on the wing had unbalanced them, and there was a short in the circuit showing . . .

The plane started to bank, and Harry knew it was hopeless, knew there was nothing he could do.

They were enveloped in a sea of blackness in the middle of nowhere. Behind him Nino, Cristina, and the navigator were in a fighting, clawing mass on the floor. Van was unconscious. Wendy hysterical. And the young flight engineer transfixed in a state of shock.

Vainly Harry tried to throttle back, attempted to bring down the landing gear. They were dropping so fast. Sinking like a stone.

Blankly he wondered where they were. It didn't matter, in a few moments they would all be dead.

☆

'Brace yourselves against the seat in front,' Cathy yelled vainly, 'head on your knees – clasp your ankles. *Don't panic!*'

Nobody was listening – they were all too busy throwing up, or screaming hysterically, or praying, or cursing.

Cathy kept repeating her instructions, while her stomach jumped into her mouth with fear.

They were going to crash. They were out of control. They were on fire.

She tried to remember crash procedure. Everyone off the plane as fast as possible. Emergency shutes down. How soon would rescue services reach them? It depended where they were, and she didn't know that.

Oh God! Why had she ever left Van? This was a punishment. This was God's way of telling her she was wrong. If only he would give her another chance . . . If only . . .

With a deafening crash the plane ploughed into something. The impact created even more chaos. Hand luggage came hurtling down from all the racks, seats were wrenched free from their moorings, windows smashed in. All the lights went out, plunging them into a murky blackness.

But the plane didn't stop. Caught up in the trees it hurtled onwards – shuddering and shaking – pitching and rolling.

And the noise. Deafening, unreal. A tearing metal noise, an exploding jagged noise, a roaring vibrating noise.

The plane was ripping through the gigantic trees, disintegrating in parts as it progressed.

First the right wing snapped off on impact – then the left wing was wrenched free.

The body of the plane careered onwards, smashing a path through the trees, and finally splitting neatly in half.

The back of the plane shuddered to a stop. The front half slid on further into the jungle, then it too finally stopped.

Miraculously both sections of the plane were still in one piece.

For a moment there was silence except for the sound of the driving rain and startled bird cries. Then a series of small explosions came from the front of the plane, and the engines burst into flames.

Next came the human sounds. Cries for help, groans, terrified screaming.

It was amazing that anyone was still alive.

The plane had come to rest somewhere in the Amazon jungle, hundreds of miles from anywhere.

After smashing through the giant trees it had slithered to a stop amidst the dense forest ground.

The storm was abating somewhat. But the rain still poured relentlessly down.

From the sky the plane could not be sighted, the huge trees, some as tall as two hundred feet, took care of that.

Al King, his plane and occupants, had vanished into the bowels of the jungle without a trace.

65

There was always a moment when Linda first woke when she wasn't sure where she was. It had happened to her since the tour, and she found it quite an enjoyable sensation.

Where am I? What city? What bed?

It was quite exciting waiting for the answers to come flooding in.

Home – schmuck. Or – with Robert Redford of course. Or – that beautiful beach bum who is quite the best lay in town.

Los Angeles. Cody. His house.

She was quite satisfied. She rolled across the bed and nuzzled his back. He wore pyjamas – very sweet. She slept nude – was there any other way?

She put her arms around his soft waistline. He was very cuddly. A strict diet could get rid of his excess flab in two weeks.

She moved her hands inside his pyjama trousers, gently holding his flaccid penis.

'Are you awake?' she whispered.

He groaned in his sleep.

She played with him. Rubbing, kneading, teasing.

He grew hard in her hands.

She slid down under the sheet and took him in her mouth. He felt so good. She used her tongue in a variety of ingenious ways.

He groaned again, this time with sleepy pleasure.

She took him deep into her mouth. Released him slowly. Took him again.

He came in lovely throbbing spurts, his liquid filling her mouth with joy.

She slid up from under the sheets.

He opened his eyes in delighted surprise.

'My morning protein,' she grinned. 'How are you this morning?'

'You're a very sexy person.' He reached for her small taut breasts. 'Very sexy indeed.'

'Oh. You think so?'

'I definitely think so. And in about half an hour I'll prove it to you.'

'*Half an hour?*'

'I'm not nineteen, you know.'

She snapped her fingers together, 'Aw – shit. And I thought you were.'

They both giggled.

'What shall we do today?' Cody asked.

'Hmmm ... Saturday ... Let me see ... How about nothing? Does that grab you?'

'It really does.'

She climbed out of bed. 'I'll make the coffee. It's actually your turn – but I'll let you off today.'

She padded in the kitchen.

Saturday – when had Paul said he would be back? Four days. He had called her on Thursday, so Sunday, tomorrow . . .

She didn't even want to talk to him, it was as simple as that. Maybe if she stayed over at Cody's she wouldn't have to. Not a bad idea.

She poured hot water onto the instant coffee, contemplated squeezing orange juice, but felt too lazy. Then she remembered the papers and opened up the front door, scooping them off the mat.

'AL KING VANISHED PLANE MYSTERY' the headline screamed.

☆

Jorge shook his wife awake.

'Where is Cristina?' he demanded.

She struggled awake. 'I don't know . . . In bed, it's early isn't it?'

'She hasn't been home all night,' his voice rose dangerously. 'Marie came running to me hysterically – "Miss Cristina's bed hasn't been slept in, has she had an accident, Senor?" I went to her room, it's true, she hasn't been home.'

Evita sat up, reaching for a swansdown bedjacket. 'Have you telephoned Carlos? Is Louis home?'

'I haven't done anything. I came straight to wake you.'

Evita picked up the bedside telephone, dialled quickly.

'Oh – good morning, Chara. So sorry to wake you this early – oh you were,' she made a gesture of impatience as Chara engaged her in conversation. 'My God, that's dreadful. Look, I know you are busy, but I must speak to Louis. Yes, I'll hang on while you fetch him.' She covered the mouthpiece and addressed herself to Jorge. The plane flying Al King to São Paulo is missing.'

'Is Louis there?' exploded Jorge, not at all interested in any other subject.

'I think so. Just a minute.' She uncovered the mouthpiece. 'Yes, Chara. Oh, I see. Are you sure? Well, do you have any idea where he might be?'

Jorge snatched the phone from her. 'Chara? I'll break his neck. He has Cristina with him.' Jorge paused to listen. 'I don't particularly *care* about Carlos' other problems. *I want my daughter back.* I *know* they are engaged, that makes no difference to me. If your son has *touched* her . . .'

He slammed the phone down.

'Chara will tell the whole of Rio,' Evita stated. 'I wish you hadn't told her.'

'What bothers you? The fact that your daughter is somewhere with the Baptista boy? Or that fat *Cona* gossiping?'

'*Both* things bother me. Does she know where they are?'

'No, she doesn't. They'll have to marry at once you know – *at once.*'

'But everyone will think she is pregnant.'

'By this time she might be,' Jorge growled. 'I never did trust that boy.'

'I thought you trusted Cristina. *You* are the one who allowed her so much freedom. *You* are the one who kept on assuring me she was such a good girl.'

'She is, she is. I don't blame her – I blame the Baptista boy. She warned me about him, warned me he had made advances towards her.'

'I'm sure Cristina can look after herself.'

Jorge stared at his wife intently. 'You can be a very hard woman, Evita – very hard.'

'Not hard, Jorge, just realistic. I told you a while ago that Cristina was a woman. She is no baby innocent being taken advantage of.'

'How can you say such things about your own daughter?'

'Making love is not a crime.'

'For children it is.'

'They are not children.'

'You can be an impossible person,' Jorge spat. 'Sometimes you are a stranger to me. I will be in my study – fetch me the moment Cristina returns – the instant.'

He marched from the room.

☆

Edna could hear the doorbell ringing, even though she was right down the end of the garden – an outside extension took care of that. She must remind herself to have it disconnected.

It chimed continually, and she ignored it. She was busy picking tomatoes. Home-grown, red, hard tomatoes. How beautiful they were. How satisfying it was to watch something grow.

She filled a wicker basket and decided to take some with her to the pottery class that evening. She would distribute them amongst her friends there – the first friends she had ever possessed. Oh – being married to Al King had produced many acquaintances, but never one true friend. They had always been nice to her because of Al. Ingratiated themselves in the hope that it would do them some good. It never did, and they dropped away as soon as they realized this.

Now she had friends. Nice people who had no idea who she was – she had joined the pottery class under her maiden name and so far her secret was safe. Yes – they would enjoy the tomatoes – Carol and Mavis, Roger and John – especially John. She blushed at the thought of his name. She mustn't keep on thinking of him. It was too early for that sort of thing. He was a nice person, a gentle man.

She headed back towards the house. The house, she had decided, must be sold. She didn't want it. It was far too big and fancy. All she wanted was a small cottage with a little garden. A private place where she could live in peace. A place where she could invite her friends without feeling embarrassed.

Humming softly to herself, deep in thought, she didn't notice the two photographers come bounding round the side of the house. She didn't notice them until their cameras flashed, and then she shouted in anger. 'What are you *doing*? How dare you. This is private property. Go away or I'll call the police!'

'Just one more shot,' pleaded one of the photographers, 'we've been waiting for hours.'

'GO AWAY!'

'How about a quote then?'

She marched towards them, shielding her face, outraged at this invasion on her privacy. 'I'm phoning the police!' she warned. But then she realized it was an idle threat. She had had the telephone cut off, she had not required its services any more. At the same time she had cancelled all the news papers, and disconnected the four television sets.

A couple of reporters had joined the photographers. They were *trespassers*. Edna ran towards the house.

'Do you think Al is dead?' one of them called. 'Who was the girl he was with? Did you know her? Is your son with them?'

Edna stopped short in her tracks. 'What are you talking about? What are you saying?'

The reporter who had yelled the questions ventured nearer. He sensed a story. 'Didn't you hear yet, Mrs King? Al's plane has disappeared somewhere in South America – he's missing – presumed dead.'

☆

Carlos Baptista had enough problems. He certainly did not need Chara yelling at him about Louis.

He took no notice of her complaints. It was perfectly normal for a young man to stay out all night. And if he had a pretty girlfriend – well, so much the better. He should have made up some sort of excuse though. They both should. Silly children. Now he would have Jorge Maraco breathing down his neck insisting on an early marriage.

But he couldn't worry about that now. He had other problems. Major problems. A disaster in fact. And it seemed no one could help him.

Fact. Al King's jet had left Rio with the famous man aboard.

Fact. Shortly after take-off it had terminated radio contact and apparently vanished off the face of the earth.

But how could a large jet just vanish? It was impossible. It had to turn up somewhere. This wasn't the Bermuda triangle.

Spotter planes had been sent out to see if it had force landed or crashed anywhere. They had no idea where to start looking. The flight path between Rio and São Paulo was clear. So where to begin the search?

The big plane had carried enough fuel to travel a long way. Who knew which direction it had taken?

Airline officials were doing everything in their power to track it down. But they had nothing to go on. Investigations were only just beginning.

Who exactly was on the plane?

Nobody seemed to know.

Airport staff on duty the previous evening were being rounded up. What had they seen? Anything suspicious? Anything unusual?

An assistant of Carlos' came rushing into the temporary office set up for him at the airport.

'The boarding officer has been located,' he huffed, somewhat out of breath, 'he has a passenger boarding list.'

'Yes?'

'It seems, Senor Baptista, that your son was aboard with Miss Maraco.'

'Whaaat? That is impossible.'

'Not impossible, Senor. Unfortunately confirmed. They boarded the plane at the last minute saying that you had sent them.'

'I don't believe it!' raged Carlos. 'Impostors.' But then he remembered Chara's phone call. Remembered the fact that Louis had not returned home. Remembered that Cristina Maraco was also missing.

Carlos buried his head in his hands.

'Oh dear God!' he mumbled, 'Oh Christ above. *Filho da puta.* What can I do? What can I do?'

66

As the plane hurtled to its death Harry Booker lapsed into unconsciousness. On the initial impact the trees smashed through the cockpit pulping Harry to pieces. He died fairly quickly.

The flight engineer was not so lucky, half his face was gouged away, he was trapped in his seat, and death did not come until the plane finally stopped and he was slowly burnt to death.

Wendy also died in the fire. Wounded and trapped beneath Van's body, she could not move. She died screaming for help.

Van, unconscious, died with her.

Nino, Cristina, and the navigator were all hurled from the plane when it split in two. The fact that they were not strapped into seats probably saved them from being burnt to death.

Nino broke both legs, and suffered a lethal-looking gash to the head. Unable to move he lay groaning on the wet ground.

Cristina was miraculously unhurt. She was thrown out of the plane like a rag doll, and a bump on the head rendered her unconscious.

The navigator landed in a tree, and hung there limply. His neck was broken. Nobody found him, and he died after an agonizing three hours.

Louis Baptista was also unlucky – caught midway down the plane as it broke in half – he was crushed to death. His last scream of *'Cristina!'* went unheard.

At the rear of the plane things were only slightly better.

The two journalists, destined never to write their story, were hurled the length of the plane strapped side by side into adjoining seats, which had cut loose on impact. They were hurled straight into nothingness, and were dead by the time they hit the ground.

Bernie Suntan had been saved by his bulk. A deadly strip of jagged-edged fuselage had bayoneted him in the chest. If he had been a thinner man it would have reached his heart, but it was embedded in fatty tissue, and although blood poured from the wound, it did not seem to be lethal.

Paul was trapped by his legs under a concertina of seats. He was extremely white and had lost consciousness.

Cathy was covered in blood. She too was trapped next to Paul, but her face had impacted with something, and blood streamed from a broken nose, and a gaping cut on her mouth.

Evan was still strapped into his seat at a crazy angle. He had been bruised and shaken, and his arm was somehow crushed beneath him. But he was alive.

Luke, however, was dead, his massive body slumped on the floor – one of his legs nearly severed by a long shard of glass. Blood had pumped from the wound forming a huge puddle. He had been smashed on the head and his skull was crushed.

The door to Al's bedroom remained closed. Twisted and crushed where the roof of the plane had given way, it would not have opened even if Al had unlocked it. It was firmly jammed.

The couch where Al and Dallas had been strapped in had

been yanked from the wall. Together they had been buffeted crazily around the padded room.

The soft walls had saved them from any serious injury, and although they were covered in bruises they had both survived. The worst injury Al had was a cut on his leg. Dallas thought she might have broken a couple of ribs – the pain was intense. But the relief of being alive was unbelievable. When the plane had started its uncontrollable, dizzying, roller-coaster drop, she had known she was going to die. *Known it.* And she hadn't screamed or cried out, but just clung tightly to Al's hand, and wished that they could have had more time together, wished that she could have trusted him sooner. Now it was all over, and at least she was going to die with him. He had made her happy in the short time they had been together, and she was thankful for that.

'I love you,' she had whispered as the plane fell, 'love you – love you – love you.' And she had meant it.

At that moment in time Al had been trying to keep up with his thoughts. Goddamn it. His plane was crashing. *His* plane. He had paid for the best – paid a fucking fortune. *How dare they do this to him? How dare they?*

Where was Paul? Luke, Bernie? Why weren't they *doing* something. That's what he paid them for, wasn't it?

Christ! Who would believe it?

He could feel Dallas' nails digging into his hand. 'Don't worry, don't worry, everything's fine,' he managed to mumble.

Seconds later they hit the trees, and the goddamn couch came hurtling away from the wall, and he thought, Sweet Jesus don't let me die like this. I don't *want* to die. I've got too many things left to do.

And they were all over the place, bumping around, smashing from one side of the cabin to the other. And he could hear himself repeating, 'Don't worry – don't worry.' And he thought how inane that must sound, how stupid, because even *he* realized that death must be only moments away. And he thought, what about Evan? And he thought of the first girl he had ever screwed. And he remembered Edna on their wedding day. And he flashed onto a memory of his first stage appearance.

And all the time he was aware of Dallas close beside him.

And he wondered why it had taken him thirty-eight years to find her. And he wondered why now that he had found her she was to be taken away from him. He wanted to scream, and shout, but he just kept mumbling, 'Don't worry, don't worry.' And when the plane finally shuddered to a stop he was still saying it.

It took him moments to realize that they had stopped. He was stunned.

He wanted to shake his head and wake up – because Jesus Christ – this had to be a nightmare – this couldn't be happening to him. Then he realized with a leaden feeling that this was no nightmare, this was *real*, it *was* happening to him. And his next immediate thought was fire – and wouldn't it be ridiculous to have made it to the ground and then to get *burned* to death.

Dallas was moaning softly. They were still strapped firmly into the leopard-skin couch – cleverly designed by some faggot designer whose balls Al would have for breakfast – the fucking thing hadn't even stayed fixed to the wall, it had come to rest against the side of the bed – and now *he couldn't get the fucking straps undone.* They were trapped.

He couldn't hear a thing. Shouldn't there be sirens and bells, for Crissake?

Shouldn't they be surrounded by rescue squads?

Why weren't they being saved?

What the fuck was happening out there?

☆

The pain in her legs was excruciating. Cathy tried to struggle up, but it was impossible. A whole section of seats seemed to have concertinaed back into a tangled mass of wreckage, and her legs were trapped beneath it.

She struggled in vain. Had to get up. Had to get everyone out of there.

It was freezing cold, pitch dark. She reached out and touched Paul, unconscious beside her. She wondered if he was dead.

Bernie was screaming with pain. 'I've been stabbed! I've been stabbed!' he kept on repeating, 'help me – help me!'

She felt for Paul's pulse. He was alive. She bent forward, and by feeling around, realized that he was also trapped.

'Can anyone help us?' she called out – but her words sounded so funny – and she realized half her teeth were missing, and the thick sticky stuff pouring down her face was blood. It was about then that she fainted.

Evan was paralysed with fear. He didn't dare to move. Yet he couldn't remain hanging nearly upside down in his seat like an inanimate puppet forever.

Feebly he struggled to free his arm twisted beneath him, and upon doing that he fiddled with the seat belt, getting it open, and falling out of the seat with a thud. He fell near Bernie, and as his eyes adjusted themselves to the dark he could make out something terrible protruding from the fat man's chest.

'Pull it out,' Bernie screamed in panic and terror, 'pull the fuckin' motherfucker out!'

Evan backed away, stumbling along the littered aisle.

He wished he had a torch. Wished he could *see* something. He heard the stewardess ask for help – then silence. He edged towards the door of his father's section, and tripped over the body of Luke sprawled outside. Suddenly his hands were covered in something hot and sticky, and with horror he realized it was blood. 'Luke?' he questioned desperately, '*LUKE?*' He pulled himself away from the body, tried to open the door to his father's room. It wouldn't budge. He threw his scrawny body against it, and started to scream hysterically. It was to no avail. Eventually he slumped to the floor, leaning his head against the door, and sobbing quietly. They were all dead. Even Bernie had stopped screaming. He was the only one left alive. He was all alone. *What was he going to do? Who would save him?*

☆

'I'm all right,' said Dallas, 'I can't believe it, but I am.'

'We've got to get out of here,' Al replied tersely, 'can you *hear* anything?'

'Nothing. Just the rain. Where are we?'

'Well, we're sure as hell not in São Paulo. Probably on the outskirts somewhere – I'm worried about the others. *We're* OK – but what about them?'

'They're probably down the emergency chutes by now.'

'Look – when I count to three push as hard as you can

against the friggin' seat belt. We can't just lie here waiting to get rescued – this whole thing could go up in flames any minute. Come on now – one – two – *three*.'

She strained with him, and a wave of sickening nausea engulfed her. 'Oh God, Al, I can't. I – I think I've broken something . . . It's my ribs . . . It hurts . . . It really hurts . . .'

He knew that every second must count. Planes always blew up. Always burst into flame. Why wasn't someone breaking in to get them out? Why wasn't anyone giving a fuck? Christ – some heads would roll for putting him through this . . . A lot of people would be out looking for new jobs . . .

'Can you help me get us over to the door – if we crawl . . .'

'I'll try.'

Together, like some monstrous snail, they managed to twist onto their bellies and inch their way towards the door, the couch still attached to them.

'Try and straighten up,' Al instructed.

She was biting her lip trying to stop from crying out. Al was so strong, so calm, she didn't feel at all afraid.

He managed to unlock the door, but it wouldn't open. If he had been able to see in the dark he would have known why – the frame at the top was crushed down – holding the door tight. It was completely jammed. 'It's no good, forget it.' If he wasn't trapped by the safety belt he could kick the goddamn door in. Thank Christ Dallas wasn't showing any signs of panic. Thank Christ the plane hadn't gone up in flames.

Then he had an idea. He would cut them free – he had a manicure case in one of the drawers – he also had a torch. If he could find both items he could cut them loose, then with the torch see their way out of the emergency exit – it was better than staying here and roasting to death.

Only one problem. The drawers had come out and splintered to pieces all over the room. On their hands and knees, with the lunatic couch attached to their backs, they would have to crawl around searching. Well, it beat the hell out of sitting around doing nothing.

☆

At first light Cristina recovered consciousness.

Slowly she opened her eyes and stared up in surprise. For a moment she had no idea where she was. Her mind seemed utterly blank. Then slowly it all started to come back. Nino. Louis. The plane. The storm . . .

She was lying in what seemed like a forest, her clothes soaking wet and torn, every bone in her body aching. She couldn't summon the strength to move, so she just lay there for a while trying to collect her thoughts. It dawned on her that somehow she must have been thrown from the plane, and gradually, tentatively, she attempted to get up – marvelling at the fact that nothing seemed to be broken.

When she stood, the world spun round. She felt very giddy and sick, and there was an empty gnawing feeling in her stomach.

She sat down abruptly, leaning against the trunk of an enormous tree. She had never seen such giant trees before and wondered where she was. Then she wondered where the plane was, and Louis and Nino and all the others.

Oh God – surely she wasn't alone out here?

She stood again, her legs barely able to support her they were shaking so much. Her shoes had been ripped from her in the fall, and her bare feet were covered in small cuts and scratches, in fact every exposed inch of her body was bruised and battered. Fortunately she had been wearing jeans, and they were intact apart from being soaking wet, but the thin cotton shirt on her top half was ripped and torn. The sweater she had worn casually tied around her shoulders was gone.

The rain had stopped, but the ground was sodden and overgrown, and she was frightened to walk on it lest she stepped on any insects – she had always had a phobia about anything creepy crawly, and the air was alive with animal and bird chirpings.

But what else could she do? She had to look for the plane. Had to hope that she wasn't the only survivor.

Resolutely she set off.

☆

Paul opened his eyes, and the pain in his legs was so intense that he shut them again and willed himself to lose consciousness. He wondered if he still *had* legs. What was the story about amputees still feeling pain in legs and arms that had long gone. 'Nurse!' he called sharply, 'NURSE!'

Cathy touched his arm. 'We're still on the plane,' she mumbled softly, 'nobody's come yet. We're trapped, can't move.'

He opened his eyes and groaned. He had thought he was in a hospital. An English country hospital.

He turned to look at Cathy. She was a horrible blood-caked sight.

It was just beginning to get light. 'How long have we been here?' he croaked. His throat felt dry, and there was a bitter taste in his mouth.

'Hours, I think. Evan's alive. Bernie was . . . I don't know if he still is. I don't know about the others . . . We're trapped. We'll just have to wait 'till the rescuers get here.'

'Al?' questioned Paul, his voice sounding unreal, *'where is Al?'*

Cathy shook her head.

Paul pushed desperately with his body, trying to shift the debris that was imprisoning them. He summoned every bit of strength he could muster, but it was to no avail.

He leaned out to look down the aisle, and was shocked to see the plane reach an abrupt and jagged end half-way down. He could see Bernie slumped in his seat with the lethal-looking metal protruding from his chest. The fat man's face was deathly pale, his mouth hanging blankly open. But he was still taking shallow breaths.

Paul looked to the back of the plane. The door to Al's compartment was badly crushed. The body of Luke lying, as if still on guard, in front of it, surrounded by his own blood. And the inert huddled shape of Evan silent and unmoving.

'Evan!' croaked Paul. Cathy had said the boy was alive. 'EVAN!'

Cathy mumbled, 'He's in shock. I tried to get him to help us before. He's in shock . . .'

'EVAN!!'roared Paul.

The boy turned slowly and regarded his uncle blankly.

'Come here,' said Paul kindly. 'Are you hurt?'

Evan shook his head.

'See if you can get us out . . . Start pulling the metal away at the front of the pile. Come on Evan, hurry up.'

'I can't do it,' replied Evan, 'I can't do it. I have to wait here for my mother. If I don't she'll be angry with me.'

'Just try,' persuaded Paul, 'your father would want you to. If you can get me out, I can go and look for him.'

Evan turned his back, covering his ears and leaning his head against the compartment door.

'He's in shock,' repeated Cathy.

'I couldn't give a shit what he's in. He *has to help us*. Evan, goddammit – get over here and *help us*.'

Evan pressed his hands tightly over his ears and closed his eyes. He wondered how long it would be before his mother came for him. He hoped she wouldn't be cross, it wasn't *his* fault.

☆

It seemed to take hours, but Al finally found the scissors, and started cutting through the thick webbing of seat belts. It took a long time, but the relief of getting that terrible contraption off their backs was worth it.

By the time he had completed the job it was beginning to get light.

Thank Christ the plane hadn't gone up in flames. If it had, they would have been finished. So much for the fast, efficient rescue teams in South America. When were they going to appear – tomorrow?

He lay Dallas on the bed. She was a mass of bruises which were starting to show up in purplish lumps.

'I'm all right,' she insisted, 'let's get out of here.' She shared his fear of fire.

He threw himself against the door in an attempt to shift it, but by this time he could see it was hopelessly jammed.

He hurried to the emergency exit.

'Christ!' he exclaimed. 'We're in some sort of jungle!'

Dallas struggled to sit up. 'What are you talking about?' Her ribs were throbbing with pain, but she had decided, after feeling them carefully, that they were only badly bruised.

'A jungle!' Al continued. 'Trees fifty friggin' feet tall! I don't believe it!'

Dallas joined him at the window.

'You're right,' she said in awe.

'How this plane made it in one piece . . .'

She nodded in agreement.

'How *we* made it . . .'

'Al – what about the others?'

He suddenly felt tired. He wanted to lie down, go to sleep, and wake up in a luxury hotel somewhere. He didn't want to start crawling out of the plane to discover – who knew what?

He wanted to pick up a phone and tell Paul or Luke or Bernie to find out what the fuck was going on.

He didn't need this whole frigging scene.

Dallas said quietly, 'At least we're alive.'

He put his arms around her and held her tightly, 'Jesus – Dallas – I don't think I can go out there . . . I don't want to find them . . . I can't . . . I just can't do it . . .'

'Sure,' she agreed soothingly. 'I know you don't *want* to go. But we have to. We have to see if they've radioed for help. We have to see if . . .' She trailed off. They both knew what they had to see. They had to see if anyone else was alive.

☆

Cristina struggled through the heavy undergrowth, stopping to rest every few minutes.

She had shut every thought out of her head except finding the aircraft. Somehow she had persuaded herself that if she found the plane everything would be all right.

As the sun got higher in the sky it started to become very warm, and her clothes dried on her.

She had discovered a massive lump on the side of her head, and it throbbed painfully.

Her feet hurt as she squeamishly picked her way along, terrified of stepping on anything that moved. Occasionally she called out in the vain hope that there was someone to hear her. But the only noises were animal ones. A monkey howling in a tree somewhere, strange unusual bird cries, the buzz of flies and mosquitoes.

She was so hungry, her stomach making angry rumbling noises. There was a tree with delicious-looking red berries growing from it, but she was frightened to pick any in case they were piosonous.

She paused by the tree anyway, but screamed in terror as a huge spider landed on her bare arm. She shook it off, screaming hysterically, plunging on through the wilderness.

Then she heard the groans. Awful inhuman sounds.

☆

They knotted the silk sheets from the bed together, and made a crude rope to lower themselves from the exit.

Dallas had dressed quickly in jeans and shirt. She went down the rope first, landing with a heavy thud on the ground.

Al followed her, having made sure the rope was secure enough, to allow them back up again. If the worst came to the worst he figured they could at least wait in comfort until the rescuers came. Who else had the luck to crash out with a double bed at their disposal?

Deliberately he tried to keep his thoughts light. He didn't even want to consider what they might be about to find.

Almost at once they saw that only the back half of the plane existed.

They struggled around to the gaping, jagged, open edge.

'Anyone there?'

Paul's voice came back faintly, 'We're trapped. Help us.'

Jubilantly Al hugged Dallas. 'They're alive!' he enthused. 'Evan – Evan – can you hear me?'

Paul's voice weakly, 'Can you get us out of here?'

'I'll try and climb in,' Dallas volunteered, 'If I can stand on your shoulders . . .'

'Forget it. We'll get some more sheets – secure them, then we can both go up.' He shouted out: 'Hang on. Is everyone all right in there?'

Paul twisted uncomfortably in his seat. 'We're trapped,' he shouted back, 'Cathy and me. Bernie's hurt badly. Luke's dead, I think. Evan's all right. Hurry up.' He could hardly stand the pain any more. Cathy's eyes were closed, she seemed to be drifting in and out of consciousness. He could understand why. She was in a worse state than he. And that cruddy kid. Nothing wrong with him – but he couldn't even help. Couldn't even get them some water. When he got free he would break his scrawny little neck.

Flies had invaded the plane, it seemed like hundreds of

them, and their main targets appeared to be Bernie and Cathy. Paul tried to keep them off her face, but every time he brushed them away they were back, settling onto her blood-soaked skin with relish. Luke was another prime target, forcing Evan to move away from his body.

'Your father is alive,' Paul croaked, 'he's coming to help. Get us some water – I can see the dispenser – it's not broken.'

Evan ignored him, huddling into an intact seat, and covering himself with a blanket.

Paul licked his dry lips. If only he was free. It was a miracle that Al was still alive. It was a miracle that any of them were.

He wondered about the fate of those at the front of the plane. He had heard the explosions last night – he didn't hold out too much hope.

It took another hour before Al was able to get a sheet-made rope and gain access to the plane. Then he climbed up.

'Oh God!' he murmured in despair, 'Oh Jesus Christ!'

Hurrying, he turned and hauled Dallas up after him.

☆

Nino was sprawled on the ground, his legs bent beneath him at an impossible angle. Across his forehead the skin gaped open exposing a deep cut surrounded by dried blood.

He was making these awful noises – a heavy groaning sound which ended up as a despairing scream.

Ineffectually he beat at the flies which buzzed around him, but he was very weak, and as soon as his arms flopped down the flies descended once more.

At first Cristina was too scared to approach him. She stood partly hidden behind a tree just watching.

Nino, her lover, her invincible strong revolutionary. Look at him now – wracked with pain, screaming in agony.

It was *his* fault she was here. Why couldn't it have been Louis she had stumbled on?

Suddenly, from the corner of her eye, she saw a movement in the long grass. With horror she realized it was a snake – a long green and black monster slithering silently towards Nino.

☆

Working feverishly with his bare hands Al pushed and pulled and tore at the debris trapping Paul and Cathy. He was covered in a film of sweat and had stripped down to his undershorts.

He had been at it for two hours, and his hands were cut and bleeding, but it didn't seem to bother him. He kept up a stream of bright conversation, making jokes, making light of their whole situation.

'We're getting there.' He paused for a moment. 'Jeeze Paul, if you think you're getting ten per cent of *this* gig – forget it!'

Dallas was busy too. They had laid Bernie out on the floor, a pillow under his head. He was in a bad way, and they both knew the jagged metal would have to be removed from his chest if he was to have any chance at all.

'We'll get Cathy and Paul free first,' Al had muttered, 'then we'll pull it out. We'll need their help. In the meantime fill him up with brandy.'

She was doing just that – sharing the one bottle that had survived the crash between Bernie, Cathy and Paul.

Evan was no use at all. Al had tried to slap him into shape, but he had merely burst into tears, and finally they had left him alone, huddled in a seat, staring into space.

Paul had told them about the hijack. Al was furious. Christ – what kind of idiots was he surrounded by? Didn't they know enough not to let strangers on his plane? He held his temper and didn't scream. What was the use of screaming? Who was he going to scream at? Paul – caught underneath a ton of fucking steel? Bernie – whose chances were about as good as Woody Allen fighting Mohammed Ali? Luke – mutilated and dead?

For once in his life he had no one to scream at. It didn't bother him. He had other things on his mind – like getting his brother free.

His hands were red and raw. But he didn't pause – he kept going. Had to get them free – had to get them out of there.

He clawed at the twisted metal – keeping up a stream of chat.

Here he was – the man who had everything. Money. Fame. Power.

Look where it got you – stuck in some asshole jungle trying to dig your brother out of the shit.

'Dallas,' he called urgently. 'I think we're getting there. Hold this back, I think I can get them out.'

She rushed to his assistance, holding on to the metal strut he had managed to lift. It was heavy, but she didn't flinch, although the pain around her ribs was agony.

Carefully Al pulled Paul free, dragging him out, leaving him on the floor, and going back for Cathy. She screamed as he moved her, and he could see why. One of her legs from the knee down was almost pulped. Blood and skin and bones. It was a dreadful sight.

He moved her into the aisle.

'It hurts, it hurts . . .' she moaned.

'Let it go,' Al instructed Dallas.

She dropped the strut and it clanged back into place.

At least they were out. He had managed that. Now all they had to do was wait for the goddamn rescue plane – and *why was it taking so long?*

☆

Cristina stood rooted to the spot. She was unable to move, unable to breathe almost. With wide eyes she watched the huge snake slither and slide its way towards Nino. It seemed to move so slowly, and there was something almost hypnotically beautiful about its measured undulations.

She knew she should do *something*. But what? How did you frighten a snake away? And, anyway, if she intervened, it might attack *her*.

At least she had to warn Nino. His head was turned away from the approaching snake, she *had* to shout, do *something*.

He let out another of his inhuman yells, and the snake paused, its tongue flicking in and out. It was only about six feet away from its human prey now.

Cristina willed it to turn and go away. But it didn't. It slithered forward, raising its head with a hissing sound, and struck purposefully towards Nino's left leg.

Simultaneously Cristina screamed out a warning. Nino rolled over, but not quickly enough. The snake had bitten into his leg, and he let out a roar of pure agony.

The snake slid quietly away, vanishing into the under-growth as silently as it had appeared.

'Oh mother of God!' Nino bellowed, 'save me – save me. Help me – please help me.'

Cristina stepped out from behind the tree. She was nauseous and hot, dizzy, and racked with stomach pains.

Nino saw her, and his eyes filled with tears. 'I'm going to die,' he said simply. 'Help me, Cristina. I'm going to die, and I don't want to be alone.'

She rushed forward and fell on him. She couldn't think about hate. She couldn't think about anything other than the fact that she wasn't by herself any more. 'I'll help you,' she promised, 'you won't die. I'll help you. What can I do?'

'Water. Do you have any?'

She shook her head. 'I've got nothing.'

He groaned. 'I can't walk. My legs are broken. You must suck out the snake venom. Do it now – do it now, please, I beg you.'

She stared at his leg in horror. The place where the snake had bitten him was already swelling into a vile purplish mound.

'I . . . I . . . can't . . .'

'If you don't, I'll die. You'll be alone out here. Suck the poison and spit it on the ground. Hurry, Cristina, it may already be too late.'

She bent her face to his leg, shushing away the flies which seemed to be everywhere. There was a bone protruding where it shouldn't. There were cuts and scratches, and in the middle of it all was the obscene purple lump of puss. He pressed near and around it with his fingers. 'Now!' he urged, '*now!*'

She put her lips over it, sucked and spat twice. Then turned away and vomited.

He let out a sigh. 'We'll know soon enough . . . soon . . . Maybe you'll end up alone after all, my little carioca – maybe . . .' He laughed bitterly. 'I nearly did it. I would have been a hero – you hear me . . .' His eyes closed.

Cristina began to sob. 'You'll be all right, Nino. I know you will. I know you will. You can't leave me. Promise. I want you to promise.'

He did not reply. He had passed out.

☆

'How do your legs feel?' Al asked anxiously.

Paul nodded. 'Not bad. I think the circulation's coming back.' He was propped on the floor of the compartment, with Dallas massaging his legs. Miraculously they seemed to be only badly bruised. It was the pressure that had been causing him all the pain.

They had cut his trouser legs off at the knee, and applied hand cream to massage away the numbness.

Cathy, however, had not fared so well. Apart from her facial injuries, which Dallas had cleaned up as best she could, her shattered legs was quite obviously useless.

The flies had invaded the plane with a vengeance. Small ones, big horse flies, tiny stinging little tics. Infection would set in at once, and there was nothing to be done.

They had covered Cathy with a blanket, but she kept on pushing it off and complaining of the heat. It was unearthly hot and humid. They were all pouring with sweat.

'You must stay covered,' Dallas warned, 'the flies will only make it worse . . .'

Cathy moaned softly, 'It couldn't be any worse . . .'

Al took Dallas to one side. 'What do you think? Shall we try and get that thing out of Bernie, or shall we wait for help?'

She gave him a strange look. 'What makes you think help is coming?'

'Don't talk crap. Of course it's coming. I'm a million dollar property, kid. They'll be searching 'til they find me. I'm sure Van must have radioed our position before he crashed.'

'Why aren't they here then?'

'I shouldn't think this is the easiest place to reach. A plane couldn't land here. I suppose they'll have to get to us by land.'

She shrugged unbelievingly. 'I haven't heard any planes flying over here today . . .'

'They'll find us,' he said sharply.

'If you say so. In the meantime if we don't pull that chunk of metal out of Bernie he's going to die.'

'Let's do it then.'

'Paul will have to hold him down . . .' she hesitated, 'If Evan could help . . .'

'I don't think so. Look – I'll pull it out, you help Paul hold him. Can you take the blood?'

'Can you? I worked with animals when I was a kid, I'm used to it.'

'I haven't always been the world's favourite superstar, you know . . .'

She pushed the hair away from her face wearily. 'Let's do it, Al. We need a towel to stem the blood.'

He held her face briefly. 'I love you,' he said quietly, 'I just want you to know that. You're not only the most beautiful girl in the world, you're also the best one to get stuck in a plane crash with.'

'You and your quickie trips to South America. Why did I ever listen to you?'

Bernie moaned loudly.

'Give him the rest of the brandy,' Al said. 'I'll be right back.'

Paul was attempting to stand.

'All right?' Al asked.

'Shaky but nothing seems to be broken.'

'I'm going to get some towels.'

'Why don't we bust through the door? Is the bed still in one piece? Maybe we could put Cathy and Bernie on it.'

'Yeah,' Al contemplated the crushed door. 'If we could get some support – take the pressure off. Shit – it would beat the hell out of crawling in and out. We'll give it a try.'

Paul stared admiringly at his brother. Who would have thought that Al had it in him? His hands were cut and bleeding. His body dripping with sweat. He hadn't stopped for a moment. And yet he was still willing to go on. *He* wasn't hurt. He could have just sat tight in his bedroom waiting for help. He hadn't even touched the brandy, although he must have been dying for a swig. 'You all need it more than I do,' he had insisted.

'I think I can walk,' Paul said, trying a few steps.

'Let's give it a try then, boyo, let's do it. You and I together, we always were a good team.' Al slapped his brother on the shoulder. 'Now, this is what we'll do . . .'

☆

Night fell quickly in the jungle.

Cristina had bodily dragged Nino up against the trunk of a tree, arming herself with a hefty stick in case of further snake attacks. She was exhausted. She knew that without food or drink she could not last much longer.

'Tomorrow,' she told Nino, who drifted in and out of consciousness, 'I'll find the plane. It can't be far. I won't leave you for long, I'll get water and come back for you.'

'Yes,' he mumbled.

She cradled his head on her lap, brushing away a spider. Her mouth was so dry. Her body ached. She had been bitten to pieces by the flies. A wasp had stung her. Her head throbbed.

Now with the darkness came the frightening noises. What other animals apart from snakes lurked in the blackness?

She clung onto Nino and tried not to think.

'I'll find Louis tomorrow,' she crooned softly, 'he will save us. Tomorrow we'll be all right.'

'I could've been a hero,' Nino mumbled, shudders racking his body.

Eventually they both fell into an uneasy sleep.

☆

On the plane, progress had been made. Between them Al and Paul had managed to get the door to the bedroom compartment open. They had half-carried, half-dragged Bernie in there, and laid him out on the bed.

Wrapping his hands in towels, Al had gripped the protruding jagged metal, and with a horrible suction sound, it had come out of Bernie's chest. Dallas had tried to stem the flow of blood with more towels. They were already soaked through, but at least Bernie seemed in less pain.

When the darkness came they were all exhausted. Their only sustenance had been water from the unbroken dispenser and a packet of dry biscuits. Al had not thought of rationing anything because he quite expected they would be rescued shortly. It occurred to him that he should have checked just how much water there was. It was too late now. Darkness had descended and the only thing to do was sleep.

Cathy and Bernie were on the bed. Evan was huddled in the seat he had not moved out of all day. Paul had chosen to sleep on the floor in the bedroom. Dallas and Al sat side by side in two intact seats near the break in the plane.

Night had brought a respite from the interminable flies, and that was a relief. But strange jungle noises were all around them, and the impossible heat of the day turned into icy cold at night.

Al slid his arm around her. 'I told you I'd take you somewhere romantic.'

She moved as near to him as she could get. 'You're not going to break into song, are you?'

'Only if you'll pay me.'

She tried to laugh, but it caught in her throat and emerged more like a sob.

'Hey – You're not going to break on me, lady? You've been pretty fantastic all day.'

'Al? We're in real trouble, aren't we? How are they ever going to find us? We're lost – even if planes *did* fly over, how would they spot us? We would be hidden from sight by the trees.'

'Don't worry,' he replied easily, much more easily than he actually felt. 'Tomorrow night we'll be at the Beverly Hills Hotel celebrating on fat juicy steaks and champagne. And if you're good – you know what?'

'What?'

'I'll take you to a party at Karmen Rush's. How does *that* hit you?'

'Like a ton of shit!'

'Oh, that's nice – really nice!'

This time her laughter stuck, and she fell asleep soon after.

Al didn't sleep. He stared out into the blackness thinking about the reality of it all.

They had been missing how long? At least twenty-four hours, and Dallas was right, not one plane had flown over, and she was also right about the trees shielding them from sight. Quite obviously the authorities did not know where to look. If they did there would have been some activity in the sky today.

The fact was it might take days before they were found. And how would they survive? There was no food, little water. Cathy and Bernie were both in a bad way   How long could they last without proper treatment?

Al swore softly under his breath. He was so used to picking up a phone and having a dozen people jumping at his every command. Somehow he felt cheated that this situation could not be taken care of in the same way.

Here he was, roughing it on a fucking aeroplane seat, whilst Bernie Suntan enjoyed the comforts of *his* bed. What a switch *that* was.

A monkey howled loudly nearby. Al jumped. Dallas mumbled something in her sleep. He stroked her hair. He loved her. For the very first time in his life he loved a woman. And he had to protect her, save her. And goddamn it he would.

Tomorrow he would find the other half of the plane, see if the radio was still working, get some action going.

Yes. And he would find some food, there must be fruit, berries . . . His eyes were closing, niggly little pains attacking every part of his body. Scratches, cuts, strains, bruises . . . He had used muscles he had forgotten existed.

'Tomorrow . . .' he mumbled. 'I'll get it together tomorrow . . .'

67

By Saturday afternoon a passenger list of those aboard the missing Al King jet was published.

Linda read it through twice.

'I can't believe it,' she said to Cody, 'I just can't believe it.'

He was stunned himself.

'How can a huge jet like that just vanish?' Linda demanded for the hundredth time.

He shook his head. 'I can only think that it must have been hijacked. If it had crashed they would have found it by now.'

'Oh God!' Linda buried her face in her hands. 'It just doesn't bear thinking about. What can we *do*?'

He had been thinking the same thing himself. It was such an impossible situation to have to garner every little piece of news from television and newspapers.

'I'm going to place a call to Carlos Baptista. If anyone knows what's going on it's him.'

☆

In New York, Melanie King licked dewey red lips, blinked baby blue eyes, and smiled into the television camera. 'Manny and I are in a dreadful state,' she said in reply to the interviewer's question. 'Paul and Manny are the best of friends. There has never been unpleasantness between any of us. After all, divorce is such an everyday happening nowadays. Paul is like ... well, he's like a much-loved brother.' She paused triumphantly, pleased with her choice of words.

Marjorie Carter, who was conducting the interview, leaned forward intently. 'How about Al, Melanie? You must know him as well as anyone. How do you think he would be able to cope if this is indeed a hijack?'

Melanie widened her eyes. 'Al King is a wonderful human being ... kind and generous. I'm sure he would react in the appropriate fashion.'

'Thank you, dear, for being with us in your time of stress.' Marjorie faced the camera straight on. 'Well, that's all for now. We will be bringing you the news as it comes in. Meanwhile, Al King, wherever you are, our thoughts are with you. This is Marjorie Carter signing off.'

The red light on the camera flicked off.

Melanie asked breathily: 'Was I all right?'

Gathering papers together, Marjorie threw her a cynical look. 'All right? You're kidding, aren't you? The sonofabitch should have you write his obituary for him! Since when has that prick been a "kind and generous wonderful human being"? Crap – pure crap. I've had him, I should know.'

Melanie dived into her bag and produced a small hand mirror. She studied her face. Petulantly she said: 'I hope I looked all right – If you need me again I'll be happy to come back.'

'Sure kid,' replied Marjorie, 'if they find the body you can come again! Oh – and give my best to Manny.'

☆

575

'She is under sedation,' Jorge said, his face grey with strain.

'I'll just sit with her,' Doris Andrews replied softly, 'comfort her.'

'If you like . . .' agreed Jorge.

He led Doris through to the bedroom. Evita lay wanly in the centre of the bed, her face a pale mask, her eyes wide open and staring.

'Doris is here,' Jorge said quietly. 'She'll sit with you for a while.'

Evita's eyes flickered slightly.

Doris took her hand and sat on the side of the bed. 'It's terrible,' she said, 'dreadful. I have friends on the plane . . .'

Jorge walked quietly from the room. Bad enough that Evita knew about Cristina and Louis being on the plane, but he didn't dare to tell her the latest news he had received. Apparently when they had boarded the plane at the last minute, they had been accompanied by a third party. A young man dressed in a mechanic's overalls. From his description he sounded uncannily like Nino.

☆

Lew Margolis said, 'What was the cunt doing on a plane with Al King in the first place?'

Cody gripped the phone tightly, trying not to lose his temper. 'She was having a rest.'

Lew snorted nastily. 'A rest? With that motherfucker? The cunt was supposed to be at the studio working for me. Remember?'

'You had fired her,' Cody reminded him.

'So I hired her again. Big fuckin' deal.'

'Will the studio release a statement or shall I?'

'We will. The publicity will give "Man Made Woman" a peachy send off. Trying to get it slotted on the tube earlier than planned. The cunt might have done us a favour.'

Cody's temper snapped. 'Don't keep on calling her that.'

'What you want I should call her? Princess?' He sniggered. 'Did I ever tell you, Cody, about how I first met your beautiful client?'

'No.'

Lew thought better of revealing the facts. 'Some other time

– remind me. By the way – you got any other girls right for the part? Looks like we might have ourselves a vacancy.'

☆

Edna sat in her kitchen sipping her fifth cup of tea in an hour. She was trying to sort out her feelings. She was grieved but not heartbroken. *And that was a horrible reaction. Why didn't she feel worse?*

Was it the uncertainty? The fact that nobody knew whether the occupants of the plane were dead or alive?

Her *husband* was on board. Her *son*. The two men she had devoted her life to. The two men who had prevented her from having any life of her own.

She had let go long ago . . . the night she had walked in on Al in Tucson. And the relief of not caring any more . . . The simple pleasure of living her life without having to put two other un-appreciative people before her.

Al first . . . then Evan. She had realized the mistake of clinging to her son. He would be better off with his father. *She* would be better off alone.

Now this . . .

The photographers and news media had descended like vultures. How happy they were that he was with another woman on the plane. They seemed to have forgotten the fact that she had previously announced she was divorcing him. That was an irrelevant fact now. It spoiled the dramatic suspense. Far better to have a 'left at home' wife while he had been gallivanting with a beautiful young girl across America.

She had sent them all packing. But they were still outside the house, waiting like birds of prey to pounce as soon as she appeared.

She had made her way across the garden and comforted Paul's two children. Nanny was in an awful state, sobbing and wailing.

'Is Mrs King returning from New York?' Edna asked.

'She can't,' snivelled nanny, 'she phoned to say it's impossible. Oh it's so awful . . . That poor, poor man . . . And to think I only spoke to him a few days ago . . . Oh it's dreadful . . . shocking . . . These poor little mites . . . What will happen to them?'

'We don't know the worst yet, nanny. The plane might be perfectly safe in some other country. Please try and calm yourself.'

'Yes,' sobbed nanny, 'yes.'

Edna phoned the telephone exchange and asked them to reconnect her phone. Then she went home and waited. It was all she could do – wait.

☆

'You left Acapulco very suddenly,' Doris Andrews whispered, 'why was that? You didn't even say goodbye.'

Evita stared at her. 'Jorge had to get back . . . Unexpectedly.'

'Oh. I see.' Doris squeezed her hand, 'I was hoping it had nothing to do with what happened between us.'

'It didn't,' Evita replied shortly.

'Good.'

The two women were silent. Evita lying wanly on the bed. Doris sitting close by.

'I thought of writing many times,' Doris confided, 'but then I would change my mind.' She laughed nervously, 'I hate rejection, you know.'

'Don't we all,' agreed Evita, sitting up to sip from a glass of water.

Doris's eyes slipped hungrily to her breasts which were softly enclosed in a pink satin nightgown. 'You are as beautiful as ever,' she murmured.

'Please, Doris. What do you want? Why are you here?' Evita's low voice was pained.

'I had to see you. I waited a year. I told Lew that you had invited me. I knew he was too busy to accompany me. I have thought about you . . . about us . . . so many times.'

Evita sighed. 'Doris . . . what happened . . . It was a slip on my part. I like you, I really do. But you must understand, I love my husband, it could never happen again. Please – would you go now. I'm really too distraught to discuss anything.'

'I know. It was selfish of me to come today. But I want to comfort you. You'll allow me that small pleasure, won't you?'

'No one can comfort me. Not until I know where my

daughter is.' Tears streamed down her face. 'This not knowing is a terrible thing . . .'

'They'll find her,' Doris assured. 'You'll see, she'll be all
right. Have faith, Evita. I promise you she will be all right.
I feel these things, I am very intuitive.'

'Are you?' Evita questioned hopefully, 'are you really?'

'Yes,' replied Doris soothingly, 'you wait, you'll see. Trust
in me. Now why don't you try and sleep, I can come back
later.'

Evita closed her eyes obediently, 'I'll try.'

☆

Saturday night there was no further news. Linda had
watched the Melanie King interview on television and she
was disgusted and despondent. What kind of a woman went
on television and gave an interview at a time like this? Why
hadn't the bitch flown back to London to be with her children? How could she be away from them at a time like this?

'I think I'll go home tonight,' she told Cody. 'I feel like
being alone.'

He understood. 'If I hear anything I'll come over.'

'Sure,' she nodded. It wasn't that she felt any differently
about Paul . . . Or was it? The fact that he might be dead. The
fact that she might never see him again . . . even if she wanted
to. It was too awful . . . And Dallas, Bernie, Al . . .

She just wanted to be alone.

The not knowing was the worst.

The uncertainty.

'We'll know something tomorrow,' Cody assured her.

'Yes?' she answered listlessly.

'Yes,' he replied positively, although he was as unsure as
she was.

It was going to be a long hard night, and one he was glad
that he would spend alone.

He wanted to think about Dallas.

He wanted to pray for her.

☆

68

Dallas was the first to wake. She ached all over, and her neck hurt from sleeping in a sitting position. She glanced at Al. He was stretched out, mouth slightly open, snoring softly. She didn't want to disturb him, he had worked so hard the previous day.

It must be very early, the sun was only just beginning to rise, and it was still chilly. At least it was daylight; the nights were so dark it was impossible to see anything.

She had woken in the middle of the night and heard noises – frightening rustles and growls. Instinctively she had know that there was some kind of wild animal circling around what was left of the plane. She had waited in horror, wondering if it would attempt to climb up, but eventually it had padded away.

She had not been able to sleep properly since then.

Oh God! What she would give for a simple cup of coffee ... A piece of toast ... A lump of dry bread – anything!

Quietly she left her seat, padding down the aisle to check out if anyone was awake.

Evan was asleep. They would have to do something about *him* today – It was wrong just leaving him alone, he would have to join in, become part of the group. After all, he wasn't hurt, he could be useful.

In the bedroom compartment Bernie lay on his back, his eyes wide open. The towels wrapped around him were stiff with dried blood. Flies buzzed everywhere. Cathy and Paul slept.

'How are you feeling?' Dallas whispered to Bernie.

The day before he had been incoherent.

'What the fuck we still doin' here?' he croaked.

'I guess we're waiting to be rescued,' she replied.

He coughed, and she was dismayed to see a trickle of blood dribble from his mouth.

'How long we been here?'

'Today's Sunday, we crashed Friday night.'

'Jeeze ... I don't remember a thing.'

☆

Al was having a beautiful dream. He was playing backgammon with the Shah of Persia, and *he* was winning. 'Hey – Shah,' he was saying, 'I won her – *you* may have more bread – but *I* won her.'

Dallas shook him back to reality. 'Al – wake up. There are a couple of cupboards in the bedroom I can't open. What's in them? Any food?'

He opened his eyes wondering where he was. Then he remembered. 'Food? I don't know . . . which cupboards?'

She took his hand, 'Come and see.'

☆

Evan sneaked a bar of chocolate out of his shirt pocket. It was his last one. He wolfed it down ravenously. Now all he had left was a couple of packs of chewing gum. If his mother didn't come soon she would be too late . . .

☆

Cathy woke up and affirmed the fact that the two locked cupboards *were* used to store supplies. She looked worse than anyone, with her poor battered face, missing teeth and crushed leg. But she refused to give in, she was cheerful and bright, and kept on saying, 'Chin up, everyone, they'll be here for us soon.'

Al smashed the two cupboards in, and they came upon a bonanza. One cupboard contained stocks of Kleenex, toilet tissue, paper towels, soap, cleaning materials, fresh towels and sheets. There were also three plastic containers of hand cream, an atomizer of perfume, and the best discovery of all – a first-aid box.

The second cupboard revealed an even more exciting array of goods. Three jars of instant coffee. Two boxes of tea bags. Four boxes of lump sugar. Three giant cans of orange juice. Six packets of crisps. Four tins of mixed nuts. Two packets of water biscuits. Six tins of the best caviar. Twelve small bottles of Perrier Water. Six large bottles of champagne. A packet of paper napkins. A packet of toothpicks. A glass jar of maraschino cherries. A corkscrew, bottle and tin opener. And finally three cans of anchovies.

'We just hit pay dirt!' Al exclaimed triumphantly, 'we can last forever on this little lot!'

'Not quite ever,' Dallas warned, 'I think we should ration it carefully.'

'The hell with *that*. I'm starving.' He was already opening up the biscuits, stuffing them in his mouth.

'Al!' reminded Dallas sharply, 'share them out.'

'Don't get panicky – there's plenty here. Everyone help themselves.'

'Look,' interrupted Dallas angrily, 'we don't know how long we're going to be here . . .'

'She's right,' Paul joined in.

Reluctantly Al put the biscuits down. 'So what the fuck do you want to do?'

'We should just make it last,' Dallas said coldly. She picked up the packet of biscuits and handed one out to everyone.

Al returned his with a sheepish grin – 'I already had two.'

She smiled at him. 'Thanks.'

'You're right,' he replied. 'I'm not going to argue when I know you're right. We could sit here for fucking ever waiting for them to come and get us. I think I'll take a little trip – see what I can find. Maybe I'll come across the rest of the plane. You feel well enough to come with me, Paul?'

His brother nodded.

☆

Cristina's own tears woke her. She had been crying in her sleep, and the tears were stinging the cuts on her face.

It was already hot. A humid stifling heat which filtered down through the tall trees.

Nino lay across her lap. He looked a very funny colour, a sort of greyish white. She tried to rouse him, but he muttered angrily and refused to wake.

They were both covered in flies and mosquitoes. The horrible aggravating things wouldn't go away. They buzzed and dived, inflicting nasty little bites on any exposed piece of skin. At least her legs were covered, but her arms were bitten all over.

She wanted to get up. She knew she *must* get up. But her strength seemed to have deserted her, and she wasn't sure if she was capable of moving.

If she stayed where she was they would both die.

That thought stung her into action, and she stumbled to her feet, letting Nino's head rest on the ground.

'I'll come back soon,' she whispered, but he wasn't listening. He was rolling around groaning.

She noticed that he still had his shoes on, running shoes with thick rubber soles. *She* was the one that had to do the walking, her feet were in such an awful state, surely he wouldn't mind . . .

She struggled to get the shoes off him and put them on herself. They were big and sloppy, but they were better than nothing.

Exhausted before she had begun, she set off to try and find the plane.

☆

Al and Paul were ready to leave.

'You've got to be careful,' Dallas warned. 'This is the jungle, there are a million and one dangers.'

'My lady – an expert on jungles!' Al laughed.

'I'm not an expert – but the only thing I learned as a kid was about animals. The big ones will leave you alone if they've eaten. It's the smaller ones you must look out for. Poisonous insects, ants, scorpions, snakes. And whatever you do – don't eat anything – no berries, plants, even flowers.'

'You know something – eating flowers just ain't my scene – and after that feast I had for breakfast – two water biscuits and some orange juice – how could I possibly think about food!'

She put her arms around him and kissed him. 'Love you,' she whispered. '*Please* be careful.'

'We will.'

She watched them set off. They had two bottles of Perrier water with them, some saccharin, and Luke's gun. They had found the gun in his jacket before burying him near the plane. They had also found a packet of chewing gum, and a hip flask of whisky. It had all been added to their supplies.

God, it was hot! How she longed for a bath, her clothes were sweat-stained and sticky. She wanted to rip them off and walk around naked, but the risk of exposing skin to the hungry mosquitoes was just not worth it. She remained resolutely covered as much as she could, and so far the only bites she had experienced were on her hands.

She had changed the towels around Bernie's wound. It did not look good at all, but he certainly seemed in better shape than the previous day. Cathy, however, was deteriorating. Her leg was an ugly open wound, and even to Dallas' inexperienced eye it seemed to be gangrenous.

There was nothing she could do for either of them, except be near when they needed her.

The first-aid box had helped. She had dabbed everyone's cuts and bruises with antiseptic cream and wrapped all the open wounds in gauze bandages to keep the flies off.

She wished that she could have gone with Al, but he had insisted she stay on the plane. 'You and I are the only two with our heads together – we can't desert them, they'll think we're never coming back. Paul's likely to fall to pieces any minute.'

He was right. Paul was making a supreme effort, but anyone could see he was on the edge of hysteria.

She could not get over Al. Spoiled superstar. Supreme user. He was a tower of strength, combining just the right amount of jokey cynicism with a strong conviction that rescue was just around the corner. He alone was keeping everyone's spirits buoyant.

She had gone to him in Las Vegas for a night of sex. They hadn't even had that, but she knew that he was the man she wanted to spend the rest of her life with.

She laughed bitterly. Perhaps she would. Perhaps the rest of her life would only be a matter of weeks . . . days . . .

Just as a feeling of despondency swept over her she heard a noise in the distance. A noise that was unmistakable.

She ran to the front of the plane, and there, as clear as possible, zooming like a bird high above the giant trees, was an aeroplane.

Frantically she waved and shouted.

'We're *here*! Down here! Can't you see us? We're HERE!'

Her yelling was in vain. The aeroplane zoomed smoothly past, a tiny dot in the sky that vanished into the distance as suddenly as it had appeared.

☆

Al and Paul heard the plane as they trekked their way through the jungle. Paul started to yell, but Al stopped him. 'Forget it,' he said. 'You think they're going to hear us? Save your breath.'

'How *will* they find us then?' Paul demanded, his voice rising hysterically.

That was a good question. Al was damned if he knew. 'They will,' he replied airily. 'Don't forget it's me they're looking for.'

'You!' spat Paul, 'if it wasn't for *you* I wouldn't be here.'

'*You* wouldn't be anywhere.'

Paul stopped abruptly. 'I've *had* that shit!' he screamed, 'had it up to *here*. You – you – you. FUCK YOU. Where would *you* be without me? I *dragged* you up to where you are today. *I* grafted the contracts, negotiated more money, *pleaded* with them to use you at first. All you were interested in was getting pissed and laid – in that order. Without me you'd be singing shit in bar-rooms for the price of a pint. I have devoted my life to you – *and I want some respect*. I'm not some ass-kissin' fan. I'm your manager, your agent, your brother, for Crissakes.'

'What the fuck are you getting hysterical about? Calm down,' Al interrupted, startled at his brother's sudden outburst.

'Don't you fucking tell *me* to calm down. I've stood in the background and let you shit on me all your life. It's over, Al, it's over. You even screwed my wife – you banged Melanie. Didn't you? Didn't you?'

For the first time in his life Al was ashamed. He had never realized that Paul harboured such resentment. And what he said was true. It was a fact that at the beginning Paul had stage-managed his success.

'Yes,' Al replied defensively, 'I laid Melanie. She wanted it. She was after me until the day she left you. It wasn't my fault, Paul, you've got to believe me on that score . . .'

'You fucking bastard. I should kill you . . . You hear me? Kill you . . .'

'Look – if you think I was the only other man in her life you're wrong. It happened once – and don't think I haven't sweated over it. I hated myself for it.'

'My brother!' Paul spat, 'my dear brother.'

'I know it's a little late to say I'm sorry, but I am. I was sorry the moment it happened.'

'Have you any idea what it's been like having you for a brother? At parties I'm dragged around like exhibit A – I don't have a name – I'm the great Al King's brother. That's enough for me to be accepted. Not as myself – as your fucking brother.'

'That's not my fault. I didn't know . . .'

'Of course not. When have *you* ever given a shit about anyone else's feelings? What *you* want – when *you* want. A fuck. A meal. A massage. Call Paul – any time of the day or night – he'll arrange it.'

'Jesus, Paul – I never . . .' He stopped talking abruptly. Staggering towards them was a semi-hysterical, ragged girl. 'Help me!' she cried out. 'Oh God! Please, please help me.'

☆

A plane would never spot them. How could it? It would be like finding the proverbial needle in a haystack. And even if by some miracle they were seen – what then? A plane would never be able to land here, not even a helicopter. The trees took care of that. Majestic giant trees – some maybe as high as two hundred feet.

It occurred to Dallas that if they were to get out it would have to be by their own efforts – and that was impossible. They had no idea where they were. No idea how far from any settlement or community. They had no compass, map, suitable clothes, or adequate supplies. To survive in the jungle was difficult enough – even with the right equipment. But without . . . It was probably impossible.

Besides which Cathy and Bernie were in no shape to travel, and they couldn't leave them.

But if they just stayed put . . .

How long would their meagre supplies keep them going? A week . . . Two weeks . . . Who knew?

Al didn't understand. He seemed to think they would be rescued. How could they be rescued when nobody knew where they were?

Angrily she swotted a mosquito away, and made her way back down the plane.

Evan still huddled in his seat. She sat down beside him.

He stunk, his clothes stained with vomit, sweat and urine. The flies were having a field day around him.

'Hi,' she said softly. 'Feeling OK?'

He ignored her, staring off into space.

'Listen,' she said gently, 'we have to get you out of those clothes – one thing we've got plenty of is clothes – a whole closet full. Come on, let's sort something out.'

He still didn't say anything.

'Did you see the plane?' she asked brightly. 'They'll be coming for us soon. You don't want them to see you like that, do you?'

'Is Nellie coming?' he mumbled.

A response at last! 'Sure she is.' Dallas took his arm. 'Come on, Evan, I'll help you choose something.'

He stood up and something fell off his lap. It was a portable radio. Dallas pounced on it. 'Does it work?'

'Don't know.'

She switched it on and was rewarded with a blurred crackle. Desperately she twiddled the tuner. Faintly she was able to receive a music station. What a find! She switched it off. Save the batteries. Maybe later, when Al returned, they would be able to tune into a news programme and find out if anyone *was* actually looking for them.

☆

Greedily Cristina swallowed the contents of one bottle of Perrier water, and munched on the saccharin tablets they gave her.

'Christ!' Al kept on exclaiming, 'I don't know how you're still alive, it's a bloody miracle.'

At first he had thought the dark-skinned, wild-haired girl was part of some Indian tribe. But Paul had recognized her as she had stumbled exhausted into their arms. Incoherently she had told them her story, finishing off with a request about Louis' safety.

'We haven't seen him,' Paul replied. 'Maybe he was lucky like you.'

'Lucky?' the tears filled her eyes, 'I have been in hell. So alone . . . so frightened. Please find Louis – *please*.'

Al glanced at Paul. They both knew she was asking the impossible.

'Let's get her back to the plane,' Al said.

'What about Nino?' she asked quickly. 'He's not far away. I can't leave him, I can't . . . I promised . . .'

'The bastard can stay where he is . . .' Paul began. 'If it wasn't for him . . .'

'Take us to him,' Al said quietly, 'I guess he's regretting the whole gig just as much as we are.'

☆

By early afternoon Bernie was feeling a lot better. His huge bulk propped up in bed he was able to flick through Evan's collection of magazines.

'What the fuck . . .' he boasted, 'tomorrow I'll be up and about. Jeeze . . . I can see it now. Goddamn press gonna accuse me of engineering the whole shitbag. They know I'll do anything for a hot story!'

'You can't help having a reputation that goes before you,' Dallas replied jokingly.

'Yeah,' Bernie mused, 'you're right. I can name my price after this. Whatcha think? Think they're gonna come for us today?'

'I wouldn't be surprised.'

He slapped a spider, squashing it on his arm, 'Goddamn insects! Gonna drive me crazy!'

Cathy, lying beside him, groaned. She had been semi-conscious all day, and her leg was looking worse than ever. Dallas did not know much about medicine, but she did know if Cathy's leg was gangrenous it would have to come off if her life was to be saved.

She only hoped that Al had found the other half of the plane, and that maybe the radio had been working, and that maybe . . .

Pipe dreams.

She lifted Cathy's head and gave her a few sips of water.

It was hopeless and she knew it.

☆

It was just beginning to get dark when Al and Paul arrived back at the plane. Between them they carried Nino, and Cristina stumbled along behind.

Dallas and Evan helped them haul Nino up into the plane, and then they assisted Cristina.

'Thought we'd never make it back,' Al gasped. He grinned at Evan. 'Hey, boyo – feeling better?'

Evan nodded.

'Did you find anything?' Dallas asked anxiously.

'Only these two. She needs taking care of – the kid's bitten and scratched to pieces. He's in a bad way. Snake bite.'

'Evan – get me the antiseptic lotion and bandages. Al, we've found a portable radio, I thought if we could tune into a news station . . .'

'Where?'

She showed him where the radio was and left him to it while treating Cristina. The girl was a mess. Dehydrated, confused, feverish. Dallas took her into the bedroom compartment, laid her on the floor, and gently got her clothes off. Then she dabbed at the scratches and cuts and bites with the antiseptic lotion. With horror she realized that whatever it was that had bitten the girl had laid eggs under the skin, and larvae were pushing their way up, horrible tiny black heads popping through the skin.

She didn't know what to do. So she just covered the girl with the antiseptic lotion and hoped that it would kill them off. Then she dressed her in a pair of Al's slacks and a shirt, and fed her a couple of water biscuits and some orange juice.

Nino was another matter. He was delirious, and seemed to be experiencing difficulty in breathing. The gash on his forehead was quite obviously infected, and his body twitched in desperate spasms of pain.

Dallas knew about snakes. They had kept them at the zoo in Miami. But there were so many different species, and she had no idea what type had bitten Nino. Without an anti-venom being administered immediately she did not hold out much hope for his chance of survival.

She fed him some water and covered him with a blanket. It was all she could do for him.

Al had managed to locate a news programme. He listened to the faint crackly newscaster intently. Paul and Dallas crowded around him.

The news was of a major earthquake in Europe, and a

terrorist group holding hostages in New York. Finally the newscaster continued, 'The Al King mystery deepens. The singer and his nine passengers and five crew have still not been heard from. The jet plane missing since Friday night on a trip between Rio and São Paulo has apparently vanished without trace. The police and airport authorities are completely mystified. No ransom demands have been received, ruling out the possibility of a hijack attempt. Search planes sent out have failed to spot any sight of the missing jet. In India, the new government is calling for . . .'

Al clicked the radio off. 'I think we're lost,' he said bitterly. 'I think we're lost and nobody gives a fuck. You know what? I could easily become the Glenn Miller of the seventies. How does *that* grab you?'

69

Juana fidgeted uneasily as she waited to be ushered in to see Carlos Baptista. It was the reward that had attracted her. Fifty thousand dollars! A fortune! Who could even imagine that amount of money. *Fifty thousand dollars!*

She glanced around the waiting room. It was crowded. Beside her sat a thin girl wearing spectacles, and next to her a young man who was not unlike Nino, only not so good-looking. He had the same untidy hair and intense eyes, but his face was longer – more horsey. No – side by side he would not be able to hold a candle to Nino.

Thinking of him she shuddered slightly. Where was he? The last time she had seen him had been at the airport when she had helped him. I'm just going to interview Al King – not shoot him – he had joked. But what *had* he done? Where had he gone? Because without doubt she knew that the disappearance of that plane with Al King aboard was Nino's doing. And she was going to tell Carlos Baptista all about it. She was going to pick up a fifty thousand dollar reward. Probably.

Didi adjusted her spectacles and edged away from the plump girl sitting next to her. The girl was fidgeting in a most aggravating way, squirming on her seat as if she had ants in her pants. Didi sighed and glanced at her watch. She had been sitting here waiting to see Carlos Baptista for one and a half hours. Her lunch hour was past, she would get back to her job as receptionist at the hotel so late that she would more than likely be fired. But if she collected the fifty thousand dollar reward who cared . . .

To think that she, an intelligent girl, had been taken in by a boy like Nino. She had given him everything. Her trust . . . Her body . . . She blushed at the intimacies they had shared together.

He had used her. He had wanted to get to Al King and he had used her. All that talk of love . . . Oh, what a fool she had been.

He had cleared out of his room, she had gone there on Sunday. He had vanished . . . What a *filho da puta*! But she would fix him. She would tell Carlos Baptista everything she knew. And she would get the fifty thousand dollar reward. Probably.

Jorge sat in a corner of the office smoking a long thin Havana cigar. He looked drawn and haggard. He had not slept since his daughter's disappearance.

Carlos was at his desk wearily interviewing the applicants who had answered his call for information. Fifty thousand dollars appeared to have attracted every nut in Rio. They filed in, one by one, with their unbelievable stories.

One woman, apparently well-dressed and respectable, claimed that Al King was under her skirt at that very moment fucking the life out of her. 'If you want him I can open my legs and reveal him,' she confided. 'But you must hand me the cheque first.'

The young secretary, taking copious shorthand next to Carlos, blushed to the roots of her hair. The police chief sitting on Carlos' other side chewed complacently on a pencil stub and ordered, 'Next one in.'

In three hours they had not received one piece of relevant information.

Then the girl came in, thin, nervous, wearing spectacles. She stated her name and address and place of work. She told them her story.

Jorge leaned forward at the mention of Nino's name. The secretary took notes. The police chief chewed on his pencil. Carlos picked his teeth with a wedge of paper.

'Is that all?' the police chief asked when she had finished.

'It's all I know. But I can assure you that Nino will lead you to Al King.' She stood anxiously. 'Do I get the reward?'

'*When* we find this Nino, *if* he leads us to Al King, *then* you get the reward,' the police chief replied.

She looked disappointed. 'I'll probably be fired . . .'

Carlos intervened, 'I'm sure you've been most helpful. Stop by my secretary on the way out and she will give you fifty dollars for your trouble.'

'Fifty? But I thought the reward was fifty thousand?'

'For information leading to Al King. If your information finds him then you get the money.'

Didi shrugged and left.

The men looked around at each other. 'It looks like Nino is the one we want . . .' the police chief said, 'at least we have a lead on him now.' He reached for the phone and issued instructions to a minion on the other end.

Jorge was not surprised. As soon as he had heard the description of the 'mechanic' on the plane he had known it was Nino. He had known he was involved. But he had been unable to tell the police anything. He was ashamed to admit that he had allowed his daughter to keep company with a boy about whom he knew nothing. Now at least they had an address.

The next person was ushered in. A plump girl in a floral dress.

'My name is Juana Figlioa,' she said, 'and I work at the airport.

I helped a boy called Nino get aboard the Al King plane . . .'

Finally they were getting somewhere.

☆

Of course the party in Doris Andrews' honour had been cancelled.

'I'm sorry . . .' Evita had apologized.

'Don't be silly,' Doris had replied, 'as if you could host a party at a time like this . . . And anyway I didn't come here for parties. I came to see you . . .'

She was by Evita's side constantly, comforting and sustaining her. It suited Jorge perfectly. He wanted to be alone with his own personal grief. He didn't want to share the misery and uncertainty he felt. He did not want to share the feeling that somehow it was all his fault ... That if he had listened to Evita ... taken more care of what Cristina was doing ... who she was seeing ... heeded Evita's intuition about Nino instead of laughing at her fears ...

In the event the two women were left alone together, and by Monday Evita was convinced she had only got through the long weekend because of her friend's support.

'How is your husband?' she finally remembered to ask.

'I am divorcing him,' Doris announced simply. 'It's not enough that he has had me watched and followed throughout our entire marriage. It's not enough that he had been unable to engage in sex. I understood. I was the perfect wife. But last week he became frighteningly violent towards me. He came home from the studio one day and beat me up. Yes – physically beat me. I don't know why. I moved out immediately. Let him have the mansion and cars for now. My lawyer will see I do not suffer. My trip here was already planned, so I came here anyway.'

'I'm glad you did,' said Evita. They sat in the conservatory, a glass-walled, plant-filled room, overlooking the swimming pool. 'What will you do when you leave here?'

Doris shook her head. 'I don't know. Perhaps a trip to Europe. Would you like to come with me?'

'I can't make any plans.'

'Of course not.' She reached for Evita's hand and squeezed it gently. 'But when you can...'

Evita allowed her hand to remain in the older woman's. It was so comforting ... It made her forget...

'Why don't you lie down?' Doris asked. 'You must be tired.'

Evita nodded. She *was* tired. The doctor had placed her on tranquillizers – a heavy dose.

Doris led her to the bedroom. 'Jorge told me he would be home late,' she remarked. 'He asked me to stay with you.'

'You don't have to ...' objected Evita.

'I know I don't have to. I want to. We're friends ... I want to help. Turn, let me unbutton your dress.'

Evita did as she was told. She knew what was going to happen but was powerless to stop it . . . She didn't want to stop it . . .

The dress slipped from her body, fell to the ground. She stepped over it and walked to her bed.

She closed her eyes and waited for Doris to join her.

She didn't have to wait long.

☆

'Do you want to fly to Rio?' Cody asked.

'No. What good would that do?' Linda replied.

'I just thought it might help to be on the spot.'

'Would you come?'

'If you wanted me to.'

'I can't eat this.' Linda pushed the salad plate away and stared around the restaurant. 'Look at them all stuffing their faces – as if they care.'

'They probably don't even know Dallas and Al.'

'Why do you always say Dallas and Al?' Linda snapped. 'Paul's on that plane too, you know. Paul and Evan. Bernie and other people. You're as bad as the goddamn television – Dallas and Al – as if no one else is with them.'

'You don't have to get mad at me. You know how I feel . . .'

She was contrite. 'I'm sorry, Cody. I shouldn't be taking my feelings out on you. It's this not knowing . . . It's so awful. It would almost be better if they were all dead. If the plane *had* crashed and been found – at least we would *know*.' She touched his arm. 'I don't mean that. I don't know what I mean any more. I'm so mixed up. It's all such a shitty game. Do you know I am making more money out of this than I ever made in my life? My pictures of Dallas are selling time and time again – the same with my stuff on Al. It doesn't seem right to make money on it.'

'That's the way it goes.'

'Oh, Christ, Cody, isn't there anything we can *do*? I feel so helpless sitting here.'

'We can go to Rio. Say the word and I'll get the tickets.'

'I don't know . . . What do you think?'

'I think we should go.'

594

'You're right. Let's do it. But I want to pay my own way. Understood?'

'If you say so.'

☆

Jorge went with the police to Nino's miserable one-roomed apartment. The two girl informants had been able to furnish them with the address.

They busied themselves taking fingerprints and searching for information. The only things Nino had left behind were a broken pair of black sunglasses, and a filthy T-shirt. The sordid room yielded few clues. A cracked ashtray overflowing with cigarette butts, hairpins scattered over the dirty grey sheet on the bed – obviously not his. And a single gold earring was discovered under the bed. A rough hoop for pierced ears – the kind Cristina used to wear.

'Does it belong to your daughter?' the police chief asked, thrusting it into his hands.

Jorge hesitated, weighing the earring gingerly. He was sure that it was Cristina's. 'I don't know,' he replied. 'I can't be certain.'

How could he admit that his daughter had been in this dirty little room? It was unthinkable that she might have lain on that filthy bed.

'Perhaps you can ask your wife,' the police chief said.

'Yes,' agreed Jorge. What did it matter anyway whose earring it was? The important thing was finding Cristina.

Alive or dead, he had to know.

70

Sunday night was the worst yet.

Nino kept everyone awake with his unearthly screams and agonized writhings. As if that was not enough, sometime before dawn, the rain started again. A heavy torrential rain that poured down spilling through the blown-out windows.

A meal of tinned caviar, maraschino cherries, and champagne seemed to have disagreed with everyone, and the toilet was occupied all night. Since the wastes could not be flushed away, a horrible stench was coming from the tiny bathroom off the bedroom.

'We'll all get sick,' Dallas told Al, 'we should never have used that bathroom.'

'So what else was there to do? Jump off the plane every time you wanted to pee?'

'Al. We've got to face facts. I don't think anyone's going to find us here.'

'I told you – tomorrow I'll search for the rest of the plane. With luck we'll be able to radio for help. If I hadn't have had to drag Cristina and Nino back I would have found it today.'

'And if you don't find it? If the radio doesn't work?'

'We'll think again.'

'We've been here two days and only seen one plane fly over. I don't think anyone's looking for us – not here anyway. We'll have to make an attempt to get out of here ourselves.'

He laughed drily. 'Are you kidding?'

'No, I'm not. I think it's our only hope. We'll all die if we stay here.'

'Worry about it when we can't use the radio.'

'But we're wasting time.'

He groaned and held his stomach. 'Christ! Remind me never to eat caviar again.'

'You don't want to listen to me, do you?'

'What makes you think you know what you're talking about?'

'I keep on telling you. I never had much education – the only kind I *did* get was about animals and survival. We have to find water – a river. If we do that and follow it, eventually we'll find people.'

'Tell me tomorrow.'

'We're not getting any stronger, we should set off soon.'

'What about the others?'

'We'll find help and send it back for them.'

'You're kidding. That lot alone out here wouldn't last five minutes.'

She sighed. 'Since when did *you* start thinking about other people?'

'Since I found you.'

☆

By morning the rain was heavier than ever. Al had set out any receptacle they had to catch it in, and it enabled everyone to have awash.

'Shit – I always did hate Monday mornings,' Bernie complained, as Dallas bathed his wound. It didn't look too bad. The skin was beginning to pucker and close up.

Cathy's leg was very infected and Dallas was convinced it would have to come off. Impossible. They didn't even have a knife. The only cure for gangrene was amputation. Cathy could barely open her eyes.

'What shall we do?' Dallas whispered to Al.

'There's nothing we *can* do. Even if we cut the leg off she'd die anyway.'

'Yes, but we would have tried.'

'And put her through a terrible scene – for what?'

'I know you're right, but I can't help feeling so helpless.'

He put his arm around her and held her close. 'I love you,' he whispered. 'Whatever happens I love you. I've been using women all my life – good for a fuck – nothing else. And then came you. I've waited for you thirty-eight years – don't feel helpless. You've made my life worth living.'

'For how long? Another week? Because if we stay put that's about all we'll have. Maybe two if we're lucky.'

'You ever tried positive thinking? I'm going to see if I can find the other half of the plane.'

'In this rain?'

'You wouldn't want me to just sit around.'

☆

He found the front half of the plane two hours later. The vultures led him to it – huge, decadent scavengers, circling above the wreck, taking their time between sweeping down and pecking at the remains of their human victims.

There was a strong smell of petrol mixed with burnt flesh. So strong that Al found it difficult to approach.

He forced himself to do so in the hope that there would be something of use he could salvage. Certainly no radio could have survived, that was obvious. But he had to look.

The nose of the plane was dug deep into the ground. Al walked around it, peering through the front aperture. What he saw made him sick to his stomach. Something that had once been a human being, now a crawling maggotty mass of open flesh and bone. He moved closer – the interior was just a charred wreck, and more maggot-ridden bodies. Oh Christ . . .

He turned and threw up, retching on an empty stomach. Then suddenly he saw a huge snake. He backed away, still sick to his stomach.

No fucking radio. What next?

The image of the maggot-ridden bodies danced before his eyes. Christ! That was one hell of a way to go.

He stumbled on through the dense undergrowth, then sat down at the foot of a giant tree and tried to shut out what he had seen, but the image would not leave him. He closed his eyes, but that made the vision worse.

It was all so frigging hopeless. Dallas was right. The only way out was if they did it themselves. Nobody was going to find them. Nobody was going to rescue them. It was yesterday's news already.

Do you remember Al King?

Who?

☆

The rain lasted until midday, crashing through the trees relentlessly, marooning the plane in a sea of mud. Then it stopped, quite suddenly, and the sun appeared almost immediately, and soon the heat was back – the humid, steamy jungle heat, which could render you exhausted in a matter of minutes.

Nino was in a bad way. His eyes and tongue protruding, his limbs stiffening, and all the while he was crying out and moaning.

Cristina sat on the floor next to him and fed him sips of water, but they all knew he was dying, and that there was nothing they could do to save him.

Since Dallas had persuaded Evan to change his clothes he seemed much brighter, and was eager to help out if he could. He didn't seem to realize where they were though, and addressed Dallas as either Nellie or Edna. He did whatever she told him, and another pair of hands was a great help.

Of course she knew he was still in shock, and suffering

from some kind of amnesia along with it, but at least he was no longer huddling in his seat incommunicado.

Paul had become very morose. He woke up complaining of stomach pains and a headache, and he was indeed very hot. Dallas got out the thermometer from the first-aid box and took his temperature. He had a fever of 105 degrees.

As if they didn't have enough problems.

She lay him down, covered him with blankets, and fed him three aspirin from their fast-dwindling supply.

How had she become den mother? She would have liked to have crawled into a corner and collapsed too – but now with Paul ill and Al away she seemed to be the one they all depended on. Not that Paul had been much help – it was Al who was keeping everyone's spirits up. He was incredible. She allowed herself a brief moment of pleasure to think about him. God, if anyone should have fallen to pieces it should have been him. So spoiled, so used to crooking a finger and having everything done for him. He had certainly come up trumps.

She remembered their time together on the plane before the storm. Lying next to each other. Exploring each other's bodies. It had all been so beautiful. Touching his naked body had been like touching a man for the first time. At last she had known what Linda was talking about. Known a feeling of such tense expectant pleasure that she had never wanted to leave his side. She had *wanted* to do things to him that she had been *forcing* herself to do to other men all her life. They had been unable to do anything except look and touch. The plane had forced them from the bed into the safety of the couch. Safety – that was a laugh. And all the time, while they had been locked in, the plane had been heading for disaster.

She sighed deeply. If they were going to die at least they would be together.

If they were going to die she wanted to possess him at least once. But how could they . . . here . . . on the plane . . . with everyone watching.

'Hey – Dallas baberooney,' Bernie's voice boomed out, 'wacha all say to a little lunch? I am personally wasting away. Can you imagine me thin?'

'Never!' she laughed. At least he was recovering; it was

more than she could say for Cathy who had lain silently all day – not even strong enough to moan. 'What's your choice, Bernie? Nuts, crisps, or a couple of lumps of sugar?'

'How many crisps?'

'Your share would be about six.'

'Sound like a feast.'

'Come on, Evan, help me prepare lunch!'

☆

Al leaned back against the tree trunk and watched the wild life. As the rain stopped, insects, birds and animals seemed to pop out from everywhere. A beautifully coloured parrot perched on a tree branch and communicated with another amazingly plumed bird. All around him on the ground tiny insects scurried around. A school of very large ants marched past. An enormous spider weaved an elaborate trap.

Suddenly a whole troop of monkeys came skipping about amongst the trees, leaping from branch to branch. Al grinned. They were all managing to survive pretty well. If they could do it . . . He stood up, feeling better. What was it Dallas had said? We must find a river. Maybe if he followed the monkeys . . . Mustn't get lost . . . Mustn't forget which direction he had come from . . .

He took a lump of sugar from his pocket and sucked on it. Instant energy. Try to forget the way your stomach really feels. The filthy taste in your mouth. The frigging flies and mosquitoes who had decided to become permanent companions. The wet clothes sticking to your aching body. Thank Christ he had been in good shape to start off with.

He thought of the others waiting at the plane, expecting him to come back with good news. He couldn't let them down. He set off after the monkeys, keeping a wary eye open for snakes. Didn't want to finish up like Nino. Dallas was right, in the jungle you had to keep your eyes open all the time.

☆

Cathy died at four o'clock. She drifted silently away, and it wasn't until Bernie noticed she wasn't breathing that anyone realized.

'We'll have to move her,' Dallas said sadly. 'In this heat her body will decompose very quickly.'

'Bury her next to Luke,' Bernie suggested. Al and Paul had buried Luke some distance from the plane.

'Yes, but I can't do it alone.'

'I'll help you,' said Evan quickly.

'I don't know ... It will be difficult. Maybe we should wait for Al.'

'Honestly, Nellie, I can help you,' Evan said earnestly.

'Yes I know you can. But I think the best thing is if we get her body off the plane, and then we can bury her tomorrow. It will be getting dark soon.'

Bernie said, 'Jesus Christ – she was a good kid. She handled the whole hijack caper magnificently – I'm gonna miss her.' His voice was all choked up. 'If they'd got us out of this piss hole she could have been saved ... Jesus ... maybe she's the lucky one ... Maybe that's what's in store for all of us ... Trash out in some friggin' jungle ...' He slumped down on the bed.

Dallas wrapped the body in a sheet, and with Evan's help lowered it off the plane. She wished Al would get back. It was almost dusk, and the deadly blackness followed soon after.

Paul was hotter than ever, the fever seemed to be getting a grip on him.

Nino's screams of agony were getting weaker, it would be him next.

'I'd better take a look at your bites before it gets dark,' Dallas said to Cristina. The girl had stayed next to Nino all day, not moving at all.

'No ... not now. Tomorrow.'

'How do you feel?'

Cristina nodded. Her face was a mass of dark purple bruises and cuts. 'Fine,' she mumbled.

'You don't look fine. I want you to have some orange juice.'

'Yes,' agreed Cristina.

Dallas walked to the gaping front of the plane and peered out. No sign of Al, and darkness was closing in. She shut her eyes tightly and said a silent prayer. If anything had happened to him she didn't want to go on. She just couldn't make it.

Evan came and stood beside her. 'Don't worry,' he said, as if reading her thoughts. 'He'll be back, really he will.'

She turned to the son of the man she loved and saw him as if for the first time. He had Al's eyes, widely-spaced pools of jet, and once his acne cleared up and he filled out a little he would be a good-looking boy.

'Thank you, Evan,' she said quietly, 'you've been a great help to me and I want you to know that.'

The darkness hid his blush. 'S'OK, Dallas, I want to help.'

He had called her by the right name. She smiled and took his hand. 'You and me and your dad, we're going to get out of this. Right?'

'Right,' he agreed.

☆

The monkeys led him to a stream. A fast-running rush of clear water that filled Al with buoyancy. He waded in, revelling in the feel of the cold water. He drank some. It tasted fine.

Now if he followed the stream it must lead to a river. Had to. And according to Dallas a river would eventually lead to people.

He was exultant. It was a way out. As Dallas had said it sure beat the hell out of sitting around waiting for some kind of slow death.

He was tempted to start on the journey immediately, and waded some way down the stream. But then he realized it was getting late, and he must go back and tell them what he was going to do. Also he should get some supplies to keep him going – who knew how long it would take? A few cubes of sugar and a bottle of water would not get him far.

It occurred to him that he should have shot one of the monkeys – he had the gun – and they needed meat. Didn't the Chinese regard monkey as some great delicacy?

He had picked up a hefty stick which he used to beat his way through the heavy undergrowth. Sometimes he could hear animals scurrying away as he approached.

He was good at directions, and hoped to Christ he knew where he was going. By the time darkness descended he knew he was not going to make it back to the plane in time, and he swore softly under his breath. Now Dallas would be worried. She would think something had happened to him.

There was nothing he could do. It would be stupid to travel in the dark.

He was mad at himself for having got caught like this. Underneath his anger he was scared. Who knew what jungle animals were kicking around out there. He leaned back against a tree and rested his hand comfortingly on the gun. He wouldn't sleep. It was too dangerous to sleep. Too fucking dangerous. Within minutes he was snoring.

The ants woke him, they were crawling all over him, biting his exposed flesh, eating him alive.

He jumped up cursing, and brushed them frantically off. They clung stubbornly. They were everywhere, they had even managed to crawl inside his clothes.

It was dawn, light enough for him to continue his journey.

He stripped off his clothes, shaking the little monsters out of them, brushing them from his flesh. He was a mass of tiny red bites. 'Fuckers!' he screamed, venting his anger and feeling better for it.

When he was sure his clothes were ant-free he put them on again, and set off. He was nearing the plane when he heard the noises. Animal noises of great ferocity.

He stopped, his blood chilling, and approached cautiously.

A few yards from the plane two jaguars tore at a human body, pulling it between them like a rag doll. Blood was everywhere as they picked and bit at the flesh.

Al's hand tightened on the gun, his only protection. He was immobilized with shock. Maybe it was Dallas ... Evan ... Paul ...

Maybe they were *all* dead.

The animals could have leapt aboard the plane during the night. They could have picked off their human victims one by one ...

He remained frozen to the spot until they finished, and strolled off fully satisfied.

Still Al couldn't move. He was paralysed with horror.

A monkey swung down off a tree, inspected the bones, squatted beside them.

Slowly Al stepped forward, the monkey skipped off. There was nothing human left to recognize.

Al hauled himself aboard the plane. Curled up in a seat at the front was Dallas. She was asleep. In the seat behind her Evan slept.

Further down the plane Nino lay on the floor, Cristina crouched beside him. Nino's eyes were wide open and staring in a sightless fashion. Al knelt, felt for his pulse. He was dead.

Cristina didn't say anything, but tears were falling down her face. She knew.

He continued through to the bedroom section where Bernie and Paul shared the bed. Cathy was no longer there. With a sick feeling he knew who the jaguars had been eating. He only hoped to God she had been dead when they had got her. Then he realized that she must have been – probably died yesterday, and been put off the plane without being buried. He couldn't help being angry. Who could have done a stupid thing like that?

He looked longingly at the bed. What wouldn't he give to just flop out and get a few hours' real kip. What was Paul doing on it anyway? Nothing wrong with him. Dallas should have the bed, She was working harder than anyone. He would soon sort *that* out today.

He went back down the plane and slid into the seat next to her. He touched her lightly on the arm. She woke with a jump, 'I knew you would come back,' she said softly. 'What happened? I was so worried. Cathy died.'

'I know.' He decided not to tell her what he had seen.

'Tell me what you found.'

'The plane. No survivors. No radio.'

'Oh . . .' Her face fell.

'But I found a stream. I was going to follow it but it was getting late. I was thinking about what you said. The only chance we've got of getting out is doing it ourselves. I'm going to do it . . . I'll find help and come back.'

'I'm coming with you.'

'No way. It's dangerous. You'll stay here.'

'Oh no, I won't. You think I can just sit around and *wait* in the hope that you'll make it. I'm coming too – there is no argument.'

'Oh yes there is . . .'

Her eyes became dangerously narrow. 'I know more about jungles than you do. I know about animals, plants. I know what's safe to eat . . . things like that. *I am not staying here.*'

'We'll talk about it.'

'Nothing to talk about. This is our fourth day here, nobody's going to come for us.'

'The others . . . We can't leave them alone.'

'We'll take them with us . . . They'll die here anyway when the food and water run out.'

'You're a stubborn bitch.'

'The hell I am. We're talking about survival, Al. *Our* survival. I want to make it – staying here means certain death. The other way there's a chance.'

'I don't know . . .'

'Well, I do.'

The rest of the day was not good for any of them. Nino had to be buried, and Cristina did not want to be parted from the body. 'He knows where Louis is,' she explained patiently to anyone who would listen, 'and I want him to tell me.'

Paul was still running a high fever, alternately hot and cold, sweating and shivering.

Bernie was coughing up blood, fat globules.

The heat was unbearable. The metal parts of the plane attracted the sun filtering through the trees like a magnet, until it was like being in the middle of a giant sun reflector.

Flies and mosquitoes were worse than ever, bothering everyone incessantly. And the larvae popping obscenely from Cristina's arms had to be dug out with a pair of tweezers while she screamed in pain.

Evan was sick and unable to stomach any food. As soon as he ate even the smallest thing he was beset with terrible cramps.

The plane's odour was getting worse, a sickening mixture of stale sweat and excrement.

'Staying here is making everyone ill,' Dallas told Al. 'The sooner we leave the better.'

He was forced to agree with her. Hellishly hot and stinking during the day. Freezing at night.

They had seen no more planes fly over. The portable radio had given one last crackle and stopped functioning.

'If everyone can walk we'll leave tomorrow,' he said.

Dallas prepared back packs for each of them to carry. A blanket, a towel, their share of food and a bottle to keep their water in. She organized a separate medicine bundle containing bandages, ointment, and the rest of the pain killers.

Wednesday Paul was not well enough to travel, so they lost another day. But by Thursday morning his temperature had receded, and although he was weak, he was able to walk.

Leaving the plane was like leaving home. They had slept there for six nights. At least it had been a base, a place of shelter. But it was now riddled with insects and unfit to spend one more night in.

They made a motley procession. Al in the lead, followed by Cristina, then Bernie, Paul, Evan, with Dallas bringing up the rear. 'If we meet any wild animals,' Al joked, 'we'll frighten them to death!'

Progress was slow, and it took them nearly the whole day to reach the stream, a journey that had only taken Al a few hours before. He detoured so that they wouldn't have to pass the nose of the plane with its maggot-ridden occupants, and for a while he thought they were lost. But his sense of direction had not deserted him, and eventually they arrived at the stream.

'We'll stay here overnight,' he said. They were all dripping with sweat and nobody argued. They dumped their back packs and collapsed on the mossy ground.'

'Watch out for giant ants,' Al warned, 'and snakes, and anything else that moves.' He felt he was becoming quite an expert after having survived one night out in the open.

'I'm going to bathe,' Dallas said. She stripped down to her bra and panties and waded into the shallow water. It was heavenly. She lay down and let her hair loose and luxuriated in the tingling freshness of the water. If she closed her eyes she could imagine she was in Palm Springs playing about in the shallow end of a swimming pool. She tried it. It worked.

She felt Al watching her, and opened her eyes and grinned at him.

'Why don't you join me?'

She didn't have to ask twice. He stripped to his shorts and was beside her almost immediately.

Cristina, swallowing her shyness about taking her clothes off in front of these strangers, followed.

Evan thought about it a bit. Should he? Shouldn't he? Would they laugh at his skinny body? Would his jockey shorts reveal anything? It looked so inviting. So what if they did laugh. He took off his clothes and got in.

Bernie, red in the face from the exertion of the trip, waded to the side, rolled his trouser legs up, and stuck his legs in.

Paul watched. His head throbbed. He wanted to join them, but he couldn't muster the strength. The attack of fever had left him weaker than he cared to admit. He kept on thinking about his children – they were both so young – if anything happened to him . . . He lay on the ground and closed his eyes. It didn't bear thinking about.

The bathe in the stream raised everyone's spirits. For a few brief moments they could forget about where they were and just relax. A large frog stood on the bank and watched them. Tiny little fishes swam about in confusion.

'Maybe we could catch a few,' Al suggested, 'I could just fancy a fry-up.'

Evan tried, but they were too small and fast for him. Cristina giggled at his efforts. It was the first time she had smiled since they had found her.

'We had better get out now, the sun's going down . . .' Dallas said.

'Wish I was,' Al muttered.

'Huh?'

He pulled her close to him and whispered in her ear, 'You're never going to believe this but I'm feeling horny!'

'Just now you were hungry . . .'

'All my appetites seem to be at full tilt! Come on – let's take a walk.'

They got out of the stream, dried off and dressed.

'Dallas and I are going to survey the scene ready for an early start tomorrow,' Al said, 'we won't be long.'

'I'll come,' Evan offered.

'No, son. You stay here – keep an eye on things. I reckon as tonight's the first step of our journey we should celebrate and have anchovies for dinner. How about that?'

'One tin,' Dallas said sternly.

'Between six of us? We'll starve to death before we get to the other two tins. I say we open all three and have half a tin each.'

'No. We've got to save what food we have.'

'Shit – we'll probably be out of here tomorrow – let's go for broke and gorge on *all* the anchovies.'

'No,' Dallas objected.

'Yes! We'll put it to the vote. All those in favour shove your hands up.'

Bernie's hand shot up, so did Evan's. Hesitantly Cristina joined them by raising her arm.

'You're outvoted,' Al said, taking Dallas by the arm and picking up his blanket, 'hey, Paul, you going to eat?'

'He's asleep,' said Bernie. 'Don't worry, we'll save his share.'

'Yeah – well, save ours too. We'll be back soon.'

Bernie shook his head in amazement. Al King was certainly to be admired. Not content with getting them all together and marching them through the jungle like some kind of Messiah – he was now ready to knock one off! Unbelievable!

But Christ – he had met his match in Dallas. She was some woman. Some incredible lady.

He sighed, and reached for the anchovies. What the fuck ... If the two of them wanted to do it in the middle of the goddamn jungle then good luck to them. Where there was life there was hope – and God knows they could all do with a little bit of hope ...

Evan watched his father disappear off into the undergrowth with Dallas, and he didn't mind. For the first time in his life he felt he was seeing Al as he really was. A man who cared about other people. He thought about all the hate he had stored up towards this man. Hate and envy ... It all seemed to have dissolved away.

It would have been so easy for Al to have left them all. He was far stronger than any of them, and not wounded. If he travelled alone he would make much better time, have a better chance. But he wasn't leaving them ... He was sticking with them ... Helping them ...

Evan was proud of having Al King for a father. He turned to Cristina, her damp curls surrounded a pinched frightened face. She probably wasn't that much older than him, he hadn't realized that before. In fact he had not taken any notice of her at all, he had been too busy worrying about himself. But she was a girl. She was alone. It must all be a terrifying experience for her.

'How are you feeling?' he asked hesitantly.

'Not so good.' Her eyes were brimming over with tears.

He put a comforting arm around her, half expecting her to shove him away. But she didn't, she moved closer to him and the tears slid silently down her cheeks. 'It's all my fault,' she muttered. 'Louis is dead and it's all my fault.'

'No, it's not,' he said in a kindly fashion. 'You mustn't blame yourself, really you mustn't. Nino would have found a way to get on the plane with or without your help.'

Her eyes widened. 'Do you *honestly* think so?'

'Yes,' he comforted, 'I'm sure he would.'

She stopped crying. 'Can I tell you about it? I must tell someone, it's driving me crazy. You'll understand, I know you will. Can I tell you from the beginning?'

'Of course you can.' Evan replied, 'you can tell me anything you want.'

☆

They didn't stray too far from the others. They just walked a few minutes downstream, and then Al lay the blanket on a soft mossy patch of ground and took off his clothes.

Silently Dallas did the same. She lay down on the blanket and stared at him expectantly. Her ribs were badly bruised, but apart from that she had suffered only a few bites.

'I'll be gentle,' Al said quietly, lowering himself on top of her. His lean body was a mass of bites, scratches, and little cuts that seemed to be healing.

'I love you,' she whispered, arching her body to meet his.

'Yeah?' he questioned. 'That's funny 'cos I love you too. Never thought I'd say that – to anyone.' He entered her, and slowly moved back and forth. She moved with him, welcoming him into her body with a passion she never knew she possessed.

'Tell me when you're ready,' he muttered, 'I'm not as strong as I used to be!'

'I love you.'

'Christ!' he shuddered, '*I love you too. Chriiistl* This must be a record! Son-of-a-beetch!' He climaxed, collapsing on top of her, his body ridden with spasms.

She came immediately after him, sighing his name, raking his back with her nails. They rolled across the blanket still joined together.

'God Almighty!' Al started to laugh. 'I haven't come that quickly since I was in *school*! I just blew my reputation in one fell swoop!'

She laughed with him. 'What reputation?'

He moved his hands appreciatively down her body, 'When you haven't eaten for a week I guess it's got to affect your sex life. I feel like . . .'

'Good I hope.'

'Pretty goddamn good. I've got sixteen flies dive bombing my ass – and hey – just a minute – how was it for you?'

'Pretty goddamn good!'

'I mean was it like you wanted it to be?'

'It was beautiful, incredible, everything I knew it would be with you from the first moment I ever set eyes on you. I'm not too mad about the setting – but the event . . . Well . . . What can I say?'

'I love you, lady. You know that? You know that's something I've never told anyone in my whole life. *NEVER.* Sex was sex. A fuck was a fuck. Women were just something to stick it into – get rid of the dirty water – a joke. Wow – I am here to tell you I have humped in a lot of strange places in my time – but this . . .'

'So have I.'

'Don't go trying to get one up on me.'

'Who's trying? I just am not very interested in hearing all about the places you've screwed in.'

'You're right. It's past news. Jesus!' He slapped ineffectually at his posterior. 'I am getting killed! I don't think these little mothers have had such a good meal in a long time. Come on, let's get dressed and back while I've still got the strength!'

They both stood up, shaking their clothes out before putting them on.

'Hey . . .' Dallas questioned, wriggling into her jeans.

'Yes?'

'If we ever get out of this . . .'

'Don't say if – say when.'

'*When*, we get out of this . . . What do you want to happen with us, Al?'

'I want whatever you want. We'll be together – buy a house together – have fun together. You name it.' He knocked a spider out of his shoe before putting it on. 'What do *you* want?'

'I'll tell you if . . . *when* we get out of this.'

He stroked her neck, and said seriously, 'I want to know now. Do you feel like I do? Do you want to spend the rest of your life with me?'

She buttoned up her shirt. 'Yes, and the way we're going it looks like I will. Come on – the light is fading and I'm not walking in the dark.'

'Don't be flip. I'm trying to tell you something. I'm trying to give you words . . . I *need you*. I *love* you. Understand?'

She nodded.

He stared at her. 'As long as you understand . . . Christ! I could get another hard-on just looking at you!'

'I look horrible.'

'You'll never look more lovely.' He took her hand and they started to make their way along the side of the stream back to the others. When they were nearly there he stopped. 'I want you to know,' he said quietly, 'that was beautiful.'

She kissed him. 'Mutual.'

He grinned. 'And now I've got a tin of anchovies to look forward to. This could turn out to be the best day yet.'

☆

Friday morning they set off early, everyone in quite good spirits.

By noon they were sweat-stained and exhausted, moving slowly through the ever-thickening undergrowth, finding it difficult to breathe, under constant attack from the vicious horse flies and mosquitoes. To make matters worse, the stream, instead of getting bigger and leading them to a river, was diminishing in size, and becoming just a tiny trickle of water.

Al knew that the whole morning was wasted. They would have to go back the way they had come, and set off down the stream in the other direction. He was loathe to suggest it. But it had to be done.

'We'll have to turn around,' he said, 'we're getting nowhere fast.'

'Can't,' Bernie gasped, collapsing to the ground, 'can't take another fuckin' step.'

'Let's have a break,' Dallas suggested.

It was hours before Al could persuade them to move again, and then it was just a question of slogging back the way they had come earlier in the day. By dusk they were back at their original camping ground. This time none of them could summon the energy to bathe. They flopped out on their blankets after sharing a precious tin of caviar, and slept.

The expectation of getting out of the steamy jungle alive was slowly dying in each and every one of them.

Except Al. Nothing seemed to daunt him. 'We'll set off tomorrow at dawn,' he told them. 'It will be cooler then. OK everyone? Want to see you ready to go bright and early.'

'You missed your fuckin' vocation in life,' Bernie muttered grimly. 'You shoulda bin' a fuckin' sergeant major!'

71

By Wednesday Cody had booked himself and Linda on a flight to Rio. He picked her up at her apartment, and they drove straight to the airport.

Cody had not been sure how to handle the hotel reservations. Would Linda want to share with him? Or would she be furious if he booked them into the same room? In the end he had decided to play it safe, and reserved two separate rooms. He made sure they were adjoining – just in case.

He wasn't quite sure how to play it with Linda. He liked her tremendously – but she was so cool and independent – and he didn't want to blow it by behaving in a way she might misconstrue. Since the plane's disappearance physical contact between them had terminated abruptly. He understood. He wasn't feeling exactly horny himself. But he hoped that eventually things could go back to the way they were. They had been at the beginning of what promised to be an exciting and maybe long-lasting affair. Relationships like that were few and far between. Hollywood was full of Carol Camerons. But how many Lindas did you come across?

The airport was crowded, people bustling back and forth – meeting, greeting, hiring cars, buying souvenirs, or just standing around. Cody saw a couple of people he knew – a fellow agent who a couple of months ago wouldn't have bothered to give him the time of day – and a minor actress who greeted him like an intimate friend. He could swear he had never met her before.

Linda walked over to the magazine stand to pick up the newspapers.

'Who's your friend?' the agent asked admiringly. 'I like her style.'

Proudly Cody followed Linda with his eyes. She *did* have a lot of style. She looked coolly chic in a white safari suit, her jet hair pulled severely back, and purple-tinted shades hiding her eyes.

'Linda Cosmo,' Cody replied, 'a photographer from New York.'

'Sure,' said the agent enthusiastically. 'I've seen her work – she's got a six-page spread in *People* this week. I never realized she looked like that . . . You want to trade numbers?' He indicated his actress, who, as if on cue, broke into a large toothy Californian grin and said in a flowing Southern accent, 'You all know if they've cast a new "Man Made Woman" yet? I don't usually test, but I got to thinking that maybe I might – you know – just for once. It's a perfect part for me.'

Cody had yet to meet an actress who didn't think every part written was the perfect one for them.

'I don't know,' he said. 'As far as I'm concerned it's a little early to start putting in a replacement.'

'Early?' hissed the agent. 'You don't think they're gonna *find* that Dallas broad do you?'

'As a matter of fact I am flying to Rio now.'

'Why – anything new happen?'

'No – but . . .'

The agent laughed. It was more of a rude sneer than a laugh. 'Chasing a dead client – come on – that ain't gonna put shekels in your pocket. She's dead, man – face it. That plane probably crashed into the sea – they'll never find it.'

It was not the first time that this sentiment had been expressed to Cody – although perhaps not in such harsh terms. His mother over a cold fish dinner the previous evening, had clutched him warmly by the hand. 'I think if she was alive they would have heard something by now,' she offered. 'Better she's dead than in the hands of those foreign maniacs.'

The two theories given wide news coverage were either that the plane had strayed off its flight path and crashed, or that some sort of terrorist organization had managed to hijack it.

The crash theory was now gaining the most strength. The plane had been missing five days. If a ransom demand was to be made it would have been done by now.

Cody bid a curt goodbye to the agent and actress, and joined Linda at the newstand.

She waved a newspaper at him. 'Page three,' she said in disgust. 'From headlines to page three.'

'It's old news,' replied Cody wearily.

'If only we knew . . . Oh God . . . If only we *knew* . . .'

☆

Jorge did not want to show the earring to Evita. Did not want to be forced to admit that perhaps he had been wrong – that perhaps Cristina *had* been sharing Nino's bed. Evita's positive identification of the earring would prove facts that Jorge did not wish to face.

Wasn't it bad enough that his daughter was missing – probably dead. He couldn't even begin to come to terms with *that*. Cristina was the best thing that had ever happened to him – an extension of his love for Evita – more, really, because while Evita was his wife, she was also a separate entity – another human being – a person from an entirely different background. Of course that didn't bother him – never had – but Cristina was his own blood. She was all he had. She was the other children Evita had not been able to have. The son that was never to be.

Jorge swore softly under his breath and turned to look at his sleeping wife lying beside him. How beautiful she was, but he was glad that Cristina resembled him and not her. It would be somehow incestous to have a daughter the image of your wife – besides which, he was proud of Cristina's dark earthy looks. She was a born Maraco through and through. No one could dispute *that*.

He had returned to the house late the previous evening and slipped quietly into bed so as not to disturb his wife. Thank God Doris Andrews had arrived when she did. She had been a tower of strength, looking after Evita day and night, moving in to the spare room to be near her. What a magnificent friend she had turned out to be.

Evita stirred in her sleep, turning restlessly and pushing the covers from her. The beige satin nightgown she was wearing had slipped from one of her breasts. Ordinarily Jorge would have been instantly aroused. But not now – in fact it irritated him, and he pulled the covers over her and left the bed.

He knew he was not being supportive towards his wife. He knew he was rejecting her at the time she needed him most – but he had to go through this alone. Cristina was somehow more his than hers – maybe it was the strong resemblance – maybe it was the fact that she was his only child. Who knew? Whatever it was his grief was personal and could not be shared – with anyone.

He shaved and dressed, then went in his study and wrote a brief note to accompany the earring which he left on Evita's bedside table. He wanted to go straight to Carlos' office. Today might be the day they got some news.

Silently he left the house, climbed into his Maserati and drove quickly away.

Doris Andrews watched him from the guest bedroom window. She waited a few minutes, then smiling softly to herself she padded along to Evita's bedroom. She locked the door and climbed into the space that was still warm from Jorge's body. Confidently she waited for Evita to awaken.

☆

Talia Antonios strode purposefully down the street. She was a tall, arrogant-looking girl clad in a smart brown linen suit. Her red hair was cropped close to her head, and she wore very little make-up.

She swept into the building that Carlos Baptista owned, and took the elevator to the eighth floor which housed his private suite of offices.

A secretary glanced up at her. 'Yes?'

'I have an appointment,' Talia said, 'ten o'clock.'

'Oh yes – Senor Baptista said for you to go right in.' The secretary indicated the way.

Talia strode through the door without bothering to knock.

Carlos, sitting behind his desk, was quite startled by the girl. For a start she was exceptionally tall, and secondly she bore down on him so intensely that he thought for a moment she was going to sweep right round his desk and hit him. She had that kind of look about her. Tough and uncompromising. Carlos was pleased that the chief of police and Jorge Maraco were stationed in an adjoining office with a tape recorder. She was only a woman – but there was something horribly violent about her – betrayed in her icy grey eyes. On the telephone he had sensed this. Known by instinct that here was someone who really did have some information for sale. She had requested that they meet alone. No police. Nobody official.

She paused at his desk and glanced around the office. 'Let's go for a walk,' she said. Hardly the opening line he had been expecting.

'A walk?' he blustered, 'what are you talking about? You said on the phone a private meeting – well, here we are alone in my office. What could be more private than that?'

'Plenty of places. The information I have for you is for your ears alone. After I've told you, then make your own decisions. For all I know this place is bugged – So we either walk – or forget the whole thing.'

Carlos hesitated. He wasn't sure what to do. But then he decided a walk would be all right – after all, as soon as he left the office the Police Chief would have his men watching his every move. The girl couldn't kidnap him – the hidden fear of every rich businessman in South America.

'If that's what you want we'll walk then,' said Carlos, getting up from behind the desk, 'but I hope what you have to tell me is worth the trouble.'

Talia nodded. 'I think you'll agree it is.'

☆

The city of Rio de Janeiro was as beautiful as Linda had always expected it to be. She only wished that she was visiting under different circumstances. Her New York agency had suggested that she do a photo story on the trip as soon as she had told them she was going. 'No!' she had protested, 'it would be ghoulish.' But she had brought her cameras anyway – she never went anywhere without them.

Why had she and Cody come there? It wasn't as though they could *do* anything . . . But somehow it was comforting to be nearer. Someone would have to identify the bodies when they were found . . . If they were ever found . . .

For the first time, sitting on the plane earlier, she had finally faced the fact that Paul, Dallas, Al, Evan . . . were all dead.

She had desperately tried to remember the last time she and Paul had been together . . . Really together. But all she could come up with was Tucson, and Melanie bursting in on them. Before that was just a blur of airports and hotels and parties.

She wanted to cry, but tears wouldn't come. And Cody was sitting beside her enquiring after her welfare every two minutes. He was starting to drive her mad with his niceness. It was too much. Right now she would have preferred a parking boy or a Rik – someone who was not personally involved and would act accordingly.

The phone in her hotel room buzzed. It was Cody. He had contracted Carlos Baptista and a car would be picking them up in an hour.

'He wants us to dine at his house,' Cody said.

'I didn't realize this was a social trip,' Linda replied coldly.

'It's not. Apparently something has come up and he wants to tell us about it.'

'They've found the plane?'

'I don't know. We'll find out soon enough. Is your room all right? Do you need anything?'

Yes – I need to be relaxed – I need to be fucked. 'Everything's fine,' she replied. She was tempted to tell him what she really wanted, but somehow she felt he wouldn't understand.

She sighed deeply. Men she could have relationships with would never understand her needs. They would be shocked at how strong her demands could be at times . . . Most men enjoyed sex. But no man enjoyed the thought that he might be used as a sexual object. Yet wasn't that the way men had treated women since time began?

She half thought that she might call Cody back . . . But no . . . he wouldn't understand.

☆

Cody replaced the telephone. It was unfair of Linda to take her rattiness out on him. None of this was his fault. He was as destroyed as anyone about it. If he hadn't sent Dallas off to Palm Springs she might never have got it into her head to go chasing after Al King in Las Vegas. And if she hadn't gone to Vegas . . . then no South America . . . No plane crash . . . Maybe it *was* all his fault . . .

Anyway, he had thought he and Linda had something good going. Had was the operative word – it all seemed to have gone sour.

He thought of banging on the communicating door – but what for? To get another knock back.

Instead he picked up the phone again and placed a call to Los Angeles – better he should take care of business.

☆

Evita examined herself in the mirror. The same ivory skin, smooth features, pale blonde silky hair. Her eyes were still blue, her breasts voluptuously full.

She looked exactly the same. Glacial, proud, arrogant. A simmering iceberg.

She stared at herself for a while longer – and she hated what she saw – hated the cool blonde perfection that so betrayed her background.

It would all come as such a shock to Jorge. He had always thought of her as so utterly and absolutely his. The thought had probably never entered his head that she was capable of being unfaithful to him. He owned her, didn't he? He had rescued her from a life of poverty? At the best – if not for him – she might have become a waitress – a shopgirl – or because of her exceptional looks perhaps – and it was only, a perhaps – a rich man's mistress or high-class call girl. At the start of their marriage he had often told her these pertinent facts. The thought of 'what a wonderful thing he had done for her' was instilled daily. After all she had so much to thank him for. He had bought her parents a house in São Paulo, and moved the entire family there. He still, even after seventeen years, paid them a monthly allowance.

Of course she never saw them. Jorge had thought it best that way. 'Forget about your beginnings,' he had told her. 'Your marriage to me is the beginning.'

'My poor little girl' was the pet name he called her as he instructed her in the intricacies of making love. 'Lie like that – legs spread – wider – wider – just like that, my poor little thing.' And he would sink his body into her, sighing with pleasure all the while.

Occasionally – if the mood took him, he would tweak her breasts for a minute at a time. But not enough to get her in the mood – never enough.

He liked her to kneel on all fours whilst he took his pleasure from behind.

He liked her to suck on his penis for hours on end.

In seventeen years of marriage he had never given her an orgasm.

Oh, he was generous in other ways. Clothes, furs, jewels. She could have whatever she wanted.

But in all these years . . . Often she had wondered what it would be like with another man . . . But Jorge loved her – in his way. He trusted her . . . He *had* saved her. How could she do that to him?

And then Doris had happened . . . Doris who caressed her body into molten liquid. Seeking and finding with her tongue every pleasure spot ever invented.

Oh God . . . Evita shuddered with joy at the very memory. And yet . . . how could she feel anything at a time like this?

She continued to stare at herself until she felt a self-hate so strong that it overwhelmed her, and she had to turn away from her own reflection.

How could a woman whose daughter was missing – presumed dead – be so heartless as to embark on a new and frighteningly exciting affair?

It was an impossible situation. If . . . when Jorge found out . . . he would want nothing more to do with her. Nothing. And she could not blame him.

Her eyes filled with tears and spilled down her naked body.

The house was quiet. Jorge had gone to an important meeting at Carlos' house. Doris was out at a dinner.

Jorge had not suggested she accompany him. Doris had.

Evita's body shook with her own sobs. She kept on thinking of Cristina – her wilful fiery daughter – a woman – but no more than a child really. That child was lying dead somewhere. Dead because of her involvement with a boy called Nino. Evita was sure of *that*. If Jorge had been firmer. If ... If ... If ...

Slowly Evita opened the bathroom cabinet and extracted the bottle of sedatives the doctor had prescribed for her. She tipped them out – all of them. There were plenty. Everyone knew Evita. They knew she was a cool, calm, intelligent woman. It would never even enter the doctor's head to limit the amount of pills he gave her.

She picked up the pills, one by one – and swallowed them down with the help of a tumbler of water. When they were all gone she extracted another bottle from the cabinet. Jorge's sleeping pills – large turquoise capsules. Methodically she swallowed every one of those. Now she was feeling tired. Her body was aching, and she felt a strange sickness.

Unsteadily she walked into the bedroom, and climbed into bed. Her eyes were blurring, distorting everything around her. She closed them, peacefully aware that she would never have to open them again.

☆

Talia Antonios had killed the hope that Al King and his plane were being held somewhere for ransom. In a brisk no-nonsense way, she had explained the situation to Carlos Baptista as they walked through the public park near his office. She had explained about the organization P.A.C.P. and Nino's involvement.

'We were expecting the plane,' she explained without emotion. 'We probably could have claimed that we did indeed have the plane, and collected the million dollars that was to have been our price. But what then? You would have paid the money – and we would not have been able to produce the goods. Not so hot for our reputation – who would have ever paid us ransom money again? We are a serious organization – dedicated to helping the oppressed and the poor. Our work is just beginning. Soon we will be famous for our deeds. We will deal honestly – and people will respect us. If we should kidnap – well – say *you* for instance – then we would demand a suitable ransom and if it was paid you would be returned unharmed. If it was not paid you would be returned anyway – in little pieces. But the point is you would be returned – either way. Are you understanding me?'

Carlos gulped. The woman was obviously mad and had to be handled with extreme caution. He glanced around, hoping that indeed the police were having him followed.

'So,' Talia continued, 'it is quite obvious what must have happened. Nino was able to seize the plane, but unfortunately it must have crashed before it reached us.'

'Perhaps Nino has taken the plane elsewhere,' Carlos suggested.

'Utterly impossible,' Talia snapped. 'Nino is – *was* – dedicated. Circumstances must have arisen to cause the plane to crash. They are all dead, Señor Baptista, and the reason I have come to see you is to know if you wish to pay for the privilege of recovering the bodies?'

'Do you *know* where the plane crashed?' Carlos asked incredulously.

'Not exactly. But for the reward money you have offered – fifty thousand dollars, isn't it? Then I could supply you with an exact flight plan. With that information it would merely be a matter of time before the plane was found.' She paused, then added meaningfully, 'I am sure that you would want to see your son have a proper burial.'

'You *cona!*' Carlos spat in her direction. 'What kind of a person are you? Do you have no feelings? Can you just talk about people being dead – my *son*. You *cona* – I will have you arrested!'

She shrugged. 'For what? You have nothing on me. I would of course deny this whole conversation. I didn't *have* to come and see you, did I?'

'I expect fifty thousand dollars was persuasion enough.'

'If you wish to accept our offer have the money in used notes by noon tomorrow. I will telephone you with further instructions. When the money is safely in our possession you will receive the flight plan.'

'I'm supposed to just trust you?'

'I told you,' replied Talia coldly, 'the P.A.C.P. is a very trustworthy organization. If we get the money – you get what *you* want.'

Carlos had related the entire conversation to the Police Chief and Jorge. They were all of the opinion that Talia knew what she was talking about.

'We will pay,' Carlos had finally decided.

'Yes,' Jorge had agreed. He wanted to recover his baby girl's body as soon as possible. Numb with shock he kept this new information to himself and did not even reveal it to Evita.

Talia had informed Carlos that Cristina had been working with Nino. Had helped to execute the whole stinking mess!

Of course Jorge did not believe it. Anyone who knew Cristina would see at once it was a bunch of lies. She had been an innocent party to a series of bizarre events. She was not to blame. No way could she possibly have been knowingly involved in any kind of terrorist plot.

☆

'It looks like a movie set,' Linda muttered, as the chauffeured Mercedes drew up outside Carlos Baptista's palatial white mansion.

'A simple palace . . .' Cody observed.

'I wonder what he is like.'

'He sounds pleasant enough on the phone.'

A butler ushered them into an ornate room and poured them drinks. Then Carlos himself appeared. He greeted them both warmly, hugging Linda as if she was an old friend. She liked him immediately – although physical contact from a stranger would normally have repulsed her.

'The news is not good,' he told them both gravely. 'I think we have to assume beyond question they are all dead.'

Jorge Maraco arrived then, and they went into the dining room and struggled through a meal that no one was really interested in eating.

'Please excuse my wife for not joining us,' Carlos explained. 'As you can imagine . . . she is . . . Louis was her favourite . . .' His voice broke. 'He was a very fine boy. Very good-looking, very intelligent—' he covered his grief with a gruff laugh, 'Not like his father, you know.'

During the course of dinner he explained the situation to them. Telling the story as he knew it, trying to piece together the bits he didn't know. 'So you see . . .' he finished off at last, 'I think we must believe this woman, and with the flight plan we will be able to trace the plane. Without the right information . . . Well – up to now our search planes have come up with nothing. Tomorrow we will pay the money. Tomorrow I think we will find them – God rest their souls.'

Linda was very depressed when the chauffeur dropped them back at the hotel. She wanted to cry, but tears again refused to come.

Cody had lapsed into his own silence.

They rode up in the elevator not saying a word to each other. Outside her door Cody kissed her absently on the cheek. 'Goodnight,' he said quietly.

Goodnight. What was so good about it? She marched into her room, slammed the door, and flopped down on the bed.

Why *had* they come here? What was the point?

Deep down she knew the point. When the plane was found – when the bodies were brought back . . . Well, she wanted to be sure that Paul had someone around who cared . . . It was silly . . . after all, he would never know . . . But all the same she felt that it was only right.

She sighed restlessly. She would never sleep. She felt strung out and tense.

The hell with it! Suddenly she didn't care *what* Cody thought of her. He could take her as she was or not at all.

She jumped off the bed and went to the communicating door. She released the lock on her side, and knocked loudly. 'Cody – hey, Cody – can you hear me?'

It was minutes before he unlocked his side and appeared, wearing a towel knotted around his middle.

'I was just going to take a bath,' he explained. 'What is it?'

'Why don't we bathe together? I've *had* being alone.'

☆

Jorge stayed and drank brandy with Carlos into the early hours of the morning. He did not want to go home. He did not want to be alone. He did not want to face what were more than likely to be proved irrevocable facts.

He dreaded telling Evita, and decided not to tell her anything definite until the plane was actually found.

Dawn was already breaking when he let himself into the house. He went straight to his study and sat at his desk for a while staring at the various framed pictures of Cristina. A pictorial history of her short life. There she was a few hours old – then a saucer-eyed four – at ten, riding her pony – at twelve, reading a book – fifteen, a formal portrait. He had no recent photos – she had suddenly become camera-shy and refused to be photographed.

Wearily he made his way upstairs. Exhaustion was creeping over him, and he wanted to be up early – perhaps go out in one of the search planes.

Evita was asleep in the darkened bedroom. He barely glanced at her. He threw his clothes off and walked in the bathroom. At first he didn't notice the two empty pill containers. Then he saw them and picked them up curiously. Wasn't one of them his ... He read the label on the side – 'Jorge Maraco – sleeping tablets.' That was strange ... He hadn't used them for weeks ...

He picked up the other empty container. 'Evita Maraco – sedatives.'

He stood very still for a moment – the full implications slowly seeping through to his muddled brain.

Sleeping tablets ... sedatives ... empty ...

He walked into the bedroom.

Evita lay very still, uncannily still.

He took her hand, it was extremely cold.

He felt for her pulse. There was none.

She was dead.

☆

Carlos paid Talia. She kept her side of the bargain and within hours a duplicate copy of the two pages of neatly scripted flight plans were on his desk.

Search planes were in the air almost immediately. For two days they scoured the route, but could spot nothing. This was not surprising because the missing Al King plane had been flying over the dense interior of the Amazon jungle, and to spot a crashed plane beneath the thick foliage was virtually impossible. Even if the wreckage was found everyone knew that by this time there would be no hope of any survivors.

On the Monday the search was called off. Al King and his plane had been missing exactly ten days.

Carlos Baptista held a news conference and revealed the facts about a mystery woman and an organization named as the P.A.C.P. 'In view of the information received we must assume that Senor King's plane did indeed crash, and that he and his fellow travellers died as a result. It would seem futile to continue the search. Al King must be declared officially dead.'

☆

Linda and Cody were on a plane back to Los Angeles the same day.

In New York, Melanie King – soon to be Mrs Manny Shorto – appeared once again on television. 'I am deeply saddened by the news,' she said. 'Manny and I will be praying for them all.' Later that evening Manny and Melanie were to be found hosting what appeared to be a celebration party, and she was joyfully heard to confide to practically everyone in sight, 'Now we can get married at once, don't have to go through all that divorce *shit!*'

In Los Angeles Lew Margolis signed a blonde amazon ex-tennis player to be the new 'Man Made Woman'. He also took a repentant Doris back and announced plans for her to star in a controversial new film about lesbianism.

In New York Aarron Mack announced his engagement to a sixteen-year-old German countess. 'She will be the new Mack girl,' he announced to the world, without so much as a word of condolence about Dallas.

At Malibu beach, Karmen Rush gave an exclusive interview to *Macho* magazine in which she revealed Al King was the most exciting lover she had ever had.

In New York Marjorie Carter snorted that Karmen Rush couldn't have had many lovers.

In London Edna King packed away the last of Al's clothes and sent them to a local charity. She was about to start on Evan's things when she realized she would be late for her pottery class – late for John . . .

Hurriedly she left the house.

In Chicago Van Valda threw a big party. '*In Memoriam Al King*', the quickly printed invitations read. 'Al wouldn't have wanted a wake,' Van puffed, his pipe lodged firmly in the corner of his mouth, 'he would have wanted all of his friends to have a good time.'

Of the two hundred and twenty-three guests, Al had personally known six – and they were only vague acquaintances.

In Long Island, Ed Kurlnik gazed out of his bedroom window overlooking the sea. He sipped at a heavy tumbler of neat scotch. His hand was shaking. There would never be another Dallas – never. She had been the sexual realization of a lifetime of searching. He regretted ever letting her go.

Meanwhile, the immaculate Dee Dee entertained a senator and a foreign ambassador to a sumptuous lunch served on the terrace. While her twin daughters, Cara and Dana, entertained movie star Ramo Kaliffe on their speed boat.

In Philadelphia the ex-'Miss Miami Beach', now 'Miss Coast to Coast' sat down to write her memoirs. She devoted two whole chapters to Al King, and their 'lasting and meaningful' affair. She devoted one terse line to Dallas – claiming she had been stripped of her title for unseemly behaviour.

In Los Angeles, Glory and Plum hung around outside a rock concert hoping to score a little coke – their new kick. 'Hey – bad news Evan hadda trash out that way,' Plum said.

'Yeah, man,' Glory agreed, 'shame he never had an address for us – he mighta laid a little bread on us in his will.'

'You think he hadda will?'

'Yeah – all these rich dudes got wills.'

'Shit! You're probably right. What a bummer. I guess we really lost out.'

In a recording studio in Memphis, Rosa and Sutch of 'The Promises' were cutting an album track.

'Mothafucker deserved to go that way,' Rosa spat, 'I hope he suffered!'

'Aw,' Sutch protested, 'don't be so hard – he had his good points.'

'Yeah – in bed. Superfuck. *Superprick* more like. Screw the motha. I'm *glad* he's dead.'

In Rio Jorge Maraco wept at his beloved wife's funeral and prepared to start his life afresh.

The past was finished.

You couldn't bring back the dead.

Headlines the world over stopped mentioning Al King.

He had been declared officially dead.

Dead people only made good headlines for one day.

His record slipped rapidly out of the number one slot.

Within days he was forgotten.

A decade later – if he was lucky – his records might be resurrected by a whole new generation. Buddy Holly. Otis Redding. Maybe Al King. Only maybe.

72

Saturday morning Dallas woke first. The pain woke her, niggly little nips of pain on her tender skin. For a moment she lay quite still, trying to get her bearings. Then she remembered – and it wasn't the nightmare she had hoped – it was real – horribly sickeningly real. Eight days of misery.

She leaped up in a hurry, and attempted to brush the giant ants from her body. They were crawling all over her – they had even managed to infiltrate under her clothes. She screamed in anger – waking the others. The ants were all over Al and Evan also. Soon everyone was standing and brushing off their clothes. Al stripped his off and doused his body in the stream. Dallas followed.

The sun was just beginning to rise, it was very early and still chilly.

Al shivered in the stream, and looked around at his travelling companions. What a motley group. Cristina with her poor bruised and cut face, her body covered in his clothes which were already tattered and torn.

Blood-soaked Bernie – the weight dropping off him at an alarming rate.

Paul – wild-eyed and feverish.

Evan – his skin red and peeling from the incessant sun of the previous day.

And Dallas – his lady – his woman. Nothing seemed to daunt her. She had screwed her luxuriant hair into a ball on top of her head. Her normally olive skin had turned a deep mahogany colour, and without any sign of artifice she still looked magnificent.

'Let's get moving,' Al said, getting out of the stream and drying off.

'What about something to eat?' Bernie demanded, his voice hoarse.

'We'll travel up stream a bit while it's still cool – then we'll take a break – eat something – and set off again.'

'What about him?' Bernie indicated Paul, who had slumped down on the ground.

Dallas knelt and felt his head. 'I think he's got the fever again,' she said earnestly.

Bernie sat down heavily. 'Aw – what the fuck ... We're never gonna get out of this pisshole. Who the fuck we kidding? We shoulda stayed with the plane ... We shoulda ...'

'Shut up,' said Al, his voice ominously cold. 'Stop bitching and get on your feet. Our only chance is to keep going – and that's just what we're going to do – even if I have to carry Paul.'

'You're not the friggin' superstar boss out here,' Bernie shouted in a burst of fury. 'I don't have to jump for you here. I can tell you to get fucked. I can tell you what I want!' He laughed hysterically. 'We're all gonna die anyway – even *you*.'

'If that's what you think, Bernie, fuck off back to the plane. I'*m* getting out of this *alive* – and I don't want anyone trailing along who doesn't have faith. You want to go – then do it. We'll give you your share of what's left of the food.'

'Aw ... shit ... I didn't mean nothin' ... course I'm with you ...'

Evan stood silently watching his father and Bernie argue. He couldn't understand how the fat man could be so stupid. Al would get them all out of it. He had *said* so. Evan had complete confidence that he would do as he said.

'I feel dizzy,' Cristina whispered, 'these ... *things* in my arms ... Oh, Evan, they're driving me mad!'

Evan patted her on the shoulder reassuringly, 'Dallas will look at them, she'll put some cream on them.'

Cristina held out her arms. The larvae from the eggs the vicious blow flies had planted were emerging like tiny wriggling worms.

Evan felt his stomach turn over with horror. Her arms were alive with the obscene larvae, digging little holes. 'Dallas,' he croaked, forcing himself not to turn away, 'can you do something about Cristina's arms?'

Dallas was immediately sympathetic, getting out the tweezers, and the cream, prising the larvae out of the girl's arms, and then bandaging them with strips of material.

Al waited impatiently – knowing that every minute lost would mean the sun getting higher in the sky – and the inhuman heat forcing its way through the tree tops.

At last they were ready to set off. Paul was hauled reluctantly to his feet, mumbling incoherently – the fever was getting a grip again. Al supported him on one side, Evan on the other. Cristina and Bernie followed with Dallas at the rear.

Slowly they began the day's journey.

The stream meandered tortuously on, twisting and turning to such an extent that an hour's walking sometimes covered only a few yards.

The mosquitoes and flies followed them – perpetual tormentors – buzzing and stinging every step of the way.

A band of monkeys joined the parade for a while, chattering amongst themselves with avid interest.

Time passed in a confused haze as they staggered and stumbled on. The humidity was so bad that it became difficult to breathe. But gradually the stream began to widen, hardly noticeable at first, but soon developing into more of a river.

Exhausted as he was, Al felt exhilaration. What was it Dallas had said? If we find a river and follow it, eventually we'll find people. He kept that thought firmly in his head as he half-dragged Paul along with him. Evan had dropped back to help Cristina.

They were all getting weaker and weaker. If they didn't get something solid to eat soon there would be no more walking – no one would have the strength. Al thought about the monkeys that had been following them earlier. Roasted monkey sounded like a treat indeed. He had the gun . . . Next time he saw them . . . and then there were many birds, frogs, probably fish now the stream was bigger. When they stopped for the day he would do some hunting.

Paul groaned and nearly fell. Al hoisted him up, 'Come on, me old son, we're going to make it . . .' he said reassuringly – but Paul wasn't listening, he eyes were glazed and staring.

Al glanced back, in a straggly line behind him the others fought to keep up. Another hour, if he could just force everyone to keep going for another hour . . .

The sun burned down. The dense undergrowth along the river bank was changing. Hard roots rose up in ridges along the ground, deep beds of decaying leaves, strange palms and tree ferns. The gigantic buttress trees were becoming less dense, allowing the sun to burn down even more intensely. Al – like Dallas – had a naturally dark skin that tanned easily – but he knew that Evan would be in bad shape from so much sun. He had suffered from sunburn all his life – he took after Edna, who always turned a lobster pink.

Edna. The name stuck in Al's mind. How was she taking it? She must be beside herself. Poor cow. He felt sorry for her. How she must be suffering. The newspapers were probably driving her nuts. The publicity alone must be forcing her into a decline. He wondered if she thought he was dead. He wondered what the world thought. Had they already written him off as dead, or were they still looking and searching? It seemed funny that in eight days he had only heard one plane fly over. But of course, they probably had no idea where to look. He shoved an overhanging bough out of the way and shouted back to the others to watch out for it.

'Can we stop?' gasped Bernie, sweat coursing down his red face.

'Let's give it another half hour,' Al shouted back encouragingly.

Bernie merely groaned in reply. Each step forward was a nightmare. He wasn't sure if he *could* proceed any further. His heart was beating so fast, his mouth was so dry. He was starting to think in terms of death being better than this. To just lie down and die . . . It would be painless . . . just like going to sleep . . .

Al knew he *couldn't* keep going much longer. The extra weight of supporting Paul was draining all his strength.

Paul. There had been no chance to talk to him since his outburst. The hate that had suddenly come pouring forth from his younger brother had shocked Al completely. He had never realized the frustration bottled up inside Paul. He had always thought of him as so together and organized. In a way he had *envied* him. And God knows he had always depended on him. He would be the first to admit that without Paul to push and promote he would never have got anywhere. He *would* have been content to piss and screw his life away.

But surely Paul had known how he depended on him? Oh yes, they had their fights, but he had always listened to him in the long run. He had never argued with his final decision on anything career-wise.

Melanie was the bitch that had forged a barrier of hate. A hate that Al had never once suspected . . .

When they got out of this Al had made up his mind that one way or another he would make it up to his brother. He would show him a love and respect and thanks that Paul obviously did not know existed.

It was funny, really. He had always looked to Paul for everything, and now here he was making his own decisions. Dragging them all through the jungle in the hope of being rescued. Maybe they should have stayed with the plane. Yeah – stayed and starved. Which reminded him, he was going hunting. The next clearing they came to he would call a stop.

☆

Cristina forced her legs to move. On and on, ignoring the cuts and blisters, and the horrible little eggs which were hatching out and eating her skin. *She was being eaten alive. Her arms were being eaten.*

She choked back a sob, and Evan tightened his grip on her. 'Can you keep going?' he questioned.

She nodded mutely. She had done enough harm, she wasn't going to hold anyone up. She would keep going until she dropped.

She thought of her mother. The beautiful blonde Evita. The

woman she had been so disdainful of – the woman she had sometimes hated.

'Don't question me, mama,' she would scream. And when her mother asked, pleasantly, 'Where are you going today, dear?' she would reply with an unfriendly sneer: 'Out.' She had thought her parents so stupid. Rich bourgois idiots. Nino had taught her that. But now she realized they had only been concerned for her welfare – they had loved her – they were worried about her. Or at least Evita had been. It was easy to fool Jorge – a little kiss on the cheek, a plaintive 'Don't you trust me, poppa?' and he was putty in her hands.

If only she had been honest with them. Told them about Nino at the beginning . . .

She thought with shame of the things she had done, and the tears rolled down her bruised cut face. If only she could wish time back, how different things would be. If only she could wish Louis back . . .

It was impossible.

☆

Dallas heard the planes first, and she called out to Al to stop so that they could listen. They all gazed skywards, and suddenly there they were, two tiny specks far up in the sky.

Silently everyone watched them. There was no point in waving or screaming. Besides, who had the strength?

Like two far-off birds the planes vanished out of sight.

'We may as well rest here,' Al said. He didn't have to say it twice, they all flopped down immediately. 'Watch out for ants,' he warned. 'Dallas, you want to take a look at Paul?'

She came over immediately, putting her hand on Paul's fevered brow, feeling for his pulse. He was shivering in spite of the excessive heat, his body shaking, his teeth almost chattering.

'I thought he'd got over the fever,' Al said. 'He seemed much better yesterday.'

'I think it's more serious,' Dallas replied quietly, 'I think it's something like malaria.'

'Are you kidding?'

'Be quiet, don't let the others hear.'

'Malaria. But that's . . .' he trailed off hopelessly. 'How can we treat it?'

'We can't. I don't know much about it – but special medicine is necessary. Quinine, I think.'

'Jesus!' Al buried his face in his hands.

'I might be wrong,' Dallas said quickly, 'it's just that malaria apparently attacks in spells. In between the victim is weakened – but all right.'

'You mean he'll be OK?'

'No, I don't mean that. It depends what type of jungle fever he's got. I remember my father – he'd had malaria in the tropics at some time – anyway he still used to get occasional attacks – an ague fit, he called it. But he had medicine.'

'How the fuck did Paul get it?'

'Certain mosquitoes carry the germ – it's not difficult to pick up in this kind of climate.'

'Shit! This is all we need, isn't it?'

Dallas felt Paul's forehead again. 'If it is malaria the attack will probably be over by tomorrow – we'll be able to go on – if we can find help . . .'

'If . . . if . . . if we could have found help Cathy could have been saved. Even Nino. What makes you think we're going to find help for Paul?'

She sighed wearily. 'What can I tell you, Al? There's nothing we can do except keep going.'

'I know.'

They lay down in the heat, trying to find a shady patch. Al let his body relax. Dallas shared out the last of the nuts and cube sugar. Now all they had left were three jars of caviar. Fortunately the river water seemed drinkable, so liquid sustenance was no problem.

Paul couldn't eat anything – but Dallas was able to feed him some sips of water. His shivering had stopped and the skin on his body was now burning up with a dry heat. He was delirious and incoherent.

☆

Al didn't know how long he had been resting. Like the others he lay in a sort of stupor – his eyes closed – his mind drifting uneasily.

He was beginning to feel so weak . . . a feeling of physical impotence so strong that to lift his arm was a major effort.

He knew they should be moving on, to stop while it was still light was stupid. Time was all important. Move in the daylight. Rest at night.

He opened his eyes and saw the monkeys – about eight of them. They were unconcernedly swinging and playing on some nearby trees.

Stealthily he reached for the gun and got up.

The monkeys moved on, and Al followed them.

They were moving away from the trees on the river bank and further into the thick foliage.

Christ! How long was it since he had fired a gun? Ten years? Twenty?

He flashed onto a memory of himself at seventeen. Battersea Park funfair, a girl on his arm, and a rifle in his hands. He had been shooting at a fixed target – a series of tin pigeons revolving in a circle. He had scored six out of six – won a mouldy pink teddy bear – and scored with the girl behind the bushes in the car park.

He could remember the scene vividly.

He raised the small gun and fired at the nearest monkey. It fell from the branch with an almost human cry, and the rest of the monkeys made off at full speed.

He hadn't killed it, merely wounded, and the small, almost childlike animal gazed up at him with bright inquisitive eyes.

He hated himself for doing it, but he finished it off with a blow to the head, and carried the still warm body back to the others.

Dallas was awake, so was Evan. They looked at him curiously.

'Did you kill it?' Evan asked.

'No,' snapped Al, 'it fell off a tree complete with bullet hole!'

'How can we eat it?' Evan continued. 'It's all covered in fur.'

'You're going to skin it,' Al said. 'You took biology at school didn't you?'

'Yes . . . But we never skinned monkeys.'

'So now's you chance to learn.'

Evan made a face, but he took out the penknife Al had given him, and squeamishly started the job.

Before nightfall they had feasted on monkey roasted over a fire Al lit with one of their precious matches. It wasn't bad at all – tasted somewhat like rabbit.

Paul still could not eat – but for the others, having a full belly was a luxury indeed.

Al looked around with a sort of pride. He had found them food. His son had prepared it – and they had eaten. It was a good feeling to know that his efforts were helping them to survive.

He slept well and woke very early to see more planes flying overhead. Three of them, in convoy, very fast and very high.

He didn't wake the others – why excite them for nothing? The planes couldn't possibly see them. But maybe at last they were searching. Maybe now search parties might come looking for them on foot.

He wondered for the thousandth time how far they were from any type of human life. Dallas had mentioned that Indian tribes were supposed to live in the Amazon – and surely there were hunters and traders.

He felt better than he had in days. It was Sunday now. They had been in the jungle for nine days. It seemed like a lifetime – six days waiting for help in the goddamn plane – and three days travelling.

A parrot had settled itself on a tree and was watching him with beady black eyes. He wondered how parrot meat would taste . . .

In the distance a huge snake slithered along. He had learned to ignore them as long as they never came too close. The danger was in stepping on one by mistake.

The interminable flies and mosquitoes had ceased to bother him. They had become a part of everyday life. Cristina was the only one that seemed to suffer from their bites. Her arms were in a dreadful state.

Paul opened his eyes and mumbled, 'What happened? Where are we? I don't remember a thing.' He was emaciated, his eyes sunken into his gaunt face, his arms almost too weak to hold the cup of water Al offered him. But as Dallas had predicted, the fever had left him.

Al explained that he had been sick, but that they were nearing help.

'How'd I get here?' Paul asked.

'He carried you,' Evan said proudly, joining in the conversation, and indicating his father.

Paul looked at Al.

'I didn't *carry* him,' Al objected, embarrassed, 'I just helped him along a little.'

'My brother – the hero,' Paul said mockingly, his voice hardly more than a whisper. But he smiled when he said it, and reached and squeezed Al by the arm. 'Thanks, brother.'

Al looked away. 'I reckon I owed you a favour.'

Dallas was moving around getting everyone ready to set off on the day's journey. Her medicinal supplies were running low. The last of the antiseptic cream was shared between Cristina's arms and Evan's badly burned face.

Foot blisters and sores – which everyone was suffering with – were tied around with strips of material.

Bernie was the last to wake. He shoved Dallas away when she asked to inspect his wound. 'I feel fine,' he snapped. But he didn't look fine. He looked extremely flushed, and his eyes were runny and bloodshot. Dallas hoped that he wasn't coming down with the fever – Bernie there would be no chance of carrying.

They set off, struggling along the tortuous path – fighting their way through the tangled undergrowth until it was almost impassable. Finally Al suggested that they wade along the shallow edge of the river. It was cooler, and the mild current would help their progress.

They had been doing this for about an hour when Al spotted the alligators – huge mud-covered creatures sliding off the opposite river bank and moving lazily through the water towards them.

'Get out of the water!' Al screamed. 'Alligators – get out! For crissakes MOVE!'

The river bank was slime-covered and slippery – it had become much steeper than when they had first entered the water.

Al hauled himself out, grabbing hold of Paul and pulling him to safety.

At the same time Evan helped Cristina out, and followed quickly.

Dallas was also able to move fast, but Bernie – his fat body half encased in the water, seemed paralysed with fear.

'Come on, man!' screamed Al – struggling back along the muddy bank to help.

Dallas leaned over and grabbed Bernie by the arm, trying to pull him. 'Move, Bernie, MOVE!' she yelled, watching in horror as the alligators glided nearer and nearer.

Bernie, stung into sudden action, attempted to climb out. But the mud was so slippery that he fell back – nearly pulling Dallas in with him. The force of his efforts caused his chest wound to open up, and suddenly his shirt was soaked with blood as he tried to stagger to his feet and get out of the water.

By this time Al was at the side to help – grabbing Bernie's arm pulling ... pulling ... but the smell of blood had attracted the alligators to move faster, and as Al pulled at one end, the first of the huge reptiles attacked at the other, its massive jaws opening and clamping its ferocious teeth down on Bernie's leg.

He screamed in agony as the alligator tried to drag him deeper into the water. Al wasn't strong enough to hold on – and Bernie's arm was snatched out of his grasp.

They all watched in mute horror as the fat man was pulled struggling and screaming into the centre of the river.

'Isn't there anything we can *do*?' Dallas pleaded. 'God! We must do *something*!'

It was too late anyway. The other alligators had moved silently in on their victim – joining in the attack.

Bernie had disappeared under the water. He never surfaced again.

They waited at the same spot for hours, huddled together. Eventually the alligators slid lazily off, climbing and slithering on to the other side of the river bank and basking in the sun's rays.

No sign of Bernie. It was as if he had never even existed.

'There's no point in staying here any longer,' Al said at last – loath to point out the very obvious fact that there was only a small river separating them from the alligators. If they decided to cross over ...

Cristina was crying. Evan put his arm around her, and she

gazed up at him with very tired eyes. 'I want to be home,' she stated simply.

'We will be,' Evan reassured, 'don't worry.'

☆

The rest of the day passed by in a haze. Blindly they followed Al, struggling along the densely overgrown river bank, too frightened to get back into the water. Driven mad by the mosquitoes and the intense burning sun. Fearful of stepping on snakes. Scratched and bruised by overhanging boughs, and sometimes being forced to wade into the water for a few yards to get round rotting tree trunks which occasionally blocked their way.

Al, in the lead, was more watchful than ever. He could only blame himself for what had happened earlier. It was he who had suggested they enter the water. If they had been on land the alligators would not have attacked.

Every bone in his body ached, and he knew that he should start to look for a suitable place to settle for the night. But when they stopped, while the others rested, he would have to look for food. All they had left was the caviar.

His head ached and his vision was blurring. Every so often he glanced behind. Paul was managing fairly well – dogging his footsteps in a dazed fashion. And behind him, Evan, half supporting Cristina, whispering encouragement to keep her going. And bringing up the rear, Dallas.

It was a horrible thought, but without Bernie they seemed to be moving faster. Had he been slowing them down? Or were they just escaping from the memory of his horrible death?

Eventually they stopped. Al was too exhausted to search for food – so silently they shared a jar of caviar and fell asleep.

In the middle of the night the rains came. Pelting great hailstones stinging them awake.

They couldn't travel, and they couldn't sleep. Huddled together they just had to accept the full brunt of the rain. It didn't stop. It was still falling heavily at the first sign of light, and they set off as soon as they could see, their path made even more hazardous by thick squelching mud.

By midday the rain turned into a storm. Ominous black clouds filling the sky, belching loud rumbles and luminous streaks of lightning.

For the very first time Dallas considered death as an alternative. Where were they going to? What were they struggling for? Perhaps Bernie was the lucky one . . .

To just lie down and sleep. Close your eyes and succumb to the temptation of never getting up again.

She thought she might suggest it to Al. If she could die in his arms . . .

She had lost all idea of time. Her clothes were soaked through, torn and tattered. Her shoes could not last much longer – soon she would have to walk barefoot. She was dizzy and nauseous.

When the rain stopped, they did also, and finished off the two remaining jars of caviar because they were quite literally starving.

Paul had the fever again. Cristina was screaming with the pain in her arms. Evan meticulously dug out the festering maggots and tried to calm her down.

Dallas moved over and lay next to Al.

He was staring up at the sky mouthing some kind of personal appeal.

She rolled close to him. 'We're going to die, aren't we?' Her voice rose hysterically. 'You can tell me, Al. I don't mind, honestly, I don't. *We're going to die* . . .'

He hit her across the face with a strength he no longer knew he possessed. 'The *hell* we are. We're going to *make it.* You understand me? *We're going to make it.*'

She understood why he had hit her, and she was glad he had. To lose control now after all they had gone through. She sobbed and he held her very close. 'I love you, babe,' he said over and over, 'and we're going to make it – you hear me – we're going to make it.'

She believed him, and once more she was calm. Held firmly in his arms she fell asleep.

☆

Tuesday. Eleven days in the jungle. Cristina whimpering quietly to herself. Stomach racked with cramps. Soon they would lose all track of time, and each day would merge into the next – fused together by the rain and the mud – the insects and blistering heat.

Dallas sat up. Insects were crawling over her – she could hardly be bothered to brush them off.

'Where is Al?' she asked Evan.

'He left early, said he was going to find something to eat. I wanted to go with him, but he said I should stay with you.'

Evan was bearing up considerably well – in fact as far as Cristina was concerned he was a tower of strength. It was funny, really – he was hardly recognizable as the surly, bad-tempered boy of days ago.

Paul was still racked with fever, mumbling to himself – his normally good-looking features changed almost beyond recognition. His face was gaunt and flushed. His eyes sunken and surrounded by deep black circles. His arms twitched uncontrollably.

Dallas missed Bernie. He had complained a lot, but he had also managed to greet each day with a wisecrack. She tried not to think about him – it was too painful.

Her clothes were stiff with dried mud, and disgustingly itchy. She removed her shoes and socks, and regarded her swollen blistered feet. It didn't seem likely that they could carry her much longer. Painstakingly she tried to bandage them with strips of material torn from her shirt sleeves. The effort involved exhausted her, and she lay back – too tired to even examine Cristina's arms. What good could she do anyway? Subject the girl to the agony of digging more maggots out when the arms were already raw and infected?

She closed her eyes and drifted back into a sort of sleep. The thought of continuing the journey today was impossible – both Paul and Cristina were in no fit state to move anyway.

It wasn't fair. It just wasn't fair. Whatever Al might say they were all going to die out here. Die . . . Death . . .

She didn't really care any more. It would be a relief really . . . A blessing . . .

☆

Al had been moving stealthily through the jungle for more than an hour. He had started off following some birds – but then he had seen the herd of wild hogs – about six or seven of them – and he had thought – Christ! If I can shoot one of those it will keep us going for days!

So he had trailed the snorting, grunting creatures, awaiting his opportunity.

They looked somewhat like ordinary pigs, only they were bigger – with a higher back and coarse long bristles. And an incredibly strong smell issued forth from them.

Al wrinkled his nose in disgust – but somehow the hunting of food raised his spirits, and he felt fitter than he had for days. He suddenly understood what survival was all about. Pitting your strength against the elements and coming out on top. Adrenalin pumped through his body at an alarming rate. Now he could understand why men climbed mountains and sailed across oceans in little boats. The excitement of conquering nature. At thirty-eight years of age he was discovering there was more to life than climbing up on a stage and singing your guts out.

Slowly he raised the gun and pointed it at the nearest and smallest hog which had paused to sniff at something.

The bullet hit it right between the eyes. A clean shot which threw the animal to the ground in a writhing fury. It thrashed around for a few minutes, and finally rolled onto its back and died.

Al leaped forward. The stinking animal was going to be too heavy for him to carry.

But he was determined. People were depending on him. His son. The woman he loved. His brother.

He took off his belt which was made of leather, and slotted it around the animal's neck tightly. He was then able to drag the hog behind him, and make his way slowly back to the others. It took quite a while, but he made it, and in no time at all Evan was dismembering the animal, and Dallas was getting a fire together.

They roasted several portions, and picked at the hot greasy flesh ravenously. It wasn't the most tempting of meals – what with the smell and the unbearable heat and the flies. But it *was* food. They cooked more than they could eat and wrapped it in one of the blankets to take with them.

Strengthened, they set off once more on their journey. Supporting Paul between them – Dallas and Al led the way.

'We won't go far today,' Al said – he estimated it was already well past noon, 'but however little – it's something.'

The river was becoming wider and wider, and they were getting quite used to the sight of the crocodiles resting on small islands in the middle. Nobody was about to forget what had happened to Bernie – so they were extra careful. At one point they came across three or four baby alligators slouched on top of each other blocking their path. Quickly they detoured further into the forest unwilling to risk upsetting the mother.

It was hard work propelling Paul along – but Al encouraged Dallas to keep going. She did so – moving one leg stiffly in front of the other. Tripping, being ripped and scratched by the overhanging boughs, allowing the filthy flies and mosquitoes to settle on the parts of her body that were exposed and lay their disgusting eggs. She was just too exhausted to brush them away.

She only kept going because of Al.

She couldn't let him down – he was so sure they would find help – so certain of being rescued. Soon he too would realize it was hopeless. Soon he would allow her to lie down and not get up again. Soon . . . Soon . . . Soon . . .

'Sonofabitch!' Al exclaimed sharply, 'what the hell's *that*?

Dallas looked ahead. She could see nothing but the river and jungle.

Al let go of Paul, his full weight came down onto Dallas, and the two of them fell to the ground.

'Wait there!' said Al excitedly.

Dallas closed her eyes. She couldn't get up again.

Evan and Cristina also sank to the ground, glad of the respite.

Al rushed ahead, spurred on by what he had thought he had seen around the next twist of the river.

He had not been mistaken. About fifteen yards from the bank of the river stood a hut. A primitive structure as he could see – but it was man-made.

He wanted to shout and scream. Yell out greetings. They had made it!

He hurried to the hut. It was empty. In fact it was hardly a hut – more a thatched roof supported on four posts, with a crude dried mud floor. There were no walls, and no sign of recent habitation. A vine was secured across part of the roof from which hung a large dead snake. Several spiders had spun their intricate webs and made their home there. A lizard stood stock still in one corner. A parade of ants marched to and fro up one of the posts.

Al squatted down on the floor, disappointment flooding through him. He had thought ... Aw – to hell with what he had thought ... At least it was a roof for the night, and at least it proved they were probably near some kind of human habitation. It proved above all that they weren't alone out here. That sometime – someone had built this shed.

He pulled the dead snake off the vine and slung it out into the jungle. It was completely dried up, must have been hanging there for quite a while. The lizard made a wild dash for safety before Al had even considered it as a possible source of food. Roast monkey – hog – why not lizard? Too bad he hadn't thought of it before.

Well, at least they would sleep with a roof over their heads tonight.

He went back for the others, and slowly they staggered to the refuge he had found for them.

'It ain't the Beverly Hills,' he quipped, 'but it beats the shit out of sleeping on the ground!'

It was sheer luxury. Ravenously they finished off the pieces of hog, and even Paul was able to chew some. Once more the fever was receding, leaving him weakened but intelligible.

They discussed the significance of finding the hut. It was a definite plus. It did mean that people had been here – in which case they must now be within travelling distance of human life.

By nightfall they settled down to sleep in comparative comfort. They even felt it safe to remove their shoes and socks and free their imprisoned feet.

In the middle of the night Cristina woke them all with some unearthly screams 'My foot – my foot!' she screamed, and a black shape fluttered away to escape her writhings. Al inspected her foot. It was spotted with blood and marked.

'Probably a vampire bat,' Dallas said dully. 'They suck out the blood ... I don't think it's poisonous.'

They tried to calm the frightened girl, while Dallas soaked a rag in water, and wrapped it around her foot.

'Maybe we should all put our shoes back on,' she suggested, 'but shake them out first . . .'

Al couldn't sleep after that. His mind was racing. If he left them at the hut and travelled on alone he could make much better time. They had plenty of water. In the morning he could find some more food to leave with them. And the gun for their protection. Yes – it was the only way. He was the strongest . . . He could move fast . . . and speed was of the essence. If Paul didn't get medicine soon . . . and Cristina was in a bad way . . . even Dallas was in a weakened state. Only Evan seemed strong enough to continue.

Al swelled with pride at the thought of his son. What a man he had turned out to be. The King blood flowed strong in his veins. And to think how disappointed he had once been in him.

By morning Al was prepared to go hunting. Quietly he woke Evan, and told him where he was going. Evan wanted to accompany him – but Al suggested it was best he stay with the others.

He set off into the jungle, feeling quite at home, and confident of a kill. He soon came across some monkeys and approached them stealthily. He raised his gun ready to fire, and the thought occurred to him that what was he going to do when he ran out of bullets? It wouldn't be quite such an easy job then. He fired, reckoning he would face that problem when he came to it. One of the monkeys fell – this time it was a clean shot, and the animal was dead. He picked it up by the legs, and carried it back to the hut.

It was ridiculous – perverse really – but he was almost enjoying himself. The challenge of getting them all out of this mess . . . and he was doing it. Single-handed. He was providing shelter and food – and soon – he was *sure* of it – he would find them medical help.

It was a great source of achievement that he had been able to accomplish this. He – who in the past had been so spoiled that all he had to do was pick up a telephone and request anything he wanted – and get it. He could not honestly remember a time when he had had to do something for himself. Now four other people's lives depended on him – and if it was humanly possible he would save them.

He told Dallas of his plan to travel on alone.

She nodded, her beautiful eyes filled with defeat.

He squeezed her hand, and was suddenly overcome with a very tender love for her. 'If I don't find anything in the next two days – I'll come back. The monkey should last that long – and you've got plenty of water. You'll be fine – won't you?'

She managed a weak smile. 'If you say so.'

'I'll leave you the gun . . .'

'I love you,' she interrupted softly. 'Whatever happens, I love you.'

'We'll make up for lost time when we get out of here. Screw work – you and I, lady, are just going to laze around making love and having good times for at least a year. You like that plan?'

'I like it . . .'

He bent down and kissed her. A long insistent kiss. And he felt the beginnings of a hard-on, and he laughed – because – shit – if he could still feel horny after all they had gone through – well, jeeze – that meant he wasn't ready to give up yet. He was a survivor. They *all* would be.

He went over to Paul and said, 'Hang on in there, brother, I'll be back before you know it. We'll bung you full of medicine – you'll be in great shape – you'd better be – there's a lot of contract-breaking I want you to do for me. You know I'm lost without you.'

Paul grabbed him by the arm, his voice hardly more than a whisper, 'I want you to forget what I said the other day – I didn't mean it. Can you forget I said anything?'

'I don't remember a thing.'

Paul nodded, the muscles in his face twitching, his eyes more sunken than ever. 'If I die,' he said slowly, 'I want you to look after my children. I want . . .'

'Don't talk such crap. You'll be good as new once they stuff some medicine down you.'

'Sure,' agreed Paul weakly, 'I know that. But if I die . . . the children . . . promise me they'll live with you . . . I don't want Melanie to have them . . . she doesn't care . . . promise me, Al.'

'I promise – I promise. Big deal. You ain't goin' nowhere.'

'And Linda . . . take care of Linda . . .'

'Jesus!' Al threw his eyes upwards in mock despair, 'dictate me your will while you're at it!'

Paul hung on to his brother's arm even tighter. 'Take it easy,' he whispered.

Al nodded, frightened of the strong emotions he felt. 'I plan to, kid, I plan to.'

Cristina was sleeping, Evan by her side, swiping the flies away from her immobile body.

'*You* look after everybody,' Al said sternly, 'you hear me?'

'Yes, dad. You can depend on me.'

Al stared at his son, hardly recognizing him. The boy seemed to have thrived on the deprivations of the past twelve days. He no longer seemed scrawny – more thin and wiry – and now that his sunburn was clearing up and turning into a deep suntan, miraculously his acne appeared to have vanished.

Emotively Al hugged him. Then he was on his way – moving quickly along the sinuous river bank, making good time. He had to. They were all depending on him.

☆

The day passed in a haze for those at the hut. They lay in a somnolent state, sweating through the day, and shivering at night.

Evan skinned and roasted some of the monkey. It didn't really matter what it tasted like, it was edible, and it filled their empty stomachs.

Paul was drifting in and out of a fevered state. He didn't want to eat. He didn't want to move. He was beginning to waste away.

Cristina, too, was in a bad way. She whimpered quietly to herself, moaning constantly about the pain in her arms.

Dallas felt incredibly weak and nauseous. She managed to eat the monkey, but after, she suffered very bad abdominal pains, and was forced to leave the hut and retch it all up.

Evan watched over everyone, clutching onto the gun, unable to help any of them, but ready to face any emergency.

Night brought relief from the heat, but it also brought frightening rustling noises and animal cries.

Evan wondered about his father, out there somewhere in the murky blackness alone. He had taken no food – no gun. How could he expect to survive and come back with help? What was going to happen to them all?

Evan tried, he tried his hardest. But all through the night tears rolled down his cheeks.

His father had left them alone. *They were all alone.* And one by one they would die.

☆

Al was amazed at the speed with which he could travel now that he didn't have to consider four other people. He stuck to the river bank for a while, but then it occurred to him that it would make his going much easier if he swam. The wide river seemed to have a strong current which would carry him along nicely. Also being in the water would protect him from the fearsome heat. Of course there were dangers. The alligators would have to be watched out for at all times. But he figured if he stayed close to the bank and was careful ... He slid into the delightfully cool water and allowed it to carry him along. It was a much easier way to travel. The current was strong and it was no effort for him to allow himself to be swept along. In fact it was rather pleasant. The first time he saw some alligators ahead he got out quickly. But they were merely lolling on an island and took no notice of him. The second time he risked staying in – they were on the opposite bank and didn't even notice him floating past. After that he stayed in the water unless they loomed ahead dangerously close.

By dusk he was starving hungry. He hadn't eaten all day, and there seemed no likelihood of any food. He looked longingly at a tree heavy with berries, but he remembered Dallas' warning about things being poisonous. It was stupid of him not to have provided himself with food, or at least the means to get some. He was no superman. He would not be able to keep going on water alone. He just hadn't thought. So sure was he of the fact that he was going to come upon human life.

He found a tree to curl up under for the night, and slept fitfully. By dawn every bone in his body was aching, and muscles were hurting that he never knew existed.

He stood and stretched, tried to limber up. It didn't help, but he set off anyway, sticking to the bank of the river until the sun became warm, and then slipping back into the current to be carried along.

His thoughts were of food. Roast chicken. Sizzling bacon and eggs. Succulent veal. Steak and kidney pud.

He shut his eyes for a moment, imagining himself sitting down for a large slap-up meal. He would drink beer ... Or perhaps champagne ... yes – certainly champagne – for it would be a celebration meal ... He grinned at the very moment his body slammed into a large tree trunk fallen across the river. He clung to it for support, his head whirling – lights flashing before his eyes. He had been knocked almost senseless.

With great effort he dragged himself from the river and crawled along the bank – collapsing in the mud.

He could feel his forehead beginning to swell where it had taken the force of the collision.

What next?

He lay very still, partially stunned. And after a while, as if in a dream, he heard voices – strange foreign sounds – and then it was all too much and he passed out.

☆

Inevitably morning dawned. The insect and animal sounds filtered through to Dallas. And the smell of four people stuck together unable to wash or clean themselves. It was a sickening smell, but one you soon got used to. If she had the strength she would go to the river and bathe – to hell with the alligators – but she felt unable to move. Her stomach was still cramping, but she had nothing left to throw up. She felt so very weak, and there was this strange euphoric feeling. A lightness of the head, an immovability of the limbs. She tried to sit up, and fell back. If a snake had entered the hut at this point and headed towards her she would have had neither the strength nor the initiative to move out of its way.

Evan offered her water. 'Shall I make a fire and cook the rest of the monkey?' he suggested.

She sipped at the water. 'No food,' she mumbled, 'don't feel good.'

He placed a hand firmly on her head, and was alarmed to

find her burning up. With dismay he realised that she too had some sort of fever. He did not know what to do. Cristina was flushed and delirious. Paul was dehydrated and possibly unconscious and he had been unable to rouse him. And now Dallas.

A black terror swept over Evan. He had promised his father to look after them all. But how could he look after them if they were going to die on him one by one?

It was an impossible situation. And one that he was powerless to do anything about.

☆

There was a moving sensation – not unpleasant. And still the strange mutterings – only clearer now – more excited.

Al opened his eyes to find himself being carried on some crude sort of stretcher – and for a moment he imagined he was being carried from the plane, and the thirteen days spent in the jungle had never happened.

His head was pounding, and he raised his hand to it, and felt something warm and sticky. He lowered his hand to find it covered with blood. He must have groaned aloud, because the stretcher was suddenly put down on the ground, and three faces were staring down at him. Three young Indian boys – perhaps sixteen years of age. They were of a deep mahogany colour, with wide, rather flattened faces, and jet black straight hair worn long and parted in the centre. They were totally naked apart from a small piece of cloth twisted around their loins. But they compensated for their lack of dress by being liberally decorated with painted symbols and designs.

They stared at Al and chatted amongst themselves in a language he had never heard in his life.

'English,' he said slowly, and then realizing he had been found, and remembering what had gone before, he raised his voice: 'English!' he yelled. 'You speak English?'

The boys jumped back in alarm.

'Christ! Am I glad to see *you*!' He raised himself on one arm.

The boys regarded him suspiciously.

'Plane,' Al said slowly, 'the sky,' he pointed to the sky, 'crashed.'

The boys exchanged glances.

'Other people,' Al enunciated carefully, 'back there.' He gestured behind him, and observed that they were travelling through the interior of the forest.

The boys jabbered excitedly together. They obviously did not understand a word he was saying. Finally one boy stepped forward and made a short speech – pointing and gesticulating ahead. Then he indicated that Al should lie down on the stretcher once more, and mimed a man much taller than himself.

Al understood it to mean that they were taking him to a person who would understand him. He complied with their wishes and lay back.

Effortlessly the boys picked up the stretcher and resumed their journey through the steamy forest. They moved quickly, weaving through the thick undergrowth at a fast pace.

Within minutes they were approaching a large clearing, where once more the boys placed the stretcher on the ground.

Al sat up, and realized that he was an expected guest. Almost an entire village of Indians had emerged from their huts to stare at him. Women, children, men – young and old. They pointed and stared and jabbered away in their incomprehensible tongue.

The women were entirely naked, the males were covered by loincloths. The huts they had emerged from were similar to the one Al had left the others at. Crude dwellings consisting of four supports and a thatched roof.

The boys, seemingly having done their part, stepped back and blended in with the onlookers. A few children ventured nearer for a closer look. Their eyes were as bright as buttons, and even they were covered in intricately painted designs.

Finally the taller man they had indicated appeared. He emerged from a hut, and everyone stood back to let him pass. He was indeed tall, and obviously someone important – for his hair was greased and coaxed into a fine tower – and some kind of stylish comb emerged from the top. Also his chest was covered by an intricately carved shield, and he wore more necklaces, bracelets and adornments than anyone else.

He approached the stretcher, regarded Al solemnly, and addressed him in a deep monotonous voice.

The only trouble was that English did not appear to be the language of the day.

'Hey—,' said Al – his initial relief at being found turning into slight anxiety – 'how about speaking a little *English* around here.'

The Chief – as Al had decided to christen him – replied in his own language, and stared – awaiting a reply to what was obviously a whole load of questions.

Al attempted to stand – realizing he must look as funny a sight to these Indians as they did to him.

He pointed to himself. 'English,' he said clearly, 'Al King.'

He was hoping that his name would cause at least a spark of recognition. After all, he was known throughout the world – his disappearance must have caused a lot of waves – maybe word had filtered through.

Suddenly he wanted to laugh. Who was he kidding? He was stuck in the middle of some dumb jungle and he actually expected a bunch of naked Indians to know who he was! It just showed how conditioned he was to his own fame. He could remember dreaming of going somewhere where no one would recognize him. Now here he was. Big fuckin' deal. Wrong place. Wrong time.

Christ! His head was throbbing, his stomach was one aching mass, and he was worried about getting back to the others. He proceeded to pantomime a series of events. A plane flying, falling from the sky, more people, a journey. He indicated strongly that they had to return down the river.

The Chief seemed to understand him – indeed he even started to mime a reply.

Al took it to mean that soon it would be dark, and they could not travel at nightfall. Early in the morning, the Chief seemed to be indicating. Then he was addressing members of his tribe, and two women came and shyly started to pull Al towards a hut.

He went with them, although there were still many questions he had to try and ask. The Chief had expressed to him that his head wound would be treated, and that then they would eat.

Al wondered how far they were from civilization. Radio contact? An air strip? When the others were rescued how long before they could all be out of here?

The women were peeling the clothes from his body, talking and giggling amongst themselves. They laid him on a rush mat, and other women appeared with an earthen pot filled with some sort of milky liquid. They proceeded to dab his cuts and scratches. It was cool, and had an almost numbing effect. His head wound they treated particularly carefully.

He tried to lie back and relax, but he was so worried about the others, and wished that they could be on their way back for them.

The Indian girls were similar in appearance. Stocky, smooth bodies, with firm jutting breasts. Greased hair. Much ornamentation. They wore beads around their necks and arms, and their lower lips were pierced and had little strings of white beads inserted, The delicacy with which they attended him reminded him of a trip he and Paul had once made to a Japanese whorehouse.

They took his filthy torn clothes away to wash, and offered him a loincloth to put on. He felt stupid in it – but what the heck – it seemed to be the thing to wear.

Dinner with the Chief was the next event. They sat on the ground in a semicircle with other men of the tribe, and the women served them a series of tasty dishes in earthenware pots.

Al did not know what he was eating, and he didn't much care. He wolfed everything down ravenously – from a mushy stuff which tasted like bananas – to a sort of sour dough bread. Not steak and champagne – but it beat the shit out of nothing!

The Chief launched into a friendly discourse about what he seemed to regard as flying birds and the stupidity of men who went up in them. He shook his head in amazement a lot – and Al noticed that the other members of the tribe copied everything he did.

'Telephone,' Al kept on repeating in pidgin English, illustrating the act of making a phone call.

The Chief nodded and smiled, but did not appear to understand.

Then it was dark, and Al was guided to a hut – where for the first time in thirteen days he had a proper place to sleep

– a most comfortable hammock. As he rocked back and forth he thought of Dallas, and the others, and could not wait until morning when he would be on his way to fetch them.

☆

Evan thought he should eat, even if the others didn't want to. He uncovered the remains of the monkey which he had carefully wrapped in a towel – and was horrified to find it crawling with maggots. He threw it out of the hut in disgust. Now there was no food at all, but he did have the gun. He fingered the weapon lovingly. He too would be able to go out in the forest and hunt like his father. He would have to.

The thought excited him. It spurred him to get up and stretch his cramped limbs. The stench in the hut was awful, even though there were no walls. He tried not to look at the others. He was frightened that one of them might be dead.

He had no idea what time it was, but maybe if he was able to kill some fresh meat he could persuade them all to eat. If they ate they would get better.

Thinking that way at least gave him something to aim for. At least he would be doing something constructive instead of just sitting there.

He set off into the jungle, filled with a sudden sense of adventure. He was like his father ⌐ strong. A survivor.

He saw some monkeys, but he decided that something different might whet the appetites of the others, he didn't know what – but it would be silly to just shoot the first animal he came across. That would be the easy way – why take the easy way?

He continued on into the interior of the forest – not at all frightened – and not taking much note of the direction he was travelling in.

The foliage was becoming sparse – the ground clearer. The area appeared to be changing in character. He noticed a huge black and green snake coiled around a tree trunk. It was a real monster, and he stepped well away from it.

Suddenly, with no warning, a large black jaguar appeared no more than fifteen yards ahead of him.

Evan froze to the spot, as did the animal. For moments

they stood and stared at each other. Then simultaneously they moved – Evan reaching for his gun, and the jaguar tensing itself ready to spring.

☆

The Indians woke Al before it was light. They were anxious to be on their way.

He wondered how they were planning to bring back the four others he had told them about. He had made them understand they would be too sick to walk. They did not seem bothered. They kitted him out in a pair of thonged sandals such as they wore, and still clad in his loin cloth he was beginning to feel almost like one of them.

They set off, trotting through the jungle, expecting Al to keep up with them. It was impossible for him, and they made faces and laughed as they had to slow down for him. Eight young men had been sent on the mission, and they talked excitedly together in their native tongue – enjoying the break in their usual routine.

Al had explained, as best he could, about the hut he had left the others at. The Indians seemed to understand him, and the Chief had indicated that it was no more than one day's journey away. It had taken him *two* days to reach them, but he didn't argue. They obviously knew best.

They journeyed to the river, where Al was shown the reason he had been found by them. The tree trunk blocking the river was a trap – set by the Indians. Nobody passed their section of the river without them knowing about it.

They set off in three canoes kept concealed in the undergrowth going against the current, but making good time anyway. The Indians were very proficient in their use of the small wooden paddles used to propel the boats along. They ignored the alligators – navigating around the islands and rocks with great skill.

The sun burned down, but Al noticed how the flies and mosquitoes seemed to have left him alone ever since his body had been bathed in the white lotion. They certainly didn't bother the Indians.

Half-way through the day they stopped and rested for no more than half an hour, chewing on raw fruits they had brought with them.

Then they were off again, the flimsy canoes moving exceedingly fast.

The knew exactly where to stop – pulling the boats up on the bank – and skipping curiously over to the hut.

Al followed. He had been gone three days and two nights – a lifetime in the jungle. But he had left them with food, water, and Evan to protect them. They shouldn't be too bad.

The Indians stood in a silent circle around the hut. Al pushed his way through them. He was horrified at what he saw. Three silent heaps – insects crawling all over them.

He went to Dallas first, feeling urgently for her pulse. She was alive, and so amazingly were Cristina and Paul. But all three of them were very sick.

There was no water left in the two leather flasks they had used to carry their supplies, and they were parched with thirst and dehydrated.

Al shoved the Indians into action – and instead of standing and staring they began to help. Running to fill the flasks with water, beating the insects off the three inert bodies.

'Evan,' Al shouted, 'where is Evan?'

He looked through the hut, there was no gun, and it occurred to him that perhaps his son had gone off hunting. But would he have left them with no water? It didn't seem likely.

Al bent to Dallas. Her face was covered in bites. So much so that her eyes and lips were swollen to a horrible degree. 'Can you hear me?' Al whispered, 'hey – beautiful – can you hear me?'

She mumbled something incoherent. She was in the grip of a raging fever.

Al turned to one of the Indians and by a series of actions tried to explain that someone was missing.

The boy nodded. He appeared to understand. He turned to one of his friends and jabbered away in the native tongue. Then the two of them rushed off into the forest.

There was nothing to do but wait. Nothing to do but feed water to Dallas, Paul and Cristina – and hope that they could stay alive another day.

One of the Indians sat quietly beside Cristina digging the maggots from her raw infected arms. She was too weak to even cry out in pain.

Another one produced the magic white lotion and dabbed it on Dallas' face.

They talked amongst themselves all the time, obviously discussing the accident, and how these people had come plummeting down into the jungle.

They went to the river and caught fish with their bare hands for dinner, which they skinned and prepared over an open fire. It was quite delicious. Al only wished that the others could taste it. He saved a piece in the hope that Evan would shortly emerge from the forest. He didn't.

It was after dark when the two Indians returned. They shook their heads and lowered their eyes. In their hands they carried the gun Al had left with Evan, and the boy's shirt – torn to shreds and covered with blood.

'Where *is* he?' Al screamed, frustrated in his efforts of not being able to understand their language.

The Indians tried to explain. With gestures they drew a picture of a large fierce animal. 'Onca,' they kept on saying, 'onca nigra.'

It meant nothing to Al. Then as they continued to try and explain to him he realized what they were telling him. Evan was dead. Evan had been killed by an 'onca nigra' whatever that was.

He could not believe it. To have gone through so much . . . it couldn't be true . . .

'The body,' he said, 'where is the body?'

They understood him. They glanced at each other and opened their arms to the sky. It was a very final gesture.

Al knew what they meant. Cathy. Bernie. The law of the jungle devoured bodies that were not immediately buried.

For the first time in his life Al cried. He could not claim to have ever been particularly close to his son – but in the past days they seemed to have developed a deep bond of mutual trust and love that had never been apparent before. The future had promised a fine relationship between them. He held his head in his hands and sobbed like a baby.

The Indians looked away in confusion.

And so the night passed.

In the morning they carried Dallas, Cristina, and Paul to the canoes and set off as fast as possible.

The journey took much less time as the river current was

with them, and the boats fairly whipped along at an alarming speed.

Al travelled in the canoe with Dallas, cradling her head on his lap. He couldn't help blaming himself for Evan's death – if he hadn't left them . . . He knew the answer to *that*. If he hadn't left them to fetch help they would all have died.

But it seemed so cruel and unnecessary. If only Evan had stayed where he was he would have been all right. Obviously he had gone to hunt for food . . . He had died trying to keep them all alive.

Returning to the Indian village was almost like returning home. The Chief himself came to the river to greet them and peer at the other white people. He clucked his tongue at their condition, and issued orders. Three of the boys were dispatched off into the jungle, three more sent off on up the river in their canoe.

Then Dallas, Cristina, and Paul were carried to the village, and whisked off by the womenfolk.

There was nothing Al could do except sip strange herb tea with the Chief, and attempt to carry on a conversation by mime.

He was weary. The strain of the past fourteen days was finally taking its toll. How long before they could get out of here? How many more had to die before they saw the light of civilization?

He tried to ask the Chief – who merely nodded and smiled.

It was unreal – the whole thing was some sort of nightmare.

He finished his tea and went to see Dallas. The women had her stripped off and were bathing her bruised, cut, scratched, and bitten body with the white liquid.

People wandered in and out of the hut to stare at her, and Al was suddenly filled with an uncontrollable jealous fury. 'Get the fuck out of here!' he screamed at two Indian males, who merely smiled politely in return, had a good look, and wandered in to stare at Cristina next door.

Goddamn savages! How many days before they could get out of this pisshole? How many fucking days?

☆

It took three. Long enough for Dallas, Cristina, and Paul to be well enough to travel.

The medicines the Indians employed were amazing. They calmed the fever in both Dallas and Paul, and treated Cristina's arms with some sort of raw plant wrapped around them.

The three of them were exhausted and weak, but no longer next to death.

Cristina was able to understand a very little of the Indians' language – it seemed several of the words were close to Brazilian or Portuguese. They were able to ascertain the fact that the only way out of this village was by river, and when they were well enough to travel a three-day journey would take them to a larger jungle settlement – and from there a day's journey would take them to a trading village which had a small airstrip. From there it was only a few short hours to the outside world.

'I guess we'll be a big surprise to everyone,' Dallas managed weakly. She was growing stronger every day. But the stronger she grew physically the more she clung to Al. He never left her side, and they talked about Evan and Bernie and why it had all happened and why they had been saved.

Paul was in a very weak state and seemed to have lost any kind of lust for life. He lay in his hammock – eating listlessly, accepting the medicines the Indians persuaded him to take.

Cristina could talk of nothing but her parents. How wonderful they were – and how she would make everything up to them. She had cried for Evan. But now her tears were dry and she was anxious to get home.

They were all anxious to get home. But where was home for Al? He kept on shutting Edna out of his head – but she was still his wife. What a shock it would be for her – she had probably resigned herself to the fact that Evan and he were dead. Now he would come strolling out of the jungle alive. What would she expect from him?

He would have to go to her, explain about Evan. Tell her what a hero her son had been. Dallas would go with him. One thing he was sure of – and that was that he and Dallas were not going to be parted – no long absences – in fact no absences at all. They had talked it over and decided that that was what they both wanted.

Thank God she seemed to be recovering. But he was still worried about Paul, and couldn't wait to get him into a proper hospital.

The Indians had been wonderful – kind and helpful – they couldn't do enough. But as soon as Al felt everyone could travel – they set off.

The Chief came to the river to bid them farewell. He seemed genuinely sorry to see them go, and in a strange way Al had grown fond of him and his tribe of gentle people. Untouched by civilization they seemed to have got human relationships together very nicely indeed. Al would have liked to have done something for them. But what did they need? They were self-sufficient – they needed none of the artifices of modern society.

The Chief and Al solemnly exchanged hand clasps – and on impulse Al took the heavy gold chain from around his neck and gave it to the Chief, who appeared delighted. He examined the various medallions and charms excitedly. A St Christopher. A small gold spoon. Brazilian hand. Solid gold tag inscribed 'Al is King', and a gold and onyx dice.

The Chief then removed his own necklace – a fearsome combination of ivory, quartz stone and animal teeth, and placed it ceremonially around Al's neck.

'I'll be back,' Al smiled. 'When I want to get away from it all I'll know where to come.'

Then they were off, in a convoy of three canoes – and their journey back to the outside world had really begun.

73

Twenty-two days after vanishing on the trip between Rio and São Paulo Al King reappeared in the outside world.

Headlines screamed hysterically – AL KING ALIVE – SUPERSTAR SURVIVES PLANE CRASH – AMAZING JUNGLE RESCUE OF AL KING.

None of the newspapers had the facts – just news of his survival through the wire services. Journalists from all corners of the world were rushed to Rio where Al was expected to arrive from some obscure jungle trading village.

Nobody had much information – only that he was alive, and had apparently survived an air crash, trekked through dense jungle, and was on his way back.

The excitement was intense. Who was with him? How had the plane crashed? How had he managed to make his way through unmapped wastes of treacherous jungle for twenty-two days?

It was the story of the year.

The world waited with bated breath.

☆

Linda was in bed when she heard. Alone. Idly watching television, flicking between 'Charlie's Angels' and an old Joan Crawford movie. A newsflash informed her that Al King had been found alive, and she sat rigidly up in bed not knowing what to do. The newsflash was so brief – it told nothing.

She leapt from her bed and frantically switched channels – nothing – commercials, soap operas, game shows, comedy, singers. No news.

Christ! Her hand was shaking as she reached for the telephone. If Al had been found alive somewhere ... What about Paul? And Dallas, and the others.

She dialled Cody's number. He would know. She had not spoken to him since they had returned from Rio twelve days previously. She had given him the speech, 'I like you a lot but...' Somehow she had not felt it was quite the right time to go falling head first into a heavy affair. If Cody had been a casual lay it would have been OK. But he wasn't. He was a kind, interesting, funny man – the sort of man she could quite consider spending the rest of her life with. And some-how ... with Paul missing – probably dead – it just wasn't the right timing.

'If you still want to we can get together in a couple of months,' she had told a puzzled Cody.

He had not understood. 'But why?' he had kept on asking over and over.

She had shrugged. 'It just doesn't seem right. Oh I know I had planned to split with Paul – but I hadn't *told* him. To be with you now ... how can I explain it? It would just be disloyal.'

'That's a load of crap – you're just opting out of what could be a very good relationship.'

'It's the way I *feel*.'

So they had not spoken to or seen each other since the Rio trip.

His phone did not answer. She kept ringing until the service picked up. 'Cody Hills,' she requested breathlessly. 'One moment, please,' the operator replied, leaving her hanging for what seemed like an endless two minutes – then – 'I'm sorry, Mr Hills is out of the country.'

'Out of the country?' Linda repeated in a dazed voice.

'He'll be in Europe for the next ten days. Would you like to leave a name and number?'

'How ... how long has he been gone?'

'I'm sorry. I don't know. Would you like me to check for you?'

'If you would.' How could he just go away like that? Without even calling her. But she had specifically requested that he did not call her. Yes ... but Europe. He *should* have called.

'Mr Hills has been gone three days,' the operator returned to inform her. 'Is there any message?'

'Do you have a number I can reach him at?'

'Sorry, Mr Hills is moving around. I'm sure he'll be calling in.'

'When?'

The operator was getting impatient. 'I really don't know that. Now – can I take your name or not?'

Linda left her name. A lot of good *that* would do. Where the hell *was* he? And why hadn't he told her? She felt strangely hurt, although he was only doing what she had asked him to do.

Shit! She kicked the side of the bed in sudden anger. Then – remembering what the phone call had been all about in the first place – she rushed to her purse. Somewhere, written on a slip of paper, she had Carlos Baptista's number. If anyone would know what was happening – he would.

☆

Cody was in London when he heard. He had just arrived back at his hotel after a pleasant dinner at Mr Chow's with his stud actor, the director of the picture his actor had just begun, and a young stoned model that the actor and director appeared to be sharing.

As he collected his room key from the desk the clerk remarked, 'Did you hear Al King's been found?'

The clerk had been volunteering this piece of information to hotel guests all evening – and reaction had varied from vague interest to an avid desire for details. Cody's reaction was the best yet. He stood stock still, went very white, and through clenched teeth muttered, 'You mean they've found his body?'

'*Him*,' the clerk elucidated, 'apparently he came walking out of the jungle. Can you imagine that?'

'Alive?'

'Well, he must have been alive if he was walking.'

'Where did you hear this?'

'Here – did you *know* him?'

'Was there anyone with him?' Cody did not realize it but he was shouting, 'Was there anyone with him?'

The clerk backed away, '*I* don't know. They didn't say.'

Cody grabbed his key and raced to the elevator.

It was amazing – a miracle. If Al King was still alive . . . What about Dallas?

He had to place a call to Carlos Baptista immediately.

☆

Edna was sitting in the front room with John and his elderly mother when she heard. She was at their house, where she had been a guest in their tiny spare bedroom for three days – ever since moving out of the big mansion she had shared with Al. She had moved out in a hurry because the Arab who had bought the house wished immediate occupation with his wife, eight children, and numerous relatives. Leaving all furniture had been part of the deal. Edna had not minded. There was nothing she wished to keep. In fact the relief at leaving the big house had been immense.

John had been so understanding and kind. She had been forced to tell him who she was because of the fact that her picture was all over the newspapers. It had been *his* idea that she move in with him and his mother.

'Nothing improper,' he had hastened to add when first mentioning the idea, 'but you will have privacy – no one will bother you.'

She had jumped at the idea – and living with them was like returning to the kind of life she had always yearned for. The kind of life she had hoped that she and Al would share. A proper cooked breakfast to see John off to his work in the morning. Housework. Tea. Six o'clock dinner, and John and his mother *loved* her cooking. Then togetherness in front of the telly before an early bedtime.

She knew that as soon as he felt a suitable amount of time had elapsed John would ask her to marry him. She was ready to say yes.

Now this. A sudden jolting newsflash that Al was *still alive*!

A newsflash that made the blood drain from her face, and sweat break out all over her body.

John was wonderful. He was calm and did not panic. 'I think,' he announced slowly, 'that this calls for a nice cup of tea.'

☆

Melanie was in Las Vegas when she heard.

'Shit!' she exclaimed, 'that's impossible.'

She was sitting in the Noshorium coffee shop in Caesar's Palace Hotel with Manny Shorto, three of his permanent entourage, two hangers-on and four interchangeable showgirls.

She was on her honeymoon, having married Manny five days previously in a much publicized midnight ceremony.

'Manny, you hear that?' she shrilled.

Manny was not hearing much of anything. He was into his sixth – or was it seventh – scotch, and he was working out the strategy he would employ in the poker game he planned to join at any minute. Meanwhile he was concentrating on a bagel – liberally spread with lox and cream cheese. 'God's food,' he called the combination – his only gesture in the direction of religion.

Melanie flapped her hands in a mild panic. 'Al King's alive!' she screeched, repeating what an alert reporter had just whispered in her ear.

'So?' munched Manny.

'If he's alive . . . well maybe . . . well . . . what about *Paul*?'

'He alive?'

'*I don't know*?'

'So worry about it when you know.'

'But Manny . . .'

'Be a good broad and cool it with the *kvetching*.'

'*Kvetching*? Are you kidding? This could be *serious*. This could mean you and I are not even married!'

Manny gazed expansively around the table – bagel hovering near his lips. 'Let's hear it for instant divorce! Think I made myself a *record* here!'

His audience laughed appreciatively.

Melanie stood up, quivering with fury. 'Fuck *you*!' she shrieked.

'Name the place, kid,' replied Manny, 'I'll be there!'

☆

The journey back to civilization was a nightmare. But a minor one compared to what they had already suffered.

The three-day journey by boat to the next village was a difficult one. As they progressed in their parade of canoes the river became wider and far more difficult to navigate. There were innumerable bends and turns, and rocks and islands abounded. The water was sometimes calm, and sometimes strong currents led the flimsy boats into whirlpools and rapids.

All the time alligators were present – lounging on their islands, sliding sinuously into the water – ready to pounce at any opportunity. And the sun blazed unmercifully down.

Al did not mind the heat any more. His body was burned a deep mahogany colour, and he wore the native Indian costume which allowed him to sweat freely. Like the Indians he accepted the heat as a fact of life. They had learned to live with it, and so would he. It bothered Cristina and Paul, though. They lay in the bottom of the little boats, uncomfortable, sweating, and weak.

Dallas had rallied wonderfully. Her swollen feet were

almost better, as was her face. She had lost a lot of weight with the fever though, and her once voluptuous body was painfully thin. 'Who needs a health spa,' she joked. 'This is instant diet.'

Al knew that a couple of weeks of proper eating was all she needed to regain her strength. The primitive medicine the Indians had given her to cure the fever seemed to have worked wonders.

After three days they had arrived at the next village – and they were left there surrounded by more Indians who came running out of their huts to form a circle and stare. Then a man had appeared dressed in shorts and a shirt. A white man – well, half white, as Al had discovered later.

He stared at them in amazement, and then in faltering English shook his head and exclaimed, 'I can hardly believe it. How long?' He gestured out into the jungle.

'Twenty-one days,' Al replied, 'and are we glad to see you!'

The man's name was Pucal. He was of mixed Indian and white blood. He was a trader who lived a nomadic existence among the Indians – only occasionally travelling to civilization to fetch supplies for himself and his Indian family.

'I have a signal you coming,' he explained. 'Cannot believe you come from jungle. Tonight we rest. Tomorrow I take you trading village – one day's journey. I radio them now you here. Small plane take you nearest city.'

He took them to his house. A more civilized affair than the Indians' habitations. It had walls, a thatched roof and a raised floor. There he gave them steaming hot coffee, mashed banana, and a sort of maize bread.

Al decided it was probably the best meal he had eaten in his entire life.

Pucal could not seem to get over the fact that they had trekked through the jungle alone and practically unarmed – and emerged still alive. He kept on staring at them unbelievingly and muttering: 'A miracle . . . God sends a miracle . . .'

The next morning they set off early – Pucal and five sturdy Indians accompanying them. Another river journey. More sun. More mosquitoes to plague them.

But nobody minded. They were on their way home. They were on their way out of the jungle.

Late afternoon they left the river and travelled overland for an hour. The terrain was smooth and flat, and rose steadily. Eventually they reached a cluster of run-down houses, and beyond them the land was more cultivated and the people that ran from the houses to stare were dressed in ragged trousers and shirts. Civilization.

A small twin-engined plane was waiting to fly them to the nearest city. The pilot, a weather-beaten American, regarded them with the same amazement as Pucal. He chain-smoked cigarettes and chewed vigorously on gum. 'I gotta message hadda fly some people out . . . Where the hell you all *come* from?'

Al tried to explain, but the American just shook his head in disbelief. 'Nobody could survive an air crash and come through that jungle alive.'

'We did,' said Al, 'I'm Al King. Maybe you read about me . . .'

'Holy mackerel!' The American peered at him intently. 'Jee . . . sus! You're that singer fella – the one the papers were full of a few weeks back . . .' Within minutes he had radioed in the news, and by the time they were airborne the rumour that Al King was still alive and had been rescued from the jungle was spreading all over the world.

☆

Carlos Baptista was as stunned as everyone else. Everything seemed to have happened so quickly. One minute Al King was dead and forgotten – the next – alive and on his way back to Rio.

The information filtering through was vague, and it had not yet been established exactly who was with him – but there were, apparently, three other survivors. And they had been transferred off the rescue plane, and were now on their way to Rio via a jet due to arrive at any minute.

Carlos waited at the airport with Jorge. Both men were silent and tense. Both men were hoping that their children were among the survivors.

Two ambulances waited on the tarmac ready to whisk Al and whoever was with him to a private clinic where Carlos had arranged for the best doctors to be standing by. Now that the singer was alive Carlos felt that he was his responsibility – besides which Al still owed him a concert – and what a concert it would be! Magnificent! The best ever! A giant tribute to Al King's return to life! Carlos' business brain was ticking over. He would use the Maracana Stadium again – but this time he would be able to charge *double* the price for the tickets. Everyone would want to see Al King. Everyone. It would be the most exciting concert ever staged.

Carlos sighed. If only Louis was alive . . .

Beside him Jorge stood stiffly to attention. He appeared to have aged ten years – his black hair – once tinged with attractive grey sideburns – had turned suddenly white. His face sagged, his whole body sagged. He was a lost and lonely man. All the money in the world could not buy back his lovely wife or return his daughter to him.

At fifty-eight years of age he found himself with nothing but an abundance of material possessions and wealth. He did not want to return to his former empty life. A different woman every week. A different party every night. A different city every month. That kind of life was for young men – men who had nothing more on their minds than how many women they could seduce in a year. Jorge had lived that life. Lived it to the hilt until Evita. Evita . . . Evita.

The jet coming into land was his last chance. Perhaps God would be kind and give him back Cristina. Although how a young girl could have survived the ordeal they must have gone through . . .

He closed his eyes and muttered a fervent prayer.

☆

Dallas held Al's hand tightly. 'What do I look like?' she whispered.

He hugged her. 'Alive. That's what you look like.'

'I never thought we would make it. I really didn't.'

'Come *on*. If it wasn't for you we would still be sitting in the wreck – dead. It was *you* who said we had to find a river . . .'

'Yes, and *you* who took us down it. Al, I'm so sorry about Evan, so very, very sorry. He was a terrific boy. I just don't know what happened that day . . . It's all a blur . . . a nightmare . . .'

'He went to find food. The funny thing is none of you

could have eaten anyway.' He shook his head in despair. 'I don't know . . .'

They had discussed it back and forth for days. How was he going to tell Edna? He just didn't know . . .

The plane touched the ground and roared along the tarmac.

'This is not going to be easy,' Al said. 'The press are going to be after us like vultures. Say nothing – whatever you let slip will be twisted – so silence. Right?'

'You make it sound as if we've done something wrong.'

'I just don't want a lot of bullshit fairytale stories hitting the papers.'

'And no Bernie to protect us . . .'

'Just remember I love you,' he squeezed her hand. 'We've come through one jungle – here we go again. Just watch out for the snakes!'

'I don't understand.'

'You will. The media is out there waiting. The real savages. They want me – they want you. We're news – the best goddamn news they've had for a long time. They'll try to tear us into shreds – so watch out, lady – they'll claw each others' balls to be the first with the story. You understand me now?'

She shuddered. 'Yes.'

'So – stay silent, and I'll protect you.'

The plane taxied to a stop.

The doors opened.

Chaos.

They were back.

SIX MONTHS LATER

74

The gates to the huge Bel Air estate opened at exactly 12 a.m. and the cluster of journalists and photographers entered impatiently.

They followed a laconic security guard up a long winding path which led them to the main house. 'Don't know why we couldn't have *driven* in,' one woman complained.

'We're lucky to be here at all,' a black girl, dressed in a jump suit and aviator shades, replied. 'I mean this is the *first* interview Al King has given in *six* months. The first since his *crash.*'

'Who cares about Al King,' sniffed the woman reporter, 'it's Dallas *I'm* here to see. *She's* the star as far as *I'm* concerned.'

'Yeah,' agreed a lanky male photographer. 'Man – she is the greatest. Hottest TV star of the season. Beeee-utiful! I am glued to my set when *she* is on – but *glued.*'

'So is every other man in America,' intoned a languid blonde, 'and who can blame them? I wouldn't throw her out of *my* bed – and *I'm* into guys!'

'Hey – Marlene – that stud you 'bin running with a guy – I thought he was a gay!' interrupted the photographer.

'Go stick it up your own ass!' Marlene replied, 'since when did *you* even know what to do with that noodle you've got hanging between your legs!'

Linda, walking at the back of the crowd, was only half listening.

Had it really only been six months since Al had come walking out of the jungle? And Dallas . . . the girl Cristina . . . and Paul.

It seemed years away. Was it really only months?

She could remember the night she had heard. The phone

671

call to Carlos Baptista. The suspense of waiting to find out who the other three survivors were.

When she had heard that one of them was Paul she had rushed to the airport and boarded the next plane to Rio.

Seeing him lying in bed in the private clinic she had thought that he would die. He looked like a man teetering on the edge of death.

She had sat at his bedside, held his hand, and willed him to get better.

Gradually he had recovered. Gradually he had begun to look human again.

Cody had been in Rio too, and if they happened to bump into each other they smiled politely and exchanged stilted conversation. They referred to nothing personal. That's the way she had stated it should be, and Cody had respected her wishes. He was still respecting her wishes. She had neither seen nor heard from him.

So – what happened? She had spent five weeks with Paul before telling him it was all over. Five weeks of having Paul behave towards her the way she had always dreamed about. But it wasn't working. It just wasn't there any more as far as she was concerned, and finally she had told him.

He had been shocked and surprised. 'But this is what you always wanted,' he had insisted, 'for us to be together, to get married. There is no Melanie to bug you any more – I'm totally yours.'

Sure he was totally hers. Melanie had publicly humiliated him. Choked when he had turned up alive making her a bigamist, she had rushed to Mexico for a quickie divorce, and married Manny Shorto all over again. The newspapers enjoyed every minute of it.

Al was not pleased when he heard Linda was taking off on baby brother. He had summoned her into his presence and screamed at her a lot. She had told him to go fuck himself – it was none of *his* business.

So she had left – returned to New York for a few months and worked and played – hard – very hard. But the playthings were not as beautiful as the ones on the coast – the bodies were not as bronzed – the muscles not as taken care of – the faces not facsimiles of Ryan O'Neal and Warren

Beatty. I mean if playthings are going to be your thing – then go for the shiniest toys.

So she had returned to California, rented an apartment in the same building as before – and thought about calling Cody. It was only a thought – she had her pride – if he didn't care enough to contact her in all these months . . . Instead she had called Julio – male hooker supreme – and they had made a businesslike appointment.

He had turned up at her apartment – white Ferrari parked rakishly outside, white teeth gleaming like a toothpaste ad in his incredibly good-looking very black face.

'Hi – I'm Julio,' he had announced very properly, very politely. Then he had removed his French trousers, silk shirt, Gucci loafers, and come into her life with such energy and expertise that she had been quite breathless.

He had been worth every cent of his exorbitant fee.

But she couldn't help thinking about Cody. Funny, sweet, kind Cody . . .

Occasionally she read about him in *Variety*. He was doing very well businesswise – and sometimes his name would appear in the gossip column linked with this girl or that. She hated them all – whoever they were.

She also read about Paul in the trades. Read that he had returned to England and was concentrating on his management company while the great Al remained in solitary exile with only Dallas for company.

Had Al King retired permanently? That's what everyone wanted to know. After his miraculous escape from the plane crash and jungle he had given one short press conference on his arrival in Rio. It was a one-liner, 'I want to thank everyone for their concern . . .' And the world waited impatiently for the story of what had really happened.

They waited in vain. No one was talking.

Cristina Maraco was offered fabulous amounts of money to tell her story. Through her father she refused. She had spent a great deal of time in and out of hospital having skin grafts on her damaged arms. In between times she devoted herself to her father – the two were inseparable.

Paul, of course, was not talking.

And Dallas had gone with Al into his self-imposed exile.

The two of them had not been seen by anyone except the small group of loyal employees who worked for them. And *they* had to sign statements that they would not write or give interviews or do anything that would infringe the privacy of their famous employers.

Of course the fact that Al and Dallas were inaccessible made everyone want them all the more. Especially since Dallas was now as big a star as Al – this due to the fact that her six hour-long segments of 'Man Made Woman' had been shown on television – and repeated almost immediately because of public demand. Suddenly she was the hottest lady on television – and nobody could get to her. Lew Margolis was tearing his hair out in frustration.

Sackloads of fan mail arrived at the studio daily. A poster of Dallas wearing nothing but a minuscule leopard-skin bikini and a smile had broken all sale records. It would seem that half the homes in America wanted Dallas on their wall.

Now – finally – the two of them had agreed to have a press conference. Public interest was to at last be sated.

Linda could not resist attending. Why not? She was press. She was entitled.

She trailed behind the others, and wondered what it was they were coming out of exile to say.

☆

Cody Hills had arrived at the Bel Air house an hour earlier. The guard at the gate had greeted him in a friendly fashion and waved him through in his car. The car was comparatively new – a sleek silver Mercedes – not rented – bought and paid for. His mother had had a fit when she had seen it – 'A *German* car!' she had exclaimed, 'I always knew you would let the family down!'

'The war was a long time ago,' Cody had patiently pointed out. He spent a lot of his time patiently pointing things out to his mother.

'So?' she replied sarcastically, 'tell your Uncle Stanley that. *He* remembers like it was yesterday!'

Cody drove right up to the main house – a sprawling building of Tudor design. He rang the front doorbell, and a thin girl, in owl-like glasses and a man's business suit, answered.

'Hi, Tilly,' Cody said. 'Are we all set?'

'Getting there, I think,' Tilly replied in clipped tones. She was the English secretary that Paul had sent over with all of Al's papers, and she had stayed on to work exclusively for Al. Paul no longer managed Al's affairs. Mutually they had agreed that it would be better for Paul to concentrate on doing his own thing. Besides which he wanted to stay in England to be with his children, and his health was not what it was – although he was better – the doctors said he could get a recurrence of fever at any time.

Al had chosen Cody to represent him. If Dallas liked and trusted him that was good enough recommendation.

Not that there had been anything to do as yet – except get out of contracts and free Al from every commitment.

Cody found himself in the position of having the two most wanted clients in show business – and not – until now – being able to set up one deal for them.

They had both wanted to do exactly nothing. They were happy just to lounge around their huge house – swimming, watching television, playing tennis, reading, listening to music – and most of all laughing, giggling, and making love.

Cody thought he had never seen two people so happy in each other's company. They glowed when they were together. They were insular – they needed no one else. He was about the only friend they allowed into their lives.

It had not been easy for Al after the crash. The newspapers had made much of the fact that his wife Edna had sold their house and *all* of his personal possessions and moved in with some nobody – all within weeks of his supposed death. She had even got rid of his clothes! It was a shock. But he had never made one public comment about it. He had made a short private trip to London to talk to Edna about Evan – tell her what had really happened and how proud she could be of her son.

Throughout their meeting she had clung nervously onto her friend John's arm, and she had refused to look Al in the eye. It was almost as if she wished he *had* died. She was not enjoying him intruding into her life again – she had found what she wanted and now she just desired to be left alone.

Al wasn't bitter. She had put up with a lot throughout the

years. He had wished her luck, and shortly after, a divorce had been arranged, and Edna had since married John.

'Can I fix you a drink?' Tilly was asking.

'Not at this time of day – I never indulge until after dark.'

'How about a coffee then?'

'That would be nice.'

Tilly went off to get his coffee, and Cody wandered into the huge comfortable living room.

The press conference had been *his* idea. It had taken him weeks to talk them into it. It had taken him even longer to talk them into doing a film together.

Lew Margolis and every other major producer in Hollywood had been bugging him to try and put a deal together. They were offering the earth. Name it. Have it. Dallas and Al King together would be the dynamite package of all time. It was too good an opportunity for both of them to blow.

'You can do whatever you want,' Cody had told them, 'brief the best screenwriter in town to do what *you* like. Choose your own director. You will have *complete* control – plus a sizeable chunk of the action.'

At first they hadn't even bothered to listen to him. Then Dallas' phenomenal success on the television series fired her ambitious streak. 'Why not?' she began to ask Al, 'it would be fun – we would be together.'

'Because . . .' Al had replied, 'this business stinks. It's a grinding cut-throat bag of shit.'

'I know that – I didn't just get off the bus, you know. But Al . . . to do something together . . . anything we want . . . It *is* a great opportunity.'

Eventually she had talked him into it. She was young, excited by her success, she had no idea what real fame was all about . . .

If that was what she wanted Al wasn't about to stand in her way. But he wondered if she realized how soul-destroying becoming public property was . . . You gained a lot. You also sacrificed your right to privacy.

Of course he could protect her. He had taken the trip before.

Against his better judgement he gave Cody the go-ahead.

Dallas was ecstatic, 'It will be wonderful!' she enthused. 'I love you, Al, I love you – love you – love you!'

He was glad it made her happy – but he was wondering what the cost would be for both of them.

The six months alone together – away from people – pressures – hassles. It had been the happiest time of his life.

Shortly after returning from Rio he handed Dallas an envelope. It was a private investigator's report on her family in Miami. Her mother, father, husband . . . Al knew that one of her main hangups was the fact that her family had never come looking for her when she had run away. It had made her feel worthless and unwanted. Secretly Al had decided to find out *why* they had never looked for their daughter – even when she was on magazine covers all over the country they had never stepped forward. And that *was* unusual – even the husband had never come sniffing around.

The reason was in the envelope.

The day Dallas had left the zoo there had been a fire. Arson was suspected, but nothing proved. Her mother, father, husband . . . all dead. And the police were looking – or had been at the time according to the press report – for a young black couple.

'After you ran off there must have been some kind of fight,' Al explained. 'The black stud you told me about must have burned the place down. Now you know why they never came looking for you.'

Dallas was numb with shock. But when the shock wore off she began to understand that perhaps after all she hadn't been abandoned – perhaps if they had been alive her parents *would* have come looking for her.

'You're not a married lady any more,' Al had joked later.

'Oh yes I am . . . Cody . . .'

A discreet annulment was arranged. Cody was just as shocked as she was. He still loved Dallas – but as a sister. Somehow it was Linda he couldn't get out of his head . . .

Tilly came back in the room carrying a cup of coffee. 'Here you go.'

Cody took it. 'Thanks. What are they doing?'

'Dallas is fiddling around with her hair, and Al's watching her. Do I have to tell *you* what they're like? Togetherness at all times. If it wasn't so sincere it would be positively sick-making!'

'Yeah.' Cody grinned. He knew what she meant. It made anyone else in the room feel like an outsider.

He thought with satisfaction of his recent conversation with Lew Margolis. Rumour had flown all over town as soon as he had put out the word that Al and Dallas were looking for the right property.

Lew Margolis had phoned him.

'So the cunt finally came around to my way of thinking,' he had bragged. 'Knew she would – and that sonofabitch she's shacking up with. You want to come over and talk terms. I can get the contracts up this week. How long before they choose a property? I'd like to start shooting as soon as possible.'

I bet you would – thought Cody. Lew had recently had a monster flop with a film on lesbianism starring his wife. '*Doris Andrews a dyke*', one of the reviews had hooted, '*it's like casting Warren Beatty as a fag!*'

'They've found the property they want,' Cody said evenly.

'Great!' enthused Lew, 'it can be the biggest piece of crap in the world – what do I care – with them in it we're going to clean up – friggin' clean up! Get your ass over here, Cody – let's hear what the cunt wants.'

Cody took a deep breath. It wasn't in his own interests to screw a man like Lew Margolis – but Jesus – if anyone deserved it . . . 'Sorry Lew,' he said smoothly, 'but "the cunt" decided to go elsewhere. Jordan Minthoff's producing.'

He hung up on Lew's explosion. It was a satisfying moment.

☆

Linda was impressed by the house. It was big and lavish – but at the same time lived-in. There was no sign of any plastic interior decorator here. They were led through the living room out to a large tented area beside the pool. A long table was set out as a bar with two virile young bartenders. Maybe later . . . Then she saw Cody. He was suntanned, his sandy hair bleached lighter and combed carefully across his forehead to hide his balding hairline. He was wearing white slacks and a blue blazer with bold brass buttons; the obligatory Hollywood tinted shades covered his eyes. He was smiling and talking to a busty blonde strung with too many cameras.

Linda hung back. She didn't want him to see her . . . and yet . . . Oh shit – they could be friends, couldn't they?

She moved nearer to him – was going to change her mind and back off – but then he saw *her*. He left the blonde mid-sentence and was by her side. 'Good to *see* you.'

'You too.' They grinned foolishly at each other.

'So . . . what are you doing here?'

'I'm a photographer, aren't I? Thought I'd see what all the excitement was about.'

'I thought you were in New York.'

'I was.'

'When did you get back?'

'Few weeks ago.'

'Can I get you a drink?' he asked anxiously, leading her towards the bar.

'No, I'm fine.'

'You look fine. I mean you look terrific.'

She laughed self-consciously. 'I cut my hair.'

'Looks nice, really nice.' He paused, at a loss for words. 'Well . . .'

'Well . . .'

'I keep on seeing your work in every magazine I pick up.'

'And I keep on reading about you – this gossip column – that gossip column – you've really been getting around.'

'Gotta fill my time.'

'Oh sure.'

'You mean *you* sit home?'

'Not exactly.'

'I didn't think so.'

They were both suddenly serious, staring at each other.

'I am here to tell you I have really missed you,' Cody volunteered, 'like *really*.'

'Yes?'

'Yes.' He fumbled for a cigarette, dropping the pack and picking it up quickly. 'I'm not nervous – really I'm not.'

She laughed softly.

'I heard about you and Paul.'

'Al was furious. You would think it was him I was

walking out on. I don't know how he'll feel about me being here today.'

'I'm sure he's forgotten all about it. Paul's doing very nicely in London – I hear he's got himself a girlfriend.'

She didn't feel at all jealous. 'That's nice.'

'Why didn't you call me?' Cody asked intently.

'Call *you*? Why didn't *you* call *me*?'

'You told me not to.'

'*Screw* what I *told* you. Oh, Cody – the trouble with you is you're too goddamn *nice*.'

'You wouldn't have said that if you'd heard me on the phone to Lew Margolis the other day. I shafted him right between the goolies. It felt good.'

Linda laughed. 'You don't have to defend yourself for being nice. I love you for it!'

'Do you realize what you just said? I think a remark like that calls for dinner tonight. I'll pick you up at eight. Where?'

'Same place, different apartment number.'

Again they both found themselves grinning foolishly.

'Hey – I've got a press conference to get on the road here,' Cody said at last. 'You're taking my mind off everything!'

'So sorry – what's it all about anyway?'

'Announce the movie . . . you know Dallas has become some huge star from that one TV series.'

'You don't have to tell me. I have made a small fortune from my pictures of her. They sell again and again and again.'

'A fortune, huh? You mean you're rich?'

'Well, you always did say I was a bright lady!'

'Ouch! You never forget.' He kissed her lightly on the cheek. 'Time to bring on my two superstars. How about you staying on after and getting some exclusive shots?'

'If you don't think they'll mind . . .'

'Mind! Dallas will be delighted, she's always talking about you.' He didn't want to confess that so was he. 'See you in a minute.'

He vanished inside the house, and Linda couldn't wipe the smile off her face. She felt ridiculous really, standing there grinning like an idiot, but there was nothing she could do about it. Seeing Cody again just made her feel *so* good.

She glanced around at her fellow photographers and

journalists. They were chatting, drinking, setting up tape recorders and cameras.

Suddenly a hush fell over the gathering. Framed in the patio doorway stood Al and Dallas.

What a couple they made. Somehow Dallas was softer than before – more glowingly beautiful. She was wearing a very simple white dress which emphasized her suntanned body. Her luxurious wild hair cascaded down over her shoulders, and her huge green eyes gleamed with a hidden danger. She looked incredibly sensual and vulnerable all at the same time. An irresistible combination. That was the new ingredient – Linda decided – the vulnerability. It had every man in the room falling instantly in love. They didn't know whether they wanted to rape or protect her. She had them bewitched.

Linda also noticed a change in Al. A big change. The arrogance had gone and had been replaced with a look of deep satisfaction. For the first time since she had known him he looked like a contented man. And who could blame him? The two of them sparked off enough electricity to light up the house. Al was thinner than she remembered, and very darkly tanned. Also he had stuck to the beard he had grown in the jungle, and it gave him the look of a gypsy. His jet hair was long and unruly, and on his forehead there was a thin scar – a souvenir of the jungle.

Whereas before Linda had always thought his sex appeal somewhat manufactured – now he looked like the real thing.

The photographers and journalists surged forward – and was it her imagination or did most of them surge in Dallas' direction? She wasn't sure but she could have sworn a look of resignation swept over Al's face.

'Ladies and gentlemen of the press,' Cody announced proudly, 'I give you Dallas, and Al King.'

extracts reading groups
competitions books new
discounts extracts extracts events reading groups
competitions extracts discounts
books new events
events extracts reading groups
extracts books
new three reading groups reading groups
interviews events new
events extracts extracts books
discounts events interviews
new books events new books extracts
events new events
discounts extracts discounts

www.panmacmillan.com

extracts events reading groups
competitions books extracts new books

Lovers and Gamblers

Jackie Collins is one of the world's top-selling writers, with over four hundred million copies of her books sold in more than forty countries. Her twenty-five bestselling novels have never been out of print. She lives in Beverly Hills, California.

Visit her at www.jackiecollins.com

'A generation of women have learnt more about how to handle their men from Jackie's books than from any kind of manual . . . She seems to know every Hollywood player and just where to find their dirty laundry basket. She is a consummate observer. An outsider with an insider's knowledge. That's her signature trick. She is, at once, both intimate and detached . . . Jackie is very much her own person: a total one off'
Daily Mail

'Jackie, we salute you!'
Cosmopolitan

'Jackie is queen of conspicuously consuming blockbusters about American high life'
Wendy Holden

'Miss Collins knows how to entertain – and that is a very precious commodity'
The Times

'She has a very sharp eye for character and situation'
Guardian

Also by Jackie Collins

Maia, Ally, Star, CeCe, Tiggy, Electra and Merope have all been found. But one member of the family is still missing. It's time to discover the truth . . .

ATLAS:
THE STORY OF PA SALT

The multi-million-copy epic Seven Sisters reaches its stunning, unforgettable conclusion.

Lucinda Riley wrote this novel in partnership with her son, Harry Whittaker.

PRAISE FOR THE SEVEN SISTERS SERIES

'Heart-wrenching, uplifting and utterly enthralling'
Lucy Foley

'There's something magical about these stories'
Prima

ictive storytelling'
oman & Home

ass in beautiful writing'
Sun

Publishing Spring 2023
Available for pre-order

THE
MURDERS
AT FLEAT
HOUSE

A masterful new suspense novel by Lucinda Riley

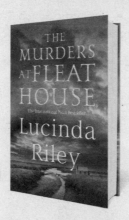

When a young student is found dead at a private boarding school, its elite reputation is at risk. The headmaster is determined to write the death off as a tragic accident – but Detective Jazz Hunter will soon suspect that a murder has been committed.

Escaping her own problems in London, the isolated, snow-covered landscape of rural Norfolk had felt like the ideal place for Jazz to hide. But when it becomes clear the victim was tangled in a web of loyalties and old vendettas that go far beyond just one student, and the bodies begin to pile up, Jazz knows she's running out of time to find the culprit.

All roads lead back to the closed world of the school. But Fleat House and its residents aren't going to give up their secrets easily – and they're more sinister than Jazz could ever have imagined . . .

Publishing May 2022
Available for pre-order

J. V. Luce, *Trinity College Dublin: The First 400 Years* (TCD Press, 1992)

Ann Matthews, *Renegades: Irish Republican Women 1900–1922* (Mercier Press, 2010)

Charles River ed., *New Zealand and the British Empire: The History of New Zealand Under British Sovereignty* (Charles River Editors, 2018)

Charles River ed., *The Maori: The History and Legacy of New Zealand's Indigenous People* (Charles River Editors, 2018)

Marianne Slyne, *Marianne's Journal* (Michael Collins Centre, Castleview, 2015)

Praise for the Seven Sisters series

'I've loved the Seven Sisters from the get-go and this
latest in the series is just as great as the rest'
Daily Mail

'A masterclass in beautiful writing'
The Sun

'A breathtaking adventure brimming with cruelty,
tragedy, passion and obsession'
Lancashire Evening Post

'An epic tale of love, loss and discovery'
My Weekly

'Heart-wrenching, uplifting and utterly enthralling'
Lucy Foley

Cast of characters

ATLANTIS

Pa Salt – *the sisters' adoptive father (deceased)*
Marina (Ma) – *the sisters' guardian*
Claudia – *housekeeper at Atlantis*
Georg Hoffman – *Pa Salt's lawyer*
Christian – *the skipper*

THE D'APLIÈSE SISTERS

Maia
Ally (Alcyone)
Star (Asterope)
CeCe (Celaeno)
Tiggy (Taygete)
Electra
Merope (missing)

Mary-Kate
The Gibbston Valley, New Zealand
June 2008

1

I remember exactly where I was and what I was doing when I saw my father die. I was standing pretty much where I was now, leaning over the wooden veranda that surrounded our house and staring out at the grape pickers working their way along the neat rows of vines, heavily pregnant with this year's yield. I was just about to walk down the steps to join them when out of the corner of my eye I saw the man-mountain that was my father suddenly disappear from sight. At first I thought he had knelt down to collect a stray cluster of grapes – he detested waste of any kind, which he put down to the Presbyterian mindset of his Scottish parents – but then I saw the pickers from the rows nearby dash towards him. It was a good hundred-metre run from the veranda to reach him, and by the time I got there, someone had ripped open his shirt and was trying to resuscitate him, pumping his chest and giving mouth-to-mouth, while another had called 111. It took twenty minutes for the ambulance to arrive.

Even as he was lifted onto the stretcher, I could see from his already waxy complexion that I would never again hear his deep powerful voice that held so much gravitas, yet could turn to a throaty chuckle in a second. As tears streamed down my cheeks, I kissed him gently on his own ruddy, weather-beaten one, told him I loved him and said goodbye. Looking

back, the whole dreadful experience had been surreal – the transition from being so full of life to, well . . . nothing but an empty, lifeless body, was impossible to take in.

After months of suffering pains in his chest, but pretending they were indigestion, Dad had finally been persuaded to go to the doctor. He'd been told that he had high cholesterol, and that he must stick to a strict diet. My mother and I had despaired as he'd continued to eat what he wanted *and* drink a bottle of his own red wine at dinner every night. So it should hardly have been a shock when the worst eventually happened. Perhaps we had believed him indestructible, his large personality and bonhomie aiding the illusion, but as my mother had rather darkly pointed out, we're all simply flesh and bone at the end of the day. At least he'd lived the way he wished to until the very end. He'd also been seventy-three, a fact I simply couldn't compute, given his physical strength and zest for life.

The upshot was that I felt cheated. After all, I was only twenty-two, and even though I'd always known I'd arrived late in my parents' lives, the significance of it only hit me when Dad died. In the few months since we'd lost him, I'd felt anger at the injustice: *why* hadn't I come into their lives sooner? My big brother Jack, who was thirty-two, had enjoyed a whole ten years more with Dad.

Mum could obviously sense my anger, even if I'd never said anything outright to her. And then I'd felt guilty, because it wasn't her fault in any way. I loved her so much – we'd always been very close, and I could see that she was grieving too. We'd done our best to comfort each other, and somehow, we'd got through it together.

Jack had been wonderful too, spending most of his time sorting through the dreadful bureaucratic aftermath of death. He'd also had to take sole charge of The Vinery, the business

Mum and Dad had started from scratch, but at least he'd already been well prepared by Dad to run it.

Since Jack was a toddler, Dad had taken him along as he went about the yearly cycle of caring for his precious vines that would, sometime between February and April, depending on the weather, bring forth the grapes that would then be harvested and ultimately result in the delicious – and recently, prize-winning – bottles of pinot noir that lay stacked in the warehouse, ready to be exported across New Zealand and Australia. He'd taken Jack through each step of the process, and by the time he was twelve, he could have probably directed the staff, such was the knowledge Dad had given him.

Jack had officially announced at sixteen that he wanted to join Dad and run The Vinery one day, which had pleased Dad enormously. He'd gone to uni to study business, and afterwards had begun working full-time in the vineyard.

'There's nothing better than passing on a healthy legacy,' Dad had toasted him a few years ago, after Jack had been on a six-month visit to a vineyard in the Adelaide Hills in Australia, and Dad had pronounced him ready.

'Maybe you'll come in with us too one day, Mary-Kate. Here's to there being McDougal winegrowers on this land for hundreds of years to come!'

While Jack had bought into Dad's dream, the opposite had happened to me. Maybe it was the fact that Jack was genuinely so enthralled by making beautiful wines; as well as having a nose that could spot a rogue grape a mile off, he was an excellent businessman. On the other hand, I had grown from a child to a young woman watching Dad and Jack patrolling the vines and working in what was affectionately known as the 'The Lab' (in fact, it was nothing more than a large shed with a tin roof atop it), but other things had caught

my interest. Now I regarded The Vinery as a separate entity to me and my future. That hadn't stopped me working in our little shop during school and uni holidays, or helping out wherever I was needed, but wine just wasn't my passion. Even though Dad had looked disappointed when I'd said that I wanted to study music, he'd had the grace to understand.

'Good for you,' he'd said as he hugged me. 'Music is a big subject, Mary-Kate. Which bit of it do you actually see as your future career?'

I'd told him shyly that one day I would like to be a singer and write my own songs.

'That's a helluva dream to have, and I can only wish you luck and say that your mum and I are with you all the way, eh?'

'I think it's wonderful, Mary-Kate, I really do,' Mum had said. 'Expressing yourself through song is a magical thing.'

And study music I had, deciding on the University of Wellington, which offered a world-class degree, and I'd loved every minute of it. Having a state-of-the-art studio in which to record my songs, and being surrounded by other students who lived and breathed my passion, had been amazing. I'd formed a duo with Fletch, a great friend who played rhythm guitar and had a singing voice that harmonised well with mine. With me at the keyboard, we'd managed to get the odd gig in Wellington and had performed at our graduation concert last year, which was the first time my family had seen me sing and play live.

'I'm so proud of you, MK,' Dad had said, enveloping me in a hug. It had been one of the best moments of my life.

'Now here I am, a year on, chucked out the other end of my degree and still surrounded by vines,' I muttered. 'Honestly, MK, did you really think that Sony would come begging you to sign a record deal with them?'

Since leaving uni a year ago, I'd slowly become more and more depressed about my future career, and Dad's death had been a huge blow to my creativity. It felt like I'd lost two loves of my life at once, especially as one had been inextricably linked to the other. It had been Dad's love of female singer-songwriters that had first ignited my musical passion. I'd been brought up listening to Joni Mitchell, Joan Baez and Alanis Morissette.

My time in Wellington had also brought home to me just how protected and idyllic my childhood had been, living here in the glorious Garden of Eden that was the Gibbston Valley. The mountains that rose up around us provided a comforting physical barrier, while the fertile earth magically grew an abundance of succulent fruit.

I remembered a teenage Jack tricking me into eating the wild gooseberries that grew in prickly brambles behind our house, and his laughter as I'd spat out the sour fruit. I'd roamed free back then, my parents unconcerned; they'd known I was perfectly safe in the gorgeous countryside that surrounded us, playing in the cool, clear streams, and chasing rabbits across the coarse grass. While my parents had laboured in the vineyard, doing everything from planting the vines and protecting them from hungry wildlife, to picking and pressing the grapes, I'd lived in my own world.

The bright morning sun was suddenly eclipsed by a cloud, turning the valley a darker grey-green. It was a warning that winter was coming and, not for the first time, I wondered if I'd made the right decision to see it out here. A couple of months back, Mum had first mentioned her idea of taking off on what she called a 'Grand Tour' of the world to visit friends she hadn't seen for years. She had asked if I wanted to join her. At the time, I was still hoping that the demo tape I'd made with Fletch, which had gone out to record companies around

the world just before Dad died, would produce some interest. Yet the replies that told us our music wasn't what the producer was 'looking for just now' were piling up on a shelf in my bedroom.

'Sweetheart, I don't need to tell you that the music business is one of the toughest to break into,' Mum had said.

'That's why I think I should stay here,' I'd replied. 'Fletch and I are working on some new stuff. I can't just abandon ship.'

'No, of course you can't. At least you have The Vinery to fall back on if it all goes wrong,' she'd added.

I knew that she was only being kind and I should be grateful for the fact I could earn money working in the shop and helping with the accounts. But as I looked out now on my Garden of Eden, I heaved a great big sigh, because the thought of staying here for the rest of my life was not a good one, however safe and beautiful it was. Everything had changed since I'd gone away to uni and even more so after Dad's death. It felt like the heart of this place had stopped beating with his passing. It didn't help that Jack – who, before Dad had died, had agreed to spend the summer in a Rhône Valley vineyard in France – had decided with Mum that he should still make the trip.

'The future of the business is in Jack's hands now and he needs to learn as much as he can,' Mum had told me. 'We have Doug on site to run the vineyard and besides, it's the quiet season and the perfect time for Jack to go.'

But since Mum had left on her Grand Tour yesterday, and with Jack away too, there was no doubt I was feeling very alone and in danger of sinking into further gloom. 'I miss you, Dad,' I murmured as I walked inside to get some brekkie, even though I wasn't hungry. The silent house did nothing to help my mood; all through my childhood, it had been buzzing with people – if it wasn't suppliers or pickers, it was visitors to the

vineyard that Dad had got chatting to. As well as handing out samples of his wines, he'd often invite them to stay for a meal. Being hospitable and friendly was simply the Kiwi way and I was used to joining total strangers at our big pine table overlooking the valley. I had no idea how my mother was able to provide vats of tasty, plentiful food at a moment's notice, but she did, and with Dad providing the bonhomie, there had been a lot of fun and laughter.

I missed Jack too and the calm, positive energy he always exuded. He loved to tease me, but equally, I knew that he was always in my corner, my protector.

I took the orange juice carton from the fridge and poured the last of it into a glass, then did my best to hack through a loaf of day-old bread. I toasted it to make it edible, then began to write a quick shopping list to stock up on fridge supplies. The nearest supermarket was in Arrowtown, and I'd need to make the trip soon. Even though Mum had left plenty of casseroles in the freezer, it didn't feel right defrosting the big plastic tubs just for myself.

I shivered as I brought the list through to the sitting room and sat on the old sofa in front of the huge chimney breast, built out of the grey volcanic stone that abounded in the area. It had been the one thing that had convinced my parents thirty years ago that they should buy what was once a single-roomed hut in the middle of nowhere. It had no running water or facilities, and both Mum and Dad had liked to recall how that first summer, they and two-year-old Jack had used the stream that fell between the rocks behind the hut to bathe in, and a literal hole in the ground as a dunny. 'It was the happiest summer of my life,' Mum would say, 'and in the winter it got even better because of the fire.'

Mum was obsessed with real fires, and as soon as the first frost appeared in the valley, Dad, Jack and I would be sent

out to collect the wood from the store, well seasoned in the months since it had been chopped. We'd stack it in the alcoves on either side of the chimney breast, then Mum would lay the wood in the grate and the ritual of what the family called 'the first light' would take place as she struck a match. From that moment on, the fire would burn merrily every day of the winter months, until the bluebells and snowdrops (the bulbs for which she'd had posted from Europe) bloomed under the trees between September and November, our spring.

Maybe I should light one now, I thought, thinking of the warm, welcoming glow that had greeted me on freezing days throughout my childhood when I'd come in from school. If Dad had been the metaphoric heart of the winery, Mum and her fire had been that of the home.

I stopped myself, feeling I really was too young to start looking back to childhood memories for comfort. I just needed some company, that was all. The problem was, most of my uni friends were either away abroad, enjoying their last moments of freedom before they settled down and found themselves jobs, or were working already.

Even though we had a landline, the internet signal in the valley was sporadic. Sending emails was a nightmare, and Dad had often resorted to driving the half hour to Queenstown and using his friend the travel agent's computer to send them. He'd always called our valley 'Brigadoon', after an old film about a village that only awakens for one day every hundred years, so that it would never be changed by the outside world. Well, maybe the valley was Brigadoon – it certainly remained more or less unchanged – but it was not the place for a budding singer-songwriter to make her mark. My dreams were full of Manhattan, London or Sydney, those towering buildings harbouring record producers who would take Fletch and me and make us stars . . .

The landline broke into my thoughts and I stood up to grab it before it rang off. 'You've reached The Vinery,' I parroted, as I had done since I was a child.

'Hi, MK, it's Fletch,' he said, using the nickname that everyone except my mum called me.

'Oh, hi there,' I said, my heart rate speeding up. 'Any news?'

'Nothing, other than I thought I might take you up on your offer to stay at yours. I have a couple of days off from the café and I need to get out of the city, eh?'

And I need to be in *it . . .*

'Hey, that's great! Come whenever you want. I'm here.'

'How about tomorrow? I'll be driving down, so that will take me most of the morning, as long as Sissy makes it, o'course.'

Sissy was the van in which Fletch and I had driven to our gigs. It was twenty years old and rusting everywhere it could rust, belching out smoke from the dodgy exhaust pipe that Fletch had temporarily fixed with string. I only hoped Sissy could manage the three-hour journey from Dunedin where Fletch lived with his family.

'So, I'll see you round lunchtime?' I said.

'Yeah, I can't wait. You know I love it down there. Perhaps we can spend a few hours on the piano, coming up with some new stuff?'

'Perhaps,' I answered, knowing I wasn't in a particularly creative space just now. 'Bye, Fletch, see you tomorrow.'

I finished the call and walked back to the sofa, feeling brighter now that Fletch was coming – he never failed to cheer me up with his sense of humour and positivity.

I heard a shout from outside and then a whistle, the sound Doug, our vineyard manager, used to alert us to the fact that he was on site. I stood up, went to the terrace and saw Doug

and a group of burly Pacific Islanders walking through the bare vines.

'Hiya!' I shouted down.

'Hi, MK! Just taking the gang to show them where to begin the pulling out,' Doug replied.

'Fine. Good. Hi, guys,' I shouted down to his team and they waved up at me.

Their presence had broken the silence, and as the sun appeared from behind a cloud, the sight of other human beings, plus the thought that Fletch was coming tomorrow, lifted my spirits.

2

'You look pale, Maia. Are you feeling all right?' Ma said as she walked into the kitchen.

'I'm okay, I just didn't sleep very well last night thinking about Georg's bombshell.'

'Yes, it certainly was that. Coffee?' Ma asked her.

'Uh, no thanks. I'll have some chamomile tea if there is any.'

'There is, of course,' interjected Claudia. Her grey hair was pulled back tightly into a customary bun, and her usually dour face had a smile for Maia as she placed a basket of her freshly made rolls and pastries on the kitchen table. 'I take it before bed every night.'

'You must be feeling unwell, Maia. I have never known you to reject coffee first thing in the morning,' commented Ma as she collected her own.

'Habits are there to break,' Maia said wearily. 'I'm jet-lagged too, remember?'

'Of course you are, *chérie*. Why don't you eat some breakfast, then go back to bed and try to sleep?'

13

'No, Georg said he was coming later to discuss what we do about . . . the missing sister. How reliable do you think his sources are?'

'I have no idea,' Ma sighed.

'*Very*,' Claudia interrupted. 'He would not have arrived at midnight unless he was sure of his facts.'

'Morning, everyone,' said Ally as she joined the rest of the household in the kitchen. Bear was tucked up in a papoose strapped to her chest, his head lolling to one side as he dozed. One of his tiny fists was clutching a strand of Ally's red-gold curls.

'Would you like me to take him from you and put him in his cot?' asked Ma.

'No, because he's bound to wake up and howl the minute he realises he's alone. Oh Maia, you look pale,' said Ally.

'That is what I just said,' Ma murmured.

'Really, I'm okay,' Maia repeated. 'Is Christian around, by the way?' she asked Claudia.

'Yes, although he is just about to take the boat across the lake to Geneva to get some food supplies for me.'

'Then could you call him and say I'll hop on the boat with him? I have some things I need to do in the city and if we left soon, I'd be back in time to see Georg at noon.'

'Of course.' Claudia picked up the handset to dial Christian.

Ma put a cup of coffee in front of Ally. 'I have some chores to do, so I will leave you two to enjoy your breakfast.'

'Christian will have the boat ready in fifteen minutes,' said Claudia, putting down the handset. 'Now, I must go and help Marina.' She nodded at them both and left the kitchen.

'Are you sure you're okay?' Ally asked her sister when they were alone. 'You're as white as a sheet.'

'Please don't fuss, Ally. Maybe I caught a stomach bug on

the plane.' Maia took a sip of tea. 'Goodness, it's strange here, isn't it? I mean, the way everything carries on just as it did when Pa was alive? Except he isn't, so there's a gaping Pa-sized hole in everything.'

'I've been here a while already, so I'm sort of used to it, but yes, there is.'

'Talking of me looking unwell, Ally, you've lost a lot of weight.'

'Oh, that's just baby weight—'

'No, it isn't, not to me anyway. Remember, the last time I saw you was a year ago, when you left here to join Theo for the Fastnet Race. You weren't even pregnant then.'

'I actually was, but I didn't know it,' Ally pointed out.

'You mean, you didn't have any symptoms? No morning sickness or anything?'

'Not at the beginning. It kicked in at around eight weeks, if I remember rightly. And then I felt truly awful.'

'Well, you're definitely too thin. Maybe you're not looking after yourself well enough.'

'When I'm by myself, it never seems worth cooking a proper meal. And besides, even if I do sit down to eat, I'm normally jumping up from the table to go and sort this little one out.' Ally stroked Bear's cheek affectionately.

'It must be so hard bringing up a child by yourself.'

'It is. I mean, I do have my brother Thom, but as he's deputy conductor at the Bergen Philharmonic, I hardly see him, apart from Sundays. And sometimes not even then, if he's touring abroad with the orchestra. It's not the getting no sleep and the constant feeding and changing that bothers me; it's just the lack of someone to talk to, especially if Bear isn't well and I'm worried about him. So having Ma's been wonderful; she's a fount of knowledge on all things baby.'

'She's the ultimate grandmother,' Maia smiled. 'Pa would

have been so happy about Bear. He really is adorable. Now, I must go upstairs to get ready.'

As Maia stood up, Ally caught her older sister's hand. 'It is so good to see you. I've missed you so much.'

'And I you.' Maia kissed the top of Ally's head. 'I'll see you later.'

'Ally! Maia! Georg is here,' Ma shouted up the main staircase at noon.

A muffled 'Coming!' emanated from the top floor.

'Do you remember when Pa Salt bought you an old brass megaphone for Christmas?'

Georg smiled as he followed Ma into the kitchen and out onto the sun-filled terrace. He looked much more collected than he had the previous night, his steel-grey hair neatly brushed back and his pinstriped suit impeccable, accessorised tastefully with a small pocket square.

'I do,' Ma said, indicating for Georg to sit down under the parasol. 'Of course, it made no difference, because the girls all had their music on full blast, or were playing instruments, or arguing with each other. It was like the Tower of Babel on the attic floor. And I adored every moment of it. Now, I have Claudia's elderflower cordial, or a chilled bottle of your favourite Provençal rosé. Which is it to be?'

'As it is such a beautiful day, and I am yet to have my first glass of summer rosé, I will choose that. Thank you, Marina. May I do the honours for both of us?'

'Oh no, I shouldn't. I have work to do this afternoon and—'

'Come now, you're French! Surely a glass of rosé will not affect you adversely. In fact, I insist,' said Georg, as Maia and

Ally walked out onto the terrace to join them. 'Hello, girls.' Georg stood up. 'May I offer you both a glass of rosé?'

'I'll have a small glass, thank you, Georg,' said Ally, sitting down. 'Maybe it will help Bear sleep tonight,' she chuckled.

'None for me, thanks,' said Maia. 'You know, I'd almost forgotten how beautiful it is at Atlantis. In Brazil, everything is so . . . *big*: the noisy people, the vibrant colours of nature and the strong heat. Everything here feels comparatively soft and gentle.'

'It's certainly very peaceful,' said Ma. 'We are blessed to live in all the beauty that nature can provide.'

'How I've missed the winter snow,' murmured Maia.

'You should come to Norway for a winter; that will cure you,' smiled Ally. 'Or even worse, you'll get constant rain. Bergen gets far more of that than it does snow. Now, Georg, have you had any thoughts on what you told us last night?'

'Other than discussing where we go from here, no. One of us must visit the address I have, to verify if this woman is the missing sister.'

'If we do, how will we know whether she is or isn't?' asked Maia. 'Is there anything that we can identify her by?'

'I was handed a drawing of a . . . certain piece of jewellery, a ring that was apparently given to her. It is very unusual. If she has it, we will know without a doubt it is her. I have brought the drawing with me.' Georg reached into his slim leather briefcase to pull out a sheet of paper. He placed it on the table for them all to see.

Ally inspected it closely, with Maia looking over her shoulder.

'It is drawn from memory,' Georg explained. 'The gems in the setting are emeralds. The central stone is a diamond.'

'It's beautiful,' said Ally. 'Look, Maia, it's arranged in a star shape, with' – she paused to count – 'seven points.'

'Georg, do you know who originally made it?' Maia chimed in. 'It's a very unusual design.'

'I am afraid I do not,' Georg replied.

'Did Pa draw this?' Maia asked.

'He did, yes.'

'Seven points of a star for seven sisters . . .' Ally murmured.

'Georg, you said last night that her name was Mary,' said Maia.

'Yes.'

'Did Pa Salt find her, want to adopt her and then something happened and he lost her?'

'All I can say is that just before he . . . passed away, he was given some new information, which he asked me to follow up. Having discovered where she was born, it has taken me and others almost a year to trace where I believe she is now. Over the years I have taken many a false turn, and it has led to nothing. However, this time, your father was adamant his source was reliable.'

'Who was his source?' Maia asked.

'He did not say,' Georg replied.

'If it is the missing sister, it's a terrible shame that, after all these years of searching for her, she's found only a year after Pa's death,' Maia sighed.

'Wouldn't it be wonderful if it *was* her,' said Ally, 'and we could bring her back to Atlantis in time to board the *Titan* and go and lay the wreath?'

'It would,' Maia smiled. 'Although there is one big problem. According to your information, Georg, "Mary" hardly lives next door. And we leave for our cruise down to Greece in less than three weeks.'

'Yes, and sadly, I have a very busy schedule at present,' said Georg. 'Otherwise, I would go to find Mary myself.'

As if to underline the point, Georg's mobile rang. He excused himself and left the table.

'May I suggest something?' Ma spoke into the silence.

'Of course, Ma, go ahead,' said Maia.

'Given that Georg told us last night that Mary currently lives in New Zealand, I made some enquiries this morning to see how far it was to travel between Sydney and Auckland. Because—'

'CeCe is in Australia,' Maia finished for her. 'I thought about that last night too.'

'It is a three-hour flight from Sydney to Auckland,' Ma continued. 'If CeCe and her friend Chrissie left a day earlier than they are planning to, maybe they could take a detour to New Zealand to see if this Mary is who Georg thinks she is.'

'That's a great idea, Ma,' Ally said. 'I wonder if CeCe would do it. I know she hates flying.'

'If we explain, I'm sure she would,' said Ma. 'It would be so special to unite the missing sister with the family for your father's memorial.'

'The question is, does this Mary even know about Pa Salt and our family?' Ally asked. 'It's not often these days that all us sisters are gathered together,' she mused. 'It seems to me like the perfect moment – that is, if she *is* who Georg believes her to be. And if she's willing to meet us, of course. Now, I think the first thing to do is to contact CeCe, sooner rather than later, as it's already the evening in Australia.'

'What do we do about the rest of the sisters?' asked Maia. 'I mean, do we tell them?'

'Good point,' said Ally. 'We should email Star, Tiggy and Electra to let them know what's happening. Do you want to call CeCe, Maia, or shall I?'

'Why don't you do it, Ally? I think that, if it's okay with

everyone, I'll go and have a lie-down before lunch. I'm still feeling a bit queasy.'

'You poor darling,' said Ma, standing up. 'You definitely look a little green.'

'I'll come inside with you and make the call to CeCe,' said Ally. 'Let's just hope she isn't on one of her painting trips in the Outback with her grandfather. There's apparently no signal at all at his cabin.'

Claudia appeared on the terrace from the kitchen. 'I will start preparing lunch.' She turned to Georg who had walked back to the table. 'Would you like to stay?'

'No, thank you. I have some pressing matters to attend to and must leave immediately. What has been decided?' he asked Ma.

As Ally and Maia left the terrace, Ally saw that beads of sweat had appeared on Georg's forehead and he seemed distracted.

'We're contacting CeCe to see if she will go. Georg, you are convinced that this is her?' Ma asked.

'I have been convinced by others that would know, yes,' he replied. 'Now, I would have liked to chat further, but I must leave you.'

'I'm sure the girls can deal with this, Georg. They are grown women now, and very capable.' She put a reassuring hand on his arm. 'Try to relax. You seem very tense.'

'I will try, Marina, I will try,' he agreed with a sigh.

Ally found CeCe's Australian mobile number in her address book and picked up the receiver in the hallway to dial it.

'Come on, come on . . .' she whispered under her breath as

the line rang five or six times. She knew it was pointless leaving CeCe a message as she rarely listened to them.

'Damn,' she muttered as CeCe's voicemail kicked in. Putting the receiver down, she was about to go upstairs to feed Bear when the telephone rang.

'*Allô?*'

'Hello, is that Ma?'

'CeCe! It's me, Ally. Thanks so much for calling back.'

'No problem, I saw it was the Atlantis number. Is everything okay?'

'Yes, everything's good here. Maia flew in yesterday and it's so great to see her. When exactly is your flight to London, CeCe?'

'We leave the Alice the day after tomorrow to head for Sydney. I think I told you we're stopping over in London first for a few days, to sort out selling my apartment and to see Star. I'm dreading the flight, as usual.'

'I know, but listen, CeCe, Georg has brought some news. Don't worry, it isn't bad, but it's big news – or at least, it might be.'

'What is it?'

'He's had some information about . . . our missing sister. He thinks that she might be living in New Zealand.'

'You mean, the famous seventh sister? Wow!' CeCe breathed. 'That *is* news. How did Georg find her?'

'I'm not sure. You know how cagey he is. So—'

'You're going to ask me if I can just pop over to New Zealand to meet her, aren't you?' said CeCe.

'Full marks, Sherlock.' Ally smiled into the receiver. 'I know it would make your journey a little longer, but you're by far the closest to her. It would be so wonderful to have her with all of us when we lay Pa's wreath.'

'It would, yeah, but we don't know anything about this person. Does she know anything about us?'

'We're not sure. Georg says he only has a name and address. Oh! And a picture of a ring that proves it's her.'

'So what's the address? I mean, New Zealand's a big country.'

'I haven't got it on me, but I can get Georg to speak to you. Georg?' Ally beckoned him over as he emerged from the kitchen on his way to the front door. 'It's CeCe on the phone. She wants to know whereabouts in New Zealand Mary lives.'

'Mary? Is that her name?' said CeCe.

'Apparently. I'll pass you over to Georg.' Ally listened in as Georg read out the address.

'Thank you, CeCe,' said Georg. 'All costs will be covered by the trust. Giselle, my secretary, will book the flights. Now, I'm going to pass you back to your sister, as I must leave.' As Georg handed the receiver to Ally, he added, 'You have my office number, contact Giselle if you need anything. For now, adieu.'

'Okay. Hi, CeCe,' Ally said, giving Georg a small wave as he walked out of the front door. 'Do you know where in New Zealand that is?'

'Hold on. I'll ask Chrissie.'

There was a muffled discussion before CeCe came back to the phone.

'Chrissie says it's way down on the South Island. She thinks we should be able to fly to Queenstown from Sydney, which would make everything a lot easier than going to Auckland. We'll look into it.'

'Great. So, are you up for it?' Ally asked.

'You know me, I love a bit of travel and adventure, even when it involves planes. I've never been to New Zealand, so it'll be fun to get a glimpse of it.'

'Brilliant! Thanks, CeCe. If it's easier, email me the details

and I'll call Georg's secretary about booking the flights. I'll fax a picture of the ring to you too.'

'Okay. Does Star know about this?'

'No, and nor do Electra or Tiggy. I'm going to email them all now.'

'Actually, Star's calling me in a bit to talk about meeting up in London, so I can fill her in. This is really exciting, isn't it?'

'It will be if it's actually *her*. Bye for now, CeCe. Keep in touch.'

'Bye, Ally, speak soon!'

3

CeCe
The Gibbston Valley

'Cee, you're holding the map upside down!' Chrissie said as she glanced over to the passenger seat.

'I am not . . . oh, maybe I am.' CeCe frowned. 'The words look the same to me either way, and as for the road squiggles . . . Jesus, when did we last see a signpost?'

'A while back. Wow, isn't this scenery spectacular?' Chrissie breathed as she pulled the hire car onto a verge and peered out at the majestic mountains that unfolded under a ponderous cloudy sky. She reached to turn up the heating as raindrops began to splash onto the windscreen.

'Yup, I'm completely lost.' CeCe handed the map to Chrissie and looked in front and behind her at the empty road. 'It feels like ages since we left Queenstown. We should have stocked up on supplies when we were there, but I thought there would be other places along the way.'

'Right, according to the directions we printed off, we should come to a sign for The Vinery very soon. I guess we just have to keep going and hopefully find someone who can point us to it.' Chrissie tucked a lock of black curly hair back

from her face and gave CeCe a weary smile. Their journey had involved stopovers in Melbourne and Christchurch, and they were both hungry and tired.

'There's hardly been a car for miles,' CeCe shrugged.

'Come on, Cee. Where's your spirit of adventure gone?'

'I dunno. Maybe I've gone soft in my old age and prefer home to sitting in a car completely lost, whilst it pisses down with rain. I'm actually cold!'

'It's coming into winter here. There'll be snow on those mountaintops before much longer. You're too used to the climate in the Alice, that's the problem,' said Chrissie as she put the car in gear and they set off once more. The windscreen wipers were working at full tilt, the downpour now rendering the mountains around them a washed-out blur.

'Yeah, I'm definitely a sunshine girl, and always have been. Can I borrow your hoody, Chrissie?'

'Sure. I did tell you, though, it was much colder here. Good job I packed a spare one for you, wasn't it?'

CeCe reached over into the back seat and opened one of the rucksacks. 'Thanks, Chrissie, I don't know what I'd do without you.'

'To be honest, nor do I.'

CeCe reached for Chrissie's hand and squeezed it. 'Sorry I'm so useless.'

'You're not useless, Cee, just not very . . . practical. Then again, I am, but I'm not as creative as you, so we make a good team, don't we?'

'We do.'

As Chrissie drove, CeCe felt comforted by her presence. The past few months had been the happiest of her life. Between spending time with Chrissie and going off on painting jaunts into the Outback with Francis, her grandfather, her life – and her heart – had never been so full. After the

trauma of losing her close bond with Star, she'd thought she could never be happy again, but between them, Chrissie and Francis had filled the bit of her that had been missing; she had found a family where she fitted in, however unconventional it was.

'Look! There's a sign.' She pointed through the driving rain. 'Pull over and see what it says.'

'I can see it from here and it's saying left to The Vinery – woohoo! We made it!' Chrissie cheered. 'By the way,' she said as she steered the car down a narrow bumpy track, 'have you told your sisters yet that I'm coming with you to Atlantis?'

'The ones I've spoken to, yup, of course I have.'

'Do you think they'll be shocked . . . about us?'

'Pa brought us up to accept everyone, whatever their colour or orientation. Claudia, our housekeeper, might raise an eyebrow, but that's only because she's from the older generation and very traditional.'

'And what about you, Cee? Are *you* comfortable about us in front of your family?'

'You know I am. Why are you suddenly being so insecure?'

'Only because . . . even though you've told me all about your sisters and Atlantis, they didn't feel . . . *real*. But in just over a week, we'll actually *be* there. And I'm scared. Especially of meeting Star. I mean, you two were a team before I came along.'

'Before her boyfriend Mouse came along, you mean? Star was the one who wanted to get away from me, remember?'

'I know, but she still calls you every week, and I know you guys text all the time, and—'

'Chrissie! Star's my sister. And you, well, you're . . .'

'Yes?'

'You're my "other half". It's different, completely different, and I really hope there's room for both of you.'

'Of course there is, but it's a big deal, you know, "coming out".'

'Grrr, I hate that phrase.' CeCe shuddered. 'I'm just me, the same as I always have been. I hate being put in a box with a label. Look! There's another sign for The Vinery. Turn right just there.'

They set off down another narrow track. In the distance, CeCe could just make out row upon row of what looked like stripped, skeletal vines.

'Doesn't seem like this place is very successful. In the south of France at this time of year, the vines are covered in leaves and grapes.'

'Cee, you're forgetting the seasons are the other way round in this part of the world, like in Oz. I'd reckon the vines are harvested in the summer, so probably somewhere between February and April, which is why they look bare now. Okay, there's another signpost. "To Shop", "To Deliveries" and "To Reception". We'll head for reception, shall we?'

'Whatever you say, boss,' said CeCe, noticing the rain had now stopped and the sun was beginning to peep through the clouds. 'This weather's just like England,' she murmured. 'One minute rain, the next minute sun.'

'Maybe that's why so many English live here, although your grandfather was saying yesterday that the biggest group of migrants here is the Scots, closely followed by the Irish.'

'Setting off to the other side of the world to make their fortune. It's sort of what I did. Look, there's another sign to reception. Wow, what a lovely old stone house that is. It looks so cosy, set in its valley, with mountains shielding it on every side. It's a bit like our home in Geneva, without the lake,' CeCe commented as Chrissie drew the car to a halt.

The two-storey farmhouse was nestled in a hillside just above the vineyard, which extended down in terraces into the

valley. Its walls were fashioned from sturdy grey rock, ruggedly cut and intricately laid together. The large windows reflected the burgeoning blue light of the sky, and a covered veranda hugged the house on all sides, with planters of cheerful red begonias hanging from the railings. CeCe could tell that the main house had been added to over the years, as the stone walls were different shades of grey, aged by the weather.

'The reception's over there,' Chrissie said, breaking into her thoughts as she pointed to a door on the left of the farmhouse. 'Maybe there'll be someone who can help us find Mary. Have you got that pic of the ring Ally faxed you?'

'I stuffed it in my rucksack before we left.' CeCe climbed out and grabbed it from the back seat. She unzipped the front pocket and pulled a couple of sheets of paper out of it.

'Honestly, Cee, they're all crumpled,' said Chrissie in dismay.

'That doesn't matter, does it? We can still see what the ring looks like.'

'Yeah, but it doesn't appear very professional. I mean, going to knock on the door of a complete stranger to tell her or someone in her family you believe she's your missing sister . . . She might think that you're nuts. I would,' Chrissie pointed out.

'Well, all we can do is ask. Wow, I suddenly feel nervous. You're right, they might think I'm crazy.'

'At least you've got that photo of your sisters and your father. You all look normal in that.'

'Yeah, but we don't look like sisters, do we?' CeCe said as Chrissie closed the car doors and locked them. 'Right, let's go before I chicken out.'

The reception – a small pine-clad showroom tacked onto the side of the main house – was deserted. CeCe rang the bell, as requested by the notice on the desk.

'Look at all these wines,' Chrissie said as she wandered round the showroom. 'Some of them have won awards. This is a pretty serious place. Maybe we should ask to try some.'

'It's only lunchtime and you go to sleep if you daytime drink. Besides, you're driving . . .'

'Hello, can I help you?' A tall young woman with blonde hair and bright blue eyes appeared from a door to the side of the showroom. CeCe thought how naturally pretty she was.

'Yes, I was wondering if we could speak to, um, Mary McDougal?' she said.

'That's me!' said the woman. 'I'm Mary McDougal. How can I help you?'

'Oh, er . . .'

'Well, I'm Chrissie and this is CeCe,' said Chrissie, taking over from a tongue-tied CeCe, 'and the situation is that CeCe's dad – who's dead, by the way – has a lawyer who has been hunting for someone who CeCe and her family have called the "missing sister" for years. Recently, the lawyer got some information that said the missing sister might be a woman called Mary McDougal, who lives at this address. Sorry, I know it all sounds a bit weird, but . . .'

'The thing is, Mary,' said CeCe, who by now had gathered her wits, 'Pa Salt – our father – adopted six of us girls as babies, and he used to speak about the "missing sister" – the one he couldn't find. We're all named after the Pleiades star cluster, and the youngest, Merope, has always been missing. She's technically the seventh sister, just like in all the Seven Sisters legends, right?'

As the woman stared blankly back at her, CeCe continued hastily.

'Actually, you probably don't know of them. It's just that we've been brought up with the myths, though most people, unless they're interested in stars and Greek legends, have

never heard of the Seven Sisters.' CeCe realised she was rambling, so she shut her mouth before she could say more.

'Oh, I've heard of the Seven Sisters all right,' Mary smiled. 'My mother – who's also called Mary – read Classics at uni. She's always quoting Plato and the like.'

'Your mother's called Mary too?' CeCe stared at her.

'Yes, Mary McDougal, the same as me. My name's Mary-Kate officially, though everyone calls me MK. Er . . . do you have any other information about this missing sister?'

'Yes, just one thing. There's this picture of a ring,' said Chrissie. She placed the crumpled image in front of Mary-Kate on the slim counter that separated them. 'It's a ring with emeralds in a star shape with seven points and a diamond in the centre. Apparently, this Mary got it from, um, somebody, and it proves that it's her, if you know what I mean. Sadly, that's the only physical clue we have.'

Mary-Kate glanced at the picture, her brow furrowing slightly.

'It probably means nothing to you, and we'd better leave,' CeCe mumbled, her embarrassment growing by the second. She grabbed the piece of paper. 'So sorry for bothering you and—'

'Hold on! Can I take another look?'

CeCe stared at her in surprise. 'You recognise it?'

'I think I might do, yes.'

CeCe's stomach turned over. She looked at Chrissie, wishing she could reach for her hand and have her own comfortably squeezed, but she wasn't at *that* stage in public yet. She waited as the young woman studied the picture more closely.

'I couldn't say for sure, but it looks a lot like Mum's ring,' said Mary-Kate. 'Or actually – if it is the same one – it's mine now, as she gave it to me on my twenty-first.'

'Really?' CeCe gasped.

'Yeah, she's had it for as long as I can remember. It wasn't something she wore every day, but sometimes on special occasions, she'd take it out of her jewellery box and put it on. I always thought it was pretty. It's very small, you see, and she could only fit it on her little finger, which didn't look right, or her fourth finger, which already had an engagement and wedding ring on it. But as I'm not about to get engaged or married, it doesn't matter which finger I wear it on,' she added with a grin.

'So does that mean you've got it now?' CeCe said quickly. 'Could we take a look at it?'

'Actually, before she left on her trip, Mum asked me if she could take it with her, as I so rarely wear it anyway, though maybe she decided not to . . . Listen, why don't you come upstairs to the house?'

At that moment, a tall, well-muscled man wearing an Akubra hat put his head around the door.

'Hi, Doug,' said Mary-Kate. 'All okay?'

'Yeah, just popping in to get some more water bottles for the gang.' Doug indicated the group of burly men standing outside.

'Hi,' he said to CeCe and Chrissie as he crossed to a fridge and pulled out a tray of water bottles. 'Are youse tourists?'

'Yeah, sort of. It's beaut round here,' said Chrissie, recognising the man's Aussie accent.

'It is, yeah.'

'I'm just going to pop upstairs with our visitors,' said Mary-Kate. 'They think I may have some family connection to them.'

'Really?' Doug stared at CeCe and Chrissie and frowned. 'Well, me and the boys will be having our tucker just out there, if ya need anything.'

Doug indicated a round wooden table where his men were gathering and sitting down.

'Thanks, Doug,' said Mary-Kate.

He nodded, gave CeCe and Chrissie a piercing look, then left.

'Blimey, you wouldn't mess with them, would you?' breathed CeCe, staring at the group outside.

'No,' Mary-Kate said with a grin. 'Don't mind Doug, he's our manager – it's just that since Mum and my brother Jack left, he's gone all protective, y'know? The boys are great actually. I had a meal with them last night. Now, come through.'

'Seriously, we can wait outside if you want,' Chrissie said.

'It's fine, although I'll admit I'm finding this all a bit weird. Anyway, as you've just seen, I'm well protected.'

'Thanks,' said CeCe, as Mary-Kate pulled up part of the counter to let them in. She led them up some steep wooden steps and along a hallway into an airy beamed sitting room, which faced the valley and mountains beyond on one side, and was dominated by a huge stone fireplace on the other.

'Please, sit down and I'll go take a look for the ring.'

'Thank you for trusting us,' CeCe said as Mary-Kate crossed the room towards a door.

'No worries. I'll tell my mate Fletch to come in and keep you company,' she replied.

After Mary-Kate left and the two of them sat down on the old but comfortable sofa in front of the fireplace, Chrissie squeezed CeCe's hand. 'You okay?'

'Yup. What a sweet girl she is. I'm not sure I would have let two strangers into my house after that story.'

'No, but people round these parts are probably a lot more trusting than they are in cities. Besides, as she says, she has a team of minders just outside.'

'She reminds me of Star, with her blonde colouring and big blue eyes.'

'I know what you mean from the pictures you've shown me, but remember, none of you sisters are related by blood, so the chances are high that Mary-Kate isn't blood-related to any of you either,' Chrissie pointed out.

The door opened and a tall, lanky man in his early twenties entered. His long, light brown hair hung down from underneath a woollen beanie, and his ears sported several silver piercings.

'Hi there, I'm Fletch, good to meet you.'

The girls introduced themselves as Fletch sat down in an armchair across from them.

'So, MK's sent me in to make sure you guys won't hold her at gunpoint over her jewellery,' he grinned. 'What's the story?'

CeCe left it all to Chrissie to explain, because she did stuff like that so much better.

'I know it sounds strange,' Chrissie finished, 'but CeCe comes from a weird family. I mean, *they're* not weird, but the fact their father adopted them from all over the world *is*.'

'D'ya know why he adopted all of you? I mean, specifically?' asked Fletch.

'Not a clue,' said CeCe. 'I guess it was probably random, like, on his travels. We happened to be there, and he swept us up and took us home with him.'

'I see. I mean, I don't see, but . . .'

At that moment, Mary-Kate arrived back in the sitting room.

'I've looked through my jewellery box and Mum's, but the ring isn't there. She must have taken it with her after all.'

'How long is she away for?' asked CeCe.

'Well, what she said when she left was, "for as long as I want to be".' Mary-Kate shrugged. 'My dad died recently, and she decided she wanted to take a world tour and visit all the

friends she hasn't seen for years, whilst she was still young enough to do it.'

'I'm sorry your dad died. As we said, so did mine recently,' said CeCe.

'Thanks,' said Mary-Kate. 'It's been really tough, y'know? It was only a few months ago.'

'Must have been a shock for your mum too,' said Chrissie.

'Oh, it was. Even though Dad was actually seventy-three, we never thought of him as old. Mum's quite a bit younger – she has the big Six-O coming up next year. But you'd never know how old she was either – she looks so youthful. See, there's a photo of her over there, taken last year with me, my brother Jack and my dad. Dad always liked to say that Mum looked like an actress called Grace Kelly.'

When Mary-Kate brought it over, both girls stared at the photo. If young Mary-Kate was pretty, Mary senior was still displaying the signs of a true beauty, despite being in her late fifties.

'Wow! I'd take her for not much older than forty,' whistled Chrissie.

'Me too,' said CeCe. 'She's . . . well, she's stunning.'

'She is, but more importantly, she's a great human being. Everyone loves my mum,' Mary-Kate said with a smile.

'I'll second that,' said Fletch. 'She's just one of those special people; very warm and welcoming, y'know?'

'Yeah, our adoptive mum, Ma, is like that – she just makes all of us feel good about ourselves,' said CeCe as she studied the other pictures arranged on the mantelpiece. One was a black and white shot of what looked like a younger Mary senior, dressed in a dark academic robe and cap, with a bright smile on her face. In the background were stone columns flanking the entrance of a grand building.

'So that's your mum too?' CeCe pointed to the photo.

'Yeah, that was her graduation from Trinity College in Dublin,' Mary-Kate nodded.

'She's Irish?'

'Yup, she is.'

'So, you really don't know how long she'll be abroad for?' Chrissie asked.

'No, as I said, the trip is open-ended; Mum said that not having a deadline on when she had to return was part of the treat. Although she did plan out her first few weeks.'

'Sorry to hassle you, but we'd love to meet up with her and ask her about that ring. Do you know where your mum is now?' said CeCe.

'Her schedule's stuck to the fridge; I'll go take a look, but I'm pretty sure she's still on Norfolk Island,' Mary-Kate said as she left the room.

'Norfolk?' frowned CeCe. 'Isn't that a county in England?'

'It is,' said Fletch, 'but it's also a tiny island that sits in the South Pacific between Australia and New Zealand. It's a beaut place, and when MK's mum's oldest friend Bridget came here to visit a couple of years back, they took a trip there together. Her friend liked it so much, she decided to up sticks from London and retire there.'

'Yup, Mum's still on the island, according to her fridge schedule,' Mary-Kate said as she reappeared.

'When does she leave? And how do we get there?' asked CeCe.

'In a couple of days' time, but the island's only a short plane ride from Auckland. I know that the planes don't fly every day, mind. We'd have to find out when they do,' warned Mary-Kate.

'Shit!' CeCe murmured under her breath. She glanced at Chrissie. 'We're meant to be flying out to London late tomorrow night. Have we got time?'

'We'll have to make time, won't we?' Chrissie shrugged. 'I mean, she's just down the road, compared to coming all this way back from Europe. And if the missing sister can be identified by this ring, then . . .'

'I'll check flights to Norfolk Island, and Queenstown to Auckland, 'cos it'd be faster to fly than drive,' said Fletch, standing up and moving to a long wooden dining table covered in papers, magazines and an old-fashioned fat-bottomed computer. 'It might take some time because the internet. around here is dodgy, to put it mildly.' He tapped on the keyboard. 'Yup, no connection at the moment,' he sighed.

'I saw your brother in that photo. Is he in New Zealand at the moment?' CeCe asked Mary-Kate.

'He is normally, but he just went off to the south of France to learn more about French wine-making.'

'So he's gonna take over the vineyard from your dad?' Chrissie clarified.

'Yup. Hey, are you guys hungry? It's way past lunchtime.'

'Starving,' both Chrissie and CeCe answered at the same time.

After the four of them had put together some bread, local cheese and cold meats, they cleared space on the dining table and sat down to eat.

'So where do you guys actually live?' Fletch asked.

'In the Alice,' said CeCe. 'But my family home is called Atlantis, which is on the shores of Lake Geneva in Switzerland.'

'Atlantis, the mythical home of Atlas, father of the Seven Sisters,' smiled Mary-Kate. 'Your dad really was into his Greek legends.'

'He was, yeah. We have this big telescope that still stands in an observatory at the top of the house. By the time we could talk, we knew all the names of the stars in and around

the Orion and Taurus constellations by heart,' said CeCe. 'I wasn't interested, to be honest, until I came to the Alice and realised that the Seven Sisters are goddesses in Aboriginal mythology. It made me wonder how there could be all these legends about them literally everywhere. Like, in Mayan culture, Greek, Japanese . . . these sisters are famous all over the world.'

'The Maori have stories about the sisters too,' Mary-Kate added. 'They're called the daughters of Matariki here. They each have special skills and gifts that they bring to the people.'

'So how did each culture know about the other back then?' Chrissie questioned. 'I mean, there was no internet or even a postal service or telephone, so how can all the legends be so similar without there being any communication between people?'

'You really need to meet my mum,' chuckled Mary-Kate. 'She doesn't half ramble on about subjects like that. She's a total brainbox – not like me, I'm afraid. I'm more into my music than philosophy.'

'You look like your mum, though,' said Chrissie.

'Yeah, a lot of people say that, but actually, I'm adopted.'

CeCe shot Chrissie a look. 'Wow,' she said. 'Like me and my sisters. Do you know exactly where you were adopted from? And who your birth parents are?'

'I don't. Mum and Dad told me as soon as I was old enough to understand, but I've always felt that my mum is my mum, and my dad is . . . *was* my dad. End of.'

'Sorry to pry,' CeCe said quickly. 'It's just . . . it's just that if you *are* adopted, then . . .'

'Then you really might be the missing sister,' Chrissie finished for her.

'Look, I understand your family have been searching for this person for a while,' Mary-Kate said gently, 'but I've never

heard my mum mention anything about a "missing sister". All I know is that it was a closed adoption, and it happened here in NZ. I'm sure Mum will clear it all up if you get to see her.'

'Right.' Fletch stood up. 'I'm gonna try getting online again, so you guys have some idea of whether you can travel to Norfolk Island in the next twenty-four hours.' He moved along the table to sit in front of the computer.

'Does your mum have a mobile?' Chrissie asked.

'She does,' said Mary-Kate, 'but if you're about to ask me whether we can contact her on it, there's only the tiniest chance that she'll have a signal on Norfolk Island. Part of the beauty of living there is the fact they're fifty years behind everywhere else, especially in the modern technology department.'

'Okay, Houston, we have lift-off!' Fletch exclaimed. 'There's a seven a.m. flight from Queenstown to Auckland tomorrow, landing just before nine. The flight for Norfolk Island leaves at ten a.m. and lands just shy of a couple of hours later. What time does your onward flight leave Sydney tomorrow night?'

'Around eleven p.m.,' said Chrissie. 'Are there any flights to Sydney leaving Norfolk Island late afternoon?'

'I'll take a look,' said Fletch, going back to his computer screen.

'Even if we can get a flight out at the right time, it would only give us a few hours on Norfolk Island,' said CeCe.

'It's a tiny island, though, eh?' Fletch commented.

'Mary-Kate, do you think you could just try your mum's mobile?' Chrissie asked. 'I mean, to go all that way and then find she isn't there would be a real pain.'

'I can try, for sure. And I can call Bridget, the friend she's staying with, too. Mum left her number on the fridge – I'll go and get it, then call both of them.'

'We're in luck!' said Fletch. 'There's a flight at five p.m.

from the island into Sydney. If you land in the morning at ten forty Norfolk time, that should give you plenty of time to meet up with Mary-Kate's mum. Who, by the way, is always known as "Merry" – she was apparently called that when she was little because she never stopped giggling.'

'That's cute,' smiled Chrissie.

'Not a nickname I was ever given as a baby,' muttered CeCe under her breath. 'Me and Electra were the angry, shouty sisters.'

'I've just tried my mum and Bridget, but I only got their voicemails on the mobile and the landline,' Mary-Kate said as she appeared from the kitchen. 'I left messages saying you were trying to get in contact with Mum about the ring and that you're planning to visit tomorrow, so if they manage to listen to their answer services, they'll know you're coming.'

'Well?' Fletch peered at them over the computer screen. 'There are three seats left on the flights to Auckland and Norfolk Island, and only two back to Sydney. Are you gonna go or not?'

CeCe looked at Chrissie, who shrugged. 'Whilst we're here, we should at least try to get to see Mary-Kate's mum, Cee.'

'Yup, you're right, even if it is an early wake-up tomorrow. If I give you my credit card details, Fletch, can you book us on the flights? Sorry to ask, but I doubt we'll find an internet café anywhere locally.'

'You won't, and course I will, no hassle, eh?'

'Oh, and just one last thing: can you recommend anywhere that we can stay the night?' Chrissie said, always the practical one.

'Sure, right here in the annexe,' said Mary-Kate. 'We use the dorms for the workers, but I'm pretty sure there's one room spare just now. It's not fancy or anything – just bunk beds – but it's the nearest place to rest your heads.'

'Thanks a million,' said Chrissie. 'We'll get out of your hair now. I'd like to take a wander outside. The countryside around here is incredible.'

'Okay, I'll just show you to your dorms and . . .' Mary-Kate glanced at Fletch before saying, 'Mum left the freezer full, and I can defrost a chook casserole for dinner tonight. You guys want in? I'd love to hear more about your family and what the connection might be to me.'

'Yeah, it would be great if you turned out to be the missing sister. And that's so kind of you to invite us,' CeCe smiled. 'Thanks for being so hospitable.'

'It's the New Zealand way, eh?' shrugged Fletch. 'Share and share alike.'

'Thanks,' said Chrissie. 'See you guys later.'

Outside, the air felt cool and fresh, and the sky was now a deep azure blue. 'It's so different from Australia here – it reminds me of Switzerland with all these mountains, but it's wilder and more untamed,' CeCe commented as they walked side by side past the sweeping acres of vines. They found a narrow path that led up an undulating hillside, and as they walked, the vegetation became coarser and less civilised. CeCe brushed her fingers over the leaves of the shrubs they passed to release the bright green scents of nature.

She could hear the calls of unfamiliar birds from the trees, and a faint rush of water, so she pulled Chrissie off the path towards it. They navigated their way through brambles – still wet from the earlier downpour and now glistening in the sunshine – until they stood beside a fast-running crystal-clear stream, splashing across smooth grey rock. As they watched dragonflies skimming over the surface, CeCe turned to smile at Chrissie.

'I wish we could stay here for longer,' she said. 'It's beautiful, and so peaceful.'

'I'd love to come back one day and explore properly,' Chrissie agreed. 'So . . . what do you think about Mary-Kate not wanting to know about her birth parents? I mean, you defo had your doubts when you went in search of your own birth family.'

'That was different.' CeCe swatted a bug from her face, panting as they followed the stream uphill. 'Pa had just died, Star had gone all weird and distant . . . I needed something – or someone else of my own, y'know? Mary-Kate still has a loving mum and brother, so she probably hasn't felt the urge to shake things up.'

Chrissie nodded, then reached out to CeCe's arm to tug her back. 'Can we stop for a second? My leg's aching.'

They sat down on a patch of mossy grass to catch their breath, and Chrissie swung her legs onto CeCe's lap. In comfortable silence, they gazed out over the valley, the farmhouse below and the neatly ordered lines of the vine terraces the only sign of human habitation.

'So, have we found her?' CeCe asked eventually.

'You know what?' Chrissie replied. 'I think we might have done.'

Dinner with Mary-Kate and Fletch that night was very relaxed, and it was after midnight and two bottles of excellent house pinot noir when CeCe and Chrissie said their goodbyes and made their way outside to the annexe. As Mary-Kate had said, the room was basic but had everything they needed, including a shower and thick woollen blankets to ward off the creeping cold of night.

'Wow, in the Alice I'm normally throwing the sheets off me 'cos I'm dripping with sweat, and here I am huddled under

the covers,' chuckled CeCe. 'What do you think of Mary-Kate?'

'I think she's cool,' commented Chrissie. 'And if she did turn out to be your missing sister, it would be fun to have her around.'

'She said she was twenty-two, which would fit in perfectly with the rest of us. Electra, who's the youngest, is twenty-six. Or maybe we're just on a complete wild goose chase,' CeCe added sleepily. 'Sorry, but I'm about to drop off . . .'

Chrissie reached for her hand from the bunk opposite. 'Night night, honey, sleep tight. We've got an early morning call tomorrow, that's for sure.'

4

'Time to wake up, Cee. We're about to land and you need to fasten your seat belt.'

Chrissie's voice broke into CeCe's dreams and she opened her eyes to see Chrissie reaching for the seat belt to strap her in.

'Where are we?'

'About a thousand feet above Norfolk Island. Wow! It's tiny! Like one of those atolls you see in ads for the Maldives. Look down there; it's so green, and the water is such an amazing turquoise colour. I wonder if Merry or her friend Bridget got our messages?'

CeCe peered nervously out of her window. 'We'll find out when we land, I suppose. Mary-Kate said she left them both details of our flight time, so you never know, they might even be there to meet us. Oh my God, have you seen that? It looks like the runway's headed right out to sea! I don't think I can look.'

CeCe turned her head away as the plane's engines roared and it prepared to land.

'Phew! I'm glad that's over,' she said as the pilot put the brakes on hard and the plane skidded to a halt.

The two of them piled off the small aircraft with their rucksacks and headed for the tiny building that was Norfolk

Island's airport terminal. They passed by a small crowd of onlookers waiting behind a fence for passengers, then through customs control, where a beagle on a lead was sniffing around the new arrivals.

'It's a bit different to arriving on the Aussie mainland, isn't it?' CeCe commented. 'I reckon the Aussie border-force guys would prefer to have you stark naked before they let you through,' she giggled, as they emerged into a small arrivals area where the same handful of onlookers had moved inside to greet their visitors.

'Remember that I've never flown into Oz before, because this is the first time I've ever left the country.' Chrissie nudged her. 'Now, can you see a woman who looks like that photo we saw of Merry yesterday?'

Both of them scanned the group, most of whom had already collected their visitors and were walking away.

'Seems like they didn't get our messages,' Chrissie shrugged. 'Anyway, Mary-Kate said it was just a twenty-minute walk to Bridget's house from here. But which way?'

'If in doubt, go to the tourist information desk, which is right over there.' CeCe nodded to a young man sitting behind a desk piled with leaflets. The two of them walked over to it.

'Hi there, can I help you guys?'

'Yes, we're looking for a road called . . .' – Chrissie pulled a piece of paper out of her jean pocket – 'Headstone.'

'That's easy enough; it's at the end of the runway over there.' The man pointed into the distance. 'Just walk round the airport perimeter and turn left. That'll take you up to Headstone Road.'

'Thanks,' said CeCe.

'You guys looking for anywhere to stay? I can suggest a few ideas, eh?' the man encouraged them.

'No, we're going back to Sydney this arvo.'

44

'A flying visit f'sure, mate,' the man joked. 'Well, why don't you check in your rucksacks now so you don't have to carry them with you? Take your togs, though, in case you fancy a dip before you leave. There's a few ripper beaches around and about.'

'Thanks, we will.'

The man pointed them in the direction of the airline desk and to their surprise, they were able to check in to the flight for Sydney immediately.

'Wow, I love it here,' said CeCe as she dug into her rucksack for swimming costumes and towels. 'It's all so casual.'

'The beauty of small-island living,' said Chrissie as they set off. 'And it's so green – I love those trees,' she gestured to the tall firs that stood sentinel in rows ahead of them.

'They're called Norfolk pines,' said CeCe. 'Pa had some planted along the edge of our garden at Atlantis when I was younger.'

'I'm impressed, Cee, I didn't take you for a botanist.'

'You know I'm not, but a Norfolk pine was one of the first things that I ever drew when I was younger. It was terrible, of course, but Ma had it framed and I gave it to Pa for Christmas. I think it's still on the wall of his study to this day.'

'That's cool. So . . . what are we meant to say when we turn up on these guys' doorstep?' Chrissie asked.

'Same as we did with Mary-Kate, I suppose. After all this, I just hope they're in. I feel wrecked from an early wake-up, two flights and now two more to go later on!'

'I know, but it'll be worth it if we get to meet Merry and see that ring. Whatever happens, we should defo go for a dip in that amazing sea before we leave for the airport. That'll wake us up.'

A few minutes later, they saw a sign saying *Headstone Road*.

'What's the house number?'

'I can't see any numbers,' CeCe said as they passed the wooden bungalows, all sitting in immaculate gardens and surrounded by manicured hibiscus hedges studded with bright flowers.

'The house is called . . .' Chrissie studied the word on the note Mary-Kate had written. 'I've no idea how to pronounce this.'

'Well, don't ask me to try,' CeCe chuckled. 'They're all very house-proud round here, aren't they? It reminds me a bit of an English village, what with all the perfectly trimmed lawns.'

'Look! There it is.' Chrissie nudged her, pointing to a neatly painted sign saying *Síocháin*.

They stood in front of the cattle grid that marked the entrance to the property. The bungalow was pristine like all the others, and had a couple of large gnomes standing guard at either side of the grid.

'Those two are dressed in the colours of the Irish flag, and I think that house name might be Gaelic, so I reckon the occupants are too,' said Chrissie as they carefully crossed the cattle grid.

'Right' – CeCe lowered her voice as they walked up to the door – 'who's going to do the talking?'

'You begin, and I'll help you out if you're struggling,' Chrissie suggested.

'Here goes,' said CeCe before ringing the doorbell, which sang a little tune that sounded like an Irish jig. There was no reply. On the fourth press of the bell, Chrissie turned to her.

'How about taking a wander round the back? They might be out in the garden – it's a beaut day.'

'Worth a try,' CeCe shrugged, so they walked round the side of the bungalow to the back of the house, edged by banana palms. The terrace, table and chairs, all protected by a sun awning, were deserted.

'Damn!' CeCe said, feeling her heart sink. 'There's no one in.'

'Look!' Chrissie pointed to the bottom of the long garden, where a figure with a spade was digging in the earth. 'Let's go and ask him, shall we?'

'Hellooo!' Chrissie called as they drew closer, and eventually a man – who was broad-shouldered and probably in his mid-sixties – looked up and waved at them from what was clearly a vegetable patch. 'Maybe he's expecting us.'

'Or maybe he's just friendly. Didn't you notice that everyone in the passing cars waved at us too?' said CeCe.

'Hello, girls,' said the man, leaning on his spade as they approached him. 'What can I do for the two of youse?' he asked in a pronounced Australian accent.

'Uh, yeah, hi. Do you, um, live here? I mean, is this your house?' CeCe asked.

'It is, yeah. And you are?'

'I'm CeCe and this is my friend Chrissie. We're looking for a woman – in fact, two women: one called Bridget Dempsey and the other called Mary – or Merry – McDougal. Do you know either of them?'

'I most certainly do,' the man nodded. 'Especially Bridge. She's my missus.'

'Great! That's fantastic. Are they in?'

'I'm afraid not, girls. They've both buggered off to Sydney, leaving me all on my lonesome.'

'You're joking!' CeCe muttered to Chrissie. 'We could've flown straight there. Merry's daughter, Mary-Kate, said she wasn't flying out until tomorrow.'

'She's right,' said the man. 'Merry was staying here, but she suddenly changed her mind and suggested that she and Bridge get the afternoon flight to Sydney, so they could spend what they called a "girls' night" together in the big city and do some shopping.'

'Shit,' CeCe said. 'That's a shame, because we've come a long way to see her and we're off to Sydney ourselves tonight. Do you happen to know how long Merry is in Sydney for?'

'I think she said she was flying out of Oz tonight. I'm due to pick up Bridge on the incoming flight this afternoon.'

'That must be the plane we're flying *out* on,' said Chrissie, rolling her eyes at CeCe in despair.

'Can I help you in any way?' the man said, sweeping off his Akubra hat and dabbing his sweating forehead with a handkerchief.

'Thanks, but it's Merry we came to speak to,' said CeCe.

'Well, why don't we step out of this glaring sun and go sit on the terrace? We can crack a couple of tinnies and you can explain why you need to see Merry. I'm Tony, by the way,' he said as they followed him back up the garden and under the cool shade of the awning. 'I'll just go grab those beers, and then we'll have a chat.'

'He seems like a good guy,' commented Chrissie as they sat down.

'Yeah, but he's not the person we want to speak to,' CeCe sighed.

'There y'go.' Tony returned and put the ice-cold beers down in front of them. They each took a grateful swig. 'So, what's the story?'

CeCe did her best to explain, with Chrissie filling in details when needed.

'Now that's a tall tale,' he chuckled, 'although I still don't fully get the connection between your folks and Merry.'

'Nor do I, to be honest, and I get the feeling we're probably barking up the wrong tree, but we thought we'd try anyway,' CeCe said, feeling deflated and exhausted.

'Mary-Kate did leave messages for her mum saying we

were coming. And one for Bridget. Didn't they get them?' said Chrissie.

'I dunno, 'cos I was out all day yesterday fixing up a bathroom for a mate of mine. To be honest, I don't know much about Merry, love. I met Bridge two years ago when she asked me to build this for her.' He indicated the bungalow. 'My parents brought me across from Brisbane when I was a kid, and I'm a builder by trade. My first wife died some years past, and when Bridge moved here, she was single too. Never thought I'd find another woman at my age, but we clicked right from the start. We got hitched six months ago,' he beamed.

'So you haven't known Merry long?'

'No, I only met her for the first time at our wedding.'

'Is your wife Irish by any chance?' continued Chrissie doggedly.

'Ya guessed then,' Tony nodded. 'She is, and proud of her heritage too.'

'We were told that Merry is originally Irish as well,' said CeCe.

'All I know is that they were at school and then uni in Dublin together. They lost contact for a long time – it happens, doesn't it, when people move away after uni? But now they're thick as thieves again. Can I get you guys a sarnie? My belly's rumbling f'sure.'

'If it's no trouble, that would be fantastic,' CeCe put in before Chrissie could politely decline. Her belly was rumbling too. 'We can come in and help you,' she added.

They followed Tony into a neat kitchen, which he proudly said he'd built himself.

'Never thought I'd get ta live in it, mind,' he said as he pulled cheese and ham out of the fridge. 'We're a bit low on supplies – everything has to be brought in by boat or plane, y'see. A new delivery isn't until tomorrow.'

'It must be amazing living here,' said Chrissie as she buttered the bread.

'For the main part, yeah,' Tony agreed. 'But like Robinson Crusoe, island living has its drawbacks. There's not much here for the young 'uns and a lot o' them leave the island to go to uni or find work. The internet is bloody terrible and unless you've got your own business like me, tourism's the only main industry. It's becoming an island of old folks, though there are changes coming to improve things, get some new blood. It's a beaut place to bring up kids. Everyone knows everyone here and there's a real sense of community. It's dead friendly and there's very little crime. Right, shall we take our tucker outside, eh?'

The girls followed Tony back out onto the terrace and launched into their sandwiches.

'Tony?'

'Yeah, CeCe?'

'I just wondered if, while she was here, you'd seen Merry wearing an emerald ring?'

Tony burst into a deep throaty chuckle.

'Can't say I look at stuff like that. Bridge says I'd never even notice if she came in dressed as Santa Claus, and she's probably right. Although . . . hang on a minute . . .' He put his fingers to his short beard and stroked it. 'Come ta think of it, I do remember a couple of nights ago, Bridge and Merry comparing rings. The one I bought for Bridge as an engagement ring had a green stone, of course . . . her being Irish an' all.'

'And . . . ?' CeCe leant forward.

'Merry was wearing an emerald ring too – they put their fingers together and shared one of those looks girls share, y'know?'

'So, she was actually wearing an emerald ring?'

'Yeah, she was. They were laughing, because Bridge said her emerald was bigger than Merry's.'

'Right.' CeCe and Chrissie exchanged a glance. 'That's encouraging,' CeCe nodded. 'Maybe we're on the right path after all. Do you happen to know where she's going after Sydney?'

'Yeah, she's headed to Canada – Toronto, I think she said, but I can check with Bridge.'

Chrissie looked at her watch. 'Thanks for your help and the sarnie, Tony. We're gonna get in a swim before we go to the airport.'

'Well, why don't we get the plates cleaned up – I don't want ta leave any mess around the place for Bridge to complain about – then you can jump in my pick-up and we'll do a quick tour of the island and finish off with a swim?'

'Wow! We'd love to,' smiled CeCe.

After a whistle-stop tour of the island, which could be reached end to end within twenty minutes, Tony drove them down a narrow road.

'Check out those.' Tony pointed at the row of ancient trees which towered above them.

'They look prehistoric. What are they?' asked CeCe.

'They're Moreton Bay fig trees; some of them are over a hundred years old,' Tony told her as the road led them past the airport runway and wound downwards, opening out at a small bridge and a cluster of stone buildings. They arrived in front of an almost deserted beach, where gentle waves lapped at the shore. In the distance a line of foaming white breakers indicated a reef. Tony led them to the hut that provided changing facilities and they emerged in their swimwear with their towels around their waists.

'Race ya!' called Tony, beginning to run across the warm

sand towards the waves. 'Last one in's a sissy!' he said as he splashed up to his waist then dived in. A few metres from the water's edge, CeCe helped Chrissie take off her prosthetic leg. Chrissie wrapped it up in a towel and placed it a safe distance from the waves.

'It always freaks me out that someone will come and steal it,' said Chrissie as CeCe helped her move towards the sea.

'Even I can't imagine anyone being mean enough to do that,' said CeCe. 'Right, off we go. Try not to leave me behind,' she called as Chrissie immediately dived in. Even though she only had one leg to propel her forwards, being an ex-champion swimmer, she always left CeCe playing catch-up within a few strokes.

'Isn't it fantastic?' Tony shouted from where he was treading water a few metres away.

'It sure is,' said Chrissie, who was floating on her back, her face in the sun. 'Wow, I hadn't realised how much I miss the sea, now that we live in the Alice,' she said as she turned to head out further.

'Chrissie, please don't go out too far!' she shouted. 'I don't want you getting into trouble, 'cos I'm not strong enough to save you.'

As usual, Chrissie took no notice of her, and eventually, CeCe swam back to shore and lay down on the sand to dry off.

'Your mate's quite a swimmer, isn't she?' said Tony, who had also come out of the water and sat down next to her. 'What happened to her leg?'

CeCe told him how Chrissie had lost her leg when she was fifteen, due to complications with meningitis, which had led to septicaemia.

'Before that,' CeCe sighed, 'she was the best swimmer in all

of Western Australia. She was about to try out for the Olympic team.'

'Life's a bitch sometimes, isn't it? It's good ta see she's still at it, though, eh?'

'Yeah, but I'm shit-scared she's gonna disappear under those waves and never come up again.'

'I doubt it, look at her go,' smiled Tony. 'Well, we should be off if ya need ta catch that plane.'

CeCe stood up and waved her arms above her head to summon Chrissie back to shore. Once they were dressed, Tony drove them the few minutes to the airport.

'If we're lucky, Bridge might come through before you're called for your flight,' he said as he parked his truck in front of the terminal. They heard the thrum of a plane coming in to land.

'How do you fancy a trip here when we're back from Europe, Chrissie?' said CeCe as they followed Tony to the terminal building. 'I love this island.'

'Okay, but let's do Europe first, eh, Cee? I can't tell you how stoked I am to see it.'

'Oh, it's very boring compared to this. Chock-full of people and old monuments.'

'Hey, I'll see it for myself and then decide what I think,' Chrissie smiled. 'Look, the plane has landed.'

'We'll go to the veranda in the viewing area, eh?' said Tony. 'At least ya might get ta say hello.'

'Okay, great,' said CeCe. The doors of the tiny plane had just opened and the first passengers were disembarking.

'Look, there she is! Bridge, I'm over here!' he shouted at a loudly dressed, buxom woman with red hair, who was clutching a number of shopping bags as she descended the steps from the plane. Tony received a smile and a wave back. 'Come on, let's go say hi.'

CeCe's heart thumped in her chest as the woman approached the fence that separated the arriving passengers yet to clear customs from people waiting to greet them. Bridget came to a halt in front of them and perched her huge sunglasses on top of her head.

'How are ya, doll? Missed ya.' He kissed her over the fence. 'Listen, I've had two young ladies visit me whilst you were away. They came because they thought Merry was still on the island. Bridge, this is CeCe and Chrissie.'

Perhaps it's just me being oversensitive, CeCe thought, *but her whole expression has changed since Tony said who we are, and she doesn't look happy.*

'Hello there,' Bridget said as she forced a smile.

'They wanted ta know whether Merry was wearing an emerald ring when she was staying with us?' Tony continued. 'I said she was. Was I right for a change?'

'I can't be remembering details like that, love,' she said, lowering her sunglasses back down over her eyes.

'I thought I heard the two of youse chatting about having similar rings?'

'I think you'd been dreaming or had a skinful that night, Tony, 'cos I'm not remembering any talk of rings.'

'But—'

'Now, I'd better be getting myself through customs. They'll probably stop me, what with all the shopping I've done in Sydney. 'Twas nice to meet the two of you,' Bridget said. 'I'll see you on the other side,' she said pointedly to Tony.

As she disappeared inside the terminal, Tony turned to the girls.

'We'd better be getting ourselves inside too, because they'll be calling f'youse ta board any second.'

The flight call was already up on the display board and Sydney passengers were beginning to queue for security.

'Can we swap mobile numbers?' CeCe asked him as she produced her phone. They did so as they drew nearer to security.

'It really was lovely to meet you and to see a bit of Norfolk Island,' said CeCe. 'And thank you so much for your hospitality.'

'It was fun ta meet you two. And if you do decide to come back, just bowl round to our place for a visit, eh?' he said.

'Bye, Tony, and thank you again!'

'Oh! How cute is this?!' Chrissie said as they reached security and she pulled out a tray that still had a sticky label on it telling the passenger it was for cat litter.

'Yeah,' commented CeCe as they watched their mobiles and wet swimming clothes disappear into the tunnel. 'Bridget wasn't very happy to see us, was she?'

'No,' said Chrissie as they passed through the scanner and began to collect their belongings. 'She definitely wasn't.'

'I wonder why?' CeCe mused. 'What does she know that we don't?'

'At this moment in time,' Chrissie replied as they walked towards the boarding queue, 'everything.'

5

Atlantis

'It's for you,' Claudia said as she handed Maia the receiver. 'It's CeCe.'

'Ally!' Maia called onto the terrace, where her sister was sitting in the sunshine, finishing lunch. 'Hi, CeCe,' she said as Ally walked inside and they put their heads together to listen. 'Where are you?'

'We're in Sydney. We're about to check in for London, but I thought I'd call before we do and bring you up to date.'

'Have you found her?'

'Well, we met Mary-Kate McDougal. We think she could be the missing sister, 'cos she told us she was adopted, which would fit 'cos we all are. She's twenty-two, by the way, so that would fit too.'

'Fantastic!' said Ally.

'What about the emerald ring?' Maia asked. 'Did she recognise it?'

'She thinks she did. If it's the same one, then it was given to her by her mum on her twenty-first.'

'Wow!' said Ally. 'Maybe you *have* found her then! Did you see the ring?'

'Er, no, we didn't, 'cos her mum, who's also called Mary,

but goes by the nickname of "Merry", asked Mary-Kate if she could take it with her on this world tour she's on. Apparently it was hers originally. We actually managed to miss her twice – the first time by just a couple of days. And the second time . . . well, Chrissie and I have discussed it, and we wonder if it was because she knew we were coming that Merry left Norfolk Island a night early.'

'Norfolk Island? Where on earth is that?' Maia asked.

'It's in the South Pacific, just between New Zealand and Australia. It's really beautiful, but kinda stuck in the past – there's hardly any phone signal,' said CeCe. 'Mary-Kate said her mum was heading to the island to see her best friend Bridget. So we followed her there, but she'd already left.'

'Damn!' Ally muttered. 'So she's in Sydney now?'

'No. Looking at the departures board here, we think her plane's just left and is headed for Toronto in Canada. We're just checking that we're okay to get on our London flight?'

'I'm totally confused,' Ally sighed, 'but if she's left, then yes, of course. Are you sure she's headed for Toronto?'

'Yup. I just called Mary-Kate, her daughter, who confirmed it was the next destination on her schedule. She said she'd try to find out where her mum is staying. Sorry to disappoint you, Ally. We did our best.'

'Don't be silly, CeCe. You and Chrissie have done a fantastic job, so thank you.'

'I think we're on the right track, but we still need to see that ring,' said CeCe. 'Listen, we have to go check in right now, but there's more to tell you, like Merry is apparently Irish, and Mary-Kate has a brother and—'

'You go,' Ally said, 'and call us when you've landed. Thanks for finding all that out for us.'

Putting the phone down, Ally and Maia looked at each other and wandered back onto the terrace.

'So . . . could you make sense of all that?' said Maia.

'Let me get a pad and a pen so we can write down what she said.' Ally darted back into the kitchen and returned with what she needed. She began to write.

'Number one: we have a young woman called Mary-Kate McDougal who is twenty-two. Number two: we've identified that the emerald ring might be the one originally owned by her mum. She was given it on her twenty-first birthday.'

'Number three, and probably most importantly: we know Mary-Kate was adopted,' cut in Maia.

'Number four: her mum is also called Mary, commonly known as "Merry",' said Ally. 'Number five: Merry currently has the emerald ring which we need to see if we're to confirm that Mary-Kate is our missing sister.'

'And CeCe said there's a brother, remember . . .'

Ally wrote that down too, chewed her pen and then wrote *Toronto*.

'So, if we find out where she's staying, who should we send to Toronto?' asked Ally.

'You think it's worth pursuing?'

'Don't you?'

Maia's eyes travelled to the path which led to Pa Salt's garden.

'Merope's name was engraved on one band of the armillary sphere along with ours,' said Maia. 'Pa wouldn't have had it included unless she existed, surely?'

'Unless it was wishful thinking. But more importantly, Georg really believes this is her. He said that the information came from Pa just before he died. The proof was that her name is Mary McDougal, who lives at The Vinery in New Zealand, which we now know is true. *And* she owns an unusual emerald ring. Which Mary-Kate thought she recognised from the picture, but . . .'

'Maybe Georg has more information. Let's give him a call, shall we?' Maia suggested.

Ally went into the kitchen and dialled the number to Georg's office. After a few seconds, she was greeted by the light voice of his secretary.

'Hello, Giselle, it's Ally D'Aplièse here. Is Georg in?'

'*Désolée*, Mademoiselle D'Aplièse, Monsieur Hoffman has been called away.'

'Oh, I see. When will he be back?'

'I am afraid I do not know, but he wanted me to reassure your family that he would return in time for the boat trip later this month,' said Giselle.

'Can you pass on a message to him, please?' Ally asked. 'It's urgent.'

'I am so sorry, Mademoiselle D'Aplièse, but I am not able to contact him until he returns. I will make sure he calls you when he is back. *Au revoir.*'

Before Ally could respond, Giselle hung up the phone. Ally returned to the terrace, shaking her head in confusion.

'Maia, Georg's gone.'

'What do you mean "gone"?'

'His secretary says he's been called away and can't be contacted. Apparently he won't be back until the boat trip.'

'He's a busy man; Pa can't have been his only client.'

'Of course, but he probably has the information we need,' said Ally, 'and he left in such a rush when he was last here. All we have is a name and a picture of a ring. Well, I suppose we'll just have to continue without him.'

'So we should try and track down Mary-Kate's mum in Canada?'

'Surely we have to at least try? What do we have to lose?' said Ally.

'Nothing, I suppose,' Maia agreed. 'But who do we send to Toronto?'

'Well, our nearest sister is Electra, but I'd have to see how far Toronto is from New York,' Ally replied.

'I don't think it's far,' said Maia. 'We could ask Electra if she can go in the next few days, but I know she's been inundated by the media since the Concert for Africa the other night. She may not have the time. When I was in Geneva yesterday, her face was all over the newspapers.'

'She certainly knows how to grab the attention, doesn't she?'

'Honestly, Ally, she's sounded so much better since she came out of rehab. I don't think her speech at the concert was about getting attention. She's serious about helping others with addiction problems and it's wonderful that she can use her fame for good, don't you think? She's become an inspiring role model.'

'Yes, of course she is.' Ally yawned. 'Forgive me; I've become a ratty old bag in the past few weeks.'

'It's only because you're permanently exhausted,' Maia comforted her.

'Yup, I am. I thought that after all I've been through in my sailing career, having a baby alone would be easy, but you know what? It's the hardest thing I've ever done, especially the "alone" bit.'

'Everyone says it gets easier after the initial months, and at least for the next few weeks, Bear will have lots of aunties around to look after him.'

'I know, and Ma has been wonderful. It's just that sometimes, well . . .'

'What?'

'I look into the future and see myself alone,' Ally admitted. 'I can't imagine meeting anyone I can love as much as I loved

Theo. I know we were only together a short time – which is what everyone says when they try to comfort me – but it felt like forever to me. And . . .' Ally shook her head as tears fell down her pale cheeks.

'I'm so, so sorry, darling.' Maia put her arms around her younger sister. 'There's no point in trying to tell you that time heals, that you're still young and of course you've got a future ahead of you, because for now, you can't see it. But it is there, I promise.'

'Maybe, but then I feel so guilty. I should just be happy because I've got Bear. Of course I love him to the depths of my soul and yes, he's the best thing that's ever happened to me but . . . I miss Theo so, so much. Sorry, sorry . . . I never normally cry.'

'I know you don't, but it's good to let it out, Ally. You're so very strong, or at least, your pride doesn't allow you to be weak, but everyone has their breaking point.'

'I think I just need some sleep – proper sleep. Even when Ma is doing the night shift, I still wake up when I hear Bear cry.'

'Maybe we could arrange for you to take a short holiday – I'm sure Ma and I could cope with Bear here.'

Ally looked at her in horror. 'What kind of mother takes a "holiday" from her baby?'

'Those that can, I should think,' replied Maia pragmatically. 'If you look back to the old days, new mums didn't rely on their husbands; they had plenty of female relatives who would support them. You've had none of that support since you moved to Norway. Please don't beat yourself up, Ally, I know how hard it is to settle in a new country, and at least I speak the language in Brazil.'

'I've done my best to learn, but Norwegian is so difficult. There were a few nice mums at my antenatal classes who

spoke some English, but since we've all had our babies, we've gone our separate ways. They have their own families around them, you know? I've begun to wonder whether it was a mistake moving there in the first place. It would be fine if I was playing in the orchestra, keeping busy, but for now I'm just stuck at home in the middle of nowhere with Bear.' Ally wiped her eyes harshly with her hands. 'Oh God, I'm sounding so self-indulgent.'

'You're not at all, and decisions can always be reversed, you know. Maybe these few weeks here at Atlantis, and then being back on your beloved ocean, will give you some time to reflect.'

'Yes, but where would I go? I mean, I love Ma and Claudia dearly, but I don't think I could ever move back to Atlantis permanently.'

'Nor could I, but there are other places in the world, Ally. You could say it's your oyster.'

'So you reckon I should just stick a pin in the map and go wherever it points to, do you? It doesn't work like that. Got a tissue?'

'Here,' said Maia, digging into a jean pocket and producing a tissue. 'Well, Auntie Maia suggests that you take a nap now, then let me and Ma sort Bear out tonight. I'm jet-lagged anyway, so I'll be up until all hours. Truly, Ally, I think that your brain has just been scrambled by exhaustion. It's important you get some rest before our sisters start arriving.'

'You're right,' Ally sighed, as she slipped a hairband from her wrist and twisted her curls into a knot on top of her head. 'Okay, if you're offering, I'll take you up on it. I'll stuff earplugs in tonight and try to ignore the squalling.'

'Why don't you sleep in one of the spare bedrooms below us on Pa's floor? That way you won't be woken if Bear starts crying. For now, I'll check flights from New York to Toronto

and then give Electra a call to see if she wouldn't mind going.'

'Okay. Right, I'm going to take that nap. Bear's bottles are all in the fridge if you need them – the nappies are on his changing unit and—'

'I know the drill, Ally,' replied Maia gently. 'Now, go upstairs and get some sleep.'

Once the internet had informed her that Toronto was under two hours' flight from Manhattan, Maia picked up her mobile and dialled Electra's number. Not expecting her to answer as it was so early in New York, she was surprised to hear her sister's voice at the other end of the line.

'Maia! How are you?'

Even her phone response is different now . . . Maia thought. Before, Electra would never have asked how *she* was.

'I'm jet-lagged from the flight here, but it's great to be at Atlantis and see Ma, Claudia and Ally. And how are you, Miss Global Superstar?'

'OMG, Maia! I never, ever expected the kinda feedback I got from my speech. It feels like every newspaper and TV channel in the world wants to speak to me. Mariam – remember my assistant? – has had to hire a temp to help her. I'm . . . overwhelmed.'

'I bet you are, but at least it's for all the right reasons, isn't it?'

'Yeah, it is, and Stella – my grandmother – has been great. She's been dealing with a lot of the charity stuff. From what she said, we've already had enough donations to open *five* drop-in centres, and there's also been tons of charities offering me seats on their boards to act as a spokeswoman and stuff. Best of all, UNICEF have been in touch to ask if I'd consider

becoming a global ambassador for them. That made Stella real proud, which was nice.'

'That all sounds fantastic, Electra! It's no more than you deserve. You're a true inspiration to those who are struggling like you have. Just make sure you don't end up relapsing under the pressure.'

'Oh, don't worry, I won't relapse. This is happy pressure, not sad, if you know what I mean. I feel . . . exhilarated. And Miles has also been great.'

'Miles . . . isn't he the guy you were in rehab with?'

'Yeah, and, well . . . we've become real close over the past few weeks. In fact, I was thinking that if he can spare the time, maybe I'd bring him along with me to Atlantis. He's a super-hot lawyer, so I can just send him into battle when I need to fight my corner against all you sisters.'

Electra chuckled, and it was a blissful, natural sound that Maia hadn't heard from her in years.

'If any of us can fight our corner in this crazy family of ours, then it's you, Electra, but of course he's welcome. I think everyone's bringing someone with them, except Ally. Her brother Thom can't come as he's on tour with the Bergen Philharmonic.'

'Well, at least she has Bear.'

'She does, yes, but she's feeling pretty low at the moment.'

'Yeah, I got that from the phone call we had recently. Never mind, we'll all be around to cheer her up and do some babysitting. So, is this just a call to see how I'm doing, or was there a reason for it?'

'Both, actually. Did you read the email Ally sent to you, Tiggy and Star?'

'I didn't. As I said, I've been inundated. Even Mariam hasn't been able to get up to date yet. What was it about?'

Maia explained as succinctly as she could the events since

Georg's surprise visit to them on the night of the Concert for Africa.

'. . . So we now know that Mary-Kate's mum, more commonly known as Merry, has apparently flown on to Toronto. She has the emerald ring with her, which Georg told us is the proof we need to identify the missing sister. We're still waiting to see if we can get an address for Merry over there, but if we can – and I'm sorry to ask you this when you're so busy – could you possibly spare a day to fly up to meet with her? It's only an hour and forty minutes to Toronto from NYC, so . . .'

'I'm sure I could, Maia. In fact, I'd actually appreciate a chance to get out of the city right now. I'll bring Mariam with me; she's great at getting information out of people.'

'Okay, well, that's fantastic, Electra! I just hope we get to find out where she's staying and then I'll be in touch.'

'Do you think this really might lead us to the missing sister?'

'I don't know, but Georg seemed certain about this information.'

'Wow, wouldn't it be incredible if we could get her to come lay the wreath with us? That would have made Pa so happy.'

'Yes, it would, and with your help, we just might. Now, I'm sure you have a busy day ahead of you, so I'll let you go. Congratulations again, little sister. What you did – and want to do – is incredible.'

'Gee, thanks, big sis. Let me know if you get that address and see you soon!'

After ending the call, Maia left the house and walked across to enter the Pavilion, closing the door behind her. Although she had chosen to sleep in her childhood room in the main house to be closer to Ally, her old home here – where she had lived alone for so long as an adult – had been kept clean and aired by Claudia. And it was where she, Floriano

and Valentina would stay when they arrived. She went into the bedroom and opened her underwear drawer. Feeling around at the bottom of it, she drew out what she was looking for, then stared at it.

Yes, it was still there. Secreting it back in the drawer, Maia walked to the bed and sat down. She thought about what Ally had said earlier; about how she felt guilty because she was low at a time when she should be happy. This was partly true of her too just now, because something she'd wanted for a long time had finally happened. Yet at the same time, it had produced a metamorphosis inside her brain, which seemed determined to drag up painful events from her past . . .

As she forced herself to stand up, she decided that she was glad she had some space from Floriano, some time to work out her thoughts and feelings before she spoke to him.

'There's no rush,' she whispered as she looked around her at the rooms she had lived in for so long. Being back here, where she now acknowledged she'd hidden herself away from the world like a wounded animal, made tears prick her eyes. Atlantis had been such a safe, secure universe where day-to-day problems were few. And just now, she only wished she could recapture that feeling, and that Pa was still next door, because she was scared . . .

6

Mary-Kate
The Gibbston Valley

As the rain lashed against the windows and a wind howled through the valley, I finally gave up on the lyrics to a new song I'd been trying to compose on the keyboard. Yesterday, Fletch and I had worked together in the sitting room as a storm raged outside.

'We could do with a fire, mate,' Fletch had said. 'Winter's here.'

I'd swallowed hard, because Mum's lighting of the first fire of the year was something that only *she* did, but she wasn't here, and nor were Dad or Jack . . .

Then I'd reminded myself that I was twenty-two years old and an adult. So, getting Fletch to take a photograph – Dad had always marked the annual occasion this way, like other families did with birthdays or Christmas – I lit the fire.

After Fletch had taken off back to Dunedin this afternoon (Sissy having needed a jump-start), I'd been determined to improve on the lyrics I'd been tinkering with. Fletch had worked on a great tune, but he said my lyrics were 'depressing'. He was right. I didn't know whether it was the fact I felt

67

so alone just now, or the general confusion after CeCe and Chrissie had left to find Mum on Norfolk Island, but nothing was coming creatively.

'What do you reckon about those girls then, eh?' Fletch had asked over a bottle of wine. 'They could be a link to your long-lost family, and they seem pretty cool – not to mention rich, if they've got this boat in the Med.'

'I don't know what to make of it. I wasn't lying when I told them I've never thought of finding my birth family. I'm a McDougal,' I'd added firmly.

But now, alone with my thoughts and rattling around in a house that was full of memories of Dad, the question of my birth family wouldn't leave me alone.

I played a dissonant chord in frustration, and looked up at the clock. It was midnight now, which meant that it was the morning in Toronto.

You have to speak to her . . .

Gulping down my nerves, I reached for the house phone to dial Mum's mobile number. *She probably won't answer anyway*, I comforted myself.

'Hi, sweetheart, is that you?' came Mum's voice after a couple of rings. I could hear how tired she sounded.

'Yes, hi, Mum. Where are you?'

'I've just checked into the Radisson here in Toronto. Is everything all right?'

'Yup, fine,' I said. 'Um, did you get my message the other day? About those two girls, CeCe and Chrissie, who wanted to meet you?'

'Yes, I did.' There was a pause on the line. Eventually she said, 'Unfortunately I'd already left for Sydney with Bridget when they arrived on the island. What were they like?'

'Honestly, Mum, they were really sweet. Fletch was here and we had them stay for dinner. They just genuinely want to

find this "missing sister", as they kept calling her. I did explain on my message—'

'Did they say if they were working with others?' Mum cut in.

'Well, yes, if you mean the other sisters helping to find you – CeCe said she had five of them. They're all adopted too, like me. Umm, Mum . . .'

'Yes, sweetheart?'

I shut my eyes and took a deep breath. 'Mum, I know I've never needed to know about my . . . birth family, but their questions got me wondering if maybe I *should* know more about them.'

'Of course, darling, I understand. Please don't be embarrassed about saying it.'

'I love you and Dad and Jack more than anything and *you* are my family,' I said quickly. 'But I've been talking to Fletch about it, and I think it might be good to know a little more about this other part of me. Oh Mum, I don't want to upset you . . .' My voice broke, and I wished with all my heart that she were here with me, to take me into her comforting arms as she had always done.

'It's all right, Mary-Kate, really. Listen, why don't we sit down together when I'm home again, and then we can talk about it?'

'Thanks, yeah, that'd be great.'

'Those girls haven't contacted you again, have they?'

'Well . . . I spoke to CeCe briefly on the phone, but honestly, Mum, all they want is to see the emerald ring – the one you gave me on my twenty-first. They've got a drawing of it.'

'You said so in your message. Did they say where they got the drawing from?'

'Their lawyer, apparently. Mum, are you all right? You sound . . . a bit unlike yourself.'

'I'm absolutely fine, Mary-Kate, just worried about you. Is Fletch still there?'

'No, he left this arvo.'

'Okay, but Doug's around?'

'Yup. And the guys doing the pulling out are in the annexe. I'm perfectly safe.'

'Okay, well, don't go letting any more strangers into the house, will you?'

'You and Dad always did,' I countered.

'I know, but you're all alone there, sweetheart. It's different. Are you sure you don't want to fly out and join me in Toronto?'

'Where's all this come from, Mum? You and Dad always said the Valley was the safest place on earth! You're freaking me out!'

'Sorry, I'm sorry. I just don't like to think of my little girl all on her own. Keep in touch, won't you?'

''Course. Oh, also . . .' – I swallowed hard because I really needed to be sure – 'just before you go, can I check that I was adopted locally?'

'Yes, you were. It was an agency in Christchurch. Green and something.'

'Okay, thanks, Mum. Well, I'm gonna head for bed. Love you.'

'Love you too, darling, and take care, please.'

'I will. Bye.'

I put the phone back on the hook and sat down heavily on the sofa. Mum had sounded so strange and tense, not like herself at all. Even if she said she didn't mind about a link to my possible birth family turning up, she almost certainly did.

We'd speak when she got home, she'd said . . .

'But when is that going to be?' I said aloud to the empty room. Given all the countries she wanted to visit, it could be

months before we could have a real conversation, and now that the spark had been ignited, I had a burning need for answers. I'd also give CeCe a call tomorrow to say Mum was at the Radisson – if that ring could be identified, it might identify *me*, and I needed to know, even if it wasn't what Mum wanted.

Coming to a decision, I got up and turned on the old computer on the table. My foot tapping impatiently as it loaded, I opened the web browser and went to Google.

Green and . . . adoption agency Christchurch New Zealand, I typed into the search bar.

Then I held my breath and hit *Enter*.

7

Atlantis

'I never thought I'd say this but, wow, sleeping is great,' Ally announced as she joined Maia in the kitchen for a late breakfast the next morning. 'You're as white as a sheet again. I'm presuming you didn't get much yourself?'

'No. I just can't seem to shake the jet lag,' Maia shrugged.

'You should have done by now; you've been back four days. Are you sure you're okay? How's the tummy?'

'Not great, but I'll be fine.'

'Maybe you should go to Dr Krause in Geneva and get checked over.'

'I will if I'm not feeling better in the next couple of days. Anyway, I'm glad *you* slept, Ally. You look like a different person.'

'I feel it. Where is His Majesty, by the way?'

'Ma took him out for a walk around the garden. You remember how obsessed she was with all of us kids being outside?'

'I do. And how much I hated walking that great big Silver Cross pram around and around the garden, trying to get Electra or Tiggy off to sleep!'

'Talking of Tiggy, I haven't heard back from her or Star

since you sent the email about the missing sister,' said Maia. 'Have you?'

'No, although CeCe said she'd mention it to Star, and you know what communications are like where Tiggy lives. She may not even have got the email yet. I just don't understand how people can live so cut off from the rest of the world.'

'You were when you were sailing, though, weren't you?'

'I suppose so, but there have been very few times when I've spent more than a couple of days away from any contact. There's normally a handy port where I can catch up on texts and emails.'

'You're a real people person, aren't you, Ally?'

'I've never really thought about it,' she mused, sitting down with her mug of coffee. 'I suppose I am.'

'Maybe that's why you find it so hard living in Norway: you don't know many people there and even if you do, it's hard to communicate with them.'

Ally stared at Maia, then nodded. 'You know what? You might be right. I'm used to living with a lot of people around me. All the sisters here at Atlantis, then sleeping with crews in tiny spaces. I don't do "alone", do I?'

'No. Whereas I love my own space.'

'You've had the opposite experience to me,' Ally pointed out. 'I've had to get used to being by myself, but after years alone here, you've had Floriano and Valentina living with you.'

'Yes, and it's been difficult to adjust to, especially as our apartment is so small and in the middle of a crowded city. That's why I enjoy going out to the *fazenda* – the farm I inherited. I can have some headspace there, some peace. Without it, I might go mad. We hope to get a bigger apartment at some point when cash flow allows.'

'Talking of cash flow,' said Ally, 'I'm going to have to speak

to Georg when he gets back, because I'm almost broke. I haven't worked for months, so I'm reliant on the small income I get from the trust. I used all my savings and sold Theo's boat to renovate the Bergen house, but the cash didn't cover everything that needed doing so I had to ask Georg for a bit extra. I feel weird about asking him for more now, mainly because of pride – I've always supported myself in the past.'

'I know you have, Ally,' Maia said gently.

'I've got no choice, unless I sell the old barn Theo left me on the Greek island he always called "Somewhere". Besides, no one would buy it until I've renovated it – which I don't have the finances to do – and I should try to keep it for Bear.'

'Of course you should.'

'I'm not even sure how much money Pa left us. Are you?' Ally asked her.

'No. Those few days last year after Pa died are just a blur, and I can't remember exactly what Georg said about the finances,' Maia admitted. 'I think it would be a good idea if, when we're all back here after the cruise down to Delos, we ask him to explain how the trust works, so we can be clear about how much we have, and what we can use it for.'

'That would be good, yes, but I still feel awful having to ask for help in the first place. Pa taught us to stand on our own two feet,' sighed Ally.

'On the other hand, when a parent . . . dies, the children get left money in the will, which they are free to spend as they choose,' said Maia. 'We need to understand that *we* are in charge now – even if we find it difficult to remember that Georg works for *us*, not the other way round. It's our money and we shouldn't be scared of asking for it. Georg isn't our moral compass; that was Pa, remember? And he taught us not to abuse what we were lucky enough to be given. Being a

single mother because your partner has died is one of the best reasons for needing financial support, Ally. If Pa was alive today, I know he would think so too.'

'You're right. Thank you, Maia.' Ally stretched out her hand to her sister. 'I've missed you a lot, you know. You've always been the calming voice of reason. I just wish you didn't live so far away.'

'I'm hoping that you and Bear will come and visit Brazil soon. It's an amazing country and . . .'

The telephone rang and Ally jumped up to catch the call.

'*Allô*, Ally D'Aplièse speaking. Who? Oh, hi, Mary-Kate,' she said as she beckoned Maia over to listen. 'It's very nice to speak to you. CeCe has told me all about meeting you in New Zealand. I have Maia – our eldest sister – here with me too.'

'Hi, Mary-Kate,' Maia said.

'Hi, Maia,' came Mary-Kate's gentle voice, 'it's good to talk to you too. CeCe left me this number and as I can't get hold of her, I hope it's okay that I've rung you.'

'Of course it is.' Ally took over again.

'I know CeCe and her friend Chrissie were trying to find out which hotel my mum is staying at in Toronto. I spoke to Mum last night and she said she's staying at the Radisson. I have all the details.' Both Maia and Ally could hear the tinge of excitement in Mary-Kate's voice. 'Shall I give them to you or wait until I get hold of CeCe?'

'To us, please,' said Ally, grabbing the pen and notepad that sat by the kitchen phone. 'Fire away.' Ally scribbled the address and the telephone number down. 'Thanks, Mary-Kate, that's fantastic.'

'So, what will you do? Will you guys fly over to see her?'

'We have a sister who lives in Manhattan. She's only a short plane ride away, so she's said that she might go.'

'Wow, your family sounds interesting. Odd, but interesting,' Mary-Kate chuckled. 'Whoops! I didn't mean to be rude or anything . . .'

'Oh, don't worry, we're used to it,' said Ally. 'I'm sure CeCe told you that if we confirm that ring of yours that your mum has got with her is the right one, then it would be fantastic for you to fly over to visit and come with us later this month on our boat trip for our father's memorial.'

'That's so nice of you, but I don't think I could afford it.'

'Oh, all costs of flights would be covered by our family trust,' Ally said hastily.

'Okay, thanks, I'll think about it. Anyway, let's see if your sister manages to hook up with my mum and ask her about that ring. Just . . . well, I think Mum's feeling a bit weird about CeCe and Chrissie turning up on the doorstep, y'know? I haven't said yet that another sister might be coming to see her in Toronto. I think that after Dad's death, she's feeling vulnerable.'

'I understand completely, Mary-Kate. We can always leave it if you'd prefer,' Maia replied diplomatically.

'I don't want to upset her or anything, but actually, I'd really like to know if I am your missing sister. Does that sound mean?'

'No, not at all. I'm sure it's a very difficult thing for the adoptive mum when a possible set of relatives turns up, especially out of the blue. That's our fault, Mary-Kate. We should have written to you first, but we were all so excited that we might have found you, we didn't think.'

'Well, I'm glad CeCe and Chrissie came, but . . .'

'I promise to tell Electra to tread carefully.'

'Electra . . . so she's the sixth sister?'

'She is,' Ally confirmed, surprise in her voice. 'You know your mythology.'

'Oh, I do. I was telling CeCe that Mum studied Classics at uni and had a bit of an obsession with all those Greek myths. Electra's such an unusual name, isn't it? There's only one Electra I know of, and that's the supermodel. I caught her speech on TV a few nights ago. That's not your sister, is it?'

'It is, actually.'

'Shit! I mean . . . seriously? She's, like, well, she's always been an idol of mine. She's so beautiful and elegant and that speech showed she's got a brain and compassion in spades. I think I might collapse on the spot if I met her!'

'Don't worry, we'll hold you up,' said Ally, sharing a smile with Maia. 'Right then, speak soon.'

'Yes. And if you do speak to Electra, tell her from me that I think she's amazing.'

'I will, and going back to what you were saying before, I do think we should give your mum some warning that Electra's coming tomorrow. If you like, I'll leave a message at the hotel reception later, saying that my sister might be visiting.'

'Okay, yes, that would be good. Thanks, Maia. Bye.'

'Bye, Mary-Kate, and thanks for calling.'

Maia hung up the phone, and stared at Ally for a few seconds.

'She sounds so sweet. And very young,' she said eventually as they walked back to the table.

'You know what? I think she sounded . . . normal.'

'Are you saying we're not?' Maia smiled.

'I think we're a bunch of women with different personalities. Just like most sisters are. And anyway, what is "normal?"'

'I am feeling guilty about her mum, though,' Maia sighed. 'It must be devastating to suddenly hear contact has been made about the possible birth family. Normally, it would have happened through official channels.'

'Yes, you're right. We should have thought,' Ally agreed. 'It

was different for us; Pa was actively encouraging us to go and find our birth families.'

'It just shows how amazing Ma has been through all this as we've found our relatives,' said Maia. 'She's loved us all like a mother. I mean, I couldn't love her more, she *is* my mother.'

'And mine,' Ally agreed. 'And a fantastic granny to Bear.'

'So . . . do you think Mary-Kate is our missing sister?'

'Who knows? But if she is, how did Pa lose her?'

'I have absolutely no idea, and I hate these conversations,' Maia sighed. 'Remember we all used to chat about why he'd adopted us when we were younger? And what his obsession with the Seven Sisters was?'

'Of course I do.'

'Back then, we could just have walked downstairs to Pa's study and asked him outright, but none of us ever had the courage to do it. Now that he's gone, that isn't an option any longer. It makes me wish I had been brave enough, because now we'll never know.' Maia shook her head wearily.

'Probably not, although I reckon Georg knows far more than he'll ever say.'

'I agree, but I guess he's bound by whatever a lawyer's oath is not to reveal his clients' secrets.'

'Well, Pa certainly seems to have had a lot of those,' said Ally. 'Like, did you know there's a lift in this house?'

'What?' Maia gasped. 'Where?'

'There's a panel that hides it off the corridor from the kitchen,' said Ally, lowering her voice. 'Tiggy found out about it when she was staying here after being so ill in the spring. Apparently, Ma said that Pa had it installed not long before he died – he'd been struggling with the stairs, but kept it a secret because he didn't want any of us to worry.'

'I see,' said Maia slowly. 'That doesn't seem too suspicious, though, Ally.'

'No, but what *is* suspicious is that the lift goes down to a hidden wine cellar that no one has ever told us about!' said Ally.

'I'm sure there's an explanation for it—'

'When Electra was here a few months ago, Ma took both of us down there. And Electra confirmed what Tiggy found when she sneaked down into the cellar when Ma and Claudia were asleep – there's a door hidden behind one of the wine racks.'

'So what's behind it?'

'I don't know,' Ally sighed. 'I sneaked down there myself one night when I was up with Bear – the key to the lift is in the key box in the kitchen. I saw the door, but couldn't budge the wine rack in front of it.'

'Well, when we're all here together we'll go and take a look. Maybe Georg knows where and what it leads to. Anyway, getting back to the missing sister, now that we know where Mary-Kate's mum is staying in Toronto, let's call Electra again,' said Maia, looking at her watch. 'It's about six a.m. in New York – that might be too early.'

This time, Electra didn't answer her mobile, so Maia left a message for her to get back to them urgently. Ma arrived in from the garden with Bear, and Ally fed him as she sat in the kitchen waiting for Electra's call.

'You can go out or upstairs if you wish,' Ma commented as Claudia began preparing lunch. 'I won't leave the phone unattended.'

'If Electra doesn't call back soon, I might,' said Ally, as Maia excused herself to go to the bathroom. 'Can I leave Bear here with you? I thought I might take the Laser out on the lake after lunch.'

'Of course. You know it is my pleasure to look after him, Ally, and I'm sure an hour or two of sailing would do you the

world of good. Maybe Maia could come with you,' said Ma, watching the kitchen door for Maia's return. 'Between you and me, she does not look well. Maybe some fresh air would do her good.'

'Maybe,' agreed Ally. 'I said she should go to the doctor if she doesn't improve over the next couple of days.'

'I hope she is better for when your sisters start to arrive. I want it to be a wonderful celebration.'

Ally caught the glimpse of anticipation in Ma's eyes.

'I hope so too, Ma. It must be very exciting for you, having all your girls back together again.'

'Oh, it is, but with all their families coming too, I must work out how to accommodate them. Do you think the couples will mind sharing the smaller beds you have in the rooms on the attic floor, or should I put them on your father's floor in the double rooms?'

Ally and Ma were discussing this when Maia walked back into the kitchen. 'Any news?' she asked.

'Not yet, but I'm sure Electra will contact us as soon as she gets the message. Ma was wondering whether you wanted to come out and take a spin round the lake on the Laser with me?'

'Not today, thank you. I'm not sure my stomach is quite settled enough yet,' Maia sighed.

'I have soup,' said Claudia from her station at the range. 'Will you eat inside or out?'

'Outside, I think, don't you, Maia?' said Ally.

'Err . . . I had a late breakfast so I'm not hungry. In fact, I think I'll go upstairs for a lie-down while you eat. I'll see you later.'

As Maia left the room, Ally and Ma shared a glance.

Having put Bear back in his pram, tucked into a shady spot under the big oak tree where Ma had always stationed the babies for a nap, Ally was just sitting down to drink her soup when the telephone rang. She dashed inside to pick it up, but Claudia had reached it first.

'Is it Electra?'

'No, it is Star. Here.' Claudia handed over the receiver and went back to her washing-up.

'Hello, Star! How are you?'

'Oh, I'm good, thank you, Ally.'

'How is Mouse? And Rory?'

'They're fine as well. Sorry I haven't replied to your email yet; we've been doing some stocktaking at the bookshop and it's been chaos. Anyway, I thought I'd call you rather than write. It seems ages since we last spoke.'

'That's because it has been,' Ally said with a smile, 'but don't worry. So you got my email?'

'Yes, and CeCe has filled me in too – we're meeting up in London in the next few days. Isn't it exciting? I mean, that Georg might have found the missing sister just in time to go and lay the wreath. Is there any more news?'

Ally explained that they were hoping Electra would go to Toronto tomorrow.

'Well, anything I can do from my end, let me know. Is it okay if I tell Orlando, Mouse's brother, about all this? He's actually a really good sleuth. It must be all those Conan Doyle stories he reads,' Star chuckled.

'I don't see why not. Have you decided when you're coming over to Atlantis yet?'

'As I said, I'll be meeting CeCe and Chrissie in London, but I won't be able to fly to Geneva with them – Mouse is very busy with the restoration of High Weald, so I don't want to leave Rory alone with him for too long. He'll only get fed

crisps and chocolate, knowing Mouse. Rory's school term finishes the day before we leave for the cruise, so I'll fly over with him then, and hopefully with Mouse too.'

'Just let us know, because it's not long now, is it?'

'No, and I'm so excited to see everybody. Goodness, Ally, it feels like so much has happened to all of us in the past year. And of course, I can't wait to meet Bear either. Keep in touch, won't you? I'm going to have to go actually – I promised to cook forty-eight muffins and a lemon drizzle cake for Rory's school fete tomorrow.'

'No problem, Star. Speak soon, bye.'

Ally wandered back outside to finish her soup, and tried not to feel envy that all her sisters' lives were so full and busy. And how all of them sounded happy.

I really do need that spin on the lake, she thought as she sat down.

Out on the water, the warm June breeze whipped Ally's curls around her face. She took in a lungful of pure air, then let it out slowly. It felt almost as if a physical weight had been lifted off her shoulders – or rather, out of her arms. She looked back at the silhouette of Atlantis, the pale pink turrets peeping out from behind the row of spruce trees that shielded it from prying eyes.

Veering sharply to avoid the path of other sailors, paragliders and holidaymakers who were cluttering up the lake on this beautiful summer afternoon, Ally guided the Laser to an inlet and lay back, enjoying the sensation of the sun on her face. It reminded her of lying in Theo's arms only a year ago, feeling as happy as she'd ever felt.

'I miss you so much, my darling,' she whispered to the

heavens. 'Please show me how to move on, because I don't even know where my home is anymore.'

'Hello,' Maia greeted her sister as Ally walked back into the kitchen a couple of hours later. 'You've really caught the sun out there. Did you enjoy that?'

'It was wonderful, thanks. I'd forgotten how much I love it,' Ally smiled. 'Is Bear okay?'

'Ma's just about to give him a bath, and he's absolutely fine.'

'Great, then I'll head up and take a shower while I can. How are you feeling, Maia, any better?'

'I'm fine, Ally. Oh, just before you go up, Electra called while you were out. I've given her the name of the hotel in Toronto and Mariam has called the private jet company, so it's currently on hold for tomorrow.'

'Okay, perfect. See you in a bit,' Ally said as she left the kitchen.

After calling Merry's hotel to confirm with the receptionist that she was still there, Maia dialled Mariam's number.

'Hello, is that Mariam? It's Maia here.'

'Hi, Maia, all okay?'

'All is fine. I just wanted to tell you that Mary McDougal is definitely staying at the hotel for another couple of nights. She was out, but I've left a message saying Electra will be in touch to confirm a time to meet her tomorrow. I didn't say her name in case it caused too much of a fuss.'

'Thank you. That'll be me making the call then. Your sister's snowed under; everyone wants to speak to her right now,' said Mariam, her soft tone like a spoonful of melting honey. 'Miles and I think that it's very important she paces herself, as it's not so long since she came out of rehab.'

'Absolutely. I said the same to her, though I'm sure Electra has other ideas.'

'Actually, she's being very calm about the situation. She doesn't want to go back to that dark place either. We've decided to pick out a couple of trusted journalists and a major chat show she'll be interviewed on, which will give the charity lots of coverage, but won't be exploitative in any way.'

'I'm so grateful she has you, Mariam. Thank you so much for being there for her.'

'It really is no problem, Maia. Apart from the fact my job *is* to take care of her, I love her. She's such a strong person and I think she's going to do great things. Now, what is the full name of the lady we're meeting?'

'Mrs Mary McDougal, also known as "Merry".'

'Great,' said Mariam. 'I'll call the hotel now, try to talk to Merry and arrange a time and a place, shall I? I would think meeting at the hotel would be the easiest as it's close to Billy Bishop airport. Do you have her room number?'

'I'm afraid I don't. I'm not sure hotels give that kind of information these days. You'll just have to ask to be put through to her room.'

'Is it okay if I use my name instead of Electra's? As you said, the last thing we want is anyone finding out she's going to be there. She hasn't been out in public since the concert. We've decided she's going to have to be in disguise.'

'What it must be like to be world famous!' Maia chuckled.

'What do I say if this Mary asks me what the meeting is about?'

'Maybe just that you're calling on behalf of the sister of CeCe D'Aplièse, who visited Mary-Kate at the vineyard, and you'd like to arrange a meeting with her at the hotel,' Maia suggested.

'Right, I'll confirm the jet, then try to contact her and get back to you. Bye, Maia.'

'Bye, Mariam.'

Claudia arrived in the kitchen, followed by Ma and a delicious-smelling Bear, fresh and clean in a babygro.

'Ooh, pass him over for a cuddle with his auntie,' said Maia.

'Of course,' Ma said as she handed a wriggling Bear to her. 'Bath-times were always my favourite moment of the day when you were all small.'

'It was probably because bedtime wasn't that far off,' said Maia. 'Seriously, Ma, now I look back, I don't know how you coped.'

'Nor do I, but I did.' Ma shrugged as she poured herself a glass of water. 'And remember, as you grew up, you kept each other amused. Is Electra going to Toronto tomorrow?'

'Yes, but I just don't know what will happen,' said Maia. 'Apart from Georg being convinced that Mary McDougal is our missing sister, plus the emerald ring, we don't have a lot to go on. And when I spoke to Mary-Kate, she was worried her adoptive mum was upset by our sudden appearance in her daughter's life.'

'I can imagine,' Ma agreed. 'But it is up to Mary-Kate to decide if she wishes to know more, and it sounds as if she does.'

'Yes. Why do you think Georg is so certain it's her?'

'I know no more than you do, Maia. All I can say is that, throughout all the years I have known Georg, he has never said that he truly believed anyone else he has investigated could be the missing sister, so he must be convinced that this *is* her.'

'Did Pa ever mention a missing sister to you over the years, Ma?'

'Occasionally. There was always a sadness in his eyes when he spoke of the fact that he couldn't find her.'

'What about to you, Claudia?' asked Maia.

'Me?' Claudia looked up from the vegetables she was chopping for supper. 'Oh, I know nothing. I am not one for gossip,' she added, and Ma and Maia shared a smile. Claudia loved nothing more than a big pile of trashy magazines, which they both knew she hid under her recipe folder if anyone walked into the kitchen.

Maia's mobile rang again, and she handed Bear over to Ma as she answered it.

'Hi, Maia, Mariam here again. Mary McDougal wasn't in her room, but I left a message with the concierge to say we were coming tomorrow. I suggested one p.m., and that we meet in the lobby. I left my cell number too, so hopefully she'll call me back. If she doesn't, do we still go ahead?' Mariam asked.

'I . . . don't know, to be honest. It's a long way to go for nothing, and that might be the result.'

'I'm up for it,' said a voice in the background.

'One moment, Maia, I'll pass you over to Electra.'

'Hi there,' came Electra's voice. 'I think we should go, even if Mary doesn't get back to us. I mean, CeCe and Chrissie turned up unannounced, and look at the heap of information they managed to get. Besides, we know she's staying in the hotel, so if she's out, we'll just ask the concierge to tell us when she returns, and we'll sit in the lobby until she does. Remind me what she looks like?'

'From the photograph CeCe saw, she's a beautiful, petite blonde who looks around forty. Like the actress Grace Kelly apparently. Are you sure you're okay to go?'

'Hey, don't sweat; it's a day trip there and back. Normally

I'm on a plane twice a week to who knows where. I'll let you know how we get on. I think we owe it to Pa to at least try to identify the missing sister, don't we?'

'Yes, Electra, I think we do,' said Maia.

8

Electra
Toronto, Canada

The six-seater Cessna jet gained altitude as it flew due north away from New York. Electra gazed out of the window and thought how, in the 'old days', she'd be itching to access the well-stocked bar and grab a large vodka tonic. The urge – the habit – to do so was still strong inside her, but she accepted that it would probably never leave her and she'd simply have to fight every day not to give in to it.

'Hey, can you grab me a Coke?' she asked Mariam, who was sitting closer to the bar at the front than she was.

'Of course.' Mariam unstrapped herself and went to open the small refrigerator.

'Get me some pretzels too, will you? Geez, have I had an appetite for junk food since I came off the booze,' Electra sighed. 'Good job I seem to have a new career ahead of me, 'cos I'm getting far too fat to shimmy down the runway.'

'Really, Electra, you don't look as though you've put on an ounce. I think you must have a very good metabolism. Unlike me.' Mariam sat down, indicated her belly and shrugged.

'Maybe it's love that makes a person hungry,' Electra said as she opened the Coke. 'Are you and Tommy good?'

'I think we are, yes. He is so happy to work for you in an official capacity and he looks so handsome in his new suits.' A gentle blush appeared on Mariam's cheeks as she sipped her water.

'He's a great guy and also perfectly qualified for the job, what with his military background. As he's my bodyguard, I know I should have brought him with us today, but it's just a short hop, and in my disguise, nobody will even recognise me. It'll be just like that night we went out together for dinner in Paris. Without the booze and drugs on my part, of course,' Electra chuckled. 'Have you mentioned anything about Tommy to your family yet?'

'No, we're going to take it slowly. There's no rush, is there? I am just happy to have the chance to be with him when I can.'

'I for one can't wait to dance at your wedding, and I know you'll have such cute kids,' said Electra. 'Miles and I were talking baby names last night. He's got some seriously bad taste – every one of his suggestions for a boy were the names of his favourite basketball players!'

'He's a good man, Electra, and so protective of you. Hold on to him, won't you?'

'I sure will, as long as he holds on to me too. The fact he's a lawyer irritates me sometimes because he's so logical, but he does talk sense. And he's just so proud, y'know? He gets paid diddly-squat because so much of his work is pro bono. I mean, you should see his apartment in Harlem; it's above a bodega and about half the size of my closet! I suggested it might be great if we bought a place together where we could spread out, but he won't hear of it.'

'I can understand why he doesn't want to feel like a kept man,' Mariam replied.

'So why is it okay for women to be "kept"? Where's the difference?'

'It's just the way some men are,' Mariam shrugged. 'To be honest, it is good that Miles refuses to take advantage of your wealth. So many would.'

'Yeah, I know, but *I'd* like to take advantage of my wealth and buy a real nice house or apartment in Manhattan that would feel like mine. I know I have the ranch in Arizona now, but it'll be a while before it's ready for me to move into and it's too far away to be a permanent home. I need a base in the city. I've been thinking lately how important home is.'

'Maybe because you are due to return to it soon. Are you looking forward to going back to Atlantis and seeing all your sisters?'

'Good question.' Electra paused. 'The answer is, I'm not sure. They all find me difficult, and I know I *have* been, but that's just who I am. Even if I'm off the booze and drugs, I'm not going to suddenly grow wings overnight and become an angel.'

'If it helps, I think you have become a completely different person since you got sober.'

'You haven't seen me when I'm with my sisters.' Electra raised an eyebrow. 'Especially CeCe. She and I have always rubbed each other up the wrong way.'

'Remember, I come from a big family too and I promise you, there is always one sibling that others struggle to get along with. I mean, I love Shez, my younger sister, but she is so patronising just because she did a law degree and I went straight into work.'

'Yup, exactly,' nodded Electra. 'So how do you cope?'

'I try to understand that she and I have always competed. I want to be better than her, and I cannot help that feeling. But if I accept why I feel that way, I can cope.'

'Maybe CeCe's competition for me too, though not in the same way as you and Shez. I mean, she can holler louder than I can, but I think I throw the best tantrums,' Electra chuckled.

'You never know, both of you could have changed in the past year. From what you've said about CeCe, it sounds as though she's much happier now. I think so many of our struggles with our siblings come from feeling insecure that they're more favoured by a parent than we are. Then we start to have lives apart from our families, we build careers of our own and we're maybe with someone we care for who is *ours*, who we don't have to share with our siblings, which makes us feel stronger and more in control.'

'You know what, Mariam? You're wasted as a PA. You should become a counsellor. I think I've learnt more from you in the past few months than from any of the therapists I've paid shedloads to talk too.'

'Well, thank you for that compliment,' Mariam smiled. 'But remember, you pay me too. And talking of which, could we go through your interview schedule for the next few days?'

'I haven't been to Toronto in years,' commented Electra as they stepped off of the jet and were ushered into a limo that was waiting on the tarmac.

'I have never been,' said Mariam, 'but I have heard it is a beautiful city. I was reading about it last night, and apparently we have to get on a ferry that takes ninety seconds to cross Lake Ontario. They're thinking of building a tunnel underground so passengers can walk to the mainland.'

'You're a mine of information, Mariam,' said Electra. 'Looking back, I now feel bad that I've never bothered to find out anything about the places I've visited for photoshoots.

One city melts into another, one golden beach looks like everywhere else, y'know?'

'Not really, but I understand what you're saying. Look, there's the ferry.' Mariam pointed towards the slim strip of water separating them from the Canadian mainland.

'By the way, you did bring my disguise, didn't you?'

'I did,' Mariam nodded, digging inside her satchel, which had begun to remind Electra of Mary Poppins's carpet bag, as it never failed to produce whatever it was she needed.

'Do you want me to help you put it on?' Mariam asked as the limo moved forward onto the ferry and then parked up.

'Yes please. If we do manage to meet this woman in the hotel lobby, it's best that I'm not recognised or we'll be surrounded. Hopefully I can explain who I really am once we get Merry somewhere private.'

'Here's the top you wore in Paris, which you can put on over your T-shirt.'

'Thanks,' said Electra as she pulled the garment over her head and put her arms through the wide sleeves. She bent her head towards Mariam so she could wrap a colourful scarf around her head and pin it into place. After Mariam had added a little eyeliner around her eyes, she sat back. 'So, how do I look?'

'Just as you should. We are two Muslim women on a sightseeing holiday in Canada, yes? Look, we're off the ferry already. The hotel is only a couple of minutes away,' added Mariam.

As they stepped out of the limousine in front of the Radisson, Electra's stomach gave a lurch. It felt like the butterflies she used to get when she had to return to boarding school. 'Which means you're nervous,' she muttered under her breath as they walked into the lobby. 'Right,' Electra said. 'What do we do now?'

'You go sit down and I'll ask the concierge if he can call Merry's room and let her know we're here. In case she's out, I suggest you find a spot to sit where we can see the entrance as well as the elevators just over there,' Mariam pointed. 'There's a free couch right in that corner which will give us a perfect view.'

'Okay,' Electra said, feeling very glad Mariam was with her. She always knew what to do and would calmly set about doing it. Having crossed the polished floor of the lobby and sat down where Mariam had suggested, Electra looked around and saw not one head turning towards her as it usually would.

Mariam returned and sat down beside her.

'No one has noticed me so far,' Electra whispered.

'Good, and I am sure Allah won't mind you borrowing the symbols of our faith occasionally, but if it's going to be more permanent, then you may have to convert,' Mariam replied. Electra wasn't sure if she was being serious or not. 'Anyway,' she continued, 'the concierge said he'd spoken to Mrs McDougal last night, and also put a note under her door, confirming we were coming and would meet her in the lobby at one o'clock.'

'I never open those notes that get left under the door, mind you,' said Electra. 'It's normally either your bill, or to say that housekeeping couldn't get access to turn down your bed. Did the concierge call her room when you were with him?'

'He did, yes, but she did not pick up.'

'Then maybe she's not coming.'

'Electra, we are ten minutes early, so let's be positive and give Mrs McDougal a chance, shall we?'

'Okay, okay, but if she doesn't show, it must mean she's avoiding us.'

'Her daughter, Mary-Kate, thinks – quite understandably –

that it might be because she is unhappy about potential relatives turning up suddenly. We must be sensitive, Electra.'

'I'll do my best, promise. Remind me what she looks like again?'

'Maia said we are looking for a small, slim, middle-aged woman with blonde hair . . . like Grace Kelly.'

'Oh yeah, I think Maia mentioned her. Who is she again?' Electra asked.

'*She* was one of the most beautiful women to ever walk the earth. My dad was in love with her for years. Here, let me see if I can bring up a picture of her.'

Mariam opened her satchel and pulled out her laptop. She typed in the password for the Wi-Fi that the concierge had given her and found what she was looking for.

'There – you have to admit she was stunning, and she even married a real-life prince! My dad was only a teenager when she got married, but he says he still remembers it because she looked so beautiful.'

'She sure is,' agreed Electra. 'And the polar opposite of me.' She gestured to her tall frame and ebony skin. 'That means that this Merry isn't genetically related to me in any way, but her colouring does remind me a little of Star . . . Now, why don't you watch the elevators over there, and I'll keep a close eye on the entrance?'

Both of them sat for twenty minutes staring at their allotted targets, until Electra shook herself. 'You know what? I'm starving.'

'Shall we order some food?' Mariam picked up the menu from the table and studied it. 'They don't have a halal menu here, so you can go veggie if you want, to keep in character.'

'Damn! I was going to have a cheeseburger, but I'll make do with a salad and French fries.'

'Okay.' Mariam checked her watch. 'It's now just after ten

past one, so she's either late or just not coming. We'll call the waitress over and order, then I'll go see the concierge again.'

Mariam did as she'd suggested, but Electra could already see from her face as she walked back to the couch that it wasn't good news. 'He's tried her room again, but no reply. I guess we're just going to have to sit here and wait.'

'If she *is* actively avoiding us, it could mean she feels threatened by us.'

'I am not surprised. She must find it strange that a bunch of adopted sisters are following her around the globe,' Mariam pointed out. 'Your family is not exactly standard, is it?'

'Well, if she actually came to meet me, then I could explain it all to her, couldn't I?'

'Explain that you need to see an emerald ring to prove that Mary-Kate is who Georg, your lawyer, thinks she is, i.e. the "missing sister"? Even that sounds odd, Electra, because none of you are your father's biological daughters. Did Georg tell you whether she has been left a legacy of some kind? Maybe that would help her think it was worthwhile meeting us. I mean, if there was money her daughter might inherit.'

'I don't know,' said Electra despairingly as the waitress brought them their lunch. 'Thanks, and can I have some extra ketchup and mayo for my fries?' she asked.

The waitress nodded and sped away.

Electra took a fry and chewed on it. 'I mean, as usual with Pa, everything is a mystery. What am I doing in Toronto, masquerading as a Muslim woman and eating fries in the lobby of some hotel? Waiting with you for someone I'd never heard of until a couple of days ago, who looks like she won't be showing up anyway?'

'You are right. Put like that, it does sound weird,' Mariam agreed, and both of them began to giggle.

'Seriously, Mariam, this is just ridiculous. If I were Mary-Kate's mom, I wouldn't show up either. Maybe you could ask the concierge if he'd try her room one last time? Then we're leaving.'

'After I've finished my sandwich, I will, yes,' said Mariam. 'And if she doesn't answer, perhaps you could write her a personal note? Then we could leave it with the concierge to hand over to her.'

'That's a good idea,' Electra agreed. 'Bring me some paper and an envelope back from the desk.'

It was almost two o'clock by the time Electra was satisfied with what she'd written.

'Right, this is the final draft,' she said, indicating all the screwed-up previous versions littering the coffee table.

'Go ahead, I'm listening,' said Mariam.

Dear Mary McDougal,

My name is Electra D'Aplièse, and I am one of six adopted sisters. Our father, Pa Salt (we're not sure of his actual name because that's all we ever called him), died a year ago. He'd adopted us from all over the globe, but had always told us that there was a seventh sister who was missing.

Our lawyer, Georg Hoffman, said that he'd found some information which proved a Mary McDougal was almost certainly the missing sister. We know from my sister CeCe's visit to your daughter Mary-Kate that she was adopted as a baby by you and your husband. The proof it's her is a star-shaped emerald ring, which Mary-Kate says you have with you.

I promise you, we are just normal women with no motive other than to fulfil our late father's wish to find the missing sister. Please feel free to contact me

*on my cell number, or the landline for our family
home in Geneva.*

*I'm sorry we couldn't get to meet you today, but if
your daughter is who our lawyer thinks she is, we'd all
love to meet her – and you – at some point.*

With best wishes,

Electra D'Aplièse

'That's perfect. It is good that you said you would like to
meet both of them,' Mariam said as she snatched the letter
before Electra could find further fault with it, then folded it
and put it, together with a card containing the appropriate
phone numbers, in an envelope. 'Should I address it to her?'

'Yeah, thanks.' Electra sighed. 'Wow, what a waste of a day.
I'm going back with nothing to report. I'm a failed detective.'

'If you are, so am I,' said Mariam as she sealed the envelope. 'Okay. I'll give the concierge the letter, then should I call
the limo to pull up outside?'

'Yes, although I need to use the restroom before we leave.'

'Sure,' Mariam agreed as Electra went in search of it.

Walking in, she saw one of the stalls was occupied, and
chose the furthest stall from the door.

'No, they're still there,' came a woman's low voice from the
other stall. 'The concierge told me on the phone my visitors
were two Muslim women. But what would they want with
me? I mean, you don't think that . . . it's *him*?'

Inside her cubicle, Electra had frozen.

Oh my God, oh my God, it's her . . . what the hell do I do?

'I came down to have a look at them. They're both young,
but no, of course I didn't recognise them . . . I'm going to go
back to my room now. I've decided to leave for London
tonight, just in case – I'm too uncomfortable to stay.'

There was another pause as the woman listened to whoever

it was she was speaking to. 'Yes, of course I'll keep in touch, Bridget. I'll call Claridge's now and tell them I'm arriving early, then ask the concierge to change my flight . . . All right then, my love, thank you and I'll speak to you soon. Bye.'

Electra heard the woman open the stall door, the tapping of shoes across the tiled floor, then the main door to the restroom opening and closing.

Trying to think fast, Electra pulled off her top and head scarf, dropping them in a heap on the floor. Then she ran out of the restroom and along the corridor back to the lobby. She spotted a petite, well-dressed blonde, still holding a cell phone in her hand, standing with others as they waited in front of the elevator for it to arrive.

'Oh my God! Is it you? I'm sure it is! Oh my God! You *are* Electra, aren't you?' Long nails dug into Electra's shoulder from behind.

'Ouch! Can you get off me, please?' she said as she turned round to find an overexcited teenager behind her. 'Look, I'm not being rude, but I need to get into that elevator—'

'It *is* her, it's Electra!' shouted another woman waiting for the elevator, and instantly a crowd began to gather around her. She tried to walk forwards as the elevator doors began to open, but again she felt a firm grip on her shoulder holding her back and her path became blocked by people in front of her.

'*Please*, Electra, I just can't let you go until my friend takes a photo of us together. You were sooo great on TV the other night!'

'Let me through!' she shouted as she watched the blonde woman walk into the open elevator. She wriggled out of the teenager's grip and reached an arm forward to try and stop the doors from closing.

'Merry!' she shouted desperately.

But it was too late, and the doors were firmly shut. Electra

looked up at the panel and saw the elevator was already on the third floor. She swore harshly under her breath and turned round to try and find Mariam, but the crowd had grown thick around her.

'Hey, Miss Electra, what are you doing here?' asked a young man as he began taking pictures on his camera.

'Yeah, we didn't know you were visiting Toronto,' called someone else. 'Can I have a photo too?'

'I . . .' Electra could feel beads of sweat gathering on her neck. 'Please, let me through, I have a car waiting for me outside. I . . .'

She was just on the verge of punching her way through the ever-deepening crowd when Mariam appeared in front of her and Electra gasped in relief.

'Hey, everyone, can you all move back a little, give Electra some space?' said Mariam in her calm, even tone.

'Yeah, ladies and gents, can we ask you to move away; you're blocking the elevator access, which could be dangerous.'

A man dressed in a black suit with an earpiece, which marked him out as security, appeared beside Mariam. 'This lady has a car waiting for her outside,' he said. 'Would you be so kind as to let her pass?'

Eventually, after Electra had posed for a number of pictures and signed autographs because she didn't want to be seen as mean or difficult, two hotel security guards escorted her and Mariam out onto the street and opened the limo door for them. It closed behind them with a bang. Inside, Electra groaned in frustration.

'Are you okay?' Mariam asked. 'Why did you take your headscarf and smock off?'

'Because *she* – Merry – was in the restroom! She was in a cubicle and I heard her on her cell phone, discussing how the

concierge had said there were two Muslim women waiting for her. She seemed frightened – talked about whether it was "him", whoever "he" is. So obviously, when she finished her call, I threw off my disguise, hoping she wouldn't run if she saw *me* as me. But then I got recognised and I just missed getting in the elevator with her by a second. Damn it, damn it, damn it!' she swore as the limo moved off. 'Merry was right there, and I can't believe I missed her. Do you think there's any way the hotel would give us her room number? Maybe if we made up a life and death situation or—'

'I'm afraid I already tried that,' Mariam cut in. 'All the concierge was prepared to do was to call her again.' Mariam suddenly let out a chuckle. 'I'll never forget his face as he came over to see what the fuss was about, and recognised you standing next to me. He must have wondered what on earth was going on.'

'I'm wondering what on earth is going on too,' Electra said. 'It's now obvious that Merry is avoiding us. She also told her friend – who she called Bridget – that she was leaving a day early and flying to London tonight.'

'Ooh, Electra! So at least we know where she's going next. Did you get a good look at her when she was by the elevator?'

'I got a back view of blonde shoulder-length hair, and I remember thinking what a neat little tush she had. From the back she could have been anywhere between eighteen and sixty, but she definitely looked smart and attractive. Oh, and she'll be staying at Claridge's Hotel.'

'That is even better! It hasn't been a waste of time coming after all. You must call your sisters and let them know what's happened.'

'Sure,' Electra agreed. 'I suppose that at least we managed to learn a bit more.'

'Oh, I think you definitely did. Now, do you have a sister conveniently located anywhere near London?'

Electra turned to Mariam and smiled. 'As a matter of fact, I do.'

Once they were settled on the jet, waiting to take off, Electra placed a call to Atlantis.

'*Allô?*'

'Hi, Ally, it's Electra, reporting in from Toronto.'

'Hi, Electra! Did you get to meet Merry McDougal and see the ring?'

'Well, I did and I didn't.'

'What does that mean?'

Electra explained the afternoon's events. When she'd finished, there was a long silence.

'Right. So, apart from the fact your day sounds a bit like a scene from a farce, at least you were able to find out where she's going next. Claridge's, eh? She must be a wealthy woman,' said Ally.

'I just want to know why she's doing her best to avoid us. None of us mean her any harm, but she's definitely afraid. She talked about "him". I wonder now if she meant Pa?'

'But she knows that Pa is dead, and can't be any threat, even if she thought he was once, which I find hard to believe.'

There was a pause on the line.

'So,' Electra sighed, 'where do we go from here?'

'I'm not sure. I'll have to speak to Maia and see what she thinks.'

'What about Star? She lives very close to London, doesn't she?'

'Good point, she does.'

'Would she mind going to Claridge's and staking out the lobby for a blonde woman with a neat behind?' Electra chuckled. 'Problem is, I'm sure that blondes with good asses are two a penny there, but maybe it's worth a try, especially as Star lives so close.'

'There's no harm in giving Star a buzz to see if she's up for it. If Merry is leaving tonight, Toronto time, she'll probably arrive there tomorrow morning.'

'If she does go, I suggest she doesn't leave Merry McDougal any messages saying that yet another of the D'Aplièse sisters wants to meet up with her,' said Electra. 'It's obviously freaking her out.'

'I agree. We have to find other ways and means of gaining an audience with her,' said Ally. 'I'll talk to Star.'

'Okay, well, my jet's about to take off, so speak tomorrow, Ally.'

'Thanks so much for your help, Electra. Safe flight.'

Electra switched off her cell phone as the engines began to roar.

9

Star
High Weald, Kent, England

'Night night, darling, sleep tight,' Star said as she both spoke and signed the words to Rory.

He did the same, then held her to him tightly for a hug, his small arms wrapped round her neck. 'Love you, Star,' he said into her ear.

'I love you too, darling. See you in the morning.'

At the door, Star watched Rory roll over in his bed, then she switched off the overhead light, leaving the small night light on. She walked down the creaking stairs and into the kitchen, which was still a mess from supper earlier. Through the window above the sink, Star could see Mouse sitting at the ageing iron table they had set up on the grass to catch the evening sun.

Pouring herself a small glass of wine, she went to join him outside.

'Hello, darling,' he said, looking up from the plans for High Weald, his family's ancient Tudor mansion that had seen so much neglect in the past few decades. She remembered how bowled over she'd been when she'd first seen it last year, and

how strange it was that she now knew every inch of decaying beam and damp, peeling paintwork inside it.

'How's everything coming along?' she asked him as she sat down.

'Slowly, as usual. I must have visited every reclamation yard in the south of England, looking for those two beams we need to replace the ones in the drawing room. But sixteenth-century beams that are the right thickness and colour aren't exactly just lying around.'

'Couldn't we do what your builder suggested, and make some that are a good approximation of the original? Giles said we could distress them and stain the wood the right colour so no one would even notice.'

'*I* would notice,' said Mouse. 'Anyway, there's an old pub in East Grinstead that's being refurbed into one of those gastro places, and they're knocking out the insides. The beams there are around the right time period, so maybe I'll find a match.'

'Let's hope so. I mean, it's fine here at Home Farm, but I wouldn't want to spend a winter here, especially as Rory is so prone to chest infections and there's no heating.'

'I know, darling.' Mouse finally looked up from his plans, his green eyes tired. 'But the point is that High Weald hasn't been properly updated in so long – and I'm talking structurally, not just a new flashy kitchen – so I want to ensure that not only is it as authentic as I can make it, but that it lasts for another two hundred years.'

'Of course.' Star stifled a sigh, because she'd heard this all so many times before. When it came to High Weald – and other houses Mouse worked on for clients – he was a perfectionist. Which was all very laudable, apart from the fact that the three of them were living in the freezing and impractical farmhouse down the lane from High Weald until the renovations were

done. *And at this rate*, she thought, *I could be drawing my pension by the time we've moved.*

'If you're busy, would you mind if I popped over to see Orlando? I have a . . . situation I want to pick his brains about,' she said.

'Oh yes? And what's that?'

'It's complicated – to do with my family – but I'll tell you when we both have more time.' Star stood up and kissed Mouse on the top of his handsome head, noticing that stress had recently brought a few grey strands to his rich auburn hair. 'Remember to check on Rory in an hour. He's been having bad dreams recently and he can't call out properly yet.'

'I will, of course. I'll take my work inside,' Mouse nodded.

'Thanks, darling. I'll see you later.'

Star walked to her old Mini, started the engine and let out the sigh she'd been holding in. She did love Mouse dearly, but wow, was he hard work sometimes.

'It's almost as if the rest of the world doesn't exist outside his sixteenth-century beams and his porticoes and . . . grrrr,' she muttered as she drove off down the country lane towards the village of Tenterden. After a ten-minute drive, she parked the car outside the bookshop and let herself in with the old-fashioned brass key.

'Orlando? Are you upstairs?' she called, as she walked through to the back of the shop and opened the door that led to the flat above where he lived.

'I am,' came the reply. 'Do come up and join me.'

Star arrived at the top of the stairs and opened the door to the sitting room. Orlando was in his favourite leather chair, a white linen napkin tucked into his shirt, as he finished his dessert.

'Mmm . . . summer pudding. I truly adore it,' he said as he took his napkin and dabbed it round his mouth. 'Now then,

to what do I owe this pleasure? We only said adieu an hour or two ago.'

'I'm not disturbing you, am I?'

'Goodness, no, although I was just about to go on a date with T. E. Lawrence and his purportedly real adventures in Arabia,' he replied, tapping the leather-bound book sitting on the table next to him. 'So, how can I help you?' Orlando wound his long, manicured fingers around each other and gazed up at her. His green eyes were so like Mouse's, and yet the two men couldn't have been more different. Star often forgot that Orlando was the younger brother, due to his penchant for dressing as if it was 1908 rather than 2008.

'I have a mystery for you: do you remember that I've sometimes mentioned Georg Hoffman, our family lawyer?'

'I do indeed. I never forget anything.'

'I know you don't, Orlando. Anyway, he arrived at Atlantis a few days ago and announced that he thought he'd found the missing sister – our seventh sister.'

'What?!' Even the usually unflappable Orlando looked shocked. 'Are you talking about Merope, the missing sister of the Pleiades? Of course, some legends say that honour goes to Electra, although your youngest sister is very much present.'

'She certainly is. You should have seen her speech at the Concert for Africa. It was amazing.'

'You know I don't approve of television – it is literal anaesthesia for the brain – but I did read about Electra's speech in the *Telegraph*. Obviously a reformed character, after her little trip into the funny farm.'

'Orlando! Please don't call it that. It's beyond rude and totally inappropriate.'

'Forgive me for my lack of political correctness. As you are well aware, my language comes from another era where

"funny farm" would be an amusing phrase for an asylum. Once upon a time they called it Bedl—'

'Enough, Orlando!' Star reprimanded him. 'I know you do it on purpose to annoy me, but for the last time, Electra was simply getting help for her addictions. Anyway, do you want to hear where we've got to with the missing sister, or not?'

'Of course I do. If you would kindly remove my supper tray to the kitchen and furnish me with a nip of brandy, using the second glass to the left on the middle shelf in that cabinet, I will be all ears.'

As Star did as he asked, she wondered whether it was Orlando who needed treatment. *He definitely has OCD*, she thought as she allowed his instructions to guide her to the right glass on the right shelf.

'There we are,' she said as she put the stopper back in the crystal decanter and passed the brandy to him. Then she sat down in the leather chair on the other side of the fireplace. She thought how this room – modelled exactly on the sitting room of his old flat above the bookshop in Kensington, with its red-painted walls, antique furniture and rows of leather-bound books upon the shelves – would be the perfect setting for any Dickens novel. Orlando lived a good hundred years behind everybody else, which was mostly endearing, but sometimes irritating.

'So, dearest Star, do tell all,' Orlando said as he laced his fingers below his chin, ready to listen.

Star did so, and it took far longer than if she was telling anyone else, because Orlando constantly butted in with questions.

'What does that razor-sharp brain of yours deduce?' she finally asked.

'Rather sadly, not much more than you already have: that this Merry of yours, who has the emerald ring which is the

clue to her adopted daughter's true heritage, does not want to be found. Or at least, she does not want to be found by *your* family. So the only question worth asking is, why?'

'Exactly,' said Star. 'I was hoping you might have some ideas.'

'I doubt it's anything personal towards any of your sisters. You say that none of you have ever met or heard of the McDougals before. So this story and the key to the mystery must go much further back in time Yes,' Orlando nodded in affirmation, 'it's definitely something to do with the past.'

'I wonder if Pa was going to adopt Mary-Kate as a baby, then something went wrong, and he lost her?' Star mused.

'Perhaps. New Zealand is about as far away as you can get,' agreed Orlando. 'At least her mother might know who Mary-Kate's birth parents are.'

'Which is why you and I need to somehow arrange a meeting with her, so we can find out. *And* finally get a glimpse of that ring to match it to the drawing Ally has faxed me.'

'Are you saying you want to embroil me in a dangerous mission to London tomorrow?'

'Absolutely, and I know you wouldn't miss it for the world,' she countered.

'You know me too well, dear Star. Now, I want to go over everything again in detail . . .'

When Star had finished and there were no more questions, she watched Orlando sitting in his chair, eyes closed and obviously deep in concentration.

'Sorry not to be able to play Watson to your Holmes for much longer, but I need to get back home,' she prompted.

'Of course,' Orlando said, opening his eyes. 'So, you're serious about meeting with this woman tomorrow?'

'You know I am. Maia and Ally have asked me to.'

'Well then, I fear it will cost your family a fortune, but you

need to reserve one suite, and a smaller single room, at Claridge's hotel.'

Star narrowed her eyes. 'Orlando, this isn't simply a ruse to spend a night in what I know is your favourite hotel?'

'My dear Star, it is you that will be making use of the luxury suite, whilst I am no doubt billeted in an attic room next to the maids. Although their afternoon tea is quite the ticket.'

'Hmmm . . . If you could tell me what this plan involves, then I could run it past Maia and Ally to see if they would allow us to spend what must be an astronomical amount for rooms there. Maia says Georg's secretary is booking anything we need. He's away apparently.'

'I am still finessing the plan, but please assure your sisters I believe it is almost foolproof. Tell them I will provide a refund of all costs if we fail in our endeavour. Now, I must get to work too; I have a lot of preparation to do overnight if I'm to pull this off.'

'What do you mean, *you* are going to pull this off? Am I not involved?'

'Oh, you are deeply involved, and must play your part to perfection. I am presuming that you have a smart dress or a suit in your wardrobe?'

'Um . . . I think I could probably pull something together, yes.'

'And any pearls?'

'I have a fake necklace and earrings that I bought once and have never worn.'

'Perfect. Oh, and of course, some heels, but not too high. Tomorrow, my dear Star, you will be Lady Sabrina Vaughan.'

'You mean, I have to act?'

'Hardly.' Orlando rolled his eyes. 'Think of it merely as preparation for your future wedding to my brother. You will be a real lady then anyway.'

'That's different . . . I'm not sure acting is my *métier*, Orlando. I've always had the most terrible stage fright.'

'You will just be playing yourself, only with more lucre, and it is I who will be doing most of the acting.'

'That's a relief. Do we need any help from CeCe and Chrissie?' asked Star. 'They're in London now, although CeCe is busy putting her flat on the market and sorting her stuff out to be shipped to Australia.'

'No.' Orlando waved the thought away. 'Under the circumstances, the last thing we require is another D'Aplièse sister. This is a delicate operation. Have the suite booked under your pseudonym, and mine under "Orlando Sackville".'

Star had to chuckle at the literary allusion. 'All right then.'

'Now, be gone and leave me to work,' he intoned. 'I shall meet you on the platform tomorrow, in time to catch the nine forty-six train to London. Goodnight.'

By the time Star arrived home, Mouse had gone to bed. She put in a quick call to Atlantis and explained the situation to Ally.

'Well, if Orlando thinks it will help, I'll send an email to Claridge's now to reserve the rooms,' Ally said. 'What exactly do you think he has up his sleeve?'

'I don't have a clue, but he's awfully clever and has helped me solve a couple of mysteries before.'

'I'm intrigued. Now, he said I should book your rooms under pseudonyms?'

'Yes. Orlando Sackville.' Star spelt it out for her. 'I'm sure he chose it in honour of Vita Sackville-West, who inspired the book *Orlando*, written by her friend Virginia Woolf.'

'Well, at least we're not the only family with obscure names,' Ally chuckled. 'And what pseudonym are you using?'

'I'm to be Lady Sabrina Vaughan. Anyway, I'd better try to get some sleep if I'm going to practise being a lady tomorrow.'

'Let's just hope that whatever your boss has planned, it works. I'll call Georg's secretary in the morning so she can arrange for the bill to be sent to her.'

'Okay. I'll keep in touch as often as Orlando allows. Night, Ally.'

'Night, Star.'

Orlando was already waiting on the platform at Ashford station when Star ran to join him, just as the train was approaching.

'Good morning. One might say you were cutting that fine,' he noted as the doors opened and they stepped inside.

'I had to take Rory to school, then hunt through my wardrobe to find something suitable to wear,' Star panted as she sat down. 'Will I do?'

'You look perfect,' said Orlando, admiring the elegant summer dress that showed off her slim figure. 'Although perhaps you could style your hair in a chignon? It might help make you look a little more stately.'

'Orlando,' Star whispered into his ear, 'we're not putting on an Oscar Wilde play, you know. These days, actresses and supermodels – common people to you – marry into the aristocracy all the time.'

'I am aware of that, but given that you told me our Mrs McDougal has lived in New Zealand for over thirty years, she, like me, may be a little behind the English times. But no matter, I think you look ravishing and will fit into our upcoming surroundings perfectly.'

'I wish Mouse could have joined me this evening. We could do with a couple of nights away together. Isn't it ironic that he is the real thing – a lord – yet not in a million years could he afford to stay at Claridge's?'

'Of course he could, Star. He has a houseful – or currently a storage facility full – of precious antiques, paintings and objets d'art that are worth a small fortune. But he, very sensibly in my book, would not think staying in a luxury hotel is worth spending his money on.'

'You're right, of course, and besides, the renovation of the house is costing everything he has. I do sometimes dream of moving into a modern semi where it's warm and everything actually works. And where my boyfriend comes home to me in time for supper and we chat about our days . . . or anything other than dado rails and RSJs – whatever they are.'

'High Weald is the other woman in Mouse's life,' Orlando declared.

'I know, and the worst thing is, I have to live with her forever.'

'Oh, come now, Star, it was obvious from the start that you fell in love with High Weald too.'

'Of course I did, and yes, it will be worth it when it's finished. Anyway, far more urgently, please tell me what exactly you have planned.'

'If all goes well, it should be a most pleasant way to pass the time,' Orlando said. 'We will arrive, unpack, then wander downstairs separately to take a light lunch in the Foyer restaurant that overlooks the entrance. Having researched all the flights that took off last night from Toronto, there are only four that our Mrs McDougal could be on. They all land between half past noon and three p.m. I have drawn a map of the ground floor at Claridge's. We will choose where we sit accordingly, so that we can espy the entrance and anyone who checks in to the hotel with luggage between those hours. Look.' Orlando dug a sheet of paper out of his ancient leather briefcase and pointed out the entrance, the Foyer and the reception desk drawn neatly onto it. 'When we check in, we

must make sure to reserve tables in the restaurant with the best view.'

'But there may be any number of women arriving in the entrance area between those times.'

'We know that Mrs McDougal is in her late fifties – although she looks younger – and is slim with blonde hair. Plus, her suitcases will have airline luggage tags on them.' Orlando produced another piece of paper from his briefcase. 'This is a picture of the tag that would indicate Merry has travelled from Toronto Pearson. The airport code is YYZ.'

'Okay, but even if we do manage to spot her and her luggage, how will we introduce ourselves?'

'Aha!' said Orlando. 'You can leave that part to me. But of course, I must first introduce myself officially to *you*,' he said, dipping once more into his briefcase and handing Star a beautifully embossed business card.

VISCOUNT ORLANDO SACKVILLE

FOOD AND WINE JOURNALIST

Orlando had put his mobile number at the bottom of it. 'Viscount?' Star smiled. 'Food and wine journalist, eh?'

'I feel I jolly well could be, given the amount of fine fare and quality wines I have ingested over the course of my life. Besides, my brother is a lord, so me being a viscount is not too much of a stretch.'

'Okay, but how is you having a business card going to help? And how did you get these printed so quickly?'

'Ways and means, my dear girl. The printing shop down the street knows me well, and as to how it will help, I simply took into account everything that you have told me. I looked up The Vinery, and it tells me the proprietors are Jock and Mary McDougal. The business was started in the early eighties and

113

is now one of the region's most successful vineyards, mainly selling wine within New Zealand, but also beginning to sell in Europe. In other words, given that New Zealand wine did not appear on any dining table further afield than Australia up until a few years ago, Jock and Mary McDougal have built up a business they must be very proud of.'

'Yes, but her husband – Jock – died a few months ago.'

'Exactly, and you have told me that their son Jack is taking over from where his father left off. If he is currently in France learning from the masters of the craft, it is easy to deduce he is aiming to grow the business further. Agreed?'

'Probably, yes.'

'Now, from what I understand of human nature, I do know that the maternal instinct normally overrides any other. Therefore, Mrs McDougal will wish to give her son any help that she can.'

'And?'

'What better than to bump into a food and wine writer whilst staying at Claridge's? Especially if he has an "in" with the well-known food and wine magazines and newspaper columns in Great Britain. *What such an article could do for our vineyard*, she thinks to herself. *And for my beloved son.* Are you getting the gist now, Star?'

'I think I am, yes. So, in a nutshell, you're going to introduce yourself to her as an aristocratic journalist – how you may get that introduction, I don't yet know – and then ask her if she'd be happy to be interviewed by you about her vineyard.'

'And her son, too, as he is the new official proprietor. It is patently obvious to me that we need to find some way of making contact with Master Jack to help establish further facts about his younger sister. For example, we have no idea if he too is adopted. Mummy dearest is bound to give me his

contact details.' Orlando clapped his hands together in glee. 'Isn't it brilliant?'

'It's pretty good, yes, but where exactly do I come in?'

'Well, I need Mrs McDougal to feel reassured that I am not some charlatan trying to gather information about her surreptitiously. Therefore, after I have spotted her, then introduced myself at the reception desk, you will stand up from your table and walk past us. I will turn and stare in surprise. "Why! Sabrina!" I shall say. "What on earth are you doing here?" I will ask as we kiss each other politely on each cheek. Then you will reply that you're up from the country with your husband, doing a little light shopping. You will ask me to join you for drinks in your suite tonight at six p.m. I utter, "Delighted to," and you go on your way, having told me which suite you're in,' Orlando added. 'If all goes well with our little charade, Mrs McDougal will be convinced of my excellent credentials and social gravitas, which will warm her up for when I ask her for an interview.'

Star breathed in deeply. 'Goodness, I really do have to act! I hope that I can pull it off without saying something that will give us away.'

'Do not fear, Star. I've made your part short and sweet.'

'But when are we actually going to get to the crux of the matter? I mean, when do I come clean about who I am and why I'm masquerading as Lady Sabrina in an enormous suite?' she asked as the train pulled into Charing Cross station.

'As you said earlier, this is not an Oscar Wilde play, dear Star, merely a real-life improvisation. We will have to see whether we get past the first hurdle, which is spotting her entering the hotel and me being able to entrap her before she can escape to her room. There are many imponderables that I simply cannot take into account, but let us go one step at a time, shall we?'

'Okay,' she sighed as they left the train to head to the taxi rank and she felt her stomach turn over.

'Oh my goodness!' Star exclaimed as the general manager – who had shown them to her suite personally – left the sitting room. 'Isn't this amazing?'

'I have to admit that it is rather, yes. I've always adored Claridge's; it's an art deco triumph, and how wonderful that they have kept it so,' Orlando said as his fingers brushed across a tiger-striped desk, before sitting down in one of the velvet smoking chairs.

'They've left us a bottle of free champagne! Can we have some? It might help to calm my nerves.'

'My dear Star, you're acting like an excited child on Christmas morning. Of course we can open the champagne if you want, although I do wish people would not regard such things as "free". You – or in fact, your family – has just paid the equivalent of your month's salary at my bookshop to stay in a set of rooms for a single night. Your champagne is not free and if you decide to partake of the other accoutrements, such as those little bottles of whatever it is you ladies need to pour into the bath, or even the towels and bathrobes, then please do so. For none of it is "free". Yet people delight in saying they "stole" things when they return from such a jaunt. Utterly ridiculous,' sniffed Orlando, standing up and walking over to the ice bucket. 'What shall we drink to?' he asked her as he lifted out the champagne.

'Either living here forever, or not getting arrested for impersonating other people; you decide.'

'Let's drink to both!' Orlando said as he popped the cork. 'There you are,' he said, taking a flute of champagne across

to her. 'I also brought you the paid-for chocolates they left next to the champagne.'

'I'm queen for a day,' Star said as she popped one of the gorgeously glazed delicacies into her mouth.

'From what you've told me of your family, you almost certainly have enough filthy lucre from your trust to live like this every day.'

'I'm not sure how much it actually is and even though it is ours, we run everything by Georg, our lawyer.'

'I have never met this Georg, but he is merely a member of staff that your family employs. It is your money, dear Star, and it's very important you and your sisters don't forget that.'

'You're right, of course, but Georg is quite scary. I'm sure he wouldn't approve of me asking him for a year's worth of money to live in a suite at Claridge's,' she chuckled. 'Besides, part of the fun is what a treat it is. It wouldn't be if I could live here every day, would it?'

'True, true,' agreed Orlando. 'Now then, while you were checking in, I was casing the joint. In other words, working out the best tables in the Foyer restaurant for you and I to sit, and I booked two. I will arrive first, then you ten minutes later. We can't be seen together by anybody before we bump into each other near the reception desk. So, you shall sit here' – Orlando indicated the position of her table on the floor plan – 'and I shall sit there, which gives us both a good view of the entrance, but means the enormous flower arrangement in the centre blocks us from each other's sight.'

'Okay, but how do we communicate? By carrier pigeon across the room?' she giggled.

'Star, I do hope that the alcohol isn't going to your head. We use the rather dull modern method of the mobile phone. If you or I spot a woman who may be Mrs McDougal, then we text each other. I will follow her progress, which will

hopefully take her to the reception desk, give her a couple of minutes, then swoop in behind her. At this point, you will stand up, and make your way slowly across to us. You will stop at the flower arrangement and admire it, while checking that I have made verbal contact with her. Then, you will walk towards us and we will enact our little play. Just remember to ask me to your suite for drinks at six p.m.'

'Right, okay,' Star breathed, taking another gulp of champagne. 'We can do this, Orlando, can't we?'

'We surely can, my dear, we surely can. Now, given it is eleven thirty, I will take a wander downstairs and leave you to titivate. Good luck.'

'Good luck to you too,' Star called as Orlando walked towards the front door of their suite. 'And Orlando?'

'Yes?'

'Thank you.'

Merry

London

June 2008

10

I sat in the back of the taxi, and even though I felt exhausted from another sleepless night on a plane, I had to give a small smile of pleasure at the fact I was actually *sitting* in the back of a black cab. All those years ago, when I had last been in London during that terrible time, it had been my dream to put out a hand and hail one. But they, like anything else that hadn't been an absolute necessity, had been completely out of my budget. In fact, I could have equally contemplated getting on a rocket and flying to the moon, which had come true for Neil Armstrong just a few years before I'd arrived here in London.

I could hardly believe how the city had changed since I'd last visited. Great flyovers led out from Heathrow, the traffic backed up in a long, never-ending stream. Tall office blocks and apartment buildings rose out of the ground all around me, and I felt tears pricking at my eyes because it could have been Sydney or Toronto, or any big city across the world. I'd held on to my vision of London for so long; in my mind's eye, I saw the elegant architecture, the green swathes of open parks, and the National Gallery, which were about the only things that had been free to me back then.

Merry, I told myself firmly, *you know very well that at least*

Big Ben and the Houses of Parliament are still there, and the River Thames . . .

I closed my eyes to block out the view, praying it would improve as we drew closer to my treasured memories of the centre of this great city. I'd hoped I would be able to enjoy it properly this time, yet since Mary-Kate had left her messages for me and Bridget, and those women had sat waiting for me in the lobby at the Radisson, I'd been taken back to the last time I'd been here. And all the fear and dread I had felt then.

It has to be him, surely . . . ?

The line repeated in my head for the thousandth time. But why? Why after all these years? And how had he – *they* – found me?

Yet again, my heart began to slam against my chest. They must be serious as well, to use so many of them and be able to follow me all the way from New Zealand to Canada.

Admittedly, I'd come on my trip partly for pleasure, but also to search for both of them, know for sure where they were. And – certainly with one of them – to finally find out *why*. I hadn't uttered either of their names since I'd arrived in New Zealand thirty-seven years ago, knowing that to survive, I had to put my past behind me and begin again. But then, after my darling Jock had died out of the blue, it was as if the buffer he had always provided had collapsed and the memories had come rushing back. When I'd seen Bridget on Norfolk Island, fuelled by Irish whiskey, we'd reminisced about the old days and I'd admitted my 'Grand Tour' contained an ulterior motive.

'I just want to find out whether they're alive or dead,' I'd said as she'd refilled my glass. 'I can't live the rest of my life not knowing, *or* hiding, for that matter. I'd like to go home to Ireland and see my family. Hopefully, by the time I'm due

to get there, I'll know. And feel it's safe, for them and me. Do you understand?'

'I do, of course, but in my view, both of them ruined your life in their different ways,' she said.

'That just isn't fair, Bridget. There *had* to be a reason why he never came. He loved me, you know he did, and—'

'Jaysus!' Bridget had studied me closely. 'You're sounding to me like you're still holding a candle for him! You're not, are you?'

'No, of course I'm not. You know how much I adored Jock. He saved me, Bridget, and I miss him terribly.'

'Maybe 'tis because he's gone that you've decided to rekindle the flame for your first love. But let me tell you, if you want to meet a man, get yourself on one of those cruises. My friend Priscilla went on one to Norway and said there were heaps of horny widowers looking for a wife,' she'd cackled.

'Looking for someone to nurse them through their dotage, more like.' I'd rolled my eyes. 'I don't think a cruise is for me, Bridget. And truly, it's got nothing to do with me looking for another man. It's about trying to find out what happened to my first love. *And* the man that I believe was responsible for destroying it.'

'Well, I'd say don't go digging up the past. Especially *your* past.'

Bridget always told it how it was and I respected her for that. We'd known each other since childhood, and despite her bossiness, which precluded anyone else's opinion being right except hers, I was very fond of her.

It was in her tiny flat that I'd stayed on the sofa during those awful three weeks in London. She'd been a good friend to me then when I'd needed her. Especially given that I'd lied and said I was going back to Ireland when I'd left her and

London behind. It was just safer she didn't know anything in case *he'd* come knocking on her door.

It was Bridget who had discovered my whereabouts two years ago, when a bottle of our 2005 pinot noir had won a gold medal at the prestigious Air New Zealand wine awards. The *Otago Daily Times* had taken a photograph of me, Jock and Jack, and printed a piece on The Vinery.

Bridget, retired and on holiday in New Zealand, had recognised me from the photograph and turned up one day, giving me a near heart attack when I'd opened the door and seen her. I'd had to tell her fast that neither Jock nor my children knew anything of my past, and, thinking she'd come to tell me of a family death, was hugely relieved when she told me it was simple serendipity that she'd seen the photograph.

I'd been thrilled when, a few weeks after moving to Norfolk Island, having fallen in love with it during our trip there, she'd met Tony – and after a short time, had decided to marry him. Given that Bridget had been a spinster all her life, I'd been very surprised.

'It's only because Tony just does whatever Bridget tells him to, Mum,' Jack had commented before he'd left for France – he was not a Bridget fan. 'I reckon she secretly beats him, then locks him in a kennel outside at night,' he'd added for good measure.

It was true that Tony was very mild-mannered and actively appeared to enjoy being ordered around. They certainly seemed very happy together anyway, though it had really put the wind up Bridget when we'd both heard the messages from Mary-Kate about the 'missing sister', and the two women who wanted to meet me.

'What did I tell you only last night about digging up the past?!' she'd exclaimed.

'But I've never even mentioned anything about all that to Mary-Kate. It must be coincidence, surely? After all, Mary-Kate is adopted, so one of these girls might just be part of her birth family.'

'They might be, yes, but I remember the "missing sister" is what he used to call you. After all these years, and Tony and me just getting hitched, I don't want anything to do with all that.'

So the two of us had decided to take the afternoon flight to Sydney, just in case. 'If these women do arrive on the island and knock on the door, Tony might spill some beans,' I'd fretted. 'Do you think we should tell him to be out?'

'No, Merry. Tony knows nothing, and if we told him not to say anything, then he'd just ask me a load of questions neither of us would have answers to. All he needs to know is we want a girls' night in Sydney. Best just to leave it and let them arrive unexpectedly.'

I could still feel the shiver of terror after hearing Mary-Kate's mention of the search for the missing sister.

I will hunt you down, wherever you try to hide . . .

Then there was the emerald ring. *He'd* hated it from the first moment he'd seen it. Because it was a twenty-first birthday gift to me from someone he loathed.

Looks like an engagement ring, so, he'd muttered. *Him, at his age, with all his money and his English accent . . . He's a pervert, that's what he is . . .*

Maybe when I arrived at Claridge's, I should just take the ring out of my bag and throw it in the River Thames. Yet I knew I couldn't, because aside from the fact it now belonged to Mary-Kate, it had been given to me by one of the most precious people in my life – by the man who had loved me unconditionally and never betrayed me . . . Ambrose.

Thankfully, the buildings around me were starting to

become lower, and some of the ones I remembered seeing from the top of a double-decker bus were appearing. The sight of them comforted me, and made the memory of the two women who had appeared in the lobby yesterday, and then the voice that had shouted my name as I stepped into the lift in Toronto, less frightening. Even though Mary-Kate, and the letter from a woman called Electra, had reassured me these sisters just wanted to see my ring, I couldn't work out how they had got to me so fast. Anyway, the good news was that the trail had ended in Canada. Not a soul other than Bridget, whom I could trust with my life, knew where I was today. For now, I was in London and there'd be no one tracking me down at Claridge's . . .

I felt a sudden and much-needed flip of excitement as the taxi pulled up outside the hotel. Porters rushed to take my luggage as I paid the driver. I'd been told about this famous and beautiful hotel by Ambrose all those years ago in Dublin, when I'd been thinking of taking an exploratory trip with Bridget to London during our summer break from uni.

'It's a magnificent city, Mary. Full of beautiful architecture and many historic buildings,' he'd said. 'If you do go, you must take tea at Claridge's, just to see the wonderful art deco interior. If my parents had to be in London for business or a social event, they would always stay there.'

So travel to London we had, but rather than Bridget and I taking tea at Claridge's, we had stayed at a grotty bed and breakfast off the Gloucester Road. Nevertheless, we had both fallen in love with the city itself, prompting Bridget to move there soon after university, and me fleeing to it when I'd needed to escape from Dublin . . .

And here I was now, being ushered through the lobby of Claridge's as a paying guest.

'Did you have a good journey, madam?' the receptionist

asked as I stood in front of the check-in desk, my eyes taking in the sheer elegance and luxury of my surroundings.

'I did indeed, thank you.'

'I see you flew in from Toronto. Canada's a country I've always wanted to visit. Do you have your passport, madam?'

I handed it over to her and watched her tap the details into her computer. 'So, your home address is The Vinery, Gibbston Valley, New Zealand?'

'It is, yes.'

'Another country I've always wanted to see,' she smiled, all charm.

'Do excuse me for butting in like this,' came a voice from behind me, 'but did I hear you say that you reside at The Vinery in the Gibbston Valley?'

I turned to see a very tall, angular man, whose three-piece suit looked as if it had been modelled on something Oscar Wilde would have worn in his heyday.

'Er, yes,' I replied, wondering if he was the manager of the hotel, because he looked terribly official. 'Is there a problem?'

'Good grief, no.' The man smiled, then reached into the top pocket of his jacket to pass me a card. 'Allow me to introduce myself.' He pointed to the name on the card. 'Viscount Orlando Sackville and, for my sins, I am a food and wine journalist. The reason I so rudely interrupted you was because only last week I was having lunch with a friend of mine. He's a wine importer, you see. And he mentioned to me that New Zealand wines were casting off their reputation for being the lesser sibling of Australian wines and producing some very good bottles. The Vinery was one of the vineyards he mentioned. I believe you won a gold medal for your 2005 pinot noir. May I ask if you are the proprietor?'

'Well, my husband – who sadly died recently – and I ran

the business together for many years. Now my son Jack is taking over.'

'May I offer you my condolences for your loss,' the man said, looking genuinely sad. 'Now, I must not take up any more of your time, but may I enquire whether you are staying here at the hotel?'

'I am, yes.'

'Then might I beg you to spare me an hour or so later on this evening? I would very much like to write a feature on The Vinery – it's the kind of thing that the food and wine pages of the broadsheets here just adore. And of course, I know the editor of the *Sunday Times* Wine Club well. I'm sure you will know that if one's wine is included in the selection, well, one is *made*, so to speak.'

'Can I think about it? I am rather jet-lagged, you see, and—'

'Sabrina! Darling girl, what on earth are you doing here?'

I turned around and saw a thin, willowy blonde, who rather reminded me of Mary-Kate, approaching before being kissed on both cheeks by my new friend.

'Oh, I'm up from the country with Julian. We're staying here for a couple of nights while he works and I do a little shopping,' she replied.

'That sounds divine, darling,' he said to the young woman, who seemed rather nervous, before he caught my eye and drew the woman in closer.

'May I introduce Lady Sabrina Vaughan? She's a very old friend of both my family and myself.'

'Hello, er . . . ?'

'Mary. Mrs Mary McDougal,' I said as I extended my hand to shake hers.

'Mrs McDougal here is the co-owner of a wonderful vineyard in New Zealand. I was just telling her how dear

Sebastian Fairclough was waxing lyrical about her wines only the other day. I am determined to entice her into giving me an interview about the vineyard.'

'I see,' Sabrina nodded. 'It's lovely to meet you, Mary.' There was a pause as my new friend eyed her.

'Oh!' she continued. 'Why don't you come to my suite for drinks at six tonight? It's room number, er . . . 106. You are very welcome too, Mrs McDougal,' she added.

'Wonderful! See you then, Sabrina,' answered Orlando.

'Excuse me, Mrs McDougal, may I take your credit card?' asked the receptionist as Sabrina walked off towards the lift.

'Why, yes, of course,' I said, digging into my purse and handing it over.

'Mrs McDougal, forgive me again for interrupting, but do come tonight for drinks with Sabrina and me if you can. Then we can discuss your vineyard and all things wine.'

'As I said, I might be a little jet-lagged, but I'll try.'

'Excellent. Adieu until then.' He began to walk away as the receptionist handed over my key, but then halted and turned back.

'Forgive me, but I didn't catch your room number.'

I looked down at the key. 'It's 112. Goodbye, Orlando.'

Upstairs in my beautiful room, with its high ceiling, exquisite furnishings and views onto the bustling London road beneath me, I unpacked a couple of summer dresses, a skirt and a blouse, then dialled room service to order tea for one. Even though there were tea-making facilities in the room, I wanted to drink it out of a bone-china cup, poured from an elegant teapot, just as Ambrose had described. It duly arrived, and I sat in a chair savouring the moment.

I studied the card that the very posh Englishman had thrust into my hand. If he was who he said he was (and the details

on the card and the fact that another woman had greeted him in the lobby surely confirmed it), then it presented a wonderful opportunity to get The Vinery some British – and perhaps international – attention.

I decided I should call Jack. Out of habit, I looked at my watch to gauge the time difference, then realised that I was no longer in New Zealand, Australia or, in fact, Canada, and only an hour behind France.

I picked up the receiver on the bedside table and dialled Jack's mobile. It took a while to connect and then gave that strange dialling tone which meant you were calling a foreign country.

'Hello?'

'It's Mum here, Jack. The phone's very crackly – can you hear me?'

'Yes, loud and clear. How are you? Or more to the point, where are you?'

'I'm well, Jack, I'm well,' I said and, hoping he wasn't familiar with either American or British dialling codes, I told my son a lie. 'I'm in New York!'

'Wow! The Big Apple! How is it?'

'Oh . . . noisy, busy, amazing!' I bluffed, because I'd never visited New York in my life. 'Just as you would imagine. Now then, how are you, sweetheart?'

'Happy, Mum, very happy. It's hard work communicating as my French is pathetic, but I'm learning a lot from François, and the Rhône Valley is something else! Just mile after mile of vines, pastel-coloured houses and blue skies. We even have mountains behind us to remind me of home. Although it's nothing at all like home,' Jack chuckled. 'So, after New York, you're off to London?'

'I am, yes.'

'Well, François said he'd be happy to host you here after

the harvest, if you'd return the favour when he and his family visit New Zealand next year.'

'That goes without saying, Jack, of course I will. I'd love to see Provence, but I've Ireland on the schedule after London, remember?'

'The big return to the homeland . . . I'd enjoy taking a trip over there to see where my mysterious mum came from. Actually, I don't think you've ever said exactly where in Ireland, other than talking about uni in Dublin.'

'To be fair, Jack, you've never asked,' I countered.

'"To be fair", is it Mum? You sound Irish when just thinking about going back! Anyway, are you enjoying your Grand Tour?'

'I'm loving it, but I miss your dad terribly. We always said we'd do this when he retired, but of course, him being him, he never did.'

'I know, Mum, but I don't like you travelling by yourself.'

'Oh, Jack, don't worry about me, I'm perfectly capable of taking care of myself. Anyway, I wanted to tell you about someone I met at the hotel . . .' – I suddenly remembered that I was meant to be in New York – '. . . last night. He's a wine writer for some big international newspapers. We got chatting and he asked me whether I'd be up for doing an interview on The Vinery, its history, and so on. What do you think?'

'It sounds exactly like what we need. Wow, Mum, we let you out of our sight for more than two minutes, and you're chatting up wine journos in hotels!'

'Oh, very funny, Jack. This man was around half my age. He's called' – I consulted the card – 'Orlando Sackville. Have you heard of him, by any chance?'

'No, but then again, I'm not exactly an expert on wine journalists yet. Dad did all that kind of thing, y'know? Anyway, it can't do any harm to talk to him, can it? You can

do the history of how you and Dad built the business up from nothing. If he needs to know the technical details of the grapes we use and stuff, then just give him my mobile number and I'd be happy to speak to him.'

'I will, of course,' I said. 'Right, I'd better leave you to get on. I've missed you, Jack, and I know your sister misses you as well.'

'I miss you guys too. Okay, Mum, keep in touch. Love you.'

'Love you too.' I ended the call, then picked up the journalist's card to dial the mobile number written on it.

'Orlando Sackville,' answered the dulcet tones of the man I'd met earlier.

'Hello, it's Mary McDougal here, the lady you met downstairs, from The Vinery in Otago. I'm not disturbing you, am I?'

'That's the last thing you're doing. What a delight! Does this call mean that you're prepared for me to interview you?'

'I discussed it with my son, Jack – the one who's in Provence – and he thinks it would be a good idea for me to speak to you. Although he's the person for any technical detail you'll need.'

'Wonderful! Six p.m. in Sabrina's suite then?'

'Yes. Although I won't stay for long, or I might fall asleep where I sit.'

'I understand completely. Sabrina is looking forward to seeing you too.'

Even though Orlando had not struck me as a man who would jump me, and was half my age anyway, I was still glad Sabrina would be there.

'I'll see you at six then. Goodbye, Orlando,' I said.

'*À bientôt*, Mrs McDougal.'

I hung up the phone, immediately taken back to my Dublin days when I'd first gone to Trinity College and encountered

similar types to Orlando and Sabrina, with their cultivated English accents and their worry-free lives.

'I'm meeting an English viscount and a lady for drinks tonight,' I said aloud, and thought how much *he* would have hated that.

Lying back on the downy pillows, I went over the facts that I'd gathered so far on both men I'd been searching for. There were certainly no males of either name of the right age living in New Zealand – I had exhausted all possibilities before I'd left. And after going through pages of marriages and deaths at the records office in Toronto had drawn a blank, the only place that was left for me to search before I headed home to Ireland was right here in London.

Come on, Merry, stop thinking about all that. It was so long ago and this is meant to be a relaxing holiday! I reprimanded myself.

I pulled my bottle of duty-free Jameson's whiskey out of its box and poured myself a finger, deciding that, having travelled across so many time zones, my body was completely confused anyway. Normally I'd never have allowed myself to drink alcohol until the evening and it was barely two p.m. here, but I took a deep swig anyway. The sudden vivid memory floated back to me of the first night I'd ever seen him. I'd looked like a complete fright, turning up at some Dublin bar to hear Bridget's latest boyfriend play in a band.

That night, he'd told me I was the most beautiful girl he'd ever laid eyes on, but I'd just taken it as part of the chat. He'd not needed to say a word to charm me, because it had only taken one look at those warm hazel eyes to fall in love with him.

Dublin . . .

How could it be that I had been drawn back into the past so vividly since Jock had died? And was it just coincidence

that, since my thoughts had travelled back in time, these women had begun pursuing me?

I'd also realised that by tentatively opening up the memories that had been sealed for so long, it had unleashed a torrent of further ones, some stemming way back into my childhood.

I remembered *him*, the young boy I'd known when we were both at school together and walking home across the fields – and how passionate he'd been even then. Fiercely set in his beliefs and determined to convince me too.

'You read this, Merry, and you'll understand,' he'd said as he'd pressed the notebook into my hands. It had been the day I'd left for boarding school in Dublin.

'I'll be after calling you the missing sister till you're back,' he'd said.

I remembered how his intensity had always been unsettling, especially as it was always so focused on *me*.

'I want you to read about my grandmother Nuala's life and see what the British did to us, and how my family fought for Ireland and freedom . . . 'Tis my gift to you, Merry . . .'

The first page of the black exercise book had been inscribed with the words *Nuala Murphy's diary, age 19*. I had kept it for forty-eight years, yet never read it. I remembered flipping through the pages when I had arrived at boarding school, but the cramped untidy writing – as well as the atrocious spelling – had put me off, besides which there had been so much else to occupy me in my new life in Dublin. And then, as he and I had got older, I had tried to distance myself as much as I could from him and his beliefs, yet still I'd taken the diary with me when I left Ireland. I had found it again in a box when I had gone about the painful process of packing up Jock's things. And instinctively brought it with me on this trip.

I stood up, opened my suitcase, and found the diary in the

inside pocket, wrapped in a canvas bag to protect it. Why hadn't I simply thrown it away, just as I had cast off almost everything else to do with my past?

Taking out my jewellery box, I went to put it in the room safe, but something urged me to open it. I picked up the ring, the seven tiny emeralds glittering in the light. Then I lay down on the bed, slid on my reading glasses and picked up the diary.

It's time, Merry . . .

I opened it, tracing my fingers over the faded black script that covered the pages.

28th July, 1920 . . .

Nuala

The Argideen Valley,
West Cork, Ireland

July 1920

Cumann na mBan

The Irishwomen's Council

11

Nuala Murphy was hanging out the washing on the line. Over the past few months it had extended to three times its size, what with all the laundry she was doing for the brave men of the local brigades of the Irish Republican Army, known as the IRA for short.

The washing line stood at the front of the farmhouse, which overlooked the valley and caught the morning sun. Nuala put her hands on her hips and surveyed the lanes beneath for any sign of the Black and Tans, the dreaded British constables named for their mix of khaki army trousers and the Royal Irish Constabulary dark green tunics that looked almost black. They trundled around the countryside in their lorries of destruction, their only mission to root out the men fighting the British as volunteers for the IRA. They had arrived in their thousands the year before to support the local police force, who had been struggling to contain the Irish uprising. Thankfully, Nuala could see that the lanes beneath the farmhouse were deserted.

Her friend Florence who, like Nuala, was a member of Cumann na mBan, the women's volunteer outfit, arrived once a week on her pony and trap with a new load of laundry concealed beneath squares of peat turf. Nuala allowed herself a small smile as the line of laundry flapped in the wind. There

was something satisfying about displaying some of the most wanted men in West Cork's underthings for all to see.

Nuala cast one more glance around her and walked inside the farmhouse. The low-beamed kitchen-cum-living area was stifling today, what with the fire burning to cook lunch for the household. Her mother Eileen had already peeled all the vegetables and they were boiling away in a pot above the fire. Heading for the pantry, Nuala collected eggs that she had taken from the henhouse earlier, along with flour and the precious dried fruit soaked in cold tea, then set about making a mixture that would provide enough for three or four brack cakes. These days, they never knew when an IRA volunteer might arrive at the door, exhausted from being on the run and in need of food and shelter.

Once she had tipped the mixture into the bastable pot, ready to be hung over the fire when the vegetables were cooked, Nuala wiped the sweat from her brow and walked to the front door to take in some gulps of fresh air. She thought how, as a child, life here at Cross Farm had been hard work, but comparatively carefree. But that was before her Irish brethren had decided it was time to rise up against their British overlords, who had dominated and controlled Ireland for hundreds of years. After the initial killings of British constables in Tipperary in January of 1919, which had sparked the hostilities, ten thousand British soldiers had been sent to Ireland to subdue the uprising. Of all the British army troops in Ireland, the Essex Regiment was the most ruthless, raiding not only IRA safehouses, but also the homes of civilians. Then the Black and Tans had joined the soldiers to quell the insurrection.

Ireland had become an occupied country, where the freedoms Nuala had once taken for granted were being chipped away at every day. They had now been at war with the might

of the British Empire for over a year, battling not just for their own freedom, but for that of Mother Ireland herself.

Nuala stifled a yawn – she couldn't remember the last time she'd had more than three hours' sleep, what with volunteers arriving at the farmhouse for food and a billet. Cross Farm was known to all of the local IRA as a safehouse, partly because of its position nestling in a valley, with the advantage of being able to post scouts at the top of the heavily forested hillside behind them, giving a bird's eye view of the lanes below. This gave the occupants of the farmhouse enough time to leave and scatter into the surrounding countryside.

'We will prevail,' Nuala whispered under her breath as she went inside to check on the vegetables. Her father Daniel and her older brother Fergus were committed volunteers, and both she and her big sister Hannah worked with Cumann na mBan. While it didn't require as much direct action as that of her brother, Nuala prided herself that their work acted as a strong foundation for the men – without the women delivering secret communications, smuggling ammunition and gelignite for bombs, or simply providing food and fresh clothing, the cause would have floundered in its first few weeks.

Her second cousin Christy had been living with the family too for almost ten years now. The Murphys had taken him in after both his parents had died, and Nuala had heard whispers that he had an older brother called Colin, who was soft in the head and up in Cork City at a hospital for people like him. This contrasted strongly with the sturdy presence that Christy brought to her life. At fifteen, he'd had an accident with a thresher on the farm, and although his leg had been saved, he now walked with a limp. Christy had carved himself a handsome oak stick, and though he was only a few years older than her, the stick seemed to lend him an air of wisdom. Despite his injury, Christy was as strong as an ox, and was an

adjutant to the Ballinascarthy Brigade of the IRA, working alongside her father. Neither Christy nor her father were on active duty, but their brains helped plan the ambushes and made sure that supplies and intelligence were coordinated. He also worked at the pub down in Clogagh, and every evening, after labouring a full day at the farm, Christy got on his old nag and rode down to the village to pour glasses of porter. There, he listened out for useful information if a group of Tans or Essexes were in the pub, their tongues loosened from the drink.

'Hello, daughter,' her father said, as he rinsed his hands in the water barrel that stood outside the front door. 'Is lunch ready? I've a fierce hunger on me today,' he added as he dipped his head to pass through the doorway and sit down at the table. Her father was a bear of a man, and even though Fergus was a tall lad, Daniel was proud he could best his son in height. Out of all the passionate anti-British feelings that permeated the very walls of Cross Farm, her daddy's ran the deepest and most vociferous. His parents had been victims of the famine, then when he was a young lad he had witnessed the Land Wars – a rising against the British landowners who charged outrageous rents for the hovels their tenant farmers lived in. Daniel was a true Fenian through and through. Inspired by the Fianna, the warrior bands of Irish legend, Fenians were firm believers that Ireland should be independent – and that the only way to achieve this was through armed revolution.

Her daddy was also a fluent Gaelic speaker, and had brought up his children with a great pride in their Irishness, teaching them to speak the language almost before they could speak English. All the children knew it was dangerous to speak Gaelic in public, lest the British heard you, so they only spoke it behind the closed doors of Cross Farm.

After the Land Wars, her grandfather had managed to buy four acres of fertile farmland from their British landowners, the Fitzgeralds. When Daniel took over, he had succeeded in purchasing another acre to expand the farm. Being free of 'the oppressors', as he called the British, was, Nuala knew, the most important thing in her daddy's life.

His hero was Michael Collins – 'Mick', or 'the Big Fellow' as he was commonly known around these parts. Also a son of West Cork, born only a few miles away near Clonakilty, Mick had taken part in the Easter Rising alongside Daniel, then after two years in a British prison, had climbed the ranks to become chief of the IRA volunteers across Ireland. As Daddy said so often, it was Mick Collins who ran the show, especially while Éamon de Valera, the president of the fledgling Irish republican government, was in America raising funds for the Irish battle against their British masters. Michael Collins's name was spoken in hallowed tones, and Nuala's sister Hannah had a newspaper clipping of his photograph pinned up on the wall opposite the bed, so she could wake to the sight of him every morning. Nuala wondered if any man would ever match up to the Big Fellow for her. At twenty, her older sister remained steadfastly unmarried.

'Where's your mam, Nuala?' asked Daniel.

'Out digging up spuds, Daddy. I'll be calling her in.'

Nuala walked outside, put two fingers in her mouth and gave a shrill whistle. 'Where are Fergus and Christy?' she asked as she returned and began to dole out the potatoes, cabbage and boiled ham into bowls.

'Still sowing the fields with winter barley.' Daniel looked up at his daughter as she put his bowl down in front of him. They were all on half-rations of ham just now, saving what they could for hungry volunteers. 'Any news?'

'Not so far today, but . . .'

Nuala turned towards the open door as she saw Hannah flying up the track towards the farmhouse on her bicycle. Her sister worked in a dressmaker's shop in Timoleague and wouldn't normally return home for the midday meal. Nuala knew something was up. Her heart began to beat against her chest, the feeling so familiar to her now it was almost constant.

'What's happened?' she asked as Hannah came in through the door. Her mother Eileen, and Fergus and Christy, followed in her wake. The door was closed tightly, then bolted.

'I've just heard that Tom Hales and Pat Harte have been arrested by the Essexes,' Hannah said, panting hard with both exertion and emotion.

'Jaysus,' said Daniel, his hand covering his eyes. The rest of the family sank down onto the nearest chair or stool.

'How? Where?' asked Eileen.

'Who knew where they were?' demanded Christy.

Hannah put out her hands to quiet them all as Nuala stood there, the bowl she'd been placing on the table frozen in mid-air. Tom Hales was the commandant of the Third West Cork Brigade – he made all the main decisions, and his men trusted him with their lives. Pat Harte, always a steady soul, was his brigade quartermaster, in charge of its organisational and practical side.

'Was it a spy?' asked Fergus.

'We don't know who informed on them,' said Hannah. 'All I know is that they were captured at the Hurley farm. Ellie Sheehy was there too, but managed to talk her way out of it. She's the one who sent me the message.'

'Jesus, Mary and Joseph!' Daniel thumped the table with his fist. 'Not Tom and Pat. O'course, we all know why. 'Twas in retaliation for Sergeant Mulhern being shot and killed outside St Patrick's Church yesterday morning.'

'And may God have mercy on his merciless soul,' said Christy.

In the silence, Nuala managed to find her wits and serve out food to the shocked gathering.

'We can't expect that Mulhern could be murdered without reprisals – he was chief intelligence officer for West Cork, after all,' said Hannah. 'To be fair, 'twas a low attack, as the man was going into Mass. 'Twas brutal.'

'War is brutal, daughter, and that fecker had it coming to him. How many Irish lives are on his conscience as he stands before his maker?' demanded Daniel.

'What's done is done,' Nuala said, after crossing herself discreetly. 'Hannah, do you know where Tom and Pat have been taken?'

'Ellie said that they were tortured in the outhouse at the Hurley farm, then led out with their hands tied behind their backs. She said . . . she said that neither man could hardly stand up. They forced Pat to wave a Union Jack.' Hannah spat out the words. 'I've been told they're held at Bandon Barracks, but I'll be betting they'll be moved off fast to Cork City, before the volunteers launch a full ambush to rescue them.'

'I'd say you're right, daughter,' said Eileen. 'Are the other brigades alerted?'

'I don't know, Mammy, but I'm sure I'll be hearing later on.' Hannah shovelled some now cold potatoes and cabbage into her mouth. 'And Nuala, I've news for you.'

'What?'

'I've had Lady Fitzgerald's maid into the shop this morning. She was asking whether you'd go up to the Big House this afternoon to mind her son Philip? His nurse has left unexpectedly.'

The whole family stared at Hannah in disbelief. Eventually, Nuala managed to speak.

'Ah, Hannah, after what you've just told me, Argideen House is not the place I'd be choosing to spend my time. And besides, why me? I've only gone up there to help out at a dinner or a shoot sometimes, and I've never even met the son.'

'Lady Fitzgerald has heard that you were training to be a nurse before the hostilities started. Someone recommended you.'

'To be sure, I can't be going up there,' Nuala replied adamantly. 'I've sheets and clothes on the line, and who will make our tea?'

There was another silence, then her father looked up at her.

'I think you should go, daughter. The fact they'll have you inside their home means we're not suspected.'

'I . . . Daddy! No, please, I can't. Mammy, tell him!'

Eileen gave a shrug. Decisions like this were her husband's only.

'I'm with Daddy,' said Fergus. 'I think you should go. You'd never know what you'll be hearing when you're there.'

Nuala glared round at her family. ''Tis nothing less than sending me across enemy lines.'

'Now, Nuala, Sir Reginald might be a British Protestant who hosts the enemy, but I'd say he's a fair man whose family have lived in Ireland a long time,' Daniel replied. ''Tis easy in these situations to tar everyone with the same brush. You all know I'm an Irish republican through and through and I want the British out, but fair play to Sir Reginald, he's decent enough, given his kind. His father gave mine our land at a good price, and Sir Reginald handed me that extra acre for next to nothing.'

Nuala looked at her father and knew there was no argument to be brooked. Daddy's word was law. She gave a curt nod to indicate her compliance, and began to eat.

'What time am I meant to be there?' she asked.

'As soon as you can,' said Hannah.

'Go and clean yourself up and put on your best cotton dress,' Mammy ordered her after she'd finished her lunch.

Giving a heavy sigh of displeasure, Nuala did as she was told.

With her mother now in charge of the laundry and the cooking, Nuala wheeled her bicycle out of the barn to join Hannah on her journey towards Timoleague.

'What will the brigade do without Tom Hales in charge of them?' she asked her sister.

'I'd say they'll have Charlie Hurley replacing him as commandant,' Hannah said as they cycled downhill, following the lane at the bottom which ran beside the Argideen River, then heading along towards Inchybridge, where they would part.

'And my Finn?' Nuala whispered. 'Any news of him?'

'I heard he's with Charlie Hurley at a safehouse, so you're not to be worrying. Now then, I'm off back to the shop. Good luck to you at the Big House, sister.'

With a wave, Hannah cycled off, while Nuala headed reluctantly in the direction of Argideen House.

The narrow track ran alongside the railway line, which in turn ran alongside the river. The birds were singing and the sun was playing through the branches of the thick forest that surrounded her. She passed the special spot where she and Finn used to meet in secret and, stepping off her bicycle, she wheeled it into the woody interior and parked it against an old oak tree. Sitting down under its protective leaves, in the very place where Finn had first kissed her, Nuala took a few seconds to herself.

She'd first set eyes on Finnbar Casey at a Gaelic football match, when he'd been playing on the same team as Fergus. He'd been sixteen to her fourteen, and hadn't given her a second glance. But she had been hypnotised by this tall, dark-haired

boy, who'd run with such grace, skilfully dodging his opponents as he kicked the ball into the goal. He had an easy laugh and kind blue eyes, and he'd stayed firmly in her memory, even after he'd gone off to complete his teacher training. They'd met again at a wedding a year ago, after he had taken up a position as teacher at the local school. Dancing together in the *ceilidh*, he had taken her hand in his, and she had known. At eighteen and twenty, the age gap hadn't mattered anymore. And that had been that. The wedding was set for August – only a few weeks' time.

'I'd always imagined we'd wed in a free Ireland . . .' Finn had said the last time they'd met.

'Sure, but I'm not waiting any longer to be your wife,' she'd told him. 'We'll fight for it together, so.'

Finn was also a committed member of the Third West Cork Brigade, alongside his best friend, Charlie Hurley. Only recently, the brigade had ambushed the Royal Irish Constabulary at Ahawadda and killed three policemen, then taken their rifles and ammunition. It was a valuable hoard as both were in short supply; while the British had an empire's worth of men and guns behind them, the volunteers were fighting with the few weapons that were either stolen or smuggled into the country from across the sea. Other men had already fallen around him, but Finn had managed to escape unharmed, which had earned him the nickname 'Finn o' the Nine Lives'. Nuala swallowed hard. He'd been lucky so far, but having been called on to tend to injured volunteers, Nuala knew all too well how luck could run out . . . . Just like it had for Tom Hales and Pat Harte last night.

'And here I am, heading up to the Big House to serve the British,' she sighed as she climbed back onto the bicycle and moved off again. As she cycled along the high stone wall that marked the boundary of the house and parklands, then turned

up the long, winding drive, she wondered what it would be like to live in a place that could probably sleep a hundred souls. The many windows of the house seemed to glint down at her, large columns flanking the front entrance, the building itself symmetrical and square in the way the British seemed to like everything.

Turning left as she approached the house, Nuala made her way around to the back to use the kitchen entrance. In the courtyard, five enormous, shiny horses poked their heads out of their stable doors.

If only we could get hold of a couple of those beauties, 'twould surely speed up the volunteers' journeys between their safehouses . . .

Stepping off her bike, she tidied her wind-strewn dark hair, straightened her dress, then walked to ring the bell at the kitchen door. She could hear the baying of the hunting dogs from their kennels.

'Hello there, Nuala, 'tis a grand day we're having for the weather, isn't it?' Lucy, one of the kitchen maids whom she knew from her school days, ushered her inside.

'I'd say any day it doesn't rain is a good day,' she replied.

'True,' Lucy agreed as she led her through the vast kitchen. 'Sit yerself down for five minutes.' She gestured to a stool by the huge hearth, a healthy fire burning within it and a pot of something that smelt delicious over it. 'Maureen, the parlour maid, is fetching Mrs Houghton, the housekeeper, to take you upstairs.'

'What's happened to the usual nurse?'

'Ah now, 'tis a good piece of gossip that's not to leave this kitchen.' Lucy pulled up a stool close to Nuala's and sat down. 'Laura only went and ran off with our stable lad!'

'And what would be wrong with that?'

'The thing that's wrong, Nuala, is that he's a local, and

she's British *and* a Protestant! Her ladyship had her brought over here especially to care for Philip. I'd be guessing they've caught a boat back to England by now. Her ladyship asked Mrs Houghton if she knew of anyone with nursing experience. Mrs Houghton asked us maids and I suggested you.'

''Tis thoughtful of you, Lucy, but I'm not properly qualified,' Nuala protested. 'I only did a year up at the North Infirmary in Cork, before I was needed to come back and help at the farm.'

'Her ladyship isn't to know that, is she? Besides, he's not sick, like, he just needs help washing and dressing himself and some company. Laura spent most of her time drinking tea and reading to him, so Maureen says. But then, she's a bit of a witch.' Lucy lowered her voice. 'Maureen's only the parlour maid, but she's all airs and graces on her. Nobody likes her. I . . .'

Lucy immediately shut up as a woman, who Nuala surmised was the unpopular Maureen, entered the kitchen. Dressed in her black maid's dress with its starched white apron, her pale face and long nose set off against her black hair, which was severely pinned back under her cap, Nuala guessed she was probably in her mid-twenties.

'Miss Murphy?' the woman asked her.

'Yes, I'm Nuala Murphy.'

'Please come with me.'

As Nuala walked across the kitchen to follow Maureen, she turned back to Lucy and rolled her eyes.

'So where did you train as a nurse?' Maureen asked as she led her across a vast hallway to the bottom of a flight of stairs so wide and big and grand that Nuala imagined they could lead to heaven.

'The North Infirmary in Cork.'

'And your family? Where are they from?'

'We live up at Cross Farm, between Clogagh and Timoleague. And you?' Nuala asked politely.

'I was born in Dublin, but my parents moved down here when they inherited a farm from my father's older brother. I've moved back to take care of my mother, who is ailing. Ah, Mrs Houghton, here is the girl who will fill the temporary nursing position.'

Nuala could hear the emphasis on the word 'temporary', as a tall woman in a long black dress without an apron, and a large bunch of keys hanging from her waist, appeared from one of the other rooms off the hall.

'Thank you, Maureen. Hello, Miss Murphy, I'll take you up to Philip's rooms,' the woman said in a pronounced British accent.

'May I ask what is wrong with the lad?' asked Nuala as she followed Mrs Houghton up the stairs.

'He was caught by an exploding mine while fighting in the Great War. He had his left leg shattered and they had to amputate to the knee. He's in a wheelchair and it's very unlikely he will ever leave it.'

Nuala hardly heard the housekeeper; she was staring at the huge paintings of people from the past that hung all the way up the stairs.

'And what are my duties?' she asked when she reached the top of the stairs and followed Mrs Houghton down a corridor wide enough to drive a Black and Tan truck along it.

'In the afternoons, Philip likes to be read to, then he will ring for tea and sandwiches around four o'clock. At seven, you will help him wash and put on his nightshirt and robe. He might listen to the radio, then at eight, you will help him into bed and he will take a hot drink and a biscuit, then his medicine. Once he is in bed, you are free to leave. Now' – Mrs Houghton turned to Nuala – 'I hope you are not squeamish?'

'I'm not, so,' Nuala replied, thinking 'squeamish' must be an English word for something she shouldn't be. 'Why?'

'Poor Philip's face was badly disfigured when he was caught in the blast. He lost one eye and can barely see out of the other.'

'Oh, that'll be no problem, I've seen the like in . . . hospital in Cork,' Nuala continued, horrified that she had been about to say 'in an ambush' when one of the IRA volunteers had been injured by an explosion.

'Good. Shall we go in?'

Mrs Houghton gave a light tap on the door and a voice called, 'Come.'

They walked into an airy sitting room, with windows facing out over the parkland beyond. The furnishings were so sumptuous that Nuala had an urge to simply run her hands over the soft silk damask that covered the sofa and chairs, and the shiny, elegant mahogany sideboards and tables that stood around the room. Sitting by the window with his back to them was a man in a wheelchair.

'Your new nurse is here, Philip.'

'Bring her over then,' a voice said in an English accent that had a slow thickness to it.

Nuala followed Mrs Houghton across the room, glad her mammy had insisted she put on her only good cotton dress.

The man turned his wheelchair round to face her, and Nuala did her best not to gulp in horror. His facial features had been cruelly rearranged: his empty eye socket, his nose and the left side of his mouth hung lower than his right. The skin in between was desperately scarred, and yet, the right side of his face remained untouched.

Nuala was able to see that, with his head of thick blond hair, he'd once been a handsome young man.

'Good afternoon, sir,' Nuala said as she dipped a small curtsey.

'Good afternoon, Miss . . . ?'

'Murphy, sir. Nuala Murphy.'

'I'm presuming you are Irish?'

'Indeed I am, sir. I live only a couple of miles away.'

'Your mother has already contacted staffing agencies in England,' cut in Mrs Houghton, 'but as Nuala has just said, she's local and a nurse.'

'As we both know, Mrs Houghton, I'm hardly in need of a nurse,' Philip shrugged. 'Come closer so I can see you properly.'

Philip beckoned Nuala towards him and only allowed her to halt when there were merely inches between them. He stared at her, and she could tell that even though he only had one eye that was apparently half-blind, there was a perceptiveness about him.

'She'll do fine, Mrs Houghton. Please' – he gave a dismissive wave with his hand – 'leave us to get to know each other.'

'Very good, Philip. Ring if you need anything.'

Mrs Houghton turned out of the room and Nuala was left alone with him. Despite her negative thoughts on coming over here, her big, warm heart immediately went out to this poor, disfigured man.

'Please,' he said, 'first of all, call me Philip, not "sir". As the staff already know, I can't bear it. Reminds me of a time I do not want to remember. Now, do sit down,' he said as he wheeled himself to the centre of the room.

Even though this was a simple request, given the fact that she had been drilled for her whole life to stand straight (and secretly proud) in front of any member of the British gentry, being asked to 'sit down' – especially on a damask sofa – was a confusing moment.

'Yes, sir, I mean, Philip,' Nuala replied, then did so. Now she had overcome the shock of seeing his face, her eyes travelled downwards to the half-empty trouser leg on his left side.

'So, Nuala, tell me about yourself.' Due to his twisted lip, she could see that it took effort for him to speak slowly and clearly.

'I . . . well, I'm one of three siblings, and I live at a farm with them and my cousin, my mammy and my daddy, Daniel Murphy.'

'Ah, yes, Mr Murphy. My father says he's a decent sort of Irishman. Sensible type,' Philip nodded. 'Not one to involve himself with the kind of activities that are going on around here and across Ireland at the moment, I'm sure.'

Jesus, Mary and Joseph! You can't let him see, I beg you, Face, don't be putting a blush up on my cheeks . . .

'No, Philip, not at all.'

He turned his head towards the windows.

'The one thing that kept me going throughout my time in the trenches was the thought of one day returning to the peace and tranquillity of my home here. And now . . .' He shook his head. 'At night I'm sometimes awoken by gunfire. I . . .'

Nuala watched his head droop, his shoulders shake slightly and realised the man was crying. She sat there, thinking she'd never seen a man cry, not even when she'd picked bits of stray bullet out of Sonny O'Neill's thigh after a Black and Tan raid on his farmhouse.

'I do apologise, Nuala. I tend to cry easily, I'm afraid. Especially when it comes to the subject of war. So many lives lost, so much suffering, and here we are in our quiet corner of the world, seemingly at war again.'

Nuala watched Philip dig into his trouser pocket for a handkerchief. He wiped his good eye, then his empty socket.

'May I get you anything, Philip?'

'A new eye and a leg would be just the ticket, but I doubt that'll be coming my way anytime soon. Until, of course, my spirit takes leave of the useless flesh it currently inhabits. I presume you believe in heaven, Nuala?'

'Yes, I do, Philip.'

'That's because you've never watched hundreds of men dying in agony, screaming for their mothers. Once you've heard that, it's pretty difficult to believe that there is a kind and benevolent father waiting for us upstairs. Don't you think?'

'Well, I . . .' Nuala bit her lip.

'Please, do go on. Nothing you say will offend me. You're the first young person I've seen in well over six months, not counting the nurse that you've taken over from – who was really quite the most stupid human being I've ever met. Mother and Father's friends are of a certain age, if you understand what I mean. You're a native of these parts, not to mention a Catholic to boot, so I'd like to hear your opinion.'

'I . . . suppose I'd say that whatever waits for all of us when we die must be so magnificent that we'd forget the pain we've suffered here on earth.'

'A true believer,' Philip replied, and Nuala wasn't sure if he was jesting or not. 'Although I can't stomach all that nonsense about being punished for sins on earth . . . What on earth has any seventeen-year-old soldier in the trenches done to deserve this, for example?' Philip indicated his face and lack of leg. 'I rather believe that the human race creates their own hell on earth.'

'War is a terrible thing, I'd agree. But sometimes 'tis necessary to fight for what is yours. Like you did against the Hun in France.'

'Of course you're right. I didn't fancy the Germans storming their way across our green and pleasant lands.'

Or you British occupying ours . . .

'I just hope it's worth all the sacrifice,' Philip continued. 'Now then, do you play chess, Nuala?'

'I don't, no.'

'Neither did the nurse before you. I did try to teach her, but she was too dim-witted to learn. Fancy having a go?'

'I'd be interested to learn a new game,' she replied, her mind scrambling to move on from the conversation they'd just had.

'Good. Then open the chess table that stands over there in front of the window.'

Philip instructed Nuala how it unfolded and she saw the top of the table was designed in a square, decorated in a dark and light chequered pattern.

'The chess pieces are in the cabinet underneath the tray holding the whiskey decanter. Pour me a drop whilst you're over there. I find the brain thinks better when it is calm, and let me tell you, a glass of Irish whiskey is worth twenty of my painkillers.'

For the first time, Nuala saw a smile appear on one side of his lips.

Nuala fetched him the drop of whiskey and a box that rattled, then wheeled him over to the table.

'Sit here opposite me; the light from the window helps me see better.' Philip dug in his trouser pocket and produced an eyeglass, which he put in place over his good eye.

'Now then,' he said as he took a gulp of whiskey, 'open the box and empty the chess pieces out. I will show you where to place yours.'

Nuala did so, and saw they were made of a black and cream material that was smooth and silky to the touch. Each one was beautifully carved, like a tiny sculpture.

'So . . . you can be white and I shall be black. Mirror your pieces to mine as I place them on the squares.'

Finally, the board was set up and after she had refilled Philip's glass, he taught her all the names of the different pieces, and the moves they could make across the board.

'Right, the only way to learn is to get stuck in and jolly well play,' he said. 'Are you game?'

Nuala said she was, whatever 'game' meant. Concentrating hard, she wasn't sure how much time passed as they moved their pieces across the board and she started to understand the rules.

There was a tap on the door. 'Damn!' Philip muttered. 'Come!'

Mrs Houghton stood in the doorway. 'I do apologise, but we were just wondering if you require tea? Normally the nurse would ring for it at four, and it is almost four and thirty.'

'That is because the last nurse was an idiot with stuffing for a brain. Whereas Nuala here has already grasped the rudimentary elements of chess. We will take tea and then continue the game afterwards.'

'Maureen will bring it up for you. It's smoked salmon and cucumber sandwiches.'

'Very good, Mrs Houghton.' The door closed and Philip glanced at Nuala. 'As we were so rudely interrupted, would you mind pushing me to the bathroom?'

Philip guided her through a door and into a bedroom with an enormous bed that had four posts, and what looked like a silk roof attached to them.

'To your right,' he ordered as he indicated another door. 'Push me in and I'll be fine from there.'

Nuala looked around in wonder at a big tub with a water pipe going into it, and a low round bowl that had a chain hanging above it from the ceiling.

'Are you sure you don't need some help?'

'I'll be grand, as you Irish say. Close the door behind you and I'll call when I'm ready.'

Standing in the beautiful bedroom, just for a moment Nuala imagined lying flat on the huge bed, looking up at its silk roof and staying here safe and sound forever. Away from the farmhouse that was under daily threat of raids, the lumpy straw pallet that formed her bed at night, and the hard work morning till dusk that was necessary just to put food in their mouths. She imagined having people to wait on her, and a bowl next door to her bedroom where she could discreetly relieve herself. And most of all, not living in fear every hour of every day . . .

But would I want to be him?

'Not in a million years,' she muttered.

'I'm ready,' came a call from the other room. Nuala shook herself and went to attend to him.

'All done,' he said as he smiled up at her. 'Would you kindly pull that chain above?'

She did so and water immediately rushed into the bowl below.

Trying not to stare at it, in case Philip were to take her for the peasant she was, she pushed him back into the sitting room, where Maureen had set up a three-tiered silver stand, brimming with sandwiches and cakes, as well as two beautiful china cups in front of the damask sofa.

'Afternoon tea is served,' said Maureen. As she gave a little bob, Nuala was sure the woman glanced in her direction and gave her a stare that was the opposite of warm.

'I hope you like fish,' Philip said as he reached for one of the sandwiches, made of a white-coloured bread with their crusts cut off.

'To be truthful, I've never tasted fish.'

'That doesn't surprise me in the least,' Philip commented.

'I've never understood why you Irish are so averse to the stuff. It is plentiful in the waters that surround us here, yet you stick to the flesh of animals.'

''Tis the way I've been brought up.'

'Well, after you have poured – tea first, milk last, by the way – I insist you try a sandwich. As you can see, there's enough for a party of ten.'

'I will so, thank you.'

Nuala poured the tea and the milk. Both teapot and milk jug were so heavy that she guessed they were made of solid silver.

'Please, pour some for yourself, Nuala. You must be parched.'

It was another word Nuala had never heard, but she was thirsty, so she did.

'Tchin-tchin,' Philip said, lifting his cup to hers, 'and well done on a couple of intelligent moves across the board. If your first try is anything to go by, we'll have you beating me in a few weeks' time.'

It was just past nine when Nuala finally left the house. Darkness was falling and she switched on her bicycle light to make sure she didn't ride into a ditch. Stopping at the same oak tree where she and Finn had always met, Nuala sat down and rested her back against the strength and wisdom of the old trunk.

She had entered a different world this afternoon, and her head was swimming with what she'd found there.

The game called chess had gone on for a fair old time after the tea (and the salmon, however pink and expensive, tasted a lot better than she'd imagined). Then Philip had insisted on

another game, in which he'd stopped suggesting moves she should make. That had only lasted ten minutes, but then the next game had lasted almost an hour and he'd slapped his good thigh with his hand.

'Well done indeed,' he'd said as his milk and biscuits arrived with Maureen. 'Do you know, Maureen, Nuala might beat me at chess yet.'

Maureen had given a curt nod, then left. Not that Nuala was wanting praise, but there was something about the woman that made her hackles rise.

Wishing she could sit here for longer to take in the past few hours, Nuala saw that darkness had truly fallen and it was time she was home. Gathering her strength, she stood up and climbed back on her bicycle.

12

That night, Nuala and Hannah lay together in the bed they shared in the tiny attic room above the kitchen. Nuala had just snuffed out the candle and tucked the diary she'd been writing in safely under the mattress, having recorded the events of the day, as her teacher at school had once encouraged her to do. She'd had to leave school at the age of fourteen in order to help on the farm, but she was proud of the fact she was still practising her letters.

'So now, what was he like?' asked Hannah in the dark.

'He was . . . nice enough,' she said. 'He suffered terrible injuries in the Great War, so he sits in a wheelchair.'

'You're not feeling sympathy for him, are you? That family stole the land that was rightfully ours four hundred years ago, then they made us pay to get a tiny slice of it back!'

'He's only a bit older than you, Hannah, but has a face on him that could earn money in one of them circus fairs. He even cried when he was talking about the Great War—'

'Jaysus, girl!' Hannah sat bolt upright, removing the sheet and blanket with her. 'I'll not be hearing you feeling sorry for the enemy! I'll have you thrown out of Cumann na mBan before daylight.'

'No, no . . . Stop that now! Even Daddy says that for

Britishers, the Fitzgeralds are a decent enough family. Besides, there's none more wedded to the cause than me – I've my fiancé this very moment putting himself in danger to bring the British down. Now, as we've no visitors so far tonight, but a meeting of the brigade in our barn tomorrow, can we get some sleep whilst we can?'

'I can't help thinking about poor Tom Hales and Pat Harte,' Hannah sighed, lying down again. 'We've already sent word to our women spies; they'll find out where they are for sure. Now so, you're right: tomorrow will be a long day. The volunteers will be fierce hungry and Daddy says we have a lot of them coming.'

'At least we've clean clothes for them,' Nuala added, not daring to tell her sister that she'd been asked by Mrs Houghton to return to the Big House until a replacement nurse had been found.

I'll talk to Daddy in the morning, she thought as her eyelids drooped and she fell asleep.

'What do you think about it, Hannah?' Daniel asked, as the family sat round the table for breakfast the next morning. Even though it was only seven o'clock, the cows had been milked, and the pony and cart dispatched with Fergus to deliver the churns to the creamery.

'I'd say she shouldn't go again, Daddy. There's plenty to do here for a start, and that's without our work for Cumann na mBan. Who'll help Mammy with the extra cooking and washing we're doing these days? Never mind picking the vegetables and helping you with the harvest coming up. I've my job as a seamstress and . . . it's just not right to have one of our own working up at the Big House.'

'I'll cope, I have Fergus and Christy after all,' Eileen said, patting Christy's hand as he ate breakfast beside her. She looked at her husband. ''Tis up to you, Daniel.'

Hannah made to open her mouth, but Daniel put up a hand to silence her. 'We've many volunteers who are spies working for us. And you women are some of the most successful, because the British don't suspect you.'

'Yet,' muttered Hannah.

'If Nuala's being offered a temporary position at the Big House, she'll be able to hear kitchen gossip from the other staff about who is visiting. Sir Reginald has plenty of military friends who might be inclined to be talking to him about any planned activities, especially after a few drops of whiskey.'

'I'm not likely to overhear chatter from the downstairs drawing room, Daddy,' Nuala interjected. ''Tis an enormous house.'

'No, but sure, your young fellow might be chatting to his daddy from time to time about what's happening. 'Twould be useful to have an ear to hear it.'

'Philip's fond of a drop of whiskey himself,' Nuala smiled.

'Then feed him extra and find out what he knows,' Daniel said with a wink. 'Besides, how would it look if you turned them down? They'd be thinking 'twas an honour for you to work so closely with the family.'

'So you want me to carry on?'

'You have no choice, Nuala,' said Eileen. 'When the Big House calls . . .'

'We jump.' Hannah rolled her eyes. 'Come the grand day when we win, we'll be having that family out of there.'

'Is the son for us or against us, Nuala?' asked Christy.

'How can you even ask that question?' cried Hannah.

'Let your sister answer,' said Daniel.

'I'd say that Philip is against any war at all and just wants it to stop,' said Nuala.

'Philip, is it now?' Hannah's eyes glinted at her sister.

'Everyone calls him that, because being called "sir" reminds him of his time when he was a captain in the trenches,' Nuala shot back. 'I won't be doing this if I'm getting this pile of shite out of your mouth.'

'Nuala!' Eileen slammed the table. 'I'll not hear that kind of language under my roof. And you, miss,' she said, turning to Hannah, 'will keep your comments to yourself. Now then, I'd better be getting started. Do we know how many men we're expecting tonight?' she asked Daniel.

'Fifteen or twenty, and I've sent word to Timoleague to get some scouts to patrol up top whilst they're all here. There's a good few of them on the wanted list,' said Daniel.

'I've rounded up some local Cumann na mBan women to help with the cooking,' added Hannah.

'Make sure they hide their bicycles in the barn behind the hay bales,' Christy reminded her.

'Of course.' Hannah stood up. 'I'll be seeing ye.'

When Hannah had gone, Nuala helped her mother clear the bowls away, leaving them to soak in one of the water barrels outside.

'I'll be in the far field if you need me,' Daniel said as he strode out of the front door.

'Daddy?' Nuala caught up with him. 'Will Finn be here tonight?'

'I couldn't say; what with Tom and Pat taken, they're all on extra alert,' Daniel said and strode off with a wave of one of his large, brawny hands.

Hannah was as good as her word, and by the time she and Nuala left, two women from Cumann na mBan were already in the kitchen helping Mammy with the cooking for that night.

Nuala's heart thumped as she cycled towards Argideen House – not only at returning to it, but at the thought of the men from the Third West Cork Brigade, which included her beloved Finn, making their way in secret to convene at Cross Farm's old barn.

'Wherever you are, darlin', I pray you're safe,' she whispered under her breath.

'Well, hello there, Nuala,' said Lucy as she walked into the kitchen. 'I'm hearing you were a great hit with the young master.'

'Was I?'

'Oh yes, Mrs Houghton told me he'd said that you had far better nursing skills than the last girl.'

'I wasn't doing any nursing,' Nuala frowned. 'He'd a way of doing most things for himself. All I did was give him a quick wash before bed, then pop him under the covers and feed him his pills.'

'Well, you got something right. Mrs Houghton's out at the moment so 'twill be Maureen taking you to him.'

Maureen duly arrived and escorted Nuala upstairs without saying a word. She stopped just outside Philip's door.

'I'd be grateful if you would ring down for the young master's tea at four prompt. The sandwiches grow stale if they're left for too long, and I've other things to be getting on with.'

With that, she opened the door to let Nuala in.

Philip was sitting by the window in the same place she'd first seen him yesterday. Remnants of his lunch were on a tray on the table facing the damask sofa.

'I'll take these out for you now, if you're finished,' said Maureen.

'Thank you.'

Philip said no more until the door closed behind her.

'A real old sourpuss, isn't she? I've been told she lost her husband in the Great War, so I try to be forgiving,' Philip added. 'Sit down, Nuala.' He indicated the sofa. 'Have you had a pleasant morning?'

She suppressed a smile at the word 'pleasant', given she hadn't stopped for a second, without time to even eat any lunch herself after she had served it to her family.

'Nuala, you look quite pale. Can I ring for some tea? Sugar always perks one up, I find.'

'Oh, I'll be grand, Philip. My morning was pleasant enough, thank you.'

'No, I insist,' he said, grabbing the bell that hung by a string from his wheelchair. 'I can see hunger and fatigue at twenty paces and we simply cannot start another game of chess until you've put some sustenance inside you.'

'Really, Philip, I . . .' Nuala could feel a blush rising up her cheeks.

'It's no problem; these days the parlour maid is hardly rushed off her feet. None of Father's English friends – or Irish, for that matter – are particularly keen to travel down here, for fear of being taken hostage or shot at by the IRA along the way.'

To Nuala's continued embarrassment, Maureen appeared at the door. 'You rang, Philip?'

'Yes. Nuala and I are about to embark on a game of chess, and I don't wish to be disturbed. So I'd like you to bring up the tea and sandwiches before we begin. Nuala is hungry.'

'Yes, though that might take ten minutes, as I always make them fresh for you, Philip.' Maureen shot Nuala a look that could kill before she left the room.

'May I ask you, Nuala, do you and your family go hungry often?'

'Ah, no, Philip, not at all. We'd be lucky in that we have a field full of vegetables, and pigs for bacon. And the potato crop is looking well this year.'

'Unlike the dreadful potato famine last century. My father was only a boy at the time, but he remembers his father doing what he could to support his local tenants. The kitchen made batches of soup and extra bread, but of course, it could never be enough.'

'No.'

'Did many of your family leave for America?' he asked.

'I know my grandparents lost a number of their own to the famine, and brothers and sisters to America. I've cousins over there now who send parcels sometimes for Christmas. Have you been there yourself? It looks like a mighty fine place.'

'I have, as a matter of fact. We travelled on the poor doomed *Lusitania* over to New York, then went up to Boston to visit some of my mother's relatives. New York is indeed a sight to behold; Manhattan Island is filled with buildings that one has to crane one's neck backwards to see the top of.'

'Do you think anyone can make their fortune there?'

'Why do you ask?'

'Oh, me and my fiancé have talked of it sometimes.'

'I doubt there is an Irish family who hasn't,' said Philip. 'Certainly for some, it has been a success, but perhaps that has to be put in context against the bleak choices available to your ancestors: starve in Ireland or make a better life for themselves in America. I do remember my father pointing out a place called Brooklyn, which he said was a vast Irish settlement, due to the fact that many of the men there who had come over during the potato famine had found work building the Brooklyn Bridge. We drove through the area and the

conditions were ... uncomfortable, to say the least. The buildings were in disrepair and the streets crowded with filthy children playing outside. In answer to your question, yes, there are a lucky few who have flourished, but given the choice between living in poverty in a tenement building in Brooklyn, or being able to grow your own food and having fresh country air, I'd opt for Ireland.'

'Finn – my fiancé – is a teacher at Clogagh School and he was thinking that he'd like to give America a try. Me? I've told him fair and square that I'd not be setting foot on a ship after what happened to all those poor souls on the *Titanic*, and then the *Lusitania* after it.'

'I certainly understand your point of view, Nuala, but you must remember that the grand old *Lusitania* was torpedoed by the Germans. I promise you it was a mighty ship that otherwise would have continued to carry its human cargo safely across the Atlantic for many more years to come.'

'When Daddy heard of it sinking, he took his horse and rode down to the coast at Kinsale to help. I'll never forget him coming back and telling his tales of all the bodies floating in the water.' Nuala shuddered. 'Even though he's as fierce scared as me of the sea, he got in a boat and went out to help bring the bodies ashore.'

'I was deployed over in France at the time, but my father was there too and said the same. Well, if the sinking of that ship did anything, it certainly brought the Americans into the war. Ah, here is the tea. Let's have no more talk of darker times, eh? Leave the tray on the table in front of Nuala. She will pour,' Philip ordered Maureen.

The woman gave another nod and a bob, then, casting a further dark look at Nuala, left the room.

'She doesn't look happy,' Nuala sighed. 'She was only saying downstairs she likes to bring tea up at four o'clock sharp.'

'Goodness, don't worry about her. She's merely a parlour maid. Now then, get on with pouring the tea and eating as many sandwiches as you can, then we can begin our game.'

To her relief, Philip had pronounced himself fatigued and ready for bed at seven thirty, so having washed him, dressed him in his nightshirt, then put him in his bed and fed him his pills, she'd been away by eight thirty.

'It's the chess that's quite exhausted me,' he'd said with a smile as she'd left. 'I haven't had to exercise the muscle that sits in my head for far too long. I really had to work to win that last game, young lady. You've got the hang of it fast, and you'll be beating me soon enough, I shouldn't wonder.'

Now in the habit of stopping by her oak tree – almost as if she needed a few minutes to turn from Nuala the nurse at the Big House, to Nuala Murphy, daughter of a fiercely republican mother and father, and member of Cumann na mBan – she sank against the trunk and tucked her arms round her knees.

Of course, she could never tell anyone, not *anyone* ever, that she'd actually enjoyed the two afternoons she'd spent in Philip's company. He had said he wasn't hungry so soon after lunch, and besides, he could always call for more sandwiches if he needed them, so she was to eat as many as she wanted. Today they'd something inside Philip called potted meat, which she decided was one of the most delicious things she'd ever tasted. There'd been scones too, which the two of them had eaten together with cream and jam after the second game of chess had ended. Then they'd gone on to play two more. Philip was still beating her easily, whatever kind words he'd said, but she reckoned if she kept going, she might be able to

hold her own in the game for longer. Having to concentrate so hard meant that all thoughts of anything else – which were mostly bad just now – had left her mind, and tonight she felt more relaxed than she'd been since before the bloody Easter Rising in 1916, four long years ago, which had been a watershed to her. It had marked the beginning of the concerted effort of the Irish to free themselves of their shackles, and Nuala had known then that her life would never be the same.

'But I like Philip, Oak Tree,' she confided to the thick, heavy branches above her. 'He's kind and gentle. And how he's suffered,' she sighed.

At least he hadn't cried today, she thought, as she got back on her bicycle, knowing she must get a spin on for home.

'It just shows that life's unfair on everyone, whether they're rich English or poor Irish,' she said to the wind as she prepared to tackle the steep hill up to Cross Farm.

'You're here at last, Nuala. We thought you might be sleeping over in one of their grand bedrooms,' Hannah commented as she walked into the kitchen.

'Jaysus, 'tis only just gone nine.' Nuala glanced around the kitchen and saw great tureens of vegetables on the table as Jenny and Lily, two women from the Clonakilty branch of Cumann na mBan, cut the ham and served it into numerous bowls.

'The men won't be coming in tonight to eat,' said Hannah, who was taking a cake off the hook over the fire. 'There was a patrol of the Essexes seen only an hour ago along the lane by the Shannons' farm.'

'Now then,' said her mother, 'we need to dole out these spuds and veg and get them to our visitors in the barn before

they get cold. And yes, Himself has arrived already, Nuala, so I'd be suggesting you run a brush through that wild mane before you serve him his meal.' Eileen patted her daughter's hand. 'Take no notice of that sister of yours,' she said, lowering her voice further. 'She's stubborn as a mule, just like her daddy.'

Nuala made her way swiftly through the kitchen and ran upstairs to use the one pane of mirror in the house that hung in Mammy and Daddy's room. Brushing her long dark curly hair, that needed a good cut and some time she didn't have to sort it at the moment, she straightened her cotton dress that she'd had to wash out last night and wear again today. After checking for smudges on her face, she ran back downstairs, her heart banging in anticipation of seeing her love.

Dusk was beginning to fall as the women stepped out of the house to walk across the courtyard with food for the men inside the barn. It was almost fully enclosed, apart from one entrance along the side. Nuala knew there were scouts up above at the top of the hill, keeping watch for any trucks approaching below.

Eileen took the lead and gave the special knock on the barn door. Receiving the coded reply, she opened it and the five women walked in.

It was almost pitch black inside the barn, with only a small area lit by candlelight at one end. Nuala could make out the shapes of men sitting either cross-legged on the floor or on hay bales placed in a semicircle around one in the centre. As the women approached, the men, who had been talking in low voices, looked up. There were faces she knew and some she didn't. She cast her eyes around the men, all of whom looked thin and exhausted, until her eyes finally settled on one.

'Hello,' he mouthed and gave her a slight wave of his

fingertips. Nuala went with the other women around the semicircle, handing out the bowls and receiving whispered 'thank you's.

'You're looking well, Nuala,' Finn smiled up at her when she reached him. 'Will we meet afterwards in the usual place?'

She nodded, then left the barn with the other women.

'Wouldn't you love to be in there with them, to hear all the news and their plans?' Nuala commented to Hannah.

'We'll be getting them soon enough when we're sent with messages, or putting on our hooded cloaks to conceal ammunition or guns,' replied her sister.

Back in the kitchen, the women sat down to eat a hasty supper of their own. 'Any news of Tom and Pat?' Nuala asked.

'Yes,' said Jenny. 'I intercepted a telegram meant for Major Percival of the Essex Regiment. The lads have been moved to a hospital in Cork City.'

As Jenny worked in the post office in Bandon, she was a valuable spy for the cause and Nuala sometimes envied her for it.

'That means they're seriously hurt, God save them!' Eileen crossed herself.

'Be grateful for small mercies, girls,' Jenny piped up. 'At least our lads are not in jail and subject to further torture. They'll be looked after in hospital by our nurses.'

'I've already dropped a message to Florence – she'll catch the train to Cork City tomorrow and have one of the volunteers take a food parcel in, to see how they both are,' said Lily.

'Nuala, you go to the outhouse and bring in that pile of laundry, ready to take to the barn after the meeting,' said her mother.

Nuala stood up. 'Are they staying the night?'

'We've some straw pallets for them if they do. At least it's warm tonight; there's few enough blankets as it is.'

Nuala walked round to the outhouse and began piling the clean underclothes, trousers and shirts into two large baskets. As she carried one across the courtyard to the house, she stopped for a while, listening. Not a sound emanated from the barn. All was as it would normally be, except plans for guerrilla warfare were being made inside it.

'Ah, Philip, what would you be thinking of me if you knew?' she muttered.

It was past eleven when Daniel, Fergus and Christy entered the kitchen. The Cumann na mBan girls had done the cleaning and disappeared into the night, so only Hannah, Nuala and their mother were left in the kitchen.

'I'm for my bed, wife,' said Daniel. He turned to Nuala. 'There's someone waiting for you outside.' He indicated the back door. 'Don't you be long, I've eyes everywhere and you two aren't wed yet.'

Nuala's heart bounced at the thought of her fiancé waiting for her outside. Her a farmer's daughter with limited education and an unfinished nursing diploma, and him with a grand job as a teacher.

I wish I could tell him I can play chess, she thought as she walked towards the outhouse they were using to store the laundry, but she knew she couldn't.

In the dark, she could only see the glow of his cigarette.

'Is that you?' he whispered.

''Tis me,' she smiled.

Finn stamped out his cigarette and pulled her into his arms. He kissed her and, as always, her legs went shaky, and parts of her burnt with longing for what could only happen after they were married. Eventually, he led her out of the courtyard

and onto the coarse grass, where they lay down and she snuggled into his arms.

'What if someone sees us here?' she whispered.

'Nuala, 'tis pitch black, but sure, I'd be more afraid of your daddy catching us like this than a whole patrol of Black and Tans,' he chuckled.

'We've no worries there, Finn, I could smell the whiskey on Daddy's breath from across the kitchen. He'll not surface until the cows are mooing for their milking in the morning.'

'Then I might just have my wicked way with you,' he murmured as he pulled her on top of him.

'Finnbar Casey! Don't you even be thinking such thoughts, so. I'm walking into that church as pure as the day I was born. Besides, what would all your schoolchildren think if they knew Mr Casey was taking a roll in the grass with his girl?'

'I'm sure they'd give me a round of applause, especially the boys.'

As Nuala's eyesight adjusted to the dimness and the moon appeared from behind a cloud, she could make out his features. She traced them with her fingertips.

'I love you, darlin', and I can't wait to be your wife.'

Some more gorgeous kissing happened, then Nuala rolled off of him and nestled her head on one of his arms, looking up at the stars.

''Tis a beautiful night. Calm, peaceful, so,' she said.

'It is, yes,' he murmured. 'And what's this I've been hearing about you nursing the Fitzgerald son up at the Big House?'

'Who told you?'

'Sure, I had a dispatch from one of the Cumann na mBan girls last night.'

Nuala sat up. 'You did not!'

'No, Nuala, I didn't, I'm just teasing you. Your daddy mentioned it earlier, said he'd told you 'twas a good idea.'

'And you, Finn? What do you think?'

'However much I'd prefer to stand waist-deep in a field of cow shite than have my girl carousing with the enemy, I think your daddy's right. What with me being a school teacher and you up the Fitzgeralds', 'twill mean we're not suspected. For now . . . The Black and Tan raids on local houses are after getting more frequent. I heard of three who had their farms searched last night, and their occupants scared half to death. The Buckleys' house was burnt to the ground. 'Twas in retaliation for the shooting of that louser, Mulhern.'

'Did Tom Hales order his shooting, d'you think?'

'I'd say he'd a hand in it, for sure. He's the commandant of the brigade – or was,' he sighed.

'What's going to happen now?'

'Charlie will take over until Tom's released. But there's no telling what kind of state the poor fellow will be in when he is. His family are all beside themselves, especially his brother Sean.'

'I won't ever let you fall into the hands of those British lousers,' she whispered fiercely to him.

'Sure, I'll be grand,' he chuckled. 'Though I'd like to see you take down the Essex Regiment, screaming like a banshee.'

'I would to save you, Finn, I swear. What else was discussed at the meeting?'

'Military business, darlin'. The less you know the better, so if you're ever interrogated, you have little to tell. One thing I will say is that Tom Barry was there tonight. You remember him, right?'

'I think so. Didn't he fight for the British in the Great War?'

'He did so, but he's one of the most committed volunteers I know. We discussed the idea of proper training,' Finn continued. 'What with Tom Barry being a military man, he'd be a good one to run it. The rest of us are amateurs at the game

of war – and that's what we're fighting: a war. We've not a chance unless we organise ourselves properly.'

'I know, Finn. I keep thinking, how can a few Irish farmers, who've only held a pitchfork or a spade in their hands before now, take on the might of the British?' Nuala sighed.

''Tis those Black and Tans who are the most vicious, Nuala. They were recruited from the British soldiers that came back from the trenches in France. They're angry and used to bloodshed, which makes them savage. I'd say they've lost their consciences somewhere on those battlefields and they've scores to settle.'

'Don't frighten me, Finn, please.' Nuala shuddered. 'And you'll be part of this training thing?'

'I will indeed. It may make the difference between winning and losing. And we. Just. Can't. Lose. To the British. Again.' He gritted his teeth. 'We've finally got our own government in the Dáil in Dublin. We voted our own in, which gives us a remit to form a republic. 'Tis our right now for Irishmen to run our country. And don't you be listening to any of those up at the Big House if they tell you different.'

'Of course not. But I don't think Philip will. I've told him all about you.'

'Me?' Finn turned to look at her. 'Who's Philip?'

'The man I'm looking after; the son of Sir Reginald.'

'Don't you be saying too much, Nuala. You never know what could slip out of your mouth. Now then, let's talk of other things, like you and me being wed. Your daddy said we'll need to be using Timoleague church to fit all your friends and family in.'

The two of them argued gently over the size of the guest list, then spoke of the little cottage near the schoolhouse in Clogagh that came with Finn's job.

'We'll be brightening it up with a lick of paint, won't we?'

said Nuala. 'And Hannah can get material cheap from the dressmaker's, so I can make some pretty curtains.'

'Sure, you'll be having it look a picture.' Finn pulled her towards him and held her tightly in his arms. 'We'll be happy there, Nuala, I know we will.'

13

Nuala's new routine settled down after a couple of weeks: she'd be up at the crack of dawn to help as much as she could around the farm, and then cycle off to the Big House after lunch. There'd been further snipes from Hannah about what she'd termed Nuala's 'easy life up with the gentry'.

'As we women race around the country delivering dispatches, strapping ammunition round our waists and doing the fellows' laundry, you're up there playing games and eating cucumber sandwiches!'

Nuala rued the day she'd mentioned what she did for all the hours she spent with Philip. Even though she had tried to make it sound as boring as possible, her mother had listened with interest, and Hannah had latched on to the sandwiches and games of chess.

'Even though Daddy excuses you by saying you're a spy, I'm not seeing how you can be spying on anyone from an invalid's bedroom,' she'd sniffed.

Nuala had begun to pray that there would be some nugget of information she could take back to justify her time at the Big House, even though both her parents said there was no need, that the extra shillings helped pay the added cost of supplying the Third West Cork Brigade with food and fresh clothing. In truth, Hannah was right; even though Nuala had

seen and reported a number of shiny black cars arriving, flanked by an Essex patrol, she couldn't identify the men inside them. All she could see was the tops of their hats or caps from her vantage point at the window above them.

'Look out for Major Percival,' Daddy had said, 'now, he's a prize we'd want to be having. He's the intelligence officer for the Essex Regiment and is responsible for a lot of the torture our lads have suffered. He's a habit of riding in his open-top car in the mornings, shooting his pistol about at farmers in the field just for the *craic*. We know 'tis him who was responsible for the capture of poor Tom and Pat.'

Through their network of female volunteers, details of the torture the men had endured had dripped out into West Cork. Charlie Hurley, now commandant of the brigade since Tom's capture, had arrived in the kitchen of Cross Farm to relay the details to the men of the family.

Banished from the room, Eileen, Hannah and Nuala had lurked at the top of the stairs, as Charlie had described the terrible beatings Tom Hales and Pat Harte had taken. The three women had wept when Charlie mentioned that Tom had had his fingernails pulled out one by one and his teeth broken, while Pat had been coshed so badly about the head with rifle butts that reports said he'd lost his brain inside it altogether. Pat was still in hospital, and Tom had been sentenced to two years in jail and shipped off to Pentonville Prison in London.

Finn had also been present that night at Cross Farm, ostensibly so they could discuss wedding plans, but their rendezvous afterwards had contained no such joy and Finn had held her close as she'd cried.

'I know what we're fighting for, Finn, and there's no one who believes in the cause more than me, but . . . sometimes I just wish I could go back to the way things were.'

'I know, darlin', but sure, doesn't it strengthen our resolve never to give in? We're in it now, and we can't give up. 'Tis a fight to the death, and that's that.'

'Please don't say that!' Nuala had begged him. 'We'll be wed at the end of next week and I'm not looking to be widowed just yet.'

'Oh, don't mind me, I'm fit enough to take on five of their side! They hide behind their weapons, but Charlie and me, we've been taking runs up and down the valley. Just feel the strength in this.' Finn had guided her hand to his thigh, which had felt like iron, but she'd quickly pulled her hand out of his grasp.

'There'll be none of that till our wedding night, remember?' She'd given him a weak smile as she'd wiped the tears from her eyes.

As Nuala cycled up the drive towards Argideen House, she prayed that one day she *would* see Major Percival, or identify *anyone* that visited Argideen House. But apart from Lucy, Maureen and Mrs Houghton, she'd not seen a single soul other than Philip since she'd arrived three weeks ago.

Parking her bicycle against the wall, she entered the quiet kitchen, feeling even more sorry for poor Philip. Nuala thought of when Christy had had his accident with the thresher, and had been laid up recovering for months.

In the heart of our home, being fussed over by everyone, not stuck upstairs with a stranger like me, she thought as she walked straight through the kitchen and up the staircase towards Philip's bedroom. It was a week ago since she'd been allowed to take herself upstairs, without waiting for Mrs Houghton or Maureen to escort her.

'That means you're trusted,' Mammy had said with a smile. 'Well done, Nuala.'

So many times she'd been tempted to dally on the grand staircase; to take in the big windows back and front that let light flood into the hall, the glass chandelier that had once held candles, which Philip said had recently been adapted for electric light. Still, to see them lit; she could hardly wait for the winter, when surely they'd have to have it turned on so you could climb safely up and down the stairs.

In truth, despite the guilt over her 'easy life', Nuala was glad of it. What with the wedding just around the corner, and all the preparations to be got on with, not to mention her household chores and her volunteer work, her hours up at the Big House were a welcome break.

'It's Nuala here, Philip, may I come in?' she called as she knocked on the door. A female voice answered that she could. Opening the door, she found a woman that she recognised to be Lady Fitzgerald standing in the room. She'd seen her occasionally at the dressmaker's in Timoleague, stepping out of a big car to choose some material or have a fitting. Even Hannah had said that she was 'not too grand with herself' considering, and spoke to the staff like they were human beings, not animals.

'Good morning, Nuala. Do come in and sit down.' She spoke in a low, warm tone, despite her crisp English accent.

'Good morning, Lady Fitzgerald.' Nuala bobbed a curtsey and did as she was bid. She looked up at the woman, who, with her blonde hair and blue eyes, was fierce pretty for an older lady. Compared to her own mammy, who must be of similar age, she looked twenty years younger. She had earrings with little pearls dangling off them, and her dress was made of a soft blue silk that matched her eyes. Nuala could only

imagine what she wore for best if this was just for an ordinary August afternoon.

'Now, Philip here has been telling me how much he's enjoyed having you as his nurse over the past month.'

'I have indeed,' said Philip. 'I told Mother how you'd become quite the thing at playing chess. She's close to beating me now, Mother, she really is.'

Lady Fitzgerald gave Nuala a smile. 'It's obvious that you and Philip get along famously, but he also says you care for his medical needs too. As you know, we were looking for a fully trained nurse—'

'Mother, we've had this discussion over and over,' Philip butted in. 'I don't need a nurse anymore. My wounds are healed, and my overall health is stable. All I *need* is someone to push me to the lavvy, wash me, help me into bed and dole out my night-time medicine.'

'Yes, my dear, but you know the doctors have said you're at risk of seizures because of your head injuries and—'

'I haven't had one so far and it's been over two years since the whole bloody nightmare happened. What I need most is company that I enjoy.'

'I know, Philip.' Lady Fitzgerald turned back to Nuala. 'You can see how persuasive my son can be when he wants something. And he's persuaded me that he wishes to offer you a permanent position here as his nurse. How would you feel about that, Nuala?'

'I . . .'

'*Do* say yes, Nuala,' Philip pleaded. 'I mean, we can't have you leaving before you've won at chess, can we?' He gave her one of his lopsided smiles that always melted her heart.

'I'm honoured that you would offer me the position, given that I'm not fully qualified. May I ask my parents if they could

spare me from the work on the farm? 'Twas the reason I came home from Cork in the first place and didn't complete my training.'

Nuala realised she was becoming more adept at lying every day.

'Of course you may.' Lady Fitzgerald gave her another of her sweet smiles that reminded Nuala so much of her son's. Even disfigured, the physical similarity between mother and son was pronounced.

'I presume you'll be wanting references?' asked Nuala.

'Mother already has those, don't you?'

'I do indeed. Your reference from the North Infirmary in Cork was glowing, although they did mention they're eager to have you back as soon as possible. *Is* that what you're planning, Nuala?'

'Oh no, your ladyship, things have changed since I left. I'm to be married this month to a teacher at Clogagh School, so I doubt I'll be leaving my husband to fend for himself.'

'Isn't that wonderful news, Philip?' Lady Fitzgerald's smile became even wider. 'About Nuala's marriage?'

It didn't look like it was much, as Philip tried his best to hide a frown. 'Then perhaps you should be asking your intended whether you're allowed to work here? He'll be in charge of you very soon.'

'I'll do that too, and have an answer for you tomorrow, I promise,' Nuala replied.

'Very good,' said Lady Fitzgerald. 'Now, doesn't your sister Hannah work in the dressmaker's in Timoleague?'

'She does, so, yes.'

'Have her take your measurements. You will need a uniform if you're staying with us permanently.'

'Mother, please, without risk of interfering in the women's clothing department, can I ask that Nuala have something

simple made for her? Some blouses and plain skirts perhaps? I have had my fill of feeling as though I'm in a hospital, surrounded by nurses.'

'Very well, darling, but I must provide some aprons for when Nuala washes you. Now then, I should be getting on. We've General Strickland and his wife Barbara coming to take tea, which means I'm going to have to entertain her while he and your father talk business. Oh.' Lady Fitzgerald paused by the door and turned back. 'You'll receive eight shillings a week, with Sundays off and two weeks' annual holiday. Paid, of course,' she added. 'And another thing whilst I'm up here: do encourage Philip to get outside whilst the weather is so clement. Some fresh air would do you good, Philip. After all the trouble we went to in order to put the lift in, it seems a terrible shame that you never use it. I'll be up to kiss you goodnight at bedtime, darling. Goodbye, Nuala, it was a pleasure to meet you.'

When she'd left, Philip looked at her. 'I do hope you will take the job, Nuala. I've fought awfully hard for Mother to offer it to you.'

'I'd love to, I really would, Philip, but I have to ask if I'm allowed to first.'

'Of course, of course,' he nodded and looked up to her. 'Do you ever get tired of the control men have over your life? You might be surprised to hear that I've got a lot of time for the suffragette movement. Father abhors them, of course, and the Cumann na mBan here in Ireland is a little too radical even for me . . .'

Nuala fought the urge to correct his pronunciation of the Gaelic words, as he had called it '*bahn*' instead of '*mahn*', but the last thing she wanted was for him to know she was an active member of the 'radical' organisation.

'Having watched women working on the front line,' he was

saying, 'it occurs to me that the fairer sex are not only equal to men, but in many ways superior.'

'I'll be honest and say that I've not thought about it much; my family all work as hard as each other on the farm, doing our different jobs.'

'But does a man have to ask his father if he's allowed to take employment before he accepts it?' Philip pointed out.

'Well now, Christy, my cousin, who works in the pub in Clogagh, did ask my daddy if it was all right for him to do so.'

'Daddy's rule is law, eh?'

'Isn't it the same for you?' she asked him boldly.

'True. Nothing much happens around here without Father having agreed to it. Anyway, I do so hope your father will say yes to you working here, Nuala.'

'So do I, Philip,' she smiled at him. 'I'd like to more than you could ever know. Now then, what's this I hear about a lift? And why have you never mentioned it to me before?'

'Because our days have been given over to turning you into a worthy chess opponent,' Philip said defensively.

'We'd have had time for a walk occasionally, Philip. It might put some colour in your cheeks.'

'The cheek that sits somewhere below my nose, and is so scarred it looks like someone has scribbled all over it with a red ink pen? No, I prefer to stay up here, thank you.'

Nuala saw pain in his gaze, and realised the real reason.

'You're embarrassed, aren't you? You don't want anyone to see you.'

There was a pause as Philip turned his face away from her, which usually meant that he was about to cry.

'Of course I am,' he said quietly. 'Wouldn't you be? How would you feel if everyone gave you one glance and you saw

the horror in their eyes? It was in yours when you first met me, Nuala.'

'Sure, I won't lie, it was. But then I got past that and saw the person you truly are.'

'That's because you're *you*. I'd have gardeners and maids screaming at the sight of me, let alone any of Mother and Father's visitors to the house. I . . . just . . . can't, all right?'

'I understand, Philip. Now then, will we be playing a game of chess or what?'

As she was cycling home, Nuala came up with what might be a plan. But first, she had to ask her family and fiancé whether they'd even allow her to stay on.

'Please, Holy Mother, let them.'

As she rode, she allowed herself to dream of a life where she no longer worked at the farm, with chickens, pigs and often cows to look after if Daddy was pushed. Just her own little cottage with Finn waking up beside her, and then spending afternoons with Philip . . .

''Twould be perfect,' she murmured as she cycled up the track to Cross Farm.

'Where are Hannah, Christy and Fergus?' she asked her mother, who was in her favourite chair by the hearth, knitting socks for the volunteers. Daddy sat opposite her, pipe in his mouth, reading a book in Gaelic.

'Christy's at the pub, Fergus is scouting at the top in case of a raid, and Hannah is after having an early night. She's to take the first train to Cork tomorrow to collect a dispatch from Dublin,' said Daniel. 'Any news?' He put his book down on his lap and looked up at her.

'Yes. I . . . well, I've been asked to stay on in a permanent

position as nurse to Philip at the Big House.' She saw the look that passed between her parents. 'I wanted to ask you whether you thought 'twas a good idea. Oh, and' – Nuala added what she hoped was the icing on the cake – 'a big fancy car arrived today. A man called General Strickland was visiting Sir Reginald.'

'Jesus, Mary and Joseph!' Daniel exclaimed. 'He's the louser that runs the police force and all military operations up in Cork. He was there today?'

'Yes,' Nuala nodded.

'Do you know why?'

'I've not a clue, Daddy, but today I met Lady Fitzgerald. She spoke to me personally to offer me the position. And 'twas her who said about the general.'

'Our girl's infiltrating the heart of that family, Eileen,' Daniel beamed.

'And I've also an idea of how to see more.'

Nuala outlined her plan to persuade Philip downstairs and out into the garden.

There was a pause as her parents looked at each other again.

'Sure, Nuala, 'tis worth sticking with the work for now. But in a week's time, 'twill no longer be our decision what you do. You'll have to visit your fiancé tomorrow and ask him,' said Daniel.

'I'd say he mightn't be too pleased if his new wife is out until nine o'clock at night. Who will have his tea on the table when he comes home from the schoolroom?'

Nuala was fully prepared for this comment from her mother. 'Finn rarely gets home until after six o'clock. I'd leave his tea ready for him, so all he has to do is take the lid off the bowl and eat it.'

'I doubt he'll be wanting cold stew or vegetables a few

hours old,' said Daniel, 'but that's for him to decide, not us, daughter. A wife's place is by her husband's side, and I'm sure he'll not be wanting you cycling home in the dark and the rain when the nights draw in for winter.'

Nuala was reminded of the conversation she'd had with Philip earlier about the suffragettes.

'I'll be earning good money, which would help us,' she persisted. 'Finn's wages don't go far and we have no land to farm on to supplement it, so. Anyway, if he's after agreeing, would you think it's a good idea?'

'I've said what I think, but 'tis not for me to decide,' said Daniel. 'Now, I'm for my bed. Leave a lamp burning in the window. We've new calves in the barn, which'll be collected by dawn. Goodnight, daughter.'

'Goodnight,' she called as her parents made their way up the stairs to the bed that sometimes creaked in an odd way a while after they closed their bedroom door. She knew what the sound was, a sound that she herself would help make when she and Finn were wed . . . She blushed at the very thought of it.

Blowing out the candles, she left the oil lamp on the window ledge and went upstairs.

Only one more week of sleeping with my sister, she thought as she undressed, then crept in next to Hannah. They took turns to lie on the lumpy bit of the covered straw pallet because it was the worst place to sleep, but with Hannah up early to go to Cork City tomorrow, 'twas only fair that tonight she had the good side. Nuala shut her eyes and tried not to think about the 'new calves' in the barn. This was code for rifles that had been passed through many hands to reach them here in West Cork, and were currently lying in a dump in the woods behind the farmhouse. If they were found by the British before they were collected, the men in the family

would be taken to Bandon Barracks to suffer the same fate as Tom and Pat. Comforting herself with the thought that Fergus was on watch up top, she did her best to go to sleep. After all, there had been 'calves' left here many times before . . .

'What's all this I hear about you carrying on working up at the Big House?' demanded Hannah the next day when she was back from Cork City. Nuala was mucking out the pigsty and replacing the straw, a job they both hated. 'What, I wonder, will Finn be thinking about that?'

'I'll be asking him, won't I? Then I'll tell you,' Nuala shot back.

''Tis all right for some: finding yourself a good husband with a proper job *and* working up at the Big House. All of this down at your cosy new cottage in Clogagh. We'll be calling you Lady Nuala soon enough, so we will. What about your volunteer work?'

'I'll take messages in the morning, and when I'm back at night, I swear. And I have Sundays off too. There.' Nuala threw in the last batch of fresh straw and moved over to the water barrel to wash the stench of pig from her hands. She'd skip eating lunch and bathe in the stream on her way to the Big House, because she'd not want to arrive smelling of pig.

'I'm sorry, Nuala,' Hannah sighed, 'I'm after turning into a grumpy old maid. I'm exhausted, I am. I had to cycle back the long way round from the station, as I saw a truck full of Tans.'

'Where were they headed?' Nuala asked as they walked towards the kitchen.

'They stopped at the Clogagh crossroads and didn't seem to know which way to turn. They were lost, since the volunteers took down the signposts,' she said with a giggle.

'I'll cook the lunch before I go, so, no bother.'

'Thanks.' Hannah gave her a wan smile as they entered the kitchen and she went upstairs.

'Did the calves leave the barn safely last night, Daddy?' she asked as Daniel arrived from the front entrance of the cottage.

'I'd say they did, yes. Now, where's my lunch?'

Having had no time to visit Finn, Nuala explained to Philip that he'd get her answer on Monday, for tomorrow was a Sunday, and her day off.

'But even if he says yes, Philip, I'd be having to take next Friday off for my wedding.'

'And I'd have thought the day after that too,' Philip said brusquely. 'Well, let me know for definite on Monday, and pity me having Maureen as my nurse all day tomorrow.'

Once she'd got that over with, they'd played their first game of chess, which took them straight up to tea time. As Nuala drank her tea, she decided to tackle him.

'I've been thinking . . .'

'About . . . ?'

'Well, what if I was to tell Mrs Houghton that you were wanting to come down to the garden but didn't want the staff around to disturb you? We could ring the bell to let her know we were coming, then I could take you out by the front entrance and into a place where the gardeners wouldn't be working. I'm sure there must be somewhere in that great big park outside where you can sit in peace? The weather's set fair for the next few days.'

'I don't know, Nuala,' Philip sighed. 'Like you, I'll think about it tomorrow and give you my answer on Monday.'

''Tis up to you, o'course, but for the love of God, you can't

stay up here for the rest of your life,' she said, trying to keep her voice calm. 'All the flowers are in full bloom, and the air smells of cow parsley and . . . I just think 'twould do you a lot of good. We could put your trilby on your head to hide your face and—'

'Have you been in cahoots with Mother, Nuala?' he interrupted. 'I'm afraid you're beginning to sound just like her.'

'No, I haven't, but maybe we're thinking the same thoughts because we want the best for you.'

'What's best for me is if I never wake up again! I don't know which is worse,' he continued. 'The nightmares full of bangs and whistles and then the thud as the shells hit the ground and explode, or this waking hell.'

'Oh Philip, please don't be saying such things! You've suffered terribly, and it's understandable you're feeling like you do, but you're still here on God's green earth and I'd say that's because you're meant to be.'

'What use can I be to anyone like this?'

'For a start, you've taught me to play chess,' Nuala rallied. 'And maybe, once you've braved going downstairs, you could be enjoying more company, like that man who visited your parents yesterday.'

'General Strickland? Good Lord, I hardly think so, Nuala. The last thing I want is to listen to Father go on about the Boer War and hear Strickland complaining about the uprising down here. Father said that they're thinking about recruiting a new division of Auxiliaries to help us "crush the Irish".' He looked at her quickly. 'My apologies, Nuala, I meant no offence.'

'None taken.' Nuala was far too pleased with herself to care what he said, as she now had information to take home with her.

'I pray for you and your family's sake that you continue to stay out of it all,' he added. 'I'm only thinking of your safety,

because Father said these new men will be highly trained and will stop at nothing to defeat this rebellion.'

'I will, so, Philip, I swear,' Nuala said, her best innocent expression on her face.

When she arrived home, Nuala was touched to see that Finn, who always came round to Cross Farm for his tea on a Saturday night, had waited for her so they could eat together.

'Hello, darlin',' he said, standing up to give her a hug as she walked into the kitchen.

'Where is everyone?' she asked.

'Oh, here and there; I'd say they're allowing us some time to ourselves.'

'Could you hang on for another few minutes before we eat?' Nuala asked. 'I've got important information to tell you all. I'll go and whistle for them.'

'What's this about important information?' said her mammy from the top of the stairs, where she'd obviously been listening in. 'Your daddy and Fergus are next door at the O'Hanlons', planning the harvest.'

'I'll go and fetch them,' said Finn, donning his cap and leaving the kitchen.

Hannah followed their mother down the stairs and fifteen minutes later the family was gathered together.

'So, Nuala,' said Daniel, 'what is it you have to tell us?'

Nuala recounted what Philip had told her about General Strickland's visit yesterday. She tried not to sound big with herself, being in possession of such knowledge before even headquarters in Dublin had sent a dispatch through about it.

'Now then, this is what I call news.' Daniel thumped the table. 'Did he say when exactly these Auxiliaries were coming?'

'No, but he said they'd be highly trained.'

'I'm assuming 'twould be soon,' said Fergus.

''Tis all we need,' Hannah sighed.

'Well done, Nuala. 'Tis obvious that you've won his trust if he's telling you things like that,' Eileen smiled at her.

'Hannah, will you write a message and get it sent off around the place?' said Daniel. 'It needs to go up to Dublin too, though I'm sure Mick Collins will already have heard the news.'

'He will, sure,' Hannah said, a glow in her cheeks at the mention of her hero. 'I'll be writing now.'

'Nuala, I'd say that decides it,' said Daniel. 'If Strickland and Sir Reginald are after discussing the British plans and Philip's being told them by his daddy, you'd be helping us by staying on there.'

'What's this?' Finn shot her a glance.

'Forgive me, Finn, I'd no time to see you yesterday,' said Nuala. 'I was going to tell you tonight that I've been offered a permanent position as nurse to Philip up at the Big House.'

'Have you now?' Finn's intelligent blue eyes appraised her.

'The money's good – eight shillings a week – and I'd reckon 'twould come in handy.'

'Though 'twould mean that you'd be missing your tea being ready on the table when you come in from a hard day's work,' her mother said pointedly.

There was a pause as Finn digested the news. Nuala felt utterly terrible and wished she'd just have said the words to him as soon as she'd got home, rather than him sitting here now with all the family staring at him.

'Sure,' he said, turning to her mother, ''tis school holidays at the moment and I've been a bachelor a while, so I know my way around a spud. Besides, if Nuala is there to help the cause, who am I to complain? 'Twill be harder for her than

me. You're having to learn to become a great actress, darlin'.' He gave her a smile.

'We're all learning that, Finn,' Hannah put in.

'I'd say Daddy and Finn are right,' said Fergus. 'You should take the job.'

The rest of the family nodded their agreement.

'That's that then, so. You have yourself a new job, daughter. Right. 'Tis time to leave these two alone to discuss wedding plans.'

As the family dispersed, Nuala rekindled the fire to warm up the pot, then served stew into two bowls, taking little for herself as she was still full from the gorgeous Victoria sponge cake Philip had insisted she try earlier. Even though it was named after a British queen and was therefore a traitorous thing to be eating, she'd savoured every mouthful. 'Can you forgive me for not telling you the moment I came through the door tonight?' she asked him.

'I'd have preferred it if we'd been able to discuss it alone but—'

'Finn, you must say if you'd rather I didn't take the position. It doesn't matter about Mammy and Daddy – 'tis you I'll be answering to this time next week.'

'And why would I be stopping you? As you say, Nuala, 'twill bring in some shillings to the household, and besides, it means your nursing training hasn't been wasted. You're doing what you were born to do.'

'Not really, Finn; 'tis hardly like I'm saving lives on a battlefield.'

'From the sound of these Auxiliaries, there might be plenty of that coming your way in the future. And isn't it you that's always said to me it's not just about tending wounds, but tending souls? Seems like you're doing that for Philip. Oh, and one more thing' – Finn took her hand across the table – 'let's have

none of this old-fashioned shite about answering to your husband. The only person you need to be answering to is yourself and your conscience. Within reason, of course,' he smiled.

She gazed at him and thought how well he and Philip would get on if they were to meet. Her heart was fit to burst with love for him.

'Thank you, though you must know I'd never do anything without discussing it with you first,' she said.

'Marriage is about being a team. We're both equals in it, and we must respect each other. I learnt that from the women up at teacher training in Waterford. I'd say half the students were women and just as bright as the men. If not brighter,' he grinned. 'Now then, with that agreed, tell me how the plans are going for our wedding?'

14

Nuala woke up on the morning of her marriage to Finn feeling as if she hadn't slept a wink. Every time she imagined taking her daddy's arm and walking down the aisle in front of two hundred souls, she thought she might be sick all over the beautiful white gown Hannah and the other dressmakers had sewn for her at the shop in their spare time.

Sitting up, she saw the sun was not yet showing its face above the other side of the valley, which meant it was before five.

Lying back down, she knew this was the last time she'd ever share a bed with Hannah. Which immediately sent her tummy into another loop of anxiety . . . She couldn't even ask her big sister what 'it' was like because she was the first to marry, and she could hardly be asking Mammy. She looked over at Hannah – she was so vivacious and quick-witted, though her temper came equally quickly, as Daddy always said. She'd had many fellows after her, but none had ever interested her.

Do you resent me for walking up the aisle before you . . . ?

Well, today, however many times Hannah would snipe at her, she'd ignore it. As Nuala had grown older, she'd also become aware that the eldest daughter had the hardest time on the farm. It was Hannah that Mammy looked to for the extra jobs, and Hannah did most things without complaint.

'I'll miss you . . .' she whispered to her sleeping sister. Hannah had inherited Mammy's pale skin, freckles and hair the colour of a shiny copper pan, whereas Nuala had her father's dark colouring. She'd always considered herself the plainer of the two, with any attention at weddings and *ceilidhs* going to Hannah. Fergus seemed disinterested in women in general, saving his affections for the cows in the field. So here she was, on the morning of her wedding, the youngest, but the first of her siblings to be wed . . .

Jumping out of bed, she decided she'd feed the hens and make breakfast just one last time.

As she crept downstairs so as not to wake anyone, she almost jumped out of her skin to see Mammy in her nightgown, stirring the pot over the fire.

'Why are you up so early?'

''Tis a stupid question to be asking on my daughter's wedding morn,' Eileen scolded her.

'I'm out to feed the hens and—'

'You'll be doing no such thing! Today is *your* day, daughter, and we'll be treating you like a princess right from the start of it. Now then, sit down in my chair and I'll be making you a mug of tea and then a bowl of porridge, so. After that, you're to be in the tub before everyone starts arriving.'

'But I—'

'None of that, miss; 'tis the last day that my word is law. For once, you'll be doing as you're told.' Then Eileen opened her hands and cupped her daughter's face inside them. 'I'm proud of you, Nuala. Finn's such a good fellow. Just remember to make the most of this time with him before the small ones start coming along, won't you?'

'I will, Mammy, I promise.'

Fourteen hours later, Nuala lay in her new bed in her new home, alongside her new husband. The sheet tucked firmly over the strange sensation of her own nakedness, she watched as her husband (equally naked) slept peacefully beside her. Even though she was utterly hanging – the most exhausted she'd ever felt in the whole of her exhausting life – she wanted to play the day back to herself so she could store it safely away in her memory without forgetting a moment.

She'd been taken to the church in a garland-streamed pony and cart, and all the way into Timoleague everyone had come out of their houses and shops and clapped her on her way. Then the walk down the aisle on her daddy's arm and the look in Finn's eyes as he turned round and saw her and whispered, 'You're beautiful,' in her ear, as Daddy had let go of her hand and had given it over to Finn's safekeeping. The fine spread laid on by friends and family, which even Finn's mammy, after a glass of sherry or two, was impressed by. The band that had struck up as the *ceilidh* had begun, with everyone in high spirits and dancing away as if they'd not a care in the world. She and Finn in the centre as he'd spun her round and round . . . Then the throwing of her bouquet, made up of wild fuchsia, violets and forget-me-nots. Hannah had been the one to catch it and everyone had cheered, especially as Nuala had seen that a young man had caught her eye.

Then the way Finn had carried her over the threshold of the little cottage that would be her new home. He hadn't put her down until he'd climbed the stairs and laid her gently on the bed. He'd struggled with all the tiny white buttons that had fastened her into the dress, but all the time he'd kept kissing her until she'd lain beneath him, and their lovemaking had begun.

She'd been amazed to find, after hearing gossip that men

liked 'it' better than women, that *she'd* liked it too. Yes, it had hurt at first, but then it suddenly hadn't anymore as she'd been swept along with all the new and wonderful sensations her body and her mind had experienced.

It has been perfect, just perfect, she thought drowsily, before she finally fell asleep.

'So, how is the new Mrs Casey faring?'

Philip looked up at her as she walked in, clad in her new blouse of white poplin and the long grey skirt of such fine fabric that it didn't itch her legs. She'd been provided with a pair of new black boots too, and a stack of crisp, starched white aprons.

'I'm well, thank you,' Nuala said. 'And yourself?'

'Oh, I'm the same as you left me. Whereas you . . . My goodness, it's a positive metamorphosis! My dear Nuala, what with the new togs and your hair pinned up like that, it seems that you've turned from a girl to a woman overnight. Now, do sit down.'

Nuala did so, feeling horribly embarrassed. Even though the tone of Philip's voice had been light, she knew what he was insinuating.

'Mrs Houghton said 'twould be more appropriate for my position if my hair was put up,' she answered defensively.

'It suits you, although I must say I rather liked it tumbling over your shoulders. At least Mother didn't insist on a nurse's cap, so I'll be grateful for small mercies. How was the wedding?'

'It was perfect, thank you, Philip. The whole day went off as well as it could have done.'

'And your new in-laws? Do they approve of the match?'

'Finn has no father – he died when he was very young. His mammy – mother,' she corrected herself, 'is a fine woman. She remarried a few years ago before Finn left to do his teaching diploma, and lives a good while away, near Howe's Strand in Kilbrittain.'

'Goodness, that all sounds very civilised,' said Philip. 'At least you don't have your mother-in-law living with you like so many Irish families do. I've often wondered how kindly my own dear mama would take to any woman I chose to marry. Not that it's a thought worth having any longer. Who would want me?'

'Many, I should think, when they got to know you.'

'You're being kind, Nuala, but let's neither of us delude ourselves. I'm a freak show, not fit to go out in public. I'll spend the rest of my days exactly where I am now. Anyway, I'm glad to see you happy, and I apologise if I appear maudlin. In truth, I can't help but feel envy for . . .' – Philip checked himself – 'for the fact that such a normal rite of passage has been denied me. Now then, I'd imagine you're quite exhausted today. So I thought I'd add in a little relief from the chess-board and teach you to play backgammon. The box is in the same cabinet as the chess pieces.'

'Whatever you wish,' replied Nuala, as she went to the sideboard to retrieve another beautifully turned wooden box full of small round black and white counters. She thought of Finn at home in their tiny cottage and, for the first time, resented being here with Philip.

Nuala would always remember those precious first few weeks after she and Finn were wed as the happiest of her life. She spent most of them in a dreamlike state of bliss; she'd wake

Mrs Houghton standing there.

'The lift door is open and I've alerted the rest of the s... to keep clear of the front hall and Lady Fitzgerald's private garden,' she said.

'Shall we go?' said Nuala.

'If I have to,' grunted Philip, his voice muffled by the thick woollen scarf in which he had buried half of his face.

Nuala pushed the wheelchair along the landing.

'Right,' said Mrs Houghton, 'there's only room for you and the chair, so I'll meet you downstairs. Press the button marked "G" and I'll close the cage.'

'I've never been in a lift before,' Nuala said. ''Twill be like flying!'

'That's the part when you come back up, Nuala,' Philip replied dryly.

The criss-crossed metal door was secured behind them and with a gentle jolt and a loud whirring noise, Nuala watched as Mrs Houghton's face disappeared from view. Five seconds later, the lift bumped to a halt. Turning round, Nuala saw the entrance hall beyond the metal grille.

''Tis magic, Philip! We've landed. What do I do now?'

'Open the cage, I would imagine.'

Nuala found the lever and pushed it back as Mrs Houghton approached from the other side.

'There we are, Philip, just a few more seconds and we'll be outside in the fresh air,' said Nuala.

She saw him slump deeper into his chair as they crossed the entrance hall. The wide front door was already open and Mrs Houghton indicated the ramp laid in front of it.

'It's not steep, but hold on tight to the chair,' she ordered.

company you, shall I?' Mrs Houghton asked.

'No need, I'm sure Nuala will not let me come to any harm,' said Philip. 'Go on then, get a move on!'

She did so, following the flagstone path around to the side of the house and arriving in a formal garden. There was a path leading through the beautifully tended beds, full to the brim with roses and other jewel-coloured flowers she'd never seen before. They arrived at a central paved area, in the middle of which was some kind of round ornament.

'Ah, Philip! This garden is just about the most beautiful thing I've ever seen!' Nuala said as she pulled him to a stop and turned around to take it all in.

'It's my mother's pride and joy,' said Philip. 'Despite the fact that we have gardeners, she's spent hours in here on her hands and knees, digging in all sorts of different specimens that Father would bring her back from his travels. She and I would sit on the bench over there and she'd tell me the names of all the things she was planting.'

'Well, you'd never have to be worried about being spotted here; what with the trees and bushes all around it, you can't be seen from the outside. 'Tis like a secret garden.'

'That's what Mother's always said. I reckon she comes here a lot to hide from Father,' he smiled.

'What is that?' Nuala pointed to the round metal ornament that stood on a plinth in the middle of the square.

'It's a sundial. Before we all had clocks and watches, it was used to tell people what time of day it was. As the sun moves around from its rising in the east to setting in the west, the shadows tell you if it is midday, or that dusk is approaching. Mother always says that when the sun is over the yardarm, it's

time for a gin and tonic, or a whiskey,' he chuckled as he tipped his head upwards towards the sun. 'Good Lord, that feels nice. Push me closer to the bench and then you can sit down by me.'

They sat in the garden for a good while. Philip didn't say much, content to simply enjoy being outside. Nuala thought how to her 'being outside' always indicated work. It was a rare occasion when the family would simply sit in the fresh air and be still.

There was a sudden rustle and the sound of footsteps along the stone path. 'Who the blazes is that?! I thought Mrs Houghton had warned them . . .'

'Philip, darling, it's only me.'

Lady Fitzgerald appeared from behind the bushes. Nuala immediately stood up and gave a bob.

'Do sit down again, Nuala dear. I just wanted to come and see how you were, Philip.'

'I'm doing well, Mother, thank you.'

Lady Fitzgerald walked round to the front of her son's chair, knelt down and took his hands in hers. 'Darling boy, I'm so very glad you decided to come outside. How do you think my garden is looking?'

'Quite beautiful, Mother. It's certainly come on in the past few years.'

'I kept busy with my planting when you were away at the front. It took my mind off things. Nuala, would you mind if I took Philip around it? I want to show him the new herbaceous border. Now, darling, can you see those sprays of mauve flowers? They're *Hydrangea aspera*, then just over there I've planted some *Rosa moyesii* to get a splash of crimson. And those are my *Callistemon linearis*, which look rather like bright pink brushes. I planted those years ago, if you remember. I wasn't sure they'd like the soil, but as you can see, they haven't just taken, they've taken over!'

Nuala sat, enjoying the sight of mother and son outside together. She was also amazed that she was yet to meet Sir Reginald; she'd only caught glimpses of a rotund figure with an enormous grey moustache when he was seeing off a guest beneath the upstairs window. She felt a distinct coldness whenever Philip talked of him. They obviously weren't close.

Philip and Lady Fitzgerald came back towards the bench and Philip yawned. 'Perhaps it's time to take him inside, Nuala dear,' said Lady Fitzgerald. 'All that fresh air must have exhausted you, Philip. Oh, and also, your father has gone to London to meet with the builders. We're having the Eaton Square house renovated: proper bathrooms installed and a telephone line. I rather thought I'd come upstairs and take supper with you later. Which means you can leave early, Nuala. I'll see Philip into bed.'

'Thank you, your ladyship.'

'Will you push Philip back in?' she asked. 'Sadly, I have letters to write.' Once upstairs, Nuala took Philip to the bathroom and then they had tea.

Afterwards, she could see how drowsy he was.

'What about we forget playing a game today, and you sit quietly and have a rest?'

'I admit the trip has knocked me out a little. And to think a couple of years or so ago, I was marching thirty miles at a stretch through French ditches and fields. Why don't you read to me instead, Nuala?'

This was the moment she'd been dreading since she'd arrived at Argideen House.

'I will try, but I'm not sure I'll be up to your standard.'

'But you can read?' he asked.

'Oh yes, so, and I know my letters, but reading out loud, I . . .'

Nuala stopped herself. She'd been about to explain that the

only books they had at home were in Gaelic. But as that would probably be seen by Philip as some kind of heresy, she managed to close her mouth in time.

'No matter, we'll start gently. There's a book of poems by Wordsworth up there,' he pointed.

Nuala turned to the bookshelf placed on the back wall of the sitting room. 'Third shelf up and just to the left. Look for "Word".'

Nuala found a slim leather-bound copy and brought it over to him.

'Now then, Wordsworth is a very famous English poet,' he said. 'His most well-known is "I Wandered Lonely as a Cloud" and it's about daffodils. Do you know what a daffodil is?'

'No, so, I don't.'

'They are rather beautiful flowers and we have them here in our garden in springtime. They look like yellow trumpets with orange centres. Now, try reading the poem to me.'

Nuala took the book and looked down at the page Philip had pointed out. She felt as if she was back at school, having been chosen to stand at the front of the classroom and read a piece aloud.

'Right, I'll be giving it a go but . . .' She took a deep breath. *'I wandered lonely as a cloud, That floats on high o – o –'*

'The word is "o'er", as in "over". Go on, you're doing awfully well.'

Six lines later, Nuala was fit to throw the stupid book onto the fire, because it was making *her* look stupid.

'I told you, Philip, reading out loud is not my favourite. Especially not with these strange words that your man Wordsworth uses. I'd do better if 'twas the Bible, or descriptions of parts of the body, or sicknesses from my nursing training.'

'It's good to be given a challenge. You challenged me today, and I took it, remember?'

'Ah, you're right; so you're paying me back for dragging you outside?'

'I am, but I'm so glad you did. It'll be the same with you and your reading. All it takes is the bravery to give something a try. Why don't you take that book home with you tonight and look over the poem? Tomorrow I'll help you with any words that you can't pronounce. And honestly, Nuala, thank you for insisting I go outside. Why don't you take a read of some of the other poems whilst I have a short nap?'

Philip's eyes were still closed an hour later, when there was a soft tap at the door and his mother walked in.

Nuala put a finger to her lips.

'The dear boy is obviously wiped out,' said Lady Fitzgerald. 'He's had more excitement in the past few hours than in the year since he came home. I cannot thank you enough for persuading him outside. He told me it was all down to you. I'm so very grateful. Here.' She pressed a coin into Nuala's hand. 'I know you were married recently, so think of it as a small wedding gift from me, and please don't tell the other servants.'

'Thank you, Lady Fitzgerald, but there really is no need.'

'Now then, why don't you get home to your husband, and I'll see Philip to bed?'

'I will, so, thank you.'

'Look at you, persuading the young master outside,' Lucy the kitchen maid smiled as Nuala, now changed into her home clothes, walked through the kitchen towards the back door. 'Everyone's been talking about it, haven't they, Maureen?'

'They have, Lucy. I'd half wonder what Nuala has been doing upstairs to persuade him.'

As Maureen turned away and walked through the door that led to the front of the house, Nuala stared at Lucy open-mouthed.

'Did she really just say what I'm thinking she said?' she breathed.

'She did, so, Nuala, but you're not to be taking any notice of the old witch. We all know she lost her husband in the Great War and her babe was stillborn, but that's no reason for being cruel.'

'Last week, she was telling me that my weight was affecting my work.' Cook turned round and shook her head. 'I told her straight, had she ever seen a thin cook?' Cook (whose real name was Mrs O'Sullivan) began to chuckle. 'And would you be trusting them if they had? Just ignore her, Nuala, she's jealous that you're in with the young master and Lady Fitzgerald.'

Having said goodnight, Nuala got on her bicycle, still seething. Under the oak tree, she let out her frustration.

'That witch knows I'm newly married! How could she even be thinking I'd be upstairs using my charms on Philip? Jaysus! I'm his nurse, 'twould almost be . . .'

The thought was so horrifying she didn't have the word for it. Her rage fuelling her flight along the valley in half the normal time, she was just leaning her bicycle against the side of her cottage when old Mrs Grady, her neighbour, appeared out of nowhere.

'Is your man sick, Nuala? I heard some talk in the village.'

'He is indeed, Mrs Grady.'

'I've not heard a peep from him since you left. I did tap on the door and look through the front window, but the curtains were closed.'

'He was probably sleeping after a bad night. I'll be up inside now to check on him.'

'If he's that sick, he shouldn't be left alone when you're at work,' Mrs Grady clucked. 'I'm happy to be popping in during the afternoons to see if there's anything he'd be needing while you're out.'

'That's very kind of you, Mrs Grady, and sure, I'll take you up on the offer if he's not improving.'

'You do that,' Mrs Grady said as Nuala unlocked the door. 'Would you like me to come inside with you? Just in case . . .'

'I'll be calling you if there's a problem. Goodnight, Mrs Grady, and thank you.'

Nuala shut the door behind her, wishing she could lock it, but knowing that would alert her friendly but nosy neighbour that something was up. Peeping through the front window and seeing Mrs Grady was still hanging around, she sighed and went upstairs to the bedroom she and Finn shared. She opened the curtains and the window to call down to her.

'He's alive and well, Mrs Grady, so you're not to be worrying now. Goodnight.'

Nuala closed the window, redrew the curtains and sat down on the bed, knowing it was going to be a long week.

True to his promise, Finn arrived home in the early hours of the following Monday. He was so quiet, she hadn't even heard the back door open.

'Finn! Oh Finn! You're home safe.'

'I am indeed,' he said as he divested himself of his clothes and slipped into bed beside her. 'Forgive me, I'm stinking from sweat and grime . . . It's been a long, hard week.'

'But you survived.'

'I did. Come here, my Nuala.' He stretched out his arm and she laid her head on his chest.

'Who was there?' she asked. 'What did you do? Were there any raids—?'

'Nuala, I'm hanging. I need some . . .'

Nuala saw his eyes had closed, but she lay awake, loving the feel of his warmth and listening to the steady beat of his heart beneath her ear. She could not be more grateful that he was home; every day she'd had the locals knocking on her door asking after Finn and when he'd be back at work. Shouldn't she call a doctor if he wasn't improving? Was it contagious, did she think? In the end, she'd cycled down to Timoleague to visit Hannah at work and explained that the locals were getting suspicious.

'I need to know the name for a bad illness that includes vomiting. I've a few ideas, but I need to pick the right one.'

'Go along to the chemist here – Susan behind the counter is a woman you can trust,' Hannah said in a low voice. 'Tell her that Finn has a vomiting bug and ask her for some powders. I'm sure she'll be able to give you a fancy name for an ailment.'

Nuala had duly done so, and Susan herself had cycled up with the powders and entered the cottage to see to the 'patient'. Her arrival and the fact that now Nuala could tell everyone Finn had 'gastroenteritis' had done nothing for her reputation as a cook, but had satisfied the neighbours. Hannah had also 'taken sick' from the dressmaker's shop, in order to assist the women cooking for the men up at the training camp in Kilbrittain, which had added strength to the myth.

The mad thing was that she knew Mrs Grady and the rest of the village would be cheering Finn on if they knew the

truth. But that knowledge would only put everyone in danger.

My life is a constant lie . . . Nuala thought, before she finally drifted into a restless sleep.

At seven a.m., she had to shake Finn awake. She'd already made him tea and porridge and took it up to him to eat in bed.

'Will you be all right to go to teach today?' she asked.

'I have to be, don't I?'

'Yes. Everyone's been asking after your health so you need to show your face. How did the week go?'

'I'd say 'twas the proper thing; we were put into sections and taught to act as if an attack from the enemy could arrive at any time. We learnt how to detonate a Mills bomb, then we practised with the new Lee-Enfield rifles, aiming and trigger-pressing, and we even slept with our rifles on us. If an alarm was given and any man in the section was not out of their bed fast enough, we'd have to do it all over again. We took turns to be in command of a section, and then in the evenings, after our tea, we'd be together in the barn to listen to lectures or do written exercises.'

'It sounds serious, Finn. Are you sure that the enemy didn't know what you were doing up there? The farm is close by the Black and Tan post in Kilbrittain.'

'The Bandon and Kilbrittain battalions fielded the scouts, and did a grand job of protecting us. We all knew the whistle that would tell us if they were coming, but thanks be, they never did. We spent a lot of time out on the land, learning how to best use natural cover and how to navigate it quietly, keeping our formation when we were ambushing a road patrol.'

'At least now you'll all be ready if there is an attack,' she said.

'We will, so, but Nuala, here's the difference: *we're* going *on* the attack. We can't just be sitting around playing defensive – we've got to organise more of our own attacks if we're ever to triumph. There have been plans discussed which will be put into action soon. I'll be needing to take more time away from the school to fight for the cause in the coming months.'

'But how, Finn? You've a fine job as a teacher; you're not thinking of leaving it, are you?'

'Not leaving, no, but if necessary, I'll need to tell Principal O'Driscoll of my involvement in the Flying Column. Perhaps my "illness" has been worse than was thought, so I might have to take some more time to rest, if you see what I mean.'

'Well, what with your pale, thin face and your red eyes, you'll be looking the part this morning,' Nuala sighed. 'Are you sure the principal can be trusted?'

'I am. He wants Ireland back just as much as I do, and has often said he'd be out there fighting with the volunteers himself if he was a younger man. I have to trust him, Nuala,' Finn said as he finished the last spoonful of porridge.

Nuala sat there, staring at him. Eventually she said, 'You know I'm as committed to the cause as you are, Finn, but if that means losing you in the process, then I'd even get on a boat and cross the sea to America to start a safer life there. And you know how much I fear the sea.'

Finn put out a hand to caress her face. 'I do know, darlin'. But this is a fight we have to win, whatever the cost. Oh, and before I forget, Tom Barry was asking whether you'd seen Major Percival up at the Big House recently?'

'There's been a few fine cars, but I haven't heard Philip talk of anyone else since General Strickland.'

'Percival's the bastard we want more than any other. And we'll have him, Nuala, we will. Tom Barry's put out the word in Bandon for his movements to be watched day and night. Once we know his routine then—'

'You'll attempt to shoot him?' Nuala looked at her husband in horror. 'Holy Mother of God . . . You'd murder him?'

''Tis not murder in a war, Nuala. Now, I must be getting off to school.'

'You'll be here when I get back tonight?' Nuala asked as she watched him dress in a smart shirt, trousers and tie.

''Twas agreed we all needed a rest this week, but . . . I can't be promising anything any longer. And remember to put it round the village I'm still suffering from the effects of my illness, and that you're worried for my health. Bye, darlin', I'll be seeing ye.'

'Will we go for a walk and a sit in the gardens today, Philip?' she asked later that afternoon at Argideen House. She had just read the Wordsworth poem he'd given her and he'd pronounced her 'word perfect'.

'No, Father has that ghastly Major Percival coming round. Mother and I can't stand him – he's an arrogant arse, if you ask me. The very worst of the British here in Ireland.'

'Have you met him?'

'No, but Mother says he'd have every Irishman – and woman – dead if he could. He's never lived here, you see, doesn't understand how you're all needed around the place, to help run our farms and houses. And that up until a few years back, we've all rubbed along together quite well. Like you and I do, eh, Nuala?'

'Yes, Philip, o'course.'

Even though Nuala knew Philip meant well, the fact he took British superiority as his God-given right irritated her.

'So, will we go out to the garden or not?' she asked him brusquely.

'Major Percival was up visiting the Big House today.'

Finn stared at her across the table, where they were eating tea. 'Did you see him? Hear him?' he asked.

'No, Philip refused to take a walk in case the major saw him. He's too embarrassed about how he looks.'

'You make sure you try and find out what the two of them were talking about. Major Percival is the number one target and is under surveillance as we speak.'

'I'll try, Finn, but Philip's never even met the fellow. He only hears bits from his mammy. His daddy hardly speaks to him.'

'Perhaps he's ashamed of his son, if you say he's so disfigured.'

'Perhaps. How were things at school today? Did you speak to Principal O'Driscoll?'

'I did, yes. We went for a glass at the pub after school. Christy was serving and looked out for anyone overhearing the conversation.'

'And?'

'O'Driscoll's said he'll help me cover my tracks. There's a doctor down in Timoleague he knows, a supporter of us volunteers. He's going to send him to me tomorrow so that the village can see I've had a real doctor come to visit, so it must be serious.' Finn gave a weak smile, took her hand and squeezed it. 'We'll get through this, Nuala, I know we will. There'll be happier days to come for our small ones.'

'Ah, sure, but with the both of us up to our tricks and

living here where everyone wants to know our business, 'tis dangerous, Finn, there's no denying it.'

'Well, we're both here and together tonight. One day at a time, eh, darlin'? 'Tis the only way to deal with it.'

With no visitors the next afternoon, Philip was happy for her to take him back into the garden. She decided it was time to press him on another point that might help in his rehabilitation.

'Philip?'

'Mmm?' he replied as he sat next to her in his chair, eyes closed as he enjoyed the glorious scent of the flowers.

'I've been thinking . . .'

Philip opened his eyes and glanced at her. 'Always a bad sign. What do you have in store for me this time? A quick spot of swimming in the Argideen River? Or perhaps taking a hack on one of the stallions in the stables?'

'Oh no, nothing as advanced as that yet. It's just, well, I'm looking at your false leg standing idle in the bedroom and wondering why you never wear it. If you did, you'd be up and walking beside me, not sitting in that chair you hate so much.'

'Nuala, I shall answer this very shortly and simply: when the doctor strapped it on to what is left of my kneecap and insisted I stand and take my not very considerable weight on it, the agony was almost as bad as coming round after the mine had exploded. Actually, it was probably worse, because I was fully conscious. So, the answer is no.'

'You say you've only tried it on once?'

'Yes. And never again.'

'But . . . the wound where they amputated your leg has healed over now. Maybe it was still raw when the doctor

asked you to stand on it before. So, yes, 'twould have been holy hell putting weight on it. I'd reckon 'twould be different now. Just imagine if you could walk again! Be independent! Wouldn't that be a mighty wonderful thing?'

'It would also be a wonderful thing if man could fly to the moon, but it's an impossibility. Now, will you please leave me alone, so that I can enjoy my time in the garden?'

Knowing Philip and his stubbornness all too well now, Nuala did not bring up the subject again. She did have something else she needed to talk to him about, and once they were back upstairs, she finally plucked up the courage to ask.

'Did your daddy enjoy his chat with Major Percival yesterday?' she said as Maureen brought afternoon tea into the room and began setting it out.

'I don't know if anyone can actually enjoy meeting the man. Mother did tell me, however, that my father said Percival was sure his movements were being watched by the IRA. He's noticed curtain twitching in the houses opposite Bandon Barracks whenever he walks a few doors down to have his evening meal. He believes the IRA are planning to assassinate him, but told my father he was prepared to send his forces to ransack every home in Bandon to find the culprits. Thank you, Maureen, you may leave us now,' Philip added to the woman. 'Nuala will pour.'

Nuala did her best not to let her hands shake as she did so.

'There you go.' Nuala handed the cup to Philip, then took a deep sip of her own tea. She'd been starving, having had no lunch again, but now she felt she might be sick if she put anything in her mouth.

'You look a bit queer, Nuala. Are you all right?'

'I'm grand, Philip, and eager to get on with that game of chess.'

Coming out of Argideen House that night, Nuala cycled to the oak tree and stood by it in a quandary as to who to take the message to, so it would reach those volunteers who were watching Major Percival the fastest. In the end, she plumped for Christy, working in the pub just across from her cottage, and cycled like a mad thing towards Clogagh.

Running into her house, she penned a quick note, then went across to the pub. Saying hello to a few of the locals hunched over their glasses at tables, she sidled up to the bar, where Christy was pouring three drops of whiskey.

'Hello, Nuala,' said Christy. 'What would you be doing in here at this time of night? Not looking for a drop of whiskey for yourself, are you?' he teased her. He'd brushed back his thick, dark brown hair today, so that Nuala could see his sincere warm brown eyes.

'There's a calf stuck in the womb up at the farm, and we'd be needing your help immediately.' Nuala used the sentence the family had constructed as code for an emergency.

'Right then, I'll speak to John; I'm sure he'll let me off early, as things aren't too busy.'

He eyed her hand as it slid across the bar to him. He put his over hers and squeezed it, then she pulled her hand away as he slid his back.

'I hope the calf survives,' she said, as she moved away back through the tables.

Heart pumping with adrenaline, she took some deep breaths as she walked back to the cottage.

'What's going on? Why did you run over to the pub?' Finn asked her as he stirred the soup in the pot over the fire.

'Philip told me that Major Percival suspects there are

people spying on him. He said he was prepared to destroy every house in Bandon to find the culprits. He knows our lot are after him,' Nuala panted, partly out of relief that she was home and able to let it out for the first time after three hours of trying to act normally in front of Philip. He said she'd played chess like a four-year-old, and to be fair, he was right.

'I'd already heard something about the house searches in Bandon, but not that they know there's any kind of a plot. We must get word to the men,' said Finn.

'I already passed Christy a note in the pub. He'll be off to Charlie Hurley's on his horse, who'll send word to Bandon.'

'Well done, Nuala,' Finn smiled. ''Tis worth all those hours of chess to think it might have saved some souls from a brutal beating and prison.'

'If we're in time.'

'Yes,' Finn agreed. 'If we're in time.'

15

Nuala heard nothing that night, or the following morning. Finn had left for school with a comforting, 'Bad news travels the fastest, Nuala,' but it hadn't eased her anxiety.

All she wanted to know for certain was whether Tom Barry – who Finn had confided in her was the one in charge of the Bandon spy party – had received the message to abort and flee in time.

'Jaysus,' she panted as she cycled up to the Big House. 'I'm a simple farmer's daughter, I'm not built for all this intrigue.'

She held her breath as she nodded to Lucy in the kitchen then headed upstairs to Philip's room. Only when he turned his wheelchair around to greet her with his half-smile did she let it out in relief.

'Hello, Nuala,' he said. 'You look as though you've been climbing Ben Nevis. Sit down and catch your breath.'

She sat down gratefully, wondering who or what Ben Nevis was.

'Today, I rather think I'd like *you* to teach me something,' said Philip. 'Refresh our minds before we play chess again,' he said.

Buoyed by relief that she'd not been found out, she smiled. 'What did you have in mind, so?'

'Have you any Irish games we could play? Although I'm

not up to hurling or Gaelic football. Perhaps a board game of sorts?'

She paused to think. 'I'll be honest with you, Philip, there's not much time for games like chess. The men sometimes play cards or drinking games but . . .'

Philip let out a chuckle. 'So did we, in the trenches. It was alcohol that kept us going more than anything else. But sadly, I don't think a drinking game will be quite as diverting with Darjeeling tea.'

Nuala tried hard to think, keen to give Philip something new that he wouldn't encounter in his small, English world, which didn't extend far beyond the borders of this parkland.

'Sometimes in the winter, Daddy used to tell us Irish fairy tales to pass the time. My sister Hannah always liked the scary tales of *púcaí*: spirit creatures who often appear as horses, then terrify any living soul who tries to ride them.'

'Let's stay away from any ghost stories, Nuala,' Philip shuddered. 'But I know you Irish believe in fairies and have a lot of tales to tell about them.'

"Tis part of our lore, of the earth and nature around us, so. I think you'd be liking Finvarra, king of the fairies. My Finn is named for him, and me for Nuala, the fairy queen.'

Nuala could not fail to note the slightest curl of his lip that she now recognised whenever she mentioned her husband.

'Well, why not regale me with the life of King Finn and Queen Nuala,' he said, giving her a thin smile.

So Nuala told him the story of how their namesakes had ruled a kingdom of fairies, or 'The Folk' as they were referred to in hushed tones. They were powerful creatures that lived close to the human world, lurking beneath fairy mounds and stone circles, waiting for a hapless wanderer to lose their way, only to be kidnapped by the all-powerful and charismatic Finvarra.

'Just as your Finn kidnapped you?' Philip put in, a hint of sarcasm in his voice.

'Ah, I was happy to be kidnapped. And just now, as 'tis close to the feast of Samhain, farmers are trying to appease Finvarra to ensure a good harvest,' she said.

'Like our druids used to in England. All humans have folklore of different kinds.'

'Do they?' Nuala asked in surprise.

'Oh yes, and this queen you've told me of – she shares traits with characters like Shakespeare's Titania and Morgan le Fay. They are all beautiful and enchanting, but clever too and often manipulative. Perhaps you are like your own fairy queen, Nuala.'

'Oh, I wouldn't be saying that now,' she countered, blushing. 'Who's this Morgan le Fay?'

'She was Merlin's apprentice in the old court of our British King Arthur. He taught her all he knew, his secret magics and ancient wisdoms. Then she betrayed him.'

'She sounds like a fierce bad woman. Our Queen Nuala would never betray Finvarra.'

'Oh, Morgan had her reasons. In fact, if you go to that shelf over there, you'll find a large green tome by a writer called Sir Thomas Malory: *Le Morte d'Arthur*.'

Nuala found it, then sat back down and opened the heavy book, internally sighing as she saw the pages covered in small text.

'I think we can skip over the Uther Pendragon stories,' he instructed her, 'and get right to chapter twenty-five – that's written XXV – when Merlin helps Arthur gain the sword Excalibur from the Lady of the Lake. Read it to me, Nuala.'

'I'll do my best, Philip.'

Having received word when she arrived home that Tom Barry and his men had escaped the clutches of the Essex Regiment in the nick of time, due to her intelligence from the Big House, Nuala walked around for the next week with a cautious optimism and pride. As autumn began and the leaves in the woods turned to red and bronze and gold, she spent her early mornings with Finn before he left for school, which provided a small window of calm in their young marriage. Then she would often cycle to other female volunteers' farmhouses to deliver dispatches – once with a pistol strapped to the outside of her thigh under her skirt – or do the volunteers' laundry. She spent the afternoons with Philip, now glad of the fire that burnt brightly in the large grate in his room as the nights drew in. They alternated between reading *Le Morte d'Arthur* (she was beginning to get the hang of the strange English it was written in), games of chess and walks around a garden rich with autumn colour.

Finn was increasingly away at night as the Flying Column gained confidence and mounted more attacks. When he arrived in their bed in the small hours of the morning, she only wished she could whisk him away to the land of the fairy folk, where the two of them ruled their kingdom together and there was only music, laughter and dancing . . .

Having had an idea about Philip, Nuala went to see Christy in the pub one night after work.

'Is all well, Nuala?' he asked, setting a drop of whiskey down in front of her with a wink.

'It is, thank you,' she said, taking a sip to warm her after her ride home. 'Christy, do you mind if I ask you something?'

'Ask and I'll answer,' he shrugged.

'Philip – the Fitzgeralds' son – you know he lost his leg in France?'

'Sure, you told me,' he nodded. 'Lucky he escaped with his

life, but I'd be thinking with all his family money, he's had the doctors at every hour and the best care.'

'He has, but . . . oh Christy, he's so stubborn! He won't take the help he's been offered. He's got a fine leg of wood made especially for him, but it gathers dust in a corner, because he won't even be looking at it. He says 'tis too painful.'

'How long has it been since it happened?' he asked as he walked around the counter and sat down on a stool beside her, easing the weight off his own bad leg.

'Over two years now. I've only just convinced him to go outside in his wheelchair. It's like he's given up, and all he wants is games of chess and his books. But there'd be so much more to life if he could only walk!'

'Sure, but you've got to be remembering that 'tis a mental wound as well as a physical one. When I had my accident, d'you remember how I was? Feeling sorry for myself, like I was no use to anyone any longer.'

'But you know that's not true. What would Mammy and Daddy be doing without you on the farm, and even more so with Fergus often . . . away. You work harder than any able-bodied man I know, Christy.'

'That may be' – Christy lowered his voice – 'but when I see Fergus and Finn going off, I feel like a useless eejit. There's not a day goes by that I don't remember the pain of my foot and shin being crushed by that thresher. I dream of it often, so, and I'm sure your Philip relives his war nightly too. I can only imagine how difficult it must have been for him to be coping with no leg, when at least I've still got use of mine. And the time it took to find the courage to stand up and use my stick.' He tapped it on the ground with a fond smile.

'So what got you to go on? To have hope?'

''Twas your family, and you, Nuala, with your care of me.' She couldn't bear the intensity of his gaze, so she averted

her eyes and looked down at the large calloused hand that rested on his oak stick.

'If it hadn't been for your cheerful smile every day,' he continued, 'I wouldn't have been wanting to even get out of bed, the pain was so fierce. But you were there, even though you were no more than thirteen. You were born to be a nurse, Nuala. And if this Philip knows what's good for him, he'll listen to you.'

'Maybe, but I'm failing so far, Christy.'

'Well now, my stick has helped take the weight off my bad leg and I've got a spare. Perhaps your man might like to try it?'

'At least I could offer it to him,' she said. 'Thank you, Christy.'

'You never let me take no for an answer,' he called after her. 'Don't let him.'

The following afternoon, Christy drove Nuala on his pony and cart to Argideen House, because she had his spare stick with her. Arriving at the kitchen door, she bolted up the stairs and knocked.

'Come in, Nuala,' said Philip.

When she entered, she noted the big book on King Arthur was placed on the side table by the damask sofa, waiting for her.

'Hello, Philip. Now then, today we'll be doing something new,' she said briskly.

'Really? Just what have you got up your sleeve?' he said, warily eyeing the walking stick in her hand. 'If it's what I think it is, then I must put my foot down – so to speak – and say no.'

Nuala sat down on the sofa, the stick in her hand. 'Do you remember me telling you about my cousin Christy?'

'Yes. The fellow who works in the pub?'

'Well, this is his.' She tapped the stick on the floor. 'When he was fifteen, he was working the thresher during barley season. A thresher is—'

'I know what a thresher is, Nuala.'

'Then you'll also be knowing how dangerous they can be. Christy's always been a strong lad, and smart too, but he slipped and his right foot and part of his leg were caught in it. I don't have to be telling you what a terrible injury it was.'

'I can imagine. Did they amputate?'

'No, they saved it, but it took near to a year for Christy to recover, and he's not been able to walk without a stick since. He'll never run, or swing a girl round the place in a *ceilidh* again, but he's walking and can ride his horse.'

'Well, good for him, but I don't see what it's got to do with me,' Philip said irritably. 'Christy's got two legs, and I'm assuming both eyes, and his whole face.'

'And you've got a fine wooden leg made especially for you just a few yards away in your bedroom,' she countered.

'Nuala, I said no and I meant it!'

She ignored him and went into the bedroom to fetch the leg. It was leaning up as usual against the wall in the corner, and Mrs Houghton had already shown her the stack of cotton socks in the dresser drawer. They would fit snugly over his stump and protect the scarred, delicate skin of the wound.

Taking the surprisingly heavy leg into the sitting room, she saw the look of abject fear on his face.

'No, Nuala, please!'

'Sure, we'll go slow about it,' she soothed him. 'But you have to try. How about we just fix it on, and you can stay

sitting with it while we have a game of chess? Just to get the feel of it, so.'

'I know you mean well, but it's no use. I'm perfectly all right here in my chair.'

'Are you, Philip?' She gave him a direct gaze. 'Every day I watch you and see how your pride is hurt by having to ask people for help. I'd feel the same way if 'twas me, and it's what got Christy out of bed and walking in the end. Besides, most soldiers I've seen in your position have little more than a wooden peg, when you have a fine custom-made leg! You've got to at least try it, so don't be letting your stubbornness get in the way of things.'

Flushed from speaking to him so forthrightly, she half expected him to fire her on the spot.

After a long silence in which neither of them moved, Philip let out a long sigh and gave a nod of acceptance.

'All right, but I'm not putting weight on it.'

'Thank you. So now, let's get going,' she said as she knelt down in front of him. 'I'll just be rolling up this trouser leg, so it won't be getting in the way,' she explained as she exposed the stump. Though he was used to being washed by her nightly, she could feel how tense he was. 'Now so, we've got a cotton sock to go on over,' she said as she slid it on. 'And I'll just be opening the clasps and bindings on it.'

The leg was made of a dark blond wood, which had been sanded, oiled and varnished. It had a foot carved at the end and leather laces so she could adjust the fit around Philip's thigh. She tried to work confidently, not betraying the fact that she'd never done this before.

Once the leg was fastened and she had checked with Philip that it wasn't too uncomfortable, she tested the hinge so it could move smoothly with his knee, and placed the foot next to his other on the wheelchair rest. Then she wheeled him

over to the window and set up the chess table without another word.

They played in silence, the satisfying click on the wooden board as pieces were moved the only sound, other than the crackling fire. Once he had declared checkmate, rather than ringing for tea, she went down into the kitchen and brought the tray up herself so he wouldn't have Maureen gawking at the leg.

As she poured him his tea, then added his preferred amount of milk, he cleared his throat.

'So, did you see many . . . amputees when you were up in hospital in Cork?' he asked.

'Yes. 'Twas the end of the Great War and we had young fellows recovering from injuries not unlike yours. I was only in training at the time, so I was emptying bedpans and the like rather than doing the proper nursing, but I saw a lot of suffering. And bravery,' she added for good measure.

He chewed on his sandwich thoughtfully before replying. 'I'm sure you did. And I know I'm luckier than most living here, but I don't think I'll ever know true peace again.'

'I think you could, Philip, if you were more independent. Yes, it takes a good deal of work and courage, but you can do it, I know you can.'

'You're so unfailingly optimistic, Nuala.'

'I don't see the point in being anything else, do you? And I've faith, Philip, and a great deal of it in you.'

'Then I'd hate to let you down, but—'

'Then don't, Philip.'

After a long pause, he sighed. 'Go on then. Let's give this a try.'

Her heart giving a bounce of joy, she wheeled him over to the long bookshelf, where there was a variety of firm surfaces to hold on to at the right height. Placing his feet on the floor

and handing him Christy's stick, she gently put her arms around his waist, as she did when she was helping him into bed at night.

'Now then, I've got you, Philip,' she said. 'We'll get you upright, and for now, balance your weight on your good leg. Once you feel comfortable, we'll try putting weight on the bad one.'

As she helped him to standing, she could feel him shaking with exertion and nerves, and saw his knuckles were white on the hand that clutched Christy's stick.

'Breathe, Philip, just in and out, so.'

With a gasp, he let out a breath and drew one in so quickly, she feared he would hyperventilate.

'Right. Hold on to the shelf there with your other hand . . .' Nuala indicated the right height. 'Now, 'tis time for you to try some weight on the leg. I promise it won't hurt as much as before,' she encouraged him.

She felt his body shift as he tentatively placed some weight on the wooden leg, and then heard another sharp intake of breath.

'How is it? Do you want to sit back down?' she asked.

'No,' he panted, beads of sweat on his forehead. 'No, no, I'm not giving up now I've come this far. It isn't as bad as it was. Let me get my balance and then I'll try standing alone.'

'Grand,' she said. 'You're being so brave. Now, when you're ready . . .'

Philip shifted about until he was comfortable. 'Ready,' he muttered.

'Balance on the stick and let go of the shelf . . . I'm here to catch you if you fall.'

He released his grip slowly, as she stood in front of him, arms stretched towards him.

'Look at you, Philip!' she said, feeling so proud of him she

was fit to burst. 'You're standing by yourself! 'Tis a breeze, isn't it?'

There was a sudden knock on the door, and it opened before Nuala could shout for them to wait.

'Philip?' Lady Fitzgerald entered the room. 'Oh – oh my . . .'

Philip had frozen at his mother's arrival, and Nuala reached out to support him, so he wouldn't lose his balance.

'It's just an experiment, Mother, to see if the leg still fits,' he said, trying to sound nonchalant as Nuala helped him sit back down in his wheelchair.

Lady Fitzgerald looked at Nuala, who gave her a meaningful glance.

'Of course,' said Lady Fitzgerald, taking the hint. 'I've just come to ask if you'd like me to join you for supper up here tonight, as our guests have cancelled.'

'That would be lovely, Mother.'

'Good. I'll come up at seven,' said Lady Fitzgerald. 'Nuala,' she nodded, and gave her a look of such joy and gratitude, it brought tears to her eyes.

Once the door had closed behind Lady Fitzgerald, Philip looked up at Nuala and gave a chuckle.

'Did you see Mother's face when she came in?! Oh, the discomfort was worth it for that alone. Thank you, Nuala. I should have tried it long ago, but I . . . I was afraid.'

''Tis understandable,' she said as she wheeled him back to the window where the sun was now setting, casting a golden glow into the room. 'I won't lie to you, there's more work to do before you can walk on your own,' she said as she knelt to unstrap the leg.

'But you'll help me, won't you, Nuala?'

'O'course I will, Philip.'

Just before seven, Nuala was just about to leave for home,

when Lady Fitzgerald stopped her at the bottom of the staircase.

'Nuala, a moment, please,' she said.

'Of course, your ladyship.' Nuala noticed that Lady Fitzgerald's eyes looked red, as though she'd been crying.

'Nuala, what you've managed to do for Philip is nothing less than a miracle,' she said softly. 'I can only thank you from the bottom of my heart.'

''Twas your son that did it,' she answered. 'Goodnight, Lady Fitzgerald.'

Nuala walked home that night not even feeling the cold wind that whipped at her cheeks. All she could think of was the look on Philip's face when he had stood by himself, unsupported for the first time since his injury. And felt determined to help him find the peace *and* sense of pride that he so longed for.

16

As autumn held West Cork firmly in its grip, the war for Irish independence went into high gear. While the British continued to ride into villages and burn down farms in reprisal for the many successful ambushes, so the IRA volunteers thwarted them as best they could, blowing up bridges, moving signposts and cutting telegraph cables wherever they could find them. Finn was away at night regularly, and Nuala busier than ever, delivering or collecting dispatches or arms.

Lady Fitzgerald had arranged for the groom who worked in the stables at Argideen House to construct a frame with two wooden bars, so that Philip could hold on to them while he practised walking on his wooden leg. The frame had been set up in Philip's sitting room, and he allowed Nuala to subject him to a rigorous exercise regime to strengthen his leg muscles.

'I'd say 'tis time for you to come off those bars and try walking a few steps on your stick,' she said one misty October afternoon.

'If I had known what a slave driver you were, I'd never have convinced Mother to employ you,' Philip had said as, his arms trembling and sweat beading his face, he held himself up on the bars and hobbled up and down the carpet.

'We'll try tomorrow, shall we?' Nuala said as she sat him down and unstrapped his leg.

An hour after she arrived home, Finn, who'd been out on Flying Column activities for the past few nights, appeared through the back door, looking exhausted.

'Hello, darlin', that smells good,' he said as he embraced her, then sniffed the pot hanging over the fire.

'And you look as if you need the stew inside you, Finn Casey. You're after losing more weight.'

''Tis all the marching around the place that's done it. I've never been fitter, I swear. I'm all brawn now, Nuala.' He winked at her.

'Any news?' she asked him.

'Yes, and 'tis good for a change,' he said as Nuala passed him the bowl of stew and he ate it hungrily. 'The Column opened fire on the Essexes at Newcestown – we've killed two officers and wounded three. Finally, we've had a victory!'

Nuala crossed herself and sent up a prayer for the dead men. Finn saw her do so.

'Darlin', the last thing we want is to cause death to other souls, but . . .' he shrugged, ''tis the only way. It's either the British or us. Some of our volunteers have been rounded up and their homeplaces have been raided and burnt to the ground. Nuala, they're arresting women too – I know of three Cumann na mBan girls that have been sentenced to jail in Cork City. I'm worried about you here alone when I'm away at night, and it's going to become more frequent. You'd be safer away up with your family at Cross Farm.'

'I've Christy across the road who'd protect me and—'

'No one can protect a woman alone from the British,

especially at night. There was a report only this week that came down from Kerry, about a woman who'd been terrorised and molested by two Tans. So, from now on, you're to go up to the farm if I'm away overnight, and not return until you have word I'm back.'

'But, Finn, what will the neighbours think if both of us are gone?'

'I've talked to Christy, and Principal O'Driscoll. Both of them are sure there are no spies in the village, only support for us volunteers and the women who are working for the cause.'

'Maybe, but we can't be endangering my position with the Fitzgeralds. If it becomes known—'

'It won't, so. We can trust O'Driscoll and our friends in the village. And, darlin', if it comes down to it, I'd have you leave your position if it means you can be safe.'

'But I don't want to leave,' she protested. 'You said yourself what I'm doing is valuable – it saved Tom Barry and his men in Bandon!'

'It did, though you're not the only spy we've got, Nuala, but you are my only wife!' He took her hands in his and softened his voice. 'We might be past trying to pretend to be a normal couple, but it's still my duty to protect you. Now then, let's eat up this stew before it gets cold.'

As October turned to November, Finn was away so often that Nuala was spending at least half her nights up at Cross Farm. Nuala noticed that Philip rarely asked after her husband, perhaps because he was kept so busy strengthening his legs. They had finished reading *Le Morte D'Arthur*. The story of the British king had turned darker towards the end of it,

although Nuala had approved of the knights' final mission to obtain the Holy Grail.

'And what is your Holy Grail, Nuala?' he had asked her as she'd finally closed the book.

Freedom for Ireland, she had thought, but instead had said, 'For you to be free of your wheelchair, so I haven't got to push you around any longer.'

Philip had chuckled and rung the bell for tea.

As Nuala lay in bed next to Hannah because Finn was away again, she thought how she'd never dreamt she'd be back here as a married woman. But at least she was kept busy: as the fighting had stepped up, volunteer casualties had grown, so she, with Hannah's help, had decided to organise a first-aid training day at Cross Farm for the women of Cumann na mBan. Aoife, one of her friends from her time nursing up in Cork, was travelling down to help her teach the basics of dressing and cleaning a wound, how to deal with an unconscious patient, and even how to extract a bullet. The women had been asked to collect as much antiseptic, bandages and basic medicines from the local pharmacies and hospitals as they could. They duly arrived and the haul was laid out at one end of the barn, with Aoife sorting it into a field kit for each woman to take away.

'I'm enjoying this,' said Nuala to Hannah as, after the first-aid training, they portioned out the stew that would be served in the barn.

'Yes, 'tis good for morale for us to gather together, *and* have the men scouting for the women for a change. Though I'd not trust them to cook for us,' Hannah chuckled.

After they'd eaten, the women, sixteen of them in all, listened

to their local captains talk on various subjects, which covered everything from how their knitting needles should be clacking away in any spare time they had as the lads were in need of socks, scarves and jumpers, to being shown a Webley revolver and a rifle. Mary Walsh of the Kilbrittain brigade gave a demonstration on how to load and fire them, explaining the different ammunitions, as well as safe cleaning procedures. There was also a call for the women to renew their efforts to fundraise.

'I'm hardly going to be holding a tea party in the middle of our village asking the locals to support our efforts, am I?' countered Florence acerbically. 'I'd be under arrest before we'd have time to clear away the cups!'

'No, Florence, you're right, but ask all the women you trust to ask the women *they* trust in their villages to give anything they can to support our brave fellows.'

'We need support too, so!' piped up another woman. 'What with all the laundry coming my way, I'm going through bars of soap like a babe hungry for her milk!'

'And food . . .'

'And wool!'

'We'll just have to do what we can, girls,' said Hannah. 'Our lads are depending on us and we won't let them down, will we?'

A rousing cheer came up in the barn before it was quickly hushed, and everyone lay down on straw pallets and huddled under blankets, as it was bitingly cold. Nuala's feet were half frozen as the rain lashed down on the roof. Thinking of how Finn and his comrades had to endure this night after night, sometimes after hours of marching or lying in a sodden ditch waiting for the enemy to approach, she felt awed by their bravery.

Once the last woman had left after breakfast the following morning, Hannah, Nuala and their mother washed out the pots.

'I'd say that was a grand thing you organised, Nuala,' said Eileen.

'It was,' Hannah agreed. 'Everyone went away with a new fire in their bellies.'

'I'm away out to feed the pigs,' Eileen announced. 'You girls sit down now and warm up after your night outside.'

'Thank you, Mammy.'

The two sisters sat listening to the crackling of the fire for a while, before Hannah spoke.

'Now so, whilst no one else is around, I wanted to tell you something. But you have to swear to keep it a secret.'

'I will of course, Hannah. What is it?'

'Do you remember Ryan, Finn's friend from Kinsale, who came to your wedding?'

'I remember him dancing with you, yes. Why?'

'I've been seeing a bit of him since then, due to him working at the post office along the road from the dressmaker's shop. He took his civil service exams and was meant to travel to England, but then when the Easter Rising happened, he decided he shouldn't go.'

'You dark horse, you. You've said nothing,' Nuala smiled.

'Because there's been nothing to tell. We've been on walks in our lunch hours, and met up sometimes after work, when I've not been away taking messages, but then . . .'

'Yes?' Nuala could sense her sister's excitement.

'Last Wednesday on our half-day, he took me for a long walk along the strand and . . .'

'Ah, stop with the suspense, woman! What?'

'He proposed!'

'Holy Mary, Mother of God! Now that *is* news! And . . . ?'

'I said yes. Oh Nuala.' Hannah reached across and squeezed her sister's hands. 'I'm so happy I'm fit to burst!'

'And I'm so happy *for* you, sister! 'Tis wonderful news, and exactly what the family needs just now.'

'Maybe, but you know what Daddy's like about these things. Ryan's homeplace is in Kinsale, so he won't know the family.'

'Ah sure, Finn's a friend of his, Hannah.'

'Maybe, but when Ryan comes up here to ask Daddy for my hand, Daddy'll spend at least an hour interviewing him like he did Finn.'

'Sure, 'tis his right as our father, and Ryan will just have to be prepared. When's he coming up?'

'Next Sunday. Can I show you the ring?'

'O'course!'

Hannah's eyes searched round the empty kitchen, as though someone might be lurking under the table. Then she reached down the front of her blouse and pulled out a ring she'd hung on a piece of thread.

''Tis in the shape of the claddagh, and only silver-plated, because his wages don't go far after he's paid for his board, but I love it.'

Nuala admired the little ring, with its silver heart cupped between two hands. She looked at Hannah's sparkling eyes as her sister gave the ring a kiss.

''Tis beautiful. Is he a good man?'

'Ryan's so good that he puts me to shame! I doubt a bad thought ever crossed that man's mind. He told me that when he was younger, he'd a notion to join the priesthood. The only problem is . . .'

'Yes?'

'He doesn't know anything of my involvement in Cumann na mBan. He wouldn't be liking it if he did. He doesn't approve of war, you see.'

'Hannah, you told me earlier that he didn't go to England to further his career there after the Rising. Surely he'd support you?'

'I'd say there was a difference between hating the British and being actively involved in fighting. He's a pacifist, which means he's against violence for any reason.'

Nuala looked at her sister aghast. 'But Hannah, you're one of the most passionate members of our cause! Are you saying you'd give up your activities for him?'

'Of course not, but after we're wed I'll be needing to be more careful. Perhaps if I explained that everything we do is for Mick Collins, Ryan might understand. I think he loves Michael Collins more than I do,' Hannah giggled. 'Ryan says he's a true politician; he believes Mick uses his intelligence and not his muscle to sort things out.'

'We both know that's not true, Hannah. Michael Collins was a fine soldier before he was a politician. He helped lead the Rising with Éamon de Valera, and spent two years in a British jail because of it.'

'True, but now he's in the newspapers, all dressed in his suit and tie, looking smart and important.'

'Does Ryan know that his hero is also head of IRA intelligence?' Nuala asked. 'That there's not a thing the IRA does in any part of the country without him knowing about it? Or often ordering it himself?'

'Maybe he does, maybe he doesn't. The point is, he'd not be pleased if he found out his fiancée was so deep into supporting the violence that she'd be drowning in it any second.' Hannah let out a long sigh and then looked at her sister. 'What do I do, Nuala? I'd die if I lost him . . .'

'I don't know. We come from a family of fierce Fenians who are all prepared to lay down their lives for Ireland's freedom.'

'I know. What if Daddy says something that gives us all away?' Hannah worried aloud. 'Ryan might turn tail and run down the valley to his lodgings in Timoleague!'

'As you say, Ryan's not local. Sure, Daddy won't give anything away until he knows to trust him.'

'You're right,' Hannah agreed. 'And it's not because Ryan doesn't believe in the cause . . .'

'Just that he doesn't believe in war.' Nuala was immediately reminded of Philip. 'At least he's not an Englishman,' she chuckled.

'Or a Black and Tan.'

'Or an Auxie.'

'Or even a Protestant!' Hannah laughed and her face relaxed a little.

'To my thinking, if you love your man the way I love Finn, there's nothing you wouldn't do to be with him.'

'I do – love him, I mean. I'd still do what I could – knit and raise money – but . . . would you understand, Nuala?'

'I would try my hardest to, Hannah.' Nuala gave a sad shrug. 'Love changes everything.'

Sure enough, a week later, the family was alerted to the fact that Hannah had invited 'a friend' to Sunday lunch after Mass.

No one was fooled, especially not Eileen, who plagued Nuala, Christy and Fergus with questions.

'Will you stop asking me! I swear I know nothing,' Nuala pleaded as her father drove his family back in the pony and

trap after Mass. Hannah was following on with her 'friend'.

When they eventually arrived, Nuala felt sympathy for the pale, slim, curly-headed man who stepped through the door behind Hannah.

'This is Ryan O'Reilly, whom you all might remember from Finn and Nuala's wedding,' said Hannah, a bright red blush travelling up her neck to her face.

Finn – who to Nuala's delight had arrived home a couple of days ago – stepped forward.

'How are you, Ryan?' he said, shaking his friend's hand. Nuala thought the poor fellow looked as terrified as if he was about to be shot by the Black and Tans.

Introductions to each member of the family were made, and they all sat down to eat. Her father was at the head of the table, silent for once as his gimlet stare fell upon Ryan, appraising him.

After lunch, fortified with plenty of porter from the barrel outside, Ryan cleared his throat and approached Daniel.

'May I have a word with you in private, sir?'

'There's little privacy to be had in here, as you can see, so I'd suggest we step outside,' said Daniel. 'The weather's set fair for a while.'

'Yes, sir.'

The whole family watched as Daniel led him outside. 'Like a lamb to the slaughter,' said Fergus.

'At least he's found a wife, unlike you, brother,' Nuala shot back, only half joking.

''Twould hardly be fair to ask a woman to be my wife when I'm not knowing if I'll see out the year,' Fergus replied. 'Besides, I'm thinking I'm happier alone. Some fellows are,' he shrugged.

'Your brother is becoming a confirmed bachelor,' sighed Eileen.

'Well, at least I don't have to put myself through all that.' Fergus indicated Ryan and Daniel talking on the bench outside.

'Ah sure, Ryan will be fine,' smiled Finn. 'He's a decent sort of a fellow, the quiet type, like none of you!'

Nuala was standing by the window, watching the two men. 'Ryan's standing up and—'

'Come away from that window, girl!' said Eileen. 'Give them some privacy now.'

All eyes turned to Hannah.

'Stop staring at me!' she shouted, and with that, ran up the stairs to her bedroom. While they were waiting, Finn, Christy and Fergus went into a huddle by the kitchen table. Nuala couldn't decide whether they were discussing the suitability of Ryan O'Reilly for Hannah, or volunteer business. Both – in their different ways – were equally important.

'Jesus, Mary and Joseph, will you be seeing the time? I'll be putting on the tea,' Eileen called far too loudly to those still gathered in the kitchen. As the water boiled, the back door opened and the two men walked in.

'I'd like to tell you that Ryan O'Reilly has asked for our Hannah's hand in marriage. And after some debate, permission has been granted,' Daniel announced.

With that, a rousing cheer broke out, and as the men shook Ryan's hand and welcomed him to the family, Daniel went to the pantry to extract the bottle of whiskey.

Nuala and Eileen looked expectantly up the stairs for the bride-to-be, who came down the steps and straight into her mother's arms.

'I'm so happy for you!' Eileen wept. 'I was worrying you'd become an old maid.'

'Jaysus, I'm only twenty, Mammy,' Hannah smiled. It was Nuala's turn to hug her big sister.

'Congratulations, sister. And don't be putting me in a gown that's pink if I'm to be your maid of honour.'

'Who says you are?' Hannah teased her then hugged her again. 'Thank you, Nuala. I don't know what I'd do without you.'

17

In late November, a day after what was already being called 'Bloody Sunday' in the newspapers, Nuala arrived at Argideen House trying to contain a fury she knew she mustn't show. Philip was now walking without the safety net of the bars, and was using Christy's stick to wander in circles around the sitting room, with Nuala at his side should he falter. It wasn't until they sat down to have afternoon tea and scones that he asked her outright if she was upset about the events at Croke Park.

Nuala took a long sip of tea to buy herself time. ''Tis tragic what happened,' she said, trying to keep any emotion out of her voice. 'Just a crowd sitting watching a game of Gaelic football, and they're fired upon by the British with no warning. We've fourteen Irish dead, including children.'

'Only the dead have seen the end of war,' Philip said gravely, which Nuala knew meant he was quoting someone she'd never heard of.

'That's no use to their families, is it?' she said, heat creeping into her voice. 'Is it a part of war to murder children?'

'No, of course not, and I'm as sorry as you are, Nuala,' he sighed. 'Like you, I simply want the British and Irish to come to a peaceful resolution. Although that might be a long way off, considering how Major Percival sounded when he was here yesterday.'

'Major Percival was here?' she said.

'Yes. Mother tried to convince me to come down and take tea with him, but I'd gladly stay in a wheelchair if it meant not having to set eyes on that man.'

'Do you know why he came yesterday?' she asked.

'From the sound of his self-congratulatory booming voice, I'd say he wanted to boast to Father about something or other. And given yesterday's horrific events, I think we can both imagine what it was.'

At that moment, Nuala decided this Major Percival deserved the most painful death that God could create for him. And knew she hated him just as much as any other of the brave volunteers who had suffered at his cruel, merciless hands.

Hannah and Ryan's wedding had been set for mid-December.

''Tisn't a perfect time to be wed, but with things as they are, the sooner the better,' Hannah had sighed.

No one understood Hannah's need for urgency better than Nuala. She'd comforted her with suggesting all the things that would make a winter wedding special. Philip had said a decorated fir tree usually stood in the entrance hall of Argideen House, and was a tradition of England's Queen Victoria, established by her German husband Albert. Nuala loved the idea, but knew it wouldn't be the right thing to have.

'We can decorate the church with sprays of holly and light candles and—'

'Have muddy puddles splashing the bottom of my white dress,' Hannah had grumbled. But it was happy grumbling, and there was a glow to her sister's cheeks that Nuala was pleased to see.

She had told Finn that Major Percival had been at the Big House again, but was frustrated with herself for not knowing more.

''Tis all right, darlin', just keep your ears pricked up,' Finn had said. He had gone out to a brigade council meeting in Kilbrittain that evening, and she knew he wouldn't be back until late. Even so, when he hadn't returned by three in the morning, Nuala's heart began to beat harder. Finally, at four thirty, she heard the back door open.

Flying down the stairs, she found Finn soaked to the skin and panting hard. Another figure stood behind him.

'Hello there, Nuala, will it be all right if I come in?' Charlie Hurley wiped his rain-matted hair from his gaunt, pale face.

'Of course, Charlie, come and sit a while.'

'I think we both need a drop of the hard stuff, Nuala,' said Finn, closing the back door as quietly as he could. Both men were still in their volunteer outfits – while the Flying Column had no regular uniform, they all wore peaky caps and long trench coats to stave off the rain and hide any weapons they were carrying beneath.

'What happened?' Nuala whispered, so as not to alert Mrs Grady, the old lady in the cottage next door.

'I'll get the whiskey first,' said Finn as he went to the cupboard, where he took out two glasses and poured a good measure into both.

As they took off their sodden clothes, Nuala ran upstairs to find shirts, trousers and socks for them to change into.

'We all started to leave after the meeting, going in parties of three,' began Finn. 'We were after getting to Coppeen and there was a truck of Auxies. They saw us before we saw them and they searched us all. Thanks be to God, none of us were carrying any papers on us.'

'We acted drunk,' put in Charlie. 'Said we'd been to the pub for a glass, but they shouldn't be telling our wives.'

'And they let you go?' asked Nuala.

'They did, so. Sean Hales and his crowd were following on, along with Con Crowley and John O'Mahoney, who had documents on them outlining what we'd discussed at the meeting. We doubled back to warn them, but we didn't get there in time,' Finn sighed. 'We hid in a ditch as the Auxies searched them. They found the evidence they needed and Con and John were herded onto the back of the truck.'

'There was nothing we could have done about it, Finn,' said Charlie, draining his whiskey and pouring himself another. 'Jaysus, those poor lads.'

'How incriminating were the documents?' she asked.

'Thank the lord Con uses code, but there's enough there to show that they're IRA volunteers, so.'

'And Sean?'

'Ah, now Sean, he has the blarney to talk his way out of Mountjoy Jail. He told Crake – that was the name of the commanding officer – that he was in the area buying cattle. He gave a false name and the eejit believed him! Said he had an honest face and wished more Irishmen were like him.'

Both Charlie and Finn laughed loudly as the whiskey calmed them. 'Shh,' warned Nuala. 'What about Con and John?'

'I'd not want to see the state of them now, if Tom Hales and Pat Harte are anything to go by.' Finn shuddered.

'These Auxies, they didn't get a good look at your faces, did they?' she said.

'What, apart from shining a torch right under our chins?' Charlie sighed. 'They saw us all right, but all we Irish look the same to them, so.'

'What do you think will happen now about what we discussed?' Finn asked Charlie.

'I'd say that Sean will be even more likely to.'

'To what?' Nuala asked.

Charlie looked at Finn.

'You can tell Nuala anything,' Finn reassured him. 'She's as good as our men any day of the week.'

'Then she'll know about it soon enough,' said Charlie. 'It's to involve all the volunteers around these parts . . . We're to blow up Timoleague RIC post and then set fire to Timoleague Castle and the Travers' house next door.'

Nuala stared at them, open-mouthed.

'You wouldn't dare! 'Tis right on our doorstep!' she gasped. 'They'll be searching every house around if you do.'

'I know, Nuala, but we've information down from Dublin HQ,' said Charlie. 'The British want to take over the castle and house and post more men in there because of the trouble we've been causing them. We can't have that happen. We'd be overrun with the lousers, so.'

'Timoleague RIC post has been evacuated already, hasn't it?'

'Yes,' said Charlie, 'but the British are looking to refill it. The company here in Clogagh will be raised, as well as others, and we're to collect gelignite from across town and hide it somewhere close. We were thinking of Cross Farm, Nuala, if your mam and dad would agree. 'Tis close enough to Timoleague.'

'But the Travers family and their servants up at the house haven't been evacuated! Will you set fire to them where they lie in their beds?' Nuala asked, aghast. She'd seen old Robert Travers from Timoleague House one day from the window of Argideen House, when he and his wife had come to visit the Fitzgeralds.

'The British would burn us in our beds and not be thinking ~~~ about it, Nuala, but no, we'll have them taken to safety ~~, don't you worry,' Finn comforted her.

She drew in a breath and then exhaled slowly.

'Now then, Nuala, go back upstairs and get some rest,' said Finn, 'and I'll be getting a pallet from the outhouse for you, Charlie.'

'Sure, I'm grand where I am in this chair . . . You two go up . . . I'll be . . .'

'He's asleep already, poor fellow,' whispered Finn. 'He's got enough work for five men. Being commandant, he takes every injury or death in the company personally.'

Upstairs, Nuala put her arms around her husband, who had fallen asleep the moment his head had landed on the pillow.

'I love you, darlin',' she said as she caressed his hair, wondering darkly how many more days and nights she had left to feel his heart beating steadily against hers.

When Nuala went into Timoleague for the next monthly fair day, when all the farmers brought cattle to sell and stallholders set up along the street, hawking everything from homemade jam to saddles, the usual jollity of the event was completely lost. The Essex Regiment were a menacing presence, marching down the streets or clearing men out of the pubs so they could sit down in their places. Hannah joined her when the dressmaker's shop closed for lunch and they wandered along the street, glancing at the stalls.

'Have you heard what's about to happen?' Nuala asked her sister under her breath.

'I have indeed. The "manure" was delivered to Cross Farm wo days ago.'

'Holy Mother of God, this will rouse mayhem around here.'

'Don't you be telling me, Nuala. 'Tis my wedding day in three weeks. I'm scared that half the guests will be locked up in Bandon Barracks, or worse, if they're caught.'

Nuala reached for her sister's hand. 'We have to believe they won't be,' she comforted her as they manoeuvred past a young bullock being walked down the street by his proud new owner.

'Now then, why don't we buy crubeens from Mrs MacNally's stall, eat them and then go to see your dress at the shop?' Nuala forced a bright smile onto her face. 'And mine, o'course, even though just the thought of it gives me the horrors!'

'I like lilac,' Hannah said defensively. ''Tis quite the thing in Paris, my magazine said.'

Nuala rolled her eyes and went off to buy their crubeens, then they sat themselves on their favourite bench overlooking Courtmacsherry Bay. The day was bright and mild, and they could see the ruins of the old stone abbey below them. The sound of the waves breaking on the shore calmed Nuala's fraught nerves.

'Does Himself know what's to happen?' she asked her sister.

'No, and I'll not be telling him,' Hannah said firmly. 'I'll be as surprised as Ryan is the day after.'

'I know it's none of my business, Hannah, but d'you think it's right to be lying about what you believe in and the brave things that you've been doing for your country – *his* country – before you're even wed?'

'This war can't go on forever, and if 'tis just a few months of pretence, I will, so. Aren't we all having to pretend?' she said pointedly.

'Not to our husbands, surely?'

'Nuala, will you leave it be for now? Everyone knows I'm to be wed to Ryan soon, so they're not asking me to take dispatches anyway. So I'm not lying to him, am I?'

Nuala wanted to say more, but knew it wasn't her place. 'Well now, will we go away up to the shop and try on that lilac rag you'll have me in?'

'Are you ready to be walking outside now?' Nuala said to Philip a few days later, as they paced around his sitting room for what felt like the thousandth time. A month of daily exercise had strengthened Philip's upper body as well as his legs, so his posture was now straighter even when sitting in the chair. Nuala had been surprised at how tall he was, standing at over six feet.

'Outside?' Philip gave a snort. 'It's December and you want to drag me into that damp, frigid air?'

'Yes,' she said. ''Twill be good for you. We'll wrap you up tight, and you'll warm up quick enough when you're walking,' she encouraged him.

'All right then,' he softened. 'After all, I did once live in a trench at below freezing point, so a walk in my mother's garden should be a breeze in comparison.'

'Right, so, I'll warn Mrs Houghton that we'll be going outside.'

'Oh, don't bother with that, Nuala, just get me ready, will you?'

She helped him dress in a woollen coat, his scarf and hat, then together they walked out onto the landing and into the lift. On arrival into the entrance hall, Maureen, who was carrying a tray across it, stopped short and looked at Philip in amazement. Nuala felt an inner sense of satisfaction.

Outside, the air was sharp and cold, and though their breath was visible in front of them, the sun had come out to shine on the barren winterscape of the parklands. With Philip using his stick, and Nuala having her arm tucked into the crook of his on the other side, they trod carefully on the path towards the garden, lest Philip slip on a patch of damp moss.

'Ahh,' Philip sniffed the air. 'The glorious Irish smell of peat fires burning. I rather think you *are* a fairy queen, Nuala,' he said as they arrived in Lady Fitzgerald's private garden, walking past stone planters full of winter pansies, which provided delightful splashes of purple and yellow against the slumbering perennials. 'I feel as if you have cast a spell on me. I could never have pictured myself walking again. Going where I please, having independence . . .'

''Tis not magic, Philip,' she replied. ''Tis your own strength and hard work.'

'And your encouragement,' he said, pausing to turn to her. 'Nuala, I can never thank you enough for what you have done for me. You have brought me back to life.' Then he took her hand and kissed it. 'Promise me you'll never leave me, Nuala. I swear I'd die without you. You've given me a reason to live again. Promise me, Nuala, please.'

She looked up at him and saw tears coursing down his face.

'I promise,' she answered. What else could she say?

With Philip declaring himself exhausted at seven that night, she changed out of her work clothes and was just about to leave for home when Mrs Houghton called her back.

'Her ladyship wants to see you, Nuala,' she said and led her across the hall into a pretty parlour, which contained a

writing desk looking over the garden she and Philip had walked through earlier. Lady Fitzgerald was engaged in reading a letter, but turned round and stood up as Nuala walked in.

'Thank you, Mrs Houghton. You may leave us. Please, sit down, Nuala.' Lady Fitzgerald indicated a chair.

'Is everything all right, your ladyship? Philip was feeling up to walking around, but if you'd rather he stayed inside in the warm—'

'Goodness no, quite the opposite, Nuala. I simply wished to thank you,' said Lady Fitzgerald. 'This wonderful change in Philip is all down to you. Not just physically, but he's been so . . . hopeful again. I can hear the two of you laughing together, and the sound makes me so happy. I—' She broke off and took a deep breath. 'As a gesture of my thanks, I would like to increase your wages to ten shillings a week. I know how hard you have worked, and I hope you will be—'

A knock on the door interrupted Lady Fitzgerald, and Mrs Houghton entered. 'Excuse me, Lady Fitzgerald, but Mr Lewis has arrived about the painting in the Lily bedroom that you want reframing.'

'Thank you, Mrs Houghton, I will come out to see him.' Lady Fitzgerald turned to Nuala. 'I should only be a moment, my dear, then we will finish our discussion.'

As the two women left the room and shut the door to keep the heat in, Nuala allowed herself a little laugh of delight.

'Ten shillings,' she breathed, thinking what she and Finn could do with the much-needed extra money. She stood up and wandered around the beautiful room, admiring the landscape paintings gracing the wood-panelled walls and the leather-topped desk.

Without stopping to think, Nuala glanced down at the letter Lady Fitzgerald had just been reading.

My dear Laura and Reginald,

Once more I write to offer my grateful thank you for dinner the other evening; a delightful harbour in what is becoming an ever more stormy sea. At least some good news on that front: two of our spies acting as deserters have gained the enemy's trust and have arranged to meet the ringleader TB on 3rd December, at which point we will arrest him.

Nuala speed-read the rest and saw the signature at the bottom:

Arthur Percival

Nuala heard footsteps approach the door and hurried to sit back down in her chair.

'My apologies,' said Lady Fitzgerald as she entered the room, then opened a drawer to her desk and took out an envelope. 'Your wages for this week with two extra shillings inside.' She pressed the envelope into Nuala's hands. 'Thank you again, my dear. Now then, get home to that husband of yours.'

Nuala cycled to Clogagh as if the devil himself were chasing her. She arrived at the cottage and was relieved to find Finn in his shirtsleeves, marking schoolwork at the kitchen table.

'Finn,' she panted. 'I've urgent news for Tom Barry!'

In between sips of water from the glass he had placed in front of her, she explained the missive from Major Percival.

Finn paced in front of the fire as he took in what she was telling him.

'Nuala, the attack on Timoleague is tomorrow, and the whole Column is in high gear, with people in secret locations . . . I don't know how to find Tom in time to tell him . . .'

'We've got to!' Nuala cried. 'Those deserters he's meeting are spies for the British! The Essex will be lying in wait for Tom and we know what they'll do to him! They know he's the brains behind the Flying Column, so 'twill be even worse than what they did to Tom Hales and Pat!'

Finn crouched down by his wife and took her in his arms.

'I'll be sortin' it, darlin', don't you be worrying. What you've found out is vital, and we've a chance of stopping the meeting. Now, please eat something before you faint from exhaustion.'

18

Finn had gone out soon after, and when he returned, he had assured Nuala he'd left word for Tom Barry with as many volunteers as he could find. The following morning – the day of the planned burnings in Timoleague – he dressed calmly in his schoolmaster's clothes.

'Now so, after work tonight, you're to cycle straight up to Cross Farm and wait there until you hear the all-clear from me or another I'll send word with.'

'Are the explosives – I mean, the manure – still in the dump?' Nuala was so agitated, she was forgetting to talk in code.

'It's been moved closer to the place it will be needed in,' said Finn. 'I'm off away to help spread it.' He kissed her hard on the lips, then hugged her tightly to him. 'Goodbye, Nuala. I love you and I'll be seeing ye.'

With that, he was gone.

Up at the farmhouse that evening, the family (minus Fergus, who was out helping to 'spread the manure', and Christy, who'd helped move the 'manure' earlier but was now working as usual at the pub), went through their night-time routine.

Though the subject was not discussed when they all sat down for their tea, the air of tension was palpable. Even her father, who was usually able to hold a conversation with a fly, was quiet. Every one of them knew how many local fellows were involved in tonight's activities. 'Will we sing some of the old songs, husband?' asked Eileen as the women finished clearing up. 'Will you get out your fiddle?'

'Not tonight; even with scouts up above on the hill, I'd be afraid of a knock on the door.'

'To be sure, Daddy, once that manure is spread, they'll all be busy down below,' said Nuala.

'I'm sure you're right, daughter, but 'tis not the night to be taking any chances. Hannah will read to us from the Bible. How about Moses parting the Red Sea, then the passage where the people are led into the Promised Land?'

Daniel offered the family a grim smile, and they nodded at the appropriateness of the suggestions.

As she sat cross-legged by the fire, with Mammy and Daddy on either side of her, she listened to Hannah's reading. And it calmed her.

Oh, dear Lord, and Holy Mother Mary, keep my Finn and Fergus safe tonight, and let all us Irish have our own Promised Land delivered back to us . . .

The family were just in the process of turning out the oil lamps when Seamus O'Hanlon, their neighbour and one of the scouts, burst through the back door. The whole family froze where they were.

'Our lads have gone and done it! Come up to the top of the hill and see for yourself!'

The family followed him out through the back door and up the steep wooded hill to the top. And there, across the valley and down the hill again towards Timoleague, they saw great yellow flames jumping into the night sky.

The family crossed themselves, then sat down in a huddle on the soaking grass.

Nuala imagined she could smell the smoke hanging in the cold night air.

'I'm just hoping the fire doesn't spread,' muttered Hannah to Nuala.

'Ryan's not in his lodgings, is he?' Nuala whispered back. 'Did you not warn him?'

'How could I? Then he'd be knowing that *I* knew.'

'Sure, he'll be fine, Hannah, he lives a way away from the targets. I'm just praying my Finn and our Fergus come home safely tonight.'

'That'll show the British we mean business and no mistake!' Daniel punched his fist in the air.

'Shh, Daniel!' hushed his wife. 'You never know who's lurking close by.'

'Tonight it's just us, woman, and I'll be as joyful as I wish on my own land.'

As they walked back down towards the farmhouse, Eileen caught up with her girls. 'I've told your father there's to be no more using us as an ammunition dump for a while. There'll be reprisals for this, make no mistake.'

'And we'll all be ready for them, Mammy,' Nuala said firmly, while Hannah said nothing and just walked off down the hill alone.

To her relief, both Finn and Fergus returned safely in the early hours, but the next morning, the main street in Clogagh was silent, everyone hiding away indoors, both from fear of reprisals and the stench of burnt timber that still hung in the air.

'Hello, Lucy,' she said as she let herself into the kitchen of Argideen House.

Lucy looked up from the floor that she was scrubbing. 'Hello, Nuala. Don't go and change – Lady Fitzgerald is wanting to see you first.'

'Really? What about?'

'I've no idea. Mrs Houghton will come and take you through to her parlour.' Nuala sat down abruptly on the nearest stool.

Lucy wasn't in the mood for talking and silence reigned as she waited for Mrs Houghton to come and fetch her.

'Follow me, Nuala.'

Crossing the hall, Mrs Houghton knocked on the door of Lady Fitzgerald's parlour room.

'Come,' said a voice from within.

Lady Fitzgerald was standing looking out of the window onto her garden, her back straight in a dark green gown.

As she turned, Nuala could see that her lovely features were held as stiffly as her body.

'Sit down, Nuala,' Lady Fitzgerald gestured, and she did so.

'Now then,' she began, 'I wish to tell you about a call my husband received from Major Percival this morning, concerning the grave events of last night.'

'Oh,' Nuala said, summoning every ounce of acting skill she possessed to hold her features steady. 'You mean the fires? Sure, 'twas terrible to see.'

'It was, yes, and my friends, the Travers, who lived in Timoleague House, are sheltering here with us. They have only the clothes they stand up in, but are at least grateful that the Irish who attacked their home allowed them to leave. Anyway . . .'

Lady Fitzgerald brushed a hand across her forehead distractedly.

'These are dark times we live in, Nuala. It has been discovered that some . . . sensitive information was passed to the IRA, regarding details that were sent to this house by Major Percival himself. The man mentioned in the letter – or at least, by his initials – did not arrive to meet the spies, but sent others in his place. They were dealt with, of course, but the man Major Percival and his team had spent months hatching a plot to entrap still remains at large to plan and commit further atrocities like last night's.'

Nuala felt Lady Fitzgerald's gaze resting upon her.

'That letter was open here on this very desk two days ago. When you were sitting in that chair, and I left you alone to see Mr Lewis for a few minutes.'

Nuala could hardly breathe. 'I—'

'And this incident had me questioning other events,' Lady Fitzgerald continued. 'A few months ago, the major foiled an attempt on his life in Bandon, but the assassin had apparently been warned and had disappeared. Not a soul other than the major, his men and my husband knew that the Essex were to break into those houses to catch the perpetrator. Except for myself, of course, and my son, whom I told in confidence. Nuala, I am asking you now to tell the truth. Did Philip discuss it with you?'

'I . . . 'tis so long ago now, but I think Philip had said that Major Percival was coming over to see Sir Reginald the day before, and that he wouldn't want to walk in the gardens whilst there was a visitor. That was all.'

'Are you sure about that, Nuala?'

'I'm certain,' she nodded.

'Sadly' – Lady Fitzgerald gave a long sigh of resignation – 'it appears that you are lying. I mentioned in passing to Philip earlier whether he'd discussed Major Percival's plan with you and he said that he had. His story was also corroborated by

Maureen, who was most distressed to report that she was in the room serving tea when the conversation took place.'

'Yes, now I think about it, 'tis true, your ladyship. Philip did mention something about Major Percival. I didn't want to say that to you, in case I got him into trouble. We often talk about the . . . hostilities. We are, well, we are friends.'

'And he trusts you. I understand,' said Lady Fitzgerald. 'Which makes this situation even harder.'

'I swear that I'll tell him in future that I don't want to discuss anything with him. 'Tis only because he seemed to have no one else to talk to, other than you, of course,' Nuala added hastily. 'And I'd never be looking into your personal things, or reading letters—'

'Forgive me Nuala, I find that difficult to believe. You see, after I spoke to Maureen and she confirmed my son's story, the poor thing broke down. She said she felt torn by loyalty to you as another member of staff, but that she felt she must tell me that your family are noted Fenians, with your brother a known IRA volunteer. She also told me that your sister Hannah is a leading light of this Irish women's voluntary organisation. She suspects that you may be too, or at the very least, support your family's . . . activities from the sidelines. What do you have to say to that, Nuala?'

'Nothing, other than 'tis true my family are made of proud Irish stock, but beyond that I know no more. Besides, I'm no longer living under their roof. My husband is Finn Casey, a schoolmaster at Clogagh.'

'I know he is, Nuala, and I also know that he has been mysteriously absent from work a great deal in the last few months.'

'He's been sick, Lady Fitzgerald, with a bad stomach. What could be wrong with that?'

'On the surface, nothing, but Maureen has a friend who

lives close to you. Apparently, she went to call on your husband in the afternoons to see if he needed anything whilst you were working here. She told Maureen the curtains were all drawn and there was no response from inside. As if the house were empty.'

'He was very sick, Lady Fitzgerald, and not up to receiving neighbours.'

'So sick that you left him all those afternoons to come here for eight hours?'

The question hung in the air for a good few seconds before Lady Fitzgerald spoke again.

'This is Ireland, Nuala, and even though I may have been born English, it has been my home for over twenty-six years. I know very well how communities look out for each other. And how a newly married wife would not leave a seriously ill husband alone without someone to care for him. There would have been someone with him, Nuala, or at least checking on him regularly.'

'I . . .'

'I am not here to judge you, your family or your husband on your activities outside this house. In fact, I'd prefer it if I didn't know, because I like you very much, Nuala. And the most tragic thing of all is that so does my son.'

Nuala watched tears come into Lady Fitzgerald's eyes.

'However, given this new information, and the devastating fires in Timoleague last night, I can no longer trust you. Or your family.'

'But I hardly know Maureen! How come she thinks she knows so much about them? The truth is that she's never liked me.'

'Now, now, Nuala, please don't be churlish. It doesn't suit you. The simple truth is, I cannot take the risk of my dear innocent Philip imparting further information to the woman

whom he believes is his friend. Therefore I am forced to terminate your employment here. You will leave the house immediately.' Lady Fitzgerald walked to the desk, opened it and pulled out a small brown envelope. 'That is your pay until the end of the week.'

Nuala stood up, open-mouthed in horror. 'May I not even say goodbye to Philip?'

'It's best that you don't. I have told him your husband is seriously unwell and you have decided you must be at home caring for him, as any good wife should.'

Nuala was crying openly now. 'Please . . . tell him that I'll miss him and thanks a million for teaching me to play chess – I never did get to beat him, because he was so brilliant and—'

'Of course I will, and rest assured that I will say nothing to anyone about our discussions this morning. Your secrets – if they are secrets – are safe with me, but know they are not so safe in other hands. Life is full of difficult choices, Nuala, and we are living in difficult times. I accept that your loyalty must always be towards your husband and your family.'

Nuala's nose was running so fast she was reduced to the indignity of wiping it on her hand.

'Forgive me, Lady Fitzgerald. You've been so kind to me . . .'

Nuala felt a hand on her shoulder. 'And you've been so good to Philip, and for that I thank you.'

When Nuala arrived home, she closed the curtains at the back and the front of the house. Then she sat down in the chair next to the fire and wept her heart out.

'Oh Philip, I'm so very sorry to have let you down. There

was no bad in you, and now I'll no longer be there to mind you.'

When she was empty of tears and desperate to talk to someone about what had happened, she splashed her face with water and tidied her hair in order to walk across the road to see Christy. No one could *ever* know how truly heartbroken about Philip she was – not even Finn – or they'd be calling her a traitor by the morning.

'Will you pop over and have a glass when you've finished here?' she asked him.

'O'course, there's few enough in today.'

Back in the cottage, Nuala forced down some bread and butter, then took out the whiskey bottle from the cupboard and found two mugs. Christy arrived twenty minutes later and she poured them both a drop.

'You on the hard stuff, Nuala?' Christy smiled.

'After the day I've had, you'll be understanding why I am.'

Then she told her cousin what had happened up at the Big House. He poured himself more whiskey.

'Jaysus,' he breathed. 'D'you think she's likely to tell Major Percival what she suspects? She'd have no reason not to, Nuala.'

'No, I don't. Maybe I'm being naive, but she was kind, Christy, even when she was saying I must leave her employment. 'Twas as if she understood and somehow sympathised.'

'She's a woman who's had a husband and a son fight through two wars. Now they're all involved in another. From what you say, seems she's the rare British person with a heart. The dangerous one is this Maureen. What a witch to be telling on you like that.'

'She hated me from the day I arrived. She didn't like the fact Philip and I were friends and she had to serve me tea every day.' That thought at least brought a smile to Nuala's lips.

'Sounds like she was jealous of you.'

'Lucy, my friend up there, told me she lost her husband and child. I reckon she's bitter, so she is.'

'War can make it that way. Listen, I need to be getting back. I'll ride over to Cross Farm later and tell the family what's happened. We'll be preparing ourselves for the worst. Finn will be back from school soon.'

'And then he's straight off out with the Column. I reckon they've something else planned.'

'You're to keep calm, Nuala. I'm across the road if you need me.' Christy stood up and kissed her on the top of her head. 'I'll be seeing ye,' he said as he walked out of the door.

The entire family were on tenterhooks in the following few days in case the reason for Nuala's abrupt departure from Argideen House reached the ears of the authorities. To their shared relief, neither Nuala and Finn's cottage nor Cross Farm were raided. When she was in town picking up a message from Hannah in Timoleague to take over to the captain of Cumann na mBan in Darrara, Nuala saw Lady Fitzgerald in the distance. She wished she could thank her for keeping her word, but instead, Nuala turned and walked in the opposite direction.

Luckily school finished for the Christmas holidays, so there was no need to give excuses when Finn announced he was off to a further Flying Column training camp.

'I'm not sure when I'll be back, darlin'. We've training and then an ambush to plan – the Auxies are moving further away from Macroom Castle and into our territory and we've to show them who's boss around here. Go up to Cross Farm with your family for a few days; I could be away for some time.'

The worry of Finn's absence was eased a little by spending her time helping to prepare for her sister's wedding and for Christmas itself. She often cycled down to Timoleague to meet Hannah at lunchtime.

'Have you been in to Ryan's lodgings yet?' Nuala asked her as they ate their lunch on the bench overlooking the bay.

'I have indeed. The house is owned by Mrs O'Flanaghan, and Ryan has the attic to himself.'

'Does it have a double bed?' she nudged her sister.

'Only a single, but 'twill do for now. We're looking for another place, as I'd like my own kitchen and facilities. With my wages and Ryan's, we can afford it, so, but there's nothing to be had in town just now.'

To while away the afternoon hours she would otherwise have spent with Philip, Nuala had embarked on making a patchwork quilt as a wedding present, using various bits of material she'd collected over the years. Never a seamstress like her sister, she was struggling, but wasn't it the thought that counted? she told herself, as she unstitched a patch for the umpteenth time. At least it took her mind off worrying if Philip was keeping up his walking practice and Finn was safe. Retribution for the burning of the barracks and castle was still taking place, and gruesome images of the kinds of torture other volunteers had suffered at the hands of the British haunted her.

If any bit of suffering was down to me being found out . . . She shuddered, then, telling herself that worrying helped nobody, she gritted her teeth and concentrated on sewing her quilt.

19

More bad news came a few days later when martial law was declared on County Cork. This meant that any man could be stopped and searched, and if he was found to have ammunition or weapons on him, he was immediately arrested and subject to a court martial. If found guilty, he could be shot. A curfew was also introduced across the county, with no resident allowed out between the hours of eight p.m. and six a.m.

'But what would happen if a family member was dying in the next village, or even in the next street?' said Nuala, showing Finn the *Cork Examiner* newspaper, in which the new laws had been printed.

'The patrols would arrest you on sight,' shrugged Finn.

'It says you can also be arrested for harbouring a suspected volunteer, for "loitering", or for simply having your hands in your pockets . . .' Nuala shook her head in disgust.

'The good news is that all the residents of the towns and villages are hating the British even more for the new ruling. Charlie told me he'd had forty new volunteers approach him, wanting to sign up. We'll win this war, Nuala, I swear to you, we will.'

Finn continued to disappear regularly after dark, despite the curfew, as the Tans and the Essexes marched down the streets of local villages to intimidate the residents. Insisting

to Finn she was going to stay at the cottage, Nuala spent most evenings alone working on Hannah's quilt. At least she knew she could always call on Christy, who was having to stay the nights up above the pub because of the curfew. She cycled up to seek solace with her family whenever the curfew allowed.

'Jaysus! Have you seen this?' Daniel slapped a newspaper down on the table and pointed with his calloused finger to the headline. 'How could he do it to us all when we're fighting to free his flock from the tyranny of the British?'

The family gathered round to read in the newspaper that the Bishop of Cork had issued a decree, saying that any Catholic taking part in an ambush would be guilty of murder, and immediately excommunicated.

'Jesus, Mary and Joseph!' Eileen muttered, as she crossed herself and sat down heavily on the stool. 'Almost every volunteer is Catholic! They're needing to feel that God is on their side as they fight, not that he'll be throwing them out of heaven and placing them in hell if they do!'

'This is what he has to say,' spat Daniel, 'after the Black and Tans have set fire to half of Cork City!'

'Do you think he'd a British rifle pointing to his back when he did this?' said Fergus.

'You might be right, but I couldn't be more sure that 'twill be him refused from entering the Pearly Gates and not our brave men and women.'

'But will they fight on?' asked Nuala.

'Will it stop you from doing what you do?' Daniel looked at her. 'Would it stop either of you?'

Brother and sister looked at each other. ''Twill not stop me,' said Fergus.

'Or me,' muttered Nuala, reaching for the comfort of her mother's hand.

Needing the security of her family after such news, Nuala opted to stay the night. Hannah arrived from the dressmaker's shop, and after tea, the two of them went upstairs to talk.

'How's the husband-to-be?' Nuala said as they lay on their bed.

'He was off to Mass when I left him earlier,' Hannah sighed. 'He said he wanted time to think about the bishop's proclamation. I've told you before that Ryan's faith puts us all to shame.'

'Does he think the decree is right?'

'He said that at least 'twould deter some volunteers from carrying on with their violent activities, and that had to be a good thing. He wants peace, Nuala, that's all.'

'Does Ryan know that most of those attending his wedding are volunteers?'

'I haven't told him, and neither has anyone else. He's entitled to his views, fair enough.' Hannah shot her sister a look. 'He still wants freedom for the Irish, but has a different way of thinking how to get that.'

'So now, let's just sit here and wait until the military kill us all, shall we? I'd like to be showing him some dispatches signed by his hero Michael Collins. 'Twas his idea originally to form the Flying Column and—'

'D'you think I don't know that?! But what can I do? I'm marrying the man in a few days' time! And that's all there is to it.'

The morning before Hannah's wedding, there was a knock on the cottage door. Nuala opened it to see her friend Lucy, down from the Big House.

'Hello, Lucy, 'tis lovely to see you. Will you come in?'

'I'm on my way to work, but I thought I should drop by and tell you before you heard it from anyone else.'

'What is it?' Nuala asked as Lucy followed her in. Always slight, today Lucy looked like a frightened, fragile bird.

'Ah, Nuala, I'm thinking you need to sit down. I've some upsetting news for you.'

'What is it? What's wrong?'

'I don't know how to say this, but, yesterday . . . there was a loud bang from the young master's bedroom. Her ladyship ran upstairs as fast as she could, but the shot was to his head, and . . . he was already gone.'

'What?' Nuala shook her head in confusion. 'Who was already gone?'

'Philip. He took his service revolver from his drawer and shot himself in the head. I'm so sorry, Nuala. I know how fond of him you were.'

'No,' was all Nuala could manage to whisper. 'Why? He was getting better, walking by himself and going outside and . . .'

'There was no more of that after you left, Nuala. Maureen was put in charge of minding him whilst Lady Fitzgerald tried to find a new nurse. She said he sat in his chair staring out of the window and not speaking to her at all. Lady Fitzgerald was worried enough to call the doctor, who prescribed some tablets for him, but . . .'

'How is . . . she?'

'She's locked herself in her bedroom and won't let anyone in. You would be knowing more than most how much she loved that boy.'

'Yes, she did, and oh . . .'

Words failed her, and she put her head in her hands and wept.

'Listen, I've got to go, but can I call a neighbour to sit with you?'

'No! I can't be seen to be grieving for the enemy now, can I, Lucy?'

'You're right, so,' Lucy agreed. 'Take care of yourself, Nuala, and I'm so sorry.'

After Lucy had left, Nuala climbed onto her bicycle and headed for the one place she hoped could give her comfort. As the cold December rain drenched her to her bones, she looked up at the barren branches of the oak tree.

'Philip, if you can hear up there, it's me, Nuala,' she whispered. 'I'm so, so sorry I had to leave you, but this whole mess meant your mammy couldn't have me stay. 'Tis my fault, this; I betrayed your trust and I'll never forgive myself for it, never.'

Soaking wet, Nuala stood up and cycled into Timoleague as the rain poured so hard on her she thought that she might drown, and didn't care if she did. At the church door, she climbed off her bicycle and walked inside. Crossing herself and curtseying in front of the altar, she knelt to ask God and the Holy Mother for forgiveness. Then she stood up and went to the votive candle stand. Taking a penny out of her pocket and putting it into the pot, she lit a candle for the Honourable Philip Fitzgerald, Protestant son of the local landowner, and her friend.

'Rest in peace, Philip, and I'll never forget you,' she muttered as the candle burnt amongst others lit for Catholic souls.

Then she turned and walked out of the church.

Merry
Claridge's Hotel, London
June 2008

20

I reached for a tissue and blew my nose hard. Then I turned the page of the battered notebook:

I cant be writin any mor.

After that, the remaining pages were blank.

I closed the notebook and lay back, thinking of this young woman who had carried the weight of the world on her shoulders, fighting a seemingly unwinnable war. She was younger than my own daughter, but had faced horrors that neither Mary-Kate nor myself, nor anyone who had never lived through war, could begin to understand. Yet I could now see that the seeds of violence that had been sown in Nuala's life almost ninety years ago had touched my own with disastrous consequences . . .

My head felt full of the voices of the past: that particular melodic West Cork cadence that Nuala had conveyed through her writing, the familiar place names that I had cut from my mind for so long.

He had given me this diary all those years ago to make me understand. And yes, if these had been his grandmother's words, it certainly explained his hatred of the British. One thing I remembered clearly about my days in Ireland was that everyone had long memories. And that old grievances were

rarely forgiven and forgotten, but passed on from one generation to the next.

I yawned suddenly, and realised I felt exhausted. The past had been a foreign country for so long but, both metaphorically and physically, I was drawing ever closer to it . . .

21

Star
Claridge's Hotel

'Where is she? Do you think she isn't coming?'

Star paced round the sitting room of her suite and looked nervously at her watch. 'It's already ten past seven. We mustn't lose her now, Orlando.'

'Don't panic, Lady Sabrina, I'm sure nothing's gone awry with my plan,' he replied, taking a slurp of champagne.

'I wish I could be as relaxed as you,' Star muttered, then picked up the receiver and dialled 0. 'Hello, is this the front desk? Could you possibly put me through to Mrs Mary McDougal in Room 112? Thank you so much, that's very kind of you.' Star waited while the receptionist connected her, raising a disapproving eyebrow at Orlando, who was pouring them both a top-up of champagne. The line rang for an unbearably long time before it was answered.

'Hello?' a dazed voice answered.

'Mrs McDougal? It's Sabrina Vaughan here. Orlando and I were just wondering whether you were still coming?'

'I – I am. Oh dear, I'm afraid I sat down on the bed and

279

must have dropped off. How rude of me. I'll be there in ten minutes.'

'No problem at all, Mrs McDougal. We'll see you soon.'

As she hung up, Orlando raised his glass to her. 'And the fish is reeled into the net.'

'Honestly, Orlando, it's not as if we're hunting her, we just want to speak to her! I'll go and tidy myself up.'

Fifteen minutes later, there was a knock on the door. Nervously smoothing down the skirt of her dress, Star went to answer it.

Merry McDougal was standing in the corridor, wearing a tasteful jade-green dress, teamed with a pair of black court shoes. Her blonde hair hung in a wavy shoulder-length bob around a fine-featured face, her sapphire-blue eyes standing out against her pale skin. Star thought how elegant she looked, despite having just woken from an impromptu nap. She was clutching a small bag, and Star gulped as she saw an emerald-green glimmer on one finger.

'Hello, Mrs McDougal. Come in,' Star said, trying to sound as natural as possible.

She led Merry into the large sitting room and saw Orlando had disappeared into the bedroom. 'Please, sit down while I fetch Orlando. He was just on the phone to a . . . wine supplier. Back in a tick,' she said, then ducked into the bedroom. He was standing by the door and had obviously been listening behind it.

'It's her!' Star stage-whispered to Orlando. 'Oh my God, I feel so nervous. And guess what?'

'What?'

'I only got a quick glance, but it looks like she's wearing the ring.'

'As they say these days, high five!' Without actually offering Star the hand-clap, Orlando swept through the door.

'Mrs McDougal, thank you so much for coming. Please, don't bother to get up,' he said as the woman prepared to stand.

'I am so sorry about my lateness. As I said to Sabrina, I'm afraid the jet lag got to me and I fell asleep.'

Star noticed she had a slight, unplaceable accent underlying her pleasant, low tone.

'Please do not apologise, Mrs McDougal. It gave myself and my old chum, Sabrina here, a chance to catch up, although it might have to be you who has to catch up on the alcohol front.' Orlando nodded at his champagne glass. 'One too many of these has gone down a treat. It's from a new *cave*, more affordable than your Krug and Dom Pérignon, and really rather pleasant. I myself am not a particular fan of champagnes, especially when the sparkling element overpowers the taste, which it does in some brands, but this is very palatable. Now, will you join us in the remnants of the bottle, or would you prefer to drink something else?'

'I may sound rather dull, but I think I'd better stick to water while we have the interview. My brain's blurry as it is. Oh, and please call me Merry,' she added as Star walked across the room to an alcove and held up two water bottles.

'Still or sparkling?' asked Star.

'I'll have the sparkling, and then I'll at least feel a little more festive.'

Once the water had been poured, Orlando sat in the velvet smoking chair opposite Merry. He indicated the dictaphone lying on the table between them. 'Would you mind awfully if I record this? My shorthand is non-existent and I'd like to catch every word that falls from your lips.'

'Of course not,' Merry said, taking a sip of water. 'What exactly is it you'd like to know?'

'Let's start with how it all began. I think I can detect from

your accent that you are not a native Kiwi. In fact, forgive me if I'm wrong,' he said, as Star sat down on the sofa, 'but I think I can hear just the slightest hint of an Irish burr in there somewhere.'

Star watched as a slight blush came to the woman's cheeks.

'You've a good ear, although I left Dublin straight after university. I've lived in New Zealand for some decades now.'

'Ah, one of the many millions of Irish emigrants?'

'Sadly, yes. We were all looking for a better life elsewhere in those days.'

'As a matter of fact, I had a couple of chums that went to Trinity College. Were you there, or at University College Dublin?'

'Trinity. I studied Classics.'

Orlando's face lit up. 'Then we may have far more to discuss than wine. Greek philosophy and mythology are great passions of mine, and I sometimes wish I'd pursued them after university.'

'They were certainly passions of mine too. I lived and breathed Greek myths when I was a child,' she said.

'It was my father who fuelled my passion,' Orlando commented. 'What about you?'

'I had a godfather who was a Fellow in Classics at Trinity when I first met him, then went on to become head of the department. Of course, he's long retired now, and may not even be alive any longer.'

'You lost contact with him?' Orlando prompted.

'Yes, I . . . well,' Merry shrugged. 'You know how it is. Anyway, shall I tell you about how my husband and I started The Vinery?'

'Please, I'm all ears, dear lady.'

'Well, Jock and I met when I arrived in New Zealand and we both worked at a hotel called The Hermitage. It's at the

base of Mount Cook on the South Island. I was a waitress there when I met him. He'd started as a waiter, but had already worked his way up to maître d' and sommelier. Even back then, he had a passion for wine. I'm sorry, I've probably gone a bit too far back for your article . . .'

'Please, the floor is yours, Merry. Spout forth for as long as you wish, I find it fascinating.'

Star listened intently as the woman talked about how the two of them had married, then how, on a trip out to the Gibbston Valley in Central Otago, they'd come across an old stone ruin of a house, which Merry said had probably been built during the gold rush. They'd fallen in love with it and it had taken years to rebuild.

'We used to travel down there at weekends and holidays. Jack was only a toddler at the time but we all loved it, and the beauty of our valley, so much that Jock and I eventually decided to put all our savings into establishing a small vineyard there.'

As Merry found her stride, telling Orlando how she and Jock had worked like the devil, bathing in streams until they had been able to build a bathroom, Star let her eyes drop surreptitiously from Merry's face to her hands, which were small, pale and delicate. One hand came to rest on her lap, and Star saw that the ring was definitely made of emeralds and arranged in a star-shaped design around a diamond. She took a mental photograph of the ring, then stood up.

'Excuse me, but I must use the bathroom,' she said as she went out of the sitting room and into the bedroom, closing the door behind her. She ran to her holdall, pulled it onto the bed and ferreted inside the net holder for the envelope containing the drawing of the ring. In the bathroom, with the door firmly locked, Star drew it out and stared at it.

It was identical.

Flushing the toilet, then secreting the envelope in the bedside drawer, she walked back into the sitting room.

'As for the details on the actual mix of grapes we use now,' Merry was saying, 'you need to speak to my son, Jack, who is currently in the Rhône Valley, studying their viticulture and looking for any techniques he can apply to our own vineyard. Otago is famous for its pinot noir, as you know. Let me write down his number.'

As Merry bent to find her mobile in the bag she'd brought with her and Orlando offered her a pen and paper from the hotel pad, Star stared at the ring again, just to make sure.

'That's his French mobile. It's best to call after four p.m. our time.'

'Thank you very much, Mrs McDougal. I think your story will make the most inspiring article. Just in case I think of any more questions, could you possibly furnish me with your own mobile phone number?'

'Of course,' Merry said, adding it to the note.

'Now, are you sure you won't have a drink with us?'

'Ah, go on then, I'll have a small whiskey,' Merry agreed.

'So' – Star took over as Orlando headed for the mini-bar – 'how long will you be in London for?'

'I'm not sure yet, maybe a couple of days, maybe two weeks or two months . . . Since Jock died and Jack took over The Vinery, I'm as free as a bird. It's a shame my daughter didn't join me. She's never seen Europe before,' Merry added as she took the whiskey.

'As they say in Ireland, *sláinte!*' toasted Orlando.

'*Sláinte!*' Merry repeated as they clinked glasses.

'So, how old is your daughter?' Star asked, even though she knew.

'Mary-Kate's twenty-two – there's ten years between Jack

and his sister. We had Jack, then struggled to conceive again, so we adopted.'

'Is Mary-Kate interested in joining the family firm?' asked Orlando.

'No, not at all. She studied music at university and wants to make that her career.'

'Well, one would hope that, with your son at the helm and this article, the legacy you and Jock nurtured can really begin to come to the attention of the wider wine world.'

'I do hope so. It was Jock's life passion.' Merry gave a small, sad smile.

'I find it interesting that you, like me, never pursued what you said earlier was your own passion beyond university,' mused Orlando. 'May I enquire why?'

'Well, I had started a Masters, thinking that perhaps I'd go on to a PhD, but . . . life had other plans.'

'As it does for so many of us,' Orlando agreed with a sigh.

'That's a very pretty ring,' said Star, knowing she must speak up before it was too late. 'The star shape is unusual.'

'Thank you. I received it from my godfather on my twenty-first birthday.'

'Are those seven points on it?' asked Star. 'It rather reminds me of the Seven Sisters – of the Pleiades cluster—'

'Yes, I've always been fascinated with their myths,' Orlando butted in. 'Particularly the story of the missing sister. I'd be delighted to chew the philosophical cud with you, if you have the time? Maybe dinner tomorrow night, after I've conducted my interviews, of course,' Orlando added quickly. 'Sabrina, you could join us, couldn't you?'

'Perhaps, although I'll have to check, um, what Julian is doing.' Star could feel her guard slipping, but while Merry was in captivity, she was absolutely desperate to ask more questions.

'Yes, that sounds lovely,' said Merry, who stood up abruptly and put her whiskey glass down on the table. 'Now, if you'll excuse me, I think I must go before I really do fall asleep here in my chair. Thank you for the whiskey and the interview.'

Star and Orlando stood up and watched her as she headed for the door.

'How does eight thirty tomorrow evening in Gordon Ramsay's downstairs sound?' Orlando called after her.

'Fine. Goodnight, Sabrina, Orlando.'

The door banged shut behind her before Star and Orlando could say another word.

They both stood there for a few seconds, staring at each other, then Orlando sat back down and took a swig of his champagne.

'Shit!' Star uttered a rare swear word in her frustration. 'The moment you mentioned the missing sister, she was spooked.'

'A miscalculation perhaps,' Orlando sighed. 'Although you had pointed out her unusual ring.'

'I had to say something, Orlando. When I left the room, I went to check that ring against the drawing Ally faxed me. There's no doubt, it *is* the ring. It's identical. She has it! I should call Atlantis and speak to Maia and Ally—'

'Hold on just one moment, Star. Let us think about this carefully. It was obvious to me that Mrs Merry McDougal has something to hide. And as her fear began the moment I mentioned the missing sister, we can surmise that it has something to do with that. One has to examine the facts: why did she leave Trinity so suddenly, before finishing her Masters?'

'I—'

'I understand it could be for a simple reason, but let me finish. This obviously highly intelligent woman moved about

as far away from Ireland as she could possibly get, then buried herself in some beautiful but off-the-map valley and never again pursued a career in academia. In my opinion, she's spent the past several decades hiding. The question is, from what? Or more accurately, who?'

'Isn't that rather a big leap, Orlando? I mean, just because she didn't want a future in academia doesn't mean anything. Maybe she fell in love.'

'Perhaps, but if you put her life's trajectory alongside the fact that she has very obviously been avoiding your sisters' pursuit of her, when all her daughter told her was that she may have found a connection to your family, with the clue of the star-shaped emerald ring, then this all adds up to a woman who is fearful of what the revelation might mean for her. And for her daughter,' he added.

'Maybe you've been reading too many crime novels, but yes, I agree, there's definitely something she's afraid of. What's so frustrating is that the woman sleeping just a few doors down from us now has the answers to the puzzle, but we daren't push her further or we'll scare her off. CeCe said that Mary-Kate has never looked into her biological family. Though as we now think she really *could* be the missing sister, maybe we could call her now and ask her on our cruise. But . . .'

'Because of Mummy Mary's obvious reticence, you feel it would be inappropriate to do so.'

'Yes. We've just lied our way into meeting her and it's . . . morally wrong to use that information to go behind her back and contact her daughter. Oh dear, Orlando, we've got ourselves into a real mess here,' Star sighed.

Silence reigned as they both thought about it.

'Perhaps there's another way of gleaning information on Mary-Kate's adoption,' Orlando said eventually. 'For some

reason only known to herself, Merry does not wish her daughter to explore her true heritage. However, we must not forget that Merry has a son called Jack. May I suggest something?'

'Go on.'

'I would call Atlantis and see if Maia can go to France to meet him. Geneva isn't far from Provence and I have the address of the *cave* he is staying at on the tape. She told us that Jack is thirty-two, and he was ten when Mary-Kate arrived in the family. He will definitely have a memory of that moment, and perhaps know more of his mother's heritage too.'

'He might, but Mary-Kate knows nothing of her adoptive parents, so why should Jack? Orlando, we can't just let Merry walk out of here without us seeing her again. I just want to come clean, tell her who we truly are. I feel terrible about all this deception. This isn't a game, Orlando, it really isn't.'

'No. Well, I promise that even if I have to sit cross-legged in front of Mrs McDougal's door all night, we will not let that happen,' Orlando said firmly. 'Now, I'm retiring to my room to think and we will speak by telephone later when I have cleared my brain. In the meantime, you call Atlantis and tell your sisters that one of them needs to get down to Provence. I will telephone you later with the exact address.'

He walked purposefully across the room, then paused at the door and turned to look at Star.

'Perchance one other question we should be asking is this: where did Merry get that ring from in the first place? Adieu for now.'

With that, Orlando left the suite.

Star heaved herself up and wearily walked into the bedroom so she could be comfortable while speaking to Maia and Ally. She tried to clarify in her mind the facts she needed to tell them.

Finding the Atlantis number on her mobile, she waited for it to connect and opened the bedside drawer to pull out the envelope with the drawing of the star-shaped ring.

'Hello, Ma, it's Star here. How are you?'

'I am well, *chérie*, and enjoying the beautiful summer weather here. And of course, your sisters' company. And you? Is all well?'

'Yes, it is, thank you. I . . .' Star stopped herself as she wasn't sure how much her sisters were telling Ma of the search for the missing sister. 'Can I possibly speak to one or both of them?'

'Of course; they are out on the terrace and I know they are eager to speak to you. I am very much looking forward to seeing you soon.'

As Star waited for Ma to fetch her sisters, she reminded herself to call Mouse straight afterwards and make sure he had fed Rory something and managed to get him to bed.

'Star! Ally here, and Maia is listening too.'

'Hi, Star,' Maia said. 'Have you any news for us?'

'I do. Orlando's master plan worked, and I've just spent an hour with Merry McDougal.'

There was silence at the other end. Then both her sisters talked at once.

'Oh wow!'

'What did she say?'

'Is Mary-Kate the missing sister . . . ?'

'Hold on, both of you, and I'll tell you as much as I can, though I'm still trying to process everything. Firstly, and probably most importantly, when she walked in, I noticed immediately that she was wearing the ring. While Orlando interviewed her about her vineyard, I went into the bedroom and checked it against the drawing you faxed me. Seriously, it's identical.'

'That's wonderful news! Did you ask her where she got it from?' Maia queried.

'She said it was a twenty-first birthday present from her godfather, who was apparently a professor of Classics at Trinity College in Dublin, where she herself did the same degree.'

'So, did you then say that the ring meant her daughter was the missing sister?' Ally cut in.

'No, because the minute I mentioned the design and how unusual it was, and Orlando said he had a particular interest in the missing sister of the Pleiades, she got up and left. She was totally spooked. Orlando and I have invited her to dinner tomorrow night – I just really want to tell her who we are – but we both think she might run again. It's obvious that, for whatever reason, she *was* avoiding CeCe and Chrissie when they went to that island, as well as Electra when she flew to Canada. And now she may well try to avoid us. Honestly, I feel truly awful for getting her here under false pretences.'

There was a pause as Star heard both her sisters whispering in the background.

'I understand, Star. The only reason we can think of is that she doesn't want her daughter to know who her birth parents were,' said Maia. 'That's got to be it, hasn't it?'

'I suppose so – but she looked genuinely frightened when she left,' Star sighed. 'Even Orlando seems stumped. He says he has a plan to make sure that she doesn't leave the hotel without him knowing about it – don't ask me how. But just in case we do lose her again, Orlando thinks that one of you two should go to Provence and speak to Mary-Kate's brother, Jack. Maybe he'll know more about his mum and her past.'

'Maybe, but how would he know any more about Mary-Kate's adoption than his sister did?' asked Ally.

'He's ten years older than Mary-Kate so he might remember

something. And also be less emotionally involved than his mum.'

'Do we know where he is in Provence?' Maia asked.

'I'll text you the address for the *cave* – Orlando has it on tape – but could one of you go? Like, tomorrow?'

'It's a good five to six hours' drive from Geneva,' said Maia.

'Send us that address and we'll get back to you in a bit when we've had a chat and sorted out the arrangements, okay?' Ally added.

'Okay,' said Star.

'And please thank Orlando for his help – so far you're actually the only ones that have managed to meet Merry face to face,' said Maia.

'Even if my Lady Sabrina acting was rubbish' – Star gave a low chuckle – 'Orlando was brilliant. You know, this sounds weird, but her face actually reminded me of someone I've seen before, I just can't think who.'

'If you do, let us know. Speak later, Star. And really, well done. Bye.'

Star ended the call, then lay back on the bed and closed her eyes for a few seconds. Then she took a deep breath, opened them and called Mouse's mobile. It rang for ages, but finally, he answered.

'Hello, darling, how are you?' his deep voice came into her ear.

'I'm fine, thanks. Just checking in to say goodnight and to make sure Rory's had dinner and you've put him to bed,' she smiled.

'Of course I did! I am capable of looking after my own child when you're not here, Star.'

'I know you are, but you're also very busy.'

'I am. So, how did the "thing" you and Orlando needed to do in London go?'

'Oh, it was . . . okay. It's complicated, Mouse. I'll explain when I'm home.'

'It all sounds very mysterious, darling.'

'As I said last night, it's just something to do with my family and organising things for Pa's memorial service. I'll be home either tomorrow or the following morning. You couldn't by any chance come to London tomorrow night, could you? The suite is just beautiful and I'm sure I could get Jenny the babysitter to stay overnight with Rory.'

'Sorry, but I'm snowed under here.'

'I . . . okay.'

'All right, darling. Well, keep in touch.'

'I will, and give Rory a hug from me. Goodnight.'

'Goodnight.'

Ending the call, Star let out a big sigh. Why did she still find it so difficult to say what she felt? Perhaps it was simply that after all the years with CeCe, it was inbuilt, or maybe it was just the kind of person she was. But keeping everything bottled up wasn't healthy and had nearly wrecked her relationship with her precious sister. She knew that Mouse loved her, but he was of that particular breed of Englishmen who were not good at expressing their feelings either. She understood that, but between her inability to say what she needed from him – that they should find even the occasional night when houses and work were forgotten and they could just be together – and Mouse's struggle with showing emotion, their communication wasn't what it should be. 'You have to try,' she muttered to herself as the room telephone rang on the bedside table beside her.

'Room 161 for you, madam. Shall I put the call through?'

'Yes, thank you.'

'Dear Star, did you manage to contact your sisters?' came Orlando's dulcet tones.

'I did and they're going to call me back when they've decided on a plan.'

'But you did insist that they went to Provence at the earliest opportunity?'

'Yes, Orlando. I'm sure Maia will go.'

'Good, good. Well, I have made sure that we will know if our Mrs McDougal exits the hotel at any point from now on. I will call you if and when I get word from my . . . contact that she is on the move.'

Star couldn't help but laugh. 'Honestly, Orlando, you've really enjoyed this, haven't you?'

'For my sins, I rather admit I have, although we are still far from solving this puzzle. Now, make sure you don't block your room telephone, and that your mobile is charged and turned on for the rest of the night.'

'I will, I promise. Oh, I need Jack's address in Provence.'

'It's the Minuet Cave in Châteauneuf-du-Pape. Now, I shall sit in my comparatively poky little room and continue to think. For now, I shall say goodnight.'

'Goodnight, Orlando, sleep well and thank you.'

After texting Ally the address, Star did her ablutions and, despite her guilty conscience, she had to chuckle at Orlando and his eccentricity. What with Mouse being so very serious and absorbed in his work, his brother so often brought a smile to her face. As she climbed into bed and turned off the light, she thanked the heavens that he was in her life.

22

Atlantis

'I found it,' said Ally, stepping through the French doors of the kitchen and onto the terrace where Maia was sitting. The sun was setting behind the mountains and turning the sky a vibrant shade of orange. 'The *cave* is in the village of Châteauneuf-du-Pape in the Rhône Valley, and the nearest airport is Marseille. Or you could just drive straight there, because by the time you've got to Geneva airport and faffed about, then hired a car from Marseille at the other end, it's probably faster.'

'Okay,' said Maia quietly.

'You're happy to go, aren't you?'

Maia let out a weary sigh. 'I'm not feeling all that well just now, Ally.'

'I told you, you should have gone to the doctor days ago. The sooner you can find out what it is, then—'

'Ally, I know what it is, that is not the problem!'

'You do?'

'Yes, I do. I didn't want to tell you before I saw Floriano next week, but . . .'

'What is it? Please, tell me, because my imagination is running riot.'

'Really, it's nothing to worry about. I am well, and—'

'Oh my God!' Ally looked at her, then threw back her head and laughed. 'It's okay, Maia, I know what it is. You're—'

'Pregnant. Yes, I am. When I went to Geneva with Christian, I bought a test and the result was positive. In fact, I bought three tests – which are hidden in my underwear drawer in the Pavilion – and they are all positive!'

'That's wonderful news!' Ally stood up and threw her arms around Maia. 'You are pleased, aren't you?'

'Of course, but it's stirred up some things from my past.'

'Oh.' Ally looked at her sister. 'I understand.'

'And apart from that, I'm feeling sick *all* the time! And when I'm not being sick, I am thinking that I will be, do you understand?'

'Of course I do, darling. I've been there.'

'And Floriano and I . . . well, we aren't married yet, and then there is Valentina to consider. How will she feel about a new brother or sister?'

'I don't think whether you're married or not makes any difference these days, Maia. You've lived with Floriano for almost a year and I've never seen you so happy. I honestly think he will be thrilled, and Valentina too. I'm certain it will bond you all even closer. If you feel it's important to get married, then I'm sure Floriano won't mind that either.'

'No.' Maia smiled for the first time. 'He won't mind at all. He proposed very soon after I moved in with him. It was me that wanted to wait. But you understand why this is sending me back to the past, don't you? I mean' – Maia bent her head and put a hand to her forehead – 'if I'm to have this child and raise it, then why couldn't I have kept my son all those years ago? Oh Ally, my head is in such a mess . . . Having all the same pregnancy sensations now just takes me back to that time at uni in Paris when I was so alone and scared. And then

giving birth to a baby who would never know me as a mother and I would never know him as my son! I . . . how could I have given him away? How could I?'

Ally took her sister in her arms as she sobbed with all the grief of the past fifteen years.

'And to top it all, the father of my child is Zed Eszu! He's an evil man, Ally. We know that he's pursued Tiggy and Electra too. Why was he doing it? It cannot simply be random that he's been obsessed with us sisters. He doesn't leave our family alone!'

'No, I've thought about that too,' agreed Ally.

'I am the only one who has borne his child, and at least he will never know.'

'You don't want him to?'

'Never! I know nothing about his business dealings, but I do know him as a human being. He gets what he wants and then moves on. He's without any kind of scruples. Or guilt,' Maia added as Ally produced a tissue from her jean pocket and handed it to her sister.

'Well, the lack of guilt or empathy is an indication of being a psychopath. Maybe that's what he is.'

'I don't know,' said Maia, blowing her nose. 'But his fascination for me in Paris, and then two of our sisters more recently, is definitely not a coincidence.'

'What makes it even stranger is that his father's boat was next to Pa's when I radioed the *Titan* to try to rendezvous with it last June. The *Olympus* was on the radar. Anyway, Maia, enough of all that. I just wish that you could be happier about your wonderful news.'

'Were you when you were pregnant?'

'Yes and no. I was conflicted, just like you are. Maybe most women are to some degree initially, even if their circumstances are less complex than yours or mine.'

'But you went ahead and kept your baby, even though you had lost your beloved Theo. My circumstances all those years ago weren't all that different.'

'Maia, please, I wasn't nineteen and just starting out on my life and career like you were. I was a thirty-year-old woman who knew that she loved the baby's father desperately, and that the baby was a gift, a chance to have a part of Theo always with me. They were completely different circumstances.'

'Thank you for trying to make me feel better about giving my baby away, but nothing can, Ally, nothing.'

'Maybe not, but equally, you can't let guilt over the past affect your present and future, Maia. This baby is the start of a whole new life for you, Floriano and Valentina. It would be very sad if you weren't able to embrace it, for them, as well as yourself.'

Maia was silent for a while, then she looked at Ally, her beautiful dark eyes still wet with tears, and nodded. 'You're right. I must embrace it for them. Thank you, Ally.'

'You know,' Ally mused, 'even though we lost Pa last year, it feels like at least we've found each other again. All those years when you never really talked to me. I missed my big sister, I really did.'

'Please forgive me for that. I was so ashamed . . . I hated myself for so long. But you're right. I must move on.'

'Yes, you must. Just one last question: would you ever think about finding your son?'

'Even though every millimetre of me yearns to know him, to hold him in my arms and tell him I love him, and there hasn't been a day that has gone past since I gave him away that I haven't thought about him, or wondered where he is and how he's doing . . . I can't. It would be for *me*, not him. I don't even know if his parents have told him that he's

adopted. Walking back into his life now could completely disrupt it. He's at such a vulnerable age – fifteen; no longer a baby or even a child. He's almost an adult. And then there are his parents: they've – or at least I hope they have – loved him like he was their own since he was a day old. How would they feel if the birth mother suddenly walked in?'

'I can't imagine, but I understand what you're saying.'

'Perhaps I'll see him one day in the future. If he wants to get in contact with me. I'm sure he could if he tried,' Maia sighed.

'Talking of that, I'm still convinced that's the problem for Merry: she obviously doesn't want to risk another family stealing her beloved daughter away.'

'I agree, but surely it's Mary-Kate's choice whether she wants to meet her birth family – or whatever we are to her? Like it would be my son's?' Maia pointed out.

'As CeCe told us, it's never occurred to Mary-Kate to search for her birth parents before. She was perfectly content not knowing about the past.'

'Then is it our place to interfere? She should talk to her mother about it first.'

'From the calls we've had with her, she now seems eager to know. Oh dear,' Ally sighed. 'I mean, from what Star has told us, that emerald ring suggests she is who we're looking for, but given she's in New Zealand and her mum's in London with no definite date to return home, it doesn't look like she'll be joining us on the cruise.'

'I'll say it for the thousandth time: I so wish Pa were here to tell us what to do,' said Maia.

'Well, he's not, and actually, before we go back to Mary-Kate and tell her that the ring is identical, I think Orlando is right: you should go down to Provence to meet Jack.'

'Ally' – Maia looked at her – 'I'm sorry, but I feel too

unwell to make such a journey. I'm sick all the time, and I just can't face the drive.'

'Okay, I understand. Well, that's that then. It's a shame, because I saw on the website that it has a very nice *gîte* set in the vineyard that visitors can rent. It's vacant at the moment. I know how much you love France, especially since you discovered your heritage there. It's part of who you are, Maia.'

'I am sorry, Ally; even though you're right, and I'd love to go to Provence, I just can't.'

'Then I'll call Tiggy and see if she can fly over. It's not that far from Scotland, is it?'

'No, but . . . Ally, why don't you go?'

'Me?! Can you imagine what Bear would be like on a five-hour car journey? I couldn't.'

'I think you could if you left Bear here at Atlantis with Ma and me for a couple of days. It would do you good, Ally. You've not been apart from him for more than a few hours since the moment he was born, and you've told me you've started supplementing his milk because he's such a hungry baby. You could express tonight and tomorrow morning before you leave.'

'Oh Maia, I couldn't. What if he got sick? Had a fever? How could I leave him here? I . . .'

'At the risk of sounding patronising, Ma brought up six babies and is quite capable of dealing with a fever and even worse. She absolutely adores Bear, and he seems to love her too. He quite likes me as well,' Maia added with a smile.

'Are you trying to say he doesn't need his mother?'

'No, Ally, of course not. What I am saying is that even *you* must admit that you've been exhausted and have found it a strain coping by yourself. I think a drive through beautiful countryside heading for a *gîte* in the Rhône Valley, and some time – and nights – alone, would do you the world of good.

It's completely normal for mothers to leave their babies in the care of a grandparent, *and* an auntie. Would you at least think about it?'

'Okay, but—'

'No buts, Ally. Just think about it. Now, I'm going to get an early night. Ma's insisted on making me a milky drink before bed like she used to when we were little,' Maia smiled. 'Have a good night's sleep, and thank you. Our conversation has really helped me. Please don't tell anyone about my news – not even Ma . . . I want to speak to Floriano first.'

'You know you can trust me.'

'Always. Goodnight, darling.' Maia kissed Ally's red curls and walked into the kitchen.

Ally sat back, watching insects buzzing around the lamps that lit up the garden. She thought about what Maia had suggested and at first rejected it out of hand because it seemed like such a foreign concept. It was almost a year now since Bear had become part of her. She'd lived every day with him either in her tummy or out of it. On the other hand, the thought of driving down to Provence alone *was* appealing. She could take the old open-topped Mercedes sports car that Pa kept in the garage just next to the pontoon in Geneva. He'd once collected her from the airport in it after a race and the two of them had driven down to Nice to meet the *Titan*. They'd played *The Magic Flute* at full blast as the wind had rushed through her hair.

'I felt so free then . . .' she murmured.

Looking at her watch, she saw it was past ten o'clock. She walked back into the kitchen to find Ma already preparing Bear's bottles.

'Ma, it's late. I could have done that.'

'It is no problem, Ally. I will do the night-time feeds again tonight. If I tell you I enjoy those moments when the rest of

the world is still and a contented baby lies sleeping in my arms, would you think me mad?'

'I wouldn't at all.' Ally took a bottle from the steriliser and put it on the table, so she could take it upstairs to express some milk for tomorrow morning.

'Maia just mentioned to me that a trip to Provence is necessary,' said Ma. 'As Maia is not quite herself, she suggested that perhaps you should go. You know I am happy to look after little Bear whilst you are away. In fact, it would be my pleasure to do so.'

'Maia seems very keen on me going, but I'm not sure I want to.'

'It is up to you, of course, but if there is someone you must meet to find out more about this missing sister, then you should consider it. I know your father wanted to find her so very badly. Ah well,' Ma sighed, 'you must do what is right for you first, Ally. And if she cannot be found in time for the cruise, the most important thing is that she *is* found.'

'But what if she doesn't *want* or need to be a part of this family? From what CeCe and Chrissie said, Mary-Kate has her own very loving adoptive family, although she too has recently lost her father. And her mum is obviously not happy about our arrival in her daughter's life either. I know it's what Pa wanted, but sometimes things just can't happen, for whatever reason.'

'I know, Ally, I know. Do not upset yourself, please, it's the last thing your father would have wanted. Now, will you come upstairs to bed with me, or are you staying down here?'

'I'll come with you.'

They switched off the lights in the kitchen, and walked up the stairs.

'Goodnight, Ma,' she said as she turned for one of the guest rooms on the first floor. 'Ma?'

'Yes, *chérie*?'

'Is there . . . I mean, do you know anything about Pa and his life that can maybe help us?'

'I know very little, Ally, I promise. Your father was a private man and he never shared any of his secrets with me.'

'But there were secrets, weren't there?'

'Yes, *chérie*, I think there were. Goodnight.'

Walking along the corridor, Ally paused in front of Pa's bedroom. She put out a tentative hand to open the door, then decided against it. She needed to sleep tonight, not have the ghosts of the past haunt her.

Inside the very comfortable guest room, she undressed quickly and slipped into bed.

'Who were you, Pa? Who were you?' she murmured before she fell asleep.

23

'I'm going to go to Provence,' Ally said to Ma early the following morning as she entered Ma's suite. As if on cue, Bear began screaming. She headed to the cot, scooped the squalling baby out of it, then sat down in the chair and began to feed him. A beautiful silence descended. Ma sat down on the sofa opposite her, managing to look elegant in her peacock-blue silk robe, even this early in the morning.

'I think that is a very good idea, Ally.'

'It's only six now,' Ally said, looking out of the window at the sun already peeping over the mountains. 'If I leave in an hour or so, I can be in Provence by this afternoon.'

'Ally, would you not like Christian to drive you there? Then you can relax and enjoy the scenery.'

'No. It's been ages since I took a road trip, and if I'm doing this without Bear, I think it would do me good to have some space and blast out tunes on the way down.'

'I will take the best care of the little one until your return,' said Ma.

'I know you will, Ma. I was thinking last night that at some point, I'll have to get back to work – but where and what that will be, I'm not sure. So I'll just have to get used to leaving him in the care of others.'

'One step at a time, Ally. You have had a most traumatic year. There is plenty of time to decide on your future.'

'Well, I'm going to have to ask Georg if I can take some money out of the trust Pa set up for all of us. I know I only need to ask,' Ally said as she moved Bear from one breast to the other, 'but all us girls find him intimidating.'

'I can assure you that Georg is one of the kindest men I have ever met. I do know that once you are all gathered on the *Titan*, he wishes to talk to you about how the trust should be managed from here on in. As he puts it, he is only the temporary gatekeeper until the six of you are ready to manage it yourselves. Now, if you are comfortable, I will go and get dressed. Shall I call Christian and tell him to bring the boat round in an hour?'

'Yes please. And also say that I'm going to drive the old open-top Mercedes.'

'Of course, Ally. I will see you downstairs with Bear.'

'So the expressed milk is in the fridge and just keep an eye on his temperature – it was raised a little a couple of days ago and—'

'Ally, please trust me to take care of your precious little one and we will see you when you're back,' said Ma. She kissed Ally's cheek and stepped back onto the grass from the jetty where the speedboat was moored.

'Bye bye, Ally.' Maia hugged her. 'Keep in touch.'

'I will. *Au revoir!*'

She waved to them as Christian pulled the speedboat away from the jetty. Normally, she would have taken the wheel herself, but today, she decided to sit back and enjoy another glorious morning on the lake. The water shimmered under the

sun as they began to speed towards Geneva. Christian knew he didn't have to worry about his passenger's sea legs, so he went full steam ahead. Ally could see how he felt in his element at the wheel of the boat, his skin tanned a deep brown and his broad shoulders relaxed.

Even though she felt choked at her first ever goodbye to Bear, being on the water comforted her and reminded her of who she had been before Bear had arrived.

This time last year, she'd been training with the crew, and at the full peak of her fitness.

And then she'd fallen in love . . .

'I will always remember those few weeks as the best of my life,' she murmured to the sky, as Christian began to slow the boat and steer it towards the pontoon. Ally jumped off to secure the ropes as Christian carried her holdall and joined her on dry land.

Parked next to the dock was the little sports car, its racing-green paintwork gleaming in the sun and its roof down. Ally watched as Christian took the keys from a young man in an immaculate white T-shirt and shorts. They chatted for a moment, then the young man waved and wandered off towards a bicycle.

'I asked Julien from the local garage to check the oil and fill up the tank,' said Christian. 'It's getting old now, but Julien says everything looks good, so you should have no problem with it.'

'It must be vintage by now,' Ally chuckled as she took the keys from Christian.

'You are sure you don't want me to drive you, Ally?'

'Quite sure,' she replied as she got in the car and turned on the engine. 'Thanks, Christian. I'll call you when I need you to come and collect me.'

'Take care, Ally, and drive safely,' he shouted above the noise of the engine as the car reversed.

'I will, bye!'

Ally made good time through Geneva and across the border into France. She'd brought a collection of CDs and spent the journey alternating between classical and pop, singing her heart out to some of her favourite anthems. She stopped at an *aire* for coffee, a baguette and to express milk – even though she was supplementing now, she didn't want to finish breastfeeding just yet.

Reaching Grenoble, she pulled off the *autoroute*, suddenly feeling exhausted. After a twenty-minute catnap, she began the final stretch down into Provence. She watched as the countryside visibly softened around her.

'It really is so beautiful here,' she murmured as she drove past a particularly lovely pale yellow farmhouse. Up a gentle slope covered in vineyards stood a grand château. The gates were open and part of her longed to drive up to the advertised *cave* to take a taste of one of her favourite wines: Provençal rosé. A road sign told her she was only three kilometres away from Châteauneuf-du-Pape. So close now, she decided to pull over and gather her thoughts. Reaching into her bag for her mobile, she saw there were a number of text messages, all from Star.

'Call me!' was the gist of most of them.

Ally rang Star's number and she answered immediately. 'Hi, Star, what's up?'

'Oh, don't worry, nothing awful has happened. As far as we know, Merry McDougal has not checked out of the hotel. She *has* left her room, however, and Orlando has followed her to see where she's going. Her bags are still here, according to the concierge.'

'Okay. I'm almost at the *cave* where this Jack's apparently staying and I've enjoyed the journey so much, I switched my brain off about what I'm going to say once I get there. I don't

know whether I should pretend to be a tourist and casually engage Jack in conversation about his family, or just come clean immediately. What do you think?'

'Oh gosh, Ally, I suppose it depends whether Merry has already told him about CeCe and Electra's visits.'

'If I somehow manage to meet him and then get him to talk to me without having to kidnap him and tie him to a chair at gunpoint, I'll do my best. Honestly, Star, you're right: now that I'm actually here, this all feels very uncomfortable. If Merry doesn't want her daughter to know about her origins, then I don't think it's right that we force it. Despite whatever reasons Pa had for wanting to find her.'

'I agree. If I were you, I'd play it by ear. Just be yourself and let things progress naturally. Good luck, Ally, and please keep in touch.'

'And you. Bye, Star.'

With a sigh, Ally started up the engine and moved out onto the road. She thought about the fact that all of her sisters had had someone with them when they'd been on the trail of the missing sister. CeCe had Chrissie; Electra, Mariam; and Star with Orlando by her side.

'And here I am, going it alone again,' she muttered as she saw a sign to the Minuet Cave. The building she was heading towards looked very much like the others scattered around the countryside: an old stone farmhouse with terracotta roofs and large blue-shuttered windows. Pausing at the turning onto a lane, which ran along a chalky path through the vines, she took a deep breath and saw an image of Theo in her mind.

'Be by my side, won't you, darling?'

With that, she pulled onto the track and drove towards the farmhouse.

'Right, here goes,' she whispered as she stepped out of the car and followed the signs to the shop. Housed in a dark,

cellar-like room at one end of the farmhouse, it was empty of people. Bottles of red Châteauneuf-du-Pape were stacked closely together, with every inch of space used. She was just about to go in search of someone when a teenage boy of around sixteen walked inside and smiled at her.

'*Je peux vous aider?*'

'Yes, I saw your sign advertising the *gîte* you have for rent and was wondering whether it was available?'

'For when, *mademoiselle?*' The teenager walked around the tiny counter jammed into a corner of the room and took out a book from a shelf beneath.

'For tonight actually.'

He thumbed through the book then nodded. 'Yes, it's available.'

'How much is it?'

The boy told her, and after saying she wanted to stay two nights minimum, she took her credit card from her purse.

'No, no, *mademoiselle*. You pay when you leave. One moment, and I will call *Maman* to come and take you down to the *gîte*.' Then he went to a small fridge and pulled out a bottle of rosé. 'Would you like a glass?'

'Do you know, I actually would,' Ally smiled. 'It's been a long drive.'

Once she had been furnished with the glass of pale pink wine, the boy walked towards the door. '*Excusez-moi, Maman* will be here soon.'

While she waited, Ally went outside into the courtyard and sat down on an ancient wrought-iron bench. The courtyard was full of wooden wine pallets, but also children's scooters, bikes and a rusty climbing frame. The sun was lower now in the azure-blue sky and Ally tilted her head back to enjoy its warmth on her face. The rosé tasted wonderful and she closed her eyes, breathing in deeply and trying to relax.

'*Bonjour, mademoiselle*, I am Ginette Valmer, and I will take you down to the *gîte*,' came a bright voice. Ally opened her eyes to see a dark-haired woman of around forty, wearing jeans, a T-shirt and a stained apron. She was carrying a small basket of food.

'I am pleased to meet you too. I am Ally D'Aplièse,' Ally said in formal French as she shook the woman's hand. She collected her holdall from the car and they walked along the chalky path towards the *gîte*, which was to the left of the farmhouse, nestled in an idyllic spot amongst the vines. She made polite conversation in response to Madame Valmer's questions.

'Yes, I live in Geneva, and I'm down here visiting for a few days.'

'To taste the wines?'

'Yes, and to also . . . look for a house round here.' The words fell out of Ally's mouth before she could stop them.

'Well, there are *immobiliers* in both Gigondas and Vacqueyras and also another in Beaumes-de-Venise. I can give you their telephone numbers or you can visit if you wish,' Madame Valmer replied as they reached the front door of the *gîte*. 'Now, here we are. It is very small, but okay for one person or a couple,' she said as they walked inside. Ally saw a basic but clean space with a small kitchenette along one side, a heavy French mahogany bed, and a sofa and two chairs placed in front of a tiny corner fireplace.

'The shower and toilet are through there,' Madame Valmer added, pointing to a wooden door at the back. She placed the basket on the small counter. 'Here is a fresh baguette, some butter, cheese and milk and there is already some rosé in the fridge.'

'Thank you, but really, I can go shopping.'

'Everything will be closed by now around here. You know

how it is in France,' Madame Valmer smiled, her dark eyes dancing. 'Nothing is ever open when you need it.'

'Then maybe you could tell me of a restaurant or a café close by where I could get something to eat? It's been a long journey from Geneva.'

'Ah, there are a few, but . . .'

There was a pause as Madame Valmer eyed her. 'Come for dinner with us.'

'Are you sure? I can easily find something in Gigondas,' said Ally.

'Another mouth will make no difference. I have three children and four hungry men who work in the *cave*, so' – Madame Valmer waved her hands at Ally expressively – 'one more is no problem. And it will be a change to have another female at the table!'

'I'd like that very much, if you don't mind.'

'It is simple food; we will eat at seven thirty. See you then.'

'*Merci, Madame Valmer, à ce soir.*'

'Call me Ginette!' she said as she left the *gîte*.

Ally went to the fridge and opened the ice-cold bottle of rosé. Walking outside, she saw an old worn table and two iron chairs placed just to the side of the *gîte*. She sat down to enjoy the sun on her face and to call Atlantis. The home number was engaged, so she rang Maia instead.

'Hi, just calling to say I've arrived safely. How is Bear?'

'In the bath with Ma clucking over him. He's fine, and I think Ma is really enjoying being in charge. So, have you met Jack yet?'

'No, just a son of the family and a woman who I presume is one of the owners of the *cave*. For some reason, when she asked me why I was here, I said I was house-hunting!' Ally chuckled. 'Anyway, the good news is, I've been invited to

dinner with them all tonight. Hopefully this Jack will be at the table, and I can start a conversation with him.'

'Wonderful! Whatever happens, staying in a *gîte* in Provence and eating a home-cooked French supper sounds delightful to me.'

'Well, it's so beautiful here, I might be serious about buying a house. The thought of another freezing and rainy Bergen winter isn't appealing just now.'

'There's no harm in looking, is there?'

'I was only joking, Maia. I have Thom and my father there. Actually, I must give Felix a call too and make sure he isn't lying in a pool of whisky somewhere. Tell Ma to give Bear a big goodnight kiss from his *maman*, won't you?'

'Of course I will. And Ally?'

'Yes?'

'Forget Jack for now and just enjoy your time there. *À bientôt.*'

Eager to stretch her legs after the long drive, Ally took herself on a walk through the vines. Not quite ready to be harvested, the grapes hadn't yet developed the dark blue hue that would produce the world-famous Châteauneuf-du-Pape red wine. Around her was the sound of cicadas and insect life that vibrated in the hot, still air. In the distance, a farm dog lay panting in the shade of a parasol-shaped pine tree, as the softening afternoon light slanted to glint golden on the vine leaves.

Ally sat down in the shade next to a wild lavender bush. She brushed her hands over the heavy purple flower heads to fill her nostrils with their calming scent. And finally felt glad that Maia and Ma had persuaded her to come.

Eventually, she returned to the *gîte* for a quick shower in the tiny cubicle (the water was only lukewarm, but the weather was hot enough for it to be refreshing) then changed into a clean pair of jeans and a shirt, adding a touch of mascara and a dash of lipstick, and allowing her hair to flow freely around her shoulders.

'Wow, it's a long time since I've been out to dinner,' she said to herself as she walked up through the vines towards the farmhouse. Glad of the glass and a half of rosé she'd had to bolster her confidence, she knocked on the front door.

'Everyone is at the back!' Ginette's head appeared from a window. 'Walk round, Ally.'

She did so, and saw a loggia hung with vines jutting out from the back of the house, which faced what she knew were the Dentelles Mountains. In the fast descending dusk, small lanterns were placed around the loggia, ready to be lit when night fell. At the table sat four men, as well as the teenage boy she'd met earlier, another boy aged around twelve, and a smaller boy of seven or eight. As Ally approached, there was raucous laughter, then all the men turned to look at her. One of them – small, but brawny – stood up.

'Excuse me, *mademoiselle*, we were not laughing at you, just at our friend's strange Kiwi expressions! Please, come and sit down. I am François, the co-owner of the *cave*. This is Vincent and Pierre-Jean who work here with me, and these are my sons: Tomás, Olivier, and Gerard. And this' – François pointed to the man she was about to sit next to – 'is Jack McDougal, all the way from New Zealand.'

Ally stood behind her chair and watched as the man she'd come here to speak to turned round and stood up. Jack McDougal towered over her. He was very fair, with piercing blue eyes and wavy blond hair cut short.

'*Enchanté, mademoiselle*,' he said in a very strange accent.

'And I apologise now for my bad French. Please' – he put out a hand – 'sit down.'

'Do you speak English, *mademoiselle*?' François, the host, asked her.

'Yes, I do.'

'Ah, Jack, then tonight you will finally have someone who understands what you are talking about!'

Everyone around the table laughed again.

'And he is not lying when he says his French is bad,' François added.

'But then, our English is worse! Would you like some wine, *mademoiselle*?' Vincent, who was opposite her at the table, tapped a bottle of red. 'It is an early sample of our 2006 vintage, which we are all hoping may be one of our best yet.'

'Thank you,' Ally said as her glass was filled to the brim. 'I'm afraid I don't know much about wine, but *santé*!'

'*Santé*.' Everyone raised their glasses, and she noticed that even the young boy Gérard had a small amount in his glass.

Ally tasted the wine, which was smooth and rich and slipped down her throat like velvet. 'You are right, this wine is beautiful,' she said to François.

'We will hope and pray that in the future, when it is finally ready, we will be winning medals for it,' he said.

Ally noticed Jack was looking in mild bewilderment around the table.

'François was just saying that he hopes this wine will win him some awards,' she translated into English.

'Ah, thanks. I've been here for a few weeks, and even though I'm doing my best to build up my vocabulary, they speak too fast for me to understand more than the odd sentence.'

'French is a hard language to learn. I was lucky because my father made sure my sisters and I were bilingual from the cradle. It's the only way.'

'I agree. My mum can speak decent French and read Latin and Greek, but it wasn't a gift that was passed on to me, I'm afraid,' said Jack. 'Sorry, I didn't catch your name?'

'I'm Ally, Ally D'Aplièse.' Ally held her breath to see if he recognised her surname.

'Jack McDougal. As you've just been told, I'm from New Zealand. And where are you from?'

'Geneva, in Switzerland,' Ally said, relief flooding through her that he obviously didn't know who she was. Ginette brought out a tray of food and Jack immediately stood up to help her, loading platters of salad and bread onto the table.

'Geneva, eh? I've never been there, or anywhere else in Europe for that matter, other than France. Is it a good place to live?' he asked as people around the table began to help themselves to the food.

'Yes, it's beautiful. We live on the lake with a lovely view of the mountains. But actually, at the moment, I'm living in Norway. Geneva is my family home,' she said as Jack offered her a platter of tuna salad. 'Thanks,' she said, taking the wooden spoon and doling a good portion onto her plate because she was starving.

'A quick warning: don't eat too much of this – it's only the starter. We have steak coming up after, and then, of course, cheese,' he grinned. 'Wow, do the French eat well.'

Ally could hear that his accent sounded vaguely Australian, but softer.

'Thanks for the warning. I'm actually really hungry. It was a long drive down here today.'

'How far?'

'Oh, it's almost four hundred kilometres from Geneva, but there's a pretty good *autoroute*.'

'So, why are you down here?'

'I'm . . . house-hunting.'

'I don't blame you. If I didn't have a vineyard to run in New Zealand and the language wasn't so hard, I'd be here like a shot.'

'How come you're such a long way from home?' Ally asked as she took a forkful of the salad – a mix of crisp green beans, tomatoes, egg and tuna, with a sharp creamy dressing.

'I'm here to learn the whys and wherefores of French wine-making to see if I can apply some of their old traditions and new ideas to our own wines. And maybe try some new combos of grapes too. I mean,' he said, taking a swig of his wine, 'if I could make something that comes even close to this, I'd die happy.'

'So you're passionate about wine?'

'Totally. I grew up on the vineyard that my father founded. He was one of the first to set up in New Zealand, and he and Mum went through blood, sweat and a load of sacrifices to get the vineyard to where it is today. It's the family legacy, so to speak. My father died a few months ago, so now it's all down to me. I miss the old boy. He might have been a pain at times, but not having him there with me has been tough.'

As he reached for the bottle to pour himself another glass, Ally could hardly believe how the conversation was flowing between them. Jack seemed so open, so natural . . . no airs and graces whatsoever.

She helped clear the plates with Ginette, and then brought out dishes of tiny roasted potatoes and broad beans, while Ginette delivered a *filet de boeuf* to her husband to be portioned out between the diners.

'*Mon Dieu!*' Ally said as she tasted the tender steak – pink in the middle, just how she liked it. 'This is delicious.'

'Everything here is, and this steak is a real treat – at home we were more a lamb than beef family,' Jack smiled. 'Mind

you, we are getting more head of cattle around the place these days. So, Ally, you said earlier that you have sisters?'

'Yes, I do,' Ally said, suddenly realising she must tread carefully. 'Five in all.'

'Wow! I've got one sister, and she's quite enough, thanks.'

'Are you two close?' she asked, steering the conversation back to him.

'These days, yeah, we are. She's adopted, actually. I was ten when she arrived so we never really grew up together, but we've got closer as we've got older. She was very cut up about Dad dying. She's only twenty-two, y'see. She feels a bit cheated, I suppose, because she didn't have him around for long. And of course, my mum misses him like crazy.'

'I'll bet she does. I managed to lose both my father and my fiancé last year, so it sounds like we've both had a bit of a time.'

'Did you? I'm so sorry, Ally. The most I can say about the past year is that it's hopefully produced a pretty good pinot noir. It'll be my first batch,' said Jack. 'Is that why you're here?'

'What do you mean?'

'Well, my mum's off somewhere at the moment on a world tour. Maybe women need to get away when something bad happens . . . not that I mean you have, or anything. Sorry, I know nothing about your circumstances at all.'

Ally saw Jack's face reddening in embarrassment. 'Don't apologise. You might be right. I think everyone reacts in their different ways to grief – all my sisters definitely did. On the other hand . . .' Ally turned to Jack and smiled in the dimming light. 'You're a long way from home, too.'

'Touché!' he said, clinking his glass against hers. 'Although my trip was actually planned before my dad died, so I have an excuse. Whatever gets you through, that's what I say.'

There was another pause as both of them helped collect the used dishes and then bring the cheese to the table. Someone had lit the lanterns, which cast a soft glow under the loggia.

'So, Miss . . . Christ, I've forgotten your surname.'

'D'Aplièse.'

'So, Miss D'Aplièse,' Jack continued as the dessert wine was being passed around, 'I seem to have, as usual, blurted out everything about myself. What about you? I mean, what's your passion?'

'I trained as a flautist, but then I got sidetracked and ended up sailing in some pretty big races. This time last year I was down in Greece in the Aegean Sea. Then I did the Fastnet and—'

'*What?!* I can't believe you were racing the Fastnet! That's like, well, the ultimate sailing challenge, and means that you're at the top of your game. Where I live in the Gibbston Valley, the lakes are where it's at, so I took some lessons and loved it. Then during my gap year, I joined a crew and took sailing trips around the NZ coast. It was nothing like proper racing, of course – just for pleasure – but there's just something about being out on the ocean, isn't there?'

'There is, yes. I'm impressed, Jack. There aren't many people who even know what the Fastnet Race is! Sadly, that's when I lost my fiancé. He was captaining our boat. We ran into stormy weather, and . . . well, he died trying to save the life of one of our crew.'

'Christ, I'm so sorry, Ally. Actually, I think I may have read about the accident in a newspaper. They always say, don't they, that what the sea gives, it takes away. And you sure lost a lot.'

'Yes, I did, but at least . . .' Ally was about to tell Jack about Bear, but something stopped her. 'I'm recovering now.'

'So, how long are you staying here?'

'I don't know yet,' she hedged.

'Well, if you're around for a while, maybe we could head to Marseille and rent a boat for a day. I'll be second mate and you can show me how it's really done.'

'That sounds appealing, although I doubt I'll have time. I love the Med – it's a breeze compared to the Celtic Sea and the Atlantic.'

'So who's at home in Geneva? Your mum, your sisters?' he asked.

'Ma's still at home, but my sisters have flown the nest.' Again, Ally purposely turned the conversation back to Jack. 'Excuse me if I'm sounding nosy, but why do you think your parents adopted your sister ten years after you? I mean . . . had they always planned to adopt, or was it some other reason?'

'I'm not sure, to be honest. Y'know what parents are like with their kids – they don't go into detail. I was only ten and didn't ask. The way I remember it is, one day I came home from school and there was Mary-Kate in my mum's arms, with my dad looking on. He was completely besotted with her actually. In those early years it used to tick me off, t'be honest.'

'Being an only child for a long time and then suddenly being presented with a new baby sister must have been tough.'

'Yeah, too right,' Jack grinned. 'Suddenly I wasn't the centre of attention anymore. But once I turned eighteen, I went off to uni and got over myself. In retrospect, it was a good thing. I was probably a spoilt brat when I was growing up, and gave my sis a bit of a hard time, y'know? Teasing her and stuff. Mary-Kate's great these days and we get on really well, and Dad's death has defo brought us closer.'

Coffee arrived, which Ally drank, along with a large glass of water from the stoneware jug on the table.

'Try a little Beaumes-de-Venise? It's local nectar in a glass, literally,' Jack asked as he lifted up his own.

'No thanks. I've already drunk far more than I normally do.'

'I've drunk far more than I normally do every night since I arrived!' He laughed. 'Wine here is simply part of the daily menu. They even make my dad look sober, and he drank a bottle of wine a day. Just out of interest, how have you ended up in Norway?'

'As a matter of fact, I was adopted too. I traced my birth family to Norway, which is why I moved there. My birth mum is dead, but I live with my twin brother Thom. My biological dad, Felix – who would think all this alcohol was paradise – lives just up the hill from us in Bergen.'

'D'you think it's a good idea? I mean, to pursue your birth family? My sis told me over the phone recently that she'd had a couple of girls turn up on her doorstep, saying there might be some connection to their family. I don't know the details, but I just wonder what you think?'

Ally swallowed and wished she *had* taken a glass of the dessert wine. Having thought she'd have to prise information out of this man, it all seemed to be coming up more or less naturally in the conversation.

'To be honest, I don't think I ever considered it until Pa died,' said Ally. 'He was . . . well, he was just enough, if you know what I mean. For me, anyway. In answer to your question, finding my birth family was fantastic, but then again, I'd lost the two loves of my life within a few months of each other, so to find I had a brother and a biological father – no matter how much of a soak he is – was wonderful.'

'Well, maybe now Dad's gone and Mary-Kate seems to have been contacted by these girls, she'll look into her birth family too. I hope she's as lucky as you.'

'So she doesn't know who her birth parents were?'

'No,' Jack shrugged. 'As I can't remember Mum and Dad going far to get her or anything, it must have been a local adoption.' He took a swig of his dessert wine. 'Wow, this is some conversation we're having, Ally. I hope I haven't said anything to upset you.'

'Not at all. Sometimes it's easier to talk with strangers about these things than it is to talk to the people you love, isn't it?'

'True, though I hope you won't be a stranger over the next couple of days. It's been good to talk to someone in English for a change,' he grinned. 'So, are you off house-hunting tomorrow?'

'I've written down the names of some *immobiliers* that are very good,' Ginette piped up in French as she poured them both more coffee. 'I'll go to the kitchen and get them.'

'Actually, I'm tired from my drive today, so I think I'll be heading for my bed now anyway.' Ally stood up, feeling her breasts heavy with milk, ready for Bear's night-time feed. 'Goodnight, Jack, it's been a pleasure to meet you.'

'And you, Ally. Hopefully I'll see you around in the next couple o'days,' he said as Ally followed Ginette into the kitchen.

'*À bientôt*,' she replied with a smile.

'There you are.' Ginette handed her an old envelope on which she'd jotted down the names and numbers of three *immobiliers*.

'Thank you so much for a wonderful evening. The food was amazing.'

'*Merci*, Ally, I am happy you enjoyed yourself,' she said as she led Ally to the front door. 'You and Jack seemed to be getting on very well,' she added, opening the door.

'Oh, that's just because we both speak English,' Ally said,

feeling her face getting hot. 'He seems like a very nice guy, though.'

'He is, and it was good for him to have someone who spoke his language. I worry he feels left out from our conversations over dinner, but what can you do? *Bonne nuit*, Ally.'

'*Bonne nuit*, Ginette, and thank you again.'

24

Ally woke up the following morning, rolled over to check the time on the old clock radio, and was stunned to see it was past ten o'clock.

She rolled onto her back, spread out her arms and legs and enjoyed the sensation of feeling rested – albeit with a slight headache from too much wine. Reaching for her mobile, she checked there had been no overnight messages from Atlantis, then saw a text from Star saying, **Call me!**

Not inclined quite yet to break the feeling of peace, she got out of bed to make coffee, then sat cross-legged on the soft mattress, sipping it and looking out of the window across the vincyard. She couldn't remember when she'd last enjoyed an evening more than last night. The gorgeous setting, combined with the convivial and welcoming company, had been a joy. There'd been lots of laughter around the table, and of course, her conversation with Jack had been a minefield, but still, a pleasure too.

They'd spoken so openly, like she used to with Theo, yet the two men could not have been more different: Theo, an intellectual at heart, despite his 'day job' as a sailor, and Jack, intelligent and obviously thoughtful, but a less complex soul than her fiancé. Even in the looks department, Theo had not been tall, even though he was strong, and his tanned skin and

dark hair contrasted completely with Jack's height and fair features. 'Ally, honestly!' she chided herself, feeling almost as if she was betraying Theo by enjoying another man's company. But it was the first time she had done so since his death, and it was okay to make a new friend, whether they be male or female, surely?

Is that all it is, though . . . ?

'So why didn't you tell him about Bear, or come clean about why you're really here?' she murmured as she stood to top up her coffee.

The truth was, she didn't know – or maybe didn't *want* to know – the reason just now.

Her mobile rang on the bed next to her, and having checked it wasn't Atlantis but Star again, Ally didn't feel up to speaking to her until she'd got her thoughts in order. Her feelings of guilt intensified as she thought about Jack's honesty, when she was here under completely false pretences.

Sighing, she picked up the mobile and placed a call to Atlantis. 'Hi, Ma, how's Bear?'

'He is perfect, Ally. I've just taken him for a walk, and now he is sleeping peacefully in his pram in the shade of the oak tree just beyond the terrace—'

'Where you used to put all of us,' Ally finished for her with a smile.

'And how are you, *chérie*? How is my beautiful Provence?'

'Beautiful indeed. The *cave* owners I'm staying with are lovely too and I slept really well last night. So thanks to both you and Maia for persuading me to come. How is she, by the way?'

'Oh, the same,' Ma said, 'but . . . well, it is the way these things are, *n'est-ce pas*?'

Ma knows Maia is pregnant, Ally thought instantly.

'She is in her Pavilion, sorting through a few things she

wishes to take back to Brazil,' Ma continued, 'and making it ready for when Floriano and Valentina arrive. She has her mobile if you wish to speak to her, but I should tell you that Star is eager to get in touch with you. Perhaps you can call her?'

'Of course.'

'When do you think you will be back, Ally?'

'As soon as possible, but I've still got some information to gather.'

'Take as long as you wish, *chérie*, I am loving my time being *grandmère* to your dear little boy.'

'Thanks, Ma. Give him the biggest hug from me, won't you?'

'Of course. Goodbye, Ally.'

Having dressed in a pair of shorts and a T-shirt, Ally munched on some now rather stale baguette with butter, and decided she must go and find the nearest supermarket to buy supplies. Pulling on a cap and sunglasses to try to stop the incessant march of the freckles across her already pink-tinged face, she went and sat outside to enjoy the mellow morning breeze while she spoke to Star.

'Hi, Ally, how are you?'

'I'm fine, thank you. You sound a bit breathless, is everything all right?'

'Yes, I just wanted to know if you managed to locate Mrs McDougal's son at the *cave*?'

'I did. In fact, I sat next to him at dinner all night.'

'Ooh! That's fantastic, Ally. Did you find out anything about Mary-Kate's birth parents?'

'Nothing, I'm afraid. Although we did have a very open conversation about adoption. He said he just remembers his parents arriving home with Mary-Kate one afternoon, so he thought it was a local adoption. His mother doesn't seem to

have warned him to avoid anything to do with us D'Aplièse sisters, but he did say that Mary-Kate had mentioned CeCe and Chrissie's visit to him when they last spoke on the phone. And that he thought she might want to find out more about her birth family. He was so friendly, I feel awful about not coming clean to him about why I'm here. What's happened at that end? Has Merry run away again?'

'We don't think so, no. Orlando followed her yesterday to Clerkenwell – she was apparently headed for the records of births, marriages and deaths. He trailed her back to the hotel, then she disappeared into her room, and I got a call to my suite at around six p.m. to say she wasn't feeling well and could we leave having dinner together. She said she was going to call back this morning to let us know how she felt and whether she could have lunch with us. The problem is, that a) I have to return to Kent to pick up Rory from school, and b) Orlando needs to get back to the bookshop. Obviously he'll stay on if Merry agrees to lunch, but . . . oh, I don't know, it just all feels wrong. Even Orlando is depressed, which he very rarely is. I just feel bad that she's scared of us and we're still pursuing her. I mean, it's not the end of the world if Mary-Kate can't be there for the laying of the wreath, is it, Ally? Having seen that ring with my own eyes, I do think it's the same one as in the picture, but maybe we should just wait until poor Merry has enjoyed her world tour and is back home with her daughter. Then they can decide together whether Mary-Kate wants to meet us all.'

'I know what you mean,' Ally sighed. 'Well, I'll call you later if I bump into Jack again, but I'm not going to engineer it, Star.'

'No. I totally understand. I've got to go now. Bye, Ally, speak soon.'

Ally came off the phone, like Orlando, feeling vaguely

depressed by the whole situation. There was part of her that just wanted to forget all about her initial motivation, and simply enjoy the feeling of calm she'd woken up with. She was about to get up and take a walk up to the farmhouse to see if Ginette could point her in the direction of the local supermarket when Jack suddenly appeared from around the corner.

'Morning. I'm not disturbing you, am I?' He pointed to the mobile still cradled in Ally's hands.

'Not at all. Would you like to sit down?'

'Sorry, I can't. I'm actually here to ask whether you need any food supplies. François is out at meetings about the upcoming harvest, so when I'm at a loose end, Ginette sends me to the village to do some shopping for her. She says it's good for my French,' he grinned.

'As a matter of fact, I was just about to go and ask her where the nearest supermarket was. And the local *immobilier*, of course,' she added quickly. 'I should get registered there at least.'

'Why don't I give you a lift into Gigondas? We can kill two birds with one stone and you can help me out in the supermarket, so I don't get my *ananas* mixed up with my *anis*!'

'Okay, but are you sure you don't want me to follow you in my car? Otherwise you'll have to wait for me to go to the *immobilier* office.'

'I don't mind. While François is out, it's either me sitting around, poring over a French dictionary to find out what a particular viticulture phrase means, or having a beer in the sun in beautiful Gigondas.'

'You could always do both at the same time,' Ally pointed out, and they chuckled.

'Right, I'll leave you to get whatever you need and meet you by the car in ten, okay?'

'Okay, thanks, Jack.'

'No problem.'

Arriving in the picturesque village of Gigondas, which Jack explained was one of the finest *appellations* in the region, Ally saw it was crammed with tourists, keen to sample the wines on offer from local *caves*. The cafés were humming with conversation, the diners seated at tables spilling out onto the pavements. They struggled to find a parking space for Ginette's battered Citroën.

'What a gorgeous little place this is,' Ally commented as they walked down the hill in the bright sunshine.

'It is, yeah. Right, let's dive into the supermarket and get the stuff from Ginette's list, shall we?' said Jack, entering a narrow shop which was like a Tardis on the inside, stretching right back and packed to the gills with foodstuffs.

'Okay, but I'm not going to help you,' Ally told him firmly. 'Making mistakes is the only way to learn languages.'

They each collected a basket and went their separate ways, before meeting at the till.

'Could you at least check that the stuff I've got corresponds with what's on the list?' he asked her as they waited in the queue to pay.

Ally did a quick search of the basket and checked the products off the list. 'Almost perfect, but she wants *demi-écrémé*, not *entier* milk.'

'Great, thanks,' he said and whizzed off to exchange the carton.

After dumping the bags in the car, Jack walked her along the street until they stood in front of the *immobilier* office. Ally tried the door, but it was firmly shut.

'Damn! It's literally one minute past midday and they've locked their door. Typical bloody French,' Jack chuckled.

'Lunch always comes first. Sorry – we're speaking in English, so I keep forgetting that you're actually French.'

'No, Jack, I'm Swiss, remember?'

'O'course, sorry,' he said as they walked back up through the village towards the car. 'Actually, I think the French have got their priorities absolutely right: enjoying the good things in life is what it's all about. You're only here once, after all,' said Jack.

'If you were my sister Tiggy, she'd disagree with you on that.'

'Really? Listen,' Jack said, pointing to an outdoor café swarming with lunchtime diners, 'why don't we hang around here until the *immobilier* reopens at two? Unless you have something else to do?'

'I don't, but doesn't Ginette need her shopping?'

'Not until later, and she's probably glad to see the back of me for a while. Shall we?'

'Why not?'

At the café, Jack indicated a free table for two and they sat down. 'Beer? Wine?' he asked. 'As I'm here, I'm going to grab some lunch too. You?'

'A glass of rosé for me, and yes, this menu looks delicious.'

'Well, if we can ever get any service, we'll order,' Jack rolled his eyes. 'I once waited twenty minutes for someone to even notice I was breathing over here. It wouldn't happen in New Zealand, that's for sure.'

'I've heard it's a beautiful country, from everyone who's been there.'

'It is, yeah, it just about has everything, y'know? Skiing in the winter, hot weather and beaches in the summer, and the interior – where I live – is sweet as. All it's lacking outside the towns and cities is people. Our nearest neighbour is a fifteen-minute drive away. So if you like solitude, it's great.'

'So, do you? Like solitude?'

'Not after I came back from uni, I didn't, but I suppose I got used to it. Then you come to a place like this, a little village that's just buzzing, and you wonder what the hell you're doing. Still, I'm not complaining. I love what I do, and I live in a stunning part of the world.'

'New Zealand's actually on my bucket list to visit one day,' she said as she raised her menu at a passing waiter, who blatantly ignored her.

'It goes without saying that we'd be happy to host you at The Vinery anytime. Another problem with the Gibbston Valley is that all the young have gone to the towns and cities, and it's mostly oldies living around me. I look forward to the company of backpackers touring the area, who sometimes hitch up in The Vinery to bag a bunk for the night.'

Ally flapped her menu at the waiter as he returned and finally, their order for beer, rosé, a jug of water and two steak hachés was taken.

'So, I presume your parents are Kiwis?' she said.

'No Kiwi is an "original", if you know what I mean, other than the Maori,' said Jack. 'Most of the population have emigrated from somewhere else. I was born there, but my dad's parents were originally from Scotland, hence the McDougal. And my mum hails from Dublin in Ireland. But yeah, I guess they'd both call themselves Kiwis, having lived there so long.'

'Do your parents ever go back to visit Scotland and Ireland?'

'I think Dad went back a couple of times with his parents, but Mum's never been back to Ireland as far as I know. I mean, there's a pic of her receiving a degree from uni there but I reckon that when people begin a new life, they want to focus on the present, not the past.'

'I'd agree,' she said as the waiter dumped two jugs, a bottle

of beer and some glasses on the table. Ally peered into both of the jugs looking for the water.

'*Mon Dieu!* One jug is full of rosé. I only asked for a glass!'

'That's not the way they do things round here,' Jack smiled as he poured her both water and rosé. 'Cheers!'

'Cheers,' said Ally, raising her glass. 'Going back to your mum, as I told you last night, when I went in search of my own heritage, parts of it were painful and parts of it were fantastic.'

'Well, Mum did mention that she's going to visit Ireland at some point on her tour.'

'Right. Is she on this holiday by herself?'

'Yeah. MK – that's what I call my little sis – and I weren't too happy about it, but Mum's pretty independent and seriously clever, y'know? T'be honest, I've never understood why she buried herself in the Gibbston Valley with my dad and didn't use her degree.'

'Maybe because she loved your father,' Ally suggested. 'Love can change everything.'

'True, but I'm yet to experience that feeling, to be honest. You obviously have.'

'Yes, and even if I never feel it again, at least I know I had it once. So your sister's holding the fort in New Zealand while you and your mum are away?'

'Not really – we have a very good manager who sorts out the vineyard. My sister's a budding singer-songwriter, and she's working on stuff with a guy she met at uni.'

'Wow. This is a terrible question, but . . . is she any good?'

'As you're never likely to meet her, I can be honest,' Jack chuckled. 'And the answer is, I haven't a clue. She's obsessed with Joni Mitchell and her type – all angsty lyrics – whereas I was born a decade before her and like a good tune, y'know?'

'I do know,' Ally agreed. 'Something "feel good" that you

can bop along to and shout out the lyrics. I was playing that kind of music on the drive down here.'

'This might be a rude thing to ask a lady, but would you be near my age? I'm thirty-two.'

'I'm thirty-one.'

'So, we're from the same generation and like a good anthem,' he grinned. The two steak hachés arrived and Jack asked for another beer.

'You are driving,' Ally reminded him.

'Yeah, but there's a lot of me to soak up the booze. They're only small bottles, Ally, and I'd never take the risk of being over.'

'I understand, and the good news is, because you are driving, I can have as much of this as I want,' she smiled as she poured herself a second glass of rosé.

'So, tell me about your sister Tiggy. She sounds interesting,' Jack said as he dug into his steak.

'Oh, my sisters are all interesting, and we couldn't be more different from each other.'

'In what way?

As she ate, Ally regaled Jack with a potted biography of each of them, being careful to use CeCe's proper name, Celaeno, in case his sister had mentioned her. When she got to Electra, Jack gave the usual response.

'I can't believe you're related to her! Her pic has been everywhere here in the past week. Wow, it makes my family seem so dull,' sighed Jack. 'Your dad sounds like he was a real philanthropist to adopt you girls.'

'He was, and an incredible man too. Like your mum, he was very clever.'

'What did he do?'

'Believe it or not, none of us are actually sure. We knew he ran a business of some kind, but what exactly, I've no idea. He was away a lot, travelling.'

'D'you think he was a spy?'

'Maybe, but I'm not sure spies make as much money as Pa did,' Ally chuckled. 'We were brought up in real luxury, although interestingly, he never gave any of us more than a basic allowance. We've all had to fend for ourselves financially.'

'Well, if it's any comfort, you certainly don't come across as a spoilt brat.'

'It is. Thanks.'

'Apart from that swanky car you arrived in,' Jack teased her. 'That's a cracker, f'sure. Is it yours?'

'It belonged to Pa, but any of us could use it if we wanted to. Of course, when Pa died, none of us wanted to deal with the nuts and bolts of our finances. Luckily, we've had people to run the trust he left for us, but we're going to organise a meeting with our lawyer in the next few weeks to have it explained to us. It's time we all grew up and took responsibility.'

'That all sounds far too complicated to me. At least when you don't have much, you don't have a lot to sort out,' Jack shrugged. 'When my dad died, the house passed to Mum, and the wine business to the three of us. End of. Coffee?'

'I think I'd better,' Ally agreed. 'The *immobilier* should be open soon, so after coffee, I'll go and register.'

'Okay, and hey, Ally, don't think I've got a problem with you coming from money or anything. It's completely to your father's credit and yours that I'd never have guessed it.'

'Apart from the car,' they both said at the same time, then laughed.

'This is my treat,' Ally said when the waitress arrived, and she slapped some euros on the table.

'Actually, little rich girl, it's definitely mine,' Jack said, slapping his euros down equally hard.

Having agreed to go dutch, they walked to the *immobilier*, where Ally registered and, given the fact she was feeling uncomfortable about Jack thinking she was a spoilt princess, made a point of looking for properties under two hundred thousand euros.

'That one's nice,' said Jack, peering over her shoulder at the listings.

'It's an old wreck and the last thing I want is to have to employ a team of builders to renovate something. What about this one?'

As they debated about the imaginary properties she might buy, Ally felt like a complete charlatan.

'Come on, let's go back to the *cave*. I'm feeling too depressed now I've seen what's available for the money I've got to spend. And no, I can't go any higher,' she said pointedly as they walked outside and along the narrow street towards their car. 'So, are you actually managing to learn anything at all whilst you're here, considering the language barrier?'

'Yeah, I've learnt a sackload of stuff,' he said as they climbed into the car and he started up the engine. 'A lot of it is watching the practical process, so you don't need words to explain what they're doing. The problem is, the soil here is more alkaline than it is back at home, but I'm definitely gonna try growing a few different vines and test out the mix of grapes they use here for the Châteauneuf-du-Pape.'

'How much longer are you staying?'

'Technically, until after the harvest. In reality, I could stay in Europe longer if I wanted, because it's the quiet period for me at the vineyard back home. So I just might go visit some other countries whilst I've got the chance. Y'never know, I might pitch up in Norway.'

'Feel free to do so,' Ally said as they arrived back at the

cave, and she got out of the car to help Jack take the shopping inside.

'Good afternoon,' Ginette said as she stood in the court-yard. 'I wondered where you two had got to. Can you take that shopping into the kitchen? I have to collect the children from school.'

'O'course,' Jack agreed.

'Oh, and Ally? You are very welcome to eat with us again tonight.'

'Thanks, Ginette,' Ally said as she followed Jack into the kitchen. The room – in fact, the whole farmhouse – was in need of renovation, she thought, as she unpacked the bags and stowed perishables into the fridge.

'Does François make any money from his wine?' she asked Jack.

'Not a lot, because any spare profit he makes is just poured back into expanding the vineyard or updating the machinery. The oak barrels down in the cellar are over a hundred years old. Last winter, they got a shedload of rain, so he's had to spend a lot of money making it watertight. That's climate change for you,' Jack shrugged. 'All right, I need a cuppa.'

'A cuppa?'

'A cuppa tea,' Jack explained as he took the kettle and filled it from the tap. 'They don't go big on tea here in Provence. I had to go and buy this myself,' he added as he switched it on. 'And the teabags. Want one?'

'Oh, I'm fine, actually. I'm going to walk back to my *gîte*. I have a few phone calls to make.'

'Okay. You coming over tonight?'

'I . . . does Ginette invite all her guests to eat with the family?'

'Only the ones she likes. So she obviously likes you.'

'I don't want to impose.'

334

'Let me promise you that if Ginette didn't want you, she wouldn't have asked. It's her that rules the roost around here, not François. Like all women, I suppose,' Jack smiled. 'See you later?'

'Okay, yes. Bye, Jack.'

Ally walked back through the vines with her own bag of shopping, which would now be redundant as she was having supper at the farmhouse. Pouring herself a large glass of water to try and ward off the headache she always got if she drank at lunchtime, she went to sit outside and dug in her handbag to check her mobile, which had been on silent ever since she'd left for Gigondas with Jack this morning. As she'd expected, there were a number of missed calls. None of them were from Atlantis, thank God, just from Star. Ally dialled her number.

'Hi, Star, it's me. I haven't listened to any messages you've left, so tell me, what's happened?'

'I'm afraid we've lost her, Ally. Even though Orlando sat in the hotel lobby all day, he nipped to the loo and came back to find she'd gone. I'm back in Kent, just about to go and collect Rory, and Orlando is following on by train. We've no idea where she's gone, Ally. The trail is cold.'

'Oh dear.' Ally bit her lip. 'I'm sorry, Star. I know you tried really hard to get her to talk.'

'We did. Orlando's furious with himself for missing her. The doorman on duty was told to watch out for her, but apparently, a big party of guests had just arrived. She somehow managed to slip out. Are you still at the *cave*?'

'Yes. I've spent most of the day with Jack – he took me to the local village so I could visit the *immobilier*, but it was shut, so we had lunch. Honestly, Star, he doesn't know anything much about his family's past. He told me that his mum was from Dublin in Ireland and had a degree from Trinity – which we already knew – but I'm afraid that's all. I'm seeing

him tonight as I'm having dinner up at the farmhouse again, but I feel really uncomfortable about probing him any further.'

'Orlando is convinced it's to do with any mention of the missing sister. Maybe you should ask Jack if that means anything to him.'

'No, Star, I couldn't. Sorry, but he's such a nice guy and I'm a terrible liar. It's now blatantly obvious his mum is avoiding us, and I'm thinking that maybe we should give the whole thing up for now.'

There was a pause on the line.

'I understand, Ally, and I agree. Anyway, it sounds like you've struck up a friendship with Jack at least. What's he like?'

'Lovely.' The word was out of Ally's mouth before she could stop it.

'Really?' Star chuckled. 'I haven't heard you say that about a man since, well . . . Anyway, just forget everything else and enjoy dinner tonight. I've got to be off now to fetch Rory. Bye, Ally.'

'Bye, Star.'

As she approached the farmhouse that evening, Ally felt totally conflicted. So much of her just wanted to enjoy the dinner and Jack's company, to go with the flow of the evening. Another part of her felt a need to tell Jack the real reason why she was here. She'd always tried to live her life as honestly as she could, albeit without hurting anyone by blurting out what she really thought, like Electra and CeCe often did. So if she were Jack, and down the line discovered that the friendly woman he had spent time with over the past twenty-four

hours had only been trying to pump him for information, she wouldn't want anything to do with that person again.

Does it matter if that happens? she pondered. *And if so, why . . . ?*

'Because he's a nice, decent guy, who treated you like a normal human being, not a victim,' she told herself as she marched up to the front door. 'Just drink wine, lots of it,' she muttered as she went to say hello to Ginette in the kitchen.

'I've brought you something small just to say thank you for being an incredible host,' said Ally. 'Sorry if it's a bit boring, but it's quite hard to think of anything to bring when you're hosted by a *cave* in one of the most beautiful places in the world. Even your flower beds are full of gorgeous specimens.' Ally pointed to a freshly picked bunch displayed in a vase on the kitchen table.

'Oh! Ladurée macarons! What a treat, thank you. Please, put them in the drawer over there so I can eat them all myself! You are leaving tomorrow?'

'Yes, sadly I must, but I'd love to come back again another time and stay for longer.'

'Did you see any houses that interested you?'

'No, it seems that properties here are far more expensive than I had thought.'

'Or maybe you were too distracted to look . . .' Ginette's eyes danced as she held up a courgette. 'I hear Monsieur Jack and you enjoyed lunch together earlier.' She smiled mischievously as she took a sharp knife to the courgette and began to chop it.

'Jack and I enjoyed talking because I speak English.'

'*Mon Dieu!*' Ginette ran a hand through her wavy dark hair. 'Why is everyone so afraid of saying that they are attracted to each other these days? It was obvious from the moment you sat down at the table last night that the two

of you had chemistry. Everyone who saw you commented on it. This is France, Ally, we invented the word "love". So what if you do want to spend a night, a week, a month or maybe a lifetime together? Those moments when you first meet someone who is as attracted to you as you are to them are so rare. And at the moment, everything is simple. No baggage has been unloaded, no soul explored . . .' Ginette gave a very Gallic shrug. 'What's not to enjoy? Now, if you are headed outside, can you take that tray of plates with you?'

'Of course,' Ally said, picking up the stacked tray, glad to have something to do. Maybe Ginette was right: she should just enjoy her last evening in the company of someone she liked. And – possibly – found attractive too.

Having received a warm welcome from everyone at the table, Ally was directed to the same seat as last night, next to Jack.

'Good evening,' he said, filling up her glass from a stoneware jug, rather than a bottle, as she sat down. 'We're on the usual Côtes du Rhône tonight, by the way. Basic table wine, but it's still a ripper.'

'Oh, I'm not fussy, I'll drink anything that's put in front of me.'

'Will you, eh? So it's vodka shots later, is it?'

'I didn't mean it like that, but if you're at sea for a while and you come into port with a load of thirsty men, you certainly learn how to handle your alcohol. *Santé.*' Ally raised her glass and smiled at him.

'*Santé.* I bet you kept them all in order, didn't you?' Jack teased her.

'As a matter of fact, I didn't at all. After the usual sexist comments, we'd push off out to sea and by the time we came back, they were calling me "Al" and barely noticed my gender.

I'd always pretend I was a rubbish cook so they wouldn't assign me to the galley on account of me being a woman.'

'And *are* you a rubbish cook?'

'Possibly,' Ally chuckled.

'What puzzles me is that in most of the houses I visited as a child, there were always mums in the kitchens, yet most of the really famous chefs are male. Why do you think that is?'

'I'm not sure I want to get into an argument about gender politics just now, Jack.' Ally knocked back another gulp of wine.

'You mean, you might end up slugging me over the head with that wine jug?'

'Hopefully it wouldn't be that dramatic, but after years in male-dominated environments, I certainly have a few things to say. Yup,' she agreed with herself and Jack poured her another glass of wine.

'Well, it's worth adding that my mum brought me up to have complete respect for the opposite sex, i.e. you lot,' he grinned. 'She taught me how to cook pasta, a roast and make a tuna salad – she said those three dishes would see me through any occasion.'

'Is she a good cook?'

'She's certainly no *cordon bleu*, but a legend at managing to produce a big pot of something tasty for large numbers from what's left lying around. Because of where we live, we can't just run round the corner to the local shop, y'know? She's fanatical about leftovers being eaten up – probably something to do with her childhood. These things usually are, from what little I know about psychology.'

'I . . .' Even though Ally was genuinely interested *beyond* gaining information on his mum, she still felt guilty for probing. 'Do you think she had a tough childhood?'

'As I said, she doesn't talk about it, and I don't think any

kid is interested in listening to the 'rents going on about their past. Now my dad is gone, and I can't ask him any more questions, I just keep wishing I had.'

'Same here,' Ally agreed as bowls of crudités and olive oil were placed on the table from anonymous hands above them. 'I can't tell you how many questions I've got now for Pa.'

'From the sound of things, you had a pretty idyllic childhood.' Jack offered her a bowl of crudités.

'Yes. We had just about everything we could ask for. A loving mother figure in our nanny, Ma, Pa's full attention whenever we needed it . . . and each other. I look back now and almost feel it was *too* idyllic. I think that's why Pa sent us all to boarding school when we were thirteen. He wanted us to know what the real world was like.'

'You're saying boarding school is the real world?' Jack queried. 'I mean, to get you there in the first place, your dad would have had to pay. Places like that were only available to the elite and still are, aren't they?'

'Yes, you're right, but mine didn't include any home comforts. It's a bit like being in a learning prison that you have to pay for, and you certainly get to know what humanity is like if you're living with it twenty-four hours a day. You have to learn to fight your own battles, without any kind of support from your parents.'

'So the rich go to boarding school to know what it feels like to be deprived?'

'I think that's a bit of a sweeping statement, but in essence, yes. Would I have wanted to go to a state-run school and be able to go home to my family every night? No matter what was on the table for supper or what kind of house we lived in? When I started boarding, I would have done. Then as I settled down to it and became more independent, I started to realise how privileged I was. The school offered me all sorts

of extramural opportunities I'd never have had at a state school.'

'Actually, my mum boarded too and said it was the making of her for the reasons you just mentioned, even though she hated it at first. I wonder what you'll do with your own kids when they come along?'

Jack was looking her right in the eye and Ally could feel a blush rising in her cheeks. Turning her head away and concentrating on her crudités, she shrugged.

'I'm not sure,' she replied lamely.

After a fantastic main course of wild boar, which no one round the table questioned the provenance of, given that shooting was illegal at this time of year, Ally went to the nearest bathroom and expressed some of the milk in her breasts to relieve the pressure and risk of leaking.

After washing her face in cold water, she stared at herself in the mirror.

'Remember what Ginette said,' she whispered, 'and just enjoy. Tomorrow, you're gone.'

'I must head for bed,' Ally said after coffee and a glass of delicious, if unnecessary, Armagnac. 'I have an early start in the morning.'

'Okay, I'll walk you home, shall I?' offered Jack.

Having said her goodbyes, left promises to all that she would return and told Ginette she'd see her early tomorrow morning to settle the bill, she and Jack walked down the now moonlit path to her *gîte*.

'If I was going to buy something here, I think the *gîte* would be almost perfect,' she commented.

'Apart from at harvest time, when it would be pretty noisy.

Plus, you'd have loads of sweaty grape-pickers peering in through your windows first thing in the morning. And spiders creeping in to join you from the vines.'

'Sell it to me, why don't you?' she smiled. 'I was just thinking how picturesque it looked in the moonlight. I wouldn't mind the spiders, after once finding a rat on my mattress on board ship. It must have scuttled in whilst we were in port and had decided to join us for the onward leg.'

'Wow! I guess even I'd have a problem with that. What did you do?'

'Admittedly, I screamed and one of the boys came to my rescue,' Ally laughed.

'Don't worry, I'd have done the same, but you're a hardy lass underneath that delicate exterior, aren't you?'

'I'm not sure about that, but there's not much that scares me these days, apart from losing someone else I care about.'

'Yeah, death puts it all into perspective, doesn't it? The thing that scares me is that I might find myself still working on my vineyard in thirty years' time, old and alone. As I've mentioned, there's not a lot of chances to meet with my own age group – there are any number of ageing single farmers and vintners living around me.'

'Does anyone ever really want to be alone?' sighed Ally.

'Well, better that than settling for someone simply for the sake of not being alone, eh?'

'Absolutely,' Ally agreed.

'Were you and your fiancé together for a long time? Sorry, I don't mean to pry or anything.'

'No, it's fine. Actually, we weren't. It was a whirlwind romance. I just knew that he was The One, and he felt the same, so we got engaged pretty quickly.'

'I get the feeling that's how it was for my mum and dad, although of course, you can never tell what goes on behind

closed doors. But when I compare their marriage to a lot of my mates' parents, they always seemed very happy. Never argued, y'know? Or at least, not within earshot of us. I worry about my mum now that dad's gone. She's almost sixty, so it's unlikely she'll meet anyone else.'

'What about all those bachelor farmers you just mentioned?'

'I doubt it. Mum and Dad were together for over thirty-five years. Talking of which, I got a strange call from Mum just before dinner tonight.'

'Really?' Ally's heart began to thump as they reached the entrance to the *gîte*. 'What about?'

'Oh, she wanted to tell me she'd flown over to Dublin earlier today, which is odd as I thought she was staying in New York for a bit to see old friends and then heading to London. I was, like, you must be excited to be back in the home country after all this time, and she was, like, yeah, well, I had to come back here, but you never know who you might meet from your past. It could have just been a joke, but to be honest, Ally, I thought she sounded, well,' Jack shrugged, 'frightened.'

'I . . . maybe everyone's nervous when they go back to the place they came from after so long?'

'Maybe, yeah, but then she said how much she loved me and how proud of me she was and all that kind of stuff. She sounded close to tears. I was wondering whether I should take a flight across to Ireland to make sure she's okay. It's only a couple of hours from Marseille to Dublin, and she just sounded . . . odd. What d'you think?'

Jack looked straight at her and Ally wanted to fall through the ground or disappear in a puff of smoke.

'Well, I – I . . . think that if you're worried about her, then maybe you should go. If it's not that far,' she stuttered.

'I'm still getting my head around the fact that nothing in Europe is that far,' he smiled. 'I'm used to it all being on the other side of the world.'

'Do you know where she's staying? I mean, with friends or . . . ?'

'Yeah, apparently the hotel she's at is called the Merrion, so she joked it was named after her – her nickname's "Merry". Anyway, I'll give her a bell tomorrow morning, see how she sounds and then decide.'

'Good idea. Right, time for my bed,' Ally said, once again feeling a blush running through her cheeks and just wanting to get inside.

'Listen, if I don't get to see you tomorrow, I just wanted to say it's been a pleasure to spend time with you. Could we keep in touch?'

'Of course we can, yes.'

'Great. I'll give you my NZ and my French mobile numbers.'

'And I'll give you my Swiss and Norwegian ones.'

They tapped their numbers into each other's phones.

'Well then, goodnight,' she said, reaching for the *gîte* key from her jean pocket and sticking it into the lock. As she turned it, she felt a pair of hands on her shoulders and jumped.

'Hey, sorry, Ally, I . . .' Jack was standing back with his hands up as though she was about to shoot him. 'I didn't mean to . . . I wasn't gonna . . . shit!'

'Seriously, don't worry. It's just, I'm not . . .'

'Ready?'

'Yes, not just now anyway, but I've really enjoyed spending time with you, Jack, and . . .' She looked up at him. 'Would a hug do?'

'O'course it would,' he smiled. 'Come here.' He pulled her

in towards him and everything about him smelt exactly as she had expected: fresh and natural and clean. She could feel the strength of him, and his height made her feel unusually like a fragile flower.

For all sorts of reasons, she pulled out of his grasp far sooner than she would have wanted to. He bent down and gave her a tender kiss on the cheek.

'*Bonne nuit*, Ally,' he said. 'I hope we meet again soon.'

With a rueful smile, he turned and ambled back up the gravel path to the farmhouse.

Inside, Ally felt short of breath and 'panty', as she'd once described the sensation to Ma when she'd had a panic attack just before she was about to sit her very first flute examination. Sitting down on the bed, she bent forward, trying to slow her breathing. Wondering exactly which part of the last ten minutes had caused this reaction, she reached for the bottle of water by the bed and took a swig from it. Finally, her breathing calmed, as did her pulse. Looking at her mobile, she saw there were no missed calls or new voice messages, which meant Bear was fine. There were texts from Star asking how the evening had gone and another from Maia saying basically the same thing.

Call me! they had both ended.

'Nope.' Ally shook her head. 'Not tonight.' She just wanted to keep the memory of the evening and that delicious hug exactly as it was for a few more hours, until she had to tell her sisters and it became another part of their joint subterfuge. Besides, she decided as she undressed, if Jack did fly to see his mum in Dublin tomorrow, she was bound to tell him about the strange women who were after her to try and claim his sister as one of their own . . .

'And he won't want to keep in touch after that, will he?' she muttered to herself as she got into bed, set the alarm and

turned off the light. She lay there staring into the darkness, remembering not only the hug but all the laughter they'd shared. It had been a long time since she'd really laughed, and even if Jack had referred to his lack of academic cleverness, it was obvious to her that he was highly intelligent.

'You don't necessarily need a stack of certificates to be wise,' Pa had once said to her when she had told him how insecure she'd felt about having a degree in music, rather than science or literature.

Jack's wise, she thought, before she drifted off to sleep.

25

Having slept badly, Ally was awake by six thirty and ready to go an hour later. She knew that Ginette would be up, preparing to drop the children at school, so she popped into the kitchen to pay her bill and say goodbye.

'It has been a pleasure to host you, Ally, and please come back and visit us soon,' Ginette said as the children ran in and out of the door, collecting lunchboxes, sports kit and books.

'I'd love to,' Ally responded as all of them walked outside and Ginette planted the region's customary three kisses on Ally's cheeks.

Glad not to have bumped into Jack on her way out, Ally set off for Geneva. Once on the *autoroute*, she pulled into an *aire* to use the facilities and to phone Atlantis.

'Hi, Ma, I'm on my way home. Is Bear okay?'

'You would know already if he wasn't. He's very much looking forward to seeing his *maman*,' Ma added.

'I'm sure that's not true, but thanks for saying it anyway, Ma,' Ally smiled. 'I'll see you later.'

'Maia would like to speak to you.'

'Tell her we'll talk when I get home,' Ally said firmly. 'I have to go now, Ma. Bye.'

Back in the car, Ally switched CDs to some of her favourite

classical pieces and relived every second of the past two days. Which for now, were *hers*, and hers alone . . .

By the time she arrived back at Atlantis, Bear was nodding on Ma's shoulder, ready for his afternoon nap. Taking him up to her bedroom, Ally put him to her breast.

'*Maman*'s home, darling, and she's missed you so much.'

Bear suckled for a few seconds, then his tiny lips let go and he lay back in her arms, fast asleep.

Logically, she was glad he seemed to have suffered no ill effects from her absence, but as she laid him down in his cot, the fact he had so easily ceased to need her still hurt.

She wished she could clamber into bed for a nap herself, but it wasn't fair on Maia, or any of her sisters who had participated in the search for the elusive Merry. She'd already waited since last night to tell them she knew exactly where Merry was. However she felt about her part in the ongoing plot, she had to at least pass on the information.

'Hello, Ally,' said Maia as her sister walked into the kitchen. 'Sorry I wasn't here to greet you when you arrived, Floriano had just called and I needed to speak to him about his flight over here. So, how was Provence?'

'Beautiful, as I said on the phone. Listen, Maia, I'm really tired after the drive, so forgive me if I cut to the chase. Jack told me that he got a call from his mum saying she was in Dublin, Ireland. She's staying at the Merrion Hotel there. The only other detail I got out of him was that she sounded, as he put it, "odd" and "frightened". Given she left London so suddenly, we've definitely scared her and I feel terrible about it.'

'Oh dear, that isn't good,' Maia agreed, 'but I understand. I'm sure it's because she doesn't want the child she's cared for

since birth to be claimed by another family. Perhaps she's scared that Mary-Kate might love them more.' Maia looked at Ally and bit her lip. 'Maybe we should just leave this whole thing?'

'That's what I said to Star last night. I mean, Jack is a decent, straightforward guy and I felt awful pretending I was somebody I wasn't – a passing tourist looking to buy a house in the area – especially when he said he was really worried about his mum's state of mind. I think we either have to come clean to Merry, or drop it completely. It's not a game, and I almost get the feeling that Orlando was treating it like one.'

'He was only trying to help, but maybe he enjoys the thrill of the chase too much. I mostly agree with you, Ally, but then again, I can't help thinking of Pa and how long Georg said he'd searched for the missing sister. I remember when I was a teenager, I asked him why our seventh sister had never arrived. And the look on his face was heartbreaking when he told me it was because he'd never found her.' Maia sighed. 'I don't know what we should do, I really don't.'

'Well, whatever it is, I think before we go any further we need to see Merry in person and put her mind at rest that we're not out to get her.'

Maia saw the tension on her sister's face. 'Oh Ally, I was hoping the trip to Provence would provide you with some time out to relax. You seem more tense now than when you left.'

'You know how I am about honesty. I'm just not comfortable with subterfuge and lies. I would have made the most terrible spy.'

'What about sending Tiggy? After all, she's the only other sister who hasn't participated in our search, and absolutely nobody could be frightened of her – she's the gentlest of us

all. If anyone can explain to Merry that we mean no harm, then it's her.'

'Yes, that's a great idea, Maia. And Scotland's not very far from Ireland, is it?'

'No, it's not.'

'All right,' Ally said with a sigh, 'let's at least ask her and see what she says.'

Maia took out her mobile and placed the call to Tiggy. To her surprise, after a couple of rings, she heard Tiggy's voice.

'Hello, Maia. I've just read Ally's email about the missing sister and had picked up my mobile to call . . . Is everything all right?'

'Yes, everyone is well here,' Maia replied. 'Ally's with me. How are you?'

'Oh, I'm good, I can't wait to see you both soon. Have you traced the missing sister and her ring yet?' Tiggy asked.

'It's a long story but . . .' Maia explained as briefly as she could what had happened in the past few days.

'We think it might be because she doesn't want Mary-Kate, her daughter, to know about her birth parents,' Maia finished.

'What do you think, Tiggy?' asked Ally.

There was silence on the line for a bit before Tiggy replied. 'It feels to me as if she is . . . frightened.'

'That's interesting, because it's exactly what her son Jack told me after he'd spoken to her yesterday. Would you, and anyone you know . . . well, *upstairs*, have any idea why?' Ally blushed as she referenced Tiggy's spiritual powers, but having witnessed them for herself in Granada, she was definitely a convert.

'I would need to think about it, and it's far easier if I can talk to the person than sense things from far away. But yes, my instinct is that she's afraid.'

'Well' – it was Maia's turn to speak – 'Ally and I were

wondering whether it would be possible for you to do just that – speak to her in person.'

'You have her telephone number?'

'Yes, Orlando got it, but we really need someone to go to see her in person and explain we don't mean any harm,' said Ally. 'We know exactly where she is, which isn't very far from where you are.'

'Everything's far from where I am,' Tiggy chuckled. 'Is she in Scotland?'

'No, Dublin. It can't be more than an hour or two's flight.'

'I probably could – I'm sure Cal can cope without me for a couple of days. It's just, well, the ethical thing that worries me. There's obviously a reason why she's running away and I don't want to scare her further by just appearing out of the blue. Can I think about it?'

'Of course,' Maia agreed, 'and if you don't feel it's right, then we'll leave it.'

'Give me half an hour. Oh, and by the way, Maia, ginger tea might help with your symptoms. Bye.'

The line went dead and both Ally and Maia sat there, staring at each other in surprise.

'I thought you said you hadn't told anybody else about the . . . you know?' Ally whispered, her hand indicating her sister's stomach.

'Ally, I haven't! Truly.'

'Well, I certainly haven't.'

'Then how does she know?' Maia asked.

'She just does,' Ally shrugged. 'In Granada, just before Bear was born, she told me things about Theo and this necklace he'd given me that she couldn't possibly have known about. She . . . she said she saw him standing there. I . . .' Tears pricked Ally's eyes. 'It was a very special moment. Our little sister has a unique gift.'

'Coming from you, Ally, who is always sceptical of anything you can't work out logically, that's saying a lot. Let's see what she's decided to do when she calls back.'

The sound of a text pinging through on Ally's mobile made her look down.

Hi, Ally, Jack from Provence/NZ here. Just checking you got back to Geneva safely. It was so great to meet you. Keep in touch and maybe we can get together in Europe before I fly home. Jack.

At the end of the text was one kiss. The sight of it made Ally's stomach flip suddenly.

'Who's that from?' Maia enquired.

'Jack, Merry's son.'

'Really? From your expression, you two obviously got on well.'

'I had to get on with him, didn't I? I had to pump him for information on his mum. I'm going upstairs to see if Bear's awake yet.'

Maia watched her sister walk out of the kitchen, then smiled. 'The lady doth protest too much, methinks,' she quoted from Shakespeare's *Hamlet*.

Later that evening, just as Ally was getting into bed, there was a knock on her bedroom door and Maia appeared.

'Tiggy's said she'll go. She's looking to get on an afternoon flight to Dublin tomorrow. It's less than two hours from Aberdeen.'

'Right. Great. Well, let's hope Merry won't have disappeared again by then, and Tiggy can get a chance to explain.'

'As Tiggy put it, "I doubt she'll have gone far." Anyway, I just thought I'd tell you.'

'I'm so glad she's going. If she does meet Merry, at least she can set the record straight.'

'Yes. Sleep well, Ally.'

'And you.'

Once the door had shut behind Maia, Ally lay back, suddenly feeling conflicted over Tiggy's decision. Morally, it was the right thing to do, but of course it would mean Jack would eventually get to hear from his mother about *her* part in the deception . . .

'For God's sake, Ally, you only knew him for less than forty-eight hours,' she told herself firmly.

But still, she spent ages agonising over whether or what she should text back, and went to sleep thinking about that kiss at the end of his . . .

26

Merry
Dublin, Ireland

I woke up with the alarm, which I'd set for nine o'clock, and lay there feeling rested after the first proper night's sleep I'd had since I'd left New Zealand. Perhaps it was partly to do with the fact that I was on 'home territory' – it felt comforting to be back in Ireland, which was ironic, given why I'd left Dublin all those years ago. Yet knowing that part of me belonged here, that I'd come from the very soil of this proud, unique and beautiful island, had made me emotional since the moment the aeroplane had touched down.

Jock had asked me time and again whether I wanted to visit my family in the 'old country', but I'd always refused. However much I missed them, I knew that they might let something slip to Jock about my hasty departure and, more importantly, because I had to protect them too. The truth was that I hadn't spoken to a single member of my family for thirty-seven years.

Lies, lies, lies . . .

'Enough is enough,' I said out loud to yet another beauti-fully appointed and furnished hotel room. Just in case there

was anyone lurking outside my door listening, I added, 'I'm not afraid anymore!'

I reached over to dial room service and asked for a pot of tea and some biscuits. Biscuits for breakfast felt indulgent, especially the homemade ones that hotels like the Merrion provided, but why shouldn't I indulge myself? I picked up one of the shiny leaflets that had been left by the phone to tempt me. I'd never been to a spa – every time I saw one in my mind, I imagined an ancient Roman bath full of ladies enjoying its restorative properties. I'd recently discovered the modern-day equivalent, which always seemed to be in the hotel basement, where long corridors opened onto treatment rooms filled with tinkling background music emanating from a discreetly hidden CD player. I flicked through the leaflets, wondering whether I would take the plunge and treat myself to one of the many massages on offer, but the menu was as varied and confusing as a Chinese takeaway.

A knock at my door caused my heart to immediately beat faster, but I took a deep breath and answered it. As a waiter greeted me, I thought that perhaps it was the lilting accent, along with the intrinsic Irish friendliness, that put me at ease. He came into the room to set up my breakfast on a small table, and asked me where I'd come from.

'London.'

'Would that be your home?'

'No, I live in New Zealand.'

'Do you now? Well, 'tis a long way you've travelled. I hope you enjoy your stay, Mrs McDougal.'

He left and I picked up the tea he'd poured and drew one of my spare teabags out of my holdall to add it to the pot. I'd decided hotel tea was watery no matter where you were in the world, but then again, I'd grown up with a brew so strong, it could strip the skin from your hands, as Jock had liked to say about the way I made it.

Back on the bed with my teacup, I thought how much I'd wanted to come out of hiding the moment I'd arrived on Irish soil. At passport control, I'd longed to announce in my broad childhood accent that I'd been born here and once held an Irish passport, but that everything about me and where I'd come from had been stripped away on purpose to protect myself and those that I loved.

Well, here I was, with a different name and nationality, returned to the land which had birthed me – and given me all the troubles that had sent me flying away from it . . .

So today, I was going in search of the one person in the world whom I trusted more than any other, but whom I'd been forced to leave behind too. I needed his help, and in light of the pursuers who had hunted me since I'd left New Zealand, I had nowhere else to turn.

I looked down at the ring my dear Ambrose had given me on my twenty-first birthday. Who would have known that something so small and beautiful and given out of love could have caused all this, simply because it identified who I'd once been?

At least, I *believed* it had been given out of love . . .

No, Merry, don't start doubting him, *because if you do, then you're really lost*, I reprimanded myself. *Now then, my girl, time for a shower and then we're going for a walk around the corner.*

At noon, I was standing in Merrion Square outside the tall, elegant town house that used to contain Ambrose's ground and basement maisonette. I checked surreptitiously through the window and saw the curtains, the lamp and the book-shelves looked exactly the same as they had when I'd last seen it.

The worst-case scenario would be that he was dead, and either a relative or a new buyer or renter had taken over his home without bothering to change anything.

'Just walk up those steps and knock on the door, Merry,' I told myself. 'He's eighty-five, so he's hardly going to shoot you where you stand, is he?'

I climbed the steps and pressed his bell, which struck the same two notes I remembered from all those decades ago. There was no answer for a while, but then a voice – a dearly beloved voice which I knew so well – spoke to me through a speaker grille above the bell.

'Ambrose Lister. Who is calling?'

'I . . . it's me, Mary O'Reilly. The girl from years ago. Ambrose, it's me!' I entreated, and by this time, my lips were virtually kissing the grille. 'Can I come in?'

'Mary? Mary O'Reilly?'

'Yes, 'tis me, even if I've lost my accent a bit, Ambrose. 'Tis me.'

Silence reigned as I gulped back tears caused by the few seconds I'd spent being who I'd been back then, and by the thought of seeing him again. Then the door opened and he was there.

'Jesus, Mary and Joseph!' I gasped. 'I'm sorry, I'm crying.'

'Goodness, in eighty-five years I haven't been so surprised. Please come in, so that we don't disgrace ourselves on this very public doorstep.'

Ambrose ushered me inside and I saw that even though he now walked with a stick, and had less hair (which hadn't been much back then) he was still completely who I remembered him as. Dressed in an old tweed jacket and a checked shirt with a dark green bow tie, his kind brown eyes seemed owlish behind thick round glasses. He was the only one to ever call

me Mary rather than 'Merry', and my heart swelled at hearing my name spoken in his clipped accent again.

Once the front door was closed, he led me along the hallway and into the sitting room. The desk in the window and two leather chairs situated opposite each other in front of a marble fireplace hadn't changed. Nor had the now threadbare sofa that sat against the wall, facing the overflowing bookshelves on either side of the fireplace. He closed the door, then turned around to look at me.

'Well now, well now . . .' was all he could manage.

I didn't do much better as I tried to gulp back my tears.

'I believe, even though it is only eleven o'clock, that some strong medicine is called for.'

Ambrose walked to one of the bookshelves and pulled out a bottle of whiskey, plus two glasses from the cupboard beneath it. As he placed the three items on his desk, I saw that his hands shook unsteadily.

'Shall I pour?' I asked.

'If you would, my dear. I find myself quite at a loss.'

'Sit down, and I'll sort us out.'

As Ambrose lowered himself into his favourite chair, I poured two generous measures, and handed one to him. Then I sat down in the chair opposite him.

'*Sláinte!*'

'*Sláinte!*'

We each took a large gulp that burnt my stomach a second later, but wasn't unpleasant. After we both drained our glasses in silence, Ambrose placed his down on the round side table next to his chair. I was glad to see that his hand was steadier now.

'I could use many quotes of renown to mark this moment, but I do not want to resort to either cliché or hyperbole,' he said. 'I will simply ask you where on earth you have been for the last

thirty-seven years? And you, I'm sure' – he put up a finger which I knew meant that he hadn't finished – 'will tell me that it's a long story. They are the best, but perhaps you could be brief initially and, as they say these days, cut to the chase.'

'I've been living in New Zealand,' I said. 'I married a man called Jock and we have two children. One called Jack, who is thirty-two, and the other named Mary-Kate, who is twenty-two.'

'And now to the most important question: have you been happy?'

'When I left, I was desperately unhappy,' I admitted, 'but eventually, yes. When I met Jock, I realised I needed to forget about the past and live with what I had found. Once I had done that, I was able to enjoy and appreciate life again.'

Ambrose paused, resting his elbows on the arms of the leather chair, his fingers under his chin. 'The next question is, whether you have the time and the wherewithal to tell me the minutiae of the intervening years. Or are you leaving again sometime soon?'

'At this moment, I have nothing planned that will take me anywhere else. Ironically, for reasons I want to talk to you about, I embarked on a Grand Tour that was meant to take me months. So far, I have been to four countries in about a week. I had planned for Ireland to be my last stop.'

Ambrose smiled at this. 'The schemes of mice and men, or should I add "and women". What matters is that you are here now, and even if my eyesight is fading fast, you look no different. You are still the beautiful young woman I loved, and last saw in this very room when she was only twenty-two years old.'

'Then your eyesight *is* fading, dearest Ambrose. I am nearly fifty-nine years of age now, and getting old.'

'So, it is possible you can spare me some time over the next

few hours – or days – to tell me why, in the first instance, you had to leave Ireland and cease all contact with me?'

'I intend to, yes. But that . . . well, that really depends on your response when I tell you about my current problem. Which has a lot to do with why I left Ireland in the first place.'

'Goodness! Are you in the midst of writing a Greek tragedy? Or are you describing the story of your life?' Ambrose raised an expressive eyebrow.

'Perhaps I am being overdramatic, but that's the reason I'm sitting here with you now. You're the only person left that I can truly ask for advice.'

'What about your husband? Jock?'

'My darling Jock died a few months ago. Which was when I decided to—'

'Revisit your past?'

'Yes.'

'And are you feeling that your past has perhaps caught up with you?' he asked, acutely perceptive as always.

'I am, yes. Completely . . .' I stood up. 'Would you mind if I helped myself to another whiskey?'

'Not at all, Mary. Pour me another drop too. I always think better when there's a rationed percentage of alcohol inside me, but please never tell any of my other ex-students that,' he said with a wink. 'There's also a tray of rather good sandwiches in the kitchen, which will soak it up. My daily, who does – or doesn't, as the case may be – everything for me, made them just before she left.'

'I'll go and get them.'

I walked down the dim corridor to the kitchen, and saw that not a single cabinet had been changed since I was last here, although there was a new cooker and even a microwave placed in one corner. The plate of sandwiches was made with soda bread and covered in cling film.

'Here we are,' I said as I returned and placed the plate on the side table next to him.

'Help yourself. One will be cheese and salad, the other ham and salad. It always is.'

'They look delicious; certainly better than anything Mrs Cavanagh ever provided,' I smiled, taking one.

'Ah, Mrs Cavanagh,' he sighed. 'Well, I may have missed out on a large portion of your life, dear Mary, but equally, you have missed out on a rather large portion of mine. And talking of portions, let us eat and continue the conversation once we have done so.'

Another silence descended as we ate the sandwiches. Ambrose had always taught me it was rude to talk with one's mouth full. And I had taught my own children the same.

'So, apart from your eyes, are you keeping well?' I asked when we had finished.

'I think the words "apart from" are the common denominator for anyone of my age. Apart from the rheumatism, and the rather high cholesterol – which I hasten to add I've lived with since my fifties – I'm as fit as a flea.'

'Do you get down to West Cork much these days?'

Ambrose's smile faded from his lips. 'Sadly I don't. In fact, I haven't been there since the early seventies, just a year or so after you left.'

'But what about Father O'Brien? You and he were such good friends.'

'Ah, now, Mary, that is a story for another day.'

I watched Ambrose's gaze move to the window and realised that whatever had ended their friendship had been a painful experience for him.

'I see you're still wearing the ring I gave you,' he said, turning back to me and pointing to it.

'Yes, although technically, it belongs to my daughter – I

gave it to her on *her* twenty-first birthday, but then I asked her if I might borrow it for this trip. I was worried that you might not recognise me after all these years, so I brought it with me as insurance.'

'Not recognise you? Mary, you are perhaps the most beloved person of my life! How could you possibly have thought that? Unless . . . ah.' Ambrose put up a finger to his head. 'You thought I may have lost my marbles, gone senile in my old age, eh?'

'To be truthful, it did occur to me that I may need something to jog your memory. Forgive me, Ambrose.'

'I will think about whether you deserve my forgiveness whilst you make us both a cup of coffee. I presume you remember the way I like it?'

'Strong, with just a hint of milk and one spoonful of brown sugar?' I asked him as I stood up.

'Precisely, my dear, precisely.'

I arrived back with the coffee five minutes later, having made myself a tea.

'So, where do you wish to start?' he asked me.

'I know it should be at the very beginning, but we may have to work backwards a little. If I give you the outline, would you let me fill in the blanks later?'

'Whatever you wish. I'm no longer needed at Trinity by my peers or students – I retired just over fifteen years ago – so the floor is yours for as long as you desire.'

'Actually, I didn't just bring the ring with me today to jog your memory, Ambrose, I brought it because it seems to have become a centre point of my problem. Back then and now.'

'Really? I'm most sorry to hear that.'

'The thing is . . . the reason I left Ireland was because I had to, well, escape from someone. I went to London first, but

then I had no choice but to move on. I decided to go further afield, first to Canada, and then to New Zealand.'

Ambrose remained silent as I collected myself to say more.

'I changed my surname when I got married – I'm now McDougal – and became a New Zealand citizen a few years later. I had a new identity, which I truly believed had freed me from the threat of him finding me. As I said earlier, I was able to enjoy my life there, running a vineyard and bringing up my family with Jock. But then . . .'

'Yes?'

'I'd only just embarked on my Grand Tour and my first port of call was Norfolk Island – a tiny isle between New Zealand and Australia. I was visiting my old friend Bridget who'd recently moved there. Do you remember Bridget?'

'How can I forget her, given we have established I am definitely not senile? Your flame-haired enemy as a child and best friend at university.'

'That's the one, yes. Anyway, there I was on Norfolk Island, drinking with Bridget and her new husband, when I received a message from my daughter Mary-Kate. Apparently, she'd had two women enquiring about her, saying she could be the "missing sister" in their family of six other girls – all adopted by a very odd-sounding man, who died a year ago. The proof of the connection was supposedly an emerald ring shaped like a star, with seven points around a small diamond.' I lifted my hand and indicated my ring. 'Mary-Kate told me she'd seen a drawing of the ring that the women had brought with them. She said she was pretty sure it was this one.'

'Really? Pray, continue.'

'Anyway, these women were so desperate to track me and the ring down that Mary-Kate said they were flying over to Norfolk Island to see me.'

'Do you know why they were so desperate?'

'Some cock and bull story about their dead father; how it had been his dearest wish to find the "missing sister". Even though it was too late for him, these sisters are having some kind of a memorial service a year on from his death, by going to the spot where they think he was buried at sea. I mean, these girls even have the same names as the Seven Sisters of the Pleiades! Have you ever heard such a ridiculous story?'

'Well, I certainly recognise the theme of the missing sister from any number of mythological tales around the globe, as you must have done, Mary. You wrote your Bachelor's dissertation on Orion's chase of Merope, after all.'

'I know, Ambrose, but the Seven Sisters were . . . *are* imaginary, not a real-life human family.'

'If you'd said that to the ancient Greeks, Mary, they'd have you left on the top of Mount Olympus as a sacrifice to their gods.'

'Ambrose, please, this isn't a laughing matter.'

'Forgive me, Mary. Do continue. I am sure there must be a method behind the madness of these events.'

'Well, when I heard that they were going to fly over to Norfolk Island, I spoke with Bridget about it, given she knew all about my past, and she agreed that I should leave earlier so I didn't have to meet them. I flew to Canada, which was to be the next stop on my tour, but on my first day in Toronto, I got calls and messages from the concierge saying that two women were coming to see me. When they arrived in reception, I asked the concierge what they looked like and he told me that they were in Muslim dress.'

'So they are not the same two women who followed you to Norfolk Island, then?'

'No. From what I briefly saw of them, they were dark-skinned, and even though I told the concierge to tell them I

was out, they simply sat there and waited in the lobby. In the end, I couldn't bear it any longer, so I came down to take a look at them for myself. One of them must have recognised me, because she called my name after she'd spotted me, as I was running for the lift. Thank God it closed before she could get to me. She also left me a letter that told the same story as the girls who had visited Mary-Kate. I was so frightened that I decided to fly straight to London.'

'Curiouser and curiouser,' said Ambrose as I took a breath and a sip of my tea.

'By chance, I bumped into what seemed like a very nice man in reception on my arrival at the hotel. He asked me whether I'd be interested in giving him an interview about the vineyard that myself and my husband built up and ran, as he was a wine journalist. He invited me to the suite of his friend, who introduced herself as Lady Sabrina. They really couldn't have seemed more above board. But then' – I took a sip of my tea – 'as this man Orlando was interviewing me, I noticed the woman was staring at my ring. Once the interview was over, she asked me about it. She said the seven points looked very unusual and then the man mentioned the Seven Sisters of the Pleiades, and the missing sister . . .' I shook my head despairingly. 'At that point, I stood up and left. And then the next day, I noticed that Orlando was tailing me when I went to Clerkenwell to look up the records of marriages and deaths. They'd invited me to dinner that evening, but I cancelled, and lay in my room that night, completely sleepless, watching the hours pass by. The next morning, thinking I'd slip out early, I saw the man was already reading a newspaper in the lobby by the front entrance. In the end, I had my baggage taken downstairs and stored by a porter. I had to wait for this Orlando to leave for the lavatory before I could slip out. And here I am! I . . .'

I put a hand to my brow, embarrassed that I felt like sobbing at his knee, as I'd sometimes done as a child when things had seemed too much. 'I'm so exhausted, Ambrose, really I am. They're after me again, I know they are.'

'Who are "they"?'

'Some very ugly, violent people – or rather a person who knew ugly, violent people and who threatened me a long time ago. He also threatened my family and anyone I loved, including you. Which is why I . . .'

'Ran away,' finished Ambrose.

'Yes. Do you have a tissue by any chance?'

'Here, Mary, dry your eyes.' He handed me his handkerchief, and it smelt so very much of my childhood with him that it brought more tears to my eyes.

'I'm just so worried for Mary-Kate. She's alone at the vineyard in New Zealand and knows nothing about my past. Nor does Jack, my son. He'd send them after my children, I know he would, and . . .'

'Hush now,' Ambrose said gently. 'Obviously I know little of the past scenario you are talking about, but—'

'The missing sister was what he always called me! Back then, when . . . oh,' I said, feeling totally out of words to describe the complexity of what had happened.

'So now, I presume you are talking about someone I knew of when you were living here with me?'

'Yes. I am, but please don't say his name. I can't bear to hear it. He's found me, Ambrose, I know he has.'

I watched as Ambrose steepled his fingers under his chin and stared at me for what felt like a very long time. A gamut of emotions that I couldn't easily read crossed his features. Eventually, he gave a long sigh.

'I understand, Mary dear, and I just might be able to allay your fears somewhat. But I'm afraid you will need to excuse

me. My one nod to my age is to take a short nap in the afternoons. And rather than doze – or even worse – snore loudly within your hearing, would you mind if I retired to my bedroom for an hour or two? Your sudden appearance seems to have rather taken it out of me.'

'Oh Ambrose, of course not. I'll leave and come back later. I'm so sorry, really I am. After all these years, I hadn't expected our first meeting to be like this.'

'Please do not apologise, Mary dear. Just accept that I am not as young as I used to be.' Ambrose offered me a weak smile as he stood up and we walked along the narrow corridor towards the back of his maisonette. 'Please feel free to stay here. As you well know, there's a plethora of books at your disposal. If you wish to go out, the key is where it always was: in the Copenhagen Blue china pot on the table in the corridor.'

'Do you need any help?' I asked as he began to descend the steps to the basement, which housed two bedrooms and a bathroom.

'I seem to have managed quite well in the years since you left, and I hope to manage a few more in the same vein. I will see you at half past four, Mary, but . . . please be assured, I believe you are quite safe.'

As he disappeared from view, I decided that perhaps I too would go back to the hotel for a nap.

Taking the key, I left the maisonette and walked the few hundred yards round the corner, breathing in the familiarity of the atmosphere and the voices I could hear around me. This city had provided the backdrop to some of the happiest moments of my life, before it had gone so badly wrong.

Stepping inside the hotel, I went to the desk to retrieve my key.

'There you are, Mrs McDougal,' said the receptionist as he

handed it to me. 'Oh, and there's someone waiting for you in the lobby.'

My heart started to thud so fast that I thought I might faint where I stood. I hung on to the desk for support and bowed my head, trying to get my breath back.

'Are you all right, Mrs McDougal?'

'Yes, yes, I'm fine. I . . . did you get a name from this person?'

'I did, yes. He only arrived fifteen minutes or so ago. Now, let me see . . .'

A hand descended onto my shoulder from behind and I let out a small scream.

'Mum! It's me!'

'Oh, I . . .' I clutched the desk tighter as the world spun.

'Why don't you take your mammy to sit down in the lounge and we'll bring some water through for her?' the receptionist suggested.

'No, I'm all right, really.' I turned towards the great, tall man I had brought into this world, and rested my head against his chest as he hugged me.

'I'm so sorry I startled you, Mum. Why don't we go to the lounge like the man said, and maybe order some tea?'

'Okay,' I agreed, and Jack manoeuvred his arm around my waist to support me as we walked.

Once we were sitting on a sofa in the quiet lounge and tea had been ordered, I felt Jack's gaze upon me.

'Seriously, I'm fine now. So, tell me, what on earth are you doing here?' I asked him.

'It's simple, Mum: I was worried about you.'

'Why?'

'You just sounded . . . odd on the phone the other day. I tried calling you again early this morning, but you didn't pick up.'

'I'm perfectly fine, Jack. I'm sorry you felt you had to chase halfway across the world to see me.'

'It wasn't across the world, remember, Mum? It only took me a couple of hours to get here from Provence. The flight wasn't much longer than going from Christchurch to Auckland. Anyway, I'm here now, and after your reaction to my arrival at reception, I'm glad I am. What's going on, Mum?' he asked as the tea arrived.

'Let's drink the tea, shall we? You pour,' I said, not trusting my own hands to hold the pot steadily. 'Add an extra spoonful of sugar to mine.'

Eventually, a hot sweet, tea and Jack's comforting presence slowed my heart rate and cleared my head.

'I'm feeling much better now,' I said, to ease my son's concerned stare. 'I'm sorry about jumping the way I did.'

'That's okay,' Jack shrugged. 'You obviously thought I was someone you didn't want to see.'

My son glanced at me through eyes that were a bright blue, very like mine. 'Yes, I thought that maybe you were,' I sighed. I'd always found it extremely difficult to lie to Jack face-to-face; his intrinsic openness and honesty – along with an acute perceptiveness, especially when it came to me – made it almost impossible.

'So, who was it you were expecting?'

'Oh Jack, it's such a long story. In a nutshell, I think . . . well, I think that someone who used to live here in Dublin – a dangerous man – may be on my trail again.'

Jack sipped his tea calmly as he took this in. 'Okay. And how do you know this?'

'I just *do*.'

'Right. So, what has happened in the last week to make you think this?'

I glanced around nervously. 'I'd prefer not to talk about it in public. You never know who is listening.'

'Blimey, Mum, you sound completely paranoid! And a little crazy, to be honest, which worries me because you've always been the calmest and sanest person I know. For now, I'm going to give you the benefit of the doubt and not drag you off to the nearest shrink to find out if you've suddenly developed delusional tendencies, but you'd better explain who this man is.'

'I'm perfectly sane.' I lowered my voice just in case the waitress standing in the corner of the otherwise deserted lounge could hear us. 'It all started when those girls came to visit your sister at The Vinery, with some story about how she was the long-lost missing sister that their dead father had been looking for.'

'Ah,' Jack nodded. 'Okay. MK told me the proof was something to do with that emerald ring you're wearing at the moment. They just wanted to take a look at it.'

'Yes. Well, since they arrived, I've had strangers turning up at every hotel I've visited, asking to see me. Then when I was in London, do you remember I called you about the man who wanted to interview me about The Vinery for his newspaper?'

'I do, yes. Hold on, you told me you were in New York!' Jack narrowed his eyes.

'I'm sorry, Jack, I knew you'd worry and ask questions if you thought I'd derailed so much from my original trip itinerary. Anyway, this man definitely wasn't who he said he was. The woman he was with saw the ring and asked about it. He even followed me the next day when I left the hotel. That's when I decided to leave for Ireland and why I sounded odd on the phone when we spoke yesterday.'

'Okay,' Jack nodded. 'And do you know why these people are following you? I mean, what do they want? Is it just the ring? It's only small,' Jack said as he stared at it. 'It doesn't

look that valuable . . . oh Mum, you didn't steal it, did you?'
He gave me a wry smile.

'Of course I didn't steal it! I promise I'll tell you the whole
story at some point – it's time, I suppose.' I sighed, then
checked my watch. 'I'm going to have to leave in a bit. I've
only popped back to the hotel for an hour while my friend
has a nap, you see.'

'Your friend?'

'He's my godfather, Ambrose, actually. I paid him a call
earlier. I haven't seen him for thirty-seven years.'

'Your godfather?' Jack frowned. 'Why have you never mentioned him to any of us before?'

'Let's just say I wanted to leave the past behind me. For
everyone's sake. It was him that gave me this ring on my
twenty-first birthday.'

'So he's involved in all this, is he? . . . Whatever *this* is?'

'No, he wasn't.' I gave my son a sad smile. 'Have you heard
from Mary-Kate, by the way?'

'No, not for the past few days.'

'This may sound ridiculous, but I'm worried about her
there at The Vinery all by herself. You haven't had any visitors
recently in Provence, have you? People asking about me?'

'No, although I did meet a very nice woman who came to
stay at the *gîte* François and Ginette own and . . .' Jack
frowned suddenly. 'Wow,' he muttered.

'What?' I asked him as my heart rate began to rise again.

'Nothing, I'm sure it was nothing. I mean, we just got on
really well. I was so happy to have someone who spoke English to talk to over dinner. She said she had adopted sisters
and, actually, I suppose she did ask quite a lot of questions
about you and MK's adoption.'

'Oh no, Jack.' I put my fingers to my brow. 'They found
you as well.'

'Mum, who are "they"?' he urged me. 'This woman – Ally – was great, and it was pure coincidence that we were put next to each other at the dinner table. Actually, it was me who offered to drive her into the village the next day, because I really liked her. She didn't mention anything about a missing sister, or the Seven Sisters, or a ring . . .'

'Okay. Well, it might be coincidence, but until we know for sure, I'm going to ask Mary-Kate to leave The Vinery and fly over here.'

'Mum, what the hell?! Are you telling me that our lives are in danger?'

'They might be, yes, and until I'm certain they're not, we need to be together.'

I looked at my beloved son's expression, which contained a mixture of shock and doubt. I knew I had to tell him something before he carted me off to the local psychiatric hospital.

'The thing is, Jack, a long time ago, someone who was in a group of very dangerous people threatened to hunt me down and kill me.' I swallowed. 'It may sound ridiculous and overdramatic, but that was the way things were here back then. He'd always called me the missing sister and hated this ring, and by extension my godfather, because he'd given it to me. This goes back a very long way, Jack, and until I can find out if he's alive or dead, I'm not going to be able to relax, okay? That's why I'm here in Ireland. I have to put this to bed for good.'

'Okay.' Jack nodded. 'So you think that he and his . . . people are after you again?'

'Until it's been proved that they're not, I do believe it's possible, yes. You didn't know him, Jack, what he believed in, the cause he thought he was fighting for. He was' – I gulped – 'consumed by it. And had been for the whole of his life.'

'All right, at least you're making a bit more sense now. Is

this why you've never really talked about your past here in Ireland then? And why you ended up in New Zealand – as far away as you could possibly get?'

'It is. Now, I need to go and see Ambrose. He'll be wondering where I've got to.'

'Can I come with you, Mum? After what you've just told me, I think I should, just in case.'

'I . . . okay. Maybe it's about time you learnt about your heritage.' I signalled for the waitress.

The bill paid, the two of us left the hotel.

'Did you bring a bag with you?' I asked my son as we walked round the corner towards Merrion Square.

'Yes, it's stored with the porter for now and they have a room for me, but I just wanted to make sure you were actually here before I checked in. This man who you think is after you, was he part of some kind of extremist group?'

'Not when I first knew him, but he was definitely involved towards the end. Jack, I swear, I'm not exaggerating. I know the organisation he was with had a network. He said he was quite high up, so one order from him and things . . . well, they happened. Now,' I said as I paused outside Ambrose's building, 'remember, my godfather is very old, but don't let that fool you into thinking he's lost one ounce of his enormous brain. Ambrose was, and still is, the cleverest man I know.'

'Well,' Jack said as he looked up at the tall, elegant red-bricked building with its old-fashioned square-paned windows, 'he must be very rich to own one of these on such a beautiful garden square.'

'He only owns the ground and basement apartment, but you're right. Even that would sell for a lot these days. He bought it a long time ago. And Jack . . . ?'

'Don't worry, Mum,' Jack shrugged affably, 'I'll remember my manners.'

'I know you will, love. Right, let's go inside, shall we?'

I unlocked the door and stood in the entrance hall, with its original black and white patterned tiles.

'Ambrose? It's Mary here,' I announced as I opened the interior door that led into the sitting room.

'Good evening,' he said, already standing up from his favourite chair to greet me. I watched his eyes sweep over Jack, who was in his usual casual attire of shorts, T-shirt and not-so-white trainers.

'And who might this be?' said Ambrose.

'Jack McDougal, Merry's son.' He held out his hand. 'How d'you do?' he said and I could have kissed him for using such a formal expression, which I knew would endear him to Ambrose.

'I do very well, thank you, young man. Well, as there are three of us, I suggest you two sit down on the sofa. Mary, you didn't tell me your son was with you.'

'He wasn't when I saw you earlier, but he turned up in search of me.'

'I see. Now,' he said, 'would anyone like a drink? I'm afraid I have little to offer but the two staples of my life: whiskey and water.' Ambrose looked at the clock on the mantelpiece over the fireplace. 'It's almost five o'clock, therefore I'll take a whiskey. Your mother knows where the bottle and glasses are kept,' he added as Jack rose.

'I'll take some water for now, Jack, thank you,' I added. 'The kitchen is at the end of the corridor, and tap is fine.'

Jack nodded and left the room as I went to retrieve the whiskey bottle and a glass.

'A fine young man, who looks very like his mama,' Ambrose said. 'And not a bad bone in his body, I'd wager.'

'There really isn't, Ambrose, though he's not so young anymore. I worry that he'll get set in his ways as a bachelor and never settle down.'

'Would any woman ever be good enough for him? Or more accurately, for his mother?' Ambrose gave me a raise of an eyebrow as I handed him his whiskey.

'Probably not. He's so completely without guile,' I sighed. 'He's had his heart broken a few times because of it.'

'I must ask you before he returns: are you happy for us to talk openly in front of him?'

'I have to be, Ambrose. I told him what I think has been happening recently and it's all because of the past. It's time there were no more secrets. I've lived with them for too long.'

Jack returned with two glasses of water, handed one to me and sat down.

'*Sláinte!*' Ambrose raised his glass. 'That's "cheers" in Gaelic,' he added for Jack's benefit.

'*Sláinte!*' Jack and I toasted back.

'Are you Irish yourself, sir?' Jack asked.

'Please, call me Ambrose. And indeed, I am Irish. In fact, if I was a stick of traditional seaside rock, it would read "Made in Ireland" down the centre of it.'

'You don't have an Irish accent, though. And nor does Mum.'

'You should have heard your mother when she was a little girl, Jack. She had as broad a West Cork accent as it was possible to get. I, of course, drummed it out of her when she came to Dublin.'

'Where is West Cork?'

'Another county in Ireland, down in the south-west.'

'So you didn't grow up in Dublin, Mum?' said Jack.

'Oh no.' I shook my head. 'I grew up in the countryside . . . We didn't even have electricity until I was six!'

'But you're not that old, Mum. You were born in the late forties, weren't you?'

'West Cork was quite behind the times then,' Ambrose put in.

'So, did you know Mum's family well?'

'In a way,' said Ambrose, casting me a glance. 'You have never told your son about your childhood?'

'No. Nor my husband or Mary-Kate,' I admitted.

'May I ask why not?' said Ambrose.

'Because . . . as I've said, I wanted to leave the past behind and start afresh.'

'I'd love to know more, Mum, I really would,' Jack encouraged me.

'Well, perhaps now might be the time to tell young Jack a bit about his heritage?' Ambrose suggested gently. 'I'm here to expand on any details you don't quite remember, Mary – I'm sure my mind will just about stretch back to my long-lost youth.'

I turned to my son, who was looking at me imploringly. Reading Nuala's diary had certainly reminded me of the familiar spaces of my childhood. Closing my eyes, a wave of emotions and memories came over me, ones I had tried so hard to forget for well over half my life.

But you can't forget, Merry, it's who you are . . .

So, I let the wave engulf me without fighting it off, and realised for the first time that here, with my son and my beloved godfather, I could safely swim in the waters of the past without drowning in them.

I took a deep breath and began . . .

Merry
The Argideen Valley
October 1955

An Cláirseach
The Celtic Harp

27

Merry started as an arm swung onto her chest. Katie, her big sister, who was only two years older than her, was dreaming again. Merry removed the arm and placed it back where it belonged on Katie's side of the bed. Her sister rolled over and curled herself into a little ball, her red curls splayed on her pillow. Merry too turned over so their bottoms were touching on the narrow mattress, and looked out of the tiny window-pane to check how high the sun was and whether Daddy would be out in the milking shed yet. The sky was as it usually was: full of big pieces of grey cloud that looked fit to burst with raindrops. She reckoned she still had an hour to stay warm under the blankets before she'd need to be up and dressed to feed the chickens.

Opposite her, Nora, who shared a mattress with their oldest sister Ellen, was snoring gently. As her brain woke up, Merry felt excitement in her tummy and she remembered why it was.

Today was the day the electricity thing was to be switched on and they were to move across the yard to the New House. She'd watched Daddy and her older brother John, and some-times their neighbours if they could be spared from their own farms, build it ever since she could remember. If Daddy wasn't in the shed with the cows, or out in the barley fields, he was across the yard, making the New House go upwards.

Merry looked up at the ceiling, which was very low and made a triangle shape (she'd learnt about triangles at her new school) with a beam through it at the top to hold it up. Merry didn't like that beam because it was dark and big spiders liked to make their homes right above her. One time, she'd woken up and seen the biggest in the world hovering just above her on its silver thread. She'd screamed and Mammy had rushed in and caught it, telling her not to be a 'silly little eejit', and that spiders were good because they caught flies, but Merry didn't think they were good at all, whatever Mammy said.

In the new bedroom, there was a flat ceiling that was painted white, which meant it would be much easier to see any webs and take them away before the spiders could build their homes any bigger. Merry knew she'd sleep much better in the New House.

There were also four whole bedrooms upstairs, which meant Ellen and Nora would have a room to themselves, so just she and Katie would share theirs. The boys – John and little Bill – would have another room, and Mammy and Daddy the biggest room. There was a new baby in Mammy's tummy and Merry had prayed to Jesus that it would be a boy too, so she and Katie could keep their new room just to themselves for always. Even though she knew she had to love her brothers and sisters, it didn't say in the Bible she had to *like* them.

And Merry and Katie didn't like Nora. She was very bossy and gave them both jobs to do that Ellen, their older sister, had given to *her*.

Mammy and Daddy were hoping for a boy too – another big strong lad to help on the farm. Merry and Katie's hands were still too small to do the milking and Ellen was only interested in kissing her boyfriend, which Merry and Katie had seen her do behind the milking shed and thought was

disgusting. There were lots of other chores on the farm and Daddy often said that John was the only useful one around, which Merry thought was very unfair because she looked after baby Bill the most. And besides, it wasn't her fault she'd been born a girl, was it?

Aside from Katie, Merry's favourite person to speak to was the man called Ambrose, who was sometimes up at Father O'Brien's house where Mammy cleaned on a Monday. Ambrose had begun teaching her letters even before she had started school last month. She wasn't sure why it had always been her who was chosen to go up to the priest's house to clean with Mammy, but she didn't mind a bit. It was better than not minding actually, because she *loved* it! Some of her best memories were sitting in front of a warm fire eating a little round cake hot from the oven, filled with strawberry jam and something that was creamy white, which tasted sweet and delicious. Now she was bigger, she knew the 'cakes' were called scones. While she was eating, Ambrose would talk to her, which made it quite difficult to answer as her mouth was so full of cake, and he didn't approve of talking while you were chewing. Other times, he'd read to her from a storybook about a princess who was put to sleep for one hundred years and only woken by a kiss from a prince.

Ambrose was very kind to her, but she didn't know why. When she'd asked Father O'Brien what he was to her, and why she was allowed to call him by his first name, rather than 'Mr Lister' like Mammy did, she watched him as he thought about it for quite a long time.

'Perhaps one could say that he is your godfather, Mary.'

She didn't like to ask what a 'godfather' actually was – Ambrose didn't look like God in Heaven *or* her father. He had round eyes like an owl behind thick glasses, and fluffs of blond hair on his head – a good deal less hair than Father

O'Brien or Daddy. He was a lot smaller than them too, but his face was always jollier and less serious.

Then, as if Father O'Brien could read her mind, he'd smiled at her. 'Think of him as your special protector down here on earth.'

'Oh. Do all my brothers and sisters have one too?'

'They all have godparents, yes, but because Ambrose is able to spoil you more than theirs, it's best you keep anything he gives you secret, or they may get jealous.'

'Mammy knows, though, doesn't she?'

'Yes, and your father, so you're not to worry you're doing anything wrong.'

'I understand,' she'd nodded gravely.

Last Christmas, Ambrose had given her a book, but it didn't have anything written in it, only lines on which she was to try practising her letters and forming them into words. Ambrose said it didn't matter if they were spelt wrong, because he would correct them and that's the way she would get better.

Reaching under the mattress, she pulled out the book. The light was very bad but she was used to it.

The cover was smooth and silky to the touch and she liked the feel of it, but when she had asked Ambrose what the cover was made of, he had told her it was leather, which came from a cow's skin. This didn't make sense at all, because all the cows she knew had hairy skin, covered in mud.

Opening it, she slid out the pencil, which had its own little band to attach it to the side of the book, and turned to the last page she'd written.

Mi familee
Ellen: aje 16. Bossi. Kisses her boyfrend.
John: aje 14. Helps Daddy. Likes cows. Smells like
*   cows. My favorit brotha.*

Nora: aje 12. Doesn't like anithin.
Katie: aje neerli 8. Mi best frend. VERRI pretty. dosnt
 help much wit babi Bill.
Me: aje nearly 6. Likes books. Not verri pretty. Caled
 Merry becos I giggel a LOT.
Bill: aje 2. Smells.
New babi: not here yet.

Deciding she should add something about Mammy and Daddy, Merry thought what she might write about them.

Merry loved both her parents very much, but Mammy was always so busy cooking and washing and having more babies, it was difficult to ever talk about the things that went through her mind. Whenever Mammy saw her she would just give her another job to do, like putting fresh straw in for the pigs or picking cabbages out of the ground for their tea.

As for Daddy, he was always out on the farm and wasn't really one for talking anyway.

Daddy: works VERRI hard. Smells of cow.

Merry thought that didn't sound very nice, so she added:

VERRI hansom.

Before she had started school a month ago, Merry's favourite day of the week had always been Mondays, when she and Mammy walked up to the priest's house together. They chatted about all sorts of things (Merry knew her brothers and sisters thought her a chatterbox, but there were just so many things to be interested in). Mammy would sometimes kiss her on top of her head and call her 'my special girl'.

Mammy, she wrote carefully, *VERRI beautiful. kind. I love*

her VERRI much. When up cleaning the priest's house, Mammy was always rushing around and muttering about Mrs Cavanagh. At home, Mammy called her 'that old crow', but Merry had been told never to repeat that outside the family, even if Mrs Cavanagh did look like one. Whenever she saw her at Mass on Sundays, perched on the pew at the front and looking around at the congregation, all beaky and disapproving, she'd see a great black bird instead. Father O'Brien had told Merry there was no need to be afraid of her; Mrs Cavanagh cleaned the priest's house every day except Monday and complained to anyone who would listen about how Mammy wasn't doing her job well enough, which made Merry even more cross.

Mrs Cavanagh often talked about having worked up at the Big House, and Merry's friend Bobby said it was because Mrs Cavanagh had worked for so long for a British family (and he said the word 'British' the same way Katie said the word 'slug') that she'd been taken over by 'colonist views' and took out her anger on the 'hardworking Irish'. When Merry had asked Bobby what a 'colonist' was, he'd gone all red, which made her think it was a word he'd heard at home but didn't really understand.

Bobby was in her class at school in Clogagh, and because his homeplace was in the same direction as Merry's farm, she and Katie walked home with him part of the way after school. As Merry and Bobby were at the same reading level, their teacher Miss Lucey, whom Merry adored because she was so pretty and seemed to know everything there was to know in the world, often placed them together. To begin with, Merry had been glad to know someone who liked reading too. Even though everyone else in the class kept away from him because of his temper and gossip about his family, Bobby could be kind when he set his mind to it. He'd given her a pink crayon

once and said she could keep it, even though everyone knew his family was very poor. His jumper was full of holes and his long dark hair looked like it had never seen a brush. He lived with his mammy and his little sister (neither of whom she'd ever seen) in a tiny cottage that Nora had said didn't have a tap or electricity.

Katie said that he was stone mad and should be taken away by the Gardaí, but despite his bad and often strange behaviour, Merry only felt pity for him. She sometimes thought that the only one who loved him was his dog Hunter, a black and white collie who had probably never hunted anything. Hunter was always waiting for Bobby in the lane near Inchybridge, his tail wagging and his tongue hanging out in a smile. Sometimes, when she and Katie parted ways from Bobby, Merry would look back to watch Hunter padding faithfully beside Bobby. Hunter could always calm him down when he was in a rage, even when Merry couldn't.

She shut her writing book carefully, replaced the pencil in its holder and put it back under the mattress. Then she sat up again and stared out of the window at the New House. It was hard to believe that today it would become their home. They would even have an inside tap, drawn from the stream on the hillside behind it. She had been allowed to try it, and it *was* like magic; the water came out when you turned it on, and disappeared when you turned it the other way. There was a range oven for Mammy to cook on so she'd no longer have to use the pot over the fire, and a big kitchen table that Daddy had made out of wood, which could seat all eight and a half of them with room to spare. And then . . . the best thing of all: a little hut which she could walk to from the kitchen. Inside it was a contraption with a seat that she'd only ever seen up at Father O'Brien's house, and a chain above to flush it.

Anyway, it meant that none of them needed to go into the fields beyond to do their 'business', as Mammy called it. How it worked, Merry didn't know, but like everything else at the New House, it was magical.

Merry shivered as a blast of wind whistled through a crack in the windowpane, so she huddled under the blanket once more. And for one of the few times in her life, other than birthdays, Christmas and when she went up with Mammy to the priest's house, Merry could hardly wait until it was time to feed the chickens, because that meant the most exciting day of all had begun.

'Merry, will you be picking up that blanket? It's trailing behind you in the mud!' called Mammy, as she and Katie followed their mother across the yard for the hundredth time to put their things into the New House.

Both girls watched as Mammy dumped the pots she'd carried onto the long table, and used an old cloth to open the small door on the new range. She and Katie had been told very sharply not to touch it because it would be too hot. A delicious smell wafted out as it opened.

'Is that brack cake, Mammy?' Merry asked.

'It is, Merry. We'll be wanting something nice for our first tea inside.'

'Does it have the little black fruit in it?' asked Katie.

'It has currants in it, yes,' Mammy answered as she drew it out and put it on a table to the side of the range to cool. 'And don't either of you be touching it yet, or I'll have you cleaning out the pigsty. Merry, get back across and see to Bill, will you?'

'Where's Nora?' asked Merry. 'She's after disappearing again.'

'I'm not knowing, but see to Bill while me, Ellen and Katie make the beds upstairs.'

'Yes, Mammy,' Merry said, rolling her eyes and passing Katie a glance. As she walked back across, Merry felt so angry with Nora, it made her heart beat faster. Nora was always disappearing when there was work to be done. And now it meant another smelly napkin to change, when it was really Nora's turn. Bill was sitting in the small wooden pen placed in a corner of the old kitchen, the only room downstairs and where the whole family were when they were not in bed or outside. For the first time she could ever remember, Merry saw the fire that had been lit earlier in the big nook that took up almost the whole of one wall had been allowed to go out.

'Bye bye, fire,' Merry said out loud. 'We'll not be needing you anymore for our cooking.' Turning her attention to Bill, who smelt worse than the fields when Daddy and John spread the manure, she took a blanket from the sideboard and laid it out on the cold stone floor. Then she picked up Bill from his pen and placed him on it. Next, she found a clean napkin from the pile in the sideboard drawer and a pail of water which they used to clean Bill's mess.

'Do you know, Bill, that you'll be two soon, and 'tis time for you to get out of napkins altogether?'

Bill, who Merry thought was the spit of Daddy already, with his dark hair and blue eyes, giggled at her as Merry held her breath and unpinned the napkin, then slid it and the mess inside it from under him. Rolling the dirty napkin up to be scraped out and washed later, she took a cloth and dipped it in the pail of water to clean his bottom. Then she expertly fastened a clean napkin around him. Immediately after she'd done that, Bill rolled onto his side and then heaved himself up onto all fours. Even though he could walk a bit now, he still preferred to crawl, and did so very fast. He knew how to

place himself under the table with the chairs about him, so hands could not easily reach him. He thought it was a grand game altogether, and would sit there chuckling as Merry had to move chairs to reach him.

'Aha!' Merry said as she dived under the table and grabbed him. 'No chairs today, Mr Bill! They've all gone over to the New House already.' Pulling him out, Bill protested heavily as she picked him up and placed him safely back in his pen. His howling grew louder, so she plucked up the empty bottle and refilled it with milk from the pail that stood outside the front door to keep it cool.

'There now, drink your milk and be good while we work away in the New House,' Merry told him. 'And there's your doggy to play with,' she said, picking up a wooden toy she herself remembered loving when she'd been little.

As Merry took the soiled napkin out to scrape away the contents in the bowl which would be disposed of later in the field, she wondered why Mammy wanted to have babies. Even though she loved her little brother, she still remembered the fierce look of fear on Mammy's face when she'd been standing in the kitchen and a large swish of water had appeared between her legs. At the time, Merry had thought that Mammy had disgraced herself, but it turned out it was the sign that Bill was on his way out of her tummy. The baby delivery lady had arrived soon after, and the family had sat in the kitchen, listening to the screaming from Mammy upstairs.

'Is she dying, Daddy?' Merry had dared to ask. 'Going up to heaven to be with Jesus?'

'No, Merry, she's giving birth to a babe, just like she gave birth to your brother and sisters.'

Merry thought now that, with the new babe coming soon, there'd be even more napkins for her to clean.

'And that's another thing that will be better, Bill,' she called

to him as she dunked the napkin in the special fluid that took most of the brown stains away. 'We have a tap over at the New House, so maybe 'twill be easier to wash these.'

Leaving the door ajar so Bill could be heard if he screamed, Merry ran back across to the New House to help Mammy.

28

'I'll be on my way now, Father,' said Mrs Cavanagh as she stood in the doorway to James's study. 'Your friend's room has fresh sheets and I've dusted round. The fire is laid and your tea is in the range.'

'Thank you, Mrs Cavanagh. Enjoy your day of rest and I'll see you as usual on Tuesday.'

'Just make sure that Mrs O'Reilly spends more time cleaning than she does yabbing. I'm getting tired of double work to do when I come back. Goodnight, Father.' With that, Mrs Cavanagh shut the door more firmly than she needed to just to underline her point. A point she made every single Sunday evening when she left for her day off. Over the last seven years, James had often wanted to tell her the truth: that young Maggie O'Reilly was a pleasure to have in the house, with her lovely smile and the way she sang in a high, sweet voice as she went about her chores. She was also a far better cook than Mrs Cavanagh could ever be, and in the few hours she spent at the house, she would leave it sparkling. However, having prayed on the subject, he'd realised that all he thought was exactly what Mrs Cavanagh knew herself if she were to look into her heart: she was threatened by the younger woman and that was why she behaved towards her as she did.

Behind his desk, Father James O'Brien stretched and

breathed a sigh of relief. His Sunday duties were over and this evening – the start of his unofficial day off (although his door was always open to members of his flock in trouble) – was made even better by the fact that his dearest friend Ambrose was on his way down from Dublin for his monthly visit.

James stood up to switch on the electric light that hung in the centre of the room.

The evenings were drawing in already, even though it was only the start of October.

Ambrose's visit prompted James to think how much had changed since he'd arrived here in the parish of Timoleague almost seven years ago. Ambrose had said then that it would take time for him to be accepted, and he'd been right. Now, he not only felt that he had been, but more importantly, that he was respected by the community he served. And rather than his youth being a negative, he had managed to turn it into a positive by lending a hand during the harvest and counselling rather than judging the wives if they came to him pregnant yet again, wondering how they could cope with another babe.

Having originally thought he'd move on to a more prestigious post in a parish with a larger flock, when one such vacancy in Cork City had been offered to him, he'd decided against it after days of reflection and prayer. He was happy here, welcomed with a smile at the homes he visited and plied with enough cakes and scones to make up for Mrs Cavanagh's lack of talent in that department.

The arrival of electricity in his home four years ago had been enormously helpful, because it had meant he could at least listen to the radio and keep in touch with what he thought of these days as 'the outside world'. When he'd taken a trip back to Dublin to visit Ambrose, the city he'd grown up in and loved with all his heart had felt claustrophobic and

noisy. He'd realised the peace and beauty he'd found here in West Cork suited his temperament. Where better to contemplate one of his parishioner's dilemmas than to drive out to the magnificent Inchydoney Beach near Clonakilty, and walk along the sand as the waves roared and the wind whipped around the skirt of his cassock. Or on a long walk along the cliffs of Dunworley, where you'd not meet another soul until you stood on a headland that looked out on all sides onto the Atlantic Ocean beneath. Unless something changed, James had decided that he suited the countryside and would probably be happy staying here for the rest of the life God might choose to give him.

Ambrose, of course, who was a Senior Fellow in Classics at Trinity College, was always trying to persuade him to return to the bright lights of Dublin, where Ambrose could walk around the corner to see him, rather than driving for four or five hours down to visit him in Timoleague. But the roads had improved between Dublin and West Cork in the past few years – they'd had to, what with the advent of the working man being able to afford a car rather than just the gentry, and besides, James thought that his friend enjoyed his road trip in his bright red Beetle. James had nicknamed it the Ladybird, as it often arrived covered in large dark splotches of mud from the many puddles it had to drive through en route. And he would be here soon . . .

While he waited, James walked over to the gramophone and pulled out a record from its sleeve. Placing the vinyl circle on the turntable, he moved the needle to his favourite variation from *Rhapsody on a Theme of Paganini*. Ambrose had told him that Rachmaninoff had turned the main theme upside down to create the extraordinary classical piece. He sat in the leather chair as the pianist played the first very simple chords . . .

'My dear boy, I've woken you, after what I know is always a long hard day for you in the "office".'

James opened his eyes, doing his best to focus, and saw Ambrose standing above him. Which was rather novel, as it was normally him looking down on Ambrose.

'Forgive me, Ambrose. I . . . yes, I must have drifted off.'

'And to Rachmaninoff, I see.' Ambrose walked over to the gramophone and released the needle from its endless circle at the end of the recording. 'Goodness, the vinyl is covered in scratches; I'll bring you a new one next time I'm down.'

'There's no need; I rather like the scratches, because it gives the piece an air of antiquity that suits it.' James smiled as he clapped his arms around Ambrose's shoulders. 'As always, 'tis a pleasure to see you. Hungry?'

'If I'm honest, no.' Ambrose removed his cap and driving gloves and placed them on James's desk. 'Not for Mrs Cavanagh's fare, at least. I stopped and enjoyed a picnic from the hamper my own daily had provided just before I entered Cork City.'

'Wonderful, then I will treat myself to a hunk of bread, ham and the homemade chutney one of my parishioners provided me with. We'll tip Mrs Cavanagh's broth into the slop for the chickens,' James said with a wink.

An hour later, with a fire burning in the grate, and a new recording of Rimsky-Korsakov's *Scheherazade* that Ambrose had brought along with him playing on the gramophone, the two men were sitting opposite each other in their fireside chairs.

'I've been looking forward to our night and day of quiet contemplation and philosophical discussion,' Ambrose said with a wry smile. 'But I always worry that you'll try to save my soul for God while I'm here.'

'You know very well that I stopped trying to do that years ago. You are a lost cause.'

'Maybe I am. However, let it be a comfort to you that I surround myself with myth and legend within my own philosophical journey. Greek mythology was simply an earlier version of the Bible: tales of morality to tame the human being.'

'And perhaps to teach him,' James mused. 'My question would be, have we learnt anything since ancient times?'

'If you're asking whether we're more civilised, given that in the past forty or so years, we've faced two of the harshest world wars in history, I'd question it. Perhaps it seems politer to use aeroplanes or tanks to spit out death to thousands. Indeed, I'd prefer being blown up by a shell to being hanged, drawn and quartered, but—'

'I believe that the answer is no,' said James. 'Look at the way the Irish suffered under British rule. Their lands taken from them, many forced to change their religion during the Reformation. Being down here amongst a far simpler population than you'd find in Dublin has opened my eyes to just how hard their lives have been.'

'I sense a glimpse of republicanism appearing in your soul, Father O'Brien, but as a large part of Ireland *is* now a republic, I'd say civilisation has moved on. I think you should read that.' Ambrose pointed to the book he'd brought for his friend. 'Kierkegaard was a religious soul and a philosopher. As he says, life is not a problem to be solved, but a reality to be experienced.'

'Then perhaps we should no longer discuss the heavenly

and human condition and both follow his lead,' James commented as he glanced down at the title of the book. '*Fear and Trembling* . . . the title does not inspire confidence.'

'Read it. I promise you'll think it rather good, James, even if the man was a staunch Protestant.'

'Then I'd also add that my bishop would find you a bad influence on me,' James chuckled.

'Then I will have truly achieved my goal. Now, tell me how little Mary O'Reilly is getting on. Have they moved into their new house yet?'

'They have indeed. Yesterday, as it happens. I went over to bless it after Mass earlier today.'

'And?'

'Considering that John O'Reilly has built it mainly with his own hands block by block, it is certainly solid enough to keep the wind out, and three times the size of their old farmhouse. The electricity is on, and the range and the kitchen tap are working. The whole family looked exhausted, but very happy.'

'Thank heavens for that. Their old farmhouse was hardly better than a hovel,' Ambrose remarked.

'Well, Fergus Murphy, the last owner, had no funds to keep up with modern agricultural methods. Poor John inherited a museum, not a farm, after his uncle died.'

'They're finally moving into the twentieth century then.'

'At least now he is able to feed his children every day, and perhaps even make a little profit from his efforts.'

'And how is Mary?'

'As bright and sweet as she always is. She told me this morning she's enjoying school.'

'I'm only glad she's going; that bright head of hers needs stimulation. How's her reading coming along?'

'I knew you'd ask that, so while I was there, I asked her to

read a few simple sentences from the "Parable of the Sower and the Seeds", which she'd been learning at school. She hardly hesitated with the words, though I worry she hasn't enough reading material at home. She's already surpassed her older brother and sisters and, to my knowledge, the O'Reillys only possess one book, which is, of course, the Bible. I told both Merry and her older sister Katie that they were to read and learn the words of the "Prodigal Son" and I'd test them the next time I visited. That way, it doesn't look as if Merry is being singled out.'

'Good man, and I know for a fact the O'Reillys have the means for her elder sisters to continue their education in future if they so desire, not just Mary. I'm sure it suits your purposes too, to know that Mary is receiving extra tuition in Bible study,' smiled Ambrose. 'It's a shame I don't see her as often as I have done due to her schooling, but I hope to see her in the Christmas holidays and it's far more important she receives at least some level of education.'

'Well, her teacher, Miss Lucey, is young and eager to bring the children on. I'd say that Merry's in a safe pair of hands. When I was last down there, she mentioned how surprised she was to see the new little O'Reilly girl already reading.'

'I only wish I could give her more reading material at home,' said Ambrose.

'We both know you can't, my friend. A gift to a child returning from the priest's house could be seen as suspicious.'

'Of course, James, of course. You know I would never do anything to compromise your position. As you have said, your parishioners have now begun to trust you.'

'I have come to understand their ways and they mine, although I did have an unfortunate incident recently with one young female member of my flock.'

'You don't even have to tell me what happened – she

caught you after Mass, seeming distressed; you took her for a walk around the cemetery. And there, she declared her undying love for you.'

James looked at Ambrose in utter astonishment. 'How did you know?'

'Because you are a handsome man in your prime, who comforts the sick and administers last rites to the dying. You act as the community's moral compass; you are approachable, yet untouchable. All that makes a tantalising recipe for young girls with no one else to idolise.'

'I am a priest!' exhorted James in frustration. 'As I said to Colleen, any special attention she told me I'd shown towards her had simply been because her mother had died recently, leaving her with five young siblings to care for at the age of just fourteen. I was being kind, nothing more.'

'I'm only surprised such a situation hasn't come up before, James. I'm sure it will happen many times more in the future, so you'd better be prepared.'

'I don't believe I handled the situation with Colleen well at all. I haven't seen her at Mass since it happened and when I went round to visit at her home, she refused to let me in.'

'Leave her be for now; she'll get over herself in time when she meets a more suitable target for her affections.'

'You're sounding like you're an expert, so,' James grinned.

'Hardly, and I'm warning you that you are starting to put the word "so" at the end of your sentences. You are becoming a true West Cork native.'

'What if I am?' James chuckled. 'It's my adopted home, where I will live for the rest of my life.'

'You also seem to have lost all ambition to move on to a more prestigious parish.'

'For now, I feel I am doing good here.'

'Well, from my point of view, even if I have to travel through the bogs of the Midlands to see you, at least I know you're close to my special little girl, and for that, I am grateful.'

That night, Ambrose settled himself as best he could on the narrow iron bed with its hard horse-hair mattress, and gave a deep sigh. Not for the first time, he wondered what he was doing, driving down every month to the godforsaken south-west coast to visit his old friend, when he could have enjoyed a far more relaxed day in his comfortable apartment in Merrion Square, perhaps sharing a light supper with Mairead O'Connell, an English Fellow at Trinity.

While the rest of the world was rocking around the clock to Bill Haley and his Comets, West Cork was still caught in a time warp, with a pig's head for a Saturday night's dinner treat. The notion of a radio in every home, or even the television screens that had started to pop up in Dublin since a transmitter had been erected in Belfast, was still far off. Let alone that, he was making the journey to visit a man whom he knew would only ever regard him as his closest friend.

Long ago, when they were at boarding school together, he had dreamt that James would see what Ambrose believed he truly was, accept it and change the course of his life plan to accommodate it. Which, of course, in Ambrose's dream scenario, would include him. But after twenty-five years, Ambrose had to accept that this was, and only ever could be, a dream because God himself was the love of James's life.

He knew he had a choice: he could give up and move on, enjoy his pleasant and fulfilling life teaching his students at

Trinity, or he could continue to hanker after something that could never be. Friendship was all James was prepared – or *able* – to offer him. But was that more painful than not having James in his life at all?

He knew the answer, of course: James loved him in his own way, and that would have to be enough, because the thought of a life without him in it was one Ambrose simply couldn't contemplate.

29

Merry woke up in her new bedroom as her stomach turned over and her heart began to beat faster. Today it was her birthday, the seventh of November, and Mammy had sewn her a special pink dress to wear to her very own party. Her class at school were coming, along with their parents.

Mammy had had them all scrubbing every surface, and even dusting the inside of the presses since yesterday morning.

'No one will say the O'Reillys are dirty,' Mammy repeated for the endless time. Merry's eldest brother John had said 'twas just a chance for Mammy and Daddy to show off their new place, but even if he was right, she was excited about the day. All her friends from school were invited, apart from Bobby Noiro, who for some reason she didn't know was never allowed up at the farm.

Merry also knew that Bridget O'Mahoney, who looked like Mammy and her sister Katie, with her pale skin and her flame hair, would be wearing a far more expensive dress than her, which would be made by the seamstress who worked for the tailor in Timoleague, like all her clothes were. Bridget came from the richest family around these parts; they lived in a house that was even bigger than the one Father O'Brien lived in. Her daddy drove her to school every day in a big shiny car, whereas the rest of her class had to walk across the fields

(which were more of a bog in the winter, when it was raining). Miss Lucey always made them take off their boots and set them by the fire in the schoolroom to dry out while she did her teaching. It was fierce kind of her to think about that, but most times they got soaked again only a few yards into their journey home.

Merry wriggled her toes. She was amazed they were still on her feet and hadn't turned into fins like the fish, given the amount of time they spent in water. Sometimes the puddles she walked through came up to the bit of her body between her ankle and her knee (she must ask Miss Lucey what that bit was called). Still, today it wasn't raining and Merry decided to enjoy every moment of it.

As it was a Sunday, the family went to Mass, and outside afterwards Father O'Brien wished her a very happy sixth birthday.

Sunday was her second favourite day, after Mondays up at the priest's house. Merry looked forward to it all week, because it was the only day that all the siblings had time to play games together after lunch was cleared away. They'd go out into the fields, rain or shine, and run wild. They'd play at hurling, trying to get the small hard ball between the make-shift goalposts that Daddy or John had erected. Or sometimes tag, or hide-and-seek, when she would always be found first because she couldn't stop giggling. Today, as it was her birthday party, she had been allowed to choose all the games.

As the family climbed onto their pony and trap to head home, Merry decided that no matter how perfect Bridget O'Mahoney's dress was, and how many layers of net skirts it had, Merry wouldn't mind a bit, because it was *her* birthday, and today was a GOOD day.

'Mammy, you look so pretty in that dress,' Merry said admiringly as her mother came into the kitchen just before the party was about to start. 'Doesn't she, Daddy?'

'You're a picture, to be sure, love,' Daddy said, putting a hand protectively on Mammy's huge tummy, as Merry surveyed the feast laid out on the long wooden table.

There were sandwiches with different fillings, Mammy's special baked ham, scones and, in the centre of it all, a birthday cake iced in pink that said *Happy Birthday Merry* on the top of it.

Lined up on another table was an array of mugs ready to be dipped into the barrel that Daddy had brought back on the cart a few days ago. Daddy didn't go to the pub much, but she'd heard him say that nothing could make a party go with a swing like a glass of stout for the men.

'Ready?' her mammy asked her daddy. He gave her one of those secret looks and a smile.

'Ready.'

'Our first guests are here,' piped up Nora, as the Sheehy family appeared in the courtyard.

'Let the party begin,' Merry heard Mammy mutter under her breath, as she touched her great big tummy full of baby.

Only a few hours later, Merry lay in her bed with Katie. Both had their heads underneath the pillows to try and block out the sound of Mammy screaming. The water had come again from between her legs just after the last guests had left, and the baby delivery lady had been sent for. Mrs Moran had arrived and shooed the family away as she'd helped Mammy upstairs to her bedroom.

'Will Mammy die?' Katie asked her sisters, and Merry

could feel her slight body trembling against her. All four girls were in Merry and Katie's room, along with little Bill, because it was furthest away from the screaming.

'No, Katie,' said Ellen, ''tis just the way. 'Twas the same when Mammy had Bill.'

'Then I'll never have babies,' Katie said, mirroring Merry's own thoughts on the subject.

'Don't worry, 'twill stop soon and we'll have a beautiful baby brother or sister to play with. Mammy and Daddy will smile and be as proud as punch,' said Nora.

'What if something goes wrong?'

'It won't,' Ellen said firmly.

'Well, Orla's mammy died having her little sister,' Katie said staunchly.

''Twill be all right, try and sleep, Katie,' Ellen soothed her.

'How can I, when all I can hear is Mammy screaming?'

'Then we'll sing, shall we? How about "Be Thou My Vision"?'

So the four girls sang their favourite hymns and a couple of the 'old songs' that Daddy liked to play on his fiddle on a Sunday evening. The agonised screaming went on long into the night. Ellen and Nora went back to their room with Bill, and Merry and Katie dozed fitfully through the dark hours until dawn, when a weak cry was heard from their parents' room.

'The baby's here, Katie,' Merry muttered, as a silence as deafening as the screams fell like a blanket over the house.

'When can we see the new babe?'

All of the children clustered around Daddy the next morning. 'Is it a girl or a boy?' asked John. 'I want a boy!'

'It's a boy,' murmured a grey-faced Daddy.

'All boys are eejits,' sighed Nora.

'All girls are eejits,' John shot back.

'Can we see Mammy?' Merry asked.

'Not for now, Merry. The midwife's seeing to her. The birth took a lot out of her,' Daddy replied.

'She will be all right, though, won't she?' Merry asked, reading the concern on her father's face.

'Sure, the midwife says she'll be fine, and we're not to worry.'

But Merry did, even when Mrs Moran eventually came down with the new baby wrapped up in a sheet. They all peered down at him.

'He's tiny!'

'His eyes aren't open!'

'He looks like Daddy!'

'Now then, would Daddy like to hold his new son?' asked Mrs Moran. John O'Reilly held out his arms and she put the baby into them.

'Would you like a cup of tea, Mrs Moran?' Ellen, the eldest girl and therefore in charge of all things domestic if Mammy wasn't here, asked the woman politely.

'No thanks, my love, I've another lady in labour in Clogagh, who I must go to check on. Now then, why don't you walk outside with me, girls?'

As Ellen showed Mrs Moran to the door, Nora, Katie and Merry followed behind.

'Your mammy lost a lot of blood whilst birthing the babe, but thanks be to God, it's stopped for now,' said Mrs Moran in a low voice. 'You'll be needing to check on her regularly to make sure it doesn't start again, and she must have complete bedrest until she's stronger.'

Ellen nodded and as Mrs Moran waved goodbye, Merry

tugged on Ellen's skirt. 'Where does she want us to check?' Merry asked her.

'In between her legs, of course!' said Ellen impatiently. 'You're not to be worrying, any of you, I'll be doing all that. Mammy has to rest for the next few days, so Nora, Katie and you will be doing more chores, understand? As well as looking after Bill and the chickens, you'll be doing breakfasts and making broth from chicken bones for Mammy, to help her get stronger, because I won't be having time for any of that.'

'But it's school today and I don't know how to make broth,' Merry whispered.

'Then you'll just have to stay home and learn, won't you, girl?' Ellen said before she turned away to go inside and head back upstairs to Mammy. 'Oh, and one of you has to go up to the priest's house to tell Father O'Brien Mammy won't be in to clean today.'

Father O'Brien was just about to leave for Mass when he heard a tapping on the front door. He opened it and saw Katie O'Reilly, a diminutive version of her mother Maggie, standing there panting, and dripping wet from the rain.

'Hello, Father O'Brien, I've a message for you. Our new brother was born in the night and Mammy is very tired from the birth and she has to stay in bed to rest and she can't come up today to clean your house and we're not to go to school so we can help and Nora's feeding the chickens but Merry doesn't know how to make broth and Daddy wanted to know when you could church Mammy and baptise the babe and—'

'Slow down, Katie,' James said, putting a gentle hand on Katie's shoulder, 'and draw breath. You look soaked to the skin. Come in for a bit and warm yourself by my fire.'

'Oh Father, I should be getting back to help my sisters.'

'I'm sure five minutes won't harm.'

James gave her a slight push and propelled her through the door to his study, where Ambrose was sitting reading the *Cork Examiner*.

'This is my friend Ambrose Lister. Ambrose, this is Katie, Maggie O'Reilly's daughter. Now then, Katie, take off your boots and we'll put them by the fire to dry out a little. You sit down there.' James pointed to the chair opposite Ambrose, who was staring at the tiny girl with the flame-red curls.

'So, your mammy has had her new babe?' said James.

'Yes, and he's going to be called Patrick.'

'A fine name that is too. And you say Merry doesn't know how to make broth?'

'No, Father. Ellen told her to make it, but Ellen's been too busy taking care of Mammy to help her, and all we know is it's got chicken bones in it, and that Mammy should have it to make her strong again, but . . .'

James's heart broke as the little girl wrung her hands.

'Well now, I've Mass at the church, but after that, why don't I come down and see what I can do to help?' he suggested.

'Do you know how to make broth, Father?' Katie asked, her wide green eyes looking hopeful.

'I'm sure that I can get some guidance to help you, and also see to having your mother churched and getting your new brother baptised. Have you had breakfast?'

'No, Father, because Merry tried to make goodie, but 'twas disgusting.' Katie made a face. 'I don't think she's a very good cook.'

'You wait there and I'll be back in a trice.'

'I'm sorry to be bothering you, Father,' Katie said as her small feet reached instinctively for the warmth of the fire.

'And you, sir,' she said to Ambrose as James disappeared to the kitchen.

'Oh, don't worry about me. I'm happy to be bothered.'

Katie looked at him, her little face serious. 'You have a funny accent, if you don't mind me saying so.'

'I don't mind, Katie. And I'd agree with you.'

'You're not from round these parts, are you, sir?'

'I'm not, no. I live in Dublin.'

'Dublin! That's a very big city, isn't it, sir? And a very, very long way away?'

'It is indeed, Katie.'

'Is that your car outside? I like the colour.' Katie pointed out of the window at the red Beetle in the drive. ''Tis a funny shape for a car, though.'

'It's called a Beetle, because it looks a little like one, doesn't it? Would you like a ride in it?'

'Oh sir, I've never been in a car before. I might be very scared of the noise.'

James walked back in with a picnic basket and placed it at Katie's feet. 'There's half a loaf of bread in there and some cheese and ham as well, which should do all of you for the morning.'

'Oh, thank you, Father. 'Twill stop Merry fretting that we've nothing to serve Daddy and John when they're in from the fields.' She stood up, then collected her boots, and proceeded to put them on. Then she reached for the picnic basket. 'I'm sure Mammy will be back next week to clean,' she reassured both of them.

'Well now, I'll be straight down to you after Mass, Katie.'

'Are you sure you don't want a ride to your house in my red car?' Ambrose asked as the little girl walked towards the door clutching the basket, which was almost as big as she was.

'No thank you, sir, I'll be grand walking home.'

Once James had seen Katie out, he came back to the study.

'What a charming little thing she is,' Ambrose said. 'It sounds like chaos at the O'Reilly farm. Surely Mary and her sisters aren't meant to run the house whilst their mother recovers from the birth? Can't the older sister take care of the household while the younger ones attend school? And what on earth is "goodie"?!'

'A cheap version of porridge using stale bread, and no is the answer. 'Tis a large farm to run, and Merry and Katie are old enough now to help.'

'The poor mites,' sighed Ambrose. 'We must do what we can to help.'

'I can certainly take up the soup that neither of us ate last night, rather than putting it in the slop. I'll be able to see the lie of the land when I get down there.'

There was another knock on the front door, then the sound of the handle turning and the familiar *tap-tap* of a pair of sturdy brogues coming along the hall.

There was a sharp rap on the study door, and Mrs Cavanagh put her head around it.

'Excuse me for interrupting, but I've heard tell that Mrs O'Reilly won't be in to do her work today. So I thought 'twas my duty to come and offer myself in her place.'

She sounds as if she's giving herself up for sacrifice, thought Ambrose as he felt her usual piercing look of disapproval fall upon him.

'That's most kind of you, Mrs Cavanagh, but I'm sure that Mr Lister and I can mind ourselves for the day, if you've other things to be doing,' said James.

'Ah, I can put them off for you, Father. Have you had breakfast yet?'

'No, but—'

'Then I'll be sorting it out for you. It's a good job I don't have small ones that are likely to mean I'll be unable to work for you if you need me, Father.'

With that, Mrs Cavanagh turned and left the study.

Rather than looking at her new blanket, knitted out of colourful squares by Mammy for her birthday, or counting the pennies she'd been given by everyone who had come to her party, Merry was having the worst day of her life.

The truly terrible part was seeing Mammy as pale as the sheets on her bed. She was too weak to even take a sip of water, let alone hold Patrick. The new babe was smaller than Katie's wooden doll and as pale as Mammy. Ellen said he didn't even seem to know how to suckle. But at least, when Merry said a prayer to the Blessed Virgin on her knees at the bedside, Mammy smiled and patted Merry's arm. Ellen entered the bedroom and pushed her out of the way to check on their mother.

'Go down to the kitchen,' Ellen barked at her.

Merry watched through a crack in the wooden door as Ellen pulled back the sheet and looked between Mammy's legs. There was no big red patch like Mrs Moran had warned about, so she gave a sigh of relief.

'Merry, I told you to leave,' Ellen hissed. 'Go and make the broth, girl.'

Merry scarpered down the stairs and into the kitchen. Daddy, who rarely drank from the whiskey bottle he kept in the press in the New Room, was now fast asleep in his chair, the bottle by his side.

Katie was also in the kitchen, with Bill asleep in her lap.

'I need to make a broth for Mammy,' Merry said despairingly.

'Ellen said I must. What if she dies in the night, Katie, because I didn't know how?'

'Father O'Brien said he'll come down to show us. I'll carry Bill up and put him in our bed, and take up a fresh jug of water for Mammy. I'll take a spoon of sugar from the pantry to put in it as well. I heard Mrs Moran say sugar water was good for keeping up strength.'

Merry stood by the range, staring down at the pile of chicken bones that she was somehow supposed to turn into the watery soup Mammy sometimes made if any of them were sick. She thought hard and remembered that carrots and spuds had been involved, so she went to find some.

She peeled and chopped a few of them, put them in the pot with the bones, added some water and put it on the hotplate of the range. She watched it come to the boil, hoping that some magic would happen, but it didn't. Instead, the water began to spit everywhere, so she had to lift it off. The pot was heavy and some water splashed onto her fingers, sending a jolt of pain through them.

'Ouch!' she cried, as she put the pan down and went to the tap to put her fingers under cold water, tears spilling out of her eyes. At the same time, there was a knock on the door and Father O'Brien appeared with another basket.

'Merry, what has happened?'

'Oh, 'tis nothing, Father,' she said, drying her eyes on the nearest cloth. 'I was trying to make broth.'

'I've brought some soup for you.' Father O'Brien put the basket down and offered her two flasks. 'With a few of the carrots and potatoes added from that pot, it should be enough for your mammy for a couple of days. Where are your sisters?'

'Ellen's upstairs with Mammy, Nora's after helping John outside 'cos Daddy's sleeping, and Katie took Bill up to put him down for a sleep and hasn't come back yet.' Merry stared

at Father O'Brien, remembering Mammy always offered him a cup of tea and some cake. But before she could, he'd picked up his basket.

'Right, if you'd be good enough to show me up to your mammy's room, I'll get on with the religious side of things.' He smiled at her, as he pulled out another flask, took the top off and sniffed it. 'I'm just checking this is the one with the holy water in it. 'Twouldn't do to be baptising your brother with soup now, would it?'

Merry giggled, and as she led him upstairs, thought how much she loved Father O'Brien because he always knew what to do.

After his arrival, the day got a lot better. Once Mammy had been churched (whatever that was), Daddy was woken up by Ellen and they all went upstairs to watch Patrick being baptised. Ellen took over the cooking after a gentle word from Father O'Brien about the dangers of small ones and boiling water, and Nora was dispatched upstairs with the soup and to sit with Mammy.

Eventually, night came and Merry and Katie were shooed up to bed by Ellen. 'Bill will sleep with you tonight – we don't want Mammy disturbed,' she'd added.

'You have him for now,' Katie said as she tucked Bill under the new blanket with Merry. Then she took the hairbrush they shared from the top of the chest of drawers. 'Count to one hundred for me,' Katie demanded, because Merry knew she got lost after the thirties.

She did so, and marvelled at the way her sister's hair shone like spun copper. 'Sure, you'll be getting yourself a handsome man to marry one day,' Merry said admiringly.

'I swear I'll be having myself a husband even richer than Bridget O'Mahoney's daddy, with a house ten times bigger than this one. Even if I don't love him and he has a nose

longer than Mrs Cavanagh's,' Katie said firmly. 'Can I see how many birthday pennies you got yesterday?'

'If you promise not to tell anyone where they're hidden. On pain of death, Katie. Swear on all the saints first.'

Katie crossed herself. 'I swear on all the saints.'

Merry climbed out of her bed and opened the drawer she used for her pants and socks. Thinking that even her sisters on the search for pennies wouldn't touch her smalls, she pulled out a black sock, then took it over to the bed and poured out the contents.

'Jesus, Mary and Joseph! I'd reckon you could buy your own cow with that amount!' Katie took one of the shiny round coins in her small palm and stroked it. 'How many do you have?'

'Thirteen altogether.'

''Tis an unlucky number, Merry. Maybe you should give one to me for safekeeping.'

'Of course you can have one, Katie, but don't tell the others or they'll want one too.'

'Will we go to Timoleague to buy some sweeties this week?' Katie suggested.

'Maybe, but I'm saving the rest.'

'What for?'

'I don't know,' Merry said, 'but something.'

'John told me a secret once.'

'What secret?'

'Oh, about how we can get more sweeties if . . .'

'What?'

'I'm not sure I should tell.'

'Katie O'Reilly! I just told you where I hide my pennies. You tell me now, or I'll—'

''Tis your turn to swear on all the saints you won't say I said.'

Merry did so. 'Come on now, Katie, tell me.'

'John told me that when he was my age, some of the boys in his class at school who had pennies took them down to the railway line when the train was due to go by. When they heard the hoot of the train, they ran onto the tracks and laid their pennies on the rails. When the train passed, its wheels ran over them. And Mrs Delaney at the sweetie shop always gave them a few extra sweeties if the boys had flattened pennies. I'd say 'twas because it makes them larger,' Katie nodded knowledgeably.

'John's never done that, has he?'

At that point, Katie's pale skin flushed a deep crimson, even as she shook her head.

'You're not to go telling Mammy and Daddy.'

'But 'tis dangerous, Katie, he could have been killed!' Merry said as she collected her pennies and put them back in the drawer.

She'd just climbed back into bed when Nora came into their room.

'Merry, go sit with Mammy while I go downstairs to the laundry with this sheet.' She yawned loudly. 'I'm exhausted, and here you two are, tucked up cosy in your beds.' Nora swung round and marched back through the door.

'All she's done is sit with Mammy for most of the afternoon,' Katie complained. ''Twas me that was washing out the new babe's napkins.'

'Well, I'd better go and sit with Mammy like she said.'

Merry walked along the narrow landing, then unhooked the latch to Mammy and Daddy's room. With relief, she saw that both her mother and the new babe were asleep, even if they were as still and pale as the grave.

Getting down on her knees, she sent up another prayer, before gingerly lifting the sheet to check for blood like Ellen had done. It was clean.

'Thank you, Holy Mother, for protecting my own,' she whispered as she replaced the sheet and then sat down in the chair to wait for Nora to return.

The week after baby Patrick had arrived felt like the longest of Merry's whole life. At least she and Katie had been sent back to school, because Nora had announced it was time for her to leave the convent school in Clonakilty. With Mammy sick, Ellen, John and Daddy needed help around the place. Besides, Nora said, what did she need with letters and numbers?

When Merry was home, it felt like the new babe cried all the time, and Ellen and Nora were only ever complaining about all the work they had to do, while Daddy grumbled that he'd hardly had any sleep due to the baby screaming. Daddy had taken to sleeping in the New Room, because he said it was quieter downstairs. The New Room was just off the kitchen and the children were never allowed in it, because it was 'for best'. It had a big fire and two armchairs for Mammy and Daddy, where he now slept while still sitting upright.

Nora handed Bill over to Merry and Katie the moment they walked through the door. He was by now moving quite fast on his chubby little legs, and the two of them spent their lives chasing after him, indoors and out.

Merry went up to see Mammy every day when she got home. She'd be awake and ask her about what she had learnt, while she nursed little Pat, who seemed to have got the hang of feeding now. She told Mammy about the new reading book she was on, and how Miss Lucey was teaching them something called geography, which was all about other countries

in the world. Then she went downstairs to start her home-work at the kitchen table.

One misty evening, Katie was sitting on the floor, throwing a ball to Bill.

'I swear, I'll never have babies. Ever,' Katie said yet again as Bill went after the ball, then fell over, bumping his head on a table leg and starting to yowl.

'But that's what God wants us to do, Katie. Father O'Brien said so. If no one had babies, then there would be no people on earth, would there? Anyway, Mammy says she's feeling much better and 'tis the last day Ellen is in charge,' Merry added, trying to cheer Katie up.

'Bridget O'Mahoney has a maid at home,' Katie said, as she gathered Bill in her small arms to comfort him. 'I'll have one too when I'm older.'

There was an unexpected knock on the front door. Merry looked at Katie in surprise, as no one ever used the front door.

'You'd better open it,' Katie shrugged.

Merry stood up and did so. Outside in the darkness stood a thin man wearing a tall hat.

'Hello there, I'm Dr Townsend,' he smiled down at her. 'And who might you be?'

'I'm Merry O'Reilly,' she replied politely, knowing his funny accent meant he was British.

'That you are, dear. Father O'Brien suggested I should call. Might I see your mother, please?'

He followed Merry into the kitchen, sweeping off his fine hat, then allowed Katie to lead him upstairs to Mammy's bedroom. He shut the door behind him.

Both Merry and Katie decided to send up a prayer to the Holy Mother that there was no bad news, because Bobby Noiro had told her that was the only time a doctor came to visit. It was a doctor who'd come to the door when his daddy

had died in a fire in their barn, but that was all Bobby would say about it.

Ellen came in to start preparing the evening meal, and Nora appeared from wherever she'd been hiding to get out of doing chores.

'Who was that man?' she asked.

'A doctor. I let him in,' Merry said importantly.

A look passed between Ellen and Nora which filled Merry's heart with fear. A silence hung over the kitchen as the four girls waited for the doctor to come down the stairs.

Eventually he did, and Nora was sent to fetch Daddy in from the cowshed. 'May I have a word in private, Mr O'Reilly?'

Daddy led him into the New Room and the door was once again firmly shut. Fifteen minutes later, the two men reappeared in the kitchen.

'Is everything all right, Doctor?' asked Katie, always first with the chat.

'Yes indeed, young miss,' the doctor said with a reassuring smile. 'Your mother will be very well and so will your little brother.'

Merry saw the expression on Daddy's face and thought that he looked as if Mammy were dead and had been sent to purgatory for all eternity.

'So now, Doctor, what's the cost?' Daddy asked him.

'As 'twas only advice, I won't be charging you. I'll let myself out,' he said. 'Good evening, everyone.'

With a touch of his hat, he was gone.

''Tis wonderful news Mammy's well, isn't it, Daddy?' said Merry.

'Yes,' he replied, but even though his mouth said the words, the expression on his face didn't change.

As the family sat down for their tea, chattering like a flock of birds, Daddy sat silently, his face like stone.

Later, after they'd finished the soup and bread, then said their prayers together, Katie and Merry went upstairs to their room.

'Daddy didn't look very happy about Mammy being well, did he?' said Merry.

'No, he didn't. Do you . . . do you think the doctor was just lying to us and Mammy's going to die?' Katie asked her.

'I don't know.' Merry shivered at the thought.

'Holy Mother, 'tis cold in this room,' Katie pronounced. 'Winter is coming in. Can I share your bed tonight?'

'O'course,' Merry agreed, wondering why Mammy and Daddy had chosen to give them separate beds in the first place, Katie was so rarely in her own.

They snuggled up together and finally the feeling began to flood back into Merry's frozen feet.

'Aren't adults a mystery, Katie?' she said aloud in the dark.

'They are indeed. And guess what, Merry?'

'I can't, Katie, what?'

'One day, we're going to be adults too!'

30

It was Christmastime and Merry had already been an angel in the little play Miss Lucey had put on in the school hall for any parents that wanted to come and watch. Katie had hated every moment of being a shepherd, but Merry had loved her own costume, even if it was only made out of an old sheet and a bit of tinsel that sat like a crown on her head. She had to concentrate hard as she'd had words to remember as well:

'And Mary will bring forth a son, and you shall call His name Jesus, for He will save His people from their sins.'

Being called Mary, she'd have preferred to be the Holy Virgin herself, but there were three other Marys in the school (which meant being called by her nickname was much better than being 'Mary M.' or 'Mary O.' or 'Mary D.'). None of the Marys had been given the part. That honour had gone to Bridget O'Mahoney. Of course, her mammy had had her costume made by their seamstress, and as Merry stared at Bridget, in a lovely blue dress that matched her eyes, she thought that if it were hers, she'd never take it off.

Mammy had come to watch, and even though baby Pat had screamed during the 'Silent Night' carol, Merry had decided she was the prettiest mother in the room. She was well now, with colour back in her cheeks and, as her brother John had said, 'a bit more meat on her bones'.

Bobby Noiro hadn't been given a role in the play, as punishment for hitting Seamus Daly on the head. Ever since, Seamus had been after saying that all of Bobby's family were traitors and murderers. Bobby would have most likely hit Seamus several times more if Mr Byrne, the caretaker, hadn't pulled them apart.

On the walk home, Bobby's favourite new thing was to disappear behind trees, then jump out shouting, 'Bang!' He told her he was shooting the 'Black and Tans'. Merry didn't know why he'd want to shoot at them, because those were colours, weren't they? Katie always got cross with him, flicking her red hair and walking faster ahead, so it was Merry and Bobby walking together and him recounting the stories of 'the old days' that his granny had told him, which were all to do with some war.

The next day, what with school being over for the Christmas holidays, she knew it would be the last time she walked home with Bobby, so she gave him the little card she'd drawn for him, spelling out the word 'Christmas' very carefully. She'd only made it because the day before, when the class had been exchanging cards, Bobby had been the only one who hadn't been given any. Even though he hadn't said, Merry could tell it had upset him something fierce.

When he saw the card she'd made him, he gave her a big smile and handed her a crumpled bit of stained ribbon.

''Tis blue, like your eyes,' he said, staring at his boots.

'Thanks a million, Bobby. I'll wear it for when Santy comes,' she said. Then he'd turned and run off with Hunter at his heels towards his cottage, while Katie made kissing noises at Merry all the way back home.

For some reason Merry couldn't quite work out, the atmosphere in the house felt different to normal Christmases. Even though the paper garlands had been made, and holly brought into the house and carols sung, something didn't feel the same.

Merry decided it was because Mammy and Daddy looked so miserable. Before Pat had been born and the visit from the doctor had happened, she'd often seen Daddy give Mammy a kiss on top of her head or squeeze her hand under the table at tea, as if they shared some secret that made them both smile. But these days, they hardly spoke and Merry had watched Daddy's whiskey bottle go down and down until there was almost none left.

Maybe I'm imagining it, she thought when she woke up on Christmas Eve and felt that lovely tingle of excitement in her belly. 'Today will be a GOOD day,' she announced to herself. This morning, she was up to the priest's house with Mammy to help her clean, because it was the Christmas holidays. She hoped Ambrose would be there as she hadn't seen him for what felt like a very long time. She loved sitting in Father O'Brien's study with the fire burning brightly in the grate. Last time, they'd had chats about how her schooling was getting on, then he'd taken a book of fairy stories by Mr Hans Christian Andersen and read her 'The Little Match Girl'. The story was all about a child on New Year's Eve, who burnt matches because they gave her light and warmth. She froze to death out on the street, but then her soul was sent into heaven and she was happy to be with her beloved grandmother.

'That sounds very sad,' Katie had pouted after Merry had told her the story. 'And it has no fairies in it at all!'

Merry heard Pat crying in their parents' room. The babe seemed to be always hungry, and sometimes Merry looked at

her mammy with Pat to her breast, and thought she was like the cows being drained of their milk morning and night.

Anxious for the day to begin, she dressed in her warmest jumper, which was really too small for her now, a skirt and a pair of woollen socks, then made her way downstairs. Since Mammy had been so weak after the babe had been born, and had to feed Pat early in the morning, she was now an expert goodie maker, getting stale bread to mix with the milk and a dash of sugar. But this morning, in honour of it being Christmas Eve, Mammy had said that it was a proper porridge day. Merry switched on the overhead light, took the oats from the pantry and filled a jug with milk from the churn. As she stirred the porridge on the range, Merry looked outside and saw the fields in front of the farmhouse were sparkling with frost.

'To be sure, it looks like a Christmas picture,' she said to herself. She had actually started to enjoy the quiet moments in the kitchen before everyone tumbled down the stairs and Daddy and John came in from the milking shed, ready for their breakfast. While the porridge simmered, Merry took the loaf of soda bread Mammy had made yesterday and put that and the butter on the table. Placing the bowls to warm on the range, she thought of the presents she'd bought with her birthday pennies for her family. Beautiful new ribbons for Ellen and Nora, a special comb for Katie's hair, and a toy rabbit and a toy mouse for Pat and Bill. She'd bought some embroidery thread to make Mammy and Daddy handkerchiefs out of squares of cotton, though the 'D's were a little bit wonky. Now she'd only tuppence left, which she'd keep for a rainy day, as Mammy always called savings. As it rained most days, she supposed those savings were important.

'Morning, Merry,' said Mammy as she walked into the kitchen with baby Pat tucked into the sling strapped across her chest.

'Sit down, Mammy. Everything is done already.'

Mammy smiled up at her as she sat in the chair. 'Pat wouldn't settle last night, so I'm a little weary this morning. Thank you, Merry, you're a good girl, to be sure.'

''Tis Christmas Eve, Mammy, the best day of the year.'

'And I must go to clean the Father's house,' Mammy sighed.

'I'm there to help you, I promise.'

'Oh Merry, I didn't mean it like that. You do your fair share here and more. And Mr Lister is such a kind man. If it hadn't been for him, then . . .'

Merry, who was stirring the porridge to make sure it wasn't getting too thick, turned to look at her mother.

'What do you mean, Mammy?'

'Ah, nothing, Merry, only that he helps you with your letters. He teaches at a famous university and you can't be getting any more clever than that. I just hope this one settles whilst we're up there, so I can get on with my work and then be back home in time to get everything ready for tomorrow.'

'I can mind Pat for you there, Mammy, you know I can.'

'I know, pet,' Maggie smiled at her. 'I'll be having some of that porridge now, with maybe an extra dash of sugar on it for energy.'

'What are you having some of, Mammy?' asked Ellen as she walked in carrying a squirming Bill.

'Never you mind,' she said. 'We were talking about Santy, weren't we?'

'Yes, we were, Mammy.' Merry smiled to herself as she sprinkled a little sugar on the bowls and brought them to the table.

An hour later, the two of them were on their way up to the top of the hill that the priest's house sat on, looking down on the village of Timoleague. When they arrived, Mammy knocked politely and waited for an answer. Ambrose opened the door.

'Good day to you both,' he smiled. 'The father's out on his rounds already, visiting the sick and giving them a Christmas blessing. You know what to do, Mrs O'Reilly. Oh, and the father said to tell you that all the ingredients you need are in the pantry.'

'Very good, Mr Lister. I'm sorry I've had to bring baby Pat along, but he just wouldn't settle and all the other girls are busy at home . . .'

'That's no problem at all, Mrs O'Reilly. Now then, I've just boiled the kettle and filled the pot. May I offer you a nice hot cup of tea after your walk? It really is biting out there.'

Ten minutes later, after a cup of tea into which Merry had poured as much sugar as she wanted from the bowl Ambrose had left out for them, she carried Pat into the study with her, while Mammy got on with her work.

'I'm sure he'll settle in a minute, Ambrose, but he's a fierce screamer.'

'That was what my mother said of me when I was a baby,' Ambrose smiled as Merry gently rocked the baby in her arms, begging him silently to go to sleep. 'Maybe the warmth of the fire will soothe him.'

'I wish something would,' Merry sighed.

'So, Mary, how has school been since I last saw you?'

Ambrose always insisted on calling her Mary, as he'd told her he wasn't fond of nicknames.

'Oh, very good, Ambrose. I'm onto reading book ten, which Miss Lucey said is normally for older children. And my

numbers are coming on well, I think, even though they're harder than reading letters. At least you don't have to add them up, do you?'

'No, you don't, Mary.'

'Look now, Pat has finally closed his eyes. I'll just lay him down on the mat over there, if you don't mind.'

'Not at all. Should we talk in whispers so as not to wake him?'

'Oh no, you should hear the noise my brothers and sisters make around the place when he's asleep. He'll be grand altogether, so.'

Ambrose watched the little girl as she laid the baby down carefully, then covered him with a worn blanket.

'And how's your family, Mary?'

'We all caught a cold a few weeks back, but we're better now, thank you,' Merry said as she sat down. 'Mammy is much better too, but this small one wants a lot of milk.'

'And your father?'

'Well, he has more glasses of his whiskey now than he used to and sometimes he looks sad . . .' Merry shook her head. 'I don't know why, Ambrose, because we're just after moving to our new house, the harvest was a healthy one and . . .' Merry shrugged. 'Sometimes, I just can't understand adults.'

'No, Mary,' Ambrose replied as he suppressed a smile, 'sometimes I can't either, and I am one! Now then, shall I read you a story?'

'Can it be "The Little Match Girl"?'

'Well now, as it's Christmas Eve, how about I read a new Christmas story to you?'

'Yes please.' Merry watched as he reached for what looked like a very old book on the table beside him.

'This story is by an English author called Charles Dickens. It's quite a grown-up story, Mary, and long too, so we may

only get through part of it today. It also has things called ghosts in it. Do you know what ghosts are?'

'Oh yes, Ambrose! Mammy's after telling us fairy stories about the old times in Ireland and there are ghosts in those. Me and Katie think they're real, but Ellen and Nora say we're eejits because of it.'

'I wouldn't call you an eejit, Mary, but my opinion is the same as your sisters: ghosts don't exist. However, sometimes it's fun to be scared, isn't it?'

'I think so, but not at midnight, when everyone in the house is sleeping except for me.'

'I think that you are clever enough to understand the difference between real life and stories. Perhaps the best thing for me to do is to start reading and you must tell me to stop if you get frightened, all right?'

Merry nodded, her eyes wide.

'So, this story is called . . .' Ambrose held out the page to Mary and pointed at the title.

'A Christmas Carol!'

'Well done, Mary. It's the story of a man called Ebenezer Scrooge. Perhaps if you think of the meanest person you know, who always looks unhappy, you can imagine what he's like.'

'Like Mrs Cavanagh, you mean?' Merry asked, then clapped a hand over her mouth as she realised what she'd said.

Ambrose gave a chuckle. 'If you wish, though Father O'Brien would call that a bit un-Christian of us. Not that it matters to me, of course.'

'What do you mean? Are you not a Catholic?' Merry asked as she suddenly realised that, even though Ambrose was great friends with Father O'Brien, she never saw him at Mass on Sundays when he was down here from Dublin.

'Ah now,' he said, taking off his spectacles and cleaning them on his handkerchief. Without them, he looked like a little mole. 'That is a big question, Mary.'

'Is it? But everyone is Catholic,' she said.

'Actually, there are many different religions around the world,' he said, putting his spectacles back on his nose. 'And Catholicism is just one of them. There are Hindus in India, for example, who believe in many gods—'

'But there's only one god!' she protested.

'There is in the Catholic belief, yes, but there are people on this earth who worship different gods.'

'Does that mean that they will all go to hell?' she asked. 'Because they don't believe in the real God?'

'Is that what you think should happen to them, Mary?' he asked her.

Merry rubbed her nose in frustration because Ambrose had a habit of asking her questions back whenever she asked *him* something.

'I think . . .' She chewed her lip. 'I think if they're good on earth, they shouldn't go to hell, because hell is only for bad people. But if you don't believe in God at all, that makes you very bad.'

'So if I don't believe in God, it must make me bad?' he said.

She stared at him open-mouthed. 'No, I . . .'

'It's all right, Mary,' Ambrose said gently, 'I'm sorry to have upset you. I'm only trying to explain to you how people believe in different things. Like you and Katie believing in ghosts, while your other sisters don't. It doesn't make any of us wrong, it just means that you have different beliefs. And that's perfectly all right.'

'Yes,' she nodded, because she did sort of see what he meant, but God wasn't a ghost.

'Now, shall we get to the story?' he said. 'So, we will begin . . .'

Merry was so gripped by the story, it took Ambrose to point to baby Pat to rouse her from her listening. 'Perhaps we should stop there, Mary dear, as your little brother seems to be hungry.'

Merry came back into the real world with a jolt; they'd just got to the part where the Ghost of Christmas Past had arrived, seeming so jolly after the very scary Jacob Marley ghost. She turned her gaze towards the wailing Pat and only just stopped herself sticking out her tongue at him.

'I'll go and find Mammy.' Sweeping up the offending baby, she marched him into the kitchen, where her mother was rolling out pastry.

'Sorry, Mammy, but . . .'

Her mother sighed and brushed a floury hand across her brow, leaving a slight sprinkling of white dust across it.

'He also smells,' Merry added as she placed Pat in her mother's arms, then swiftly turned towards the kitchen door, eager to get back to the story.

'Now then, girl, would you not be changing him for me before you go? Unless you have better things to do.'

Merry rolled her eyes then turned back to her mother, resigned. 'O'course, Mammy,' she said.

It was almost time to leave for home when Ambrose beckoned Merry back into the study. She was still holding a grizzling Pat in her arms. Every time she'd put him down,

he'd start up the racket all over again, so they hadn't carried on with the story.

'Today I'm nearly hating you, Patrick O'Reilly,' she whispered to him as she walked down the corridor towards the study.

'Why don't I take Pat for a while?' suggested Ambrose, and promptly took the babe from her. Pat stopped fussing immediately and just looked up into Ambrose's owl eyes. 'What a good boy he is,' said Ambrose. 'And that touch of dark hair, just like your daddy.'

'I was hoping he'd be blond like me, so I wouldn't be the only one in the family,' she said. 'Katie says 'tis because I'm the youngest sister. God ran out of colour and that's why my hair is so light.'

'Katie certainly has an imagination,' Ambrose chuckled. 'Now then, Mary, I'll be here with Father O'Brien over the next few days, so perhaps it will be possible for us to continue *A Christmas Carol* before I leave. But for now . . .'

He pointed to a flat package on Father O'Brien's desk that was wrapped in bright red paper with Santys all over it. It was proper Christmas paper, not the plain brown stuff that her family used for presents.

'Ooh! Ambrose, I . . .'

'Perhaps you should open it now, so your brothers and sisters don't get jealous, eh?'

'Do you think it's all right to do that before Santy comes?'

'Yes indeed, because this is from *me* for Christmas. Now then, sit down and open it.'

Merry did so, quivering with excitement about what could be inside, although from the shape and feel of it, she'd a pretty good guess. She undid the ribbon and the wrapping carefully, because if Ambrose would let her, she wanted to keep it and use it for some of her own presents. Peeling it back, she stared at the words on the front cover of what she'd already known was a book.

"Tis beautiful. Thank you, Ambrose.'

'Can you read the name of the book, Mary?'

'Um . . . could I have a go?'

'Please do.'

'*The My-thes and Leg-ends of the Gre . . . Greek Gods!*' Merry looked up at him to see whether she'd got it right.

'That was a very good try indeed. It's actually *The Myths and Legends of the Greek Gods*. Myths and legends are similar words for the old Irish tales you've heard from your parents. These stories are about gods who lived in Greece long ago, on top of a mountain called Olympus.'

Merry was still transfixed by the front cover. The letters were all made of gold and she traced her fingers over them. The figure on the front was a man with a bare chest, but at least he had material covering his middle parts, so he looked like Jesus did on the cross. Except he had a pair of wings on his back, which Jesus didn't have, because wings belonged to birds and angels.

'We have to go home now, so maybe I could leave it here with my other books and then 'twould be a treat to look at each page slowly and read it when I come back to visit.' She stroked the front cover lovingly. 'Thank you, Ambrose, 'tis the most beautiful thing I've ever seen.'

'It's a pleasure, Mary, and a very merry Christmas to you.'

Walking home with Mammy, Merry tried to understand what Ambrose had been telling her about God. In fact, her mind felt overcrowded with new thoughts to think.

'You're very quiet, Merry, 'tis unlike you,' Mammy said, smiling down at her. 'Are you thinking of your Christmas presents?'

'I'm thinking that Ambrose told me he doesn't believe in God. Does that mean he'll go to hell?' she blurted out.

'I . . . did he really say that?'

Merry could tell Mammy was shocked. 'I think so, but 'twas a bit confusing.'

'I'm sure he didn't mean it.'

'I'm sure too. Ambrose is a good person, Mammy, and always so patient with me.' 'Patient' was a word Mammy liked, because she was always telling her and Katie to be it.

'He is, Merry, and he's been so kind to you, helping you with your letters and giving you books. I've known Mr Lister since you were a little baby, and he *is* a very good man. Remember, he's from Dublin, and up in Dublin people think funny things, maybe different things from us, but I'm sure he has God in his heart.'

'Yes, so am I,' Merry nodded, feeling relieved that she could continue being Ambrose's friend without making God angry. Besides, she really wanted to hear the rest of *A Christmas Carol* . . .

'Dear little Mary had tears in her eyes when she looked at the book. She caressed the letters as if they were made of solid gold. It brought tears to my own eyes, James, it truly did.'

James sat opposite Ambrose, nursing a mug of tea, as Ambrose drank a large whiskey. It had been a long, busy day, as Christmas Eve always was, and James still had Midnight Mass to go. His stomach felt heavy from the amount of Christmas treats he'd been plied with by the kind parishioners, which he'd felt he must eat gratefully and comment on their wonderful flavour.

'Is all quite well in the O'Reilly household?' Ambrose was asking. 'I had the distinct feeling from Merry that her parents

were less than happy. And her poor mother looks far too thin and completely exhausted.'

'I sent the doctor up to see her as you requested. He reported that Maggie O'Reilly's fatigue is simply the result of too many babies. I don't know the exact medical details, but the doctor has told both husband and wife that young Patrick must be their last child. Apparently, it's doubtful that Maggie could survive another pregnancy.'

'What does that mean in practice?'

'I'm sure you can understand what that means, Ambrose. 'Tis our Catholic ways; nothing must prevent God's children coming into the world, other than nature.'

'So in short, all conjugal rights have now become wrongs?' said Ambrose.

'Yes. Maggie and John can no longer indulge in the natural pleasures of the flesh, because any resulting child would surely kill her. Neither can they take safeguards to stop that happening, or they go against God and everything their faith stands for.'

'No wonder even a six-year-old has noticed her father is taking a nip of whiskey more often than he used to,' Ambrose remarked. 'Six years ago, Maggie O'Reilly was a beautiful young woman, and her husband a strong, handsome man. Now she looks as though she carries the weight of the world on her shoulders.'

'They both do,' sighed James. 'Sadly, they are just one of many young couples in the parish in the same predicament.'

'Do you think I should offer some extra support? If the family were able to employ domestic help, then—'

'No, Ambrose. No one except the richest farmers and trades-people, and myself as a priest of course, can employ domestic staff. It would be seen as a move far above the O'Reillys' station, and would alienate them from their community.'

'Then there's nothing we can do?'

'I must leave now to prepare for Midnight Mass. We'll talk more when I'm back, but no, I don't think there is.'

Ambrose watched as James left the room to go and celebrate one of the most holy nights of the year in the Christian faith. He'd said before that the majority of his flock were even less well off than the O'Reillys. Hope of a heavenly existence beyond the hardship of their lives on earth was an easy myth to peddle to the poor.

The question was, was he himself playing 'God' with Mary, due to his fondness for her?

As a child, he'd been presented with his own first book of Greek fables, like the one he'd just given Mary. He'd read it with fascination, and it could be said that the book had brought him to where he was now: a Senior Fellow in Classics at Trinity College, Dublin.

Then, he'd imagined the gods on the top of Mount Olympus as puppet-masters: each one in charge of a few million human beings who lived like ants below them on the earth.

'The gods' games,' Ambrose muttered as he poured himself another glass of whiskey. Yet now he was a human god, capable of using money he'd never even earned himself to change the life of one young child. He was becoming sure that Mary had a bright academic future, but was he like all parents – albeit a quasi-one – and trying to model Mary in his own image?

His Greek philosophers had plenty to say on that score. But for once, Ambrose preferred to think for himself.

As the clock struck midnight, Ambrose crossed himself out of habit. James was right: they must trust the O'Reillys to be the reliable and steady cradle that Mary needed until she was older – and if fate took a hand he could step in sooner.

31

'I wish I'd lived in the days of the War of Independence against the British,' Bobby said as he and Merry walked across the fields from Clogagh to home. Her little brother Bill, who had started school last autumn, was following on behind, holding on to the hand of Bobby's little sister Helen, a quiet, shy girl who had Bobby's colouring, but none of his anger.

'Then you might have been shot, Bobby Noiro,' Merry replied as she watched him stop suddenly. His latest game was shooting stones from his slingshot, pretending he was something called a 'volunteer'.

'One day, I'll show you the gun my granddad used to kill the British colonists,' he said as he caught up with her.

'What's a colonist?' she asked him, just to test whether he really knew.

'Britishers who stole countries for themselves. My granny told me,' he said importantly.

Merry sighed and shook her head. As Bobby had grown, so had his aggression *and* his hatred for the British. And as she knew Ambrose came from a British family originally, even

433

if they had arrived here hundreds of years ago, which really made him Irish anyway, she didn't like it when Bobby gave her the chat about the British being evil.

'Bang!' he shouted suddenly. 'Got yer!'

Merry looked on horrified as he started taking shots at the cows in the O'Hanlons' field.

'Stop that, Bobby!'

''Tis just target practice, Merry,' he protested as she pulled him away from the cows, who were lowing in distress. Helen had started to cry and looked genuinely frightened. 'They're for the slaughter soon anyway.'

'You can't be hurting creatures for sport,' she reprimanded him, taking Helen in her arms and grabbing Bill's hand. 'There's no reason for it.'

''Tis what the British did to us,' he muttered darkly, but he moved away from the cows and walked next to her the rest of the way.

Merry knew it was best not to talk to him once he went down this path. In the years that they'd been at school together, she'd learnt he was a boy whose moods could change like lightning. Even though the rest of their class barely acknowledged him anymore, due to his violent attacks if the boys were playing football in the playground and someone called his tactics 'foul', Merry still saw a different side to him when they were alone. In the classroom, he was the only one who was up to her reading standard and took an interest in the world beyond their small farming community. Bobby *wanted* to learn like she did, and that bond, and seeing the gentler side that the others didn't, gave Merry hope that Bobby would grow out of his bad behaviour. Besides, she felt sorry for him, what with him having no friends and having to be the man in his family because he'd no daddy.

She would never forget the day he'd cried like a baby on

Merry's shoulder. His dog, Hunter, had been shot by mistake by a neighbouring farmer out after rabbits. He'd crowed in delight when the farmer's pigsty was mysteriously set alight a few days later.

'"An eye for an eye" is what the Bible says, Merry,' Bobby had concluded, even though she'd endlessly tried to explain that Hunter's shooting had been an accident.

Yet however strange and sometimes downright cruel Bobby was, Merry knew she was his only friend, and she couldn't help her heart going out to him.

What made it worse was that Katie, now thirteen, had left school last Christmas, declaring herself 'bored of learning'.

'Besides, what with Ellen away and married, and Nora working up at the Big House during the shooting season and when the family are there in the summer, I'm the eldest girl and Mammy needs my help at home,' Katie had said.

Bobby had been scared of Katie, who always said exactly what she thought, so now it was just Merry and the little ones who walked home with him.

Since leaving six months ago, Katie never read anymore and was only interested in putting her hair up in different styles, or listening to loud music by someone called Elvis on the radio Daddy had bought a year ago. She and Nora often practised new dances together in the kitchen, and Merry felt left out, even though Katie insisted she was still her best friend.

'And I don't like you spending so much time with Bobby Noiro,' she'd said to Merry. 'Your man is mad as a box of frogs.'

'No, he isn't, he just has a vivid imagination, 'tis all,' Merry had defended him, but inside, part of her agreed with her sister. She'd found that the best way to calm him when he got into one of his moods was to tell him a story. She'd been

telling him Greek myths and legends from the book Ambrose had once given her for Christmas. While Bobby enjoyed the violent tales of gods wreaking vengeance on other gods most, Merry's favourite was that of the Seven Sisters, as she was one of seven siblings herself.

'You know that the IRA stored arms in my family's barn during the revolution,' Bobby continued as they walked. 'My granny told me they were always gone by morn. She hates the British and so do I,' he added, just in case she hadn't understood from the thousands of times he'd told her before.

'Bobby, we shouldn't hate anyone. The Bible says that—' Merry began.

'I don't care what the Bible says. The British Protestants have ruled over our country for too long. They stole our lands, treated us like peasants and starved us! Granny says in the North they still do.' He turned to Merry, his black hair grown so long it blew in the wind, and his heavy dark eyebrows fierce over his blue eyes. 'You would think that any good god wouldn't have made us suffer like that, wouldn't you?'

'No, but to be sure, He had his reasons. And look! Ireland's a republic now, Bobby. We're free!' she said.

'But the English are still here, in the country that should be ours, *all* ours, even the North.'

'The world isn't perfect, is it? Besides, take a look at where we live,' she said, turning round and stretching out her arms. ''Tis beautiful!'

Merry stood looking down over the fields, as Bill picked up a ladybird and handed it to Helen, who immediately screamed and dropped it.

'Look at the lady's eardrops growing everywhere' – Merry pointed – 'and the coppertips in the woods. And then there's the green fields and the trees and the blue sea just beyond the valley.'

''Tis the trouble with girls,' Bobby grumbled. 'Your heads are in the clouds, dreaming the day away. That's why we men have to fight the wars and leave you behind at home with the babes.'

'Not fair, Bobby Noiro,' Merry retorted as they set off again towards Inchybridge. 'I'd beat you in reading any day. I bet you wouldn't even be knowing who Charles Dickens is.'

'No, but I'm sure he's a Britisher with that name, so.'

'And what if he is? Shakespeare, the greatest writer in the world, was an Englishman too. Now then, we're here,' she said with relief as they reached the narrow bridge that crossed the slim strip of the Argideen River. 'I'll be seeing you tomorrow, Bobby. Eight o'clock, or I'll be gone without you. Bye, Helen,' she said to the little girl, who nodded and trotted off behind her big brother. Merry felt sorry for her too – she was desperately thin and hardly ever said a word.

'I'll be seeing ye,' Bobby said as he turned and marched off along the lane to his homeplace further along the valley. Merry walked on with Bill, loving the rare feeling of sun on her face. There was a smell of what Merry could only describe as a freshness in the air, and the fields were dotted with daisies and dandelions. She sat down where she was and laid flat on her back, and Bill, who adored his older sister, followed suit. She was sad that there were only a few days to go before the end of term. Next year would be her last with Miss Lucey, because she would be eleven. After that, she didn't know where she would be sent to school; maybe St Mary's Convent in Clonakilty, where her sisters had all gone for a while.

'The nuns hit you with a ruler if your skirt's not down to your ankles or your shoes don't shine,' Katie had declared when she'd been there. 'And there are no boys,' she'd added with a sigh.

Merry had decided no boys sounded like a good thing, but the nuns definitely looked scary, and 'twas a long walk to meet the school bus every day.

As Merry stood up, she decided that, unlike Nora and Katie, she didn't want to grow up at all.

'Phew, 'tis hot in here!' Merry commented as she threw her satchel on the kitchen table.

'Don't be complaining it's too hot when you spend all winter complaining about the cold,' Katie reprimanded her.

'Want some bread and jam?' Merry asked her sister as she cut herself a slice and covered it in the rich strawberry preserve Father O'Brien had given Mammy last week. Merry thought it was the best thing she'd ever tasted. 'Where is Mammy today? Has she taken Pat out visiting?'

'I'd say she's resting. She's exhausted all the time, so 'tis a good thing I'm here to keep house.'

'I'm here, girls.' Their mammy gave a weak smile as she walked through the kitchen door.

'Where's Pat?'

'In the fields with Daddy and John,' said Katie.

Merry studied Mammy and thought she looked as wan as she had after Pat was born. She'd seemed better in the last few years, but as her mother turned towards the range to boil the kettle, Merry's own tummy turned over as she saw the slight outline of a bump.

'Katie, will you go call the boys in for their tea?' Mammy ordered her. Katie gave a toss of her flame-coloured curls and went outside.

'Mammy,' Merry said, lowering her voice as she walked towards her, 'are you, well, are you having another babe?'

Maggie turned to her daughter, then stroked the top of her blonde head.

'There's nothing you don't notice, is there, Merry? Yes, I am, but 'tis a secret from the rest of your brothers and sisters.'

'But, I thought the doctor had said no more babies, because then you'd get sick again?' Merry felt the panic rising inside her – she still remembered the time after Pat's birth as the worst few months of her life.

'I know, but sometimes, these things just . . . happen. God has put new life there and' – Merry watched her beloved mammy swallow hard as her eyes glinted with tears – 'if that's what He wants, there's none should say 'tis wrong. Now then, Merry,' Maggie said as she put a finger to her lips, 'shhhh, promise?'

'I promise.'

That night, Merry didn't sleep a wink. If anything happened to Mammy, she thought she'd die.

Please God, I'll do anything, anything, *even kill Britishers, but please let Mammy live!*

'Maggie O'Reilly is expecting again,' James sighed as he and Ambrose enjoyed a rare sunny day in the pleasant garden of his house, which overlooked the whole stretch of Court-macsherry Bay below.

Ambrose looked at him in horror.

'Surely that's a disaster! She's just written herself her own death sentence.'

'We'll all have to pray that she's stronger now than she was the last time. The doctor might be wrong.'

'James, you know what this might mean for Mary, and she's doing so well at school.'

'She is indeed, and what makes it worse is that Miss Lucey came by only the other day to talk with me about her. Merry is in desperate need of superior teaching. She's surpassed everyone in the school and Miss Lucey is in a quandary as to what to do with her next year. After that, well,' James concluded, 'if her mother is having another baby, her help may be needed at home.'

'What can I do?'

'Very little for now,' said James. 'I can at least make sure the doctor puts Maggie in a hospital to have this baby. Then, if things go wrong, she has professionals around her.'

'Mary *must* continue her education, James,' Ambrose urged him. 'She's read the entire works of Charles Dickens, and last time I saw her, I gave her a copy of *Jane Eyre.*'

'Would you not think that the . . . romance side of it was a little grown-up for her?'

'There's nothing of the physical side of love in that story, James.'

'No, and we must both remember that Mary has grown up watching bulls mount cows. The children round here are innocent in many ways, yet at the same time they have to grow up so fast.'

'Not as fast as young women are growing up in Dublin. Have you heard of this new book, *The Country Girls*, by a young writer called Edna O'Brien? It's just been banned in Ireland because it talks openly of women having sex before marriage. There's been an outcry from the church, but my English Fellow friend provided me with a copy,' Ambrose grinned.

'And?'

'It's a triumph, if one is eager to break boundaries and move Ireland – and the lives of women here – forward, although I doubt it would be your cup of tea. We also have

the imminent prospect of a national television service, which will again change the country as we know it.'

'Have you seen a television?'

'Yes indeed. I have a friend who lives up close to the border with the North and is able to get a picture from the British transmitter there. It's like having a miniature cinema in your own sitting room.'

'I'm sure 'twill be years before such a thing makes its way down here to West Cork,' said James.

'Are you glad about that, or not?'

James gazed down over the fields, the town beyond them, and the bay. 'I'd certainly like my flock to live above the breadline and to have advances in medicine . . . I'm all for that.'

'Even contraception?'

James saw his friend had a mischievous glint in his eye. 'We both know the answer to that. As a priest, how can I be in favour?'

'Not even when it would have safeguarded Maggie O'Reilly's life?'

'No, Ambrose. Wilfully stopping human life arriving goes against every Christian belief. It must be God's decision to give life or to take it away. Not ours.'

'This from a man who, after a few drops of whiskey last month, agreed that more wars have been fought and more millions of lives lost in the name of religion than anything else.'

James couldn't deny he'd agreed, so drained his teacup and placed it back in its saucer.

'Anyway, dear boy, we have veered heavily off track,' said Ambrose. 'Whether we like it or not, Mrs O'Reilly is having her baby in – what? Six months' time? And Mary's fate will then be known. I suppose all we can do is wait.'

'And pray for them both,' whispered James.

As the glorious summer months descended into autumn and then into winter, Merry watched as her mother's stomach grew large and sapped her energy. Dr Townsend had been to visit only last week and had advised, to everyone's relief, that mother and baby were doing well.

'However, given the damage inflicted on Mrs O'Reilly during her last labour and the fact that she's underweight herself, I must advise complete bed rest. This will give her a chance to save the energy she needs for when her time comes.'

Merry had looked at her father aghast, but he'd hardly seemed to hear what the doctor was saying. These days she rarely saw him, nor he his family. He'd be out all day on the farm, come in for his tea, then be off to either the Henry Ford pub or the Abbey Bar in Timoleague to chat with the other farmers. Merry didn't like the sound of Pa Griffin, the owner of the bar. When he wasn't pouring the stout or whiskey, he'd be off taking in dead bodies and making the coffins to bury them in, because he was also an undertaker. Merry was long in bed when she'd hear Daddy arrive home. In the mornings, when he came in for his breakfast, his eyes would be red, like he was the devil.

'What will we do, Daddy?' she'd asked him once the doctor had left. 'While Mammy has to be in bed,' she'd added in case he didn't understand.

Daddy had shrugged. 'Well so, you, Katie and Nora are the women of the house. Sure, you can sort it out between yourselves.'

When he left the kitchen, Mammy appeared from upstairs. She looked even paler than before the doctor had arrived, and sat down heavily in the chair by the range.

Katie glanced around helplessly at them all.

'Don't look at me, Katie,' said Nora. 'I'm away up at the Big House most of the time, skivvying in the kitchen.'

'You could leave your job and help me,' put in Katie.

'What? And lose the few shillings they pay me?' Nora shook her head. 'I'll be working for free here doing the same thing.'

'Your wages don't help us, do they? They just pay for your fancy clothes and your trips up to Cork City to buy them, while I do everything here,' Katie spat back.

'Girls, please!' Mammy said as Nora and Katie eyed each other furiously. 'Sure, we can work something out.'

'At least Bill will be coming to school with me,' put in Merry. 'And I'll make the breakfast before I leave.'

'But there's minding Pat, an' all the washing and the cooking and the cleaning and the pigs! Who'll do the pigs?' Katie's eyes were full of tears.

'We won't be taking every word the doctor said seriously,' said Mammy. 'I can rest when Merry and Bill get back from school.'

'Mammy, we must do as the doctor has told us, mustn't we, Katie?' Merry implored her.

'Yes,' Katie replied reluctantly. 'But, Nora, you have to be helping when you're here.'

'Are you saying I don't help now? 'Tis a lie, Katie O'Reilly, and—'

'I—'

'Stop!' Merry butted in before another argument could start between them. ''Tis only a few weeks until the babe is born, and I've the Christmas holidays from school too. I'll help all I can, I swear.'

'I'm not having you doing housework instead of homework, Merry,' said Mammy firmly. 'I'll ask Ellen to come in every day to help us.'

'Oh Mammy, she'll be bringing her own babe up here and then 'twill be a madhouse,' Nora complained.

'Will all of you stop it!' Mammy said, and Merry saw tears in her mother's eyes. 'Now, can one of you be laying out the plates for our tea?'

Later, up in their bedroom, Merry and Katie discussed the situation.

''Tis all very well Mammy saying she'll find a way, but for a start, she can't be working on a Monday for Father O'Brien,' said Merry. ''Tis a big old house and Mrs Cavanagh gets so cross if she doesn't leave it sparkling. *And* spreads gossip around the place about how bad at cleaning Mammy is.'

'Oh, don't you be minding her; everyone knows she's an evil old witch. One day her cold heart will turn her to stone and she'll be in hell for all eternity.'

'Maybe I could do the cleaning at Father O'Brien's house,' Merry thought out loud. 'Just one day of missing school wouldn't be too much of a bother. Our John left at my age to help Daddy run the farm.'

'But farming's what he's born to do, Merry. Everyone knows you're cleverer than anyone else around these parts. And how much you love your learning. Father O'Brien wouldn't be hearing of it.'

Merry sighed, then turned out the light on the little wooden night stand that Daddy had made for them one Christmas.

'Merry?' came a voice out of the darkness.

'Yes?'

'Do you . . . do you think Daddy is a drunk?'

'Why are you asking?'

'Only 'cos I heard Seamus O'Hanlon laughing about Daddy being too fond of the bottle. You know 'tis often John that's up and into the shed to start the milking. And he's driving the

cart with the churns to the creamery most mornings, because Daddy's still asleep downstairs.'

Merry lay there thinking how Katie always said out loud what she only dared to think. Of course she'd noticed, but what could she do?

Nothing, was the answer.

During the next two months, Merry and Katie did their best to help Mammy rest. They shared the early morning chores, making sure everyone was fed before Merry and Bill left for school. If Nora wasn't working up at the Big House, she would mind Pat, although, as usual with Nora, she often couldn't be found when she was needed.

'I'd reckon she's meeting a fellow on her way home,' Katie told Merry. 'That Charlie Doonan lives near to the Big House, and she's always been sweet on him.'

Mammy would sit in the leather chair next to the range and teach her younger girls how to make soups and stews from the vegetables they grew in the field. Merry decided that when she grew up, she'd never cook another turnip again as long as she lived. They'd also had to learn how to break a chicken's neck, which was awful as the girls fed them every morning and had named them all. Even though Mammy had also been teaching her how to make sweet things like brack and scones, Merry despaired as all her mixtures came out of the range wrong. So she left Katie to take over those because she was so much better at it.

Often, Mammy insisted on coming downstairs more than she should to supervise them.

'I'm your mammy, girls, and I'm not ill, just carrying a babe,' she'd say when they chastised her for being in the kitchen.

Ellen had temporarily taken on Mammy's duties at Father O'Brien's house, so Mammy could return to the job once she'd had the new baby.

'I need that job, girls,' she'd said one night as the three of them had sat in front of the fire in the New Room, knitting booties and bonnets for the babe. 'See, the wages I've saved have paid for the wool to make sure this babe never goes cold.'

Now it was the start of the Christmas holidays – the baby was due during Christmas week itself – and Merry despaired that there was no walking up the hill to the priest's house with Mammy, to sit in front of the fire with Ambrose to talk and read. All the books he'd given her were still there in Father O'Brien's study, and she'd read everything they had at school, which were mostly books for babies anyway.

Please come soon, Baby, Merry thought miserably as she dragged herself out of bed one rainy morning to go downstairs and cook the goodie. As it was thickening, she crossed the hallway and went to peep in at the New Room. Since Mammy had got pregnant, Daddy had again taken to sleeping downstairs, because now he had a long sofa to stretch out on. Sure enough, there he was, snoring away with his boots still on and the room smelling like a whiskey bottle. She'd heard John earlier, getting up to milk the cows and the clop of the donkey and cart as he took the churns to the creamery.

'Daddy?' she whispered, but got no response.

'Daddy! Will you not be getting up now?' she asked more loudly. 'John's away up with the churns already.'

He stirred, but stayed asleep. Merry sighed and rolled her eyes. At least, she thought, as she closed the latch behind her, John was steadfast and hardworking and never complained about all the extra work he had to do. The family didn't speak

about Daddy's fondness for the bottle, but Merry always made sure she gave John an extra spoonful of sugar on his goodie in the morning. It was hard on him too.

Katie arrived into the kitchen yawning, with Pat and Bill in tow.

'Pat bangs that drum Ellen got him for his birthday the moment he wakes,' Katie grumbled as she looked out of the window. 'It doesn't feel like Christmas is coming, does it?'

'Everything will be better once the babe has been born, Katie.'

'Why does it have to be due at Christmas?'

'Maybe 'tis the new baby Jesus,' Merry giggled. 'This farm will become like Bethlehem, and we'll be charging thousands to pilgrims wanting to see where he was born.'

'That'll be at the Bon Secours Hospital then,' Katie replied pragmatically.

'Holy Mother, I'd not want to go and have my babe delivered by nuns!'

'There's doctors there too, Merry, and it's safer for Mammy.'

'Talking of Christmas, have you been adding the whiskey to the fruitcake every day?' Merry asked her.

'I've tried, but every time I go for the bottle, 'tis always empty. Where is Daddy now?'

'Asleep in the New Room. It might as well be called Daddy's Room these days.'

'Could you not wake him up? 'Tis past seven,' Katie suggested.

'I tried, but he wouldn't wake, so,' Merry shrugged. 'He'll be in when his tummy is growling.'

'Daddy should be out there with John. His son should be helping *him*, not the other way around. Like Nora should be up helping us.'

'I know, Katie, but 'twill all be sorted again when the babe comes, I swear.'

'As long as nothing goes wrong,' Katie said, a grim expression on her face as she doled some goodie into a bowl. 'I'm off to take this up to Mammy and fetch the washing from the boys' room. You should see the state of it – those boys live like pigs. I'll give Nora a kick too,' she called as she left the kitchen.

As Merry gave the goodie another stir, she thought that her sister had unknowingly voiced exactly why it didn't feel like Christmas: everyone in the family was holding their breath until this baby was safely born.

With only a week to go until Christmas, Merry let Dr Townsend in.

'Good afternoon,' he said as he took his hat off. 'I'm here to see your mother. How has she been?'

'I . . .' Dr Townsend frightened Merry, even though he was perfectly nice and Father O'Brien had said he was to be trusted. 'She's been all right, sir, although she did say she was suffering a bit from headaches and complaining her ankles were swollen, but that's just the weight of the babe, isn't it? Would you like a cup of tea, sir? And a mince pie, maybe? My sister made a batch this morning.'

'That would be excellent, thank you, Katie. I'll go up and see your mother first, and be down for one after.'

Merry didn't correct him on confusing her name with her sister's. The fact he'd bothered to try made him a little more human in her eyes.

Ten minutes later, just as she was taking the warmed mince pie out of the range and the tea in the pot was perfectly brewed, Dr Townsend came into the kitchen.

'There you are, Doctor,' she said, pointing at the cup and saucer (Mammy had said they must serve him tea in one of the two china cups they owned). 'Please, sit down.'

'Thank you, Katie. Is your father around?'

'I'd say he's in the milking shed,' Merry answered as she poured the tea for him.

'Good. While I drink this, would you be able to run and fetch him? I need to speak to him.'

'O'course. Is there something wrong with Mammy?'

'Nothing that we can't sort out, so please don't worry. Off you go, there's a good girl.'

A few minutes later, Merry was back with Daddy and John, and Bill and Pat in tow. Katie appeared from the scullery, and Nora arrived from work. Merry was only glad that it was early enough in the evening so that Daddy hadn't disappeared off on his nightly trip to the pub.

'What is it, Doctor?' Daddy asked, and even though the worry in his eyes frightened her, there was a part of her that was glad to see it, because it meant he wasn't drunk. She handed him a mug of tea, then poured some for the rest of the family.

'Please don't be alarmed, Mr O'Reilly. As I said to your daughter, it's nothing that we can't sort out. And by the way, Katie,' Dr Townsend said, turning to Merry, 'you were right to mention your mother's swollen ankles. It's a condition called oedema and is very common in a lot of women when they are near their time. However, given the fact Mrs O'Reilly is also suffering from headaches and has a previous history of problems, I'd like to make arrangements to take her into hospital now, so that we can monitor her closely up to the birth. If it's acceptable to you, Mr O'Reilly, I'll drive up to Father O'Brien's to use the telephone and let the hospital know Mrs O'Reilly is coming in.' He turned to Merry again. 'Perhaps

you could pop upstairs and pack a bag of things your mother might need, like a nightgown, slippers and a dressing gown. And, of course, things for the baby. I'm presuming you have no transport?'

'No, sir, only a donkey and cart and a tractor,' Daddy said.

'Then I'll be back in an hour to drive your wife to Cork City. I'll see you later,' Dr Townsend said, then left.

A silence hung over the kitchen.

'I'll be running upstairs to sort out Mammy's things,' Merry said. Reaching the door, she glanced back at Daddy's face. He looked terrified, because everyone around these parts knew that you never went into the hospital unless you weren't going to come out again.

Stop it, Merry, you always knew Mammy was having the babe there. She's just going a little early, that's all.

She tapped lightly on Mammy's door before walking in. Her mother had hauled herself upright and was sitting on the side of the bed, cradling her huge tummy. She was deathly pale and her forehead was beaded with sweat.

'I've come up to help you pack your bag for hospital.'

'Thank you, Merry. My spare nightgown is in the press over there, and . . .' She directed her daughter around the room to collect all the items she needed.

'Have you ever been in a hospital before, Mammy?'

'No, but I went once to Cork City with Daddy. 'Tis very big.'

Merry thought she looked like a frightened child.

When the bag for her and the baby was ready and she'd helped Mammy into one of her smock dresses, Merry came to sit on the bed next to her and took her hand.

''Tis good you'll be looked after, Mammy.'

'What will those grand city women think of me?' Mammy swept a hand down her old maternity dress.

'It doesn't matter. All that does is that you and the babe are safe and well. Father O'Brien says 'tis a very good hospital.'

Maggie took Merry's head in her hands and kissed the top of it.

'You're a good girl, so, Merry. Whatever happens to me, you must listen to Father O'Brien and Mr Lister. They'll help you, I know they will.'

'Yes, Mammy, I will, o'course, but you'll be home soon enough.'

Maggie took her daughter in her arms and held her tight, like she couldn't bear to let her go.

'Just remember to follow your dreams, won't you? You're special, Merry, and don't you go forgetting you are. Promise?'

'I promise.'

It was the last conversation that Merry would ever have with her beloved mother.

32

It was a bitterly cold January day when Maggie O'Reilly was buried with her newborn baby in the graveyard at Timoleague church. Father O'Brien took the service, and Merry held Pat on her lap, her brothers and sisters tight around her, all numbed with grief. Pat still hadn't understood that his mammy had gone; the rest of the family had been unable to explain to the five-year-old what had happened.

Merry was relieved when Nora took him from her during the wake up at the farm, and carried him upstairs. She could still hear Pat screaming his little lungs raw, asking where his Mammy was.

'I can't bear the noise,' muttered Katie, as she put out another plate of scones for the mourners. 'What'll we do now, Merry? What'll happen to our family?'

'I don't know.' Merry scratched distractedly at the high neck of her black funeral dress, too devastated to think straight.

'Did you see all the people in the church?' said Katie. 'I've never seen some o' them before in my life. Who was that old man walking with the stick? And that fierce-looking lady on his arm? Did Mammy know them?'

'Katie O'Reilly, keep your voice down,' hissed Ellen as she came up behind them, holding her two-year-old daughter,

who she'd named Maggie after their mother. 'I think that lady was Mammy's mother,' she whispered.

'Our grandmother, you mean?' Katie asked in shock.

'I remember seeing her once in the street years ago, when I was with Mammy in Timoleague,' said Ellen. 'Mammy looked at her, and just as the lady was about to walk straight past her, she called out to her and said, "Hello, Mammy." The lady didn't answer, just carried on walking.'

'She didn't say hello to her own daughter?' Merry breathed in disbelief. 'Why?'

'I'd not be knowing,' Ellen shrugged, 'but the least that woman could do is to come to her daughter's funeral,' she muttered angrily, then turned away to fill the mourners' glasses.

Merry stood where she was, too numb to summon up the energy to ask more. It felt like the house was stifling hot and full of people. While all their friends and neighbours had come, Bobby hadn't. He had caught her at Inchybridge the day before on her way back from getting some shopping in Timoleague.

'I'm sorry about your mam, Merry. I wanted to tell you that my mammy said my sister and me are to stay at home. Maybe 'tis since my daddy died that she's not been wanting to go to any funerals. 'Tis no disrespect to your mammy, Merry, or your family.'

She'd nodded, close to tears for the thousandth time since Dr Townsend had arrived with Father O'Brien to tell them all the terrible news.

'It doesn't matter, Bobby. 'Tis kind of you to explain.'

''Tis to do with our families, I think. Something that happened a long time ago, but I don't know what. I'll be seeing ye.' Then he'd given her a hug the only way he knew how, squeezing her hard round her middle.

Merry felt as though she might suffocate where she stood. She needed to get away from the crowds of people that were milling around the New Room and the kitchen. Outside, she could hear the cows lowing in the barn, continuing on as though everything was normal, when it really wasn't. And never would be again, because Mammy was never coming back.

'Good Lord, what a wretched day,' muttered Ambrose as he looked out of the window, the sky pendulous with heavy grey clouds. Like most people in northern Europe, he'd always loathed January. As a child, going back to school after the Christmas holidays had always been the most miserable journeys of his entire life. Nothing to look forward to, the weather dreadful, just as it was outside now. Up to his knees in mud as he staggered across a rugby pitch, waiting to be attacked by one of the larger boys, which, given how short he was, meant just about everyone on the pitch.

And now, all these years on, he had different reasons for feeling as miserable and helpless as he did today.

'So, where do we go from here?' Ambrose said as he sat down and stared at James, sitting opposite him in front of the fire in his study. It was a week since Maggie O'Reilly's funeral, which he'd been desperate to attend, but James had said his presence would attract too much attention in the close-knit farming community.

'Sadly, I doubt there's much we can do, Ambrose,' said James.

'The family must be heartbroken.'

'How else would they be? 'Twas Maggie who held that household together. Especially after John O'Reilly began drowning his misery in whiskey.'

'How is he now?'

'I tried to speak to him at the wake, but he wasn't saying much.'

'Does Mary know what it will mean for her?' said Ambrose.

'Ah, sure, all the girls know there'll be hard work ahead.'

'But what about her schooling, James?'

'I'm afraid that round these parts, education doesn't win over two little boys needing care, let alone feeding the chickens, doing the washing, shopping and cooking, tending the cows and helping to bring in the harvest.'

'But . . . it's mandatory for all children to go to school.'

'Only to primary school, up to the age of eleven, which Merry is now. And even then, especially down in a rural place like this, teachers would be expecting a number of absences from children of Merry's age.'

'What you're saying is that Mary's formal education could stop in six months' time, when she finishes primary school?' Ambrose shook his head in despair. 'To see that bright, enquiring mind reduced to baking cakes and washing the family's smalls is simply a travesty! And I won't have it!'

'Of course I agree, but I can't see how it can be averted,' said James.

'James, in my role as quasi-godfather, all I wish to do is to protect her and educate her. Do you understand?'

'I do, of course . . .'

'You know I have the funds to help. Can you see any way in which I could?'

'I'd say that any money you handed over to John would only be used for one thing, and that would not benefit Merry or the rest of her family.'

'Then what if I took her back to Dublin with me and put her into school there? Surely Mr O'Reilly couldn't complain?

I'd be taking one of his children off his hands, relieving him of an extra mouth to feed . . .'

James took a deep breath to calm himself and gather his thoughts before he spoke. There had been many times the two of them had disagreed over the years, but the subjects that provoked those disagreements, such as politics or religion, did not take the form of an eleven-year-old child *or* her family, who were part of his flock.

'Ambrose, would it not occur to you that John O'Reilly might actually love his daughter? That Merry's brothers and sisters love her too? And, even more importantly, that she loves *them*? She is grieving for her mother. From what I've seen, Nora, the eldest sister left at home, is a self-absorbed young lady, who finds a way out of everything that needs to be done. Which places the burden of running the house and looking after the younger brothers squarely on Katie and Merry's shoulders. Is it fair on Katie to remove Merry from her home? I too love her dearly, but I must consider all members of the family.'

'Is there not a relation who could step in at this point? Surely John O'Reilly has an extended family? Everyone in Ireland does, especially down here.'

'There is family on both sides, but they are . . . estranged. 'Tis a long story, but like most things around these parts, it goes back a long way,' sighed James. 'I've learnt in my time here that old wounds run deep. It is, after all, the area where Michael Collins lived and died.'

'I see, but what about friends and neighbours?'

'We'll not get friends and neighbours to take on another family's domestic situation, Ambrose. They've enough managing their own.'

Ambrose took a sip of his whiskey. 'It makes me wonder when Ireland will stop looking to the past, and begin to see the future.'

'I'd say it will take a good few more years than we have now. Tales are told of family heroes in the War of Independence to the young seated around the hearth, which often sows the seeds of hatred in the next generation.'

'Still, none of this solves the problem with what to do about Mary,' said Ambrose.

'I think you must accept that for now, there is nothing you can do. Merry is still grieving; she needs her family around her and they need her.'

'But if she misses out on her education now, she'll have no chance of getting the university degree I know could be within her grasp. It would change her life, James.'

James reached out a hand and placed it on Ambrose's. 'Trust me, leave it for the moment.'

There was a tap on the door as it opened, and Mrs Cavanagh appeared. James immediately pulled back his hand.

After a moment's pause, Mrs Cavanagh's beady eyes pulled themselves up from James's hand to his face. 'Excuse me if I was interrupting, but I was wondering what time you wanted your tea?'

'Mr Lister will leave to drive back to Dublin in twenty minutes or so. I can make myself a sandwich later,' James said abruptly.

'Very well,' Mrs Cavanagh nodded. 'I'll be off then, and we'll be having to find a permanent replacement for Mrs O'Reilly soon. Ellen O'Reilly isn't reliable, in my opinion, and I need my day off. Goodnight, Father,' she said, then nodded at Ambrose and added, 'Sir.' The door shut behind her with a thump.

'That woman never ceases to remind me of Mrs Danvers in Daphne du Maurier's *Rebecca*,' Ambrose sighed. 'And you're right, my friend, I must be off.' Ambrose stood up. 'Will you telephone me as soon as your thoughts on Mary have coalesced?'

'I will, and please try not to fret. I won't be letting your beloved girl's brain stultify,' he said as he followed Ambrose out of the study and to the front door. 'May God take care of you until we meet again.'

'And may you take care of Mary,' Ambrose muttered under his breath as he climbed into his Beetle, ready to drive through the West Cork rain and home to Dublin.

James left the conversation he needed to have with John O'Reilly for another two months. In that time, he consulted with Miss Lucey at Merry's school, who was also anxious to see her star pupil continue to blossom.

'She's a gifted child, so, Father,' Geraldine Lucey said, as James sat in her parents' parlour eating what he considered (and he had extensive knowledge of the subject) to be excellent brack cake made by Miss Lucey's mother. He understood now why all seasoned priests were carrying extra weight.

'She's still coming to school with her little brother Bill, but she looks like a ghost. I'd say she's taking on extra chores at home, because her homework is never done. That's all right for now, Father, she's ahead anyway, but if she stops school in June to help on the farm full-time, all her potential will be wasted.'

'Yes, it would be tragic,' James agreed.

Geraldine shook her head and exhaled in agitation. 'I understand how it is here, but . . . this is 1961, Father! The dawn of a new decade. You should see some of the pictures in magazines of what the girls are wearing in London, and even in Dublin! Trousers, and skirts above their knees! Emancipation is coming, it truly is, and I believe that Merry O'Reilly has the makings of a fine school teacher in her, and perhaps more. She has a brain that needs stimulation.'

'I agree, Miss Lucey, but emancipation has yet to reach the south-west of Ireland. Well now, perhaps I could help for the foreseeable future.'

'How? As I mentioned to you before, Merry's after reading through every book in the school library.'

'I'd be willing to lend you some from my own library. I've Lamb's *Tales From Shakespeare*, some Austen and Brontë. And what do you think of introducing her to some modern poetry? T. S. Eliot, perhaps?'

'I'd say she was ready for it, Father, and I would, of course, take great care of them, and lock them up in my office after Merry has read them.'

'I'd only be able to do this if the books were to be offered to every other child in her class.'

'They would be, Father, but there is no eleven-year-old who'd want to take them; most of them are still struggling to put their words into a sentence. Other than one boy: Bobby Noiro is as bright as a button, but what a troubled soul he is,' Miss Lucey sighed.

'He comes from a troubled family, as you know. Anyway, regarding the books, there's no harm in offering them to the other children at least.' James gave Miss Lucey a smile. 'Now, I must be off, but I'm grateful for your support and your discretion on this matter.'

Climbing onto his bicycle, James rode away from the gaily painted house that stood halfway up the hill along the winding streets of Timoleague. Looking at the steep slope and then down at his bulging stomach, he pedalled with determination up the rest of the hill to home.

Ambrose arrived for his monthly visit, bringing all kinds of books to help further Merry's education.

'She must learn of the world around her,' he said, as he stacked the last of several leather-bound volumes onto James's desk. 'This is the full set of the *Children's Britannica*, only published last year. They are for children aged seven to fourteen – an offshoot of the adult encyclopaedia – and I had them sent from Hatchards in London. They cover most subjects and will help feed Mary's enquiring mind.'

James studied the title and gave Ambrose a wry smile. 'I'm not sure the word "Britannica" will go down well around these parts.'

'Goodness, James, this is the most comprehensive compendium of collective knowledge it's possible to read in English! Surely no one need worry about its nationality? The Irish have their republic now, and they still speak the same language after all!'

'I shall leave it up to Miss Lucey's discretion. Perhaps she can keep them in her office, and the children can read them when they wish.'

'Whatever you and Miss Lucey think best. Now then, how is Mary?'

'Still devastated by her mother's death, as is all the family. Last time I saw her, she told me that school was all that was keeping her going. At least the older sister Nora is back full-time at the farm, because the shooting season is over and she's no longer needed to help in the kitchens at Argideen House. And . . . I did hear something that may be of use. Bridget O'Mahoney, who's a classmate of Merry's, is being sent to boarding school in Dublin next September. Her mother is originally from Dublin and went there herself. The family is wealthy and they want Bridget to have the best education money can buy.'

'Ah . . .' said Ambrose as he sat down in James's study and looked up at his friend expectantly.

'Now, the fees are exorbitant, but the school does offer scholarships to bright Catholic girls from poor backgrounds.' James looked at Ambrose. 'What do you think?'

'I think . . . I think that you may have just solved the problem, James. You are a genius!'

'Hardly, Ambrose. For a start, Merry has to win the scholarship. Added to that, she herself must want to go. And then there's the issue of her father agreeing to it, although the fact Bridget will be attending will help enormously. The O'Mahoneys are very well respected around these parts.'

'As I said, you're a genius, James. So, what happens next?'

A week later, James had gone for his regular visit to the school. Afterwards, he'd summoned Merry into Miss Lucey's office. The child looked exhausted and had lost weight, so her huge blue eyes stood out in her pale, gaunt face.

He explained the idea to Merry, and watched her expression go through a gamut of emotions.

'What do you think, Merry?'

'I'd say 'tis not worth thinking about it, 'cos I'm not clever enough to win anything, especially against girls from Dublin. They'd be far cleverer than me, Father.'

'Well, Miss Lucey, Ambrose and I all think you are quite clever enough to give it a try, Merry. 'Twill be just like a test that Miss Lucey gives you. And she'll make sure you have lots of practice.'

'But even if I did win a scholarship, I'd not want to be leaving everyone here, Father. I'm needed to help at the farm. And Dublin's a long way away.'

'Ambrose lives there, as you know, and I used to as well. It's a beautiful city too. And remember, Bridget O'Mahoney will be going.'

'Yes, but . . .'

'What, Merry?'

'Nothing, Father.'

James watched Merry bite her lip, and knew, of course, that the child did not want to speak ill of a classmate in front of him.

'Might I suggest that you have a try at the scholarship? After all, if you think you will fail anyway, then what do you have to lose?'

'Nothing, I s'pose,' Merry whispered. 'But if Bridget knew I hadn't passed, she'd be teasing me, because she's going anyway.'

'Well, why don't you keep this test a secret for now? Then, if you don't pass, nobody has to know.' James realised that he was stepping out of his remit as a priest to suggest this, but needs must.

'Yes, Father. That would be a better idea. Thank you.'

During the next few weeks, helped secretly by Ambrose to compile what Merry should be studying, Miss Lucey set her star student to work.

Merry had never felt so exhausted. Every day, she was taking books home to study once she'd finished all her chores.

'Why is your satchel so heavy?' Bobby asked her one rainy afternoon as he held it while she climbed over the fence. 'You got some ammo in here or what?'

'You say some really stupid things, Bobby Noiro,' she said as she snatched her satchel back from Bobby, once she'd

helped little Helen and Bill over too. 'Who'd I be trying to kill?'

'The British doctorman who sent your mammy into that hospital to die?'

'He was trying to help her, not to kill her! Will you shut up with your stupid talk?'

'You can say 'tis stupid, but I've been reading my granny's diary, written during the War of Independence and—'

'I said, stop your chatter about wars! Come on, Bill,' she said, grabbing her brother's hand and pulling him off across the field.

'See you tomorrow, Merry,' Bobby called, and Helen raised her small hand in a wave.

Merry didn't bother to respond.

The day of the scholarship exam came, and Merry was put in Miss Lucey's office to take it.

'There you are, Merry,' Miss Lucey said when she arrived, 'a nice hot cup of tea with sugar, and one of my mother's homemade shortbread biscuits.'

'Thank you, Miss Lucey,' Merry said, her hand shaking so much that she had to put the cup down.

'You try and drink up now and eat that biscuit. You need the sugar for your brain.'

Merry said a quick prayer before it was time to turn the test paper over. When she did so, she was surprised to see how easy many of the questions were, and she finished with twenty minutes to spare.

Miss Lucey walked in. 'All done, Merry?'

Merry nodded, and quickly wiped her eyes with her hands. 'Ah now, was it very hard?'

'No . . . I mean, I don't think it was, because I finished ages ago and . . . I must have answered them wrong or something,' Merry sobbed.

'I doubt that, Merry,' Miss Lucey said as she collected the papers from the desk. 'Sometimes, things are easier than you'd imagine them to be. Now then, dry your eyes and eat that biscuit. You've done your best and we can only wait and see.'

'What were you doing all morning in Miss Lucey's office?' Bobby asked her that afternoon.

Merry had the answer all prepared. 'I was in trouble for stealing Bridget's rubber, so I had to do lines.'

'Don't believe you,' said Bobby, as he waited for her, Helen and Bill to catch him up.

'I don't care what you believe, Bobby Noiro,' she said, too tired to argue with him.

'Well, I know you and I know when you're lying, Merry O'Reilly. You an' me, we're the same, we are.'

'No, Bobby, we're not the same at all.'

'We are, Merry, you'll see. We'll be knowing each other for a long, long time!' he shouted at her as she took Bill's hand and, using up the last strength she had left, marched on towards home, not looking behind her.

33

On a bright March morning, James opened his front door to find Geraldine Lucey standing outside.

'Hello, Father, sorry to be bothering you, but I've news about Merry O'Reilly.'

'Right. Do come in.' James ushered her through to his study, then indicated one of the leather armchairs by the fire.

'From the look on your face, I suspect it's not good news.'

'Oh, it is, Father, I mean, Merry has won the scholarship, but . . .'

James found a lump in his throat. He swallowed hard, knowing it would be inappropriate to show such emotion over one young member of his flock.

'That is wonderful news, Geraldine! Just wonderful. So, what is the problem?' he prompted.

'The problem is, Father, that even though the scholarship covers the school fees, there's nothing there for extras. Look.' Geraldine pulled an envelope out of her satchel. 'Her uniform's included, but she'll be needing a whole long list of other things: a gym kit, all kinds of shoes, a camogie stick, nightgowns, a robe, slippers . . . never mind the train fares from here to Dublin. Oh Father, we both know John O'Reilly barely has the money to feed his family, let alone to buy Merry all this!'

'No, he doesn't, but . . . Listen, would you be so kind as to give me some time to think about it? There may be a way to find the money needed.'

'Really? From where?'

'As I said, leave it with me. Don't say anything to Merry just yet. We don't want to raise her hopes, only to have them dashed.'

'Of course, Father. Shall I leave the paperwork with you? We have to tell them whether Merry will accept within fourteen days.'

'Yes, thank you,' he said as Geraldine stood up and he walked her to the door.

'Oh Father, I so hope she can go. She deserves the best teaching there is.'

'I know, and I shall do my very best to make sure she gets it.'

'Well, of course I will pay! Good grief, James, you didn't even have to ask,' said Ambrose on the telephone later that day. 'I could not be more delighted Mary has won the scholarship. We should be celebrating her success, not worrying about details.'

'They might be "details" to you, Ambrose, but to her father and her family, Merry's possible departure most definitely isn't. I have to find a way to convince John O'Reilly this is the right thing to do.'

'I know, James. Forgive me, but I can't help but be utterly relieved and thrilled. So, how do you plan to go about it?'

'I'm not sure yet, but I shall pray for guidance as always.'

'Well, if God suggests you throw in a new tractor to help heal the pain of John losing his daughter, then please do let me know,' Ambrose chuckled.

Having prayed, but found no direct answer, James decided he must let his instincts lead the way. The following Sunday after Mass, he asked a bleary-eyed John whether he'd be able to call on him the following evening.

'Six o'clock would suit, Father. I have . . . things to do from seven. Is anything wrong?'

'Not at all. In fact, it's very good news.'

'I'll be needing some o' that just now. Goodbye, Father.'

James watched the man wander over to the long line of O'Reilly graves in the cemetery surrounding the church. The rest of his family were kneeling over the plot where their mother and her tiny newborn baby had been interred. It was still waiting for a headstone and the sight of Maggie O'Reilly's children placing posies of spring flowers picked from fields and hedgerows brought tears to his eyes. Even Bill and little Pat had laid a squashed handful of wild violets upon the mound, still yet to grow a full head of grass.

'I trust you, Lord, but sometimes, I'm not understanding the way you work,' James muttered as he walked back inside the church.

'So, that's the situation, John. The question is, what do you think? As Merry's father, it's ultimately your decision.'

James watched as various emotions passed across John O'Reilly's face. It was a long time before he spoke.

'Is it your friend Ambrose Lister who'll be paying?'

'No. Merry won the scholarship fair and square. It's a huge achievement, John, and all credit to her.'

There was another long pause.

'I – and Maggie – we love her so much. Maggie always said she was special. Merry has the brains, but a kind heart too, and some fierce strength inside her. She's the one who's comforted the small ones and slept with them in their beds when they've been crying for their mammy. Nora and Katie might be better at the washing and the cooking, but 'tis Merry who's kept this family's spirit going since . . .'

James could only watch as John put his head in his hands.

'Sorry, Father. I loved Maggie from the moment I laid eyes on her at a *ceilidh* in Timoleague. Our parents weren't for the match; her mammy and daddy refused permission, but Maggie and me, we married anyway. She gave up everything to be with me, and what did I give her? A life o' hell, that's what! Her life was no better than if I'd chained her in a cellar on rations. And then . . . Jaysus, Father, I killed her by putting that babe inside her, but me and Maggie, as well as love, that . . . side of us was one thing we always had in our marriage.'

'You also have seven beautiful children that were made out of that love,' James said quietly. 'And you must thank the Lord for that.'

John looked up at him. 'I don't want to lose Merry, but is it my decision to make?'

'You're her father, John, so yes, it is.'

'What does Mr Lister say?'

'That she should go. But then, he's all for education, teaching as he does at a famous university. He thinks it's an opportunity for Merry to better herself.'

John paused again before he spoke. 'Then better herself she should. It's what my Maggie would have wanted. Even though 'twill break my heart.'

'She'll be home for the holidays, John. And Bridget O'Mahoney is joining her there, so at least she'll be going

with someone she knows. They can ride to Dublin on the train together. Do you want to tell her, or shall I?'

'You, Father. I'd not be knowing what to say.'

As James left the room, he caught a glimpse of John reaching down the side of his chair for the whiskey bottle. And felt such sorrow for a fine, good man, broken by the harsh life God had chosen for him to live.

Merry and Katie were in the kitchen setting out the table for tea when Father O'Brien came in and asked to speak to Merry outside. He beckoned her to sit down on the bench in the courtyard.

'Have I done something wrong, Father?'

'No, no, Merry, not at all. Quite the opposite in fact. You've won the scholarship.'

'I've what?' Merry stared at him as though he'd told her she was about to be shot.

'You've won the scholarship to the boarding school in Dublin.'

'I . . .'

Then she burst into tears.

'Merry, please don't cry. It's wonderful news. You beat girls across the country to win it. It means you're very clever.'

'But . . . but there must be a mistake! I know I failed. 'Tis a mistake, Father, really, it is.'

'No, Merry, it isn't. See, here's the letter.'

James watched her read it, her expression changing to astonishment, then back to misery.

'So, what do you think?' he asked.

'What I think is that 'tis nice of them to offer it to me, but I can't go.'

'Why not?'

'Because Nora and Katie and the small ones need me here. I wouldn't leave my family. What would Daddy be saying?'

'I've spoken to him and he's said yes to you going. He's as proud as punch of you, Merry.'

'He wants me to go?'

'Yes. He thinks it's a wonderful opportunity. Like I do, and Ambrose,' he added.

'But it's Dublin, and so far away.'

'I understand, but you'll be back in the holidays, and . . .' James paused, wanting to choose his words carefully. 'Merry, the world is so much bigger than down here in West Cork, and it is becoming even more so for young women. With a proper education, you could have a wonderful future ahead of you. Ambrose has always believed you do.'

'Can I . . . can I think about it?'

'Of course you can. Let me know when you have decided.'

In bed that night, Merry confessed to Katie what Father O'Brien had told her. Expecting her sister to react with rage, declaring that she wouldn't let her leave because she would have more work to do, Merry was shocked when Katie nodded calmly.

''Tis what you need, Merry,' she said.

'No! I need to stay here and help you and Nora take care of Pat and Bill and Daddy and the farm . . .'

'And you'll do that by going off to Dublin city and becoming even more clever than you already are, and making this family rich,' she said. 'Ellen showed me some of her magazines – Merry, girls in Dublin drive cars! And dance at rock concerts, not *ceilidhs* . . . Maybe I could even come and visit you sometimes and see for myself. We'll be grand here without you. We'll miss you something fierce, but we'll have you back plenty enough in the holidays.'

'Oh Katie, I'm scared. Dublin is a big city and I know I'd be getting homesick for all of you.'

'I know,' she said, taking her sister in her arms. 'But I'll be telling you something, Merry O'Reilly: when I grow up, I'm not staying in this life we have now. Mammy died 'cos of it, and look at Ellen: she's married a farmer's son, and already has one babe and a second on the way. She's swapped one hard life for another and I'll not be doing that. My way out is my looks and yours is your brain. Use what God has given you, Merry, like I will, and then neither of us will be spending the rest of our lives cleaning out pig shite. Think what Mammy would have wanted for you. I know she'd say 'tis the right thing for you to do.'

With her beloved sister's approval, and her father, Miss Lucey, Father O'Brien and Ambrose all saying she should go, Merry finally agreed.

A celebration was held at the farm and, for once, Merry didn't mind Daddy drinking whiskey, because he took out his fiddle and played as the children danced around the New Room.

Little Pat didn't really understand why everyone was happy and dancing, but it didn't matter, Merry thought, because it was the first time she'd seen her family smiling since Mammy died. All except Nora, who'd glared at her when Daddy had announced the good news. But everyone knew she was a jealous eejit, so Merry ignored her.

At the beginning of September, dressed in her new school uniform, Merry went out into the courtyard to say goodbye

to all the animals. Bridget's daddy would soon be arriving in his car to drive them both to the station in Cork City so they could take the train to Dublin together. It would be Merry's first ever time on a train, and when she had confessed this to Bridget, she hadn't laughed at her as she'd expected, but had said that they would have a grand time, as her housekeeper would pack her a picnic with plenty of sandwiches to eat, and a big bar of chocolate for afterwards.

'There'll be enough for the two of us to share, promise.'

Perhaps they could be friends after all, Merry thought.

It was warm in the cow barn, and there was the familiar rustling of young calves.

'Merry!' shouted her brother, who was changing the straw. 'Don't you be getting any muck on your fine new clothes. Get on with you, out of here!' He shooed her into the courtyard, then gave her a big hug. 'You're not to be taking on any airs and graces now and coming back with a soft Dublin accent,' he said. 'You take care of yourself up in the big city.'

'I will, John, I'll see you soon.'

After she'd said goodbye to the pigs and the chickens, Merry walked across the field to say goodbye to the cows, then climbed up on a fence and looked over the valley. She tried her best not to feel frightened at the thought of her new life in Dublin, because at least she knew that Ambrose would be there. He had said she could stay at his home during what the school called 'exeats'. Ambrose had explained it meant pupils were allowed out of school for the weekend, and 'twould be too far to travel home.

'I've been waiting for you, Merry.'

She jumped as she heard a voice from behind her.

'Bobby Noiro!' She turned round to look at him. 'Why can't you be saying hello like a normal person?' Merry complained.

'You're leaving today?'

'Yes, Bridget's daddy is driving us to the train station in Cork.'

'He's a British sympathiser,' he scoffed. 'That's how he made all his money.'

'Might be, but 'tis better than dragging my case to the station on foot,' she said, by now immune to his barbed comments.

'I've got something for you,' he said and reached inside his trouser pocket to pull out a small black book. ''Tis a very special book, Merry. 'Tis my grandmother Nuala's diary. The one I told you about. You read this and you'll understand.' He put the book in her hands.

'Oh Bobby, I can't be taking this! It must be very precious to you.'

'Well, I'm giving it to you because I want you to know about her life and see what the British did to us, and how my family fought for Ireland and freedom. 'Tis my gift to you, Merry. Read it, please.'

'I . . . thank you, Bobby.'

He stared at her for a while, the irises of his dark blue eyes almost black. 'You'll come back, won't you?' he asked eventually.

'O'course I will! I'll be home for Christmas.'

'I'll be calling you the missing sister till you're back, like in the Greek story you told me once about the Seven Sisters and Iron,' he said. 'And I'll be needing you back here, Merry. You're the only one I can talk to.'

''Tis Orion, and sure, you'll be grand without me,' she replied.

'No.' Bobby shook his head fiercely. 'I need you. We're different to everyone here. Bye now, Merry. You take care of yourself up there in Dublin city. And remember, you're mine.'

With a shiver, Merry watched him run off across the field. And for the first time, felt glad she was going far away.

Hearing a car, Merry saw Bridget's daddy driving up the hill towards the farm, so she jumped off the fence and ran back across the field.

John, Katie and Nora had come out to say goodbye with Bill and Pat, the younger boys' hair brushed and their faces scrubbed so they wouldn't embarrass themselves in front of Emmet O'Mahoney. Merry felt tears prick her eyes as she saw that Daddy had come out of the house in a fresh shirt too. He walked towards her and placed a rough kiss on her cheek.

'Your mammy would be proud of you, Merry,' he whispered in her ear. 'And so am I.'

She nodded, not able to reply because she was too choked up.

'You take care of yourself in Dublin city, and make sure you do lots of learning.' She felt him slip a coin into her hand and hug her, and she suddenly wanted nothing more than to stay at home.

She got into the car, sitting on the plush leather back seat next to Bridget, and trying not to cry. As the car drew out of the courtyard and she waved goodbye to her family, she remembered her mother's last words to her:

You're special, Merry, and don't you go forgetting you are. Promise?

She had made her mother a promise. And she would do her best to keep it.

Merry
Dublin

June 2008

34

'And from then on, when I went home for the holidays, Bobby always called me the missing sister,' I sighed. I felt exhausted; I had been speaking for over two hours, with Ambrose helping by filling in the gaps about the part he and Father O'Brien had played behind the scenes.

'It must have been devastating when your mum died.' Jack shook his head sadly. 'You were so young.'

'It was. I still think about her every day, even after all this time,' I admitted. 'I adored her.'

'Maggie was a truly remarkable woman,' said Ambrose, and I saw that his face looked grey. 'Seeing your family grieve, and knowing there was so little I could do to help you all . . .'

'But you did help me, Ambrose, and I'm only starting to learn how much. So it was you that gave Miss Lucey the *Encyclopaedia Britannicas*? I always wondered.'

'Yes, and it was a pleasure, Mary. You were such a strong, cheerful little girl, and you grew by leaps and bounds once you were at boarding school in Dublin, with the right teachers and resources to help fuel the fire of your curiosity. Although I have often wondered if it would have been better for you to stay with your family, with the love of your brothers and sisters around you.'

'Ambrose, I have no regrets about going to school in Dublin,' I reassured him. 'I know I was only eleven, but I did have a choice even then and I know I made the right one. Had I stayed in West Cork, I never would have gone to university. I would most likely have married a farmer and had as many children as my mammy,' I joked weakly.

'I'd love to meet your – *my* family,' said Jack. 'It's so weird to think that a few hours from here are people who share our blood.'

Ambrose stood up and began clearing our glasses.

'Don't worry about all that, Ambrose,' I said. 'I'll wash everything up before we leave.'

'Mary, I'm not that decrepit yet,' he said, but I could see that his hand was shaking as he picked up my empty water glass. I stood and gently took it out of his grasp.

'What's the matter, Ambrose?'

He gave me a sad smile. 'You know me well, Mary. I . . . there are . . . aspects of your past that I know I should have discussed with you when I gave you that emerald ring all those years ago. Back then, there was always tomorrow, but you disappeared for thirty-seven years. And now, here we are, and I am still to explain to you all that occurred.'

'What do you mean?'

'Oh dear, as you can see, I do indeed feel very weary. Why don't you and Jack return tomorrow, when all our minds are refreshed?' he suggested. 'As long as you can promise me you'll be back?'

'Of course,' I said, and drew him into a hug, feeling the guilt of having left this man, who had been nothing less than a father to me, weighing heavily on my shoulders.

Once Jack and I had washed up the glasses and cups from the sitting room and made sure that Ambrose was settled back in his chair, we stepped out of the house and into the warm

evening air. Merrion Square was quiet and the streetlights had only just come on, the long summer evening light still casting a gentle glow.

Jack and I had a quick meal of fish and chips in the hotel restaurant, my mind so full of memories of my family that I barely heard Jack speaking.

'Mum, you know what?' he said, breaking into my thoughts. 'You're right: I think Mary-Kate should be here in Dublin with us. I reckon we're going to be in Ireland for a while, and you should ask her if she wants to fly over. Whatever this puzzle of the missing sister is, I'd feel a lot better if we were all here together.'

'Yes,' I agreed, 'you're absolutely right. She should be here, just in case . . .'

'In case of what, Mum? Won't you tell me what it is that has so frightened you? You stopped your story just when you went to boarding school, so what happened after that? Was it something to do with that weird Bobby character who called you the missing sister?'

'I . . . you wanted to know about my childhood, Jack, and how Ambrose fitted into it. I've told you now. So, no, Jack, I can't tell you any more. Not until I've found out some facts for myself.'

'But if Ambrose hasn't seen or heard from you since you left, there must be a reason for it?'

'Please, Jack, that's enough questions, I'm very weary too and I just need some sleep. As my darling mammy used to say, things will be better in the morning.'

We finished dinner in silence, then walked towards the lift together. 'What floor is your room?' I asked as we stepped inside it.

'It's just down the corridor from yours, so any problem, just give me a buzz.'

'I'm sure there won't be,' I said, 'but will you give Mary-Kate a call and ask her if she'd be able to fly over as soon as she can? Here.' I dug in my bag, fished out my purse and handed Jack my credit card. 'Pay for the flight on that, and whatever you do, don't panic her.'

'As if.' Jack rolled his eyes. 'I'll just tell her that our mum's going on a journey of self-discovery and she should be here to see it. Night, Mum.' Jack kissed me on the forehead then turned along the corridor in the direction of his room.

'Sleep tight!' I called.

'And don't let the bed bugs bite,' he chanted, as he had since he was a small one.

I went into my room, undressed, did my ablutions and climbed into the marvellously comfy bed. I made a note to change the thirty-five-year-old mattress the moment I returned home to New Zealand – I still had the one Jock had bought just after we were married. I lay there and closed my eyes to try to sleep, but there was so much buzzing around my brain, it felt like a hive of bees had colonised it. I realised that there were names that had been mentioned in Nuala's diary that I was now remembering from my own childhood.

There's no point in trying to work it all out tonight, I told myself, but still, sleep did not come.

I used the relaxation techniques I'd gleaned over the years, even though they left me more tense because none of them ever worked. In the end, I got up to find my bottle of duty-free whiskey, and drugged myself into an uneasy slumber.

'Right,' said Jack as he joined me downstairs for breakfast the next morning. 'MK's flight is already in the air, and what with

all the stopovers and the time difference, she should be here sometime after midnight,' he said as we sat down to eat.

'The wonders of the modern age,' I smiled. 'All that way across the world in a day. How far we've come as human beings. In my childhood, that would have been regarded as a miracle.'

'From what you told me yesterday, it sounds as though you had a very tough upbringing,' Jack said tentatively as he stood next to me at the buffet and piled bacon and eggs onto his plate.

'We certainly never had breakfasts like these, but we never went hungry either. Yes, life on the farm was hard and we all had to do our chores, but there was a lot of love and laughter too. I missed it so much when I went away to boarding school, even though there wasn't pigs' muck to be cleared out of the sty on wet winter mornings. I could never wait to get home for the holidays.'

'Did your brothers and sisters not resent you for having a better education than them?'

'No, not at all. I think they all felt sorry for me. I had to be careful not to come back from Dublin with any "airs and graces" on me, as they put it. It was Katie I missed the most,' I sighed. 'We were very close when we were young.'

'It sounded like it, from what you said. Yet you haven't kept in touch. You just dropped everyone from your past when you left. Why, Mum?'

My son looked at me, his blue eyes urging me to explain.

'As I said, I will tell you everything, just not yet. Now, let's go and hear what Ambrose has to tell me.'

'Okay. I'm quickly gonna grab my mobile from my room and call Ginette at the *cave* in Provence, to tell her I'll be away for a while.'

'Please, Jack' – I caught his arm before he left the table – 'if you're needed back there, I promise I can do this alone.'

'I know you can, Mum, but the harvest isn't for over a month, and this is much more important. I'll meet you in the lobby in fifteen, eh?'

As we approached Ambrose's front door, I had a premonition that he wanted to tell me something important – even life-changing. I rang the doorbell and felt a surge of trepidation run through me.

Ambrose welcomed us in, but as he led us into the sitting room, I thought he looked every one of the eighty-five years he'd spent on the earth.

Jack and I settled ourselves onto the sofa as we had yesterday.

'Are you feeling well today? You look a little pale, Ambrose,' I said.

'I admit to not sleeping as soundly as I normally do, Mary.'

'Could I make some coffee for you? Tea?' offered Jack.

'No, thank you. I have water, which, after the amount of whiskey I drank yesterday, should reinflate the vital organs that we're all so reliant on. Putting it bluntly, I have no ailment other than a mighty hangover,' he smiled.

'Would you prefer us to come back later? Give you some time to sleep it off?' I offered.

'No, no. I feel that whilst I have breath left on this earth, and you are actually here, I should tell you the truth. The alternative being a letter sent by some nameless solicitor after my death. Which is what I was planning to do until you turned up on my doorstep,' he chuckled.

I reached instinctively for Jack's hand, and he squeezed mine. 'Ambrose, whatever it is, it's best said, isn't it?'

'It is, my dear. When I heard you speak so lovingly of your

childhood and your family yesterday, I knew that what I had to tell you would be so very difficult, but—'

'Ambrose, please, we've agreed, no more secrets,' I entreated him. 'I mean, there's nothing that you could tell me or Jack that I don't already know, is there?'

'As a matter of fact, there is. When I gave you that ring on your twenty-first birthday' – he gestured to my hand – 'I'd sworn that I would tell you the truth about its provenance. But, at the last minute, I did not.'

'Why? And why is the ring so important?'

'I am about to tell you, but I rather fear that the story you told me yesterday about the people you believe are following you from hotel to hotel has something to do with it.'

'I'm sorry, Ambrose, you're not making sense.'

'Try to understand that objects can become symbols of importance to different factions. These women who arrived on your daughter's doorstep in New Zealand, talking of Mary-Kate being the missing sister of the seven, is not, I believe, directly to do with your time here in Dublin before you left.'

'Ambrose, you can't know that . . .'

'My dear Mary, it may or may not come as a surprise to you that I had an inkling of the situation you had got yourself into. Especially during that last year. You were living under my very roof, remember?'

I had the grace to blush. 'Yes. I'm sorry, Ambrose. But this ring . . .' I held up my hand for Jack to see. 'You told me that the seven points around the diamond were for each of us seven sisters and brothers, with our mother sitting in the centre.'

'I did, but sadly, Mary, and to my eternal shame, it was a lie. Or more accurately, I invented a story about its design that I knew would appeal to you, because of your fascination with

the Seven Sisters myths and the fact you were one of seven siblings.'

I stared at him, shocked to the core that this man whom I had so adored and trusted above any other had lied to me.

'So' – I swallowed hard – 'where is the ring from?'

'Before I tell you both how I came by it, I should set the scene. Perhaps the first thing that you need to understand, Jack, is that even though the Irish were victorious in achieving their dream of independence, it was on the British government's terms. They partitioned the country into the British-run North and the Irish Republic in the South. Not a lot had improved for the poor on either side of the border. By the time you were born in 1949, Mary, Ireland had just become a republic, but the levels of poverty here were more or less the same as they had been in the 1920s. Many had immigrated to America, but those who stayed were suffering from the effects of another depression, which hung across Europe after the Second World War. They were dark times in Ireland; as you experienced, families like yours lived on subsistence levels only – in other words, using what they grew to feed and clothe their families. And for Irish women in particular, almost nothing had changed.'

'You're saying that Ireland was stuck in the past, even though things had changed politically,' said Jack.

'It was certainly true of rural areas such as West Cork,' Ambrose nodded. 'At the time of your birth, Mary, I'd just completed my DPhil here at Trinity and had only just been promoted to Research Fellow. As you heard yesterday, I regularly travelled down to Timoleague to see my dear friend James – Father O'Brien – who had recently taken his first position as priest of a parish that encompassed Timoleague, Clogagh and Ballinascarthy. I had few friends and even less family, and James was my closest friend and confidant.'

'It was a long drive for you, wasn't it?' I put in.

'Even longer before you were born, my dear, as I didn't have my red Beetle then. I took the train down, and I remember Mrs Cavanagh, the housekeeper at the priest's house, greeting me as if I was a stinking bundle of seaweed washed up on the shore,' he chuckled.

'Mrs Cavanagh didn't like anyone,' I said with feeling.

'Indeed not. Now, Mary, it was on one such visit to see James that my life changed. So, let me take you back to West Cork and the time that was then, to the moment of your birth in November 1949 . . .'

Ambrose and James
West Cork

November 1949

An Cros Cheilteach
The Celtic Cross

35

Father James O'Brien jumped awake and sat upright. A crying baby had filled his dreams and, as he listened, he realised he could still hear it. Pinching himself to make sure he wasn't still asleep, and realising he wasn't, he stepped out of the warmth of his bed, walked to the window which faced the front of the house, and pulled back the curtains. He could see no one on the path or in the garden – he'd been expecting a young mother with an already big brood to look after, who had come to him for comfort because she was finding it difficult to cope. Pulling up the sash, he leant out and looked down in order to make sure there was no one at the front door, and then let out a gasp of surprise. Lying in what seemed to be a wicker shopping basket was a wriggling bundle of blanket. Which was most definitely where the crying was coming from.

James crossed himself. Babies had sporadically been left on the presbytery doorstep in Dublin, but Father O'Donovan, his priest there when he'd been a deacon, had always dealt with them. When James had asked him where they were taken, he had shrugged.

'Down to the local convent orphanage. The Lord help them all once they're there,' he'd added.

With Dublin being the size it was, it was hardly uncommon for such things to happen when young ladies got themselves

into trouble, but here in such a tight-knit community, where James had learnt in the six months he'd been here that everyone knew everyone's business better than they did their own, he was surprised. He dressed hurriedly, pulling on a thick Aran jumper to ward off the West Cork winter, then did a mental check of his parishioners. Yes, there were a number of young women expecting, but they were all married and resigned to the prospect of their new arrivals. As he opened his bedroom door, walked along the corridor and then downstairs, his mind ran through any teenage daughters in the parish.

'Dear Lord! Where is that squalling coming from?'

James looked behind him and saw his friend Ambrose standing at the top of the stairs, wearing a pair of checked pyjamas.

'There's a baby been left on the doorstep outside. I'm just about to bring it inside.'

'I'll collect my robe and be down in a jiffy,' Ambrose said as James unlocked the bolts and drew the front door open.

The good news was that at least he already knew from the screeching that he would not pull the blankets from a child already blue and lifeless. Shivering in the chill wind, he picked up the wicker handle and lifted the basket inside.

'My, my. Now, this package might be even more interesting than the parcels of books I'm sent from Hatchards,' Ambrose said as the two of them stood over the basket.

'Right then,' James said as he took a deep breath and prepared to uncover the baby, only hoping the poor creature was not so disfigured that the mother had abandoned it.

'There's a thing indeed,' Ambrose said as they both stared down at what looked like – even to two amateurs – a perfectly formed, if rather red in the face, newborn infant.

'Girl or boy, I wonder?' mused Ambrose, pointing to the piece of cloth covering the child's genitals.

'We shall find out, but before we do, let's take it into my study and light the fire. Its tiny fingertips look blue.'

As James laid the basket on the mat in front of the hearth and lit the fire, Ambrose continued to stare down at the baby, whose screaming had now abated to the odd yelp of displeasure.

'There seems to be something rather wrong with its belly button,' said Ambrose. 'There's a bloody grey stalk sticking out of it.'

'Don't you remember your biology classes?' James clucked. 'That is what remains of the umbilical cord which attaches the mother to the baby.' He knelt down by the basket. 'From the look of it, this little dote is no more than a few hours old. Let's see whether it's a girl or a boy.'

'I'd bet a few punts on it being a girl. Just look at those eyes.'

James did so, and even though the skin around them was blotched red from crying, the eyes were huge – of a deep blue, framed by long dark lashes.

'I'd say you were right,' James agreed as he timidly pulled away the damp, soiled cloth to reveal that yes, the infant in the basket was female.

'What a shame, now you can't name the child Moses,' Ambrose quipped. 'You think she's a newborn because of the umbilical cord, but she's really rather large. Not that I'm any expert on these kinds of things,' he added.

James looked at the plump little arms and thighs – babies' legs always reminded him of frogs' – and nodded. 'True, this child does look more well nourished than most of the scrawny mites I baptise around here. Now then, can I trust you to mind her while I find a cloth from the kitchen to replace this sticky mess of one?'

'Of course. I've always loved babies, and they like me too,'

said Ambrose. 'There now, little one,' he soothed the child as James left, 'you're safe with us now.'

By the time James returned, having resorted to the hot press and tearing apart one of Mrs Cavanagh's immaculately laundered sheets, the baby was staring up at Ambrose as he muttered softly to her.

James chuckled as he listened. 'You're speaking Latin to her?'

'Of course. It's never too soon to start learning, is it?'

'As long as it keeps her quiet and calm, whilst I deal with the other end of things, you can use any language you want. We need to lift her out and put her on the towel so I can clean her.'

'Let me hold her . . .'

James watched in genuine surprise as Ambrose took hold of the baby's head with one hand and slipped another under her lower back, then placed her gently on the towel that James had laid out close to the fire.

'Seems like you do have a knack with the small ones,' James commented.

'Why on earth shouldn't I?'

'True. Now, I'll do my best to make a napkin, although it'll be my first time.'

As Ambrose continued to talk to the baby – this time in Greek – James struggled to clean and then secure the piece of torn sheet around the baby's plump little bottom.

'That will have to do,' he said as he tied a knot just below her belly button.

'Was there a note of any kind left in the basket?' Ambrose asked. 'Or some clue as to who the mother might be?'

'It's not likely there will be, but . . .' James shook out the blanket that had accompanied the baby, and a small object fell to the floor. 'Oh my,' James gasped as he bent to pick it up.

'Is that a *ring*?' said Ambrose.

Together, they went to the light on the study desk to inspect the item in the palm of James's hand. It was indeed a ring, unusually made in the shape of a star, with emerald stones set around a central diamond.

'I've never seen anything like it,' Ambrose breathed. 'It's got seven points, and the colours of the emeralds are so clear and vibrant . . . it can't be costume jewellery, James. I'd say that this is the real thing.'

'Yes.' James frowned. 'You'd think that someone who could afford this kind of ring would be able to keep their baby girl. Rather than answering questions, the ring has simply raised more.'

'Perhaps she's from a well-to-do family, the product of a forbidden love, and the mother had to dispose of her lest she face recrimination from her parents,' Ambrose suggested.

'You've obviously been reading too many romance novels,' James teased him. 'For all we know, the ring might be stolen. Whatever its provenance, I shall keep it in a safe place for now,' said James. He fetched a small key and the leather pouch in which he kept the silver cross his parents had given him on his confirmation from his desk drawer. He slipped the ring inside with the cross, and then went over to his bookcase to unlock a cupboard set under one of the shelves.

'Is that where you hide your whiskey from Mrs Cavanagh?' Ambrose chuckled.

'That, and other things I don't wish her to find,' said James, as he slipped the leather pouch into the cupboard and locked it.

'Well, one thing's for certain,' Ambrose said, gazing down at the baby, who was now lying quietly on the towel, 'it appears that our little girl is special indeed. She's very alert.'

However, even Ambrose's gentle attentions no longer held

sway as the baby realised her tummy remained empty and she started to scream again. Ambrose swept her up into his arms and rocked her gently, to no avail.

'This girl needs her mother's milk, or anyone's milk, for that matter,' said Ambrose. 'And that's not something either of us can provide. What are we to do now, James? Kidnap the nearest cow and stick an udder in her mouth?'

'I've no idea,' James sighed helplessly. 'I'll need to send word to Father Norton in Bandon and see what he would suggest.'

'I'm not meaning what will happen to her eventually, I'm talking about now!' Ambrose raised his voice. 'Ah, baby, how can a tiny mite make such a loud noise!'

Just as both men were on the verge of panic, there was a knock at the study door.

'Who on earth is that at this time of the morning?' Ambrose demanded.

'It must be Maggie, my domestic help on Mrs Cavanagh's day off. Come in!' called James.

A pair of large, emerald-coloured eyes, set in pale Irish skin dotted with freckles, appeared around the door. She had glorious red hair that tumbled across her shoulder in ringlets, held back by a headscarf.

'Hello, Father . . .'

'Come in, Maggie, come in,' said James. 'As you can see, we have a guest. She was left in a basket on the doorstep some time in the night.'

'Oh no!' Maggie's eyes opened even wider in shock and surprise.

'Did you . . . do you know any young women locally who may have, um, well . . .'

'Got themselves into trouble?' she finished his sentence.

'Yes.'

494

Maggie frowned as she thought about it, and for the first time, James saw the beginnings of lines etched on her young face – brought there by the sheer physical hardship of the life she lived. He knew she had four small ones at home and was pregnant again. He noted also that the skin around her eyes was reddened, as if she had been crying recently, and there were dark patches of exhaustion underneath them.

'No, Father, I can't think of anyone.'

'Are you sure?'

'I'm sure,' she said, looking him straight in the eye. 'That young 'un needs feeding,' she commented on the obvious. 'And that cord needs seeing to.'

'Do you know of anyone who is nursing presently around these parts? And would be prepared to take on another just until we find a place for her to go? That is, if we can't find her mammy.'

There was a pause as Maggie stared at James. 'I . . .'

'Yes, Maggie?'

'Oh Father . . .'

James watched as Maggie put her face in her hands. 'My babe passed into God's hands only yesterday, so . . .'

'Maggie, I'm so very sorry. I'd have come up to give last rites. Why didn't you tell me?'

When Maggie looked up again, James could see the fear in her eyes.

'Please, Father, I should ha' told you, but me and John, we couldn't afford a proper burial. She came a month early, see, and she . . . she breathed her last inside me, so . . .' She took a deep, gasping breath. 'We . . . put her in with her brother who died in the same way, under the oak tree in our field yesterday. Forgive me, Father, but—'

'Please.' James's ears were beginning to ring from the racket the baby was making, and the horror of what Maggie

had just told him. 'There is no need to ask my forgiveness or God's. I will come to the farm and say a Mass for your baby's soul.'

'You would?'

'I would.'

'Oh Father, I don't know how to thank you. Father O'Malley would have said the babe's soul was damned to hell for not being buried in hallowed ground.'

'And I will tell you, as His messenger on earth, the baby's soul most assuredly is not. So now, Maggie, are you telling us that you have . . . milk?'

'Yes, Father, it comes as if she's here and waiting for it.'

'Then . . . would you be prepared to feed this child?'

'To be sure I would, but I haven't lit the rest of the fires, or the range, or—'

'Don't worry about any of that. I am sure we can manage for a while whilst you take care of the baby. Eh, Ambrose?'

'Of course. Here.' Ambrose handed Maggie the baby. He watched as Maggie looked down at the child with such devastation that it almost broke his heart in two.

'I'll take her to the kitchen to feed her, so,' she said, recovering herself.

'No, the kitchen is freezing,' said James. 'You sit there in the chair by the fire. Let us know when she's had her fill.'

'Are you sure, Father? I—'

'Completely. We'll see to everything, won't we, Ambrose?'

'Of course. Take as long as you need, my dear.'

The two men left the study.

Ambrose sat in a chair in the kitchen, a blanket wrapped round him as James re-stoked the range and waited for the kettle to boil so they could have a cup of tea.

'Are you all right, my friend?' James asked him. 'You look quite pale.'

'I confess that I'm shocked by the morning's events. Not only at the arrival of a baby on your doorstep, but young Maggie . . .' Ambrose sighed and shook his head. 'She buried her newborn only yesterday, and yet here she is at work, despite what must be considerable physical exhaustion and inexorable grief.'

'Yes.' James warmed his hands on the range as he willed the kettle to hurry up and boil. He too needed solace, and it could only come in a cup of hot, sweet tea. 'Here, human life is cheap, Ambrose – you must realise that you and I are very privileged in our different ways. At my church in Dublin, I was protected by my priest, whereas out here, I'm on the front line. And if I'm to stay and survive, I must understand the ways of the flock I serve. And that flock is mostly poor and struggles to stay alive.'

'From what I've seen this morning, surely it will test even your faith in God?'

'I will learn, and hope I can bring solace to those affected by situations that I can't even begin to imagine. It does not test my faith, Ambrose, it strengthens it, because I am God's hands here on earth. And the little I can do for them, I will do.'

The kettle finally gave a weak whistle and James poured hot water over the tea leaves.

'And what of the baby? That precious new life?'

'As I said, I must send a message to Father Norton; he will know the local orphanage, but . . .' James shook his head. 'I was once sent to administer last rites to a child dying of tuberculosis at the convent orphanage close to my old Dublin parish. 'Twas a dreadful place; I can't say it wasn't. The babies were three to a cot, filthy from their own mess, their skin alive with lice . . .'

'Maybe couples should desist from the activity that brings

them here in the first place,' said Ambrose as James put a mug of tea in front of him.

'I'd hardly say that could ever be the answer,' James cautioned. 'It's a natural human instinct, as you well know. And the only form of solace some of these poor young couples have.'

There was a timid knock on the kitchen door.

'Come in,' James called and Maggie appeared with the baby fast asleep in her arms.

'She's taken a full feed and is quiet now. I was wondering, Father, whether I may take some salt from the pantry, and some hot water to bathe the babe's cord, lest it turns septic.'

'Of course. You sit down, Maggie, and I'll find a bowl and mix some salt water in it.'

'Thank you, Father.'

'Ambrose will get you some tea, Maggie. You're very pale, and only a day after giving birth yourself, never mind the grief of losing your child. You shouldn't be here.'

'Oh no, Father, I am well and healthy and able to work today, so.'

'How are your children coping?' James asked.

'They don't know yet. When I felt the babe was coming and that something was wrong, I had my eldest, Ellen, take them to our neighbours. I . . . I haven't fetched them back yet to tell them as I was up here working today. I'll get right back to the cleaning, Father.'

'Please, rest for now,' Ambrose said to her as he placed a mug of tea in front of her and James went to the pantry in search of the salt. 'Why don't you give me the baby, whilst you drink it?'

'I am well, sir, really,' Maggie reiterated.

'Even so, I'd like to hold her.'

Ambrose took the child from Maggie's arms, then sat down and cradled her in his arms.

'She's very beautiful,' he said as he looked down at the sleeping baby.

'That she is, sir, and big too. Fatter than any of mine, so. Must'a been a difficult birth for the mother.'

'You have no idea whose baby it could be?'

'None, sir. And I'd be knowing every pregnant mother round these parts.'

'Then the baby must have come from outside the village?' Ambrose queried.

'I'd say so, yes.'

James came back with salt and a basin and followed Maggie's instructions to take a little hot water from the kettle and mix it with cold. He was amazed as Ambrose insisted on holding the baby for Maggie while she tended to the cord.

'There, it's clean now. 'Twill dry out in a week or so, then drop off,' she said, re-covering the baby in the blanket. 'Now, if you don't mind, I must get on with my work, or Mrs Cavanagh will have words with me next time I see her.'

Maggie gave a small bob and left the kitchen.

'Surely she should be in bed resting, just a day after burying her child? She's terrified of losing her position here, isn't she? And of Mrs Cavanagh,' commented Ambrose.

'She is, yes, and we will both try to make her rest as much as possible today. Of course, those few extra shillings she gets for her one day a week could make the difference between her family being fed or going hungry.'

'I wonder who minds her children when she's here?'

'I dread to think, Ambrose,' James shuddered. 'They probably mind themselves.'

'How she could hold this perfect healthy baby in her arms and let it feed on the milk meant for her own dead child is truly beyond me. Such bravery, I . . .'

James could see tears in his friend's eyes. He'd never seen

them there before, even when he'd been badly bullied at school.

'Is an orphanage really the only route for this poor, innocent child?' Ambrose looked up at him. 'I mean, you saw that ring, perhaps we could find out who it belonged to, track down her family . . . Or if not, there are childless women, desperate to adopt – my English Fellow friend was telling me that American couples come over here to adopt from the orphanages.'

'Well, if the Irish are normally good at one thing, it seems to be giving birth to fine healthy children. Shall I take her from you? I can lay her upstairs on my bed, and I'm sure Maggie will be able to feed her again later.'

'What will you do now, James?'

'I will speak to Father Norton after Mass to find out the protocol on these things down here.' James lifted the baby out of his friend's arms. 'There now, I'm taking her away before you adopt her yourself.' With a sad smile, he left the kitchen.

36

While James went to Timoleague church to perform morning Mass, Ambrose took himself off for a walk down the hill, to Courtmacsherry Bay below it. Today it was filled with millpond-still water, and the breeze was gentle as he walked along the seafront. It was a crisp, bright November day – the kind Ambrose loved – and even though he could not imagine how faith alone in an invisible being could tempt his soulmate away to this godforsaken part of Ireland, he could occasionally appreciate its raw natural beauty.

Ambrose had known since the day he'd met James – even at eleven, tall and almost roguishly handsome – that this boy who would become the beautiful man he now was had promised his life to God. He remembered sitting on the hard, uncomfortable pew of Blackrock College chapel, always with a slim paperback to hand in order to surreptitiously read all the way through the endless dirge of Evensong. He'd sometimes glance at James sitting next to him in the pew, his head bowed in prayer, with a look on his face that he could only describe as ecstasy.

Ambrose knew that he could never talk about his lack of spiritual belief in public; after all, he was at a Catholic boys' school and taught by devout monks. The Holy Ghost Fathers, the order that ran the school, were preparing their pupils to

become missionaries in West Africa. Even as a young boy, the idea of travelling far across the seas to an unknown land had terrified him. If he mislaid his glasses, he was immediately tumbled into a blurred, indecipherable world. Unlike James, whose constitution could withstand the wettest, coldest days on the rugby pitch, after a single match, Ambrose could be laid up in the sanatorium for days with a bad chest.

'Be a man,' his father was always saying, especially as Ambrose was the heir to an Anglo-Irish dynasty, or at least what was left of it. The family had once owned half of Wicklow three hundred years ago, as the masters of the Catholic poor. But through his ancestor's philanthropic work for the tenants and their farms at that time, the family had come to be loved. Lord Lister had passed the ethos on to his son, who had taken it one step further and in his will had left the land to his tenants. This act had left future generations of Listers with only a vast mansion and little means of supporting it. Yet that generosity had saved the place from being burnt to the ground like so many other grand houses had been during the War of Independence. And there, his father still lived to this day. Ambrose was technically an 'Honourable' as heir to the dynasty, with only a gold signet ring given to him on his twenty-first birthday to mark his noble ancestry. His father also rarely played on his own heritage, unless he needed to impress an Englishman, who he joked may regard him as an 'Irish navvy'. Ambrose always chuckled when his father returned from England and said this, because despite everything, he had a cut-glass English accent.

Ambrose wouldn't be at all surprised if Lister House wasn't mortgaged to the hilt. At the age of eleven, he was certain already that the Lister dynasty was doomed to end with him, because he would never marry. His mother had died young, leaving him a substantial trust fund, inherited through

her own family. With his father still alive and drinking through what remained of his Lister heritage, she had sought to protect her son. Ambrose harboured dreams of selling Lister House to some *nouveau-riche* Irish family who'd made money out of the war, and buying himself a small, cosy apartment near Trinity College, where he could surround himself with his books and, most importantly, be warm . . .

Which he definitely wasn't now.

'Oh, how I hate the cold . . .' he muttered as he turned back towards the village, with its pretty pastel-coloured houses, many of whose owners earned their keep from the shops they'd established on the ground floor within them. As always, the Catholic church towered over the village – there wouldn't be a soul in Timoleague or its surrounds that would miss Mass on a Sunday. Often, James said, there'd be standing room only, even though the church could seat at least three hundred people.

Ambrose then looked down to his left at the far smaller Protestant church, built just below the enormous breadth of the Catholic church of the Nativity of the Blessed Virgin Mary. Here for certain, a very unholy war had taken place and still rumbled on. Even since Partition, when Northern Ireland had been split from the rest of the new Republic of Ireland, there was anger that the Protestant British ran part of the island. And yet, wasn't the act of Communion at the centre of both Catholic and Protestant communities?

'Dear James,' he breathed, 'I do love you so very much, but I also fear you've wedded yourself to an empty promise.'

However, Ambrose accepted that, like the Franciscan monks who'd built Timoleague Friary over seven hundred years ago, his beloved friend wished to do good while he was here on earth. As he thought about that precious newborn baby – the way he'd felt as he'd held her in his arms, knowing

he would never hold one of his own – Ambrose felt a tug at his heart.

Turning back and bracing himself for the rest of the walk up the hill, he headed back towards the priest's house.

'How's the little one?' James asked Maggie as she set the table for lunch.

'Grand altogether, thank you, Father. I fed her again and she's sleeping tight on your bed.'

'And you, Maggie? You must be exhausted.'

'I am very well, Father,' Maggie replied, although her face told another story. 'Have you spoken to the father in Bandon?'

'No, I'm only in from Mass for a few minutes. Do you happen to know where the nearest orphanage is?'

'I believe 'tis in Clonakilty. There's a convent there and they take in babes like ours . . . yours,' Maggie blushed.

James could see she was close to tears as she stirred the soup on the hob. She opened the door to the range and pulled out a tin of something that smelt delicious.

'I've made you a brack, Father. I found some dried fruit in the pantry and thought you could have it with a cup of tea this afternoon.'

'Thank you, Maggie. I haven't had a brack cake since I was in Dublin. Ah,' he said as he heard the front door open and close, 'that'll be Ambrose. Please, serve up.'

Ambrose entered the kitchen, breathing heavily.

''Tis a steep climb indeed from the waterfront,' James said. 'Are you all right, my friend?'

'Yes, just unused to walking up hills, that's all,' Ambrose said, sitting down and drinking some water from the glass Maggie had set on the table. 'How was Mass?'

'Busy for a Monday morning. And there were a number for confession after.'

'I would guess that was to do with taking drink on God's Holy Day,' Ambrose smiled as Maggie placed a bowl of soup in front of him.

'There is also bread and butter for you both. I'll be getting on with my chores now, if you have everything you need.'

'Thank you, Maggie. This smells delicious.'

''Tis only turnip and potato, but I added an apple from the windfall pile you have in the pantry. Lends a touch of sweetness, I always think.'

Giving a bob, Maggie left the kitchen.

'This actually tastes as good as it looks,' said James as he blew on a spoon and took a sip, then cut himself a thick hunk of homemade bread and laced it with butter. 'Bread for you, Ambrose?'

'Indeed. And the soup *is* good. What a shame you couldn't get the girl to replace Mrs Cavanagh completely.'

'If only,' James sighed. 'But there'd be riots in the hierarchy, I can tell you. She looked after my predecessor for years.'

'Maggie is a real beauty too, if only she wasn't so thin,' Ambrose commented. 'Listen, dear chap, I've been thinking while I was out and about on my walk.'

'I know that is a dangerous thing,' James smiled.

'For some reason, I was pondering my own family genealogy, back to Lord Henry Lister, known in our family as the Great Philanthropist. He near bankrupted the Listers through his generosity. I was also thinking about that baby sleeping upstairs. And how you know better than I that the best she can hope for, *if* she survives childhood, would be a menial education, which would only fit her for a future in service or some other low-paid job.'

'And . . . ?'

'Well, getting to the point, I have money, James. And as I know, I will never have a family of my own—'

'You simply cannot know that.'

'I *can*,' Ambrose replied firmly. 'I'm fully aware I cannot change the world, let alone save it, but perhaps a small act of charity *could* change one life at least.'

'I see.' James sipped his soup thoughtfully. 'Does this mean you are intending to adopt the baby currently sleeping upstairs? You certainly seemed to bond with her this morning.'

'Lord, no! I wouldn't know where to begin,' Ambrose chuckled. 'However, it does seem to me, that with my help from the sidelines, a solution to this puzzle appears to be sitting right under our roof.'

'Which is what exactly?'

'We have a woman who has just lost a beloved baby. And a newborn orphan who needs a mother and her milk. The only thing stopping them from being joined together is money. What if I suggested to Maggie that I would cover all costs for the baby, and add a little bit extra to help her and her family too? What do you think?'

'I'm not sure what I'd be thinking, to be honest. You're saying you will pay Maggie to adopt this baby?'

'In essence, yes.'

'Ambrose, that sounds like bribery. For a start, we don't even know if she would want someone else's child.'

'The look in her eyes when she tended to her tells me she would.'

'Maybe, but Maggie also has a husband, who may well have other views.'

'You know him? What is he like?'

'From what I've seen of him at Mass, John O'Reilly is a good God-fearing man. There's certainly no gossip of trips

down to the village to haunt the pubs, and trust me, I would have heard about it. All the same, bringing up an unknown man's child may not be an idea he would be willing to consider.'

'Then we must speak to him. What of the rest of her family? What are their circumstances?'

'They have their eldest, Ellen, who is ten, their son John, who is eight, then two girls of six and two. I've heard chatter that Maggie and John married for love, against both their parents' wishes, and they are devoted to each other.'

Ambrose smiled. 'Fortune and love favour the brave.'

'That's as may be, but it doesn't help put food on the table. The family has some pigs and chickens and a few cows on a couple of acres of land. They live in a dark, cramped cottage with no electricity or running water. Ambrose, I don't know if you appreciate the stark poverty that some families hereabouts have to endure.'

'James, I know that I am privileged, but I'm not blind to the deprivations of others. It seems to me that however poor, the O'Reilly family have the foundations that would enable them to give this child a stable future, with a little help from me. And we must act fast. Maggie said this morning she's told no one of the death of her baby, and has not yet collected her children from their neighbours. If we act quickly, we can make this all happen privately. As I said, I'm prepared to pay. Whatever it takes,' Ambrose added firmly.

James surveyed his friend thoughtfully. 'You'll have to forgive me, but your talk of a philanthropic ancestor is not going far enough to convince me of your sudden need to perform an act of charity.'

'Maybe the Holy Ghost Fathers never convinced me to believe in a God, Catholic or otherwise, but the simple innocence of that newborn girl sleeping upstairs has done more for

my charitable sensibilities than they could have managed in a lifetime. I feel I've done nothing particularly good in my twenty-six years, unlike you, who does good every day. And I want to help, James, it's as simple as that.'

'Ah, Ambrose,' James sighed. 'You'd be asking a lot of me, in my position here as a priest. The babe should be legally registered in my church notes as being abandoned, and—'

'Would we be incurring the wrath of the Lord if we tried to find a better life for her than the one on offer through the church?'

'Who says 'twill be better? Maggie and her husband John are very poor, Ambrose. This new child will be amongst a number of siblings who may not even have enough to eat. She will be asked to work hard on the farm, and given no better an education than she would receive if she went into the orphanage.'

'But she will be *loved*! She will have a family! And let me tell you, as an only child, with a father who could barely acknowledge me, I'd take the harder life with a family around me, always. Especially as you – and I – will be here to watch over her as she grows.'

James stared at his friend and saw tears in his eyes. In all the time he'd known him, he'd never heard Ambrose talk of his father like that.

'Can I take some time to think, Ambrose? Maggie is not due to leave here until six o'clock, after she's served our supper. I must go to my church and pray on what you have suggested.'

'Of course.' Ambrose cleared his throat and took a freshly laundered handkerchief out of his trouser pocket to blow his nose. 'You must excuse me, James. The arrival of that baby has quite disconcerted me. I do understand that I'm asking a lot of you.'

'I'll be back in time for tea and a slice of Maggie's

delicious-smelling brack cake.' With that, James nodded and left the kitchen.

As always in a crisis, Ambrose went to his room and took out his volume of Homer's *Odyssey* from his old Gladstone bag. Its deep wisdom from many hundreds of years ago comforted him. Back downstairs, as Maggie tended to the baby, he told her to rest by the range in the kitchen and made her a cup of hot, sweet tea. He went into James's study, stoked the fire and sat in the leather armchair to read. But today, even Homer's words could not bring him solace. With the book open on his lap, he questioned his own motives for helping this child. When he'd fully understood the answer, he then asked himself whether, even if the motives were intrinsically selfish, the result was any the worse for it?

No, he was convinced it was not. The child needed a loving home and one was possibly available. And there was nothing morally wrong with that.

'How did your prayers go?' he asked as James appeared in the study an hour later.

'We spoke very well together, thank you.'

'Did you come to a decision?'

'I think we must first talk to Maggie. If she and her husband are against the idea, then there is no decision to make.'

'She is resting by the range with the baby – I insisted.'

'Then I shall go and get her.'

James left the study as Ambrose stared into the fire. For once in his life, Ambrose actually felt the urge to pray too.

James returned with Maggie in tow. She had used the other half of the torn sheet to make a sling around her, so the baby could lie tucked up close to her breast.

'Have I done something wrong, Father?' she asked as James offered her the armchair by the fire. 'The babe was fretful and I was after needing to cook your supper, so I took the sheet and—'

'Maggie, please don't upset yourself. Ambrose told you to rest,' James said as both men looked down at the little fists and feet that were appearing from the sling. 'Now,' James continued as the baby made small mewling noises not unlike a kitten, 'the thing is that . . . I'd better leave Ambrose to explain.'

'I know you've just lost your own baby, Maggie, and that she was a girl,' Ambrose began.

'Yes, sir, she was.'

'I'm so sorry for the pain you've been through. And here you are, nursing a newborn.'

Tears shone in Maggie's eyes. 'She's so much heavier than my poor babe was. Mary – me and John named her before she was born – was only a little wisp of a thing . . .'

Ambrose handed Maggie a handkerchief and let her collect herself before he continued.

'Now then, we all know where this poor child will end up if Father O'Brien contacts Father Norton,' continued Ambrose.

'I've heard orphanages are terrible places, so,' agreed Maggie. 'There was an outbreak of measles in the Clonakilty one not long ago, and many of the babes died.' Maggie looked down tenderly at the baby, then took a finger and stroked her cheek. 'But what's to be done?'

'You said you haven't told another soul about poor baby Mary's death?' James cut in to confirm.

'No, Father,' she gulped. 'As I told you, it all happened so suddenly, we decided 'twas best not to, given as we couldn't afford the wake. We're not heathens, I swear. We said prayers over her once we'd laid her to rest and—'

'I understand, Maggie, and I'm sure you are not the only parents to do the same around these parts.'

'The thing is,' said Ambrose, 'I was wondering whether you – and your husband, of course – would be willing to adopt this little one?'

'I . . . of course I'd take her in as mine if I could, but' – Maggie blushed to the roots of her beautiful red hair – 'we already have four hungry small ones, and 'tis difficult enough as it is . . .'

'Maggie, please, don't be upset,' James comforted her, seeing her embarrassment and distress. 'Listen to what my friend Ambrose has to say. This was his idea, not mine, but I said he should put it to you at least.'

Ambrose cleared his throat. 'I understand your financial predicament, and if you and your husband would consider taking her in as your own, I would be more than happy to cover any costs the baby incurs until she reaches twenty-one. That includes her education if she wishes to go further than secondary school. This amount would be paid in a lump sum to you every five years. I would then add on another sum, payable immediately for your trouble, and also for your discretion. Your friends and family must believe that the baby is one and the same as the child you were carrying. Otherwise it would put Father O'Brien in an intolerable position for not reporting her arrival through the correct channels. Now, this is the sum I am prepared to give you to cover the child's costs for the first five years of her life.' He handed Maggie a sheet of paper on which he'd written down a figure earlier. He waited until she'd looked at it, then handed her another sheet. 'And that is the lump sum I will pay you and your husband immediately for your trouble, and for any extras along the way.'

Both James and Ambrose studied Maggie as she deciphered the figures. It crossed James's mind that she may not be able

to read, but the look of utter shock on Maggie's face as she glanced up at Ambrose was enough to tell him she could.

'Jesus, Mary and Joseph!' Maggie put her hand to her mouth as she looked at James. 'Forgive me, Father, for using such language, but I'm, well, I'm in shock. These numbers, have you perhaps added an extra nought to them by mistake?'

'No indeed, Maggie. Those are the sums I'm prepared to pay for you to take the child.'

'But, sir, the first amount is more than we could think of earning in five years or more! And the second, well, we could begin to build a new home, or buy a few more acres of land . . .'

'Of course, you must consult your husband, explain what I'm suggesting. But if he did agree, I could go to the bank in the village tomorrow and pay you the cash in full. Would he be at home now?'

'He'll be in the milking shed, but I know he'll think I've gone stone mad if he sees these numbers.'

'All right. Well, why don't you go home now, explain what Ambrose has proposed and, if you wish, bring your husband here so I can confirm everything?'

'But your supper, Father, I've not yet served it, or cooked the cabbage.'

'I'm sure we can see to ourselves,' said James. 'If this is to happen, it's vital the baby leaves with you tonight. We wouldn't want Mrs Cavanagh knowing about it, would we?'

'No, Father, we wouldn't. Well, I'll be off home to see Himself, if you're sure.'

'I'm sure,' said Ambrose. 'We'll take care of the baby until you're back.' He stood up to collect the child from the sling.

Once Maggie had left, the two of them plus baby went to the kitchen where James took what smelt like a meaty Irish stew out of the range.

'If it's all the same to you, I won't be cooking cabbage. 'Twill be good to have a night off from it,' said James. He looked at his friend, whose attention was focused on the baby as he rocked her gently in his arms. 'May I ask how much you offered her?'

'You may not.'

'The only reason I ask, is I'm thinking that there is a possibility they may take the baby simply for the grand sum.'

'It certainly is enough to encourage them to take the baby, and for Maggie to put some weight on that frame of hers, yet not deck it out in grand clothes. And yes, to help them live a slightly more tolerable life. The baby is really quite beautiful, isn't she?' he murmured.

'You're smitten, Ambrose. Perhaps she will finally change your mind about having some children of your own.'

'Impossible, but I'd certainly want to keep a fatherly eye on her as she grows. And so must you when I'm away in Dublin.'

'Of course, but first, let's see if the husband agrees. Now, come and try this stew. It tastes delicious.'

An hour later, Maggie was back with a brawny, handsome young man by her side. He'd obviously put on his best clothes for the occasion and was wearing the peaky, flat cap that most of James's male parishioners wore to Mass.

'Please come in,' James said as he ushered them inside and quickly shut the door, glad of the five windswept acres around the priest's house, which meant no nosy neighbours. He took them into his study, where Ambrose had placed the baby in the basket she'd arrived in. He knew that the husband might think it strange to see a man tending to a newborn.

'This is my husband, John,' Maggie said shyly.

'And this is my Dublin friend, Ambrose Lister, a Fellow at Trinity College.'

'Tis a pleasure to meet you, sir,' mumbled John.

James could see how uncomfortable he was – so many of the farmers around here spent much of the day outside on the land, and often only spoke to others beyond their immediate family for a few minutes after Mass on Sunday.

'Good to meet you, Mr O'Reilly,' Ambrose said, noting John's body stiffen instinctively at hearing his English accent.

'Shall we all sit down?' James suggested. 'John, you and Maggie take the chairs by the fire.'

James went to sit in the chair behind his desk, actively separating himself from Ambrose and the two prospective parents, because it was vital that this 'deal' did not include him. Ambrose sat down in the wooden chair in front of the desk. He saw husband and wife sit down tentatively beside the fire and stare down into the basket.

'Please, Maggie, take the baby out if you wish to,' said Ambrose.

'No, sir, I'll leave her there until . . . well, for now.'

'So, Mr O'Reilly, Maggie will have told you of my thoughts,' he began.

'That she has, sir, yes.'

'And what are yours?'

'I suppose I'd be asking you why you'd do such a thing for the babe?' John didn't meet his eyes.

'Well, that, Mr O'Reilly, is a very good question. And the simple answer is, I am a bachelor who lives in Dublin, and am lucky enough to receive a private income that supports my current studies at Trinity College. Before you ask, I am Catholic,' Ambrose added hastily, realising that even though John O'Reilly was a simple farming man from West Cork, he may

well have heard that the famous Trinity College had been originally founded in the Protestant faith.

Ambrose braced himself to continue, knowing he must choose his words carefully: 'As such, I have disposable income. When this infant turned up on Father O'Brien's doorstep this morning, and he told me her fate would be an orphanage, I found myself wondering what I could do to help. And then, of course, your wife arrived and told us of your tragic loss . . . Put simply, I saw a way that the baby could be helped to receive a family upbringing, and at the same time, could perhaps relieve a little of the grief you both must feel over your loss.'

There was a pause as John pondered what Ambrose had said. Maggie was looking at her husband with nothing less than blatant hope in her eyes.

As the silence continued, Ambrose felt he should fill it.

'Of course, neither of you are under any kind of pressure to agree, but I thought that there was no harm in suggesting a possible way forward that might suit all parties. Both Father O'Brien and I were educated by the Holy Ghost Fathers, who taught us to be charitable. I have recently felt that I have not done enough to help others less fortunate than I, being busy with my studies in Dublin as I am.'

John looked up and met Ambrose's gaze for the first time.

''Tis an awful lot of money you'd be offering us, sir. What would you want in return?'

'Nothing at all. In fact, as Maggie has explained to you, any transaction that happens between us must never be spoken of again. For both your sakes, and the father's,' he said, indicating James. 'Father O'Brien cannot be seen to have had anything to do with this, and indeed, he does not.'

John's attention moved to James. 'You went to school with Mister . . . ?'

'Lister,' James confirmed, 'and, yes, I did. I can vouch completely for his character and tell you that this is nothing more than an act of charity towards a motherless child.'

'And towards us,' muttered John. 'We don't need to take that much for one small babe.'

The baby in question had been mewling all through their conversation and now burst into full-throttled screeching.

'May I pick her up and take her to the kitchen for a feed?' Maggie's eyes beseeched her husband.

John nodded his consent. Maggie swept up the child and almost ran from the room, as if she was unable to hear any more.

'I think that before you even begin to discuss the finances, the most important thing is to decide whether you are willing to take her,' James cut in from behind his desk.

'You can see already that Maggie has her heart set on the babe,' said John. 'It nearly broke in two when she lost our Mary only yesterday. And only a year since we lost the babe before that. O'course, we'd be hoping there'll be more babes of our own to come. Is this child healthy?'

'I'd say so, from the size of her,' James answered. 'And your wife certainly seemed to think so.'

John O'Reilly sat in silence for a while before he spoke. 'You're certain you'll be wanting nothing more from us?'

'Nothing,' confirmed Ambrose. 'I'm sure Father O'Brien will keep me updated occasionally on her progress, and that will be payment enough. I simply want to see the child brought up in a family and taken care of.'

'We'd do our best, but we can't guarantee to keep her safe if the measles or influenza are making the rounds.'

'I do understand that, Mr O'Reilly, I only meant that I would take an interest from afar. But if you prefer, no interest at all.'

'Well, as to the money . . . You told Maggie 'twould be in cash? And we'd have it tomorrow?'

'Yes.'

'Then I must tell you that we are a God-fearing family, and if my wife had come home and told me of the babe, and what with her still in milk, I might ha' been persuaded to take her in without your offer.'

Ambrose could see from the set of his shoulders that the man might be poor, but he was proud in equal measure. Ambrose liked him even more.

'I believe you would, Mr O'Reilly. I can see that you love your wife very much, so perhaps the best way to look at the amount you will receive is that it can be used to make her and your family's lives more comfortable than they have been.'

''Twould certainly do that, sir. The damp in our place is something fierce. I may be able to fix it, or even begin on a new farmhouse for us all. Not too fast, mind, or the neighbours would start to wonder where the funds had come from. I'd be wanting no gossip over this.'

'I'm sure you are both sensible enough to make sure that won't happen,' James interjected. 'We must remember that at the heart of all this is a newborn child who needs a home and a family. Everyone involved is performing an act of charity.'

'Yes, Father, thank you. And I'll be wise over how the money is spent. Slowly, over time, so.'

There was a knock at the door and Maggie appeared round it with the baby in her arms.

'She's sleeping now,' she said, then looked at her husband. 'See, John? Isn't she beautiful?'

John got to his feet to look at the baby and gave a small smile. 'That she is, love.'

'And?' It was as if Maggie couldn't bear to ask.

John turned back to Ambrose and James. 'Would we be taking her straight home with us now?'

'Good Lord,' Ambrose said as James returned to the study, having said goodbye to the young couple and their brand-new child. 'I feel quite overcome.'

James watched as Ambrose pulled out his handkerchief and mopped his eyes. 'What is it?'

'Oh, I'm sure it's a mixture of things,' said Ambrose. 'But mostly it's John O'Reilly: as poor as your poorest church mouse, and yet so proud.'

'He's a good man,' James agreed. 'And worships the ground his wife walks on. Which is good to see, given the amount of marriages I've conducted that feel more like joining acre to acre rather than man and wife. That is a love match for sure.'

'Would you mind if I helped myself to a whiskey? After all that excitement, I feel I need one to calm my nerves.'

''Tis a good thing you've done today, my friend. *Sláinte*,' James said as he accepted a glass of whiskey from Ambrose and toasted him. 'Here's to you, and the baby.'

'Who will be called Mary because that's what they want, which is rather a pity. I have a whole host of Greek names I rather like. Athena, perhaps, or Antigone . . .'

'Then I'm happy she was already named after the Holy Virgin,' smiled James.

'Mary is special, James, I feel it. She was sent for me to watch over.'

'I'd be agreeing that God does move in mysterious ways.'

'I'd call it fate, but I must admit the chances of my taking a

trip down here, combined with the absence of Mrs Cavanagh, together with a mother who had recently lost a child herself, does make me feel as if it was all destined.'

'I'll make you a believer yet,' smiled James.

The next morning, Ambrose walked down to the village and stepped into the bank. He drew out the amount he'd promised Mr and Mrs O'Reilly, then walked back up the hill. Taking two envelopes from James's desk, he separated the amounts, then sealed the envelopes. The withdrawal would not even make a dent in his trust fund, yet to the O'Reillys, it represented financial security for the next five years at least. Mrs Cavanagh was bustling about the house, complaining at anything and everything she could find to suggest that 'the O'Reilly girl' had not been thorough in her duties, so he stuffed the envelopes into the desk drawer.

There was a knock on the study door. 'Come,' he said.

'Will you be staying for luncheon, Mr Lister?'

'No, Mrs Cavanagh. My train leaves at noon, so I'll be off to the station in fifteen minutes,' Ambrose said, checking his watch.

'Right so. Safe journey then,' she said and almost slammed the door behind her as she left. He could feel the animosity that emanated from her. Even though he'd accepted the woman was not a lover of the human race in general, her dislike for him – though he was, after all, a guest of the man she worked for – was palpable. It was obvious she thought it somehow inappropriate that the priest should have a male friend who visited him every month. He'd done his best to be as polite as he could, for James's sake at least, but he could smell that the woman was trouble.

James walked into the study and gave him a weak smile.

'You look weary, dear boy,' Ambrose observed.

'I admit to not sleeping well last night, after all the . . . activity yesterday.'

'Does it concern you?'

'Not the act itself, but the deception of it worries me. If anyone found out that I was associated with this, then . . .'

'No one will; the O'Reillys won't tell, I'm certain of that.'

Ambrose put a finger to his lips as they both heard footsteps along the corridor. 'I must be leaving now,' he said in a normal voice as he went to the drawer to show James where he'd put the envelopes.

James nodded. 'I'll give them to Maggie next Monday when she's in for work, as we agreed,' he whispered.

There was another knock on the study door, and Mrs Cavanagh appeared around it again.

'Don't forget, Father, you're due at choir practice in ten minutes – the organist changed it from Thursday, because it's fair day in town and he has to take two of his heifers along to it.'

'Thank you for reminding me, Mrs Cavanagh – I'd quite forgotten. Ambrose, I'll walk with you as far as the church.'

The two men left the house and walked the short distance to the front of the church. Already, the sound of the organ could be heard inside.

'Thanks a million for coming, Ambrose. I'll write to you.'

'Of course, and I'll do my best to come down at least once before Christmas. Keep a watchful eye over our Mary, won't you?' Ambrose whispered.

James touched him on the shoulder. 'Safe journey, my friend. Thank you.'

Ambrose watched as he swept into the church. Then he turned away to walk down the steps and head for the tiny

railway station. He was always filled with a sense of loss when he said goodbye to James, but at least now, through a motherless newborn abandoned on a doorstep, Ambrose could comfort himself that they shared a secret that would last a lifetime.

Merry
Dublin

June 2008

37

As Ambrose finished his tale, I found I couldn't speak. I didn't have the words to describe how, within the space of less than an hour, everything that I thought I had known about myself – my childhood, and journey into adulthood – wasn't real.

'So, Ambrose,' the calm voice of my son spoke for me. I hadn't let go of his hand since I'd taken it as Ambrose had begun to tell me who I was. Or, in fact, who I *wasn't* . . . 'What you're saying is that Mum isn't actually related by blood to either of her parents, or her sisters and brothers.'

'That is correct, Jack.'

'I . . .' I cleared my throat, because it was dry from shock and emotion. 'I don't know what to say.'

'I'm sure you don't,' said Ambrose. 'You must feel as though your entire childhood was a lie. A lie, which was perpetrated by myself for far too long. My dearest Mary, I can only offer my abject apologies to you, because it is I who was the coward. I should have told you the truth on your twenty-first birthday when I gave you that ring. Please believe that, however misguided, I continued to lie out of love for you. I simply couldn't bear to destroy your love and belief in your family. I never once thought that we'd all be sitting here now, so many years on, with you in unnecessary pain because of my continued deception.'

Jack turned to me. 'Mum, I know it must feel terrible at the moment, but you have to remember that you and Dad adopted Mary-Kate. She's not related by blood to any of us either, but do you love her any less because of it?'

'No, of course I don't. And nor did your dad. We both love her as our own.'

'And so do I. She's my sis, and always will be.'

'But the difference is,' I said, 'as soon as she could understand, we *told* her that we had adopted her. So she'd never grow up thinking we'd deceived her in some way. It was something that your dad and I felt strongly about.'

As I spoke the words, my heart clenched again. I knew *I* had kept *my* past a secret from my husband and my children. So did that make *me* a hypocrite . . . ?

'Mary, I understand that you must be so very angry with me, but I beg you to forgive me for what I failed to tell you when I gave you that ring. You were off to visit your family to celebrate your twenty-first, and receiving your first-class degree in Classics. How could I have spoilt your happiness?'

Even though my entire view of myself had just been whipped from my grasp, I could see Ambrose was close to tears. I was angry – of course I was – but remembering the way I'd walked out and left him thirty-seven years ago, I stood up and went over to him, then knelt down and took his hand in mine.

'I understand, Ambrose, really I do. Maybe we all lie to protect those we love. Or at least, don't tell them things that we feel might hurt or frighten them.'

'That is most generous of you, dear girl. I expect I would have told you eventually. But then you disappeared from my life so very suddenly. I had no idea where you were. As I said, I was planning to leave a letter explaining all this to you in the hope that a solicitor could trace your whereabouts. You

are the sole beneficiary of my will to this day. I . . .' Ambrose removed his hand from mine to take the immaculate square of handkerchief from the top pocket of his jacket. He blew his nose hard.

'Well, as you just said, Jack, even if I wasn't their blood, the O'Reillys will always be my family.'

'You must know that I loved you from the first moment I set eyes on you,' said Ambrose.

'And I often wished that you *were* my father, darling Ambrose. What you've told me is a huge shock, but you weren't to know I was going to vanish for so long. I have to believe you would have told me sooner. Besides, you saved me from an orphanage.'

'Thank you, my dear, it is so very magnanimous of you to take the news as you have. But I also fear that I'm partly responsible for what made you leave Dublin. I was aware of what was going on, but felt it wasn't my place to intervene. You were all grown-up, an adult.'

'Shall I make some tea?' Jack asked, obviously keen to break the subsequent silence.

'Perhaps a little whiskey would be better?' I said, indicating the bottle.

'You'll have me turning into a lush! It's only just past noon,' said Ambrose, looking at the clock that had always stood in the centre of the mantelpiece. But he didn't refuse the glass that Jack offered him. He took a few sips and eventually, I saw some colour appear back in his cheeks. I went to sit next to Jack.

'Better?' I asked Ambrose.

'Much.'

'Of course, Mum, this means that if you *were* adopted, it could be either you or MK that Ally and her sisters are searching for,' Jack said.

I looked at him in surprise. 'My goodness, you're right. *If* these women are actually telling the truth about why they are hunting me down,' I added. But it did prompt me to ask Ambrose an important question.

'Do you . . . I mean, would you have any idea who my birth parents were, Ambrose?' I asked tentatively.

'None at all, Mary, none at all. You were what was once known as a "foundling", and because you replaced the Mary that had died, there was never any gossip about you. No one except the unknown person who brought you knew that you *had* been left on James's doorstep.'

'Do you . . . well, do you think my parents took me in because of the money you paid them?'

'Of course that was a worry to begin with, but I remember so vividly the look on your mama's face when she held you in her arms for the first time. And your dear papa was so very much in love with her that he'd do anything to make her happy. I watched as he grew to love you. You were very easy to love, Mary,' he smiled.

'Perhaps you'll never find out who your birth parents were, Mum,' said Jack. 'Does it matter if you don't?'

'Under normal circumstances, it might not,' Ambrose cut in, 'except that there seems to be a search taking place by a group of sisters who are determined to look at that ring of yours. As it is the only clue to your original heritage, it does indicate that they may well be genuine. Mary, might I suggest that you actually consider meeting with one of these women to discover what it is they want?'

'I think Ambrose is right, Mum,' said Jack. 'I could certainly contact Ally.'

'But you're not even sure whether she *is* one of the sisters, are you, Jack?' I said.

'The more I think about the conversations we had, the

more I think she sought me out on purpose. Anyway, there's only one way to find out.'

'I've just realised something,' I said with a shudder. 'That man I met in London – Orlando Somebody-or-other – I told him which *cave* you were staying at in Provence, and even gave him your mobile number, in case he wanted some further technical details about our vineyard.'

'Well then,' Jack sighed sadly, 'that settles it. That's how she found me.'

'It seems that these sisters are certainly resourceful.' Ambrose gave a weak smile. 'Despite your fear that their motivation is connected to your past here in Ireland, perhaps either yourself or your daughter *is* their missing sister.'

I could feel every nerve in my body tingling as I thought of the connotations of me being the missing sister. Even if Ambrose said he had an inkling of why I'd run away all those years ago, and he was certain that these women looking for me were not connected to it, I was still not convinced. I stood up suddenly. 'Would you mind if I took a walk? I need some fresh air.' With that, I turned, made my way to the entrance hall and left the house.

Outside, I took in some long, deep breaths of Irish air, then I walked determinedly through Merrion Square Park, past the couples and groups of students having summer picnics in the shade of the large trees, just as I'd once done. Walking past the Oscar Wilde statue, I followed the same path I'd trodden in my uni days. When I emerged onto the intersection between Merrion Square West and North, I saw that even though the streets were now packed with cars, and the odd new building had popped up along the way, it was otherwise unchanged. I'd always loved how green everything was here in the city centre, having missed the wide-open spaces of West Cork, and in a daze, I automatically walked down the road, past Lincoln's Inn,

which had always been a popular student watering hole, then around College Park, where men in whites were practising cricket. I arrived at the smaller green of Fellows' Square and remembered how I used to meet Ambrose outside the School of Humanities to walk home together.

I saw tourists were lined up outside the Trinity Library building, waiting to view the famous *Book of Kells*, and continuing onwards, I arrived in Parliament Square and looked up at the central campanile tower, its white granite facade still as imposing as I remembered it. I smiled weakly at the tourists posing underneath it for photographs, thinking of the student superstition that if one were to walk through it while the bell was tolling, you would fail all your exams.

Student life had been full of superstitions, ancient traditions, balls, house parties and anxiety over exams, all accompanied by a good quantity of alcohol. Being here at the beginning of the seventies, a bright new decade when the youth were finding their voice, had been exhilarating – Parliament Square had frequently been filled with students protesting against apartheid in South Africa, or the republican student clubs rallying for support.

I went and sat on the chapel steps and I shut my eyes, overwhelmed by the memories evoked. I remembered sitting on these steps with my friends in my first ever pair of Levi's jeans. I'd started smoking, just because everyone else did then – we'd even had our own brand of Trinity cigarettes, sold by a man at the college front gate, who'd always flirted outrageously with any girl he saw. It was here that I'd celebrated the fact that I'd won the Classics scholarship at the start of my second year. It meant that I wouldn't have to worry about tuition fees, accommodation or meals, they were all provided for me by the college. It had been fiercely competitive, and after months of studying, I'd rarely felt more elation than I

had then. We'd all drunk beer out of bottles, then gone to the student café in New Square for some more. The Beatles' 'Hey Jude' and 'Congratulations' by Cliff Richard had been on the jukebox, and we'd played them over and over. It had been one of the happiest days of my life. I'd felt young and free, as if anything was possible.

'If only life could have been frozen there,' I murmured as I watched the students coming and going, their exams over for the year and as carefree as I'd been back then, before everything had changed. Sitting here now all these years on, I simply didn't know where to turn for comfort. My mind – usually so clear and organised – was in turmoil.

'I'm falling apart,' I whispered, on the verge of tears. 'I should never have left New Zealand.'

'Mum?'

I saw Jack standing at the bottom of the steps looking up at me. I hadn't noticed his approach, because he'd blended in with the rest of the young faces milling about.

'Are you okay?' he asked.

'Not really. I just needed . . .'

'I know. I understand. I can leave you be if you want?'

'No, come and sit up here with me.'

He did so, and we sat side by side, our faces tipped up to the sun, which had just appeared from behind a grey and very Irish cloud.

'What a beautiful place. You must have loved being here at uni,' he said.

'I did.'

Jack knew me well enough not to push for any further information; he just sat quietly beside me.

'Is Ambrose all right?' I asked him eventually.

'He is, but obviously pretty devastated about upsetting you. I took him the sandwiches his "daily", as he calls her, left

531

for his lunch. He's a nice man, I like him a lot. And he adores you, Mum, he really does.'

'He was like a father to me, Jack, and a mentor academically, not to mention that I now know he was my financial benefactor. He had great things planned for my future.'

'It sounds as though he and this priest – James – were very close.'

'They were. I asked him how Father O'Brien was, but he said he hadn't seen him for years.'

'That's sad. I wonder why.'

'Who knows?' I sighed. 'I just hope it was nothing to do with me. Father O'Brien was a very good man, Jack. Some priests, certainly back in the day, could be so frightening, but Father O'Brien was approachable. He had humanity.'

'Maybe we should take a walk and find a pub where we can get some lunch? I wanna try my first pint of proper Guinness,' Jack smiled as he stood up and offered me his hand. 'Any suggestions?'

'Definitely,' I said as I took his hand and let him pull me up. And I thought how I had never loved him more.

I took him to the Bailey pub in Duke Street, where we had gone as students. I was shocked to see how much it had changed: tables were set up outside, and men and women were eating fresh seafood in the sunshine. Luke, the dour doorman of my time, was of course no longer there, and the inside of the pub had been completely refurbished, the once battered tables and worn leather banquettes replaced by sleek new fittings, the only nod to its history being the pictures on the wall. The air smelt of delicious food, rather than stale beer and male sweat.

Jack pronounced his Guinness the best he'd ever tasted and I insisted he had colcannon and ham for his lunch.

'That's my kinda grub,' Jack said as he put his knife and

fork together, having finished the succulent ham and creamy mashed potatoes mixed with cabbage in record time. 'It reminds me of your cooking, Mum.'

'Well, Ireland's where I learnt to cook.'

'Yep. Er, Mum?'

'Yes?'

'I was thinking that maybe we should think about travelling down to where you were born. I mean, we're here, aren't we? In Ireland? It might be good to meet up with some of your family again.'

'Go down to West Cork?' I rolled my eyes. 'Oh Jack, after this morning's revelations, I'm not at all sure I'm up to that.'

'Apart from seeing your family after all these years – and they *are* still your family, even after what Ambrose told you – it's the only place you're going to get any answers about who your birth parents are. There must be someone who knows how you came to be left on Father O'Brien's doorstep.'

'No, Jack. I mean, even if somebody did know something back then, they'd be dead now, wouldn't they?'

'Ambrose is still alive and kicking, Mum, and there'll be plenty more like him still left.'

'Maybe, but I'm not sure I want to know. Would you?'

'It's a question I've never had to think about, but yeah, if I was in your shoes, I guess I would. Come on, Mum,' he urged, 'I'd love to see where you came from and meet your family – *my* family.'

'Okay, okay, I'll think about it,' I agreed, just to shut him up. 'Shall we go?'

Strolling back through the city, we walked into the lobby of the Merrion to pick up our keys, and the concierge turned round to take a note out of a pigeonhole.

'Message for you, Mrs McDougal.'

'Thank you.'

As we headed to the lift, I looked at Jack. 'Who would be sending me messages? Nobody knows I'm here.'

'You'll have to open it and find out, won't you?'

'Can you open it?'

'Okay,' he said as we entered my room.

I sat down in the nearest chair, my nerves yet again jangling. At this rate, I thought, I'd be dead from a heart attack soon and joining Jock. Bizarrely, I felt comforted by the image of my earthly remains spread across the vines with his, always together at the safe haven we'd created.

'Right.' Jack tore open the envelope and removed the short note inside.

Dear Mrs McDougal,

My name is Tiggy D'Aplièse, and as you might know, my sisters and I have been trying to track you down to talk to you. I don't wish to disturb you or, more importantly, frighten you, but I am staying in Room 107 and my mobile number is below. I can be contacted at any time.

With best wishes,
Tiggy D'Aplièse

'Well.' Jack eyed me as he handed me the note. 'One thing I can confirm is that Ally and Tiggy *are* sisters, because Ally mentioned a sister called Tiggy. It's not a common name, is it?'

I glanced up at him and saw the look on his face. I'd been so taken up with these women pursuing me, I hadn't put two and two together.

'You really liked Ally, didn't you, Jack?'

'I did, yeah, even if she was only there because I'm your son and she had a hidden agenda,' he said ruefully. 'I did text

her, but I haven't heard back. I don't seem to have much luck with women, do I? Anyway, apparently we have another of these sisters right here in the hotel with us. What do you want to do, Mum?'

'I . . . I don't know.'

'Well, I don't know what it is that made you leave Ireland, or why you've been scared ever since, but the one thing that I *do* know, having met her, is that Ally is a good person.'

'That's what James Bond thought about Vesper Lynd in *Casino Royale*,' I smiled weakly.

'For goodness' sake, Mum, we're not in a fictional thriller!'

'As a matter of fact, Ian Fleming based his spy stories on fact. Trust me, I know how these organisations work.'

'Maybe soon you'll tell me all about it, but for now, I've had enough of this subterfuge. Let's find out for sure, shall we? I'm gonna call this Tiggy's room and arrange to meet her. You can stay safely up here until I give you the all-clear, okay?'

'Look,' I sighed, torn between looking like a total fruitcake in front of my son, and protecting him. 'I know you think your old mum is losing her mind, but I swear, Jack, there's a good reason why I'm frightened.'

'Which is why *I* will meet this newest member of the family. Enough is enough, Mum; I can see you've lost a load of weight since you left home, and you're in a right state. Dad's not here to protect you anymore, so I'm going to.'

I watched my son stride over to the phone that sat by the bed and pick up the receiver.

'Hello, could you put me through to Room 107, please? Yes, my name is Jack McDougal.'

We both waited as reception transferred the call, me in an agony of tension, Jack perfectly calm.

'Hello, is that Tiggy D'Aplièse? Yes, hi there. I'm Jack McDougal, Merry McDougal's son. I was wondering if we

could meet down in the lobby and have a chat whenever you're free?'

I watched Jack nod and give me a thumbs up. 'Right, I'll see you there in ten. Bye now.' He hung up the phone. 'So, I'm going downstairs to meet her – I doubt she'll be shooting me in the middle of a public lounge with people taking afternoon tea. I suggest you have a lie-down while I suss her out. I'll give you a call on the mobile to update you.'

'But—'

'No more "but"s, Mum, please. Trust me. For everyone's sake, we need to get to the bottom of this, okay?'

'Okay,' I nodded. What else could I say?

He strode out of the room, and even though part of me wanted to call him back because of the danger he could be in, I had never felt prouder of him. He had his father's clear, calm demeanour, and every day, he reminded me more of my beloved husband.

'Oh, Merry,' I said as I followed Jack's advice and lay down on the bed. 'What a mess you've made of your life . . .'

Of course, I couldn't sleep, so five minutes later, I was up and pouring myself a cup of tea, waiting tensely for Jack to call.

Fifteen very long minutes later, he did.

'Hi, Mum, it's Jack. I've just talked with Tiggy, and I promise, you're totally safe to come down.'

'Oh Jack, I don't know.'

'Well, I do, Mum, and you're to come. Are you wearing that emerald ring?'

'Yes, why?'

'Because Tiggy has a drawing she wants to show you. I swear, Mum, she's lovely. Want me to come up and get you?'

'No, no. If you're sure it's safe, I'll come down. See you in a minute.'

I tidied my hair in the mirror, applied blusher to my pale cheeks and some lipstick. Jack was right: I had to stop running away and face my fears. Taking a deep breath, I left my room and headed for the lift.

Downstairs in the lounge, I saw my son's blond head immediately, then took a few seconds to study the woman sitting with him. She was small-boned and slim, with a head of thick, wavy mahogany-coloured hair that fell prettily around her shoulders. As I approached them, they both stood up, and I felt instinctively that this young woman had a fragility to her, her expressive tawny eyes dominating the rest of her face.

'Hi, Mum, meet Tiggy D'Aplièse, who is number . . . ?' Jack looked at Tiggy for confirmation.

'Five of my six sisters,' she said in a soft French accent. 'I'm so pleased to meet you, Mrs McDougal, and I just want to say that really, we mean no harm.'

Tiggy smiled at me, and even with my paranoia, it was difficult to believe that this gentle young woman was here to harm me.

'Thank you, Tiggy. And please, call me Merry.'

'Sit down, Mum.' Jack patted the space on the sofa next to him.

As I did so, I felt Tiggy's eyes travelling from my face to the ring on the fourth finger of my left hand. I instinctively put my other hand on top of it.

'So, Tiggy has been explaining exactly what MK told us both after the visit she had from Tiggy's sister, CeCe, and her friend, Chrissie. If you wouldn't mind, Tiggy, maybe you can tell Mum yourself?'

'Of course I will, but I want to apologise on behalf of all my sisters. I totally understand why you must have been frightened by us trying to find you,' said Tiggy. 'I'm so sorry,

Merry, I really am. It's just that, well, as your daughter probably told you, our father died a year ago, and the six of us
are all going on a cruise to where my sister Ally – who Jack
has met – thinks she saw him being buried at sea. Recently,
Pa's lawyer received some information on someone who my
family nicknamed the "missing sister". Pa named us all after
the Seven Sisters of the Pleiades, you see, and of course, the
seventh would have been—'

'Merope,' I finished for her.

'Yes, and whenever any of us asked him why there wasn't
a seventh sister, Pa said that he never found her. So, when we
got this information from our lawyer, our two eldest sisters
contacted the rest of us to see if we could help find her. And,
if she was who we've been told she is, ask her to join us on
our pilgrimage to lay a wreath on the sea at the spot where
we believe he was buried.'

Of course, I knew this story already, but I felt calmer hearing it from this sweet girl, whose eyes shone with what I could
only describe as a kind of goodness.

'It wasn't well planned or anything,' she continued. 'We
just sent the sister closest to where Mary-Kate had said you
were travelling to. Electra lives in New York – that's the
woman Jack said you noticed in your hotel lobby in Toronto.
She discovered you were going to London next, so my third
sister, Star, was sent.'

'Yes. I did meet her. She called herself Sabrina. Is she
blonde, thin and tall?'

'Yes. That's Star. She was with her almost-brother-in-law,
Orlando. He's a little on the eccentric side, and came up with
a plan to entice you to meet him and Star by saying he was a
wine writer.'

'Well, he did fool me, so it was a good plan.'

'But it scared you too, didn't it, Mum?' Jack cut in.

'Yes, because even if he'd concocted a plausible story, he doesn't blend into a crowd. I saw him following me around London the next day.'

'Oh dear.' Tiggy gave an embarrassed chuckle and sighed. 'I can only apologise again for the disorganised and thoughtless way we've gone about this. You must have felt as though you were being hunted.'

'That's exactly how I felt, yes.'

'And then there was Ally,' Jack said. 'She had me completely fooled, until Mum told me about the other women who'd arrived everywhere she was going, and I put two and two together.'

'Now you are here, Tiggy,' I said. 'Does that mean that between us McDougals, we've met all of your sisters?' I briefly counted up on my fingers. 'Yes, what with the two Muslim women in Toronto, that makes six. Was the other one Maia?'

'You know her name?' Tiggy said in amazement.

'Mum did her dissertation on the myths of Orion. Part of that was to do with the Seven Sisters of the Pleiades, and Orion's obsession with Merope,' said Jack. 'Other kids got Snow White or Sleeping Beauty as their bedtime stories, while we got Greek legends. No offence meant, Mum,' he added suddenly. 'Or to you, Tiggy.'

'None taken,' she smiled, and as her eyes swept over me, I had the strangest feeling that I was being X-rayed. 'We obviously grew up with the stories too,' she continued. 'By the way, it wasn't Maia with Electra, it was Electra's PA, Mariam. Maia is holding the fort in Geneva at our family home which, by the way, is called Atlantis.'

'Wow.' Jack shook his head. 'I mean, isn't it a coincidence that both sets of us kids grew up with a parent obsessed by Greek mythology?'

'I don't think that coincidences exist,' Tiggy replied, as she looked at me steadily again.

'So you believe in destiny, do you, Tiggy?' I said.

'I do, yes, but that really *is* another story. Anyway, Mrs McDougal, the reason all of us sisters have been trying to get to see you was because of your ring. Here.' Tiggy pulled a sheet of paper off her knee, turned it over and placed it on the coffee table in front of me. 'That's the drawing our lawyer gave us. Star confirmed it was identical to the one you were wearing. Would you agree?'

I stared down at the drawing and then reluctantly unclasped my left hand from my right. I stretched it out so that Tiggy could see it. All three of us looked down at the drawing and the ring.

'They are identical, Mum.'

Jack spoke for all of us because, down to every detail, the ring and the drawing were the same.

We all sat there in silence for a few seconds, none of us knowing exactly what to say.

Then Tiggy put out her hand and took mine very gently in hers. She looked at me and I saw her eyes were full of tears.

'We've found the missing sister,' she said. 'I'm sure of it.'

The touch of her small hand, and her obvious emotion and conviction blew away the last remnants of any fear I had left.

'Tea anyone?' said Jack.

We drank the tea and, sensing the fact that I was overwhelmed, Jack took over the conversation, chatting about how this was his first visit to Dublin, and how he wanted to explore the city before he left. Both Tiggy and I replied monosyllabically; we

were each lost in our own worlds, trying to make sense of it all. Or at least, I was, especially after the news I'd received from Ambrose earlier today . . .

I could hardly keep my eyes off the girl sitting opposite me. I felt connected to her somehow, and even though she was obviously very young, there was a wisdom, a depth to her that I couldn't put my finger on, as if she somehow knew all the answers but wasn't telling.

'Can I ask you where this information about the ring came from, Tiggy? I mean, your lawyer's source?' I asked.

'All I can say is that he told us that he'd followed many false leads over the years, but he'd been assured by our father that this ring was definite proof.'

'And what was your father's name?'

'He was always called Pa Salt at home. I think Maia or Ally named him, because he always smelt of the sea. And he did.' Tiggy nodded. 'It's a shame about the "P" for Pa in the name, because I've marked out the rest as an anagram of "Atlas".'

'Perhaps the "P" might be for Pleione, the mother of the Seven Sisters?' I suggested.

'Oh!' Tiggy clasped her hands together and tears welled again in her huge brown eyes. 'Of course! Of course. Now I have serious shivers.'

'So do I, and I'm not a "shivery" person these days,' I smiled at her.

'Well, I'd love to meet Mary-Kate, but I totally understand if you're not comfortable yet with this situation,' she said.

'As a matter of fact, Tiggy, she's arriving here tonight,' said Jack. 'Mum was worried about her, and didn't want her by herself in New Zealand whilst all this was going on . . .'

I sat there and gave my son a look that could kill. It was okay for *me* to trust this woman, but Mary-Kate was my

daughter and this was information I hadn't yet wanted to divulge.

'Oh, how wonderful! I do hope I can meet her,' said Tiggy. 'CeCe said she was lovely. She fits the age perfectly; she'll be the youngest of us seven sisters.'

'I was one of seven children,' I said, trying to change the subject.

'Really?!' Tiggy's eyes lit up. 'What number where you?'

'Number five.'

'So am I! How marvellous,' she added. 'I've never met a fifth sister before.'

'Well, I had three brothers, so it's not quite the same as you.'

'No, but it feels nice anyway,' she smiled. 'One day, we'll have to talk about our shared mythology.'

'I already know the legend of Taygete. Zeus pursued her relentlessly,' I said.

'He did, yes, and, oh, it's a long story but . . .' Tiggy shrugged. 'I hope we can speak for longer some time.'

'Yes. I'd like that.'

Jack looked at me. 'Mum, you look exhausted. I know I am, and I've only sat on the sidelines of all of this. Go and get some rest before Mary-Kate arrives.'

'Yes, you should.'

Tiggy's tiny, calming hands were once again placed on mine, and I felt my heart rate slowing. This girl, whatever and whoever she was to me, was magical.

'Yes, I think I need to sleep,' I agreed, standing up. 'Would you excuse me?'

'Of course,' Tiggy said as she stood up too, 'and thank you for trusting me today. I know it's confusing, but my instinct tells me that everything is as it should be.' Then she enveloped me in a big hug. 'Sleep well, Merry. I'll be here when you need me.'

'Would you like me to come up with you, Mum?' Jack asked.

'No, I'm fine. Why don't you amuse yourself in the city this afternoon? I can recommend the *Book of Kells* in the Trinity College Library.'

'That's been on my list forever,' said Tiggy. 'Are you up for it, Jack?'

'I sure am, Tiggy. See you later, Mum.'

By the time I entered my room, I could hardly stand from exhaustion. Having put the *Do not disturb* sign on, I closed the curtains – I was never one for sleeping during the day – undressed and sank under the duvet.

'Who am I?' I whispered drowsily.

For the first time in my life, I realised I didn't know.

38

Tiggy
Dublin

'Maia? It's Tiggy here.'

'Hi, Tiggy! Ally's here, and CeCe and Chrissie have just arrived from London. Have you found her?'

'I have.'

'More importantly, have you managed to speak to her and explain everything?'

'Yes.'

'And?'

'I think I managed to reassure her. I showed her the drawing of the ring and she agreed it is identical.'

'Fantastic. And what would be your feeling about Mrs McDougal?' said Maia.

'Oh, she's lovely, although I don't think our rather slapdash undercover tactics helped – her son said she literally thought we were some organisation hunting her down, but I hope I convinced her that's not what we were trying to do.'

'What about her daughter, Mary-Kate? Like, how does Merry feel about her meeting us all?' CeCe butted in.

'We haven't discussed it yet. The good news is, Mary-Kate's

landing here in Dublin tonight, so hopefully I'll get to meet her.'

'How exciting!' said Maia.

'Please say hi to her from me and Chrissie,' said CeCe.

'You're the one with the instincts, Tiggy. Do you think we've found the missing sister?' came Ally's voice.

'Definitely, but . . .'

'What?' said all three sisters at the other end of the line.

'I need to think about something. I'll tell you once I have. Her son Jack is also lovely.'

'Hey, he's not adopted too, is he?' CeCe chuckled. 'Wouldn't it be weird if the missing sister was a guy?'

'Merry certainly didn't say he was. He talked a lot about you, Ally.'

'Did he?'

'Yes.'

'I bet he was cursing me, because now he knows I lied to get information out of him,' Ally sighed.

'He didn't do that at all, I promise you. When we went to see the *Book of Kells* together this afternoon, he said he wished that you could have seen it too.'

'Oh, come on, Tiggy, he must hate me,' Ally persisted.

'He may feel many things about you, Ally, but hate is definitely not one of them.'

'Anyway, well done, Tiggy. I'm so glad you've been able to reassure her,' said Maia. 'Do you think it's possible that Mary-Kate might be able to fly over from Dublin to join us on our cruise?'

'Let's wait and see, shall we? If it's meant to be, then—'

'It's meant to be,' chorused her sisters.

'Even though my instincts tell me that we're completely on the right track, do you think you could contact Georg to say

I've found Merry and the ring? I'd really like to speak to him about something.'

'I'm afraid Georg is away,' said Ally. 'I've already tried to reach him, but his secretary told me he won't be back until the boat trip.'

'Oh dear, that makes things more difficult,' said Tiggy. 'I mean, it's all very well us trusting him and his information, but others might not. All we have is the ring.'

'When I discovered my ancestors, apart from the likeness to my great-grandmother Bel in a painting, it was a piece of jewellery – my moonstone – that convinced me that I genuinely was her great-granddaughter,' Maia interjected. 'Maybe it's the same with the ring.'

'I know, but we don't have a painting and there's no one on earth that can actually confirm that Mary-Kate is who we think she is, is there?'

'Unless she finds out who her birth parents were,' put in Ally.

'True,' Tiggy agreed, 'which is why I could do with some help from Georg to find out if he knows any other details. Please, try contacting him again for me, if you want me to convince Mary-Kate and her family to come with us on the cruise.'

'You're saying that Merry and Jack should come too?'

'I think they should all be there,' Tiggy said firmly. 'Right, I'll keep in touch if there's any news. I'll have to go with my intuition on this one.'

'Do you ever live any other way?' Ally smiled. 'It would be so amazing if we could have her with us.'

'I'll do my best, promise. Bye, everyone.'

Tiggy ended the call and then dialled Charlie on his mobile. These days, he was spending much less time at the hospital in Inverness, as the Kinnaird estate needed every hand to the pump. Even though he'd moved to a three-day week, if there

was an emergency, he'd still get in his beaten-up Defender (Ulrika had the new Range Rover *and* the family house in Inverness, negotiated in a separation agreement) to drive the two hours to the hospital. His voicemail kicked in as it usually did, and Tiggy left a message.

'Hi, darling, I arrived safely in Ireland, and I've managed to meet with Merry. She's lovely, as is her son, Jack. Anyway, her daughter's arriving tonight, so I'll try and get back home at some point late tomorrow. Love you, miss you, bye.'

Tiggy laid her head back on the soft hotel pillow, sighed in pleasure and wondered if there was any money in the coffers to buy some new ones for her and Charlie. They'd rented out the luxurious lodge to wealthy families for the summer and were reduced to living in the poky gatehouse where Fraser had once lived. Not that she minded – but every penny that came in from the guests was going towards planting saplings, fencing and the re-stocking of indigenous wildlife, such as the European elk she and Charlie's daughter Zara had their hearts set on.

Her greatest triumph so far was that her Scottish wildcats had managed to produce a healthy male kitten in April. She'd been tempted to pet it, but of course, she knew she mustn't; if the cats were ever to be freed from the pen they currently lived in and released back into the wild, then any human contact was a no-no.

'Perhaps I'll ask Georg if I could have some money from Pa Salt's trust to help us,' she mused. At least it looked like Ulrika had decided against trying to snatch the Kinnaird estate, but she was still demanding a huge divorce settlement. When Charlie died, the estate would pass to Zara. Her step-daughter-to-be was so passionate about it, and Tiggy thought how terrible it would be if the estate had to be broken up to pay for her mother's taste in designer clothes.

'All things do pass,' Tiggy murmured as she closed her eyes

and breathed in deeply. Since her heart scare, and discovering the condition she would live with for the rest of her life, she'd become much more aware of her heartbeat. And it was definitely raised at the moment.

She'd felt something so strongly when she'd met Merry, she could hardly describe it. And her son Jack too . . . As for Mary-Kate, she'd meet her later tonight, but Tiggy was fairly certain she knew the answer already.

'Am I right, Pa?' she asked.

Yet again, there was no reply from him. Was it because he hadn't settled there yet, or was it her own emotions crowding the usually clear line between heaven and earth? There was always silence when she asked her father for help; like a void, as if he wasn't there . . .

'Maybe one day you'll speak to me, Pa,' she sighed, before turning to one of her other relatives who had passed on. She thought about the question she needed the answer to, then asked it.

'*Yes*,' came the reply. '*Yes*.'

Jack had spent the evening in his room at the hotel, jotting down notes on all he had learnt so far. He liked order, not chaos, and this situation with his mum and sister was unsettling him. How could it be possible that two worlds, which both included the Seven Sisters in one way or another, had collided? Or was it just coincidence . . . ?

Tiggy had said coincidence didn't exist. He wasn't so sure.

Shared interests, he'd written in his notebook.

Did Mum once know the sisters' father? he wrote (*which would explain shared interests*).

Ambrose?

Father O'Brien?
Proof? The ring. (Is this enough?)
Ally: why do I keep thinking about her?

'Yes,' he said out loud, 'why do I? I mean, I must be . . . Damn!' Jack threw the notebook down on the bed in frustration. He was glad Mary-Kate was arriving soon, because he sure needed somebody to talk to about all this.

'Why is Mum so scared?' he asked the wide-screen television on the wall.

Surprisingly, it didn't answer.

'Time for a beer and some grub, Jack,' he said as he rolled off the bed, put on his trainers, and headed downstairs to the bar.

Just as he was ordering, a text message pinged on his phone.

On the 10 pm flight to Dublin. I'll get a taxi to the Merrion Hotel. C u soon, bro. MK xx

Sitting at the bar having a beer, he listened to the hum of Irish voices and wondered if this small island made up any part of his genes. If the DNA ran through his mother, it must run through him too. But given she'd just found out she was adopted, who was to know?

Ah, I miss you, Dad, he thought, *you were always the voice of reason, and boy, do I need that right now . . .*

Seeing it was past nine o'clock, he went to reception and asked them to call his mother's room to see if she wanted to join him for something to eat while they waited for Mary-Kate to arrive.

'I'm sorry, sir, but Mrs McDougal still has her room phone on "do not disturb",' said the receptionist.

'Right, okay, thanks.' Jack wandered away from the desk, wondering if he should go upstairs and knock on her door.

Deciding to leave her be – she'd looked so very pale earlier – he wandered into the restaurant and saw Tiggy sitting alone at a table.

'Hi,' he said.

'Hello there, Jack,' she replied, smiling her sweet smile. 'Want to join me? I was just about to order something for supper.'

'Thanks,' he said, sitting down opposite her. 'Me too.'

'Is your mum not hungry?'

'I think – or at least I hope – that she's sleeping. She's been through a lot in the past few days.'

'Because of us trying to find her?'

'Partly, yes, but also because . . .' Jack sighed and shook his head. 'Let's order, shall we?'

'I'm having the butternut squash soup.'

'I'll have the steak, with a side of fries,' he added.

The two of them ordered, Tiggy having a glass of white wine and Jack another beer.

'Cheers,' Tiggy said as they clinked glasses. 'Here's to new friends.'

'Yes. Although, it's just that, well, the whole thing's a bit weird. No offence to you and your sisters, but who was this man who adopted you all?'

'That is the burning question,' said Tiggy. 'None of us ever really knew – not where he came from or even what he did for a living. I think it's human nature to believe that the people you love will just live forever, so you never ask the questions that you should have done until it's too late. I think all of us sisters regret it now: that we didn't ask Pa more about himself, or why he adopted all of us specifically.'

'Do you mind me asking how old he was?'

'Again, we don't know, but I'd guess that he was well into his late eighties. How old is your mum?'

'Fifty-nine in November – and I know that for sure,' said Jack with a smile. 'She had to renew her passport last year, so that would put, what? Twenty-five, or even thirty years between him and my mum.'

'What are you thinking?'

'Only that, well, I was wondering if the two of them—'

'Could have got together at some point in the past? I've thought about that too. But then . . .' Tiggy eyed him.

'That would make *me* the missing brother!' Jack grinned. 'I'm joking. My mum and dad were devoted to each other, and I'm definitely my father's son.'

'Well, the one thing that my father was was specific. It was absolutely the missing *sister* he was looking to find.'

'Then it has to be Mary-Kate, doesn't it? She's the one who's adopted, but . . .'

'Yes?'

'Nothing,' said Jack.

'Does Mary-Kate know, or in fact, does your mum know who Mary-Kate's birth parents were?'

'I've no idea, but these days, it's probably easy for Mary-Kate to find out if she wants to.'

'And does she?'

'Tiggy, I honestly don't know, but as she's arriving in a couple of hours' time, I'll ask her.'

'And what about your mum? Who were her parents?'

Jack took a sip of his beer, knowing it was not his place to tell what Ambrose had said this morning. 'They were Irish, I think.'

'Jack, was your mum adopted too?'

He stared at Tiggy in disbelief as she calmly ate her soup. 'Christ! How did you know? My mum was only told that this morning! Who told *you*?'

'Oh, nobody, it was just a feeling,' she said. 'I have a lot of

those, Jack, and when I met your mum earlier today, I *knew*.'

'Knew what?'

'Just that she was. Now it all makes sense.'

'Well, at least I didn't tell you. Seriously, Tiggy, this must stay a secret from everyone, including your sisters. Mum was pretty devastated, y'know? Even if she's never talked about her past to us kids, knowing where you come from and believing your family is your family . . . it identifies you, doesn't it?'

'Yes . . . but being adopted myself, I firmly believe that if you grow up in a loving environment, it doesn't matter what your genetic make-up is.'

'Yeah, but like Mary-Kate, you always knew you were adopted. And you made that a part of your identity. Mum has thought she came from her Irish family the whole of her life. And now, at not far off six decades, she's just been told it was all a lie.'

'That must be so very hard for her to come to terms with. I'm sure it will take her some time. Please don't worry, I'm especially good at keeping secrets. I won't say a word until I'm allowed to, but it does mean that we might have got it all wrong.'

'About what?'

'Oh, just assuming things. Anyway,' Tiggy shrugged. 'It doesn't matter.'

'Everything's a bit crazy just now, eh? Especially for Mum. I don't like craziness.'

'Perhaps there has to be a moment when everything is thrown up in the air before it can settle again, then maybe it can be even better than before. Tell me if I'm wrong, but I get the feeling your mum is frightened of something else, other than us sisters tracking her down. Is she?'

'Yeah, she is for sure. Wow, Tiggy, are you a mind-reader or what?'

'I just sensed it. Now then, shall we look at the dessert menu? I'm still hungry.'

After they'd eaten, Tiggy and Jack sat in the lounge having coffee and chatting about both living in far-flung, isolated locations when Jack's mobile rang.

'Excuse me,' he said as he answered it.

'Hi, Jack! I'm here!' came Mary-Kate's bright voice.

'Where is "here"?'

'I'm standing in the lobby, idiot! Where are you? You're certainly not answering the phone in your room.'

Jack looked at the time on his watch and saw it was after midnight. 'O'course! Sorry, I'd lost track of the time. I'll come and get you.'

'Mary-Kate's here,' Jack said as he stood up. 'I didn't realise it was so late,' he added as he began to walk towards reception.

'Jack!' Tiggy called. 'I'm going back to my room now. You need some time with your sister.'

'Okay, but why don't you come and say hi? After all, she might be your missing sister . . .'

'If you're sure.'

Tiggy stood up and followed Jack into the lobby. She saw a young woman dressed in black jeans and a hoody, her fair hair scraped up into a topknot. She watched as brother and sister embraced and felt the easy warmth and affection between the two of them.

'Tiggy' – Jack beckoned her over – 'this is Mary-Kate, more commonly known as MK. MK, meet Tiggy D'Aplièse, the fifth sister.'

'Pleased to meet you, Tiggy. Sorry I look such a wreck; it's a long way from NZ to Ireland, and I left in a huge rush to make the flight.'

'You must be exhausted, but it's wonderful to meet you,

Mary-Kate. My sister CeCe said you were very hospitable to her and Chrissie when they visited you.'

'Us Kiwis are just brought up that way, eh, Jack? But yeah, they were great and we had a fun night together.'

'Right, I'll leave you two to it and say goodnight.'

'Night, Tiggy, and thanks for the chat,' Jack called to her as she walked towards the lift. After Mary-Kate had checked in, he took her rucksack. 'Let's get you upstairs to your room, so you can get some shut-eye.'

'I'm not sure I can sleep, y'know?' said Mary-Kate. 'I'm wired; my body has no idea what time it is or what it's meant to do. Where's Mum?'

'Sleeping. I haven't woken her – I know she'll be mad at me tomorrow morning, but she's had a helluva day today.'

'Really? Is she all right?'

'I'm sure she will be,' Jack replied as they went up in the lift, then headed for Mary-Kate's room. 'Coming back here to Ireland has been a bit like pricking a boil: you gotta get the poison out before it starts to heal.'

'Lovely analogy, Jacko,' Mary-Kate commented as her brother opened the door to her room for her. 'What kind of "poison"?'

'It's all to do with her past. I'll let her tell you. Anyway, it's good to see you, sis. I'm glad you came.'

'I didn't think I had a choice, Jack.' Mary-Kate climbed onto the bed and leant back against the pillows. 'What's been going on?'

'I wish I could tell you, but at the moment, I can't. Basically, there's something – or someone – Mum is frightened of. And when this family of sisters kept turning up at her hotels trying to speak to her, she got really spooked.'

'They only wanted to meet her and identify that ring, Jack. Why would that scare her?'

'I haven't a clue,' Jack sighed. 'All I've managed to get from her so far is that *she* used to be called the "missing sister" when she was younger. Listen, I've had a long day too, even if I haven't travelled round the world like you, and I'm beat. I think we should both get some shut-eye; if tomorrow's anything like today, you'll need your wits about you.'

'Bad stuff?' Mary-Kate asked.

'Just . . . stuff. Put it this way, after years of never mentioning it, Mum's on an odyssey into her past, and it's complicated.'

'So it's nothing to do with me then? Or the fact I might be this missing sister? I was thinking on the plane that maybe she's scared she's going to lose me to some other family.'

'Maybe, yeah, but as all the rest of the sisters are adopted and their dad is dead, I'm not sure how you'd be related to them anyway.'

'What about the adoptive mum? Who's she?'

'I don't think there ever was one. Tiggy told me that some nanny brought them all up. It's all a bit weird, to be honest, but she and her sister Ally, who I met in Provence, are lovely and seem pretty normal.'

'CeCe and her friend Chrissie were great as well,' Mary-Kate agreed. 'Anyway, I've got something to tell you and Mum tomorrow. Right, I'm taking a shower and then I'll try to get some sleep. Night, Jacko.'

'Night, sis.'

39

Merry
Dublin

I woke up and lay there in the dark, thinking I was at home. I reached out for Jock's comforting bulk, but found emptiness next to me.

And remembered.

'I miss you, my love, every day more, and I'm so sorry if I never appreciated you properly when you were with me,' I whispered into the darkness.

I felt tears prick my eyes as the nightmare of my current existence began to flood back into my brain. I reached to turn the light on to stop the bad thoughts. And was shocked that the clock was saying it was ten to nine.

'At night?' I muttered as I staggered out of bed to open the curtains. I was amazed to find the sun shining high in the sky. Partly because it was rare to see such a clear sky in Dublin, but also because it meant it was morning, and I'd managed to sleep for almost fourteen hours straight.

'Mary-Kate!' I exclaimed out loud as I remembered. Reaching over, I dialled Jack's room.

'Hi, Mum. Sleep well?'

'I did, yes, but did Mary-Kate arrive? Is she okay?'

'Yeah, she's fine. I left her in her room at around one a.m.'

'Why didn't you wake me?'

'Because you needed to sleep. You had quite a day yesterday. Fancy some breakfast?'

'I need to come to first, Jack. I feel like I've been drugged. It's tea and a bath for me, but you go ahead if you want.'

'I can wait. Just give me a call when you're ready to come down.'

'You're sure Mary-Kate is okay?'

'Totally, Mum. See you in a bit.'

I lay in the bath, drinking tea and thanking God and the heavens for the gift of my two children. Coming from a big family myself, I'd hoped for more babies, but that wasn't to be.

'But you weren't from a big family, Merry, you just *belonged* to one,' I whispered to myself.

However, the thought of Mary-Kate, my precious daughter in all but blood, lying a few feet away from me, stopped me from self-indulgence. Jock and I could not have loved her any more than we did. We were her mum and dad and Jack her brother, no matter whose genes she did or didn't have.

Out of the bath and feeling calmer, I dried my hair and thought about the reason – the *real* reason – I'd decided to embark on my tour of the world. Now here I was in Dublin and even though it frightened me, I knew exactly where my children and I needed to go next.

'But first . . .' I said to the mirror as I applied the usual dab of pale pink lipstick, 'I must visit my godfather.'

'Mary-Kate, it's so good to see you!' I said as she reached our table in the dining room.

'And you,' my daughter said as we hugged. 'You look well, Mum. I was worried when Jacko called and told me to jump straight on a plane.'

'I'm fine, really, sweetheart. Fancy some breakfast?'

'Weirdly, I'm craving a glass of our Kiwi wine, preferably red.'

'Your body clock hasn't caught up yet,' Jack grinned. 'It's evening wine time in NZ. Some of this fantastic Clonakilty black pudding will have to do.' Jack indicated his plate.

'Ewww. It looks disgusting. What's it made of?' Mary-Kate asked.

'Mum says pig's blood mostly, but it tastes great, I promise.'

'I'll grab some toast, if they have anything like that here,' she said as she began to walk to the buffet.

'Oh, they do, try the soda bread with some jam!' I called. 'You'll love it.' Mary-Kate gave a thumbs up and I took a sip of my steaming cappuccino. 'They never had coffee like this when I was growing up. Ireland, or at least Dublin, has changed so much, I can hardly believe it.'

'In what way, Mum?' Jack asked me.

'In every way. I mean, Dublin always was ahead of the Irish curve, so it would be interesting to see what West Cork is like these days, but—'

'No wonder your fry-ups have always been good, Mum,' said Mary-Kate, returning with a fully loaded plate. 'I've got some toast, eggs and bacon and a bit of that pudding stuff. I'm actually starving.'

I watched my daughter as she ate hungrily, just enjoying the sight of her here with me.

'That bread is delicious, Mum,' said Mary-Kate in between bites. 'And the pudding thing is really good, even if it's full of

stuff I don't want to think of.' She put her knife and fork together and looked at me. 'Jacko says you've been on a voyage of self-discovery since you've been here. What's the news?'

I looked at my watch. 'Actually, there's somewhere I need to be.' I stood up from the table abruptly. 'I'll only be gone an hour or so, and I'll tell you everything when I'm back. Feel free to go out and explore the city while I'm gone.'

'Okay,' said Jack, and I saw my children exchange glances.

'See you later,' I said, then I walked out of the hotel and headed back to Merrion Square.

'Mary, come in,' said Ambrose. He led me slowly through to his sitting room and eased himself into his leather chair. 'How are you, my dear? I've been so concerned for your state of mind after what I told you yesterday. Again, I beg your forgiveness.'

'Ambrose, please, you mustn't worry about me. Of course I was shocked. But firstly, I met Tiggy, the fifth of the six sisters who have been chasing me. She arrived at the hotel yesterday afternoon.' I explained the conversation we'd had and how it helped ease my mind. 'Then, after a surprisingly good night's sleep, I woke up feeling much calmer. Truly, I understand why you hadn't told me before. My daughter Mary-Kate arrived from New Zealand too, and having her here with me – especially as she's adopted herself – has really helped.'

'I'd very much like to meet her.'

'I'm sure you will. Ambrose . . .' I paused for a moment, collecting my thoughts. 'You know I've always come to you for help and advice, or at least I used to. And . . . I need some now.'

'Fire away, Mary, and let us hope my advice to you is better than the advice I gave to myself all those years ago, when I neglected to tell you about how James and I found you.'

'I . . . well, after Jock died, I decided that it was time to finally put my past to bed. So when I went to visit Bridget on Norfolk Island at the start of my Grand Tour, I wanted to know if she'd seen . . . well, *him* in Dublin after I left. I think you know who I mean.'

'I do, my dear, yes.'

'She said she hadn't, because she'd moved to London and, like me, hasn't returned to Ireland since, as her parents sold their business and moved to Florida. She told me it would be better to let sleeping dogs lie. Especially when the two girls showed up to see Mary-Kate at The Vinery and used that phrase, the "missing sister". And then said they wanted to see the ring.'

'I think I understand, Mary, but surely now, having met Tiggy, you can see that your past problems in Dublin have nothing to do with the sisters who've been trying to find you?'

'I'm starting to believe it's coincidence, but I can't tell you how terrified I've been. As far as *he's* concerned . . . I decided that I had to find out what happened to him. I've been searching for his name in public records offices in all the countries I thought he might have gone to if he was following me. So far, I've found no trace of him.'

Ambrose paused before he spoke. 'Mary, you never told me the whole story, so I cannot claim to know exactly what happened, but I will say that after you left, I had a visit from him here.'

'Did you?' My stomach turned over. 'Did you speak to him?'

'Briefly; he was thumping so violently on my front door that I rather felt I had no choice but to let him in. He obvi-

ously wanted to know if you were here. When I said I hadn't seen you for two days – which was the truth – he didn't believe me. He tore through here, looking under beds, searching in all the nooks and crannies and out in my tiny back garden, in case you were hiding under a pot of begonias! He then caught me by the lapels of my jacket, making threats of violence if I didn't tell him where you were.'

'Oh, Ambrose, I'm so, so sorry, I—'

'It was a long time ago, Mary, and I'm only telling you this to assure you that I understand why you left. Luckily, I'd already seen him lurking out on the street before I let him in, and had the foresight to call the Gardaí. A patrol car arrived in the nick of time and he made a run for it.'

'Did they catch him?'

'No, but he never came back here again.'

'You got my note saying that I had to leave for a while?'

'I did. Your Greek was almost impeccable; only a couple of small grammatical errors,' he said with a sardonic raise of an eyebrow. 'I still have it to this day.'

'I'm so sorry he came here, Ambrose. He'd made the most terrible threats against me, my friends, my family . . . everyone I loved. And he hated you most of all, and that ring you gave me. He called it "obscene", said it was like an engagement ring and that you were in love with me. In the end, I decided that all I could do was to disappear and cut off all contact with everyone. They weren't idle threats either; he'd told me he was involved with some violent men and, given his republican extremism and what was happening here in Ireland, I believed him. Oh dear,' I sighed, feeling dizzy as I said the words I'd kept to myself for so long, but I had to continue. 'The point is, Ambrose, I have to know if he's alive or dead and end this thing once and for all. Even though I've changed my name, my nationality and lived in the safest place you

could possibly imagine, I still jump whenever I hear a car coming down the track towards our house. So the question is, do you ... do you think I should go back to where it all began?'

Ambrose steepled his fingers and thought for a while. It was such a familiar gesture, it brought a lump to my throat.

'In my view, it's always beneficial to rid oneself of one's demons, if at all possible,' he said eventually.

'But what if he went back home to West Cork and is living there now? I think I'd die of fright if I actually saw him.'

'Do your children know your ... situation?'

'No, nothing, although after the past few days, I know Jack's aware something's not right.'

'I'm sure he is. I presume they would accompany you?'

'Yes.'

'And you'd visit your own family?'

'I'd hope to. I don't even know if they're still there,' I sighed. 'One of the reasons I came to see you originally was because of your friendship with Father O'Brien. I always thought that would endure the test of time, and if anyone would know if *he* was still around down there, it would be him. He was the parish priest, after all.'

'Ah, sadly, that was not to be,' Ambrose replied quietly.

'May I ask why?'

'You may, and the answer is two words: Mrs Cavanagh.'

'How can I forget her? With that long, pointed nose of hers, she always reminded me of the Wicked Witch of the West in *The Wizard of Oz*. What did she do?'

'Well now, from the moment she set eyes on me, I felt her utter dislike. She didn't approve of me or my visits, and most of all, the friendship I had with dear James. After all, I was a single man with a British accent, and I was labelled by her the moment I opened my mouth. Ironic, really, considering she

worked as a housekeeper at Argideen House, and was the most out and out snob I'd ever met. Well, there we are.'

'But what did she do to end your friendship?'

'Oh Mary, she was merely waiting for her chance to destroy it. When she was around, I took every precaution I could to make sure she had no ammunition. Then my father died a few years after you had left Dublin. Even though my father and I had a difficult relationship, it was the end of an era – I sold our family house only a few months later, after four hundred years of Lister occupation. I went down to see James after the funeral, and I admit to breaking down and crying in his study. James put his arms around my shoulders to comfort me, just as Mrs Cavanagh opened the door to tell us that lunch was served. The following morning, when James was out holding Mass, she cornered me and told me that she'd always felt our relationship was "inappropriate", especially for a priest. Either I left and never came back, or she would tell the bishop what she had seen.'

'Oh Ambrose, no,' I said, my eyes filling with tears. 'What did you do?'

'Well, both you and I know what a devoted man of God Father O'Brien was. If there had been any words whispered in the bishop's ear – words that she was sure to embellish – his priestly journey would have been halted then and there. It would have destroyed him; not just his career path, but spiritually too. So, when I arrived back in Dublin, I wrote to James telling him that, due to my new appointment as head of the Classics department, the workload would prevent me from coming down regularly to see him.'

'Surely Father O'Brien must have contacted you after you did?'

'Oh, he did, and I evaded and evaded, with excuse after excuse as to why I couldn't spare the time. He even came up

to Dublin to see me, so I invented a lady friend.' Ambrose chuckled sadly. 'Eventually, he took the hint and I heard from him no more. Of course, now that I'm retired, I have far too much time to look back on things I'd rather not remember.'

I watched as Ambrose took his handkerchief from his pocket and dabbed his eyes.

'You loved him, didn't you?' I whispered.

'I did, Mary, and you're the only person in my entire life to whom I've admitted that. Of course, I was aware from the start that he could never love me, not in the way I wished at least. For me, it was the love that dare not speak its name, and for James, the true embodiment of my precious Plato's platonic love. Still, just seeing him regularly was a gift. I treasured our friendship, as you will remember.'

'Yes. He was such a very good man and even I could see how much he cared for you. If only—'

'Sadly life is filled with "if only"s, my dear, but there's never a day that goes by when I don't miss him.'

'I suppose you have no idea where Father O'Brien is? Or even if he's alive?'

'No. Rather like you, I felt that cutting off contact was the best thing for us. And if he *is* with his beloved God now, then I am happy for him. Well,' Ambrose sighed, 'there we have it.'

'I'm so sorry for asking you. The last thing I wanted to do was to upset you.'

'Goodness, no; as a matter of fact, it's rather a relief to speak it all out loud to someone who knew him. And his goodness.'

'Ambrose, I've just discovered that if it hadn't been for the kindness of you and Father O'Brien, I'd have ended up in an orphanage. And we all know now how terrible most of them were.'

'Luckily, James knew that already, having seen one for himself in Dublin.'

'At least Mrs Cavanagh must be a few feet underground by now. Frankly, I hope she rots in hell, and I don't think I've ever said that about another human being,' I added staunchly.

'Anyway, we've veered off track, Mary. Do continue with what you were telling me.'

'Well, only recently I read the diary *he* gave me as a parting gift when I left for boarding school. He wanted me to understand why I must hate the British too and continue the fight for a united Ireland. He told me it was written by his grandmother, Nuala. She'd given it to him apparently, so he'd never forget. Of course, I never read it back then, but given my current odyssey into my past, I decided I should. So I did, a few days ago.'

'And?'

'Well, it certainly didn't make easy reading, but it's obvious where *he* got his republican leanings.'

'You should hold on to that diary, Mary. There are so very few documented first-hand sources about the fight for Irish independence. Everyone was far too frightened of being caught.'

'You can read it if you'd like. There were names and places mentioned in it that make me think there was a family connection between us. For example, Nuala talks about her home being Cross Farm, and her brother being Fergus. Well, our family lived at Cross Farm and I know my Daddy inherited it from our great-uncle Fergus.'

'I see. So you're thinking that *he* may have been a relation?'

'Yes.'

'Well, that's hardly surprising – everyone was related to everyone down in West Cork.'

'I know, and I'm wondering if he knew too. He was never

565

allowed up to our farm and I'm thinking that maybe there had been a falling-out long ago. And that's why he behaved so oddly with me when I was a child. He seemed to love me and hate me in equal measure.'

'Maybe,' Ambrose agreed. 'There's only one way to find out and that is to go back to where it all began.'

'That's what I came to ask you: should I travel back to West Cork?'

'On balance, I think you should, yes. You have your son and daughter to protect you, plus a family there, who I'm sure will be delighted to welcome you back into the fold.'

'Oh Ambrose, I don't know. What if he *is* there? It would be a lot easier just to get on a plane to New Zealand and forget all about it.'

'You will find out very quickly if he is, Mary; we both know how everyone knows your business there before you do. And the young woman I once knew you to be was brave and strong, and would face her foes head on. Besides, surely now there is another reason to travel there?'

'What?'

'The fact that it's the only place to discover your original birth family. As I explained yesterday, you couldn't have been more than a few hours old when we found you on the doorstep, Mary, so your birth parents must hail from somewhere very close to the priest's house in Timoleague.'

'I suppose so,' I sighed, 'but I'm not sure I want to find them. My head's so full at the moment, I hardly know which way to turn.'

'I'm sure you don't, Mary, but my belief is that in the end, we must all go back to where we began in order to understand.'

'Yes, you're right as usual,' I smiled.

'One thing I must ask you is what happened to that nice

young man you were seeing before you left? Peter, wasn't it?'

'I . . .' For some reason, I blushed, simply at the sound of his name. 'I don't know.'

'Right. He also came to see me after you'd left. He seemed distraught – he said he hadn't received a reply to letters he'd written to you in London.'

'Did he?' My heart began to thump again against my chest. 'Well, I certainly didn't receive any. Actually, he . . . *that* situation is something else I wanted your advice on . . .'

I arrived back at the hotel and was handed a message at reception from Jack to say he and Mary-Kate had gone on a wander into the city and would be back in time for a late lunch.

Upstairs in my room, before I could even begin to process the conversation I'd just had, I did as Ambrose had suggested. I went to a leather folder on the desk, drew out some hotel notepaper, found my pen from my handbag and sat down to write.

'Jesus, Mary and Joseph!' I murmured. 'What on earth do I say?'

In the end, I decided that less was more, and what did it matter, as the chances of finding the other 'him' were tiny anyway?

I read it through once, then signed it and sealed it in an envelope before I lost my nerve. I quickly packed my suitcase and threw some essentials in my holdall, then stood up to leave the hotel and give the letter to Ambrose before I changed my mind.

'If you could store my suitcase for me until I'm back, that

would be wonderful,' I said to Ambrose as he met me on the doorstep. 'And here's the letter,' I added.

'Right,' he nodded. 'I will do my absolute best to locate him, and will let you know if I do.'

'Thank you, darling Ambrose. Oh, and I brought you Nuala's diary to read. I'm afraid the writing isn't very clear and the spelling is sometimes phonetic rather than accurate,' I said, handing him the small, black exercise book.

'Exactly what I need to keep my brain active,' Ambrose smiled. 'Now then, Mary, go with your children and try to relax. As Jean de la Fontaine said, a person often meets his destiny on the road he took to avoid it. Or she, in your case. Please keep—'

'. . . in touch,' I parroted as I walked down the steps. 'I promise, Ambrose, truly, I do.'

Then, seeing I had just enough time before the children were back, I headed for the Dublin records office.

'Hi, Mum, sorry we're late – we got lost in a few alleys off Grafton Street,' said Jack as he and Mary-Kate appeared in the hotel lobby a few minutes after me.

'Oh, don't worry, I had bits to do myself.'

'Well, I'm starving,' Mary-Kate announced.

'Then let's go and grab a quick sandwich in the lounge, shall we?' I suggested. 'The train leaves at four,' I added.

'The train to where?' asked Jack.

'To West Cork, of course. The county where I spent my childhood. You said I should go back, Jack, so we are.'

Jack and Mary-Kate glanced at each other as we sat down on a free sofa. 'Okay,' they chorused.

Once we'd ordered, I saw Mary-Kate give Jack a small nod.

'What?' I enquired.

'MK has something to tell you.'

'I do, but . . . well, I know you've had a tough time recently, Mum, and I don't want to upset you any further,' said my daughter, who could hardly look me in the eye.

'Whatever it is, just tell me, or I'll worry anyway,' I said.

'Well . . .' She looked at Jack and he gave a nod of encouragement. 'You remember we had that conversation after CeCe and Chrissie had been to see me?'

'We had a few, so remind me which one?'

Again, I saw her look at her brother, who offered his hand to her.

'The one when I asked if you knew who and where my birth family was.'

'Yes,' I nodded as I wondered how much more stress my soon-to-be fifty-nine-year-old heart could take. 'I said that we'd talk about it when I got home.'

'Yeah, well, the whole thing had obviously got me thinking, so I found the adoption agency you mentioned in Christchurch, and they had my details on file. I made an appointment last week to go and see the guy there who runs the records department. I explained the situation to him – that a woman saying I might be related to her family had turned up on my doorstep, and I wanted to know if she really was who she said she was.' Mary-Kate eyed me, obviously trying to gauge my reaction. 'I'm sorry I couldn't wait for you to come home, but, well, seeing as it had come up, I couldn't think about anything else, y'know? You're not angry or anything, are you?'

'Of course not; I'm just sorry I wasn't there with you.'

'Mum, I'm twenty-two – I'm a big girl now. Anyway, the guy was great. He said I'd have to fill out some consent forms if I wanted to trace my birth parents and they'd have to be

asked as well, assuming they could still be found.' Mary-Kate let go of Jack's hand and put hers on mine. 'I swear, this will make no difference to the way I feel about you. Or Dad. I mean, you *are* my mum and always will be, but what with all this missing sister stuff, I just want to know who my birth family is and move on, y'know?'

'Of course,' I nodded. 'So, what happened next?'

'Well, I filled in all the forms, then I faxed them a copy of my birth certificate and passport. The guy – Chip – said it might take some time, so I wasn't expecting to hear anything back any time soon, but . . .'

'What?'

'I got an email a couple of days ago. They've found her! I mean, they've found my birth mum!'

'Right,' I nodded, instinctively wanting to cry, because those two words hurt my soul so much. 'And?' I said lamely.

'I typed out a quick email to her as Chip had asked me to do, saying I'd like to get in touch, and guess what?'

'You got a reply,' I said.

'Yeah. Last night, when I was at Heathrow airport. Obviously, it's all going through the agency at the moment, but I know her name is Michelle, and she's going to email me back. She wants contact. Mum, is that okay with you?'

'That's great, yes, great,' I replied, not having it in me to step up to the plate and look happy for my daughter. *My* daughter . . . The waitress appeared and I was relieved that the sandwiches had arrived to give me something to concentrate on. 'These look good,' I said as I picked one up and took a bite, even though I felt sick to my stomach.

'I think what Mary-Kate means is that at least, if this woman does email back, maybe we can get to the bottom of this whole missing sister thing,' Jack said gently.

'Completely. We all want to know whether I'm related to

those girls in some way. One thing I have thought about, Mum,' Mary-Kate said between munches, 'is whether there were other people trying to adopt me. Chip mentioned that there's not usually many Kiwi newborns going spare in the region. I wonder whether this dead father – Pa Salt, or whatever silly name those sisters call him – applied to get me and lost out to you and Dad. Or something,' she shrugged.

'That's certainly another theory,' I nodded, trying to look enthusiastic. It wasn't Mary-Kate's fault that I felt emotionally conflicted about this news, as well as just about every other thing in the current maelstrom of my life. 'So, have either of you seen Tiggy this morning?'

'Yeah, she came down to breakfast after you'd left, so she joined us for a tosh around the city,' explained Jack.

'Where is she now?'

'I think she went up to her room to pack. She's on the afternoon flight back to Scotland.'

'Right. You have my credit card, so would you pay the bill for all of us, Jack, and ask them to get a taxi to pick us up in twenty minutes?'

'O'course, Mum.'

'You come with me, Mary-Kate,' I said as I signed for lunch, then made for the lift as Jack headed for reception.

'Are you okay about all this, Mum?' Mary-Kate asked me tentatively.

'Of course I am,' I said as we walked out of the lift and along the corridor. 'I'd always known it was a possibility that one day you'd want to meet your birth family.'

'Hey, slow down, Mum. We're only going to email at the moment,' said Mary-Kate. 'The last thing I want to do, especially after losing Dad, is cause you any more pain.'

'Come here.'

I pulled my daughter to me and hugged her. She snuggled into me, just as she'd done when she was a tiny newborn of only a couple of days old.

'Right,' I said, knowing I was close to tears, 'pack up your stuff and I'll see you downstairs in twenty minutes, okay?'

'Okay. Love you, Mum,' she said as she wandered along the corridor to her room.

Just as I was about to go downstairs, there was a knock on my door. I opened it to find Tiggy standing there.

'Tiggy, come in!'

'Hello, Merry, I just wanted to come and say goodbye. Jack said you're leaving.'

'Yes. I mean, we're not leaving Ireland, just travelling down to West Cork where I was born.'

She stared at me. 'Are you looking for answers?'

'I suppose I am, yes, but whether I'll find them or not is another story. I have no idea what to expect.'

Tiggy walked over to me and again took my hand in hers. 'I'm sure you will, Merry. All of us sisters were sent on a journey into our past after Pa died last year. It was scary at times, but we each found what we were looking for and it made our lives much better. It will for you too.'

'I hope so.'

'I can feel you're frightened, but wouldn't it be so much better if you were finally freed from that fear?'

I stared at this young woman who looked so fragile, yet seemed so wise. Every time she held my hand, I felt a sense of calm sweep over me.

'I've written down my mobile number,' she said as she released my hand to reach into her jean pocket and give me a piece of paper. 'Any problem, call and leave a message and I promise I will get back to you as soon as I can. The signal's patchy where I live,' she explained. 'I've also written down my

big sister Maia's number, and the landline at Atlantis, our house in Geneva. Any help you need, just call.'

'Thank you,' I said. 'When are you all leaving for your boat trip?'

'One week on Thursday. Some of us are flying to Geneva and others straight to Nice, where the boat is moored. We'd love for you to join us. All of you,' Tiggy added firmly.

'But . . . we don't even know for sure whether Mary-Kate is the missing sister, do we?'

Tiggy looked down at my ring and brushed a finger over it gently.

'*That* is the proof. Seven emeralds for seven sisters. The circle is complete. Goodbye, Merry, and I hope to see you all again very soon.'

On the two-and-a-half-hour train journey down to Cork City, I slept most of the way; just the touch of Tiggy's hands seemed to have that effect on me.

'Mum, we're pulling into the station.' Mary-Kate shook me gently.

I came to and looked out into Kent station, which I had come to know well between the ages of eleven and twenty-two. It had been modernised, of course, but it still had that grand old air of the past about it, with its vaulted iron ceiling and echo of voices and footsteps. In the early days, I'd been glad to arrive back here with Bridget for the holidays from boarding school. Her father had collected us in his shiny black car with the big leather seats, and driven us back to West Cork, because the old railway line that served it and had once taken Ambrose almost to the doorstep of Father O'Brien's house had been shut down in 1961. I remembered how I'd

always let out a breath of relief when climbing into that car, because I was on my way home. Then, when I went to Trinity College at eighteen, everything had swapped around, and on my return to Dublin, I'd seen Kent station as a gateway to my freedom.

'So,' Jack said, looking at me as we stood on the main concourse, 'where to from here, Mum?'

'The taxi rank,' I pointed.

'Hello there,' said a cabby as we reached the front of the queue for a taxi. He opened the car doors and gave us all a smile. 'Welcome to the city of Cork, the finest in all of Ireland. My name's Niall, so,' he added as he stowed my holdall and the two rucksacks into the boot, then climbed behind the wheel and turned round to me. 'Now then, where'll I be taking you?'

The sound of his lilting West Cork accent brought a lump to my throat. I took my purse from my bag and handed him the piece of paper with the address of the hotel on it.

'Ah, the Inchydoney Island Lodge and Spa. 'Tis a grand hotel altogether,' he added. 'I don't live so far from it myself – it's near the town of Clonakilty. Will you be on your holidays here, sightseeing?'

'Sort of,' said Jack from the front seat. 'It's me and my sister's first time down here, but Mum used to live here, didn't you?'

I saw Niall glance at me in the rear-view mirror. 'Whereabouts would that have been?'

'Between Clogagh and Timoleague, but it was a long time ago now,' I added hurriedly. I knew how local gossip could begin with a whisper of someone's arrival, and be trumpeted around in the space of a few hours.

'I've cousins in Timoleague,' he said. 'What's your family name?'

'I . . . well, it was O'Reilly.'

'Sure, there are a few O'Reillys down in those parts. What was your homeplace called?'

'Cross Farm,' I said.

'Ah, I think I know of it, so, and I'd be betting we have kin in common. Everyone does down there.' Niall turned to Jack. 'So, 'tis you and your sister's first time here, to see where your mammy grew up?'

'Yes. We're looking forward to it, aren't we, Mary-Kate?'

'We are,' she agreed.

'You'll be staying in one of the grandest spots on the coast, but if you fancy a trip out, I'd recommend you see the Galley Head Lighthouse, which isn't so far from your mam's homeplace. Then there's the friary in Timoleague, o'course, and you should go to the Michael Collins Centre in Castleview.'

As Niall regaled my children with what to see and do, I gazed out of the window in amazement, not only at the number of cars, but at the roads themselves. We were on some kind of dual carriageway and the surface beneath us was completely smooth as we drove along. Journeys home from Dublin, even in Bridget's daddy's big comfortable car, had been bumpy to say the least. It was obvious that West Cork had finally joined the twenty-first century.

'There's the airport,' Niall was saying. 'The new terminal was only opened a couple of years back, and 'tis grand altogether! I often pop in on my way back from Cork City for a coffee, so.'

As we arrived at Innishannon, I was relieved to see that the main street of the village hadn't changed much.

'Oh look, Mum!' said Mary-Kate. 'The houses are all painted in different colours! It's so pretty.'

'You'll be seeing a lot of those around these parts, and

other villages in Ireland too,' cut in Niall. ''Tis something bright to look at when the rain's tipping it down in the winter, or on any day of the year.'

We entered Bandon, which Niall duly announced was the 'gateway to West Cork', and again I recognised some shops that still had the same family names painted above their doors. Then finally, we were off and out into the lush and unadulterated countryside I remembered so vividly. Gentle slopes on either side of us were peppered with grazing cows, and I caught sight of fuchsia bushes coming into bloom. The only change was the number of bungalows that had replaced the old stone ruins of cottages.

'Wow, it's so green here,' said Mary-Kate.

'Well, it is called the Emerald Isle,' I smiled, looking down at my ring.

'Am I ever going to get that back from you, Mum?' she teased me.

'Of course you will. I just needed it in case anyone I met from the old days didn't recognise me.'

'Mum, you look exactly the same now as you did in that black and white photo of you when you got your degree,' said Jack.

'Flatterer,' I said. 'Look! We're at Clonakilty Junction. There used to be a train line down here, which serviced West Cork. My older sisters used to get on it if they were off for a day of shopping or a dance in Cork City.'

'My daddy used to cycle up if there was a big GAA match at the Park,' said Niall.

'You cycled all the way we've just driven?' Mary-Kate asked.

'And many miles more too,' Niall confirmed.

'I rode everywhere on my bicycle when I lived here; it was just the way we got around back then,' I added.

'Sure, we all had calves the size of body-builders in those days, didn't we, Mrs O'Reilly?' Niall laughed.

'Please, call me Merry,' I said, not bothering to correct my surname.

'Now then, look to your left, at the car up on that plinth. This is the village where Henry Ford himself's parents lived, before they followed half o' Ireland across the Atlantic to America.'

I looked over at the stainless-steel replica of a Model T car, standing on a plinth just across a lane from the Henry Ford pub. It was a lane I knew well, for further on, it would eventually bring us to our own farm.

'So now, we're heading into Clonakilty,' said Niall. 'If you've not been here for a good few years, Merry, I think you'll spot some changes. We've a new industrial park with a cinema, and a sports centre with a swimming pool these days. O'course, Clonakilty is most famous for being the nearest town to Michael Collins's homeplace.'

'Michael who?' said Jack.

'Is he a film star?' Mary-Kate asked. 'I'm sure I read somewhere about him being in something.'

'Ah now, I think you mean you read of a film *about* him,' Niall corrected my daughter. 'The young ones don't know their history these days, do they, Merry?'

'To be fair, they were both brought up in New Zealand,' I interjected. 'What happened here and who Michael Collins was didn't really feature in their history lessons.'

'And you're telling me that you were born here and never told your small ones about the Big Fellow?'

'To be honest, Niall, Mum didn't tell us much about anything to do with her childhood,' said Jack.

'Well, I'll be tellin' you that Michael Collins was one of the greatest heroes Ireland has ever bred,' Niall said. 'He led us towards independence from the British and . . .'

Welcome home, Merry, I thought, as we turned off towards Inchydoney and I let Niall's history of Michael Collins wash over me.

Five minutes later, Niall pulled the car to a halt in front of the entrance to the Inchydoney Lodge.

'Now, Merry, what do you think of this?' he asked as he got out of the taxi and the three of us opened our doors too. 'I bet you're remembering that old shack that used to be here when you were a girl.'

'Yes, I am,' I agreed, as I admired the big, smart hotel, then turned to face the magnificent stretch of white sandy beach with the waves crashing onto it and felt the wind whip through my hair. I took in a lungful of fresh, pure, West Cork air, smelling its unique scent of sea and cow.

'So what will you be doing for transport whilst you're here?' Niall asked as I paid him in euros, rather than the shillings I'd so carefully counted when I was growing up.

'I'll rent a car,' I said. 'Where would be the nearest place?'

''Tis Cork airport – you should have mentioned it and we could have sorted it out on our way here. Never mind, I can help you until you get your own,' Niall said as he picked up my holdall and we all walked into the lobby.

'This is stylish,' Jack said as he looked around the spacious, modern reception area. 'I was expecting something beamed, like a farmhouse, y'know?'

We checked in, with Niall chatting away to the staff behind reception, who gave me the number of a hire car company based at the airport.

'Sure, I can be taking you back there early tomorrow morning. Just give me a call,' said Niall. 'Anything else you need, you have my number. I'll be seeing ye,' he said with a wave as he walked off.

'Everyone's so friendly here, Mum. Was it always like

this?' Mary-Kate asked me as we followed the porter to the lift.

'I suppose so, yes, but it was different for me living here. We were all more worried about what everyone was saying about *us*.'

'Well, they're certainly chatty,' said Jack as we walked along yet another hotel corridor.

'Here now,' said the porter, taking us into a room still flooded with soft, early evening light from the glass sliding doors, which led onto a small balcony. 'You've a grand view of the ocean.'

'Thank you,' I said as I tipped him. 'You can leave the rucksacks in here.'

'Anyone for a cup of tea?' I asked my children when he'd left.

'It's almost eight, so more beer time for me, thanks, Mum,' said Jack.

'I could kill for one too,' agreed Mary-Kate.

'Then let's treat ourselves to room service, shall we? We can sit out on the little balcony and enjoy a sundowner,' I suggested as I walked towards the phone.

'Why don't you sit down, Mum? I'll get the drinks in,' said Jack.

'What number hotel is this one, Mum?' Mary-Kate asked me as we slid the door open to the large balcony.

'I've lost count, to be honest, sweetheart,' I said as I pulled out a chair and sat down.

'You were meant to take months to do what you've actually done in the space of less than two weeks.'

'I wasn't counting on being followed, was I?'

'I still don't understand why you were running away, when I'd told you the sisters just wanted to see the ring and—'

'Could we leave it for tonight, Mary-Kate?' I sighed. 'I'd like a breather from the whole thing, if you wouldn't mind.'

'Of course, but wasn't Tiggy lovely? She was so sweet to me. She said that even if it turned out that I wasn't related to them, she'd love for me to stay in touch and to come and visit them at Atlantis whilst I was here in Europe.'

'She was lovely, yes,' I agreed. 'She even invited all of us to go on this boat trip down to Greece.'

'Well, hopefully Michelle will get in touch with me via the agency soon, and we'll be able to find out more about who I am. Chip also said that it's easy enough to do a DNA test.'

'I don't doubt that you're her daughter, sweetheart. Maybe it's just whose daughter *she* is. Or in fact, who your birth father is. He might be the one who's related to this mysterious Pa Salt.'

'Do you know what, Mum?' said Mary-Kate as Jack brought the tray of drinks out onto the balcony. 'You're right. I hadn't thought of that.'

'As I said, shall we leave all that for now? And just enjoy us all being here together in West Cork; a moment I never thought would happen,' I said.

'I'm really glad it has, Mum,' said Jack. 'Cheers!'

'Cheers,' I toasted, as I took a sip of the strong tea that tasted so much better than any other I'd tasted since I'd been on my travels. Sitting here with my children, it suddenly felt very good to be back home.

After supper in the relaxed Dunes pub downstairs, we all opted for an early night.

I climbed into bed and switched off the light, leaving the door to the balcony open so I could hear the waves crashing onto the shore.

It was a beautiful sound, and one that had been heard by

humankind since we'd begun to populate this earth of ours. And by other creatures for billions of years before that. No matter what happened to any of us in our small lives, that tide would come in and roll out, and continue until the moment when our planet and everything on it ceased to exist.

'So why *do* the things that happen to us in our small lives matter?' I murmured. 'Because we love,' I answered myself, 'because we love.'

40

Niall picked us all up at nine the next morning to drive us to the airport. Having collected the hire car, and put myself and Jack on the insurance, I took charge of the steering wheel.

'Where are we headed to, Mum?' asked Mary-Kate from the back seat.

'To my old family home,' I said, glad that I was driving so I had to concentrate on signposts rather than the final destination. Just after Bandon, I swung a left at the signpost for Timoleague and headed along what had once been a narrow lane and now was – at best – a wider lane.

'Did you live in the back of beyond here as well, Mum?' Jack asked.

'Not like we do in New Zealand, no, but on a bicycle, it certainly felt like that.'

I turned left at the Ballinascarthy crossroads, and then took a right in Clogagh village and wound my way through the country lanes completely by instinct. We ended up turning a corner near Inchybridge and almost driving into the Argideen River.

'Jesus, Mum!' Jack said as I slammed on the brakes to stop us going bonnet-first into the water – there was no protective barrier or warning sign, which actually made me smile.

'You might find it funny, Mum, but I really don't,' muttered

Mary-Kate as I reversed into a ditch on the side of a field filled with maize, which had obviously replaced the barley of my era.

'Sorry, but we're not far away now,' I reassured her.

About ten minutes later, I saw the high stone walls that surrounded Argideen House in front of me, and knew we were getting close.

'Who lives inside there, Mum? It looks pretty overgrown.'

'I've no idea, Jack. My sister Nora worked there for a while, but I'm sure the occupants are long dead. Now, let me concentrate; the farm is up here somewhere . . .'

A few minutes later, I turned into the track that led up to it. Even though I was glad the children were with me, I wished I could have taken a moment to stop the car and draw breath before my arrival was noticed. Taking the drive as slowly as I could, I saw very little had changed, only the odd concrete bungalow peppering the valley, where before there had merely been the uninhabitable stone ruins of cottages abandoned during the Great Famine.

Arriving at the farmhouse, where the washing still hung out like flags on the line, and cows were grazing in the valley that led down to the slim sliver of the Argideen River, it was almost exactly as I remembered. Apart from the modern car parked in front of the house.

'We're here,' I said, stating the obvious.

'Hey, Mum, I thought you said the house you grew up in had really low-beamed ceilings? This farmhouse looks quite modern,' said Jack, disappointment on his face.

'This is the new farmhouse that we moved to when I was six. You'll see the one we used to live in behind it.'

Looking at it now, I agreed with Jack that it was an unre-markable and small square house. Yet, moving from one side of the courtyard to the other, with all its space, light, and

modern conveniences, had been a revelation for me back then.

'Okay, why don't you two stay in the car while I go and see who's home?' Before they could answer, I was out of the car and walking round the back towards the kitchen door, because I couldn't ever imagine walking in through the front entrance. Only the priest or a doctor or a British person had ever done that.

The kitchen door was made of PVC now, not wood, and I saw that all the windows had been replaced in a similar fashion too.

'Here goes.' I held my breath and forced my fist out to knock on it, because I had no idea who would answer.

There was no reply, so I knocked louder. Putting my ear to the door, I heard a noise coming from within. Testing the stainless-steel door handle, I found it was unlocked. Of course it was, I told myself; on a farm, there was always someone in. Pushing the door open, I stepped into the kitchen and looked around me. The only thing that was the same was its shape and the old press holding tableware that still stood against the wall. The rest of the room had been filled with modern pine kitchen units, the old stone floor now tiled in an orangey colour. The range had gone, and instead there was an oven with an induction hob over it. The long table in the centre was also made of pine.

I walked to the door that opened onto the narrow hall which led upstairs, and realised the noise was of somebody hoovering above me.

The door in front of me led to the New Room; the over-riding memory I had of it was of Daddy in his chair, with a glass in one hand and a bottle of whiskey in the other.

The open fire had gone, and a wood-burning stove stood in its place. There was still the long leather sofa and a box of children's toys was stowed in one corner.

Walking back into the corridor, I heard the hoovering noise above had stopped. 'Hello?' I called.

'Hello there, can I help you?'

An unfamiliar woman stood at the top of the stairs, as I stood at the bottom.

'Er, yes, my name's Mary, and I used to live here with my parents, Maggie and John. And my brothers and sisters, of course,' I added, trying to work out whether the woman could be one of my sisters grown older.

'Mary . . .' the woman said as she came down the stairs towards me. 'Now, who would you be?'

'I was the youngest of the sisters – Ellen, Nora and Katie. John, Bill and Pat were my brothers.'

Having reached the bottom, the woman stared at me. Eventually, realisation appeared on her face.

'Jaysus! You mean, *the* Mary, who everyone called Merry?'

'Yes.'

'The famous missing sister of the O'Reilly clan! Well now, what a gas! If I make one phone call, we'll have them that are here out within the hour. Come into the kitchen and we'll have something to drink, will we?'

'I . . . thank you,' I said as she led me back into the kitchen. 'Um, sorry to ask, but who are you?'

The woman laughed suddenly. 'Well, o'course, considering you've been missing for all these years, you wouldn't be knowing, would you? I'm Sinéad, John's – your eldest brother's – wife.'

Now she was close up, I glanced at her again. 'Did we ever meet?'

'I doubt it. I was in John's year at Clogagh School. We started courting a year or so after you disappeared. He dragged me down the aisle a few months later. Now so, what can I offer you? I'd say we should be opening a bottle of

something that sparkles, but I don't have any in stock just now,' she smiled and I thought what a lovely warm woman she seemed.

'Um, tell me if it's too inconvenient and you'd rather not, but I've got my two children with me,' I said. 'They're waiting in the car outside whilst I found out whether the house was still owned by our family.'

'O'course, Mary, or are you still called Merry?'

'I am, yes.'

'Sure, I'd love to meet them!' she said, so I went outside and beckoned Jack and Mary-Kate in.

After the introductions, we all sat down with a cup of coffee.

'I'll be telling you, John'll fall to the ground in shock when he sees you, Merry. You haven't changed at all from the old photos I've seen of you, whereas I' – Sinéad indicated her curves – 'have filled out.'

'Do you have any children yourself?' I asked.

'We have three, so, two of them married already, and just the young fellow still at home with us during his hols from uni. He wants to be an accountant,' she added proudly. 'Either of you two wed yet? Givin' your mammy some grandchildren to play with?'

Both of mine shook their heads.

'We've four from our bunch now,' Sinéad continued. ''Tis good to have small ones around the place again. They'll often come and stay over too. Will you be joining us for lunch? Both you and John will have a lot to be talking about.'

'Really, Sinéad, don't go to any trouble for us.'

'As if it would be, Merry. 'Tis not every day a missing member of the family appears out o' the blue. 'Tis like the parable of the prodigal son, so you're getting fed the fatted calf. And it's beef and Guinness casserole for lunch!'

'Can I ask you how everyone is, Sinéad? All my sisters? Bill? Pat?'

'The sisters are grand, so; all of them married, and Pat too, though Nora's on her second husband and lives in Canada these days. She always was a flighty one, wasn't she? Ellen, Katie, Bill and Pat – who runs a farm of his own these days – are all still local and some have grandchildren of their own too. Bill's in Cork City, working for the council, no less. There's a rumour he'll be running for election for Fianna Fáil soon.'

I struggled to picture my little brother being all grown-up, with a responsible job.

'And Katie? Where is she?'

'Katie?' Mary-Kate queried.

'My sister closest in age – she was two years older than me,' I explained. 'And yes, I named you after her,' I smiled.

"'Tis normal to name our kids after their families here, especially their parents,' Sinéad explained to my daughter. 'It gets complicated at family parties, mind, when everyone's shouting for a John and four of them appear,' she chuckled. 'Ah, here's your man coming up the drive. Himself will be knocked over by a feather when he walks in, just you wait.'

As I heard the door to a truck slam and footsteps walk towards the back door, I didn't know what to do with myself. In the end, I stood up as John opened the back door. He had filled out since the last time I'd seen him, but in a brawny way, and his curly hair was peppered with grey. I looked into his green eyes, inherited from our mother, and gave him a smile.

'Hello there, John,' I said, feeling suddenly shy.

'Guess who it is?' chirped Sinéad.

He stared at me, and I finally saw recognition dawn on his face.

John took a step forwards. 'Jesus, Mary and Joseph! Merry, is it you?'

'You know it is,' I said, my eyes filling with tears.

'You come here, girl, and take the first hug I've been able to give you in over thirty-five years.'

'Thirty-seven,' I corrected him as we walked towards each other and he took me in his big strong arms. He smelt comfortingly of cow and it made me want to cry.

The others in the kitchen remained silent until John unclasped me. 'I've missed the sight of you, Merry.'

'Me too,' I gulped.

'And are these your young ones? They're the spit of you!' he said, turning his attention to Jack and Mary-Kate. 'Where've you been all these years?'

'We've been living in New Zealand.'

'Well now, I'd say 'twas the moment to open something to welcome you back home. What'll you be drinking? Beer? Wine?'

'I'll have a beer, please, sir,' said Jack.

'And me,' volunteered Mary-Kate. I saw that both my children looked dazed at what was going on in front of them.

'White wine would be perfect,' I said.

'Right then, Merry, I'll be having one too,' said Sinéad. 'Beer, John?'

John nodded as he sat down, hardly able to take his eyes off me. Sinéad brought the beers and two glasses of wine to the table.

'To my missing sister, safely returned. *Sláinte!*' said John.

'*Sláinte!*' we toasted, as Mary-Kate frowned.

'It's the word for "cheers" here,' I told her as we all took a sip.

'Don't tell me your mammy hasn't been educating you in the Irish ways,' John said to my daughter.

'She never said much about her childhood until recently,' Jack said. 'All we knew was that she went to university in Dublin.'

John paused for a moment, then looked at me before he answered. 'Sometimes 'tis better not to dwell on the past too much, isn't it?'

'Yes,' I said gratefully.

'So now, tell me about your life in New Zealand. Plenty of sheep there, I've heard?' he said. 'Not as good for the milk as cows, mind,' he added with a wink at Jack. 'Have you a husband? Where is he?'

I hardly ate a mouthful of the delicious beef stew as John and Sinéad fired questions at all three of us. My kids did me proud, sometimes answering for me when they sensed I was overwhelmed.

After a homemade chocolate cake with cream was offered for dessert, and Sinéad was chatting to Mary-Kate and Jack, I leant over to John.

'How's Katie? Do you see much of her?'

'Ah, she's busy working up at the Clonakilty old folks' place. She cares for the old people around these parts that have dementia or can't cope in their own homes.'

'She has a husband?'

'She does, so. Connor was in construction and when the Celtic Tiger began to roar here in Ireland and the boom came, he made a good deal of money, that's for sure. He's retired now, sold up his firm. And lucky for him he did, what with the recession starting here. I'd be saying some of the lads that went on to work for the new boss will find themselves out of a job soon enough,' John sighed.

'The economy's not good here?'

'No. There's been a big downturn in building round these parts during the last few months. You know, I'd look at Connor sometimes, with the big smart house he built for himself and Katie, and the summer holidays they took to Tenerife, and I'd wonder what I was doing up at five every

morning to sort the cows. The good news about my animals and their meat and milk is that the world continues to need them, whatever's happening in those stock market places.'

'Have you expanded the farm since I was last here?'

'We have indeed. Do you remember our neighbours, the O'Hanlons, who owned the few acres next door to us?'

'I do, of course.'

'Well, he was old and wanted to sell up, so I bought the land.'

'What about Daddy? Sinéad didn't say when I asked, so . . .'

'Ah now, I'm sure it won't be a surprise to you to learn that the drink got him eventually. He died in eighty-five. He's buried with Mammy and the rest of our family in Timoleague graveyard. I'm sorry to be the one to have to tell you.'

'Don't be, John. It was me who left, and it was you that had to pick up the pieces here. You were virtually running the farm by the time you were sixteen.'

'I can't lie and tell you it wasn't hard, but it hasn't been a bad life, Merry. Me and Sinéad are happy, so. We've all we want and need, and have our family around us.'

'I'm desperate to see Katie, and, of course, the rest of the family. Could you give me Katie's number so I can call her?'

'I can, and once she's over the shock, sure, she'll be delighted to see you. How long are you thinking of staying?' he asked.

'A few days, or maybe longer . . . I haven't got any definite plans.'

'I'll get Katie's number for you.' John stood up and went to the telephone that sat on a chest of drawers. He pulled out a black leather-bound book from one of the drawers, which I recognised immediately.

'You still have the same address book that Mammy and Daddy used?!'

'We do, so, yes. We hardly needed it in those days; we knew where everyone lived, but now 'tis useful for the mobile phone numbers. There's Katie's.'

'Thank you.'

'I'll be putting your number in the book now, just in case you're thinking of disappearing for another thirty-seven years.' He winked at me.

I recited my number and he wrote it down. Then he gave me the landline here so I could do the same.

'I can't be doing with mobiles even though I have one,' said John. 'It means that if I'm out in the meadow on a sunny day having a snooze, Herself can call me,' he sighed. 'Now then' – John raised his voice so everyone could hear – 'I've got to be off back to my tractor, though I'll be seeing you again soon, I hope.'

'I was just saying to the kids that we should have a family get-together, so they can meet all their aunties, uncles and cousins,' said Sinéad.

'Apparently we have about twenty in all, Mum! But some of them are in Canada,' said Mary-Kate.

'Don't you worry, there's enough of them to be getting on with right here,' Sinéad smiled. 'How about this Sunday coming?'

'Can we, Mum?' asked Mary-Kate.

'I'm sure we can, and it's very kind of you to offer, Sinéad. Right, kids, let's be off,' I said. 'Thank you for lunch and being so hospitable.'

'Ah, 'twas nothing. I just can't wait to tell all my sisters-in-law that I met you first!' she giggled.

All three of us had a big hug from her, then climbed into the car and followed John's tractor down to the lane. I felt so proud of my children, especially Mary-Kate, who ironically, although she didn't know it yet, shared the same circumstances

as me: we both knew that those we'd just visited were not our blood family. Yet her obvious excitement at having 'cousins' meant she hadn't even thought about it.

Maybe it was simply because she'd spent twenty-two years being loved by her parents, as I had been loved by mine.

Would I tell John and the rest of my siblings that I had been 'dropped in' as a replacement for a dead baby?

No, I thought, that didn't matter. Love *did*.

'Where to now, Mum?' asked Mary-Kate.

'Back to the hotel, I think.'

'Well, as it's such great weather, I wouldn't mind seeing whether that surf school we spotted on the beach hires out their equipment,' said Jack. 'It's ages since I last surfed. Join me?' he asked Mary-Kate.

'If Mum doesn't need us, then yeah, I'd love to.'

'I'll be fine, you two go and enjoy yourselves. The sea's always freezing, mind you,' I warned them with a smile.

Back at the hotel, the kids walked off to enquire about hiring surfboards, and I went back to my room and immediately dialled Katie's number. There was a voicemail telling me to leave a message, but I had absolutely no idea what to say. I dialled the number for Cross Farm and Sinéad answered.

'Hi there, it's Merry here. Katie's not answering her mobile, so maybe I'll just turn up at her door. Where exactly does she live?'

'In Timoleague. Do you remember where the GAA pitch is?'

'I do.'

'Well, 'tis a grand big house on the other side of the lane, just beyond the pitch. You'll see it because it's painted bright orange. Wouldn't be the colour I'd choose, mind, but at least you can't miss it,' chuckled Sinéad.

Leaving a message at reception for Jack and Mary-Kate, I got back into my car and headed for Timoleague. Like Clonakilty,

the village had expanded upwards and sideways, but the main street remained more or less as I remembered it. As I drove, I looked across the magnificent Courtmacsherry Bay. Passing the GAA pitch, where I could see boys practising Gaelic football, bringing back vivid memories of watching my brothers playing in the field with Daddy, I saw the big house standing up on a slope just beyond it and agreed with Sinéad that the bright tangerine colour was not one I would have picked either. 'Look at me,' the house was saying. It was obvious Katie had done very well for herself.

I headed up the drive, admiring the pristine gardens and the carefully tended flower beds. There was a Range Rover parked outside which was so shiny, the sun glinted off it and half blinded me. Bringing the car to a halt, I turned off the engine and gathered my nerve to get out and knock on the front door.

It was opened by a slim, greying but still handsome man dressed in a pink shirt and chinos.

'Hello there, can I help you?' he asked.

'I'm looking for Katie.'

'Aren't we all,' the man shrugged with a grim smile. 'She's at work as usual. And who might you be?'

'My name is Mary McDougal, and I'm Katie's sister.'

He looked at me for a while, then nodded. 'You'll be the one that disappeared then?'

'I would, yes.'

'Well, she's due back around four, in about twenty minutes. I'm Connor, by the way, Katie's husband. Do you want to come in and have a cuppa? I was just making one for myself.'

'Thank you,' I said as he ushered me inside and into the kitchen. 'Sit down, take the weight off your feet.'

I did so, looking round at what was obviously a state-of-the-art kitchen, with no expense spared.

'I can't be saying she'll be home on time,' he said as he put

a cup of tea in front of me and sat down. 'As you can see, she doesn't need to work, but no matter what I tell her, her old people up at the home come first. Dedicated, she is. So, can I be asking you where you disappeared to for all these years?'

'I moved to New Zealand.'

'Now that's a place I'd love to visit, if I could ever get my wife to take a holiday. Whereabouts are you? The North or South Island?'

I told him and we chatted pleasantly about the country and the vineyard, until I heard the sound of a car coming up the drive.

'Must be your lucky day. My wife is home on time for once.' Connor stood up. 'Why don't you go and sit in the lounge across, and I'll tell her you're here, prepare her, so. 'Twill be a shock for her; I wasn't around when you left, but I know how close the two of you were.'

'Of course.' I went into the room he'd indicated, which looked more like a showpiece in an advertisement than a home. Everything, from the cream leather sofas to the faux mahogany side tables and grand marble fireplace, was immaculate. I heard low voices beyond the door, and finally my sister came into the sitting room. She looked exactly the same as I remembered her: slim, elegant and the spit of our mother. Her red hair was piled up on her head and as she came towards me, I saw her lovely pale skin was clear of wrinkles, as if she had been held in aspic since I last saw her.

'Merry.' She studied my face carefully as I stood up. 'It really *is* you, isn't it?'

'It is, Katie, yes.'

'Jaysus, I don't know what to say.' Her voice trembled. 'I feel like I'm in one of those reality TV shows where two long-lost sisters meet again.' She started to cry. 'Merry, come here and give me a hug.'

We hugged for a long time, until she finally pulled away and indicated the nearest sofa.

'My legs are shaking. Let's sit down,' she said.

We did so, and she reached towards the glass coffee table to pull a wad of tissues out of a box.

'I'd always wondered what I'd say if you ever turned up; I hated you for going and not even leaving me a note to say why or where. I thought I was your best friend? We *were* best friends, weren't we?'

Katie wiped away her tears harshly.

'I'm so sorry, Katie,' I said, gulping back my own. 'I'd have told you if I could have, but . . . I just couldn't tell anyone.'

'Not true,' she said, her voice rising. 'You left a note for that Ambrose of yours, didn't you? I know because I got hold of his telephone number and called him. The note said you had to go away, but he wasn't to worry about you. And then you disappeared for thirty-seven years. Why, Merry? Please tell me why.'

'I had no choice, Katie, believe me. I never meant to hurt you or the rest of our family. I was trying to protect you.'

'I knew you were keeping secrets from me, Merry, but I'd have never told. Ah, Jaysus, I can't stop crying.'

'I'm so, so sorry, Katie.' I put my arms around her and hugged her again as she wept.

'I'd have done anything to help you, you know I would. Come with you if that was what you needed. We shared everything, didn't we?'

'We did, yes.'

'I hate that Ambrose; 'twas him that stole you away from us all in the first place. Getting Father O'Brien and Daddy to agree to send you to that fancy boarding school in Dublin, then you staying with Ambrose all the time when you were up there. It was like *he* was wanting to be your daddy, even though he wasn't. He wasn't, Merry.'

'No, he wasn't, but the reason I left has nothing to do with him, I swear.'

'Have you seen him since you came back?' she eyed me.

'I have, yes.'

'He must be very old these days.'

'He is, but he still has his wits about him.'

'And what did *he* say when you turned up out of the blue with no warning?'

'He was shocked, but happy to see me. Katie, please don't cry anymore. I'm here and I promise, I'll tell you why I had to leave, and I just hope you'll understand.'

'I've had so long to think about it, and I'd reckon I have an idea. I think—'

'Would it be all right if we talked about it another time, Katie? I've my children here with me and I haven't told them anything about it either.'

'What about your husband, assuming you have one? Does he know?'

'My husband died a few months ago, he didn't know. Nobody did. When I left, I forgot the past. I made a whole new life and got myself a new identity.'

'Then I'm sorry for your loss, Merry. But . . . well, I've some things to tell you about *our* family, some things we didn't know as children, but that make sense now, looking back. Especially for you.'

'Then you must tell me, Katie.'

''Tis not a pretty story, Merry, but it explains a lot.'

I was just about to mention I'd read Nuala's diary, when there was a brief knock on the door and Connor appeared.

'Sorry to interrupt, but will we be having something for our tea tonight or not, Katie? There's nothing in the fridge that I can see.'

'No, Connor, I need to go shopping. I just came back here

to take a shower and change out of my uniform.' Katie stood up. 'What about I come to see you tomorrow?' she said to me. ''Tis my day off. Where are you staying?'

'The Inchydoney Lodge Hotel.'

'Oh, 'tis a lovely place that, with a beautiful view.'

'It is,' I said, sensing the tension that had appeared in the room with the arrival of Connor. 'Well, I must be off anyway.'

'Would eleven o'clock suit?' she said.

'It would. I'll be down in the lobby to meet you. Bye, Katie. Bye, Connor.'

As I drove back to the hotel, I decided that, despite the car, the perfect home and the handsome, rich husband, my sister was not a happy woman.

That evening, Jack, Mary-Kate and I enjoyed a relaxed supper at a pub in Clonakilty. Afterwards, we went to listen to some Irish music at An Teach Beag, once a tiny cottage that had now been turned into a pub. The traditional band played the old ballads, bringing back memories of my father playing his fiddle. Then we headed back to the hotel.

'Looks like the weather is set fair for some good surfing tomorrow, Mum,' said Jack, 'so if it's okay with you, MK and I will get our togs on after brekkie.'

'I'm seeing one of my sisters anyway, so that's perfect.'

'I really love it here, Mum,' Mary-Kate said as we kissed goodnight. 'Everyone is so friendly. It's like NZ, with a different accent!'

I was happy that my children liked it here, I thought the next morning, as I donned a pair of jeans and a blouse for Katie's imminent arrival.

At eleven o'clock prompt, she arrived in the lobby. Yesterday

she'd been in her navy-blue nurse's uniform, but today she was immaculately dressed in tailored trousers and a silk blouse.

'Katie,' I said, standing up to hug her, 'thank you so much for coming.'

'As if I wouldn't! I might have been shocked and upset yesterday – who wouldn't be? But I know you must have had your reasons, Merry, and 'tis so grand to see you! Where are your kids?' she asked.

'Out there, braving the waves. They're both mad for surfing, so.'

I listened to what I'd just said and had to smile because, with the West Cork accent all around me, I was slipping back into it myself.

'Is there somewhere we can talk? I mean, privately?' Katie asked me.

'Is here not private enough?'

'You need to remember that walls have ears here, and my husband, well, he's well known round these parts.'

'Are you saying you're ashamed to be seen with me?' I giggled.

'Of course I'm not, but what I want to tell you . . . well, we might not be comfortable being interrupted.'

'Okay, let's go up to my room.'

We ordered cappuccinos from room service and chatted away about how modern this part of the world had become.

'Don't I know it – until recently my husband had one of the biggest construction companies here, so he's been kept very busy in the last few years,' said Katie. 'Now there's a downturn, but he saw it coming and managed to sell the business last year. He's sitting on a fortune, whilst the new owner and all those fellows who worked for him will probably watch the whole thing go down the drain. He's always been lucky that way.'

'Or a clever businessman?'

'I suppose, yes,' she agreed with a weary smile.

'Can I ask you something, Katie?'

'Of course you can, Merry. I'd never be keeping any secrets from you, anyway.'

'Touché,' I said with a slight grimace. 'Are you happy with Connor?'

'Do you want the long or the short answer to that?' she replied with a shrug. 'I mean, there was me pulling pints at the Henry Ford pub and he waltzed in one evening and swept me off my feet. Even then his company was starting to do well, so he'd all the luxuries. He showed me plans to build a grand house on land he'd bought in Timoleague, took me driving in his flash sports car and then presented me with a big rock of an engagement ring when he asked me to marry him.' Katie shook her head. 'You'll be remembering what our childhood was like and how I'd sworn I'd not repeat it, so to have a rich man offering to marry me felt like a miracle. Of course I said yes, and we had a big wedding up at the Dunmore House Hotel, and a honeymoon in Spain. He spoilt me rotten with clothes and jewellery, said he wanted me to look the part on his arm.'

'Were you happy?'

'Back then, yes. We were trying to grow a family. It took a long time, but I managed to produce a boy and a girl – Connor Junior and Tara. It wasn't long after Tara was born that I got wind of my husband's first affair. He denied it, o'course, and I forgave him – and then it happened again and again, until I couldn't any longer,' she shrugged.

'Why haven't you divorced him?'

'Knowing Connor, he'd have found a way to wriggle out of me getting much in any settlement, so once the kids had left home, I decided to go to college and take my nursing

exams. It took me three years of driving back and forth to Cork City, but I got my qualifications, Merry,' she smiled proudly. 'So, for the past fifteen years, I've been working up at the old people's place in Clonakilty, and I love it there. I'm happy enough, Merry; I've learnt we all need to make compromises in life. What about your hubby? Was he a good one?'

'He was, yes,' I smiled. 'Very good. I mean, we had our ups and downs as any marriage does, and went through some very hard times financially when we were building up our vineyard—'

'Vineyard, is it? Remember how we used to steal Daddy's homemade porter? A couple of sips of that could pull the skin off a cat!'

'I do! It tasted disgusting.'

'But we still drank it,' Katie giggled. 'Sounds like we've both come a long way since our childhoods.'

'We have. Looking back, we lived close to the breadline, didn't we? I remember walking to school with big holes in my boots because we couldn't afford new ones.'

'We'd definitely be described as deprived kids these days, but then, 'twas half of Ireland at the time,' said Katie.

'Yes, and after all that suffering our ancestors went through to fight for their freedom, nothing much had moved on in reality, had it?'

'As a matter of fact, that's what I wanted to talk to you about.'

'Our past?'

'Yes. You'll be remembering that we never had our grandparents round to visit us, or any cousins either?' said Katie.

'I do, and I could never understand it.'

'No, but when I started working at the old people's home in the early nineties . . . let me tell you, you learn a lot about

the old stories there. Maybe their folks have stopped listening, or maybe they tell you things because you're a stranger. Anyway, I'd one old lady who was in our special care unit, as we called it, which meant those who didn't have long left on this earth. I was on a night shift and went in to check on her. Even though she was in her nineties, she'd all her faculties on her. She stared at me and said I was the spit of her daughter, then asked my name. I told her I was Katie Scanlon, but then she asked what my maiden name had been. I told her it was O'Reilly and tears appeared in her eyes. She grasped my hand and said she was my grandmother, Nuala Murphy, and her daughter had been named Maggie. She told me she'd a story she needed to get off her chest before she met her maker. It took her three nights to tell it, because she was so weak, but she was determined to do so.'

I stared at Katie in disbelief. 'Nuala was *our* grandmother?'

'Yes, the one we never saw, apart from that once at Mammy's funeral. After what she told me, I understand better why we didn't see her. Merry, what's wrong? You're a strange colour.'

'I . . . Katie, I was given her diary a very long time ago, by someone we . . . both knew.'

'Who?'

'I'd prefer not to say just now, or we'll be off down another track and—'

'Well now, I can guess who gave you that diary. Why did you never tell me?'

'Firstly, because I only read it myself a few days ago – I know that might sound odd, Katie, but I was only eleven when it was given to me and I wasn't interested in learning about the past. Then when I got older, because of who gave it to me, I never wanted to set eyes on it again.'

'But you still kept it?'

'Yes, I did. Please don't ask me why, because I honestly couldn't tell you,' I sighed.

'Sure, I won't, but since you've read it, I'm guessing you've made the family connection?'

'No, because the diary stopped in 1920. Something happened to Nuala and she said she couldn't write anymore.'

'Maybe you could show it to me sometime. I heard the whole sorry story from beginning to end. Where did you get up to in the diary, so I won't be repeating myself?'

'I . . .' I cleared my throat. 'It was just after Philip – the British soldier – had shot himself.'

'Right. Nuala was still upset by that, along with a whole lot more that came after, including the reason why she never came to visit when our mammy married our daddy.'

'Katie, just tell me,' I said in a burst of impatience.

Katie drew a folder out of her smart Louis Vuitton shopper and flicked through a large sheaf of pages. 'I wrote it all down after she told me, so I wouldn't forget it. So, you already know the part up to when Philip killed himself.'

'I do.'

'Well, the War of Independence went on for a good deal longer after that. Finn, Nuala's husband, was a volunteer, as you know, and they were dark times as both sides stepped up the violence. Now then, let's start when Hannah, Nuala's sister, married her fiancé, Ryan, soon after Philip met his end . . .'

Nuala
Clogagh, West Cork
December 1920

Irish Claddagh Ring

41

The wedding of Hannah Murphy and Ryan O'Reilly took place in Clogagh church, in a very different atmosphere than that of Nuala and Finn's. They had wanted something small that befitted the sombre mood that hung in the air.

Decked with holly and a candle set in each window, the church looked festive, but Nuala walked through the wedding in a fog of grief she couldn't seek comfort for. No one could know how devastated she was at Philip's death.

At the party afterwards, held in the church hall, Sian, one of Hannah's dressmaker friends, leant over to Nuala.

'Is Herself not interested in helping the cause now she's a married woman?'

'What do you mean?'

'Well, she used to be the first we'd all go to if a message needed sending somewhere. Now she says she hasn't the time.'

'I'd say her mind was on her wedding, Sian,' Nuala replied. 'Sure, she'll settle down once it's all over.'

'Maybe, but . . .' Sian had to put her mouth to Nuala's ear to whisper over the sound of the little *ceilidh* band. 'I'd reckon her man doesn't want her to be involved in our activities.'

Sian was pulled up to dance a few seconds later, but as Nuala sat and watched the bride and groom take their places in the centre of the group, she wondered whether love really

was blind after all. As hard as she tried, she could not see what her strong-minded, passionate sister saw in the quiet, self-proclaimed pacifist she had just wed.

The year 1921 dawned, and over the following few months the brave volunteers did all they could to thwart the British. There were whispered reports of IRA victories, that the boys were slowly winning with their clever use of guerrilla tactics and knowledge of their own land, but the reprisals for British casualties were harsh. Nuala found relief in keeping busy running messages and helping those whose homes had been turned upside down and often set alight by the British in retaliation. There was many an elderly couple who had been forced to live in their chicken coops, too frightened to come out. Nuala rounded up as many Cumann na mBan members as she could and they met one night at a safehouse in Ballinascarthy to draw up a list of temporary accommodation for the poor souls to be billeted at. There was an air of positivity and hope that the conflict would soon draw to a close, but Niamh, their brigade captain, urged caution.

''Tis not over yet, girls, and we mustn't let our guard slip too soon. We've all lost people dear to us in this battle and 'twould be good not to lose more.'

'What about those in jail?' asked Nuala. 'I hear the conditions there are terrible, and they say they're worse up in Mountjoy Prison in Dublin. Is there a plan to get our fellows out?'

'They're under lock and key day and night,' said Niamh. 'They're the Britishers' prized possessions; they know our volunteers will think twice before launching an ambush, for fear of one of their comrades being shot in reprisal.'

She was almost numb these days to hearing terrible things, but the death of Charlie Hurley, Finn's closest friend, hit her hard. He had been shot at point-blank range at Humphrey Forde's farmhouse in Ballymurphy. Finn was devastated but could spare little time for grief. A few days later he went deep undercover with the Flying Column and Nuala didn't know when she would see her husband again. She knew that Charlie's body had been carried out of the workhouse morgue in Bandon by the women of Cumann na mBan. He'd been buried in the graveyard in Clogagh in secret at night, so that all the volunteers who had loved and respected him as commandant of the Third West Cork Brigade could be present.

The thought of all those she and Finn had lost in the fight to secure Ireland's freedom fuelled her determination to help as much as she could, which was more than she could say for Hannah. Even though she did her best to accept that Hannah had no choice but to follow her husband's lead, her sister's now open refusal to have anything to do with the cause she'd once been so passionate about cut her soul in two. The fact Hannah had told her Ryan condemned the volunteers' bravery, in the name of pacifism, had caused a deep rift between them. Often, when she was in Timoleague and saw her sister emerging from the dressmaker's shop, Nuala quickly turned and walked the other way.

The farming seasons carried on despite the war, and still no sight of Finn, apart from the odd message passed by Christy to say he was alive and sending her his love. Nuala spent time up at Cross Farm, and threw herself into any job she was given. As spring progressed, golden gorse filled the valley, the barn was full of newborn calves, and the days lengthened. At least, in the fear and grief that cast a shadow over everything, Nuala had a special secret that lit a spark of joy within her.

'Soon enough, you'll be showing yourself and there'll be

nothing can hide it,' she said as she looked down at her tummy. By her estimation, she was about two months gone, and due sometime in late December. Now over the worst of any sickness, she felt renewed vigour to win the war for her and Finn's child. She told nobody, wanting her husband to be the first to know, but was sure her mammy had guessed her secret.

As spring turned to summer and with fewer British troops visible on the roads – wary of ambushes from the volunteers – Nuala also did the rounds of those wounded in action or injured during a raid on their homeplace.

All of the fellows and their families poured gratitude on her head, offering her whatever they had to eat as a thank you. Most of her patients were barely more than boys, who'd had their bodies and their lives blown apart by the cause. They and their families humbled and moved her.

I've learnt more about nursing in the past year than I could ever have learnt from books, she thought as she cycled home one evening.

What with all she was doing, she fell asleep easily at night as the summer wore on. The talk was that the British had retired to their barracks, if they'd not already been burnt down by the volunteers. She'd heard from Christy that Michael Collins himself had sent a personal message of congratulations to the West Cork Flying Column. Next time she saw Hannah in town, Nuala invited her to sit and eat lunch with her. She wanted to tell her sister about the message to the lads, and have Ryan know too.

'Imagine that!' Hannah said to her dreamily as they sat on their favourite bench overlooking Courtmacsherry Bay. 'A message from the Big Fellow himself!'

'He's behind the boys and all they're doing, Hannah,' she said pointedly. 'I hope you'll tell Ryan that.'

Hannah had ignored her sister's comment, instead going on to confide that she was expecting. Nuala had shared her news too, but sworn her to secrecy until she was able to tell Finn. The exchange had engendered a few moments of their old closeness, as the sisters had imagined their babies playing together in the future.

Then Nuala had asked whether she and Ryan were coming up to Cross Farm for lunch on Sunday.

'We've not seen the sight of the two of you for weeks,' she'd added.

'Sorry, we can't. Ryan's taking me on a vigil over by his homeplace near Kilbrittain. We're praying for peace.'

'And your prayers will be needed, if this war is ever to end,' Nuala had muttered.

She'd just made a brack for poor Mrs Grady next door, who was now confined to bed as her arthritis was so bad. It was an unusually sweltering June day, and she stared at the dry, unkempt patch of earth at the back of the cottage, which she'd had no time to do anything with since she'd moved in. She was just wondering if she could tidy it up and plant some pretty flowers when there was a sudden tap on her shoulder.

'Jaysus, Christy! You made me jump,' she gasped as she turned round.

'Sorry, but I thought you might like to hear the news: last night the volunteers burnt down Castle Bernard up in Bandon and took Lord Bandon hostage.'

'Holy Mother of God! They did *what*?! Were any of them hurt?'

'Not that I've heard, no. Are you feeling all right, Nuala? You're swaying where you stand.'

'Let's go inside, where you can tell me more,' she whispered nervously.

Once Christy had furnished her with a glass of water, Nuala looked at her cousin, her expression a mixture of horror and amazement.

'I can't believe they did that!' she said. 'Castle Bernard is centuries old, and Lord Bandon is surely the most powerful man around these parts. The volunteers have him as a hostage, you said?'

'Yes. And I've been sent here because he's being kept not far from where we sit, and you're trusted by the volunteers. Let's just say that currently he's a neighbour of poor Charlie Hurley, lying in Clogagh graveyard.'

Nuala opened her mouth to speak, but Christy hushed her.

'Lord Bandon needs feeding; we'll not have him reporting back that we treated him badly, like so many of ours have been when they've been "guests" of the enemy. Can you be making some food for him?'

'Me? Make food for Lord Bandon? The man is used to the finest salmon, fresh from the Innishannon River, and freshly slaughtered meat from his herd of prize cattle. I can hardly make him turnip soup now, can I?'

'I'd say that some well-cooked Irish food is exactly what the man needs. Just be remembering that he's human and shits and pisses like the rest of us, despite his grand life. I'll be taking that brack cake away up, if that's all right with you.'

Christy scooped it off the cooling tray.

'Get your filthy hands off that!' Nuala grabbed it from him, then found a square of muslin to wrap it in. 'Will I be adding a pat of butter to go with it?'

'Whatever you think is right. 'Twill do for his tea at least. I'll be back tomorrow for his lunch. Bye now.'

Christy left and Nuala watched him walk towards the schoolhouse, then turn right by the church.

Nuala reckoned she knew exactly where they were hiding Lord Bandon. The question was, was her husband with him?

That afternoon, using her precious supply of flour, Nuala made a potato and ham pie. She was nervous about the result because she was unaccustomed to making pastry, but the top came out as golden as you'd like. She'd just set the pie down on the kitchen table to cool when there was a knock on the door.

'I'm here, Christy. Just let yourself in, will you?' she shouted as she concentrated on trimming the extra crust off the pie.

'Hello, Nuala.'

She turned round, the knife still in her hand.

'Nuala, please, I come here in peace, I promise. And in secret.'

The woman removed the hood of her long black cape from her head. 'Lady Fitzgerald?' Nuala whispered in utter shock.

'Please, don't be frightened, I'm not here on business of my own, I'm here to pass on a plea for mercy from a very good friend of mine.'

Lady Fitzgerald set a wicker basket down on the table as Nuala, still holding the knife, went to the front window to check there were no military using Lady Fitzgerald as a decoy, waiting to break down the front door and arrest and torture her until she told them what she knew about Lord Bandon.

'I have come alone, Nuala, I swear. I even walked here all the way from Argideen House, so that none of my family or servants would know of my movements. May I sit down?'

Nuala gave a slight nod and indicated the one comfortable chair they owned.

'I know you have me down as the enemy, and have learnt to trust no one, but please, I beg you, you are the one person who understands what I've been through.' Lady Fitzgerald's eyes filled with tears, and Nuala knew she was thinking of Philip. 'And I'm here to talk to you today because of the bond that we forged, woman to woman. We are both risking a lot by my being here, I know, but in my cape, with my hair unpinned' – Lady Fitzgerald gave a sad smile – 'I'd doubt even my husband would recognise me.'

Nuala thought Lady Fitzgerald looked so very pretty, with her long blonde hair falling in waves on either side of her face. Her lack of make-up or jewellery showed off her natural beauty, making her look younger and more vulnerable.

'I am begging you to trust me,' Lady Fitzgerald continued. 'And you should know that I have tried to protect you and your family. Even though you and your husband are suspected, your cottage has never been raided, has it?'

'No. Well, if that's to do with you, then thank you.'

Nuala stopped short of saying 'your ladyship', and showing the appropriate courtesy to an English gentlewoman. Even if Lady Fitzgerald had been kind to her, the atrocities committed in her and her husband's and every other British person's name made the words stick in her throat.

'What can I be doing for you?' she asked.

Lady Fitzgerald eyed the pie. Then her eyes moved back to Nuala.

'A very good friend of mine came to visit me this morning. She told me that her husband had been taken hostage by the Irish, and was being kept by them in retaliation for the executions of IRA prisoners in both Cork and Dublin jails. She said that an ultimatum has been issued by the IRA, saying

that if there are any further shootings of their volunteers, they will kill her husband.' There was a slight pause before Lady Fitzgerald said, 'I think we both know who I'm talking about.'

Nuala sat in silence, her lips pinned together.

'That's a very fine pie, Nuala. Are you expecting company, or is it for . . . another?'

''Tis for my neighbour, who is bedridden next door.'

'Well, she is a very lucky woman, and I'm sure she will enjoy the pie. Nuala, I come to you on behalf of a wife who is sickly and, like yourself, desperate for her husband's safe return. If there is anyone you know who might be holding Lord Bandon, could you please send her plea for clemency?'

Again, Nuala sat poker-faced, saying nothing.

Lady Fitzgerald indicated the basket. 'Inside are foodstuffs from my own pantry, which will feed the hostage in the manner to which he is accustomed. There is also a note from his wife.'

Lady Fitzgerald searched her face for a reaction. Nuala was now struggling to keep her expression plain.

'Perhaps there is someone you know who could get the basket to him. There is nothing within it that could be seen as incendiary; it merely contains love, support and comfort from his wife. May I leave it with you?'

This time, Nuala gave a slight nod.

'Thank you. I must also tell you that my husband and I are leaving Argideen House. We are packing our trunks and closing the house as we speak, then returning to England. After what happened to my friend's husband two nights ago, and the burning of the Travers' house in Timoleague, it is clearly unsafe for us to stay any longer.'

Lady Fitzgerald stood up and began to walk towards the front door. Then she turned back.

'Goodbye, Nuala. May your side prevail and your husband be safely returned to you. This is your land after all.'

With a sad smile, Lady Fitzgerald left the cottage.

After her departure, Nuala finally found the strength to move from where she sat and turned to the basket. Her fingers inched so tentatively towards the cloth that covered it, it could have contained a Mills bomb.

'And it might still, so,' she muttered.

Inside were tins of things from a shop called Fortnum and Mason's. Biscuits, Earl Grey tea leaves and a tin of salmon. There were also chocolates and a box of tiny speckled eggs that the writing on top said were apparently laid by a quail. Right at the bottom of the basket was an envelope addressed to *James Francis*. Nuala turned it over and was just about to open it when she saw Christy coming across from the pub towards her cottage. Putting everything back, she covered the basket with the linen cloth, then ran to dump it in the outhouse.

'That pie is looking fit for a king, Nuala,' Christy said as she stepped back into the kitchen. ''Twill keep his lordship going for a couple of days, so.'

'I'm sure he's used to better than spuds and ham, but 'tis all I have.'

'Right then, I'll be off.' Christy picked up the pie.

'Is he a still a neighbour of Charlie Hurley?'

'The fellows are moving him around.'

'Have you seen him?' she pressed.

'No.'

'Do you know who's guarding him?'

'The lads are taking it in turns.'

'Is Finn one of them?' she asked.

Christy stared at her, and even though he didn't answer yes or no, she knew her husband was involved.

'If you see him, say his wife loves him and is waiting for him at home.'

'I will so, Nuala. Now you take care, and if any British patrols come a-calling, act innocent.'

'Would I be doing anything else? I know nothing,' she shrugged.

'I'll be back at the pub in half an hour, so you know where I am if you've any trouble. Bye now.'

'Bye, Christy.'

He gave her a wink and she watched him limp back across to the pub, thinking how glad she felt that he was only a stone's throw away. She didn't know what she would have done without him.

She poured herself a glass of water and went to sit in a shady patch in the back garden. It was plain that, despite Lady Fitzgerald's plea to deliver the basket, she could not risk passing it on.

'Forgive me, Philip, but I can't be seen to have anything to do with your mammy,' she whispered, raising her eyes to the sky.

Making a decision, she stood up and went to the outhouse to collect the basket.

An hour later, she had decanted the contents of all the tins and boxes into either bowls or brown-paper packages. Collecting the discarded wrappers, she knelt by the fireplace and burnt each one of them. Lastly, she put the letter on the flames and watched it burn. Even though she could have opened it, she hadn't. What was in there was for 'James Francis's' eyes only, and she respected that.

When she had burnt all the evidence, Nuala stood up and cut herself two healthy slices of bread, and had a delicious salmon sandwich for her tea.

The following day, she gave the same to Christy for Lord Bandon's lunch.

A week had gone past and Christy was still coming to collect food, and every day, Nuala would use a little of the foodstuffs Lady Fitzgerald had sent to salve her conscience.

'How long will they be holding him?' she asked as she and Christy drank a mug of tea together.

'As long as is needed. Sean Hales, who was in charge of the burning of Castle Bernard, has made sure that General Strickland up in Cork knows we have him. He was told that unless he stopped the executions of our fellows in prison, Lord Bandon would be shot. Not a single execution has taken place in Dublin or Cork since,' Christy grinned. 'We finally have the British by their balls.'

'So you won't be killing him anytime soon?'

'Not unless the British execute any more of our own, but I'm guessing they won't. Sean says Lord Bandon has friends and relations in the British government. They'll not see one of their own murdered by the Irish. All of us are praying they'll offer a truce.'

'As long as they don't find him first, Christy.'

'Ah now, they'll not be doing that, however hard they look,' he chuckled. 'He's never in the same billet twice, and we've scouts and guards on him night and day. So now,' Christy said, standing up, 'I'll be seeing ye, Nuala.'

Christy left with the basket Lady Fitzgerald had brought, the linen cloth covering the food. She was glad to have it out of the house.

'Can you imagine?' she said to her unborn baby in wonder. 'Peace might be coming.'

It was ten more days before Christy burst into the cottage and enveloped her in an embrace.

'It's happened, Nuala!' he said as he finally let her go. 'We've a truce agreed with the British! It's over, 'tis really over. Now what do you think of that?'

'But . . . just like that? What will happen to Lord Bandon?'

'It's been agreed by our side that he'll be returned safely to his home tomorrow.'

'He has no home now.'

'No, the castle is burnt to the ground, so maybe he'll feel the pain thousands of us Irish have felt as they burnt our homeplaces and left them in ruins.' Christy looked at her. 'You're not feeling sorry for the man, are you?'

'Of course I'm not . . . I just can't believe it, so.'

'Come outside and see what's happening.' Christy offered her his hand, and the two of them walked out of the front door. Nuala saw the residents of the village opening their front doors timidly and standing in the street, dazed from the news that had obviously spread like wildfire.

There was a lot of hugging and kissing, and nervous glances to either side in case the whole thing was another British joke on them, and they were going to be shot by the Black and Tans or the Essex Regiment, rumbling into the village on their death trucks.

'Is it true, Nuala?' asked one of her neighbours.

''Tis true enough, Mrs McKintall. It's all over.'

John Walsh at the pub came out to announce free beer for all and the little village gathered together outside and in, toasting the victory with glasses of porter.

''Tis a victory, isn't it?' she asked a filthy, pale Fergus, who had appeared out of nowhere to join in the celebrations.

'It is indeed. Sean Hales said the truce will hold for six months, and in that time men like Michael Collins and Éamon

de Valera up in Dublin will be negotiating with the British on how things will work.'

'I just can't take it in! Will we have a republic? I mean, are they really giving us our own country back?'

'They are, Nuala. Ireland is free! It's free.'

Later that day, Fergus drove her and Christy on the pony and cart into Timoleague to collect Hannah, so that the whole family could be reunited at Cross Farm to celebrate the victory together. Even Ryan had agreed to come, and there was much whiskey drunk and laughter and tears and toasts for all those who had contributed so much to the fight, but were no longer here to celebrate with them.

Even though Nuala had joined in with the celebrations, she felt distracted.

'Do you mind if I drive the pony and cart back home now, Christy?' she asked her cousin, who'd had a good few too many whiskeys.

'O'course. I'm in no fit state to drive the cattle into the barn, let alone a pony and cart,' he chuckled. 'But I'll come back down to Clogagh with you. Sure, John will need some help clearing up in the pub tomorrow morning.'

Nuala left the rest of her family to their joy, and was glad to see Ryan chatting away happily to her father about how Mick Collins would sort everything out for Ireland peacefully.

On their journey down to Clogagh, there was a strange hush on the roads, and they did not meet a single car or truck.

Nuala released the horse from the cart and took the animal into the field next to the pub. Christy was still punching the air, and swaying as he sang an old Irish ballad.

'Time for your bed, Christy, but I'll be seeing you tomorrow,' she smiled.

'Goodnight, Nuala, and I'm sure your man will be back with you soon,' he said, as he leant heavily on his stick, then

staggered through the pub door, the place still full with customers.

'I can only pray he will be,' she murmured as she let herself into the cottage.

For the next twenty-four hours, while it seemed like the whole of Ireland was letting out its breath, Nuala was still holding hers. She'd hardly slept a wink, listening for the sound of the back door opening. But it hadn't come.

By the evening, she was beside herself with worry as she watched thin, dishevelled volunteers appearing back in the village and embracing their loved ones.

'Where are you, Finn?' she whispered. 'Please come home to me soon, or I'll be losing my mind.'

By bedtime, Nuala was too exhausted to change, and fell asleep in her clothes on the bed. She didn't hear the back door open, or the footsteps up the stairs.

Only when his voice whispered in her ear, then took her into his arms and held her close, did she know her prayers had been answered.

'You're home, Finn. God love you, you're home.'

'I am that, darlin', and I swear I'll never leave your side again.'

42

Over the following few months, the atmosphere in Ireland was jubilant. The British troops moved out, and life resumed a semblance of normality. As Nuala's pregnancy progressed, Finn went back to teaching his children at Clogagh School. Summer turned into a wet and windy autumn, which couldn't dampen Nuala's spirits.

In November, during Sunday lunch at Cross Farm, all talk was of the truce negotiations currently happening in London between Michael Collins and the British Prime Minister David Lloyd George, supported by his team of seasoned politicians. Collins had been sent as Ireland's advocate and had promised to bring back a treaty that would give Ireland their republic.

'I'm surprised Éamon de Valera didn't go himself to negotiate with the British,' said Finn as he tucked into the beef and stout stew Eileen had made. 'After all, he's our president, and more experienced at all that than Mick.'

'Mick Collins will bring us the peace we've been yearning for,' said Ryan tersely, and Nuala could still feel the underlying tension between the soldier and the pacifist.

'I'd reckon that de Valera is after using Mick Collins as a scapegoat. He's always been good at making sure he's out of the way of things when they go wrong, then taking the credit

if they go right,' said Daniel. 'Look at how he left Mick to fight the British while he sailed off to America to raise funds. I'd not be trusting that man an inch. I'm glad 'tis Mick who's there for Ireland.'

Nuala saw Finn about to speak and put a hand on his leg under the table to stop him. The war was over, and Nuala wanted peace at the family lunch table as much as she wanted it for Ireland.

By the beginning of December, Nuala was heavy with child, and eager for the babe to arrive. She was glad that her sister was only a month behind her, and the two commiserated over their aches and pains.

"'Tis only a few more weeks.' Nuala gritted her teeth as she lowered herself into a chair. She was up in the kitchen of Cross Farm with Hannah and her mother, knitting hats and booties for the two babes. A gust of cold wind blew in as Daniel swept through the kitchen door, waving a newspaper over his head, with Fergus behind him.

'We've got a peace treaty!' he cried. 'Mick's done it for Ireland!'

As the family hugged each other and cheered at the news, Daniel opened the *Cork Examiner* and began to read out the terms of the Treaty. As he read, the excitement in his voice turned slowly to anger. When he'd finished, he sat down heavily at the table, the family crowding round him to read the details for themselves.

'This can't be true,' Daniel murmured.

'It is, Daddy. It says here that Ireland is to be a "self-governing dominion" of the British Empire,' said Hannah.

'But we wanted a republic,' said Nuala. 'Does this mean

we'll still be swearing allegiance to the feckin' King of England?'

'Nuala!' her mother reprimanded her. 'Well, Daniel, does it?'

'Yes,' said Daniel, his excitement completely vanquished. 'And that part of the North of Ireland is being kept under British control.'

'Jaysus Christ!' murmured Fergus. 'How can Mick Collins have agreed to this?'

'I don't know, but surely they can't carve up our country?!' cried Nuala.

''Tis a travesty,' said Daniel, slamming his fist on the newspaper. 'Mick Collins has had the wool pulled over his eyes by the British negotiators.'

'He calls it "a stepping stone to Irish peace",' said Hannah. 'Maybe he always knew he couldn't get a republic out of the British immediately. At least this is a start, and we'll have our own legal government here in the South.'

'Yes, and the British will govern part of the North! 'Tis a stepping stone to hell more like, Hannah,' raged Daniel. 'Seven hundred years of British dominance, and it seems we're no further on.'

'De Valera should have gone to London,' said Nuala. 'Mick Collins wasn't the right man for it.'

'You say that now, but you were cheering him on during the summer when we got our truce!' said Hannah, still loyal to her hero. 'He's done his best to protect us, bring us peace and an end to the killing!'

'And at what price?!' Nuala retorted furiously. 'Having part of *our* island chopped away, and the South still a dominion of the United Kingdom?!'

'Girls!' said Eileen. 'Calm yourselves. The Treaty hasn't been approved by the Dáil government. The newspaper says

de Valera is against it and will put up a fight. Just be glad the war is over.'

But what was the point of it all if we don't have our republic? Nuala thought as she watched her red-faced Daddy reach for the whiskey bottle.

The plans that had been made to celebrate not only peace but the first Christmas free from British occupation were put on hold, as Ireland became a divided nation once more. The chatter in the villages and pubs was all of who was for Mick Collins and his pro-Treaty followers, and who stood firm with Éamon de Valera and his anti-Treaty faction of the Sinn Féin party.

'Hannah just told me she and Ryan are staying home for Christmas lunch,' Eileen said to Nuala as she dropped in to see her at her cottage for a cup of tea.

'What was her excuse?' asked Nuala numbly.

'Well, she's close to her time and—'

'Mammy, so am I! Closer, in fact, and I'm still riding up with Finn to Cross Farm to spend the Holy Day with my family! 'Tis that Ryan; he's knowing we're all anti-Treaty and for de Valera, while he's for his precious Mick.'

'They are for peace, Nuala, as are many others. You can't be blaming them for that,' said Eileen.

Finn and Nuala welcomed their daughter Maggie safely into the world just after Christmas. Hannah and Ryan's son John was born at the beginning of January, amid Irish politicians shouting furiously as they debated the Treaty in the Dáil.

Despite her new babe, and the happiness she felt at being a mother, Nuala feverishly followed the news, praying that de Valera's anti-Treaty faction would triumph. When Mick Collins and the pro-Treaty lot won the vote in the Dáil, Éamon de Valera stepped down as president, in protest at parliament approving it, and was now putting his full energy into physically fighting it. An election was looming, the first of this strange new 'Irish Free State' that the South had become. Political turmoil continued in Dublin throughout the spring, and the IRA, which had ballooned with new recruits during the months of the truce, was now turning against itself, as weary soldiers declared which side they were on. Led by de Valera, anti-Treaty soldiers began to take matters into their own hands and seized state buildings, including the central Four Courts in Dublin, where the Easter Rising had begun in 1916.

'How dare they act against the law like this?' Hannah fumed, as she and Nuala sat on their bench overlooking Courtmacsherry Bay, John and Maggie on their laps. 'Can't they see that this Treaty is giving us the freedom to achieve freedom?' Hannah parroted the slogan that Mick Collins had been spreading to garner support.

'He's in the pockets of the British now,' Nuala scoffed. 'Finn told me he heard what Collins said after he'd signed the Treaty – that he'd just signed his own death warrant. He knew true Irish republicans would denounce it, so.'

'Are you saying I'm not a true Irish republican?' Hannah bristled. ''Twas me who brought you into Cumann na mBan if you remember, sister.'

'And 'twas me and Finn who fought to the very end of the war,' retorted Nuala. 'I can't be talking to you any longer if you insist on swallowing Mick Collins's propaganda.' With that, she stood up, put Maggie in her sling and walked home, fuming all the way.

It was in June, when little Maggie had just started on solid food, that Nuala read the newspaper with a sinking heart.

'De Valera and the anti-Treaty representatives have lost. The pro-Treaty Collins lot have won the election!' she cried out to her husband, who was coming down the stairs, doing up his tie in readiness for his day at Clogagh School. 'The Irish people voted for his despicable Treaty, Finn! How could they, after all they've – *we've* – done to fight for a republic?!'

Nuala laid her head on the table and sobbed.

'Ah, Nuala, darlin', I know 'tis a disaster. But if politics fail—'

'War begins again, and this time 'twill be brother against brother. Jesus, Finn, I can't even think of what that'll mean. Families around these parts are already divided over the Treaty. Look at our own,' she added as she stared up at him, tears still streaming down her face. 'Hannah told me proudly she and Ryan had voted for Michael Collins! She'd better not be showing her face round here after this! I'll drag her up to Cross Farm and get her to curtsey to the King of England in front of her Fenian father! And her brother Fergus, and you and our friends and neighbours who risked their lives for a republic!'

'I know, Nuala, I know . . .'

''Tis even worse than fighting the British! Now we're a land divided against ourselves.'

'Well, at least *we're* not divided. Now then, try and keep calm and see to that babe of ours over there. She's wanting her breakfast.'

As Finn doled out some porridge from the pot sitting warm on the hearth, Nuala swept up six-month-old Maggie and

placed her in the wooden feeding chair Finn had made during the Easter holidays.

Maggie smiled at her, which melted her heart. She was a beautiful babe – the irony being that she'd inherited her Auntie Hannah's red hair, and was the spit of her.

'Pass me her porridge, Finn.'

Finn did so, hoping that their daughter would act as a calming influence on his distraught wife.

'So now, I'll be seeing you both later,' he said and, placing a kiss on the top of the dark head of his wife and the red-gold of his daughter's, he left the cottage.

'I'll tell you, Maggie,' said Nuala, 'if that sister of mine comes round here crowing about the pro-Treaty lot winning the election, I'll be having to slap her hard.'

Maggie gurgled and opened her tiny mouth for more porridge.

'Maybe later we'll walk across to see your Uncle Christy, will we? He'll be feeling it like I am.'

Just as she'd laid Maggie down for a sleep, Christy arrived on her doorstep. 'Have you heard the news?' he asked as he walked in.

'I have indeed. Maggie's asleep with a tummy full of porridge, so shall we take a glass outside?'

'Of what?'

'Whatever you want.' Nuala lifted up a bottle of whiskey, as Christy took his arm from behind his back to raise a bottle of porter.

'I brought my own,' he said and followed her outside into the garden. 'Thought we might be needing it after what's happened.'

'Remember walls have ears,' Nuala whispered nervously.

'Unless poor Mrs Grady next door will rise from the grave we both saw her buried in three days ago, I'd be thinking

we're all right.' Christy gave her a weak smile. 'If we're worrying about that, then we really are back to the old days.'

'I'd say with the pro-Treaty lot winning the election, we are.'

'Yes,' Christy agreed. 'There's fellows in the pub already this morning, so I'll not be here long, but they are singing the same song as us, and it isn't in support of Mick Collins. There's a lot around here who'd fight on for the republic we dreamt of. I've been hearing tales that Protestants round these parts are already packing and heading up to the North. There's talk of closing the border.'

'We won't be allowed into part of our own country?' Nuala gasped as she took a sip of whiskey.

'Ah now, I don't know how 'twill work, but many will go, just in case.'

'But what about the Catholics living across the border in the North?'

'They'll be trying to come south if they can, but like our own family, many will have land they farm to survive. What a bloody mess it all is.' Christy shook his head and knocked back a great gulp of porter straight from the bottle.

'How will we ever start a war against ourselves? Would you be willing to fight your friends? Your kin? I . . . don't know.' Nuala put her head in her hands. 'With Daddy being a Fenian, he'd continue the fight for a republic to the death, and Mammy would support him as she always has. Fergus would too, but Hannah . . .'

'Don't be too hard on her, Nuala. She has to stand by her husband, and there's many around here that were voting for peace, not war, whatever the consequences.'

'We had peace before with the British ruling us, and where did that get us? We were so close to being free and we lost so

many doing it. Surely we owe it to those who died to continue the fight?'

'Even though 'tis an unbearable thought, I'd agree, and 'tis one we volunteers will all be debating the next time the Third West Cork Brigade meet. Sean Hales won't be present – he's already made it obvious he's pro-Treaty, the traitor! He's even in Dublin working with Mick Collins to recruit a national army. Tom Hales will stand with us and support fighting on.'

'How can Sean Hales support the Treaty, when his own brother Tom was beaten and tortured by the British?!' Nuala raged.

'Look now, we're not there yet. Try not to worry, Nuala. Mick Collins doesn't want war against his own just as much as we don't. Let's see if he can work his magic politically, and we'll take it from there.'

It was only ten days later that newspapers reported that the Dublin anti-Treaty headquarters, set up in the Four Courts with Éamon de Valera at its head, had been attacked by Michael Collins's new National Army.

After requests for the anti-Treaty men to surrender their position at the Four Courts, the order was given to attack. Pro-Treaty forces bombarded the building with heavy artillery.

Rather than slamming her fists on the newspaper, Nuala took it in her hands and began to rip it to shreds. Finn walked in from his day in the schoolroom to his wife tearing paper and a screaming child.

'Have you heard? Collins has attacked the Four Courts! The fighting's still going on, but the paper says Collins has

got help from the British, with them supplying cannons and artillery and . . . Oh Finn, please tell me I'm dreaming,' she said as she walked into the comfort of his arms.

'Nuala, we triumphed before and we can do it again. Christy just told me there's a meeting for our brigade tonight. Now's the time to show whether a man is with us, or with the pro-Treaty government. Darlin', we'd not be wanting Maggie upset, would we?'

Nuala shook her head and went to calm her crying babe.

'You're to concentrate on being a mammy, Nuala, and leave the rest to your husband, all right?'

'But if things get difficult, sure I'll have to work with Cumann na mBan again, and—'

'No, Nuala. 'Tis one thing risking your life when you've no one depending on you, another when you've a family. This time, you're to leave this to the men. I'll not have us leaving Maggie an orphan. D'you hear me?'

'Please don't say that! I'd rather me die than you.'

'And leave me to change Maggie's napkins?' Finn chuckled. 'Now, is there a bite to eat in this house of ours before I go out?'

Finn came in late that evening, but Nuala was still awake. 'What happened at the meeting?'

''Tis looking good, Nuala,' Finn said as he undressed and climbed into bed next to her. 'We've almost everyone with us, so it's the pro-Treaty lot who should be watching their backs in these parts. I've heard that Rory O'Connor himself is coming down from Dublin to Cork to take control of our anti-Treaty forces. We have to defend ourselves against this new Irish National Army that Mick Collins has recruited. I

hear him and his government are calling *us* the republicans these days!' Finn shook his head and grimaced. 'It has to be faced, and we will face it; we've experience on our side, and men like Tom Hales with us.'

'With Sean Hales in charge of this new army?'

'Yes. Ah, Nuala, it looks like we're headed for more difficult times. Let's get some sleep while we can.'

As Finn disappeared off again to volunteers' meetings and drills, Nuala read that the Irish National Army, headed by Sean Hales – who'd fought side by side with Finn and been responsible for burning down Castle Bernard, which had brought about the truce – was travelling by boats supplied by the British to make landings on the southern coast. Aware of the way that the volunteers had blown up bridges and railways when Sean was fighting with them in the last war, landing the National Army by sea was a clever ploy.

She was only thankful for Maggie, who kept her busy. She was on tenterhooks every moment Finn was away. It felt like the nightmare was happening all over again. With Maggie strapped to her chest, she drove the pony and cart into Timoleague. In the shops, there was nothing but talk of what was happening, most of the residents horrified by the new turn of events. There was a palpable air of uncertainty and fear.

''Tis civil war now and there's no denying it,' said Mrs McFarlane in the butcher's. 'I've heard that Sean Hales landed the army in Bantry yesterday and they're marching towards Skibbereen. What will it all come to?' she said as she handed over the stewing steak and some bacon to Nuala.

Walking down the high street, Nuala saw that the pubs, which had been full since the truce had been agreed and the

British had withdrawn from the area, were now empty, apart from old men drowning their sorrows. On the way to collect her pony and cart, Nuala saw Hannah come out of a shop right in front of her.

'Hello there, Nuala, how are you? And the little one?' her sister asked.

'We're grand altogether. How's your small one?' Nuala replied, as if she was addressing a stranger.

'Sure, John's coming on well, thank you.'

'Well, 'tis a while since we've seen you up at the farm for Sunday lunch. Will you and Ryan be joining us?' Nuala asked.

'Ah now, with feelings running so high, Ryan says 'tis best if we stay back till the whole thing's sorted. He knows too well how my family feels about the Treaty.'

'And how do you feel, Hannah?'

'I just want peace, like Ryan. Now, I need to get back home to my babe. Goodbye, Nuala.'

Nuala watched her sister turn away from her and walk down the street towards the little house she and Ryan had moved into just after John had been born. There was no more watching their babes grow up together; all that had stopped since the fighting had begun.

'All because of Uncle Ryan,' Nuala said to the sleeping Maggie, cradled peacefully against her chest. As hard as she tried, she could not forgive her sister for what she saw as nothing less than treachery.

Luckily, the school holidays had just begun and Finn was free to join the other anti-Treaty volunteers in the fight. He had said the National Army were now heading towards Clonakilty.

'The home of Michael Collins himself,' Nuala said to Christy when he popped over for a chat.

'Is Finn going there? I'd be worried if he was, for even if they're anti-Treaty, there's many in Clonakilty that'll come out in support of the Big Fellow. He's one of their own.'

'No, Finn's on his way up to Bandon with the rest of the brigade. They think that's where the army will head next.'

'Well, the lads know what they're doing, and they're on their own territory,' said Christy. 'Try to remember, the National Army are just ordinary Irish folk like us, in need of a wage to feed their families. Besides, whatever we may feel about Sean Hales being pro-Treaty, he's a man of peace. He doesn't want to kill his fellow men in the same way as the British did. He'll show mercy, Nuala, especially in West Cork where he and his brother Tom were born.'

'I can only hope you're right,' Nuala sighed. 'Are you joining us for lunch at the farm after Mass on Sunday?' she asked him.

'Sure, and we'll listen to a few Fenian songs of your daddy's on the fiddle, to remind us what we're fighting for, eh?' Christy smiled. 'I need to be getting back. I'll be seeing ye, Nuala.'

As Christy left, Nuala pondered why a man who – apart from his bad leg – was such a fine figure of a fellow, and so kind and clever, had never found himself a wife.

The following Sunday, with Finn away fighting to hold Bandon, Christy drove Nuala and baby Maggie in the pony and cart up to Cross Farm after Mass. It was a beautiful July day, and Nuala looked up at the blue, blue sky above her.

Wherever you are, Finn Casey, I'm sending my love and all my blessings to you.

Talk at Cross Farm was all of the battle in Bandon. News had filtered through to her father that despite the anti-Treaty volunteers defending it bravely, the National Army would take the town.

'At least the loss of life was far less than it would have been if we'd been fighting the British, and we must thank God for that,' her mother commented as she and Nuala served lunch.

'Ah, but there were still some casualties, and what's your man Sean doing using British warships and artillery to fire on his own?' Daniel roared from the end of the table. 'And Mick Collins sanctioning it?!'

''Tis a tragedy and that's all I can say,' sighed Eileen.

'The enemy know our tactics, because they once used them themselves not so long ago. They're taking West Cork easily, and we're sitting around and watching it happen!' Daniel continued in his rant.

'Finn isn't sitting around, Daddy,' said Nuala defensively. 'He's out there fighting for our republic.'

'That he is, Nuala, along with our Fergus,' said Eileen. 'And may God bless both of them.'

After lunch, Daniel took out his fiddle and played some rousing ballads from the old times, then newer ones he'd learnt, like 'The Ballad of Charlie Hurley', Finn's closest friend, who had died so tragically during the last war. As his rich voice soared through the moving words, Nuala felt calmer. They weren't just fighting for their republic, but for all those who had lost their lives to the cause.

Finn came back from Bandon a day later, exhausted but unharmed.

'Towns across West Cork are falling to the National Army

– towns where we won against the British to get the truce for Ireland. But are we now to go in and blow up a garrison full of our Irish brothers?' he sighed. 'Word is, the National Army are off to take Kinsale, and unless we start putting up more of a fight, they'll have that town and the rest of Ireland surrendering before the month is out.'

'Will you continue, Finn?'

'To the end, Nuala, you know that.'

'Did you ... did you kill anyone during the Bandon battle?'

''Twas dark, and I couldn't be seeing, but yes, there were some men lying injured in the street, but I've no idea whose they were, or which gun fired the shot. Jaysus, I'm tired and for my bed. Are you coming?'

'Of course, darlin'. I'll take all the chances I can to hold you safe in my arms,' Nuala whispered as she snuffed out the oil lamp and followed Finn miserably upstairs.

43

By the middle of August, the National Army had Cork City and all the major towns in the county under their control. Michael Collins and his pro-Treaty government were triumphing.

'If they've taken Cork, what's the point of continuing?' she said to Finn, who had arrived home, filthy and dejected from another fruitless fight. 'We've lost, and that's all there is to it. And if there's no hope, I'd be preferring to live with this travesty of a Treaty than without my husband.'

'Nuala,' Finn said as he knocked back a drop of whiskey, 'we all agreed we'd fight for a republic, didn't we?'

'Yes, but—'

'There *is* no "but". If you asked all the people around here to put their hands on the Bible and say what's in their hearts, they'd all be for saying no to the Treaty. And we're all Ireland has left to make that happen. I couldn't live with myself if I didn't give my last breath to the cause.'

'So you're saying you'd prefer to die, Finn? That the cause is more important than me or your daughter?' she demanded.

'Now then, where is this talk coming from? There was none of it last time. You stood with me, and 'twas your love and belief that got me through.'

'Yes, 'tis true, but our lives have changed. Look at you,

telling me I wasn't to be involved with Cumann na mBan because of our Maggie. We're a family now, Finn, as you said yourself. That's what matters most, isn't it?'

Finn looked at her and sighed. 'I'm too tired for this, Nuala. I'm off to clean myself up.'

Nuala took the sleeping Maggie from her cradle and hugged her to her breast, looking down at her young daughter's face.

'What's to become of us, little one?' she whispered. Maggie continued to sleep peacefully in her arms.

It was decided that all members of Finn's brigade should once more take to the hills and become the shadows they had been last time around.

'Are you saying the pro-Treaty lot will come and arrest you on your doorstep like the British did last time?' Nuala asked Finn when he came home.

'Some of ours have been arrested and thrown into the jails by the National Army during the skirmishes, but if they want to push further to clear out the troublemakers, well, they'll be knowing where we all live, won't they?' he pointed out. 'And where our safehouses were, because they used them themselves in the old days.'

'How many of you are left, would you say?'

'Enough,' said Finn. 'But there's news come down from one of our spies in Dublin that the Big Fellow might be planning to pay a visit to West Cork.'

'Mick Collins would come here?!'

''Tis where he was born, Nuala. 'Tis his place, and there's many around these parts that might be anti-Treaty, but still see Mick as a god, the hero that saved Ireland. 'Tis ironic, isn't it?'

'What?'

'West Cork and Kerry probably contributed more to the winning of a truce with the British than any other part of Ireland. We all fought for Mick, believed in him because he was one of our own, but that passion makes us the most anti-Treaty area in Ireland. 'Tis madness, it really is. Anyway . . .' Finn tied the belt of his trench coat and heaved his haversack onto his shoulder. 'I'll be off.' He took her face in his hands and kissed her gently on the lips. 'Remember how much I love you, my Nuala. And how I'm doing this for you, our small ones and their babes to come.'

'I love you too, and I always will,' she whispered as she watched the door close and her husband leave her again.

Two days later, Nuala saw a number of villagers walking down the street or on their ponies and traps.

'Where are they going?' she asked Christy, who had popped over for his now habitual cup of tea before the pub opened its doors.

'The talk is that Michael Collins will be in Clonakilty this afternoon. I heard some chat last night in the pub that he'd passed through Béal na Bláth. His convoy had to stop and ask directions outside Long's pub from Denny, who works there.'

'What!' Nuala put her hand to her mouth. 'Did Denny tell them the way?'

'Sure he did,' nodded Christy. 'There were a few of our boys in the pub, as there's a brigade meeting later at Murray's farmhouse nearby. Tom Hales was up there, and I also heard that de Valera himself was travelling down from Dublin for the meeting. 'Tis said they're deciding whether to continue with the war or not. And there, bold as you like, our sworn

enemy, Mick Collins, passing by just a few miles from where they all were, not suspecting a thing.' Christy shook his head and chuckled.

'Are you sure Denny saw Mick Collins in the car?'

'Yes, Denny would swear on the Bible 'twas him. He was sitting in an open-topped car, and now half of West Cork has got wind that he's down here. Word has it he'll be visiting all the towns that the National Army has taken, and everyone has taken a bet he'll stop at Clonakilty near his homeplace.'

Nuala watched the flurry of activity in the street gaining momentum.

'You'll be giving it a miss, will you, Nuala?' asked Christy with an ironic smile.

'I will indeed.' There was a pause as Nuala took in the ramifications of what she'd just been told. 'If our lot know he's here and will most likely return the way he came, will they be planning anything?'

Christy turned his head away from Nuala. 'I'd not be knowing. Seems to me that today, all the chickens have come home to roost.'

It was late evening by the time Nuala saw the villagers and those who lived beyond Clogagh returning. They obviously had drink in them and wanted more, as many of them parked their carts, bicycles and themselves outside the pub. Unable to resist, she opened her front door and listened as the crowd milled about outside with pints of porter or drops of whiskey.

''Twas at O'Donovan's Mick bought me a drink . . .'

'Ah now, it was drinks on the house at Denny Kingston's place. He waved at me!'

'Mick asked after my small ones, he did!'

Nuala recognised men and women who'd been passionate IRA volunteers during the revolution. With a sad shake of her head, she closed the door. Then she poured herself her own whiskey.

At just past midnight, Nuala was roused out of a whiskey-induced slumber by the creaking of the back door opening. She heard footsteps coming upstairs and sat up, holding her breath until she saw Finn enter the room.

'Nuala, oh Nuala . . .'

She watched as Finn staggered towards the bed, then almost fell forward onto her and began to sob.

'What is it? What's happened?'

'I . . . what a mess, Nuala, what a mess.'

Nuala could do no more than wait for her husband to stop crying. Then she handed him some whiskey from the bottle and he drank it straight down.

'Can you tell me what's happened?'

'I . . . can't speak the words, and I've run many miles through the night to get back to you. Let me sleep in your arms, Nuala, and I'll tell you in the . . .' Finn fell asleep mid-sentence, his head on her chest.

Whatever it was he had to tell her, she didn't care, for her husband was safe home.

The following morning, Nuala left Finn in bed and went downstairs to feed Maggie. Finn joined her an hour later, looking gaunt and haggard, as if he'd aged ten years since she'd last seen him.

'Porridge?' Nuala asked.

Finn could only nod as he slumped at the table.

'Get that down you,' she said quietly.

He finished the bowl in a few gulps and Nuala, who'd been too exhausted herself this morning to bake bread, used the rest of yesterday's loaf and lathered it with jam.

'Ah Nuala.' Finn finished the bread and jam, then wiped his hand across his lips. 'My head is spinning this morning, I . . .'

'Tell me, Finn, you know 'twill go with me to the grave if that's what you ask. I heard chat from Christy that Mick Collins was expected in Clonakilty yesterday. Was an ambush planned on his convoy?'

'It was. Me, Tom Hales and the boys were up at the Murray farmhouse for a meeting with the Cork brigades. When we heard from Denny Long that Collins was likely to come back along the same route he'd arrived by, Tom directed that we should plan an ambush. We laid in wait for hours around the crossroads at Béal na Bláth, but the convoy didn't appear. Tom decided we should call it off because of the weather – we were soaked to the skin from the rain. So me and some of the other men left, but there were a few who stayed just in case, including Tom. I was coming home across country when I saw the convoy beneath me. I crouched down in case they saw me, and then, about ten minutes later . . .'

He stopped and took a shuddering breath before he was able to continue.

'I heard shots ring out from where I knew some of the men were still waiting. I began to run back to find out what had happened, and met a couple of volunteers sprinting towards me. They told me that the weather was too bad to see who they were firing at when the convoy passed, but that Collins had gone down. The rest of the convoy had fired back, but had soon stopped when they'd seen Mick lying there.'

Finn looked up at her, his blue eyes filled with tears. 'He was dead, Nuala. The only one in the convoy that was.'

'Mick Collins?! Dead?! I . . .' Nuala stared at her husband in shock and disbelief. 'Do you know who shot him?'

'The man I was talking to – and I'm giving no names now – was hardly making sense, other than to keep repeating that "Mick's dead, Mick's dead!" Jesus, Mary and Joseph, shot by his own down here in West Cork.'

Finn began weeping again, and all Nuala could do was to stand up and put her arms round him.

''Tis one thing to fight for a proper republic, but another to be part of an attack that killed the man that originally led us to victory and a truce. God only knows what will become of Ireland now, without the Big Fellow.'

'Where was de Valera? Did he know about the ambush?'

'I'd say he did, yes, but he left West Cork early yesterday to get back to Dublin for a meeting.'

'Did he order the attack on Mick?'

'Word is 'twas Tom Hales, who cried like a baby when he found out Mick was dead. You know what good friends they once were before the Civil War.'

'I . . . just don't know what to say.' Nuala shook her head, unable to stop her own tears from falling. 'Where will we go from here?'

'I don't know, but there's not many around these parts, whatever side they were on, who won't be shedding a tear today. I tell you something, Nuala, 'tis over for me. I've not the stomach for any more now that Mick's gone.'

'I understand, Finn,' she replied eventually. 'I wonder how many others will feel the same, so.'

'Most of us. I'm frightened, Nuala, for the first time; I'm frightened that people will find out that I was part of the ambush that killed Michael Collins, and that they'll come after me.'

'But you weren't part of it, Finn; you told me just now that you'd already left and were coming home to me. There were so many out on the streets last night, who'd travelled back from Clonakilty with a bellyful of porter, so drunk they could hardly stand up. They'll not be knowing where you were. If anyone asks, you were here with your wife and child last night. I'll swear to it on the Bible if I have to. Sure, there'll be Masses said for Mick all over Ireland and we should go.'

'We should, yes, and I'll say a prayer for a man that I didn't kill with my own hands, but will forever feel as if I did.'

'Well, you didn't, Finn, and you must try to remember that you were just following orders, like any soldier in battle.'

'You're right, of course.' Finn wiped his hands harshly across his streaming eyes. 'I'd doubt Tom Hales or a single one of us thought for a moment 'twould be Mick that would get it. We just wanted to have a go at the Dublin lot, remind them that there were many of us still out here, fighting for the republic we'd dreamt of. Jesus, Nuala, Mick was the head of our new government! Why was the man riding around in an open-topped car? And where were the soldiers who were meant to protect him when they were needed?'

'I'd say that Mick didn't think anyone down here in West Cork would want him dead. He was amongst his own, wasn't he?'

'Yes, or so he thought.'

'And from the state of those back from their drink with him last night, he and the soldiers must have downed a few with them. They weren't on the lookout, were they?'

'You're right, Nuala. Mick was always one for the party and a drink. Whatever their politics, people loved him down here. *We* once loved him; he was one of us . . .' Finn began to cry again.

'Now then, how about I fill the tub with some nice warm

water and you go clean yourself up? Then I'll lay out a shirt and some trousers and you, me and Maggie will take a walk outside, so our neighbours can see that you're here and mourning for Mick with them. You're respected, Finn, you teach the children at the village school. Sure, no one's going to want to see you harmed.'

Nuala spoke with a confidence she didn't feel, but whatever it took to console her devastated, frightened husband, she'd do and say.

As she made to move, Finn caught her, drew her roughly into his arms and kissed her hard on the lips. When he eventually pulled away, his eyes were wet again. 'God help me, Nuala Casey, I'm spending the rest of my life being grateful for the woman I have for my wife.'

The mood in the week after the ambush that killed Mick Collins was sombre. Everywhere she went, Nuala saw windows hung with the black of mourning, and grown men weeping in the streets. The newspapers were full of tributes to the man who'd been born on West Cork soil. There was a great deal of local upset when Michael Collins's body was buried in Dublin, rather than locally where he'd been birthed.

Nuala, Finn and Maggie joined a Mass held in Timoleague church on the day of his burial. She had never seen the church so full, and recognised many of the men who had been fighting against him. Her whole family was present, joined together in grief for a man who'd given them the belief, strength and courage to begin the revolution. And had now made the ultimate sacrifice himself, aged only thirty-two, and already Chairman of the Provisional Government of Ireland.

Outside the church, both Hannah and Ryan were inconsolable. As Nuala passed her sister, Hannah reached out and grabbed her to whisper in her ear.

'I hope you and that husband of yours are happy. You've both got what you wanted, haven't you? Don't be telling me Finn wasn't involved in the ambush – I know very well he was and so do many others around these parts. *He's* the one who deserves to be lying in a grave, not the saviour of Ireland,' she hissed through her tears.

Nuala didn't tell Finn what her sister had said, as there was no point worrying him any more than he was already.

Two nights later, he told her he was going out to a brigade meeting.

'You're not to be fretting, Nuala, I'm telling them the fight is over for me. I'll not put you and Maggie at risk any longer for a cause that's already lost.'

As it was a warm August evening, Nuala sat outside in the garden. Maggie – who was just sitting up – sat on a blanket, playing with the toy dog that Finn had carved from a piece of wood.

'Perhaps that'll become Daddy's new hobby now he's retiring from war,' she said to her daughter. Despite the tragic events that had occurred, and the fact they'd lost the dream of their beloved republic, part of Nuala felt relieved. Ireland's path was still unclear, but she could now imagine a more peaceful future, without the terrible lump of fear that had sat in her stomach for so long. At last, the three of them could concentrate on being a family, and with the prospect of Principal O'Driscoll at Clogagh School soon retiring, Finn would take over and they'd have more money to spare.

'Maybe your mammy could think about getting a part-time job in the local pharmacy, what with her nursing training,' she cooed to Maggie, as she picked her up to get her ready for bed.

Finn had not arrived back by eleven, but Nuala did her best not to panic.

He's probably got caught up chatting, she told herself, as yet again she mounted the stairs alone to bed.

Exhausted from the past few days, Nuala fell asleep easily. It was only when she heard a loud banging on the front door that she woke with a start.

Looking out of the bedroom window, she saw Christy with Sonny, another man from the village, standing below.

Running down the stairs, she opened the door.

With one glance at the expression on their faces, she knew.

'Finn's been shot, Nuala, up near the Dineen Farm,' said Christy.

'I found him in my field as I was walking home from the meeting. He'd been thrown into a ditch,' said Sonny.

'I . . . is he alive?'

The men bowed their heads. 'Nuala, I'm so sorry,' said Christy.

Christy caught her before she fell. She could hear someone screaming from far away. Then the world went black.

Finn's funeral took place at the little church in Clogagh, the day after he had been waked. If she could have done, Nuala would have only allowed her family to be there to support her, as they prayed for his immortal soul. No one had come forward to confess to shooting her husband, and even though there'd been plenty of rumours as to who it might have been, Nuala had ignored them. Her husband's murderer was probably sitting

right here in the church, pretending to be sorry for not only ending Finn's life, but her own and her daughter's too.

On the journey up to Clogagh graveyard, which sat in an idyllic spot at the top of the Argideen valley a good half-mile away from the village, the coffin was borne by the volunteers Finn had stood side by side with. Nuala walked in front of the coffin, supported by Christy. With his volunteer's cap on the top of it, Finn had been interred into the ground next to Charlie Hurley, his closest friend. Then the Clogagh company had fired off a seven-gun salute to their fallen comrade.

At the gathering afterwards, held up at Cross Farm, Nuala had smiled and nodded at the condolences from friends and neighbours.

Realising who was missing, she excused herself and went to find her mother. 'I didn't see Hannah and Ryan at the church. And they're not here either.'

'No, they didn't come.' Eileen did her best to control her anger. 'Don't blame your sister, Nuala, 'tis that husband of hers who's the problem.'

'Well, she married him, didn't she?'

In that moment, in a heart already scarred with loss, Nuala felt a part of it turn to stone.

That night, staying in her childhood bedroom, with Maggie lying next to her in the bed she used to share with Hannah, she came to a decision.

'God save me, but I can never forgive Hannah for this. And I never want to see her again for the rest of my life.'

Merry
West Cork, Ireland
June 2008

An Crann Bethadh
Celtic Tree of Life

'There now, that's the story that Nuala told me only hours before she left this earth,' said Katie. ''Twas emotional for both of us when she told me the family connection.'

I did my best to come back to the present, still enveloped in the utter tragedy of Finn's death, and all that Nuala had suffered.

'So Nuala was our mother Maggie's mum . . . our grandmother? The one we never saw when we were growing up, apart from at Mammy's funeral? And what about our grandfather? Finn died. So who was that man with her, who walked with a stick?'

''Twas Christy, her cousin who worked at the pub across the road. She married him a few years after Finn died. You can see why she did: Christy was always there for her. They had shared experiences,' Katie replied, then paused as she stared at me. 'Christy's surname was "Noiro".'

I stared at her in utter shock. 'Noiro?'

'Yes. As well as her daughter, Maggie, Christy and Nuala went on to have a son, Cathal, who married a woman called Grace. And, well, they had Bobby and his little sister, Helen.'

'I . . .' My head was swimming. 'So we shared a grandmother with Bobby Noiro?'

'We did, yes.'

'But why didn't Bobby ever say?'

'I don't think he knew, to be fair.'

'Why didn't Nuala and Christy ever visit us?'

"Tis complicated,' Katie sighed. 'Our great-uncle Fergus was running Cross Farm before our daddy; he inherited it when Fergus died.'

'Fergus was mentioned in the diary I read. He was Nuala's brother. Did he ever marry?'

'No, so the farm went to our daddy as the eldest boy of the clan. We never met his parents – our other grandparents – because they both died before we were born. Our grandmother was named Hannah, and our grandfather was called Ryan.'

Katie gave me a meaningful stare as I tried to compute what she was saying. 'So now, Nuala was Mammy's mother and Hannah was Daddy's! Our grandmothers were sisters! Which means . . .' Katie produced a sheet of paper. On it was a family tree. 'See?'

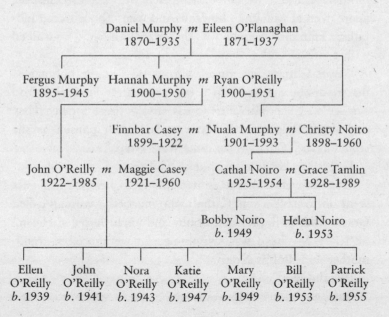

Daniel Murphy *m* Eileen O'Flanaghan
1870–1935   1871–1937

Fergus Murphy   Hannah Murphy *m* Ryan O'Reilly
1895–1945   1900–1950   1900–1951

Finnbar Casey *m* Nuala Murphy *m* Christy Noiro
1899–1922   1901–1993   1898–1960

John O'Reilly *m* Maggie Casey   Cathal Noiro *m* Grace Tamlin
1922–1985   1921–1960   1925–1954   1928–1989

Bobby Noiro   Helen Noiro
b. 1949   *b.* 1953

Ellen   John   Nora   Katie   Mary   Bill   Patrick
O'Reilly   O'Reilly   O'Reilly   O'Reilly   O'Reilly   O'Reilly   O'Reilly
b. 1939   *b.* 1941   *b.* 1943   *b.* 1947   *b.* 1949   *b.* 1953   *b.* 1955

I took it from my sister to study it, but a raft of names and dates danced in front of my eyes and I looked up at Katie for guidance.

She pointed at two names. 'John and Maggie – our mammy and daddy – were first cousins. It isn't illegal here in Ireland, even these days – don't worry, I checked. With such big families often living in isolated communities, 'twas common, and still is, for cousins to mix socially and fall in love. And after Hannah didn't turn up for Finn's wake or funeral, Nuala never spoke to her sister again. You know 'tis an awful thing not to pay your respects to the dead, especially here in Ireland, and 'twas the icing on the cake, after her sister had said such terrible things to her.'

She raised her eyebrows at me and I nodded in agreement. It was one thing that had struck me when I had moved to New Zealand – that there didn't seem to be any long-running family feuds that had been passed down through the generations, just because a great-grandfather had once insulted his cousin's fiddle-playing.

'Old wounds run deep here,' I murmured.

'They do,' Katie agreed. 'Now, when our parents – Maggie and John – met and fell in love, Nuala and Hannah must have been horrified. 'Twas like *Romeo and Juliet*. Nuala said she'd told her daughter that she'd disown her if she married John, but Mammy loved Daddy so much, she went ahead. Ah, Merry, Nuala couldn't stop weeping as she told me how she had cut our mammy out of her life. And how much she regretted it looking back, especially when Mammy died so young. She said she just couldn't bear to set eyes on Daddy – Hannah and Ryan's son. She asked my forgiveness for not being there for all of us kids after Mammy died.'

'Oh my God . . .' I muttered, tears springing to my eyes as I thought about the diary I hadn't read for all those years. The

story of a brave young woman who had been my grandmother, who through the pain of war had lost her husband, but who had also been prepared to cut not only her sister but her beloved daughter out of her life.

'So now, I went to Timoleague church to look through the records and put the tree together.' Katie pointed to it.

'There's Bobby,' I whispered. 'All those stories he used to tell of his grandparents fighting the British in the War of Independence . . .'

'Yes. I remember, Merry,' Katie nodded grimly, 'and I think it explains why Bobby was the way he was. With Nuala and Christy as his grandparents, Bobby would have been brought up as pro-republican as you can be. Nuala's hatred for the British, for Michael Collins and "his gang", as she called them, passed down through the generations. After all, the Treaty that Mick Collins signed with the British government in London sparked the Civil War, which killed her husband, Finn. He was the love of her life.'

'Yes.' I spoke quietly, as my chest felt so tight I could hardly breathe. 'Which must also mean that I – *we* – are closely related to Bobby and Helen Noiro.'

'We are, yes. He's our first cousin. And o'course, his daddy, Cathal, was half-brother to Mammy.'

'We knew that Bobby's daddy, Cathal, died in a barn fire, didn't he? So Nuala lost her son as well,' I sighed. 'What a sad life she led.'

'I know so, 'tis tragic, but it's interesting working with the old folks. They took death to be part of life back then, because they were used to it. These days, with all the new-fangled medicine, 'tis a shock when anyone dies, even if they're very old. What I've learnt is that life was cheap back then, Merry. I went to Nuala's funeral at Timoleague church. There

weren't many there, just a couple of old friends and Helen, Bobby's little sister.'

'Bobby wasn't there?' I held my breath for an answer.

'No, he wasn't.' Katie eyed me. 'What happened in Dublin, Merry? I know 'twas something to do with Bobby. He was obsessed with you from the first moment he set eyes on you.'

'Please, Katie, I can't talk about it now, I just can't.'

'But he was why you ran away, wasn't he?'

'Yes.' Tears jumped into my eyes as I spoke the words.

'Ah, Merry.' Katie took my hands in hers. 'I'm here now, and whatever happened then is long in the past. You're safe back home with me.'

I put my head against my sister's chest, gulping back the tears because I knew that once they began, they'd never stop. I needed to hold it together for my children. There was one last question I needed to ask.

'Has he . . . have you seen him around here since I left? I was wondering whether he comes back to visit his mum. She was called Grace, wasn't she?'

'Helen Noiro told me at the funeral that her mammy was long dead, and as for Bobby, I've only seen him once, and that was soon after you'd vanished from the face of the earth. He came tearing up to the farm, wanting to know if we'd seen you. When we said no, he didn't believe us, and went raging through the house, opening all the presses, looking under beds until Daddy came along – he had to threaten him with his rifle . . . Bobby was frightening, Merry. The rage on him . . . 'twas like he'd been possessed.'

'I'm so sorry, Katie. He did the same at Ambrose's flat too.'

'But you weren't there?'

'No, I'd already gone. I had no choice, Katie.'

'Well, part of me is glad you disappeared, Merry, because

I thought to myself then that if he found you, he'd kill you. Though I'd have liked to have known whether *you* were dead or alive sooner, so.'

'It wasn't just me he was threatening to kill, Katie, but . . .' I shook my head. 'I promise I will tell you everything, just not now, okay?'

'O'course, and I hope what I've told you today has helped in some way. Old scars never seem to heal here, do they? And 'tis so unfair when they're inflicted on the next generation. Ireland's been too good at looking back at its past, but now I'd say we're getting better at looking to the future. Things have finally moved on.'

'Yes,' I agreed as I dug in a pocket to find a tissue. 'I really feel that. Even though part of me still wants to see the ponies and carts on the roads and the old cottages rather than all the modern bungalows, progress is a good thing.'

'So you don't know where he is, Merry?'

'No. I've checked the records in Dublin and London to see if I could find out whether he was still alive, but there wasn't a single Robert or Bobby Noiro registered as dying since 1971. So, unless he moved somewhere else abroad and died, he's still alive, out there somewhere.'

'And that frightens you?'

'I can't tell you how much, Katie. He was partly the reason I decided to come on my Grand Tour after my husband died. I thought it was time to put the past to rest.'

'Did your husband know about it?'

'No. I agonised about telling him, but knowing Jock, he'd have gone to hunt him down and the whole nightmare would have begun again. I just wanted a completely fresh start. I haven't told my children either, but I'm going to have to tell them now, Katie. They both think I've lost it, which I have a bit recently. The strange thing is, as I set out to find Bobby,

some other people were trying to find me too,' I confessed. 'And I thought . . .'

'That Bobby was after you again. Jaysus' – Katie raised her eyebrows – 'you've certainly led a more interesting life than I have. So, who are these people trying to find you?'

'That really *is* a story for another day.' I checked my watch. 'My kids will be back at any moment. Please don't tell them what we were discussing this morning. When I find out what's happened to him, I will.'

'I'll just say we were talking of the old times, which is true. Take that with you, Merry,' she said, pointing to the family tree. 'Have a look at it in more detail another time . . .'

There was a knock on the door. 'Come in!' I called.

'Hi, Mum, the surf was fantastic out there!' said Jack, walking into the room with Mary-Kate. His eyes fell on Katie, who smiled and stood up.

'Hello there, you two. I'm your long-lost Auntie Katie, and you are?'

'I'm Jack.'

'And I'm Mary-Kate. So you're the sister I'm named after?'

'She is,' I smiled as Katie embraced Jack and then Mary-Kate.

'What a legacy you've been given: named after the both of us. Sure, you've the best qualities of your auntie, and the bad ones of your mammy.' Katie winked at my daughter.

'I don't have any bad qualities, do I, kids?'

'Of course not, Mum,' said Jack as he and Mary-Kate rolled their eyes.

'Maybe you two can tell me more about what my naughty little sister's been up to in the past few years,' Katie chuckled.

'We'd be up for that, wouldn't we, Jacko? I love the colour of your hair,' Mary-Kate added.

'Ah, thanks. I'd be having to get the red roots from a bottle

these days, mind. I always wanted the blonde curls of your mammy when I was younger. Now so, I'm starving. Shall we treat ourselves to some freshly caught fish at An Súgán in town?' she suggested.

Over lunch, at a lovely pub-restaurant in Clonakilty, Katie regaled them with stories of our childhood, some of which Jack had heard already.

'She was always the clever one, see, and she won a scholarship to go and be educated properly at boarding school in Dublin.'

'When she got older, did she have many boyfriends?' Mary-Kate asked.

'I'd say your mammy was more for her books than she was boys.'

'But your auntie always was a one for the lads, weren't you? There was always some fellow hanging around,' I teased her, relishing the relaxed atmosphere after the tension of our earlier conversation.

By the time Katie had dropped us back at the hotel, I felt utterly exhausted.

'So, your Uncle John's already been in touch – all of us who are here around these parts are invited up to the farm on Sunday night, including grandchildren. No sign of kiddies for you yet, Jack?' Katie asked.

'I just haven't found the right woman to be their mother yet,' Jack shrugged. 'Bye, Katie. It was a pleasure meeting you.'

'And you. Never thought I'd see the day.' Turning to me, she said, 'Call me, Merry, and we'll talk some more, okay?'

'I will, thanks, Katie.'

Inside the lobby, I told the kids I was going for a rest, and handed Jack the car keys.

'Go and explore, but stick to the main roads for now. They're not big on signposts around here.'

'Okay. Are you all right, Mum?' asked Jack.

'Yes, I'm fine, sweetheart. See you later.'

Up in my room, I took the family tree out of the file Katie had left for me. Taking it over to the bed, I studied the names on it. Even now, knowing that I wasn't blood-related to any of them, I realised that the dreadful legacy of war and loss that Nuala had passed down had radically altered the course of my life.

Then I thought of Tiggy; how she had said that even though it had been hard sometimes to come to terms with the journeys she and her sisters had taken into the past, it had changed their lives for the better. I only prayed it would be the same for me, because every instinct in my body told me the answers to the questions I had lay down here in West Cork.

If only I knew where *he* was, then . . .

The hotel phone rang by my bed and I picked it up.

'Hello?' I said tentatively, doing a mental tally of the people who knew I was here.

'Mary, my dear girl,' came Ambrose's clipped tones. 'How are you finding being back in your homeplace, as they say down there?'

'Grand altogether,' I said, smiling into the receiver. 'I've just been with Katie . . . oh Ambrose, it's been so wonderful to see her.'

'I'm happy for you, Mary. This call is simply to tell you I located the address you were after. And it was quite a surprise, let me tell you,' Ambrose chuckled. 'I posted your letter to him immediately. Let's see if he replies.'

'I . . . oh my goodness! Thank you, Ambrose, I can't believe you found him!'

'It's the least I can do for you, Mary. Do let me know when you are returning to Dublin.'

'Of course I will, Ambrose, and thank you. Bye.'

Putting the receiver down, my heart racing, I once again longed for Jock to be here beside me. But . . .

Why did you never tell him, Merry?

You saw him as second best, a safe haven . . .

In retrospect, I could see that I'd been too preoccupied hankering after a love I'd lost, a love that had been so passionate and exciting and forbidden that I truly believed there was nothing that could ever match up to it. And because it *had* been lost, I'd built it up into some grand *coup de foudre* . . .

I'd counselled and consoled both my children through their own various break-ups with people they'd believed were the love of their lives, but eventually they'd recovered and moved on.

When I'd been their age, no one had been there to counsel me – Ambrose had not been a person I could turn to on affairs of the heart. And as for Katie . . . I knew she and my family would never approve because of who he was. And because of what had subsequently happened, I'd had no 'closure', as the kids would say.

And all along there'd been Jock, who had loved me deeply and always protected me.

Now here I was, missing him so desperately that it physically hurt.

Well, I thought, the closure I'd always wanted might possibly be within my grasp . . .

Yet the truth was, it wasn't true love for *him* I'd discovered since I'd left New Zealand; it was for my husband.

45

'Any news from Ireland?' CeCe asked as Ally walked into the kitchen.

'No, nothing. Merry, Mary-Kate and Jack all have the Atlantis number and our various mobile numbers, so the ball is in their court.'

'But, Ally, you said we had to leave next Thursday morning at the latest to have any chance of getting down to Greece to lay Pa's wreath next Saturday. Which means they all need to be in Nice by the middle of next week to join us on the *Titan*. Can't we contact them?' CeCe urged.

'No,' Ally replied firmly. 'Tiggy said that there's things both Merry and Mary-Kate need to find out, and we shouldn't interfere.'

'To be honest, I think we probably have to accept that we're not going to have Mary-Kate with us,' Maia sighed.

'Besides, there's only one person who can confirm it's her and that's Pa. And he's dead.' CeCe looked up at her older sisters' faces and saw them cringe. 'Sorry, but he is, and this cruise is all about us saying goodbye to him properly. I mean, Chrissie and I really liked Mary-Kate; she was lovely and the right age to be the missing sister. But she – and her family –

659

never even knew him and . . . Hi, Ma,' CeCe said as she walked in.

'Hello, girls. I . . . oh dear, Claudia's been called away to visit a sick relative. Christian's taken her to Geneva on the speedboat. Which means we'll have to cope here domestically without her.'

'That shouldn't be a problem, Ma,' said Ally. 'We're all completely capable of cooking for ourselves these days.'

'I know, but with the others arriving, well, I don't know how I'll manage without her,' Ma admitted. 'It could not be worse timing. If all your partners come, there will be at least eleven of you, plus Bear, Valentina and Star's little Rory . . .'

'Really, Ma, we'll be fine.' Maia offered a chair to her. 'Sit down, please, you look very pale.'

'I feel it. I don't think any of you realise how much I – and this household – depend on Claudia.'

'Remember, most of the others will be joining us directly in Nice,' said Ally. 'I'm sure Claudia will be back by the time we're home at Atlantis after the cruise.'

'It'll be fun, Ma,' CeCe put in. 'We can have a rota on the fridge, like we had for the washing-up when we were kids.'

'Which you always managed to get out of, CeCe,' Maia teased her.

'She still does, don't worry,' remarked Chrissie.

'I think we should each take a night and make a dish from where we all live now,' suggested Maia.

'Which means we'll get a hot dog from Electra,' giggled Ally. 'See, Ma? It'll be fun. Anything you need us to do?'

'No, thank you, Ally. All the rooms have been prepared and are ready for the guests and Claudia said she'd left a salmon out for tonight.' Ma looked round at the four women. 'Does anyone know how to cook it?'

'I think that's my night on the rota,' Ally smiled. 'Fish is what you might call a Norwegian staple.'

'I just wanted you all to have a rest from your busy lives, be looked after here at home,' Ma sighed.

'Maybe it's you who should be taking a rest,' Maia replied, putting a hand on Ma's shoulder.

'Chrissie and I are going for a swim in the lake. Anyone want to come?' CeCe asked. 'Chrissie used to be a state champion!'

'I might take the Laser out and race you,' challenged Ally. 'But first, let me help you with the dishes, Maia.'

Alone in the kitchen, the two sisters fell naturally into the rhythm of washing and drying up.

'When does Floriano leave Rio with Valentina?' Ally asked.

'The day after tomorrow. It's ridiculous, I know, Ally, but I'm nervous about seeing him.'

'Why?'

'Because we discussed getting married and starting a family, but not, well, immediately. I'm not sure what he'll say. And then there's Valentina. She's been so used to having us to herself that she might not like the idea of a younger sibling.'

'Maia, I understand why you're nervous about telling Floriano, but I can't believe there are many seven-year-old girls who wouldn't love having a real-life baby to play with. I'm sure she'll love it.'

'You're right, Ally, and forgive me for worrying about this, when you couldn't share your pregnancy with Theo.'

'Don't apologise, I understand. Although as I admitted to you before, now all the partners are about to arrive, I wish I had one of my own . . . Someone in my corner, you know? I called Thom today to check on Felix – who is fine – but Thom definitely can't make the cruise. Anyway,' Ally said, changing

the subject, 'isn't Chrissie great? And she puts CeCe in her place when she needs to.'

'She does, and CeCe seems far more relaxed than she's ever been.'

'It's going to be quite a gathering, isn't it?' Ally smiled. 'Let's hope everyone gets on okay.'

'We've all got to accept that we won't get on with some of them as well as others, but that happens in all families. Pa would have loved to have seen us all here together. It's just so sad he won't be there.'

'Yes, but not wanting to go all Tiggy on you, he'll be there in spirit, I'm sure,' Ally comforted her.

46

Merry
West Cork

I had just started to stir awake when my room phone rang.
'Hello?'

'Merry, it's Katie. I haven't woken you, have I?'

'Yes, but that's all right. What is it?'

'I'm just about to go in to work for my shift, but I had a
couple of thoughts last night after we'd spoken. About Bobby,
and you wanting to find out what's happened to him. I still think
it's worth contacting his younger sister, Helen. When I saw her
at Nuala's funeral, she told me she'd moved to Cork. Noiro isn't
a common name, so you might find her in the telephone directory. Sure, you could ask reception – they're bound to have one.'

'Thanks, Katie.' I could hear my voice already wavering
with nerves at even the thought of it.

'Strikes me that you need to put this to bed now, Merry.
Let me know how you get on. Bye now.'

'Bye.'

Just after I'd finished dressing, there was a knock on my door.

'Who is it?' I barked.

'It's me, Jack.'

I opened the door and he came in, shaking his head.

'Honestly, Mum, who were you expecting, other than me, MK or housekeeping?'

'I'm sorry, I'm just a little paranoid at the moment.'

'You're telling me. Now listen, the sooner you explain what is spooking you, the better.'

'I will, Jack, I will. Are we going down for breakfast?'

'We are, but I just wanted to tell you something first. Last night, MK checked her emails and . . . well, she found one from her mum. I mean, this woman that—'

'I know what you mean, Jack, it's all right. I suppose you're here because she's worried about upsetting me?'

'Yes.'

'Right, I'll go and speak to her.'

I brushed past Jack and walked down the corridor to Mary-Kate's room.

'Hi, Mum,' she said, lowering her eyes as she opened the door to me.

'Jack's just told me your news. Come here,' I said as I stepped inside, then opened my arms to wrap them around her. When I finally pulled away from her, I could see her eyes were wet with tears.

'I just don't want to upset you, Mum. I mean, the only reason I decided to find out in the first place was because of the whole missing sister thing.'

'I know, sweetheart, and you absolutely do not need to feel guilty about it.'

'You mean, you don't mind?'

'I'd be lying if I said I wasn't apprehensive, but our relationship has always been special, and I have to trust that. Hearts are big spaces if you let them be. If your birth mum wants to be part of your life in the future, then I'm sure yours can make room for her in there too.'

My daughter's gaze finally met my eyes. 'Wow, Mum, you're amazing. Thank you.'

'Please don't thank me, Mary-Kate, you don't need to. Now then, what did this email say?'

'Do you want me to read it to you?'

'Why don't you just give me the general details?' I said as I walked over to a chair and sat down in it. Despite what my mouth was saying, I only hoped that my heart really could be as generous as I was telling my daughter it was. Jack stepped into the room, obviously having waited outside in the corridor until he could hear that our emotions had settled down. He sat down on the bed beside his sister, who had opened up her laptop to find the email.

'Well, her full name is Michelle MacNeish, and she's of Scottish heritage originally, like Dad. She lives in Christchurch and was seventeen when she got pregnant with me. The long and short of it is, she ignored it for the first few months and was too scared to tell her parents. At the time, she was about to go to uni because she wanted to train to be a doctor . . .' Mary-Kate consulted the email. 'She says, "I did tell my parents eventually, but because they are quite religious we had a massive showdown. In the end, they agreed to support me through university as long as I had the baby, then gave it up for adoption."

'She goes on to say that she didn't feel that she was equipped to have a child so young, especially as the dad – her boyfriend at the time – wasn't interested in having a family with her. They split up soon after and apparently my biological dad is married and works as the manager of a hardware store in Christchurch. Michelle's a fully fledged surgeon these days, Mum. She's also married with a couple of young kids.'

'So . . . how do you feel?'

'About the fact she gave me up? I'm not sure yet, but to be honest, if that had happened to me at seventeen, just when I

was on the verge of leaving home and going off to uni, I don't think I would have been too chuffed to find myself pregnant either. I guess I understand why she did it. At least she *had* me,' Mary-Kate shrugged, 'she could have got rid of me.'

'Yes, she could have, sweetheart, and thank God she didn't. Does she want to meet you?'

'She hasn't said. She just asked me if I'd like to email her back and tell her a little about myself. But she says there's no pressure or anything. I mean, if I don't want to.'

'Do you think you will write back?'

'Maybe, yeah. It might be interesting to meet up with her eventually, though I'm not, like, desperate or anything. But what that email also means is that I'm probably not the missing sister that CeCe and the other sisters were looking for. Michelle is definitely my biological mother and my biological father is local too. She says there are hospital records of my birth and everything. It makes me a bit sad, actually; I'd got into the idea of being part of that big family of adopted girls.'

'So, you're not blood-related to the sisters' adoptive father, even if they thought you might be. Of course, as you said before, it's possible this Pa Salt guy wanted to adopt you too, but Mum and Dad got there first,' Jack shrugged.

'You mean, perhaps Jock and I were approved by the agency and he wasn't?' I asked.

'Something like that, yeah,' said Jack, 'but who knows? And I'm getting to the point where I want to say, who cares? It's only relevant if this Pa Salt is a proper relative, isn't it?'

'True,' said Mary-Kate, biting her lip. 'And I suppose I do have new siblings now through Michelle . . . How weird.'

'It's okay to take all this slowly,' I said to her, 'and as a matter of fact,' I added, making a decision, 'I have something I need to tell you. About me, I mean. It's nothing to worry about, but after what you've just said, it's relevant. So why

don't we go and have some breakfast and I'll tell you while we eat?'

'Hold on a minute' – Mary-Kate's forkful of bacon and egg hung suspended between her plate and her mouth – 'you're telling me that you were dumped on a priest's doorstep as a newborn? And then this priest and a man called Ambrose gave you to their cleaner, whose baby had just died, to save you from life in an orphanage?'

'That's about the size of it, yes. I was only called Mary because the poor baby I'd replaced was too.'

'And they pretended that you were her,' Jack added.

'Which was a good thing actually, or Ambrose would have chosen some outrageous Greek name for me,' I chuckled.

'So, Mum, how are you coping with the fact that your family isn't your family, after all these years of thinking they were?' Mary-Kate asked.

I smiled inwardly, because it was the one area in which my daughter had far more experience than I did. And I'd taken a chance that sharing the fact I was also adopted might help her too.

'It was a shock at first,' I said. 'But a bit like you, when I met my brother and sister again after all these years, the blood bit didn't matter.'

'See, Mum?' said Mary-Kate. 'It doesn't, does it?'

'No, and especially because I have no idea – and nor does Ambrose or anyone else – who my biological family are.'

Mary-Kate gave a small chuckle, then wiped her mouth with her napkin. 'Sorry, Mum, I know it's not funny but, like, how the tables have suddenly turned. I now know where I came from, but can we help you find out who you really are?'

'At nearly fifty-nine, sweetheart, I think I know who I am. Genetics aren't important to me. Although looking back now, I knew that I was different. When I went away to boarding school and then university, everyone back in West Cork used to tease me about being the missing sister, not because of the Greek myth like Bobby, but because I wasn't at home anymore. And then I really was missing for thirty-seven years.'

'It's all a bit of a coincidence, isn't it?' countered Mary-Kate. 'I mean, this whole family that thinks I'm related to them in some way, but it's actually you who really *has* been the missing sister.'

'Yes,' I sighed, 'but for now, I suggest we forget all about them. Let's try and actually enjoy the three of us being down here in this lovely part of the world and getting to know my family again.'

'Will you tell your brothers and sisters, Mum?' asked Jack. 'About you being parachuted into their family?'

'No,' I said, with surprising certainty. 'I don't believe I will.'

The three of us spent the rest of the day driving along the coast, then enjoying a relaxed late lunch at Hayes Bar overlooking the almost Mediterranean-looking Glandore Bay. We returned through Castlefreke village, where the ruined castle stood in its dense forest, and I recounted the ghost stories my parents had told me about it. Taking the byroads along the coast, we found a tiny deserted cove near a village called Ardfield, and both my kids immediately put on their swimming gear and ran into the freezing cold sea.

'Come in, Mum! The water's fantastic!'

I shook my head lazily and lay on the pebbles looking up at the sun, which was so graciously making a rare appearance.

I'd never told my kids I couldn't swim and was hideously afraid of the ocean, like many Irish of my generation. But so much of what was then wasn't now, and after hundreds of years of stagnation, it seemed that Ireland was reinventing itself in every way. The mass poverty and deprivation I'd known when I was younger seemed to have lessened considerably. The Catholic Church – such a huge part of my upbringing – had lost its claw-like grip, and the hard border between the North and South had come down after the Good Friday Agreement was signed in 1998. The Agreement had even been voted for in a referendum across Ireland. And – mostly – it had held for ten years.

I picked up a pebble from beside me and, sitting up, clenched it in both hands. Whoever I really was, there was little doubt I'd been born here on this land. For better or worse, there was a big part of me that would always belong right here, on this beautiful but troubled island.

'I have to know what happened to him before I leave,' I muttered. Then I saw my children running towards me, so I collected their towels and walked to meet them.

Back at the Inchydoney Lodge, as the kids went off to find hot chocolates in the pub, I asked the receptionist if I could borrow a telephone directory. I took it over to one of the comfortable sofas and, with trembling hands, found the 'N's.

N-o . . . N-o-f . . . N-o-g . . . N-o-i . . .

My finger landed on the one and only 'Noiro' listed. And the initial was 'H'.

My heart beating fast now, I scribbled down the number and the address. 'Ballinhassig,' I said to myself, the name sounding familiar. Handing the telephone directory back to

the receptionist, I asked her if she knew where Ballinhassig was.

'Sure, 'tis a small village – well, not even a village really – this side of Cork airport. Here now.' The woman, whose name badge said she was called Jane, took a map of West Cork and pointed it out.

'Thanks so much.'

Then I went into the pub to join my children and have a cup of tea.

'MK and I were thinking we might go up to Cork City and look around tomorrow morning if that's okay with you, Mum,' said Jack. 'Fancy coming along?'

'Maybe. There's actually a friend I want to visit who lives near there. I'll give her a call, then I can drop you two in the city and go and see her. Okay?'

They both nodded and then we all went upstairs to our rooms to freshen up before dinner. Taking the piece of paper out of my handbag, I sat on my bed and laid it nervously by the phone. As I picked up the receiver to dial Helen Noiro's number, I could see my hands were shaking.

She probably won't even answer, I told myself. But a female voice did, after only two rings.

'Hello?'

'Oh, er, hello,' I replied, wishing I'd rehearsed what I was going to say. 'Is that Helen?'

'It is indeed. Who's speaking?'

'My name's Mary McDougal, but you might remember me as Merry O'Reilly. We used to live quite close to each other when we were younger.' There was a pause on the line before Helen answered.

'I do remember you, o'course. What can I be doing for you?'

'Well, I've been abroad for a long time and I'm looking

up . . . old friends. I'm coming up to the city tomorrow morning and I wondered if I could drop in?'

'Tomorrow morning . . . Hold on whilst I check something . . . Okay, I have to be out of the house by noon. How about eleven?'

'That sounds perfect.'

'Grand. If you're driving, it's easy to find; as you're coming down from Cork past the airport and into the village, look for the garage on the left-hand side. I'm the white bungalow next to it.'

'Okay, Helen, I will. Thanks for that, and see you tomorrow. Bye.'

I put down the receiver and scribbled the directions underneath the address. I didn't know what I'd been expecting, but it wasn't the casual reaction Helen had just given me.

Maybe she didn't even know what had gone on between me and her brother. Or maybe she did and thought I was just a girl from the past that Bobby had long since forgotten.

'Maybe he settled down and is married with a few kids,' I muttered to myself as I stood up, applied a little lipstick and left the room to go and have supper.

Having dropped the kids off in the centre of Cork the following morning, I headed back towards the airport. As we'd gone through the village of Ballinhassig on the way there, I'd glanced around and noticed the garage Helen had mentioned. It took no longer than twenty minutes before it came back into view.

There was a small, white-painted bungalow next door, and I pulled into the drive that had an attempt at a patch of garden to one side of it.

Switching off the engine, I suddenly wished someone was

with me. What if Bobby actually *lived* with his sister? What if he was inside this nondescript bungalow and would come for me, then hold a gun to my throat . . .

I sent up a quick prayer begging for protection, then opened the car door and walked to the front entrance. I tried the bell, but it didn't work, so I knocked instead. A few seconds later, a woman dressed in a smart navy-blue suit, her shiny dark hair cut into a bob and her make-up perfect, answered the door.

'Hi there, Merry . . . Everybody called you that in the old days, didn't they?' she said as she ushered me through the door.

'They did, yes, and still do.'

'Come through to the kitchen. Is it coffee or tea you'd be wanting?'

'A glass of water will do me fine,' I said as I sat down at a small table. The kitchen was as nondescript as the bungalow and not nearly as smart as its resident.

'So, what brings you to these parts after all this time?' Helen asked as she poured some coffee from a machine into a mug and came to sit down next to me, handing me a glass of tap water.

'I thought it was time I visited some friends and family. And, well . . .' I brought out the family tree that Katie had given me. I'd decided that the familial connection between us should be the initial pretext for my visit.

'Ah, don't tell me you've been living in America and wanted to come back to explore your roots? A good few tourists that pass through the duty-free shop are after that *craic*.'

'That's where you work?'

'It is indeed. I do all the promotions for them, like hand out tasters of whiskey or portions of a new local cheese we're selling,' she shrugged. 'I enjoy it and I'm after meeting some interesting people there too. So now, what have you to show me?'

'Maybe you already know this, but it looks like we shared the same grandparents.'

'Yes, my mammy told me before she died. She said that your mam and my dad were half-siblings.'

'They were.' I turned the tree around and pointed to Nuala and Christy's names. 'If you follow the tree, there's your daddy's parents and there's you. And Bobby.'

Helen's glossy nails traced a path down the tree.

'It means we're cousins. Mind you, 'tis hardly surprising, is it? Everyone in that area is a cousin of someone.'

'I only ever saw a glimpse of Nuala, my – *our* – grandmother, once. And that was on the day of my mother's funeral when I was eleven. Nuala and Hannah were estranged.'

'Oh, I know all about that. We saw a lot o' Granny Nuala when we were younger,' said Helen. 'She and Granddad Christy were always up at our cottage, singing the old Fenian songs. When he died, and then my daddy, Granny came to live with us. What a load o' chat she filled Bobby's head with,' she sighed. 'You remember those walks home from school.'

'I do,' I said, hardly believing we'd moved on to this topic so quickly.

'Would I be remembering right if I said that you were at Trinity College, while Bobby was at University College, in Dublin?'

'You would be,' I nodded.

'And wasn't he always sweet on you?'

'Yes,' I said, feeling like the mistress of understatement. 'Um, how is he?'

'Well, 'tis a bit of a story, but sure, you'd already be knowing that he got mixed up with the republican crowd at university?'

'I would, yes.'

'Jesus, the venom inside him and the stuff he used to come out with . . .' Helen gave me a direct gaze. 'Do you remember

how angry he got? He was so passionate about "the cause", as he called it.'

'Is he dead, Helen?' I asked, not able to bear the suspense any longer. 'You talk about him as though he's in the past.'

'No, he's not dead, or at least he hasn't left this earth. But to be honest, he might as well have done. I thought you were up in Dublin in the early seventies? Surely you'd have heard?'

'I left Ireland and went abroad in 1971. Bobby told me he was going on protests in Belfast with the northern Catholics. I even heard a story that he was shielding a Provisional IRA man on the run down in Dublin.'

Helen looked at me uncertainly, then sighed. 'Listen now, it isn't a subject I'd be wanting to talk about to just anyone, but seeing as you're family . . . Wait there.'

I did, because even if she told me to leave, I wouldn't have been able to. I felt weak all over, and though my body was still, I could feel the blood rushing through my veins.

'There now, read that,' she said as she returned and handed me a sheet of paper.

I saw it was a page photocopied from an old newspaper, dated March 1972.

UCD STUDENT JAILED FOR ARSON ON PROTESTANT HOUSE

Bobby Noiro, a twenty-two-year-old student of Irish Politics at UCD, has been sentenced to three years in jail for attempting to burn down a house in Drumcondra. Telling the court he was a member of the Provisional IRA, Mr Noiro pleaded guilty to arson. The house was unoccupied at the time.

During sentencing, Mr Noiro had to be restrained as he attempted to break free of the guards. During the struggle, he shouted IRA slogans and made threats against leading members of the Democratic Unionist Party, the DUP.

On sentencing him, Mr Justice Finton McNalley said that he was taking into account Noiro's youth and the fact that he may have been influenced by his peer group.

Judge McNalley also cited the fact that nobody was injured in the fire. The Provisional IRA has denied any part in the attack.

'Helen . . .' I looked up at her. 'I don't know what to say.'

'Does it surprise you?'

'If I'm honest, no. Was he released after his three years?'

'Well, when Mammy first went to visit him in prison, she came back in bits, crying buckets. Said Bobby had been ranting and raving, and the guards had had to take him away. "He's not well in the head, like your daddy," I remember her saying. And sure,' Helen sighed, 'he caused so much strife in the jail that they moved him to a high-security prison where he could be better controlled. When he was released, they tried to re-introduce him to society, but he accused one of the men at the halfway house of being a "bastard Proddy" and tried to strangle him. After that, he was assessed and diagnosed with paranoid schizophrenia. He was moved to the psychiatric hospital in Portlaoise in 1978. He's never come out,' she said grimly, 'and nor will he. After Mammy died, I went up to see him. I'm not sure he recognised me, Merry. He sat there and cried like a baby.'

'I . . . I'm so sorry, Helen.'

'Turns out the madness runs in the family. You won't be knowing this, but Cathal, our daddy, committed suicide; he set fire to our barn, then hung himself inside it. Mammy also told me that our Great-Uncle Colin – Christy's brother – was stone mad too, and ended up in an asylum. That's why Christy came to live on the farm after his mammy died of influenza and grew up with Nuala and her brothers and sisters.'

'Bobby told me your daddy had died in a barn fire, an

accident,' I breathed. 'Maybe that's what he was told by your mammy.'

'Yes, we both were, Merry, though I was just a babe when it happened. Did Bobby ever . . . how can I put this? Hurt or threaten you?'

'He did, yes,' I said, and the words came out of me like a boulder that had held back a river of emotion. 'He'd found out about . . . something I'd done that he didn't approve of. He had a gun, Helen, which he said had been given to him by the Provisional IRA. He put it to my throat . . . and . . . and said that if I carried on seeing this boy he didn't like, h-he'd have him and all my family sh-shot by the people he knew in his terrorist organisation.'

'And you believed him?'

'Of course I did, Helen! Back then, the Troubles were just beginning. Tension was running high in Dublin, and I knew how passionate Bobby was about the North being returned to the Republic of Ireland, and his anger at the way the Catholics were treated across the border. He'd joined one of the more radical student groups at UCD and was always asking me to go with him on his protests.'

'Merry, I think he must have used the old pistol that had belonged to Finn, our grandmother Nuala's first husband. She kept it and passed it on to our father, Cathal. When he committed suicide, it passed into Bobby's hands. So now, I suppose he wasn't lying to you if he said that it had been given to him by the IRA, but it certainly wasn't during the recent Troubles. 'Twas ninety years old, Merry, and I doubt Bobby knew how to load it, let alone fire it.'

'Are you sure, Helen? I swear he was involved with what was going on at that time.'

'As a student rebel, maybe, but no more. If he had been, the Provisional IRA would have taken great pride in announcing

they were responsible for the burning of that Protestant house in Dublin. When I came up to support Mammy during the trial, I met one of his friends from UCD. We went for a chat and Con told me that everyone who knew him had been worried about his mental state. He'd lost his girl; I'm realising now he might have meant you . . . ?'

'I . . . I think he probably did but, Helen, I was never "his girl". I mean, Bobby was a childhood friend,' I sighed, 'but everywhere I went, he seemed to be there. My friend Bridget used to call him my stalker.'

'That would be Bobby, all right,' said Helen. 'He'd have fixations and would have believed that you *were* his girl, and that he was part of the Provisional IRA. But it was all in his mind, Merry, and as the psychiatrists I've talked to since have told me, it was part of the delusions.'

'I never, ever gave him any kind of sign that I wanted to be with him in a romantic way, Helen, I swear,' I said, gulping back tears. 'But he wouldn't take no for an answer. And then when he found out about me and my boyfriend, *and* that he was a Protestant, he said he'd kill us and our families. So I left Ireland and went abroad. Ever since then, I've lived in fear, because he told me he and his friends would hunt me down wherever I tried to hide.'

'Leaving was probably the sensible thing to do,' Helen nodded. 'There was no doubt Bobby was a violent man when he was in the grip of one of his episodes. But as for his IRA terrorist friends hunting you down – 'twas all nonsense. His friend Con confirmed that. When the police interviewed one of the real Provisional IRA mob after the fire, he swore blind he'd never even heard of Bobby Noiro.' She took a sip of coffee, sympathy in her eyes. 'So you left, but what about your boyfriend? Him being Protestant and all – now that was like a red rag to a bull for Bobby.'

The boulder had settled back in my stomach again, and I could barely speak. 'We lost touch,' I managed, because that was a different story. 'I married someone else and was happy in New Zealand.'

'Ah, 'tis good you found a home and a husband, so,' said Helen. 'There now, Merry, you have every right to be upset,' she said, reaching out to put her hand over mine. ''Twas terrible what Bobby put you through,' she continued, 'but the signs were always there, weren't they? Like on all those walks home, he'd be racing like a mad thing across the field ahead of us, hide in the ditch, then as we passed by, spring out and shout, "Bang! You're dead!" 'Twas a childhood game that became a lifelong obsession, fuelled by our grandmother and all her talk of war. I don't often go to see him, but now Mammy's dead, 'tis me who gets the reports from the hospital. He still talks about the revolution, as if he's part of it . . .' She shut her eyes for a moment and I took a deep breath, simply glad to be with someone who understood exactly who the person that had haunted me for so long actually was.

'Did he harm you, Helen?'

'No, thanks be to God, he didn't, but I'd learnt from the cradle to be invisible. If he was in one of his tempers, I'd take myself off and hide. Mammy protected me too; what a terrible life she had, what with Daddy not right in the head, then her son. I do remember her saying . . .'

'What?'

'Well, how upset she'd been that your mam, Maggie, hadn't come to Daddy's funeral. He was her half-brother after all – Nuala's son with Christy. I'd reckon that was the reason we were never allowed to come near Cross Farm.'

'Family members not turning up for funerals has caused a lot of grief in our family,' I sighed.

'Listen now, Merry,' Helen said, 'I have to be off soon – my

shift at the airport starts at one – but would you be able to come back and see me? I'm happy to answer any more questions you might be thinking of, so.'

'That's very kind of you, Helen, and I can't thank you enough for being so open and honest with me.'

'What's there to lie about? All these years you've been living in fear, thinking that real terrorists were after you, and yes, Bobby *was* a threat to you then, but if only you'd known that a year later he got locked up and will stay that way for the rest of his life . . .'

'It would have made a huge difference.' I gave Helen a glimmer of a smile.

'I'd no idea he'd been after you, but I moved away up to Cork City after Mam died,' she said. 'I wanted to make a fresh start. You know how it is,' she added as we walked to the door.

'I do. So, you live here alone?' I asked.

'I do, so, and 'tis just fine by me. I've a way of picking the wrong fellow, but now I've my work, my girlfriends and my independence. You take care now, Merry, and give me a bell if you need anything.' She gave me a brief but firm hug.

'I will, and thanks a million, Helen.'

I walked to my car on wobbly legs and sat down heavily behind the steering wheel.

Bobby's securely behind bars, Merry. He can never hurt you again, I told myself. *He never* was *able to hurt you for all these years, and everything he told you was a product of his imagination . . .*

I steered the car out of the drive, then took the first lane I saw. Parking my car between two large fields, I climbed over the fence and walked fast and hard between grazing cows. Rain was threatening, and grey clouds were hanging low overhead, but I sat down on the rough grass and began to sob.

It's over, Merry, it's really over . . . He can't ever hurt you again. You're safe, you're safe . . .

It took me a long time to cry out all the tension, after holding it in for thirty-seven long years. I thought of all that had been lost because of it . . .

'And found,' I whispered, thinking of my beloved children and dear, dear Jock, who'd swept me up in his capable arms and put a blanket of security and love around me.

Looking at my watch, I saw it was almost one o'clock and I was late to meet the children for lunch. 'Children!' I muttered to myself as I brushed myself down and headed for the car. 'Jack's thirty-two, for goodness' sake!'

Deciding that he really was a big boy now and perfectly capable of getting them both back to the hotel in a taxi, I called him and said I had a migraine – which wasn't a lie as my head was thumping – and drove slowly back to Clonakilty. As I passed Bandon, I saw the turning to Timoleague, and on instinct I took it. There was somewhere I wanted to go.

I wended my way through the familiar streets and parked the car next to the church. It was a huge building for such a small village and there was something moving about the tiny stone-built Protestant church just below it and then the ruins of the Franciscan friary standing right out into the water.

'What suffering has come from the differences in how we worshipped our God,' I said out loud. Then I walked into the church where I had prayed and taken Mass every Sunday, and seen my mother lying in her coffin.

Walking down the aisle, I genuflected and curtseyed automatically at the altar, then turned to my right where a frame full of votive candles stood, their flames flickering in the draught creeping through the old windows. Whenever I'd come back from boarding school, I'd always been comforted by lighting one for my mother. Today I did the same, then

dropped some more cents into the box as I lit another one for Bobby.

I forgive you, Bobby Noiro, for all you put me through. I'm sorry for your continual suffering.

Then I lit one for Jock. He'd been a Protestant by birth, coming from a Scots Presbyterian background. We'd married at the Church of the Good Shepherd by Lake Tekapo, under the magnificent Mount Cook. It had been interdenominational, welcoming people of all faiths through its door. At the time, I could hardly believe such a thing existed, but the fact that it *did* had made the day even more wonderful. We'd invited a small group of friends and Jock's sweet and welcoming family, and the ceremony had been simple but beautiful. Afterwards, there'd been a drinks party on the Hermitage Hotel terrace, where we had first met and worked together.

I went to sit down on one of the pews, and bent my head in prayer.

'Dear God, give me the strength to no longer live in fear, and to be honest with my children . . .'

Eventually, I stepped out into the church graveyard, where generations of the family I'd believed was mine by birth had been buried. I went to my mother's grave and knelt down on the grass. I saw that a spray of wild flowers was arranged in a vase and presumed it was one of my sisters or brothers. Beside her was my father's grave, the stone less weathered.

'Mammy,' I whispered, 'I know everything you did for me, and how much you loved me, even though I wasn't your blood. I miss you.'

Wandering along the lines, I saw Hannah's and her husband Ryan's graves, then Nuala's. My grandmother had been interred alongside Christy and the rest of our clan, not with her beloved Finn up in Clogagh. I sent up a prayer, hoping that all of them rested in peace.

After meandering through the family graves, I looked for Father O'Brien's headstone, but couldn't find it. Eventually, I drove home, my mind feeling curiously empty. Maybe by allowing myself to acknowledge the trauma I had been through and its physical and mental effects on me over the decades, now I could finally begin to heal.

'No more secrets, Merry . . .' I said to myself as I arrived at the hotel, parked the car and walked inside. A note in my pigeonhole told me the children were already back from Cork. I went up to my room and downed a finger of whiskey. It was time. Summoning Mary-Kate and Jack to my room, I closed the door behind the three of us.

'What's up, Mum? You look very serious,' Jack queried as I indicated they should both sit down.

'I feel it. This morning I went to see somebody, and after I talked to her, I decided that, well, I needed to tell you a bit more about my past.'

'Whatever it is, Mum, don't worry, we'll understand. Won't we, Jacko?' said Mary-Kate.

'Course we will,' Jack smiled at me encouragingly. 'Come on then, Mum, get on with it.'

So I told them the story of Bobby Noiro, and about how he'd come up to uni in Dublin while I'd been at Trinity.

'Trinity was, and still is, a Protestant university, and University College was Catholic,' I explained. 'These days, of course, it hardly matters, but back then, when what the Irish have always called "the Troubles" were beginning, it mattered a lot. Especially to somebody like Bobby Noiro, who had grown up in a household with an intrinsic hatred for the British, and what he and many Irish republicans saw as the theft of Northern Ireland for their Protestant citizens. Catholics who ended up stuck across the border in the North often weren't well treated and were always last in line for new

housing and any jobs on offer.' I paused, struggling to simplify what was such a very big story. 'Anyway, I settled into university very well, and absolutely loved it – what with Ambrose teaching Classics there, and me studying the same subject, it was what you two would call a no-brainer for me to follow in his footsteps. However, Bobby didn't approve – I think I mentioned him to you when I was telling the story of my childhood in West Cork, Jack.'

'You did. He sounded like a really weird kid.'

I then told them what had happened in Dublin.

'All these years, I've lived in fear that he'd find me, or send his friends in the IRA to hunt me down. I know it sounds ridiculous, but he was terrifying,' I gulped. 'And as I told you, he was imprisoned for burning down a Protestant family's house. Well, that's why I left Ireland and ended up in New Zealand.'

Mary-Kate came and sat down next to me on the edge of the bed where I'd been perching and put her arm around me.

'It must have been terrible for you, thinking that he was after you for all these years, but it's all over now, Mum. He can never harm you again, can he?'

'No, he can't. Today is the first time I actually know that.'

'Why didn't you tell us any of this before?' asked Jack.

'Let's be honest, even if I had, would you have been interested in listening? Is any child ever really interested in hearing stories of their parents' past? I used to hate it when Bobby went on about the Irish revolution, singing those Fenian songs. My mum and dad never said anything about their past, because of the family rift.'

'What family rift?' asked Jack.

I was very tired now. 'It's a long story, which if you *are* interested, I'm happy to tell you one day. However, tomorrow morning, I'm packing both of you off to the Michael Collins Centre up at Castleview. At the very least, you can learn about

the local hero who originally released Ireland from the grip of the British.'

Mary-Kate rolled her eyes, which made me smile.

'See?' I said. 'You're not interested. But as he did have a big impact on my own upbringing and subsequent life, you'll just have to put up with it for a couple of hours.'

'Was this Michael Collins Bobby Noiro's hero?'

'As a matter of fact, Jack, quite the opposite. Anyway, let's get something to eat, shall we? I'm starving.'

When I returned to the room, I saw the message light was flashing on my phone. It was from Katie, just asking mc how I'd got on, trying to track down 'your friend', as she put it.

I dialled her mobile number and she answered on the second ring. 'Well?' she said.

'I'll tell you when I see you, but the good news is, that even though Bobby isn't dead, he's certainly never going to come after me again.'

'Then I'm so happy for you, Merry. You must feel quite a weight off your shoulders now.'

'Oh, I do, Katie, yes. Also, while you're on, I popped down to the church in Timoleague this afternoon and I was wandering round the family graves. Then I looked for Father O'Brien's, but I couldn't find him. Do you know what happened to him?'

'I do indeed, Merry. As a matter of fact, I saw him myself only this afternoon.'

'What?! How?'

'He lives at the old people's home in Clonakilty where I work. He never budged from his Timoleague parish, even though I know he was given offers of promotion. Anyway, he

finally decided that he was getting too long in the tooth to carry on, and he retired five years ago when he turned eighty. You'll be remembering that draughty old presbytery he lived in, so a year ago, despite protesting he could take care of himself and he wanted to die in his own bed, he was brought to us. Would you like to see him?'

'Oh, Katie, I'd love to see him! Is he . . . all there?'

'You mean, does he have all his marbles? He does, 'tis only his body that's after letting him down. Riddled with arthritis, he is, God bless him, from all those years o' living in that house, I shouldn't wonder. They've built a new one for the next priest, which is sheltered from that evil wind which rattled through the panes.'

'I'll come to visit him tomorrow morning then.'

'Grand job. I'm up at John and Sinéad's, baking for the family hooley on Sunday.'

'Katie, please, there's no need for everyone to go to a lot of trouble.'

''Tis no trouble. A family get-together is long overdue anyway, and there'll be plenty of room for all the kids to run around outside.'

'The forecast is for rain tomorrow.'

'Ah, sure it is, but 'twill be warm rain at least.'

'Oh, just before you go, I was wondering if I could invite Helen Noiro to the party. I mean, she is related to us and—'

''Tis a grand idea, Merry. Bye now. I need to go check on my pie.'

Going over to draw my curtains and seeing there was a puddle of water on the floor from the rain blown inside by the wind, I shut out the roar of the waves. In bed, I tried to file away everything that I'd learnt today, but I was so exhausted, I fell asleep immediately.

47

The old people's home was light and airy, even though that particular hospital smell of disinfectant lingered strongly in the air. I asked for Katie at reception and she bustled through, giving me a big smile and a hug.

'He's in the day room, and look now, I haven't said who his visitor is. I'd say he's in for a grand surprise. Ready?' she asked me as we stood outside the door.

'Ready.'

We threaded through the chairs occupied by elderly men and women who were chatting or playing board games with their visitors. Katie pointed to a man looking out of the window.

'See him there in the wheelchair? I've put him in the corner, so you two can have a little privacy.'

I studied Father O'Brien as I approached. He'd always been a handsome man, as my mammy and the rest of the young women used to whisper to each other. His thick head of dark hair had turned white and had receded somewhat, but he still had a good amount of it. The lines etched onto his face gave him an added air of gravitas.

'Father, here's your visitor,' Katie said, ushering me forward. 'You might remember her.'

Father O'Brien's still brilliant blue eyes gazed up at me and

slowly, the look in them altered from disinterest, to puzzlement, and then eventually to amazement.

'Merry O'Reilly? Is that you?' Then he shook his head as though he was dreaming. 'Sure, it can't be,' he muttered to himself, turning away from me.

'It *is* me, Father. I was Merry O'Reilly, but I'm now Mrs Merry McDougal.'

I squatted down so I could look up at him, just like I'd done when I was a little girl on the visits to his house that had meant so much to me. 'It really is me,' I smiled, taking his hands.

'Merry . . . Merry O'Reilly,' he whispered, and I felt his warm hands tighten on mine.

'I'll be leaving you now to chat,' said Katie.

Still clasping his hands, I stood up. 'I'm sorry if I've given you a start.'

'You've certainly got my heart beating faster than it has done for a while.' He smiled at me, dropped my hands and pointed to one of the plastic-covered easy chairs. 'Please, pull that chair closer to me and sit down.'

I did so, gulping back the tears as I felt his wonderful calm and secure essence wash over me. I realised it reminded me of the way Jock had made me feel: that I was totally safe in his presence.

'So, what brings you back to these parts after so long, Merry?'

'It was time to come home, Father.'

'Yes.'

He gazed at me, and in one glance, I felt as if he knew everything he needed to know about me. I supposed that he'd spent so long both contemplating and dealing with the human soul and its complex emotions that he could probably see into my mind.

'Unfinished business?' he said, confirming my theory.

'Yes. I'm so very happy to see you, Father. You look well.'

'I am very well, thank you.' He cast an arm around the room. 'Sadly, many of these dear people have no idea whether it's 1948 or 2008, so it doesn't always make for good conversation, but all my needs are taken care of,' he added quickly. 'And the staff here are wonderful.'

There was a long silence as both of us struggled to know what to say. I'd no idea whether I'd meant as much to him as he had always meant to me.

'Why didn't you ever come back, Merry? I know you were in Dublin, but often visited your family here. And then suddenly, you didn't.'

'No, I moved away, Father.'

'Where to?'

'New Zealand.'

'That *is* a long way away,' he nodded. 'Was it because you were in love?'

'Sort of, but it's a very long story.'

'The best ones usually are, and I've heard many of them in my confessional, I can tell you. But of course, I never would,' he said with a wink.

'From what Katie said, it's obvious you're very well loved around here, Father.'

'Thank you for saying that, and sure, I have plenty of company still coming to visit me here, but it's not my home. Ah well, I mustn't complain.'

'You're not, Father. I understand.'

'I've nowhere to put my books, you see, and I miss them. They were a love that both myself and my friend Ambrose shared. You remember him?'

He looked at me and my whole heart almost broke in two at the yearning in his eyes.

'I do, Father, yes. Where are your books?'

'In a storage facility in Cork. Never mind, I always have the good book at the ready if I need it.' He pointed to the low table between us and I recognised the small leather-bound copy of the Bible that he'd never been without. 'So, tell me, did you ever marry? Have children of your own?'

'I did, and they're both here with me. I've sent them off to visit the Michael Collins Centre. It's about time they learnt of their mother's history.'

'That man and what he did for Ireland were certainly part of yours, Merry. I was saddened to bury your grandmothers Nuala and Hannah. They both pleaded for God's forgiveness over their feud at the end. 'Tis a sad story.'

'It is. I only know of the rift between them since my sister Katie told me about it yesterday. I finally understand a lot of things,' I added, 'and I'm so glad I came back.' A tea trolley was being brought round and the echo in the room seemed to grow louder. I wanted to tell him I knew what he'd done for me all those years ago when I was a tiny baby left on his doorstep. But this was not the place or the time to bring up such a subject.

'How are you both doing?' The tea lady, with her jolly smile, had reached us. 'Tea or coffee for either of you?'

'Nothing for me, thank you. Father O'Brien?'

'Nothing, thank you.'

There was a pause as she wheeled the trolley away and we collected our thoughts.

'I'd love to meet your children,' he said.

'I'm sure that can be arranged, Father. I'd love you to meet them too. I—'

It was Katie's turn to bustle over. 'All good here?'

'Yes,' I said, wishing she would go away and give us some peace to continue the conversation I felt we both wanted to have.

'I'm sorry to interrupt but 'tis time for your physio session, Father,' she continued.

Father O'Brien's eyes filled with resignation. 'Of course,' he said. 'Can you come back another time, Merry? Bring your children?'

'Definitely.' I stood up and kissed him gently on the cheek. 'I'll be back, I promise.'

I collected the children outside the Michael Collins Centre.

'Wow, Mum,' Jack said as he buckled his seat belt and we drove off, 'I've learnt so much. I had no idea about the Easter Rising of 1916 that sparked the Irish revolution against the British. Ireland finally became a republic in 1949 – the year you were born! Did you know that?'

'I did, yes, but I wasn't old enough to take in its significance at the time.'

'I understand now why so many Irish people were angry back then,' Mary-Kate put in from the back. 'Jacko and I went halves on a book and we're both going to read it, aren't we?'

'We are. I didn't realise how much religion played a part in it all. We never even think about whether we're Protestant or Catholic, do we, MK?' said Jack. 'It doesn't matter in New Zealand.'

'Well, here there's still die-hard Catholics and Protestants on both sides,' I said.

'What's amazing is that everyone here seems so happy and friendly. You'd never know what the country's been through from the people you meet,' commented Mary-Kate. 'The suffering was so terrible – I saw the stuff about the potato famine and . . .'

I listened to my children chatting about my homeland and

the turmoil it had been through in the past. And suddenly felt an enormous pride in just how far it had come since I was born.

Back in my room at the hotel, I sat out on the balcony, having a cup of tea. A thought had come to me since my meeting with Father O'Brien.

The question is, is it really my place to interfere?

Then again, Merry, you've spent your life hiding behind your husband and your children, never making decisions for yourself . . .

'Come on, Merry,' I told myself out loud, '*do* something for a change.'

I walked inside, telling myself the worst that could happen was that he would say no. Picking up my mobile, I dialled the number.

The phone rang three or four times before it was answered. 'Ambrose Lister here. Who's speaking, please?'

'Ambrose, it's Merry. How are you?'

'Very well indeed, thank you. And you?'

'I'm fine, thanks. Ambrose. Actually, I was just wondering if you were busy in the next couple of days?'

'Mary, I'd be lying if I said my calendar was full, but Plato awaits, as he always does.'

'I was wondering if you would consider coming down to West Cork. I . . . well, I need your help.'

'West Cork? I don't think so, Mary, it's a long journey for these old bones.'

'I promise you, Ambrose, things have improved since the last time you drove down here in your bright red Beetle,' I smiled. 'It's motorway or dual carriage and certainly tarmac all the way. How about I book you a taxi? I have a man here who I'm sure would be delighted to come and get you.'

'Mary, I would rather not, I—'

'Ambrose, I *need* you. And we're staying at the most wonderful hotel overlooking Inchydoney Beach. You remember, the huge one near Clonakilty?'

'I do remember it, yes. And the shack that stood above it. I wouldn't say it looked terribly inviting.'

'Well, this hotel is modern, with every facility you could imagine. It would also give you a chance to meet my daughter before we go back to New Zealand. Please, Ambrose, there's a mystery I need solving and only you could possibly know the answer.'

I'd now run out of ammunition to persuade him. There was a pause on the line. 'Well, if you really need me to come all that way, I have to believe that it's for good reason. What time would this taxi collect me?'

'I still need to confirm it, but how about we say eleven o'clock tomorrow morning?'

'And I shall no doubt arrive in time for a cup of bedtime cocoa.'

'Nonsense, Ambrose. It'll take you three hours at the most, so I'd hope you'd be in time for afternoon tea, taken with a gorgeous view of the Atlantic. I shall book you a lovely room and look forward to seeing you tomorrow.'

'Very well, Mary. I will see you then. I have something to give you that arrived here only this morning. For now, I will say goodbye.'

Switching off my mobile, I threw it down on the bed and then gave a little whoop of triumph. There was a knock on my door and I went to open it.

'Hi, Mum, you look happy,' Mary-Kate said as she wandered inside.

'I feel it, actually. Or at least, I think I do,' I shrugged. 'I've just done something that I hope will make the lives of two people I love very much better. Anyway, are you okay?'

'Yeah, I'm good. Listen, Mum, I was just having a chat with Jack and . . .'

'What is it?'

'Well, we both feel we should let Tiggy and her sisters know that I've found my birth family. And it's unlikely that I'm the missing sister they're looking for.'

'You don't know that for sure, Mary-Kate. Your birth parents could have some connection to this dead father of theirs.'

'Maybe, but the point is, I feel I should at least give them the name of my birth mum. Then they can investigate themselves whether there's a connection. It's obvious they're desperate to find the missing sister so she can join them on their cruise. Would you mind if I gave them a call?'

'Of course not, sweetheart. It's your decision to make, not mine.'

'Okay, thanks. And . . .'

'What is it?' I asked. I could see she was about to broach a sensitive subject by the look in her eyes.

'Would you mind if I also told them that you were adopted too? I mean, Jack and I were saying that the emerald ring was yours originally and . . . Mum, the missing sister could be you.'

'I doubt it – those adopted girls are all a similar age to you and Jack. No.' I shook my head. 'I realise you'd like to have a connection to them, but unfortunately for you, I'm not it.'

'So you don't mind if I tell them you were adopted then?'

'Go ahead,' I sighed. 'It doesn't matter to me one way or the other. I'm sorry, sweetheart, but seeing they've managed to ruin my Grand Tour, in truth, I just want to forget all about them.'

'I understand, Mum, but thanks anyway. See you at dinner.'

Giving me an apologetic smile, Mary-Kate left my room.

48

Atlantis

'I have news,' said Ally, arriving on the terrace where Maia was serving up a Brazilian stew.

'What?' CeCe asked.

'That was Mary-Kate. She called to tell us that she's found her birth parents.'

'Wow, that *is* news,' whistled Chrissie.

'It is and it isn't, because obviously, until Mary-Kate has established proper contact with her mum, I don't think it's our place to start investigating her parents, and she won't do that until she's back home in New Zealand.'

'Which will be way after the cruise,' said Maia. 'Sit down, Ally, before the food gets cold. Maybe if we could get in contact with Georg, he'd at least be able to make some discreet enquiries.'

'I tried his mobile earlier and he's not picking up,' CeCe shrugged. 'Maia, this is delicious. Thanks, Ma,' she added as Ma poured wine into the women's glasses and then sat down herself.

'It is,' said Ally. 'There's also something else Mary-Kate told me.'

'What?' Maia asked.

'She told me that her mum, Merry, has just found out that she was adopted too.'

The entire table looked at her in total silence.

'How come?' said Maia. 'Tiggy said they were off to visit her long-lost family in the south-west of Ireland.'

'Mary-Kate didn't go into detail, but Merry was apparently found on a priest's doorstep and replaced a baby that had just died.'

'Right. Well, does that mean it could be her that's the missing sister?' CeCe asked.

'But she's old, isn't she? Far older than you guys anyway,' Chrissie pointed out.

'Be careful, Chrissie, Merry and I are only middle-aged these days,' Ma smiled.

'Sorry, but you know what I mean,' Chrissie blushed.

'Of course. But we must remember the ring was Merry's originally,' Ma added.

'You're right, Ma,' Ally breathed. 'So, do we have two possibilities for the missing sister now?'

'Maybe, but with two Marys, who have both owned the ring, we need to speak to Georg.' Maia took a sip of her water.

'So, do we hold to our invitation and have Merry and her two children on the cruise anyway?' Ally asked the table. 'I mean, if the ring is the proof – and Georg was adamant it *was* – one of them has got to be the missing sister.'

'I don't know,' Ma said softly. 'This is a very big occasion for all of you. And these women—'

'And Jack, Mary-Kate's brother,' put in Ally.

'Well, the three of them are strangers.'

There was silence around the table as the girls ate and thought.

'Ma's right,' said Maia eventually. 'We knew and loved Pa

so very much, and they didn't know him. It will be an emotional time for everyone.'

'Does that mean Chrissie and the other partners who didn't know him aren't welcome, then?' CeCe fired back.

'Don't be silly, CeCe, of course Chrissie is welcome, as are all the partners of you girls, and the children,' said Ma. 'There will be quite a crowd on board.'

'There's plenty of room at least,' said Ally. 'It's what the boat was made for, and the McDougals are only a short flight away. Personally, I'd like them to come.'

Maia studied Ally. 'Why don't we all think about it? Maybe call the other sisters tomorrow and see what they say?'

'Tiggy invited them all in Dublin and Star was definitely up for it when I last spoke to her,' said CeCe.

'So that only leaves Electra,' said Ally.

'Let's sleep on it, shall we?' suggested Maia.

CeCe and Chrissie followed Ma upstairs after supper, while Maia and Ally tackled the washing-up.

'What time does Floriano land tomorrow?' Ally asked her sister.

'He and Valentina will land in Lisbon tomorrow morning. As long as they make the connection to Geneva, which they should, Christian and I will pick them up from the airport after lunch.'

'Fancy a nightcap on the terrace?' Ally asked as Maia turned on the dishwasher. 'I think I'll have a small Armagnac – I have a taste for it since I came back from France. You?'

'Just water will be fine. I love it here in the evening,' Maia said as they sat down. 'It's always so calm and quiet and safe.'

'It was only a year ago that you were living here full-time. Look at you now.'

'I know. Ally, can I ask you something?'

'Of course you can.'

'This Jack . . . You got on well with him, didn't you?'

'I did. He was a genuinely nice guy. I mean, he's still single and in his thirties, so maybe there is something wrong with him.'

'Excuse me,' Maia reproached her. 'I am also approaching my mid-thirties and have only just found the one.'

'And I found mine and lost him.'

'I know . . . but at least you have Bear.'

'I do, and you know what's odd? I feel ashamed to tell you this, but . . . for some reason, even though I told Jack about losing Theo, I didn't say that I'd had his baby.'

'Right. Do you think maybe that's because – subconsciously, of course – you were worried that he might be put off by it?'

'Yup, and how awful is that?' Ally sighed.

'Not awful at all. It just meant that you *did* like him, that there was a connection.'

'Maybe there was. I've definitely thought about him a lot since, which makes me feel even more guilty, like I'm betraying Theo as well.'

'From everything you've said about him, Ally, I'm sure that Theo would want you to be happy. What happened was so terrible, but for both you and Bear, at some point you must take the decision to live again. Please, don't do what I did and make the mistake of shutting yourself and your heart off from love. I wasted years because of Zed, although I'm glad that I was here for Pa, at least.'

'Yes. It meant we could all go off and live our lives, knowing you were at Atlantis with him.'

'Ally?'

'Yes?'

'You would like it if the McDougals came on the cruise, wouldn't you?'

'Yes, though Jack will probably never speak to me again after he's found out I didn't come clean about who I was.'

'He's probably guessed already, after speaking to Tiggy,' Maia pointed out.

'Maybe,' Ally sighed. 'Anyway, I don't want to talk about it, to be honest.'

'Okay, I understand. I just wish that Georg were here to tell us which of the two Marys she is. It's just bad luck he isn't available to ask.'

'Well, he isn't, and you also have to remember that we're not in control of this situation – Mary-Kate and her mum are. Now, I'm going upstairs to try to get some sleep before my usual early morning call,' said Ally. 'Coming?'

'I'll be up in a minute.'

'Okay, night, Maia.'

Maia sat there a little longer, thinking of Floriano arriving tomorrow and how exactly she would tell him he was going to be a father again.

And where . . .

The thought carried her along the softly lit path to Pa's garden. She went and sat on the bench in front of the armillary sphere, and took a deep breath of the still warm summer air, scented with the roses that grew on the arbour all around her.

'Maybe here,' she whispered to herself. Standing up, she walked towards the sphere. Uplighters had been placed around its edges since she'd last been here, which meant it glowed against the darkness of the garden. She ran her fingers over the bands, then she stopped and leant down to see her own inscription.

'*Never let fear decide your destiny* . . . Oh Pa, you were so right,' she whispered. She was just about to walk away when something odd caught her eye. Leaning down again, she checked the name on the band and what was below it and gasped.

'*Mon Dieu!*'

Without pausing, Maia turned tail, ran as fast as she could into the house, then raced up the stairs to the attic floor.

'Ally! Are you asleep?' she panted as she knocked on her sister's bedroom door, then opened it.

'Nearly . . .'

'Sorry, Ally, but this is important.'

'Shhh . . . don't wake Bear. Let's go outside,' Ally whispered, collecting her hoody from the back of the door. 'What is it?'

'Ally, you've been here quite often in the past year. When did you last look at the armillary sphere?'

'Um . . . I don't know. I do sometimes take Bear to sit in Pa's garden, so maybe a couple of days ago?'

'I mean, looked at it really closely?'

'I don't understand what you're saying. Of course I've looked at it, but—'

'You have to come with me. Now.'

'Why?' asked Ally.

'Just come!'

Back downstairs, Maia collected a notepad and pen from beside the phone in the kitchen and the two of them ran towards Pa's garden.

'I hope this is worth only having two or three hours' sleep for,' Ally complained as Maia led her towards the armillary sphere.

'Look, Ally, look at Merope's band.'

Ally bent down to see what Maia was pointing at.

'Oh my God!' she said as she stood upright and gazed at her sister in shock. 'Someone's added a set of coordinates to it. But when?'

'I don't know, but more importantly, Ally, where in the world do they point to?'

'Pass me that pad and I'll write them down. My laptop's on the kitchen table. Let's go and see where they lead, shall we?'

Back in the kitchen, while Ally fired up the laptop, Maia paced up and down. 'Ma must know when that inscription was put there, Ally.'

'Surely if she did, she would have told us.'

'She must know far more than she's telling.'

'If she does, she's a very good actress. Ma's the most honest and straightforward person I know, so I'd be surprised if she is keeping anything back from us girls. She'd want to help us in any way she could. Okay, so . . . here we go.'

Maia stood behind her sister and watched as Google Earth did its miraculous thing.

'Oh, wow, how interesting, it's not gone to New Zealand, it's closing in on Europe, on the UK and . . . Ireland!' Maia gasped.

'And down in the south-west too, where the McDougals are now. It's closing in on what looks like a lot of farmland – oh! There we go. There's the house.' Ally picked up her pen. 'Argideen House, Inchybridge, West Cork,' she read. 'So.' Ally looked up at Maia. 'It looks like our missing sister is Irish and not a Kiwi, which means . . .'

'It's Merry. It's Mary-Kate's mother! She's our missing sister.'

49

Merry
West Cork

That evening, Niall drove us up to Cross Farm in his taxi so
we could all have a drink. As the taxi turned up the lane
towards the farmhouse, I could see that the drive was already
full of cars and a hubbub of laughter and conversation rang
out through the valley from the open windows. As Jack,
Mary-Kate and I stepped out of the car, John and Sinéad came
out to greet us.

'So now, I'll be back to pick you up later,' Niall said to us
with a wink before driving off. As we entered the kitchen, the
crowd in the room turned to look at us.

'Merry!' came a voice, and a plump woman with steel-grey
hair emerged from the crowd. 'Oh Merry, 'tis me, Ellen!'

'Hello,' I gulped as she engulfed me in her arms and hugged
me tightly.

She pulled back to look at me. 'You haven't changed a bit
and I've missed the sight of you,' she said with tears in her
eyes. 'Do you still giggle like a mad thing?'

'Yeah, she does,' Jack put in, and so followed a chaotic
round of introductions as Ellen and John guided us round the

party. I was speechless to see my baby brothers Bill and Patrick grown into tall, burly men, like my father had once been, their dark hair now greying. Katie waved at me from where she was putting the finishing touches to a table groaning with food; the sights and smells of home-cooked cakes and bottles of stout, sparkling wine and whiskey laid out in a corner of the kitchen sent me falling back in time to my sixth birthday party.

'. . . And this is little Maeve, my first granddaughter,' said a red-headed woman called Maggie, holding a toddler in her arms. 'I'm Ellen's eldest daughter.'

Maeve reached out to grab a strand of my hair, and I giggled at the sweet child with green eyes so like my mother's.

'I remember when you were little, Maggie,' I said to my niece. 'And here you are, a grandmother!'

'I remember you too, Auntie Merry,' she smiled at me. 'I can't tell you how delighted Mam was when Uncle John rang to tell her you were back.'

A glass of whiskey was pressed into my hand, and I was introduced to so many children and grandchildren of my brothers and sisters that I gave up trying to work out who was whose.

I found my own children in the New Room, where Jack was chatting to a crowd about rugby, while Mary-Kate was talking to a handsome young man.

'Mum,' she called to me, 'this is Eoin, who's your brother Pat's son.'

'Will you be joining us in a song, Mrs McDougal?' he smiled at me, taking his fiddle out of its case.

'Please, call me Merry. It's been a long time since I've sung the old songs, but perhaps after a few drops of whiskey,' I said.

Bill came up to me, his face already flushed pink from the drink, and flourished his mobile phone at me.

'Merry, 'tis Nora! She's on the phone from Canada!'

I pressed the phone to my ear and immediately removed it when I heard a familiar high-pitched shriek of excitement, as if Nora was trying to shout across the Atlantic Ocean.

'Hello there, you eejit! Where have you been all these years?' she cried.

'Ah Nora, it's a long story. How are you?'

I let her chatter wash over me, as Eoin struck up a tune on his fiddle. More people gathered in the room, their feet stamping and hands clapping along. My little brother Pat pushed his two young granddaughters into the centre of the circle, and they began to dance, their identical curls bouncing as their legs performed intricate steps and hops.

'Oh my God, Mum, that's just like *Riverdance*!' Mary-Kate smiled. 'Aren't they sweet?'

'We never had the money to go and learn properly, but be glad I never sent you to Irish dancing lessons, it's brutal,' I giggled.

John offered me his hand and led me into a dance, and I was surprised as muscle memory took over and I remembered all the steps. Ellen and her husband were dancing beside us, and with a hop, we switched partners.

'Ah, 'tis the song they played at our wedding,' said Ellen's husband Emmet. 'You were only a slip of a thing back then.'

As invisible hands poured drops of whiskey into my glass, the dancing, singing and laughter went on, and my heart felt fit to burst with happiness, surrounded by my family and my own children in the house that I had grown up in, the music of my homeland thumping in my veins. And knowing at last that I was free from the man who had haunted me for thirty-seven years . . .

Later, needing some air, I pushed through the crowded rooms and made my way out of the kitchen door. Facing me across the courtyard was the old farmhouse where I'd lived

up until the age of five, and where I now knew Nuala and her family had lived before us. The barn next door to it had obviously been recently rebuilt, but the sound of young calves still emanated from within it.

'What troubles this place has seen,' I whispered to myself as I wandered across to the side of the courtyard, beyond which we used to hang the washing every day. Now the area had been lawned and turned into a garden, with flower beds and a thick fuchsia hedge growing along one side to give shelter from the winds that swept along the valley. There were some children playing on the swings and slide in one corner, and I sat down in one of the ageing wooden chairs placed around a table. The view down the valley towards the river was quite beautiful, not that I'd ever fully appreciated it as a child.

'Hello there, Merry. Mind if I join you?'

I turned around to see Helen, looking as immaculate as the last time I'd seen her.

'Of course not, Helen. Sit down.'

'Thank you so much for inviting me tonight. Everyone's been so welcoming, treating me like a long-lost relative.'

'You *are* a long-lost relative,' I chuckled.

'I know, but 'tis still strange that we lived not far away from you, went to school together, and yet I've never set foot in this house before tonight. Mammy would have strung me up if I had.'

'I don't think it's possible for us to begin to know what our ancestors went through,' I sighed.

''Tis only sad that no one talked of it much outside their own families, because they were too frightened. Some of them wrote about it when they were older, or made deathbed confessions, but 'tis important for the young to know what their forefathers *and* mothers did for them and understand how long-held family grudges began.'

'I agree. I wonder what Hannah and Nuala would think if they could see us sitting here right now?' I said. 'In an Ireland that feels to me as if it's being modernised by the day. I was only reading this morning that there's been a move to legalise gay marriage.'

'I know! Jesus, who'd have thought it? I'm hoping Hannah and Nuala are sitting up there together and feeling proud of what they began. 'Twas the start of a revolution in all sorts of ways.'

'Helen? Can I ask you a question?'

'O'course, Merry. Ask away.'

'I was wondering why you've never had children.'

'Apart from never finding the right fellow, you mean?' she chuckled. 'I'll let you in on a little secret: after I researched the mental illness that ran through my family, I've discovered there's a genetic component that mostly affects the male line. So I'm glad I never did have children. The Noiro line will die out with me, and I'd have no regrets about that. Sure, 'twasn't Bobby or my Daddy or our Great-Uncle Colin's fault, but 'tis better to let the genes die with them.' Helen gave a sad sigh. 'Anyway, I'd better be off now, so. I've an early shift at the airport tomorrow morning. Nothing like the smell of whiskey at seven a.m. to turn your stomach.' She raised an eyebrow. 'But 'tis amazing the amount of people who'll take a free sample. Can we keep in touch, Merry?'

'I'd love to,' I said, as she put her arms around me. 'If you ever fancy a trip to New Zealand, I'd be so happy to have you visit.'

'Well now, being young, free and single and all, I might take you up on that. Bye, Merry.'

'Bye, Helen.'

I watched her wander off towards her car and thought how I'd never have believed before a couple of days ago that

communication, let alone a warmth and potential future friendship, could be established with Bobby Noiro's younger sister. She'd said little about what she'd suffered because of him, and that made me warm to her even more. She was made of strong stuff – and I needed to take a leaf out of her book.

I heard a rousing round of applause as everyone cheered and stamped for my brother John to play his fiddle – the one that had once belonged to Daniel, the proud Fenian and the great-grandfather Helen and I shared – and I went inside to join the party.

I woke up the following morning with a thick head, which was all of my own making. I only hoped Niall had made it up in time to go and collect Ambrose from Dublin, because it had been past two in the morning when he'd picked us up from Cross Farm.

After a cup of tea and a hot shower, plus a couple of para-cetamol, I called Katie on her mobile, wondering how on earth she was at work this morning. She answered after a few rings.

'Hi there, Merry, 'tis all organised this end. I'll be bringing him over to the hotel at two p.m. He's very excited about meeting your kids.'

'Perfect, I'll speak to you later.'

As I ended the call, I saw I had a missed one, as well as a voicemail. Pressing the right buttons to retrieve it, I sat down on the bed to listen.

'*Hi, Merry, it's Ally D'Aplièse here. You met my sister Tiggy in Dublin, and she gave us your number. Could you possibly call us on the home number at Atlantis? You've probably got it already, but if you haven't . . .*'

I *did* have it already, so I didn't worry about writing it down.

'*There's some new information that's just come to light, so*

call us as soon as you can. Thanks, Merry, and I hope you're okay. Bye.'

My mobile then rang again. I saw it was Niall the taxi driver, and answered it immediately.

'Hello?'

'The cargo's on board and ETA is around two fifteen.'

'Thanks, Niall. See you then.'

I sat there, debating whether to phone the Atlantis number back before deciding not to. Just now, I had more important things to think about than any tenuous connection to some strange dead man and his adopted daughters.

There was a knock on the door.

'Hello, Jack, how are you feeling?' I smiled as my son came into the room.

'I'm upright, so that's something,' he said. 'That was quite a piss-up last night. The Irish sure know how to enjoy themselves. Maybe a fry-up would help.'

My own stomach turned at the thought. 'Maybe. Have you heard from Mary-Kate?'

'Not yet. She was in a worse state than I was. Even you were a bit tipsy, Mum,' he grinned.

'I admit that I did knock it back a bit.'

'Well, it was great to see you relax and laugh like you used to when Dad was alive. Besides, it's known across the world that the Irish can drink, so we couldn't really leave without participating, could we? Right, I'm off down to brekkie. You coming?'

I nodded and Jack led the way.

After some coffee, toast and jam, I felt better. It was a sunny day again and Jack decided that an hour on the waves would clear out any cobwebs.

Back upstairs and seeing the time, I called Mary-Kate's room.

''Lo?' said a muffled voice.

'It's Mum, and it's almost noon, sweetheart. Time to get up.'

'Mmph . . . Not feeling well.'

'Okay, well, sleep a bit longer and I'll give you a call in an hour. Remember, my friend Ambrose is arriving this afternoon, and I don't want him to meet my daughter for the first time with a hangover.'

''Kay, Mum. Bye.'

'I only hope I've done the right thing,' I muttered as I took myself off for a walk across the dunes.

At two on the dot, Katie's car drew up in front of the hotel.

'Right, Father O'Brien is here,' I said to my children as we stood up from the sofas in the reception.

'I thought it was Ambrose we were meeting?' Mary-Kate queried.

'It is, but Father O'Brien was a big part of my childhood too. I'll go and help him inside.'

I hurried outside and saw Katie unfolding the wheelchair from the boot.

'Hello there, Father, isn't it a beautiful day?' I said as I opened the front passenger door.

'It is indeed,' he answered.

I watched Katie expertly manoeuvre him out of the car and into the chair. She wheeled him into the hotel as I walked alongside him.

'Remind me of the names of your children?' he said.

'Jack and Mary-Kate. I'm afraid they're not feeling too well this morning. My brother John and his wife threw a party up at Cross Farm, so we could meet up with everyone again.'

'And sure, a good time was had by all?' Father O'Brien chuckled.

'Exactly. They're over there,' I pointed as we wheeled him over.

'Hello there, I hear you've been given a baptism in how to enjoy yourself the Irish way. I'm Father O'Brien and 'tis a pleasure to meet you. You're the image of your mother,' he added to Mary-Kate.

'Thank you.' My daughter threw me a look and I gave her a slight shake of my head. There was no reason for him to know just now.

'Why don't we go up to my room and I can order some tea up there?' I said. 'It's a bit more private, isn't it, Father?'

'Ah, I'm just as happy down here, Merry. Please don't go to any bother.'

'It's no bother. You go with Katie and we'll follow.'

I handed Katie my key card, then she pushed Father O'Brien into the lift. As the doors shut behind them, my mobile rang.

'Hello there, it's Niall. We're just approaching the hotel. Will I bring your man into the lobby?'

'Yes, perfect timing. I'll meet you there. Kids, go up and chat to Father O'Brien and order some tea. Don't say a word about Ambrose arriving, okay?'

'Okay, Mum,' Jack shrugged as the two of them took the stairs.

Hurrying towards the lobby, I saw Ambrose being escorted through the entrance by Niall. He looked his usual dapper self in a checked jacket, pressed twill trousers and shiny black brogues.

'Here he is, Merry, safely transported from Dublin. There now, it wasn't as bad after all, was it, Mr Lister?'

'No, although it's still an awfully long way,' said Ambrose. 'How much do I owe you for the ride?'

'It's all taken care of,' I said as I slipped Niall a wad of euros. 'I'll let you know when he's returning.'

'Grand job. We'd a good chat on the way, didn't we?' Niall smiled as he headed off. 'I'll be seeing ye.'

'I'd query the fact we had a good chat. That would take two of us, after all, and I hardly got a word in edgeways,' muttered Ambrose.

'You must be exhausted,' I said as I linked my arm through his.

'What I could do with more than anything else is a nice cup of tea. It is that time of day, after all.'

'That's perfect then,' I said as we stepped into the lift and I pressed the button to take us upwards. 'I've just ordered some to my room. Jack and Mary-Kate are up there too.'

'Well, even if you have dragged me halfway across Ireland, it will be a pleasure to see Jack again and to meet Mary-Kate.'

'What do you think of this hotel?' I asked him as we emerged onto the second floor and walked slowly along the corridor towards my room.

'It's certainly a step up from the shack that used to be here,' he agreed as we came to a halt in front of my door.

Feeling breathless with nerves, I knocked and waited for Jack to open it.

'Hi, Mum. Hi, Ambrose. It's good to see you again. We're just pouring the tea to take out onto the balcony.'

'Perfect,' I nodded at him.

Katie gave me a nod and I saw that Father O'Brien's wheel-chair was on the balcony, partly concealed behind the curtain at the window.

'This is my sister Katie, and my daughter, Mary-Kate,' I said to Ambrose. They all said hello, and then Katie looked at me for instructions.

'Now, Ambrose, why don't you come and sit outside? We'll bring your tea out to you.'

'I might as well make the most of the sea air before it starts bucketing down with rain, which is what it usually does here,' he commented as he refused my arm and walked with his stick towards the open glass door. I followed him, not wanting him to trip on the ridge between the room and the balcony, and held my breath as he stepped across it. I watched as he turned towards the man sitting in the wheelchair.

Both men stared at each other for some time, and from my vantage point hidden behind the curtain, I could see Father O'Brien's eyes filling with tears. Ambrose took a step closer, as if his already compromised sight was playing tricks on him.

'Ambrose? Is that really you? I . . .'

Ambrose staggered a little and caught hold of the back of the chair in front of him.

'It is, indeed. Dear James . . . I can hardly believe it! My friend, my dear, dear friend . . .'

Ambrose held out his hand across the little table. Father O'Brien raised his to meet it.

'What's going on, Mum?' Mary-Kate whispered. 'Do they want some tea?'

'I'll take it out to them, and then I think we should leave them alone. They have a lot to catch up on.'

Armed with two teacups, I stepped out onto the balcony and placed one in front of each man. They were still grasping each other's hands, so lost in a lifetime of memories that they didn't even notice me.

I stepped quietly back inside and ushered my children and Katie out of the room.

'Are they okay?' Katie asked an hour later as I joined her back in the lounge downstairs, having discreetly checked on the two men.

'They seem fine. I asked them if they wanted anything and they said no. Where are the kids?'

'In their rooms. I think they're still getting over the hooley last night,' she smiled. 'So, why did Ambrose and the father's friendship end all those years ago?'

'Do you remember that old battleaxe of a housekeeper called Mrs Cavanagh, who used to work for Father O'Brien?'

'How could I forget her?' Katie rolled her eyes. 'A fierce old witch she was, for sure.'

'She threatened Ambrose with the fact that she'd seen them hugging just after Ambrose's father died. Father O'Brien was simply consoling his beloved friend after his loss, but she said she was going to tell Father O'Brien's bishop of their "inappropriate behaviour".'

'So the old bat was twisting it into something more than it was?'

'Exactly,' I sighed. 'Ambrose had no choice but to walk away. He knew any sniff of scandal like that would end Father O'Brien's career. I believe it broke Ambrose's heart, Katie; every time he was there at the presbytery, the two of them would talk for hours, mostly arguing about the existence of God. Ambrose is an atheist, you see.'

'Do you think that, well, there *was* anything inappropriate going on?'

'No, I don't. Absolutely, categorically not. I know that you've never liked him, but Ambrose always knew and respected that the love of Father O'Brien's life was God. And he could never compete. Who could?' I shrugged.

'Well, whatever I feel about Ambrose, 'tis a beautiful thing you've done, Merry, bringing the two of them back together.

'Tis hardly much of a life for the father up at the old people's home, that's for sure. Now then, I'll be having to take our fellow back before they call the guards out for him. I hate to break them up, but . . .'

'Of course,' I agreed. 'I'm sure that Ambrose will stay on down here longer now he knows why I asked him to come in the first place.'

Upstairs, we both crept into the room, feeling almost as if we were voyeurs. I was only relieved to hear laughter coming from the balcony.

I stepped out onto it and looked down at both at them.

'Have you had a good catch-up?' I asked.

'We have indeed, Merry,' said Ambrose, 'and may I say that you're a very naughty girl, bringing me here under false pretences. My poor old heart almost stopped when I saw James here.'

'Well, you'll just have to forgive me, won't you? Now, Father, I hate to break up the party, but it's time for Katie to take you back home.'

'I'd hardly be calling it home,' Father O'Brien shrugged sadly.

'You'll be here tomorrow, won't you, Ambrose?' I asked him. 'He wasn't sure whether he actually wanted to stay down here overnight,' I said as an aside to Father O'Brien.

'As we've only reached 1985 so far, I rather feel I must,' said Ambrose. 'What time are visiting hours?' he asked as he stood up and stepped back to make room for Katie to wheel Father O'Brien inside.

'For the father, any time you please,' said Katie with a smile.

'Until tomorrow then, dear James,' said Ambrose, stepping into the room. 'Until tomorrow.'

The look in Ambrose's eyes as Katie wheeled Father O'Brien out of the door brought a lump to my throat.

'Good grief! Well, that certainly got the blood racing around my old veins,' he murmured. 'I feel quite wrung out.'

'You must be hungry, Ambrose. Shall I order you something?'

'First of all, Mary dear, please escort me to the nearest facility. I haven't used the bathroom since we stopped off in Cork three hours ago!'

Having taken Ambrose to his room, he opened his Gladstone bag – a relic I remembered from his days with Father O'Brien – and pulled out a letter.

'This is yours, I believe,' he smiled, as he handed it to me.

I looked down at the writing, feeling I should recognise it, but I didn't. Why should I? There had been no need for correspondence between us all those years ago.

'Thank you. Why don't you have a lie-down and call me on my room phone when you want to have supper?'

'I will. Thank you, my dear, for what you did today.'

'Ambrose, it was a pleasure.'

Back in my own room, I put the letter to one side and sat on the balcony to check my mobile. Three voicemails had been left for me.

I listened to them, finding they were all from Ally D'Aplièse, and urging me to call her back. With a sigh, I found the Atlantis number and did so; after all the anticipation and emotion of the afternoon, I really wasn't in the mood for any further drama.

'Allô? C'est Atlantis.'

The unfamiliar voice speaking French threw me for a second and I hunted around my brain for the words I needed to reply, as I hadn't used French for so very long. In the end I gave up.

'Hello, this is Mrs Merry McDougal here. I've had a message from Ally D'Aplièse to call this number.'

'Ah! Of course!' the woman replied immediately in English. 'It is a pleasure to speak to you, Mrs McDougal. My name is Marina and I have looked after all the girls since they were small. I shall just go and find Ally for you.'

As I waited, I could hear the sound of a baby crying in the background, and wondered whose it was. At the same time, there was a knock on my door. I ran to open it and saw Jack standing there with his mobile phone in his hand.

'Mum, I've just had a text from Ally. She's desperate to get in touch with you,' he said as I sped back to pick up the receiver.

'Hello?' said a voice at the other end. 'Is anyone there?'

'Yes, sorry about that, Ally. It's Merry here. I got your messages and Jack's just come in to tell me you sent him a text too.'

'Yes, I did. I'm so sorry if you feel hounded, but we didn't want you to leave West Cork before we'd spoken to you.'

'Oh, why would that be?'

'Because, to cut a long story short, some information has just turned up that we wanted you to know about.'

'What is it?'

'Well, it sounds a little strange, but each of us were given a set of coordinates telling us where we'd originally come from, so we could go back and trace our biological roots if we wanted to. All ours have been accurate so far. Last night, we found the missing sister's coordinates, and they pinpoint a place in Ireland. So, we believe it must be you rather than Mary-Kate who they refer to. Shall I confirm with you where they lead to?'

'Go on then,' I sighed, 'surprise me.'

'Mum!' Jack frowned at the cynicism in my voice.

'Well, it's in an area called West Cork. I'm not sure where exactly you are at the moment, because I know the region

covers a large area, but the address the coordinates lead to is called Argideen House, near the village of Timoleague. Does that mean anything to you?'

I gulped in astonishment and sat down abruptly on the bed. How *could* she know?

Eventually, I found my voice. 'I . . . yes it does. My family home here was originally part of the Argideen estate, so maybe that's what the coordinates point to.'

'We can see on Google Maps that the Argideen estate still covers a few hundred acres, but the coordinates we have point specifically to Argideen House,' Ally replied.

'Right. Okay.' For some ridiculous reason, I wrote 'Argideen House' down on the pad next to the phone, as if I might forget it. 'Well, thank you for telling me. I'm sorry I haven't got back to you sooner, but it's been a very busy day. Goodbye.'

I shuddered suddenly, hating the thought of this unknown, dead man telling his adopted daughters the whereabouts of *my* birthplace.

'Mum, what is it?' Jack stared at me.

'They've had some new information and apparently they know where I was born. How do they know? How *can* they know, when even I don't?'

'I dunno, but where is it then?'

'It's very near here actually, only a couple of miles from where we were last night – the farm where I was brought up. Which means they could have made a mistake with the coordinates, as I told her.'

'What's the name of the place?'

'It's called Argideen House, but in my day it was always known as the "Big House". My grandmother Nuala worked there for the rich Protestant family who owned it during the revolution. And actually' – I frowned and cast my mind back – 'so did Nora, my older sister, for a while when I was young.'

'I suppose it makes sense that it's local, doesn't it? I mean, is this house close to Father O'Brien's house in Tim . . .' Jack looked to me for help.

'Timoleague. Yes, it is. Very.'

'Who lives at Argideen House now?'

'I've absolutely no idea. And do you know what, Jack? After this afternoon and last night, I feel too exhausted to even think about it.'

'Of course, Mum.' Jack came to sit on the bed next to me and put his arm around me. 'All this has been really hard on you. We can talk about it tomorrow maybe. But whether or not you decide you want to have anything to do with Ally and her gang in the future, surely for your own benefit, while you're here, it might be interesting to find out a bit more about this Argideen House?'

'Maybe,' I sighed. 'I feel awful now for being rude to Ally. Could you speak to her and apologise, say I've had a long day, or something?'

'O'course, Mum. And you've had a helluva time in the past few weeks. I'll explain that to her, don't worry. I guess you're not up to eating downstairs tonight?'

'No, and the good news is that this is one of the only hotels I've stayed at where the room service menu has sensible things on it, like toast and homemade jam. I'll give Ambrose a call and see if he wants any company tonight, but I somehow doubt it. It's been a very big day for him.'

'Yeah, and you made it all possible.' Jack hugged me. 'You just take it easy, okay? Give me a call if you need anything, but otherwise, I'll see you in the morning. Love you, Mum.'

'Thanks, Jack, love you too.'

As the door closed behind him, I found myself on the verge of tears again.

Simply because I felt so lucky to have given birth to such a wonderful human being. 'Now all he needs is the love of a good woman,' I muttered as I went to start the bath running. But for now at least, I was glad to have him by my side.

Having taken a bath, I called Ambrose, who said that he felt too exhausted to do anything more than have some sandwiches in his room, so I ordered a platter for him, and toast and jam for me. Then I switched the television on and watched a bad Irish soap in an attempt to turn off my brain.

However, it didn't work, and as I slid under the duvet, I couldn't shake off what Ally had told me:

Argideen House . . .

Countless times on my cycle rides to Timoleague and walking home from school, we'd gone past the never-ending stone wall that cut the Big House and its residents off from the rest of us. I'd never seen the house myself; the chimneys were only visible in winter when the trees that shrouded its perimeter had shed their leaves. I knew my brothers had often climbed over the wall, looking for the apples and figs that grew there plentifully in the autumn.

Then I suddenly remembered the letter Ambrose had handed me was still sitting in my bedside drawer, as yet unopened.

Why are you so frightened? He loved you . . .

Yet, the whole point was that maybe he hadn't, and I'd spent thirty-seven years picturing a thousand versions of a tragic love story that never was . . .

'Just open it, you silly woman!' I told myself, as I sat up and opened the drawer next to me. Tearing the envelope open, I took a deep breath and read the letter inside.

He had responded in the same guarded way I had written to *him*. Except he had included a telephone number.

Please do call me with a suitable date and time for us to meet up.

I stuffed the letter back inside the drawer, lay down and switched off the light.

But sleep wouldn't come, and why should it? I'd just had contact with the man who had haunted both my dreams and my nightmares for so long.

Then a thought made me giggle out loud. Wouldn't it be the most ironic thing if I, brought up in a staunch Catholic family, whose life had been under threat because I'd fallen in love with a Protestant boy, had been born into a Protestant house myself?

With that thought, I finally fell asleep.

'Would you kindly give me a lift up to this old people's home where James lives?' Ambrose asked us over breakfast the next morning.

'Of course we will,' I said.

'I must admit, I've rather a phobia of such places,' he said with a shudder. 'Dear James did say – in confidence, of course – that half the residents are often chatting away to him as if they are still living in the 1950s. At the very least, both of us have our little grey cells still intact, even though our bodies are failing us by the day.'

Jack agreed to run him in to the home, saying he had a couple of errands to do in Clonakilty. So Mary-Kate and I sat finishing our coffee together.

'Feeling better today?' I asked her.

'Yeah. You know I don't drink much usually, and certainly not whiskey. Oh, by the way, Eoin, one of the cousins I met at the party who played the fiddle the other night, is a musician and songwriter, and gigs around the local pubs. He says I should come down and join him one night at the open mic

session they have at a pub called De Barras. He's just lost his female singer apparently, because she went off travelling.'

'That's wonderful, Mary-Kate. It's traditional Irish music, is it?'

'God no, Mum,' she giggled. 'It's modern stuff. Eoin says that there's a huge live music culture down here and across Ireland. I suppose it helps that there are so many pubs. We have nothing like this in NZ.'

'Certainly not in the Gibbston Valley, no. Will you take him up on it?'

'I can't, can I? I'm presuming we'll all be heading back to Dublin soon. Have you thought about when?'

'To be honest, I'm just living from day to day at the moment, but there's no reason why you couldn't stay on here for a bit, Mary-Kate, even if Jack and I leave.'

'Maybe,' she shrugged. 'Who knows? If someone will give me a lift at some point today, I might go to his studio and listen to the type of stuff he writes. Oh, and changing the subject, Mum, I had another email from Michelle yesterday. She's sent a photo that was taken of the two of us just after I was born. I . . . well, if it wouldn't hurt too much, would you mind taking a look at it for me? I just want to make sure that the baby in the picture looks the same as the ones you have of me at that age. So there's no doubt or anything. I mean, I know all babies look the same but—'

'Don't worry, darling, I'll know immediately if it's you or not,' I confirmed. 'Whilst we're waiting for Jack to come back, why don't we go up to your room and you can show it to me?'

Upstairs, it took me one glance to know that the newborn child lying in her mother's arms in the photograph was now my daughter.

'You were even wrapped in the same pink blanket when you were given to me and your father.'

'How old was I?'

'No more than a few hours, sweetheart. That photograph was probably taken just before she had to say goodbye to you. It must have been very hard for her.'

'She said in the email that the weeks afterwards were terrible – that she coped by thinking I would be given a better life than she could have given me at the time. I think she feels really guilty, Mum.'

'Do you resent her for making the decision she did?'

'I don't think so, but that's partly because I was lucky enough to come to you and Dad and have such a great upbringing. She wants to . . . well, meet up whenever I feel ready to.'

'Do you think you will?'

'Maybe, yes, but I don't want to become part of her family or anything; I have my own. I know it sounds weird, but she was so young when she had me – if I do end up having any kind of relationship with her, I'd see her more as an older sister. I mean, Jack's only a few years younger than she is. Sooo . . .' Mary-Kate looked at me with a glint in her eye. 'Seems like I'm out of the running for being the missing sister, Mum. Jack told me last night about the coordinates that had appeared on Merope's band of the armillary sphere at Atlantis. They're close to where you were brought up as a child, apparently.'

I stared at Mary-Kate in confusion.

'Sorry, I've no idea what you're talking about.'

'Surely Ally told you about the armillary sphere that appeared at the sisters' home just after their father had died?'

'I vaguely remember her mentioning it, but can you explain again, please?'

'Well, CeCe told me that their father had a special garden at their house in Geneva, and this armillary sphere appeared in it overnight, just after he died. There were bands on it for each of the sisters, and each of the bands had a quotation

engraved on it and a set of coordinates to where they were found by their father.'

'And . . . ?'

'Ally told Jack that Maia – the eldest, and the sister who none of us have met so far – was wandering about in the garden a couple of days ago, and saw that a set of coordinates had been engraved on Merope's empty band.'

'What?! This whole thing gets more far-fetched by the second.' I rolled my eyes.

'Oh, come on, Mum! Stop being such a cynic. You're the one who's been a self-professed addict of Greek mythology the whole of her life. Obviously their dad was too, and the armillary sphere was his way of passing on information. As Ally said to Jack last night, it was what they all needed if they wanted to find out where he'd found them. Maia was adamant that unless this information was completely accurate, it wouldn't have been engraved on the armillary sphere.'

'So when did this information appear?'

'Jack said Ally wasn't sure. I mean, she said that both she and Maia and the other sisters had gone to sit in the garden where the armillary sphere is, but none of them had studied it closely for a while, so it could have been months, or just a few days ago. I'm not sure that's the point, though, Mum. The more important thing is that it can't be complete coincidence you were put in a basket on a priest's doorstep, which is only a mile or so from where the coordinates said you were born.'

I felt my daughter studying me, waiting for a reaction.

'So this father – with no name other than a nickname – apparently found me there? If he did, why on earth did he then put me on a priest's doorstep?'

'I don't know, Mum, and nor does Ally or anyone else. But taking Pa Salt and the sisters aside, wouldn't it be interesting

to find out who you really are? Who your birth parents were?'

'This from the child who told me only a few minutes ago that she wasn't bothered about meeting her own birth family?' I smiled.

'Yeah, but the difference is, I can if I want to,' Mary-Kate countered. 'You're frightened, aren't you, Mum? Of knowing the truth?'

'You're probably right, Mary-Kate, but the past few weeks since I left home have been rather a roller-coaster. Perhaps one day I'll want to know, but like you, it's only those that I love and that love me – my family – that really matter, and I'm quite happy with the one I've got, especially after just meeting them all again.'

'Yeah, I understand completely, Mum.'

'I'm sorry if that sounded like I was commenting on any feelings I have about you and your adoption,' I added quickly. 'I swear that these are completely my *own* feelings. Even if this bunch of sisters has a missing one, which they now think might be me, I can't cope with another family just now.'

'I get that, Mum, and please don't apologise. It's actually Jacko that seems keen to find out stuff. Remember, if you *are* related – or your story is anyway – to this other family, then he might be too, because he's your and Dad's biological son.'

'Actually, you're right,' I said, suddenly feeling terribly selfish. 'Just because I'm not interested in knowing, doesn't mean he isn't. Thank you, sweetheart, for pointing out that this is Jack's history too. And yours.'

'No problem, Mum. Well, I'm with him – I'd like to get to the bottom of all this. It's like the best mystery ever! I know exactly where Jack is at the moment, and it's totally up to you if you want to come along and see this house. We're gonna go take a look – whoops! That must be Jack, checking in from Clonakilty.' Mary-Kate swooped to answer her mobile. 'Hi,

Jacko, yup. Okay, I'll ask her. I'll be in the lobby in half an hour.' She put the phone down.

'So, we're off to see Argideen House. Wanna come along?'

'Why not?' I answered with a grim smile.

'I know exactly where it is,' I said to Jack as we set off. 'We don't need the satnav.'

'Okay, I just got the feeling that maybe you weren't up for it. Sorry, Mum,' he added, turning the satnav off.

'No need to apologise. How was Ambrose?'

'Much more jolly than he was when I first met him in Dublin. You did a good thing there, Mum. I saw our Aunt Katie when I arrived at the home and she said she'd call when Ambrose wanted to be collected.'

'Okay. Turn right here, Jack,' I directed. 'Where were you this morning?'

'Oh, just around Clonakilty.'

'How is Ally? Mary-Kate said you spoke to her last night.'

'She's good. All the rest of the sisters are arriving for the cruise in the next few days. Their boat is sailing down from Nice to Greece on Thursday morning.'

'That's nice,' I said. 'Okay, right round the roundabout and then follow the road until I tell you different.'

We sat in silence for a while, so I looked at the countryside speeding by. I felt numb, as though my brain had switched off, because it simply did not want to know or be involved with the place where I was being taken. As if somehow, seeing it and knowing that I was connected to it would change my life forever. That it mattered.

And I so didn't want it to.

'Turn right here,' I almost barked at Jack.

Stop it, Merry! Remember, you're here for Jack, for your son. It's his story too . . .

The lane twisted, turned, then became narrower as we drove towards Clogagh.

At this moment, I felt it was a metaphor for my life:

What if I was to turn left instead of right in my own life at this moment? Is all life simply a series of twisting and turning paths, with a crossroads every so often when fate allows humanity to decide their own destiny . . . ?

'Mum, where to now?'

The road had narrowed even more as we arrived at Inchybridge and I told Jack to keep going a little further, then turn right.

'That's the stone wall which is the boundary to Argideen House,' I announced.

'It goes on for miles, Mum,' said Mary-Kate from the back.

'They wanted to make sure they kept us peasants out,' I smiled. 'The main entrance is just up here on the left.'

Jack slowed down as he approached. Opposite, a field of maize was growing high in the fertile soil that took nourishment from the Argideen River below it.

'That's the entrance,' I said.

Jack slowed down and then parked in front of it. The majestic old iron gates were open and the driveway beyond was covered in weeds. The trees surrounding the border of the property inside the stone wall had turned into a forest. It reminded me of the enormous thorn bushes that had grown up around Sleeping Beauty's castle.

'Shall we get out and take a look?' asked Jack.

'We can't! We might be trespassing,' I replied.

'I spoke to a local this morning and they said no one's been living here for years. It's empty, Mum. Promise.'

'Well, it's still owned by someone, Jack.'

'Fine, you stay here then.'

I watched Jack climb out of the car.

'I'm coming too,' said Mary-Kate as she opened the back door.

'Oh, for goodness' sake,' I muttered as I got out too. We all circumnavigated the huge nettles that had sprung up along the drive. Ironically, I found it comforting how, without human interference, nature would so quickly start taking back its own.

'Ouch!' Mary-Kate winced and hopped as a nettle found its mark between her trainer and jeans.

'The house should come into view at any minute,' I said from behind them. And a few minutes later, it did. Like all Protestant houses around here, it was a squarely built, elegant Georgian building. Its frontage was vast – eight windows wide on both the ground and the upper levels and surrounded by what would once have been beautifully manicured parkland. As it was, even if the facade was still standing, I could see the rotting wood around the windowpanes, and the ivy on its constant crawl upwards from the base of the house. The feeling of neglect was palpable.

'Wow!' said Mary-Kate as she looked up at the front of it. 'This must have been amazing in its day. Do you know who lived here, Mum?'

'I can tell you who it was one hundred years ago, but I know the Fitzgeralds returned to England during the revolution. They were English, you see. And Protestant,' I added. 'I'm sure someone else bought it just after the war. The Second World War, that is. One of my sisters, Nora, worked here in the kitchens during the shooting season, but I don't know what the family was called.'

'You're right, Mum, the Fitzgeralds went back to England in 1921, and the house was empty for a while.'

'How on earth do *you* know that, Jack?'

'Because Ally, who's a bit of an expert in researching family histories, suggested I looked up solicitors' practices locally, as they would probably have handled any sale of the property. The solicitor I found in Timoleague told me it wasn't him who had dealt with the sale of Argideen House, but he gave me the name of who had. So I visited them in Clonakilty earlier.' Jack shook his head. 'This area is amazing, Mum; everyone knows everyone else, or knows someone who does.'

'And?'

'The guy I spoke to made a call to his dad, who made a call to *his* dad, and apparently the house was sold by the Fitzgerald family in 1948 to a new buyer.'

'Who was that buyer?' Mary-Kate butted in.

'He doesn't know. Or at least, his grandfather doesn't. He was asked to send all the title deeds and related documents to London.'

'Do you have an address for wherever they were sent?' I asked.

'Apparently it was a post office box address, and I've no idea what that actually is.'

'We'd have called it a PO box,' I explained. 'It basically means envelopes or parcels go to the post office to a locker with a specific number attached to it, and the recipient collects them from there.'

'So it means that the person wants to remain anonymous?' said Mary-Kate.

'Yes, in essence, it does.'

'Do you have the PO box address?' I asked Jack.

'I do, and it's a place in somewhere called Marylebone. I checked out the post offices there online and called around them all. Basically, the number doesn't exist anymore.'

'Surely they had the name of whoever had opened that PO box account?' Mary-Kate asked.

'They did, but as Mum just explained, the whole point of having a post office box is to remain anonymous. They weren't going to give the owner's name out to a stranger over the telephone, that's for sure,' said Jack.

'This is such a beautiful house,' Mary-Kate said dreamily.

'My grandmother Nuala looked after a young British officer who lived here and who'd been injured in the First World War. She talked in her diary about how wonderful the gardens used to be. Sadly, he committed suicide soon after Nuala left.' I shuddered then and turned away from the house. 'I'm going back to the car. I'll see you there.'

As I trekked through the undergrowth, I could hardly believe that the story which had moved me so much and had taken place here had possibly been part of *my* history too. Yet, there was just something about the house, an atmosphere – an energy – that was unsettling me.

Not prone to anything spiritual, even I felt as if a darkness hung about Argideen House; although there was no doubting it was – or had once been – beautiful, I knew that tragedy had taken place within its walls and still left its mark until this day.

I began to run, tripping over the weeds and the roots that had pushed up along the drive, until I passed through the gates panting, and taking gulps of fresh air.

Whatever my connection was with Argideen House, I knew I never wanted to pass through those gates again.

50

Having dropped Mary-Kate off in Clonakilty, where she'd arranged to meet her new friend Eoin at his studio, Jack and I went to collect Ambrose.

'You're upset, aren't you, Mum?'

'A bit,' I admitted. 'I can't really say why. But seriously, Jack, it's nothing you've done. I just don't like Argideen House, that's all.'

'But you've never been inside the walls before today?'

'No, never.'

'By the way, when are you thinking of leaving?' he asked me.

'I haven't thought about it, to be honest. I think it depends on Ambrose. We can take him back to Dublin with us.'

'Okay. Well, if it's all right with you, MK and I are thinking of going to Dublin tomorrow, then flying on to Nice via London. You know that all of us have been invited on the cruise down to Greece. I get that you don't want to go, but . . .' – Jack shrugged – 'I'd like to. Maybe I could investigate for you, Mum, find out what all this missing sister stuff is about, if that's all right with you?'

'Of course it's all right, Jack. You're a grown man and you can do what you want. As Mary-Kate pointed out to me, if I'm related to them in some way, then so are you.'

'Yeah, I would be.'

'So, be honest, Jack, how much of your eagerness to go is to do with Ally?'

There was a pause as he thought about it. Or at least, thought about what to say to *me*.

'Quite a lot, actually. I mean, I'm obviously interested in finding out more about the whole situation, but yeah, it's been a long time since I met a woman who I just felt . . . well, an immediate bond with.'

'Do you think she feels the same way about you?'

'I don't know; she might just be texting me because of the whole missing sister thing, but when we spoke last night, we laughed, y'know? I get her and she gets me and that's all there is to it.'

'Then you absolutely must go, Jack. Right,' I said as we pulled up in front of the old people's home. 'I'll go in and get Ambrose.'

Katie came out to reception to meet me. 'How have they been?' I asked her.

'Ah now, I'd say they haven't stopped chatting since Mr Lister sat down.'

'They've had a lot to catch up on.'

'They have, so. I'll go fetch him now.'

'Oh, by the way, Nora worked at Argideen House when we were younger, didn't she?'

'She did, yes.'

'Do you think you could ask her if she remembers the name of the family she worked for?'

'I will. If I remember rightly, 'twas some foreign couple,' said Katie. 'I'll give her a bell when I'm home tonight.'

'Thanks,' I said, as she gave me a smile and walked off. As I stood in reception waiting for Ambrose, I thought about the six sisters' strange surname, which I'd already worked out was an anagram of 'Pleiades'.

D'Aplièse . . . I pulled a pen out of my handbag, asked the receptionist for a piece of paper and wrote the word down.

As Ambrose appeared with Katie, there was a definite spring in his step that hadn't been there in Dublin.

'Good day?' I asked him.

'Apart from the less than private surroundings, it's been most pleasant. Thank you, Katie, it's been a delight to make your acquaintance again, and rest assured, I'll be back soon,' he said to her.

'Can you check with Nora that this wasn't the name of the family up at Argideen House?' I said to her, handing her the slip of paper.

'Of course,' she said as she tucked it into her uniform pocket. 'Bye now.' She gave me a smile and walked off.

'I don't know how James copes with living there,' said Ambrose as I helped him into the car and we drove off. 'And yet somehow he bears it. I'd rather be with my maker.'

'I didn't think you believed in God?'

'I said "my maker", dear girl, which could technically be my parents, and therefore, at the very least, my earthly remains will lie with theirs.'

'You're splitting hairs, Ambrose.'

'Maybe so, but . . . Merry dear, would you be available for a chat once we get back to the hotel? I've drunk more tea today than I think I've drunk in a week, and I may treat myself to a glass of whiskey.'

'I'll go and collect Mary-Kate when she calls,' said Jack as we parked in front of the hotel. 'See you later at dinner.'

'Your children are utterly delightful, by the way. Now then,' he said, as Jack moved off to find a parking space, 'how about we sit outside on the café terrace, whilst the sun is gracing us with an appearance?'

Over a pot of tea for me and a whiskey for Ambrose, we

sat enjoying the sound of the huge waves breaking on the shore below us.

'What is it you wanted to talk to me about?' I asked him.

'It's about James, of course. I mean, I know he is in a wheelchair and needs help with his daily ablutions, but I don't feel he should see his golden years out in that home. So I was thinking . . .'

'Yes?'

'Well, I'm hardly getting any younger, am I? And even though I hate to admit it, I'm beginning to struggle with the stairs down to my bedroom and bathroom. I've been thinking for a while that I should sell the flat and move to a modern apartment block with a lift, and everything I need – including a walk-in shower – all on one floor. Let me tell you, there are plenty of those types of places available in Dublin these days.'

'I see. And?'

'You can imagine that selling the home I've lived in for so very long will be something of a trauma. But seeing James's current situation has given me the spur I needed. So when I get back to Dublin, I intend to put my little half of a house on the market and buy something more sensible with three bedrooms. One for myself, one for a live-in carer and, well, one for James.'

'Goodness!'

'What do you think, Mary dear?'

'I think it's a wonderful idea in theory, Ambrose. However, it would be a huge wrench for Father O'Brien. He's lived down here for most of his adult life, and even if his living circumstances are not quite what they should be, he has many of his old parishioners popping in to see him.'

'Parishioners who he's seen every day for the past sixty odd years. He might be glad of a change.'

'Have you actually asked him?'

'I have, yes, as a matter of fact. Or, putting it another way,

I've hinted at the idea to him. My plan is that I make the move, and then have James up to visit me when I have found a carer who can live in with us. And perhaps—'

'He will never want to return to West Cork,' I finished for him.

'Exactly. And there's no reason why we couldn't take somewhere down here every summer, if he felt the need of some fresh sea breezes.' Ambrose pointed to a separate building adjacent to the hotel. 'I've enquired and discovered the apartments are let out to families needing a self-catering space.'

'Goodness, Ambrose, you've certainly got it all worked out,' I smiled. 'I do know that he misses his privacy and his books around him.'

'I shall, of course, have shelves made especially for those. Truth to tell, I'd move down here if that is what he wished, but no doubt tongues would wag. Whereas in Dublin – the big city – no one would notice or even care about two old friends seeing out their twilight years together. Would they?'

Ambrose looked at me for reassurance.

'I'm sure they wouldn't, although you'd better make sure the apartment's near a church. I'm sure that James will wish to keep in touch, so to speak, when he's in Dublin.'

'Well, the moment I get back, I shall begin to put my plans into action.' He smiled, then turned to me. 'Thank you, dearest girl, for what you have done. I will remain eternally grateful,' he added, his eyes full of tears. 'You've given me a reason to live again.'

'Oh Ambrose, don't thank me, please. After all you've done for me, there's no need to say anything.'

'I wanted to say it anyway. Also, Mary dear, have you read your letter yet?'

'Yes.'

'And?'

733

'And . . . I don't know. I mean, it was quite formal, like mine to him. He left me a telephone number that I could contact him on, but—'

'Mary, for goodness' sake, go and see him! He – and the other one – have haunted you for all these years! If there's one thing life has taught me, it's that it's too damned short!'

'Yes. You're right, of course. Okay, I will. And while we're here, I should tell you all about "the other one", as you've just called him . . .'

Forty minutes later, Ambrose had gone for a nap and I was back in my room. He'd listened intently as I'd told him what had happened to Bobby, then placed a hand on my arm.

'So, finally the past has been put to bed and you can start to breathe again,' he said.

'I can, yes.'

'Dear Mary, if only you'd have told me at the time, I might have been able to help.'

'No, Ambrose. Nobody could,' I'd sighed. 'But at least it's over now.'

'And just this to go,' I murmured as I took out his letter and dialled what I knew was a British code. He answered after a few rings and the two of us made an arrangement. Very formally, like we were having a business meeting. Putting the receiver down, I folded the piece of paper on which I'd written down what time and where, and put it in my purse.

'Why didn't he sound guilty?' I asked myself. The answer was, I didn't know.

'So, Mum, how long are you going to stay in Ireland?' Jack asked me that evening as we all ate in the smart restaurant upstairs, which had a panoramic view of the sea.

'I'm coming back to Dublin with Ambrose and you two tomorrow, then after that, I want to spend some time with my family down here.'

'Are you sure you won't come on the cruise, Mum?' asked Mary-Kate. 'You've always wanted to see the Greek islands – the birthplace of all your beloved mythology. Ally sent Jack a picture of the boat – it looks amazing!'

'You should think about it, Mary dear,' Ambrose piped up. 'Your daughter is absolutely right. I haven't been back to Greece since my last trip to Sparta, over twenty years ago now. The theatre is something to behold at sunset, with Mount Taygetus forming the backdrop.'

Ambrose gave me one of those looks I remembered so vividly from my student days.

'Named after Taygete, the fifth of the Seven Sisters of the Pleiades, and mother of Lacedemon, sired by Zeus,' I parroted, just to assure him I hadn't forgotten. He gave me a slight nod of approval. 'Tiggy's name is short for Taygete – she's the fifth sister in her family,' I continued, 'and ironically, I'm the fifth child in my adoptive family.'

'Or maybe the missing sister in Ally's family,' said Mary-Kate. 'Oh Mum, please come,' she urged me again.

'No, not now, but maybe I'll add Greece to my list of places to see on my Grand Tour. So, anyone for dessert?'

When I arrived back in my room, I saw the red message light was flashing on my hotel telephone, and that there was a

voicemail on my mobile. Picking up my landline message first, it was Katie asking me to call her back.

Turning to my mobile phone, I listened to my voicemail messages. The first was – coincidentally, after our dinner conversation – from Tiggy, asking how I was and saying that she was hoping to see me on the cruise with Jack and Mary-Kate.

I then called Katie.

'Hi, it's Merry. Is everything all right?'

'Yes, grand altogether, thank you. I just wanted to let you know that I spoke to Nora, and she said she couldn't remember the name of the family that she worked for up at the Big House, but she'd have a think. Then she called me back to say she'd remembered it. I was right, 'tis a foreign sounding name, but not the one you gave me. I'd better spell it out for you. Got a pen and a pad?'

'Yup. Fire away,' I said, pencil at the ready.

'Right, she thinks she's got the correct spelling, so it's E. S. Z. U.'

I read the letters back to myself.

'Eszu,' I said. 'Thanks a million, Katie, and we'll speak tomorrow.'

51

Atlantis

'Have you heard anything back from Jack about who owned Argideen House, Ally?' asked CeCe, walking into the kitchen, where Chrissie was preparing a supper of steak, with all the Aussie-style trimmings.

'No. I asked him to let me know if Merry's sister remembered what it was. Obviously she hasn't,' Ally sighed.

'Did he say if his mum's still refusing to come on the cruise?' said Maia, who was sitting in front of a laptop, checking her emails.

'She wants to stay longer in Ireland, apparently. Well, I think we all have to accept we've done our best to find the missing sister. If the ring's the proof, plus the fact Merry was adopted, along with the address of where she was found being so close to the priest's house, we've found her. But if she won't come on the cruise, we can't make her.'

'No, but it's such a shame, because everything fits,' Maia said.

'Apart from her age,' Ally countered. 'We all presumed we were looking for a much younger woman. At least we'll have her children with us, which will just have to be good enough.'

'Right,' Maia said, jotting down some notes on a pad

beside the laptop. 'Tiggy and Charlie's flight lands in Geneva at eleven thirty on Wednesday, Electra's confirmed that she's going to fly straight to Nice, and so will Star, Mouse and Rory. Then there's Jack and Mary-Kate, who are yet to confirm when they'll arrive.'

'So how many bedrooms do we need for tomorrow?' said Ma, who was ferrying glasses and cutlery out onto the terrace.

'Just one for Tiggy and Charlie,' Maia said, standing up. 'Please relax, Ma. You have to remember we're all here to help you.'

'We sure are,' Chrissie said as she turned round from her station at the range and smiled at Ma. 'Although how anyone can cook anything on this ancient gadget, I have no idea. Good job we decided to have a barbie and cook the steaks on that, isn't it, Cee?'

'Ma, why don't you sit down and we'll get you a glass of wine?' Ally steered her towards the table and pushed her gently into a chair. 'Let us look after you for a change.'

'No, Ally, that is not what I am paid to do, and I cannot bear it,' Ma protested.

'You were never paid to love us, but you did for free, and now we're loving you back,' CeCe said as she plonked a glass of wine in front of Ma. 'Now drink it,' she ordered, 'and stop flapping, okay?'

'As I said to Star when I visited her in London last year, without Claudia by my side, I fall apart; she is truly the engine of Atlantis.'

'Well, maybe we never appreciated her enough,' Maia said, then smiled as she saw Floriano and Valentina walk in through the doors from the terrace. They had both been taking a short nap in the Pavilion, having only arrived from Rio de Janeiro via Lisbon that afternoon.

Ally studied Floriano as he held tight to his daughter's

hand. He had tanned skin, dark hair and expressive brown eyes, his teeth flashing a smile on his handsome face. Valentina looked up at all the adults, her huge brown eyes wide, shyly twisting a strand of her shiny long hair around a dainty finger.

Ma stood up immediately. 'Hello, Valentina,' she said, walking over to the little girl. 'Are you feeling better after your sleep?'

'Yes, thank you,' the little girl answered in thickly accented English. Maia had said that, being bilingual himself, Floriano had taught her English from the cradle.

'Would you like a drink? Coke, maybe?' Ma continued, looking up at Floriano for guidance.

'Of course she may have a Coke,' agreed Floriano.

'I am *verrry* hungry, Papai,' she said, looking up at her father.

'Supper won't be ready for perhaps thirty minutes, so why don't you come with me and we'll see if we can find a snack for you, to keep you going until then?' Ma offered her hand to Valentina, who took it willingly. The two of them walked in the direction of the pantry.

'Straight back into mummy mode,' Ally smiled as she rolled her eyes.

'Where she is happiest,' said Maia as she went to Floriano and gave him a kiss on the cheek. 'Would you like a beer?'

'I could kill for one,' he said as he put his arm around her shoulder.

'One for the chef too, if there's any going, please,' called Chrissie.

'I'll get them,' said CeCe, heading for the fridge.

Ally poured a glass of wine for herself, and when everyone was furnished with a drink, raised it. 'To Floriano and Valentina, for making it all the way here from Rio to join us on this very special occasion.'

Everyone toasted, and Ally thought how wonderful it was to see the Atlantis kitchen not only full of her sisters, but also their new partners and family.

She watched Valentina spot Bear, who was lying on his playmat in a corner of the kitchen.

'*Aí que neném bonito!* May I play with him, Maia?'

'Of course you may,' Maia said, looking at Ally as Valentina put down her Coke and made her way over to Bear. She knelt down next to him, then gathered him up in her small arms. The two sisters shared a smile.

'Would it be okay if I took Floriano to see Pa's private garden?' Maia asked the kitchen in general.

'Of course,' said Ma, moving towards Valentina and Bear. 'I will watch over the children, don't worry.'

'Thank you.' Maia took Floriano's hand and led him out of the kitchen.

'We'll whistle when it's ready, Maia,' CeCe shouted after them. 'I should think the barbie's nearly hot enough to go now, Chrissie.'

'Well, I'll come with you, otherwise you'll burn the steaks to a crisp as usual,' Chrissie quipped as the two women walked outside.

'Isn't it wonderful to see CeCe so happy?' Ma said as she sat down in the easy chair, next to where Valentina was playing with Bear.

'Absolutely, and just look how maternal Valentina is.'

At the mention of her name, Valentina looked up at Ally questioningly.

'You like babies?' Ally asked her.

'I like babies *verrry* much,' she agreed as she gently put a wriggling Bear back onto his mat.

Fifteen minutes later, CeCe gave a shrill whistle to let Maia and Floriano know that supper was ready, as the rest of the

girls took the bowls of salad and a large tureen of French fries onto the terrace table. Ally sat down, watching for any signs of Maia returning. She knew why her sister had wanted to catch Floriano alone as soon as she could. Eventually, she saw them walking hand in hand towards the terrace. Maia's head was resting on Floriano's shoulder and just before they reached the table, he stopped, turned towards her and put his arms around her so tightly that he lifted her off the ground. He kissed her on the lips, and the beam that spread across his face meant that Maia's news had been received more than positively.

As everyone sat down and Chrissie began to serve the steaks, Ally heard her mobile ringing in the kitchen. Dashing back inside, she saw it was Jack.

'Hi there.'

'Hi, Ally,' he replied as a burst of laughter came from the table outside. 'I'm not catching you at a bad moment, am I?'

'Actually, we're just sitting down for supper.'

'Okay, well, very quickly, I just called to say that Mum's sister, Nora – the one that worked at Argideen House – has remembered the name of the family that owned it. It's a weird one, I can tell you, something foreign. I'm not even sure how to pronounce it properly.'

'It isn't D'Aplièse, is it?'

'No, no, it's . . . well, I think I'll spell it, rather than say it. Have you got a pen?'

'Yup,' said Ally, reaching for one. 'Fire away.'

'Okay. It's E-S-Z-U.'

Ally wrote the letters down, and it was only when she looked at the word on paper that she struggled to gulp in air. Jack was saying something, but she wasn't listening as she mouthed the surname to herself.

'Ally? Did you get that? Did you want me to repeat it?'

'No, I got it. E-S-Z-U.'

'Yup. Told you it was a weird one.'

'It is . . .' Ally sat down heavily in a chair.

'Hey, Ally, you okay?'

'I'm fine.'

There was a pause on the line before Jack spoke. 'That name means something to you, doesn't it?'

'I . . . yes, it does, but how it fits into everything, I really don't know. Listen, I've got to go and have supper now, but I'll speak to you later.'

'Okay. Speak later.'

Ally stood up and realised she was sweating with . . . what? Surprise, or fear . . . ? Deciding she wouldn't share the news with anyone just yet, she went to the sink and splashed her face with water, then stepped outside to join the diners.

After supper, everyone except Ma, who was upstairs putting Bear to bed, joined in with the clearing up.

'I guess it went well, then,' Ally whispered to Maia as they stood side by side, drying the saucepans as CeCe and Chrissie stacked the dishwasher.

'It did,' Maia whispered back. 'He was thrilled, Ally, and I'm just so relieved!'

'I certainly don't think you need to worry about Valentina's reaction either, given the way she already adores Bear. I'm so happy for you, Maia, I really am. I just hope you can be happy for yourself.'

'Now I've told Floriano, maybe I can be. I'm not going to say anything to anybody until we're all gathered together on the boat, although I think that—'

'Ma already knows,' they both whispered together, then smiled.

'Was that phone call earlier from Jack, by the way?' Maia asked.

'Yes, it was.'

'Any news?'

'Yes, but it wasn't important,' Ally lied. 'You go off with Floriano and Valentina and enjoy your special evening, okay?'

'Okay. I'll see you tomorrow.'

'Sleep well, Maia.'

'I think that finally I will. Goodnight.'

Taking Valentina by the hand, Maia and Floriano left the house to head for the Pavilion.

'I think we'll have an early one too,' said CeCe. 'It's gonna be a busy day tomorrow. Night, Ally.'

Chrissie and CeCe left the kitchen and Ally watched as Ma entered it and began preparing Bear's bottle for the night-time feed.

'Honestly, Ma, I'll do tonight. I think you need a full night's sleep before tomorrow. I'm feeling so much better since I came back from France. Seriously.' Ally almost grabbed the bottle from her and put it on the table. 'I'll do it,' she repeated.

'Perhaps a night's sleep will do me good. These last few weeks have made me realise I'm getting old, Ally. When you were younger, I could exist on almost no sleep and did for years. But now . . . well, it seems I can't.'

'Ma, you've been absolutely wonderful and I don't know what I would have done without your help with Bear. Now, go to bed and enjoy the peace while you can.'

'All right. Will you come up with me?'

'I . . .' Ally was desperate to confide in someone. 'Ma?'

'Yes?'

743

'I need to get hold of Georg, but he's just not answering his mobile. Do you know for sure when he'll be back?'

'As he is coming on the cruise with us, it must be tomorrow. May I ask why?'

'I . . . oh Ma, Jack told me something earlier and it's really shaken me. Normally I'd tell Maia and we'd work out what to do. But under the circumstances, I just couldn't tell her. Especially not tonight.'

'Tell me, *chérie*. You know it will go no further. What did Jack say?'

'That Argideen House, which is the place the coordinates for Merope point to, was once owned by a family called Eszu.'

Ally registered the shock on Ma's face. 'Eszu?'

'Yes. Jack spelt the name out for me. It's identical, Ma. I mean, over dinner I was thinking that maybe it could just be a coincidence, but it's such an unusual name, isn't it? Especially in Ireland. Do you know if there was any connection between Pa and the Eszu family in the past?'

'Truly, Ally, I have no idea. However, I do know that you believe you saw Kreeg Eszu's boat close to where you think your father was buried. And then, of course, his son, Zed . . .'

'The father of Maia's child,' Ally spoke in a whisper, just in case CeCe or Chrissie came down for a mug of something to take up to bed. 'I hope you understand why I didn't want to say anything about it tonight.'

'Of course I do. She told Floriano she's pregnant, didn't she?' said Ma.

'She did. But you mustn't tell anyone, Ma.'

'Of course I won't. I'm so very happy for her.'

'Do you think that Georg might know anything about the Eszu connection?'

'Ally, please believe me, I know no more than you, but he worked so closely with your father, so he might well, yes.'

'You really don't know where he's gone?'

'I swear, I have no idea. I am sorry I cannot help you further – I would if I could. I'm going up to bed. Goodnight, Ally.'

'Goodnight, sleep well.'

Ma left the kitchen just as Ally's mobile rang. 'Hello?'

'Hi there, Jack here again. You're not in bed or anything, are you?'

'No, not yet. How's things in Ireland?'

'They're well, thanks. The taxi's booked to take me, Mary-Kate and Ambrose – my mum's quasi-godfather – and Mum, of course, back to Dublin.'

'Are you sure you can't persuade your mum to join us? I'm hoping that our lawyer, Georg, will be back tomorrow and then hopefully he can confirm for certain it is your mum who is the missing sister.'

'No can do, I'm afraid, Ally. She's adamant that she wants to spend more time here in Ireland. Mary-Kate and I will fly from Dublin to London tomorrow afternoon, then our plane for Nice leaves early the next morning. We'll meet you on the boat, is that right?'

'Yes, I'll send a car to pick you up from the airport, then I'll see you aboard the *Titan* with . . .'

Ally stopped herself, realising she hadn't yet told Jack she had a baby son. 'With the rest of the sisters,' she added quickly.

'Okay. Well, sounds as if it's sure gonna to be an adventure. Mary-Kate's excited to meet the rest of you girls.'

'And I'm excited to meet her. Okay, let me know if there's any delays, and if not, I'll see you in Nice.'

'Yeah, and I'm really looking forward to seeing you again, Ally. Night.'

'Goodnight, Jack.'

Grabbing the milk bottle from the table to take upstairs in case she needed to supplement for Bear, and switching off the kitchen lights, Ally headed for bed. As she lay down, ready to sleep, she thought about her conversation with Jack.

I'm really looking forward to seeing you . . .

Ally felt a little bump of excitement at the fact Jack had said that, but then squashed it immediately when she heard Bear give a tiny snore from his cot.

'Even if he does seem to have forgiven me for not coming clean on who I was, he's hardly going to be interested in a single mother, is he?'

Doing her best to push down any silly flutters in her stomach, Ally fell asleep.

52

Merry
Dublin

I sat in the back of the taxi next to Mary-Kate, with Ambrose on the other side of me. We'd offered him the front seat, but he'd declined, saying that Niall might talk him into an early grave, so that honour had gone to Jack. Yet again, my children had tried to persuade me to come on the cruise, but given that the meeting I had waited thirty-seven years for was only hours away from happening, I had yet again declined.

'Another time,' I'd said, 'but you both go and have a wonderful holiday. It all sounds very glamorous.'

Reaching Merrion Square, Jack helped Ambrose out of the back of the taxi, as Niall collected my own and Ambrose's luggage from the boot.

''Tis a pleasure to have met both of you,' Niall said. 'You have my card now, Ambrose, so any time you're wanting to come down to West Cork again, you be giving me a ring, so.'

'I will, and thank you again,' Ambrose said as he turned and, using his walking stick, manoeuvred his way up the steps to the front door.

'Bye, Mum.' Both Jack and Mary-Kate hugged me – they

LUCINDA RILEY

were going straight off with Niall to Dublin airport – and I felt tears prick the back of my eyes.

'You two keep in touch, won't you?'

'We will,' said Mary-Kate. 'And if you're down in West Cork when the cruise is over, I might come back and join you.'

I saw the faintest hint of a blush appear in my daughter's cheeks and knew immediately the meeting with her new musician friend, Eoin, had obviously gone well.

'If you change your mind, Ally says there's plenty of room on the boat,' Jack urged for the last time.

'No, Jack. Now, you'd better get back in that taxi or you'll miss your flight.'

I said goodbye to Niall and stood on the pavement waving them off, then followed Ambrose inside.

'Cup of tea?' I asked him.

'My goodness, I could murder one,' he said.

Fifteen minutes later, we were in his sitting room drinking tea and eating a slice of a very good fruitcake his daily had left for him.

'So, are you still set on selling this, Ambrose?'

'Absolutely. Even though I love the dear old place, and whether or not James will join me somewhere new, it's time.'

'I'm sure he won't take that much persuading, Ambrose. It was wonderful to see the two of you reunited after all this time.'

'It felt wonderful, too, Mary. I'd forgotten what it was like to laugh. We did an awful lot of that. So, I shall invite some auctioneers to come and value this and up for sale it shall go. Now then, and far more pressingly, are you sure you want to go tonight? You're most welcome to stay here, Merry.'

'I know I am, but I've never been to Northern Ireland before and I feel I'd like to see it.'

'As you are aware, the last time you were in Ireland, Belfast

wasn't a safe place to visit, but recently, I hear there's been major regeneration in and around the city.'

'You know,' I said quietly, 'if any Provisional IRA bombings were reported on television or in our New Zealand newspapers – which, as you know so well, happened a lot in the seventies and eighties – I wouldn't look. Or read. I just . . . couldn't. But then in 1998, I actually sat in front of my television in Otago and cried my eyes out when I saw the *Taoiseach* sign the Good Friday Agreement. I couldn't believe it had finally happened.'

'It did indeed, but of course, it will never be enough for some republicans, who won't stop until Northern Ireland is reunited with the South and back under our Irish governance, but I *do* believe the next generation have been brought up to define themselves as human beings first, rather than Catholics or Protestants. That certainly helps, and a broader education too, of course,' he added. 'I find it quite amusing that I'm one of those rare old people who doesn't look back to the past and think how perfect it was, and despair of the world we live in now. In fact, quite the opposite. The human race has taken quite remarkable strides in the past thirty years, and I rather envy the young, who live in such an open society.'

'Both of our lives would have been very different if we were young in this generation,' I agreed, 'but, well . . . I'd better be thinking about leaving soon. I'll pop downstairs and get changed.'

In the basement, I opened the door to the bedroom that had once been mine. And felt choked when I saw that Ambrose had not removed my books or the bits and pieces I'd collected as a teenager. The wallpaper – which he had had sent over from England for when I began to stay with him – was of the flowery pink variety, and the same lace counterpane lay neatly across the bottom of the wrought-iron single bed. I remembered that when I'd first seen the bedroom, I'd almost

cried in pleasure, not only because it was so very pretty and feminine, but because it was all mine. Certainly through all those years of boarding school when I had a short weekend exeat and it was too far to travel home to West Cork, this bedroom had provided a refuge. Then I'd moved in fully when I'd started my Masters, which I'd never completed . . .

I opened the wardrobe, wondering if all my clothes from the early seventies – mini-skirts, bell-bottomed trousers and tight, ribbed polo necks – would still be hanging there, but they weren't. Of course they weren't. I'd left decades ago, so why should Ambrose keep them?

Shivering suddenly, I sat down on the bed and my mind immediately sped back across the years to the last time I'd been in here and Bobby had arrived on the doorstep. He'd banged so hard and was shouting so loudly that I'd had no choice but to let him in.

With his long jet-black hair and intense blue eyes, along with his height and muscled torso, he'd been a handsome man. Some of my friends who'd met him when he'd gate-crashed our group having drinks in a pub had found him attractive. But to me, he was just Bobby: the angry, mixed-up but highly intelligent little boy I'd known since childhood.

As he'd pinned me against the wall, I'd felt the chill of steel pressing into my neck.

'You'll stop seeing him, or I swear I'll kill you, Merry O'Reilly. And then I'll go after him and his family, as well as yours. You're mine, do you understand? You always have been. You know that.'

The look in his eyes and the sour smell of stale beer on his breath as he'd pressed his lips to mine would never leave me.

With my life under threat, of course I'd promised him that I'd stop seeing Peter, that I'd join him in his terrorist crusade against the British.

I'd been terrified out of my wits, but at least I knew how to calm him down – I'd had years of practice after all. Finally, he'd removed the gun from my neck and let me go. We'd agreed to meet the following night and I'd just about managed to stop myself from vomiting when he'd kissed me again. When he eventually walked towards the door, just as he was about to open it, he turned round and stared at me.

'Just remember, I will hunt you down, wherever you try to hide . . .'

It was after he'd left that I'd decided I had no choice but to leave. And I'd come down here to my bedroom and begun to pack . . .

'It's all over, Merry, Bobby can never hurt you again,' I told myself as I tried to quell the familiar panic attack symptoms that had begun automatically for thirty-seven years every time I'd thought of him. I was sure, given the hundreds of times I'd relived that moment, that a psychiatrist would tell me that I was suffering from post-traumatic stress. I had no idea whether coming back to where it had happened would actually help, but I had to believe that one day, I'd manage to convince my brain that it was all over and I was finally safe.

I heaved the large suitcase I'd brought with me on the Grand Tour onto the bed, opened it and tried to concentrate on what to wear to my 'meeting' tomorrow.

Not that it matters, Merry . . .

I pulled out some clothes. Should I look sophisticated? Casual? I just didn't know.

In the end, I plumped – as I usually did when I wasn't sure – for my favourite green dress, folding it carefully into my holdall, alongside my black court shoes. After changing into my usual travelling attire of jeans, a shirt and a Chanel-style bouclé jacket that added a touch of class and just seemed to

go with everything, I packed my washbag, some clean under-wear and a book for the train, then zipped up the holdall.

Back upstairs, I left it in the corridor and went into the sitting room to say goodbye to Ambrose.

'I've left my big suitcase downstairs, along with a pile of laundry which I'll sort out when I'm back tomorrow. I hope that's okay?'

'Of course it is, dear girl. It means that you must return to collect it, though given you left a wardrobe full of clothes last time, I suppose that's no guarantee. They're all here, by the way.'

'What are?'

'The clothes you left behind. I packed them into a suitcase and put it in the bottom of one of my wardrobes, just in case you might be passing one day.'

'Oh Ambrose, I'm so, so sorry.'

'Don't be. *Je ne regrette rien*, as the French say so suc-cinctly. You are back now and that is all that matters. Oh, and with everything that has happened recently, there's something I keep forgetting to tell you. I've read Nuala's diary. Your grandmother was a very brave young lady.'

'Yes,' I said as I watched him tap it gently on the round table next to his leather chair. 'She was.'

'It was a struggle to make out some of the misspelt words, but goodness, what a story. It moved me to tears at certain points,' Ambrose sighed. 'One thing I must tell you is that Nuala writes about the parlour maid, Maureen.'

'The one who betrayed her?'

'Yes. Now then, you remember Mrs Cavanagh, James's famous housekeeper? He told me she worked at Argideen House before she kept house for James. Guess what her first name was?'

'No, Ambrose . . .'

'Maureen. Maureen Cavanagh. One and the same woman who betrayed young Nuala, and who also betrayed myself and James years later.'

'Oh my God,' I breathed.

'What a sad, bitter woman she was. Poor James told me he had the job of presiding over her funeral. He said that only three people attended, and you know how many people usually turn up for such events here in Ireland. She lived alone and died alone. And perhaps that was her punishment.'

'Perhaps, but if I had ever met her, then I couldn't be held responsible for my actions,' I replied fiercely.

'Dear Mary, you could never hurt a fly, but I appreciate the sentiment,' Ambrose chuckled. 'Although perhaps one day you might think of publishing Nuala's diary, especially as you now know the end of her story. There aren't enough factual accounts of that moment in time, and the anguish it caused so many families afterwards, and certainly very few written from a female perspective. The role Cumann na mBan played in freeing Ireland from the British barely gets a footnote in history.'

'I agree, and maybe I will. In fact, confronting my past has also made me remember my love for academia. I was thinking downstairs that I never finished that Masters I started, because I had to leave . . .'

'I still have your half-finished dissertation in there.' Ambrose indicated his desk. 'It – and you – were becoming something quite brilliant. Now then, shall I call you a taxi to take you to the station?'

'I'll walk down to Grafton Street and find one. I shall be back tomorrow, Ambrose darling. Wish me luck, won't you?'

'Of course. I can only pray that you will finally be able to put the past to rest.'

'I hope so too. Bye, Ambrose,' I said, then picked up my overnight bag and left the house.

The train to Belfast – which was rather aptly named the Enterprise – caught me by surprise, as it was so modern and comfortable. I watched as countryside flew by, wondering if I'd see a sign when we crossed the border into Northern Ireland. In the old days, there'd been border controls on all forms of transport. Yet today there was nothing, and just over an hour into the two-hour journey, we were stopping across the border at Newry, a place I knew had seen such violence during the Troubles. In August 1971, six civilians, including a Catholic priest, had been shot dead by the British army in Ballymurphy. News of the massacre had only added another spark to light Bobby's already flammable touchpaper. I had realised that that incident, plus the fact he'd seen me in a bar with Peter, had almost certainly been what had sent him over the edge, and it had happened very close to here.

Today, it looked like any other station that serviced a small town, but back then, it had been the scene of an old conflict brought back to life by extremists like Bobby. So many times he'd set off at me in the pub, raging about the plight of the Northern Irish Catholics and how the IRA would bomb 'the bastard Proddies' into extinction. I'd said to him over and over that the way forward was negotiation, not war, that surely a way could be found to make the situation better through diplomacy.

He'd accused me of sounding like Michael Collins himself.

'That traitor spun us all a tale, told us that signing the truce would be a stepping stone to an Irish republic. But the North is still in British hands, Merry!' he'd railed at me. 'You watch and see how we'll fight fire with fire.'

I had watched, as the Provisional IRA had done as Bobby

promised they would, bombing targets in the North and then heading to the British mainland. 'The Troubles' had lasted for almost thirty years, and all through them, I had imagined Bobby being part of the death and destruction that the new war had wrought.

No wonder I couldn't watch the news bulletins on television . . . they had fuelled my own fire of fear. Yet all those years, Bobby had been sitting in an institution, believing he was back in 1920 . . .

Well, here we were in 2008, and yes, Northern Ireland was still part of the United Kingdom, but the fact that I had just sailed at high speed across the border had to be a sign of progress, surely.

It felt ridiculous even to myself when I looked out of the window and was surprised to see that the surrounding landscape looked very similar to that south of the border – *As if a manmade line could change anything*, I thought – but coming here to the area that had seen so much bitter conflict was yet another demon in my head that I was trying to tame by facing it.

The train arrived exactly on time at Lanyon Place station in Belfast. Walking through to the exit to look for the taxi rank, I heard the lilt of an accent that was familiar, yet unique to this Northern Irish part of the United Kingdom. Climbing into a taxi, I directed the driver to the Merchant Hotel which, so my guidebook told me, had once been the headquarters of the Ulster Bank.

I looked out of the window fascinated, as we drove into the city that no longer showed any signs of its terrible wounds, on the outside at least.

'Here you are, madam,' the driver said, pulling up in front of the Merchant Hotel. 'It's a fine wee establishment.'

'How much do I owe you?'

'That'd be ten pounds, please.'

Pounds . . .

I hunted through my purse for what was left over of my British money from my London stay.

'There you go, thank you.'

I walked up the steps and into a very modern lobby. I checked in and the porter took me and my holdall up to my room, which was beautifully decorated in a cosy, rather chintzy way.

'I'll certainly have had my fill of hotels by the time I get home,' I sighed as I lay down on the bed.

I checked the time and saw it was past seven o'clock. Calling down for room service, I ordered the soup of the day and a bread roll. I then had my usual moment of feeling bad for spending so much money on smart hotels, but then, what were savings for? Jock and I had put a bit aside every month for the past thirty years and, given we had never taken a holiday outside New Zealand, I didn't think he'd mind.

'But he might mind about tomorrow,' I muttered.

I hung up my dress to take out any creases, then I switched on the television as I ate my soup. BBC One was showing *EastEnders*, a British soap that Mary-Kate had found on a channel of our satellite package back home.

It all felt very strange here, to still be on the island of Ireland, and yet so definitely in a tiny parcel of land that was distinctly British.

I took a long, leisurely bath in the free-standing tub and wondered how I'd feel when I was back in my farmhouse in the Gibbston Valley, which was certainly homely, but had none of the fine furnishings or modern appliances I'd become used to.

After my bath, I watched a terrible romcom about a bridesmaid, trying to do anything to distract myself from thinking

about tomorrow. I took out my bottle of Jameson's, which was now three-quarters empty due to me plundering it each time there had been a new revelation to deal with. Just maybe, after tomorrow, I could get back on that train to Dublin, knowing that I'd finally put my past to rest. Slipping under the crisp white sheets, I set my alarm for nine o'clock, just in case, and lay back on the soft pillows. Lying there in the dark, my arm instinctively reached out towards Jock.

'Please, darling, forgive me for never telling you about any of this, and for meeting him tomorrow . . .'

I woke with a start to the sound of the alarm clock. I had tossed and turned into the small hours, wondering how I'd feel when I saw him, and thinking about all the things that I wanted to ask him, but equally knowing there was only one question I needed answering.

'In under an hour's time, you'll be finding out,' I said as I reached for the bedside telephone to dial room service for a cup of tea and some toast.

While I waited, I dressed and gave myself a quick wash and brush-up, then put on some mascara, adding a little blusher to my cheeks. My hair was doing what it always had done, waving in places it shouldn't wave – oh, how I had always longed for straight, easy to manage locks – but having tried it in an elegant bun and then some combs, I gave up and let it hang naturally in a wavy bob around my face. Last time I had seen him, my hair had been long – almost reaching to the bottom of my back. My 'mane', he used to call it. I drank the tea, but I was so nervous that I almost choked on the toast and gave up on the third bite. I checked my watch. A quarter to ten. In less than ten minutes, I needed to walk downstairs.

'Calm down, Merry, for goodness' sake,' I told myself as I applied my usual pink lipstick and gave my hair a last quick brush. 'The onus is on him, not you, remember?' I said to my reflection.

I walked to the door, opened it and headed for the lift that would take me downstairs to meet him for the first time in thirty-seven years . . .

The receptionist pointed me in the direction of the Great Room and I walked towards it, my legs like jelly beneath me. As I entered, I saw the most enormous chandelier hanging down from a high atrium in the centre of an incredible room. Pillars bedecked with cherubs and golden cornicing held up the intricately decorated ceiling. I was still gaping up at it when I heard a voice from behind me.

'Hello, Merry. Amazing, isn't it?'

'I . . . yes.' I dragged my eyes away from the chandelier and turned to look at him.

And . . . he looked exactly the same: tall and slim, albeit with grey peppering his sandy hair and a number of thin lines etched across his face. His brown eyes were just as mesmerising as I remembered and . . . here he was, standing next to me after all these years. The world spun as a wave of dizziness engulfed me. I had no choice but to reach out a hand to his forearm to steady myself.

'Are you all right?'

'Sorry, I'm feeling a little dizzy.'

'It's probably standing there, craning your neck back to look at that chandelier. Come on, let's get you sat down.'

I half closed my eyes as further waves engulfed me. I clung on to him as I felt his arm go round my waist to support me as we walked.

'Can you bring some water over?' I heard him ask, as I felt him sit me down.

I'd broken out in a sweat and I sucked in some air to try and steady my breathing. 'Sorry, sorry . . .' I muttered, hardly believing that, after all this time, my plans to be cool, calm and in control had gone out of the window before I'd even begun.

'Here, drink some of this,' he said and I felt a glass being thrust between my lips. My hands were too shaky to hold it myself, and he emptied so much water into my mouth that I choked and began coughing and spluttering.

'Sorry,' he said, as I felt a piece of cloth being dabbed round my mouth and then patted down my neck. At least the water on my skin cooled me down, even if I wanted to die of embarrassment.

'Can you bring us some hot tea?' I heard him say. 'Or maybe a whiskey might help more? Tell you what, bring both.'

I laid my head back against the soft covering of the banquette that I'd been placed on and took some long, deep breaths in and out. Finally, my body stopped doing the strange tingly thing and the black spots in front of my eyes began to recede.

'Sorry,' I said again, pointlessly.

'Tea with plenty of sugar, or whiskey?'

I heard that familiar ironic smile in his voice. I shrugged.

'Right, whiskey it is. Can you hold the glass?'

'Maybe.'

He placed it into one of my hands and then steered it towards my mouth. I took a small sip, and then a larger one.

'Honestly, Merry, any excuse for an alcoholic drink at breakfast.'

'That's me,' I agreed. 'I'm a lost cause, but at least I'm feeling better.' I opened my eyes fully and the world finally stood still. I placed the whiskey glass on the table in front of me,

then looked down at my front, which was spattered with water.

'I'll pour you some tea too, in case you want that.'

'Thank you. I apologise again.'

'Seriously, there's no need. It's actually very muggy in here as well, not a feeling we tend to be used to in Ireland, is it?'

'No.'

'Global warming and all that . . . A few offices I know are beginning to put in air conditioning. Can you believe it?'

'No, considering I spent most of my childhood not being able to feel my toes. Anyway,' I said as I turned to him, unable to keep my own eyes away from his, yet terrified that if I looked into them again, I'd be as lost as I had been the first time I'd met him.

'Anyway,' he smiled. 'It's very good to see you after all these years.'

'And you.'

'You haven't changed a bit, you know,' he said.

'Thank you, but I doubt you'd be saying, "Jaysus, Merry, you've turned into an old bat!" now, would you?'

'I suppose I wouldn't, no,' Peter chuckled.

'Just for the record, you haven't changed either.'

'That's an out and out lie. My hair is almost entirely grey—'

'At least you have some, which is more than can be said for a lot of men your age.'

'My age, is it, Merry?'

'You are two years older than me, remember? In your sixties . . .'

'Yes, I am, and feeling every bit of it too. I may look all right on the outside, but I certainly can't run around a pitch kicking a ball like I used to do. Now I have to hit it against a wall in a squash court – the game of city-dwelling old men,' Peter added as a waiter approached our table.

'Can I offer you any breakfast?' he asked us. 'It's last orders, I'm afraid.'

Peter looked at me and I shook my head.

'No, thanks.'

'Are you sure?'

'Positive. I'll nibble on the biscuits they brought with the tea.'

'I'll have a croissant and a double espresso, to soak up the whiskey,' he said with a raise of his eyebrow as he reached for his glass. '*Sláinte!*'

'*Sláinte*,' I parroted without picking mine up. My head had spun once this morning and I certainly didn't want it to happen again.

'So, how have you been?' he asked me.

'I . . .' We caught each other's glance and, given the situation, we both began to chuckle at the ridiculous inanity of the remark.

'I've been . . . well, I've been fine, really,' I said, and then we chuckled some more, which turned into a good few minutes of uncontrollable laughter.

We both ended up wiping our eyes on our napkins, which meant I had probably smudged my mascara all over my face, but I was past caring. One of the reasons Peter had so attracted me in the first place was his sense of humour, which, levelled against the intensity and seriousness of Bobby, had been a relief. Peter had worn life lightly back then.

When the waiter returned with the coffee and croissant, we both tried to get ourselves under control.

'Do you think he's going to chuck us out for bad behaviour?' I whispered.

'Possibly. My reputation here will probably be destroyed – it's close to my office, so I use the hotel for the occasional meeting – but who cares?'

'What do you do?'

'Why don't you guess, Merry?' he challenged me.

'Well, you're wearing a suit and tie, which wouldn't mark you out as a circus performer, so we'll cross that one off the list.'

'Correct.'

'You have a leather document holder with you, that's useful for putting papers in when you have meetings.'

'Correct again.'

'And the third and most important clue is that you were studying law at Trinity, then doing your articles when I last saw you. You're a lawyer.'

'Correct. You could always read me well, couldn't you?' he said as he picked up his espresso and eyed me with amusement over the top of the cup.

'Perhaps, but why don't you try to do the same with me?'

'Ah, now that's far harder. So . . . let me see.'

I felt his eyes scan over my face and my body, and for my sins, I blushed. 'Clue number one: even though women tend to age far better and are able to keep themselves much fitter than they could in the old days, it would not strike me that you followed your own mother down the path of having nineteen children, or however many it was.'

'Seven, actually. Correct. Continue.'

'Given the fact that you are wearing a wedding ring, I assume you're married.'

'*Was* married. My husband died some months ago, but I'll give you that.'

'I am sorry, Merry. I had a similar tragedy when the woman I'd lived with for ten years died. Anyway, given I already know you haven't been resident here on the island of Ireland for many years, or London in fact, or ended up in Canada as we'd planned – I've checked the register – I'd reckon, taking

all the circumstances of thirty-seven years ago into account, that you went elsewhere. Somewhere far flung, like Australia, maybe.'

'Ooh, you're hot,' I replied, then felt a further blush rise to my cheeks, as it wasn't appropriate to call someone 'hot' these days.

'New Zealand then.'

'Correct. Very good.'

'Perhaps you pursued an academic career at one of the universities over there?' he said. 'It was certainly where you were heading in those days.'

'Wrong, completely wrong. You've failed, Mr Lawyer,' I smiled. 'I actually built and then ran a vineyard with my husband down in the back of beyond on the South Island.'

'Okay, even if I couldn't have ever guessed that, I suppose it does sort of fit,' he said. 'I mean, you were brought up on a farm in West Cork. That was the back of beyond too, and you're certainly used to working on the land, although it's a shame that you didn't pursue your academic career, Merry. You were destined for great things.'

'Thank you for that. Life had other plans, but yes, I'd be lying if I said I don't sometimes regret not following my dream.'

'If it makes you feel any better, I *did* follow mine and – especially recently – I've begun to regret it. Don't get me wrong, it's provided me with a very good income and quality of life.'

'But?'

'When I qualified, I chose to go into corporate law, which was the golden nugget financially. I moved to London and worked my way up to being an in-house adviser at a large oil and gas company. Spending my days telling them how they could achieve X-million pounds in tax breaks every day for

twenty-five years was probably not the right career choice for a self-proclaimed aesthete, but hey, it bought me a nice suit, didn't it?' Peter gave a 'grin-mace', as we'd always called his ironic smile.

'I thought you were all set on becoming a barrister?'

'I was, but my father talked me out of it. Said it wasn't secure in comparison to taking articles and becoming a solicitor in a nice steady job, not just being as good as your last case in court. Everybody has regrets, I fear, by the time they get to our age. I was pensioned off at fifty-five, so I decided that I'd finally do my bit for my fellow man and ended up here in Belfast.'

'Really? And what do you do here?'

'I've actually been working in an advisory capacity for what's now known as the Titanic Quarter of Belfast. There's a massive regeneration project in progress on Queen's Island, and in fact, not that you'd probably know about it, as you haven't been around in Ireland recently, the tourism minister, Arlene Foster, has just announced that the Northern Ireland Executive is going to provide fifty per cent of the finances for the Titanic Signature Project, with the other fifty per cent coming from the private sector. We've got an incredible American architect who will come on board and hopefully create something to reflect the great shipbuilding history of the city. You know, of course, that the *Titanic* was built here,' he added.

'Somewhere in the back of my mind I did, yes. Wow, Peter, that all sounds fascinating.'

'And a bit weird?'

'No, not at all,' I said.

'Well, you might remember I've always been a hybrid – English Protestant mum and Irish Catholic dad – born in Dublin, following my mother's line and being baptised as a Protestant. Not that either of them were interested in their

religion, just their love for each other,' he shrugged. 'The good news is, I've now lived and worked in England and in the North and South of Ireland, and after years of struggling with my identity, especially during the Troubles, I've arrived at my own personal – and very simple – conclusion: that who you are has everything to do with whether you're a decent human being or not.'

'I totally agree, of course, but extremist indoctrination from the cradle can definitely hamper one's personal develop-ment, can't it?' I said.

'It certainly can, and let's face it, there aren't many of us who can live without a cause of some kind, be it work or family. I made work my cause for far too long. At least now I feel I'm using my experience to make a difference to a city that was in such desperate need of regeneration. If in some small way I can provide – through my knowledge and skill set – help to make that happen, it'll make all the years of grind worthwhile.'

'I'm sorry you weren't happy, Peter, I really am.'

'Oh, I was fine, Merry, just playing it safe, which was my *own* family form of indoctrination. Everyone from my lower-middle-class background was told by their parents to go into a profession that would see them safe and secure financially. Doctors and lawyers were where it was at, unless you were aristocratic, of course, and there were certainly a few of those at Trinity, weren't there?'

'There were, yes,' I chuckled. 'Do you remember that guy who drove around Dublin in his open-topped Rolls-Royce? Lord Sebastian Something-or-other. It was awfully smart at Trinity in those days, wasn't it? All those wealthy, bright young things who were there for the social scene rather than the degree.'

'Well, I'm pretty sure my mum always thought that I'd

meet some Anglo-Irish heiress and end up living in a draughty mansion, surrounded by dogs and horses, but—'

'I've always hated horses,' we both said at the same time and laughed.

'Where did we both go wrong, Merry?' He shook his head in mock-sorrow. 'I mean, the British and Irish are obsessed with the nags.'

'Only if they're groomed to a shine by a minion, who will also muck out the dirty hay when the wealthy behind has had its ride and leads it back into the stables.'

'Or when the owners are holding the Winner's Cup on Derby Day, when it's the trainer and jockey who have done all the hard work.' Peter rolled his eyes. 'Or maybe that's just jealousy, Merry. Both of us were bright, of course, but from poor backgrounds and had to work. So, how is your family?'

'They're mostly well, but I hadn't seen them since the last time I saw you, up until a few days ago. My daddy died over twenty years ago of the drink, which was sad. He was a good man, destroyed by a hard life. Though actually, I found out recently that they weren't my blood family. I was simply dropped into their midst as a newborn, but that really is another story.'

Peter looked at me in shock. 'You mean, you were a found-ling?'

'Apparently I was. It was Ambrose who told me – remember him?'

'Of course I do, Merry, how could I forget him?'

'Well, he and his friend Father O'Brien persuaded the O'Reilly family to adopt me. Or in fact, take the place of a dead baby they'd lost. Called Mary,' I added.

'Goodness, I don't know what to say.'

'At this moment, Peter, nor do I, so let's not talk about it, shall we? What about your family?'

'My mother's still alive, but my father died a few years ago

of old age. I think he lost the will to live when he retired from the railways. He loved that job so much. Apart from my old mum, that's it. I have no family.'

'You never had children of your own?'

'No, and that's another regret I have. But for some of us, it just isn't to be. After my girlfriend died, I took a company transfer over to Norway to make a fresh start and I was briefly married to a Norwegian girl there. It didn't last long – in fact, I think the divorce process lasted longer than the actual marriage, but hey, that's life, isn't it? We all make mistakes. Do you have kids?'

'I do, two of them. One boy and one girl.'

'Then I'm envious. We always wanted kids, didn't we?'

He looked at me and I knew that the game of pussyfooting around was now at an end. However much we'd both enjoyed it.

'We did. I think we named them something ridiculous,' I responded.

'You mean, *you* named them something ridiculous. What was it now? Persephone and Perseus, or some such. I was quite happy with Robert and Laura. Ah,' he said as he picked up his whiskey glass and drank the remains of it, 'those were the days, eh?'

I couldn't answer then, because yes, they had been 'the days', but I needed to ask the question.

'Why didn't you come and meet me in London as you'd promised to, Peter?'

'So . . .' He eyed me. 'Here we are, finally on to the meat of the matter.' I watched as he signalled for the waiter and ordered two more whiskeys.

'Will I need another?'

'I don't know, Merry, but I certainly do.'

'Please, Peter, just tell me what happened. It's a long time ago and whatever the reason, I promise I'll understand.'

'I think you're clever enough to know what happened, Merry.'

'Was it him?' I forced the name onto my tongue. 'Bobby Noiro?'

'Yes. After you left for England, I'd done as we agreed that night and made a point of being seen in that bar where he'd first spotted us together, to make sure he didn't think I had anything to do with your disappearance. I don't know whether he saw me, but then, just the day before I was about to get on the boat to England, he turned up at my parents' front door – he must have followed me home from the bar – pinned me against the wall with a gun to my throat and told me that if I disappeared too, he'd make sure Mum and Dad wouldn't live to find out where I'd gone. That he and his "friends" would make sure of it by burning down the house. He said he'd be keeping a watch on it to make sure I was there at home every day, going out in the morning and coming home at night. And he did, Merry, for months.' He took a sip of his whiskey and gave a deep sigh. 'He made sure I saw him too. What could I do? Tell my parents they'd been targeted by the Provos? A terrorist gang that, as we both know and history can attest to, would stop at nothing to get what they wanted.'

'I waited for three weeks in London at Bridget's place. And heard nothing from you. Why didn't you *write* to me, Peter? Let me know what had happened?'

'But I *did*, Merry, and I even have the proof. Let me show you.' Peter reached for his leather case, unzipped it and pulled out a bunch of old airmail envelopes. He handed them to me and I stared down at the top one.

My name and the address in London were crossed out, and in big letters was written *Return to Sender.*

Then I looked at the address he had sent it to.

'See? Look at the stamp at the top,' he pointed. 'It's dated August the fifteenth, 1971. Turn it over, Mary.'

I did so. It had Peter's Dublin address, in his neat handwriting, and a note beneath it: *Person not known at this address.*

'That isn't Bridget's writing,' I said. I frowned and, turning it over to the front, I reread the address.

'Oh no!' I gulped in horror and looked up at him. 'You got the address wrong! Bridget didn't live in Cromwell Gardens. She lived on Cromwell Crescent! I told you that!'

'What?! No!' Peter shook his head. 'I swear, Merry, as you were packing to leave, you told me it was Cromwell Gardens. It was indelibly inked on my heart – why would I ever forget? When we decided we needed to go, that address was the only means of communication we had. I swear you told me it was Cromwell Gardens . . .'

'And I swear I said Cromwell Crescent.'

I forced my mind back to that night, when Bobby had paid me a visit and threatened me and mine. Peter had arrived an hour later and I'd taken him down to my bedroom to tell him we'd been seen by Bobby in a pub the night before. I'd been hysterical, as I'd sobbed in terror and thrown God knows what into a suitcase.

'Did I not write it down for you? I'm sure I wrote it down,' I said, desperately trying to recall the details of telling Peter I was going to Bridget's flat in London on the morning ferry, and parroting the address she'd given to me when I'd called her earlier.

'Merry, you know very well you didn't. You were in a terrible state, and to be fair, so was I.' Peter gave a heavy sigh. 'Well, one of us made a mistake that night,' he shrugged. 'And ever since, I've never known whether that maniac had caught you, murdered you and thrown you into the Liffey, or whether you had just decided it was best if we ended it.'

'You know I'd never have ended it, Peter! We were secretly engaged, had all our plans set out for a new life in Canada . . . It was a decision that was only pre-empted by Bobby and his threats. I thought *you'd* changed your mind, and as I knew I could never come back to Ireland because of Bobby, I had to go on. Alone,' I added.

'So you went to Toronto as we'd arranged?'

'Yes. After delaying my passage three times to see if you'd come. The fourth time, well, I got on board.'

'And how was it? Canada, I mean.'

'Terrible,' I admitted. 'I headed for the Irish Quarter in Toronto as we'd agreed – Cabbagetown, it was called. It was little better than a slum and there was simply no work available other than literally selling my body. A girl I met there told me she'd heard that they were desperate for young workers in New Zealand and there were plenty of jobs, so I used the last of my savings and went with her.' I looked down at the letter that I was still holding in my hands.

'Can I open it?' I asked.

'Of course you can. It was written to you, after all.'

I looked at it again and then at him. 'Maybe I'll save it for later. What does it say?'

'It says what I just told you – that your Bobby had paid me a visit at home and threatened to burn down my parents' house. That I had gone to the police to tell them about him and his threats, and that they said that they'd look into it. I was hoping that they'd take him in for questioning and charge him with threatening behaviour, but I didn't even know where he lived.'

'If I remember rightly, he was squatting at the time, with his fellow "comrades".'

'Exactly. So I wrote that I'd have to wait before I came to London, but that I'd write as often as I could.' Peter shook his

head sadly. 'It seems ridiculous, doesn't it, in the age that we live in now, that my parents didn't even have a landline installed in their house, because they simply couldn't afford it? In all the panic, I hadn't given you my address either. I said I'd write to you with it, and I did.' He indicated the pile of letters.

'The schemes of mice and men . . .' I said quietly.

'I did all I could to find you, Merry. I went to visit Ambrose and he said he'd had a note written in Greek telling him you were going away. He knew no more than I did.'

'Oh God, Peter,' I said. 'I . . . don't know what to say. But even if you knew where I was, what could we have done? You couldn't have left and put your parents at risk. That was the point – Bobby had threatened to kill everyone I loved. And I believed him.'

'No, but at least when the situation here really started to heat up, Mam wasn't comfortable with staying in Ireland any longer – there were bombs going off in Belfast constantly and even Dublin was under threat. They were vulnerable anyway, what with their "mixed" marriage, so she persuaded my dad to move to England. I moved with them to Maidenhead, where Mum had relatives, and managed to find a job at a solicitors' practice there, where I could continue my articles. Of course, I went to up to London and to Cromwell Gardens, but they'd never heard of either you, or Bridget. I swear, I was half out of my mind with worry.' Peter gave me another 'grin-mace'. 'I then heard a few weeks later that some madman called Bobby Noiro had burnt down my parents' old rented house, and that they'd locked him up for it.'

'When Bobby's sister Helen told me only a few days ago about Bobby being imprisoned for burning down a Protestant house, it did cross my mind it could have been your parents'.'

'At least no one was hurt,' Peter sighed. 'He really was a

total headcase, wasn't he? Him and his friends in the Provisional IRA.'

'He was a headcase, yes, but he didn't have friends in the Provisional IRA,' I sighed, suddenly feeling completely exhausted. 'What a mess it all was. One stupid, misheard word, and here we are thirty-seven years later, thinking the other had . . . well, I imagined just about everything, that's for sure.'

'So did I. But at least I knew my family was safe when Bobby Noiro was put behind bars, but not you. I never forgot you, Merry . . . A year on from the burning, someone at my law firm recommended I find a private detective. I saved up to pay for a company to look for you in London and Canada. To be honest, I assumed the worst. Merry, there *was* no trace of you.'

'Forgive me, Peter, that's how I needed it to be. For the safety of everyone I loved. I didn't even know that Bobby had been locked up until a few days ago, when his sister told me. Maybe if I had, I'd have come back. But who knows?'

There was a pause as both of us sat, lost in thoughts of the past and what might have been.

'At least it sounds as though you've been happy, Merry. Have you been happy?'

'Yes, I think I have. I married a lovely man called Jock. He was a good few years older than me and, if I'm honest, I do think part of the initial attraction was the fact that I felt protected by him. But as the years passed, I honestly grew to love him, and when he died a few months back, I was completely devastated. We were together over thirty-five years.'

'Far longer than I ever managed.' Peter offered me a wry smile. 'But I'm glad you found someone to care for you, I really am.'

'And I cared for him. With the kids coming along too, I was

contented. Yes, I was,' I said out loud, mainly to myself. 'But I also realise now I was always holding something back from him emotionally, and that was because of you. I learnt from my kids that first love can be overwhelming – a grand passion, if you like – but often that love comes to its natural conclusion. Ours never did; in fact, quite the opposite. There was always the "what if" scenario. And because it was forbidden, what with you being Protestant and me a Catholic at that moment in Ireland, not to mention Bobby . . . Well, it gave the whole thing the feeling of an epic romance, didn't it?'

'You're right, it did, and it has continued to do so for the whole of my adult life,' he agreed. 'I admit to not sleeping properly since I received your letter, or being able to concentrate on anything much. I could barely speak when you called me and I heard the sound of your voice, so forgive me if I sounded formal. When I saw you here earlier, actually in the flesh, looking up at the chandelier, I seriously wondered if I was dreaming.'

'Oh, I know, I was completely terrified! Yet, when you think about it, we were only actually together for six months and never out in the open. You never met my family and I never met yours.'

'Well, if you remember, I was planning to introduce you to my parents, who wouldn't have minded in the slightest about our different religions, as they'd intermarried themselves. I've spent the last thirty-seven years kicking myself for not being more together that night. I should have given you the telephone number at my lawyers' practice, but we didn't think about all that, did we?'

'No,' I sighed. 'I was in complete shock, so it was probably me who gave you the wrong address. I did pick up the receiver in a call box in London a couple of times to dial Ambrose and see if he'd heard from you, but then I remembered how Bobby

had threatened to hurt him too and I felt I just couldn't put him at risk. If he'd have known where I was, I'm sure Bobby would have beaten it out of him, so I thought it was safest not to contact him at all, then he'd have nothing to tell. The bottom line was that I just never thought you wouldn't come,' I shrugged. 'It was as simple as that.'

Peter took a sip of his whiskey and looked at me. 'I've sometimes wondered if it would have lasted . . . you and me.'

'That's something neither of us will ever know the answer to, isn't it, Peter?'

'Sadly, yes. So, wanting to meet up with me today, is this all about what they call "closure" these days?'

'Yes; I left New Zealand on a mission to try and track down both you and Bobby. It was time, if you know what I mean.'

'I understand. You really did lose everyone you loved when you left, didn't you?'

'I did, but remember, I'd known Bobby since I was a little girl, and he and his obsession with the Irish Revolution – and *me* – had always frightened me. It actually turns out that we shared the same grandparents – we were cousins through our grandmothers, who had been sisters. But they were estranged – as many families were – during the Civil War of 1922. It turns out mental illness ran in the family. I'd always been told about Bobby's crazy dad, then I met up with his younger sister Helen, as I said, who told me their great-uncle, Colin, ended up in an asylum. She decided she didn't want any children, so that she couldn't pass whatever gene Bobby and his forefathers shared on to the next generation. All that talk about him being in the Provisional IRA was rubbish. It all came out of his psychosis. The whole thing's so, so sad.'

'Psychosis or not, it didn't make him less dangerous. He was an extremely violent man. As a matter of fact, I went to visit him at St Fintan's some years back.'

'Did you? Oh my God, Peter. That was brave of you.'

'Well, he was handcuffed to an iron bar on the table and I had two burly guards in there with me. I suppose I too wanted to put the past to rest, after he'd terrified the life out of me and then tried to murder my family. I actually walked out of there feeling sorry for him. I remember thinking he'd probably be better off dead than in that living hell. He was so drugged up, he hardly knew his own name. Anyway, what's done is done. Life's about the future, not the past, isn't it? Now, how long are you staying in Belfast?'

'As long as I'm here with you. Then I'm on the train back to Dublin to spend a little time with Ambrose. After that, I'm going to go back down to West Cork to get to know my family again.'

'That'll be nice, and so long overdue.'

'Well, there was a lot of us to begin with, but now they've all had families of their own, it'll take me a good couple of weeks to get round to see all of them,' I smiled.

'And then?' he asked.

'I don't know, Peter. I've only thought as far as meeting you today, to be honest. I'll go back to New Zealand eventually, I suppose.'

'If that's the case' – Peter looked down at his watch, then back up at me – 'could I take you to lunch? I'd love to hear more about your life and this journey you've been on in the last few weeks.'

'Okay,' I smiled at him. 'Why not?'

53

In transit: Geneva to Nice

The private jet touched down smoothly at Nice airport, as its occupants looked out of the windows in either anticipation or trepidation.

'We've landed,' Maia said to Valentina, who was strapped into the seat opposite her, her eyes wide as she continued to grip the armrests. 'What did you think?' she asked in Portuguese.

'I preferred the bigger plane, but this is nice too,' she said politely.

Ally was sitting opposite Floriano, with Bear strapped into his child safety harness on her knee. She was very proud of him, as he hadn't cried once.

'The key is to feed him a bottle as we ascend and descend, because the sucking stops the air pressure hurting his little ears,' Ma had advised her before they'd boarded, and sure enough, it had worked. As the plane taxied to a halt, Ally's nerve endings jangled. Only a short ride away sat the majestic *Titan*, anchored just outside the port and ready for its last guests to be ferried out on the gig to join it.

Waiting on board would be Star, Mouse and his son Rory, Mary-Kate *and* Jack.

Ally's stomach turned over and she grimaced at the mere thought of the look in his eyes when he saw her. *Yet another lie . . .*

'Anyway, why should it matter what *he* thinks,' she whispered to Bear as she unstrapped his harness and lifted him into the papoose.

The doors opened and the friendly ground-staff officials welcomed them all to Nice. Ma walked towards the front of the cabin and greeted them both as Floriano and Charlie – who had arrived with Tiggy at Atlantis last night – helped everyone reach for their bags.

Ma was led down the steps by the ground staff, followed by CeCe and Chrissie.

'Can I help you with anything, Ally?' Charlie asked her.

'Could you take that nappy bag?'

'Of course,' he nodded as he picked it up.

The fact that this man had delivered Bear into the world a few months ago made Ally feel comforted by his presence.

'Ally, are you okay?' Tiggy asked as Charlie descended and they were left alone in the cabin.

'Yes, why?'

'Please don't worry,' she smiled at her as she indicated Bear. 'I promise Jack won't mind at all. Now, you two first.'

Ally descended into the gorgeous light, warmth and smell that was so intrinsic to the Côte d'Azur, with Tiggy bringing up the rear. After a short walk through passport control, their bags were loaded into two limos and they were whisked out of the private terminal and into the Nice traffic.

'Where's Electra?' Ally turned to Maia. 'I'm sure she said she was meeting us here, not at the boat.'

'I just got a text to say her plane landed early so she's – or should I say *they*, as Miles is with her – have headed straight for the port.'

'So she's brought her man with her – isn't it wonderful?' said Ma.

'It is,' Maia agreed, as she put a protective arm around Valentina and smiled at Floriano, sitting opposite them.

Forty minutes and a serious amount of traffic congestion later, they arrived at the Port de Nice. Ally felt her blood pound in her veins, awash with conflicting emotions. As a child and then a young woman, the annual summer voyage on the *Titan* with her sisters and her father had been the moment she'd looked forward to more than any other. Now, the person that she'd loved most in the world was gone, as was Theo, who hadn't lived to see this day. Yet now, someone who seemed to matter to her far more than he should was waiting for her to arrive.

Shaking herself, she turned to Ma. 'Will Georg be there?'

'I hope so,' Ma said. 'His secretary said he would meet us on board.'

'Please, Ally, don't stress.' Maia put a hand out to her sister, sensing her obvious tension. 'Everyone who needs to be there will be there.'

'I'm sure you're right, Maia. It just all feels a bit odd, doesn't it?' she sighed.

'It feels different, yes, and sad too, because this was always the moment when we were reunited with Pa from wherever we were. But we must try to celebrate his life, and also the many positive things that have happened to all of us in the past year.'

'I know,' Ally replied, experiencing just the slightest sense of irritation as she felt her older sister was patronising her. Which was completely unfair, as Maia could not have been sweeter in the past few weeks. 'Where are we meeting everyone?'

'On board,' said Maia. 'It's all organised, as it always is.'

Their limo, and the one behind them carrying the other sisters, drove through the harbour to a pier, at the bottom of which floated two gigs that would take them out to the *Titan*. Given

the time of year, the port was packed with boats bobbing on the water, and many larger craft were sitting out in the bay.

Stepping out of the limo, the heat of the day hit Ally and she pulled Bear's tiny sun hat down over his eyes.

'*Bienvenue à bord du* Titan.' Hans, the captain who had skippered the boat for as long as Ally could remember, greeted them as their bags were unloaded by two deckhands, smartly dressed in white. Everyone was offered a cooling towel and led along the pier towards the gigs.

'Can I take your arm, Ma?' said Charlie, sweeping in from behind, as she attempted to descend the steps.

'Thank you. I should have remembered to leave my court shoes at home and put on a pair of deck shoes, shouldn't I?' she said, as she did every year.

Once everyone was on board the gigs, the engines were started and the short trip out towards the *Titan* began.

'Wow,' said Chrissie, as the gigs navigated out of the harbour then picked up speed on the blue of the Mediterranean Sea. 'This is the way to travel!'

'Pass me those binos, Ally,' CeCe called to the front of the gig.

'The *Titan* is just over there,' said Ally as she did so.

CeCe fixed the setting on the binoculars and then passed them to Chrissie, who looked through them.

'Oh my God! You're actually joking, aren't ya? That's not a boat, it's a cruise liner!'

'Yeah, it's pretty big,' CeCe agreed as they drew closer towards it.

'Now that,' said Charlie, indicating the *Titan* to Tiggy, 'is what my father would have called a floating gin palace.'

'I'm not sure if that's a compliment or an insult, but yes, we do have an occasional gin and tonic on board,' Tiggy grinned.

'I don't ever think I've properly realised until coming to

Atlantis last night and now seeing this today just how rich your father was.'

'Yes, he was,' Tiggy agreed.

'Do you know what makes me really happy?'

'What?'

'That my dear ex-wife would have probably given up anything to be invited on one of these for a summer cruise on the Med. And as it turns out, it was the "hired help" – as she always calls you – whose father actually owns one.' Charlie gave a chuckle. 'We'll have to take lots of photos and leave them lying around the next time Ulrika arrives to collect Zara, just to annoy her.'

Tiggy looked up at the *Titan* as they drew alongside it, and realised that yes, it did indeed look majestic. At over seventy metres long, the Benetti superyacht rose four levels out of the water, the radio tower reaching into the cloudless azure sky.

A deckhand helped Ma on board first, followed by the rest of the passengers. Two very excited faces stood on the aft deck to receive them.

'Hi, guys! Star and I were thinking about not waiting for you all and just sailing off, but hey, here you are!'

And there was Electra, looking as insouciantly beautiful as she always did, in a pair of denim shorts and a T-shirt.

'I love your short hair,' said Maia as she took her turn to hug Electra.

'Yeah, well, it's a new me in all sorts of ways. Now, come and meet Miles.'

'You're here!' Star said from behind her, as CeCe and Chrissie stepped onto the deck. Star put her arms around both of them. 'It's so good to see you both. Hi, Tiggy, and this is?'

'I'm Charlie, pleased to meet you, Star.' He shook her hand.

'And you, Charlie,' Star smiled. 'This is Mouse, my other half. Now, have a glass of champagne and make yourselves

comfortable,' Star continued. 'Rory, Mouse's son, has been taken off by our first mate to see the bridge about twenty minutes ago, and we haven't seen him since.'

The sun deck, with its comfortable canvas-covered soft furnishings, was suddenly full of milling people. Out of the corner of her eye, Ally spotted Jack and a young blonde woman standing slightly apart from the rest of the sisters and their other halves.

'Okay, Bear,' she whispered to the baby fidgeting in his papoose. 'Here goes.'

'Hi, Jack, how are you?' she said as she walked towards them.

'I'm good. This is Mary-Kate, my sister, and . . . ?' He looked down at Bear, surprise in his eyes. 'Who is this little guy?'

'My son, Bear. He's just about four months old.'

'Hi, Ally,' said Mary-Kate, 'nice to meet you. Jacko's told me a lot about you. And oh,' she said as Bear continued to wriggle, 'he's sooo cute! Isn't he, Jacko?'

'He is, yeah. Very.'

'He's getting hot and bothered in his papoose,' she said. 'Could you lift him out for me, Mary-Kate?'

'I'll do it.' Jack reached his big hands into the papoose and pulled Bear out of it. 'There you go, little one. That's better, isn't it?' he said as he gave Ally a quizzical look over the top of Bear's head.

'Jacko's very good with babies, aren't you, Jack?' said Mary-Kate. 'He had a summer job as a manny to one of our neighbours when he was eighteen.'

'Yeah, I did, for my sins,' he said, 'and I detect a familiar pong from this little guy. Which, from my expertise, I deduce belongs to a full nappy,' he chuckled. 'Here you go, Mum,' he added, handing him back to Ally.

'Thanks. I'll take him downstairs and change him. Maia?'

Ally called across the deck. 'Come and meet Jack and Mary-Kate.'

With her sister taking over the helm, Ally walked into the main salon, where the bedroom plan was always pinned to a cork board inside a metal case.

Deck Three, Suite Four, she read and went down a flight of stairs to find it. Having changed Bear and given him a quick feed, they were just leaving her cabin when she saw Georg walking along the narrow corridor towards her, still dressed in a suit and tie. He was on his mobile and looked agitated. Spotting her in front of him, he said something in German, then ended the call.

'Ally! How are you?'

'I'm well, thank you, Georg. How are you?'

'I'm . . . well. Many apologies for having been absent in the past weeks. I had matters to . . . attend to.'

Ally studied him, thinking he looked suddenly older. His skin was grey and there was a gauntness to his face that suggested he'd lost weight since she'd last seen him.

'I'm glad you're here, Georg. You look exhausted, if you don't mind me saying. Hopefully you can take off your suit and tie and start to relax.'

Just as she and Bear were about to ascend and join the others, Georg put a hand gently on her shoulder to stop her.

'Ally, may I have a word? In private?' Georg indicated the door that led into what they called the Winter Salon, which was a cosy lounge used when the weather was bad.

'Of course.'

Georg opened the door into the salon, and both of them moved to sit on a couple of sofas placed on either side of a low drinks table, with lovely views through the portholes onto the sparkling Mediterranean Sea.

'What is it, Georg?'

'Well, I have met both Jack and Mary-Kate upstairs on deck, but I hear that Mary-Kate is not the "Mary McDougal" you originally thought she was?'

'No, she's the adopted daughter of her mother, who is also Mary McDougal, or Merry, as she's more commonly known.'

'Atch!' Georg said in frustration. 'We – I – did not foresee such a thing. All I'd heard was that Mary had been located and had agreed to join us on our cruise.'

'Yes, but in the past few days, Mary-Kate has made contact with her birth mother, and it turns out that her mother Merry was actually adopted too. Well, she was a foundling, anyway.'

'So, let me get this straight.' Georg pulled out a miniature leather-bound notepad and a fountain pen from the inside pocket of his jacket. 'The daughter, Mary-Kate, is how old?'

'Twenty-two.'

'And born where?'

'In New Zealand.'

'And she has recently identified her birth mother and father? Who are also from New Zealand?' he asked.

'I believe so, yes.'

'And Merry, the mother, how old is she?'

'Fifty-nine this year.'

'And she has just discovered that she was adopted?'

'Yes. Merry just found out that she was put in the place of a dead baby, and brought up as part of that family. But that originally, she'd been a foundling.'

'From the south-west of Ireland?'

'Yes. We did try and contact you, Georg, because we needed more information about Mary McDougal and which one of them it might be, but we didn't hear anything back from you. Then, just by coincidence, Maia happened to be in Pa's garden and saw a set of coordinates had been added to Merope's band on the armillary sphere. I looked them up on

Google Earth, and it turns out that they pointed to a big old house, very close to where Merry was put on the doorstep of a local priest down in West Cork.'

'I . . .' Georg looked up at Ally in horror. 'You mean, you had only just seen that set of coordinates?'

'Yes. I'd been in the garden sometimes when I was home, sitting on the bench under the rose arbour, and looked at the armillary sphere, but never that closely.'

'*Mein Gott!*' Georg thumped the table. 'Ally, those coordinates have been on the armillary sphere for months. I myself gave orders to have them engraved only a few weeks after we all saw the armillary sphere for the first time. I'm amazed that none of you girls had noticed them. And when I came to see you . . . I took a call, if you remember, and had to leave immediately.'

'But why would we have seen it, Georg? Maia had left for Brazil and the rest of us were only going home sporadically. If we did look, it was only at our own band.'

'Then this is all my fault,' he said. 'I assumed that you *had* noticed it, and to be perfectly honest, my mind was on other things. So why is this Merry not here with her son and her daughter?'

'Jack told me she didn't want to come,' Ally shrugged. 'I'm not sure of the reasons why. Georg?'

'Yes, Ally.' Georg had stood up and was pacing around the salon.

'So, the mother of Mary-Kate – Merry – is definitely the missing sister?'

'As far as I am aware, she is, but after all this, she is not here! And neither is the ring. This is all my fault, Ally,' he said again. 'In recent weeks, I have been . . . distracted, but still, I should have told you how old she was, checked if you had seen her coordinates on the armillary sphere. But I wasn't

expecting that there would be *two* Mary McDougals. I . . . aatch!'

Ally watched him, this man who had always seemed so cool and calm, never showing any emotion. Yet now, she saw that he was utterly beside himself.

'Do you know who used to own that old house in West Cork?' she probed. Georg turned round, stared at her and nodded.

'Yes, I do.'

'Then why didn't you tell us?'

'Because, because . . . Ally, as always, I was only following orders . . .' Georg sat down opposite her and wiped his sweating brow with his white handkerchief. 'Giving you that information from the start might have upset certain . . . members of the family. It was thought best for you, or in fact, Mary McDougal, to discover it for yourselves.'

'You mean, because Maia's son is Zed Eszu's child? And because he pursued Tiggy and Electra?'

'Exactly, but still, this is all my mistake, Ally, and I must rectify the situation immediately.'

'Why? I mean . . .' Ally's head was spinning. 'How?'

'Where is Merry now?'

'Jack said she was staying in Ireland to spend some time with her family.'

'So she is still down in West Cork?'

'No, I'm pretty sure she travelled back to Dublin with Jack and Mary-Kate, but we can ask them. She has a godfather there apparently, called Ambrose.'

'Right, then I must sort this out before it's too late. Excuse me, Ally.' Ally watched as Georg marched out of the salon.

54

Merry
Belfast, Northern Ireland

'More wine? Or maybe an Irish coffee to finish? I bet it's a long time since you had one of those,' Peter said to me across the table.

'It was, at least up until a few days ago when I treated myself and the kids to one down in West Cork. Anyway, the answer is sadly no; I've drunk far more than is good for me, especially at lunchtime. I'll end up sleeping the afternoon away.'

'Well, it's not every day you meet a long-lost love again after thirty-seven years, is it?'

'No,' I smiled.

'It's been so wonderful to see you again, Merry, even though I was dreading it.'

'That makes two of us, but yes, it's been wonderful. Now I really must go, Peter. It's half past three already and I have to get myself back to Dublin.'

'You can't stay on another night?'

'No, I promised Ambrose I'd be back, and given that he's paranoid I may suddenly disappear again, I must. I wasn't even intending on staying this long.'

'He knows where you've been?'

'Of course. It was him I asked to try and help trace you after I could find no records of you in Ireland, England or Canada. He suggested he contact an old student of his who works in the records office at Trinity, to see if you still had a subscription for *Trinity Today*, the university alumni magazine. He took a look at the records of subscribers and there you were, with an address in Belfast!'

'Full marks to Ambrose for excellent sleuthing,' said Peter as he signalled for the bill. 'It's a real shame you can't stay longer, as I'd love to have shown you around more of the city. Everything you remember from your TV screen in the seventies and eighties is not how it is now. It's beginning to thrive, and once the Titanic Quarter is completed, Belfast really will be a destination city.'

'I'm so happy it will be, and that old wounds are beginning to be mended,' I replied, as I took out my wallet and offered Peter a credit card. 'Let's go dutch?'

'Don't be silly, Merry. I've waited a very, very long time to take you out for lunch – besides, you put the whiskeys and my coffee and croissant on your hotel bill this morning.'

I agreed, and ten minutes later, we left the restaurant and wandered past the great mass of St Anne's Cathedral.

'It's very impressive,' I commented. 'What is that long steel pipe coming out of the top?'

'That was installed only last year, and it's called the Spire of Hope. It's illuminated at night, and actually, I love it, and what it stands for. Merry?'

'Yes?'

'I . . . I mean, obviously it's up to you, but I'd love to see you again before you go back to New Zealand. Today has just been, well, fantastic. It was so good to laugh like we used to.'

'It was, yes. As I said, I have no real fixed plans yet and I'm still getting over the loss of Jock, so . . .'

'I understand,' he said as we entered the hotel. 'But this time, we'll take out our mobiles, swap numbers and emails and addresses, then double-check we both have them written in correctly, deal?'

'Deal,' I smiled as I walked over to the porter's desk and handed in my left luggage tag.

While we waited for them to retrieve my holdall, we did exactly as he'd suggested.

'Do you need a taxi, madam?' asked the porter.

'I do, yes please.'

Peter and I followed the porter back down the steps outside, and watched as he whistled to attract a cab's attention.

'I hate saying goodbye when we've only just said hello. Please think about coming back here, Merry, or I can come to you in Dublin. In fact, anytime, anywhere.'

'I will, I promise.'

He took my hand and kissed it, then enveloped me in a hug. 'Please, take care of yourself, won't you?' he whispered gently. 'And don't you dare lose touch!'

'I won't. Bye, Peter, and thank you for lunch.'

I climbed into the cab and waved at him as we set off into the traffic.

Due to the build-up of tension, the emotion of actually seeing Peter again after all these years, plus the amount of wine I'd downed over lunch, I slept for most of the journey back to Dublin, only waking up when the man next to me nudged me to let him out.

In the taxi to Merrion Square, I felt half drugged, and

could hardly believe that I'd actually just been with Peter after all these years.

Letting myself into Ambrose's flat, I put down my holdall and walked into the sitting room, where he was in his usual chair.

'Hello, Ambrose, I made it back safely,' I smiled at him.

'All went well then?'

'Oh, it did! I was so unbelievably nervous, I literally fainted into his arms and . . .'

I suddenly became aware of the fact that we weren't the only two people in the room. I turned to look behind me and there, sitting in the corner of the sofa, was a man I'd never seen before. As my gaze fell on him, he stood up. I saw that he was very tall, immaculately dressed in a suit and tie, and probably in his early sixties.

'Do excuse me, sir, I didn't notice you were there. I'm Merry McDougal, and you are?' I asked him as I held out my hand.

For what seemed a very long time, the man didn't answer, just stared at me as if he was mesmerised. His grey eyes looked a little wet, as if they had tears in them. My hand still reached towards him, but as he didn't seem inclined to take it, I let it fall. Eventually, he seemed to shake himself out of his hypnotic state.

'Do forgive me, Mrs McDougal. You bear a striking resemblance to . . . someone. I'm Georg Hoffman, and I am so very pleased to meet you.'

The man spoke perfect English, but with a pronounced accent I placed as German.

'And . . . who are you?'

'Please, won't you sit down?' Georg indicated the sofa. I looked over at Ambrose for reassurance.

'Do sit down, Mary. Can I offer you a whiskey?' he asked me.

'Goodness, no, I've had far more than my fair share of alcohol today.'

I sat down tentatively, as did Georg Hoffman. I saw that he had a slim leather case very similar to the one Peter had brought with him this morning. He pulled a plastic file out of the case and laid it on his knee. I sighed, because after the day I'd had, I simply wanted to have a quiet cup of tea and a sandwich with Ambrose, tell him of my meeting with Peter and then slip down the stairs to bed.

'Are you here to see me, or do you and Ambrose know each other?' I asked.

'Mary, Mr Hoffman is the lawyer of the dead father of all the sisters that have been trying to trace you recently,' said Ambrose.

'Please, call me Georg. I believe it was Tiggy you met here in Dublin.'

'Yes, it was. But I've also met other sisters and their . . . partners around the world. That is, they've been trying to track me down.'

'Yes, they have. And I'm here tonight because I now realise it should have been me who came to you in the first place, because I had more . . . details of your origins than my client's daughters. But when the girls – as I call the sisters collectively – came up with a plan to track their missing sister down, I took the decision to let them find you. They had been very successful in finding their own birth families, you see, and I had other matters to attend to. Let me now apologise for any inconvenience or worry I – and they – have caused you in the process.'

'Thank you. The situation has caused me some distress, especially as I booked a Grand Tour to try to get over the loss of my husband.'

'Mary, my dear, do forgive me, but that isn't quite true, is it?'

I looked at Ambrose, wondering why on earth he was defending the behaviour of a set of sisters whom he knew had completely terrified me.

'What I mean, Mr Hoffman, is that at the same time, Mary – and I do hope you don't mind me speaking for you,' Ambrose continued, 'was also on a search for her *own* past. Ironically, as the sisters were trying to find her, she was searching for someone too. Someone that frightened and terrorised her as a young woman. Unfortunately, the two lines of enquiry became confused. Do you understand?'

'Not completely, but enough to know that you, Mrs McDougal, did not welcome the sisters' pursuit of you.'

'Please, call me Merry, and no I did not, but you still haven't answered the question: why are you here tonight?'

'Because . . . forgive me, Merry, if I sound as though I'm talking in riddles. To be honest with you, I never expected this moment to arrive. I have worked for the girls' father—'

'Whom they call Pa Salt,' I butted in.

'Yes. He's been like a father to me ever since I have known him. I have worked for him for the whole of my career as a lawyer, and he has always talked of the fact that there was a missing sister, one he could never find, however hard he searched. I joined him in that search when I was old enough to do so. Occasionally, he would call me with a promising lead as to her whereabouts and I would employ a trusted team of private investigators to follow that lead up. Every time, they led to nothing. And then, this time last year, finally, my employer discovered new information, which he assured me was almost certainly accurate. I had very little to work on, but work on it I did.'

I watched the man pause for a moment, then lean forward to pick up the glass of whiskey on the table in front of him. He drained the glass, put it down and looked at me.

'Merry, I could sit here and tell you the pains that I and the private investigators went to in order to discover who you had become, but . . .'

I watched him as he shook his head and put his hand to his brow, obviously embarrassed to be showing deep emotion.

'Excuse me one moment . . .'

He fumbled in the file on his knee. Accepting and rejecting various pages, he finally drew one out and turned it round to face me.

'If only I had known how simple the puzzle of identifying you would eventually be, then I could have spared you all you've suffered during these past weeks. After all this, we didn't even need that emerald ring.' Mr Hoffman pointed to it sitting on my finger, then handed me the sheet of paper. 'Look,' he said.

I did look, and once my brain had made sense of the image, I performed the cliché known as a double-take, because I looked again in disbelief.

On the page in front of me was a charcoal portrait of *me*.

I looked closer, and discovered that yes, maybe the shape of my jaw was heavier and my eyebrows were a little lighter than the drawing in front of me, but there was no doubt.

'It's me, isn't it?'

'No,' Mr Hoffman whispered, 'it isn't you, Merry. It is your mother.'

In the following twenty minutes, I couldn't remember much about what I'd said or what I'd done. That face, which was mine yet wasn't, stirred in me some primeval reaction I'd been unprepared for. I wanted to stroke the drawing, then I wanted to tear it into shreds. I accepted a whiskey that I didn't want

but drained the glass, and then I cried. Torrents of tears for the mess my life seemed to have become. Whatever I thought I had solved, each time a new puzzle had appeared in its place, along with a gamut of emotions that ended with me in Ambrose's arms on the sofa, and the lawyer watching from the leather chair.

'Sorry, sorry,' I kept saying as I dripped tears all over the charcoal drawing of the me that was my mother.

Eventually, I stopped crying and with Ambrose's handkerchief, dried my eyes, my cheeks and then patted the photocopy of the face that had apparently borne me into the world. Which was now smudged and ugly.

'Please, do not worry about that. It is a facsimile of the original,' said Georg.

As my senses began to return to normal, I moved out of Ambrose's embrace and sat upright.

'Merry, if you please, could you give me a little tug upwards?' Ambrose asked. 'I think some tea is in order for all. I shall go and make some.'

'Ambrose, really—'

'My dear, I'm perfectly capable of making a pot of tea.'

Georg and I sat together in silence. There were so many questions I wanted answers to, but I struggled to know where to start.

'Georg,' I managed as I blew my nose for the umpteenth time on Ambrose's sodden handkerchief. 'Could you please explain why, if you knew which year I was born, you pursued – or the sisters pursued – my daughter, who is only twenty-two?'

'Because I had no clue that your daughter would be called Mary too. And that you would have passed the ring on to her on her twenty-first. During the past two weeks when the search for you was continuing, having established that they

had found Mary McDougal, I was then . . . unavoidably detained elsewhere. Out of contact with them.'

'I'm very sorry, Georg, but there are so many things I don't understand. You say that this charcoal drawing is of my mother?'

'Yes.'

'How do you know this?'

'Because of the drawing that has hung on the wall at Atlantis, my employer's house in Geneva, for many years. He had told me who it was.'

'Did she die? Giving birth to me, I mean?'

Yet again, I could see the man's indecision at revealing what he knew and didn't know.

Just as Ambrose brought the tea in, Georg stood up and went to retrieve his leather case. I watched as he removed a padded brown envelope from inside it. He sat down in Ambrose's chair and laid the package on his knee.

'Do you take sugar, Georg?' Ambrose asked.

'I do not drink tea, thank you. Merry, this package is for you. I believe it will answer all the questions that I cannot. But before I give it to you, I entreat you now to come with me and join your children and the sisters on the *Titan*. You will be fulfilling their father's long-held dream, and I cannot leave here without begging you to come. A private jet sits on the runway at Dublin airport, waiting for us to board and fly to meet the boat.'

'I'm so tired,' I sighed. 'I just want to go to bed.'

I turned to Ambrose as I sipped my tea, at nearly fifty-nine years of age, still looking to him for guidance.

'I know, my dear, I know,' Ambrose replied, 'but what is the price of a night's sleep, as opposed to discovering your true heritage?'

'But it's all so surreal, Ambrose.'

'That is simply because so far, your experience of the sisters has been so fractured. Plus the fact that you have had so much to contend with recently, but even your own children are on the boat. They are sailing towards Greece, the land that you never visited, but always wished to, and from what Georg has said, where you may find the answers that you seek. I too, as the man who first laid eyes on you at only a few hours old, then watched you grow into a remarkable young woman with a passion for philosophy and mythology, beg you to go and discover your *own* legend. What do you have to lose, Mary?'

I stared at him, wondering how much had been discussed between him and Georg before I'd arrived. Then I thought of my children, already ensconced in this strange, disparate family, somewhere on the sea sailing towards Greece, the land that had always held such a special, magical place in my mind . . .

I reached for Ambrose's hand. And took a deep breath. 'All right,' I said, 'I'll go.'

An hour and a half later, I was on the kind of private jet I'd only ever seen in movies or magazines, sitting in a leather-covered seat, with Georg opposite me on the other side of the slim aisle. At the front of the plane, I could see the two pilots getting ready for take-off. Georg was on his mobile, speaking to someone in German. I only wished I could understand what he was saying, because it sounded urgent.

A male steward appeared and asked us both to fasten our seat belts and turn off our mobiles. The plane began to taxi, and then within the space of perhaps only a few seconds, the jet picked up speed and we were suddenly airborne. I gazed out of the window, wondering what madness it was that yet again, I was abruptly leaving the land where I had been born

and raised. The lights of Dublin twinkled below me, and then almost immediately there was darkness as we began to cross the Irish Sea. I closed my eyes and tried to focus on the fact I was flying *to* my family – Jack and Mary-Kate – and not away from it, like the last time I had left Ireland.

There was a ding from above me, then the steward arrived and told us we were free to take off our seat belts.

I watched Georg as he reached for his leather case. He pulled out the brown padded envelope.

'This is yours, Merry. Inside, I hope you will find the answers to the questions you have asked me. For now, I will leave you to take some rest.'

As he handed it to me, I saw the glimmer of tears once again in his eyes. He then summoned the steward. 'Mrs McDougal wishes to have some privacy and sleep. I will move forward.'

'Of course, sir.'

'Goodnight, Mary. I will see you when we land,' Georg nodded.

The steward duly pulled out two panels from either side of the cabin, which formed a partition between the back and front of it. He then handed me a blanket and a pillow and showed me how to form the seat into a bed.

'How long is the flight?' I asked him as he placed a glass of water in the holder beside me.

'Just over three hours, madam. Would you like anything else at all?'

'I'm fine, thank you.'

'Please press the bell beside your seat if you need anything. Goodnight, madam.'

The panel doors slid closed behind him and I found myself in total privacy. I experienced a moment of sheer panic, because I was flying to God knows where and had a brown

package on my knee that apparently contained the secret of my true heritage.

'Ambrose trusted Georg, and so must you, Merry,' I murmured to myself.

So here I was, suspended somewhere between heaven and earth. The Greek gods had chosen Mount Olympus, the highest mountain in Greece, as their home, perhaps wishing for the same feeling. I looked out of the window at the stars, which seemed so much brighter up here, shining down like astral torches.

I turned my attention to the parcel on my lap and stuck a finger under the seal to pull the large envelope open. I reached inside and took out a thick and somewhat battered brown leather book, and an accompanying cream vellum envelope. Placing the book on the little table in front of me, I looked down at the envelope and read the three beautifully scripted words on the front of it:

For my Daughter.

I opened it.

> *Atlantis*
> *Lake Geneva*
> *Switzerland*

My darling daughter,

I only wish I could address you by your given name, but sadly I do not know what it is. Just as I have no idea where in the world you might live. Or if you still live. Nor do I know whether you will ever be found, which is an odd thought for both of us if you are reading this, because it means you have been, yet I am gone from this world. And the two of us will never

meet on earth, but in the next life, which I believe in with all my heart and soul.

I cannot voice or begin to explain the love I have felt for you since I knew of your imminent arrival. Nor can I tell you in this letter the lengths I took to find you and your mother, who were both lost to me so cruelly before you were born. You may well believe that you were abandoned by your father, but that is far from the truth. To this day – and I write to you as I have written to my six other daughters, because I am close to death – I do not know where your mother went, or whether she lived or died after you were born.

How I know you were born is also a story that can only be explained in more pages than I have the energy to write here.

However, write it I did, many years ago, in the journal that I have instructed my lawyer, Georg Hoffman, to give to you. It's the story of my life, which, if nothing else, has been eventful. You may well have had contact with my adopted daughters and I would ask that, once you have read it, you share my story with them, because it is their story too.

Read it, my darling girl, and know that there hasn't been a day that has gone by without me thinking and praying for both you and your mother. She was the love of my life . . . everything to me. And if she has passed on to the next life, which some deep instinct tells me she has, know that we are reunited and looking down on you with love.

Your father,

Atlas x

Author's Note

I'd always known that I would set *The Missing Sister* predominantly in my home territory of West Cork, Ireland. Given the coronavirus pandemic, it was as if it was meant to be: I'd already secretly visited Central Otago in New Zealand and Norfolk Island before Christmas 2019. Then, only a few weeks later, I was locked down in West Cork with the research I needed for once at my fingertips. I'd believed I knew quite a lot about the past turbulent one hundred years of Irish history, but as I began to do my usual in-depth research, I realised that I'd only scratched the surface. I also noticed that the scarce personal accounts of those who were directly involved in the Irish War of Independence were written by men, and mostly penned many years after the fact. I decided that, to get as true a picture as possible, I'd need to turn to my family, friends and neighbours, whose ancestors had fought for freedom at the time. Out of this, a picture of wartime West Cork and the huge contribution its brave volunteers – nearly all rural farming people, mostly aged between sixteen and twenty-five, with no fighting experience and outnumbered in their thousands by trained British soldiers and police officers – made to winning what, on paper, was an impossible fight.

It is only due to all the locals prepared to give up their time

to help me that I was able to write what I hope is a relatively accurate portrayal of what happened in West Cork back then and throughout the rest of the twentieth century. My biggest thanks must go to Cathal Dineen, who (when we were 'unlocked') drove me all over, into the *back* of the back of beyond to meet men like Joe Long, who Cathal had heard still had Charlie Hurley's original rifle, which he did! Then up to the remote Clogagh graveyard, to show me the vault beneath an enormous Celtic cross sitting on a gravetop, where Lord Bandon had reportedly been placed when he was held hostage for two weeks. My spine tingled when I looked around and saw bones visible in the eroded coffins still lying on the shelves around me. Nothing was too much trouble for him or anyone he contacted, and if they didn't know, normally there was a grandparent or older relative available to ask who'd had parents alive at the time or had kept newspaper cuttings. Tim Crowley, who runs the Michael Collins Centre at Castle-view, is a relative of the Big Fellow himself. He and his wife Dolores were not only able to help factually, but actually let me hold the very briefcase that Michael Collins had used for his papers when he journeyed to London to negotiate the long and rocky road to eventual Irish independence with the British.

I'd read of Cumann na mBan, but again, there were and still are few books/papers published on the organisation, and they didn't relate specifically to West Cork. Through my friend and owner of my local bookshop in Clonakilty, Trish Kerr, I contacted Dr Hélène O'Keefe, an historian and lecturer at University College Cork, who put me in touch with Niall Murray, a long-time journalist with the *Irish Examiner*, historian and current PhD candidate at the university, researching the Irish Revolution in urban and rural districts of County Cork. He suggested visiting the Irish Government's War Pension Files website to discover who from Cumann na mBan in

my local area had applied. This opened the door not only to how many local women were involved in providing invaluable support to their men, but also to the real and present danger they were prepared to encounter, while still working on their farms and in the local post office or dressmaker's. I can only pay tribute to each and every one of these unsung heroines.

My wonderful friend Kathleen Owens also went in dogged pursuit of the smallest details, aided by her Mammy, Mary Lynch, her husband Fergal, and her son, Ryan Doonan. Mary Dineen, Dennis O'Mahoney, Finbarr O'Mahony and Maureen Murphy, who wrote to me from New York where her family had emigrated after the Civil War, are just some of those in my kind local community who contributed so much colour to this book. However, this book is categorised as a work of fiction – but peppered with real historical figures and set against an all-too-real fight to the death to achieve freedom from the British. As always, history is subjective, being reliant on human interpretation and, in many cases throughout this book, memory. Any 'mistakes' are mine and mine alone.

Also, in New Zealand, heartfelt thanks go out to Annie and Bruce Walker for their tour around beautiful Norfolk Island and their stories of NZ and island life, plus, of course, a taste of true Kiwi hospitality.

Huge thanks must go to my 'home' team, who have given me amazing support in their different ways. Ella Micheler, Jacquelyn Heslop, Olivia Riley, Susan Boyd, Jessica Kearton, Leanne Godsall and of course my husband Stephen – agent, rock and best friend – have all been there when I've needed them. Tribute must also go to all my many publishers around the world, who have walked the extra mile to get the books out to their readers, especially in these unprecedented times.

My tight cluster of close friends, who all know who they are and never fail to spur me on with honesty and love. And of course my children – Harry, Isabella, Leonora and Kit – who will always remain my greatest strength and inspiration.

On another point, I imagine that some of you might be sitting reading this letter in shock and perhaps disappointment that so many of the underlying mysteries throughout the series remain unsolved. This is simply because, as I started to write *The Missing Sister* and her own story grew, I realised that there just wasn't the space to tell the 'secret story' properly. So yes, the eighth and truly final instalment of *The Seven Sisters* series is yet to come . . .

Thank you for bearing with me, and I promise to begin writing book eight as soon as I've put *The Missing Sister* 'to bed', as they say. It's been in my head for eight years, and I can't wait to finally get it down on paper.

Lucinda Riley
March 2021

To discover the inspiration behind the series and to read about the real stories, places and people in this book, please visit www.lucindariley.com.

Bibliography

Munya Andrews, *The Seven Sisters of the Pleiades* (Spinifex Press, 2014)

Sebastian Balfour ed., *Trinity Tales: Trinity College Dublin in the Sixties* (Lilliput Press, 2011)

Tom Barry, *Guerilla Days in Ireland* (Mercier Press, 2013)

Alan Brady, *Pinot Central: A Winemaker's Story* (Penguin, 2010)

Tim Pat Coogan, *Michael Collins: A Biography* (Head of Zeus, 2015)

Dan Crowley, *My Time in My Place* (Michael Collins Centre, Castleview, 2013)

John Crowley, Donal Ó Drisceoil and Mike Murphy, *Atlas of the Irish Revolution* (Cork University Press, 2017)

Tim Crowley, *In Search of Michael Collins* (Michael Collins Centre, Castleview, 2015)

Liz Gillis, *The Hales Brothers and the Irish Revolution* (Mercier Press, 2016)

Da'Vella Gore, *This Blessed Journey* (Da'Vella J. Gore, 2009)

Patrick Radden Keefe, *Say Nothing: A True Story of Murder and Memory in Northern Ireland* (William Collins, 2018)

Anne Leonard ed., *Portrait of an Era: Trinity College Dublin in the 1960s* (John Calder Publishing, 2014)

Ken Loach et al., *The Wind that Shakes the Barley* (London: Sixteen Films, 2007)